SOUTHSIDE HOOKER SERIES

BOOKS ONE — FIVE

BAER CHARLTON

MORDANT MEDIA ™℠
A Division of Charlton Productions

Compiled by Rogena Mitchell-Jones, Literary Editor | www.rogenamitchell.com

Published by Mordant Media, Portland, Oregon

Published 2019 — 10 9 8 7 6 5 4 3 2 1

CONTENTS

ABOUT THE STORIES

Just as not all mysteries are killings, and not all killings are mysteries, not all mystery stories are told the same way. These are the stories of an ordinary group of people involved in extraordinary circumstances. Hooker, Hieronymus Octavius O'Keefer, is a tow truck driver with a collected family of retired detectives, cops, radio dispatchers, blind disc jockey, nurses, and a twenty-pound cat named Box.

DEATH ON A DIME — BOOK 1

A classic who-done-it of a serial killer with a shotgun, loaded with dimes, killing cops.

NIGHT VISION — BOOK 2

A psychological thriller with a psychopathic mutilator killing innocents in a ritual of world-building.

UNBIDDEN GARDEN — BOOK 3

A 20-year-old cold case focuses on procedural step-by-step case-building and the painstaking research of 1973.

BOOMTOWN — BOOK 4

A 50/50 split of telling the story from both sides as an explosive-for-hire expert destroys businesses and creates mayhem.

ONE DAY UNDER THE GRASS — BOOK 5

A psychological thriller of multiple personality disorder. One person does the killing, and the other buries the bodies in the seagrass of the south San Francisco Bay.

DEATH ON A DIME

A SOUTHSIDE HOOKER NOVEL — BOOK 1

1

The fork was a burning accusation firmly planted by the steel-like fist through the bony hand with one finger touching the dollar and change tip. The pain seared the rims of the young punk's sunken eyes as his mouth opened slowly in a breathless silent scream. Pinpricks of strain-induced sweat ruptured around his temples, and his body froze against the pain as his brain told him what was happening.

The cold gaze of the gold-flecked green eyes slid slowly from the interrupted book, locking onto the frightened brown eyes twitching on the young street tough. The quiet leather-jacketed avenger slowly swung his face closer to the blanched face of his captured prey. The young man's inner soul was clearly quaking as he took in the fierce scarred face.

"Did you think you worked hard for that dollar?" The chilling voice was barely louder than the young man's breathing.

The eyes on the young man grew even wider as his face started a shudder of denial.

"Did you run your ass ragged all night until the drunks come in to steal your tips because they think you would never miss it?" The vise grip on the fork wavered ever so slightly, grinding the points of the fork, buried in the offending hand along the Formica counter of the all-night diner. "Did you ever think the waitress just might need the dollar more than you do?"

Less than six inches separated the two faces as the tension built. The trapped thief now wondered if his hand was only the beginning of what could happen to him this night. A distinct aroma started to emanate from his lap as he lost any decency of control he may have previously had back when the other dude was still reading his book and eating his dinner.

"Hooker!" the woman screamed from the other end of the counter as she flew out of the kitchen. Rushing to the counter, she tried to stop what she was afraid would happen. "Hooker, stop!" She slid to a stop and placed her hand on the fist and the fork handle. "Stop," she pleaded. "He didn't mean it."

Hooker turned his gaze from the kid to the woman. "He was going to steal your tip, Candy," he rumbled. Slowly, with both of her hands guiding his, he withdrew from the fork.

The mousy blonde's shoulders slumped as she saw the tines of the fork buried fully in the boy's hand. She reached out, grabbed his jaw, and shook it toward her. "Johnny, don't move. I'll be right back, but don't move." She shot Hooker a cold look as he returned to his dinner, borrowing another fork from the place setting on the other side of him. Picking up his book and turning it over, he stole a glance at the now rushing waitress as she pushed through the door to the back. Glancing at the kid, he saw the scared child he hadn't noticed when the hand crept across the counter toward the tip.

"Johnny, huh?" The kid nodded numbly as a tiny bit of drool snuck out of the side of his drooping mouth, still blinking at the blinding sear in his eyes, a low painful moan quietly bubbling up from a deep, primal place in his belly.

The scrawny waitress banged through the swinging door and rushed back in as she folded a couple of clean towels. She started and stopped in hesitation, considering what to do next. She gingerly rolled the hand over to see the points of the tines making four pimples along the palm, bumping out, but not penetrating all the way through.

Hooker reached over without looking and grabbed the fork. "Hold his hand." Turning the page with his other hand and chewing, he continued to read.

"What are you doing?"

"Hold his hand down tight, or it will hurt worse." Hooker made a mental note of where he had stopped reading and looked up at Candy's face. Despite the freckles, her two decades of hard life lay carved deep. With grim determination, she pushed the hand back down into its original position and pushed down with both of her hands. The fork flashed out of the hand as she reached for the towel to stanch the bleeding.

"What were you thinking, Johnny?" She scolded as she tied the towel in a knot. The white Turkish towel was stark against the long-unwashed skin. "I've told you a hundred times if you need money, come ask me. We don't steal." She reached out and ran her fingers through his hair trying to straighten out the mess crowning the shrunken boy caved into the chair in front of her. "What am I ever going to do with you until the Navy or somebody takes you?" She fussed.

The kid slowly rolled his shoulders and mumbled, "I don't know."

The waitress mirrored her younger sibling, and then, shaking off the sorrow and resuming her bravado armor of the late-night waitress, she turned on the leather-jacketed man quietly reading. "As for you, you're done," she demanded. "Pay the bill and go back to work."

Hooker looked up, pained. "But I wanted some—"

She cut him off. "Not tonight, mister. You're done." She waved the back of her hands at him. "Shoo, you can have apple-pie tomorrow night." Still shooing him, "Tonight, you've done enough damage. You'd better leave a big tip though, because tomorrow I'll have to take him up to the clinic, and I don't have the kind of money they want."

Hooker withdrew from the counter seat and started to protest but was shut down by a snap of her head and a single hard glare. Knowing defeat, he fished a twenty-dollar bill out of his wallet, thought about it, added a five for the meal, and then slipped both under the edge of the coffee cup. He caught the kid, Johnny eyeing the largess of tip, and pointed at him as he closed his left eye and sighted down the pointed finger at the kid, who sunk even deeper into the chair.

As he started to walk off, he caught the hurt and stern look on the face of his favorite waitress. Slapping the kid gently on the shoulder, he parted with a half attempt to make up with the server by saying, "Do what your sister tells ya, Johnny, and stay out of trouble." Turning, he took three steps and pushed through the glass door into the damp, chilly night.

Glancing at his watch, he noted the five minutes to midnight as he opened the door and clambered up into the large yellow and blue tow truck. He leaned across to the glove compartment and hit the upper corner to make the door open. Fishing in the sizable dark maw, he withdrew a half-empty pack of unfiltered cigarettes. Absentmindedly, he tapped a single cigarette on his watch face as he stared across the empty street at the dark shops. His mind was a million miles away. His hand fished the keys out of his leather jacket and then turned the square silver key in the switch. Hooker listened to the turbo wind up, and then pushed the small silver start button. The largest, fastest tow truck in the five counties of the bay area rumbled to life.

Looking in the long side mirror, he smiled and rolled down the window, as the oldest street urchin in the city came drifting along the side of the truck like so much night mist. Delicate fingers, like those of a concert pianist, lightly danced and walked along the edge of the steel working bed of the tow truck. Hooker absently counted the touching pattern. It never changed. Always three, then a skip or hop, then two, a midair twist, a middle finger bounce followed by a midair flare of the whole hand flat and spread, and then dropping into a repeat for the next three feet of the truck. Every night, it was always the same time, always the same Peter, and always the same finger-dance of touches working their way along the twenty feet of truck bed.

"Good morning, Peter." Hooker greeted the man who was little more than a walking pillar of filthy rags.

"Oh," the man feigned being startled. "Oh, it's you. Good morning, Hooker." He stopped but looked back at the restaurant.

Hooker chuckled. He had never seen the street urchin look directly at anyone, or even face them.

"What's the word?"

The bum compulsively washed his face with his right hand as he almost slurred, "Thunderbird."

"Half the price," Hooker recited in the ritual.

"Twice as nice." The man giggled in his pride of having a special connection with this man in his big working truck. "H-h-h-hey H-h-hooker?" Peter stammered. "Do you have a s-s-s-st-stick I could b-b-b-bum?" He looked across the street as his right hand rose above his head, and like an elephant's nose, the hand searched the air and then retreated to the safety of his head and repeated the ritual.

"Let me look around here, Peter. Maybe somebody left something from the day shift." Hooker would never tell Peter the truck was his and his alone, or he stocked the cigarettes in the boot just for these shared moments, but he thought about the moment as he continued to strike the end of the cigarette on the watch face.

"Well, th-th-that would be g-g-good." The elephant nose rising a little higher was rewarded with the 'cancer stick' and retreated.

"Do you need a light there, Peter?" Hooker pushed in the as-yet unused lighter on his dash. "I have a great lighter right here on the dashboard."

"N-n-no thanks, I-I-I'll use it l-l-la-later," Peter responded, completing the ritual as he wandered off back the way he had come out of the dark.

Hooker watched in the mirror as the migrating heap of rags slowly dissolved into the dark of the night. He reached for the radio's microphone, silently reciting a small prayer for the homeless man. Take care, Peter, and may you sleep without your demons tonight and find peace in the morning. Hooker moved the mic near his mouth and keyed the red talk button.

"Dispatch, this is unit 1-4-1. Show me 10-8," letting them know he was back in-service.

"10-4, Hooker. All we have hanging is a 1971 white El Dorado with a flat tire, southbound 101, just north of Pearl."

"Sure," Hooker responded. "I'll take it. Show me five minutes out."

"10-4, showing 1-4-1 on call number 0-0-2, ten minutes out at 12:06. And Hooker, no speeding. It's only a flat tire."

"10-4." Hooker hung the auto club yellow microphone over his disused rearview mirror facing the towing mechanism behind him and chuckled at the mother-hen routine. Hooker checked both side mirrors, and down both ways of the empty boulevard. Robotically, he jammed the gears into the first of six gears of the main transmission. His right hand reached slightly back to the second gear shifter, selecting the second gear of the four-gear 'crash box' or transfer gearbox gaving him twenty-four gears in all. Hooker liked to think of the gearing as zero to one-twenty in twenty-four. Slowly, the eleven tons of giant truck nosed out onto Winchester Boulevard and headed for the freeway on-ramp three blocks away.

2

Hooker, born Hieronymus Octavio O'Keller, loved the giant truck as much as he loved anything. The body of the machine once worked as a Marmon logging truck with an oversized conventional snout. The snout didn't need to be so long, so Hooker and his uncle had chopped it down to the needed length. The cab was roomy and easily fit the extra radios—the lifeblood of a freelance tow-trucker. The engine was a special. It had started life as a 900 horse-powered dragline winch on the back of a logging truck. It could winch a forty-ton tree trunk up a thousand feet of steep mountainside until a falling boulder had killed the owner and destroyed the front half of the dragline truck.

Flipping the truck through a few of the twenty-four gears and winding through the streets to the on-ramp was second nature for Hooker. The roll and rumble of the engine were what he liked to think his blood sounded like rolling and rumbling through his veins. Flipping the blinker, he downshifted and wound the steering wheel as the giant lumbered lazily around the corner and began to drop down onto the I-280.

His right foot feathered back slightly, and as the needle he wasn't watching dropped just under 2,100 rpm, his right hand popped the shifter out of fourth, and he palmed the nob up into fifth and danced his toes on the gas pedal as the giant began to roar down the on-ramp. The now

1,200 horses roared up the twin stack pipes just behind the cab as Hooker bypassed sixth and seventh and jammed the gearbox straight into the eighth and rolled out on the freeway dressed for dancing—empty and under a full moon. Fifteen seconds later, eleven tons of yellow and blue steel was rolling toward Highway 101, twenty-five miles per hour over the limit and still climbing.

"Hooker?" He ignored the sideband radio behind his head.

"Hooker, you had better answer me, or I'll start calling you by a different name." The sweet voice oozed from the speakers directly behind his head and could not be missed.

He rolled his eyes, reaching behind his head where the microphone hung. "Go ahead, Momma."

The woman was as much his mother as his Uncle Willie was his real uncle. But they were a significant half of the only family he ever really had.

"Sugar, there is a little birdy out there talking about a big truck not obeying the speed limit."

Shit! Sheriff Deputy Podell, hated by 'most everyone. They called him Poodle behind his back. "Is the dog huntin' or leashed to a tree?"

"Running wild in the street, darlin'—just thought you'd want to know, and you still have plenty of time to make your flat tire. Please don't ruin my evening, sweetheart. You know I worry about you." The voice was soft and sweet and sounded like a young Marilyn Monroe or the best wet dream you could think of. But the voice didn't match the woman as she put down the desk stand microphone and slowly rolled her extra heavy-duty, custom-made, oversized, all-steel chair back around to her main desk.

The dark room was punctuated by the small pools of light from the tiny desk lamps. Three women wrangled most of the radios operating in the entire South Bay area surrounding San Jose and Santa Clara. The business was simply called 'Dispatch.' Some called it Night Dispatch. Either worked for Dolly as long as they called her. Even though some traffic came in from plumbers and alarm companies during the day, the bulk of the business came after the sun went down. By three am, even the police radios were handled through dispatch. The city and county quite literally went through Dolly's switchboard.

Of the near half ton of female flesh occupying the room at the moment, almost half sat behind the large, custom-made black walnut desk. There lay one chief adornment on the desk: a large, highly-polish tree limb paperweight carved to read *The Stick*—meaning, *the stick you stir stuff up with*—and Dolly was the only person allowed to touch it, much less use it.

The buck started and stopped with the giant woman affectionately known as *Momma* by many of the 'homeless waif' young tow truck drivers who learned fast: at least one person in their world cared about them —Dolly.

"Think he listened?" The voice floated from the younger dispatcher, Dina, who could still possibly buy her pants at a regular store if she were lucky. The business of answering service and dispatching is a nonstop eight-hour torture of doing nothing but sitting, talking, and eating. Between calls, Dolly occupied herself in dispatch's large kitchen to satisfy her passions for cooking, eating, and feeding the multitudes at her twelve-person table.

"If he knows what's good for him," Dolly growled as she picked up her pen. "Call him for an ETA." Estimated time of arrival was the lifeblood of a defensible dispatch log.

The middle dispatcher keyed her headset microphone, "Unit 1-4-1?"

"1-4-1, go."

"ETA?"

The radio squawked, and then a short bark as Hooker was down-shifting with an open keyed mic, "Um, got a little traffic out here. Probably be about another six or eight minutes, over."

"10-4, Hooker. Just let us know when you get there."

She side glanced over to Dolly to see the woman nodding her head as if listening to some unheard melody. Confirmation of Hooker behaving himself was music to Dolly's ears like none other. The dispatcher smiled as she flipped another switch and plugged in a line, answering, "South Bay Alarm, how may I help you?"

The dimly lit dispatch room was brighter than the dark along the side of the road where Hooker rolled up behind the Cadillac El Dorado. The flat tire was on the right rear, the one in the mud.

Not thinking, Hooker pulled his mic from behind his head instead of the yellow towing radio's microphone. "1-4-1, show me 10-97. I don't see a member anywhere. Didn't you say this was a club call?"

Dolly looked up at the two dispatchers, then back around at the radio. Spinning her girth around with unnatural grace, she grabbed the *lollypop* or desk stand microphone. "Hooker, you stay in the truck. We'll try the callback number." She thought about it a second. After being in the business for so many years, all of her internal alarms were going off at once.

"Hooker?"

"Yes, ma'am."

"Son, why don't you back away from the car until we straighten this out?" She took a large breath. "Just give it about a hundred yards, would you?" She knew there should have been a highway patrol or someone standing by at 12:30 in the morning.

There were two clicks on the radio as Hooker acknowledged by keying the mic with a double tap.

The young dispatcher Patty leaned back, looking at Dolly. She shook her head to confirm the *no answer* to the number she had dialed. Her much larger boss held up her hand with four fingers in the air, as a visual confirmation as she spoke into another microphone. "10-4 unit 7-1-9-Kilo, tow truck is standing by about one-hundred yards north."

Dolly muttered under her breath the holy prayer of all-night dispatchers: *And now we wait.*

The California Highway Patrol car glided past Hooker and eased over to the shoulder as it approached the large white car. The red lights were flashing, casting eerie shadows as another car slid by in the fast lane as far away as it could get from whatever was going on at this time of the morning.

Dolly's voice whispered from the speakers, "Hooker, the chip just called ninety-seven. Do you have eyes on him?"

Hooker whispered back, even though his truck's twin pipes and giant engine could never be classified as stealthy, "Be vewy vewy quiet... we're hunting wabbits," he called back in his best Elmer Fudd imitation. He watched as the officer slipped slowly out of his door with his right hand on his service pistol.

Hooker nodded to himself as the officer slowly eased the door almost closed. The dome light was off, the interior of the patrol car dark to prying eyes. Even Hooker couldn't tell if a second officer was in the car or not, usually not.

The officer inched along the driver's side of the Cadillac, almost running his butt along the chrome strip presenting the smallest target, and yet getting the best view of the interior. As he reached the backseat window, he rotated and gave his front to the car as he leaned down to get a better look at something in the back seat.

Hooker jumped as the officer buckled in the middle and jerked like a marionette as his back exploded through his highly starched shirt. The rag doll, once a police officer, was thrown six feet out into the traffic lane.

Hooker's right hand slammed down on the large red brake disengage button and dropped the gearshift as his left foot engaged the clutch. As the shifter snicked into the reverse cog, Hooker dumped the clutch and floored the gas pedal. The rear window of the Cadillac exploded into a crazed pattern, and then a large hole appeared. The eleven-ton monster roared backward up the freeway as all eight drive tires threw dirt and gravel.

Six pits appeared in Hooker's windshield-turned-target. The engine screamed as it hit well into the redline, and Hooker still didn't let up on the gas.

Buckshot, or what he thought was buckshot, rattled off the windshield a second time but left no pits. So Hooker jumped on the brakes, opened the clutch, and whipped the steering wheel a flick to the right and then harder to the left as the giant truck's tires all howled in a ten-part harmony as the vehicle slewed around and was now faced the wrong way up the freeway. Hooker slammed the gearshift into high second and dumped the clutch and worked the truck back up toward the get-outta-Dodge gear. He thought he might have heard more of the heavy buckshot rattle around in the tow rigging, but he also figured it might just be his imagination.

Letting the truck run itself down the main lane of the 101, he reached back with his left hand to grab his microphone from behind his head, as his right hand slapped its way through to the last gear in the second tier of gears.

"Dolly, the chip is dead," he called. "Shotgun with a double aught buck is my guess. The license plate was Charlie Adam X-ray Niner One Five."

"Got it, Hooker. Officers on the way," said the consummate professional, but then the mother took over. "Are you okay?"

"Dings in my windshield, but I'm okay." His hands were starting to shake. "Mom, it was a set-up."

"Doors open, Hooker. Coffee is always on." She knew when a driver had crossed a line of comfort, or worse, tolerance, the office was a safe haven for Hooker. "The Chips will want to be able to find you soon, and probably the sheriff, as well. I'll call the captain and get him over here. Careful coming down Story. The boys have been out tonight. You don't need a 45 or 9mm round through your cab, too."

Hooker clicked the mic key twice, downshifting as he surged the wrong way up the long straight ramp. A hard right, back over the overpass, and he felt the powerful ass-end drift out screaming of hot rubber sliding sideways on the only slightly damp night asphalt. Stomping on the accelerator, he powered back up through the second gear of the third tier and 70 mph. *Let the boys try to hit this moving target,* he thought as he hit the city street's 35 mph speed zone and pushed the truck up through the eighty mark, roaring past a collection of Asian street punks standing gape-mouthed on the corner. Hooker laughed a sardonic deep-throated chuckle when, out of the corner of his eye, he caught one of the kids reaching under his shirt for what had to be a pistol tucked in his waistband. *Been tried before, buddy.* He pulled the chain for the air horn and gave it two short blasts in salute. The kid was not earnest about shooting the highballing truck—he was just posing for his gang brothers.

Hooker rode the brakes instead of using the noisy air brakes in deference to the neighborhood. As he brought the rig quietly around the corner, he drifted the shifter into eighth gear, or semi-low third, as he pulled up into the large parking lot.

Grabbing the microphone behind his head, he squeezed the key. "Coming in."

As the engine rattled down to silence, and he slipped down out of his door, the heavy steel-plated door swung open and a very large shadow stood backlit, waiting.

As Hooker approached the doorway, Dolly quietly stated, "Plates were on a Ford half-ton in Gilroy this afternoon. The guy didn't even know they were gone." She stepped back a few feet then turned on her bare feet and waddled back toward the kitchen. "This sort of thing happens when you're pushing ninety-two and still driving into town without a license. The daughter he lives with didn't even know he had gone into town." She looked back at Hooker. "That happens when you drink heavy before noon."

Dolly stuck out her left arm and stopped herself on the door jamb with her right. She waved the great left wobbling arm and hand toward the two dispatchers huddled in the two pools of dim light. "Patty, Hooker. Hooker, my new girl Patty." She turned to give him a hard look. "And no sniffing her neck until she has gained at least forty pounds. She's my brother-in-law's baby girl, and he has a bad temper and several shotguns."

The young girl plopped her face into her hands.

"Hey, Patty, nice to meet you."

In a good imitation of her aunt, she waved a wobbling but slightly smaller arm at Hooker. The glow of the dim light didn't do much to hide the burn of the blush on her face and ample upper chest.

Dolly moved farther into the kitchen and came to rest in front of the stove as Hooker quietly quick-stepped over to the two dispatchers and nuzzled into the large neck of the quiet bleach-teased blonde wearing a well-stretched tank top T-shirt. She softly giggled as he nuzzled near her ticklish ears.

"And don't you be nuzzling Dina's neck either, young man. She's getting married in two months," Dolly continued from the stove.

"Yes, ma'am, just congratulating her, Dolly." Stepping around to face her, he mouthed, "Really?" She nodded as she rubbed both hands on her belly, and then put her finger up to her lips and nodded toward the kitchen. Hooker's eyes went up a notch. As he passed around the back of her, he nuzzled back into her neck, whispering, "Pregnant women are so very sexy." He danced away from her horrified slap and jumped over to

Patty for a quick nuzzle; making her jump as he whispered, "I just couldn't wait a whole month."

The young girl had a horrified, offended look on her face as he strolled back to pay attention to Dolly. She looked at the older operator, and then they both grabbed at each other as they broke-up into fits of giggles.

Dina leaned over to the younger girl and confided, "He's always this bad, but when you need the shirt off his back, it's in his hand before you can ask." She smiled at the thought of Hooker without his shirt, and then realized the younger gal was having the same thoughts as she watched him walking back to the kitchen. She giggled and playfully slapped the new sister in lust. "You are so bad." The two giggled as they turned back to the large board of holes and lights, and then stole a last glance at the retreating hind end of male, which led to more giggles.

The giggles stopped only when they heard a throat clearing in the kitchen. Dolly did not need to look to know what was going on. She had been doing the job longer than the two girls had been out of diapers.

3

The young man stood behind the large woman stirring the sauce in the pot and reached around and gave her a long soft hug, almost hanging on for support, his trim bearded jaw resting on her shoulder.

"Are you going to be okay?" She continued to stir so she didn't have to look at him and expose the wet red eyes she had been wiping.

He leaned his head against her head and rested. "I guess." He took a deep quick breath and sighed. "I think it was John Senol."

She sagged, and was quiet for a moment, weighing the information. Quietly, she confirmed it with a slow nod.

Hooker's eyes stung at the confirmation as he whispered more to himself, "His little girl just turned two this last month." Dolly just nodded. Turning to the cupboard for a glass, he added, "I don't think I'd want to be the captain this morning."

"Nope." She raised her head and stared at the wall behind the stove, seeing too many other things. She called out, "Dina, any word on Captain Davis?"

"He just passed King and Story, so about two minutes." She plugged in a cord and keyed the boom mic at her jaw. "10-4 3-7-8, we have you 10-8. You'll be looking for a 1978 Gold Pacer with a flat tire. Let me know when you get there, Danny." She looked over at Patty and mouthed the word 'newbie.' The younger girl made large eyes and rolled them as she planted her face in her right hand and began to giggle in quiet laughter.

Dolly tasted the sauce from the spoon she was blowing on, nodded and put it down, and then headed for the door. As she cleared the kitchen door, she glared at the two dispatchers. "You two better not be making fun of the new kid Danny. He's very sweet, and I want him around for a while."

"Yes, ma'am," they chorused.

Opening the door as the knock came from the outside, she stood there with her left fist buried deep in what was probably her hip. Slowly shaking her head, she backed up and let the highway patrol captain into the hallway. "Sauce is done, and I'll be starting the pasta directly. Coffee is at least four hours old, and Hooker's in the kitchen. Why don't you two go use the office? I'll bring you the coffee."

The officer removed his hat as he crossed the threshold, revealing the gray flattop haircut standing ridged from the decades of brushings. His craggy face, abused by teenage acne, softened as he leaned over and kissed her on the cheek. "Thanks," he muttered softly as he kept moving.

She quietly closed the heavy armored steel door standing between her and her 'girls' and the not so nice world a few feet away. It had not always been this way, but over the years, the neighborhood changed, and after one harrowing night of blazing guns, the steel door was installed. As was her habit, she touched her two right fingers to her lips in a kiss, and then pressed them on an escutcheon directly above the doorknob—a badge with the number 701 on it—the same badge number of the officer who died that night.

Hooker stepped out of the kitchen and took the officer's hand. The captain greeted him. "There is a juvenile over at county with a fork in his hand. Know anything about it?"

Hooker just looked him in the eye and weighed his options. "There's a young officer lying dead on southbound 101, too. Who do you really want to talk about?"

"In the office," growled the older man. Looking back over his shoulder at Dolly, "Double the sugar, please." Nodding at Hooker's back, he continued, "It's going to be a long night."

A snap glance over at the dispatchers across the room, and he was turning into the office behind the young man in the leather jacket. He was already loosening his tie.

"10-4, Danny. I'm showing you 10-97 on call number November Delta 0-2-1."

The older officer closed the office door slowly as he weighed the young man before him. He had heard about Hooker but had never met him. Mainly, he looked like a street tough: a curly mop of black hair, tight and trimmed to the jawline beard, and a white T-shirt and raked jeans over the engineer boots favored by most of the hard-core bikers. With over thirty years as a highway patrol officer, he also knew his background was coloring his perception of the kid. But if Dolly said he was her golden child, then it was her church, and he would just have to tread lightly until he understood the liturgy.

Placing his hat upside down on the table, he lowered himself into the chair across the table from Hooker as Dolly pushed her way through the door.

"Why, it's pitch-black in here. Let me turn on some lights," Dolly fussed as she set the large mug of coffee in front of the officer who was trying to wake himself up by washing his face and hair in his hands.

"Please don't," Hooker, responded softly. "The extra light would disturb the girls. It reflects off the notes on the board, and they can't see the right holes for the plugs." Dolly and he both knew it was a bullshit reason, but she nodded and backed out.

"Chet," she added, using his shortened family name, "I have pasta with meat sauce ready when you want it."

"Thanks, Dolly, but let me wake up first," he said as he registered it was only 2:20 in the morning. He groaned inwardly and looked over at Hooker.

"No, I'm good, Dolly, thanks anyway. It did smell great, though. Maybe reruns tomorrow."

She slowly closed the door with a quiet click and padded back to her desk as the yellow pool of light and mounds of paperwork hid the romance novel, she knew she would never get to tonight or any time soon. She looked over at the two girls, the older could feel the heat of her look, wagged her head, meaning still no word from the officers at the scene. She creaked down into her custom steel welded chair, and for the first time, regretted making the office soundproof.

The two men sat silently sipping on the steaming thick, gutsy coffee, each busy with their own thoughts, and neither much thinking about the events earlier in the night. A dim light glowed through the soundproofed windows from the small lamps in the dispatch room.

Looking for answers in his mug of coffee he knew were not there, the officer rumbled a low throat-clearing rasp. "You look after people because you really care." The officer watched the young man with his one eye as the other closed against the steam from the coffee.

The kid shrugged with a roll of his left leathered shoulder. His face was a clear statement of 'Yeah, so what?' But there was a slight hiccup in the movement of the mug to his lips as if he suddenly realized it was indeed something he did.

Slowly setting the mug down as if he weren't sure he wanted to let go of the security of the warm stoneware handle, Hooker looked up into the eyes of the officer. "And your point would be?" He presented a full press of street tough, with a twenty-mile stare of pure cold steely-green eyes, the heat just below the surface singeing the edges of the eyes and words.

The eyes held for a few seconds before the older acquiesced and passed back a low shrug of his own. "Just saying." The much older officer knew you don't work a lifetime in the gutter without some of the gutter getting on you, even on the relatively clean streets of the Golden State's highways. But a caring person on the streets was a good thing to have, and even better to know. He had his confirmation about Dolly's *golden child,* and it was good enough for him.

Another sip of coffee and he dove into the debriefing, even as informal as it was. "You were the first there." He put his mug down and folded his hands together on the table in front of him. "What made you back off?"

Hooker started to shrug but thought more about what had warned him. "When you roll up on a member… auto club member," the officer nodded in understanding, "there is always a person who is happy to see you, waving with at least one hand and sometimes two, big smiles, especially in the middle of the night. But tonight, there was nobody there. No one was standing on the side of the road, jumping up and down waving their arms. It was just—I don't know—wrong." He stopped drawing patterns on the table with his finger and looked up. "And I didn't see the flat tire. They had called it in as a rear right flat. It was in the dirt, but not flat. It looked as if they were ready to drive off."

"Did you see anyone in the car?"

"No, the dome light was off, as were the headlights, but I think the car was still running. I mean, who waits in the pitch black of night, and not put some kind of light on?"

The captain nodded, and scratched the middle of his flattop, nodding as he thought for a moment before he stated, "You're right, they don't."

4

Dolly knocked on the door and opened it. In her right hand, she carried a tray with a plate of food and a carafe of more coffee. Placing the tray down on the table, she set the plate in front of the gray-haired officer. "I know you won't have time later to get any food, and I remembered you don't like pasta, so I made you an omelet and toast."

Captain Davis looked at the huge omelet. Probably at least four eggs or more, with what looked like Linguica sausage slices, and a white cheese oozing out around the mushrooms falling out of the open mouth of the omelet. All smothered with a long-simmered meat sauce. To balance the plate, Dolly had stacked four pieces of wheat toast. "Whoa, Dolly, what about my diet?" he complained half-heartedly.

Pouring the man more coffee with one hand, she reached over to pick up the top piece of toast, took a bite out of it, and replaced the remainder to the stack. Dolly then offered the carafe to Hooker with a twinkle of the devil in her eye. "There, now you have the diet platter," she teased with a giggle, as she nudged the older man almost off his chair with a side push of her plentifully padded hip.

"Hooker?" Dina called from her station.

Laughing at Dolly's ideas of *diet*, the young man stiffly unwound himself from the straight chair he had been sitting in for what seemed like hours. "Yeah, baby?" He wandered toward the door with his mug held out to Dolly for a refill.

"I've got Manny on the phone."

Stepping into the larger darker room, he glanced over at the large school clock hanging with its own pool of light on the wall. Calculating distance and time, he replied, "Tell him I'll have his jump-start at quarter after five. And remind him he owes me a ten-spot," pointing at the dispatcher with his finger like a gun and snapping his thumb down. Then realizing what he had just done, he apologized.

Turning, he handed the mug of coffee back to Dolly. "Here, finish this for me. I have to go get me some jelly donuts, and don't you dare tell Stella." He kissed her on the cheek and was out the steel door before she could protest or feed him.

She just rolled her eyes and slumped into herself and quietly mused to herself, "Kids. It's a wonder he has any meat on his bones at all." She looked at the mug of coffee, and kind of snarled like a dog not trusting the food in front of it. She raised the cup, took a sip, and cringed. "Needs some cocoa," she muttered to herself, looking back into the office to make sure her other man was still busy with his food. She then shoved off for the kitchen. "Girls, I'm making cocoa."

"Sounds right," followed by, "Ditto," was acknowledged with a nod from the queen bee. Caffeine and calories kept the night shift running.

Humming a senseless tune—one she probably learned in the kitchen from her mother or grandmother—the queen bee was where she loved to be... cooking for others and being the center of the universe for things going on in the South Bay.

5

The black-clad shadow strolled across the parking lot. It usually had no more than a few cars in it, except during New Year's Eve, when the lot could be holding upwards of thirty tow-trucks, and a few police squad cars. It's hard to look at the seemingly small puma-brick building and imagine it could hold over fifty drivers and their wives or girlfriends, or just someone who was riding around with them, but Hooker had seen a packed house before. Two years ago, a call for a tow-truck had come in, and the dispatcher realized there wasn't a single truck out in the over four hundred square miles of the greater San Jose area—everyone was at Dolly's.

Unlocking the door, he stood back as the large orange tabby erupted out of the cab, bouncing off the side fuel tank and into the grass. He waited for his partner, as he knew it would only be a minute or two at the most. He turned and saw the beat-up one-eyed street-tough cat starting to go into a crouch. Whether it was a mouse, bird, or a fight, Hooker didn't have time to indulge his cab mate.

"Come on, Box." He snapped his fingers. "Gotta go get some jelly donuts for Manny."

At the sound of one of the few humans he could tolerate, the cat broke from the grass and shot over to the truck. Bouncing off the tank, off the door, slipping through Hooker's legs and past the front of his seat, he was in his box before Hooker even had the door closed or the truck fired up, purring the whole way.

Hooker just wagged his head as he turned the key and hit the start button on the side of the dashboard. The giant engine fired back to life and shook the cab. The radios all lit up, and the eight-track came to life as Tennessee Ernie Ford moaned about a giant of a man buried in the bottom of a mine. It was almost enough to make Hooker purr. His right hand reached down and scratched the twenty-plus-pound ball of fur behind what was left of a scarred ear, "Maybe Manny will have something meaty for you this morning, eh, Box old buddy?"

His hand shoved the small shifter into the second range, and moved the large shifter into first, as he eased out the clutch on seventh gear. The large truck rolled forward into the last of the dark night.

Reaching up behind his head, he clicked the key on the microphone twice, as he shifted up to eighth, and the double clicks returned. The traffic light was still glowing cherry red as the big yellow truck slid through the intersection at fifteen over the speed limit, and as Hooker again shifted into the next higher gear, and swept the behemoth up the ramp and onto the 101 headed north toward the only donuts he would allow in his cab.

The night air would have been nice, but there was just a tinge of a morning fog putting a bite in the freeway wind, so his window was uncharacteristically rolled up. It was common enough for Hooker to show up at a wreck in the middle of a cold winter night eating an ice cream cone. The many times he had stood looking at bodies smeared through bad wrecks on Blood Alley could have garnered him a nickname from the officers who work the night shifts, but his name was enough. Mostly, the officers were just glad to see him. Whether he got a tow or not, he was always the first to pop flares, direct traffic or break out his broom and trash can to help clean up the mess. Many times, it netted him tows that were not his, or at least a much-appreciated unopened box of CHP 30-minute flares left on the rear working deck of his truck.

The low rumbling hum of the engine combined with the muted whine of the tires wasn't enough to drown out the almost whisper of his least used radio—a small ham sideband walkie-talkie he had reworked into a static radio. "Hooker, are you out there?"

Hooker flipped the switch over his head to engage the same microphone. Reaching back behind him, he grabbed the mic and squeezed the key. "Go ahead, Sweets."

The whisper persisted in an eerie, surreal way. "Bad vibes, man, really bad vibes. All night, I have had bad feelings, man. All night, I've seen things about you."

"I'm fine, Sweet. What did you see?"

"Can't talk about it on the waves, man. Come by the house for breakfast when I wake up. We'll talk then, man." The voice was as smooth on the radio's scratchy little speaker as it was on any stereo listening to KLIV from midnight until the sun came up with Sweet Sam at the helm.

"Three pm it is, Sweets, three it will be. Get some sleep." Hooker hung up the microphone and switched the toggle back to its regular setting connecting him directly to the radio on the credenza behind Dolly. The radio link had meant the difference between work and going broke many times. It was probably equal amounts of her having a soft spot for him and she knowing he could be counted on to do some of the tougher jobs in towing. It also had a lot to do with the fact on any given day, he spent twenty hours or more in the cab or within earshot of his radios... or told her where she could call him. Either way, she had a direct line to him rivaling an umbilical cord.

He downshifted for the steep off-ramp turn that would dump him onto the parkway and four blocks from the Whole Donut, as he muttered to himself, "Sweet, sweet Sweets." Shaking his head, he shifted again and hit the street still about twenty over the limit but slowing as he bled off speed with the Jake brake, rattling windows in the business district.

Sweets and Hooker went back many years from when Hooker had first started towing with a bogus driver's license at the age of fourteen. Hooker had rolled up on a jump-start in the early morning at the radio station. It was a 1959 Buick La Sabre with huge wings spreading out and away from a large rear deck. All Hooker could think about at the time was what a great car it would be to take to a drive-in theater. The back seat was as big and roomy as a queen-sized bed.

The lanky black man had been standing there next to the driver's side door, and as Hooker got out of the truck and walked over, Sweet had started slowly shaking his head and clicking his tongue. He was dressed in an all-white linen suit with a red tie as if he were going out clubbing up in the city on a Saturday night with a couple of fine ladies on his arms. His appearance was complete with a white linen fedora and dark glasses. As Hooker got closer, the slender black man started humming, "Humm uhn ahh, they do make them younger and younger every day."

Hooker ignored the *younger* remark and asked what the problem was and not really paying any attention to the white cane in the man's hand stretched along his body. At fourteen, and trying to appear twenty, who's tallying up the dark glasses and a white cane in the middle of the night and a car that won't start?

"I think it's a dead battery, man," the dapper dude said with his head rolled back almost like he was looking more at the tops of the trees than at Hooker.

Hooker just shrugged and popped open the hood. With his flashlight, he looked over the battery and checked the connections. Wiggling the cable, he whipped out his small wrench and tightened the connection. "Go ahead," he called.

"Go where, man?"

"Try it."

"Try what?"

Hooker looked around the hood to see the man still standing where he had first met him. He hadn't moved a step. He wasn't even trying to open the door.

"Get in and try to start the car," Hooker explained shortly, if not a little testy.

"No can do, Roger Roo," the guy rhymed.

"Why not?" Hooker asked.

"Don't know how."

"Isn't this your car?" Hooker was now very confused and was just starting to wonder about the dark glasses and the guy's behavior.

"Sure it is. Paid cash for it three years ago."

"Then why don't you start it?"

"I don't know how."

Just as Hooker was starting to figure he had been played for a sucker, another much larger black guy came out of the building saying, "Oh great, you're here." Walking over and taking Sweets by the elbow, he started to guide him around the car to the passenger side. "Let me get Sweets in his seat, and we'll be set to start it."

Hooker was stunned and stood there saying nothing.

Sweets turned his head in Hooker's general location. "You didn't know I was blind, did you."

Hooker, now embarrassed, swallowed, "No, no I didn't."

"It's okay, daddy-oh. I didn't know you were white either," and smiled with his hallmark ten-megawatt smile. "But I did know you're not old enough to drive."

Danny, Sweet's brother, driver, and caretaker helped him in the door, so he didn't hit his head or crunch his hat. Danny was the stereotypical linebacker turned bodyguard, with the nice suit pants and a leather jacket for a sport coat. The only difference with Danny was he had never done anything except take care of his brother since Sweets was in high school and a welding tank in the metal shop had exploded. A large piece of steel had hit Sweets in the head, taking his eyesight, but leaving him with a couple of quirky gifts.

One was the ability to remember every song he had ever listened to—who the artist was, the recording company, how it had done on the charts, and any residual effects the song had on the artist or music in general. With that ability and a deep voice like honey in the summer sun, a very lucrative career in radio had supported him and his brother, along with their mother.

The other gift, if you could call it such, could cause sleepless nights and unidentified anxiety: a quirky gift of seeing things—not necessarily in the future, but just things. Sometimes he just let it go because it didn't mean anything to him, but sometimes he knew who it was connected to, and that was when he called Hooker.

Sweets never told anybody Hooker's real age, but on his real twenty-first birthday, the three of them had a quiet dinner together to celebrate his majority.

Danny didn't say very much, but when he did, it was important. The night in the parking lot as Danny closed the door behind Sweets, he walked to the front of the Buick and gently lowered the hood until it quietly caught with a dull metallic click. Turning to Hooker, he shared the truth of the night. "My brother told me about you yesterday. There was nothing wrong with the car. We just needed to meet you." Handing him a simple white card with two phone numbers on it, he said, "The top number is the house, the bottom is here, both are unlisted. Don't lose the card."

Hooker nodded as Danny slipped a fifty-dollar bill into his hand. "Don't write this call up. You were never here. This call only went through Dolly at Night Dispatch. If you ever have a problem, talk to Dolly. If you're ever hungry, go see Dolly. If you need money, come see me." He turned and walked to the open driver's door. As he started to fold his towering mass through the doorframe, he paused, "What's your name?"

"Hooker."

"Fair enough, Hooker. We'll be in touch."

Hooker blew two sharp blasts on the air horn as he pulled in behind the Whole Donut. The rear parking lot was a field of concrete with random parked tractor-trailers and cars. Out front, there was the obligatory early morning clot of San Jose PD squad cars.

The back screen-door screeched as the human form of twisted wire stepped a foot out. "Hey, Hooker, how's it hanging?"

"Choke and puke, with cream on the side, Ralph. Same as it always is, same as it always will be. How are you and the missus?"

"Fighting like cats and dogs as usual. She's top dog, and I'm as pussy whipped as I wanna be." He rubbed the last of his unfiltered Camel straight out between his fingers as he field stripped the butt, a habit left over from his three tours of duty in Vietnam where he had left half of his guts and was forced to come home, bringing home a just turned sixteen-year-old girl he married on her eighteenth birthday. The two had less than nothing, but by leveraging some help with his army buddies and the VA, he sunk their life into the Whole Donut, and the community never let them down.

"What can I get for you this morning?" Looking at his watch, he then added, "Oh, at this hour I'm guessing you're picking up a jump-start for Manny?"

"Yeah, his wife is down south, so he needs his fix."

"Coming right out!" He shuffled back into the kitchen, calling out the order to his wife in Vietnamese. The hum of the fans on the roof was a dull massage as the day prepared to wake up and take notice of the sun. The air over the South Bay was taking on the special glow the thin hanging fog would get about an hour or so before dawn.

Hooker's right hand dangled down between the seats and absently twiddled with the larger intact ear as Box's purr echoed the deep quiet rumble of the turning idle of the lopping engine. The eight-track clicked into the next round as the New Riders of the Purple Sage softly harmonized about tumbling tumbleweeds. Hooker let his eyes close and drifted across the desert, and the boys from another time crooned in a bygone way.

The screen door squealed, and Mai Lin walked out, wiping her left hand in her apron. The shy smile on her face could light up Spartan Stadium in Hooker's opinion. He opened the door and reached down with a five-dollar bill. Mai Lin handed him the box of donuts and pursed her lips with a "pfut" at the money. Smiling, she instructed Hooker, "You give Mr. Manny a big hug for me. You tell him, he is no good not to come around here and see his goddaughter, Mai Lin."

"Okay, Mai Lin, I'll tell him, but I will leave the hugging thing up to you." Closing the door, he watched her laughing and walking back to work where she would put in an eighteen-hour day and never complain. She was in a good home, with a good husband who worshiped the ground she walked upon—she would tell you she was blessed, and Hooker didn't doubt it, but he knew it was Ralph who was the blessed one.

Sticking the transmissions in seventh gear and shoving the box of donuts down deeper in the passenger seat, he let out the clutch. As much to Box as himself, said, "Let's go see Manny, Box."

Two blocks over and he took a left leading to a right, and another left and would become Almaden Expressway, named after California's first commercial winery—or as the lower life would raise a glass to, the first winery to put out wine in a box.

Hooker chuckled at his old joke and looked down at his constant companion. "Should we get a little Box down in the Almaden Valley, Box?" Hooker was known for a few sips of a beer a couple of times a year, but because he always considered himself to be on duty, he never really drank, so the *Box* was in reference of where he had found his companion—half-dead in a box behind the Almaden Winery. It was the only fight Hooker had known Box to lose. He had been one torn up kitty.

The street flowed out into the expressway, and Hooker wound the truck up into a higher gear. Glancing at his watch, he shifted again and laid the hammer down, as the white lines became just a little more solid-looking as they blurred together. *Where does the time go these days, where does it go?* Arriving at five-fifteen at Manny's was important, and it was going to be close.

6

J ust off the Almaden Expressway, deep in the Almaden Valley, the big yellow truck roared around the sweeping curve leading into what Hooker thought of as the *Hill of Stupid.* In homage to California's roots, the developer, or someone equally as stupid, had started naming a series of streets 'Calle de' something. So giving directions to places like Manny's home for the last twenty years, which had been as simple as turn left on Sage Road, then left on Rim Drive, and go about a mile, look for the pinkish building on the left with the red tile roof, had turned into right on Calle de Dios, left on Calle de Verde, right on Calle de Verde Gras, right on Calle de Altos, left on Calle de Suenos, right on Calle de Alta Verde, left on Rim and look for the pinkish house that doesn't look like the rubber stamp houses.

Hooker couldn't help but hate the developers who had no idea what the names meant, and the people who bought the ticky-tacky claptrap soon-to-be shacks encouraging the developers to cross the small valley and start crawling their way up the other side. Some days his favorite fantasy was a horrific wildfire—to scorch and cleanse the earth. But he knew there would be no stopping the rape of the valley. He was just thankful for the few orchards still lining Blossom Hill Road, as well as the bean fields.

Turning up onto Rim Drive, he let the engine roar for the last quarter mile with the twin pipes rattling the windows of the overpriced wannabe fake Tudor manors, with the two and three-car garages poking out like a dog's snout, and two cars parked in the driveways because you know the garage is stuffed full of crap.

The only hand-built adobe plastered hacienda in the whole valley came into view. The wheelchair-bound figure waved as Hooker pulled up across the driveway. The driveway led down and around to the garage hidden from the street. Only the giant gate in the front pierced the front wall rising ten feet to the red clay hand and leg formed barrel tiles on the roof. A much younger and able-bodied Manny and his wife Estelle, had gathered the clay, mixed, and shaped the barrels to be dried in the hot summer sun, and then carefully stacked around a bonfire made of wood and coke. They set the fuel ablaze and fed it for ten hours, firing the clay tiles in the traditional way.

As Hooker slid down out of the cab, holding the box of jelly donuts, Box bounced down to the tank and shot out toward the small patch of grass beside the driveway. For not the first or hundredth time, Hooker admired the deep thick walls he knew contained stacked bales of straw to create the two-foot mass. The concept of the super-insulated walls came from the prairies of Nebraska. Manny had grown up first in a dug-out hole in the ground, covered over with two feet of sod cut from the prairie floor while his father and mother built a house out of straw bales and plaster. They had lived in it for the rest of the forty years of their lives.

"That Box does like my grass," Manny commented.

"Well, it beats pissing in his box in the truck, eh, Box?" Hooker chuckled as Box shook first one hind leg then the other—shaking off the dew from the taller grass he had just stepped on.

Passing Hooker a disgusted look for his insulting talk, he took two bouncing jumps then into the man's lap with a roaring purr. Settling into a furball facing forward, Box was ready to be carried into the house on four wheels instead of something as pedestrian as walking.

Bombastically, Manny rolled his eyes and lolled his head, looking at Hooker. "Nah, he's not spoiled at all, is he?" They both chuckled at the running joke about the cat's habit for the last few years of hitching a free ride in the wheelchair, since a bullet in his spine had robbed Manny of his mobility.

As they moved through the thick medieval-looking gate, hand-hewn from junipers found on the property twenty years before, their talk was relaxed and casual. The fountain in the center of the inner plaza tinkled with lazy music Hooker always found relaxing, but not enough to take up Stella on her offer for him to come live full-time in the north wing of the hacienda. Manny would even pay to have his small lawn turned to a concrete apron to park his truck on, but the thought of cruising up and down the Hill of Stupid was just too much for Hooker to even contemplate, even as seductive as the offer was. He also knew in his heart of hearts; he would end up weighing a hundred more pounds with Estelle's great cooking.

"So Stella trusted you and ran off."

"Trust schmust, hell, she just stocked plenty of insulin before she left." He grinned back at Hooker, who was still holding the box of forbidden fruit. Well, fruit filling at least.

"That reminds me, your goddaughter gave me hell about you never coming to visit." Hooker pushed open the eight-foot matching doors to the front gate door, running his hand over the adze marks on the iron-hard aged black walnut.

"Screw them, both of them," Manny said without conviction, as he rolled through the doors onto the honed slate entry floor. "Those two haven't stopped long enough these last three years to come up here for even a late-night dinner." Hooker sensed an edge of truth and even a certain underlying hurt and anger from the man who had sponsored not only Mai Lin's citizenship but the founding of the Whole Donut. But he also understood the dangers of not taking some downtime and being consumed by one's profession.

"Have they ever come up here since the shooting?" Hooker laid the box on the giant granite-topped island and looked out the wall of windows over the sink and countertop running along the east-facing wall. The sun was just a half ball of fire with streaks of rays caused by the unseen bits of clouds.

"Screw it. I don't want to ruin a perfect morning. Grab the coffee pot.

The mugs are out here." The older man grabbed the box of contraband and headed for the adjoining sunroom. Wheeling past Box, who was face down in a bowl of his favorite food, he reached over and scratched the cat's back and gently curled his hand into a cone running up the thick meaty tail to the one-inch crook at the end. His ministrations were greeted with a deep appreciative rumble sounding more like Hooker's truck than a cat's purring—or Box was just growling with him mouth full. Manny chuckled as he kept on rolling into his favorite room. The cat was very picky, but when it came to Manny, it was an on-again/off-again relationship changing with the day.

Two hours later, the sun was well up. Box was snoring in a pool of sunshine on his pad made from old down pillows. The two men sat lounging around the table with the empty box and tiny traces of the omelet Hooker had whipped up to help counter the sugar shock to the diabetic system. Manny's injection kit with the spent ampule lay on the table among the carnage.

"So you never saw anyone in the car?"

Hooker shook his head. "No, it was as if the shooter was invisible." He cocked his head, thinking. "In fact, I don't even remember seeing a muzzle blast either."

"If it was a shotgun, and it was a full choke on a long barrel," Manny scratched his chin by rubbing it between his fingers and thumb. "or maybe it was just below the window or something so you couldn't see it." He looked up into the young man's eyes. "I don't know, but it's curious."

"Even if it were below the window, the muzzle blast would have lit up the interior like a bolt of lightning."

"True," the former police officer acknowledged.

"I know my truck isn't quiet, but the window was open, and I didn't hear any gunshot either." He raised his mug and sipped the last of his coffee.

"Hmm," the mind of the older man churned as he looked out across the valley, and back on over thirty years working a beat solving crimes. It was there, he could feel it, and it frustrated him. He just couldn't see the answer—yet.

He looked over at the young driver, whose hand still held onto the handle of the mug on the table and was slumped just a little more as he had fallen asleep sitting up. Manny's heart ached, as he knew the boy probably had been in the truck for at least the last twenty-four, if not forty-eight, hours without any real sleep, just a little shut-eye here and some closed eyes there. He reached across the table and poked at Hookers hand. "Hey."

The head came up, but the eyes were only at half-mast. "Hmm?"

"Go climb into bed. I'll call Dolly's and let them know you're here." He waved the back of his hand at the young man. "Go on—and I mean get naked under the sheets sleeping. Enough of this fully dressed, just stretching out crap. Your eyes are bleeding out of your head, and you need to stop for some downtime." He shooed him some more as Hooker slowly pulled himself up and lumbered off back down toward what was kindly known as 'his room'—a suite with its own living room, master bath, and kitchenette.

"Come on, Box."

"No, leave him be. He's already smart enough to be asleep." The older man just shook his head at the closest thing to a son they had ever had. "I'll wake you if you get a call," as he thought to himself, *Like hell I will—if it's before dinnertime maybe!*

Turning, he sipped on his coffee, watched Box's side slowly move up and down, and thought about a shotgun blast with no sound or muzzle blast in the night. In his experience, it was impossible to silence a shotgun, and hiding the muzzle blast on a dark night would be almost impossible, too.

Softly, he muttered more to himself than the cat, "It just can't be done, Box, it just can't be done. But it was." His body was broken, but his mind was better than ever.

He reached down absently and grabbed his large wheels as he slowly moved toward the phone with the coffee mug jammed between his paralyzed legs. Time to make a couple of calls—calls he could never have made when he was an officer, to people who would never speak to a person in uniform. But first, he had to call Dolly. He glanced over his shoulder at the large schoolhouse clock matching the one in her dispatch room. He pushed a little harder so he wouldn't miss his sister-in-law.

7

Hooker had sat bolt upright at the sound of the silent shotgun as he watched the officer lift off the ground and sit down in the road, slumped like a rag doll. The time telescoped as the body slowly rolled back spinelessly to lay crumpled on the asphalt as Hooker blinked a third time and washed his hands over his face. Stretching his eyes out away from the vision, he knew no matter how much time passed, it would always remain vivid. He only wished for it not to be in his sleep.

The shadow cast by the fountain in the courtyard was on the wrong side of the patio. His mind tried to make sense of the meaning until it finally gelled. It was already afternoon. And then he remembered his lunch date at Sweets' house.

Throwing the covers to one side, he swung around and looked at the clock—two forty-three pm. He folded over and reached for his jeans and caught a strong whiff of his body. Quickly he sat back up with his lip curled, thinking. The math came down to well over forty-eight hours since he had last danced in the water locker, and there was no way he would be allowed anywhere near Sweets smelling like a herd of banded sheep in heat.

As he finally turned off the shower, he heard the distant phone ring.

Intermittent with the rubbing of the plush terry towel bath sheet, he could hear Manny arguing with someone on the phone. The one thing you never wanted to do was argue with Manny, especially on the phone. Hooker chuckled as he remembered a time when he had witnessed Manny in the heat of his favorite battle—on the phone.

It had been about the easement running along the bottom of their property. The conditions of the easement would have prevented Manny from having a barn or raising chickens or even a single horse. Now, Manny could care less about having livestock. Life in Nebraska in general, and one horrible particular memory (having to go to school after plucking hundreds of frozen chickens when the power failed the night before) had cured Manny for life about keeping any kind of livestock, even a family dog. Box was a very special case, and Box knew it.

Manny had been bounced from one functionary to the next higher, all not really understanding Manny had worked longer for the city than they had worn long pants. Manny knew exactly *who* he needed to talk to and who had the authority to rescind the easement. He could have just called his office, and be done with it, but where would the fun be in that? So, Manny, writing down every name and asking for exact spelling and job title along with their direct phone number, would once again go through his entire song and dance. The results were always the same—a transfer to someone with more authority.

With each new person, Manny would roll his head with a beaming toothy smile, and wink at Hooker who was relaxed in the warm afternoon sun of the sunroom. Manny was in heaven, his favorite room, his favorite cat sleeping and purring in his lap, and his favorite game of warfare.

Finally, the game came down to the final showdown. The county commissioner had been his former partner when they worked as beat cops. Each knew more about each other than their own wives ever would. They both knew where the bodies were buried. They knew the other knew it as well, because they had buried them together. When one had been reprimanded, the other was standing right there getting the same. When they were honored by the mayor, and eventually the Governor, they were honored side by side. But only one had taken the bullet. Giving him the edge forevermore.

As the commissioner had answered, Manny changed his tone. The nice guy was gone. The bad cop was out, and he was stomping through the unmarked graves, kicking the thin dirt covers off all the bones, and doing it in full sunshine. He rampaged for almost exactly five minutes with his partner unsuccessfully trying to wedge in a word. Finally, he stopped. In the middle of a sentence, he just stopped. Winking and smiling at Hooker, he held up his thumb, the one finger, then two, then a third and finally, the fourth, and on the other end of the phone was the question.

"Are you done?"

Manny didn't say a word. The silence was deafening, and you knew his former buddy could taste it along with the bile building up in the back of his throat. Manny in his wheelchair with flaming wheels like the chariot of Apollo had come to call, and he wasn't happy—not one bit.

The commissioner had started the county line of song and dance. Manny let it run for almost thirty seconds before he started pounding the speaker part of the phone on a board he had brought in just for the purpose. Ten whacks, ten seconds, and then he counted to three and quietly said, "Paul, you haven't been listening."

Manny quietly read his list of notes, and the names, titles, phone numbers, and responses he had been through that afternoon. At the end, he told the commissioner he had missed his lunch (the remains littered the table between him and Hooker, which required another smile and wink), and he, the commissioner, should check into this miscarriage of the taxpayers, and especially the staunchest of supporter's trust and get back to him in say, about an hour? Then, without waiting for an answer, he had quietly hung up while writing down the time.

The phone had rung about forty-two minutes later. There would be no easement. Manny was free of the county ever annoying him again. Manny's favorite phone sport was winning.

Shaking his head at the memory, Hooker shrugged his leather jacket over his shoulder, and checked the room to make sure there was no real evidence he had been there, he turned and walked down the hall to the main living space. He was rounding the corner as Manny hung up the phone. Hooker walked over to his favorite chair and lowered himself in slowly, as he studied Manny's concerned and concentrating face.

Finally, Manny focused on Hooker. "That was a buddy of mine, a weapons expert." He looked out over the valley as he raised his glass of iced tea and took a long slow pull. Carefully putting the glass back down on the roughhewn table, he looked back at Hooker. "It seems there is a way you could shoot a shotgun at night, and hear nothing, as well as see no muzzle flash."

Hooker's eyebrows rose.

"It matches the strange things the coroner found in the wound, as well."

"You spoke to the coroner?"

"We play poker every Wednesday night, and we've been masonic brothers for well over twenty-five years, why wouldn't I talk to him?"

Hooker just shrugged and rolled his eyes wide to look at the floor and Box soaking up the sun. "So what did he find so strange?"

Manny edged forward, knowing he never had to swear Hooker to confidentiality because he was now in his element as a detective. "The wound had fibers of stainless steel, and there were fifteen dimes in the body cavity."

Hooker frowned. The stack of dimes in a 12-gauge shotgun was an old trick. The sawed-off pump in the cab of his truck was just such a case, but there is only room for fourteen dimes in a standard shell unless you shaved the wadding the extra dime's worth. But why?

"Who would shave the wadding down, just to have an extra meat cutter?" Shrugging his hands in askance, "I mean, if the first buck forty didn't get the job done, what's a cup of coffee extra going to do?"

"Good question," the detective mused. "Good question. And it probably goes to motive," he concluded as he reached for his iced tea, with his mind's eye a hundred miles away.

The two sat thinking as Box rolled over for some more sun on his belly.

"Oh, Karen called. There are a couple of commercial tows waiting for you this afternoon, so when you're ready, give her a whistle."

Hooker smiled and nodded as he pushed himself erect. "Did she mention what or where?"

"She said they're for the Fly, and one was up in Contra at an impound yard, so you can go do it before or after the traffic clears. Maybe it's something for the dead time from seven to nine."

Hooker nodded. "I've got to go over to Sweets' for lunch. He was doing the freaky thing this morning and wants to talk…" he said as he pointed down to Box.

"Oh, sure, leave the mange bucket here. We'll throw together something for him to do." They both looked at the topic of conversation ignoring them. "But make sure you pick him up for the night shift, or he will be pissed all night long, and I'll get the short-end of the stick for it all."

"Deal," Hooker nodded as he strode toward the front door.

As if as an afterthought, Manny mentioned, "Oh, your ten-spot is there on the hall table."

Hooker glanced over and saw a wadded-up bill with a ten showing just a little too obvious. He nonchalantly grabbed it and shoved it in his pocket, feeling it was more like a couple or three bills wadded together. "Thanks, Manny," and he was out the giant door.

As he walked around the fountain toward the front entry gate, he withdrew his hand from his pocket and peeked at the money. As he suspected, there were two bills wadded in the center, a C-note and a Grant. He shook his head and looked back at the front door as he slipped out through the gate.

Typical Manny, he thought, but he also knew the twin saddle-tanks on the truck were getting low, and Hooker was a strictly-cash-for-fuel kind of guy.

As he fired up the monster, his right hand reached down and back, finding the handle that fit only his hand. It was matched up to eight dollars and change in dimes, stacked in the sawed-off pistol-gripped Mossberg. His thumb rubbed the walnut grip as he thought about the fifteen dimes in the dead highway patrolman's body. *Why the extra dimes?*

The truck eased forward and headed back down the Hill of Stupid, but only going through the back way where there were no houses thus far, but just little orange ribbons tied to stakes seeming to migrate a bit more with the passing of each Friday night.

Hooker reached behind his head and double keyed the microphone. A few seconds later, there was a return double click. Dolly was back at work, and Hooker would talk to Karen the day dispatcher later, but first fuel and lunch at Sweets or vice versa.

8

Driving through daytime traffic is in a completely different category than driving the empty streets in the middle of the night. Mr. Obvious would point to the hundreds of cars flowing around the big truck, but that's not it. It's the mix of cars, the light, and the many things vying for one's attention. The first couple of billboards ever put up got a person's attention, as did the first few neon signs, or red signs, or the kind where the lights jump around. But when you line a street with billboards every hundred feet, all filled with red neon lights jumping around, then you just have a mass of oddly pulsing color and light. In that universe, the muted small sign doing nothing glaringly stands out or is totally missed. Much is the same with the little old lady standing stoically on the side of a busy expressway with no car.

It didn't sink into Hooker as his reflexes took over. The left ring finger flexed and triggered the right turn signals as Hooker checked his mirrors, clearing the lane change. He would miss the lady, but it only meant he would have to put the truck in reverse and back up on the shoulder for a few hundred feet. As he changed lanes and got closer to the lady, his mind caught up to what his eyes were seeing.

About sixty feet off the side of the expressway, parked in the cull de sac of a side street, was a light-colored Cadillac de Ville. The lady was wearing a hat with a lace veil and matching white gloves holding a pump shotgun rising to aim at Hooker. The long dress and flat chest weren't the giveaways, but it was the black *men's* shoes and the left hand jacking the pump on the shotgun. His mind may have even missed the first muzzle blast, and because Hooker was engaging all ten sets of brakes, the shooter had misjudged the lead, and the dollar and change of dimes had twirled away across the high hood of the truck. But at point-blank range, the next shot would be different.

A normal person would probably try to swerve away from the pending danger, but Hooker was more a part of the mass he was herding like an elephant down the road and swung even harder toward the shooter. The sudden change in the demeanor caught the shooter off guard, and the flurry of dimes rattled noisily in and around the towing structure on the back bed as the figure in the dress still holding the shotgun became unbalanced and tumbled backward down the small embankment. Hooker stomped harder on the gas pedal and roared away, as he grabbed at the second microphone hanging lower and unused under the dashboard—the microphone he would never have touched under any other circumstances.

"All units in the area of Almaden Expressway and Seneca Street, be on the lookout for a light-colored late-model Cadillac de Ville. Driver was last seen wearing a hat with a white lace veil, long dark grayish granny print dress, white gloves, and men's black shoes. The shooter is also packing and using a pump shotgun. I repeat: the driver is armed with a 12-gauge shotgun and is using it. Armed and very dangerous; approach with caution. And do NOT approach alone, get backup." Hooker let go of the key on the microphone as he shifted into the next higher gear.

The radio squawked. "10-4 units Adam 12 and Bravo Zero-4... Hey, who is this? Unit, identify yourself."

Hooker grimly slowly wagged his head and gave the illegal radio a cold stink-eye as he muttered to himself, "Not on your life, dude."

"Reporting unit, identify yourself." Hooker just kept driving.

As he pulled into the truck stop, he thought more about the coincidence of the shooter. Was he the target? If so, how had the shooter known to be there at that random time of day? Or was it just a cop they were looking for? Or just anybody who would pull over for an old lady on the side of the road, same as Hooker had? And, more importantly, was this the same six-bit killer from this morning, but five miles away from the original kill zone?

Hooker stuck nozzles into the two saddle tanks and climbed up onto the working deck of his truck. Slowly going over every inch of the lift rigging exposed to the shotgun blast, Hooker checked for paint chips or dimes. There were a few old chips he made a note to do some touch-up paint on later, but no obvious new chips, but several white or silver marks where the soft silver dimes had rattled around among the uprights, boom, and cables. Looking around, Hooker almost missed the tiny edge of the little silver disk peeking out from under the edge of a bolted flange.

Taking the point of his pocketknife, he teased the dime out into the open. The trademark icon of the burning torch stared back at him—a 1960 Mercury head dime.

"Hey, Hooker, your tanks are full."

Jerking erect, he looked at the attendant in the door of the control doghouse. "Hey, Billy, do you have an envelope or something like it I can have?"

"How big do you need?" The lanky kid leaned against the door jam, with both hands jammed down in the pockets of his one-piece uniform with the cuffs rolled back almost to the elbows, his only allowable nod to looking cool and pumping gas at the pimple-riddled age of twenty.

Hooker, looking down at the evidence on the deck floor, replied, "Big enough to hold a dime."

Smiling a little too big, the kid withdrew his right hand and held a tiny piece of paper folded into an envelope the size of a thumbprint. "I can finish this off and let you have the paper."

Hooker looked up and realized what the kid was holding would also contain trace amounts of illegal drugs. "It's a perfect size man, but could you make me a fresh one?"

Ducking into the doghouse shed, the kid called back. "Sure. Just give me a minute."

True to his word, he walked out with a fresh yellow envelope made from a legal pad. "Your total comes to ninety-three dollars and sixty-four centavos senor. The envelope is on the house."

Hooker traded the Benjamin Manny had given him earlier for the envelope. Carefully unfolding the envelope, he reached down with his knife and tried to lift the dime, only to have it skate around the bed of the truck.

Seeing he was having trouble, the kid reached out toward the dime. "Here, I'll get it for you Hooker."

"Stop! Don't touch it."

The kid froze.

"Thanks, Billy, but there might be some fingerprints on there we need." The kid backed off. Finally getting the dime against a welded foot flange, Hooker got the blade and paper under the dime and refolded it back into the needed envelope.

Securing the knife blade and stowing the knife in his front pocket, Hooker pulled out his large wallet chained to his belt. Opening the zipper pocket, he stuffed the bindle in and secured it all back into his rear pocket. Taking the receipt from Johnny's hand, he looked at the change, knowing it would soon be a white powder in the kid's nose. Hooker ignored something that was not his business. "Keep the change, man. Today you earned it."

The kid was confused but smiled and stashed the money in his overalls. "Thanks, Hooker, you're the best."

Hooker gave one last glance around the working deck and then jumped down. Reaching into a welded cup of a recess, he withdrew the lead hammer he kept there. Bouncing the hammer on all ten tires, Hooker checked the air pressure. He made his way around his rig as he visually checked the condition of the tread, mentally making notes. If he was lucky, the expensive set of tires might make it to the end of summer.

Returning the tire hammer to its hole, he traced his way back to the nose of the truck. The hood was a split affair with a continuous hinge running the length. Unlatching the one side, Hooker raised the hood, and folded it back on the top of the other side. With a grease rag in his left hand, he withdrew the long spring steel rod that measured the life's blood of the beast, the oil. Wiping the oil off the rod, he reinserted then withdrew the rod and examined the level and color of the oil. Again wiping the oil from the rod, he restored it cleanly to its hole. With deft fingers and an eye for the unique truck engine, Hooker went about his daily engine check.

"Billy," Hooker called to the kid now back to reading the paper in the doghouse, "put me down for two cases of oil for next week."

"You got it, big daddy," the kid called out. "Are you going to need some new filters this time?"

Hooker thought a moment. "Nah, I still have some of the last case left." Stepping over to the door, and looking in, Hooker saw the nudie magazine the kid was hiding in the newspaper. "You'll go blind reading those magazines," he said softly, startling the kid.

Snapping the paper shut around the magazine, with the horror of being caught, he jerked his head around and looked at Hooker with his mouth hanging open. Seeing Hooker with his silly sidelong smile, he knew his secret was safe, and Hooker was just funning with him.

"Can I just read them till I need glasses?" he goofily asked as he pushed the thick-glassed offenders back up his nose.

Hooker laughed. "Too late." They both chuckled as the kid waved his fist in front of his crotch and made a squinty buck-toothed face.

Hooker turned to go with a roll of his eyes. "Put me down for a case of air filters, though. I've got an itchy feeling I may be doing more work down in Gilroy or somewhere as screwed up hot and dusty as Salinas this summer." As he walked back around his truck, he thought about the summer heat in Salinas as he shuddered and stuck his tongue out with a *blaah*. Hooker hated the heat, and San Jose was bad enough, without the extra manure and then rotting vegetable smell in Salinas and Hollister through the planting and growing seasons.

Firing up the monster, he eased out of the truck stop, blipped his air horn, and was vapor in the wind as the kid returned his attention to the naked girls he would only ever dream about.

9

For as dapper a dresser, and as nice a car as Sweets ran around in, the neighborhood he lived in confirmed his blindness. Modest mid-century homes, the hallmark tacky look of hasty post-World War II construction, lined the quiet streets of the Willow Glen neighborhood where mostly both parents had to work to make ends meet. Hooker pulled up in front of the primped and trimmed, model home of the neighborhood with an immaculate charcoal gray 1968 Lincoln Continental with suicide doors, parked in the curved driveway at the front door. The front door opened as Hooker walked up the drive, and the mass of Danny filled the doorway.

"You're late," he growled. "I was forced to eat your share so Sweets wouldn't know you never showed up."

"Yeah," Hooker teased back, "otherwise, you would have probably starved to death and looked like the poster child for Biafra." He cocked his head and made huge eyes as he then lolled his head around on his neck.

Danny laughed through his nose as he tried to maintain his stern bodyguard/bouncer look, grabbing the much smaller man and enveloping him in an almost acceptable shoulder man hug. Squeezing him through the doorway, he groped the iron-hard six-pack body and chided Hooker about being underfed with his oversized clothes hanging off his coat hanger frame of a body, an accusation belied by Hooker's bulky muscles gained from pushing more than his weight around in the garage gym at Manny's. Neither man looked like he had missed a meal, and both had nothing to do with looking like a poster child for a starving country or a coat hanger.

There was a loud squeal from the kitchen, and a pleasantly padded good-looking older black woman came rushing around the corner wiping her hands in her apron. A palm-width shock of white hair waved through a still massive headdress of salt and pepper that was more like a lion's mane than the lioness. Her eyes crinkled over a megawatt smile of large beautiful teeth. The spray of darker freckles folded into the warm, reassuring laugh-lines pressed into her face from a lifetime of the joyful celebration of life as the mother of two boys she was proud to call her own.

Her arms flew open as she reached to fold Hooker into her bosom. "Oh, my ghost child has finally returned." She giggled as Hooker nuzzled in her neck, as was his signature in making larger women giggle and squirm.

Deep in her neck, he muttered for only her to hear, "You are keeping yourself pure for me, aren't you, Tilly?"

Giggling until she jiggled all over, she pushed him back and gently slapped his chest. "Why child, of course, I am… But you can't keep me waiting too much longer." She pushed up on her mass of hair with the flat of her hand and posed with her other hand on her bouncing out-thrust hip. "After all, a girl in her prime of life is a much sought after commodity."

Laughing and squealing, she spun her arm into his and guided him into the large kitchen and family room combination. "Come on in, and let's get you fed before my other babies die of starvation."

Danny snorted softly through his nose and followed them deeper into the house.

Sweets lounged in his large chair near the sliding glass door, with his signature two-toned patent leather shoes crossed on the leather ottoman. On his head was a pair of professional-grade headphones as he listened to something on the large reel-to-reel tape recorder. His face was slightly furrowed in concentration as he listened.

"Sweets!" Danny barked, then continuing the now running joke, "Hooker is finally here, the famine is over."

The slender hand with long musical fingers slowly reached over to the machine. The body flowed forward as the man sat up. Hovering over the buttons, there was a pause, and then a single finger made a choice and depressed the lever, stopping the tape from scrolling. The other hand reached up and whipped the headphones off his head as the feet popped off the ottoman and Sweets stood up. "Hooker," he started toward them as his right hand came up as if to shake. "How good to see you, my man," he gushed as he moved across the empty room.

Watching Sweets move about his familiar territory, one would not know he was blind, other than his eyes were perpetually closed, and he held his head as if he were always watching the ceiling above you or slightly behind you. Hooker detected the soft little ticking that Sweets made with his tongue, like a bat locating his surroundings. Discounted in America as nonsense, Sweets had taken the family to Switzerland for a year while he had learned the echolocation system. It wasn't infallible, but it was impressive to watch Sweets do it.

Looking back at Tilly as she worked at the cooking island, Hooker smiled and played the theme song. "Sweets, good to see you, man, and I'd love to talk to you, but I'm starved. Can we just eat first?"

A small bit of celery hit Hooker in the back of the head as Tilly softly laughed and reached over with the long French knife and poked Danny in the behind as he stood before the open door of the refrigerator, sneaking a drink of milk straight from the gallon jug. "Hey, mister," she cried, "what do you think I am, blind?"

Chagrined, Danny put the jug back and closed the door. Turning, he whined like a pre-teen caught with his hand in the cookie jar, "Mama, I was thirsty."

"Then get some class and get a glass." She waved the knife in his face, and then lowered it to below his belt, "Or next time I may just do more than poke."

Turning on Hooker, she asked, "Are your hands clean, young man?" Pointing the knife at the sink, she sniffed the air and scowled as if offended. "You can wash the diesel I smell off them before you carry some of *my* dishes into the table." Ever the queen of the castle and the Sweets Empire, Tilly Sweets trucked no back talk or accepted any contradiction to her velvet-covered iron fist.

An hour or so later, the shards of a traditional Tilly meal lay scattered about the table like bodies on a battlefield. Danny picked at the remains like a vulture. A peck here, a peck there, and after a while, clean bones and a happy grown boy named Danny. Sweets didn't have to see to know what his brother was doing, as he had been doing it all his life. Tilly sat quietly, but inwardly was in horror at what Hooker took so coolly as just part of his day, or so he seemed to project.

"I didn't see her or him in a dress, just all black except the throat." Sweets continued. "The throat was definitely white. Like it was missing on a photograph or something. It was also strange that I saw the rage of the gun, but not the fire." Sweets picked at his own plate with slender piano player's fingers. They seemed to sense where the little bits of food were still hiding as they played around and across his place setting.

Putting his mug of coffee down, Hooker stared at the table as if the answers would be written in the grain of the wood. "Manny was confused about it too, but he has some theory about some kind of silencer over the end of the gun to suppress the muzzle flash as well as the noise. But this afternoon, there was just a raw naked shotgun, and it was barking just fine."

Even without sight, Sweets looked toward where he knew his brother to be.

The older brother simply said, "I'll check around."

Nodding acknowledgment, Sweets looked back toward Hooker, as he asked, "But the cars were either the same or similar?" He scratched his left palm in a nervous habit of thinking. "Sounds like the shooter is either stupid or has a fixation on that car and color."

Hooker shrugged and leaned back in his chair, and with his one eyebrow arched, he fiddled with his empty coffee mug and stared. "Yeah, well, it is a very common color for a couple of years in the de Ville line."

As they all sat in a post-lunch torpor thinking about the shooting, or not, the phone rang, and Tilly got up to answer it as Danny turned to Hooker and quietly asked, "Now what?"

"I don't know." Hooker shrugged as he still stared at the mug. "I'm just the tow driver." There was something there, and he just couldn't put his finger on it. "But I'm not going to go into hiding." Looking up at Danny, he then looked further up at Tilly, who stood there with her hand covering the phone.

"You just may want to do that." She held the phone out for Hooker as she finished with a concerned look on her face. "It's for you—and she is all kinds of pissed off."

Hooker's eyes went big as they rolled into the look of shame. What now?

Taking the phone from Tilly's outstretched hand, he hesitated to answer. "This is…"

"Yes."

"Yes, ma'am."

"No, Dolly, I didn't mean to…"

"Yes, ma'am. Right this second, ma'am."

"Yes, ma'am?"

"Did they say how much?"

"Just a moment." He covered the mouthpiece and looked at Danny. "$400?"

The large guy just scoffed, snarling the one side of his lip, flared the nostril, and nodded, as if to say Hooker was talking about chump change.

"Yes, ma'am, I'll be in the truck in five minutes…"

"No, ma'am!" he snapped.

"Yes, ma'am, I've got my foot out the door as we speak."

As he hung up the phone, Danny had a wad out and was peeling off Benjamins. Tilly saw her chance and stuck her hand out, too. There was only one heartbeat of hesitation, and she was holding two more of the Bennies.

Hooker snatched his jacket with one hand and the bills in the other. "Tilly, hug Danny for me." And true to his word, he was out the door as he cleared his last command. "And Danny, give Tilly a kiss."

Tilly stared at the doorway, then out the window with wide eyes. Turning back and blinking at Danny, she asked in a stunned voice, "Did you know he could move that fast?"

Danny and Sweets both chuckled as Danny stood and started to clear the dishes as he had done since the job had fallen to him in high school, and after the great experiment of Sweets learning how to do so with the fine China they no longer had.

Tilly stopped the large man with a hand dwarfed on the giant chest. "Hey, mister, you heard the man." She turned her cheek and opened her arms wide.

"Ah, mama," the embarrassed little boy whined as Sweets just steepled his hands to cover his silent laugh at his brother's discomfort.

The sound of the monster truck vibrated into life and then faded off down the street, and the sounds of birds and afternoon lawnmowers returned to the quiet neighborhood.

10

Valley Medical Center, known locally as Valley Med, hulked in the waning afternoon sun, crouching like a vulture overlooking the freeway. Occasionally, the vulture's pickings were slim, but most days, when people forget how to drive, the freeway turned into a human smorgasbord. The 280 Freeway was the hallmark of insanity of state or county highway planners who lived elsewhere. Planners who didn't understand the impacted nature of the area were responsible for designing a lack of off-ramps with direct access to the medical center, the final destination of the many ex-drivers and walking brain donors who tended to park creatively on or around the network of the southern bay area freeways. The nearest off-ramp to the medical center and emergency treatment was half a mile away from the door to the ER.

Parking his rig in the larger lot fenced off for county vehicle use only, Hooker locked the door and took a deep breath as he hung from the key in the door, gaining inner strength. Resolved, he slowly pulled the key and turned to face the music.

A *normal* hospital's emergency room at its busiest is quietly filled with those with broken arms or bodies who can't wait to see their family doctor in the morning. The patients sit in quiet stupors, waiting for their names to be called as the system slowly makes its way through the caring of those in medical distress. Triage is performed on those who walked in from the bus stop, those who drove themselves, those who somebody drove, and those who were admitted directly through the large double doors by two uniformed medics who drove them there with a very loud obnoxious noisemaker and pretty flashing lights on the front of a one-ton van with extra headroom. Usually, these were not the brain and organ donors from the freeways—those go directly to Valley Med.

The ER at Valley Med is on the other channel of the TV steeped in the reality shows of man's stupidity to himself, man's cruelty to others, and man's incestuous flirtation with his own mortality or those close enough to be infected with or by the same stupidity. If there were one summation of all the carnage and semi-breathing cordwood shoveled into the county emergency hopper, it would bear the honest title of operator error. Rare was the case of a non-provoked or a non-self-inflicted wound in the county grinder.

The blonde, cute in a cowboy/horsy sort of way, with her ponytail down past her seat cushion, looked up and slumped back relaxed in her chair. "Well, if it isn't Hooker." She smiled a sarcastic yet friendly exhausted smile. "And look, he doesn't have something wrapped up in a greasy rag needing stitches."

Hooker stood leaning against the intake secretaries' cubical wall, knowing he would never be able to get past the friendly ration of crap he so well deserved for the seeming nonstop summer of not-so-minor gashes and lacerations he had brought into the ER—not all on his own body. He also knew 'Cynthia Eye Candy' was just getting warmed up, and she would never cut Hooker any slack for the onetime slip of his nickname for her to one of the EMTs.

"Connie, come look," she called her best friend and head nurse. "It's Hooker, and he doesn't have a box with ice and body parts in it." She cackled her throaty high smoker's laugh. "So, what can we do for you, slick?" She rolled forward toward her armament of an IBM Selectric II typewriter she could fire faster than Al Capone's Tommy gun could go through a barrel of bullets on a Valentine night. "And, no, I won't go out with you, so don't ask."

Hooker considered a few sarcastically funny responses, but none would be appropriate or conducive to getting what he needed, so he just played it straight. "I understand you have a young kid named Johnny. He came in last night with a fork in his hand, and you're holding him for ransom."

Hooker couldn't have gotten a more stunned, wide-eyed response from the secretary if he had slapped her face. Slowly she rose with her mouth pursed in an open oval the size of a dime. Her blue eyes were like hot daggers as she examined his soul through his eyes and kicked it down the rotting stairs of purgatory. "You... you're the one who..." she drew the words out in a long breathy whisper. "You..." Her mouth snapped shut, and she spun around. "Connie," she called into the nurse's office with her sarcasm freezing hot as dry ice, "the child stabber is here. And I'm taking my break." She stormed off, looking back twice, scandalized, with hot daggers for eyes, at Hooker.

The stocky older nurse stepped sternly out of the small office and surveyed first the retreating secretary and then Hooker. Her face was a motionless tableau of concrete, all mixed up, and set for life, making her unreadable to Hooker. Silently weighing the balance of the circumstance, she stepped over to the folders on the duty shelf. Pulling one, she glanced at it and looked up at Hooker. "You are here to pay for this?"

Hooker looked down the hall where the secretary had gone, thinking, then returning the nurses gaze, "Yeah," he sighed. "I sure am." He reached deep in his jean's front pocket.

The nurse held up her hand in a sign of stop. "Oh no. I'll give you the bill, but you have to go pay up at accounting." She withdrew the triplicate form from the folder and gave it to Hooker. "I believe you know where it is?"

Hooker nodded. Looking back down the hall again, he knew he would be *paying for it* for a very long time to come.

"When they are finished with you, come on back here, because we aren't done with you yet."

Hooker looked at her stern face, weighing the intent, nodded, and turned toward the hall to the elevators. *I'm sure you aren't... not by a long shot.*

As he stood waiting, a familiar dark specter, accompanied by an adjunct figure, wandered down the hall toward the elevators and Hooker. The standard uniform was a little crumpled as if it had been a long night or day spent sitting uncomfortably at the bedside of someone in need of a kind voice, a warm hand, and an attentive set of ears. As long as Hooker had been stopping by Valley Med, the man clad in black from shoes to neck was a familiar and warm sight, who had always been topped with a massive head of wavy, but now thinning, snow-white hair matching his huge pearly white smile. His green eyes were always sparkling.

"Father McBride," Hooker greeted him as he also nodded to the nun walking with the older priest. "You look like you've had a long day already."

"I think, Hooker, at eighty-seven, I may be getting too old for this duty," the smile widened. "So, it's probably a good thing I'm only eighty-five." Taking Hooker's extended hand and shaking it as vigorously as a scared young teen trying to impress his date's father.

"Well, Father," Hooker looked him up and down, "You don't look a day over eighty-three to me."

They both laughed as the elevator dinged, and the doors opened to let a family out before they stepped in. The nun touched the priest on the elbow with her hand bound excessively with an extremely long rosary. "Father, I'll meet you later to take you back to your parish in time for vespers."

The priest jerked up his head and looked at her as if she had just appeared. "Oh… oh, yes. Thank you, sister," then he remembered social protocol and introduced the nun to Hooker. "Ah, sister, I'd like you to meet my good friend Hooker. Hooker, this is Sister Mary Michael Frances. She's over at Holy Redeemer," turning for confirmation, "Am I right?"

The sister nodded but offered no hand. "Yes, I believe I have seen you before, but we weren't introduced." Nodding to the older priest, she confirmed his memory. "Yes, I've been in sanctuary for the last two years now."

As she turned to go, she nodded again to Hooker as her hands wound even more vigorously about the binding rosary. "Nice meeting you, Hooker. I'm sure we will see more of each other."

Something about the extra-long rosary was familiar, and it bothered him at the back of his memory as he watched her walk away. He marveled, not for the first time, how a nun was able to seemingly blend or disappear in a busy hallway, much like a chameleon on a branch.

Turning to poke at the numbers as they stepped into the open elevator, the priest grew sober, and with downcast eyes, shook his head. "You know, Hooker, it's a sad world this has become." He raised his eyes to the ceiling and crossed himself slowly and dramatically, then looked back down as if studying the floor for answers. "I've just spent the better part of the night and morning with a poor young fellow brutally attacked over a single dollar bill."

Without thinking, Hooker commiserated, "Father, that's terrible."

The elder's right eye slid sideways and looked at Hooker through the shaggy bramble of his bushy eyebrows. "Aye, 'tis now and the saddest part is if the young man had asked for the dollar, explaining his plight, the attacker would have probably given him the dollar and maybe even more." He shook his head again as he eyed the floor counter, blowing out his breath as the elevator came to a stop on the third floor, and the doors whooshed open.

As Hooker moved to the door to leave, the priest dropped the other shoe. "At least he wouldn't have gotten the four tines of a fork through his left hand."

Hooker froze, and slowly turned and looked at the priest whose lower lip was curled up against his upper lip and nose, with his left eyebrow arched high over the mischievously twinkling eyes. "It wasn't the kindest of things to do, Hooker. Not kind at all."

Hooker stepped his black engineer boot into the opening to stop the automatic door from closing. He thought a few seconds, and then asked, "Is there anyone left in this building who doesn't know about what happened at Bob's last night?" His shoulders sagged as the wind was rapidly leaving his sails. His head slowly cocked to one side.

The priest suddenly jerked and held up his index finger. "Oh, thank you, young Hooker, I nearly forgot," as he reached out and pushed a low button on the panel, "Walt! Walt doesn't know, but he will in a few minutes."

"Walt? Walt, the janitor in the basement?" Hooker was horrified as the doors slid shut on the priest's enormous smile and a wave from the tip of his brow with his right hand.

The seconds ticked as Hooker stood looking at the stainless-steel panels of the elevator doors. A blurry visage stared back. *What did I ever do to deserve this?* He knew there were some events and actions that could never be recalled, no matter how much a person wished or wanted to recant or make new. Finally turning, he looked across the hall, directly into the billing and cashier department. There standing was not one, but five women behind the counter, glaring at him, trying oh, so hard not to laugh at the squirming familiar friend.

As he slowly staggered across the hall, as if to the gallows, he began to hear the low humming of a disapproving Claretta Nightingale Johnson. "Um mmm um um ummm," she mouthed as she wagged her large head and larger afro. This was a woman not to be trifled with, but to be reckoned with, especially now with the fierce backup squad at her side.

"Mis-ter Hook-er," she stated, enunciating every syllable to its fullest.

"Yes, Miz Johnson?" Contrite, Hooker bowed his head.

"Don't be tryin' no sweet talk on me, young man. This one is going to cost you." Her puffy fists were buried in the bum-rolls of her hips.

Hooker thought a second. "French chocolate pie or Black Forest cake?"

She looked to her posse, and they nodded. They turned to face the young man and laid down the rules, "Both. One tomorrow, the other on Friday," she started. "Better make the cake on Friday, and it better be large, because we have a couple of birthdays this week."

"Yes, ma'am," Hooker saluted. "Cake on Friday, it is."

"And," she stuck her scolding single finger-facing palm out toward Hooker, "no nuzzling necks for a week."

Hooker collapsed for dramatic effect into the plastic chair and the posse all feigned horror at the tough sentence laid down by their leader. Reconsidering the harshness, and the joy it brought the entire five, "Well, maybe not until Friday with the cake."

Hooker and the posse wiped their brows, as the girls giggled and went back to their work answering the phones still buzzing the entire time.

As Claretta jockeyed her ample body into her business chair, she reached out and slammed her right hand down hard on Hooker's left hand on the low counter. Her eyes were all business and steel cased. Low and quiet, she clenched out her edict. "What you did was wrong. No matter what your gut was telling you that you were protecting, it was still wrong. That boy is scarred for life. You may as well have pulled the shotgun of yours and taken his life. It would have been more merciful. Now he must live out his life with four scars the size of his conscience, forever reminded of last night." She gently shook his hand. "And that, young man, is just wrong."

Hooker just sat looking into her eyes. She was not telling him anything new or anything he did not know. It was just one of those bits of the universe giving you feedback you really didn't want to hear. His nod would have been nothing more than a light breeze ruffling a few of his hairs, but she noticed, and the subject was now closed, almost.

Swiveling the chair in a high-pitched squeal she didn't seem to hear or just ignored, she deliberately walked her fingers over the hanging charts in the stack-rack in front of her. Each finger step was an excruciating eternity for Hooker. "Humph." The large black woman's face scrunched up in consternation and confusion. She glanced over at Hooker, who was all but squirming at the delay. Looking at the side counter, she glanced back at Hooker and then picked up the manila folder as if to say, "Oh look what I found!" It couldn't have looked any more contrived.

Without even glancing in the folder, she pronounced his sentence. "You owe us $382.25. The extra $17.75 will go toward the uninsured children's fund." She reached out her left hand toward Hooker as he rose up on his left butt cheek and fished into his front pocket withdrawing the four Benjamins Danny had given him earlier. There was nothing Hooker could say or do; he had been neatly backed into his own corner.

Finally opening the folder, she withdrew the bill marked "PAID" and handed it to Hooker. "You go show this to Connie. And while you're at it, let her know you are bringing cake on Friday." The large dark brown eyes were orbs of steel—warm steel, but steel, nonetheless.

"Yes, ma'am." Hooker rose to leave. "Thank you, Miz Johnson. I'll see you tomorrow with the chocolate pie."

She waved her hand, dismissively. "Oh, forget the pie!" Her hand turned into an index finger gun of vengeance. "But you best not forget those *two* cakes on Friday."

"Yes, ma'am. I will order them today and have them hand-delivered or bring them myself on Friday." He saluted as the elevator door opened, and he made his escape. Thinking about the current tone of the medical staff, he knew he would have those cakes delivered. It was just safer that way.

11

The emergency room had gotten much busier with the end of the school day and other injuries. The bedlam was palpable as Hooker swung out of the elevator and headed toward the intake area. The blonde's anger was still smoldering as she looked past the old man with the bloody towel held to his forehead. Hooker knew it would take weeks or months to mend the woman's attitude.

Connie stepped out of her glassed-in office, pointing to a phone on the counter. "Line five."

Hooker frowned in confusion, picked up the phone, and poked at the blinking button of line five as directed. "This is Hooker."

"Don't say a word." Dolly's voice had an edge Hooker rarely heard. "You know you screwed up, and I don't even want to talk with you right now, but I have to. So shut up and listen. The boy—what's his name?"

"Johnny?"

"Johnny. And I said shut up, and I meant it. The boy, Johnny, is there at the ER. And Connie will show you. You take him with you, and you watch out for him. If you get the chance, you can go drop him off with Manny, but if it's getting close to seven before you can drop him off, you better feed him. And I don't mean some shit burger on State Street. You go get him something good for him." Stopping to think, she continued. "In fact, just swing by Togo's now, get some dinner, and then call Dina. She's holding a call for you, and it's already five away." The five she was referring to was the call was already five out of the twenty minutes allowed for a driver to respond to an auto club call for roadside assistance. "So get moving, mister!"

Hooker hung up the phone as he looked to Connie for directions. She was pointing behind him, and the young boy was rising as Hooker turned. The entire left hand was wrapped in gauze, and it looked more like the hand of a snowman. He kid was obviously gun-shy with Hooker, and Hooker gave him some distance. He waved for the kid to follow. "Come on, let's get you fed," as he turned to Connie waving and mouthing a thank-you as he knew she had gone a lot easier on him then he deserved. The blonde followed him with an icy glare that sent shivers down his spine as the men left. *A very long time,* Hooker thought.

Arriving at the truck, Hooker unlocked the passenger door and watched protectively as the boy climbed up clumsily into the high cab. Hooker had seen older women in high heels and tight skirts make the entry with more grace. He shook his head as the side of his mouth pulled back in wonderment and amazement mixed with disgust. Gently closing the door, he walked completely around the truck with the bang hammer checking his tires. Even with the time ticking, there were lifesaving habits you never shorted. He was aware of the set of eyes watching in the mirror as he performed the curious ritual.

Finally climbing into the cab, Hooker fired up the giant engine and waited out the radio tubes to warm up as he fiddled in the box without Box, touch-stoned the shotgun and reached behind his head, keying the mic twice. He didn't expect the two return clicks, but reassuringly they were there. Some rituals transcend even a pissed-off woman.

Jamming the gears into first over second, he eased out the clutch, checking the mirrors all around as he oozed the yellow monster truck out of the lot and onto the side street. Reaching for the radio with the yellow microphone, he pulled the mic, shifted up twice, and keying the mic, calling the regular auto club daytime dispatcher. "1-4-1, show me 10-8 at Valley Med."

"10-4, 1-4-1, be advised I have a T-3 'can't start' on a 1968 blue Chevy

Nova, on Eighth Street. Member is in front of Togo's sub-shop. Call is now fourteen minutes old." The crisp tenor voice of Randy had just the hint of being in on the 'Let's mess with bad-boy Hooker day' joke.

Hooker smiled at being toyed with. "Ten-four, 1-4-1 out." Turning to the young kid, he asked, "You up for a foot of a Togo's sandwich and some chocolate milk?" Re-keying the mic, Hooker ordered meals for the two of them. "Dispatch, could you double my usual on eighth?" The yellow radio just stutter-sparked with the answer. The auto club favored shorthand acknowledgment was just a swift-key double-tap.

The kid just blinked, as Hooker shoved the gears up, and around into the higher transfer case and back to the bottom of the main transmission. The old system of a four-gear transmission backed with a four-speed transfer box gave a truck a lot of pull at different speeds and conditions with the result of sixteen gears. But not being satisfied with just pulling power, Hooker and his uncle had found a rare 6-speed transmission that worked with the engine and the transfer case. This resulted in a set of gears left over at the top for speeds to take the enormous Marmon tow-truck roaring down the night highways faster than most standard police cars. Hooker frequently arrived at crash sites even before the fire or medical first responders.

This resulted in Hooker being given tows even when they weren't supposed to be his but was issued for expedience sake to clear a street, road, or freeway. This also caused much consternation among the ranks of his slower competition. They coupled his moniker to that of a prostitute and hung the term *Southside Hooker* on him as a name of shame—until he had the Fly and her paint shop letter both sides of the truck with the signature name. Additionally, the lettering ran up the large giant booms of the largest Holmes towing rig you could have installed on a truck of any size. The subtext was Hooker's proudest addition: *When you need a quickie.*

Turning right down Eighth Street, Hooker started looking for the blue Nova needing the jump-start. Looking for the darker B5 blue, he almost passed the custom powder blue car with the jacked-up rear-end, large meat tires, and tiny kiddy wheels in the front. Hooker looked for a zit faced know-nothing rich kid of an owner and was surprised as a graying husky, bearded guy in a Grateful Dead T-shirt waved from the porch of Togo's among the co-eds standing in line.

Hooker fished a ten-dollar bill out of his pocket and handed it to Johnny. "They probably already have our sandwiches and cows ready." As they opened the two doors, sliding out, Hooker flicked on the unneeded but required strobes and flashing lights.

As he came around the rumbling nose of his rig and approached the auto club member, he couldn't help but notice the stacked six-pack of carburetors poking through the hood and topped with a mechanical blower ram scoop. The hood was up, hiding the large mill and true hot-rod stack on the labor-intensive engine of a true muscle car.

As the member stepped off the curb and joined Hooker, he held out his card. Hooker absently took the card as he examined every inch of the spectacular engine. "You put in a lot of late nights under this hood." Turning to the guy, who now was smiling at the well-deserved knowledgeable compliment, he took in the unassuming nature.

"It sounds like you have a few of those nights under the hood of your truck, as well." The man leaned back to look around Hooker, who was leaning in to look closer at the header system. "What is it, about a 1956 Diamond Reo cab?"

Hooker looked up and smirked in camaraderie, "Close, but no cigar. It started life as a 1959 Marmon hauling logs in Oregon, but we shortened the nose about four inches to bring the dual radiator closer to the fan."

"It doesn't sound like a stock Detroit in there, either."

With the pissing on the backside of the barn and measuring of manly parts, Hooker continued. "The mill was a wildcat Marmon engine used as a logging pony on a high wire show in Oregon, but we pumped about 300 more ponies in her when we went through it and worked her over for power and speed." Hooker was having fun talking in the shorthand of gear heads but forgetting that not all gearheads also knew the shorthand of the loggers in Oregon, but the guy got the gist and nodded.

"So," Hooker got back to business, handing back the member's card, with the name Roth not lost on Hooker, pointing to the line on the form for him to sign, "...what could ever go wrong under your hood, that you would need a jump start?"

Signing and handing back the clipboard and form, he said, "Nothing, and you were never here." The man laughed. "So I will never have to admit I stuck an underweight battery in her." He smiled conspiratorially at Hooker, who noticed the folded bill peeking out from under the form on the clipboard.

Tearing off the receipt part and handing it to the now fully recognized man, Hooker turned to the jumper cables wound above the large push bumper. "Works for me... Mr. Smith." Hooker smiled and clipped the cables to the battery as he also held the cables off the custom paint job. He admired the probably several pounds of mother of pearl that was a dying talent to paint just right. The *rat* engine rumbled to life. Standing and admiring the engine and hard work, Hooker waited a few minutes before unclipping the cables, knowing his rig would do more toward recharging the small battery than the guy's car would do with an hour of driving.

Winding the cables back up, Hooker noticed the kid climbing back into the cab as the man gently lowered and then pressed his hood closed with an unheard click. "You probably want to either charge this battery or just get a properly sized one or two installed."

Slipping Hooker another tip, "I hadn't thought of using a dual battery, but I guess it would make a lot of sense. I think I'll look into it. Thanks for the jump."

"No problem." Hooker pocketed the extra tip. "If you want the dual, you might stop by and see the Fly on San Jose Avenue. She puts them in the highway pursuit cars all the time. Those beefed up Magnum four-forty engines matched up to the Torque Flight and three-ninety-one limited-slip Posy rear-end chew up batteries as fast as they do tires."

"Thanks for the tip," the man waved and smiled as he eased himself back into the hot rod. Revving it a couple of times, then pulling out and rumbling down Eighth Street, Hooker followed the sound and sight as he felt sorry his uncle hadn't seen the engine or the *man*. He would have really enjoyed talking steel and iron for hours.

Shaking his head, Hooker turned and walked around the truck and climbed into the cab to find Johnny halfway through a sandwich and one dead brown cow lying in his lap. Hooker snorted and looked for his sack as he reached for the yellow microphone.

"1-4-1, show me 10-98 at Togo's."

"10-4, Hooker. Call your base."

"10-4, 1-4-1." Hooker switched to his commercial radio and checked in. "Base, 1-4-1."

There were a few moments hesitation, as Hooker knew this time of day was a busy time for police, plumbers, and other tow companies. "10-4, 1-4-1, standby." The gentle static of a half-keyed mic, or one shared, softly filled the cab as Hooker turned right and settled alongside a naked shady stretch of curb. Opening his sack and withdrawing one of the twin six-inch torpedo sandwiches, he unpeeled the paper and took a large bite into the beef, turkey, and Provolone cheese with salad and balsamic vinegar, and a dusting of raisins. Opening the small shaken carton of chocolate milk, Hooker took a pull on the brown cow as the radio squawked back to life.

"Thanks for holding, 1-4-1. We have a multi-car pileup, southbound 101 at Coozer Road, CHP standing by. Fire and ambulance are on their way. You are requested to see the CHP officer, Larson, for your tow. I'm showing you 10-8 at 17:27."

"10-4, 101 and Coozer Road, 1-4-1 out."

The sandwich hit the sack, as the last half of the brown cow hit the back of his throat, and the carton landed in the same sack. Jamming the truck into gear, Hooker cleared his left mirror and left about twenty feet of black rubber at the curb as he headed for the on-ramp eight blocks away.

Flipping on all his rotating lights, he glanced at the kid who had gone somewhat white and had stopped eating. "Put your seat belt on." Hooker didn't even want to watch as the kid fumbled the procedure, as the truck ground its way through the city street traffic and finally roared up the on-ramp onto the 280 headed for the commute jammed 101. Hooker swore his usual silent tirade about those few hours he worked during the daylight hours where it was traffic, not the work wearing at his soul.

True to form, the 101 was at a standstill, probably because of the accident nine miles away.

Reaching under the dashboard, he flipped a hidden switch, and a bank of multiple red and blue strobe lights flashed from inside the grill at the right height to be seen in rearview mirrors.

If he thought he could get away with a siren, Hooker would have installed one too, but the lights would just have to do for now. Hooker maneuvered onto the shoulder. The combination of flashing lights and the monster truck's scary front bumper with its grill looking like the mouth of a chromed shark did the trick. He inched past the nine-mile clot of cars along the south county's only artery. On any given day, a quarter-million cars and trucks passed over any mile of this freeway.

As the giant yellow truck glided past the same spot where Hooker had witnessed the highway patrol officer being killed, his mouth froze with the last bit of sandwich stuffed halfway in. The vivid image replayed in a snapshot of time sent a chill down Hooker's spine and caused him to twitch enough to shake the wheel.

Johnny looked over, "Are you all right?"

"Yeah." Hooker passed it off as he checked his side mirrors. He also scanned the field beside the road. Shoving the last wad of sandwich in his mouth, "Just something that happened last night," glancing over at the kid's hand, "after I was finished with you."

The kid raised his left hand and large mitten of white gauze. Looking at it, he slowly turned it examining the wrapping. Softly, he commented, as much to himself as to Hooker, "Yeah, it was a bit scary there."

Hooker felt like the ass he wasn't going to admit to. Again clearing his mirrors to see an ambulance about a mile back slowly making the same slow trek, he glanced over at the kid with the still unkempt hair. He thought about not saying anything, but as it was his nature, he prodded anyway. "Well, I hope you learned your lesson of asking if you need something, instead of just stealing it." The kid nodded slightly and looked out the window as Hooker continued. "I bet you caught hell from stealing stuff out of your mother's purse as a kid, too."

The young man, turning an even more childlike face to Hooker, admitted quietly, "I never really knew my mother. She left us when I was three." He blinked back the sting in his eyes as he kicked the dam of his life open a little more. "Our dad couldn't take it and left on a ship two years later. Candy and I have been on our own since she was fifteen." Staring blankly out of the front windshield, the kid blinked back tears and wiped them with the large bandaged mitt. "I try to help," he sighed. "But I just don't know how to do anything, so nobody will hire me."

Hooker shifted into the higher gears as the shoulder widened and flattened out where the valley spread into more traditional farmland. Hooker knew very soon the smell of freshly harvested garlic and onions would fill the valley air and push its way as far north as Fremont and Menlo Park. It was Hooker's favorite time of year, but it wasn't starting out well.

"Holy crap!" the kid exclaimed as they crested over the last low rise. They could see the mass of fire engines, ambulances, and police vehicles had already arrived on the scene from San Martine and Gilroy from the south.

Hooker quickly surveyed the scene from his professional perspective. Pointing with his right hand and finger, "You see the larger fire truck near the right side? Not the farthest, but like the third over from the right—the one with the door open?"

The kid nodded. "The one with the guy just getting in?"

"That's it," Hooker continued. "I'm going to park right behind him. In the very back of the truck are a ten-gallon tin pail, a broom, and a shovel. I want you to get them and meet me at the front of our truck."

"In the back of the fire truck?"

Hooker shot the kid a frown.

"The pail and shovel—they're in the back of the fire truck?"

Hooker was stunned at the lack of understanding in the kid. "No—*my* truck." Slowing and working into the mass of the disjointed parking lot of emergency vehicles, Hooker continued. "You'll have to keep up, but I just need you to follow me as I sweep the glass, plastic, and guts."

The kid was horror-struck.

Hooker didn't have to look over, because he could sense it. "If you have to throw up… you run for the grass. Don't you dare throw up on any of the fire trucks, cop cars, or most of all, this truck, and just in case it's a crime scene, not on the highway. You got that?" Hooker pulled to a stop and looked at the now blanched face of the kid.

The kid only nodded with big eyes, afraid to trust his stomach by opening his mouth.

"It's not so bad, kid, you'll get used to it." Opening the door, "Now come on, time is ticking. Get the pail, broom, and shovel, and meet me right over there." He pointed.

The kid fumbled with the door getting out. He found the pail, broom, and shovel, arriving at the back of the fire truck only seconds after Hooker showed up with his two brooms from his side panel contained everything else he might need.

The CHP officer turned as Hooker, and the kid walked up. Jerking his chin at the kid, he asked, "Hey, Hooker. Is he with you?"

"Yeah, for this accident at least. His name is Johnny, but you can call him Squirt." They both eyed the large white billboard of the wrapped hand. Hooker blushed slightly. "He stuck it where it wasn't supposed to be, but he won't bleed on your scene."

The officer thought about it but thought better about a snide remark. Glancing one more time at the hand and kid, he turned to Hooker and pointed out the scope of the accident. "The car is still pinned in the side of the jack-knifed truck, but fire is getting the driver out, and then they will see if the passenger is even alive." He pointed along the innermost lane. "We want to clear number one as soon as you can jerk the truck back off the side, but we have to wait out the fire guys. So, the sooner you and the Squirt can start scraping the crap up, the sooner we can clear this mess."

A fire crew in turnouts came over on his way to the truck. "We're about five away from getting the passenger, and then we'll know about the other."

"Ok, we'll have Hooker pull the rig when you guys give the okay." The officer turned to confirm with Hooker, but only addressed empty air as the fireman jerked his thumb back over his shoulder toward the two moving out into the fast lane. The fireman just chuckled as the officer muttered, "Damn, he's fast."

"Okay. I'm going to sweep the crap into small piles with the push broom," as Hooker started. "All you have to do is shovel it into the bucket. Use the whiskbroom to get the last pieces. It has to be entirely clean, or they will never let you work another accident. Got me?"

The kid nodded as Hooker shoved the handle of the whisk broom into the kid's back pocket. "Keep up."

The two swept and shoveled like the devil was behind them. There was not a lot of accident detritus on the highway but combined with the usual small stones, washers, a nut or bolt here or there it all added up. Soon the pail wasn't the light tin pail anymore. The weight tipped the scrawny kid as he moved it from rapidly appearing pile to two more, as Hooker wielded the broom across and around the contaminated area.

A sharp whistle split the air from the direction of the pinned car under the truck's trailer. Hooker's head popped up to see one of the firemen circling his finger in the air. Hooker waved and turned on the kid. "Squirt! Leave it, get to the truck now." Seeing him struggle with the can, Hooker stepped over, handed the broom to the kid, and grabbed the now heavy can as they ran to the truck. Stowing the can and throwing the brooms on to the back of the truck, Hooker pointed to a fence post. "I want you to go stand there, and don't move until I call for you."

Hooker's left foot hit the step on the large 100-gallon saddle fuel tank as he rocketed into the cab. Hitting the large red three-inch button—releasing the air brakes. Jamming the truck into gear, he closed his door. As he slowly wound his way along the scene, he eyed the trailer and tractor to see how he wanted to position his rig to pull them out of the hot lane and over to where he could hook up and then tow them. But first, he would have to turn the tractor back over onto its tires.

Leaning out of the cab window, he called to one of the firemen standing by. "Do you know if the trailer is loaded?"

The fireman nodded and held up four fingers, meaning it was a full load or four quarters. Hooker groaned and wheeled the giant truck for a straight shot from the back end at the tractor.

Setting his brakes, he jumped down and headed for the rear towing deck. Dropping one of the many doors on the side, he reached into the now exposed controls. As he flicked at the main switch, he could hear the truck's engine increase by the needed hundred RPMs he would need to drive all of the hydraulic pumps on his towing deck.

Pulling out one of the levers, he actuated his outrigger legs as they slowly slid out from just in front of the rear sets of tires. Pushing down, the legs extended and planted on the asphalt, pushing the rear end of the truck off the ground. The truck now couldn't roll and would be a dead 22,000-pound anchor for his winches.

Setting another lever to neutral, Hooker watched as the thirty-pound hook slowly dropped from its own weight. Grabbing the hook, he fed the line into a pulley assembly called a 'snatch block,' which he attached to an iron ring on the back of the deck. Walking over to the wrecked truck tractor, he carried the hook as he spooled out the five-eighths-inch winch cable of stranded steel rope.

The frame of the wrecked truck was twisted, but Hooker knew from experience the twist could be taken out and the rig salvaged, but the kink where the left front end had folded during the process of jack-knifing, was another story. Hooker knew he didn't have to be careful with this rig; it was now just scrapped iron. But he still had to get it out from under the trailer in such a way as the trailer could also be towed.

He kneeled down and looked at what was left of the fifth-wheel connection on the bottom of the trailer. There was a gaping hole where a round tongue should be sticking down. The trailer was, essentially, untowable. It would have to be loaded onto a flatbed trailer. Not his problem. Hooker didn't do flatbed work.

Standing, he spotted the CHP officer in charge. "Hey, Mike," he called.

The officer turned. "Yeah, Hooker. What have we got?"

"Dead trailer and it's full." Hooker dragged his index finger across his throat. "You can put a call into the brothers. It's going to need their flatbed and a crane, but I'll jerk the tractor. It's toast, but the Fly can strip it for the insurance."

Nodding, the officer started to turn and then looked back. "By the way, just so you know, there is something wrong with your front grill the watch commander coming up from Gilroy won't like."

Hooker thought a moment then grimaced as he headed back to the cab to turn off the completely illegal emergency lights.

Letting down the landing gear of the trailer would help stabilize the trailer once Hooker jerked the tractor out from under the leading end. It couldn't be towed by the gear, but it would stand on the gear statically until Hooker could get his sling under the nose to coax it to the side of the highway where it would have to be unloaded into another trailer, then pulled up onto a flatbed lowboy trailer, and hauled away.

Hooker looked south down the highway as the flashing yellow lights on two approaching trucks caught his eye over the mass of the first five cars who started the entire mess. Hooker's mouth pulled back to one side in a sardonic grin of self-satisfaction, knowing it was never unnoticed when he was first on an accident by many minutes. In this case, almost a half-hour had passed.

Turning back to the tow buckles common in rigging sea-going barges to each other, but only Hooker used in towing and recovering wrecks, he worked the clasping buckle to the lower frame as the cable passed up and over the higher frame. In the initial pulling of the cable, the entire tractor would be pulled out from under the trailer, but once free, the buckle would create leverage, and flip the tractor back upright. In theory.

Hooker waved to the other tow truck drivers as they began the ugly and low-paying task of sorting out the mangled cars. Hooker could tell, that unless the lower ends of the two cars were put on dollies, (a small low-laying on-site constructed rig with four wheels that made the wreck roll straight), the towed cars would be wobbling down the highway sideways—expedient, but not a professional sight to display in front of officers who may just choose someone else the next time, with or without a rotational system in place.

Hooker, watching how the other driver worked, cranked down the landing gear on the trailer. Slowly, it lifted the weight somewhat off the tires of the tractor. Returning to the controls on his truck, Hooker began to take up the slack on the cable, then watching the flipped rig as he increased the tension, he increased the load until he saw the truck begin to slide. After about a foot, he stopped and walked over to check the trailer. Satisfied the truck would slide out smoothly from under the trailer, he continued pulling the tractor out. As the hind end of the tractor cleared, the trailer clunked down the last few inches and rocked back and forth but sat solidly on the tires and metal landing gear.

Stopping the pull, Hooker ran another cable out and buckled it to the truck's front bumper, to stop it from swinging away from the pull. This stabilized the front, and he went over to the rear set of tires lying on the asphalt and kicked what looked like an oversized doorstop called a chock between the lower tire and the highway to stop the back end from swinging. Returning to the controls, he slowly took up the tension one last time and was rewarded with the truck slowly flipping back into an upright position with a sick squishy crash with chunks of the fiberglass fenders and front hood shattering into shards and crumbling down onto the engine and highway.

A couple of the firemen standing around watching clapped in an unsolicited show of appreciation for the performance. Hooker smiled shyly and gave a mock bow. Assured the trailer and tractor were now safe, he turned and whistled, waving the kid over. "Grab the broom and shovel, don't worry about the can," he directed. "Sweep it as best you can with that gimp burger of yours into a pile near the front end of the trailer."

Turning back to the controls, he started dragging the rear end of the tractor around as he reached over and whipped the stay cable out of the way. Running the stay cable back into its small hidden spool under the bed, he let the main winch gradually drag the tractor back toward the tow truck, and out of the way.

One of the Garcia brothers walked over from his truck. "Hey, Hooker, where you at?" he greeted. Hooker never understood the question of *Where you at?* but understood it meant the same as *How are you?* or *What's going on?* but it didn't stop him from verbally kicking the older Garcia brother in the mental shin.

"I'm right here in front of you, Joe." He smiled stupidly as the man became a little flustered for probably a fifth dozen time. They just never learn.

"No, I mean… oh, never mind." The tow driver caught himself, and half-heartedly mock swung his big meaty fist at Hooker's shoulder. "Hey," as if he just thought of it, "if I sling a dolly and lift balloon under the trailer, do you think you could pull it out of the fast lane at least?"

Hooker looked at him with the still goofy face. "Sure. Let me hook them both up, and I'll even haul 'em all the way to Gilroy for you." Sarcasm was the trade money between the two drivers, but Hooker knew it was only logical as he was already in position to pull the trailer and clear the lane, and it would also build cache with the highway patrol.

Joe shot him a snap double-take look and then started off toward his two trucks. "Thanks, Hooker, we'll get it set up."

Hooker dug in a little more. "Just hurry it up. I have a date tonight, you know."

The giant of a man just waved with all five fingers, hinted at becoming less. "I know, I know—with my skank sister," the man called over his shoulder. The non-existent sister was an old joke going back to the older Garcia's high school days, long before Hooker had ever heard the joke and started in on the now ineffective teasing. It was just now a running joke among most of the drivers who towed the south end of the Santa Clara valley.

Thirty minutes later, with a 'case of toast' hanging off the back end of Hooker's truck, he turned right onto the narrow rural highway leading the back way to the lower Almaden Valley. The kid was kind of quiet as Hooker sat chewing on the last of the second half of his sandwich.

Shoving the wad of sandwich to one cheek, he looked over at the kid. "What's wrong, Squirt?"

The kid gave him a hard look, and finally replied, "That."

"That? That what?" Hooker went back to chewing and driving.

"Squirt." The kid sighed. "Where the heck did you get that for a nickname?"

Hooker thought about it as he chewed. He swallowed and downshifted for a sweeping curve then upshifted as the road straightened back up. "I don't know, but I bet I was just preemptive."

"What's that?"

"What?"

"The pre-whatever it was."

"Preemptive? It just means I did it before someone else does." He took another bite of his sandwich and washed it down with more milk from the second carton of brown cow. Looking back over at the kid watching him, he chuckled. "It just means before the day is out, someone else will probably be calling you Squirt also."

"Won't neither," the kid defied.

"They won't either," Hooker corrected his grammar, "and yes they will."

"Nobody even knows me."

"It doesn't matter." Hooker pulled the turn indicator and downshifted twice. "I'll make you a bet—nobody calls you Squirt in the next five hours, and I'll pay you double. But, if you get called Squirt, you work the next few weeks for me, for free."

"You can't tell anyone."

"Deal?" The truck eased into the back road leading up to Rim Road. Hooker smiled, knowing he was stacking the deck unfairly in his favor.

"Deal." The kid leaned back in the satisfaction he might have just gotten a job.

Ten minutes later, they walked through the massive twelve-foot tall doors of the hacienda. As they crossed the patio, the kid's eyes were the size of baseballs as he marveled at the large hand-hewn beams protruding from the stucco walls, the fountain completely set with colorful tile, and the repeat of the massive double five-foot wide and twelve-foot tall doors letting into the house.

"You're too late," Manny called from the sunroom as they stepped into the clay-tiled entry and gently closed the door.

They walked in through the kitchen toward the sound of the small TV playing in the corner and the older man lying on the large leather couch with a lap and stomach covered in a purring orange fur rug. Looking up over his reading glasses, he took in Hooker then noticed the young man standing behind him.

"Who's the squirt?" the old man caustically called out.

Hooker gave the now dejected kid a knowing smile. Slowly turning back to Manny, he jerked his left thumb back over his shoulder. "He's my new free worker for the next few weeks while his hand heals, and he stays out of trouble."

Manny turned his attention back to the TV and a commercial he could care less about. The sound was turned too low for anyone to make heads or tails about what was being said. "So, you got a name, Squirt?" he asked seeming only to be paying half attention.

The kid started to answer, then closed his mouth twice. Manny finally looked over at him from over his glasses. "Well?" he asked softer.

Quiet in resolve, the kid's shoulders slumped as he answered, "Squirt, I guess."

Manny studied him, looked at Hooker who was half-smiling and shrugged with his face as he turned toward the kitchen. "Yeah," Manny stated, looking back at the TV. "Good name, it suits you pretty good." The old habits of a cop holding a straight face, and delivering an even straighter line, were evident to only those around the person a long time. Hooker was beating a fast retreat and hiding his quiet laugh in the lower section of the freezer.

"You leave the orange sherbet alone in there, Hooker."

"Just looking for the Rocky Road, Manny." The ongoing joke. There was no Rocky Road, and Manny wasn't allowed any sweets, but would sneak little balls of sherbet kept there by Manny's wife 'in case Hooker might want some.'

Hooker pulled out the sherbet and got down three bowls. In the small bowl, he placed about as much as two melon balls worth.

Handing a larger bowl and spoon to the kid, they walked back out into the sunroom where Hooker placed the small bowl down on Manny's chest in front of Box. "Don't gorge yourself, Box. Leave a lick or two for Manny." Turning, he sat down and watched the last vestiges of the sundown leave the sky before Manny reached up and turned on the lamp behind him.

"Slow day," Manny observed, as he indeed shared the dish with the cat.

"Yeah, picked up a commercial rig down in Blood Ally. It's out on the hook. We'll go drop it at the Fly in a few minutes."

"I heard it on the scanner." Manny ran his finger in the bowl and stuck it in his mouth, looking over at Squirt. "Any guts?"

"I saw two tarps in the cars out front." Hooker glanced at the kid. "But I didn't let him near it." As he pushed the last bit up onto his spoon, "I figured I'd break him in slow."

Manny nodded as he put the bowl down on the side table. Box stretched then jumped down, headed for the dog door just big enough for him. "What did Sweets have to say?" He pulled his legs over the edge of the couch and sat up.

"Not much." Hooker stood and collected the bowls and handed them to his new employee. Johnny headed back into the kitchen.

"He said he saw the person dressed all in black. All in black except the throat—which was white."

"Hmm." The detective rubbed his chin, then washed his face with his palms. "That would account for not seeing the shooter at night."

"Yeah, but I know what the SOB looks like in a dress." Hooker remembered the afternoon event and was amazed at how it seemed like weeks ago.

Manny looked up, frowning, with a question on his face.

"I was shot at from the side of the Expressway just up from Blossom Hill." Hooker continued to relay the events of the afternoon and fished the dime out of his pocket in its envelope.

As Hooker continued telling about things in the hospital and picking up Johnny, Manny carefully picked out the dime with a pair of tweezers and examined it with a magnifying glass he got from his side table by the couch. Looking at an oblique light, he was looking for possible fingerprints.

As Hooker admitted to the conversation in the elevator, Manny stopped and looked up at Hooker. The ever-present detective gears were grinding away.

"What?" Hooker asked as Johnny rushed back into the sunroom.

"I think there is someone outside, messing with the truck."

Hookers chair was empty as the front door swung open and he ran outside. Six long strides across the ten-stride piazza and Hooker's warning sense slowed him down, and he veered left and stopped just behind the closed half of the thick oak front gate. Peeking around the corner, he saw the front blossom of the muzzle blast as a buck and change slammed into the two doors just missing his head.

As Manny wheeled out the front door, hell-bent for leather, and armed with both of his nine-millimeter pistols, they heard the squealing of tires as a car left in a hurry. Hooker looked around the corner, and he saw a light shadow, but no taillights, as the car crested over the first slope and was gone. "Damn!" he spat.

Turning back to Manny and the kid, he was seething, and Manny read his mind and put it into words. "It just became personal." They all turned and strode out to check the truck over.

"What exactly did you see, Squirt?" the detective asked.

The kid thought. "It was more of a moving shadow." He struggled for an explanation. "I kind of felt it more than saw anything." He looked back at the kitchen window and back through the front gate. "I know!" snapping his good fingers and pointing at the gates. "It was this—this side of the gate was closed. It was open when we got here."

Deep in thought, Hooker raised an eyebrow. "Good memory, kid. I don't know if I would have caught that." He looked at Manny as he sat thinking.

Turning, Hooker reached up under the seat of his truck and pulled out the large flashlight police issued for a reason. Switching on the bright light, he began to examine the truck in close detail while Manny and the kid stood watch.

Finally returning to the house, Manny was quiet and pensive. Something hid behind the curtains of his mind, and he couldn't draw them back. Frustrated, he wheeled past Box as the cat came out to see where everyone else was.

Hooker headed for the bathroom as Box watched after his buddy and his usually free lap ride around the house. He was now ignored. Miffed, Box looked past the wheeled meal ticket and turned his attention to the new person standing in front of him.

Johnny didn't know what to do with a cat almost as big as some medium-sized dogs. He stood frozen.

Box, sensing this uncertainty, casually walked over for a good sniffing session. Finding nothing truly offensive, he decided ignoring this person until he went away would be a good enough tactic. Besides, it was time to hit the streets and log some *box time*.

Hooker came around the corner and was slightly amused at the sight of the kid being cornered by Box. "Careful, he can take your hand off in a heartbeat." He smiled as Johnny responded with an appropriate blanching as he slowly drew up both hands to his chest.

Hooker opened the door, and Box shot through first, followed with trepidation by the kid as Hooker called out over his shoulder, "See you in the morning, Manny, I'm locking the door."

The detective responded with a distracted grunt and wave. His mind was grinding, and it wasn't looking good.

1 2

———————

Hooker keyed his mic twice as he turned down the dark street and pulled into the large parking lot in front of Night Dispatch. Setting the air brakes, Box was already under his feet waiting for him to open the door. Hooker chuckled as he opened the door, and the orange streak flew from the cab, hit the asphalt maybe four times in the twenty yards to the door, and with one last bound, he was nestling in the large chest of his truest affection in the world. For all of her cooking, Dolly was the one person who never fed Box a single thing. She didn't have to.

Hooker slapped the back of his hand gently on Johnny's arm and pointed at the two in the large doorway. "Box only pays me attention because I feed him and haul his ass over to see his girlfriend." He laughed a low evil chuckle, as he got close enough to Dolly to nuzzle his nose in her rolls of the heated neck.

Dolly pushed him away, laughing in mock disgust, as she turned on her bare feet and padded back down the short hallway. "You are such a slut, Hooker. You'd stick your nose in any fat woman's neck just to make her giggle." She lifted Box to her face and nuzzled the purring mass of orange, and adding over her mound of a shoulder, "Who's the Squirt?"

Hooker turned back to smile at the kid who was standing in the open doorway with a gaping mouth of indignation. Hooker rolled his eyes as if to say, *What can I say?* But told the kid, "Shut the door. You'll let the bullets in."

The kid sneered at what he took as a joke until he spotted the five slugs buried in the outside steel plate of the door. His eyes popped and his butt poked forward as he pushed the heavy door closed behind him. "Really?"

Hooker nodded and proceeded into the dark room, punctuated by the pools of dim light. He walked toward the dispatchers, asking about the second commercial tow they were holding, but when he got close, he got the giggles he was looking for as he nuzzled their necks.

Dolly sat and leaned back so she could apply both hands on the large cat nestled between her ample breasts. Watching Hooker, she grumped in mock disgust and turned her attention to the kid. "Do you have a real name, Squirt?"

The kid hesitated and looked to Hooker for guidance. Dolly noted the subjugation and told the kid it was her house, and to just ignore Hooker. Besides, he was busy.

"Johnny," he told her quietly as he slicked back his hair with his large white gauze mitten.

The penny dropped, and Dolly dove in predatorily to catch it. "So you're Candy's little brother."

"You know my sister?"

Dolly snickered in one breath—pay dirt! "No, son, I truly don't." Glancing toward the figure bent over into the other small pools of light. "He doesn't respect me enough to bring her by."

Standing, Hooker smirked, "I heard that." Walking over, he placed his hand on Johnny's shoulder. "Johnny, this is Dolly, she runs the city and county by night, then loans it back to other people during the day." He patted the shoulder lightly. "If you ever get in a bind, you tell them you need to talk to Dolly Dispatch, and they will bend over backward to help you not be pissed enough to talk to Dolly."

The kid stood looking at Hooker, just soaking it up. Turning to the large woman and cat, "Is it true? What he said about getting in a bind and all?"

Dolly quietly examined the kid then asked, "Do you have a wallet?"

Confused, he nodded, fishing the wallet out of his jeans.

She held out one hand and took it. Her other hand fished in one of the drawers as the fur chest warmer complained about the movement and lack of attention. Finally, she withdrew three business cards and held them up for him to see. "Don't ever lose these. One is mine, and the other two belong to the Police Chief and the District Attorney... with mine being the most important."

The kid just nodded, and with the *bunny in the headlights* look on his face, returned the black leather wallet to his hind pocket. "When are you here?" He looked around the gloom of the cavern-like room, trying to squint into the dark recesses. "Don't you have any real lights?"

Hooker laughed as he turned toward the kitchen to see what was on the stove or in the refrigerator he could grab a mouthful of before he got his hand slapped. "She does," he called back as his head got lost in the lower section of the large commercial refrigerator. "She actually uses them." He poked open a large Tupperware container with a smile. "New Year's Eve the place is lit up blindingly with all two of the sixty-watt bulbs she keeps in her bottom..." as he stepped back out into the main room, and handed the kid a couple of sticks of homemade beef or elk or deer jerky, "...drawer." Smiling with a self-satisfying smirk at his crude joke, he looked down at the oversized woman as she slowly, lovingly stroking the deep purring chest of a very contented cat, searing the air between her and Hooker with her scowl.

The kid chewed hesitantly on the dried meat as he looked from the one dangerous person to the other and wondering if either was having an effect on the other, or whether they were even dangerous. Deciding food was a better topic of conversation, he held up the now half-chewed stick of jerky. He glanced in Hooker's direction. "This is good, what kind of meat?"

The large woman shook from the poke of mirth starting somewhere from deep inside, as she and Hooker both said 'roadkill' at the same time. The kid's head snapped around and his eyes the size of hubcaps fixed in the disbelief of please let it not be so. "Yup," she continued. "Best not to ask the gift horses in their mouths. They carry *big* guns." Her body quivering and rolling from her captured laughter was now enough to disturb her chest heater. Box almost stopped purring as he complained with a mouth full of white teeth and a silent cry. She petted him back into supplication and just kept jiggling silently with a twisted smile.

Hooker took over with rolling eyes. "Chip's bribe her with the stuff they clean off the highways." He jerked his head at her while enjoying the view of the kid's squirming war between being repulsed and the addicting flavor and finished with, "They figure with her southern background, she would love to get fifty pounds of dried possum or raccoon, so the regular roadkill is as close as it gets." He laughed as he ripped another chunk off in the side of his mouth. "The joke is, she hates the stuff, but keeps it for the tow truck drivers who are so starved we don't care anyway, as long as it wasn't once human or dog—we hope."

The kid blanched from white to almost transparent, as both of the dispatch gals had to release their microphones and stop talking before they broke the cardinal Dolly rule of no laughing over the radios. Never!

Hooker deadpanned the kid as he watched him near his stomach's limit. The young hand began to shake and quiver as the fingers all but let go of the offending meat. Hooker stood quietly chewing and slurping with relish on the hunk in his mouth. Slowly in a classic John Wayne voice, Hooker told the kid, "Suck it up, Squirt, this is some of the best the street has to offer. From here on out, it's all downhill." The tip of his tongue slowly traced his lips as he finished the swallow and readied himself for the next bite if only to keep his face straight, as he twisted the knife a little harder into the young kid's mind.

Dolly, who normally enjoys a little mischievous humor of her own, took pity on the kid. "Okay, Hooker, enough. It's all right, Johnny. He's just pulling your leg. They buy several bags of Grumpy's Jerky from the mini-mart around the corner, take it out of the bags, and stick it in the Tupperware, just to see if it will get a rise out of me." She waved the back of her hand at the jerky in his hand as she tried to reassure the kid. "It's all good and safe, go ahead, and enjoy it."

Returning to petting the cat, "The only reason I don't eat it is because Hooker keeps putting the container on the bottom shelf of the reefer where I can't get it, and he isn't gentleman enough to bring me some." She smiled innocently as she batted her eyes at Hooker.

Slowly the kid moved the meat back toward his mouth. Hooker leaned over and placed a stick of jerky directly in front of the woman. She shoved one eyelid half-shut in heated disdain and glared at Hooker, causing him to smile sweetly back at her—the line of bullshit busted.

"Come on, Box, it's time to go." Hooker turned to head for the door.

The cat slowly opened one disinterested eye and snuggled down even deeper into the large billowy-soft bosom. "Pick my boy up on the way back, Hooker," Dolly growled as she snuggled Box deeper on her chest. "He needs some time with class."

Hooker rolled his eyes and put his hand on the large door's knob. Dolly looked over at the small black & white TV's seemingly static view of a parking lot and the large tow truck sitting there. Thinking as she looked, she finally looked back at Hooker and nodded. He opened the door and waved the kid out with his sticks of jerky.

As the door was closing, Dolly leveled with one last shot of the running joke about the jerky in her care. "If it were human or dog, you wouldn't be able to tell by taste, because it all tastes like beef anyway." The heavy door clicked shut with a rumble concealing her outburst of laughter. Hooker was having more trouble controlling his.

As they neared the truck, Hooker snuck a peek at the kid, and as he raised the jerky into his mouth, Hooker looked away saying, "She's right, you know, about the taste. You can't really tell because the pepper and stuff are all you can taste." The kid's mouth hung open around the slowly retracting jerky. While the kid was thinking, Hooker continued. "The Cannibals call it long pig, but only because they've never tasted beef or deer," grinding the blade a little deeper.

As they climbed into the cab, Hooker was proud of the kid, as he noticed the last of the jerky was still in his hand, and he was chewing—thoughtfully, but still chewing.

1 3

Hooker jumped in the truck and looked at the kid. "What do you think, kid, should we go north?" Silently, the kid just nodded and kept chewing as he closed the door and rolled down his window. Then he went back to staring strangely at the jerky in his hand, still undecided whether it really was roadkill or not, or if he should even care.

Pushing the small silver button Hooker lit up the monster with his left hand, as his right hit the air brake release. Jamming the truck into gear, they slowly rolled out of the parking lot. In the gathering gloom, the giant yellow truck slowly loafed its way down the streets as the street punks looked on. Picking up speed, Hooker turned onto the highway roaring up the on-ramp and dropping down onto the northbound 101. The longer stroke gave the heart of the beast the slow throaty growl, but the custom oversized pistons gave it the unique and distinct bark. Hooker started skipping gears and leapfrogging into lower edges of the higher power bands, as the giant mill made full use of its massive torque and the unladen truck.

Mae West was nothing more than a yellow streak passing an over-confident red Corvette in the second lane as they roared passed in the *slow* lane. Snapping his fingers, Hooker remembered he needed to stop at the restaurant. Shooting a quick glance at the kid, he took the northbound 280 transition ramp toward Winchester Boulevard. The kid gave him a strong look, not sure of where they were really going. As far as he knew, they were headed north and inland of Fremont, not toward San Francisco. Hooker just shrugged and said he had something to do first.

By nine o'clock, San Jose normally half-asleep, traffic on the 280 northbound was light and dry, and Hooker just rolled along, letting himself mentally drift over the day's events. Less than twenty-four hours had passed, but it seemed like two weeks. Something someone had said knocked on the back of Hooker's head—not quite remembered, but not forgotten either. It frustrated Hooker that he couldn't pinpoint it. Whatever it was hadn't been important at the time, but now maybe it could be. He mauled the roadkill of his memories, searching for the tasty morsel to fulfill his need.

The small square of a dirty yellowish-white Toyota or Datsun car drifted right, languidly across the front of the truck and slowly made its way up the dark off-ramp. Something about the small cubic spot of light color in the dark of the night worked on Hooker's mind, but it wouldn't come. Shrugging, Hooker downshifted the truck and slowed for the next off-ramp. Double clutching, his two feet worked back and forth in the synchronized dance of teamwork as his right hand worked, blurring back and forth between the two gearshifts as he transferred the main transmission to the lower tier of street gears. Some days, the possession of twenty-four gears spread through two transmissions could be a headache, but generally, it was just so second nature for Hooker he never gave it much thought.

Hitting the top of the ramp, Hooker drifted his left foot across to the brake pedal in-between the dance of the clutch and gears. The yellow hulk loomed up off the freeway just as the light turned green for his left turn, and Hooker left the last downshift undone as he manhandled the large steering wheel, swinging onto Winchester Boulevard faced west toward the creepy tourist attraction of the Sarah Winchester house. Hooker was convinced it was the color of the house that had influenced the florid choice of yellow and blue as the California choice for the auto club trucks.

At least with his uncle, and some creative thinking and exceptional paint job, the converted monster former 1959 Marmon logging truck was barely in the realm of the vapid scheme of the other trucks in California. The sixteen pounds of crushed reddish-pink mother of pearl had just happened to fall into their possession when they were thinking of what to do to the primed gray hulk parked under the army of long florescent lights in his uncle's barn. The 1932 deuce coupe hot rod in the corner under the tarp with the sixty-eight layers of hand-rubbed lacquer in candy apple blue had provided the other half of the equation.

After six long weeks and many sleepless nights of sanding, the yellow truck shimmered in waves of pearl, pink, and red with the nose on fire with a cold-hot candy apple and blue flames reaching back to lick at Mae West on the driver's side. A WWII scoreboard of five Volkswagen bugs, two Toyota Corollas, one deer, and three rabbits gracing the passenger side. Under the scoreboard was the ribbon saying, 'Caution: You may be next,' and under the much-revered Ms. West was the old railroad slogan 'It's what's up front that counts. Everything else is behind.'

Mae West waved at the rest of Winchester Boulevard and the Winchester house a few blocks farther on as Hooker swung the massive truck into the back driveway to the parking lot of the diner. Pulling to a stop in the empty area of the lot, he looked at the kid. "You can come or stay. It's your choice," he said as he opened his door and started out. The kid rolled his eyes and slid out his side and caught up to Hooker at the door. Mae West purred in the lot with a husky heavy drinking and smoking kind of throat as the two men walked past the large fiberglass statue, and his ever-present plastic smile. Hooker pulled open the glass doors and walked into the bright lights of a twenty-four-hour restaurant in its slow 'catch a breath' period of the late evening.

A couple of regulars took up the pews at the altar of mediocre coffee and food. But unlike other discerning diners, many of these had no other choice other than to return to something heated over a tenement hot plate. At least with the counter, there was usually Candy, who was not only gentle on the eyes but also had a kind heart, if not a soft spot, for the less fortunate in the world—something Hooker had an entirely new understanding and respect about.

The two men stood halfway down the long counter as they waited for

Johnny's sister to finally finish with the small deuce table and see them. The smile faltered as she turned and saw who it was. The pause was telling as she weighed the possible meaning of Hooker bringing her brother into the restaurant. Slowly she came toward the two with a deadpan 'I can take anything' face.

"What?" She asked the two quietly, looking like a stern mother from Hooker to Johnny to Hooker again.

"I just wanted you to know the Squirt will be with me for the next couple of weeks so I can keep an eye on his hand." Hooker ignored her stare and attitude.

"Would you stop calling me that," the kid protested under his breath as he hung his head looking around to see if anyone had heard.

"Shut up, Squirt!" his sister snapped quietly. His head jerked to look in horror at the betrayal from his own flesh and blood as she gave him a hard look before refocusing on Hooker as he was nonchalantly finger-combing his waves of dark curly hair—something she down deep wished she was doing instead.

"Is it going to be okay?" she asked as if the kid wasn't even there.

Hooker glanced at the object of the discussion. "Yeah, I'll feed him, and we'll pick up some more clothes later, but he lost a bet, so now Johnny has to work for free for a couple of weeks." He nodded his head at the white mitten—now a little soiled. "Besides, I've got a lot invested in his hand healing right." He was smiling his silly smile—more goofy than self-satisfied. "So it stays where it belongs and away from other people's property."

The older sister weighed the value of the offering as her eyes slowly slid through a blink into looking hard at her little brother who was now looking anywhere but at his sister. Quietly she asked, "Are you going to behave?"

The now very red face nodded and mumbled acquiescence, "As long as he stops calling me Squirt."

She looked silently at her troubled brother and took a deep breath, sighing out, "Shut up, Squirt." Turning to Hooker, she glanced at her watch. "A little early for lunch."

Hooker quietly snorted his acknowledgment of the new treaty. "I just wanted you to know I had him and he wasn't lying dead up some alley. I need to jerk a truck up north, but we'll be back for lunch. I need to ask Peter some stuff when he comes around for his midnight cigarette."

"Where's Squirt going to sleep? In the truck with you?" She watched the kid squirm at the new name, but it appeared he was getting used to it for some reason.

"We'll hole up out at Manny and Estelle's place, and I'll give you the phone number when we get back for lunch, but you always have Dolly's number at dispatch. Or worst case, you can just tell any cop you need to get ahold of me." He backed out of the restaurant dragging his new charge.

Candy laughed and waved them to leave as she turned to grab a fresh pot of coffee and restart her rounds of the sparsely occupied booths and counter. "Hey, Hooker," she called out.

He stuck his head back in the closing door.

"Bring me a donut."

He shot her with his right-hand finger gun and a wink and was gone.

14

Running loose up the 680 on the backside of Fremont, Hooker let the monster get out and breathe. Some days it just seemed like the 1,200-horsepower that finally arrived at the twin axles was somehow restrained by the slow chugging around from jump-start, to flat tire and the occasional tow.

The original engine had started life as a Wildcat towing winch of a different type in the wild woods of Oregon logging. As steam engines and trains were pushed out of the great forests of the Pacific Northwest, gas and diesel-powered machines took over many of the jobs. And as companies became more about the owners and shareholders in the east, instead of the wood-wise loggers in the forest, newer and wilder machines and techniques were tried until something went wrong and one or more died. So was the story of the 1,200-hp engine now hidden under the large nose of the monster truck, nicknamed Mae West.

One of the crazier reckless forms of logging was reaching down into draws and valleys and pulling the logs up the hill or mountainside to the logging road and staging area above. With much of the timber ranging in butt spreads or girth, the size of a man's height or larger logs could commonly weigh into the many tons in a single lift. This load required a lot of bulk power but also needed speed. Three-speed slip gears driven by huge engines seemed to be the answer.

The story goes that the *high wire* on the *Show* (logging company) was over a mile long and as thick as a good woman's wrist, (one who could milk eight or ten cows twice a day and run a bunkhouse of a hundred loggers.) The rip-line rode up and down the high wire with a hundred-pound pulley and at the end were a set of collars to strap onto or choke the end of the sixteen to twenty-four-foot-long log. When the rigger blew his whistle to tell the high-top the log was choked, the high-top man at the *donkey* engine would pull on the accelerator, slip the brake on the take-up reel, and the log would lift from the forest floor and fly up the hill at speed approaching eighty miles per hour. Lighter logs had a nasty habit of completely leaving the ground and indiscriminately whipping about in the air over the logged off mountainside. Standing or walking anywhere within a hundred yards of a high wire was known suicide. But then standing at the top of a high wire with five tons of log flying at you at four times faster than you can run, isn't always a guarantee for long life either, and was how the donkey ended up in a salvage yard, sitting next to a 1959 Marmon conventional tractor. They were two castoffs of a changing world, both in need of a loving home.

Hooker was working on his third-year towing and was finally a legal age to go get a real driver's license, and it might as well be a commercial towing license. So they looked around, and they found a Holmes 950 extendable split-boom towing rig and began building the custom working bed.

Uncle Willy wasn't really Hooker's uncle, but more of the guy who grabbed him by the ear one night, hauled him home, and kept his nose somewhat clean since Hooker was fourteen. Having this home kept Hooker out of the system and off the streets as a runaway from the ninth foster home in six years. William Hollister was a man caught in a time and at an age when you were supposed to marry a woman and build a family —not shack up with another man, at least not if you are a high ranking officer in the Naval Intelligence. The occasional houseguests of his 'uncle' never bothered Hooker, as all the men were nice and respected the law that Hooker was off-limits and would one day find a nice girl to 'make him happy.' Sadly, Hooker observed happy was something eluding Willy except when he was black with grease to his elbows, skinned knuckles, and listening to the hum of a perfectly running engine. Even if it was only a lawnmower, it did not stay stock past its first winter.

Hooker could not stand the silence of having a living, breathing person in his cab, one who could talk but did not. He didn't want a chatterbox, but just some talk. "So where did you two live after your old man bailed on you?" He grabbed a glance at the kid with his head against the window, watching the night go by. He was not the first, as everyone got the *stare* the first time they rode ten feet above the highway.

The kid had a kind of dreamy far off look to his eyes when he finally focused forward. "I remember living in a garage for a while, and then there was a guy who took us in when I was in the fourth grade. He was nice enough to me and helped me with homework, but I think he was, you know, with Candy. So when summer came, we left. Candy got a job in Turlock waiting tables in a breakfast diner, and we did laundry at night. I ran back and forth with dimes keeping the machines going, and Candy would iron the sheets and stuff."

"How did you end up in San Jose?"

The kid just looked out the window, chewing on what he could or shouldn't tell. Looking down at his hand, and bandages, he kind of shuddered. "One night the owner cornered Candy in the back room of the Laundromat and was starting to…" the kid's eyes glistened and reflected the oncoming lights. He chewed as he sucked both of his lips in working on pain to stop from crying. He probably had never really faced the scene he was replaying in his mind.

"Hey," Hooker offered quietly. "It's okay. You don't have to…"

"No." The kid shook and wiped his face. "It's okay. If Candy goes out with you, it's something you have to understand. She's not… she's, um… things haven't been very nice for her." He took in a huge breath and slowly let it out. "And you might be something good in her life finally."

"She's a nice lady, Squirt. You could have gotten a lot worse." Hooker grabbed the mic from behind his head and pulled it around as he keyed the red button. "Dolly?"

He waited. The silence was the volume of the monster engine and the whine of the giant tires in the night air. Hooker looked to the left as he caught the last sight of the bay lights before they were cut off by the hills as he dove into the rolling hills to Pleasanton.

"Go ahead, Hooker," the radio squawked.

"10-4, sweetie. Can you please call Contra yard and tell them I'm about thirty minutes out and ask them in your Dolly-by-golly way you have to get the truck ready to roll?" Releasing the key, he smiled with the knowledge she had her ways of getting people to do things, and he had his way of asking her for the help.

"You mean you don't have a phone in that super-truck of yours? The girls tell me you have everything else."

"None of your girls have been in my truck, Dolly. The bed is too small." Out of the corner of his eye, he saw the kid looking back into the single sleeper—a very comfortable thirty-two inches wide.

"And you better keep it that way, mister." The thud of the microphone key was followed by silence. Hooker knew there was nothing but mock-offended giggling going on at dispatch. The silence was broken with a terse "Stand by."

Hooker turned toward the kid laid up against the window rolled down to just above his ear. The longish hair whipping around in the open air. Hooker knew the look; he had felt it hundreds of times—the edge of despair where it just aches, no thought, just the ache.

"You going to be all right?" he asked.

"I stabbed him." The small voice drifted mournfully in the buffeting wind and was gone.

"What?"

The kid sat up and leaned his head back over the top of the seat. "He had his hand up her uniform and was pulling her panties down." The horror he was reliving was written all over his face. "There was an old knife, like a kitchen knife or boning knife they used for opening boxes. I grabbed it." His eyes were big and wild, his mind almost out of control as that night seared in his veins, unrelenting. "I stabbed him." He looked to Hooker. "I stabbed him in the back."

Hooker glanced at the kid, and then just stared down the highway as his vision tunneled for a few seconds. So much was just too close to home for Hooker—he had to take a couple of breaths. He felt his heart climb back down his ribs and retake its proper seat.

"Hard?" Hooker croaked, "I mean—did you stab him very hard?" He glanced over and then checking the gauges and meters on the dash and then he cleared his mirrors.

"I buried the blade till it stopped at the handle." He took a sharp breath and slowly let it out as he tried for a better grip on his life. "We didn't know if I killed him or not, so we ran." He looked over at Hooker. "We came here."

Hooker thought about the impact of such an event, and not knowing the extent of what you had done. "How old were you then?"

The kid's head flopped forward as he resumed looking down the highway. "Twelve. We had celebrated my birthday the night before. Candy had bought two cupcakes, and we rolled up some paper to look like candles and lit them." He looked out the side window as they crossed the bridge over a dry riverbed. "It was the first birthday I had ever got any kind of cake."

The silence stretched on as the big truck wound its way through the hills and up the backside of the east bay. The moon was just coming up over Livermore as Hooker turned left and started the back way into the Contra Costa Impound Yard where a stolen 1975 Peterbilt waited to be hauled back to the San Jose Police yard for processing.

15

The towing yard was like most others—bright stadium lights in the front, but not so well lit near the rear where the dogs usually hung out. It was one of the few things Hooker hated about the job, the dogs. You never knew if the owner was just seeing if you were stupid enough to test the yard and the free-running dog, or if the dog was really trained enough to be completely on off-leash command. Contra Costa was the latter. Hooker even knew the two dogs, Mutt and Jeff, and more importantly, they knew him. They also liked him because he kept Box in the truck so Box couldn't come tear them up as he did the first time they met.

As Hooker squatted down to look at the undercarriage of the diesel truck, Mutt came around the backside of the truck and nuzzled up under Hookers arm. "Hello, buddy." Hooker grabbed the head and shoulders of the large Rottweiler with his right arm and gave the head and ears a rough rubbing down with his left. The dog's hind end wiggled wildly as his rear feet lost traction. "What do you think of this piece of shit truck? Huh? Should I tow it on out of here?" The dog backed out and away from too much affection as he heard his yard mate returning from doing his business out in the darkest part of their fenced world. Hooker went back to looking at the condition of the rig he was going to tow, and he wasn't pleased.

Standing up, he looked at the huge man in the grease splattered one-piece jumpsuit. "Jesus Mike, what the heck did they hit with the front end? Those tie rods must be at least fifteen degrees out of whack." He shook his head.

"The police said they left the highway doing about seventy and the riprap, those great big rocks along the stream bed, was what stopped them." The towheaded, goofball-looking guy with one crossed eye said as he reamed his left ear with his pinky while his right hand was busy scratching his butt through the jumpsuit. For once, Hooker was thankful for the man's uniform. He didn't want to think what the guy would have been doing with the easier access regular pants would afford.

Hooker looked back at the twin driver sets of wheels. "Well, I'll have to pull her with the ass down, and I didn't bring anything to pull the axles." Returning his gaze to the large man, he found him examining the interesting artifact he had found in one end or the other, and Hooker didn't want to know which. "Can you pull those, Mike?"

The man looked up with a startled look as if Hooker and his truck had just materialized in front of him. "Huh? Oh… uh, yeah. Sure, Hooker, I can do that. But it will cost you extra." The guy kind of sidestepped and kicked the dirt. Hooker knew the 'extra' wasn't an extra charge on the bill.

Lowering his voice, Hooker looked around the empty yard like a conspirator. "What do you need, Mike?" He slumped down on the truck's tire with one hip as if he were bored already.

"While I pull those axles," the man nodded and pointed at the obvious, "maybe you could run into town and get me some dinner?"

Hooker looked at the man well past the 300-pound setting on the scales. It didn't take a genius to figure out what was going on. "She still has you on a diet, does she?" The man just caved inside of himself and nodded.

"Would a couple of bean burritos with extra cheese do it for you?" Hooker sympathized with the guy. The man had fought the battle all of his life. Now his wife was determined to hold him to a thousand calories a day. And for her, it meant driving him everywhere so he couldn't stop for extra food.

The man's face brightened into a gratifying smile. "That would be great, Hooker. You're my hero, and I'll have those axles out by the time you get back." The man turned toward the small mechanics shop he maintained behind the office.

Hooker let himself out of the gate and climbed up into the big truck. Gently closing the door, he sat quietly for a moment with Johnny watching him. It was like a ritual of prayer. He took a couple of slow deep breaths and finished with a soft 'thank you.' Looking over at the kid, he reached forward as he laid the gears in the right alignment and pushed on the big red parking brake button to release it. The air hissed loudly in the night as he flicked his head at the kid. "What?"

"You just... sitting there," the kid waved his finger at Hooker's seat, "are you okay?"

Hooker chuckled as he let out the clutch and the truck lurched into the street. "Oh, yeah. Just keeping clean by being dirty, is all." The monster 1,200 horse-powered engine loafed down the street toward the local Pup & Taco with bean burritos the size of a large cat's head. Hooker's mouth folded up in a wince as he remembered Box was not in his box where his idle right hand was feeling for an ear to scratch.

The light changed to green and Hooker shifted back up the gears as he continued his mission. Back in the yard, he knew the large man was swiftly getting greasy and dirty without a care, except for the reward coming back with Hooker. In a way, it just wasn't a fair trade. Hooker knew he was the winner, because it's a disgusting job pulling the axles on all four of the drivers, but he also knew Mike would say he was the winner, as he buried his face into the warm bean burritos as if they were manna from heaven.

The low-sodium stadium lights turned the parking lot around the eatery into daylight, except unlike the warm sunlight, these lights turned make-up into garish Halloween war paint leaving attractive young girls looking more like vampires, ghouls, or zombies, which of course they found unacceptable, so they stayed away. And without the girls, the boys didn't hang out either. With the parking lot not full of teens hanging around, it cut down on the criminal activities and made it a lot more attractive for the straighter elements of society to frequent the twenty-four-hour establishment in the middle of the night. Knowing he could never fit the Marmon through the drive-through, he parked out in the far corner and set the truck into a stable idle as the giant motor loped in a deep-throated rumble. "Just hit the lock button, as you get out." he nodded at the door to the kid. "I need some coffee, and we may as well wait inside." The two doors clicked shut, and they walked across the tarmac.

Uncomfortable with constant companionship, Hooker fidgeted with the conversation. He looked at the kid. "So what do you want to be when you grow up?"

To the kid's credit, he didn't answer fast but kept walking. Finally, he looked up at the night sky just above the burrito shack. "I haven't thought much about it, but it's more like what can I do?" He looked over at Hooker. "I didn't finish high school, so someone like the cops won't take me."

"Does it appeal to you?" Hooker held the door open. "Being a cop?"

The kid shrugged. "They kind of get respect, they make good money, and they help people." The kid stood for a second waiting for Hooker to laugh at his simplistic view of the world, but when no laughter came, he continued into the restaurant.

Hooker looked back at the truck waiting like a hulking behemoth in the night under the sodium lights as he thought of his own choice and of the Manny he had met seven years before, and the Manny of today in his wheelchair with a wife he could never take dancing again. "There is the respect thing," he said softly. "There is that." Turning, he followed the kid into the restaurant, resizing his opinion of the conflicted young man.

The Peterbilt rode behind the Marmon like a pregnant salmon, large but docile on the hook, as they wound their way back down the backside of the east bay. The crescent moon was a rusted orange sliver coming in from the central valley above the inner coastal hills behind Livermore, as the large yellow and blue-flamed nose of the giant Marmon pushed through the gathering moisture of the night air. Hooker listened more to the heartbeat sound of the throbbing oversized engine, and then he paid attention to the several dials meant to monitor the life of the stroked and bored out engine—an engine that started life as the most powerful engine to come stock in any truck—even before his Uncle Willie and he had stripped it down to parts of bare metal.

Hooker flexed the fingers of his right hand, remembering his fifteenth birthday. He had never seen inside the large bore of a diesel engine before, and he was totally captured by the size of the bore, as he stuck his hand with fingers spread loose down into the port to the top of the piston. That was the moment he knew he was destined to be the master of the monster, and if it could be made even fiercer, he wanted it. And so the research had begun.

The research nature of Willie had forced the young Hooker to get a library card and sift through hundreds of books, searching out the engineering that would justify the machining and sizing of the engine's basic body, commonly referred to as the *mill*—the working core. At first, Hooker rebelled at what he thought was weird punishment and resisted really reading the books or taking the time searching the bibliographies. His gut felt the way to build the engine was just make things as big as you could buy them, and it would all work out.

He had silently chuckled at the tiny sweater-clad librarian with the tight bun of newspaper gray hair coming over and sitting down at the table across from him. She looked at him with the eyes of a teacher he was trying to lie to. She studied him for almost a full minute before she snapped quietly, as only a librarian could, "You don't deserve this opportunity." Her eyes burned, stone-cold, through his.

"Excuse me?"

"God knows you may or may not deserve it, but you have been given an opportunity many other people would give a left leg to be even allowed to glimpse. And here you sit pissing it away."

"What do you know?" The defiant street-forged tough surged to the surface.

"I know you have someone who loves you and cares about you, like the son he thought he would never have. I know that when the man does his research, he has ten times as many books, real books." She dithered her finger at the few books scattered on the table. "Not these kiddy books. I also know if you don't square away your research, you will end up building a monster who will eat you alive and blow up in your face." She started to rise. "Get squared away or quit wasting your time."

"You're just a stupid old woman who doesn't know squat!" He lashed out from a place of being caught doing exactly what she said… and it hurt.

Her head snapped back at him, the eyes burning, as she slowly sat back down. "Do you know what it feels like to drive a 1932 deuce coupe with a 380-horse flathead Lincoln motor, at a hundred thirty miles per hour across a salt flat? No. Have you ever held onto the handlebars of an over-sized Indian Chief doing over a hundred miles an hour down the coast highway on a moonlit night, and you have no lights? Do you know what it feels like when a piston pulls out of the bore and punches out the side of your fresh engine because you may or may not have built it wrong? No, because you're just a kid with more sperm and little boy bravado in your pants than experience." She rose back up with seething indignity and fired her parting shot. "When you can tell me why you need a new transmission in the truck instead of a larger bore, I'll respect you and tell you the four books you need to read cover to cover. Until then, you don't need to come back in here."

Hooker had watched as the tiny woman walked away with a certain pained bowlegged wobble hinting at some of the past she had spoken of. He thought about what she had said, and even more importantly, had implied, as he replaced the books on the shelf. He left the library, shabbily wrapped in his battered pride.

He had finally asked his uncle about the little bird lady at the library and then sat transfixed, as Willie had spewed forth the longest string of stories about her father and three brothers who were the biggest rogue racers along the central coast.

The *little sister*, Madeline, was barely distinguishable as such, as she had been drawn into their world of gas, grease, and hot metal without a mother to provide any alternative rearing. She had been the first woman to drive over two-hundred miles an hour at the Bonneville Salt Flats in Nevada and had an oversized Indian Chief Motorcycle engine blow-up during a drag race, sending her to the hospital for most of a summer racing season. They put her legs and body back into only some kind of usable order. She had gone to college and tried to teach auto shop, but the men of the world wouldn't allow it, so she resigned herself to the library, where she guided those who would listen to the education they wanted or needed. Which is where a young Navy officer Willie had found her again and rekindled their mutual affliction or addiction to metal and grease.

Hooker eventually learned his answers and even came to the revelation about the new transmission on his own. Long before he had the nerve to go back to her branch of the library, he had made friends with the diesel mechanic at the Fly's truck repair. The mechanic, to his surprise, handed him a few books from a shelf Hooker hadn't noticed before, and referred him to many books for the answers to his questions.

Finally armed with expanded knowledge and understanding of the huge torque power band, and lack of ability to rev to high revolutions because of the mass of metal being moved in the engine, he walked into the library and up to the desk of the seemingly distracted and very busy librarian. He stood silently waiting his turn as she shuffled papers and books while making notes.

After a few minutes, as he started shifting his weight from leg to leg, she looked up over her half glasses. "And what kind of transmission have you decided you need?" she asked flatly as if the conversation of seven months earlier had never ended.

"A six-speed Torque Master."

She thought about it with a twisted turn to her pursed lips. "Hmm," she decided. "And is it going to match up to the Bell transfer box?"

"With an adapter ring, we are going to mill."

"And, so I would assume Willie is in agreement with this choice?"

"Yes."

"Anything else?" She drilled him with her intensity.

"We're going to expand the range in the primary for a wider range, that is possible with the eight extra gears." He recited with a bit of attempted self-satisfaction.

"Which, Mr. Hooker, the word is 'which,' not 'that'... is possible," she corrected, nodding. "And what do you plan to gain by the new added and adapted gears?"

"We've got all the bottom end pull and muscle we will ever need, so the change will all go into expanding the top end. The truck, stock, would probably top out at seventy, but with the change, it should be capable of a hundred and fifteen to a hundred and twenty miles per hour."

"And why would you want to ever drive such a huge CHP target at those kinds of speeds?" She slowly removed her glasses and began to polish the lens with a fold of her dress. "Is there a racetrack I don't know about?"

Hooker laughed, understanding they were now reading from the same book. "I drive tow trucks for a living. Sometimes in a wreck, a wrecker is a critical piece in saving lives, especially a large recovery wrecker that can pull a tractor-trailer off a car."

She nodded as she reached low under the counter and retrieved a small stack of books. "I believe these are yours now to check out." She pushed the stack toward the young man with a small smile of pride.

He quickly reviewed the titles and handed one of them back. "I read this one and then bought it last month." He smiled with well-deserved satisfaction. "I think these others are on Uncle Willie's shelf. I'll check tonight, and if they are, I'll return them tomorrow."

Ever the librarian, she admonished, "You may want to check the publish date of your uncle's books, and the revision date of these before you so hastily return them." She reached up and pulled the half-glasses from the end of her nose, letting them hang from the chain about her neck. Looking up warmly at the much taller young man, she shared her wisdom of the book. "Just because you are talking about 300 cubic inches of 1930 and 300 of today, doesn't mean you are talking about the same dynamics of energy."

Understanding that he had overstepped just a bit, Hooker backtracked into the line of grace. "Yes, ma'am, I will bear it in mind in the future."

"You are welcome here anytime, Hooker, to do research or to even just say hello and keep me appraised of the project truck."

Turning to leave, the young man ran his fingers through a much-needed haircut. "Yes, ma'am."

Just before he touched the door, she called out one last admonishment. "And Hooker..." He looked back. "I do plan to get a ride in the new Speed-wagon when it's finished."

"It's a Marmon, ma'am, not a Reo."

"Yes, Mr. Hooker, but I suspect between you and Willie, it will most definitely be a 'Speed' wagon of a truck." She smiled, with a slight pull of stiff skin to one side of her face.

He nodded as he now understood and smiled broadly as he pushed through the glass door, thinking of an old line in a Mae West movie—*it's what's up front that counts.*

What was up front protested as his reminiscing had caused his attention to drift and the pyrometer was registering near the danger zone. Quickly he backed off the throttle, but also shifted to the higher gear, dropping the RPMs, letting the engine relax back to a cooler running temperature. He looked over at the passenger who was leaned against the window napping from exhaustion. A small trace of drool ran down his chin, reflecting like a Christmas tree the many lights of the dashboard and its many dials and radios. What Hooker had misheard as Box purring, was a low, quiet snore coming from the young man.

Hooker smiled as the slow sweeping curve brought them out of the hills, and for a moment, into an expansive view of the South Bay area. The lights of Moffett Field, twenty miles across the back-bay mudflats, twinkled as a small red light lifted off the ground. The P-3 Sub-chaser airplane ascended to its flight duty for the next long day over the Pacific Ocean. On top of Hanger One, the giant former dirigible hanger, red lights slowly strobing on and off, were both a warning to aircraft and the pulsing heart of the South Bay.

Hooker slowly reached for the radio behind his head to report to Dolly. Thinking, and then looking back over at the kid, he relaxed, letting his hand fall. The kid needed sleep and Hooker would call her in about a half-hour when they dropped the truck off at the San Jose Police impound yard.

16

"Hey, Hooker," the first cop said as the two slid down next to him at the counter. "Who's the squirt?" The two officers smiled with big goofy smiles.

Hooker looked over as he chewed on his sandwich. He swallowed and turned to the kid, waving his sandwich at the two cops. "Johnny, I'd like you to meet Officers Asshole and his partner Dickhead." Looking back at the two now laughing officers, he prepared to take another languid bite. "Who let you two out together?"

Sobering, the taller redhead offered, "Until they solve this cop killer stuff, every car in the South Bay is on doubles now. Which is why we stopped in to talk to you. You were there when the Chip got it, right?"

Hooker nodded as he chewed.

The second of the twin brothers asked, "Is it true you couldn't see the shooter? That it was all just black?"

Again, Hooker nodded confirmation.

"When the shooter shot at you, there was no muzzle blast?" The slightly taller brother, beefier by at least fifty pounds, was trying to get his mind around a night firing with no muzzle flare.

Hooker, reliving the scene, laid down his sandwich and wiped his hands on the paper napkin in his lap. Looking with a squint at the pie cupboard, but seeing that night again in vivid detail, he spoke, "No... no, it wasn't totally dark. From head-on, the flare was maybe of a twenty-two or a thirty-eight, but definitely not a shotgun." Shaking, he looked back at the twin Irish cops. Walking stereotypes, even down to them being fourth-generation cops, but two of the smarter street cops in the city. They were the same two who busted him for stealing a car when he was fourteen and told him he should be driving for a living, but only legally. When he showed up driving a tow truck three months later, they turned a blind, but friendly eye to the fact they knew his true age, not the twenty years on the totally fabricated driver's license in his jeans.

They were looking at each other in the silent communication exclusive to twins. Hooker raised the cup of coffee and sipped while he waited his turn in the silence. The Squirt, not understanding any of it, just quietly ate his sandwich and fries.

"So it's probably what Manny was thinking," the larger one said turning back to Hooker. "A two-liter coke bottle stuffed with steel wool, taped to the end of the barrel."

"It makes a lot of sense," the other continued the train of thought. "It would suppress the noise and the muzzle flare at the same time, and then it's totally a throwaway."

"So," Hooker swallowed, "a smart shooter, but not a professional who is going to do this on an ongoing basis." The two cops nodded. "And they found nothing on the car they recovered?"

"Wiped clean with white gas." The two shrugged with wide eyes and contorted faces at Hooker's furrowed brow as if to say *Who knows?*

Hooker looked back at the pie case as Candy came down the counter with more coffee. "Are you gentlemen here to harass customers, or just arrest Hooker and his squirt to put me out of my misery?" The Squirt flinched and didn't even look up at his sister.

"Special duty tonight, ma'am," the smaller, and married one chimed in. "Harass and to lust after the most beautiful coffee packer in the three counties." His brother looked at him, askance. In his defense, he whined back at him, "What? A guy can't even flirt?"

Candy leaned over, and in a voice reserved for a small baby or adored puppy, she patted him on the cheek saying, "It's okay, little wubby, we wuves you any way Puddin'."

He flushed bright red but returned, "I'm Cup Cake," pointing his thumb at his brother, "and he's Puddin'."

The larger just rolled his eyes in mock horror and slowly planted his face in his open hand.

Returning to business, she started to turn a mug over. "Coffee?"

They both shook their heads. "No, we just needed to check in with the mayor here," jerking a thumb in Hooker's direction.

She nodded and turned to Hooker and giving no options just poured, as she dropped the check on the counter. Nodding toward her sibling. "Is he behaving, at least?"

Hooker frowned as one side of his face pulled back, deliberately drawing out his answer, "I'm afraid not." Wagging his head. "He goes to wrecks and just stands there."

The kid looked up in horror, coming to his own defense, "You told me…"

Ignoring the kid, the waitress turned and quipped as she wandered off down the long counter, "Then don't stab him this time. It didn't work before. This time just shoot him." She didn't laugh, and everyone but the kid was amused. He just collapsed more into himself as a tiny rivulet of catsup ran truant at the corner of his mouth.

Hooker reached over and patted him on the shoulder. "Relax, kid. You have thirteen days more to redeem yourself. And wipe your mouth," pointing at the corner of his own mouth. The two cops quietly snickered at the kid's expense.

Pivoting back to the cops, Hooker turned serious. "So what about the guy in the granny dress who shot at me on Almaden Expressway?"

"When was that?"

The day was rapidly running into a week's worth of memories. Hooker had to stop and think what day it was. "This afternoon, as I was coming up from Manny's, where the two bean fields are split by the cul-de-sac at the embankment. A little old lady was just standing there, just watching the cars go by, and then as I approached, I saw a raised shotgun, which pumped out about two or three shots as I hammered it and flew by. The shooter was knocked ass over teakettle, too. The car in the cul-de-sac was cream-colored and was either a Cadillac or a Cordoba. The jerk also showed up at Manny's place about sundown, and if it hadn't been for Squirt here, would have probably gotten a fair piece of me."

"You say the berm at the cul-de-sac between the bean fields?"

"Yeah, I called it in."

The two cops did the twin look thing and then turned to Hooker as they rose. "We've got to go," the one started. "We'll find you tomorrow," the other finished as they were out the door.

"Clear it first through Dolly."

The twins smirked knowingly and waved as they pushed out through the glass door.

Hooker turned back around to the kid, who was still blinking at the door where the cops had been, processing things a little slowly, or too much, so Hooker asked him, "Did you fart?" The kid looked horror-struck and then realized Hooker was joking with him and began to laugh uncontrollably.

Candy stepped around the corner from the manager's station and gave him a stern look. "Hey! No laughing in here." Resulting in the kid giggling all the harder. She rolled her eyes. "Hooker," as she held the phone out to him.

Hooker got up and snapped the kid on the top of his head. "Knock it off, or you'll get us kicked out." Looking at his watch, he saw it was five of midnight—must be Dolly. He took the phone from the waitress. "Thanks."

"This is Hooker." The voice was not the one he expected.

"Stella's home and she said to come now, not in the morning."

"Yes, sir. We were just walking out the door." Hanging the phone, Hooker fished in his pocket for a ten-dollar bill and a one. Handing them to Candy, he told her they had to go. Gathering the kid on his way, they were walking across the parking lot as Hooker thought about how Manny had sounded, very distant and very serious. But it was almost midnight.

As Hooker sat in the quiet cab, the kid didn't say a word as he fished the pack of cigarettes out of the glove box, tapped out one, and threw the remainder back in as he shut the box. Hooker stared out the rear side mirrors as he tamped the tobacco stick on the large white Bakelite steering wheel turned ivory and brown with age. Very low, the AM radio played country-western rock. Almost more of a white noise than it was music. Sweets wouldn't be on for another thirty minutes, and then the tone of the music would change.

Hooker looked out at the left side mirror and watched as a smudge of the night moved and materialized again alongside the truck. When he opened the door and stuck his foot out, the smudge stopped, and then stood wearied and still. Speaking softly in a soothing, casual tone, Hooker said, "Hello Peter." The smudge was torn between the confrontation and the offering of a cigarette. The ritual had changed.

"Hooker?" The sound was like a wisp of fog off the bay that had lost its way and rasped along the rocks of the Santa Clara fields.

"Peter, I need to talk to someone." His right hand was fishing back and pointing to the glove box he had just closed. Snapping his fingers and pointing until he heard Johnny move and open the box. "Peter, I have two cigarettes if that makes it okay." He held up one finger, and he felt the kid slip one more cigarette into his hand.

"I… I don't know Ho… Hooker." The man was out past the edge of where he was comfortable. "I just don't know… I've never had two ciga-rettes before Hooker."

"It's okay, Peter. I'm not going to make you take it. I was just offering it."

Relieved, the man sighed and took another small step as he felt along the edge of the familiar truck bed. The torn, dirty fingers were street thin and as sensitive as a surgeon or concert pianist. The man *felt* his way as much as he saw his way. Everything was a touchstone in his life as routine ruled his being.

Quietly, Hooker cajoled him forward. "I'm not getting out, Peter. I just need my other foot here in the door," as he moved his foot. In the small fisheye mirror he had installed months before on the inside of the door, he saw the shadow of a man hesitate, so Hooker offered out the routine cigarette. He saw the shadow resume, and a lighter colored patch of smoke snaked out, and the cigarette was gone from Hooker's hand.

"Peter?"

"Hooker?" the night-shaded smoke whispered back as the cigarette was slowly passed directly under the man's nose.

"I need to talk to the Mouse."

Silence.

"Peter?" Hooker restarted the slow dance with the street urchin grown old.

A moment of silence then the whisper. "Hooker?"

"Peter, I need to talk to the Mouse. Do you know where she is?"

The man was in conflict now, and it upset his world. "The... the Mou... Mouse isn't very... very nice." Hooker knew Peter and the Mouse had history. But it was why he knew Peter would know where the Mouse was at all times, just to avoid her.

"Peter, I know she isn't very nice to you. Peter, I know, but I must talk to her. I need to see her. Peter, I need her help."

"Hoo... Hook... you need help?"

Hooker was amazed the deranged street waste was grasping the concept. "Yes, Peter, I need help. The kind of help only the Mouse can help me with." He let the concept rest a moment.

"The... the rock." He stumbled. "The rock."

Hooker thought about what rocks, and which one could be *the* one. "You mean the rock near the big church, Peter, or the one between the college and the stream?"

The mist looked back toward his safety zone of the dark, "Hoo... Hooker?" He was torn between his friendship and his need to be only a part of the fabric of night—friend or flight.

"The church or the stream, Peter, and then you can go." Hooker watched the mirror.

The words choked in his mouth, "The stream..." And the mist was a vapor, and the vapor was air.

Hooker slowly pulled his feet in closing the door, looked at the kid, shook his head scowling, and shooed the pack of cigarettes to be put back in the glove box. Turning the key, he listened to the turbo turn as the starter whined up to speed until he hit the start button firing the glow plug firing the monster engine into life. Thinking about the rock and the stream, he absently stuck the truck in seventh gear and rolled out of the driveway, heading south on Winchester Boulevard toward the backway into the Almaden Valley.

Shifting up into tenth, he looked over at the kid who had a look on his face as if he wanted answers but was afraid to ask. "Peter?"

The kid nodded. "He's not all there, is he?"

Hooker had to think about it, and he wondered if Peter had ever been *all there*, but maybe in another time or place with people who cared for him. Hooker thought he would like to believe that—that at one time, life was better for the man who now walked the streets at night dressed in only rags. "No, no, he's not." He thought about what Peter would occasionally say. "But some days, he has more."

They rode along in silence, each man thinking about his own realities. The asphalt drummed against the tires as the lights clicked by and the gears changed up and down as the night wore on.

Halfway down the long boulevard, Hooker glanced over at his passenger. "A cop, eh?"

The kid nodded absently. "If I could."

Hooker thought about it as he shifted down, approaching a flashing signal light. To his right, he could see headlights coming, and he knew they had a flashing yellow, so he eased on the brakes and dropped the truck into the lower ranges, but not choosing a specific gear, he just let it drift. A little white Toyota wandered across the midnight intersection, and the driver turned and looked at the large truck slowly rumbling his way still a hundred feet or more away. Hooker could see the guy's eyes get larger and his mouth making an "O" of surprise. Even from the nearly half a block away, Hooker could plainly see the man's face. *So why couldn't I see the shooter's face from the same distance away?*

Hooker glided across the intersection and looked down the street as he watched the white square box of the Toyota become just a patch of light in the dark of the night. Something about the square bothered him, something about *something* someone had said. The big truck had almost glided to a stop before the kid dug Hooker out of his thoughts with a short stage cough.

Embarrassed, Hooker glanced at the kid. "Umm, sorry. I was just thinking, I guess." He jammed the shift into eighth gear and ramped up the speed. As he swiftly passed through the next four gears, he continued to sort through the various things he knew… or didn't know.

"Can I ask a question?"

Hooker looked over at the kid, stunned he had initiated conversation. "Sure, any time."

"Everyone we have run into today has asked you the same thing, everyone."

"Yeah. So what's the question?"

"What is it with everyone and the name Squirt?"

Hooker looked at him and started to laugh.

"I'm serious," the kid whined. "Every single one of them—we walk up, and they asked you 'What's with the squirt?'"

This made Hooker laugh even more. It was so pitiful it was hilarious, and it became funnier because the more Hooker thought about it, the more he couldn't explain it because he was laughing. Finally, he pulled the truck over and got out to take a walk. Finally, the kid slid down from the cab and joined him.

Hooker stood on the edge of the hill looking northeast across the lower southern half of San Jose. The twinkling lights represented all the people who were snug in their beds, peacefully sleeping, and staying out of Hooker's way. It was a dark bucolic scene Hooker never got tired of. Without looking at the kid, for fear he would just start laughing again, he told him the word 'Squirt' was more of a term for the new guy, instead of a name. The 'Squirt' in a patrol car was the newbie, except the term FNG wasn't for nice company, especially as there were more new officers who were female, so the term Squirt, meaning the small guy on the pecking order was more acceptable.

"So, are we good now?"

The kid hung his head. "Yeah, we're good."

"Ok, then, because we need to fly like the wind. We're late, Squirt!"

Hooker reached out, tousled the kid's hair, and jumped back as the big white mitten waved threateningly. Sobering, Hooker thought about the kid and what it must be like to be outside of the know, only looking at the curtain, and never getting to sit in the theater and to see the show, even though he bought the ticket. He looked at the kid. "Sometime when we have time, I'll tell you about Peter."

Hooker looked at his watch as he ran the truck up through the ninth gear. 12:38—perfect. Reaching back behind his head, he grabbed the microphone and keyed the mic as he brought it past his face. "Sweets, you got your ears on?" He reached down with the mic in his hand and pulled the shifter out of twelfth gear into neutral, double-clutched and shifted the transfer case from second to third, clutched again as he revved the engine, and pushed the main up into thirteenth gear as the radio squawked.

"Danny, Hooker. Sweets is OTA (on the air)." The voice could have been a professional DJ as well, but Hooker knew Danny was the kind of guy who only had about seventy words a day in him. If he hits the limit, that is all you'll get out of him until the next day.

Hooker thought about it for a moment, and then keyed the mic. "Danny, I'm about five out from Manny and Stella's place. So have Sweets call me there. But first, the question is, 'Who dresses in all black?' You got that? Who dresses in all black? Have him call me at Manny's." He let go of the microphone and waited. It wasn't that Danny was dumb, far from it. It just took him time to process things back into words.

"Four," came back the reply. Hooker knew Danny hadn't 'swallowed' the 'ten' which should be in front of the four, but it was just Danny's shorthand.

"Thanks, Danny. Dolly, I know you heard us. I'll be 10-7 in two." He re-hung the mic as the radio clicked twice. Some nights Dolly was as talkative as Danny was, but he was surprised she didn't remind him to come get his *mangy partner.* But he was pulling up the hill, and started working down through the gears, before he remembered to actuate the mufflers, or a set of baffled chambers he could divert the exhaust through, therefore quieting the thunder from the giant engine.

As the two men were climbing out of the truck, the radio squawked,

"Hooker, don't forget you left a demanding package of mange lying around here." Hooker laughed and closed the door, then opened it back up and reached up to push the lock button down. He looked over and saw the kid had remembered, too. *There might be some hope for him yet,* Hooker thought as he headed for the house, and the kid followed.

17

"Sweets, honey, I just heard the truck pull up. So let me put Manny on. You two can brainstorm while I go hug my baby." She nodded and listened. "I love you too, baby, here's Manny." As she handed her husband the phone, she kissed him on the top of his head.

"Sweets!" Manny bellowed. "It's been way too long since you boys brought your mother out for Sunday dinner. Stella is home now, so we won't take no for an answer."

Stella chided, "Manny, he's blind, not deaf." As she reached the front door, she called back, "She can bring dessert, anything she wants to dream up." The door opened, and she was rushing across the plaza for the front gate.

"Yeah, that's what she said, anything Tilly wants to dream up," he laughed. "I for one hope she dreams in raspberry and chocolate, they're kosher, you know. Well, in this house at least." He smiled as he missed the free-loving energy Stella always brought to the house or wherever she was.

"We'll be there, and I'll make Danny wash the car, so it doesn't stink up the neighborhood." Sweets' voice oozed through the phone. "But listen, my man, I've got to hop out for a moment and spin up another record. I wish I were throwing down rock. I could spin out Iron Butterfly and go for a walk in the park and be right back."

Manny leaned back into the wheelchair as the country music came on the line as the hold music. He thought about how different his life had turned out from what he had thought it would be as the only Jewish boy growing up in a cow town in Montana. His father was the government-appointed doctor for the Indian reservation and by proxy the only doctor in the small town.

His father had been a joyous man who wasn't what anyone would have called a devoutly religious man, except he loved his holiday confections. Like Stella, his mother was an amazing cook and could care less about keeping kosher except when their parents would come to stay. She would do crazy things, like set up a kitchen in the ranch's guesthouse, and then run back and forth to serve the dinner. Finally, one year when both sets of parents were visiting for Passover, and they sat down for the Seder dinner, his mother's father-in-law had asked his mother for a large glass of her buttermilk he had heard so much about. Then her father, looking at the meat, said buttermilk sounded splendid and it would help settle the whiskey he planned to have later with a nice cigar.

Manny chuckled to himself, thinking it just might have been the last strictly kosher dinner he would have had until he married his Stella. She was the only woman who could cook kosher so good even a cowboy would ask for seconds.

Outside, Stella stood in the gate under the light with her arms akimbo as she watched with a mother hawk's set of eyes the young man who had become so special in their lives. She thought back to the night Hooker had been the knight in shining armor for her and her best friend, Claire, in the middle of the night on Christmas morning. As she watched, the two men climbed out of the truck and locked it up. Hooker called softly for the new kid to do something on his side of the truck.

Finally, they started across the front yard. "This must be the squirt," she called.

"Yes, ma'am." The kid didn't hesitate to answer. "The fun new guy."

Stella laughed and shook her head. "Oh good lord, you've already spent too much time with Hooker." She grabbed Hooker and squeezed as if she were afraid to let go. "You weren't hit anywhere, were you?" She nuzzled in his neck so the Squirt couldn't hear her being a baby or a fussing mother.

"No, ma'am, but I can't say the same for Mae. She might need some new glass and some touch-up paint." He nuzzled back, still hugging the zaftig woman with the bottle-blonde hair.

She pushed him back, more to get a good look at him but also to tease. "I'm hugging you, and you're talking about another woman. I never…" Turning to the kid, she put her arms out and moved a large-chested hug on the much confused and embarrassed boy. "It's good to meet you, Johnny. Don't let my Hooker work you too hard, you hear?"

The kid felt sort of strange about the older woman, but it did make his tummy feel good, as well as deeper inside where he hadn't been touched for a long time.

Sensing his unease, she turned and hooked her arm in both men's arms and started through the gate. "Sweets is on the phone, and they will be here for Sunday supper, and so will you two." The matter was settled before the subject was discussed. Hooker smiled deeply—*his* Stella was home.

They busted through the front door bubbling with laughter. "Just a minute, Sweets. They just walked in." Manny covered the phone as he barked, "Hooker! Sweets is waiting."

Hooker strode into the kitchen, taking the phone, "Where you at, Sweets?"

Stunned, Sweets was at a loss for words for a second, "I'm… I'm at work. Where did you think I was?" Hooker could hear the consternation in the man's voice at being thrown for a loop by a slang usage he never heard from Hooker. Hooker smiled at getting the older friend.

"Now you know why I hate that greeting. It just sounds stupid." The two laughed in agreement.

"Danny told me what you were thinking. But man, you forget I told you about the figure being all in black." Hooker could hear the edge of indignation creeping into Sweets voice. "But I know you remembered but had something else in mind."

"Very perceptive, my good brother, very perceptive." Hooker eased over the ruffled feathers. "And with that, I'm assuming you came up with a list?"

"The man is hot tonight. But I need to jump out and do some work with our sponsors for a bit and earn our keep, so I'll call you back in about fifteen or twenty minutes," and hung up with no more dismissal. Hooker, used to the working ways of Sweets, hung up the phone without thinking anything more.

Turning, he found the soft brown eyes of Stella boring into his soul through his eyes. "You know, Stella, you're just a bit creepy when you do that to me."

Manny laughed from the archway as he rolled into the sunroom. "Hah, try being married to her and rolling over in the middle of the night, only to find out she wants something." He picked up the TV remote control. "Go ahead and ask her what she wants… if you have the guts."

The object of his derision and his undying affection slid her eyes sideways as the lids lowered to the hooded eyes of a hunter. She harrumphed as she slid her eyes back to Hooker, quietly starting to confide in him, and then seeing Johnny, she stopped. "Squirt, why don't you go watch a little television with the cranky old man. It'll probably do you both some good."

The kid knew when it was in his best interest to become vapor, and in the clearing wisps of his presence, Stella turned her attention to Hooker. Putting her hands on his shoulders, she moved in closer. "I just wanted to hear from you that you were all right. I don't just take Manny's word for things. He's still a cop. Even though they took the man off the force, the macho stuff is still in his belly, and they will never be able to pull the detective badge out of his pants—it's attached." She smirked at her slightly crude joke.

"I'm fine, Stell," nodding his head. "Really, I'm okay. Well, other than I have a kid to drag around for a while." He rolled his eyes with a little too much drama.

"Yah, and Squirt is another thing." She looked with a sudden hardness in her face. "Really? Putting a fork through a kid's hand?" The fact the two sisters talked about everything had stopped surprising Hooker a long time ago.

"It wasn't all the way." He shrugged. "Just most of the way." His face looked up at her from a sideways boyish half-smile showing he knew the punishment would come but knew it would be bearable; but just maybe he could weasel out of it.

Her finger flashed up into his face as her nose came within two inches of his. Her whisper had a bite as well as bark. "Don't you dare try to give me those big weaseling green eyes. This time it won't work." She poked his chest, driving home the guilt she had no reason to inflict. "You had better pay for his doctor bills!" she whipped around to the sink. "Doing some foolish street punk thing like that. What were you thinking?"

He opened his mouth, and she jumped right back into his face with her finger and all. "Shut it." She glared hard, and a lesser man would have wet himself. "Anything you thought you were going to say, you better think about for a day or so."

The phone rang, and Manny picked it up in the sunroom as Stella just stood with silent eyes locked on her knight in shining armor, and the child they never had. Every bit of motherhood was being used up in heaps and loads far beyond mortal woman, and Hooker was the beneficiary, and he knew it.

"Hooker!" Manny called.

She poked her finger one last time for emphasis and let him go. Hooker slid from between the stone island and an even harder object.

"Yeah, Manny?" he asked as he walked into the sunroom. The kid was staring at Manny who was drained of all color and still listening as he wrote on one of the legal pads always within reach of Manny, as well as not one but three pens in his shirt pocket, and even his T-shirts were pocketed. Hooker thought, *once a detective, always a detective—it's attached.*

"Okay, here's Hooker," he said, handing over the phone. "It's Captain Davis."

"Yeah, Captain, what can I do for you?"

"Hooker, we have another officer down. I want you to handle the tow, but you're going to need a flatbed."

"I don't have one, but I can get one. Where's it at?" The officer told him as he looked and saw Manny already had it written down.

"I need you to bring Manny out with you, can you do it, or should I send a patrol car?"

"No, I can handle it." He looked at the small man in the chair. "But why Manny?"

"He knows more about what we're up against. Just bring him and fast. This one is going to be hard to keep a lid on."

"We're in the truck, sir." Hanging up and then picking the phone back up again, and dialing a number from memory, he turned to Manny. "You need anything else?" The man nodded and headed into the office he almost never used anymore.

From the office, he called out, "Hey, Squirt, can you give me a hand in here?" The kid was last night's vapor as he reappeared on the way to a place he was needed.

The ringing on the other end of the phone stopped, and a groggy voice answered. "Si, this is Jose."

Hooker's head snapped around at the sound of the older Garcia answering. "Jesus, Joe! You sound like shit."

"Miguel is in worse condition. He's been throwing up since last night. Hooker, I tell him to go to the medico, but he is one giant pendejo. What I gonna do with such a stupid brother?" The older brother was now starting to sound almost alive. "What you call for, Hooker? It's the middle of the night, you know. Not every people be a vampire like you."

"Joe," Hooker didn't know how to phrase his request. "I need a flatbed right now."

"You no have one, senor."

"Joe, I know that. You didn't get this call, but I'm going to give you the whole tamale. But I don't know where the tow is going, and you probably never saw it, but I need your ass up here and don't worry about a ticket. There isn't a cop between you and this address, trust me."

"Where you need it, man?"

Hooker gave him the address and then told him what was there. The man gave a low whistle and told him fifteen minutes. Hooker hung up knowing the man lied because, with his trucks, it would take him at least thirty, and the clock was ticking.

Walking out into the entry vestibule he called for Manny, and the man rolled out of the office. "Hey, Squirt. There are those two black bags in there, too. Can you go place them… not throw them like Hooker would, into the back of the truck?"

The kid slid by confidently. "Sure, Manny." Then he saw the *bags.* "Do you have dead bodies in these coffins?" He started lifting the large black crime scene bags.

Hooker glanced in and saw the bags. "Good gosh, Manny, I thought they took those away from you when you got your ticket clipped."

"Shut up!" the man barked. "The less you see and know, the better."

Stella, the guardian, stood by the door and kissed each on the top of the head or cheek as it was presented in passing. As Hooker followed up the rear, she rolled her eyes and hissed. "Retired my aunt Sarah's behind!" She kissed his cheek. "You're still on my shit list, but you watch out for the old battle-ax. I still might want to have him around."

"You've got it. Don't wait up."

She stood stoic in the doorway, watching the three traverse the court-yard as the watery lights cast giant shadows along the walls. Three decades of marriage had tempered her steel, but only to the point which was visible on the outside. The young girl, quaking on the inside was about to go call her little sister who was busy pampering a battle-worn furball on her chest, purring contently with the smell of pure white Alba-core tuna on his breath. Spoiled would be too mild of a word when it came to the relationship of Box and Dolly.

The kid hoisted each of the large squared-off black ballistic nylon bags up onto the back of the truck. Each got its own grunt from the young man. Finished, he came around the right side of the truck to see Hooker with Manny slung over his shoulder, climbing up into the cabin.

As he flipped Manny down onto the seat, he looked down at the kid. "Go get up through my side and climb into the sleeper." Climbing down, he collapsed the wheelchair, placed it effortlessly on the back work-deck of the truck, and strapped it down with bungee cords.

Climbing into the cab, he looked at Manny in the passenger seat. "What do you think, back route or down Blossom Hill?" He fired up the monster and stuck it in seventh gear.

Manny leaned over and felt for the hidden switch he knew was there as he sighed. "Why waste time, lets fly." The flashing red and blue lights lit up the neighborhood as the truck began to roll down the road. "At this hour, you won't need a siren." He smiled over at the man he always thought of as *the kid,* but then looked back at the very young face of the new squirt.

The asphalt stretched out and was consumed by the giant Marmon truck and the oversized engine as it slung the monster down the road like a Corvette in a tailwind. The denizens of the night and drunks coming out of the closing bar of the steakhouse could see the swirling yellow lights on top and the alternating blue-red hiding in the oversized grill from many blocks away. The street itself was all but empty as the three men rolled across the bottom of the valley to the other side.

Reaching back, Hooker grabbed the mic and keyed in. "10-8."

The radio squelched and then cleared. "About time. You left the house seven and a half minutes ago." Hooker could hear the constant purring of Box through the radio.

"Box must not be massaging you in the right places, because you sound like your panties are in a twist, Dolly. What's up?" Hooker was actually concerned.

"It's not going to be a pretty sight when you get out there, Hooker. You keep Squirt away from it, you hear?"

Hooker looked over at Manny, and the man nodded in understanding and agreement. Hooker just double-clicked the mic and hung it back up. He cleared his mirrors and looked back over at Manny as he downshifted for the red light at Snell, but instead of stopping, merely turned right. "Was there something you were going to tell me?"

The former detective glanced and nodded back at the kid in the sleeper.

Hooker glanced back and gave Manny a look of exasperation. "He's a grown-up, for God's sake. What can be so bad?"

Thinking for a moment, Manny finally spoke. "They think it was a flame thrower, both officers were killed, but it wasn't instant." The older man looked out the forward window. "Captain Davis said it likely won't be very pretty."

Hooker weighed what the man was saying and started downshifting to turn left. Across the broken fields a half-mile away, Hooker could see the flashing and rotating lights of police and fire trucks. He manhandled the large truck around the corner and reached over and down under the dashboard to switch off the highly illegal red and blue lights.

Parking Lot B came up first as they slowed and made the turn into the giant lot where you could park four aircraft carriers while leaving a lot of room between the ships, or two thousand cars and trucks. But, at two o'clock in the morning, there were just police and fire department vehicles with one burned-out car in the middle, all under one of the large floodlight poles marching across the parking lot.

Hooker nosed in as close as he could without being intrusive. He'd leave that department for Manny to handle later. Unloading the wheelchair while the kid clambered out of the sleeper and unstrapped the large crime scene bags, Hooker climbed up to catch Manny as the man literally rolled out of the seat seven feet above the asphalt.

"Holy moly, Hooker. Any slower, and I'd be picking myself up off the grinder by myself."

"Here, let me put you back. This I want to see." Hooker gave just as he received the friendly caustic sarcasm from the man he loved deeply, and who had been like a father or favorite uncle to him.

"Just try to get me in the chair without sticking the back-rest up my butt."

Hooker smudged a bad imitation of Mae West as he slowly lowered the older man— "Excuse me, but is this seat taken or just filled." The two snorted with the bad old line they relished anytime Hooker helped him with a transfer to his chair.

Hooker straightened to find an officer standing at casual parade rest, waiting for the center of attention to be readied. "Officer Aligo, how good of you to join us." Hooker joked but got no rise to levity from the usually humorous or near to large humorous Filipino.

"Sorry, Hooker, but there is no humor here tonight." Looking from the driver to his passenger, he asked, "Do you have everything you need, sir?"

"I think so, James. If you could help carry the bags, I think Squirt would appreciate it." As the officer started to turn to the bags, Manny cautioned, "But first I want the lay of the land. I take it you were the first responder?" He caught himself. "I mean, of course, after the other two."

"Yes, sir. Basically, what you will see, other than some parts still with bits of fire still present, is exactly what I rolled up on."

"Did you deploy any fire extinguishers?"

"No, the small flames were already guttering, and I wanted the scene as uncontaminated as possible, sir." He looked over his shoulder and thought aloud, "There was one thing, though."

"What?"

"While it was settling down, a round cooked off and punched a very large hole in the front windshield, sir."

"About the size of a dime?" Hooker injected.

The officer thought about it as he looked at his fingers. "No, but close, more like the size of a nickel or quarter."

Manny looked back at Hooker. "The close range would also be capturing the energy of the explosive wave. Therefore, I would expect it to be a little larger."

Hooker nodded. "That's why you have a higher pay grade."

Manny's head snapped back toward Hooker with his most 'nail them to the wall' look. Then turning back to the uniform, he asked, "Did you hear anything landing?"

"Dimes, sir. Marked them all, I think. How did you know?" His face became a mass of confusion.

Manny gave him a side-stare as he began to push toward the scene stinking up the neighborhood like a luau gone horribly wrong. "It's what I get paid the big bucks for." Throwing a call in Johnny's general direction, "Punjab, bags," he rolled away, consummately taking command of the scene. "Officer Aligo, where's my path in?"

The officer pointed out the two small cones, "Straight into the driver's door."

As he cleared the vehicles and came to view the entire scene, he noted the small yellow cones on the asphalt. He thought a moment and spun the chair. "Officer Aligo?"

"Sir." The man hustled overhauling one of the large, heavy bags.

"How many dimes did you find?"

"Twelve."

"Hmm..." Manny spun his chair back to look at the yellow cones standing like little soldiers. Something was wrong, and then he saw the pattern.

"Hooker?"

"Yeah, Manny, right here."

"What was the farthest you ever shot a dime load and hit anything?"

The young man looked at the officer of the law and hesitated only a moment. "When Betsy was Betsy Ross McWhole, it would be the day you and I shot and killed the barn. That would be almost what, a hundred feet? But as she is now, about fifty or sixty feet at the most."

"What if you shot it almost straight up and through a windshield?"

Hooker looked out across the parking lot and now understood what the little yellow cones were. "I would guess there are probably one or two more dimes lying under those two cars and the fire truck."

Turning his chair back to the officer, he agreed. "My thinking exactly." Pointing to the three vehicles and a couple of others, he told the officer how to back them away from the scene. "Everyone is to be in latex gloves. I want no chance of getting someone's fingerprint or jelly donut leftovers. I want an officer on each tire, as the vehicle backs out in creep mode. I want four hands floating on those tires. If they feel or see a dime, they call a halt. We'll place the dime, and mark it, and then keep going. But in the end, I want all five of those vehicles backed off about one hundred feet."

"You've got it, sir." The officer took off jogging toward the cluster of other officers, both San Jose PD and CHP.

Soon the three stood watching a slow, painful process unfold which, in the end, yielded four more dimes. Manny looked up at Hooker with a question on his face. Then looked back at the scene. "What's wrong here, Hooker?"

"Too many dimes, Manny, too many dimes." The young man stood slowly shaking his head, trying to make it understand the evidence.

Johnny cleared his throat, and Hooker looked over, jerking his head as if to ask what was on the kid's mind. The kid cleared his throat again. "Why are sixteen dimes too many?"

Hooker stared at the scene with his eyes twitching, taking in the information more than they were swiveling with surveillance. Finally turning to the kid, he asked, "Do you know anything about how a shotgun shell is put together?"

The kid nodded. "Yeah, kind of. There is a metal back end and plastic front. There are the powder and little BBs in it."

Hooker took over the simplistic explanation. "Once you put the powder in, you pack it with a small disk of felt, and then there is a thicker felt pad called the compression pad, and then a plastic cup with the shot in it. All of it has to sit at such a point the top can get crimped over and formed into place." The kid was nodding along, until Hooker added, "Take out the cup, and a standard two and three-quarter-inch shell only holds fourteen dimes, not sixteen," as he extended his arm and waved it across the now expanded crime scene.

Manny was slowly rolling into the scene, yelling for the officer. "Aligo! Have them look for the wadding and plastic cup also. I seriously doubt they'll find any, but it's worth a look." As he rolled up to the side of the car and the open driver's door, he viewed what he could have the interior. Everything appeared charred but was really just smoke-blackened. Manny's nose was working overtime as, once again, he was back in the middle of what had been an inferno.

As he looked across the dashboard, his eyes stopped. Even if he had been a religious man, he would have stopped when his brain caught up to what the eyes were seeing. "Hooker?"

"Yeah, Manny?" Hooker called back from over a hundred feet away. "Got your back, you need your bag?"

"Come in slow, straight at me. Oh, yeah, and bring the smaller bag." Manny was still focused on the interior, trying to make heads or tails of the object on the dashboard.

Hooker kneeled down to Manny's height. "What am I looking at?"

"Look along the dash for two things, one the condition, and two, what the hell is standing in the middle—because it sure as hell isn't a Virgin Mary."

Hooker studied the dashboard and its strange swirling of burn marks. Thinking about what could have caused the pattern, he also started putting himself in the place of the shooter turned fire bomber. He stood and looked at the almost untouched back seat. And other than the smoke damage, and secondary, the front seat was all but pristine.

"What do you see?" Manny, in educator mode, stirred the pot.

"When they pull the residuals, my guess is the dashboard was wiped down with gasoline, but why?"

"What is on the dash?"

Hooker now stepped around the man in the wheelchair and crouched in the doorway. He then stood over the windshield and then walked around the car, trying to get a better look but to no avail. Finally, he arrived back standing next to Manny, who handed him some rubber gloves and some stick swabs. "Go ahead and climb in, there is nothing on the seat or anything you might touch, but I want a swab of the residue just down from that object."

Hooker obeyed and climbed in. As he got close to the object, he could see what it was.

"It's the brass butt of a 12-gauge shell, isn't it?" Manny swore.

Hooker nodded.

"Get the swab, and then here is a bag."

Hooker poked at the remains of the shell, and it moved. Taking the swab, he wiped it along the area just below the shell. Retracting the swabs into the protectors, he traded Manny for the baggie and removed the shell.

"How did you know it wasn't glued down?"

Manny focused on writing the pertinent data on the containers and baggie they went in. "I didn't, but I know you would have found a way to give it to me."

Hooker climbed out of the car and handed the baggie to Manny, who slapped the prepared tape on it—sealing the top. Slipping the baggie into the container in the one bag, he looked up, saying, "Are you up to this?"

Hooker just stared at him thinking a moment. "I saw my first dead body at fourteen, and my first dismemberment the same summer. Shake and bake I didn't get until the nine-car in Blood Alley the next spring when IBM laid off all of those whack engineers who decided crossing the center line was better than going home to the wife and kids." He slowed the recitation of his resume in gore as he remembered whose parking lot they were standing in. "So, does anybody ever get to the point of being *up to it?*"

The man stared up at the angry young man from his wheelchair. Manny had forgotten just how much Hooker had seen and never brought home with him. Personally, he didn't know why the boy never suffered from nightmares. Only Stella knew of Manny's. After six years off the force, he still woke more nights than not in cold sweats she had to wipe down with the towels always handy by the bed. He nodded, "Good point," and as he turned toward the back of the car, he caught sight of the young boy thirty feet away, standing ready with the other bag, the one he would need now. "Hooker?" he asked softly.

Hooker looked toward the kid. "Yeah, I know. I was thinking about him." He stepped in front of the wheelchair. "But there is something you might want to consider."

"What? He's a kid."

"Yes. But he's a confused kid who has never found a place to fit in. Today, he has busted his hump, and in his own way, managed to fit in." Hooker didn't know why he was riding to the kid's defense so hard, but he had decided it really didn't matter, because the kid deserved a break, white mitten hand and all. "Besides, he thinks he wants to be a cop." Hooker's shoulders sagged with the weight of sharing something he didn't know if it was his to share.

Manny thought more about what he was seeing in Hooker, and then what he said. He turned and whistled, waving the kid forward. "Bring the bag. Watch where you walk, and follow where Hooker came in," he instructed the kid. "And walk slowly, for Christ's sake."

They watched as the kid performed an exact duplicate of Hooker's path and approach. Manny looked at Hooker, who just looked away so Manny couldn't see the growing smile of pride. The three moved to the rear of the car.

The two officer's bodies were draped with yellow tarps. Manny looked at the lumps and back at the trunk lid. He rolled close to the bumper and investigated the deep trunk where he saw the remains of two mangled five-gallon cans with blown off lids. Manny thought he knew what he was looking at but wasn't sure. The paint on the inside of the trunk was blistered across the entire trunk-lid. There were no hot spots. The bottoms of the cans had been blown apart, most likely, Manny thought, by det-cord (detonation cord used as a fuse and igniter because it burned at 700 mph.) The cord probably was used to first cut the bottom off from the sides of the cans, creating a plunger. Then there would be a larger charge in the center of the can bottom to push both the can bottom and the contents out. A last trailing bit of the explosion would ignite what was probably homemade napalm as it hit the trunk lid and splashed out onto the two officers in a wave of sticky gelatinized gasoline. It would have first robbed them of oxygen, and then cremated them alive as they fell screaming in silence from the lack of air and their bodies melted from the extreme heat. Manny had seen it before as a liaison officer in a country known as Vietnam. Only, there it was called Foo Gas, and it usually came in fifty-five gallon drums instead of five-gallon cans.

"Squirt," he asked quietly. "Look on the top of the trunk lid. Don't touch it, just look." Manny turned to see the kid staring at the bodies under the tarps. "Johnny, I need you here with me now." The kid kind of shook. "Johnny!"

The kid snapped out of it, and turned toward Manny, "Sorry, I was just…" he looked back at the tarps. "They didn't know what hit them, did they?"

Manny's shoulders caved-in, ever so slightly. "No," he said sadly. "They had no idea what they were up against."

The kid, turning to the requested task, spat out almost sub-vocal, "We really need to nail this asshole to the ice-house wall." Looking at the top of the lid, he scanned the wide expanse of scorched and blistered paint. "What am I looking for?"

"What do you see?"

"It's scorched."

"How? In one spot, all over? Is it sunburned or seared like a steak on the Fourth of July? Look at it, and just tell me what you are seeing. Don't tell me what you think you see."

The kid backed off and looked at Manny for a moment as if he were crazy and could do some serious damage to a few million brain cells, and then he eased back over and started looking at the lid with a more critical eye.

"At first glance, it just looks burned all the way across, but then if you look at the top at an angle, you see there are two areas—kind of round, and the metal is a little more rippled like it got more heat or something."

"Good, Johnny, go on. Tell me about the colors." He sat with his eyes closed, seeing through the kid's eyes.

The rings are full black metal, there is no paint there, but there's like an outer ring. It's white, like chalk. Maybe the paint burned up and…"

"STOP!" snapped Manny. "Don't do that."

"Do what?" The kid was only a little defensive and more wanting to do it right.

"Don't think. Don't conjecture about what could or couldn't have possibly happened. Just tell me what you are seeing. Okay?"

Hooker stepped over to the other side of the car and looked at the lid, also.

"Ok," the kid resumed. "There is about a two-inch ring of white chalky substance where the deformed metal ends."

"Good, that's good. Keep going."

"There are some small red areas, but they don't appear to have anything to do with the initial burn areas. In fact… just a moment." He leaned into the trunk before Manny could stop him. The kid looked up under the rear deck for a moment then stepped over and took the flash-light away from Manny and leaned back into the trunk's more intimate reaches up under the back panel. Looking about for a moment, he gave a grunt and withdrew. Handing the flashlight back to Manny, he said, "The red is from the iron oxide undercoating they primed it with." Pointing back into the trunk, he explained, "When they shoot the final color, they always skimp, and so the final paint doesn't really cover the primer."

Manny sat with his mouth open.

The kid was offended. "Hey, I know things, okay? I worked in a body shop for a short time, and they are always cutting corners." He stood with his arms somewhere between fists on his hips and fists in the air.

Manny held up both of his hands. "Peace, peace. No, I'm impressed. I would have never thought to look under there. How about you, Hooker?"

Hooker came around the edge of the car. "Hey, I'm sitting in your chair."

Manny considered the new information, and slowly spun his chair around, looking at the slain officers and the trunk lid back and forth. "Guys, do me a favor and peel back the tarps, go easy though, they may be stuck to the burned flesh. But I want you to start from this end—feet first."

The remains, Hooker was thinking, because from about mid-thigh up, there wasn't enough left to call them corpses, were seared into a tableau of horror and surprise. "They must have died almost instantly," he sighed.

"One would hope." Ever professional, Manny leaned in close to look at the cremation.

Johnny stepped around the end of the car, careful not to touch anything and staring at the two still somewhat smoldering cenotaphs of a pair of cops who gave their all to protect and serve the citizens of San Jose. Gently he asked, "What am I looking at, Manny?"

The older detective looked up at the kid and saw he was serious in his request. Nodding, he turned back to the evidence. Pointing to the thighs, he indicated the burned edges. "If this had been just gasoline, the splash would have at least taken the entire pants from the knees up. But what we have here is napalm. It's gelatin and very sticky, so where it landed is where it burned."

He looked back up at the kid. "What we probably have is homemade napalm, not much more than a bunch of Styrofoam or polystyrene mixed into gasoline. The gas melts the foam, but the foam changes the gas, and eventually, it thickens or gels until you have napalm." Seeing if the kid was following, and seeing his eyes were clear, and his head was nodding, he continued. "The nasty thing about napalm is the foam chemicals mixed with the gas form a hydrocarbon which burns much, much hotter than gas alone. In fact, gasoline doesn't burn, just the fumes. But with napalm, the heat quickly reaches an intensity to allow the liquid itself to ignite. With the liquid burning the temperature turns left and goes straight up and burns at temperatures approaching five-thousand degrees. Because it is so sticky, it's impossible to get it off." Turning to indicate the former officers, "but these guys were ambushed, and I'm willing to bet a steak dinner at the Bold Knight when the flaming mass came at them, they took a very large suck of air, drawing the flame right down into their lungs, searing off any oxygen exchange."

"They didn't even have a chance." The kid sagged.

"No, no, they didn't." Manny grimaced and turned back toward the kid. "It sucks, but it's kind of the way the job is. You get the test, and if you're lucky, you pass well enough to then learn the lesson."

They worked for another thirty minutes taking samples and lots of pictures until the medical examiner showed up to take over. The ME walking up to the perimeter was an old friend of Manny's, and he guided him down the already known pathway to the car.

They shook hands. "Hello, Frank. I bet they got you up from a sound sleep."

"Manny," the man grumped. "It was supposed to be my night off. They can't seem to find my understudy, for some reason." Looking about, he asked in the shorthand coming with working close together for years. "Run it down, will you?"

"Two officers, my guess seeing the open door on the empty car, they come to investigate. They see the trunk lid cracked maybe an inch or so and open it. Inside are two five-gallon cans full of napalm and rigged with det-cord. Opening the lid pulls the wire that triggers the mechanism. The napalm is ejected from the cans, straight up, hitting the lid and forcing it fully open. The napalm is ignited by now and starting to hit temperature as it hits the stops on the lid and bounces out hitting the two officers. The initial strike is down the bronchial, searing the membrane into Saturday night's steak. They're dead standing at twelve-thirteen a.m."

The ME is still nodding as he follows the pattern as Manny describes it. "Um-hum, yes, yes. How did you get the twelve-thirteen? Why not twelve-fifteen?"

"Because *twelve-thirteen*," pointing to the all-metal dive watch on what was left of a wrist, "is when the guy's watch stopped."

The ME leaned over and examined the watch. Standing, he dusted off his hands. "I don't know why they even called me."

Manny turned to the Squirt. "Pull the small plastic box out of the smaller bag and give him the evidence, and give me the paperwork right beside it, would you please?" Turning to the ME as he pointed at the cops walking a grid, "Frank, those officers are looking for a 12-gauge shot cup, some dimes, and the wadding. I rather doubt they will find the cup. I don't think he used one. There are sixteen dimes out there. But I'm very curious about the wadding. Let me know what you find. If you could call me later this morning, I'd like a full rundown. You have my phone number. Just so you know, I'll be running a board of my own at the house. I'd appreciate it if you would call me with any info before you kick it upstairs."

"Are you on the clock now, Manny?"

"No. Chet called, and this is personal," he jerked his head in Hooker's direction. "They shot at my boy—twice." He started rolling around toward the pathway. "Bags, boys. We're going home. We still have a beating from Stella coming. I smelled pineapple upside-down cake earlier."

Hooker put the bag down on the working bed of the truck and turned to the kid. "Strap these down, Squirt, and if you're feeling strong, you can stow Manny and strap his chair down, too." Turning to Manny, "I need to go arrange things with Jose, and I'll be back in a few minutes. Don't do anything stupid while I'm gone." He reached into the cab and grabbed his leather jacket against the chill of the early morning air.

Manny watched as the young man walked away like the man he had become. Manny thought about the night he and Stella had met such a young kid. For a Jewish couple, it had been quite the Christmas present, even though they hadn't known it at the time; but then, a lot can change in a decade or so. He just shook his head and looked over at the new kid. Maybe not so fresh-scrubbed, but he definitely had the hot and eager look in his eye.

"Don't even think about it, Squirt. I'd crush you like a June bug on a two-step line dance floor in Gilroy on a Saturday night." The two laughed at the funny saying, but more as a relief from the horror they had just spent nearly three hours with. "I've got to say, kid, you handled yourself well out there. There are plenty of rookie cops, and some older ones too, who see something like and just start puking their last Sunday's dinner all over the crime scene." He nodded and watched the kid turn darker in the dark, but Manny knew the kid could tell he wasn't just blowing smoke up his skirt. The kid really did have potential.

"So, are you going to tell me about the hand, or do I have to have Stella beat it out of you?"

The kid passed the now dirty gauze mitten back around behind him, and the night darkened even a shade deeper around his ears. "It's nothing," he lied quietly.

Manny looked at him for a full minute, and when he realized the story wasn't forthcoming, he looked away from where Hooker was arranging the tow with the flatbed truck. "It's okay. When we get home, I'll just loan Stella my belt, and she can beat the story out of you." He could feel the horror in the kid's eyes on the back of his neck and smiled inwardly as he watched Hooker direct the action needed to happen in scraping up the mess.

Hooker pointed out the alignment for getting the car. "We'll have to use the inflate bladder to get the back part up high enough to slide the dolly under those rims." He looked at the melted tires and turned back to the large Latino with graying at the one temple where he had been hit by a wreck recovery gone bad. Other than that, he was a handsome man—if you liked gold teeth. "Do you have some heavy plastic or Visqueen? Because we're going to want to line those tires, or you'll never get the gooey rubber off your dolly."

"My dolly?" The man slurred in one of his favorite movie lines... "We don't need no stinking dollies!"

"Okay." Then Hooker pointed out, "My dolly. And I don't want it all covered with fung." He made a face at the larger driver. "But my point is, the ass-end of the car is toast, so you can't jerk from it, or it would fall apart, and if you snatch from the front, the car will just break up, and there goes the crime scene, and then we're both out of business. So, we have to dolly the butt and pull the dolly from the front. Comprende, amigo?"

"Si, si, si, si." The man nodded, then jerked his head as he saw the cop approaching.

Hooker turned. "Ready for us, Aligo?"

"About five minutes. The ME is done, but we need to figure out how to scoop the bodies and still have them hold together."

"Sure, no problem." Hooker nodded as the officer strode off to arrange a few last details on his crime scene, like the three news reporters who had shown up in the last thirty minutes.

Turning back to the larger Garcia brother, he finished going over where the tow would go, and how to deliver it and who got the bill. "The captain requested it, and he knows what the bill should be, so don't be bashful, but don't slam them either, or I'll come after you." Hooker hiked up his left eyebrow for emphasis, and the driver got the message.

"No problem, jefe, I do the tow, drop it and bill it. No hard skin on my back, but what about the dollies?"

"Don't worry. I'll pick them up tomorr…" Hooker caught himself and looked at his watch, "…later today. Don't even bother with them, because they will need the bladder to get them off anyway. So I'll just do it all at once." Turning toward his truck, he waved at the officer who was circling his hand in the air for the sign to circle the wagons and get things done. Dancing backward, he pointed at the burned-out hulk. "Go ahead and back into it for a front snatch, and we'll be right over with the dollies and bladder." He then turned and jogged for the giant truck and smiled at seeing Manny still sitting in his chair. He chuckled and thought *smart kid*.

As the first pink tinged the gray of the last night air, the tall nose of the big truck followed the flatbed truck up to Blossom Hill. Then as the smaller truck continued to the forensic lab's barn of a garage, Hooker flicked his blinkers and turned left across the south end of the valley, and the smell of rich loam soil turned to plant beans and strawberries. Hooker always thought he had the best territory in the South Bay area basin. Just along Blossom Hill Boulevard itself, there were orange, apple, and cherry orchards, and then there were the back reaches stretching down through San Martine, and onto the Garlic Capital of the world, Gilroy. And if there wasn't enough food, there were truck farms running all the way down to King City until they stopped at the great expanse of Fort Hunter Leggett.

The sun was searing the frothy wisps of clouds as Hooker pulled Manny out of the truck, and they all headed toward the end of the very long day which felt more like a week. Even the woman, standing with arms akimbo in the front gate doors, would not have a shot at them until about three pm and a pot or two of coffee.

18

The phone wouldn't stop ringing. The answering machine should have picked up, or at least some other person in the house, but the phone kept ringing. Then it stopped. Silence. Then broken again as the jangling ring of the phone continued.

Hooker didn't care what time it was, but he felt like someone on the other end of the phone needed a piece of his mind. Rolling out of bed, he stuck his stocking feet in the boots captured at the side of the bed by his pants legs. Grabbing the belt, he pulled them up and buttoned the fly as he expanded his eyes to make them focus.

Shuffling across the room, he opened the door. The strong midday sun poured into the darkened room, and semi-blinding him as he made his way to the still incessantly ringing phone. Waking up amicable was not one of Hooker's strong suits. "Hello," he answered curtly.

"Hello, princess," the voice oozed.

"Oh, hi, Willie."

"My, we are so chipper this morning. Did you have a lousy night last night?"

"Yeah, we were out on a burn job till sun-up. What do you need?" He started looking around for a note or something to explain Stella or

Manny not answering their phone. Distracted, he missed his uncle's statement. "Wait. What did you say?"

"I said it was all over the front page of the Star this morning. Imagine my shock to see not only you but also Manny at a crime scene. I thought the old fart retired and got a life."

"At seventy-four, I would be careful who you called 'old,' you old fart."

"Stop it. I'm only seventy… one." The silence was palatable as Willie waited for a reassuring compliment he knew all too well wasn't coming. "Speaking of the child, why isn't he answering his phone?"

"I don't know, Willie. Stella came home last night; then we rolled on the fire call… What does it say in the paper?"

"Oh, plenty, but you know newspapers. They always get things wrong then they must retract them the next day, except it takes them a week. But they think they are still right, until they say their wrong, so they put it off as long as they…"

"Willie!" Hooker grabbed his forehead with his whole hand in an effort to stop the coming headache. He loved his uncle dearly, but there were days…

Quieter and calmer, he asked the now silent phone, "Willie, what does the paper say?"

"Well," ignoring being yelled at, "Hmm… responded to a call from security… blah, blah, blah… two officers… found a 1968 Coupe de Ville… anda, anda… oh, here it is, and it appeared a firebomb killed the two officers on contact." Hooker could hear the man put the paper down in quiet exasperation. He asked softly, "Hooker, is it true? About two officers killed?"

Hooker sunk against the kitchen island, and the cold granite felt good across his upper buttocks. He sighed. "Yeah, Willie. Unfortunately, this time they got it right." The headache wasn't going to stop today. "Did it say anything about them finding anything else?"

"Oh, yeah, they are calling him the 'Dime-Load Killer.'"

"Oh, Christ on a crutch—who is?" Hooker looked out the window into the courtyard.

"The Star, silly," the man exclaimed. "The police would never use such a stupid name."

As his uncle had broken him of swearing out loud, Hooker swore under his breath.

"I heard that, Hooker. That will be a nickel in the jar when you get home, you naughty boy."

Hooker rolled his eyes. "Anything else, Willie? I've got to get some more sleep."

"No, just checking in. And letting you know about the article."

"Great, thanks." He started to hang up and then remembered. "Hey, Willie, would you make up the bed in the guest room, please?"

"Male or female?"

"What?"

"Is our guest a male or a female?"

"What's it matter what sex the person is?"

"It matters, trust me. If it's a female, I need to use the nice sheets and some throw pillows. If it's just one of your tow truck buddies whose wife threw him out for being drunk or farting in the fresh sheets…"

"Male."

"Who-ooo?" he singsonged tauntingly at Hooker.

"My new employee, and be straight with him, he's only eighteen, I think."

"Spoilsport. When are you coming home?"

Sniffing his T-shirt and twisting his face up. "Sooner than you think."

"Okay, Big Stuff, I'll make up the guest bed and lay out some towels and such. See you later."

"Bye." Hooker placed the phone in the cradle. Now it was really bugging him that nobody was there, and no note.

As he shuffled back toward his room, he noticed Manny's office door was closed. He opened it quietly and saw why Manny hadn't answered the phone. He couldn't hear it. The man sat in his wheelchair staring at two large pinboards with photos and cards tacked to them. On his head was a pair of commercial recording headphones covering most of each side of his head. Hooker looked at the twelve-inch commercial reel-to-reel tape deck Sweets had gotten for him years before, slowly turning. Hooker's guess was Vivaldi or Brahms.

Manny noticed a shift in the light and turned his chair around and raising the headphones to the top of his head so he could hear Hooker. "Stella went to the grocery to restock the fridge and should be back soon. The kid is in the sunroom, and when I last checked on him, he was curled around Box."

Hooker snapped his fingers and silently swore. "Bean burritos on a stick!"

"It's okay. Dolly figured we were coming straight home and dropped him off around seven this morning, but he probably won't be talking to you for a few days, so you may as well leave him here for Stella to chase around, or vice-versa."

Hooker was looking at the boards. "When did you do all of this?" Then he realized. "You haven't been to bed at all, have you?"

Manny waved the back of his hand. "Blah, sleep is overrated."

Hooker yawned and thought about the time. "Well, I'm not as old, so I need more sleep. Wake me about two or so, would you?"

"Sure," the detective was already turned around and looking at his board. Vivaldi softly filtered from the top of his head.

Hooker shuffled back to his dark chamber and closed out the light. Dropping his pants down around his boots, he slipped out of the boots and fell back into the bed.

Not working set hours and being on-call 24/7 had put craters the size of New Jersey in his internal circadian clock but did make it easy to drop into a deep sleep before his wavy head of hair hit the pillow. This time was no exception. The only thing that caused a few seconds hesitation was the tiny spot of white among the complete background of black. The white had meaning, and a part of Hooker knew he knew what it was.

But old habits took over, and Hooker was dead to the world until a shotgun blast would rip his sleep apart a few hours later.

19

The shotgun blasts were silent and in very slow motion. Hooker woke because of too many. When they should have stopped at five or six, they kept exploding out of the dark from a light-colored car. Shotgun flash after shotgun flash silently ripped through the dark of night, and then the last one made a sound—the sound of terra-cotta plates landing on a granite island.

Hooker rolled over and looked at blurry red numbers that made no sense. There were three blobs of red, and he could have sworn when he had laid down, a few moments before, there were four. The light taps on the door confirmed there were really three and it was two in the afternoon.

"Thanks, Stella," he mumbled, wondering if he had even said it out loud.

The ocean waves roared in his head and ears as he slung his legs over the edge of the bed and sat up with his eyes closed. Washing his face and eyes with his palms, he raised erect and silently stumbled toward his bathroom. Flicking on the shower faucet, he walked past and sat on the throne while the water warmed up, trying to remember what was so important when he lay down. The fog was thick, and he was unsuccessful. Flushing, he counted to five and got up, grabbing a towel as he shuffled into the shower room big enough for a party of four to eight, or a caretaker and a wheelchair.

Hooker sat on the cedar bench under the water as he filled the wooden bucket with some water, squirted liquid Castile soap into the bucket, and stirred it with the long-handled brush. Absently, he thought of the design features Manny and Stella had incorporated into their dream home... back when Manny was a virile police detective with his legs working under him. Two months, seventeen days and three hours remained until his retirement. No one ever thinks they will be the one needing extra wide doors or bathrooms large enough for a wheelchair and a caregiver—no one. But it had not been very long after they had finally moved out of the trailer at the bottom of the driveway and into the house when a drug bust gone wrong left Manny in the wheelchair, he had only thought his father would need. Forty-three weeks later, Manny had left the hospital for the first of five times over the next two years, and came home to a loving, carefully thought out home that would be fully supportive of his needs. Life is funny that way sometimes.

Starting with his feet, he began to scrub his entire body with the Japanese scrubbing brush. He chuckled as he wondered how it now seemed so natural for him to sit in a Jewish couple's home, built like a Mexican hacienda, taking a shower in this huge room, scrubbing down with a traditional Japanese cleaning tool. It is so natural to adapt to things outside of our nature, and in so adapting, making them our nature. Even though people on the outside make assumptions about only what they see on the surface, like the neighbor across the street for years assumed Manny and Estelle were Mexicans, he was surprised when Stella whipped up some killer latkes and kugel after they finished the building and held an open house the first Christmas. Maybe it was Manny's Italian name of Romero that threw them off.

Hooker smirked under the foaming head of bubbles and then his hand froze on the handle of the water control. The deck of information and conversations over the last few days suddenly shuffled, and Hooker's dealt hand was a full house flush of black knaves.

The chill ran down his spine had nothing to do with the hot water now flooding over his head, and then a flash as he rinsed his body: he knew who the ninja in black was… or could be.

Flipping the water lever off and grabbing the large bath sheet, Hooker toweled down as he stepped over to the door and yelled for Manny. The clock was now ticking, and a very large train wreck was headed toward San Jose. "Manny!"

"Coming, I said," as he wheeled out of the office toward the glassed hall down the guest wing.

Hooker pulled his pants up, ignoring their four-day filth on his clean skin. Grabbing his T-shirt, he caught a strong whiff of his odor, once again wishing he packed a small bag of spares in the truck.

The wheelchair appeared in the doorway. "What?" The headphones hung about his neck impotently as the wire and jack-plug dangled down his chest to his lap.

"Sweets said ninjas wear all black. You said they make napalm different ways, but you thought our napalm smelled like the kind used in Foo Gas." Hooker was pounding out the words to match his racing heart, "A dollar sixty in dimes… The dimes are the only coin that fits in the shotgun. It's not about the dimes. It's about how many. We know only fourteen fit in a cup, but they found sixteen and no cup."

The man looked at him with stone-hard eyes, the mind running faster than the eyes could keep up. Hooker knew the look was one not of stupidity but just the opposite. "So…?"

Hooker jammed the bottom of the starched T-shirt into his jeans. "So, if the killer uses sixteen, the carrier for the dimes is specially adapted. The focus is on sixteen for some reason, not the dimes."

Manny's mind was now catching up and running at top detective level. "Or maybe, it is about the dimes *and* how many."

Stella called from the kitchen. "If you boys don't come now, I'm giving it to Box and the Squirt."

Hunger overtook Hooker and Manny at the same time, and they moved to the kitchen, both lost in thought. Manny had long ago taught Hooker the power of pushing out thoughts to a group and watch for the answers taking shape from the collective. He could never imagine what kind of collective group Hooker could or would create. Sometimes the kid flat-out amazed him.

As the large terracotta dishes sat in front of the four humans and one content cat in Manny's lap, Johnny tippy toed into the idea pool. "So, if the message is about the dimes and how many, could the dates or mint mark have any meaning, too?"

"Sure," mused Manny as he morphed into teaching mode. "Let's say you were killing people who did you wrong in 1970. So to get your message across, but you are the only one who understands the message, you load the rounds full of 1970 dimes. Also, let's say this happened in Philadelphia, so you use all dimes minted in Philadelphia in 1970."

Hooker sat looking in the coffee mug only inches away from his mouth. Then looking up, he furrowed his brow and looked over at Manny. "Do we know if the dates or mint are all the same?" His eyebrows raised, and his eyes rolled. "I mean it is a pretty 'out there' kind of idea."

Manny just sat and stared at Hooker.

Finally, Hooker asked, "What?" shoving his hand out palm up.

Manny just stared, and then said quietly, "That's just it. I don't know."

Hooker now stared at him then held up his hands and asked with a shrug, "And?"

Stella rolled her eyes as she got up and looked at the kid. "Would you please clear the plates, Squirt? I need to get my husband his tools." Giving Manny a look, which he knew all too well, she turned toward his office. "Anything else you need besides your cordless phone, legal pad, and a pen?"

"No, dear." He flashed Hooker the wounded husband goofy face, and then called after her, "You are not only my hero but the love of my short-ened life."

She scoffed as she sauntered into the other room to retrieve the items.

Manny quietly planted his face into his right hand as Hooker began to chuckle. Manny muttered into his hand as he slowly shook his head, "I'm so very glad I didn't marry the fine little Italian girl, Virginia Pipeline." Referring to a very bad old joke about three octogenarian Italian men, which made Hooker laugh even harder as he rolled over and buried his face in a throw pillow.

Several minutes later, he thanked the medical examiner and hung up the phone. He sat, staring at Johnny, who silently started to fidget and blush. Quietly, Manny bounced the back of the pen off the legal pad. "How old did you say you were?" Manny asked.

"Twenty."

"Hmm." Manny closed his eyes and laid his head back, thinking. The music of Stella's humming in the kitchen was soothing, but Hooker was getting a little impatient. Manny opened his eyes and looked at Hooker and Johnny. "The ME said he was just about to call me. All of the dimes they recovered from both scenes were dated 1958... and minted in San Francisco."

Hooker looked at the Squirt and smiled at the kid whose mouth was gaping open.

"He also said they were all in mint or uncirculated condition. So they were probably, or at least possibly, bought as a collector's roll."

Johnny added quietly, "Or bought as new rolls of dimes at a bank in 1958."

Manny smiled as he turned to the kid. "How does it feel to have cracked a major break in a high stakes case, kid?"

The kid was trying to breathe or catch his breath. "Pretty cool, but do you think it really means anything?" Looking from Manny to Hooker and back, "I mean, like Hooker said, it really is pretty far out there."

Manny thought about what the kid was really asking, and what he really needed. "I think it is the kind of thinking that could lead to cracking the case."

The kid just sat looking at Manny with a stunned look on his face. Box jumped up on the couch, ignoring everyone, crawled into the kid's lap, and curled up for a nap. Hooker's eyes grew big and looked at Stella, who had just walked back in as she was wiping her hands on her apron.

Stella looked over at Box and the kid, then back at Hooker. "Oh, this is nothing. They were curled up together all night and Box never stopped purring, even when he was snoring." She chuckled. "It was really quite adorable."

Box cracked open one eye and gave Stella an unappreciative look. *Adorable* was not a Box kind of word.

Hooker, reading the cat's look as a great time to escape, stood up. "Manny, we're out of here, but if you can keep working the angle on the dimes, I'm sure something is there. Later, I'm going to try and get some heartbeat from the street, if she's there." Raising his T-shirt's armpit closer to his nose, he winced. "And we are both going to get some fresh clothes."

Stella caught the slight wince out of the corner of her eye as Johnny stood up and had a suspicion of her own she decided she was going to act upon. *And things were going to change around here,* she thought.

As the kid walked past, she reached out and grabbed him by the back of the belt. "Hold on there, cowboy. I'm a checking your brand." As she turned down the belt to reveal the label and the size of the pants, then she let him go.

It was only a half-second, but it made him jump, "Wha... what brand?"

Hooker slapped him gently on the back of the head, "Don't ever ask a woman what she's doing." He leaned over and gave her a buzz on her neck. Even though she wasn't one of his plump gals, he still liked the reaction he got as she melted into his sideways hug.

Her finger reached over and poked him in the chest with each of her words. "You behave and be careful out there." Looking after the kid who was making his escape with the orange furball alongside, she added, "And you take care of him."

Hooker broke the seriousness with a tease. "Box can look after himself."

She slapped his chest and shook out her graying red hair. "You know who I mean, jerk." As he slipped out of her arms, she thought of something else, and she checked his brand, also. "Make sure you give your uncle the same kiss and remind him he is supposed to come help cook on Sunday... and he can bring the blonde friend of his who *really* knows how to cook."

Hooker laughed. "I'll kiss him, I'll tell him, and I'll even tell Hank he has to drag Willie over here, but if Willie touches the brisket, I'm not eating. He would use too much axle grease." Waving at the office door, he yelled at the man with headphones on, "Later, Manny!" but there was no response. Closing the door gently behind him, he could hear Stella laughing about Willie, and it put a big smile on his face to match the sunny day.

As he walked out of the gate, he smiled even harder as he watched Johnny checking the oil on Mae West, knowing he wouldn't stop until he knew everything he needed to check on the rig before starting her up. The kid *was* a fast learner.

Jamming his hand into his pants, looking for his keys, he felt a small envelope. "Shi… eets of rain on the freeway!" He turned back to the house to leave the found dime with Manny. Opening the small packet, he looked at the mintmark—San Francisco 1958. The hairs stood up on the back of his neck and an icy chill shot down his spine. Too close—too, too close.

2 0

____

Box jumped out the door before the truck engine finished shuddering to silence. Striding to the middle of the large lawn, he looked around to make sure any and all were paying attention, and then peed standing straight-legged. No sissy squat-sit for the Box, he was a full-on *man*. Hooker would be the last to remind him of the little 'sleepy time event' occurring in the early days of their relationship.

As Box finished and started kicking the grass, he looked over at the neighbor's yard a hundred feet away and the large bulldog lounging in the sun. Box's grass kicking changed ever so slightly until Hooker called from the truck, "Box, leave Coco alone. You already beat him up this year, and once a year is enough." The cat looked offended and turned his gaze to the street like he was thinking, and to make it clear, he was completely ignoring any contemptuous noise coming from the truck he couldn't see. Sighing, he kicked one last grass tuft in Hooker's direction as he strolled off to see if there might be any fresh food in his dish in the very large garage barn where he heard Willie rummaging around banging metal.

"Wait a minute," Hooker stopped Johnny from getting out.

"Yeah?"

Hooker curled his lower lip in against his teeth, and then looked over at the kid. "Have you ever had any dealings with queers?" This was a tough thing to cover for Hooker. For him, it was just everyday living, but he understood other people had different feelings.

"Once." The kid thought. "I think, why?"

"They aren't called queers. They prefer the term gay. The irony of the term and the life many have been beaten up or killed over is not lost on them. But it is the way they are." Hooker looked through the window into the dark of the shop and watched a small, very bright light spring into being accompanied by the static snarling of the welding. Turning back to the kid, "Some, you would never know they were gay, others are... well, let's just say, a bit more flamboyant." The enormity of introducing someone to one of the most important people in his life had caused his mouth to go dry.

"Willie is the greatest man in the world to have in your corner when the chips are down. If I ever had to choose between Willie and Manny & Stella, I think I would rather just shoot myself." Hooker fidgeted with the keyring in his hand. "Manny and Stella are like the folks I never had, but Willie... well, Willie is the kind of uncle you can talk to about everything. You have a question about cars or trucks? He's your man. You have a question about understanding girls? Well, he's your girl. He's not the best cook, but we're still alive, so he's not going to kill us."

"Okay," Johnny stated as he blinked a few times.

Hooker looked over at the tense young man and realized just how on the edge of becoming a good-looking man he actually was, or at least he could clean up good. Reassuring, "It's okay, he won't touch you unless you tell him you're gay and you want him to touch you. He's kind of in a new relationship right now with a very nice guy."

Hooker was relieved as he watched the tension wash out of the kid's shoulders, and the rigidity disappeared in the set of his jaw. "Okay," the kid started with a sigh, and then his eyes flashed big with horror. "I mean, it's not okay. I mean, I'm not that way, so it's okay that he is, but I'm not, so it's not okay for... oh shit." He collapsed against the door. "I'm just screwing this up, aren't I?"

"Naw, you're doing fine." Some movement caught his eye in the large shop as the man walked across one of the columns of light from the skylights. "Oh shit." It was Hooker's turn to slump. Turning to the kid, he shared the last secret. "Just so you know—he sometimes wears a dress around the house."

The kid looked at him, and then a smile tugged at one corner of his mouth. "He's wearing one now, isn't he?" Hooker rolled his eyes down and twisted his mouth as he nodded his head. Johnny continued, "It's not a pretty one, is it?"

Hooker looked out of the side of his eye at the kid and grimaced in a gimpy smile. "Not on your life. It's the ugliest rag he owns, but hopefully, he will light it on fire from the welder." As they laughed a mutual laugh of camaraderie, they rolled out of the respective doors and strolled into the unavoidable.

"Uncle Willie, I've told you a hundred times not to wear your good dress when you're welding," Hooker called out at the man working halfway into the very large barn of a garage shop strewn with trucks and cars in various conditions of assembly or disassembly.

"Hooker, damn it all! Its laundry day, so what's a girl to do?" The man in the long granny dress so popular with young ladies a quarter his age, walked toward them as he worked his hands out of the large welding gloves and pushed the large mask deeper back on his head.

Extending his firm mechanic's hand, trying hard to keep the Nancy suppressed while he stood in a flowered dress, combat boots with no laces, and a large black leather smithy's apron with decorative studs arranged in a heart shape in the crotch area, he lisped ever so slightly, "William Nest, but just call me Willie."

The kid engaged him firmly and shook. "Johnny, but everyone is calling me Squirt."

"So good to meet you, John," giving Hooker an evil look. "Ignore the Cretans. They can be horribly cruel."

Hooker leaned over and gave him one of his signature big kisses on his neck. "Stella sends her love, even if you are an ass sometimes. Which reminds me, Sunday dinner is at the hacienda."

The older man leaned over and sniffed, "Eww, good thing I'm doing laundry. And stop nuzzling my neck, I'm not one of your fat ladies."

Hooker leaned back and looked at the slightly overweight, but very much in shape older man in the dress, as he raised his eyebrow. "Really?"

Willie slapped at Hooker's chest with his gloves, "Stop it! You'll embarrass your young man here." Then realizing what he had said, he fumbled. "That's not what I meant," as he put a hand out toward Johnny. "I didn't mean to offend you. I mean I just…"

Johnny smiled and clapped the man on the shoulder. "It's okay, and there was no offense taken." Patting him on the shoulder, he started off to follow the way Hooker had taken. "And it may just be my opinion, but really?" He held out his hand palm up as he moved it up and down at the dress while screwing up his face in a disgusted grimace. "The floral pattern is just wrong with the leather. I think maybe a nice patchwork quilted jean dress would be so much more 'go to town.' And, it *is* a more slimming look." Turning before he busted up laughing, he stepped through the doorway into the hall-breezeway leading into the house, catching up with Hooker.

Just inside the door leading into the giant playpen of pure testosterone, with its mix of steel, grease, and gasoline, was the only thing adorning the walls of what Johnny could see to be a sparely appointed living quarters. The kid stopped to look at the photograph and document placed side by side in a simple reddish wood frame. The black and white photo had been taken in a hospital. President LBJ was laying some kind of medal with a long ribbon on the chest of what Johnny assumed was a younger unconscious Willie. The tubes and bandages made it kind of difficult to tell for sure.

Hooker looked up from the open door of the white refrigerator. Seeing the intent concentration on the young man's face, he anticipated the questions. "Manny says the medal is a Congressional Medal of Honor, but Willie won't talk about it. He just says it's his three pieces of silver. The document is a DD-214, his separation papers from the Navy. He calls them his 'slave papers of freedom.' Those two things mean he never has to be anybody but himself, and he never has to answer to another person for who he is.

"One of his longtime friends up at the Navy yards made the cherry frame for me. I had a picture framer in Willow Glen do the rest. The cherry is because of the old story about not telling lies and chopping down the cherry tree. I hung it there to remind him every day to be honest and proud of the man he is."

The silence fell as Hooker felt a rising stiffness in his throat. He realized this was the first time he had ever really vocalized how he felt about his adoptive uncle, and how proud of him he was. Not for his past heroic service for his country, but the man he was today, and every day. The weight of the story hanging on the wall wasn't lost on the kid.

A few minutes later, as they stood in the kitchen draining the gallon container of milk, and the last of a bag of cookies, Hooker stared at the kid. The mischief in his eyes he couldn't hide, so he just let it play. Finally, it was too much, and he started to chuckle. "Really?" He made a goofy face at the chuckling kid. "More slimming?"

"Well?" The kid laughed with his palm up. "Wouldn't it?"

Hooker rolled his eyes to the side and lolled his head over to one side. "Umm, maybe. But, come on, 'more go to town'? I'm trying to discourage him from flaunting it about downtown."

The kid just sliced his head in a sweep as he looked at Hooker. "I don't know, but I do kind of think it's his life, and he should do what makes *him* happy."

"The guy used to get the snot beat out of him for wearing a satin jacket and talking different. What do you think his wearing a dress at Safeway would get him?"

"Probably not a discount, but he might get some better melons." Hooker saw the kid was having fun but was also serious. "Look, I'm just a kid, but this isn't the 1940s or 50s when you couldn't be different. They used to beat a black guy to death for even whistling at a white lady, but now we have marriages. This is the 1970s. We've been through the Flower Power and the Summer of Love. Who says an old guy can't wear a dress— the Scottish guys do."

"Well said." The man in the dress now stood there in just his white boxers with red hearts.

Hooker almost lost a mouthful of milk and cookies back up his nose. Swallowing, he choked out, "Where's your dress?"

Jamming a thumb back over his shoulder, Willie responded, "Out there in the shop, probably still burning." Turning to the kid, he asked, "Newer darker denim, or the worn faded look with some colored patches?"

Now it was the kid's turn to almost lose his food but chuckling as he recovered. "The darker would be more slimming, but the faded with patches would be more funky, and compliment your hair." He gave the man a serious look. "Besides, with the patches, you could do a red bandana heart where it counts and drive Hooker nuts." Blinking, he waited for the man to step up to the plate, but he wasn't going to flinch.

Finally smiling, the man clapped him on the shoulder and turned to Hooker. "You found a good kid, and you can bring him around more often. But you really need to do something about the one white mitten. In a neighborhood like this, it could give people something to talk about." Pointing at the offending hand, the Nancy came out just a bit too much. "It is supposed to be white, isn't it?" Turning, he scratched at the words on the backside of his boxers as he walked back down the hall, past the framed photo and document. Hooker could just make out the words *Kiss Me Hard.*

"Oh, and Stella said to remind you you're helping cook this Sunday, and just so you don't poison us, bring Hank."

The man called back from the hall as he continued to walk out the door, "Yes, dear. Hanky Panky it is, and I'll wear my new jean dress." Waving his hand in a loose wavy kind of flounce as the industrial fire door closed softly behind him.

Hooker leaned over and planted his face in his palms, shuddering. Looking out with one eye between his fingers at the kid, he mumbled into his hands, "See what you started?" His hands dropped to his sides, and his head bounced off his chest and then just hung there as he sniffed and snarled in disgust. "Laundry, I need to do laundry."

Looking up at Johnny, he pointed toward the large adjoining room. "Living room, TV, magazines, but they're all car stuff, and books which are more car stuff, or just hang out with Box. I'll just go change, and we can get over to your place and get you changed."

"Can't."

"Can't what?"

"Can't get changed," the kid slumped against the large island as he nibbled at the last cookie.

"Why not?"

"The only other pair of jeans I have are ratty, and the knees are blown out." Looking in the direction where the older man had gone, "Torn, I meant to say ripped out." He smiled shyly. "You don't want me working for you looking that way."

"Then buy another pair." Hooker was having a little trouble getting his mind around the concept of only one real pair of jeans.

The kid said it all by pulling his pockets out and palming the three pennies and a nickel.

Hooker was going to get a headache. Finally, he waved at the kid. "Okay, come on. What size do you wear?"

"Twenty-eight waist and a thirty-two leg."

Reaching into the drawer, he pulled out the only two pair of jeans there were in the drawer. Too many foster homes, and always a fist swing away from the next, Hooker wasn't big on having a lot of clothes to pack. He handed one pair to the kid. "Thirty—thirty-six. You can pull them in with the belt and cuff them up inside the leg."

Reaching into the closet, he pulled out two white T-shirts pressed to the flatness of a linoleum floor. "Large is large." Pointing across the hall, "Towels on the towel bar are clean and for you. Use anything you see, except my toothbrush. There should be a new brush in the drawer to the right of the left sink. When you're done, just hang the towel on the bar, it's yours. Then come on out. My office is off the living room."

The kid looked at the clothes and turned a half shade of red. Quietly he nodded. "Thanks."

"They're only for today or so. We'll work things out. Willie did more for me than a cheap pair of jeans and a white shirt." Turning to walk away, he added, "I'll see you in a bit. There is plenty of hot water, so take your time and relax."

Hooker walked into the large garage and looked around. The welder was shut down. Willie was nowhere to be seen, so Hooker strolled out to the one place he knew the old man couldn't resist—Mae West.

The bright sunshine did nothing but stir up the fire in the radiant red pearl over the yellow paint and candy-apple blue flames. Willie had the right hood up, and Hooker figured he was sniffing the oil to see if the driver had highballed the rig into hard-on-the-engine territory. Hooker smirked as he rounded the huge chrome front bumper. The old man had his head buried deep down in the front of the engine compartment. "You got lucky this time, junior." Pulling back out and jumping down to face Hooker, Hooker was at once glad the dress was a long dress because, on a warm day like this, he suspected the old guy probably was going commando underneath. The fact he had been wearing boxers a few minutes before meant nothing.

"The oil is ready to change, but you haven't been scorching it." The old man wiped his hands on the red grease rag.

"Then why am I lucky?"

The old guy eyed him with his good eye, as the other was squinting against the glare from the sun. "Dolly called."

"Oh shit," Hooker muttered as he walked back around the truck to go call her on the radio.

"It's okay," Willie stopped him. "I talked her down off her pity party. It's a slow day. There wasn't anything out there, but Stella stopped in, and so she knew you were up and out but didn't call in." The old man leaned against the bumper as he absently rubbed the chrome.

"So what did you tell her?" Hooker looked off down the valley to where he knew the dispatcher was sitting.

The old man shrugged with a conspiratorial smile. "I told her the truth."

Hooker gave him a hard look the old man ducked. "I told her I needed to change the oil and fix a few other things, but I would have you down in her loving arms by six this evening when your shift starts."

"What other things?"

"A couple of things come to mind." Hooker watched as the usual Uncle Willie slipped smoothly back into the career officer of Naval Intelligence and spy. Willie had a jagged scar running from below his left ear, down his throat and hooking out to the end of his chin where the meat hook used on him as a POW in North Korea had stopped and caught hold of the jawbone before it ripped out four days later. Never invisible, the scar was now shining extra white from lack of blood. Hooker knew it meant his blood pressure was up about whatever came out of his mouth next.

"What's on your mind right now, sir?" Hooker stood a little straighter out of respect for the man.

"Maddie also called. Your paper was due yesterday."

Hooker sank mentally into the depths of the well of I-screwed-the-pooch. "Yes, sir, it was," knowing there were results, and then there were stories. He knew neither his uncle nor the librarian would be willing to listen to stories.

"I explained you'd worked hard lately, precluding you from logging some time with the history books. She agreed with me about rounding out the discussion to include the piston shape of the side draft flathead. You could give a better understanding of the dynamics for an early muscle car. We assumed you could get it done in twenty pages instead of a cheap note of twelve." The white brush-cut hair stood stiff as the man's stare. The muscles rippled along his jawline, daring the least whine or complaint from his ward.

"When would she want the paper, sir?"

The soldier softened some as he turned back to the truck and knelt to look under her. "I'm sure Sunday would be the most appropriate time."

"Before or after the barbecue, sir?"

Muffled as he looked along the length of the undercarriage, "I would supose when you get there, you two can find a few minutes to review the merits of your continuing education, Mr. Hooker."

"Yes, sir."

Standing and cleaning his hands in the grease rag, the calm softer uncle had returned, within reason. "You have a leak, tiny, but a leak in the lower radiator hose," and bending over, pointing under the truck, "and I know that spot of oil wasn't there this morning."

Standing up, he looked hard at Hooker and let his jealous girly side slip out a tiny bit. "Just what have you been up to with my girl, young man?" A father with a sixteen-year-old girl couldn't act more protectively. His rag filled fist rested on the now out-slung hip as he raised one eyebrow.

Hooker's eyelids slowly lowered in the challenging look of an older teenager… a sure-fire way to knock the old man off his game.

Willie struck out with the rag as he softly waved it across Hookers chest and quietly giggled. "Oh, just never mind. I'm sure it is something a girl in my delicate years shouldn't even want to hear." Moving off toward the large barn doors, he swayed his hips in an exaggerated flounce. Dropping his voice back into the deep serious register of his mechanic's voice, he directed Hooker. "I'll move the Speedwagon out of the way, and you bring Mae all the way back and over the pit."

Hooker swung up into the cab, and as he turned the engine over, he reached left-handed for the microphone. "Dolly, sorry about the no-call, but as Willie told you, I'm down for maintenance this afternoon."

"10-4, Hooker, just wanted to know where you were."

"If you need me for something small, I've got the Ford here."

"10-4. Just take care of Mae, and we'll see you for lunch. We are expecting two of you correct?"

"Negative. Box will be with us too… set the table for three."

"I meant Johnny."

"10-4. He's my slave for twelve more days."

"10-4. Get your money's worth."

Hooker double-clicked and hung the mic as he eased the beast through the large barn doors. Slowly creeping down the glass-smooth shop floor, the giant truck was more like a dutiful puppy following the flour-sack dress over lace-less army boots. As the old man walked down the stairs into the grease pit, Hooker drove on over the top of him until the windshield just touched a tennis ball hanging on a cord from a rafter thirty feet above.

Mae West shuddered to silence as Hooker set the brakes and arranged all the gears to neutral. The voice giggling up from under the truck was partially amused and half-nervous. "Oh dear, you are not going to believe this." Hooker slid out of the cab and walked to the set of stairs at the front end of the pit.

Looking up at the large radiator hose, Hooker eyed the slight nick, and then the oil pan where the maker of the nick had come to be buried. The dime had punctured halfway into the large front face of the pan. Completely in awe of the amazing trajectory, the dime must have taken to nick the heavy hose, and still have the energy to bury itself deep into the heavy steel pan, he turned to the older man and wailed in a whiney voice, "My… my baby is… is… WOUNDED!"

The two could laugh now, but both knew this was not really a laughing matter. The older man carried five major scars he had acquired during his thirty years in Naval Intelligence. Hooker's mind still playing the other night's event overlaid with helping Manny process the crime scene through the night and morning. Hooker remembered his times with Manny. "Don't touch it." To which the man just raised his palms up next to his face in a *stick 'em-up* formation of submission.

Hooker climbed back up into the cab and grabbed the mic, "Dolly?"

"Go, honey."

"Can you find Captain Davis and have him bring an evidence kit up here to the house?"

"Is someone shooting at you up there?" Her voice immediately took on the protective edge of someone in control of calling out first responders.

"Negative. We just found some evidence from the other night that Mae wants to give up. He also needs to bring a camera."

"10-4. I'll find him."

Hooker double-tapped the mic and left it lying on the seat.

Walking back under the truck, he found Willie looking up at the front of the giant radiator. Hooker walked over and looked up. The silver flame on the tails side of the Mercury-head dime was just peeking out of the fins in the radiator.

Hooker clapped the man on the back. "Great work, Unc, great work." He then held him out at arm's length and looked him up and down. "You might want to go change. There should be a CHP captain pulling in the driveway in a little bit."

"Is he cute?"

Hooker gave him a stern look.

"I'm going, I'm going!" he said as he waved his hands above his shoulders. "Just asking, just asking."

Hooker chuckled silently and shook his head as he looked back up at the dime buried in the fins.

"Hey, Hooker!" The fresh-scrubbed kid called down from where he was busying himself by polishing every piece of chrome he could find. "Do you have any fingernail polish?"

Willie froze, and then looked longingly at Hooker. Mouthing the words, "This is the stuff fantasies are made of," with a huge smile as he batted his eyes.

"Stop!" Hooker mouthed back. Turning toward the front of the truck where both men could see the young man's spread legs straddling the concrete stairwell, Willie elbowed Hooker and nodded toward the kid as if to say 'see, see.'

Hooker rolled his eyes closed, then buried his face in his right palm, saying, "No, but I know a nasty old man who should be acting his age. Why?"

The legs straightened and the kid bent down to look at the two men dressed in identical white T-shirts, jeans, and dirty sneakers. He ignored the goofy lascivious moon-dog look on the old man's face as he blandly explained, "There is a good-sized gouge here in the face of the bumper, and it looks to be down to the steel. I thought maybe some nail polish would keep it from rusting."

Hooker screwed up his face in askance at Willie muttering incredulously, "A gouge? In the bumper?" The two scrambled out of the dark hole to look with wonder at the custom-made armor-plate steel bumper. Unlike most bendable modern piece-of-shit bumpers Willie and Hooker had considered when they were building Mae West, the chrome beauty gracing the intimidatingly massive front end was made entirely from the same armor-plated steel used to make battleships, courtesy of the local Navy repair yard. The steel had been chrome plated to a military 'work' thickness and maybe a squidgy point beyond. As Willie always said, "It pays to know people who know you."

"Huh?" Hooker looked at a narrow divot no longer than a half-inch where a dime had given up its useful life. Turning to the older and wiser man. "Got any better ideas?"

Willie stared at the dime edge mark. "Heck no, it would have just rusted on me." Turning to the kid, he gently slugged him in the shoulder. "You're worth keeping around here, Squirt." Stepping over the open stairwell, he headed toward his boudoir, stating, "I'll go get you some nice pearl pink I have been dying to get rid of."

Hooker shot him a glaring look, knowing full well the man was joking. Taunting the old friend, Hooker shot back as the man reached the door, "Knowing you, if you have wanted to get rid of it, then it must be 'pussy pink.'" The old man responded by scratching the back of his head with his middle finger. Hooker and the kid laughed as they also heard a car pull up and into the barn.

Rounding the nose of the large truck, Hooker saw the captain standing up out of the California Highway Patrol cruiser. Hooker grabbed a fresh red grease rag off the large commercial bundle and wiped his hands in the cloth as he sauntered across the rest of the 10,000 square foot car barn. "Any trouble finding the place, Captain Davis?"

The man reached into the open trunk, withdrawing the large black case of a field exam kit. "No, Hooker, it was a piece of cake. Dolly brought me up here a number of years ago for your uncle to fix my truck." Looking around at the size of the barn and the height of the unsupported arched roof, he marveled and wondered. "Of course, the little three-car garage has kind of grown since then." Turning a full three-hundred sixty degrees, "I understand having all the real estate, but why the air space?"

Hooker snorted a laugh, remembering his second summer with Willie. "Willie bought it from the Navy as surplus. It was a smaller 'Battle Balloon' repair barn they never erected, and it was just sitting up at Moffett Field, so they sold it to him." Hooker was kind of proud of the building, too. "When they brought it up, Willie looked at the piles and piles of materials, and then told the commander they forgot to include the directions for assembly. I guess it was slow at the base that summer, so they sent a crew along with four cranes, and the building was up on the five-foot deep footing foundation in less than two months." He winked. "Of course, it was summer, and with the swimming pool and all, there were many details which dragged on for the next three months."

"But how do you heat something like this?"

"Hot water," Hooker started. "The first well Willie drilled hit water at 140°F. The second well went almost horizontally into the mountain and hit an artesian aquifer, but it is very cold water for drinking."

"Aquifer?"

Hooker stopped, never realizing he might know something others didn't.

"Actually, it's called a 'confined aquifer,' which means the water is under pressure… about a hundred pounds constant to be more exact," Willie explained as he walked up, sticking his hand out. "Good to see you again, Chet." They shook, "It is Chet if I remember right?"

"Nobody but Dolly and family calls me Chet anymore, but sure, you're close enough to family." The captain smiled, remembering his real family.

"Still have the 1952 Chevy Step-side with the straight-six?"

The officer chuckled sadly, putting down his case as if it were just another heavy burden. "Nah, I sold her paying off the cancer bills, along with the fishing gear."

Willie waved off the sad memories with a loose hand. "Nah, we don't have any fishing gear around here, but I'm sure anytime you need a truck and or a beer, we can rustle up something."

The officer weighed the offer.

Willie quickly added to put the man at ease, "You can even bring a lady friend up if you want. Hell, we even let Dolly come up on some occasions when she promises to behave herself."

Agreeing to the now specified terms of the offer, the officer relaxed. "Sounds good. In fact, I'm having some troubles with my new car."

"I hate new cars!" Willie snapped.

"1955 MG TD."

Willie softened. "Well, in that case…" smiling then snapping his fingers, "as long as you let me rip out all the Lucas electrical crap."

"Done!" Chet smiled broadly sardonic with the side of his mouth. "That's the problem I'm having—electrical." And just to solidify their friendship, he threw in, "And maybe we can look at how to stick a small block in it?"

Smiling at Willie's gone-goofy-in-lust smile, he picked up the case again and asked, "What am I processing here?"

Hooker scooped the air with his hand as he turned. "It's in the truck, over here."

The two older men followed. "So how do you heat with the hot water?"

Willie pointed at the glassy floor they were walking on. "We run it through a series of copper pipes buried in the sixteen-inch thick concrete floor. I change the mix to heat about the middle of September. By October, when it starts to get cold, then the floor is radiating about ninety degrees. It keeps everything in the building about seventy-three to seventy-five degrees in here, just right for T-shirts or a dress." He looked over for a reaction, but there was none. "Best of all, every tool or piece of steel is all the same temperature. So it makes it a real pleasure to work out here all year long."

"But what about when the summer is over a hundred?"

Willie reached out and stopped the man. Kneeling down, he placed his palm flat on the floor. "Feel." The officer did, and his eyes arched. "Fifty-one-degree water, straight out of the mountain; but right now I'm throwing a mixed temperature of about sixty degrees to match the nice weather, but I'll go straight cold by the end of the month."

They rose and continued toward the truck. "So, what about the house?"

"Oh, there too," he continued. "I actually tore down the old shack, after

Hooker burned it down, and started over. So by then I knew about the hot water and buried the pipes in the house pad, too. Although, it's only six-inches thick."

"How did you ever figure this system out?"

Willie waved his loose hand. "Wasn't me. The Romans did it two thousand years ago, and they learned it from the Chinese." He pointed at the divot in the chrome bumper. "After World War II, they built a whole community in New York called Levittown, and every house is radiant heat."

The captain leaned in closer to the divot. "Holy catfish! That is one hell of a dime load." Looking up at Hooker, "I'm assuming one of the dimes did this."

"I think it may have been when I was a lot closer on the Almaden Expressway and those two or three shots came from the side."

"There are two more," Willie added.

"Dings?"

"Nope. These two stuck around." The older man giggled at his little joke. Then he remembered something more and turned to Hooker. "I guess I have to date Jeff for a pair of dimes."

Hooker rolled his eyes. "I think Mae can forego your suffering with Jeff for a couple of simple dimes painted on her side," in reference to the tote board of 'kills' on the truck's side. The drama of Willie and Jeff's breaking up was what drove Hooker to seek refuge in one of Manny and Stella's guest rooms.

The other room had become the 'catch-all' as everything, not in use was moved into the room at the end of the hall and farthest away from the kitchen. Stella had joked off and on it was where she should store Manny on most days. Then she would snuggle down on his lap, as he would explain there really was a defining difference between abuse and use. Hooker had never heard them having even a half-heartedly angry word for each other, even though they referred to each other in such terms as *useless old man, good for a doorstop,* and *old woman.*

Willie, on the other hand, had been in a few relationships less than good for him or anyone around him, but he was learning. His recent lover was a more staid plodding kind of guy who would just lean back in his chair and chuckle at Willie's blustering and cackling, and it was having a very good settling effect on the old warhorse. He was finally sleeping more nights than not, and his high blood pressure was coming down into some semblance of control. He had even finally started going up and talking to a shrink at the VA about his years as a spy.

"Maybe after everything is done, they will give us the dimes back, and we can just epoxy them on," concluded Hooker.

Johnny eyed the tote board, and quietly remarked, "Candy could paint a pair of dimes better than that Volkswagen."

"Really? Candy paints?" Hooker's antennas were twitching at the mention of the kid's sister. "Well, maybe someday when she has time…"

The two older men were under the truck with the captain taking photos before they could pull the dimes out. Hooker looked out the rear barn doors at the large lawn needing a good mow now as spring was encouraging it to grow. A klaxon horn sounded from one of the timbers running like soldiers along the wall separating the house from the garage —the phone was ringing. Hooker looked at his watch. "Willie! Don't pull the oil yet. I've got a bad feeling about this," as he ran to the phone.

They finished the photos and took some measurements as Hooker talked on the phone. "Got it, Dolly." Hooker started to step away toward the truck. "Yeah, he's here. I'll let him know. Love you," he concluded as he slammed the handset down on the receiver.

Running for the truck, Johnny saw him and responded by throwing the rag and polish in the bucket and heading for the passenger door. "Box! Go time!" Hooker called. "Chief, we have a nineteen pileup at Blossom Hill and 101 northbound. A flipped fuel tanker gushing its guts onto the 101."

He hit the side of the truck, bounced through the door as he scooped up the microphone, and keyed it left-handed as his right turned the switch, hitting the start button without waiting for the turbo to wind up. The still-warm engine fired into life as he slung the gears into reverse then looked in the mirror. Seeing the captain struggling to run with the case for his car blocking the front door, Hooker shifted into seventh and yelled out the window, "Willie! Down!" The giant truck rocketed forward over the grease trench, and Willie's head as Hooker roared out of the rear doors and wheeled across the rear lawn. Cutting deep trenches in the soft spring turf, out around the swimming pool, throwing sod and any small animals caught in the grass, as he cleared the end of the house and dropped down the old access dirt road leading out to the street.

As he fishtailed onto the street, headed down the hill, he peeked at his large rearview mirrors and saw the patrol car swerving out on the street behind. The light bar and siren erupted to aid their rush down the quiet mountain street. Hooker threw on his legal set of flashing emergency lights and kept the lead. In theory, the Pontiac should have been able to overtake the large truck, except Hooker skipped gears, and he used all 1,200 horses, as the drop of the hill helped. The accident was still almost two miles away.

Realizing he still had the microphone keyed open to talk, he simply called "1-4-1, show me 10-8 in route, ETA two minutes."

Moments later, the speaker from the main radio confirmed as Karen's voice was all business, "10-4: 1-4-1, we have fire and police in route with an ETA of an additional five. CHP unit is on-site and advises 5-Delta-Bravo, 1-2-3-4-5-Delta-Bravo. There is fuel from the tanker in the entrance of the transition from northbound 101, they have asked for you to come in from Coyote Road or Silver Creek and snatch roll it back. The rupture is near the top."

"10-4. We are on Silver, and I can see it. They are about to lose some fence."

Turning to the kid, he checked his seat belt, as he hit a short straight away and snapped his, pulling it tight. "Box, get in the sleeper." The cat didn't hesitate—the orange streak shot for the only safe and secure padded hole in the truck.

Hooker hit the Jake brake and flooded the giant engine with air, creating backpressure, and providing a warning horn of sorts as they approached the accident, and the backed-up traffic. The truck eased into the empty oncoming lane and continued the approach at about fifty miles per hour as Hooker let off the fuel pedal, allowing air pressure again into the engine, and the Jake brake slowed the rig.

By the time they got close to the berm of the off-ramp, they were down to twenty, and Hooker swung the wheel as they hit the scrub desert along the backside of the berm. The mass of the truck and its custom front bumper peeled about sixty feet of freeway marker fence like a banana. Bouncing along the top of the berm, Hooker watched the tanker and figured how best to set the truck up for a snatch to roll the trailer back over onto its wheels.

The 22,000 pounds of bucking steel and rubber jumped and slew all over the sand berm. The only thing the truck had going for it over the sand was the talent of the driver. Even when a lesser man would have had his hands full with just the steering wheel, Hooker, working the *dance of the two levers,* dropped the rig down through the bottom of the second tier of gears into the bottom end as he slowed to the last crawl along the top of the berm.

"I can't see that side of the berm. Open the door and swing out and tell me how steep it is."

Without hesitation, the kid pulled the handle and with his right arm in the window hole, pushed out and hung over the edge, then swung back in. Holding his arm at an angle of about thirty degrees, he showed Hooker what he needed to know.

Hooker laid the hammer down, and the truck vaulted forward as he whipped the wheel right and then spun it hard left as he revved the motor into the red, the ass end slewing around. When the truck came to a stop, it was straddling the berm with the working deck pointed directly at the middle of the tank. Hooker set the brakes as the kid jumped back out of the truck.

They met at the back as Hooker pulled the working deck's control panel open and jerked the releases to let the lines free-feed. The weight of the sling pulled the two snatch hooks down from the twin booms. Hooker unhooked the sling and fed the lines through the snatch-tag ring hooks welded to the back of the deck. Handing one of the hooks to the kid, they ran down the face of the berm and crossed over to the belly of the tank trailer.

The stench of the spilled fuel burned their eyes with creosote acidity. "From here on out, do not rub or touch your face, no matter what, you got me?" Johnny nodded. "Ok, now pull an extra twenty to thirty feet of cable and lay it in a loop like this." Showing him the large six-foot wide loop on the ground. "Good, now all I want you to do is throw the hook as far as you can over the tank."

The kid had a good arm, and Hooker wasn't about to admit it, but he might have thrown the hook and cable a good two or three yards farther than Hooker. "Great, now on your side of the deck, the second box back from the cab, there are two short brass chains with funny looking hooks on each end," showing the length with his two hands held about as wide as his shoulders. "I want you to bring me one on the other side and drop the second one here."

There was a loud whistle, and Hooker looked up to see an officer pointing toward the fuel. Turning to the kid, "Hurry, we need to turn this before some idiot lights up a cigarette in San Jose and blows us to Gilroy."

Johnny ran for the rig, and Hooker hustled over to the officer. "About ten minutes and we can start pulling the trailer. How are we doing on the spill?"

"I wish the fire guys would hurry up and get here. They're sending a foam truck up from San Martine, maybe in ten, but if we wait much longer, it's going to get to the gray car, and there is a woman trapped in there."

Hooker looked over the carnage of vehicles. "Am I the only one here?"

"Yeah, and am I ever glad to see you." The officer leaned back and looked past Hooker. "Oh great, the captain is here." Hooker could hear the dread in the young officer's voice.

"It's okay. He's with me." Looking back north up the freeway, he could see yellow lights flashing. He slapped the officer lightly on the chest to get his attention, and then realized the man's shirt had blood soaking out from under his protective vest. "How did you get here?"

The officer pointed to the middle of the mass of twisted metal. With the four tires of his cruiser getting some unneeded sunshine, Hooker understood the blood.

"Great, an eyewitness." Pointing back north, toward the still approaching tow-truck, he snapped, "When that tow-truck gets here, have him drag the car and woman over to the center grass." The officer nodded and winced at the effort, Hooker gave him a look of two counts, then, when the officer waved him off, headed for the snatch hooks as Johnny came running with the short chains. The fuel was everywhere, and Hooker had to walk slowly and carefully.

As Johnny approached, he held up the short chain with a question on his face. Hooker reassured him. "Yup, those are the right ones. The brass won't cause a spark and ignite the fuel. There is nothing we can do about the snatch hooks and cable." Grabbing the short chain, Hooker wound the pigtail hook onto the one cable and then the other end onto the second cable. "Here." He held the chain. "Hold this here while I secure the hooks."

The kid took the chain as Hooker grabbed the first snatch-block hook and walked to the one end of the trailer. Feeding the cable under the edge, he reached and looped the cable around part of the undercarriage of the trailer. Finishing doing the same at the other end with the other cable, he went back to the kid.

"I want you to hold your chain until the cable draws it up to about as high as your head, then let it go and get the heck back to the truck. Just don't slip in this shit, and don't wipe your face." The kid had just tried to wipe the sweat from his forehead on his shirt. "Your shirt is now soaked with the fumes of the fuel and will burn your eyes until you are blind." He slapped him on the back. "Got it?" Johnny nodded as Hooker nodded and walked back around the end of the trailer.

At the end of the trailer, Hooker met back up with the captain. Looking back, he saw the other officer was telling the small truck to pull the car away from the fuel. Turning back toward the captain, he assessed the situation. "I'd rather wait for the foam truck before I lift, but there is already about a thousand gallons on the road, and with every minute, the tank is bleeding another hundred or more."

"Go ahead and pull it. Hopefully, by the time you get her up, the cavalry will be here."

Pointing toward the gray car and tow truck, Hooker asked for the officer's help. "I won't be able to see him, so signal me when he starts pulling her. Once she's safe, I'll go ahead and pull the trailer up." The captain gave him a thumbs-up, and Hooker headed back to the truck.

Dancing with the two levers controlling the twin pulley winches,

Hooker carefully took up the slack on the towing cables. As the bronze chain Hooker could see began to pull taut, the kid came back around the trailer. Taking one last look, he turned and shook the captain's hand then started back toward the truck.

"The other tow truck just finished setting the hooks in the car and should be pulling her away about now." A low whistle from the captain and a spin of his finger in a circle above his head confirmed the kid's report. Hooker tightened the cables until they were straight as rods.

"Watch our rear tires. Let me know if we slip more than six inches." He continued the dance as the tanker started to twitch. Hooker was relieved to see the captain moving off to a safe distance in case the fuel ignited.

Slowly, the trailer shifted into a roll and stopped sliding its metal along the asphalt, which was the most dangerous part of this kind of situation. As the trailer tipped closer to upright, Hooker slowed the progress to let the fuel settle into the new attitude, but then he noticed the one thing he didn't want to happen—the rubber tires started to slip in the fuel.

"Johnny, grab those wood chocks and bring them," as he lowered the trailer back down until the metal touched and stopped the sliding. Hooker reached over and grabbed the tin pail used for picking up glass and wreckage and stopping long enough to scoop up a bucket full of the decomposed granite sand making up the berm, he ran for the trailer.

Throwing sand all over the fuel-soaked road, and on the tires them-selves, he began soaking up fuel and providing a base for traction. Taking the first two chocks from the kid, he kicked the thin end of the wedge under the tires touching the ground. Then stomping on the asphalt about eight feet away, he instructed the kid. "Go get the shovel, and take some sand dirt there on the shoulder, and make a pile about two feet high, here and here." Johnny took off for the truck, and Hooker turned toward the other end of the trailer.

The trailer had 'airport' legs he could crank down for the trailer to stand on by itself without a tractor. Jumping up on the trailer, Hooker grabbed the crank and turned it. Turning easily, he continued until the lower foot was almost touching the asphalt. Throwing the rest of the sand in the bucket in a pile at the contact point, he was assured there would be some traction, but not a height to off balance the trailer when it finally tipped upright.

Looking back to where Johnny was piling his second pile, Hooker smiled. The kid was shoveling at a fevered pitch, and the left mitten looked more like something a zombie would wear to the prom. "Good enough, Squirt. Clear out." And they both headed back to Mae West and the working deck.

"Is that so the tanker won't just continue to roll our way when she comes over?"

"Yeah," Hooker smiled. "The sand will crush but absorb the blow enough to stop the rocking. I'll still be able to pull her off there, but at least we don't get a back flop." Johnny put the shovel in its holder, and Hooker pitched the can into its respective hole and grabbed the levers to start the pull. "If that happens, the tank will rupture from one end to the other, and we are ground zero for the wave of fuel, so don't light a cigarette."

They watched as the trailer shuddered and slowly began to rise. Hooker watched the airport landing gear for any slipping, but they followed the lead of the tires and held steady in place as the weight began to transfer onto the balance of two tire edges and the half-inch wide edge of the steel foot.

Not taking his eyes off the tanker, he warned the kid, "Squirt, if you see the tanker start to double over, you run south as fast as you can. You hear me?"

"Got it! Make like a bunny."

The tanker groaned as the stress of the steel tank and its contents, in relation to their connection to the trailer frame, transferred weight. Hooker watched the landing gear to see if it were threatening to buckle, or if it would hold. In his peripheral vision, a part of his mind registered the Garcia brother's trucks had arrived and were hooking up or pulling cars from the south end. The rig from Central Tow had pulled the woman's car out of the fuel patch, and the fire crew was setting up a Jaws of Life to take off the car's top and door to free the woman. The warm sun overhead could have been a lulling factor in a lazy snooze in the hammock out by the pool, but right now, it was just manufacturing hot steel and slippery sweat.

The one cable started to lose its tension, and Hooker squeezed the lever controlling the cable's winch, causing it to turn slightly faster than its twin. The cable tightened to match the other. Hooker watched the bronze chain holding the two cables and the draw point it created about twenty feet from the tanker.

"Pay attention, Squirt!" He could feel the kid's head had been scanning the southern area of the carnage now snap back to the cables. "Watch the bronze chain, and when you see it stop being a hard bar between the cables, it means the tanker has reached the balance point." Hooker slowed the winches to a crawl. "See it?"

"Yeah, the links in the middle just came back together."

"Get ready to run. She's coming over now." Hooker let go of the controls, and with his eyes on the tanker, turned his feet into a running position. The kid, also paranoid, looked more like a baseball player ready to steal to second base with a ten-foot leadoff.

Slowly, with a drawn-out groan and a shriek of complaining steel, the tanker rolled upright and as the tires hit the sand, crushed it to a flat cushion. The top rocked side to side with a bit of lift-off the tires on the far side, but then the trailer settled back, and Hooker relaxed.

From somewhere behind the tanker, an arch of white foam laced into the air and fell into a blanket, covering the tanker and the giant pool of spilled fuel. The foam contained tri-sodium phosphate to break down the slippery oil of the fuel, and nitrogen to stop any ignition of flames. Hooker thought about how the very green grass at Willie's was thanks to a couple of well-placed BBQs for the fire crews resulting in a demonstration of the foam. The soap breaks down the surface tension in the soil, and the grass loves the nitrogen and turns an unrealistic green, but then you have to start mowing the yard twice a week. Driving the small tractor around the three acres was more fun for the man than work.

Hooker pointed at the foam and noted to the kid, "Grass along the side of the off-ramp is going to grow like crazy until the summer heat kills it."

Slipping around the ends of the tanker, they unhooked the cables and pulled everything back to the upside to wind it back onto the spools.

"Here, put these gloves on and use the rags to clean the cables as I draw them up. Just let the cables run loose in the rags and wipe the worst off." Hooker knew a true full cleaning and re-application of white lithium would come later. "We'll clean it up later. Right now, we need to rock and roll."

Grabbing the bronze chains, Hooker went back to the rig. Stowing the chains in the second side box, he thought about the last time he cleaned all the gear and boxes. It would be a great job for the kid to do while Willie worked on the engine and Hooker touched up some paint. Maintaining a large tow rig was a full-time job. From just the daily washing to cable and equipment cleaning, Hooker really understood what firemen in a firehouse really did for a living, and it wasn't putting out fires.

Hooker jockeyed the giant truck down off the berm and brought it back around to conventionally tow the trailer and tractor. "Are we going to pull the tractor and trailer at the same time?"

Looking at the kid with a smile, "I wish, but no, even if it were legal." Pointing with a thumb jerk, "The tractor can't safely re-hook anything on its fifth wheel until it's been reapproved." Pointing to a large flat space of dirt about mid-way up the off-ramp, Hooker explained the process. "We'll drag the tractor out of the way, over there and haul it up to the Fly later, but we need to get this," indicating with a jaw nod toward the trailer, "to the county yard so they can safely drain the fuel that's left."

"Why the county yard?"

"Because of the crack. Some of the foam might have gotten in and contaminated the fuel. So, right now, it's just considered to be 10,000 gallons or so of toxic waste."

The tractor they had been pulling back upright finally flipped and rocked on its tires. "It won't go to waste. All of the fuel will get used by the county, cleaned up and run through lawn mowers, used in weed burners, or used in their burners for torching asphalt and striping." Resetting the hooks on the sling, "Nothing goes to waste anymore—not with fuel at sixty-nine cents a gallon." Pointing at the tanker. "That right there, the fuel company's insurance will pay them for the loss, and we taxpayers get about eight thousand dollars relief on our county taxes." Heading for the cab, "Everything helps these days."

Later, as they cleaned up for an early lunch at six PM, Willie dropped a stack of clean jeans and freshly ironed T-shirts in Hooker's room. "I've got gauze and stuff out in the first aid kit in the shop." Addressing the kid, he asked, "How's the hand?"

The kid looked at the stitches as he flexed his now clean hand. "It feels kind of silly to wrap it up in a bunch of cloth," as he brought the fingers into a fist and then back flat several times.

Willie stepped over and looked at the stitches. "Hmm, maybe just a jumbo patch will do for now." He looked up at the kid in the eye. "But don't pull a Hooker and go without a cover on it for at least a few more days."

The kid held his gaze, and then slowly broke into a smile and a chuckle from the insight into the enigmatic, seemingly together, older young man, "Got it."

Hooker turned into the room, followed closely by Box. "You ready? We need to get down the hill or Dolly will be hell on wheels if we're late for dinner," as he looked at his watch.

The kid nodded, but the older man interceded. "He needs a square patch and some ointment first." He gave Hooker a stern look which looked funny on the old drag queen, back in a pink flowered muumuu and bunny slippers this time. "I'll deal with Dolly, but first things first."

"Come on," he waved at the kid. "We'll grab several patches, and you can put them in the truck as spares."

The old man shot Hooker a hard look. "Maybe you're getting old enough to start packing a first aid kit in the rig."

As they clambered into the truck with some added oil at least, Box jumped into Johnny's lap and settled down with a purr. Hooker gave him a stern look as he turned the key then pushed the small silver start button. "Traitor."

Shifting into reverse, they glided out of the barn with the kid and Hooker both laughing at the fickleness of the large cat. Petting the lap-full of fur, Johnny observed, "I take it Box is pretty selective?"

"Fickle is more like it." Hooker swapped gears, and they began to roll down the hill. "Almost becoming a slut." The kid laughed, and Box changed position so his back was to Hooker, which made the two men laugh even harder. "He almost took Stella's hand off the first time they met." Hooker danced the gears to the next tier. "Even today, she can feed him, but not pet him."

They chuckled and purred, respectively, down the hill as they headed to dinner at Dolly's place.

2 2

The home-baked sourdough rolls hadn't quite mopped up all of the evidence. Reddish smears remained on the plates, the last traces of the *Dolly made* fresh spaghetti with handmade Sicilian style sausage from Chiaramonte's on North 13th Street. Everyone around the table sat back with satisfied expressions as well as tummies. Mike, the diminutive driver from Fremont, who had made the stop on North 13th for the sausage and other things on Dolly's standing order at Chiaramonte's, burped quietly, and said it all, "As usual, Dolly, it was terrible." And with a slightly louder burp, "Luckily, there were just enough of us to hide all of the evidence."

"Good thing I brought Squirt," Hooker jibed the older driver. "Otherwise, you might have had to let out your belt some more." They all laughed at the gentle ribbing common around Dolly's Wednesday night dinner tables, open by invitation only to tow drivers, officers, the occasional fireman, and a rare elected official.

Hooker's presence at the head of the table was mandatory. All other chairs cycled through the county based on a priority which was secret to all but the queen of the county. It was rumored more promotions, jobs, contracts, political alliances, and elections were formed or destroyed around her table than in any county office. Only Dolly and Hooker knew its truthfulness.

"Well, I'm sure glad you boys could come to this girl's rescue." Barefooted, she hovered around her table tending to the men of her world, with coffee, hair tousles, and the occasional hug.

Getting serious, the small driver leaned forward with his elbows on the table, straddling his clean plate, "Any word on the funerals yet?" The table sobered.

Dolly stopped and looked back toward Dina, unplugging a wire and hanging up on a call at the switchboard. Without turning around, Dina acknowledged the question, "The CHP will be on Saturday at two PM. Services are closed to all but family and CHP. The procession will be open for law enforcement only. Interment will be on the hill at about four PM. I haven't heard on the second officer, but the one PD was Jewish and kosher, so he was quietly laid to rest this afternoon."

The table stared at things in front of them but were many miles away. Over the years, everyone had accumulated the ghosts to haunt them. Some lost friends while others, well, are 'others.'

Hooker looked over at the walnut-colored face of his longtime CHP friend Micha Jawolinski as the not-so-young-anymore officer looked up from picking at the small red stain on his *Fishermen Don't Lie* T-shirt. The two shared a common ghost from the night they first met. There were no smiles between the two. Just the flat look acknowledging to each other they were thinking about the same night; it had been a bad night, in a rare soft drizzle on the 101, under the 'Altars.'

It was one of those freak October nights when the humidity from the bay meets the cold air pushed over the Santa Cruz Mountains. It wasn't enough to even call a rain, but drivers react to what is on their front window long before the squirm of their tires, so most had ignored the thin layer of wetting on the summer's built-up oil on southbound 101 Freeway.

In the prosperous times under Governor Reagan, many highway construction projects had been started. A very large and high Los Angeles style interchange of the three freeways of 101, 280, and the 680 had begun construction. First raised were the over-passing exchange stands. Then another election cycle had swept the new junior Jerry Brown into office. The very large infrastructure war chest had evaporated in a matter of weeks. The shrine-to-Moonbeam Brown was a stack of two four-lane transitions, one on top of the other. Hovering thirty feet above the 101, where the 280 would become the 680, was a northbound 101 transition overpass to northbound 280 capping it all forty feet higher.

Besides being the butt of every joke known to transportation about being an *altar, still looking for a virgin to sacrifice*, the structures were also the source for many wrecks on the 101. Some involved gawkers or the occasional idiot who tried to take a picture while driving, but more wrecks happened as the dangerous rain season started.

Under the stacked altars, the surface is protected, so the oil builds up throughout the summer is the last to dissipate or be washed away. More specifically, on that fateful night, the already wet tires of many cars ran over the oil at speed and started slipping. Emerging from the underpass onto the truly slick entertainment field of four lanes of water over oil, the hydroplaning tires never stood a chance. What should have been an orderly progression of cars ended up looking more like a yard sale on a late Saturday afternoon. CHP called out seven tow trucks for seven cars. By the time they arrived, there were fourteen to be towed.

Hooker hadn't been called out, but he had simply been returning to his territory when he saw the mess. A tall CHP officer had been standing along the side, waved him over, and pointed at a creative cluster which may have started as three or four cars, but was by then just a mass of mangled colored steel and rubber. Not knowing what else to do, and not having been called out, he began sweeping the traffic lanes while the other drivers hooked up in a ceaseless leapfrog of blow-and-go. As things cleared out, and his pail got heavier, Hooker just dumped it in the others' pails and kept sweeping. His service in the wet, cold, dark night did not go unnoticed.

Mike, one of the older and more observant drivers, brought down from up north, had stashed two cars in a parking lot within a mile. He was hooking up his third as he slipped Hooker the keys to an AMC Pacer and told him where it was. It was a *dead bone* or worthless, but it was at least a tow.

As Hooker was pulling out so the Chip could clear the scene, he noticed a red 1952 Chevy pickup with baby-moon hubcaps and an expensive paint job. The truck was over in the shoulder, facing up the small berm. It didn't seem to have been part of the massacre. Hooker had watched the red truck as his wipers clacked an ominous counting of time, as time suspended. Something about the truck tied itself to Hooker, and he felt it was worth pointing out to the officer, and who knew? He might even throw Hooker the tow.

The officer had told Hooker to go over and check it out to see if it was part of the night's mess, or if someone had just parked a break-down at a strange angle. As Micha cleared the traffic, he was only seconds behind when Hooker opened the driver side door.

As Hooker approached the truck, he had seen the driver, a young blonde. She was the kind of girl any red-blooded American boy with a pulse would have been proud to take to the prom and who, he later discovered, had been the prom queen just the year before. She turned her face toward him. "Are you all right?" he asked as he reached over and opened the door.

The gorgeous beauty blinked her powder blue eyes once and then slumped out of the truck and into Hooker's arms. He barely caught her as she sighed, "Don't let me die." Then, she was gone.

Stunned, neither Hooker nor Micha moved. It was all just too overwhelmingly surreal for either to think about performing CPR. The wet turned to rain as the two soaked men stood on the side of the highway, washed in the red and blue flashing lights, and wept. It would be many minutes before the last paramedic came to check on the two standing off in a dark corner. Nothing was ever really said after that, but the two men knew they shared a commonality going far beyond anything they could ever say to each other. Several years later, Micha had bought Hooker a shot of whiskey in the bar at the Bold Knight on Monterey Highway. Hooker didn't understand the unwarranted gesture until the man had clicked their two shot glasses and said quietly, "Here is to beauty queens in pickup trucks. May they always be remembered for their laughs, smiles and the way they make their daddies proud, and may there always be many more."

Hooker looked down Dolly's table at the older CHP officer, then raised his water glass to the man, who returned the subtle toast, and they sipped their water and drank deeply once again their shared brotherhood. Since that night, both had seen more than their share of bodies, but you never forget your first.

Dina's voice broke the revelry. "Mike, your boss, just called, and she said if you're not back in your territory in half an hour, you can find another couch to be in trouble on." The men all started chuckling about the driver who had married the boss after she had gotten the company in a divorce.

"Ace, you just had a T-1 go live in Willow Glen, I'll give it to you in the truck." She continued, "Hooker, I'm still holding the commercial reefer needing to go down to Monterey, and if you want it, they have a service truck needing to be in Santa Cruz and will drop you a couple of twenties to get it there. Micha, you were 'on-call' as of fifteen minutes ago... Go home and sleep. The rest of you, tonight I need you to clear the dishes and wash them. I need Dolly at her desk." Turning back around to her desk of slips of paper, lights, and corded plugs needing to be inserted into magical sequences, she galvanized the group. "Jump to it before I hold you all ten minutes on your next calls." Minutes were everything to a driver, and when it came to whether you run clean or run late, Dina and the other dispatchers had the power of a god over your life.

Chair legs scraped as the men rose from the table. They shuffled into their orders of doing as Dina's added command bumped the group into smiles and a detour. "I'm getting married next month. I'm pregnant and expect extra hugs and kisses. So nobody has any excuse for not giving me presents or being at my wedding."

The men responded by lining up for hugs and kisses as they headed for the door or to clean up the dinner. Dolly stood command at the door after checking the security TV. As Hooker and Johnny passed review, she stopped them. "Do the loop, and then head for Stella's. You two need the sleep. And in case I forget in the morning, there are twenty pounds of Chiaramonte's sausages in the fridge you need to take to her for Sunday's dinner." She kissed both on the cheek.

"Yes, ma'am," they responded in unison. She swung at Johnny's behind but missed by an inch. The kid looked back with a smile and laughed. It was the best thank-you she could get. She loved her men well-fed and happy.

Box stood in the window as Hooker climbed up into the truck and started the beast. Thinking a moment, he turned Mae back off.

"What's wrong?"

Extending his left leg out of the now open door, Hooker looked back at Squirt. "I think I want to check the oil before we haul a heavy refrigerated truck down to Monterey." Climbing out, he grabbed a fresh rag out of the side box.

"What do you think?" Johnny asked as Hooker looked at the long spring steel dipstick.

"We're fine, but I think we'll swing by and pick up a few extra gallons. I also forgot my jacket," Slipping the tongue back in the tube and closing the hood, he turned on the kid, and questioned, "Speaking of which, don't you have a jacket?"

Turning a little red, the kid lied, "Sure, at my house."

Hooker gave him a hard look of a few extra seconds, and when he saw the kid start to squirm, he broke and walked back around the truck. As he got on the other side, he swore under his breath—*Fucking kid is just like me at that age.* He failed to realize he truly had never been *that age.*

It was a long, silent, dark ride back up to Willie's and the garage, and Hooker was not going to be the first to blink. The kid needed to learn not to lie to him. When you are spending almost twenty-four of the twenty-four hours each day together, you must be as honest as Box with each other.

"What did you forget this time?" The disembodied question came out of the dark. Hooker looked around the black volume of space. No work lights burned under any number of hoods of vehicles to be worked on. The moon having set almost an hour before didn't help seeing into the tar-black shop area.

The voice was definitely Willie's, so Hooker simply stated, "I have a tow down to Monterey, and then up through Santa Cruz and back to Manny and Stella's, so I figured I'd pack an extra gallon of oil, at least till we patch the oil pan."

There was some low muttering in the dark, so Hooker figured Willie had company, probably Hanky Panky. If so, with them out here in the garage, who knew what games they were up to in the dark, so he was glad there were no lights.

"Good thinking. It's why I left you two one-gallon jugs there by the door, to your right." There was more muttering in the dark, but with a very feminine giggle at the end. "We were wondering if you would figure that much out."

Hooker was almost afraid to ask, but his curiosity was up and about to get the best of him when Johnny stepped through the door and asked, "We?"

Hooker stiffened, and his shoulders sunk in on themselves as he felt more than heard the small click. A small 60-watt work light went on near the rust-red REO Speed Wagon with its hood completely off from work being done. Hooker was afraid to look.

Willie and the female with him were sitting in the padded chaise longues, fully clothed. "Madeline, I'd like you to meet a very nice young man. Madeline, this is Johnny," pointing to the kid. "Johnny, this is Madeline—or Maddie to her family and friends."

She raised a pint-canning jar half-full of clear liquid, "Nice to meet you, Squirt."

Hooker chuckled, more at the fact Willie and the librarian were nine-sheets to the wind than her pegging the kid and the nickname he hated. He turned and smiled at the kid's face.

The kid looked at him in disgust. "That isn't *even* funny anymore."

Hooker pointed with his open hand at the librarian, as if to say, *she's a guest, and you should answer her.* He arched his eyebrows and nodded his head at the older couple. "Well?"

The kid's shoulders slumped in resolve. "Very nice to meet you, Madeline." He reached out with his right fist and almost connected a solid punch to Hooker's arm.

"Oh, please, call me Maddie," she slurred back. Looking at Willie with a short giggle, "We're all among friends here. I mean, we're not naked, or nothin', but we are... we'll, otherwise in-car-pass...erated." She hiccupped and then ripped out a definitive belch that could have come from a man twice her size. Her hand came up to almost hide the self-satisfied smile, but then she quietly said, "Oh, my. Excuse me, if that was rude... unless you have one hiding that's better?" She then broke down laughing as she rolled on to Willie's lap as he tried to belch but just farted.

Hooker looked at Johnny and rolled his eyes, saying quietly, "The good news is one, she won't remember any of this in the morning, and two, we won't be here to remind her." Pointing at the two cans of oil, he told the kid, "Grab those and stick them in the second side-box on my side. I think there should be enough room. Then open my door and call for Box so he can hit the lawn." Starting toward the door to the house, he added, "I'll just grab the jackets."

The kid picked up the two cans and headed back out to the truck. Securing them in the second side-box, he turned to the driver's door. As he opened the door, the orange streak slipped out and passed him. He turned back to look at the garage, scowling in curiosity, "Jackets?"

He watched Box do his manly evening constitutional. It was more of a ritual a dog might do than a cat. The stance was definitely not cat. As he thought, *but who am I to understand what a cat wants to do.* Box was almost the sum of his experience of cats, and up until now, he felt it was kind of a nice experience. Little did he know how *chosen* he was, but then, he had yet to experience the tattered, one-eyed street warrior take apart a 150-pound dog like a three-year-old kid ripping into presents on Christmas morning.

"Box! Go time!" Hooker called as he walked back out of the dark garage interior, calling back over his shoulder at the dark, "Willie, Stella said she would castrate you if you even thought about not showing up Sunday for dinner. Make sure you bring Hank. He can help with the cooking. And Maddie can be my guest. So twist her arm." Heading for the truck, he carried a large fist-full of leather sort of matching the newer jacket he was wearing over his fresh white T-shirt. Throwing the extra eight pounds of leather at the kid, he instructed, "Here, see if this doesn't keep you warm while we eat some ice-cream."

The kid didn't question it but slipped it on. The leather was some of the softest he had ever felt, much less worn. It fit him almost like it was custom made, which is exactly what it had been for Hooker almost ten years before when he laid down two crisp Benjamins at the Just Leather store up on Steven's Creek. Hooker watched as he walked around the front of the truck and smiled. He had been pretty sure it would fit. Maybe, if anything, it was about an inch too long for the slightly shorter kid, but then if he got a motorcycle, the fit would be perfect on those cold winter nights.

"Thanks," the kid acknowledged, climbing into the cab. "It fits almost like it was made for me, except a little loose," as he rolled his arms, feeling the fit.

"It's loose like that," Hooker started the truck and set it in seventh, "so you can wear a sweatshirt or heavy Pendleton flannel shirt under it."

Glancing at the side mirrors, he let out the clutch and rolled down the driveway.

Smiling as he looked back at the kid's mock horror on his face. The Squirt threw his hands out and asked in mock sarcasm, "What, and spoil the look?"

Hooker rolled his eyes back into his head with a mock pained look. "Just don't start wearing penny-loafers." He jumped the gearbox from eighth to eleventh and let the truck drift down the hill he had let-her-roll down at least a few thousand times. He knew every twist and bump of a turn so well one very dark night he had bet Willie he could take it all the way down to Coyote Road without any lights. They never spoke about hitting the family of raccoons.

Where the kid thought they would go straight out to the freeway, Hooker turned right and headed west. As he looked at Hooker with a question mark carved in his face, Hooker turned a couple of head snaps to give him a goofy look. "What? Are you going to tell me you don't even like ice cream?"

"Sure, I like ice cream, but what's it got to do with going to Monterey?"

Hooker's eyes got huge as he stared out of the front window. "Everything!" he exploded. Looking over at the kid, the older and wiser street-tough explained with a lascivious smile, "It means we can have triple cones. It doesn't get much better than that." At the kid's confused face, Hooker frowned languidly and smacked his lips flatly as if he were bored. "You'll see."

Fifteen minutes later, they were climbing back into the truck with two triple cones and a little red dish, stored in the truck for just such occasions, with a scoop of French vanilla for Box. The kid's tongue swirled around the top plug of ice-cold delight. Frozen tongued as they rolled down Monterey Highway to pick up the new freeway extension near San Martine, the kid said, "Who would have guessed there was ice cream available at every hour of the night." With the windows wide open to the still cold spring night air, the crooning of the Texas Boys' Choir gently swirling around the cab, the giant homage to Mae West rolled effortlessly southward.

Nodding his head as he licked his lips clean, Hooker agreed, "Yup, best thing Thrifty did besides those dumb Twin-Pics and dumb ads." As they drifted up onto the freeway, Hooker took a quick lick and reached back for the microphone behind his head.

"Hooker, base?"

There was a minute of hesitation, and then Dolly's voice cut through the night. "I thought you would be in Monterey by now. Well, at least as far as Prunedale." Hooker could hear the laughter just behind the scolding.

Rolling his eyes as he keyed the mic, "I felt it would be prudent to pack an extra gallon of oil or two, so I stopped up the hill."

The silence was longer this time as Dolly was either laughing or busy. Finally checking back, the digging voice was even deeper and sharper. Hooker could feel her eyes on him. "Uh-huh, right. You know when you eat ice cream, your voice gets deeper and bed-roomy and drives Dina crazy." She had to stop to laugh. "And you better have thought of the mange bucket with some French vanilla."

Hooker glanced down at the topic of conversation already finished and settled back in with a deep purr to last all the way to Monterey. As he slowly reached for the yellow microphone on the dashboard, Dolly fired her final shot. "And—don't you dare even think about calling Dina right now. She's busy, and I need her concentrating on real things. Besides, she's pregnant, and it's not yours. And she's getting married."

"Yes, Momma," Hooker chuckled. "We're clearing Gilroy, and you're all broken up, 1-4-1."

Lowering his voice in an even deeper register, he keyed the yellow microphone, "1-4-1, southbound to the deep loins of Monterey."

The regular auto club dispatcher, Jake, startled Hooker and replied with a laugh, "10-4, 1-4-1, showing you out of area until tomorrow. I will advise Night Dispatch in 5-4-3-2- I'm gone."

Dina's voice, ever professional, filled the space between Jake's laughter and Hooker's, "Dispatch showing 1-4-1 Zero-Zero-Alpha, deep in the loins." Laughing, Hooker knew he would be paying for it on Sunday with Dolly teaming up with her unstoppable sister Stella, but sometimes, it's just worth it to stir the pot.

Hanging up the mic, he looked at his watch and realized what stretch of road was coming up. Getting the evilest wide-eyed maniacal look on his face, he looked at the kid and asked in a cackling crazy voice, "What's the fastest you've ever ridden in a truck before?" He danced the clutch and sticks, shifting into the top tier of gears as he slid north of eighty.

Johnny thought about it a moment as he watched Hooker slip the truck into its twentieth gear, with four more to go. Looking out at the night ahead, he weighed how much he trusted the person he was with— "Probably not nearly as fast as I think we will be going tonight."

Hooker laughed as he shifted through the last four gears of the giant truck. Eleven tons of rolling stock highballing down a dark moonless highway—these were the nights Hooker lived for, these were the times for which this truck was built. Smiling, he glanced down at his street-tested partner. "Hang on, Box—we are headed for Dead Man's Curve."

He glanced over to see if he had any effect on Johnny, but the kid was just snuggling into his new jacket and enjoying the ride. His head turned toward the open window as he watched the night fly by. He didn't have to look at the speedometer to know they were well north of the 100mph mark on the dial he knew went to 140 mph. Well past.

The five-ton refrigerated truck just followed along like a happy little puppy behind its momma in the scintillating starlight as the boys from Texas crooned about tumbleweeds and scudding clouds on the dusty trails. These were the moments Hooker lived for; the defining moments of calm with activity, and the reasons he worked the night, instead of the day.

"You didn't have to slip me the forty," Johnny half complained as they slid out of the truck, now ticking as it began to cool from the hard run over Highway 17 and the Santa Cruz pass. "It's not like you haven't been feeding me or anything."

Hooker smiled, thinking how he had probably said something similar in the first year or four living with Willie. Looking across the working deck as they each locked up their side panels and boxes, securing for the night. "I'll tell you what—you buy breakfast."

Snorting from the last turn of the key, Squirt just nodded. "Sure, and how exactly was I supposed to pay Estella for cooking breakfast… clear the table and wash the dishes?"

Hooker pursed his lips and lolled his head to one side with a shrug. "It's a start." Reaching out and slapping a hand on the kid's shoulder. "It's a start."

"Hardly seems like enough." The kid mumbled as he opened the large portico gate door. "Jeez Mareez," he stood looking at every light in the house turned on.

"Oh, shit!" Hooker pushed past him and strode quickly toward the front door. The door opened as he touched the knob.

Stella stood in the way, then stepped aside, her face a swirl of worry, anger, and sorrow. Nodding her head at the office, "A deputy has been killed, down at Calero Dam, at the boat ramp." Her lower lip quivered almost imperceptibly, something Hooker had only seen once before when Manny had been shot. Then, as now, it was only for a second before the iron and steel renewed, and she was her usual self again. She sucked in a deep breath. "He's in talking to the sheriff himself."

"How are you holding up?" Hooker looked deep into her face.

She hesitated a moment. "We don't know many deputies anymore, but they are all family." She sucked her lips in hard against her teeth, then nodded as if to change the subject. Turning to the kid, she patted Johnny on the chest and asked in a too-casual tone for the hour, "How was your day today, dear?"

The kid started to talk, but froze with his mouth open, looking to Hooker for guidance.

"Don't look at me." Hooker short-laughed. "Answer the lady." Kissing her on the top of her head, he squeezed Stella's arm. "I'll be in listening to the master when you run out of places to beat the kid." She slapped at his butt, which he bent forward out of the way.

She turned back to the kid, still standing open-mouthed. "Come on. I've got some things you need to see while you think about it." She pulled him through and closed the door. Taking him by the arm, she started him down the hallway of the guest wing. "Did I ever tell you about when Hooker came to camp with us?"

The kid just smartly shut his mouth, wagged his head, and allowed himself to be towed down her memory lane. "Well, it was several years ago…" She wound her arm in his, and they walked slowly down the guest wing hall, toward the end room.

Hooker slumped into the large soft leather easy chair in the darkest corner of the office. As he listened to Manny work his favorite tool, the phone, Hooker carefully scanned the boards for the new details that hadn't been there the day before. Each of the new pictures had at least one or three 3x5 cards next to them with details and questions. It was always the questions with Manny. As long as Hooker had known Manny, a question or a picture or a piece of a puzzle had always poked Manny to spew out at least as many questions. He called it his 'Solving Problems with

Socrates and Sherlock,' his two most favorite people to read or read about.

"Listen, Ted, Hooker just got home, and there are a few things I want to go over with him before we all go to bed." Manny held up his other hand with his index finger extended, "Sure, give me a call in the late afternoon about four. Sure, that would be even better. We'll see you for dinner. Goodnight, Ted." He dropped the phone in his lap as he thumbed the button to hang up.

Turning toward Hooker, he studied the young man's face and body language. "Boy, did you ever need this early night, you look like something Box was finished with."

Hooker's face rolled into a deep tired smile pulling up along his right side. "I think that *something* would be looking better than I feel. It's been a long week." He rested his head back along the chair as he softly blew out his breath. Waiting a three count, he nodded forward and looked at Manny. "A deputy, this time." The small statement carried more weight than the words.

The tip of Manny's tongue snuck forward and licked the center of his lower lip. Then as his lips drew back like steel bars, the tongue tip slid into retreat. "I heard Stella fill you in." He swiveled the chair back around to face the boards. He pointed to the new section. "He was ambushed at the boat ramp down at the dam." Manny slumped back into his chair. "He was supposed to have a partner, but the guy was sick, and the only other person for the right seat was a fresh cadet who didn't have his weapon clearance yet." The retired detective's head kept scanning back and forth as he talked—almost as if the talking wasn't connected to the head. "They found all sixteen dimes this time—the four in the door, and the twelve in the deputy."

The two men sat silently, staring at the large roll-around pinboards with writing, pictures, and lines drawn where the battle raged, and there were no answers coming as fast as they were wanted.

Deliberately, Manny rolled back around to face Hooker, quiet in his thoughts. He morosely watched the young man's face as the eyelids caught up with the slouched body in the soft, comforting chair. "On your way to your room, you might want to go see the end room."

Hooker looked up with leaded lids. "Hmm?" The message slowly pinballed around his brain and came to rest in the pocket labeled *We Have a Winner*. He rose and waved goodnight to Manny, who was just chuckling.

Shuffling down the hall, he noticed the light on in the back room. As he turned the corner, he saw a cleared-out room now semi-squared away as a sleeping room. Johnny sat on a bed Hooker had never even seen before. The kid looked like a fresh poleaxed steer.

"Did you know about this?" The kid could barely control his quivering voice.

Hooker just shook his head no. "Looks good. Goodnight." Turning, he left the kid to his new digs. Hooker figured it would all be sorted out in the morning. If Stella wanted another waif in their lives, far be it for him to stand in their way. His mouth stretched in a small smile as he laid his head down on the pillow. Hooker had been there before, and he knew the kid would be all right.

Moments later, the large diesel engine rumbling in his ear was not Mae. The sun was shining, but it was night, and the engine needed a tune-up something fierce, as the lope in its idle was very erratic, and then Box stuck his ice-cold nose into Hooker's right ear.

Blankets and sheets exploded about the room as Hooker turned inside out with the shock. Box, who was used to even more violent reactions than this, just sat purring and staring at Hooker with his one good eye. Something told Hooker it was late, and either Box needed to be fed or let out.

Giving the tough cat a cold look, only a close partner could and did ignore, Hooker shoved his legs into his pants, bypassing the boots as he pulled the jeans together around his waist and buttoned the fly closed before cinching the belt. Box, now satisfied things were going his way, slithered down from the low bed and marched through the doorway now being held open by Stella.

"Sorry about that," she reached out and hugged Hooker with a kiss on his neck. "I told him to let you sleep in, but you know how the mange bucket can be." They both looked at the closed door at the end of the hall as they cleared Hooker's room.

She looked back at Hooker and pulled on his arm as she nodded at the kitchen. "Let's give him some time to get used to it." She didn't have to remind Hooker of his first week of unease with his new room that was every bit as much a sanctuary as his room at Willie's house had been… until the screaming and tempers that went with a very serious and emotional break-up of Willie and his longtime boyfriend. It wasn't until a year later Hooker found out it was really about the friend dying, and he was breaking up with Willie because he didn't want to be a burden on Willie and Hooker. If Hooker had known, he would have stayed and fought to keep the men together, but he hadn't known. Instead, he found his other half of the family.

As the two of them turned the corner into the foyer area, Hooker took one last glance back down the hall and stole the opportunity to kiss Stella's cheek. "Thanks." She just squeezed him a little harder and nodded her head. She knew she couldn't trust herself to talk at the moment.

"Jesus, Mary, Joseph, and Rex!" Manny loudly started from the sunroom, "I thought you were going to sleep the clock around."

"Love you too, Manny." Hooker and Stella veered off for a stop at the large coffee pot before Hooker had to engage more torment at Manny's mouth. Hooker squinted at the clock to make sure it was still running because the time was way out of whack.

Stella just nodded as she grabbed a set of hot pads and opened the upper oven. "Brunch is in about forty or fifty minutes. So if you're going to horseplay with the frisky old fart and get a shower, I'm going to vote for the water locker first."

Still a bit foggy, Hooker nodded as he medicated his coffee with sugar and cream. "Has the kid even made any noise yet?" Sipping from the large mug, Hooker's eyes slowly slid closed in *first sip of coffee* ecstasy.

Dusting her hands with the pestle-ground rosemary over the chickens for dinner later, she shook her head. "You might want to kick his door and get him moving, too."

"Okay." Stepping into the archway to the sunroom on his way to the shower, Hooker took a glancing stab at the man relaxing on the couch with a large book in his lap. "Sorry, Manny, but Stella says I either have to take you out and hose you down along with Box or take a shower myself. I voted for me in the water. You lose." Looking about, he spotted the orange topic of derision waiting impatiently at the front door. "I'm coming. I'm coming."

Opening the door, the orange doorstop became a bullet across the plaza. Hooker sipped on his coffee as he watched the big cat hit the grass, do his thing, and then begin to look for something to beat up. "Come on, Box, no fights today. Not on the Sabbath." Hooker could hear the dual snorts of laughter from the kitchen and sunroom. The furry ball of macho stalked back across the plaza and through the closing door.

Slipping his way to the far door, Hooker knocked. "Squirt, dinner is in thirty minutes, be showered and don't be late, or you have to answer to Stella." Listening, he heard movement, then a groan, so he headed for his shower room and ritual. Sundays could be a total relaxing bust, business-wise, or Hooker could be back up at the crack of noon and run himself ragged until well past midnight or beyond. Sometimes, it was nice to wake up and find out you're eleven-plus hours into the day, and only having to look forward to a shower and dinner with loved ones.

25

ooker padded back down the hall and tapped on the still closed door listening to Johnny respond he would be out in a few minutes. Hooker threw back the last of the coffee in the large mug and headed for a refill. As he walked past the open office door, he saw the pinboards as he remembered the news from last night about the sheriff's deputy. He scowled at the thought of another cop taken down in his prime because only the prime work the street—even the ones who are only days away from retirement.

Manny was at the large table, going over some notes. Estella's dining table was sacrosanct: for eating and talking—no radio, TV, newspaper or books. Manny was allowed notes, but only if he were working on a case, and only if he was alone. Hooker poured himself some more coffee and stayed away from the table until Manny put down the notes, stacked them in a neat pile, and looked up.

"Another week and you're standing upright." Manny rolled out their old standby joke as Hooker brought over the coffee carafe to fill the other man's oversized mug. The joke was the evolution of Hooker's first comment to the detective when he woke-up in the hospital paralyzed from the waist down. 'How are you supposed to be an upstanding guy if you're just laying around all day?' had become a myriad of comments to each other about standing and up—but mostly it became about still standing after a grueling week, as well as standing this side of a dirt blanket.

"At least I'm standing on this side of the dirt," Hooker mumbled with a slur matching his still blurry eyes.

Returning to the long counter, he plugged the carafe back into the wall cord. Hooker turned and leaned his lower back against the cool stone and asked his friend, "Anything new?" As to what he was asking about was completely unnecessary. There had been only one thing consuming Manny's attention night and day.

Grabbing his own large mug, Hooker returned to the table and took a seat at the other end. He closed his eyes and sipped the nectar of the morning as if it were mother's milk fresh from the breast.

Manny shook his head, his mind still many miles away from the table. "They thought they had a partial print on one of the dimes, but it was just a greasy print of a latex glove. Not much help, unless the grease is unique." Slowly coming back to the reality around him, he noticed some movement in the window through to one of the hall windows in the guest wing. "The Squirt's up," he softly commented.

Hooker didn't even have to look as he could hear the slight squeak of bare feet on the red terracotta tiles of the entryway. "Mugs are above the coffee pot, choose any but the black one or the flowered one, those are Dolly's and Stella's respectively." Smiling as he added, "Only Sweets can get away with saying he didn't know."

The kid grabbed an oversized stone mug, and as he poured, asked with a muffled voice, "Sweets? There is someone I haven't met yet?"

Hooker raised his eyes to look at Manny as they shared a large smile, "Yeah, and trust me; he won't call you Squirt." Manny pursed his lips as he sipped his coffee and nodded in agreement. "In fact, you're going to like him a whole bunch. But if he doesn't like you, then... well, we'll just have to take you out and shoot you... leave your body for the wolves."

The kid slid into one of the side chairs. "Now I know you're fibbing, cuz there ain't no wolves around here."

Manny's left eyebrow slid up into an arch. "You sure?"

The kid looked the man in the eye. "Yeah."

Hooker continued with the mutual digging on the unsuspecting victim. "Would you bet your life on it?"

The voice of reason was issued from the sunroom. "You boys leave the kid alone."

The two men chuckled and sipped their coffee, wisely not willing to risk any comment that may cross the queen of the house, especially on a Sunday morning.

Johnny ventured a bit of humor that played well with the playful nature of their morning. "Stella," he whined in a drawn-out child's voice, "they… they're picking on me."

"Shut up, and drink your coffee," the reply came, as there was also an irritated shake-ruffle of the Sunday paper as she shook out the turned page, and to reinforce the information the men were messing with the sanctity of her *Sunday morning paper time.*

The kid tucked his chin back into his chest and stared with huge chastised eyes at Hooker, then Manny, as they nodded their heads knowingly and quietly sipped their coffee. As the kid started to say something, Manny held up his right index finger into the air between them to stop him from vocalizing. The paper shook one more time, and then there was a smoothing out and a final flip of paper folded length-wise, the silence of the woman sipping her own coffee, and the click of the matched flower mug clicking down on the glass-topped end table.

Manny withdrew his finger and looked at the kid. "You were saying?"

The kid just shook his head. "Wasn't important."

Hooker put down his mug and stretched his lanky legs under the table as his arms reached for air behind his head. Yawning, he asked, "So, how was your new bed?"

Snickering, the kid put down his empty mug. "It was great until I had to share it with Box." Looking over at Hooker. "Did you know he likes to steal blankets?"

Hooker, unsure if he should feel betrayed by his partner or enjoy sharing the cat, chuckled silently. "What part of my door being closed did you not understand?" He looked down the table and rolled his eyes at Manny in a knowing manner. "You either learn, or you learn to suffer, but I can guarantee you this—Box isn't going to be changing anytime soon."

The kitchen timer dinged. The paper only ruffled a tiny bit, and the two men knew she was turning down the one corner as she assessed the next movement in the house.

The gentle, commanding voice carried from the sunny morning room, any other day, the sole bastion of Manny. "Hooker, show John where the place settings are, so he can learn to set the table. Then take the baked French toast out of the upper oven. The quiche needs about five more minutes. I can't smell it yet." She flipped the corner of paper back and resumed reading the morning horror stories, or as other people called them, the obituaries. "There is a new bottle of berry syrup in the pantry, as well as the standard. Get them both, please." She shook the paper to enforce her will, and the two younger men rose from the table.

Hooker turned to the kid. "Stick with me. I'll teach you everything you need to know about Sundays around this house." As they moved into the kitchen area, he added, "If you ever end up at Willie's on Sunday... just start pouring the cold cereal in anything you can find clean or looks clean."

An hour later, the two were standing at the sink, Hooker washing as the kid dried and stacked the colorful Fiestaware pottery dishes, as well as all the rest of the large cupboard full of dishes—every shape and size fulfilling several full sets.

"How many people are coming to this barbecue?"

Hooker cocked his jaw as he chuffed a deep laugh. "Let see, there are about twenty pounds of Chiaramonte's Sicilian sausage, about three gallons of marinated chicken breasts in the bottom of the fridge, what looked to be about three or four gallons of different salads, and doesn't even start to include what Dolly and Tilly will be bringing. So just off the top of my head, I would say about a good hundred humans, and then there's Danny and Box."

The back of Hooker's head stung as the tips of Stella's fingers snapped off the back of his scalp where it was most sensitive. "Don't you dare be inferring Danny is an animal, he's just a growing boy who likes to eat... and I like watching him enjoy himself." Winking at the kid, "The mange bucket, on the other hand..." She rolled her eyes as she lolled her head to her shoulder, stuck out her tongue, and hung her head back in her *zombie* pose.

Once Hooker was cleaned up, and as squared away as the morning's kitchen, he sat down with Manny and Johnny for a chalk talk. Manny was not happy but understood, but the kid was just upset.

"Why can't I come?" The nonplussed youth paced with exaggerated hands, well, hand and arms. "Who's going to have your back?"

"Box," Hooker shrugged.

The kid was incredulous. "A cat?" It stopped him dead in the center of the office with arms at both extremes. "A cat is going to have your back? What's he got, an Uzi?"

Manny's lips were a grimaced taut line and slowly raised his eyes to engage the kid standing above him. "Don't count Box out. Where Hooker is going, he'll be more than enough." Manny thought for a moment before he continued. "Probably more than the shorty 12-gauge he'll be carrying." He looked at Hooker for confirmation.

"Look, Johnny," Hooker confided adult to adult, "These people are like Peter, spooky and superstitious. They semi-understand the shotgun, but it's being loaded with silver makes it very scary to them. Box isn't like a regular cat. He comes when I call. He is larger than most." The kid's eyes got big with expression as he nodded. "And most of all, he has my back. Anybody tries to sneak up on me, Box will bushwhack them. He's done it before with this group.'

"But…"

"No," Hooker finished as he stood up. He looked at Manny. "I'll check in through Dolly as soon as I get there, and when I clear."

Manny nodded agreement. "And we'll find something around here for Squirt to do on his day off." Turning his chair to look squarely at the beaten kid, he continued. "I think it might be time to clean out the office area in the garage level."

"Yeah, right. Like you have a garage level," bracketing the *garage level* with quoting fingers he could now use, and a heavy sluicing of sarcasm.

Hooker snorted. "You're going to wish you had said that with a lot more respect when you see his cars… which you now don't get to drive."

Grabbing up his leather jacket, he turned for the door. "Keep him working, Manny. I'll check in and be home by dinner."

As he stepped into the foyer, there was a toll to pay. He gave the best he could with what he hoped was a reassuring hug and smile. Stella ran her warm hand down along the side of his face. "Don't let your sister get to you. She's gone to this world, and there is no redemption to ever put the genie back in the sister you knew."

Hooker's face pulled back in a grim frown. "I know. I just miss her and knowing she's out there still doesn't make it any easier."

"Both of you made choices when you ran from the last foster home. You turned out, and she, well, just turned…"

"I had a lot of help. She didn't." He studied her eyes of concern.

"You offered, just like Willie did, and like we did. Beyond that, it's all up to the person being offered the hand as to whether they take it or not."

Hooker settled into silence and just looked at her face. For a moment, he thought if he had been looking into it all his life, things might have turned out differently, and then again, maybe not. He kissed her on the cheek and turned the doorknob.

Turning back, he called to the sunroom, "Box. Go time." The streak was almost to the front gate by the time Hooker closed the house door. Some things, you just didn't have to tell the cat a second time. Picking a fight, Hooker knew, was another.

The road out to the rock wasn't exactly much of a road as much as it was an ignored or abused track in the South Bay scrub and sand marsh pan. From his advantage of ten feet above the pan, Hooker could see almost anything moving within a half-mile—but the operative term was *moving*.

Hooker knew and could feel, the small army of creatures *The Mouse* had gathered around her. They were hidden across the pan, watching his slow approach. Although, their mothers had thought at their births they were all humans, time, and the warping nature of mental illness, had created changelings only the most creative 'things that go bump in the night' storytellers could even begin to imagine. And mostly, they would be sorry to have imagined. And more beyond… something even the most creative would never get close to imagining in this universe.

Even the Mouse had been 'human' at one time. Even though the times weren't the best, she had occasionally worn a dress, gone to school, and talked about 'when she grew up.'

Then there was the change in the foster homes, from purgatory to nothing less than perdition itself. The incarnate was not another foster child, but the foster family themselves. The same family Hooker had beaten on his way out the door at age fourteen, two very long months after the Mouse had taken a razor blade to the couple as they had proceeded to rape her one more time before they turned her over to their even more sadistic mentally retarded forty-three-year-old son to 'play with for the night.'

Even in the heat of the day, on the flat pan with the sun reflecting from the brackish waters of the muds and the back bay, the thoughts of their childhood made Hooker's spine sub-zero and froze his resolve to see her. As he drove closer to the distant wavering knot of dark clay rising from the pan, his usual green hazel eyes slowly drained of color on their way to aqua-white ash. This would not be a day of emotion. This would be a day of pure nerves—and the cold of blue-white steel was his only way to stay alive.

The truck nudged up within fifty feet of the large rock of clay towering close to the height of the forty-foot telephone poles in the distance. The giant motor rattled and shook in protest, on its way to silence. Box stood as tense as the strained cord on a war bow drawn tight with an arrow—all anticipation and potential of death. If the large deep dashboard had been anything softer than steel, his claws would have dug in as the experienced paws of death extended and retracted in anticipation and reflex.

"Ready for this, buddy?" Hooker asked quietly as his eyes scanned the dead scrub, barren of any signs of life.

The tip of the cat's tail kinked, and then the whole swept in an expressive arc of 'Let's go.'

Checking his side mirrors, where he had thought he had seen a flash of movement, there was nothing there. He reached for the door handle and released the chrome lever, silently swinging out the door as his left foot slipped out and sought the step on top of the saddle tank.

Leaning back and twisting right to reach the shotgun in its wall-mounted holster, Hooker felt the cat hit his left shoulder for a brief second as he catapulted through the open door. The resulting scream, animal as it was, was not Box, but Box's prey. Hooker jacked the action on the pump shotgun and spun out of the door to face any other idiot who didn't understand who they were dealing with.

Out of the corner of his eye, Hooker could see a large chimera of rags, that may or may not be a man, writhing in the dust dealing with over twenty pounds of orange hellhound in a cat's body. The face and two hands were rapidly losing the battle. "Mouse?" Hooker called out to the rock and pan, "Your dutifully stupid underling is rapidly losing his face and hands." He collected his thoughts. "In a minute or less, the only recourse will be for me to put an ounce of silver through his brain."

"Call off your beast!" The diminutive woman stepped out away from the bush where she had been hiding. "Call it off. He was only doing what he thought would make me happy."

Hooker stood his ground and after a slow count of three, called softly. "Box, come."

The cat stood up on the man's face and took tearing swipes at the offending hands hovering around him, flaying the palms, and calling forth a fresh scream of anguish and pain from the form under him. One last deep shearing sweep of the quad swords of pain and the man's nose was a spread deck of cards. Turning, Box sprayed his way slowly off the hunter-turned-catch, marking his kill, or at least establishing grounds for territory.

The cat passed behind Hooker's legs, rubbing to let him know he was there, and then settled down and cleaned his paws as he sat next to Hooker and acted as if he were uncaring or even unnoticing of any minor stuff happening around him. Hooker could feel the slow rhythmic breathing as the cat leaned against his leg. The twenty-plus pound cat wasn't even breathing hard, having just taken out a 140-pound man—a tough act to follow.

The small woman calmly walked forward as other entities began to materialize out of the dirt and brush, her cold blue eyes never leaving the matching steel of Hooker's. As she reached within ten feet, her eyes slowly drooped. She broke eye contact and looked at the man holding his destroyed face in his wounded hands.

She looked toward someone off to one side who was out of Hooker's vision, but probably not Box's vision, or at least attention. She flicked her head and made a subtle sign of her hand, and two came forward to collect the suffering, sacrificial mound of flesh.

Hooker didn't have to look. "You didn't have to test me, Sissy."

The woman reared back and hissed silently like a vampire Hooker had just tossed holy water on. "That name is not used anymore, Hooker."

"Too bad. Those were better days for both of us."

"Maybe because only you think so." She still circled around like a large wary cat.

"At least you slept in a bed with a roof over your head."

"Some beds are better left unmade," she shot back. "Some look better but are wastelands of pain and suffering, or just worse than hell itself."

Hooker sighed. "Mouse, we can argue this until we are both old and dead, but it's not why I came here to see you."

"You didn't come just to be neighborly, Hooker." She pointed at the shotgun at his side. "You bring the viper of silver and the beast of hell. What happened to the trust of a brother?"

"It disappeared with the knife through my back, and the five broken ribs your tribe gave me many years ago."

"You shouldn't have come." She fidgeted, trying to see where Box was without being obvious.

"I need your help." He knew he had the upper hand if he didn't stop to look around, as more of her minions slithered out from under the cover where they had been hiding. If she was the one worried, he could get what he wanted, or at least needed.

The heat of the pan beat harsh on the denizens who usually only moved about in the cool of darkness. The constant buzz of marsh flies and sand fleas intensified the perception of an intense heat, which Hooker experienced as mild. Hooker knew the sun on the thin milky skin of his redheaded, borderline-albino, foster sister, must be searing and painful. She would pay for days for the few minutes she had been exposed today.

"There have been killings…"

"There are always killings!" she snapped, now impatient.

"These have to do," Hooker lifted his shotgun by the barrel, "with a weapon like this." A sharp intake of breath hissed from the unseen collective. These hidden denizens knew of the silver the gun contained.

The Mouse weighed her options and the value of information. "We have heard."

"I need to know what you have heard so I can stop this killer." He studied, from the dozen or so feet away, the flush of heat along her right cheek.

"What is it worth, this information?"

Hooker had been thinking about this for most of the previous day, knowing this meeting would come down to what she was going to get out of it. It had to have a certain tangible value to her, and yet be an intangible item he would not have to produce or carry back to her. But instead, it would have to raise her standing as a leader.

"Who is the killer killing?" he asked.

"Pigs," she hissed.

"Police," he corrected.

"Pigs. Pigs—those who harass us and stop us because we are not like them, and who prevent us from going where we need to go for food and clothing. Pigs, who force us to live in this hell, because the people in their washed clean city are offended by seeing someone who must climb through their garbage because they don't want to give us their leftover garbage—their rotting fruit and vegetables or bread which is already molding. Pigs." She picked at her arms in an old habit of irritation that had garnered the nickname of Mouse. The dead gray skin covered her arms and hung like fur.

"Don't pick, Sissy," Hooker said very quietly, almost to himself, an old habit of his own from better times, or not.

Her head snapped up, unsure if she had heard the name she now could not tolerate, a name which could denote a connection that would belie her position of supreme leader. She glared at Hooker, and she slowly withdrew her hand from her somewhat furry arm.

"Okay, but they are still the police. They are my people. I can talk to them. Maybe some kind of accommodations can be made. A blind eye turned, as it were—but only if you can truly help me." For the first time, Hooker allowed himself to slowly look about at some of the now visible walking wounded of the night. She was right. They lacked any decent food—or any food at all. "I'll also see what I can do about getting you some food before it's rotten. I don't know what I can do, but I will try. And maybe some kind of medical help…" His voice trailed off as he knew they would never trust another doctor in their short lifetimes.

She thought for a moment. "Sanctuary and redemption."

"I don't know where they could give you… " Hooker started.

"No, stupid. Not for us, the killer. The killer is in the sanctuary and has eaten the meal of redemption and salvation."

"I'm not sure I understand, Mouse. I need for you to talk to me in plain talk, not riddles. We aren't ten years old anymore." He could see she was at the end of what she could stand. "Please, my time is up, and I have to go. What are you trying to tell me?"

"The person you seek is one of the blessed and forgiven of *His* army. But the person you seek is not the person you think you seek. Look to the killers of nature, and you will find your answer in the garden."

"Mouse, you're not being…"

"Your time is past. Now take your beast of evil and go." She violently fluffed the rags of her clothing like they were a multitude of wings, and the fine dust filled the air enough to obscure her passing to under, behind or into one of the bushes, or even somewhere else. For all Hooker cared or understood, she could have successfully disappeared, and as he turned around, there were no others but him standing on the pan next to the giant truck. The heat and the flies were the only sound.

Hooker slowly raised his right hand up to the grab-hold beside his door, still looking about across the pan. Hoping what she had said would have some meaning for someone—and soon. He turned up into the cab. "Box, go." The orange streak tore from the lower brush, into the cab through the small space under his feet, and into his box.

Stowing Betsy in her holster, he sat in the silence thinking, his right hand hanging and finding the one almost whole ear to slide between his fingers. He gently massaged his knuckle in the cat's ear and was rewarded with a deep, contented purr. All around a good day when you can take on an advisory ten times your size and come away the untouched victor.

Turning the silver key, and pushing the small silver button, the massive engine matched the purr in the cab. Hooker had a lot to think about, but with a quick glance at his watch, knew he would have no time to casually drive and think. Pushing the gears into reverse, he checked his side mirrors as he began the half-mile of backing out of the Mouse's domain. Hooker had no idea where her people were, or slept, and he didn't want to find out a three-point turn-around had been a three-person kill as he ran over them. So for future's sake and out of respect for his sister, he could do a little backing up.

The alkali-dusted tires were just starting to spin back to black on the asphalt as Hooker keyed the mic behind his head. "Hooker, 10-98, and safely heading home. Please make the call and advise Dolly and Stella their chubby little neck nuzzles are safe."

The radio squelched from being picked up too fast and over modulating with a mouth too close to the sensitive lollypop microphone. "You had better be safe, young man."

"I am, Dolly." *Shift on a biscuit,* Hooker thought, *what the heck is she still doing there?* "I would have thought you would be out helping your sister already."

"Nice try. But now we can both go on out. Oh, and Hooker... I'll take the sausage you forgot."

"Shi...ift in deep sand," he thought. "Thank you, Dolly. See you there."

"10-4, base out."

Hooker looked down at his companion, who was now sound asleep. "Careful when we get home, Box, your girlfriend is in one of those rare moods." He meant *motherhood.* A small warm smile washed his face as he pushed south into the top of the city, clearing his side mirrors and looking at the sparkle of the last visible vestiges of the San Francisco Bay sparkling in the late afternoon sunlight unique to the bay area in the late spring.

Over the years, people had told him about Paris in the spring, and how over there, the evening light was different and magical like nowhere else. He had heard stories about London, New York, and even Los Angeles and

San Diego, but for Hooker, he would rather have the spring light in his hometown that bounces off the bay, or the ultra-glow lighting up the sail-boats. This was to Hooker like the sprinkles on a cupcake—one of life's little quiet pleasures. He was a simple man who took his real pleasures in the little things.

His right hand hung down along his seat in the off chance Box might just sit up and stick an ear in twiddling range. The smile seemed stuck on the left side of Hooker's face as the hulking truck dropped down the last slide onto the Almaden Expressway, the yellow brick road to home.

The large flashes of emerald green, mixed with the lines of golden-brown, crept back in over the powder-gray in his eyes. The closer to home, the more there were, and the larger the flashes of green would appear. Purring deeply, Box rose up and stuck his ear in between the prof-fered fingers. Box would purr for the two of them, as the large engine harmonized and carried the tune.

Johnny stood beside Stella as they rewashed already clean dishes. The two were looking at the growing crowd. Both were futzing around, but with different motives—the kid was intimidated by the growing mass of people he didn't know, and Stella was waiting for it to be just the right amount of people for her entrance. Inside, she was worried sick about Hooker, and she wouldn't be able to settle down until both he and her sister had walked through the gate.

Johnny was admiring how good Willie looked in his new patchwork jean bib-overalls, a consideration to convention, and that others might just be a little uncomfortable around a white-haired man in a long dress. A small self-satisfied smile crept across his lower face.

"Did you make that suggestion, too?"

He looked over at Stella with confusion then understood she was talking about the same thing he was looking at. "Naw—you're looking at pure Willie. I suggested he would look better in faded denim instead of the flower dress he was wearing the other day." He shot her a shy side-glance. "I was talking about another dress. The bibbies were something he found."

"Or had sewn." She bumped her hip into his. "Don't count the old man out—he has amazing connections."

Thinking a moment as he dried another plate, he asked, "How did he and Hooker meet?"

Stella laughed a low rolling chuckle starting from deep and far away. "That story, you should hear first-hand from Willie. Hooker tells a decent rendition, but the better telling is from William himself."

The kid dried another plate, stacked it, and reached for another. "I guess it will just be a story I'll never hear then." He looked back out at the man standing near the giant open grill as he watched his friend play the fire and steel like it was a violin. "It just sounds too personal of a story for me to ask to hear."

"Pfft," Stella chided. "Nothing so personal."

The kid just shrugged one shoulder and reached for another plate.

"Okay, wimp," she shot him an indulging motherly look, "but as I said, this isn't nearly as much fun as when Willie tells it," nodding her jaw toward the window, "especially when he's gone past the second beer and a shot of moonshine or two. Because then he slips a little and his Nancy comes sliding out…" She giggled. "First time I heard him tell the story, I wet myself just listening to him."

"I'll settle for a version where I don't have to change my pants."

"Version of what?" Hooker asked as he strolled out of the pantry, having used the secret stairway up from the garage.

"Well, it's about time!" Stella turned on him with her arms up for a hug.

"I had to park in the lower pasture. There's no room up here." He nuzzled in her neck in a perfunctorily distracting buzz. "Dolly here yet?"

"No, honey, but I expect her along any time now."

"She's probably out circling around looking for a parking place. I'll go find her."

"No, I'll go whistle my little sister up. You tell Squirt how you met Willie."

Hooker looked at the kid who was trying to act busy at the sink. Hooker smirked. He knew the kid deserved to know the story. It was all part of becoming one with the family. As Stella moved through the plaza like a winter tornado, Hooker clamped his right hand on Johnny's left shoulder, making the kid jump.

"Don't worry, kid. I'm not going to bore you to tears." He stepped closer to the counter and looked out at his uncle. "Willie will be primed and perfect by about seven tonight, and by midnight, you might have recovered." He chuckled at the wide-eyed look the kid now wore. "For now, you're off the hook. I need to talk to Manny."

The kid turned his head, facing Hooker. "You got something?"

As Hooker moved toward the office, he called back, "Maybe."

Johnny wiped his hands in the dishtowel, and then on his new jeans as he followed Hooker into the office in search of the detective.

Forty minutes later, Stella knocked and opened the office door. "Hank says you men have only five more minutes for your man bonding thing. So beat your drums faster."

Sweets being the fastest with the mind and lips answered for the eight men. "Thank you, my love. We were just wrapping up the details and preparing ourselves to partake in the radiance of your beauty and hospitality."

"Awe, thanks, Sweets. It's just so sweet for you to say such a thing—but it doesn't mean you're clear of slinging bullshit. Hustle them along." Giggling, she quietly closed the door, and then called through the thick wood. "You now have four minutes."

Manny rolled his eyes. "So if all of the saved, redeemed, forgiven, and sanctuary stuff is about a priest, why are we looking for the wrong guy?"

"I'm not so sure we are." Hooker scratched at the back of his left ear. "I think Sissy was being obtuse, but I also think she tried to direct me, but not to appear so in front of her clan."

Danny grunted and shifted uncomfortably, giving Hooker the eye.

Hooker looked at him a second, and then asked, "What?" with his hands out and shoulders in a shrug to say, "What did I do wrong?"

Danny half-rolled his eyes. "She's right. You need to stop using it."

"What?"

"Sissy. It's demeaning and doesn't help her or you."

"It's short for Lucinda, her middle name. Claire is her first. It's the only name she went by for years."

"No, it's about being a sissy. It's not who she is. She is not your sister anymore, nor a Lucinda or a sissy. She is the commander of an army. If they catch a whiff of weakness, they will turn on her and eat her alive, man."

Sweets perfunctorily stood up and raised a hand. "Danny is right. Hooker, you need to respect the Mouse's right to be the Mouse, even if she is surrounded by rats." Lowering his hand as he aimed his open palm in the direction of the doorway in which Stella had appeared. "Gentlemen, our time is up. The ladies and a gentleman await our presence."

The remainder, grousing, rose from the places they had come to roost on in the office. Danny, ever being Danny, groused the loudest. "There better still be some food left."

Hooker grabbed at the big man's tummy and shook it. "Mihito, tus flaco." (Little one, you're skinny.) The three laughed as they walked out of the office pushing Manny—Danny being one of the few people who had ever been allowed to push him.

The roar of the ongoing conversations flowing about the large patio was a wash of topics with varying levels of mirth and merriment. It was a much-needed salve for Hooker and most of the rest in the crowd who were all somehow connected to the law enforcement industry. Manny held court from his massive *special* table, the large round one he had built even before they started raising the adobe walls.

Manny and Stella had known, even before starting this house, they wanted a place where many could gather or just a few for an intimate dinner. The patio which spread out from the house was larger than the footprint of the large sprawling hacienda, fully taking advantage of the nine months of outdoor entertainment weather enjoyed by the trapped heat in the Almaden Valley. It was the main reason for originally buying the land—other than the knoll being their favorite picnic spot for many years.

Manny looked around the several tables where many still picked at the remains of a food orgy which would have made the ancient Romans proud. Others, who had reached their limits, were merely in resting or relaxing as they enjoyed the group dynamics. Seeing the tell-tale signs, he quietly touched Stella's hand and minutely jutted his jaw toward the other oversized table containing Willie, Hank, and Johnny, as well as other unsuspecting members who were about to receive 'the story,' as it had come to be known.

Johnny needed a point cleared up. "Wait, wait… why, was he stealing your car in the first place?" He wanted to make sure he wasn't getting only the partial story, but his loud question stopped many conversations at other tables. Some wondered what was going on about a stolen car, and others who knew the story and the storyteller had quieted the rest so they could hear it, too.

"Well, silly," Willie's hand flopped languidly out in the air as the many shots of Madeline's family moonshine worked its magic on his inner Nancy, "because he was hungry, of course." The final 's' was drawn out into a little giggle that needed a wee bit more moonshine.

"But who was he going to sell it to?"

Hank laughed as Willie sipped. "That's the best part— the kid didn't have a buyer."

Willie put down his half-pint canning jar and reinserted himself back into his proper role as the storyteller. "He hadn't thought so far ahead. Little Hooker had only thought up the idea the moment he saw my unlocked car." Waving his hand about to wash the air in front of him and his stage as he winked. "We'll just forget about it being a convertible with the top down."

Pulling himself up to show up-rightness and respect, he would imbue in the character of the *young* Hooker. "I'm sure he's been able to break into many tougher cars since then." He got the much reached for laugh from almost the whole crowd as he now raised his voice in the knowledge he was the entertainment for the entire large patio.

"So, as I came back out of the hardware store with my purchase, I'm greeted with a tiny little butt, wiggling in the air as he's trying his hand at figuring out which wires to pull and cross to hotwire my car." Full into his Nancy now, he waved his spread right hand across the stage in the air above his face, so everyone could see the panorama he was seeing.

"As delightful as it was at the moment, I knew he was about to start ripping into wires which would take me a full day or two to reinstate. So I popped him one on his cute bottom!" Willie was giggling in his own fantasy.

Hooker growled from a distant table. "Will-ie."

"Spoilsport," Willie stage muttered under his breath. "Well, as much as I wanted to—I just cleared my throat instead. I said in my deepest cop voice I could, *'I've got a 357 here that wants to know what the hell you think you are doing in my car.'* Well, you have never seen a kid flip over and get so big-eyed in your life."

Danny elbowed Sweets in the arm, and quietly muttered, "Except when mom caught you stealing those cupcakes, she had baked for the church bazaar." The two men chuckled at the common memory as their mother gave them a stern look from two tables away.

"Now, Hooker is a pretty quick thinker, and on occasion, he's even smart." He sipped as he milked the chuckles from the crowd that almost all knew the man being roasted, and he returned the jar of moonshine to the table with his two smallest fingers stretched slightly out. "So he looks at my hand, and says, *'You don't have a gun.'* My Hooker... so quick. He figured it out all on his own. So I told him never to bet his life on it and told him to scoot his ass over," motioning with his fingers and two hands. *"'We're going to lunch,'* I told him because obviously, he was hungry. Of course, it never hurts to use a situation to your advantage, and turn it into a teachable moment, so I did."

He leaned back as if he were driving the 1952 DeSoto Sportsman. With his right arm stretched out, and his wrist draped over the large French ivory steering wheel and moving lazily back and forth as he steered, he turned his head to look at Johnny. "The first thing you need to know about stealing a car is you don't hotwire the radio first."

The eruption of laughter at Hooker's expense carried out across the valley to the very tips of the hills barely lit by the setting sun. With good food and good friends, Stella and Manny sat back and took it all in as this was their entire intent when they had first sat on a knoll in the dry stub-grass overlooking a then sparsely populated little valley. Someday, they would have friends to come and enjoy the same view and plenty of good food for all to share.

As the evening dimmed, and the talking quieted, Johnny busied himself by carrying in dishes to the sink. Some of the guests had left, begging early shifts or pressing business, but the general mass was talking over coffee.

With one load, he found Dolly already at the sink absently washing the colorful heavy dishes, looking out at the crowd who were as many members of her fiefdom as they were her sister and Manny's.

As Johnny set the stack down on the sideboard, he noticed her watching Hooker making rounds among the guests. He stopped briefly to kiss Stella on the top of the head as he smoothed his hand across her shoulders. Her right hand caught his and gave it a small squeeze, as she never broke eye contact with the young couple she was listening to.

"So I know how Hooker met Willie, and I think I understand knowing you just came with the job, but how did he meet Stella and Manny?"

Dolly stopped washing but kept watching her sister and the young man. Thinking, she heaved a deep breath. "That would have started Christmas Eve, 1942, at the Alameda air station." She pushed softly to turn and lean her backside against the counter. Her mind and sight were many miles and years away.

Johnny started to protest Hooker not being so old when her finger rose to silence him.

"They were just a couple of crazy kids. Manny was fresh out of the police academy and had even taken a few tours of downtown as a foot patrol squirt. But the war was the war, and when Pearl Harbor was hit, it was everybody in. But by December 7th, Manny was already in San Diego learning how to chip paint on a destroyer expecting to go kill Germans.

"After his weeks of boot camp, he had five days of leave before shipping out to Pearl. He called Stella and said he was catching a train up the coast and they could take the bus over to Reno to meet his folks who were coming down from Montana. The long ride over to Nevada was enough to convince her she would never find anyone else. On the way back, he asked her to marry him. But they were out of time, so they got the base Chaplin to marry them there on the dock in front of five-thousand other sailors waiting to ship out.

"Stella had called when the bus stopped in Sacramento and asked her best friend Ruth to come be her bridesmaid. Somewhere, Ruth had even found some fresh flowers. So there they were married for all of five minutes, and Manny got on the troop ship. Some wedding night. He didn't come home for two years."

"But…?"

Up came the finger again, as she turned to pour a mug of fresh coffee. Sipping, her eyes closed languidly, either enjoying the drink or remembering. The mug hovered a moment at her lips as she continued. "Well, it was wartime, Christmas Eve, and two young girls. They coaxed the coxswain on a Navy man-boat to ferry them across the bay to the Tenderloin in San Francisco where they had dinner and danced with any and every sailor. By the end of the night, Stella and Ruth had a fist full of men's names and addresses. I think, by the end of the war, they were writing about a hundred letters a month between the two of them.

"But back to Hooker—so by the time Manny gets back, Ruth and Stella have celebrated not only the wedding night but two anniversaries while Manny was away. So, being the smart man, he was, and is, Manny sends them off to San Francisco every Christmas Eve to light up the town. Except for the night they met Hooker, they didn't make it back so easily. Their car broke down on the 101 in a rather unsavory section of Santa Clara.

"Hooker was on his second or third year of driving then and could have even had the night off. But Hooker being Hooker, took the backup position because he and Willie had baked chocolate chip cookies, and whipped up gallons of hot chocolate.

"He'd just headed out with a big batch of warm cookies and cocoa to give to all of the other drivers working the night shift when Manny called me at two in the morning. He explained where the girls were, and how they were dressed to the nines. So I called Hooker. He always had the fastest truck and was near the area anyway.

"Hooker found them, but I didn't tell him who they were. I kept checking in with him like a mother hen. He couldn't get the car running, so he needed to tow it back to the dealer up in Palo Alto."

Taking a sip of the coffee, she shook her head. "It wasn't an easy thing like now. No freeway then. So he had to drag it back up the 101, and then back into the Camino Real. Meanwhile, he has to put up with me on his case, asking where he is, how Mrs. Romero and Mrs. Steinberger are doing, are they hungry, or need something to drink—anything to keep his mic open so Manny, on the line with me, could get a kick out of this kid, too."

Danny brought in a huge stack of the remaining plates, and put them on the counter, nodded and headed for the bathroom. Stella and Johnny just watched the silent juggernaut move with the grace and silence of a cat. Dolly quietly observed more to herself than the kid— "If I didn't know and love that boy, he would be one of my biggest nightmares. The man is flat scary how silent he moves—like a whisper of fog in the night."

Shaking herself, she took a sip, and with a last look at the hall Danny had disappeared down, she resumed her story. "So unbeknownst to Hooker, Manny basically had the same front row seat I had. In between radio checks, I filled him in about Hooker and Willie, and as much of Hookers back-story as I knew.

"Just about the time the sun is getting ready to pop over the east hills, Hooker is finally pulling the grade on Stupid Hill. Only it wasn't stupid yet. Manny and Stella's was almost the only house on the hill back then." Dolly glanced back through the front window as if she could see the lines of tacky houses now blanketed the north side of the hill.

"In the half-light of Christmas morning, they pulled up out front, and Manny was standing in the upper driveway. Being the gentleman he is, Hooker got out to open the door for the girls. As they get out, heading for the house, they leaned over on both sides of the kid, and plant a big kiss with fresh lipstick on his cheeks. Stella says he was redder than a tomato.

"After the girls had said their thank-yous and had gone inside, the men start the dance about getting paid or in this case, not. This was Hooker's only tow for the evening. On commission, it's his choice to charge or not. Manny and Hooker just stood watching the sun come up. It was Christmas morning. Manny said he guessed Hooker wouldn't accept a tip either, but would he take a Christmas present they had got for him?"

Johnny noticed the reflections on Dolly's eyes were wetter.

"Hooker figured because they didn't know him, he was safe there. He didn't know Manny, either. Manny reached in his pocket as he told Hooker Stella had gotten it for Hooker the year before, so Manny was just holding it for him. He pulled out a money clip with a few bills in it. When

Hooker started to take out the bills, Manny instructed him there are two places you don't count your money—at the poker table, and in front of the person giving you a present. Hooker only saw the five-dollar bill facing out, and felt he was okay with it and let it go."

The kid laughed. "But... he didn't know Manny." Stella nodded, and they both laughed.

However, the joy, mirth, and camaraderie of the day were not shared seven miles away. Ivory chopsticks moved by the slender fingers of a killer as they carefully inserted a stack of sixteen 1958 San Francisco minted dimes down into a shotgun shell, one dime at a time. Each dime was like a bead on a rosary, receiving a ritual mantra prayer. A latex-sheathed index finger slid in, as the whole was picked up ceremonially and tamped back down on the table. Sixteen times before the top was crimped back over and sealed with a spot of wax from a burning votive candle.

Carefully, the especially loaded shell was placed in a hollowed-out space in the pages of a book. The killer slowly closed the Bible on the six freshly re-packed shells. Kissing the first two fingers on the right hand, each pad was placed on the chests of the two young men in a small framed photo on the nightstand. The drawer was opened and the Bible, likewise kissed, placed inside and the drawer closed. The night's ritual of revenge was done—just in time for vespers.

2 7

"**I** had a long talk with Box last night, but he isn't talking either."

"Squirt, sweetie," Stella turned toward Johnny and placed both of her hands on the sides of his face, patting the right hand slowly. "In life, there are things you want to know and can't. There are things you need to know and don't. There are even things you know and wish to hell you never did or even were in the same state as knowing. Hooker's relationship with his sister is one of those things you can count your lucky stars you don't know. It's bad enough you even know about her."

The hard-drawn lips on the young man were a tough thing for Stella to see because it meant indecision and pain in someone she had come to care about. It's hard to be a mom or even a 'not-mom' when someone is hurting, and all you can do is just stand there and be with them. Throwing caution to the wind, she just went ahead and hugged him. By the slow count of five, and one deep sigh, she could feel the bristling steel melt into the soft stuffing in a favorite teddy bear.

"It's okay, honey. Things are just not very usual right now." She pushed back from him and holding his arms, she admitted, "It's never really 'usual' around here with Manny and Hooker and all of our extended family, but it can become a wonderfully boring routine… for a day or so." She smiled as a thought struck her. "Did those jeans fit okay?"

He took a moment to shift from the one topic to the half a dozen pair of jeans, and a drawer full of underwear along with the dozen starched white T-shirts hanging in the closet that had rocked his world a couple of days ago. He tried to swallow the golf ball-sized lump in his throat. "Fine," he squeaked.

Stella smiled knowingly as she patted her warm palm of a wrinkled life-worn hand on his chest then rubbed it back and forth. "Don't sweat the small stuff, kid. Life is short enough, and then we can't do for others, as we wanted." She quick hugged him for reassurance and grabbed his hand, pulling him toward his new bedroom and past the closed office door where the four other men were talking. "Come on. I want to show you something."

Hooker could hear them walk past as he was leaning up against the wall next to the door. Manny was on the phone and listening to someone he had called in Sacramento. It never ceased to amaze Hooker the names Manny could pull out of his Rolodex on his desk. If he had said he was calling the White House or a personal line to President Ford at Camp David, Hooker would have just sat back and listened to the conversation and asked how the president was after Manny hung up.

"Okay, then, we'll see you when you come through padre. Just make sure to give Stella some heads-up, so she can go to the market and buy some hot dogs or something. You know how she is." The man laughed with the person on the other end of the conversation. "You too and have a great night with the Reagans next week." He nodded. "I'll pass it along. Thanks again and goodnight." He hung up the phone and silently sat, studying it as if he didn't know what it was.

The antique Register hall clock ticked with a deep wooden drum sound in the quiet of the office. Manny's right ring finger tapped imperceptibly, keeping time with the clock. To think his mental pace was in the same register would be to make a grave mistake. The mind was stirring then re-parsing the case from hour zero to the moment. The only things slow about Manny were the blinking of his eyes and the beating of his still athletic heart.

"And?" Hooker wasn't as patient as the two older officers relaxing in the armchairs were.

Manny's eyes refocused and slid over to Hooker, who was leaning back in his chair against the wall with his hands out and palms up. "Don't lean the chair, it weakens the joints," Manny chided quietly as he turned to the police detective with the iron ridged flattop haircut the color of the aircraft carrier it was named after. "Do you know a priest named Father Damian Garza y Espinosa, Mike?"

"Sure, he's the new priest at Saint Mat's… hmm… about a year or so. Why?"

"The Archbishop said he is the only priest in the area under fifty and only one other than Father McBride who saw military duty."

"But a Chaplin doesn't carry a gun or…"

"As Special Forces, Recon," Manny cut him short. The other three sucked in a breath as one.

"Jesus," Chet Davis muttered.

"Something else." Manny paused as both cops raised attentive eyebrows. Manny looked toward the PD. "The Archbishop confirmed your lab's suspicions. The oily residue was in fact not only holy oil but a very specific holy oil."

"Most of the holy oil the church uses is virgin olive oil made from green olives, with a trace of balsam added. The balsam of choice is camphor, but due to cost, occasionally frankincense or myrrh is used."

Hooker twisted his face. "As in, the tree kings?"

Manny pointed his finger at Hooker. "Good boy, you've been doing your homework!" He rolled his eyes and planted his face down in his palm. "Yes, one and the same.

"But our little dime shooter is using one of the rarest holy oils of all. It's made locally, and as your lab determined, the oil is olive oil made from the Russian olive, and the balsam is from the juniper trees up on Mount Madonna."

Manny leaned in. "But here's the kicker. There are only five parishes using this holy oil, and because it is only used for baptisms and consecrations, it is only handled by the priests.

"And, our boy Damian…" he stopped to check his notes, "…Garza y Espinosa is one of those priests."

"But come on, a priest?" Chet held his hand out evidentially. "It just doesn't make any sense."

"I don't want to think he had anything to do with these killings, Chet. But, other than the oil, he has served in Vietnam as a Ranger where he would know how to make and use Foo Gas. I don't see any rational connection here. But when does murder, especially seemingly random serial murder, make any rational sense?" Looking down at his notes, and then glancing over at the pinboards, he concluded. "Right now, he's the best suspect we have. And as for fitting the profile, how many people would know anything about how to use Foo Gas as effectively as in the car?"

"Then why… I mean, why become a priest after you've done that job?" Mike scratched his head then slicked the rumpled single hair back into formation. "Usually, those kinds of guys go on to do sedentary things like working for other governments with trouble or start racing stock cars around large dirt tracks… you know, safe and quiet." His sarcasm was syrupy thick.

"I don't know." Manny shook his head. "But I think I do know someone who may have a take on him," he said, looking over at a now properly seated Hooker. "Doesn't the Squirt need to have his stitches taken out today?"

"Probably, but I just figured I'd let Willie or Stella do it. They both have more experience than most doctors." Hooker referred to Stella's nickname for Manny as *Mr. Zipper*. He had more yards of scars from being stitched up than all the balls in major league baseball and Little League combined.

Manny wagged his head. "No, I think you need to take him back to Valley Med."

"They don't do check-ups. You're supposed to go to your regular doctor."

"And… Johnny has a doctor?" The old man gave him the questioning eye and a smirk. "Look, I'll make a call to Connie. Maybe she'll have to take them out herself, but I need you to have a reason to be down there. It's the one place we can all agree Father McBride will be."

Looking at nodding heads, "And it is the one place and with you being the one person who can talk to him on his turf, as it were, where he would be willing to open up. You can tell him everything. We just need to know where this young priest is coming from and about his background." He hunkered in his chair like a coach with his fingers interlaced. "Are you up for it, or not?"

Hooker nodded. "Okay, but I have to get rolling here real soon if I'm going to blow part of the payday in the Med." Hooker looked at his watch. "And speaking of which, I need to go check in with Dolly. She was holding some long commercial run for me."

Pointing his finger at Hooker, Manny finished with a reminder. "You need to get a new pan on Mae. Willie told me at the barbecue, and it slipped my mind until now."

The highway patrol officer snapped his fingers. "I need to grab those dimes out of the pan and radiator before," jerking his right thumb at the other officer, "his evidence team has me forfeit at least a pizza lunch for being late harvesting evidence."

"Ah, it's okay, Chief, the evidence isn't going anywhere," Hooker laughed and waved his hand, looking at his watch again, "...for at least another two minutes."

The four laughed at the pressing nature of the evidence versus Hooker's need to continue working as they broke up. Manny grabbed his phone and dialed a direct line to the nurses' station on the third floor at Valley Med, as he called out to Hooker, "Grab the kid, but see me before you leave. Gentlemen, thanks for seeing me on my turf. I really appreciate it."

The officers waved as Manny started grilling one of his favorite nurses. Chief Davis turned quietly to Hooker. "I'll come out and get the evidence tomorrow evening when you break for lunch at Willie's. Hank told me he'd show me how to do the sauce he had on the pig steaks Sunday, and I think Willie mentioned some nice cold beer or something."

Hooker smiled and slapped him gently on the side of the arm. "Yeah, sure. Barbecue sauce and beer, sure." He patted his arm patronizingly. "Let's face it, Chet. We both know you're coming out to see if the Speedwagon is ready for a test drive." The two smiled largely at the man's love for older trucks. "And, if I know Willie, he's probably busting his hump right now trying to make it happen just for you."

Laughing, and heading down the hall, Hooker stopped, thought a moment, and smiled deeply. Turning back, he added, "And I wouldn't be surprised if there wasn't a cute little-butted moonshine-running someone all greasy and sweaty going elbow to elbow with him... and she might even be out there tomorrow night." He smiled as the other man blushed.

"Now you're just teasing me." Chet coughed as he grabbed at the imaginary stake through his heart. "You are just a cruel person, Hooker—toying with a man's heart."

The two laughed as Hooker headed back down the hall. "Squirt! Go time."

Reaching the young man's room and finding it empty, he was confused. Checking the bathrooms, he found all empty, making him even more confused, so he headed for the deck. Stepping through the sliding glass door, he looked around the basketball court-sized three-level deck, all of it empty. Then he noticed Box hadn't taken the opportunity to slide out through the door toward the small knoll of grass, so he must be with the kid. Leaning on the railing, he called out, "Hey Squirt? Stella?"

"We're down here in the garage, Hooker," Stella's answer drifted up from under the deck.

Closing the glass door against the heat, Hooker walked over to the pantry, and sure enough, the secret door stood wide open. Grabbing a jar of home-canned pears, he headed down the stairs opening the jar and fishing out a pear-half with his fingers. "What's up, guys?"

The two turned where they stood between a 1963 Corvette and a 1966 Dodge Dart GT. Stella spied the fingers in the jar, reaching for the second half. "How many times do I have to tell you when you open a jar, there might be other people who want some, and using your fingers is not the most sanitary option?"

Hooker walked up and offered the jar to her. "Want some, Stell?"

"Of course," as she grabbed the jar and fished out a half and passed the jar to the kid. "You into pears from our garden?"

The kid didn't have to ask, nor did he need to be pushed. He understood this was the test, the trust only coming from fingers stuck in a jar and drinking milk directly from the gallon jug passed around true friends or family. Stella warned him, laughing, "Just don't use your bunged-up hand."

They laughed as they finished off the jar while leaning against the cars.

Squirt wiped the back of his arm across his mouth. "My gosh, those are good."

"Come this August, you can help us put up a couple of hundred more jars of them," Stella recruited him. "We usually take a week and can about 1,200 gallons of donated fruits and veggies from around the valley, and we can use all the help we can get."

Hooker leaned conspiratorially and stage whispered, "She's not joking. Run—while you have a chance!"

The kid thought about the number of jars it would be. "What do you do with all the food?"

Hooker and Stella both pointed at a set of double doors along the wall of the fourth car bay. "It's all in there," Stella started, "or what's left from last year. Mostly empties in there now, waiting for the harvest."

"But you can't eat that much?"

"No, no, it's not for us. Well, some, but most of it goes to officers who are hit with some hard times and need some food to tide them through. And then there are other people we find out about who need some extra help. A few jars here and there aren't much, but a single jar of handmade preserves will always be worth more than a case of store-bought junk. It's the love in the jar that counts."

The kid looked askance at Hooker as Hooker held up his hands. "Don't look at me. I usually take some long hauls or hide out with Willie during their cook the jars fest." Hooker lolled his head in the zombie roll and winked at Stella as he smiled.

The woman slapped at his shoulder and confided with the kid. "Hide out my Aunt Judy's patootie! Those two hauled most of the fruit up from the lower valleys. Then they would dip and peel into the middle of the night while Willie would sing the worst sorry sounding cowboy love songs." Holding her hand on the kid's shoulder, she continued. "If Willie ever starts singing in a *twangy* sort of voice—run! Because to stay around is to risk wetting your pants from laughing too hard."

They turned and were headed for the stairs. "So what were you two doing down here?"

The kid snuck a peek back over his shoulder at Hooker. "She wanted to know which car I wanted."

Hooker laughed as they headed up the stairs. "I'm taking you to the hospital to get your hand checked, and then we need to make some money before you even consider owning a car like either of those two."

Stella commented at the top of the stairs as she reached the pantry, "I don't know about the Corvette or Dart, but I do know he's going to need a car to get around." She thought a moment. "Manny is never going to use them again, and I certainly can't drive either one of those monsters, so why not?"

"Why not what?" Manny asked as they emerged from the pantry.

Stella turned. "Let the kid use one of the cars."

Manny thought a moment. "I'll tell you what: you drive the Dart to San Francisco and back without a scratch, and no ticket, then say that again." The serious look on his face stopped the conversation and any possible argument.

The kid leaned over to Hooker. "What's so special about an old granny car?"

Hooker smirked. "The old granny car, as you so ignorantly put it, was built by Willie." Knowing the concept meant nothing to the kid, he continued. "Willie stuffed a 340 Hemi engine with pistons twenty-thousandths over, with a twitchy five-speed transmission, and Posi traction rear end." Seeing the blank, uncomprehending look on the kid's face, he finished. "It's a ten-second car."

"What's a ten-second car?"

"It's a car that can run the quarter-mile drag in ten seconds or less."

"Is that fast?"

Hooker gave him a blank stare, and then said, "About a hundred and fifty miles an hour, but that's just the first quarter mile, then she opens up…"

As the kid's eyes grew, Hooker reminded him they needed to leave. Turning to Manny for a situation report, he called for Box.

"The good father is there, just got back from lunch, so he's in for the long run." Pointing toward the kid, he said, "Drop Johnny off with Connie, she'll take care of him and pump him for information about how bad you have been abusing him. So just go talk to the good Father."

The two men and cat were out the door and across the plaza under the watchful eye of Stella as she slowly closed the door. She knew better than to call after them something like 'be careful' or 'watch yourselves'— she had been married to Manny too long and knew it wouldn't do any good. The door quietly clicked shut, and she held her hand flat against the edge with her other on the handle, a short quiet prayer. Turning, she looked at the man she had shared life and death with too many times to count. He pulled his hands up out of his lap and wiggled his fingers for her to come and sit in his lap. The two stayed cuddled until long after the sound of Mae had faded down the hill with her head resting on his large shoulder, his safe arms around her.

Finally, she quietly spoke. "We were looking at the apartment downstairs. Squirt thinks it would be more than enough room for his sister. She wants to study to be a nurse."

The silence from Manny was a reassurance he was thinking about what she was saying and knew the story about the car was just about pulling Hooker's chain.

The low rumble in his chest preceded his speech. "You're right. It's time to sell the cars. The space could be used by something a lot more useful." He petted her hair. "I'll talk to Willie and make some arrangements."

The afternoon sun was starting to pour into the sunroom, and the urge to take a nap in the warm breeze coming in through the lower apron windows moved the two. It was one of those little things the two liked about the house... a house made for naps.

2 8

"Look, Manny isn't stupid." Hooker continued the argument about why Johnny wasn't getting a car. "Neither is Estella. She's just going through one of her 'new mother' stages." He looked over at the kid who was studying a bug on the windshield very hard. "Look, relax. You're around a week, and you already have new jeans I bet you wish she'd washed first."

The comment drew a tiny smirk and a bump up in the body, or just a lump in the road, but only on the kid's side.

Hooker softened. "Look, tomorrow we'll load it all in a go-bag and shimmy it over to Willie's and let him do the laundry. Of course, if you wear boxers, his heavy hand with starch and the military crease down the two cheeks will really make you remember him."

The chuckle started low, and with a lot of resistance, built to a full-on foot-on-the-dash-so-you-don't-fall-over belly laugh. Even Hooker almost passed a little yellow VW under the wheels of Mae before he gained control.

"She means well, but she has no idea why Manny even had those cars."

"Why did he?" Slowly getting some control back.

"To keep Willie alive." Dead serious, Hooker glanced over at the kid.

"What was he dying from?"

Hooker thought about the question for a few minutes as he wound his way through the south end of Willow Glen. He wanted to see if something was still there. The streets were all residential, and as a tow truck, he was marginally okay to be there—but if a cop wanted to be hard-nosed about it, he could get a ticket for what he was doing.

They turned a left corner, and Hooker pulled over to the side and parked along an empty lot where two houses had burned down the winter before. He set Mae down on a low loping idle and turned in his seat. Leather draped over the seat back-rest, across the open window and over to the steering wheel as his left first fingers bounced a stiff finger tap dance on the French ivory wheel.

"Speed. He was dying from speed, as well as a love he had but couldn't have."

"Huh? I don't…"

Hooker held up his right hand in a stop. "You have now met Maddie under two conditions. Drunk off her butt and ready for a Sunday barbeque." The kid nodded. "The Maddie you haven't met is the one he is madly in love with. The one he would have married if things had been a lot different."

Hooker looked about the old burn and sniffed. The smell of the gelatinized gasoline was still gooey in the air, even months later. Putting the truck back in gear and heading for the hospital, Hooker thought about how much it smelled just like the burned-out car in the IBM parking lot, but he also knew the bomber was dead. He swung the giant beast right onto Winchester Boulevard and shook the chill in his spine.

Looking over at the kid, he remembered where he was in the story. "Back in the day, her father and three brothers were the biggest moonshiners in the entire upper central coast. They even ran a fair portion down as far as Bakersfield and Wasco to the Kentucky and Arkansas transplants, all who had come out during the dust bowl but still had a taste for White Lightning. I don't know if it's true or not, but the story goes they were always getting stopped just outside of Stockton by the same cop, four times a year, for the same three cases. Rumor had it those bottles stood on the top of the liquor cabinet within easy reach at the

Governor's mansion in Sacramento. Maddie will only tell you 'whatever you heard, is probably true.'"

"The other more public side of the family business was racing. They were the fastest rogue racers in Central and Northern California. If it ran on wheels and gasoline, they drove it in a race—even Maddie. When it came to iron and hot grease, it was spread thick across the five of them. Their mother had died with Maddie's birth. Her father never even tried to be a mother to a little girl. She was just thrown in with the other three boys.

"Willie used to hang around their garage almost as much as the boys and Maddie, so he was kind of like the fifth boy, except he was a little different. As girly as Willie is, Maddie was a tomboy. I don't know if she likes girls or men, but I do know if you see a dress on one butt in the air, and bib-overalls on the other, with the upper bodies down in the motor area of an old car or truck... the bibbies are the only butt connected to female parts."

"But what's Maddie got to do with Manny saving Willie?"

Hooker uncrossed his eyes from looking at a memory.

"The Corvette—right." Gathering his story, he continued. "Willie built the 1963 Vet from what was called a *Killer Engine*—it was a 375-horse-powered, 327-cubic-inch engine. By the time Willie was done, it was up over 500-horses, ported, polished, and strapped to a matched gearbox and positive rear end. The car could tear up a drag strip or dance down the freeway. He tried to give it to Maddie as a gift."

"And...?"

"She wouldn't take it. She said no self-respecting librarian would be caught dead driving to work in such a flashy car. So he built her the granny car."

"But the car is just as fast?" The kid was resting his tousled hair in his hand, sticking out of the leather jacket—a mirror to Hooker's.

"Faster and lighter." Hooker looked out the front windshield at the hulking concrete and glass mass of Valley Med. "Much faster." Turning back to the kid, he finished the story. "One night, they ran down to Monterey for dinner, and they were on the way back. They told the police they were only doing about eighty, but the twirling skid marks for almost a quarter-mile told a much different story… and luckily, ended up two-hundred yards into a soggy freshly plowed field." Nodding at the large building in front of them, "They both got here by helicopter." Hooker stared at the gray building housing so many stories.

He turned back to the kid. "It took Maddie almost a year to walk again with a cane. Willie was only a little luckier."

"So Manny offered to buy the cars." The kid was beginning to understand the family dynamics. "But wasn't the granny car wrecked?"

"Not too bad. But by the time Willie got around to fixing it, I was in the house, so things changed quickly. By the time the Granny was up and running again, we already knew Manny, and he had bought the Corvette and had his eye on the Dart."

Hooker turned in the seat toward the door and rolled up the window. "I don't think Manny even drove the cars more than a few dozen times before he got the bullet in his back and ended up here, too." He looked down at his hands for an answer that wasn't there. Quietly, he looked up, and then at the kid. "Let's go and get your hand taken care of."

As they climbed out of the truck and locked her up, the kid complained. "I still don't see why I can't just take the stitches out by myself. It's not so hard."

Hooker braced him in front of the truck. "It's not about you. You are just the excuse and diversion here. What Connie says you need, you seriously need. If she says x-rays, you get x-rays. If she says enema, you get two of them—you hear me?" The kid was nodding. "Until I come back for you, you do everything Connie says for you to do—except talk to little Miss hair-to-her-ass Loretta Lynn at the front desk. If she asks you anything, you just tell her I'm beating you, working you all hours of the night, and I make you sleep in the puddle of oil under the truck. You got it?"

The kid snickered. "There's no pool of oil under Mae. She wouldn't allow it."

Hooker snarled. "Pretend there is."

The kid nodded and shrugged, and as they started walking off toward the ER entrance, he turned his head back toward the truck, and in a very bad John Wayne imitation said, "Sorry Mae, but a man's gotta do what a man's gotta do."

They walked about another hundred yards, and just as they were about to get to the entrance, Hooker growled out of the side of his mouth. "You're a really weird kid. You know that? You know? You are really weird."

"Yeah," the kid agreed. "I get it from my sister and you."

Hooker clipped the top of his head with a slap. "Don't be bad-mouthing your sister. She's nowhere near my class of weird."

He followed it up by flipping his foot up and slapping the kid's new jeans in the seat. The kid laughed.

The force of a busy morning at the ER hit them full force as they walked in at four in the afternoon. Many of the brain and parts donors had been there since the wee hours of the drunk-shift, or when the bars closed, and the stool drivers became Mario Maladroit. This would back up the morning catastrophes, which blended into the hangover morning rush, leading up to the after-lunch industrial fell-asleep-into-the-machine crap filling the void until the late evening bar fights.

Hooker motioned the kid to follow him and wound his way through the walking death traps and sick people. As the mass moved in a slow drunken dance, the way to become noticed was to either shoot off a gun or just stand still within the eye range of the person whose attention you needed to attract. The blonde sensed the calm in the stormy sea of humanity and jerked her head up.

At first, she was trying to remember who the kid was, and then she noticed the shit-eating grin next to him with the tight thin beard wrapped around it. "Oh jeez, what now?" Turning only halfway, she kept her eye on Hooker as she called for backup. "Connie, we have trouble."

Connie exploded out of her stupor of going over charts and shuffling schedules. She grabbed the doorjamb to stop from continuing out into the typing pool. *Hooker*, she thought, and then stepped back into her office for a clipboard, although it contained nothing but blank paper and used up forms, made for a good cover.

She waved toward the end of the long desk of typing stations, as she whispered out of the side of her mouth. "We'll be back in operatory number six."

Cynthia whipped around. "We don't have an operatory number six—we only have five. Connie Lynn Nichols, what are you up to?"

The head nurse ignored her as she split the crowd like a battleship on a mission, and then turning to Hooker and the kid. "You two, come with me." At the end of the hallway, they turned down another smaller hall stopping into an exam area to grab a blue cloth wrapped roll of triage supplies. Shooting the nurse a hard glare to stop any protest, they continued down the side hall and into a small break room where a large nurse was stuffing the first of three donuts in her mouth as she scanned through the latest trashy tabloid.

Connie leaned over and took the two donuts from the box and shoved them into the two gaping mouths of Hooker and the kid. Then spinning around before the nurse could make a sound, she braced her with her eyes. "Weight Watchers wouldn't approve of your diet, and neither do I. Be glad I didn't take the one out of your mouth, too." The nurse's eyes bulged at Connie's audacity. "And your break was over almost twenty minutes ago. So now you get to run all over this hospital looking for Father McBride." Putting up her hand with the index finger up, she snapped. "Now scoot! I want him in here in less than the time it takes me to remove these stitches."

The nurse had disappeared before the chair had bounced off the floor, or the half of a donut had bounced a second time on the plate. Hooker stuck his head out the door, watching the sizable woman make a sizable amount of haste.

He stepped back into the room as Connie gently pushed the kid down into a seat and took a seat, too. Hooker peeked back out the door, and then looked at Connie. "Could you talk to Mae West that way, when you get a chance?"

The head nurse ignored Hooker as she started removing the bandage. "Shut up, Hooker, your truck is fast enough as it is." She began to hum to herself as the bandage came off and she could view the stitches. Muttering to herself as much as to the kid, she complimented his hygiene and care of the wound. Occasionally, she would look up with one eye cocked and give a hard look at Hooker. But she kept humming as if she had all the time in the world. When two nurses started to bubble their way into the room, they took one look at her and went back to work.

She chuckled softly to herself as she commented, "I ought to bring my work in here more often. It seems there would be a lot more staff on the floor."

Father McBride strolled into the room, and without acknowledging anyone, went straight to the coffee urn as he decanted a large mug. Taking a hesitant sip, he relaxed and turned so he could lean up against the counter. "I haven't removed stitches since I left the old neighborhood." His brogue fell from his lips a little thicker than usual.

Connie raised one eyebrow and looked at the old friend, then smiled broadly, as she opened her arms and spread them, draped back across the chair and table. With a very good thick imitation of the man's affected accent, she asked, "And tell me, Father, would that be Dublin or Boston?"

Caught at his own game, "Nay, it would be lower west side... Berkeley. Well, Emeryville." He smiled his warmest smile at a shared jest. "How can I be of help?"

Connie jerked her head at Hooker. "For all of the sakes involved, talk to this man honestly and spare nothing."

The priest looked at Hooker and then Connie and understood the gravity of the conversation to come. He nodded his head and the mug of coffee toward the hall. "Let's take this down to the chapel. I can almost guarantee we won't be interrupted there unless it's a couple of Connie's hot-blooded nurses having a little rendezvous."

Twenty minutes later, having shared their thoughts and concerns about a priest who fit the killer's profile right down to the use of Foo Gas, Hooker had more than his answer, but less than he wanted.

"The traces of holy oil are worrisome, I'll grant you, but I'm positive you gentlemen are barking up the wrong tree." He slowly scratched his head of thinning white hair. Looking up, his eyes pierced the air between them. "Look, son, if I knew more, I'd tell you. I know you think Father Damian could be this person they are calling the *Dime Load Killer,* but I really don't think so." He reached out and placed his wrinkled hand on

Hooker's knee. "I'll tell you what. Do you still have lunch at the place up on Winchester Boulevard?"

"Sure, almost every night."

"Let me go talk to the young priest and explain the circumstances. At worst, I'll come buy you and the kid lunch. It's the least I can do."

"It's a date, sir." Hooker stood and held out his hand. "I'll see you there about eleven tonight."

The Father remained seated but shook his hand. "I'll see you there." Nodding toward the small altar, he made his apologies. "I'd walk you out, but I think I need to have a bit of a conversation here right now."

Hooker looked at the cross. "I understand. Just don't let Him get the upper hand."

The old man chuckled. "Son, He always has the upper hand."

Hooker, looking back, watched the man. With his body riddled with arthritis, he took a while to get down on his knees and then began to talk to his boss. Hooker looked about the room and felt the silence of peace—so very different from his world.

Returning into the insanity of the ER, he looked around and then headed down the hall toward the break room. Just before he entered, he could hear the kid's voice talking about how he and his sister had gotten to San Jose. Hooker smiled inwardly. For all the iron tough and brass Connie pushed around, she could also get to the heart of a story faster than anyone Hooker knew—other than the interrogation sisters, Dolly and Stella.

Hooker cleared his throat as he walked the last several feet to the doorway of the break room. As he turned the corner into the room, Connie was standing and cleaning up the small mess they had made of eating something. "Well, it's about time you got back, this young man has work he needs to get to, and it doesn't include lounging about in some chapel swapping lies with an old man in his dotage."

Hooker looked at the kid who looked a little like his hand was still in the cookie jar. "If she says we're good to go, we're gone." Turning to an equally caught red-handed Connie, he continued. "Thanks for this, I think we got more than we came for," looking back at the kid, "in many ways." Turning on his heel, he strolled back out the door and down the hall, paying attention to, but ignoring the sound of starched white uniform hugging leather and a mumbled votive of assurance. *Jeez mareez, this kid gets more mothering than I do.* Hooker smiled, thinking it was starting to be a good day.

He was wrong. So very wrong.

29

The chopsticks methodically pulled apart the roll of extra-fine steel wool. The killer had become adept at using chopsticks with both hands at an early age while helping cook. Working at pulling out wisps of steel wool, then inserting them into the plastic 2-liter bottle, was child's play.

A web of half-inch holes drilled in the bottom of the bottle. A staggered double row of holes stitched their way down the four sides of the green plastic cylinder. The web pattern, in the end, creates a barrier for the steel wool, but not the dimes. It would break away easily and be destroyed with the third shot. A fourth shot would be lacking the silenced effect of the contraption but couldn't be helped. It was unnecessary. The rows of holes along the side were pressure relief for the expanding gasses pushing out the air between the steel wool. The term 'silencer' was a misnomer. It should be called simply a 'muffler' as it just muffles the sound of explosively expanding gasses by rerouting and slowing them down until the concussion shock sound wave is diminished as close to nothing as possible.

The sound of the old record played so softly in the background as to not be heard by the other residents in the building. Jefferson Airplane's *White Rabbit* would have been severely frowned upon. Lips followed each word carved indelibly in the killer's heart along with memories of a happier time, and also the beginning of the horror.

The click of the four chopsticks working to tear apart the puffy cloud of warm steel wool echoed the sound of the tiny click as the needle slid back and forth in the never-ending loop of the finished record. Both hands moved adroitly pulling and pushing the wool.

The final piece of wool is inserted, and the chopsticks are all brought together and carefully laid to rest in a case with an extra pair. A set of three ivory chopsticks with three names hand engraved in the sets. A thoughtful gift brought back from Vietnam, an offering of family and love from a place of horror, hatred, and destruction.

The delicate two right fingers, index and ring, were ritually kissed, and then placed on the photograph, each finger in the middle of the bare chests of two young smiling males bracketed with arms draped across the shoulders of a younger happier killer. The fingers lingered—much happier days.

The killer slowly tried the snug fit of the bottle on the barrel of the shotgun. The new form used to warm and expand the mouth of the bottle had worked perfectly... lessons learned so many years before... with a different gun, and a different kind of bottle.

Hunting close range at night was so much different from hunting long-range in the light of day; so much different.

The latex-clad right hand slowly slid the bottle off the barrel and set it aside. Wrapping the bottleneck to the barrel with tape would come later in the night—after prayers. There would be plenty of time before the midnight meeting. All the time in the world.

30

The two priests sat at the back of the booths, quietly talking shop. They were dressed in black with small white squares at the throats of their rabbinical shirts. The small number of neighborhood denizens sat scattered like leaves tossed about by a gust of breeze. The two waitresses didn't really mind having their quirky customers scattered about, or as the ladies would say *separated,* it was easier to maintain the peace.

The various diners stole surreptitious glances at the men in the back booth. Some were not sure as to why these two were here on their turf. Others just worried about the diner becoming a soup kitchen where they would have to listen to some preaching just to get a meal. A few just stared drunkenly slack-jawed at the apparition they knew were just 'vapors' of their breath.

The glass doors swung open as the two leather-clad, almost twins, walked into the diner and headed for their section of the counter. Jerry, who was always in seat 107 (seventh seat along the counter) looked up in his best Annie Greensprings fortified wine sort of way. "Hey Hooker..." and was then stuck for any more scintillating conversational contribution.

Hooker spotted the older priest waving from the back booth and walking past the counter crustacean, patted him on the shoulder. "Hey,

Jerry, good to see you up and around this side of the dirt blanket. You holding your own on your Thunderbird diet?" He continued toward the back.

Dazed and confused, Jerry tried at a response. "No… ah, um, Thunderbird, Hooker…" Then he realized he was talking to himself, so he returned to his original conversation. It seemed to be more personally meaningful anyway.

"Hooker." Father McBride stood up, leaving the younger seated. "So very good to see you. And this must be the young man I have heard so very much about." Reaching over, he shook the kid's hand. "Johnny, isn't it?"

"Umm, yes, sir."

"Please, no 'sir' here, just us padres, or Father Mike, if you want." Turning to the quiet young priest still sitting, he introduced the man. "Hooker, Johnny, I'd like you to meet the newest member of our clergy here in San Jose, Father Damian Garza y Espinosa." Looking hard at the young priest, he asked, "I did get that right, didn't I?"

The young priest nodded his head as he reached across himself and the table with his left hand as he leaned slightly forward to shake hands. "You did fine, Mike." Turning to Hooker and Johnny, "Please, you can call me Damian or Dan. I just don't respond well to being called late for dinner."

The kid leaned in and shook the offhand clumsily. "Squirt, everybody just calls me Squirt."

The young priest smiled a small smile then grew a larger one as he asked, "Is it because you were small once, or because you're the fucking new guy?"

The term was like a grenade. The silence stopped the other three men dead in their tracks. Candy, who was walking up to their booth, was also silenced. Then she shoved her brother into the booth and hip-checked Hooker out of the way. "Yup, same as you, Dan, but for stunning the words out of Hooker's mouth, the pie is on me tonight. You can pay tomorrow night."

The young priest laughed. "You have a deal, Candy. Make mine French apple."

"It's called Dutch. Dutch apple pie."

"Mmm, it's all European and delicious to me."

The other men settled in and placed their orders, all as Hooker kept sneaking looks at the waitress, trying to figure out what was going on. The left-handed shake had also unsettled him, but he wasn't going to say anything yet. There was just too much at stake.

The waitress read back the order. "Okay, then, I have one chick plate mashed with ranch, a burger with a salad for the growing kid—no fries, four coffees and two pieces of Dutch apple pie." She looked up from her book to see if there were any other items she had missed. She nodded and spun on her heel, as she smacked the book on the top of first Hooker's head, and then backhanded her brother. "Behave, you two. You are out to dinner with some nice guys." Then she caught one of the other regulars doing something. "Fester, I have my eye on you. I'll cut you off for a week if you don't sit back down and behave."

Father McBride watched her as she worked the room full of less than desirable customers and did so as if she were their mother—a firm yet caring hand. He smiled at some inner thought or memory and then looked at Johnny. "Now I see how you have survived."

The kid glanced at, as much as listened to, his sister, "Yeah, she's hard sometimes, but she's soft where it counts, I guess." Then realizing what he had just said turned beet red. "I… I didn't… I meant…"

Hooker put his hand on his arm. "We knew what you meant." But it didn't mean they couldn't laugh at his expense. It was as good an icebreaker as was the young priest busting him with the rougher street vernacular of the term FNG.

Turning to the young priest, he tried to be subtle. "So Father Dan, what brings you to San Jose?"

The priest looked Hooker in the eye measuring where to go with everything he knew about why he was there, and about Hooker's place in the entire scheme of things. "I had a calling, and then I was assigned here." He said this with the blank straight face he had learned in the seminary but had perfected with real-life experience in the military. "But it's not what you meant, is it?" He didn't blink. It wasn't so much a challenge, as it was a notice he knew what was going on and wasn't shying away from addressing things as they landed on the table.

"Hooker," Father McBride interceded. "I took the liberty to confide in Dan what this is all about. He is here to help to the fullest of his ability."

"I didn't intend to ambush him…" Hooker tried to explain himself.

"Look," the young priest reached across his body and rested his hand on Mike's arm. "I'm not a child. I can look after myself." Patting the arm. "It's okay. I'm a big kid now."

McBride looked him in the eyes, and the young priest engaged him and nodded. The older man turned toward Hooker and rolled his eyes. He raised his eyebrows, and pressing his lips taut, he smacked his tongue against his teeth with a click. "Okay." He jerked his thumb at the other man in black. "He's all yours. Have at him."

The young man sat back as Candy brought the coffees. "Jeez, I didn't mean to let him just shoot me in the booth. At least give me a running start."

Candy put the coffees down and looking at the young priest quipped, "No can do, Kemo Sabe. You no can run anymore." This raised a smile on the priests' face.

Hooker pointed back at the retreating waitress. "You know Candy from before?"

"This is my parish, Hooker. So, yeah, I know her from before." He leaned forward with his hands in his lap. "I know all about you and how deadly you are with an unloaded fork, too." He smiled as Hooker's eyes popped open even wider. "Yeah, you're kind of famous around here in the middle of the night."

Hooker started to ask a question but was stalled as the 'w' froze on his lips as his open pointing finger stopped in midair. His mind was chugging along, but the gears weren't engaging. He literally didn't know where he wanted to go in gathering information.

The young father continues. "What shift do I come in on? I roll in here about the time Jerry sobers up enough to go home, and Mac decides the worms in the parking lot will leave him alone for one more night. About two-thirty or so in the morning, when I wake up with cold sweats from being back in Vietnam and don't dare go back to sleep." He took a bite of the pie and chewed slowly, savoring the fruit flavor, and then pointing with his fork at the table. "This is my assigned table. This is my library, and I'll be here reading for a couple of hours while she does all of her side work."

"The Bible?"

He turned an eye on Johnny, then a quick glance at the older priest who was smiling and looking at his pie, purposely ignoring him. "Not usually. Mostly science fiction or trashy magazines about hot rods and street machines," he said as he looked at Hooker.

Hooker didn't know if he was being set up or just getting his chain yanked, but he did like the man's style. "Big block or small?"

"Truth be known, I'm kind of a die-hard Mopar kind of guy. There has never been an engine that will out endure and perform like a Hemi." He smiled as his eyes hooded with memory. "Personally, I would go for a Dart stuffed with a 318, six-pack, and Max Wedge front clip with a shaker hood."

"Not exactly a typical priests ride." Hooker smirked, thinking about the convertible granny car in Manny's garage.

"Yeah, but it would be grand to drive again."

"Speaking of cars, what about Cadillac?"

The man turned serious but quiet as Candy arrived with the plates of dinner for Hooker and Johnny. As she placed the plates, the young priest took another small bite and chewed slowly.

"Okay, two tow driver dinners," as she poured refills on the coffee, "and everyone is fueled up. I'm going to go take a fast break, so no fist-fights or stabbing small children while I'm gone." The men all smirked and nodded their devotion to her directions.

As she left, the young priest put down his fork, thought a moment, and then looked at Hooker. "Didn't you really want to know about shotguns and Foo Gas?"

Hooker took a bite, as his stomach turned over like a large fish rolling in the sun of his abdomen. He realized there was not one punch this man would pull, so he thought about how he could ask what he needed and not sound like he was judge and jury. He thought about the background he knew. "Experience?"

Relived the conversation was now out in the open, the priest took another small bite and dabbed at his mouth with the napkin at the end of his right arm. The silver glint off the pincer hook was not lost on Hooker. The conversation just took a huge leap sideways. The young priest missed nothing—the change in Hooker's eyes told him everything he needed to know.

"If you look over there in the shadows, that's my ride. I had Candy put it over there out of the way." Hooker could see the wheelchair. "After I lost my hand, some of my hearing, half my guts, one leg just below the knee and the other at the ankle, I spent a lot of days in the hospital thinking about what I had done, and why I was still alive. It wasn't self-pity, it was soul searching to figure out where I would go from bed and into the future.

"There was a padre who came to Letterman Hospital every day. One day I asked him if he could just shove me out the door, so I could look up at the Golden Gate Bridge. He ended up pushing me to the middle of the bridge and asking me if I wanted his help in shoving me over the side. We didn't say a word for about an hour—just sat looking at the bay. I had never thought about suicide, but he knew somewhere inside, I was weighing the option.

"We ended up doing a lot of talking in the next year as I got my rehab and learned to walk on the plastic legs and sticks. These days it's just easier to ride," he held up his hook, "even with this little gem."

Hooker put down his fork across his empty plate and wiped his mouth. Clearing his throat, he thought about what the man was saying… or what he wasn't. "I don't know what to ask anymore. I mean, obviously, you couldn't have been standing on the berm and shooting a shotgun at me with your right hand."

"But I do know a lot about guns, and more importantly, Foo Gas." The man mirrored Hooker with his fork and wiped his mouth. The napkin returned from his lap but was deposited on top of the plate with still half a piece of pie underneath. Seeing Hooker's quizzical look, he explained. "I wasn't joking about losing half my guts over there. I can only take so much food at one time, and sugar is even more restricted. I'll be paying all day tomorrow for the little bit of heaven."

"That munches the big one."

"Yeah, but then it is what helps me maintain this girly figure." He smiled. "But seriously, getting back to the Foo Gas. Did they ever get the spectrum analysis back on what was in the gasoline?"

"You can check with Manny, but I'm pretty sure it was Styrofoam."

The priest became pensive. "Describe the set-up, or can you?"

Hooker looked at the kid who had been silent the entire time, as he looked up at Hooker, who nodded at the priest. "Walk him through it, newbie, same as you did for Manny. No analysis, no thinking—just what you saw."

The kid nodded, and it was almost as if his eyes rolled up in his head. He wasn't in the booth but was back at the scene. His description was scarily accurate and so exacting Hooker could smell the burned-out car and cremated bodies. Hooker hadn't remembered the kid going over the mechanism so meticulously with Manny. But he had something then and was doing something now, which Hooker had never seen done before— the exacting total recall of what he had seen.

About halfway through Johnny's recall, Candy quietly walked over and touched Hooker on the shoulder and motioned him to follow her as she put her hand up to her head with the little finger and thumb extended. He had a phone call. As they walked away, Hooker asked her if she had seen the kid do the detail recall before.

"Sure, that's the problem. He does it in his sleep."

"Why's it a problem?"

"Because what he sees, he never forgets. Trust me. There's a lot of shit he should forget." She handed him the phone. "There's a lot I'd like to forget also. It would do us both a lot of good."

Hooker nodded in understanding. "This is Hooker."

"I'm sorry to have to break up your little love fest, but CHP needs you right now above the Cats, about the five-mile curve with the bad drop off. They have a set of doubles jack-knifed, and the cab is over the edge..." Dolly quit talking when she realized she was talking to a dial tone.

"Excuse me, but we've gotta go," Hooker rushed as he reached over the kid and grabbed his jacket. "Can we pick this up in the morning or something?"

"Sure. If I'm not here between two and four, Candy will have my phone number. Just call, I'm two blocks away." He wiped his mouth. "And,

Hooker, it sounds like Special Forces, but with more of a secondhand domestic twist to it. I'll kick around what I might be able to help you with."

Hooker stuck out his left hand as an offer of peace. "Thanks."

Father McBride interjected. "I'll get the check, Hooker. You be the Samaritan."

The two leather jackets were racing for the door as Hooker called back, "Thanks!"

The doors, key, brake, clutch, silver button, seventh gear, and they bounced west out onto Winchester Boulevard. Grabbing back at the microphone behind his ear, Hooker keyed the red button as it passed his head on the way to shifting up into ninth. Pulling it back, he checked in. "1-4-1, 10-8 for the Cats."

"10-4, 1-4-1, dispatch shows you 10-8 at twenty-three forty-two. CHP is advised. You're free to rock and roll. Your cross over will be at the pass-through at the south end of the reservoir. They would suggest Summit Road and then backtrack the mile, but things are already wall-to-wall. See Officer Schwindler. Chief Davis says if you need to remove any center fence, try to keep it less than sixty feet this time. Cal Trans seems to be having a little fence budget problem lately."

"10-4." Hooker hooked the mic back on the slide mount and reached to drop the two gears as he slid around the corner onto Hamilton Avenue, goosed the power, then used the Jake brakes down around the cloverleaf to the mid-point, and then it was gas and gears all the way up to 'rock-and-roll' speed. Hooker loved the middle of the night in the early part of the week. One car went past on its way back into San Jose. Slowly, Hooker rolled the window down and settled into eighteenth gear, which would take them up the lower part of the Highway 17 mountain pass into the Santa Cruz Mountains. Hooker's right hand dropped down as it turned up the eight-track, and then fondled Box's ear. As his fingers found the top of Box's head, he could feel the purr harmonizing with the throbbing coming from under the hood.

Go time. Hooker's drug of choice, and Box would second it.

Hooker glanced over at the kid chewing on something as he watched the world fly by through his open window with his leathered arm cocked out the hole. "What are you thinking?"

Without really looking at Hooker, the kid gave it a moment to gel, then supposed. "I think he may know something." The kid looked out the open window to the side, watching the city end and darkness fill the night. Turning he finished, "As I was talking, I could feel him going through a mental checklist. Then… I don't know, his face maybe, it changed… something I said, hit the bell for him."

Hooker glanced over as he took the transmission down to lower gears. "We'll stop by when we're finished with this mess and see what he thinks."

Shifting down again for the grade, Hooker saw the reservoir off to the left and knew the pass-through would be coming up soon. He reached back to the mic and keyed it at his cheek. "1-4-1, I'm 10-97 at the reservoir. Was there going to be an officer standing by at the pass-through?"

"They didn't say, Hooker."

"10-4." Hooker knew it would most likely be something he would have to feel for in the dark. CHP rarely had the extra manpower in the middle of the night to stand by at a pass-through for a tow truck, or even an ambulance, for that matter. As he reached back to hang the mic, he glimpsed a lone flashing red light, and as he got closer, a matching yellow light in the back seat of a cruiser. He shifted down three more drops and gently threaded the needle and waved at the officer who had the forethought to help. He would have to put in a good word with the chief.

31

The night breeze blew the dust, bits of wastepaper, and leaves, in a swirl behind the darkened car sitting backed into the far dark corner of the parking lot. The black Buick La Sabre sat, the engine compartment still ticking as it cooled down. The swirl of dust stopped and seemed to settle behind the car trunk. The occupant looked in the rearview mirror, seeing nothing but the lights in a building two blocks over through the trees. The two hard locust trees bent over the car had helped confuse any glancing eye which may have strayed its way, much like the duck blinds and deer perches of the killer's youth.

The sound of the giant yellow tow truck was still fading as the killer silently pounded slender fists on the steering wheel, seething at the missed opportunity with the stupid tow truck driver.

Calming down, the killer leaned back against the headrest, right hand searching for, and then softly stroking, the hand-carved stock of the shotgun. The delicate fingers found the tiny lines of the aged black walnut from the tree in the yard back home. The light of a turning car triggered the memory of the lightning hitting the tree—splitting it down the center all the way to the ground. Their father had cut out the blanks for four matching shotguns. Then, two years later, he began to carve them. This gun was the oldest brother's, the first to shoot, and the first to die. The hand rubbing on the wood was like a calming blanket. The strokes became slower and shorter as the killer remembered everything they had lost, and the reason for being here tonight.

The light breeze stirred the leaves and dust, but one pile of dust stayed behind the car—painstaking writing, letter by letter and number by number, with a nub of a pencil found years before on the northern end of Stevens Creek Boulevard. The paper delicate, and easily punctured, but the dust was the epitome of patience, each letter, and number exacting in the detail of an engineer writing the most important notation of his career.

Slowly, the dust and dirt swirled and collected in the space of the dark of the trees. The dark was protective, and the tiny touches of fingertips felt the way, guiding the eyes needed to see and to gather what was needed by his friend. The shreds of the night hung from the dust's shoulders and head, the perfect blending of the night. The wisps of what could have been, blending with the shadows of what was impossible in the dark of imagination, had gone rapidly beyond the usual. In the middle was the calm of the man who lived his life in the middle of a maelstrom.

Slowly, with the wind and movement of shadows, the dust moved, bobbed, and weaved as the eyes, missing nothing, took in the shotgun, the bottle attached at the end, the extra shells, and the hair of the killer, as well as the unusual clothes. The dust now knew the identity of the killer and the possible reason for tonight's vigil. The dust was making connections like he hadn't in many years. Why, just now, he had written like he hadn't in so many years? Something he didn't think he would ever do again, but this was for his friend.

The driver suddenly realized the dusty shadow of the night was a *human being* and quickly muffled a scream. In this startled state, the killer started the car, slammed it into drive, and shot across the parking lot lurching out into the boulevard and racing away. Just when the front doors of the diner opened, and a wheelchair emerged.

The young priest turned to the elder and smirked. "Hmm, I didn't know we were powerful enough to drive the devil away in a Buick." The two chuckled about working in mysterious ways as they crossed the lot toward Father McBride's twelve-year-old Ford Falcon.

Stopping at the side, the elder padre patted the old friend on the rear quarter panel. "If only we could instill a little more fire and brimstone in old Lazarus here. He's been a good trooper, but at nigh-on hundred and twenty thousand of the long miles, he's asking for deeper rest than I can grant at this time." Turning to the younger priest, "and you, we should find you one of those new vans with a power lift or something, so you can get around."

The seated man waved his last hand. "Mike, it's why I have this small parish. My wheels can make it to anywhere I need to be, even down to your bulwark, the medical center." Shaking his head. "No, I haven't a need for a van or even a car. Any time I have needed to get around, I have a list of volunteers willing to take me anywhere but to heaven's gates."

"But then isn't the po…" He hesitated, looking up at the apparition approaching them from along the bush line. He bent and squinted as he wasn't sure what he was seeing, and if it were real or imagined? "What have we here…?" As his Irish burr thickened, his heart started beating a bit faster than usual.

"What is it, Mike?" Father Damian pushed back away from the car so he could see a broader view of what the elder was looking at. Looking along the bush line, his well-trained eyes caught the slight movement, and then, in the slightly lighter patch of dappled night, a face among the dirt and trash carried with the shard of a defensive life on the streets.

"Peter?"

"Hmmm."

"Peter, meet Father McBride. He's a very close friend of mine." He palmed a stay motion to the elder padre as he carefully started rolling toward the street urchin. "Peter, Peter, are you all right?"

The small voice in the bushes was pained as well as frightened, "N…nnn… no."

Damian stopped.

"Ho… Hook… Hooker is… oooohhhh," the man wailed pitifully as if in pain.

Damian edged closer, and spoke lower, "Hooker is what, Peter?

Hooker was just here, but he had to go somewhere and help people who needed him."

"Y… yes, Hoo… Hooker helps p… p… people."

"Yes, he's a very good man."

"But… but he… he, he is in danger."

Damian edged the last ten feet and stopped within an arm's reach of the man. Quietly he asked, "How is Hooker in danger, Peter?" He folded his hand and hooked them together and leaned forward in supplication. "What do you know about Hooker being in danger?"

"The d… dev… the devil!" The man was clearly agitated, and Damian had never seen him shudder and stutter so much. A small cloud of dust vibrated and floated about him. Clearly, something had happened, and it had him very upset.

"What did you see, Peter? What about the devil?"

"She was he… he… was here."

Ignoring the 'she' reference, the padre bore in. "Where was the devil?"

The man licked a finger and made some kind of sign or wrote something in the air only he could see, and then pointed at the dark back corner of the parking lot.

"It was in the trees?"

The man nodded, "Sh… she… she was parked, parked in the dark. Parked in the dark with a dog no bark, watching for the cat with no hat— leather. She waited with hell, ready by her hand, for the Hooker come walking to send to the promised land."

Damian sat stunned. He had never heard the street urchin say more than a few words at a time, much less spew out a string of words in a rhyme precluding his agitated stuttering. "You said the devil was a woman?"

"Y… yes, ev… yes, an evil woman." The man was looking around everywhere but at Damian, as he reached out with a cigarette in his extended fingers. "Evil… evil woman with a dog, no bark." He waved the cigarette, "M… m… mus… must Hooker. Must tell Hooker. Mu… must warn Hooker. Devil."

Damian took the cigarette Peter offered as he did most nights. He knew Peter bummed the cigarette off Hooker just so he could give it to him a couple of hours later. It was their ritual, a touchstone for common ground. "Yes, I know this came from Hooker. Thank you."

"N… no… not that one."

Damian realized he was holding a filtered cigarette, not a Camel straight. He looked closer. There in pencil, inscribed by a very finely trained hand, were perfect letters and numbers written in the font used by engineers. Reading the series, he realized what he was looking at. "Peter, is this the license plate number of the woman's car?"

The man nodded. Strangling to be talking so much but torn by his emotional ties to what he had left, and with a touch to humanity, he croaked, "Mu… must warn Hooker. Sh… she… she has a dog with no… wi… with no bark."

The meaning slid in from Damian's past as he remembered some of the guys in Vietnam had referred to their rifles as their 'dog' and if it jammed or the sights got mangled, about how 'their dog don't hunt,' but he couldn't understand the term of not barking.

"You mean she had a gun. Yes, we know about the shotgun." Then it dawned on him. "You mean the gun had a silencer on it, don't you, Peter?"

The man nodded.

Looking at the cigarette with the license number, he looked up. "Do you know what kind of car it was?"

Father McBride spoke quietly from his car. "Probably the black Buick tearing out of here like the devil himself was after it." Licking just the center of his lips, the man sadly added, "But I guess it was the devil *herself* driving."

Damian turned back to look for confirmation from Peter, but Peter was gone. All they had were the numbers penciled on a cigarette… a cigarette Damian so much wanted to smoke at that moment. Turning back and deferring to the elder, he held up the cigarette. "Who do we call about this, and how do we explain my friend Peter?"

Father McBride thought for less than a second then waved the young priest back toward the diner. "I believe I know just the person to call, who can handle all of the bases at one time," and as he opened the glass door, he turned and pointed at the young priest, "and, if you plan to stay in this town for very long, someone you need to know."

As they walked back into the light of the diner, Candy came walking out of the back. "Candy, my dear, I need to trouble you for the use of your phone. We need to call Dolly."

Candy's right hand came out from behind the prep station holding the phone.

3 2

"Hooker?"

The whisper carried like a deathly smoke across the highway from the external speakers and fell down the side of the embankment. The two young men covered in dirt, mud, and other fung, looked up at each other. It sounded almost like the wind calling Hooker's name. Hooker thought a moment, *Sweets*. The last thing he needed right now. If Sweets were calling him now, there was trouble, and he didn't think he wanted to know about it.

"Hooker? If you are out there, you need to be careful. The evil is on the move, and it is full, man, so very full." The voice melted over the rocks and oozed down into the soul. Hooker shivered.

Johnny looked at Hooker and saw the slight blanching along with the light flush of green just below the tightly trimmed beard and jaw. "He's right, isn't he?"

Hooker nodded. "It's what he does."

"Creepy."

"Even when you get used to it." Hooker reached over and buckled the snap hook around the cable. "Done. Now let's go pull this bad girl back to the land of the safe."

They climbed the embankment to the highway. "Why are they always female?"

"Why are what always female?"

"All the wrecks we recover. You always call them a female."

"No, I don't."

"Yes, you do. They are 'bad girl,' or 'sweetie pie' or even a 'prom queen'—every one of them."

Hooker dodged the truth, realizing he did, and he knew why. He shrugged it off. "I don't know…"

Scowling, he thought about needing to be as honest with himself and the kid, as he wanted the kid to be with him. He drew his lips tight across his teeth, looking over the entire set-up as he held the winching controls. Focusing on the cable strung in a curved configuration to twist the tractor as it pulled it up to the highway, he suddenly thought about Box. He could feel the cool ear between the knuckles of his right hand. He knew it was just a transit thought, but he knew what it meant… so as he pulled the levers out, which made the controls live, he glanced over at the kid and confided. "Maybe I'll tell you about it sometime," and pulled the levers up and started the winch pulling.

Thirty minutes later, the tractor was sitting righted on the side of the highway, and the first trailer was following Hooker like a fish on a short line. They would stash the trailers, first in a parking lot where they looked innocent, and go grab the tractor, and start the first of three tows back to San Jose and the Fly's yard.

"Why spend the time stashing the trailers? Why not just leave them on the side of the road?"

Hooker smiled as he thought of an incident in his early years. "There was a guy, several years ago, who moved a trailer to the center dirt divider out on one-oh-one while he hauled the tractor back to his yard. When he got back an hour or so later, the trailer door was open. The broken lock just hung there. Nine black and white TVs sat in the trailer, but not a single one of the one-hundred and fifty-three of the color TVs. The cops found no truck tire tracks, just several dozen car tire tracks."

"Whoa. Fast."

"A gypsy bobtail is faster. It would take less than two minutes for a lone trucker with no trailer to just back right into a trailer, raise the airports, hook up the air, and be gone."

"So we just go hide the trailers."

"Yup, in plain sight, but logical, like where they're an empty trailer waiting for pick up... such as the Safeway down here." Hooker pointed toward where they were headed. "That's why it's so important to know where things are. The right business with a large lot where some trailers or cars can park overnight are prime places to stash two or three tows you can do in a few minutes to clear a wreck.

"Knowledge is the power to get your job done. For my territory, knowing all the back roads and ways to get around a wreck or another way in is crucial. I cover over five-hundred square miles down here. Only about thirty or forty of it is what we would call city streets. There's a popular motor boating lake down here called Calero Dam. Most people get there from the south or north on one road. I know all five ways to get in there.

"If I can get in fast while everyone else is taking the long way around, I can get the tow. If I can stash a tow and get back before any other driver has gotten there, I might get two or three tows on a large wreck. Know your roads, and where you can stash a paycheck, and you're in business."

"Meanwhile the chips are still working the wreck and clearing the traffic..."

"... And, watching over my other trailer." Hooker smiled at how quick the Squirt was learning.

"That's pretty slick."

"I didn't think of it but learned it from the Ace himself."

"Ace? The guy at Dolly's dinner?"

"The very same."

"Who did he learn it from?" They unhooked the trailer behind the Safeway.

Hooker chuckled as he lowered the cables and settled the trailer on its landing gear. "From the people who stole all of those TVs."

They were still laughing as they climbed back up into the cab of Mae West. Striking the large red button released the air brakes as Hooker reached back and grabbed the mic from behind his head. "1-4-1, 10-8 for second trailer."

Hooker eased the clutch and started rolling.

"10-4, Hooker. Be advised we have a description and license number of the car the shooter is now driving, and she is armed with the shotgun and soda bottle silencer."

Hooker looked over at the kid in surprise. He slowly brought the mic up to his mouth and thought a moment with a frown before depressing the red button. "Ayah, 10-9?"

"I said—we know who she is, and what she's driving. It's a black sixty-six Buick La Sabre."

"She?"

"She." Dolly's tone was one of 'and don't argue,' a tone very familiar to Hooker, so he didn't.

"10-4." Hanging the mic, he looked at nothing out of the windshield. "Well, that's weird."

Johnny had big eyes as he looked forward. "Man, I'll say... about as weird as it gets."

He was wrong.

Dolly was back after a few minutes. Hooker knew she had weighed who might be on the air, and then Dolly being Dolly, threw caution to the floor, stomping on it, and pickled her lollypop mic. "I doubt you would have any reason to know her, but it's Sister Mary Margaret Joseph at the Holy Redeemer." She keyed off, then back on with a bit of motherly nudging. "Just watch for a Buick with a nun in it, and be very careful out there, Hooker."

Hooker almost bit his tongue, but then she would know he was concerned anyway, so he shrugged and said it anyway. "You threw me out of the nest years ago. Don't start reeling me in now, Momma." It was the closest to a hug he could muster over the air.

The return double-click rattled around the cab like a dog snapping his teeth—cold and hard, but with meaning.

Dina keyed in on the yellow radio quietly, but with her teeth clenched. "I am so going to smack the back of your head if you don't behave. And if you get yourself killed, I'll... I'll kill you myself."

Johnny looked over at his boss with a refreshed light. "Boy, they sound pissed off."

"Worried." Hooker downshifted and threaded through the pass-through as he waved to the officer still standing by with his rotators lighting the way.

Johnny looked back out the side window hole as he checked the mere inch or three Hooker had cleared the fence post by. Reflecting on the two comments, he dittoed. "Yeah, that's what I said."

Both worked the next hour in their own silence. Hooker, a couple of times, started to direct Johnny but turned to find the kid already doing what was needed, or the next thing. *There's hope for this kid yet, but I'd kick his ass if he settles for tow driver,* Hooker thought.

As the tractor followed along backward, with a slight cock due to the need for the belt to be tied off with the steering wheel slightly out of center, they headed for the yard. Hooker was pretty happy the rig had some tin damage, but not real serious stuff. An easy turn with some good profit would mean a nice commission back to Hooker in the form of a full set of tanks or more, as he was thinking about some of the paint chips on the working bed.

"We could just make a diner stop before Candy goes off shift," Johnny offered.

Checking his watch, Hooker figured the time they would also need to retrieve the two trailers. "As long as we make it sort of quick. Those trailers need to go up to Palo Alto, and I want to do it before the traffic starts to build on the 280, much less the 17 crush."

"Actually, I just wanted to tell Candy something before she goes home. Food can wait."

"How about you go visit with your sister. I'll run back up and grab the first trailer, and then pick you up on the way back through. The north ramp is right there, and Hamilton has a sweeper ramp making it easy to get off. I'll just blow the horn from across the street, you can run out, and we'll be in the wind."

Jumping out of the rig twenty minutes later, the kid turned. "I'll give it about forty-five then have them make you up a sandwich or something to go."

"Great." Hooker cleared his mirrors of traffic behind him. "Just have her put it on my tab."

As the door clicked shut, Hookers left leg rose as he eased down on the gas. Mae West roared down Winchester Boulevard past Sarah Winchester's house sitting quietly in the dark waiting for the hundreds of tourists who would wander its halls with their mouths hanging in stark wonder.

Hooker's eyes scanned the instruments lit up on the dashboard. The head temperature had been a little high earlier but was back down to her usual location of the needle. Hooker downshifted and turned onto Hamilton and then cranked down around as he corkscrewed the cloverleaf on-ramp to Highway 17 and back out to Los Gatos. Slowly easing his right hand forward, he turned up the eight-track a few notches more and slipped in a new tape by Elton John. The cab filled with the song Hooker was hoping was going to play first as he and the giant yellow missile rocketed down the freeway.

The wind was a gentle chill as it blasted through the open window where his elbow was cocked out and resting on the sill. The needle on the big dial flirted between the seven and the zero, as Hooker reached back and flicked the switch to broadcast on the sideband of the radio. Keying the mic, he reached out to Sweets and Danny.

"It's okay, kid. He understood when you didn't answer. You were probably working."

Hooker downshifted as he approached the off-ramp for Los Gatos, a nice sweeper he wouldn't have to stop on. "So did he share what he's been seeing?"

"No, man. You know how he gets about stuff."

"Okay. Well, tell him I have to hook this trailer, and I'll call him back in about fifteen minutes."

"Will do, Hooker. Stay safe." The big man signed off.

Great, Hooker thought as he hung up the mic and switched it back to the Dolly side, *now even Danny is worried.*

A few miles away, a black Buick slowly drove through a residential neighborhood. Slender self-manicured fingers drummed a tattoo of irritation on the steering wheel. The right hand slid for the fifth time in two minutes back down to check the custom stock of the old Mossberg pump shotgun. The fingernail traced the fine crack that had been there since it had fallen out of the tree with the young boy as they tried hunting pig with a solid-slug shell. The recoil of a quarter pound of solid lead was something her brother had not expected. It had dislocated his shoulder as it knocked him off the small perch in the elm tree, dropping him to the ground sixteen feet below, and in the path of a very pissed-off wounded 300-pound European sow protecting her brood of suckling piglets. The pig's rampage had cracked the black walnut stock and put her brother in the hospital for a couple of weeks. Not the fall.

The sister thought about her two brothers more than the nun did about God. Even as a novice in the convent, her rosary wasn't beads supposedly blessed by the Vatican, but beads she had made herself out of rolled tissue paper glued together by the blood of her brothers. Over the years, she had collected the tissue paper used to stop their bleeding as she sewed up their cuts and scrapes and had then secretly made them into hard beads. These beads had become her personal rosary of the two brothers she loved more than anything. As she drove slowly, looking for the small house, her left hand thumbed and fingered the beads as she named each brother. She touched each bead made of their blood. "Timothy, pure of heart, Matthew the protector, Timothy, pure of heart, Matth… ew…" She had found the house.

It had taken her months to find out which officer had stopped the car that night, and which had pulled the trigger. The officer who had pulled the fifteen-year-old car thief over had been taken care of first.

The power of the simple black dress and coif of a nun had always amazed her. How trusting trained police officers and county clerks were, people who were trained to ferret out the truth, and to be untrusting. She had learned the true power of the habit several years before when she had hunted down the recruiter who had enlisted her older brother, than talked him into serving, not only a second, but a third tour of duty as a Special Forces LURP, or Long Range Reconnaissance Patrol, a duty from which he had never returned. He had stolen half of her life, so she had stolen all of his in a bathtub in a hotel who charged by the hour on the seedier side of Monterey.

As she sat in the idling car, in the early light of the day, she thought of their growing up. Their father had taught her and Matthew, and later little Timothy, how to hunt for food. Their practice training had been carefully walking up to deer in the southern Santa Cruz Mountains, and touching them on the nose, or slapping them on the rump. She had almost always been the better of the three at the game, and at the frontal approach, she was the master. Unassuming, unthreatening, just another plant in the meadow or forest. A trick she had found even easier with humans once she had graduated from the convent.

Her pulse rate was slowing. She focused on the surroundings of the neighborhood. The light was still on over the porch. She knew if she went up and rang the doorbell next to the oak and glass door, there would be nobody coming to answer the door. There was nobody home. Her prey was still running for several minutes more. Only when the officer returned from his daily five-mile run would he open the front door, turn off the porch light, and enter the small light green depression-era composition shingled bungalow with the yellow trim. Exactly thirty-eight minutes later, the widower would step out of the house, lock the door, and drive off in his duty cruiser. She knew he owned a private car, but it didn't run very well… not since she had poured lapping compound in the fuel tank a couple of months before.

As she sat there, she watched the cross street three blocks ahead, and checked her side mirror, specifically the cross street two blocks away. The officer had fallen into the worst trap of complacency—routine. From watching and following him over the months, she knew he ran only four routes, all of them exactly five miles from his front door. She would kill him at the fifth mile, just as he had done to Timothy, shooting him at mile marker five on the Watsonville highway. The image of the grainy black and white photo printed in the Mercury News of a small crumpled body seemingly wrapped around and hugging the mile signpost, burned forever in her mind.

She saw everything else through the image, much like looking through sheer drapes to the world outside. You can see the world, but it is always filtered by the veil of the drape. Only her training as a nun, and losing her older brother years before, had prepared her not to react other than a mourning sister over the tragic loss of her brother. Retribution would come later, and as she glanced in the mirror, she saw the gray sweat suit-clad man turn the corner. He had run course number C, and her lips pulled back in a small mirthless smile, as she knew retribution was at hand.

The elder officer plodded along, one athletic shoe in front of the other. The five miles each morning cleared his head as he first ran and then jogged around certain courses. Each had its purpose. One had hills to work his upper legs, and then stretch his shins. Even though it killed him for an hour after, the net gain was a more limber leg set, which was something he didn't get behind the desk. Today had been what he called his *heart through the chest run.* For the first three miles, he wound down through the southern tip of Willow Glen known as the Hollows. It didn't seem like much of an elevation change until near the end of the third mile when he turned up a forest trail climbing the thirty-eight floors of elevation in less than three blocks, and then there was the last mile left to run back to the house. All the routes were the same five miles. They represented the five years of happiness he had enjoyed in his marriage before the cancer had begun.

Five hundred feet from the front door, across the final street crossing, and as he made the little jump over the water running down the gutter as the sprinklers at the yellow house ran out of control and broken with five geysers fountained in the yard, he scowled with his eyes as his mouth hung gaping open, sucking the air as he jogged past the corner, and turned his attention to the street in front of him.

The quiet of the neighborhood was what had attracted him. The early morning, in a community dominated by retirees, was his personal silent gym. Even the many dogs seemed to be retired or at least didn't care, as the slapping of his rubber-soled shoes padded by every day. As he trotted past the driveway of the house three doors from his own, he noticed the black car idling at the curb across the street from his house. Somewhere buried in the fuzzy gray of runner's hypoxia, an alarm bell was sounding. An alarm bell that should have awakened the neighborhood but was more of the sound a gopher makes as he scurries along in his holes under the lawn.

The door of the black car opened as Chief Davis made his way past his neighbor's driveway and sixteen feet before Chet would turn left up his walkway and take the last eight steps in a faltering pace reducing to a walk. The gopher stopped as time telescoped for the gunmetal gray-haired officer.

A nun was exiting the black car, but it wasn't a Bible she was carrying in her right hand.

A police car with flashing lights silently slammed around the street corner ahead. Chet knew there should be a sound of screaming tires, protesting against sliding sideways fast enough to produce smoke as the car slew right in his vision.

The sunny day had become a dimmed moving tableau of gray as the scene before him moved with the precision of a large watch ticking off each second. As the scene slowed down for each facet to be examined, sound became nonessential.

The nun raised the shotgun with some large object on the end looking more like a small watermelon than something life-threatening. As the gun came up, the cop car came to a halt, and an arm extended out of the window. Sound erupted back into Chet's world as the police revolver fired and the yellow flame licked out three feet from the end of the barrel in the morning light and drove birds from their safe roosts in the trees. The second shot galvanized the nun as she swung the barrel of the rifle toward the car forty feet away and fired. Sound had stopped again. There was no sound other than something sounding like a grunt at any gym. The large green melon on the end of the shotgun burped bloated, and the sound returned as the windshield of the cop car exploded.

Chet felt the doorknob in his hand before he realized he had taken the last twenty feet to his door. Hitting the door with his shoulder as he turned the knob, he slid in past the oak planking as fourteen dimes found their last burial in the grain of the hardwood door.

Stumbling past the small table near the door, he reached into the drawer and grabbed the Colt 45, the one his father had carried in the *War to End All Wars*. He pulled the slide as he took the two steps across the large front window exploding in shards right behind him. Turning, he aimed in the general direction of the black car and fired five fast shots, not thinking about the house across the street or anything else. He was fighting for his life.

The window jam near his head exploded, and the shards and dimes peppered the side of his face, chest, and shoulder. As he fell, he finished the clip in the general direction of the black car.

The colors around him fuzzed and lost shape as they turned grayer and grayer and Chet heard the car door slam. The squealing tires were reassuring as his world turned black. The model 19 fell empty to the floor. Silence settled back down on the street, and even the dogs, of which there were many, seemed to be retired and uncaring.

33

"Sugar in the sunshine!" Hooker cursed.

"What?" Even Box looked up at Hooker's uncharacteristic outburst.

"We forgot to grab your stiff-as-a-board pants and shirts to wash."

Johnny thought about how uncomfortable his new jeans and starched T-shirt had been all day—or was it night? "Screw it. I'm too tired to care at this point."

The large ball of gaseous fire blazed over the east hills and seared their unaccustomed eyeballs. "I really need just to break down someday and buy a pair of shades to leave in here." Hooker reached forward and pulled the visor extender down, which only tempered the heat of the spotlight, which they were driving directly into.

The kid fumbled with his and looked at Hooker's—there was no extension on the passenger side. "Yeah," he grumped as he leaned back and just closed his eyes. "Speak for yourself."

Chuckling with more than a bit of punchy sleep-deprived humor, "I just did." Hooker giggled, and then slapped his right hand over his mouth. *Thank goodness,* he thought, *it's time for bed.*

The sweeper down on southbound 101 was as clear as he could expect for the early morning commuters. Most of the commutes had shifted to the northbound since Silicon Valley, as they were now calling it, had moved most of the jobs away from IBM, and had grown exponentially in Santa Clara along the new expressways. Hooker drifted the giant into the second lane as he closed on a slow-moving high-cube box pulled by a Peterbilt. The older truck was having a struggle keeping up with the flow of traffic. The black smoke pouring from the top of his twin stacks told Hooker the rig didn't have much farther to die. He chuckled as they swept past, and the kid looked at him and jerked his chin askance.

"Old truckers never die," Hooker explained, "they just get a new Peterbilt."

The kid either didn't get it or was too tired to laugh. Whichever, Hooker didn't care either.

"Hooker?"

Hooker reached behind his head and grabbed the mic. He didn't like the sound of Dolly's voice and glanced at his watch. She should have gone home an hour ago. "Yeah, baby."

The squelch couldn't hide the tattletale of her grabbing the lollypop mic too hard. "Do you have your No-No radio on?"

"No, baby, I'm behaving myself."

"Well, stop it. Turn it on and turn it up. The bitch just shot Chet."

Hooker almost hit the Dodge next to him but recovered. Both drivers were wide awake now. Reaching over, he turned on the police band radio—highly illegal, but sometimes very useful.

Making sure he wasn't about to hit some other car, he keyed the mic. "It's warming up. What bitch and when did she tag Chet?"

The police band surged into activity as Dolly answered. Hooker turned the police down and asked, "10-9... the other radio walked all over you."

"About twenty minutes ago." He could hear the quivering in her voice. "PD had sent a cruiser by the house, but he was out for his morning run. The cruiser went looking for him but had a bad feeling and came around the corner as the bitch was about to plug him. The officer got off some shots, but she riddled his car and him with dimes. The guy got the call in, but he's going to be touch and go for a while."

"So who's the ... female?"

"I told you, a nun, or someone in a nun's habit."

Something wasn't connecting, and the important ends were hanging in front of Hooker's mental eyes, but he couldn't see how to put it together. "Do they know where she went?"

"We're trying to follow it, but it doesn't make much sense. They're chasing her down the Almaden Expressway."

"But that is pretty much a dead end... oh shit."

"Hooker..."

"Sorry." He let go of the key. He needed to think. If she really knows the territory, she might know about Hicks Road...

The map played out in Hooker's head. He knew every square mile of his fiefdom. Technically, the auto club said his territory was only forty-seven square miles. But Hooker knew he was the only rig to call for many of the recovery jobs in an area more like *six hundred* forty-seven square miles with well over a thousand miles of freeways, expressways, streets, lanes, roads and tracks from highly maintained Cal Trans freeways to dirt tracks which were at one time either logging or fire roads left to return to nature.

Hicks Road was one of the more interesting back ways few people knew about, and even fewer used. Where Almaden Expressway with its almost straight smooth four lanes ran out, Almaden Road took over as a twisting snake, sometimes slowing to twenty miles per hour through little shanty towns of recluses. The extremely rural road ran through deep forest, tiny horse properties, and other falling down shacks barely surviving better than the road. Where it dead-ended was at Hicks Road, where she could turn right and wind up and over the twisting dragon run of the pass to Highway 17—not far from where they had been all night. At that point, she had a choice of running down to the coast or back into San Jose.

If she turned left, she would be at the 101 freeway in less than twenty minutes and could run north to Frisco or south to any choice of locations on the freeway, including the giant of all hiding places, Los Angeles. The other option, but not the most likely, was to go over the hills to the central valley. Everything was about what or where she would feel comfortable running to, and what roads she knew to take. Hooker only needed to know which choice she was hopefully making to get there first. He downshifted and slowed the truck as he too was rapidly approaching his decision point.

He raised the mic and keyed it. "Dolly, how close are they following her?"

"Aren't you listening to the radio?"

Hooker looked bug-eyed over at the kid who just rolled his eyes and then closed the lids and laughed. "I can't talk to you and listen at the same time." He off-keyed, took a deep sigh and keyed back. "How close are they? Do they have her insight?"

"Yes," she confirmed, and through her open mic, Hooker could hear she was listening to their scanner. "It sounds like she's got a fast engine in her car because she is slowly pulling away from the officer."

Hooker upshifted again as he triggered all of the flashers on the front of Mae. This was when he wished he had a siren. And seeming like he had the power to snap his fingers and get his wish, a siren started wailing to his right. A CHP cruiser dropped down the on-ramp as Hooker went by. He couldn't tell at a glance, but with luck, it would be Micha now closing on his tail.

Hooker hoped the cruiser wasn't closing on his six to write him a ticket, because it just wasn't in the cards today. The low-slung, specially rigged chippy pursuit cruiser sidestepped over two lanes and was now in the center or hot lane and moving up rapidly. The simple fact of it being one of the few hot-rodded pursuit cars in the state almost guaranteed it was Micha. As the cruiser came alongside Hooker running at eighty down the freeway, the officer keyed his outside speaker. "Hooker, go to Tack three," blared across the lanes of traffic—it was Micha.

Hooker leaned over and switched the selector on the radio match of the radio in Micha's cruiser. He clicked the key twice.

Immediately the radio responded, "Hotel 1-4-1, this is Charlie 3-4."

Hooker now had his call tag. "Hotel 1-4-1, go ahead, Charlie."

"1-4-1, you are apprised of the situation?"

Remembering Dolly, Hooker returned, "10-4. Stand by one."

He keyed the other mic. "Dolly, I need to know if she takes McKeon Road or goes on down Almaden road to Hicks."

"10-4, Hooker. She's approaching the break point now. Stand by."

As Hooker raised the second mic, Micha called back, "We need to get to Bailey Road or Morgan Hill, stay behind me, but keep up." Hooker double keyed the mic and shifted up another gear, thinking to himself, *Keep up?*

There was a snort from the other seat, "Keep up?" Johnny observed. "Does this person even know you?" He snorted again. "It's more like, 'Please don't run me over!'..."

Dolly's voice came across. "She took McKeon, Hooker."

He raised the mic. "Okay. This is the important part. The officer needs to stay with her no matter what." He reached over and danced his way into the top tier as they flirted with 90 mph. "The next decision point is Bailey Road at Calero. If she stays on McKeon, then it will become Uvas. From there, she only as two real options—she turns at the Chesboro reservoir or stays on Uvas and heads for Watsonville highway."

Grabbing the other mic, he passed the information and game plan. "Charlie, suspect just turned on McKeon. The pursuing officer is falling behind, but we need to know if she turns on Bailey or heads for Uvas or Chesboro. Tell the Chip to man-up and keep up."

"10-4, Hotel. We will head for Bailey and wait." The pursuit car pulled a small bit ahead until Hooker eased down on the pedal and shifted one more time. He still had four more open gears in the box.

"Where do you want to catch her?" Johnny was sitting up and cinched his belt tighter for the fifth time in fewer minutes.

Hooker, out of habit, checked his mirrors for anyone trying to keep up. The tiny smirk on his face was more about the kid and his belt than it was about anyone who could hit a flat hundred on the 101 South at this time of the day. He was sure if any drivers in the light traffic ahead of them looked in their rearview mirrors, they weren't going to argue with a highway patrol wailing down the highway. Especially one being followed by an even larger truck with flashing lights looking like a shark chasing a small tuna for lunch as the freeway portion of the 101 ran out onto the Monterey Highway, more commonly known as *Blood Alley*—a two-lane cluster fuck any time of the day.

The old highway worked fine for its first seventy years when two lanes handled the farm traffic just fine, but now the two flashing and screaming vehicles couldn't maintain the high-speed. Micha dropped to a reasonable seventy. The new slower speed made Hooker antsy.

The morning traffic heading south was scattered along the edge of the highway under the row of trees on the dirt shoulder. The heavy north-bound commute was separated from this by only a little asphalt and two highly effective lines of paint less than six inches wide. A look of fear was plastered on almost every face as the highballing freight train of car and truck barreled past at a wind rocking speed made all the scarier by the keening of the siren.

The cruiser started to slow, and then resumed speed, as they blew past the turn for Bailey Road. "Hooker, she's still headed south. Let's just hope Strombeck can grow a pair for the curves ahead."

Hooker thought about the sweeper curves on McKeon-Uvas Road. They weren't exactly treacherous, but they could take you by surprise when they weren't banked right or worse, not banked at all. *Maybe we'll get lucky, and she'll pile it into one of the sandhills down near Casa Loma Drive, or spin it out into one of the many small farm fields or pastures,* Hooker thought to himself, but he knew with a car like that, she most assuredly knew how to drive it.

He muttered out loud to himself as he reached back for the micro-phone, "Who the hell is she?"

"Dolly?"

"Hooker."

"Has anyone found out anything about this nun?"

"All they know is she is local somewhere."

Hooker knew who would know. "Have Dina call McBride, but you call the Archbishop." He snapped off the mic and was immediately back on. "Please."

"That's my boy, I have the card right here, and I'm half dialed."

"Hooker?" The wane voice seeped through the cabin from the secondary two-inch tweeter monitoring the non-active band of his personal radio behind his head. Hooker wasn't even sure Sweets was even on the radio. He should have been home in bed with this much sunshine.

Flipping the switch to change the active band, he keyed the trigger on the mic. "Go, Sweets."

"I've got a bad feeling, Hooker."

"Sweets, at a hundred miles an hour, I'm kind of busy here."

"Hooker, I keep seeing motorcycles, leather jackets, and an angry mob. It doesn't make sense, but I also see a nun."

Hooker keyed the mic and then released it. Thinking about angry mobs and motorcycles and what it could mean. He keyed the mic. "Where is the nun, Sweets?"

"In the middle of it all," Sweets moaned in his ethereal voice Hooker knew he was seeing it all now. "She is in the middle, but it's not about her —she's connected, but she's not touched by it, just standing there… in the middle. It's just raging all around her, the mob and flames. Hooker, they are taking the town apart."

"Who is, Sweets? Who's destroying the town? He looked over at the kid and back down the highway, as he shifted down again as the daily traffic was building approaching Morgan Hill. If it weren't for the start of the bypass at Tennant Road, then by Gilroy they would be doing good to maintain an even fifty.

"The leather crowd on the motorcycles."

"It's a gang?"

"I don't know. I don't feel it's a gang."

Hooker swore internally at being stumped. So close, and yet a gray fog. "Do you see anything else, Sweets?"

"Just the water towers."

Hooker jumped on the information. "What's it say on the tower, Sweets? Those towers always have the name of the town on them."

"Nothing, my man, nothing. Just the two gray towers standing out in a field." Sweets moaned in the far off but coming back way of his meant he couldn't see anything more.

"Okay, thanks, Sweets." He keyed off. "Shit!" Hooker wanted just to throw the microphone through the window, or at least do some bodily harm. He hung the mic behind his head and danced down to the next lower tier of gears. The farm traffic of Morgan Hill wasn't going to let them just fly low down the two-lane highway of Blood Alley.

"Where do you think she might go?" Johnny asked, still white-knuckled with his right hand on the door handle.

Hooker was thinking the same thing. "Dolly said local, and most people will run to where they feel safe, where home is or was."

Hooker's right index finger beat a fast tattoo on the ivory of the steering wheel, his eyes blinking and almost keeping up as he tried to see the answer. *But which town?*

"She didn't go for Hicks Road, so I'm thinking she's running south. If she takes the Chesboro turn onto Oak Glen, she's coming out to the highway to get lost in the city streets or hit the freeway and run flat out. I'm guessing with the mill she's got we may not be able to keep up with her."

Squirt was learning on the fly. "And if she doesn't take the turn?"

"Then she is headed for Hecker pass and over to Watsonville."

The Squirt frowned out the front window. "What's in Watsonville?"

"Nothing but a clean shot at the coast highway and all points south, including the one-oh-one or the coast highway." Hooker dropped a gear and kept the motor revved higher.

"Which means…?"

"We're screwed. We can't get from here and up Hecker pass fast enough. We'd have to know where she is headed first." Hooker was thinking of divine intervention, but he knew something that was almost as good.

Grabbing the mic from behind him, he checked the selector switch was toggled correctly. "Momma, how we coming with the divine intervention?"

"Nowhere, Hooker. He's in a meeting and can't be disturbed."

"Okay, I need you instead." He snapped the mic down onto the shifter and dropped another gear. "What town got torn apart by bikers in leather?"

The silence was the longest three ticks of a secondhand Hooker ever wanted to experience.

"I'm assuming there is a point in asking about old movies?"

"Movies?" Hooker was confused.

"Marlon Brando and the *Wild Ones*," she retorted.

"Who?"

"Smartass… Marlon Brando… *The Wild Ones* was a movie about bikers tearing apart Hollister back in the late forties."

Hollister! Hooker lightly banged his fist on the steering wheel. Keying the mic, "Do they have twin water towers?"

"I don't think so, but they do have a lot of grain silos."

Of course, silos. They would be just naked concrete cylinders Sweets would confuse for water towers, but they almost never have the name of the city—just who owns them or an old ad for Mail Pouch tobacco.

He grabbed for the lower mic under the dash, "Charlie…" forgetting what the call numbers were, "…whatever. Micha, she's headed for Hollister, so she will have to come out on Chesboro and head south on Oak Glen, or whatever the road is at that point. We can take Tennant Avenue, and it runs right into it."

"You're right. Strom just called, she's coming out." The cruiser surged a bit ahead as the traffic was lighter and the road was straighter, allowing people to see the cruiser's lights from farther away.

Hooker pushed the gears to the higher, and his right hand dropped in habit to the lower side of his seat. The furry head was braced full upright. Box loved a good fight, even if it was from inside the hulking truck. Hooker scratched the top of his partner's head and fingered the ear. "Box, you need to be in the sleeper hole, buddy."

The orange cat understood the sleeper hole command, no matter how it was given. Bouncing off the side of Johnny's leg, Box hit the large archway leading into the sleeper. Hiding over in the one corner, was a padded hole slightly smaller than his box. Hooker and Willie had built it as a bed, but the cat had dragged a cardboard box up into the cab for his continual use. The other was for just when things might get rough.

The cruiser's brake lights flared as Micha braked for the hard right turn onto Tennant Road. Hooker steered for the left side of the two-lane highway and downshifted in preparation to drift the eleven-tons of truck. "Grab on!" as he snapped the wheel left then pulled hard right as the rear-end's eight large tires broke away from the hold on the asphalt. Wailing like a large pack of injured dogs in heat, the back end slewed and came around, lining the truck up facing west on Tennant Road. Hooker stomped on the gas and danced with the gears to keep his giant chrome bumper mere yards from the back of the wailing cruiser and his friend.

"Hooker, the Archbishop just called back. The nun, Mary Margaret Joseph, grew up in Hollister."

Thank you, he thought as they ran down the middle of the four-lane street, *but you are just a few minutes late.*

Sadly, Dolly added, "Her real name was Anna Rose Stillman."

For some reason, the name rang a bell, but he was a little too busy to try to remember why. As it was, it wouldn't matter anyway.

The radio burped. "Timothy Stillman was the kid Chief Davis killed this last winter after he blew up the ATF guy and his family in Willow Glen."

The dominos began to fall for Hooker.

The kid had blown up or burned an ATF officer who had been investigating several pockets of anarchists and other right-wing extremist nutjobs living up in the hills. The groups saw themselves as the last hope of the dying America. They dealt in growing marijuana, running moonshine, and dealing in illegal guns and explosives. The kid had learned about bomb-making from his older brother, who was a decorated soldier in Vietnam. Hooker was sure everyone else, same as he, had forgotten the quiet, mousy nun, hands clasped in her lap fingering a long rosary wrapped in and around both hands, praying continually. She had been as easily ignored as the potted plant in the corner—until today.

Hooker double keyed the mic and slid it back behind his head.

Anna Rose was beyond caring who knew her or remembered her. The events of the last eight hours, one accidental intervention after another, made her guts seethe as she threw the car around the tight bend in the road. The same bend in the road she had spun out on ten years before as her big brother had taught her to drive the hot-rodded Buick.

She could hear Matthew's calm voice as he guided her through the driving, shooting a gun, or making a bomb—all of it was the same to Matthew. Everything was a preparation for the inevitable, the crumbling of society when every family would have to fend for themselves. Except it wasn't the way things had turned out. Anna Rose fingered the rosary of blood and tissue wrapped around her arm and hand and fed through her fingers.

Matthew was supposed to return home from the far-off land of heathens, having served his country's masters for a third and final time. He had learned much, and in turn, taught it all to her and Timothy, so they would all be ready. But who is ever ready for a mere child, a girl of six or eight with a live grenade in an outside bar in downtown Saigon? She fingered the rosary faster as she chanted her mantra, as ingrained as breathing for her now.

The Buick, with its reworked 340 engine, roared down the pass road toward the stop sign. Anna Rose glanced in the rearview mirror for the CHP officer who dogged her since Willow Glen. How they had figured her out and prevented her from removing the last person on her list was beyond her, but right now she was looking back up over a quarter mile of empty asphalt, and she was happy. Happy, but not enough to worry about running the stop sign. For just one moment, she considered running the sign over, but she knew the dangers that could stop her meant caution and attention to details.

She slid the medium-sized car around the corner as if it were the bicycle Matthew had trained her and Timothy to ride. The large twenty-six-inch balloon tires turned only a couple of feet from her face as she rode down the dust-laden back roads of Hollister—home.

They say home is where the heart is, but for Anna Rose, it was where the soul was. It was where the gang of motorcycle hill climbers tore apart the town, and the older deputy sheriff, her grandfather, had tried to stop them. His widow had followed him, but only after a long interlude being a mother—first while she raised their daughter, and then again when her grandchildren needed her in 1961. Three orphaned children after their parents were taken from them by a hail of bullets from a posse of revenuers' intent on shutting down all of the stills in the upper central coast area.

The new decade had been only days away when Anna Rose lowered the guiding light of her life into the family plot next to her husband. And then it seemed like she had just clapped the dirt from her hands, and she was digging again for her older brother, and then once more only a year later. Now, just one more space remained in the family plot, and she was determined to leave it empty for as long as she could.

Unknown to her, eleven tons of destiny rolled only six miles away—and closing in fast.

The giant engine was just hitting the power band as Hooker pulled the mic out from between his legs. Keying the mic, he reached out to the car in front of him. "Fall off, Micha. You can't go head to head with her and survive, but I can." He danced the gears up another notch and closed on the police car's rear end.

Hooker heard the officer key his mic, and say nothing, then watched as the car snuggled right and out of Hooker's way. Hooker mouthed a small grunt of satisfaction. *Nobody argues with twenty-two thousand pounds of steel and chrome—nobody!*

As Hooker pounded up into the next gear, Johnny squealed in a high girly voice, "You can just let me off anywhere along here is fine."

Hooker shot him a look of question and amazement, to which the kid just waved his two hands in a forward shooing motion as he chunked out in a newfound husky voice, "Kidding, just kidding."

The time for kidding was rapidly coming to a halt.

Tennant Road takes a slight rise before it turns into another name nobody ever cared about, but today, as Hooker cleared the rise and made the almost imperceptible veer to the left, he looked ahead along a tree line of old oaks for any movement. As the large truck settled down from the low rise, a fast-moving shadow among the morning shadows of the trees alongside Oak Glen Road caught his eye. Hooker knew the the fast-moving car was no granny out for a Sunday drive. Morning sun flashed a Morse code off the glass and chrome of a black Buick La Sabre, and Hooker began to adjust his speed.

The slightly curvy section of Oak Glen would keep her from moving faster than about ninety, whereas the straight shot of the road Hooker was on would allow him any speed he needed for the next ten seconds and closing.

To have two vehicles meet from a right angle, the cars need to look like they aren't moving. It's an optical illusion and has fascinated many who forget how it culminates. But the culmination was what Hooker was looking for. A permanent stop to the Buick—and he wanted it at the intersection.

Time telescoped for Hooker as his foot feathered back and forth taking commands from the eyes and brains as they raced for the end of Tennant Road where it *T'd* with Oak Glen. Where Hooker was sure minutes were crawling by, the tenths of seconds were flying past. Johnny now understood what he had signed on for, and where it was headed. Reflexively, his hands sought to pull just a tiny bit more slack out of the belt already restricting the blood flow to his legs.

The intersection was just out beyond the end of the giant hood.

In her side vision, she had caught the flicker of a large yellow truck. For hundreds of yards, she refused to admit it could be the pesky tow truck. But as they drew closer, the blue flames were more than distinct enough to tell her Moby Dick was highballing down the very road she would need to use, unless she continued for about a half-mile more and went around on Sycamore Road. Every second counted, but the road had just straightened, and so she pushed the gas pedal to the floor. The 383 engine, which had been rebuilt as a 455, growled and surged.

Out of the corner of her eye, she knew she was too late as the chrome grill and giant bumper loomed large, and then was the cause of a sickening crunch as the rear half of the car was sheared away and collapsed sideways, much like an origami construct under a large hand slapping it to the table.

The world spun for Anna Rose. The strike was little more than a tug for Hooker and Johnny. The truck took away the back half of the car as it made its way into the field of torn-up grass and little stakes with orange ribbons. Mae started to become mired in the soft mud as Hooker spun her steering wheel to make headway back to the road before they became totally stuck.

Throwing mud balls, streamers, and any other form of yuck and guck in a soggy field, Mae fishtailed around and reached out for the safety of the asphalt. The front tires had just touched solid pavement when the truck halted suddenly. Hooker's will, gas, jockeying gears to rock her— nothing would move the truck.

Hooker sat back as he put the gears in neutral and pulled the large red button—setting the brakes. He looked down on what had once been the front half of a Buick La Sabre. Everything behind the back of the front seat was gone and now sat in the middle of the field. The shearing force had been so almost perfect only a hacksaw and a lot of sweat could have done a cleaner job. An older car with a frame and body would have created more of a crumpled mess, but the unibody construction had sheared away at the swipe of the massive bumper and eleven tons of avenging angel. The front seat now sat a couple of inches above the asphalt where it had spun to a stop.

Reaching for the door handle, Hooker kept his eyes on the front of the car. Nothing was moving except the now released driver's door sprung open with no post left to latch onto. In the distance of the small valley, Micha's siren ricocheted about the hills and forest as a dull keening wail from a dying beast.

Hooker slipped his feet out of the door and jumped down to the roadway as Johnny started out of the other side. Hooker, as if in a daze, cautiously started for the backless car. He could hear the kid get back in the cab and tell Box to stay in the hole. Some part of him wondered why, after such a wild ride, the cat couldn't get out and prowl in his favorite turf of tall grasses.

He blinked, and another piece of the rapidly changing scene clicked into place but seemed unimportant as the habitual side was already turning his body to tell Johnny to let Box out. The mind is an amazing item—sometimes it's in control, and sometimes it goes on vacation. The bee sting at his neck, back, and butt, also didn't make any sense.

The leather-clad man flying out of the door eight feet above him in the air only made sense if this was a comic book and he was Superman. But then, it wouldn't explain the shotgun aimed at just above Hooker's head when a buck-thirty came blazing out of the end of the barrel. Time was collapsing, and Hooker's hearing was starting to synchronize with his shock-stalled brain.

The elongated "Noooooo!" from Johnny was punctuated by four explosions, but Hooker only saw two come at the mouth of his shotgun as the Squirt pumped the second rack of change down the retribution-pipe. As the second flare of heat, fire, and silver slid across the air by Hooker's head, the bees stinging him were relentless as they picked him up and twirled him about, stinging his shoulder and side as he lost his battle to remain standing.

The flying body of the avenging new kid was rapidly becoming twisted into a non-returnable, no-refund heap of meat chewed through with silver tumbling through avenues where there shouldn't even be pathways. The mass, missing the body it was intending to knock out of harm's way, rebounded off the asphalt a couple of skidding times and came to rest just past the body of the man he had tried to protect.

Leather oozed red life into the cracks of the warm spring highway. The sound of birds had stopped many long seconds before, as silence except for the incessant cry of a siren now harmonizing with three more in concert across the small valley.

Too late, much too late.

A few dimes lay about where they had spent themselves beating off a hard surface and bouncing back to die from use. These would now become just evidence.

A Raven glided overhead, a symbol of the end of life. The morning sun was warm on the black leather and denim crumpled in twin heaps along the pitted macadam of Oak Glen Road where it was met by a road nobody remember except it was the last part of Tennant Road—a fitting meeting for the last part of a brief but explosive event.

The door on the Dodge Polaris characteristically screeched its hard wail of steel on steel as the tall California Highway officer stood up stunned from his seat. The sunlight twinkled off the high polish of his calf-high boots with their military spit-shine. His right hand rested on the butt of his service revolver as he cautiously stepped around his door and approached the puddle of black cloth of what was once a nun. A pistol-gripped pump shotgun with the tattered remains of a green plastic soda bottle taped to the end still clutched in her right hand.

Standing over the body, Micha reached forward with his boot and kicked the shotgun several yards away. Routine, but by looking at the missing parts and what was left of the head, he knew the 'SOP' was a 'WOT,' but then a lot of standard operating procedures were just a waste of precious time.

The officer looked about the silence of the scene. Since the day standing in the rain behind his friend cradling the prom queen, he had never felt so useless. The officer and friend fell to his knees and wept.

35

The high-pitched squeaking of white rubber-soled shoes on polished linoleum floors were almost the only sound changing in the room. They would approach, pause, and then fade away, leaving only the soft hiss of the oxygen in the nose, and the occasional tick of a monitor. The turning of another page was regular like the step of the minute hand on the large wall clock over the head of the bed.

The soft sunlight fell lightly on the tipped-up blinds holding the room somewhere between dimmed and almost lit. The low ambient white noise of the pulsing city, washing the glass of the window, ebbed and flowed as the day followed its course. The clock ticked, the page turned, a monitor blinked, and the soft breathing rose and fell almost imperceptibly as the man waited.

The approaching footsteps were not of a nurse. The footsteps slowed and stopped outside the door. The sound of the chart being turned and shuffled through then returned to the chart rack by the door indicated a doctor or an intern. The black-clad man stepped into the door. "Damian, I'm going down for some coffee, son. Would you be up to join me?"

The young priest moved his marker and closed the book and laid it on the small table. For some reason, the trashy action novel just wasn't getting his attention or enjoyment. He looked over at the form lying in bed, unmoving. Inwardly intoning a short prayer, he turned toward the other priest. "Wail," he intoned a truly awful fake imitation of his friend, "as long as the good father is buyin', 'ho am I ta be sayin' no?" He pushed on the wheels in his own special way with two appendages of disparity, but nonetheless, propelled the chair toward the door.

The two chuckled softly as they progressed down the hall of the intensive care unit. "Any change?" Father McBride looked down in hope. The other shook his head.

"Nothing yet, at least from where I'm sitting." He thought as they turned the corner and stood waiting for the elevator. "But you know, I was in a coma for over six months, and they weren't really sure I was going to ever wake up."

The steel doors opened, and a young woman started to get off but stepped back. "Well, if it's both of you, then it must be time for the morning coffee." Candy reached over and pushed the large button with the *B*. The coffee urn they all knew they were headed for wasn't in the cafeteria, but rather in the basement, and was the personal fiefdom of Walter Green himself. Janitor coffee is always the best in the house. She looked at the two men's faces, but they didn't have to say a word. At times like this, it was always a waiting game.

Three floors above, a warm hand took the slender hand of the young man, and carefully started clipping the fingernails. The clucking of the tongue was the ticking of a clock as she finished the one hand and moved to the left. "Umm mmm mmm, amazing how time does fly when you are lazing about in a bed," Stella hummed to herself as she slowly moved the large soft nail file over the freshly cut nails. Her left thumb rubbed gently over the four tiny pink dots on the back of the hand. "At least those are healing nicely."

"Is there a sponge bath in the offering, too?"

Stella didn't have to even look up or turn around at the voice she had listened to all her life. "I hope you at least put some shoes on this time."

Dolly let go of the door-jam and wandered into the room looking for a place to settle. "I certainly did not."

Stella leaned back and caught a glimpse of the ubiquitous flip-flops, which to her sister were the closest to footwear you would ever get her to don. She knew when she died, Dolly was to be buried barefoot, but with a pair of flip-flops in the coffin, just in case there was a dress code at wherever she ended up.

A large black woman in blue scrubs came through the door pushing a very oversized wheelchair. "Miss Dolly, I am so very sorry. I didn't expect you for at least another hour."

Dolly turned around and raised her arms for a hug, "Katie Did. Honey, how have you been?"

Muffled by the large hugging the larger, "Great, and you?"

"Hmmm, you know—same old day, just a different shift." She gratefully eased herself into the chair. "How is that Marvin of yours?"

Laughing, "How in the world should I know? You talk to him more than I do."

Dolly gave her a look of question. "How would I talk to him?"

"He's working nights for the county now. I think his call number is Alpha thirty-two, or something like that." She tossed her hair about. "I don't keep up on the detail stuff, you know. He goes to work, and I cash the checks," laughing.

"Alpha 3-2 … but wait." She adjusted herself up on one elbow. "That is a guy named Mark or Marcus, or something like that."

"Marcus Ulysses Nims. We just called him Marvin Gardens like in Monopoly, because his momma did. She loved the game, always winning, too." Touching Dolly on the hand, "Listen, honey, I love chatting with you, but I need to get back down to the ER. We are full of brain donors today." Pointing at Stella, "How's the boy today?"

"No change."

"It be okay, trust me. The boy's a fighter. He's no donor," and she was gone in a blue whirl of scrubs and squeaking white shoes.

The two ladies sat quietly, each humming and reading their own brand of trashy novels. Stella liked the manly swashbuckling science fiction of discovering other planets, whereas Dolly was more down to this earth and was rereading James Michener's *The Drifters*—something she never did, nor had the desire or weight to do.

"Where's Box?"

Dolly looked over at her reading sister. "At Willie's."

Her sister looked up. "What's at Willie's?"

"Box." She looked at her sister's questioning face. "You asked."

Stella laid the book down into her lap and gave her sister the kind of hard look only a sister could give and get away with. "Have you been smoking bat shit again?"

Her sister mirrored her with laying her book on top of her chest, which was on top of her belly, which was filling her lap. "I am not being batty. I was sitting right here and as clear as day, you asked where Box was."

"I certainly did not."

"I did."

The two women looked at Johnny. Dolly, always being the *Dolly-who-never-cut-a-driver-slack-when-she-didn't-have-to*, snapped, "Shut up, Squirt. My sister and I are having an argument here!"

"Okay, but can I get something to drink here first?" The whisper was weak and scratchy, but the fight was good to hear after two weeks of coma, five surgeries, and two shunts in his head.

"Anything you want." Stella was by his side and patting his left hand.

"Anything he wants, except moonshine. Maddie and Willie are down in Bakersfield racing the car or truck, or whatever it is." Dolly's voice was starting to crack as she struggled to get out of the wheelchair. "Oh, hell, just ring the damn buzzer, would you."

Laughing, Stella held up the plunger for her sister to see.

"It isn't working fast enough!" Dolly stormed. Facing the door, "WE HAVE AN EMERGENCY HERE!" she bellowed loud enough to make the deaf in the ER jump.

The little blonde nurse came skidding around the corner, expecting to see blood and mayhem, or something equally traumatic, but only found two women and a patient. Looking from one woman to the other, "What's the emergency?"

The woman standing next to the coma patient nodded her head toward the patient. "He's awake, and would like to know what you have to drink…"

"… As well as a couple of steak dinners," her sister finished. Then as an afterthought, added, "…and some Jell-O for the kid."

The nurse approached the bed and took the right hand, all the while watching the monitors. "But the main monitors at the nurses' station didn't register any changes in his heart rate or breathing."

The face swathed in gauze quietly responded. "Yeah, I'm sneaky like that. But, when you're finished holding my hand, can I get something to drink, please?"

The nurse was flustered, but Stella calmed her down with a quick, "He did say *please.*"

The nurse gave up trying to find a pulse and rushed out.

Dolly settled back with a satisfied smile. "Well, that ought to change the look on the day."

Stella patted and rubbed Johnny's hand. "It is such a shame Hooker couldn't be here to see this." A lone tear crept out of the inside of her left eye, the matching one on the right wasn't far behind in falling.

3 6

"Hey, Squirt, wake up and smell the coffee."

The blinds were still dark, and the dim blue night light was still on. The hallway was still in the dimmed night mode so as to not wake the patients as the nurses and staff came and went in the rooms, checking vitals, swirling thermometers in the ice water before taking rectal temperatures and other things going bump or squishy in the night.

Johnny looked around the room and saw the dark figure sitting in the darkest corner. Slowly, the figure glided out of the corner, pulled by the single barefoot leg not in a cast. Hooker took shape.

The bottom of a hospital gown, barely hiding the required dignity, peeked out from under the black leather jacket over the ubiquitous starched and ironed white T-shirt. The left arm of the jacket hung empty and impotent while the arm rested in new surgical wrapping and a sling under the bulging leather jacket. The silly grin was optional with Hooker.

"At least you're growing the beard back," Johnny croaked. "You looked really creepy without any hair on your face and head."

Hooker ran his palm over the half-inch of new hair and beard. His fingers picked up the empty patches where the scars would grow instead of hair. "Yeah, I considered going Yul Brenner for a while, but then it might be a little cold during the winter and ice cream season." He continued to push and pull the wheelchair closer.

"So what is with the wheelchair?" The kid was sensitive to the various changes he and Hooker had both been going through on the road to recovery.

"It helps with your birthday present, dufus."

"But my birthday isn't until Octo..." he paused, trying to do some mental math.

"Don't even try it, Einstein... today, it's your birthday." Hooker got close to the bed and unzipped the top of the zipper from almost at his neck. Reaching into the jacket, he pulled out a pint bottle with no label. Reaching into his jacket pocket, he produced two small empty jelly jars. Handing them out to the kid. "Here, hold these a second." He handed them off then unzipped the rest of the jacket to reveal a large patch of orange fur.

Box's head popped out from under Hooker's arm and looked at the kid in the bed. Nobody had to tell him twice where he was to go. Hooker stood up as the cat stretched out and lightly jumped onto the bed, purring like Mae West after a bad tune-up. Hooker unscrewed the cap and poured a couple of fingers worth into each jar. "Maddie says *hi*." Replacing the cap, he laid the bottle on the bed and reached for one of the jars. "Hmm what should we drink to? If it's not your birthday, we need something to celebrate."

"How about the fact we're both alive?"

"Nah, we were both that before."

Johnny sniffed at the moonshine. "How about friends?"

Hooker thought a second. "How about, here's to friends who look after you when you can't."

"I'll drink to that," as the kid raised his jar to his lips and sipped his first taste of moonshine. Hooker watched over the edge of his jar as he sipped from his. The show was well worth the admission. He imagined he was looking at something similar to his face at age sixteen when Willie had finally let him try a sip of Maddie's best. It's truly amazing a human face can make those kinds of changes in such a short time.

The kid's voice was strained and sounded more like chalk on smooth steel, "Smooth."

Hooker laughed and reached in his jacket and pulled out an envelope as thin as one piece of paper can get and laid it down in the kid's lap. "Maybe the second sip will be rougher."

"What's this?"

"Just an offer…" Hooker sat back down in the wheelchair. "…you might want to consider."

The kid looked at the envelope, then placed it in his lap as he took another sip of the moonshine and thought. Letting the fire subside a moment, his hand lowered into his lap with the jar as he leaned back into the hospital bed and pillows propping him up in a semi-sitting position relieving the pressure of the eleven wounds where the dimes had entered, and the longer scars where the doctors had done the same, chasing all but three pieces of them. Quietly as his left hand stroked Box curled beside his uninjured leg, he tipped his head back and asked the ceiling and Hooker, "So, why would a nun kill people she didn't even know?"

Hooker sipped on his jar. "There's the answer. She did know some of them. Chief Davis and the first CHP officer had been the ones who had stopped her little brother this last winter and killed him in a firefight at the IBM parking lot. Everyone else, it seems, was just collateral damage along the way."

Johnny slowly rolled his head forward and took another sip as the medicinal factors of the clear liquid were starting to take effect. "For what?"

"Remember the burned-out lots in Willow Glen?" The kid nodded. "One of those had been the home of an Alcohol, Treasury and Firearms agent and his family, along with their neighbor's home. The agent had been getting too close to his operation of selling stolen guns and running moonshine, so he killed them in the middle of the night with a Foo Gas bomb."

The kid frowned with his swollen left cheek scrunched up. "But a nun?"

Hooker shrugged, and his eyes rolled large as he looked down at the moonshine, thinking about another woman who had come from a local family of moonshiners but had seemingly turned out for the better. "It seems the family wasn't all to stable anyway. The older brother had volunteered into the army and served three tours of duty in Vietnam, just so he could learn more about guns and explosives. When he was home, he put his sister and the little brother through the intense training he had learned the previous year."

The kid thought about things he knew, and things he thought he knew, but didn't have much of an equation of an answer. He swallowed another tiny sip. "So she…" he squeaked, and then cleared his throat, "so she was really only a nun from the clothes out."

Hooker nodded and took another sip and then poured them both some more. "It would appear so."

The night duty nurse walked by, then stopped, and returned. Coming into the room, she whispered, "Visiting hours were over several hours ago, young man." She came around and saw who was sitting in the chair, and as she was about to say anything else, her eyes adjusted as she saw Box and the bottle.

She turned and walked toward the door, adding curtly, "There better be a little left for me when I get off in another hour."

"Oh, there is plenty of Box to go around, if he'll let you touch him."

"The cat is not what I meant, young man!" She stopped and returned to the door, asking quietly as she looked back down both ways of the hall, "Does the third floor know where you are?"

Hooker nodded. "Uncle Willie and Maddie are up there directing traffic."

She stepped in the few steps to rub Hooker on his good shoulder. "It's good to see you two finally moving about." She kissed him on the largest pink scar on his head. "I'll be back for some of the bottle in an hour."

Hooker chuckled. "Bring your own Dixie cup, Celeste."

"I will honey, I will," and she was gone down the hall.

Hooker looked back at the kid who was looking at the letter, but not understanding what his eyes were reading. He even started rereading it with his lips moving, but the two short paragraphs still meant nothing to him. Or, maybe they did, and it was the damp eyes which were the problem.

The kid put the letter down and looked at Hooker. "I don't understand."

Hooker shrugged the leather jacket against the large itchy bandages, which weren't covered by the lightly starched T-shirt and tipped his patchwork head of shaved surgical scars and hair. With the quirky little smile of his when he was having fun, he grumped warmly, "It basically says your family: Dolly, Manny, Chet, and others, think you should wait until you're physically able to enter the academy, but you've been accepted to the Police Academy for San Jose Police or California Highway Patrol— your choice. It means you get to be a cop."

The new scar rippling along Hooker's cheek and running back to his ear made him a matched set with the cat snuggled by the kid's lap. Smiling until the scar buckled, Hooker thought, *the kid is really going to have to work on the goofy stunned look.* It just wasn't real cop potential. He sat back and enjoyed another sip. *So much for having a free employee.*

NIGHT VISION

A SOUTHSIDE HOOKER NOVEL — BOOK 2

FIRST KILL

In the dark of night, red looks black, and the white of freshly exposed bone appears gray. Nothing is truly black and white. All is a variegated palette of grays. The evil actions of humans fall likewise into the palette between, and are rarely at the extremes—except, of course, when they are.

There is an old tale about a man wandering in the wilderness with a staff and a lantern. The lantern had no candle, and yet there was light. The light, it was said, could illuminate the darkest corners of a man's soul—an ancient story for an ancient and simpler time. Today it was as simple as the light from a passing truck spilling between the slats of a freight car shoved off on a rail siding waiting for its next train. Or perhaps it was a forsaken crucible for the unspeakable.

In the dark night, a truck rolls to a stop at the stop sign by the highway. The driver gazed across the highway to the field of broken earth beyond. Sparse clumps of tall grass were the only audience to the dilapidated, faded red-brown freight car. The man had noticed it Monday night as he headed for work at the Gilroy's spice plant. He didn't remember the door on the side as being open.

"*Kids,*" he thought as his right hand reached across the metal dashboard. The cigarette lighter popped back out from the hole in the dashboard and into his yellow-stained fingers. The glow from the hot metal flared as he lit his cigarette. His eyes were on the door across the highway as his right hand found the hole in the dash from years of habit. The smoke seared sweetly as he took the first deep draw of the morning. His wife had never liked him smoking, but his truck was his kingdom. He confined the habit to his work commute each day, where there would be no dispute.

He absentmindedly fingered the turn signal and slowly eased the '52 Chevy pickup out onto the empty highway. Turning left, he headed for work on the graveyard shift. The rail car was no longer even a memory as he turned up the radio. The sounds of Tennessee Ernie Ford sang to his truck driver's soul as they crooned together about another sixteen tons of coal and being deeper in debt.

The light had swept along the walls, illuminating a Rorschach of bloody red flesh and white neon bone framing a silent scream and horror-frozen blue eyes. As the light disappeared back into the blackness of the railcar, the scene faded quickly to gray on gray. Life-giving air ebbed and flowed with a high-pitched whistle from the slit in the throat pushed and pulled by lungs nearing the end of their journey from life into death.

The slender claw of a hand weighed the long thin bone bound with human hair and flesh at the end. The movement was slow as if it were the balance of life itself being weighed.

The brush dipped again into the dark cavity of the body pinned like a bug to the wall of the railcar. Small crescent cuts opened into cups to pool the blood, marching down both sides of the torso. As one fountain congealed, a fresh one was cut—to renew the flow.

The killer hummed tunelessly, contentedly, in the thick silence of the night. Feeling the added weight of the loaded brush, the strong, boney hand moved carefully to the wall and continued the curious twists and turns, creating a terrible tableau. Drawings and glyphs stretched around the walls of the railcar. Quarts of blood turned into a maniacal scribe's ink or an artist's paint.

The gibbous moon played hide and seek with a handful of late summer clouds. Far in the distance, a lone coyote howled his tortured call of solitary desperation. Summer's last crickets were ominously silent.

The killer gave a little giggle at the final pass of the bloodied brush. Throwing the now useless tool over his shoulder, he sat down on the floor to watch this latest life drain away. To feel the essence of the spirit as it flowed from the old vessel to the newer, more deserving.

His left hand silently withdrew the short-bladed knife from the scabbard on his belt. His right hand dreamily plucked a hair from his head. The edge of the sharp blade slid along the hair in the moonlight, slivering it.

Without thinking, his right hand placed the hair in his mouth as his left hand returned the knife to the scabbard. His right fingertips danced delicately along the edge of his left Killing Boot in delicious anticipation. He could feel the stirring of his penis as the time drew near.

With satisfaction, the killer eyed the lacey fringe hanging from what once was a face. Every slice had been a symbolic stripping of the identity. Every strip had been a morsel for the killer to ingest the power and strength of the victim's essence. Each strip sucked of its delicate copper and salty nature before being swallowed. Every finger pad had been a delight of sensual touch on the tongue.

The hollow whistle of the shallow breaths now drew shorter and more rapid. Soon, the killer knew they would catch, stop, and catch again. This one was strong. This one might actually take a try at a third breath.

The moon slid behind another cloud as the blue eyes grew flat and dull. The catch in the breathing rattled one last time. The killer smiled at the strength and determination residing in the heart and spirit.

Dark eyes flared with a red heat, then lidded and rolled upward as the killer reached release. Breathing rapidly, his chest fluttered. He moaned.

Out in the field, a lone cricket rubbed its legs with the heat of the night. A fast hand pinched it to silence and then passed it to a faster death between yellow and black molars. The tiny juicy feast was much smaller than the Master's but no less satisfying. The small figure shifted back into the small gully and became one with the tufted grass in the night.

The silence of the night was complete.

Most in the South Bay Area slept. However, tonight, one had died as another renewed his power.

1

If you're in your mid-twenties, at the peak of condition, with mornings beginning with a fast routine of weights and martial arts, the mind remembers. When mountains of soap bubbles applied with a Japanese wooden brush in a large shower follow, the memories are ingrained. The mind will even remember what breakfast for you might be dinner for them, before you start a long hard night of muscle-wrenching work.

However, getting up in the morning can be a bitch after three surgeries, two broken ribs, a cracked hip, a dislocated shoulder, a broken arm, and holes where the surgeons followed the eleven dimes shoved through your body from a twelve-gauge shotgun at the hands of a revenge-driven killer.

Your only salve for inching to the toilet is the knowledge the man who saved your life is also alive, and in the hospital, recovering from fourteen dime holes and more surgery holes getting most of them out. He will undergo his fifth surgery while you sit on the porcelain easy chair playing with your cat's only ear with your left hand because your right is still in a cast.

Box slid around the corner from his sandbox. Straight and bold across the tiles, he strutted his full twenty-some pounds of pure orange tabby male muscle. Hooker recognized their relationship as one of equals. He had seen what the cat could do to a grown man.

Box leaned his head into Hooker's better leg and smeared his scent from the side of his cheek along the calf. As the warmest part of the body reached the calf, he stopped and leaned in. Hooker's left hand fumbled down and found the ear. The instant purr resonated off the tiles and echoed in the battered chest above. For Box, life was good.

Hooker's blurred vision refocused on the crosshairs of the bathroom tiles. The cool of the ceramic reassured him he could feel his feet. Well, at least better than he could the week before. His left hand was getting better at playing with the fuzzy ear. He rolled slightly on the toilet as the one thigh twitched and jerked with a spasm.

Four dimes had sliced his jeans and then flipped and tumbled their way through his upper leg and hip. As each had twisted and turned, they had cut muscle, tendon, and nerves. The surgeons hadn't been sure he would have much feeling in his right leg and foot for the first week. Once the feeling had started back, they started reconstruction, another operation in the basement of Good Samaritan.

The long operation had gone well, putting torn holes back together. Everything except two dimes and a piece of a third had come to rest close to the spine, a major artery, and nerve cluster. The dimes were close enough to pure silver, allowing the surgeon to leave them in place. The change was close enough to twenty-five cents. The surgeon made some 'two-bit' jokes with Hooker during visiting rounds. It hurt Hooker too much to laugh now, but he knew, in the future, he would get some good mileage out of the same jokes.

As he swallowed the last of the glass of water washing down a dozen aspirin, Hooker looked at the wild pinto blotching of yellows, reds, pinks, blacks, and blues, which splattered his torso from the last round with the surgeons.

His hair was becoming almost long enough to cover the two long scars along his scalp where the hot silver had sliced open his head like a surgeon's scalpel. The left eye was still not totally focused but was doing better.

"You would make one ugly date right now," he said to the young man in the mirror. But inwardly, he was happy his facial hair was taking shape again, or at least, enough to shave it into his signature beard tracing his narrow square jaw. He did his best with his left hand, and Stella cleaned it up when it was too messy.

The green that had danced in his hazel eyes was now missing, leaving only a washed-out gray. The return of green would signal his return to health and happiness. This color change in his eyes was something the two sisters and matching mother hens, Stella and Dolly, monitored to check his progress.

He snapped off the lights and slowly limped toward the closet where he knew two dozen, more or less, starched and ironed white T-shirts were ready for him, thanks to Stella. He struggled into one of the masses of white. He could hear terra-cotta plates being set down as quietly as possible on the granite countertop in the kitchen. He heard muffled conversation between the couple who were the closest thing to parents Hooker had ever had. This sense of *home* did more to ease him than the massive doses of aspirin.

Hooker tugged at the bottom of his T-shirt as he limped slowly toward the open door of his bedroom. "Come on, Box. Let's go see what Stella and Manny have whipped up for breakfast." The large, one-eyed, battered, and scarred cat purred as he followed his partner in life.

The two had been almost inseparable since the day Hooker had found the almost-dead orange tabby kitten in a box under a car in the alley behind the Almaden winery. He had apparently been savaged by more than one dog. The vet had strongly suggested euthanasia, but Hooker could only think of how the cat, with the last of its strength, had purred the entire way to the vet's office. He insisted she do everything she could to save this fierce little life and watched as she sewed him back together.

"Good morning, sunshine," Manny called from his wheelchair at the breakfast table. He put down his pen alongside the pad of yellow legal paper and reached for his large stoneware mug of coffee. He watched the shuffling mass. "And good morning to you, too, Mr. Zombie."

"Hello, sweetie." Stella reached her cooking arm, spatula in hand, around Hooker's shoulder as he leaned in for a side hug from his left where it would not hurt. "Go sit down," she muffled into his hair. "I'll bring you fresh coffee when it finishes."

He nodded as he turned taking in the fresh pot still brewing. "Box, out," as he lumbered over to the front door and opened it. The yellow cat sauntered out the door, as Hooker reminded him, "And leave Mike alone. He isn't old enough to know you can beat the snot out of him. Let him turn two in peace." The cat shot a sultry look back at his partner, but also the alpha of the team, and headed for his own yard of grass.

Hooker closed the door softly and rubbed his face with his left hand. Rolling his eyes wide, he commented to nobody in particular, "Why, oh, why, does Box love to beat up on dogs so much?" He padded his way to the table.

Manny watched his movements with an experienced eye. During his twenty years as a cop and detective, he had suffered many broken bones, more than a hand-full of gunshot wounds, and several knife scars at hands other than surgeons. All totaled, enough scars for his wife of even more years to nickname him 'Mr. Zipper' long before the final gunshot split his spine and ended his police career.

"We need to get you down to the whirlpool today. The scar tissue on your hip is stiffening."

Hooker looked at the short silver hair over the reading glasses perched on the bent nose. Manny's liquid brown eyes danced with an inner light which could only be described as gold. "Yeah," he nodded, "I was thinking the same thing. I felt it tear a bit when I rolled out of bed." He dropped his right eyelid and let it flutter to describe the pain he had suffered earlier. "Please, tell me it gets better," as he dropped and slumped down into the chair, "or just shoot me now and be done with it."

Stella came over and kissed him on top of his head as she set the large mug of coffee down in front of him. "Oh, no, honey," she chuckled, "it gets worse. Just wait until you turn sixty, and you start to really fall apart."

Hooker heard the flapping of the cat door in the sunroom. Box jumped up on the back of the long custom-made couch. Hooker leaned back and watched his partner saunter down the entire fourteen-foot length. The world was his empire and his to command. The kinked tail swayed like a slow metronome as he made his way to the end. Front paw out, he rotated off the end, just a longer step to an almost silent landing. It still amazed Hooker that a cat with no depth perception could still know exactly where the floor was.

The proud tabby sauntered into the kitchen and dining area. He sat down to watch Stella. Box always kept his eye on her but took nothing—no attention, no food—from her.

If Manny happened to be lying on the couch in the sunroom, Box would occasionally honor him with a sniff or allow a brief pat on his head, but for the most part, Hooker was his only real friend in the house.

Stella reached in the refrigerator. The small white bowl had a rubber hood on it. She took off the hood and calmly walked over and set the small dish of chopped tuna on the table. Hooker frowned at the strange breakfast food.

Manny sipped his coffee and made a couple of more notes in the Manny style of shorthand. He looked at his watch and leaned back to quietly sip more coffee. "I think we might build the barn this year."

Hooker had heard about 'this' barn—a family joke—for years. Manny had browbeaten his ex-partner on the phone about this barn just so a right-of-way would not go through their acreage. Once Manny had landed in the wheelchair, any need for a horse barn had become moot.

"Are you planning to get small horses to pull your chair?"

Manny gave Hooker the 'deadpan homicide detective' look, which quickly morphed into rolling his head back, open-mouthed in imitation of a zombie. It was the family joke for asking a stupid question—being as stupid as a zombie.

Hooker snickered as he watched Manny lean forward and pick up the small white bowl. Leaning sideways, he placed it on the floor. In the dining area—Stella's dining area—the cat stood, stretched, and approached the bowl. He started delicately licking at the tuna.

Hooker could not see Box, but he could hear him. The cat was eating his tuna in the same reverential way he ate the small dollop of ice cream Hooker always shared with him in the cab of the truck. Even on the coldest winter nights, Hooker was known for arriving at the scene of a wreck with his windows rolled down and polishing off a sugar cone with French vanilla.

Hooker looked at Manny. "When did that start?"

Manny thought about it. It had become an unconscious routine. He looked to his wife. She leaned against the stone-topped counter, raising the hand still holding her spatula. She scratched her hair with the back end of the handle. "After you died."

Hooker chuckled. He joined in as all three went zombie. Box just kept on eating. The tuna must have been fresh.

Stella turned, still chortling over catching her favorite child with his mouth open and speechless. The scrambled eggs were just at the perfect stage. She lifted the pan and upended the contents onto a large serving plate. The pinion pine nuts were perfectly roasted to tan with tiny bits of darker brown. The tiny Canadian bacon strips were cooked just short of crisp and looked just like they were supposed to look. She stirred the grated mozzarella and parmesan cheese into the mix. She tasted a small bite—perfect.

With a stack of toast in one hand, rattlesnake hearts and flank steak with yellow guts omelet in the other, she returned to the table. Placing the food in front of her men, she stepped back for the fresh carafe of coffee.

"Oh, gosh, my soul, pioneer breakfast, and it is not even close to a special Sunday." Manny reached for the serving spoon.

Hooker held out his arm, and Stella leaned into his hug as she poured him more coffee. "Any day this side of a dirt nap and having breakfast with you two is special enough for me."

Stella topped off Manny's mug and sat. "Hear. Hear."

Manny raised his mug. "I'll drink to that."

They each took a bite of the omelet and leaned back to savor their favorite breakfast. "This is heaven," Stella said as she sighed, ignoring her usual rules about talking with food in your mouth. "Well cooked food, my two men both with smiling faces and a peaceful morning in which to enjoy them."

The two men raised their mugs, lightly tapped them together, and sipped on the great coffee.

In Manny's office, the phone rang. The ring echoed from the sunroom where the cordless extension sat next to Manny's place on the couch.

Stella almost spat her coffee. Her head whipped around and looked at the wall clock near the office door. Seventeen past nine. Not a good sign.

The phone would ring through another five rings before the tape machine would pick up.

Manny deliberately focused on his food and continued chewing. Hooker, ever the tow truck driver—who never got a slow meal, was torn between staying calm and shoveling in the only chance he may get before the machine answered.

Stella, too long at being a cop's wife, leaned forward and rested her elbows on the table and sipped her coffee with her face in the steam. The first ring had killed any appetite she had for any food. The world was holding its breath.

The tape machine in the office clicked. There was the five-second silence, as they all knew Manny's terse greeting was going out. *"Romero, you know the drill."*

The machine clicked again, and then there was a two-second tone. The voice was a not so disjointed spirit. "Manny Romero, if you still value anything between those legs, you will push back from my sister's table and pick up. You have five seconds."

Manny was already pushing toward the office at the first word out of Dolly's mouth. Stella looked at the clock again. She knew her sister should have been deep asleep until about five in the afternoon.

Hooker knew he was now in a time constraint. He started shoveling as his right hand reached for a second piece of toast.

Stella reached out and calmed his right hand. "Slow down. They can't get here that quick, and with your bum arm in a cast, you can't drive." She tilted her head and looked at him through the top of her left eye and raised an eyebrow. "Besides, you look ugly enough eating with the fork in your left hand, but when you hurry, even the kids in Africa lose their appetites."

They both strained to try to hear what was going on. Manny was too subdued for them to hear. It was not a good sign. Nor was Dolly calling in the middle of her night. Her days were running the city of San Jose from the night dispatch, an answering and dispatching company in the roughest neighborhood of the city from her custom-built oversized steel desk chair made to hold her quarter ton of boss. She knew where all the bodies were buried, and who had bones left to rattle. Nobody who was anybody disputed she was the heart and soul center of the city.

On her desk was a large tree limb with two words, *The Stick,* carved into it. It was a large stick the large woman stirred shit up with, and only Dolly ever touched it.

Manny rolled out of the office as he stuck the pen back in his shirt pocket.

He took a sip of coffee and loaded his fork. He looked up at his wife of twenty-three years. "They called her at home."

Hooker ate faster.

Stella put her coffee mug down and picked up her plate of food as she stood. She turned and then looked back at Manny. "Shit." She turned in disgust and went to scraping the good food into the garbage.

The temperature rose with Stella's anger. Manny looked over at Hooker. "If you're going to get a shower, now is the time. A deputy will be here with a van in about fifteen minutes. Dolly said the guy knew the way. He helps with the canning."

Stella stood leaning against the apron of the large farmhouse sink. Her arms were crossed over her large chest. "It's okay, Hooker. Just leave the dishes. I'll clean them up." She glared at Manny. *This crap was supposed to be over.*

He closed his eyes and stretched his eyebrows as his head tilted as if to say *these things happen.*

Her lips curled as she turned her head and looked out the window. The valley they loved stretched out for miles. What was once a green valley was now dotted with new homes. The developers had discovered heaven in the Almaden Valley.

She turned back. "How bad?"

He weighed what to tell her. Only one victim killed was not bad, but nobody in their right mind would call a retired detective in a wheelchair out for just a single dead body. He knew it, and he knew Stella knew it, too. It was the nature of the killing. It was the killer. And there lay the problem.

Manny looked in his mug as he took one last imaginary swig of coffee. He was stalling. He knew his time was up.

Quietly he placed the mug back on the table. He straightened his plate and the silverware.

Stella cleared her throat.

He looked at her. It was going to break her heart, and he knew it. Their eyes were locked.

Stella turned suddenly, raising her head. "Oh, shit, Manny." She stood holding onto the cold porcelain of the sink. "That asshole is back, isn't he?" Stella would have to pay heavily into the swearing jar before it was over.

Manny's voice was small. "Yes."

She stared out the window at the fountain in the entry. "Who?"

Manny chewed on the information. "A man." He chewed on his upper lip. "They haven't identified him yet. They may never. He has started peeling. He peeled the gloves and mask."

Over the years, Manny had learned Stella was a strong person. He had shared much about his job. It had helped her understand as the night-mares came and went. This killer, the one who had been nicknamed the Cowboy, still visited Manny and Stella on an almost nightly basis.

This was the killer who had put him in the chair seven years before. The killer had shot Manny in the spine to incapacitate him. Fortunately, Manny's partner had reached him in time to save him from becoming the killer's latest statistic.

Manny's mind raced where he didn't want it to go. They had stopped to check out an open door in an alley and had heard a noise. His partner was calling for backup, and Manny had stepped down the alleyway. Suddenly, there was a blinding flash, and his head hurt. As he wavered from the blow to the head, there was a pop, and his back was on fire. His last thought was how mad Stella would be. Him being getting home late to dinner, and the muddy water he was falling into would ruin his new shirt.

His partner had found him five minutes later, stripped naked. An 'X' of black electrical tape held a wad of cotton over the bullet hole to stop the bleeding. The eight-inch spikes used by the killer to nail up his victims were lying by Manny's side.

Manny and Stella jumped at the knock on the door.

Hooker, now showered and dressed, opened the door for the deputy.

2

The railcar stood shabby and sun-scorched in the late summer sun. It looked as if Butch and Sundance had robbed the train and cast this car aside.

The sheriff deputy pulled the van off the side road, easing it in next to the patrol cars and blackouts from the medical examiner's office. All the usual suspects were here.

Seeing the blacked-out Cadillac meat-wagon, Manny moaned quietly. "Oh, great, Doctor Doom is here." It was anybody's guess as to whether the county medical examiner got along with anyone, but the general feeling among the rank-and-file was a crime scene was more pleasant without him showing up in person. Not that any bloody crime scene could ever be pleasant, but it was the thought. The mere fact of him thinking to show up personally meant there would undoubtedly be some other high-profile brass standing around with their thumbs up where no tan lines existed.

Manny reached out and grabbed Hooker's arm as the young man groaned his way out of the back of the van. Hooker turned to look at his mentor and father figure. He very slightly jutted his chin out and up as if to say *What?*

"Never mind... You already know. I shouldn't have thought otherwise." The man's shoulders collapsed ever so slightly in resolve.

"Manny. I've got this. I have your back. Anything I say only goes to you. This is your domain, man. I'm just the Fun New Guy."

The older man scoffed. "Right, a newbie with two bits buried in him from taking down a serial killer. You may be young, but there's nothing newbie about you."

They held the look of mutual respect that was their bond. Slowly, a tiny curl began at the corner of Hooker's mouth.

Manny grumped to hide his smile. "Oh, shut up. Get me the hell out of here."

Hooker pulled the chair out, set it up, and then reached in and leaned into the other man's lap with his good shoulder. Manny reached out and grabbed, two-handed, at Hooker's belt. With his legs, Hooker dragged the man out of the back of the van. Manny knew the pain on Hooker must be intense, but he also knew Hooker was relentless—only Hooker touched the older detective.

The deputy who could have been there a few minutes earlier to offer some help started to say something. Manny snapped his head at the man and gave him his *you are so dead meat* burning eye. It was a look he had perfected over a couple of decades as one of the top detectives in the city.

The deputy withered and backed away.

Manny pointed to an unoccupied area. "Let's get back up on the asphalt and go over there. I want to look at this from along the road first."

Hooker and Manny moved along the road cautiously. The communication was perfect between them. Not a word was spoken. A nod of a head, a finger here, and a hand spread there. It was silent but rich in the depth of looking, instead of just seeing. It was one of Manny's favorite approaches to teaching.

Looking is what you do at a crime scene. Seeing is looking, but with an overlay of judgments, wants, needs, beliefs, and prejudices. The talent is just to look. Gather all the information you can before you start assuming.

They could feel most of the eyes watching them, wondering what they were doing eighty yards away from the crime scene. One voice called out, and it was calling Manny.

Manny didn't flinch, didn't even look up. He kept doing his job. His left hand rose with one finger up, and the middle finger going up and down. His old friend Paul Tanner knew the finger was Manny's code for *'be with you in a few minutes.'* For anyone else, it may have meant *'shut up and go away,'* but for the county commissioner, it was the former. He and Manny had been partners, walking a beat together back in the bad old days.

Had they known each other back then, he would have been Manny's best man when he married Stella on the dock beside the troopship, he then boarded ten minutes later. Ten minutes after Manny had boarded the ship bound for Pearl, he met the man on the top rack of the bunks, and they had become good friends. When they returned, Manny had convinced Paul the only place to live was in San Jose.

The soft-spoken eighth-generation Minnesotan hadn't even gone home to collect his belongings. He had his folks bring them out when he and Manny graduated from the police academy. The folks stayed for a month and then went home to sell the family farm. They had lived near the coast in Watsonville ever since.

The soft crunch of hard soles on gravel and sand let Manny and Hooker know from forty feet away they had company. The steps stopped, and Manny made one more critical scan of the field.

The fingers on his right hand kept slowly drumming. Drumming... And then they stopped. There was a slight intake of breath, and Hooker squatted down beside him.

Nodding out with his chin, Hooker knew the mentor was asking for his take. He gathered his thoughts and mapped the area. He nodded slightly toward their right. "There was no evidence of a car, but he came in carrying along that depression. He then moved left to about where Doctor Doom, in the stupid black suit, is standing. After t, he circled to see if the area was clear. But I don't see that he came out this way."

Manny nodded as he raised his left hand slightly and waved his old friend Paul in. Still, only to Hooker, Manny continued Hooker's evaluation. "The bent grass suggests you're right about him carrying the vic. But I think the deep weight-carry damage masked them leaving."

"Them?"

"Look along the sightline where the depression becomes a berm. There is some grass flattened there, too. I think we'll find a footprint, or at least a toe print along there before it becomes hard-packed and railroad ballast. The line you see off to the left is the lookout. Last night, the breeze was coming up from Gilroy, so the lookout took station downwind while our killer walked straight in with the vic on his shoulder."

"What do you have, Manny?"

Without looking up at his friend, he took in the entire scene. "Well, Paul, to gild the lily and put it in terms little schoolgirls like you and the stupid suits out there can understand, we have a cluster fuck." He folded his hands in his lap. "Ask Doctor Doom out there not to take a step. Then have your brightest boy go snoop around his feet for the barefoot prints I think he will find.

"As for the royal fucking, the prize would have to go to the two idiots standing at the end of the railcar drinking coffee. They've been milling around the past twenty minutes all over the tracks of your killer. The blond one even didn't like his coffee, so he threw it out, probably along the best place we could have pulled a pure boot print."

He turned around and looked up at the man. "But if you want to save anything from here, you can ask Hooker here to show your best caster where he can get an un-fucked-up print. Why the fuck would you guys come down here, dance all over the evidence for hours... and then call me? Do you really hate me so much for raping you at the last poker night?"

The man growled back with a deadpan face. "Fuck you, too, Manny. I would have called you three hours ago, but it was some tit-head in City Hall who thought it would be improper to have a civilian here."

He held Manny's stare until Manny nodded in understanding. They had both worked against the machinations of those in City Hall, who had no clue about how things ran in the real world of the street.

Sighing, Manny returned his gaze back over the tableau.

Turning to Hooker, the commissioner acknowledged him. "Hooker, it's always good to see you son. How is the body coming along?"

"Stiff and hurts, but then again, there are the not-so-good days." They smiled at something all too true about the wounds only coming from being shot, stabbed, or beaten. The commissioner had his fair share of scars, also.

Pointing, "You see the guy in the gray jumper? His name is Harold. He is the best and brightest we have. Go see him about where you want him to cast. We still have to figure out how to get the deadweight up onto the railcar," he finished as he jerked his thumb at his former partner.

Manny grumped, "At least you didn't call me a sea anchor," referring to a bad comment made years before that had become a running joke.

They both watched as Hooker made his way across the field, scanning the entire time—something the police had failed to do.

The commissioner squatted down and rested his right arm on the wheelchair armrest, pushing off Manny's arm. It was the most extreme invasion of personal space for a person in a wheelchair, but Manny made no protest. They had too much history for privacy.

"He has turned into one fine young man."

Manny chuckled. "Between Willie, Stella, and Dolly, the kid didn't have a chance."

"Would you have pegged him for only sixteen the Christmas Eve he towed Stella and her girlfriend, Claire Osofsky, off the Guadeloupe Parkway?"

"I could tell he was young, but we all thought he was maybe a youngish nineteen or twenty. Only Sweets knew right off the bat, but then Sweets is Sweets."

Paul laughed. "I still wake up in the middle of the night. I'll get up and sit in the den and turn Sweets on and listen to the cowboy music of his and read. He even got me reading Louis L'Amour and the whole Sacket family stuff."

Manny looked sideways at him.

"Don't look at me that way. I know for a fact you have more than a handful of his books in your office."

"Reference books," Manny defended with a faux grump. "All two-hundred books as well as some Zane Grey."

The two continued to banter and stab at each other like puppies who had gotten too tired or too old to play the physical rough-and-tumble.

The two smiled proudly as they watched Hooker walk straight up to the most loathed man on the county payroll to tell the medical examiner not to move an inch—until he was released. He pointed out the man had accidentally stepped into the middle of the most important section of ancillary evidence.

The two old friends watched Doctor Doom stiffen in his jet-black sharkskin suit. However, he didn't even turn his head as the tech took castings mere inches from his shoes. He knew he had screwed the pooch. As a very senior person, he had made a mistake usually marking newbies for their entire careers.

This will be the last crime scene he comes out to for a long time, Manny thought as a wry smile crossed his face and was matched a couple of feet away.

A large box delivery truck with county markings stopped on the high-way. Shortly, as the two watched, it carefully started backing its way toward the railcar. On the back was a lift gate.

The commissioner rose stiffly. "I think your elevator has just arrived."

Manny reached out and gently backhanded his old partner's sleeve. The silent communication had the man follow as Manny wheeled along the road to the depression at the edge. He pointed at an unmistakable cowboy boot print, size ten or twelve, undisturbed in the sand about five feet away from them.

The toes pointed away from the railcar.

The two men turned and looked across the narrow-asphalted lane. The field beyond was a good hundred acres of burned off stubble from some crop that had failed a few years before. Manny guessed a poor try at winter wheat or sorghum. They moved for a closer look.

There was nothing there.

"A car would have been obvious sitting out here at night." Paul scanned about. "So, what are you thinking, they were dropped off?"

Manny's eyes searched the side of the field, looking at the dirt clods for thirty or forty feet in each direction. "I don't know yet." He looked up at the commissioner. "I'll let you know once I see the body."

"Body is gone. It left almost an hour ago." He knew what Manny was after. "Male, about five-nine, and hundred-twenty or thirty pounds. An easy carry."

Manny weighed the information. Turning the chair, he studied the road.

"Then get some cops out here and have them comb this line for at least a quarter-mile."

He held his hand up to shade his face. He looked across the field to a small stand of low trees in the distance. "What's out there, Kooser Road?"

"More like Santa Teresa." Paul saw what Manny had spotted. "I'll have a team check around those trees and make sure they park a hundred yards off."

Manny spun and gave a hard push, still thinking. "Let's go look at the art gallery."

The sand and broken field weren't easy, and Manny had to let his old partner tilt him back on the large wheels and then drag him backward to the waiting truck. It was the worst insult for a person in a wheelchair. Surrendering control and doing it so completely they are moved like a broken stove on a hand truck. The commissioner never said a word, but both knew it was something that would always be between them. The same as the bullet in Manny's spine—he would forever have the upper hand.

Hooker pushed the button, and the motor whined as the three rode up the approximate level of the railcar. The driver had done an almost perfect job of lining up the liftgate until there were only a few inches of separation. This distance was nothing for Hooker and Paul. They each took a side, and they were in.

The walls were solid graffiti in blood.

Hooker and the commissioner stood, with respect, in the doorway. They looked at the horror as Manny unhurriedly rolled the length of the railcar, his eyes cataloging every sweep of the brush strokes.

Manny gave a low whistle. "This is a hell of a lot more than he had to say eight years ago." He gradually pushed his wheelchair down the railcar.

"Did they find the brush hairs?" It was almost a distracted comment. Paul knew it came from the second side of Manny that was just gathering the information.

"Over here by the door."

"Were they still bound?"

"Yeah." Paul shuddered.

"With what?"

"They will have to look at the lab, but they think he peeled the skin off the vic's penis."

Manny kept moving and cataloging. He sounded distracted, but both men in the railcar with him knew what they saw were the two heads of Manny. One, looking and recording, and the other, asking questions. When Manny and Paul had been working crime scenes together, Paul had always joked they were the Three Musketeers—Manny, Manny, and him.

Manny stopped. He sat a moment, and then spun the chair around, frowning. "What were they bound to?"

Paul scratched his head. "We're not sure. It was a small bone of some kind. It was very light and about six inches long."

Manny didn't even turn. "It's a wing bone from a raven. One showed up with the young girl. It just wasn't attached, so nobody thought anything about it. I always figured, because of the three days it took to find the body, a mouse or rat had separated it from the hair bound to it and moved it just enough away to appear as if it were outside the kill zone." He turned around, thinking about crows and blackbirds. "Hooker, do we have ravens here?"

He had caught Hooker unaware, and the young man had to do some mental gymnastics to catch up. He knew it was a trick question of Manny's to bring him back into the investigation instead of just standing in repulsed awe of the writings on the walls. "Um, no... We have crows and blackbirds. Many people think the crows are ravens because they are large. A crow is much larger than our blackbirds, but the raven is even larger still."

Manny put his index finger in the air. "Paul, did you know that?"

The larger man looked at Hooker with a frown. "You sure they aren't ravens?"

Hooker nodded. "Ravens have a diamond-shaped tail when they fly, but our crows have a blunt square tail. People confuse them because they both have black beaks, as where the blackbird has a brown beak."

"Where are ravens found, Hooker?" Manny smiled to himself. He was now having fun with his former partner. He leaned in to look closer at a few of the writings in the darker areas. Only half of his mind was paying attention to the lecture path he had sent Hooker down.

"They should be here, but the crows and blackbirds seem to have pushed them out. Going south, there have been sightings down in Salinas, but more down near San Louis Obispo. In the temperate spring, you might find some venturing into the upper bay, but mostly they stay over in the Central Valley. There is a lot more grain over there, but the crows and blackbirds like the roadkill, and we have it in spades on Blood Alley."

Paul stood with his mouth open. He thought a moment and closed it. "How do you know all of this?"

Manny laughed. "How long have you been clearing bodies and stuff off Blood Alley, Hooker?"

"Ten years... thereabout."

Manny looked at his old detective partner. "It's like working the streets, Paul. Some things you learn in books, and then you learn the more important stuff by just doing it in the street."

"But how did you know he knew it?"

It was Hooker's turn to laugh. "One day, we caught Dolly out on something. And I'd never tell a soul what it was... just because. But I shot three or four birds. Maddie told me I had the wrong ones. They were only large blackbirds. She told me she would pay me a dollar if I could kill a crow. But then she added she would pay me a fifty if I could bag a raven. She knew there weren't any ravens."

"So how many crows did you get?"

Manny laughed. "None."

The commissioner frowned and looked back at Hooker.

Hooker rolled his eyes and shrugged. "Crows are smart. They can count up to three. So if you sneak up on them, they know it. They also know what a gun or rifle is."

"They can count?"

"Yup," Hooker nodded. "They count one... two... three... many. So if five men walk into a blind, they are many. If four walk out, they are many... and the blind is empty. But if four men walk in, and three walk out... the crow knows there is at least one still in the blind."

"So, you never got close enough to shoot one."

Manny was laughing even harder now. Hooker glared and then laughed, too.

"Oh, I did... once... I reloaded Betsy with hard bird buck, which is between the size of double ought with nine pellets in the shell and standard bird which is twenty-four or so. I had sixteen BBs. And I spent the day walking around the field with Betsy under my coat."

"So, what happened?" Paul frowned, getting a little antsy about telling war stories instead of solving a crime.

Manny *harrumphed* a snort. "He was right underneath the bird when he shot it."

Paul thought a moment. His imagination shifted from information to imagining. He chuckled. "Was there anything left?"

Hooker shrugged and rolled his eyes. "A few feathers."

Paul laughed, and then looked out at the other people looking in at the three laughing at a crime scene of a brutal murder.

He frowned as he thought it. "What did this have to do with Dolly?"

Manny smiled. "Stella was going to bake a pie for Dolly."

The penny finally dropped for Paul... "So she could eat crow."

The young tow driver and the man in the chair just smiled.

Paul smacked his face with his hand. "Oh, brother, she would have been on the warpath for sure."

Hooker nodded his head as if to say *do you think so*.

Manny wheeled back and down to the other end and returned, and then circled his finger in the air. "You think they got plenty of good photos of all this?"

Paul frowned. "Sure, why?"

"Because I need to go down now, over near the highway."

Hooker didn't have to ask. He pulled the chair up on its back wheels and jumped it down onto the liftgate and into the box of the truck. "Hold on to the bang boards," he directed Manny and then leaned out and around the edge of the truck. He whistled to the driver. "Take us out to the highway and stop on the side."

The driver fired up the truck, and it started to roll as the commissioner jumped over with a question on his face.

Hooker didn't have to look at Manny for clearance. "He's going to throw up."

The ex-partner looked around Hooker to see Manny grabbing the sideboards with both hands and had pulled his body out of the seat until his head was hard against the boards. His knuckles were as white as his blanched face.

Paul watched his old partner and still best friend.

It was a rare cop or detective who ever had a personal stake, much less personal experience in a murder. This one was too close for Manny. Manny and Paul had drawn this killer over a period of five years when he started.

The controlled violence of a true psychopathic killer is like no other killer. Most kills are classified as a cold-blooded kill, such as a hit with a single gunshot wound, or GSW, to the head or heart. These are usually from someone who knew the victim, and the victim is usually found in bed with another person to whom they aren't married.

The next step up in violence and gore is the crime of opportunity. This spreads a whole class of gore. The cleanest is an armed robbery gone south. It is usually the nervous young gang punk who empties a gun into a liquor store owner and then runs, leaving the money lying on the counter.

The bloodiest is the wild bar fight that goes wrong if there is such a thing. A good bar fight is just fists and kicking until someone breaks it up. When things get out of control, bottles are broken and used as weapons. These usually result in ambulances and time in jail. The ones Paul and Manny saw were the ones starting with bottles and pool cues but soon turned to knives and a rare gun.

None of them is more than heated blood.

The psychopath plans and is metered. How the crime is performed is like a fingerprint. The fingerprint of this killer was a small four-inch scar on Manny's lower spine where the surgeons removed the bullet but couldn't repair the spine.

Several minutes later, the three stood on the side of Monterey Highway looking across a small field at the rail siding. Manny grumped quietly. "We need to contact Southern Pacific and find out how long the car has been there."

"But this is a Northern Pacific and Burlington Northern line. Southern doesn't run up this far."

"That may be true, Paul, but look at the undercarriage. It's not made for snow country. It's a Southern." He looked up at his ex-partner. "I don't know if it makes any difference, but I want to know why it's here, how long it has been here, and when it was supposed to move next. I want all the information I can have on the car. I also want to know how often this siding is used. The ballast is all washed out, and I don't think the bed would hold much weight."

"I'll get them rolling on it. Anything else?"

"We need the officer and van for a few more hours. And I'd like copies of everything you find as well as all the photos out to the house this evening."

Paul smiled. "Is Stella home?"

"Call her and give her your request. If we need to pick anything up, like Sicilian sausage from Chiaramonte's, then she can get ahold of us through Dolly and the radio."

"I'll have it all at the house by dinner." He turned to leave and looked back. "I'll have the deputy bring the van over here to pick you up."

"Thanks, Paul. We'll see you for dinner. You can even bring a date. It'll give Stella someone to talk to who isn't talking about killing and blood."

The man waved his hand over his head as he walked across the field toward the rest of the circus. The troops had thinned out, but there would still be some kind of presence until they figured out how to move the railcar to an evidence barn.

"What do you think?" Hooker squatted and steadied himself by putting down his fingertips of his left hand.

"I think it's going to be a happy tummy dinner." Manny smiled at the young man.

They both knew Stella loved cooking extra special when there was a guest at the table, and the last guest had been Hooker's slave for two weeks. Squirt, was a young kid who saved Hooker's life a couple of months before, and who was having the fifth and hopefully, final operation this morning to remove some excessive scarring restricting the blood flow and use of his right arm.

"I was talking about this," Hooker pointed to the railcar and surrounds.

Manny pointed out across the fields. "I think they parked over there in the little clump of low trees. I think the killer did all the carrying. The other guy is just the watcher. I think he carried the vic all the way over here, and then I think the vic took a very long time to die, probably hours. This asshole has expanded, and he had a lot to say this time." He thought, and then looked over at Hooker as they saw the van arriving onto the highway. "And I think we need to go see your girlfriend."

"Uncle Willie or Dolly?"

"Both."

"I take it we're going up to William's first?" The deputy didn't even look in the mirror. His turn indicator started to click.

Hooker sunk back into the seat, and zombie rolled his head into the window. "Of course, you know Uncle Willie." Manny shot him a commiserating grin. Just when he thought Hooker had figured out how everyone in law enforcement knew everyone else, he made these little surprise discoveries.

The deputy looked in the mirror at the tow truck driver sidelined by a handful of dimes delivered by a twelve-gauge shotgun a few months before. "You know the 1952 Hudson Hornet over in the far corner under the green tarp? It's mine. I'm still looking for a Lincoln flathead sixteen to jam up to the fluid drive and pozzie rear end." He took the right turn to head up the hill to the house connected to the oversized barn of the garage he was talking about, and he glanced back at Manny. "But until then—William and Maddie are finished racing the convertible Dart GT that was yours—so I'm thinking of buying it."

"What the hell are you going to do with a nine-second car?"

"We thought we could get her down into the low eights... but instead, we're going to pull the 340 Hemi and stick a 318 in her, so I have a nice dependable daily runner." They didn't have to see his face to know he had a love-struck smile on his face.

Manny looked at Hooker. "I thought Willie didn't have any kids."

Hooker laughed. "It looks like Willie has been duping us all these years." As they pulled into the driveway, the subject of their derision strolled out into the sun in all of his glory. Hooker groaned.

His uncle's florid blue granny dress had a large burn hole at thigh height. It was high enough to see Willie was taking the day commando. The dress stopped short of the battered engineer boots with the bands of silver Concho hearts over the instep. The welding helmet was thrown up over his head, which pulled the skin on his face and accentuated the jagged scar started under the right side of his jaw and ripped a pinkish-white highway across the throat and up the side of his face in front of his left ear. The scar with its final star pattern was a souvenir of the meat hook from which he had been suspended for three days, before it finally ripped across his throat, tore through his shattered jawbone, and out of his face.

Ten minutes later, he had killed seven of his Viet Cong jailers, and then led and carried six other men through the jungle to freedom, a hundred and forty kilometers and seventeen days later.

Willie removed his large leather welding gloves and opened the side door. The deputy came around to help get Manny out of the van.

"Jeez, Willie, this one has got to be the ugliest dress you have ever dragged home." Hooker half covered his face in mock terror.

The deputy smiled and leaned in toward Willie and stage whispered, "He hasn't seen the pink and lavender one, has he?" Willie started laughing and slapped the man on the chest with the gloves.

"Ssstop!" he lisped.

Hooker knew Willie only let his Nancy come out and dance when he was among trusted friends and those he considered family. Hooker groaned more and held his head as he lay forward onto Manny's shoulder. "Oh, Gawd, Manny, the kid actually *is* his."

Manny sat stoically. He let Hooker play, but he had things more serious on his mind.

Willie sobered and looked at the detective. "You're coming from the railcar?"

Manny nodded.

"Chet stopped by about an hour ago. He's not officially back to work, but he was down there, too. They hadn't cleared the car yet. How bad was it?"

"He got worse." Manny thought about it. "They are bringing duplicate photo sets of everything out to the house tonight. Paul is coming over for dinner. Why don't you join us unless you have a date?"

"Hank and I were just going to grill some roadkill here, but I can bring him and give Stella someone to talk to about cooking."

Manny hiccupped a laugh. "Oh, that's even better. She's getting the outside kitchen ready for the annual canning. I'm sure it's about time Hank receives the final indoctrination into the perverse side of this family."

They both smiled as Hooker buried his face in his left hand. The cast on his right kept his dominant hand away from his face.

"Perfect. Hanky can schlep canning stuff with the best of them." Willie turned toward his ward who was eyeing the large burn hole on the dress. "Do you need anything from your room, Hooker?"

"Willie, I spend my days barefoot in jeans and a T-shirt. But if there are any jeans here near wearing out, I could cut them down for shorts." He put his hand along his face and turned it to hide the dress.

The three laughed at the slapstick humor as the deputy joined in.

Willie hung his hand on his now out-thrust hip. "Don't knock the coolness of a chintz dress, young man." His Nancy was in full steam.

The other three men groaned and then laughed.

Hooker shot back. "But those boots and gloves offset any advantage you get from the dress."

Willie lifted the hem of his dress. "Not this advantage."

Manny just looked at the deputy with a pleading look. The deputy sprang into action and rounded the van. Climbing in, he acknowledged with a train conductor's voice. "All aboard! Next stop, Dolly's Dispatch."

The van nosed around and out of the giant driveway. Halfway down the hill, the deputy broke the silence. "If I may ask, why does he wear those dresses? He only destroys them with the welding and all."

Hooker chuffed with a short laugh. "It's economics. He buys them by the bagful at the Goodwill. They would cost him fifty cents each, but by the bag, they cost about a quarter. A pair of bib overalls, if you can find them, would run upward of two or three bucks. So, its dresses by the bagful or go pay retail for work pants. The pants wouldn't last as long as a shopping bag of dresses, and he doesn't buy them by the shopping bag—he uses the thirty-gallon trash bags."

"Hmm, I'll have to remember that."

Hooker and Manny both buried their faces in their hands. *He really must be Willie's love child.*

"Oh, I didn't mean for me. I meant for when I need to bribe him, I should make a run-through the Goodwill first." He rolled the steering wheel right and eased around the ramp onto the freeway. "Do you know what size he wears?"

Hooker growled back. "Anyone at Goodwill can tell you. They probably set those ugly dresses aside for him. Nobody else would be caught dead in something so visually abusive."

The rest of the drive was thankfully in silence.

Dispatch was a gray cinderblock building hunkered down in the corner of a large parking lot. As per normal, there were only three cars in the lot. But Hooker had seen many New Year's mornings when the overflow of tow trucks, plumbing trucks, security vans, and cop cars turned the quiet side street into a parking lot.

As they got Manny settled in his chair and started toward the steel-plated door, it swung open. A quarter ton of Florida orange muumuu over bare feet walked out into the sunshine. Dolly lifted a large arm and shielded her eyes from the painful light.

"Who the hell are you two?"

Hooker took the lead and walked into the large hug and buried his nose down into the woman's fat neck. "Hello, sweetie. Miss me?"

Her right arm came up and trapped his head hard into her neck as she giggled. "Don't you dare tickle my neck like you do your fat girlfriends, you little pervert, just give Mama a hug. And don't talk. It will ruin the fantasy of you being a perfect child." They laughed together. Dolly was the surrogate mother for many young tow truck drivers who had no one else to care about them. Three weeks after Willie had caught Hooker trying to hotwire his car, she had taken over the duty of putting him to work. He was only fourteen but lied and had a bad fake driver's license saying he was twenty. She found him a better-looking license and a job jump-starting cars and running parts for a tow company. He had now been connected to them for over ten years. He let go of her so she could hug her brother-in-law.

She didn't have to say a word as she swooped down on the man in the wheelchair.

After a minute, Manny told her, "In nineteen states, this would be seen as a mugging. In two others, it would be seen as rape. In Arkansas, they would just call it incest, and it would all be good. But you would have to explain things to your sister."

Dolly backed her shaking jello into the shade of the door. "Get in here. I'm not going to stand out here in this heat." She looked out at the deputy. "Steven, are you coming in or are you standing out there like a stupid or crazed dog?"

"Coming, ma'am."

"Coffee is fresh, just made it last night."

The deputy doubled his walk. "Perfect, ma'am."

She shot him a stern eye for his obvious sucking up.

The three sat near Dolly's desk. Dolly held court from her custom oversized welded steel office executive chair that had four pneumatic rams instead of the usual single one that was only rated for two-hundred pounds. Her bare feet were crossed on the desk near The Stick.

"Chet stopped by earlier."

Manny sipped on his coffee. "He gets around for a guy who is supposed to be recovering from a gunshot wound."

She looked at Hooker, who was paying close attention to the coffee in his mug. "Hmm, yes—seems to be going around lately."

She looked back at Manny. "How's my sister doing with all this extra work?" She referred to taking care of Hooker while he too recovered from gunshot wounds on top of tending to Manny.

Manny ignored the jab. "Oh, the canning is coming along just fine. We have a new tent that will be about sixty feet long by the same twenty. It should give plenty of shade when you come to peel potatoes. And with the Squirt out of the way, she's almost bored and looking for something to do."

She gave him a deadpan look before her head fell back into the zombie-head family response to dumb questions or statements.

The deputy giggled. Hooker looked over, and the word *Nancy* drifted through his head.

Manny braced his forearms on the arms of the chair and rocked forward to adjust the pressure on his rear end. To those who knew him, it was also his way of clearing his throat.

"Willie is coming over for dinner, along with Paul. I think it would be good to tap into Willie's Naval Intelligence thinking. With all that time he spent in the jungles of Vietnam, I think he might have a better take on some of this aboriginal mindset. Maybe we can finally get a grasp on all this message shit the asshole is writing."

Dolly, ignoring Manny's language and venting, snapped her fingers and pointed to Hooker. "That reminds me, Father Damian has a message for you. Said that any night you could make it up for dinner at your usual time, let Candy know. Oh, and don't bring cigarettes, he's quitting."

"Maybe I can get up there tonight after we go over this stuff. If Stella won't loan me the Caddie, she can schlep me. She wants to meet Squirt's big sister, anyway. I think she's working on trying to get Candy a slot at the college for nursing school."

Dolly made her living listening to people and more of how they said things than what they said. She was listening to the tension in Hooker's voice.

"How long before you have your girlfriend back?" She was referring to the eleven tons of steel that were Hooker's tow truck.

Hooker sunk into his seat. She had scored a direct bull's-eye.

"Willie said that he couldn't even get three of the pistons out of the case because they were seized in there so bad. He'll have to drill and shatter them. The case will have to be sleeved to a larger bore, which means that we have to figure the stroke to balance her out. The pistons may have to be custom cast, and that would take until fall. So all told, I would say Mae West might be a Christmas present all over again. He was referring to the Christmas that they had found her in Oregon, and then the next Christmas when she became a tow truck. But to get me back on the road, Don is going to put me in a one-ton and have me just run service calls until the doc says I can pull regular duty."

Dolly looked at Manny with the same look that Manny knew all too well from his wife. The look that said *I lay this at your feet. You're the man. It is all your fault.*

Manny put up his hands. "I have nothing to do with this. Stella works his physical therapy, and what she says, goes in the house. You know that, I know that, and he knows that. Hell, even Box knows that... but he just ignores it. And he is the only male who can get away with it, too."

Dolly didn't have to say not to be trash-talking about her favorite fur chest warmer. She was the only person who could pick Hooker's cat up other than Hooker, and even Hooker avoided that kind of contact as much as possible. He had seen what the burly warrior cat could do to a human face or hand.

Hooker calmed the tension. "The truck he has is an automatic. I could drive it with one hand. So even with a cast, I can run service calls. Dolly, trust me. I won't lie to you or Stella if I am in pain. I am not a stupid kid... most of the time. I'll take it easy. I'm in for the long haul here, and I need my body to be right as much as I need Mae's engine to be right."

She watched him for a minute as she sipped her coffee. She looked at her coffee and then she looked over at the two women wrangling with the phone lines. Dispatch, being the answering service for most of the businesses in the San Jose area, was also the dispatch for all of the alarm companies, and most of the plumbers and electricians. They were the only dispatch for all of the independent tow companies, and after midnight, the only dispatch for the auto clubs, sheriff, highway patrol, and ambulance. Most calls for the city police and fire department went through the city dispatcher but could switch over after the ten o'clock shift change if they needed it.

"Karen, is this coffee the new beans I ordered in from San Diego?"

"Yes, ma'am, they are."

"Don't let me do that again. There is absolutely no kick in this coffee at all. I'm falling asleep just sitting here listening to Hooker drone on about his girlfriend."

The two women at the switchboard looked at each other and smiled. "Lucky you, we think it would be yummy to fall asleep with Hooker." They giggled like schoolgirls.

Dolly ground her head around and glared at Hooker.

He raised his hands and cast. "Hey, you saw. I didn't get anywhere near them, much less nuzzle their necks."

"You three are incorrigible." She looked back at the two giggling girls. "Dina, you should be ashamed of yourself. You're newly married and pregnant to boot. Karen... Karen, you're just being nasty. Wait until I get home tomorrow and tell your father."

It had been a running joke for many years that she looked like Dolly's husband even though he could never have kids. However, the family that was made was every bit as strong as the family that was born. Only Dolly and Hooker knew that if Dolly passed away, Karen would own dispatch with Hooker as a partner. Hooker knew that he never wanted Dolly to leave him four walls and no window. He'd rather have the grief and love she handed out in fair amounts.

"Well, we ought to let the young deputy get back to real work, and I'm sure it's getting close to time to set the table or take a nap." Manny stretched as he spoke.

Remembering, Dolly snapped her fingers. "Hooker, there is a box of Chiaramonte's Sicilian in the fridge. I had it towed down when Stella called. Mike had to come bring me some new information for the company, so I had him run by."

Hooker got the ten-pound box of sausage as Dolly rose to get hugs all around. Each person always got a hug and a *'stay safe'* when they walked out the steel-plated door that had five bullets still stuck in it. It was a rough neighborhood, and Dolly knew, sometimes an even rougher city.

As she let Hooker go, she reminded him to call Candy and to go meet with Father Damian some night around midnight soon.

4

Coffee was fresh and steaming in the office. The three older detectives and their protégé were pinning up photos on the large movable boards.

Paul explained the larger crime scene board and the eight-by-ten photos. "We had these re-cropped to the most salient information. The four upper rows are the corresponding symbols starting with the first known kill site and working down to last night along the bottom.

"In these file boxes are the close-ups of each overview in case they can help. Today they shot the six large areas, which you see here, and then sectioned them off into twenty-four sections each. Those sections are in each of these six binders and are marked to coordinate to each of the overview shots.

"There is still no identity to any of the victims except for the second, which was the college girl hitchhiking down the coast."

"Melody Richards," Manny offered.

"Thank you." Paul moved to the other board. "This is what we have so far on this one.

"We think they got there sometime around midnight. By the dried blood on the hands and legs, we figure about twelve-thirty when he nailed the victim up to the wall.

"The gunshot wound was consistent to a twenty-two short, the same as you got in your back. The bullet was too deformed to pull barrel marks, which is consistent with all four, or five, counting Manny. The perp used a chunk of the vic's shirt to stop the blood flow and taped it on with electrical tape, consistent with the others. The lab is trying to see if there are any prints, but unless he got sloppy this time..." He looked at Manny, who was slowly shaking his head.

"After what you said today, we went back over the first three and did find a bird bone in the general cataloging of items in the kill zone. But because nobody gave it any credence, it was held into evidence as 'other.' But it was consistent with the one you picked up and had identified. I also noticed in the first case, they didn't even figure out the bloody bunch of the vic's hair was also the paintbrush."

Willie had been staring at the photos of the print castings. "What do we know about the barefoot prints?"

"This was the first time we had soil, so we got lucky on the lookout. The print indicates fine bones, and the weight to be under a hundred pounds. The shoe size would be about a men's size six. However, we really don't know if it is a small man or woman's print. We did determine, with the flattening of the arch there was no hesitation on walking on either the sand or stubble—they are always barefooted."

"Because of the desensitization of the footpad... as well as sandals being an unnecessary expense," responded Willie with a nod. "We saw a lot of it in Nam."

Hooker mused, almost to himself, "It would be consistent with any of the Mouse's tribe."

Manny nodded and looked back at Paul. "What did they find in the tree line over on Santa Teresa?"

"Good call there. We have tire tracks, the boots on what we assume was the driver side, and the barefoot was the passenger. The boots made for grinding of small stones to create trace grind marks, but there were none on the passenger side. There was a weight load shift, resulting in grind marks at what we believe was the trunk. After, we found they led off into the field. The field is being guarded tonight, and forensics will start working it with a group search tomorrow to see if there is anything else we can find."

"What about the tire tread?" Hooker leaned forward.

"Firestone 575-16 series, consistent with every small Ford, Dodge, Mercury, Chevy you can think of from 1962 forward, they all used this tire. It was the number two best-selling tire in America for over the last decade or more. Sorry, but we have a dry well there unless we find the car and match some unique tread wear."

"So the only thing new is we now know the raven bone is a part of the package." Manny leaned back and stretched.

Paul pointed at him, and then at the footprint castings as he sat down on the corner of Manny's desk. "And we know we have a lookout."

"And the cowboy boot prints are consistent?"

"They may be new boots or soles, but same make and model, and by the footprint, we don't think his weight has changed by more than maybe ten pounds heavier." Paul finished his coffee.

Willie frowned. "Why not a woman? Do you have evidence the killer is male?"

Paul's eyebrows rose as he set the mug on the desk. "Good point. It's the nature of the kill making us assume it's a male. In the Navy, you didn't have to deal with this kind of stuff, so this psychological profiling may sound a little out there, but it bears up.

"In the rare instances of a serial killer being female, they don't do it up-close and personal. They will use either a gun or something that doesn't make a mess, like poison. Also, female serial killers are about the kill. It's almost always a sexual thing, and they get a release. With guys, it is a very personal ritualistic thing."

The old Navy Seal snorted. "*Arsenic and Old Lace* syndrome."

"Exactly."

Willie nudged his chin toward Hooker. "So your explanation for the dime...?"

"The exception to the rule—it was an anomaly." Referring to the Dime Killer, Hooker continued with, "It was a shotgun but with overtones of personal and rituals."

Paul glanced at his watch. "This is all we have at this time, and if there are no other thoughts, I have an early meeting with probably the mayor and some other bite-in-the-ass in the early morning, if I don't have reporters camped out on my doorstep."

Manny hunched on his elbows translateing into a slight hop in his chair. It was more of him shifting mental gears than any kind of adjustment in his seating. "No, we're good here, Paul. Thanks for all of the information and the briefing. If anything comes in, give me a call, and you know what time dinner is."

Hooker sat quietly. Something was just too familiar, but he couldn't put his finger on it... just yet.

"Hooker... have you got something, son?"

Hooker looked up at the commissioner as if he had just suddenly materialized. "Wha—? Uh, no... Just thinking."

Paul stuck his hand out. "Dolly can find me night or day. Since my Patricia passed, she has become my guardian angel." He sighed. Two years since he had lost his wife to cancer and the pain was still fresh. "If you get a thought, just give a holler... night or day. It doesn't really matter anymore. I don't really sleep much these days."

As the detective collective invaded the kitchen area, they were greeted by two grown children powdered with flour. The entire large square island was taken up with making food. More specifically—exotic cultural confections.

A very happy, but slightly embarrassed Hank, smiled sheepishly. "Hello, boys."

Willie eyed his partner, whom he had never seen wear anything more feminine than a white shirt but was now down to his jeans and barefoot with a frilly pink apron covering his wife-beater undershirt. The apron might have gone without comment except it was the joke apron Manny had gotten for Stella as a housewarming. The large bold letters relayed the sentiment: *If you don't like my food, you can kiss my grits.*

Willie cleared his throat. "And which part exactly *is* your grits?"

Hank turned red as a barn. Stella interceded. "Don't you boys have some toys to play with? Hanky and I are making kugel, and if any of you plan to have any on Saturday for dinner… you will shut up and go away."

Stella had spoken.

Hooker turned to Willie as Paul squeezed Manny on the shoulder and slipped out the front door. "Willie, I need to go meet Father Damian at eleven, and if we go now, we can stop in and check on the Squirt."

Willie's right hand came up in a silent goodbye as he turned away from the force, he knew not even decades of being a tough Navy Seal could have prepared him for. He slapped Hooker lightly on the chest and pointed at his bare feet.

Hooker stopped by the door and tried on a pair of Stella's flip-flops. A wee small, but close enough, and he didn't want to spend another moment in the eye of Stella's storm. Manny was already beating a fast retreat to his office and the two doors, front and office, snicked shut at the same time.

Willie stopped halfway to the fountain dominating the center of the hacienda entry plaza. "Don't you want to bring Box?"

Hooker thought a moment about opening the front door, and then just stared at his uncle as he barked loudly. "Box. Go time." He smirked at Willie.

As they both turned to walk around the fountain and out the tall hand-hewn black walnut front gates, they could hear the SNAP-snap-snap of the plastic door on the other side of the house. Box had his own door but usually refused to use it for anything other than a necessity. Two things you never had to tell Box twice—*dinner* and *go time*. Of course, he was always ready to beat up another dog, too.

The large orange tabby was standing straight-legged on his small patch of grass between the driveway and the promenade walkway leading up to the front gates and entry into the traditional hacienda with its two-foot thick straw stucco walls. Hooker had never seen any other cat pee standing like a horse. Even dogs made arrangements, but it was as if Box was proud of what he could and was doing. Box was Box.

The cat scratch-kicked a couple of divots in the grass and looked to see what vehicle had replaced the giant tow truck.

Hooker opened the passenger door to the 1952 DeSoto convertible. It was the very same car Willie had caught him trying to steal over a decade before. Hooker wasn't sure if Willie held onto the car because he really loved it or it reminded him of where they had started. Either way was fine with Hooker; he had long gotten over the embarrassing story Willie loved to tell about finding Hooker hot-wiring the radio instead of the ignition. Hooker had come a long way. He now stood at the door. "Box."

The cat seemed to shrug as if to say, *I guess this one will have to do.*

The late evening was a joy in the top-down roadster. Even Box was enjoying the wind as he stood on Hooker's lap with his front paws on the windowsill and his face in the breeze. His one good eye was closed, but Hooker and Willie could tell the unique cat was in heaven with new smells coming at him at forty miles an hour.

The large old Detroit V8 engine rumbled and echoed in all three hearts. Hooker looked across the lights of the valley. He missed the much higher perch and deeper rumble of his true love, the eleven tons of his Mae West.

The 1959 Marmon truck was Hooker's first vehicle and first major love. He and Willie had rebuilt her up from scratch, so to speak. They had torn the old truck down to just the frame and built from there. The front nose of her was the largest ever made commercially. The engine was almost double the size and power of any other big rig in the San Francisco Bay Area. She was the fastest tow truck in five counties. Hooker floated her over the 120mph mark on a regular basis. With Hooker at the wheel, she ruled the night.

5

The halls of Good Samaritan Hospital were clear of the usual flurry of family members coming and going, soothing or irritating the patients, and testing the patience of the nursing staff who were hoping to get their charges settled down to sleep through the night. The third floor was almost all post-op recovery and was usually a mausoleum by eight at night.

The two men walked quietly down the linoleum hall looking into dimly lit rooms with monitors blinking or the bluish-gray wash of color from televisions hung from the ceilings. The large shopping bag hung heavily from Hooker's left hand. The occasional movement in the paper bag was lost in the gait of his injured leg.

The doorway was lit, and the two entered single file. The nurse was holding the young man's wrist, taking his pulse. Her back was to the door. She stiffened at the sound of the hushed voices.

"I hope this means he still has a pulse."

"He looks like something even Box wouldn't chew on."

"Do you think he's still in a coma?"

"Was he before?"

"Well, he was stupid enough to dive in the way of a buck sixty in change."

"He must have been hanging out with you."

"Are you saying I'm brain dead?"

"Well, you are nothing more than a two-bit survivor of the same killer."

"You do know he has the same amount of change still stuck in him, don't you?"

"Are you calling him a two-bit zombie, also?"

A low moan came from the bed. The nurse was both amused and annoyed at the two characters for disturbing her patient. "Nurse, can I get a better room with intelligent conversation?"

Hooker laughed. "Squirt, you better stay here. Your nurse is the best looking one on the whole floor. But if you want us to leave you two alone, we can close the door and go talk to Helga, the night duty nurse, who has been known to twirl rectal thermometers in ice water before administering them."

The young nurse opened her mouth in shock. "She does not. I will have you know his night nurse is kind and caring."

"Must be you," Willie was warming up to the young lady. He wasn't attracted, but he did have a knack for drawing the best out of people.

"Well, um, yes. Yes, it is." She blushed slightly.

The smooth talker moved in close to her. Draping a gentle avuncular arm around her shoulder, he led her to the door.

"Well, we are glad you will be taking care of our young friend tonight after we are done with him. He will probably need a nice long sponge bath, as well as a very long special massage." He winked at her and smiled his winning smile. "But first, so you don't lose your job, and we accomplish what we need to do to the young man, you need to go find something else to do."

She turned and looked over Willie's shoulder as Hooker opened the top of the bag as a large orange missile ejected from it. "Is that a..."

Willie turned her out the door as he swung it shut. "Goodbye."

The cat stalked up the young man's chest as he sniffed around and between the hospital smells for a hint of his young friend. Only Hooker and Dolly had ever been allowed the privilege of touching him—until this scrawny kid walked into Hooker's life, and the picky cat had added him to his social circle.

"Hello, Box," the voice groaned from the large white ball of a bandage wrap. "Good to see your mangy butt—or is this your face?"

The cat stood on top of his chest and touched his nose to what should have been a human nose but was just an opening in the gauze. Box took in a long breath. Somewhere between the conflicting acrid and sweet odors of medical pollution, he found the familiar scent of his young man Johnny —who had become known as the Squirt, shorthand name cops usually hang on any new guy. The cat relaxed and lay down on his chest and began to purr his signature uneven rumble.

Hooker looked at Willie and smiled. All was right with the world.

The young man moved his one un-bandaged hand onto the cat and was soon asleep. The two older men sat quietly soaking in the tableau of their friend and the cat. They also needed the calming coming from such a strange yet familiar place.

A while later, the light from the hall split the gloom of the room as the young nurse silently slipped in, and upon seeing the cat, closed the door.

Willie leaned his head back and saw the concern on her face. "We're sorry, but he was uncooperative, and we had to knock him out."

At first, she looked shocked, and then she realized Willie was joking. "It looks like you did a good job of it. Why... he looks almost... um... catatonic."

Hooker groaned. "Oh, you went just a bit too fur."

Willie choked, and then offered, "I had to paws and think about that."

Hooker rose, putting an end to the *punishment*. "Seriously, we would leave the mange bucket here all night, but you will probably have to give the kid some more drugs later, and Box wouldn't let you near him. But for now," he looked at the drool coming from the kid, "I think he's good for a few hours."

He held the bag open for Box, who lay ignoring him. "Box, come on. We've been busted, so it's go time."

The cat jumped off the bed, grudgingly crawling into the bag, which Hooker picked up and carried. Turning back to the nurse, he shrugged. "It's a medicinal cat."

The two men walked down the hall. They had not gone far before the giggles settled in. The wiggle in the bag didn't help. The cat in the bag routine just barely made it to the elevator.

Box may have had only one eye and one ear, but his deadly claws were all intact. The bottom of the bag hung in loose shreds as the doors of the elevator closed on the three standing males.

Willie giggled. "Left him catatonic…"

6

The two priests sat uncharacteristically at the last table in the front window. Father Damian's usual table was in the back room. It was a quiet corner where he sought refuge from the daily noise. In addition, it was where the street urchins and crustaceans who washed along the great way of Winchester Boulevard knew they could find an open ear and a kind word. Some nights he heard more confessions in his middle-of-the-night booth than he did all week in the confessional.

The new location was Father Damian's choice for two reasons. The first was to create more seating, the restaurant had removed the four large booths and replaced them with five tables. This provided Damian easy wheelchair access by simply having a chair removed.

The second reason was he could see out the window and view most of the parking lot, an important aspect this night.

Father McBride, the old man at the watch, leaned back in his chair.

"Long day at the hospital, Father?" Damian knew the sun was barely up when Father McBride started his self-appointed rounds at the Valley Medical Center, the catch-all for the county derelicts and those who could pay very little or nothing at all.

"Aye, and not a good day, as it were." The balding man slumped into his chair. "We lost another of our flock this morning. I think it was one of the lads who occasioned his way in here. It doesn't feel cold, but sometimes when they lay on the concrete, it sucks the heat and life right out of them." He closed his eyes as he shook his head in denial. The heart-wrenching decades had taken a toll on the man, but even well past retirement age, he refused to stop. The younger priest prayed that one day, he too would find such strength in his faith.

The low rumble of a deep, powerful engine caught the older man's attention, and his eyes opened as he saw the large chrome front end of the DeSoto as it nosed into the driveway. He sat up for a better look. "Now, here is a real car."

The scars on the younger priest's face crinkled as he saw who was in the passenger seat. "It looks as if our young friend Hooker has secured the services of a chauffeur."

The man whose business it was to know or find out who people were, drew his smile up tight on one side. "I believe, my friend, this is the young man's adopted uncle. You two have a little history in common. You were Ranger, and he was Navy Seal. He also served in Korea, and then in the early years of Vietnam, he was captured and held captive for almost a year before escaping.

"I'm sure he talks just as freely about his service experience as you do. So I would say if you want him to talk at all, stick to what he really loves."

"And that would be...?"

"Why, Hooker or cars. Unless you are inclined toward his life's sexual nature or his predilection for..."

"Hooker, so good to see you."

"Father Damian, Father McBride, this is my uncle, William Knight."

Willie leaned forward with his right hand. "Please, call me Willie." He shook with McBride and turned to the younger priest.

Father Damian stretched out his left hand and right hook from his body and wheelchair. "Excuse me if I don't stand."

Willie said nothing. His right hand remained extended over the chair. His eyes and smile never wavered. "Hooker tells me you were also Special Forces."

The priest examined the large 'J' scar covering the man's throat and up the side of his face. Slowly, Damian moved his right hook into the hold, and they shook. "Father McBride was just giving me the sit-rep briefing on you, too." They both smiled. Everything was in the open now, and any pissing on the back of the barn was unnecessary.

Hooker passed around the back of the younger priest and pulled out the chair next to the window. Father McBride cleared his throat and looked behind Hooker. Willie had sat down but leaped to his feet.

Hooker froze and then rolled his eyes. "I'm in trouble, aren't I?"

The soft voice behind him was pure warm biscuits and honey. "Only if you don't turn around and give me a hug, you big goofball."

He turned, and the scrawny, freckled waitress flowed into his arms. They stood silently. Neither knew what to say in front of the two priests or Uncle Willie. Finally, they separated enough for Hooker to give her a quick kiss before turning a tiny bit red. "I missed you."

"Well, mister, I've been right here. First, you get my brother shot up, and then you two just lay around like two big fuzz balls of gauze for months. What is a girl to think?" She gently dug her finger into what she hoped were ribs more ticklish than painful. Hooker winced and squirmed anyway. "If it wasn't for running into Willie and Hank occasionally, when I sat and watched you two drool into your bandages, I would have never been entertained."

She released Hooker and stepped back around the table. "Hello, Willie." She folded into his arms as well, and when she kissed him on the cheek, he didn't blush. "How is Hank?"

"Hank is a little sassy, but I try to keep him in line. I'll tell him you asked for him. He would have come, but Stella seduced the young boy away, and they're cooking as we speak. It was something disgusting with sugar, cinnamon, dough, and several other things to ruin a girl's figure."

"I'm sure you will survive."

Willie leaned back toward Hooker, and in a staged whisper shared, "Oh, and I forgot to tell you—don't ever play gin with her for real money. She's better than Hankie."

As Willie took his seat, Candy drew a finger gun bead at Father McBride. "Coffee and cherry pie…." Placing her hand on Damian's shoulder, "Coffee and Dutch apple. Moreover, Willie, what can I get for you? I already have Hooker's water and stale bread."

"I'm an apple man, Candy, and I guess I can indulge in one cup of black."

"Great, I will leave you gentlemen to your man talk stuff. Just remember—keep it clean. Hooker is still a virgin." She spun on one heel and with great drama, huffed off like a steam engine.

Willie laughed at her playful, dramatic movements. "Such a refreshing child!"

The other three chuckled. Sometimes it took a fresh set of eyes to remind you what it is you enjoy about something. Hooker smiled as he watched Candy's ponytail flip as she walked. The warmth in his chest moved north.

As the coffee flowed and drained away, and the dishes of food became just dishes ready for a wash, the conversation was light.

"What time do you have, Hooker?" Father Damian leaned forward.

Hooker looked at his watch. "11:48."

Damian's eyes were focused just slightly over Father McBride's shoulder. "Hmm, interesting. A little early, but drawn in."

"What's early?"

Damian studied the young man's face. He hadn't really gotten to know him before, but could now see under the young face, the eyes and soul belonged to someone twice or three times his age. Softly, he confided, "Why, the reason you are here tonight, your important message." Looking out the window at Willie's parked convertible, he lowered his voice as it drifted off. "But let's give them a few minutes alone."

Hooker followed the priest's gaze. At first, he only saw the large blue car. As he looked closer, he noticed there was a large orange cat lying on the tan boot covering the folded down top. A second, careful look found the small whirlwind of dust and scraps of paper and street flotsam. This whirlwind wasn't moving with the wind. This one moved by its own volition. This bit of the night air and grit was named Peter, a man whose previous assistance had helped to save Hooker's life.

Peter was one of the lost people who floated in the world between reality and one they felt more comfortable in because they made it up. A former engineer of some sort, but now just a shattered soul. Most days, he found his way by touchstones, such as a midnight conversation with Hooker, and a bummed cigarette he had later passed to Father Damian.

Hooker watched the smudge in the air and his cat who could fillet a hand in one swipe. "What is Peter doing?"

Willie turned and watched the scene for a moment. "My dear boy, it would appear your feline juggernaut is becoming a true slut."

"Maybe we should go talk to him before there is trouble." Damian pushed back from the table and turned his chair. He pushed out toward the large glass doors.

Slowly opening the doors, Damian came out first. In a soft, reassuring voice, he attempted to calm the man from the streets. "Hello, Peter."

The standing swirl of dust and detritus turned his head. His hand continued to rub the ear and neck of the large purring cat. "He... hello... fa... fa... fa... Damian."

"Peter?"

"H... H... Ho... Hook... Hooker?"

"How are you, Peter?" The two carefully approached the midnight swirl of dust around the side of the car.

"G... Go... Good Ho... Hooker." The man continued to pet Box, who continued to purr loudly.

"You seem to like my cat. And more importantly, Peter, he seems to like you."

"Th... This... is a n... ni... nice cat." The man spoke as he continued stroking the cat. "Thi... this is... yo... your cat... H... Hooker?"

"Yes, Peter. He is my partner. His name is Box."

The man thought but didn't laugh. "B... Box... Box is a... v... very nice n... name. He is a v... very n... nice cat."

The three men watched the man's hand pet and scratch, rub, and smooth the cat's one ear and neck.

"H... Hoo... Hooker?"

"Peter?"

"Wha... wha... where... is y... your truck?"

"It's broken right now. It's getting fixed."

"L... li... like... like your arm?"

Hooker raised and looked at the cast. "Yes, Peter, like my arm."

"I... I... I'm so... I'm sorry you got shot."

Hooker looked at Damian. Damian just shrugged.

Hooker just had to accept things and information were passed on the network of the streets.

"Peter?"

"H... Ho... Hook... Hooker?" "Did you have a message for me?"

"H... Ho... Yes."

Hooker was used to the tiny steps as well as the missteps it took with Peter to get a discussion handled. The shattered mind flowed like the wind he seemed to exist in.

"Did you want to give it to me?"

The man stopped petting Box. He seemed to just freeze for a long moment. Hooker suspected it was for more than a few of the man's heart beats.

With exact movements, the man stepped back a step and then side-stepped once, and then once more. Hooker could feel the counting.

Peter turned slightly and then began to hum, but with an open mouth. The hum rose and fell, and then he spoke. "The killer is known. The dog gets a bone, Secure the death, but only when the debt is paid. They meet they will, on Fox's Eve, be by the old mill when the moon hits the trees."

Hooker wasn't sure he had actually heard the man rhyme and not stumble or stutter. It was the most amazing thing he had ever heard Peter say in the ten years they had known each other.

"Who gave you this message, Peter?"

"Th... the... Mo... The... Mow... The Mouse."

Hooker thought. He knew his sister. Or at least what was left of her inside the tortured body of what she had become—the leader of a gang or tribe of mentally unstable and barely human entities. They lived in the dark shadows of the land or city. They floated up and down in the lower half of the San Francisco Bay Area. But they were trapped from roaming farther by their own fears of crossing over open water, even on a bridge. In the south, the strong permanent smell of garlic kept most of them at bayside or at least from traveling south.

"Peter, I know the Mouse. She won't send me a message of a rhyme unless she also sent a side message that would guarantee the rhyme was true. Did she send a side message along with it, Peter?"

The man thought by looking at the stars. Hooker didn't think that was where his memory box was, but he knew Peter was obsessive-compulsive, and he would only do things if there was a touchstone for his compulsions or at least made sense once he finished.

He pointed to the sky. "Th... the d... the dog."

Hooker tried to help. "The Dog Star, Peter?"

The man nodded. "Trav.... traveler... traveler cross d... dog." His left hand pointing to Sirius, the Dog Star, as his right pointed east and moved across the other finger to the west.

Hooker saw the ancient art of storytelling in the man's hands. He knew there was more trapped inside of Peter than would ever get out again. "When the bright traveler crosses the dog, what will happen, Peter? What did she say?"

The man fell in on himself. "Yel... Hoo... Hooker? Yell... yellow ha... yellow hair." The man was very agitated, but Hooker needed to know.

The calming voice of Father Damian interceded. "Peter? Peter?"

The dirt swirl rallied. "Fa... Fath... Damian?"

"Peter, you are among friends here. Even the cat likes you. You are safe." He let those last two bits of information transfer. Box even stood and leaned toward the inhabitant of the night air.

Damian relaxed in his chair. "Peter, the cat's fur feels good, soft, and safe. Box likes you. You have a new friend." The slow, softer pacing had calmed the man, and he even reached out and ran his one hand along Box's head and back.

Damian and Hooker waited out the man and the cat. Finally, Peter took the critical steps back to the side of the car, so there was more contact with the cat.

Damian's voice was as soft as a summer breeze in the treetops. "Peter?"

"Da... Damian?"

"Peter... can you tell us what yellow hair is?"

The man continued to pet the cat, but his right hand rose near his ear and then fluttered as it moved downwards.

Hooker watched. He whispered, "Long hair... it's a woman." That was the complete confirmation Hooker needed the message was from his sister. The sign language was how they had spoken to each other as kids. Partly real deaf sign language they had learned from the other kids, mostly what they made up. The fluttering open hand was Hooker's sign for his sister's long hair that he loved.

At one foster home, the woman was jealous of her long hair, so she cut it and shaved her head. That night, as they sat on the opposite ends of the bunk beds, Hooker signed to his crying sister. He would always love her and in his eyes, she would always have her beautiful hair.

Hooker looked at the priest in the wheelchair. The man nodded. "Peter? What will happen to the woman?"

Peter petted the cat one more time, and then with his other hand, he reached out slightly to his side, and spreading his fingers, as if taking in the night air, he closed the hand violently into a white-knuckled fist.

Then there was nothing in the air. Not even a hint he had ever been there.

Damian and Hooker stared at the empty air. The two were still thinking as Box jumped down and headed across the parking lot toward the small bit of lawn surrounding the restaurant.

The glass door sucked open, and the two older men walked out. Father McBride stopped to put on his black fedora. Willie softly asked as he approached, "Well?"

Hooker thought as he turned. He looked up from the pavement into his uncle's face. "I think I need some help from your old work."

"What kind of help?"

Hooker pointed into the air. Willie looked up.

Looking back at Hooker, he chuckled. "The sky covers a lot."

"I need to know what satellite we have visible to the naked eye which Peter could see, and when it will be crossing Sirius from our viewpoint."

The older man washed his hand over his silver brush cut. He smiled. "The answer may be closer to home than you think. Hanky is more than just a starry-eyed young lad. He even has a large telescope in his garage. He eats this stuff up like you chew up large engines." The man leaned his head and gave Hooker a serious stink-eye.

"Ohhh shhhhift into third gear." Hooker saved himself from another quarter in the swear jar. He knew Willie was talking about the blown-up engine in the giant tow truck.

Turning around to shake hands with Father McBride, Willie stuck his hand out. "Father, it was grand to meet you and your associate finally. I will see what we were talking about and get back to you by the end of the week. Then we will have you two out for a Sunday dinner." Turning, he took in Damian. Once again taking the man's hook, he secured their bond. "We will have plenty of times to chat and get to know each other. But for right now, I need to get this boy home to his bed, and hopefully, rescue my boy from the grips of a woman who cooks."

The DeSoto nosed out of the driveway and headed south as the two priests waved goodbye. Box settled down in the middle of the front seat between the two laps and closed his eyes as he began to purr. Willie reached over and turned on the radio. The tubes warmed up as the second refrain began about tumbleweeds tumbling in the blue shadows—the kind of music only Sweets played. With a glance at his watch, Hooker confirmed the disc jockey friend was indeed working his shift.

A powerful old car, great music, his cat next to him, and one of his favorite people at the wheel—Hooker's left hand found the cat's only ear and absently rubbed it gently between his knuckles. He put his chin up and into the wind as his right arm in the cast rested on the windowsill. The temperature was T-shirt under leather jacket weather—if he still had a leather jacket. For now, the faded yellow-tan work jacket would do. All was right with the world.

Except for the rhyme was now rolling over again and again in his head.

7

The big car barely changed its tone while climbing the hill. Hooker finally broke the silence. "How bad?"

Uncle Willie thought for a moment. "Remember those pieces of bread you put in the toaster back when you were fifteen? The ones when you thought the toaster wasn't working right, so you batted the flipper down a third time?"

Hooker rolled his eyes and looked over his shoulder back at the lights of San Jose twinkling in the distance. "The ones that caught fire and burnt the house down?"

The older man stuck his index finger into the air. "Just the kitchen, young man, it was just the kitchen. I had to use a cutting torch to get the rest of the house to go up."

"But kind of like the toast, huh?"

Willie nosed the large car into the driveway and brought it up to the gates. He set the brake and turned off the ignition. "Not just like the toast, but exactly like the toast."

"Toast."

"You may say so."

"So the block is..."

"Cracked." The man opened the door and stepped out. "In five or six places I can see with my naked eye, two I can stick my thumbnail in. There is one crack I stuck a dime in, just for you." The man's humor could run to the macabre. Hooker had destroyed the engine in an effort to stop the killer who had nearly dimed him to death.

"What are the chances of finding another Marmon engine these days?"

"Working on it." They walked through the outside gate to see the house lights were still very much active. "Oh, Gawd, help me wrestle Hanky to the ground and drag him out of here."

The two were still laughing as they entered the quiet house. "Hello?"

"We four are in here."

Willie looked at Hooker and mouthed the word *four?*

The two empty wine bottles on the island were an indication. The empty quart Ball jar with the characteristic reusable glass and wire top was the final giveaway. Stella and Hank were lounging in the sunroom, plowed.

As the two men entered, the two drunks chorused, "Hello, dear."

Willie looked at his cross-eyed partner as he leaned over to Hooker. "I'll bet they see more than two of each other."

Hooker giggled. He had never seen Stella so plowed. "Two bottles of wine, and then a quart of Maddie's moonshine.... It's amazing they are anything short of catatonic."

"What about Box?" Stella slurred.

"Nothing, dear." Hooker leaned into Willie. "I'll help you with Hank, and then I'm just going to throw a blanket over the other body."

Box entered through the cat door behind the large couch. Sensing all the activity was on the couch, he jumped up onto the back. He took one sniff and headed for the sanctuary of Hooker's bedroom.

The two men watched the orange commentator as he stalked from the room in stiff-legged disgust. Willie commented about him being a very smart cat, and then they laid-to on the aqueous body of Hank.

Hooker returned and locked the door. As he heard the big V-8 leave down the hill, he started turning off lights.

He stood in the archway of the sunroom. Stella was already snoring lightly. Hooker brought a light blanket and tucked her in on the couch.

"I don't think she has been tucked in since she was maybe twelve."

Hooker turned to find Manny sitting in the archway. "I'm sure she was looking after other people long before she was twelve."

The old detective pursed his lips as he thought. "I can't remember which, and I would be stupid to ask, but Dolly is three years older or three years younger?"

"Dolly is the older, and it's five years." Hooker leaned over and turned off the three lights on the wall switch. He looked at the surprised look on Manny's face. "You didn't hear that, and certainly not from me."

"I was just curious as to how you knew."

"I saw a photo of when Dolly was six and holding Stella. If I hadn't loved them both already, I would have fallen in love with them then. Of course, neither one resembles those two little girls in any way, shape, or personality."

"And you would probably get slapped on the back of the head for even mentioning the picture."

"Got that right, buster," slurred from the couch.

They both froze and then listened to the resumption of snoring before they moved into Manny's office.

"How does she do that?"

"Scary, isn't it?" Manny forced his eyes open wall-eyed and crazy. "She's been scaring me since we first met. The scarier thing is she will never mention it again. I don't know if she doesn't remember, or if she just holds onto it until it's the right time to bring it back up."

Hooker shook all over and closed the office door behind them.

He walked to the chalkboard and wrote:

"*THE KILLER IS KNOWN. The Dog gets a bone.*
  Secure the death, but only when the debt is paid.
  They meet they will, on Fox's Eve,
  Be by the old mill when the moon hits the trees."

AND THEN ON the other end, he wrote:

. . .

WHEN?

When the satellite crosses the Dog Star, Sirius?
What day?
A blonde woman will be killed.
Who? Where?

MANNY READ and then leaned back in his chair. "This is your sister."

Hooker nodded. "Even more interestingly, she fed me the message verbally through Peter."

"He's the night dweller you see at midnight and give a cigarette to?"

"The same."

"But I thought he was afraid of her? She beat him or terrorized him or something."

"I don't think she does any of it personally. I think it would be more of a psychological threat if it came directly from her. But it could have been one of her thugs. I think they are all afraid of her, anyone on the streets. I have no idea what the size of her tribe or army is, but I know it is more than a few dozen... um, bodies."

"So what do you think?"

Hooker sat in the large barrel chair. "Manny, I'm not really sure what to think." He leaned forward and laid out his right hand from the cast. "I've known Peter going on ten years now. I know when he tells me something, he has read... it's dull and flat. He is just reporting. But this was a rhyme. He recited it in a sing-song fashion. I could almost hear my sister's voice telling him the rhyme."

He pulled his hand and arm back in and chewed on his thumbnail. "And if she taught it to him, she would have had to go over it and over it many times."

Hooker's eyes were pointed at the desk, but his focus was a long way away and a long time ago.

Manny watched the young man think and then turned his chair to study the rhyme and questions.

"You capitalized the word 'Dog.'" He sat thinking about it.

"It was the way Peter sang it. It sounded like more of a name or title. I think it may mean something about the knee slave who is never more than a few feet from her knees. I seem to remember her calling him Dog. The whole tribe is about animals because they live like them."

Manny nodded. "Do you think she might be talking about the killing in the railcar?"

Hooker stopped chewing at his thumb. He rested it gently on the chair arm, thinking.

He looked up at Manny with a question on his face. "I don't know. For someone who is always on foot with no means of communication, she has always impressed me with how connected to everything she is. It is like every street bum and night dweller is her personal radio station."

"Do you think she is asking you to meet her on this Fox's Eve at some mill?"

"The meet and the mill, I am sure of. I've met her there before. It is one place she can be sure we're not being observed by her people. But what I don't get is this Fox's Eve. Huckleberries, we don't even have any fox in this area."

Manny chuckled to himself. It always amazed him how the young man caught himself from swearing.

Manny considered the lack of foxes. "We don't have any ravens either."

Hooker stood up and wrote on the board *Raven bone.*

"Put a question on that—*how close.*" Manny looked at the last line. "And I guess that would be moonrise?"

Hooker looked at the corner where the large bookshelves met the ceiling. "Moonset if it's in the next couple of weeks. The moon has been rising in the afternoon lately. And the trees are to the southwest of the mill so they would be moonset." He turned and made the notation followed by *when does the moon set.*

"So now we come to the satellite?"

Hooker chuckled as he collapsed back into the chair. "We'll get the information when Hank sobers up in the morning. Willie said he's an amateur astronomer who has a large telescope." He widened his eyes and made an 'O' of his mouth. The joke was lewd, crude, and exactly the kind Willie would make.

The two laughed.

"Have you ever seen your wife that plowed before?"

"Years ago." His lips sucked hard against his teeth. "When Paul and I worked the King and Story area. It was hard on her.

"When she kissed me goodbye in the mornings, she never knew if I would come home at night, or if she would have to go identify my body. When I made detective, it went in waves. She never had a drinking problem. It was more of a 'holding it all in' problem. Sometimes the dam or wall would crack, other times it would flat break." He leaned on his elbows and rocked his butt off the cushion. "After I got shot, and it looked like I would survive, and you decamped from Willie's, she got some relief. Her only fear was you might knock up some nice girl or something."

"But what about you?" Hooker asked.

Manny scrunched his face and farted. "I was out of the picture then. Get me up and dressed in a clean diaper. Feed me and keep me from drooling in my gruel. Stuff me in a corner for the day and put me back to bed with clean diapers. There was nothing to worry about anymore."

"So it was just me?"

"Kid, you were usually one glass of wine kind of worry. By the time you came to us, you were legal for driving. You hardly ever drank. You never smoked. Hell, I never asked—did you ever do drugs?"

"Is this the dad talk? Because if it is, then you're years too late." Hooker thought a moment. "So this nice girl she was worried about, did she have anyone in mind?" His smarmy grin turned into a full Hooker smile, the one he used to get out of most trouble, even with Dolly and Stella.

"Boy, if you have the balls, ask her. But you better do it before Squirt and his sister move in." He slapped his forehead. "Shoot, I forgot. Put 'Trace Van De Camp' on the corner where I'll see it in the morning."

"You're tracing people now?'

"No. His name is Trace. Used to work bunko on the north end, but now he does small construction. I've forgotten to call him these last couple of months—what with you in and out of the hospital and all."

"So you two are serious about Candy and Squirt?"

"Why not? Stella and I could never have kids. We didn't even know we wanted any. Now, after inheriting you and Willie, we think we did all right. So why not rear up two more? All it would be is a reach back with a hand up. It's not as if we have to grow them through diapers or pay for their school or anything. And in the end, we are rewarded with a daughter who is a nurse, and we finally get a son who's in the family business."

"What, wearing diapers?"

Manny had felt the jab coming. He already had his hand on his tennis ball he used to squeeze all day for muscle tone in his hands and arms. The fuzzy ball hit Hooker square in the forehead and resulted in fits of laughter from both men.

Box scratched on the door.

A still laughing Hooker pushed himself out of the chair and opened the door just as the phone rang.

It was 3:37 in the morning, hardly ever a good sign.

Manny picked up the receiver. "Hello?" His tone was terse and short. He listened and hung up.

Manny turned and looked at Hooker who hung in the doorway. "Go to bed. Danny is picking you up for breakfast."

8

Danny was a force of nature. At six foot five, he was built like the most frightening lineman the Forty-Niners could ever dream of having. Incongruously, he was also the most settled person one could be around. His movements were spare, and he was the kind of guy who had about seventy words a day in him. Get to number seventy, and you'll have to see him tomorrow for the rest of the sentence. Unless, of course, if he is met at the door by Stella. She could make the dead talk like they were at a Toastmaster's meeting.

The door flung open, and before he could take evasive action, he had a large soft chest shoved into his lower half where other people would have a belly. Danny had a six-pack made more from steel than aluminum, but it was susceptible to being made happy with a very full-bodied hug from Stella or his mother, Tilly.

"Danny, Danny, Danny. You get better looking every day. So much so, I just can hardly wait until next Sunday when you bring," Stella pushed back from him and gave him the eye, "your mama and Sweets out for dinner."

Danny stumbled through his memories. Not finding an appointment involving a Sunday dinner, he quickly made the notation. "Yes, ma'am. You can expect us about...?" he fished.

Stella flirted with a passing slap across his white shirt and chest. "Oh, shucks, Danny, any time after four is all good. I know Sweets sleeps until two or so. Now, come on in and have some coffee while you tell me how your mama is." She grabbed his hand before a *no, thank you* could escape his lips.

On seeing the giant black man in tow, Manny greeted him from his throne of the sunroom. "Danny!" he yelled with his arms raised.

Stella waved with her palm facing down. "Manny, I have told you a thousand times. The boys are black, and Danny's brother is blind. Neither one of them is deaf. But with your yelling at them, they will get there soon."

Danny leaned over and side hugged her as he kissed her on the top of the head. "I've got this, Mama." He strode into the sunroom.

Manny frowned with an ugly face. "Oh, lawd, you been losing weight?" Same old joke.

Danny pulled his custom-made shirt away from his sides near his belt line. "A little." Looking up with a worried face, he asked, "You don't think it looks good on me?"

The two laughed and shook hands. Old school respect—no thumb jig, none of the hand jive—just shook. It was the sign of the straight, simple respect the two had for each other—no fluff.

Danny sat at the other end of the couch where Manny was reclining. Hanging out on the couch was Manny's one vacation from the constant reminder he was not the man he used to be.

The couch was custom built for the sunroom when Manny still walked the halls of San Jose Police Department as a senior detective. On his days off, he enjoyed reading the paper in the sunroom with Stella. The length of the couch allowed both to stretch out reading or dozing.

They had designed the entire room around napping and enjoying the morning overlooking the Almaden Valley spread out below. The sunroom was the kingdom Manny and Stella took turns ruling, but on Sundays—it was a shared domain.

Manny sipped from his mug, the one with the gold detective badge molded onto it. Quietly, he asked about Danny's brother. "How is Sweets these days?"

Danny took the large mug from Stella as she sat on the ottoman to listen. He took a long sip and closed his eyes. The soft smile warmed and softened his face. It was the face of the man Stella liked best and held in her heart.

His life was of driver and bodyguard for his little brother. Blind since high school, his brother Sweets was now a night disc jockey for the local radio station. His popularity was legion. He could have had the more prestigious day shifts, but the night and the people who were awake and working then were what Sweets called *His People*. The simple fact was he knew he was allowed more leeway in the music he chose to play—even though it was against the company's programming.

Danny forced his eyes open and licked his thinned lips with just the tip of his tongue. Spare movements. "Sweets is doing okay. It's the end of a cycle, so he has to memorize the next eighty songs and their colors." He was referring to the new program routine where the owners of the company send out a new list every ninety days, and the DJ plays the songs by their color. Sweets had to have the list memorized because of his blindness. But he also played the music he wanted to play, a country-western sound, but more like a cowboy-who-likes-rock-and-roll kind of sound.

"Do you help him with that?"

"Not for the last few cycles. The East Coast finally got their heads around Sweets being blind, so they sent the list in braille. Mama helps him with the colors. The idiots still stick the color dot next to a line of braille." He did a fair imitation of Stella and Hooker's favorite physical commentary on all things dumb—he rolled his head with his tongue out in an almost perfect zombie roll. He ended up looking into the eyes of Box on the back of the couch. They held each other's stare.

Danny had never figured out whether Box was friend or foe. Box kept him guessing. Danny's calm disguised any fear, or maybe respect. The only thing he truly feared was his mother, Tilly Sweets, a force of nature to be reckoned with. Be on her good side, and life was glorious. Be on her bad side, and hell would be a nice vacation.

Box slowly closed his eye in measured disdain, walked along the couch back, and headed for the kitchen. He passed Hooker. Hooker only glanced at his partner and smirked. He knew there had been a face-off, and once again, the smaller fur man had won.

"Hey, big guy. I saw someone come in, but you've lost so much weight, I didn't realize it was you."

Danny stood and glared at the famous Hooker smile. In the last seven years, neither one had won this face-off. Once Hooker turned eighteen and was legal to tow, he stopped backing down from anything—tow or fight.

The two laughed and hugged. Danny growled like he hated it. It was a standing joke.

"We need to go. Mama put the quiche in as I was leaving."

Stella grabbed the man's tree of an arm. "What kind?"

"Don't worry. If it don't kill us, she'll bring you the recipe on Sunday."

Hooker called down the hall as they opened the front door. "Box, stay. Torment Stella and Manny." The cat stuck his head out of their bedroom door. The single eye was noncommittal, but the ear twitched. Hooker pointed his finger at him from the cast. "Behave. I'll be back soon and bring you some roadkill from Tilly."

Hooker had long admired the perfectly kept suicide-door Lincoln from the outside. The engine surged quietly as they headed down the hill of stupid to the Sweets home in Willow Glen. Hooker looked around the interior. His left hand stroked the soft leather.

Danny's eyes missed nothing—a small smile slid across his face. He settled back into his place in the world. This was his domain. Sweets may own the car—but Danny ruled it.

"Nice, huh?"

Hooker's eyebrows went up in appreciation. His hand did not hesitate its stroking of the smooth coolness. "It's softer than my jacket." He thought a moment and remembered what was left after the emergency medical units had finished cutting him out of it. He almost chuckled at the eight pieces of leather held together with surgical tape so he could wander around the hospital in his signature leather jacket—until Willie, in disgust, took it and burned it. "Was."

Danny frowned and then remembered, too. His right eye slowly closed as he made a mental note about birthdays. A few years before, his brother

Sweets and he had taken Hooker out to dinner and his first truly legal drink. The date was in October, and it would be in his past datebook.

Hooker leaned against the door and looked out the window listlessly. "What?"

Hooker looked back through the front glass. "I was thinking how nice the leather would feel in Mae when we get her rebuilt... then I was just thinking about Mae." He looked over at Danny. "Willie says I baked, raked, and snaked the engine. We have to find a new one."

The large man looked over at the depressed young white kid. He needed to be kicked in the ass and cheered up at the same time. Danny growled his throat clear. "Your scrawny bone for an ass would have torn up this sort of leather inside of a month. Probably wouldn't make it through the first week and a good fart. If you're going to have leather seats, you need some tougher stuff than what you get in your jackets. You'll need oil-tanned boot leather.

"Go over the hill to Santa Cruz to the tannery and pick up some yellow and blue leather so it looks right for that rig of yours. Any of the upholstery shops in town can reupholster the seats for you."

Hooker looked at the big man and laughed. "Danny?"

The man nosed the large car into the neat driveway with a perfect lawn on each side. He followed the short curve to the front door. "What?"

"Did someone adjust your word limit to a higher count?"

The big V8 burbled to silence. Danny stared at the front of the long hood. Slowly his head ground its way around to look at Hooker, who was on the verge of laughing. "Fuck you, fool." His imitation of an angry man made the response even more hilarious for Hooker.

Hooker rolled out his door, laughing. Danny steamed.

The front door opened as Danny made it there first. "What is going on out here?"

Danny squeezed past his mother. "Ain't talking," he grumped.

She turned to see her adopted white son. He was laughing so hard she knew it had to be something to do with her oldest and largest. Her fists found their usual resting place on her hips. "And what is so funny about you harassing your big brother?"

Hooker pulled himself together enough to stumble into her arms. He loved hugging her. There was no halfway or sort of with Tilly. When it came to hugs, she was in all the way. You knew when you were hugged by Tilly Sweets.

As they started to break apart, Hooker whispered in her ear. "Try to get him to say two more words today."

She knew her son. She rolled her eyes and then gave Hooker a 'Tilly' look as she slapped his chest with the hand towel. "Hooker, you leave your brother alone, or I will withhold dessert from everyone, including Sweets."

"Did I just hear my name being taken in vain?" The smooth-as-silk voice came from the front room.

Hooker closed the front door as Tilly headed back toward the kitchen.

"No, Sweets." Hooker strolled into the living room and was met in the middle by the slender man. There was a soft ticking sound coming from the man, and Hooker knew it was his sounding for objects around him, much like a bat. He put out his hand as he crossed into the room. "We were just commenting about being so late. We just knew you were probably starved and chewing on the furniture."

He took the outstretched hand and stepped in for a hug. If you hug one of the Sweets family—then you hug all three.

Tilly sang out from the kitchen. "Quiche."

None of the four was bashful around food. Amazingly, for the size of him, Danny ate little more than Sweets did. But the pie dish was showing nothing but the glass at the bottom. The biscuits had been the most amazing, as they were sourdough without any mistakes.

Hooker pushed back from his plate. He was too full to get up and clear his dishes just yet. Tilly followed suit, and Sweets still had a few bites to go. Danny got up unbidden. Without a word, he cleared all the dishes. He returned with a fresh carafe of coffee and poured his mother's cup full. He likewise filled Sweets and his, and then set the carafe in the middle and sat down.

Tilly gave him a hard look. He just sat with a deadpan look. "Danny, be a dear and see if there is any milk in the fridge?"

Danny looked at Hooker. He shook his head.

"Is that a *No*, there isn't any or no, I won't do what my dear sweet mother who carried me for nine and a half months, breastfed me until I was..."

Danny bolted up. He returned with the half-gallon of milk and placed it beside the only person he knew who used it, Hooker. He went into the living room, leaving the three alone to talk.

Sweets looked to a place just above Hooker's head. "Did I miss something?"

Hooker folded his napkin and placed it on the table. He confessed contritely, "I asked him if someone had upped his word allowance. He was unusually chatty. I guess he got mad." He started to get up.

Sweets reached out to the air near Hooker. "Leave him be. He's a big man. The conversation you entered started several days ago. It wasn't even your conversation, and you are right, Danny is a quiet man. He always was a man of few words. But this fight, you didn't start.

"About a week ago, I had Danny going through some old records back in the cold storage room. He overheard one of the engineers at the station explaining to someone else the reason he was so quiet was he didn't have much in the way of brains and had nothing to talk about or say."

"But that isn't even half true."

"You know it, I know it, and Mom knows it, but the engineer hasn't spent any time with Danny, and so he doesn't know it. But in his world, it is all about his perception, not ours."

"It's still a mean thing to say."

"True, but I doubt if I approach the man, he will ever see Danny as anything but a giant black man, and in his mind, that means Baby Huey." Sweets got a thoughtful look on his face. "As I said, the man has spent no time getting to know Danny, but you teased him because he had something to say."

Hooker had known it was wrong the moment he had said it, but he didn't know how to make it right. "And I feel like the stink on the bottom of a misstep on the lawn."

Sweets smiled his megawatt smile and made things all right. "I think you two are both man enough to get over it."

Hooker thought as they all three sipped. He noticed Tilly, the consummate mother hen, quietly watching over her brood.

"So what do you think his opinion of Sweets is?" Hooker smiled even though he knew Sweets was blind. He also felt Sweets could feel or hear he was smiling.

"I don't have a problem with, or from, the man. So I would be prejudiced if I tried to put words in his mouth. They might be right. They might be far wrong. I'm just not going to do it."

"This brings up something else I have wondered about for years—the name Sweets. It's your last name, but Danny and even your mother here call you by it."

Sweets' chuckle grew into a belly laugh. Tilly had tears squished from the corners of her eyes she was laughing so hard. Hooker joined in the infectious laughter with no inkling of what they had found so hilarious.

Danny walked in from the living room where he had been reading. His index finger marked his place in the middle of the book. He frowned at the other two and turned his glare on Hooker. "What?"

Hooker smiled, he had at least one more word out of the big man. "I only asked why you two call your brother by y'all's last name. You are all Sweets, but with you two, only Sweets is Sweets."

Danny thought a moment and looked at his family. The giant man softly shushed his chinos onto the chair and poured himself some more coffee. "It's his name." He glared at his brother and mother who were now laughing even harder. Sweets had even stopped making any noise. He was in silent convulsions. Tilly was threatening to bash her chin with her undulating chest. Danny sipped his coffee and growled.

Knowing he wasn't going to get any help or contradictions from his family, he put his coffee mug down and looked at Hooker.

He jabbed his right thumb toward his brother. "It started at the hospital. The wimp was in welding class in high school. Some ass..." He looked to see if his mother was listening. "Some ass-wipe dropped an oxygen bottle. The steel table sheared off the head. The bottle became a missile, and after bouncing off two walls and taking out four welding booths, it hit Sweets in the head." Hooker nodded. He had heard this part before.

Danny sipped calmly on his coffee. The memories made the vein in his forehead swell and pulse. "When I got back up here from USC, where I was on scholarship, I went right to the hospital from the bus station. His head was just a big ball of white wrapping, just like you were a few months ago. We still didn't know if he would live or die. Hell, I didn't even know for sure it was even him. All I could see was a big white ball with two scrawny little black arms hanging out down the sheets. They had tubes going in and more coming out. He looked like a Boy Scout knotting class gone wrong.

"Being the only smart guy in the room, I grabbed the medical chart off the end of his bed. Some ignorant fuckhead…"

Tilly reached out and backhanded his shoulder. He turned on her.

"Then you tell it."

She laughed harder and rolled her hand in the air. She couldn't stand it. She leaned over and hugged her arms around his big arm and pushed her cheek into his shoulder. The left hand rolled again in the air.

Danny gave her a sympathetic look of disgust and turned back to Hooker. "They had him on the chart as Sweet Christopher. Not even Christopher Sweet… but Sweet Christopher—no comma."

Hooker frowned. His left index finger extended open from his hand. "His first name is Christopher?" His other hand took up the load of the mug, the cast working as ridged scaffolding.

"No. That's the point. They had him all screwed up. It was after visiting hours, and the head nurse came trotting down the hall to shoo me out. I spun on her like she was a right tackle. She might have outweighed me, but I had her by at least a head and shoulder. I put my finger on the name and quietly explained to her the grievous error of her ways and the ways of the hospital. I had her backtracked and hard up against the nurse's desk.

"I told her the name was Sweets—plural. Not rock candy, not gumdrops, not gooey cinnamon rolls, but all of them—Sweets. And when she started to point to the name Christopher, I snapped. I yelled his name was not Christopher… it was Sweets. She asked what the last name was. I guess I growled or something. I told her in no uncertain terms… Sweets."

The whole table chorused. Then they all started laughing.

Finally, Hooker got enough control. "Then what is your first name?"

The three chorused the same. Hooker raised his hands in surrender. And laughed. He was sure he knew who the charge nurse was on the fateful night. He knew all the important fat necks to nuzzle. He rubbed his scars on his right side. They were still tender.

Sweets was first to break the contemplative silence. "When do you get the cast off?"

Hooker looked up. "One more week. They say the pain will be worse once I start moving those muscles."

Danny leaned forward. "I'll come rub the knots out. I can work out some stretches for you, too. I notice when you walk you're still bound up on the right side."

"I'd like that, Danny." He smiled. "So we're good now?"

"No." The twinkle danced in the whole family's eyes was there. "You're still underfed."

"Yeah, well, it's Stella's cooking. She has me on some crazy restrictive diet and all."

The two jabbed with the verbal sparring dance that happens with brothers. Tilly cleared the last of the serving dishes and unused silverware. Puttering around in the kitchen, she made a fresh pot of coffee.

Hooker noticed first. "You're awful quiet there, Sweets."

The man turned his face to where Hooker was. "When did you last talk to your sister?"

The laughs were over. The meal was eaten. The pleasantries were finished. It was now time for the work. It was time to get down to the real reason Hooker was in Sweets' domain.

"The Mouse? Just before I got shot. Why?"

"Any contact from her lately?"

Hooker's mind raced. *How does he do...?* It had long since stopped being creepy or even scary. It was now a great curiosity.

"Last night. She sent a rhyme puzzle. Actually, it was two of them."

"How did you get them?"

Hooker pointed into the air between them. "And there is the curiosity. She sent it verbally through an intermediary she used to torment. He's very afraid of her and her gang. But the way he recited it, I could tell she worked with him personally until he had it perfect. It was very strange."

"She needs your help."

"The Mouse. We're talking about my sister, The Mouse. The Mouse—

the evil queen of all the night creatures and things crawling on two or four feet in the dark of the world. Help? Her?"

Sweets nodded. "She reached out through someone who would rather die than deal with her. You know that, and she knows you know that. That's why she used him."

Hooker knew Sweets' injury was a give and take sort of thing. His sight had been taken from him. But in exchange, he had been blessed with an enhanced ability to remember every song, artist, producer, and other liner note information about music. But he had also been cursed or gifted with another kind of sight—he could 'see' images. Sometimes they were just wild extraneous stuff he couldn't attach to anything or anyone. Other times, they were very vivid and exact, meaningless to Sweets, but important to the person in the vision.

"What did you see, Sweets?"

Sweets sat stoically and then washed his hands over his face as if to clear his vision. "It was like Dorothy in the Wizard of Oz. She's running here and there with her little dog. In the air, I could sense the dark bird or birds. They were chasing her. She knows they will kill her, but not yet. So she is searching for you..." He sat back in silence, his face blank. If he could see, Hooker would have said he was just staring.

"What else, Sweets?"

He slowly shook his head.

"What?"

"It doesn't make sense."

"What doesn't?"

Sweets struggled. His voice was strained. "You had a big gun. A very big gun."

"Betsy. My sawed-off twelve-gauge."

Sweets thought a moment. "Maybe."

"I protected her."

"No." He shook his head. "You shot her... and she smiled. Then the whole area just turned to flames and exploded."

"You mean exploded and then turned to flames?"

"No. Everywhere was one big fireball... and then there was an explosion." He leaned toward Hooker. Danny was frowning as he watched his brother. He had seen this intensity overcome Sweets before.

"I told you it didn't make sense."

Hooker shook his head. "No. What does *not* make sense is me shooting Sissy."

Danny growled at Hooker. "I told you before not to call her by that name."

Hooker ignored Danny's anger.

"It's what I saw. You shot them both, her and the dog. And she smiled when you did it. It was like a relief. You were setting her free."

"Death is not freedom," Hooker growled.

Danny growled reflectively. "It is to someone who is truly committing suicide."

9

ooker found Manny in his office. The large professional headphones covered the sides of his head. He was humming with the music and staring at the boards. The man was most alive when there was a problem in front of him to solve. Murder was the ultimate problem. Manny was at his best. He was at his most aware. It was as if every one of his senses was on hyper-overdrive.

Manny raised his right hand and then raised his index finger. Without turning around to see who was in the doorway, he called out loudly over the music only he could hear, "I figured out Fox's Eve."

Stella came up behind Hooker as he stood in the office doorway. Hooker turned to her. "How does he do that?"

She shrugged. "One of life's little Manny mysteries. You need anything to eat or drink?"

He smiled and shook his head. She knew where he had been. He was more ready for a nap. Instead, he walked over to the oversized black walnut desk. He sat on the corner and waited.

Manny took off his headphones. "How was breakfast with the Sweets?"

"Good. Disturbing."

The man thought about the dichotomy. "Yeah, I guess it can happen with them. I can imagine the good. What was disturbing?"

"Danny talked straight for almost five minutes. It had to be over a few hundred words."

The man did not laugh. He grabbed his pursed lips, and his eyes roamed about the desk and walls. "He's worried about something. Did he say anything?"

"Sweets did. It was about some ass-jerk engineer at the radio station. Danny overheard the guy say the reason Danny didn't say much was because he wasn't smart enough to have anything to say. I just made it worse because I teased him by asking if someone had bumped up his daily word allowance."

"I thought you said he had run his mouth for five minutes."

"He ran his mouth after I had teased him."

"If he was pissed off, why was he talking? I would think he would just clam up for a few days."

"He did. He was in the other room reading Plato's *The Cave*. I recognized the book. It should be right there in the hole in your shelf."

Manny glanced over at the large bookshelf with the four holes. "Hmm, I would have thought he would have read the Dostoyevsky first. Interesting... So what was the long speech about?"

"I asked why they called Sweets 'Sweets' when they are all Sweets." Hooker's eyes went up. "Yeah, it does sound silly when I put it that way."

"So why was Danny elected to be the mouthpiece?"

"He was the only one who could talk. I thought Sweets and Tilly were going to just blow gaskets right there from laughing so hard. I guess they thought maybe I knew."

"...about Danny marching Wanda Cutter backward down the hall?" Manny and Stella both chuckled.

"Now, there is an image." Hooker now had confirmation on his guess at it being Nurse Cutter. "A destroyer backing an aircraft carrier back across the ocean."

"I don't think even your Uncle Willie would have the balls to back-march Dolly or even Stella, much less Wanda Cutter."

Hooker laughed. "Oh, he has the balls. He's just not stupid." Hooker jabbed his finger at Manny. "You know, when I was on the third floor, and they would come to visit, I thought it was kind of strange Nurse Wanda 'I rule the world' Cutter would all but disappear."

Manny stroked his pursed lips and chuckled at the thought of her giving anyone a wide berth.

Stella rolled her head and leaned her hip against the door. Both men knew this was her giveaway tell she was going to stir up some fun stuff. "You know why they built Good Sam, don't you?"

"Because they needed another hospital?"

"No, silly. It was because they needed at least two miles of turf to separate Wanda and Connie." She was referring to the other strong nurse in the San Jose area who ruled the Valley Medical Center from her glass booth overlooking the emergency room—the place everyone joked was Hooker's second home.

They all laughed and then thought about what it would be like having the two domineering women running a hospital from the ground and third floors. The mental image made them laugh even harder.

Hooker shifted and stood.

"Well, it's been fun, but I need some aspirin and a nap. I'll talk to you in a few hours at dinner."

Manny hid his smile. "Sure thing, kid. I'll wake you when it's time." He silently counted three. "Oh, Hooker?"

The mop of curly black hair and droopy eyes looked back around the corner. "Yeah, Manny?"

"Have you ever heard the song... and I can't think of how the music goes... but the words are something like: *The fox went out on a chilly night. Prayed to the moon to give her light. Many a mile to go that night, before she reached the town-o, town-o, town-o. Many a mile to go that night before she reached the town-o.*"

Hooker frowned, thinking.

"Heard it before?"

Hooker thought blurrily. Shaking his head, "No, Manny, I haven't. Why do you ask?"

Manny waved his hand. "Nothing kid. Just thinking... Enjoy your nap."

He listened to the kid pad his way down the hall. Stella watched from the door. There was a muted conversation with Box, and then the silence. The man smiled and noted the time.

"That was evil, Manny Romero." Stella pushed off the door and headed for the kitchen. "I'm proud of you," she added with an evil smile. The constant take-no-prisoners and give-no-ground approach kept everyone in the family on their toes. It was refined to a very high and talented game. Most days, Manny was the Master, with Stella and her sister not far behind. If anyone were close to Manny, it would be Dolly—she practiced the game deftly with those who were in charge of her city.

The house settled into silence as Stella leaned over the island, sipping coffee, and reading the paper. This was her time of the year to scour the want ads for used canning jars for sale. One year she wrote directly to the Ball jar company, but the closest they could come to the prices she normally paid was a small discount off what the large chain supermarkets paid. Most of what she acquired was paid for in canned fruit or vegetables.

Manny opened one of the books he was currently reading. He had started back through the classics written in the nineteenth century. Sir Arthur Conan Doyle was one of four books he was dipping into, back and forth. Keeping the four-complex story-lines straight was his defense against boredom.

Manny looked at the clock when he heard the scream.

"Holy Chry... Sothamnus Nauseosa... on the desert floor!"

Manny smiled, *twenty-eight minutes*. Good recovery too... The Latin name for rabbit brush. The kid might have even hit REM sleep before the bomb hit his subconscious. He slipped the headphones back over his ears and chuckled. Some days he just loved being an evil man.

Hooker slid to a stop when his shoulder hit the doorjamb. "Damn it all, Manny, that was not nice."

He strode into the office in only his boxers and socks. "And knock it off. I know you can hear me. The tape isn't even running."

Manny swore under his breath. He knew he should have turned the reel-to-reel back on. It was obvious when the huge professional twelve-inch reels were moving. He looked up at the young man as he chuckled. Hooker was now very much awake.

"Yes. It was a nursery rhyme or something. She sang it to me when I was a kid."

"Full moon is Tuesday."

"I've got to call Willie."

Manny raised his open hand. "Telstar crosses Sirius every seventeen days in its orbit. The next from our point of view is Sunday morning at 1:17."

Hooker slumped back against the desk cursing. "Beans and wienies!"

The man in the wheelchair echoed him. "Correct, the pooch is fucked."

"She told us when. She even told us who... or what she will look like. But she held back the where." The two men thought about what all those points meant. "She did not intend for us to stop the kill, just to know she has the inside track on everything. Whatever she wants will be huge."

Hooker had grown up in seven foster homes with her. She had run away for good on her sixteenth birthday.

The foster parents had decided to have some fun with her for her birthday. The mother held her down while the father raped her front, top, and back. When they were finished with their fun, they turned her over to their mentally challenged adult son who was more violent and sexually sadistic than they were.

This was not the first time she had been abused in the homes. However, when it started, she knew this time, it was up to her to make it the last time.

During the exchange of the prisoner, she had made an escape, taking her to the sanctuary of the kitchen. She had started on the dim-witted son with a paring knife. As he sprawled screaming and bleeding from multiple minor cuts to the face and hands, she turned on the parents. The father had suffered the most with slashes to his crotch and face. The mother received only minor but painful cuts to her breasts.

Four months later, when they began to take their anger out on a thir-teen-year-old Hooker, he finished what his sister had started. After no charges were filed, and during a transfer to a new home four states away, Hooker lifted the wallet out of the purse of the woman transporting the poor child and disappeared from the Greyhound station. Later, through some research about the homes they had been in, they realized he and his sister had always been *sold* to the next home. It had been a secret network of pedophiles and sadists. To Hooker's horror, he discovered the sexual abuse of his sister had been going on for many years and homes since she was nine.

Finding her had only been a matter of walking out of the bus station. She was waiting with a few new friends in the shadows. If he had gotten on the bus with the woman like planned—it would have been the end of their family.

Three months later, they had wound up in San Jose and were separated. She kept to the streets and the night, and Hooker had found Uncle Willie's car.

She had taught Hooker the power of the underground or street telephone, the passing of information from one denizen of the night to another—from the bum on the corner to the alcoholic in the alley. As their worlds separated with time, there was still a connection. They each knew they could somehow send a message to the other.

Just as she ruled a tribe of the creatures of the night, Hooker also knew and used the powerful tools of knowledge flowing openly in the street. For Hooker, it could be as simple as knowing where a derelict car was parked—no longer good for sleeping in. But on a more personal level, it was his lifeline to the only sister he had—even if she was not blood-related.

He looked at Manny leaning back in his chair, studying him. "What?"

"Care to share?"

"Share what?"

"You've been gone off into that head of yours for the last ten minutes."

"I was thinking about Sissy." He caught himself. He could hear Danny yelling at him to stop calling her childhood name. It was a name of derision, not just what a little boy calls his older sister. "... The Mouse."

"What about her?"

"She wants something. And if Sweets is correct, I'm not going to like it." He told Manny about Sweets' vision. Stella wandered back into the room with mugs of fresh coffee.

The two parents listened as their kid peeled the onion of his knowledge and of his pain. There can be no harder job than to be a parent who can't fix the tough boo-boos in life. Manny and Stella could only sit and listen and watch the slow train-wreck as it happened.

The afternoon sun lay slanted along the floors.

"Do you think there's any chance what Sweets saw could have been misinterpreted? I mean, he might have seen one thing and thought it was something else?"

Hooker pushed at the last bite of the afternoon snack. They had been talking for hours—over and over, all about the same things. They had looked from this angle or that. His eyes were blurry as he looked at his plate, but his focus was miles away. He was trying once again to read his sister's mind. Something they had laughed about as children—their ability to know what the other was thinking, without verbal communication.

"It's not how Sweets operates. He describes exactly what he is seeing. He can't interpret it, so he just describes the pictures. It's always as if his is in a museum or looking at *National Geographic* or *Life*. There are pictures in front of him, and he will tell you what he sees in detail. But he doesn't know it's a cow or car or building." Hooker looked up. "I guess he does know what things are and look like, but he saw a whole lot of flames as the world blew up. However, there is no perspective. If I were Box and sat next to the fireplace in there, it would be a big fire. Nevertheless, for us, and many feet away, it's just a fire in the fireplace. So he does not know if it's a campfire, a bonfire, or half of San Jose blowing up. He just doesn't know."

Manny moved his index finger along the grain of the table. His focus was closer and farther than Hooker's. "Let's hope it's just a campfire."

Stella cleared her throat but still croaked her words. "But he saw you shoot your sister."

Hooker slumped and nodded. "That's the part that scares me. He does know what that would look like."

"No doubt..."

"He was very clear about it—right down to my shotgun."

A heavy silence hung in the air. They were all talked out. It was now time to realize it and do something about it.

Stella watched as Hooker's jaw slid open and his head hung lower. The soft snoring sound effects were supplied by her husband. If she hadn't been so tired, it would have been funny.

Her chair purposely scraped, and the men jerked. Without spoken directions, plates were cleared, and the three headed for their respective beds.

The warm afternoon sun slanted across the dark slate floor. In the center of the warmest part, there was no cat to soak up the heat.

Life was twisting.

10

The quiet was a pressing gray noise, and the heat was building. Hooker knew he should look behind him but could not bring himself to turn. He was searching. What he was looking for, he couldn't find. You have to know what you are looking for in order to know when you have found it. The buzz of the heat reflected off the hot sand. Hooker could not feel his feet in the sand.

He knew he needed to turn around. He just did not have the strength to push his will.

The heat seared until everything was just white. Hooker looked for something. He knew he had to find it, whatever *it* was.

He knew he should turn around, but he didn't want to. He was afraid of what was there. He kept searching.

The white began to take parts of Hooker. He had to find it. He looked harder.

His legs ended at his ankles in the white of the sand. He wiggled his toes. He could feel the toes were now part of the sand. "I won't need boots next year."

The white sand washed against his legs and bound them together. The heat intensified. He pushed forward, searching for what he needed to find. He was trapped, but he had to find it.

The white around his legs drew snug. What was behind him drew near. The voice was urgent. He needed to find the thing and make the voice stop.

With a rush of adrenaline and determination, Hooker turned. He screamed as the shotgun exploded.

The expanding cloud of hot orange gas enveloped him and reached for his soul. He recoiled.

Hooker physically screamed, and as he recoiled in his mind, he jumped backward in the bed. He was suspended in midair for a moment. Then, in his mind, the shotgun blast hit him in the back and head.

His scream was cut short as his head and back hit the concrete floor.

Stella's shoulder slammed into the doorjamb and the half-open door. The door slapped against the wall, burying itself on the stopper. The noise was loud and explosive, like a shotgun blast at point-blank range.

Hooker's heart skipped a beat, and he passed out. His terrorized mind was certain he had been shot again.

Moments later, Hooker's eyes fluttered, and then he blinked. He was lying on the hard floor. His pillow was under his head. His blankets were neatly over him, and he was staring up through the spokes of Manny's wheelchair at the man himself.

"Just lay there. Stella is getting the ice pack."

Hooker closed his eyes. He tried to pull himself together, tried to remember. "Sorry for waking you two up."

"You didn't." Stella's face appeared over him, looking down. She knelt with a wince as her knees groaned and popped. "Why do you guys always have to end up on the floor? I'm truly getting too old for this nonsense." She placed a cold ice bag under Hooker's head.

A warm purr moved along his right arm. His arm and cast felt funny. Hooker wondered if a person could break an arm when it is in a cast.

Box placed a tentative front paw on Hooker's chest. Meeting no resistance, he placed the other on the chest and then sat down in the open armpit. It was warm and snuggly, but without the fuss of climbing on the chest.

Hooker frowned and rolled his eyes up to Stella. "What time is it?"

"A little past three."

"Day or night?"

Manny moaned, "Night."

Without looking, Stella reached over and rubbed Manny's hand. "It was one of those nights again."

Hooker looked through the spokes. "Getting shot again?"

Manny winced with a drawn back lip. The nod was almost imperceptible in the dim light from the hall. The man was embarrassed this kind of crap could go on for so many years. He looked out of the room's door at the black wall of glass and dim night lights in the courtyard fountain.

Hooker thought about how tough the man was, and how such a little thing could cause so much havoc in a life. He sighed deeply. "So, I guess this is never going to just go away."

Stella silently stroked his forehead and slowly shook her head.

Hooker smiled weakly. "So we are all up. I guess some hot cocoa would be out of the question?"

Manny harrumphed. "It tastes like crap with moonshine in it."

Stella rolled her eyes as she pursed her lips and nodded in agreement. "Guess I'll have to find where I hid bottle of dark rum."

Hooker sat up carefully.

"You dizzy?"

"Naw, I'm fine, just the bump hurts."

Stella stood. "Keep thet ice on it."

Manny chuckled. "Check the floor and see if there is a divot or dent?"

Stella tapped her husband's head as she walked out. "He's not your blood relative."

They all three laughed at the hard-headed family joke.

Hooker leaned back against the bed platform. He held the ice bag on his head. His eyes closed sluggishly, but without a sign of sleep. He was thinking.

Manny watched him attentively, deep in thought, immersed in his own brand of hell.

Hooker opened his eyes. He looked up at the detective.

Manny rocked forward on his elbows splayed on the chair arms. It was his way of preparing to talk. "The shotgun?"

Hooker nodded.

"It's strange, even if you are looking at the person who shoots you, in the night terrors, you never see the person... only the end of the gun, and a blast."

Hooker let the ice bag slide down his head, as he drew it out in front of him. He surveyed the cast. There were some cracks. It was at the end of its usefulness. The elbow had been feeling mushy for a few days.

"Have you ever figured out why people kill people they don't even know?"

Manny rocked back gently as he pursed his lips. "There is a belief in the Jewish religion that most people are good at heart. But there are a few who are evil incarnate. What makes them evil is anyone's guess. They are evil from birth. Maybe this guy is one of those. I don't know. All the years on the force, I saw a lot of bad things. But down deep, few of the people were bad themselves. Their circumstance may have been. They may have felt they had no other choice, but they weren't evil in the root."

Hooker slowly slid back up onto his bed. "I don't think mine was evil. He just didn't know any other way."

"Maybe you're lucky, and it won't follow you for long."

Hooker looked at his friend. "But you don't believe it."

Manny shrugged and closed his eyes. "There is always hope."

Hooker scratched his curly hair and finished the smartass remark. "Hope is a diamond."

Stella called from the kitchen.

Manny laughed. "Speaking of real diamonds..."

The three mugs were on the table. Stella sat at her place, shuffling a deck of cards—something Hooker had never seen her do.

He sat down as Manny slid into his area at the head of the table. Hooker watched her continue to break, separate, pile, and reshuffle the cards. She focused on the deck as if she were mesmerized by the moving pieces of card stock.

Hooker raised his mug and sipped at the heat and vapor of chocolate powder. As a kid, he had never tasted chocolate or hot cocoa. He had first tasted it at one of the other tow truck driver's houses. They had made it for the kids, and Hooker had taken a sip. He had almost given up coffee. The next morning, he was back to his old ways, but forever changed. He had stopped on his way home and bought some powder mix. When Willie had caught him, he threw the powder down the toilet. Hooker, red-faced with indignant anger, had stood the man up against the wall. As he was about to scream his venting spleen, Willie calmly shuttered his eyes and stated, "If you want hot chocolate, I will make you some. But it will be real hot chocolate. Never settle for an imitation. Always remember you are worth the real stuff."

A warm flood washed through Hooker. He realized now Willie had been speaking about a lot more than just a mug of hot chocolate. He was talking about love and family and relationships, and basically, anything in life. It was about finding value within you. And, as Hooker realized the next day, Willie was reminding himself of that, too.

That was the day Hooker pulled the Congressional Medal of Honor out of the second drawer on the left under the sink. He had hunted around and finally found the photo to go with it and had taken it all up to the Phoenix Frame Shop. A few weeks later, he hung the framed medal, photo, and ribbon by the door. Every time they passed it, it reminded both Hooker and Willie—Willie had paid the price to be the man he wanted to be.

Willie had watched Hooker hang the frame. As he walked past, out into the shop, he commented in a grump, "At least you could have found a picture showing my better side."

Two days later, Hooker found a photo of Willie in the naval hospital with tubes and bandages covering most of his face and chest. Hooker had thumbtacked it to the wall beside the other, but recently, Hank had taken it down, stating how disgusting it looked. Then he had it framed to match.

Hooker sipped on the hot chocolate, thinking about how hot chocolate and chocolate chip cookies on a Christmas Eve was how Hooker had finally met Stella, and then Manny. Who could have known that two months later, he would be taking refuge in their home?

"Hey... Hooker?" Stella sat ready to deal.

"What?"

"I asked, are you in?"

Hooker looked with a frown at Manny and Stella. He was lost.

Manny leaned back. His right eyebrow rose. He summed up the situation. "We're playing gin until dawn."

"Gin until dawn?" Hooker was now really confused. He had never really played card games at all, and so this was a new game to him. "Is it like regular gin?"

Stella started to laugh, but Manny put his hand on hers and frowned.

"You were always working or over at Willie's. That's why this seems strange to you."

"Well..."

Stella rested her hands on the table, still holding the cards. "When Manny wakes up with the terrors, we get up and have hot chocolate. It always reminds us of the Christmas Eve you came into our lives. And we play gin... a penny a point. Manny owes me a million dollars he'll never pay. So we can start fresh with you and just play for points."

Hooker looked at Manny. "A million bucks?" He laughed. "You really are bad at this?"

Manny shrugged his eyes and shoulder as he raised his mug. "To Christmas and forgiven debts."

They laughed, and Stella dealt.

"So, what is the dawn part?"

Manny was looking at his cards. "The sun comes up."

Stella drew a card and discarded. "The terrors stop, and he can sleep again."

"Aha." Hooker nodded and thought about his cards. He was so savagely screwed. He drew and discarded.

The large clock in Manny's office could be heard ticking between the ticks of the cards. The night rumbled on with the soft thumps of the mugs of chocolate landing absently on the large table. Hooker could feel the soft soothing calm coming with the mindless play.

Softly, Stella laid out her cards. "Gin." She pulled the score sheet toward her and drew vertical lines.

Manny leaned toward Hooker. "I don't know why she draws those lines. Other than it gives us hope, maybe just one hand, we might put some points up."

Hooker laid out his hand. It was still a mess. At least Manny's was close.

The hands moved on. As Manny had predicted, numbers only filled one column—but it didn't really matter. Hooker realized he had spent very little time doing nothing with Manny and Stella. In fact, he and been a non-stop whirlwind since he first met Willie.

"What was it like growing up in the wild west of Nebraska?"

Manny stopped and put down his cards. He thought about the question. He rocked forward on his elbows, metering out a deep sigh.

"Main Street was a patchwork of concrete, board, and dirt sidewalks. Dad had a Model T truck we went to town in. He had paid a man twenty-two dollars for the truck and a battered trailer carrying a horse. The man saddled the horse and rode off down the street.

"I remember another day coming out of the dry goods store. The day was high heat, and there was a horse tied up to the rail on the bed of the truck." Manny looked at Hooker's frown of confusion.

"A horse?" Hooker nodded.

Manny snorted. "Don't worry about it... they were everywhere, and this horse was standing there tied to the truck with its tongue hanging out. My dad didn't say anything. He untied the horse and led him about a block down the street to the gas station. In those days, there was a large pan full of water to check tires and tubes for leaks. He led the horse to the pan.

"I remember my father standing there in his wool suit pants and a white long-sleeve shirt. His tie was one of those ribbons they just tied in a bow. His cowboy hat was pushed back on his head so he could scratch at his forehead. The back of his white shirt was stained into a gray cross from the sweat.

"He stood there, waiting for the horse to drink his fill. Then he led him back up the street. He tied the reins to the car behind us, and we drove off to home. I asked him why he had watered the horse. He didn't even think about it. He just told me it was because the horse was thirsty. He meant anyone else would do the same thing because it was what neighbors were for. Nebraska was that simple. You just looked after what needed to be done."

Hooker thought. "Like the canning."

Stella nodded and laid down her cards. "Gin."

Hooker thought about the horse and about the canning. He looked at Stella shuffling. "What about you?"

She laughed loosely. "The kibbutz?"

"What's a kibbutz?"

"It's a Jewish collective farm where many families live and work the same farm as a common family."

"I thought it was just your family?"

"Oh, it was. But with Dolly and me, it felt like a collective farm. For as unorthodox as we were Orthodox, we still got all of the lessons and stories as if my father were a rabbi."

"But he was a farmer."

"Farmer, lay veterinarian, furniture builder, substitute teacher, even a cop for a while." She looked over at Manny.

Manny laughed. "That's how we met. He arrested me for stealing a watermelon in the middle of the night."

"He caught you stealing?"

"Oh, heck no." Manny laughed. "He was the gym teacher. He knew it had to be one of the boys in the gym class. He just didn't know which one he had shot full of rock salt the night before. So he had both classes of gym running wind sprints up and down the football field. Pretty soon, the blood pressure is up, the scabs are weak, and were being rubbed off. I started bleeding. It was just small dots here and there… but he knew the pattern. He walked up behind me and slapped the cuffs on me. When I asked what for, he pulled the shirt up my back."

"What happened?"

"I served my sentence—the rest of the harvest was spent in his fields. I was very thankful someone took pity on me and brought me cooled tea."

"Stella."

She harrumphed.

Manny laughed and waved the back of his hand at her. "Oh, heavens no. She only had eyes for the Grader kid."

"Ralph."

"Yeah, Ralph. What a screw-up he turned out to be."

"Prison?"

"Nah, Congress." The two laughed.

They played cards for almost an hour in silence. 'Gin' was the only word spoken, other than when Stella stood at the stove and asked, "More?"

Stella sipped on her fresh mug as she reviewed her cards. She mused. "You know what would go good with this?"

Without looking up, Hooker replied distractedly, "Chocolate chip cookies."

Stella laid her cards face down and looked at Hooker over the rim of her mug. Manny decked his cards because he knew the look. They weren't going to be playing cards for at least a few minutes.

Hooker started to reach for a drawcard, and then realized he was the center of attention. Stella's face was completely unreadable, and Manny's was of light amusement. Hooker slowly withdrew his hand. He knew something was up, and it didn't feel good.

"What?" Hooker's breath was almost as loud as his word. He was rapidly reaching panic under Stella's pressure.

Stella let him stew and worry a few seconds more. "What exactly *were* you doing out there that night with hot cocoa and fresh-out-of-the-oven cookies?"

Hooker had to replay what she had said a few times in his head. It didn't sound right. There was no trouble, no threat, and no condemnation, nothing… No trouble of any kind.

He swallowed and then cleared his throat. "It was Christmas Eve."

Her face was as animated as the stone fountain out front.

He laid his cards on the table and then slowly raised the mug to his mouth. Almost a decade playing this game with the two sisters had taught him the tricks. He sipped, never breaking eye contact. He sipped again, and then quietly placed the bright aqua blue mug on the thick walnut table. There was no sound from the placement.

Stella cocked her head slightly. Her eyes didn't betray her amusement at how well he had learned the waiting game. Rule one: whoever speaks first loses.

Hooker picked up his cards as if to resume the game. He moved two cards.

Stella smiled as she pushed back in her chair. "Really?" She laughed as Manny chuckled. "You won with the second sip with an empty mug. If I weren't rationing Manny's sugar, I would have sworn you had cocoa left to drink."

Hooker smiled softly at the acknowledgment of his prowess at the game they all played—he took the win. But his voice was soft as he spoke.

"Most people think the drivers volunteer to work the holidays for the extra pay. The truth is, there is no holiday pay, especially nights. The club calls pay a flat $7.41. $7.41 for a jumpstart, $7.41 for a flat tire, and $7.41 for a tow, even if it's a roll-over wreck down a cliff—$7.41 and the drivers get half if they're lucky. Most drivers came from situations not much different from mine. Most of those have a weekend or three to look forward to throughout the year." He laid down his unneeded pass cards.

"Even the summer I first started, I heard what the drivers looked forward to every year. It was your sister's ham hocks and black-eyed beans on New Year's Eve. Nobody ever asked what part of the South Dolly was from. She just said it was a family tradition and they didn't care. What they looked forward to is the confirmation that someone cares.

"Most of the older drivers can tell you how many days are left in the year. After turkey awful, Ace can tell you exactly how many hours until that midnight. It's a small thing for Dolly to do, but for them, it's the biggest thing all year."

He looked in his mug and started to get up. Stella waved him down and grabbed his mug. "Time to switch to coffee."

Hooker looked at her backside as she drew the coffee mill toward her on the counter. He frowned at Manny, who was relaxed in his posture.

The man smiled and nodded his head behind him. He didn't have to look, and neither did she. Hooker looked into the sunroom. The previously dark windows were now a soft gray of fog. Soon they would be pink.

"I didn't stop listening." The antique mill growled as she turned the crank.

Hooker collected his thoughts. "Willie wasn't dating anyone then, so Maddie had come over and brought a bunch of fixings. We were baking up dozens of cookies, and there was at least a gallon of hot cocoa. I knew we would never eat and drink all of it, so I packed up the picnic basket and was out looking for the other drivers."

Stella plugged in the percolator and stood leaning with her hands on the counter. Her focus was hundreds of miles and years away. She was seeing a snapshot of her father taking the family and their Christmas dinner down to the Sheriff Station and county jail. There were two officers and the town drunk. The seven of them ate together in the larger holding cell because they couldn't let Junior Dirken out of the cell. The deputies had thanked her father for the best kosher Christmas dinner they had ever had.

Two weeks later Junior had come around to the farm. He told their father he was tired of being the town drunk and asked for his help. Their father had given him a job on the farm and made a place for him out in the barn.

Many years later, Junior still lived in the barn when he delivered their father's eulogy. He had recalled the dinner. Sometimes, it is not the big things that make the difference, but the little ones.

She turned and sat against the counter. "So you were bringing them Christmas."

Hooker nodded. "For once, I had too much. It was my turn to share."

He turned toward Manny. "And I still have the Zippo money clip you gave me that morning."

Stella chuckled. "Was it the one I gave you the year before?"

He smiled wetly. "I was holding on to it for Hooker."

Stella croaked just as wet. "If there was ever any doubt about who is a member of this family... There is none now."

The percolator bubbled its finish as she collected and rinsed out Manny's mug and filled all three. Placing the two mugs on the table, she turned back toward the refrigerator. She took out Manny's insulin, and drawing out a larger dose, she said to herself. "I feel like pancakes are in order."

She walked over to where Manny was holding his undershirt up. She swabbed the alcohol pad over the area and pushed the needle in. "I'm feeling like chocolate chip pancakes."

11

———————

Stella walked into the gym room Hooker had set up years ago. She watched the giant black man from the back. Bored, Danny had stripped to the waist and was absent-mindedly curling the largest stack of dumbbell weight he could make as he watched Hooker struggle with the small kettlebell with his right arm.

Something was wrong with the picture. It took Stella a minute. "Where is your cast?"

Danny froze.

Hooker jerked at being caught and looked up sheepishly. "It got wet last night. It was falling apart in the sheets." He sat back up, resting the small weight on his knee. "I took it off before the sheets all turned to plaster concrete."

She cocked her head slightly sideways and gave him the eye. He smiled. "I put them in the washer. They should be dry by now. I'll put them back on the bed this afternoon before I take a nap."

"Hmm." She cocked her hip. Finished with him, she turned to Danny. She stepped over and rested her hand lightly on his massive shoulder. He twitched, unsure of what was coming. She bent over and kissed the top of his head. "Thank you for bringing your mama and Sweets out last night. I swear, I would have Tilly at my table any Saturday or Sunday you can spare her."

He looked up and around at her. "You can have her. But then her two foundering children would starve."

She leaned on him as she laughed. "I can see that."

"Danny is going to start dropping Sweets off, and then come out and work me over until I can work again. We might get Manny down here and work his upper torso, too."

Danny turned slightly toward Hooker. "You should have an upper torso like his. The man just needs to work on what he can't move." He turned back to Stella. "I've been reading some books about massage and stretching for better blood flow. I'll work on him and show you what you can do for him in bed."

Realizing what he had just said, he flushed. Stella felt the quick heat in his neck more than she could see any blush in his walnut skin. She hugged him. "I know what you meant. You don't have to do anything for us, Danny, and you and your family are always family and welcome for any dinner that doesn't have you two running off to work halfway through the evening."

"Speaking of work," she turned back to Hooker, "a deputy just dropped off four large boxes. I have to get Manny up and through the shower. Paul is coming over for breakfast. So, you two have about ten more minutes, and then get cleaned up for breakfast."

She looked around the large unfinished room. The wall of windows looked out across the valley and the lower driveway. The door entered from the garage, but there was all the plumbing for an apartment with two modest-sized bedrooms. The high ceiling matched the garage area, which was built to accommodate a commercial car lift in one of the three bays. Across the garage was a large storage room which over the next few months, would become stuffed with tons of canned food. It was Stella's personal food bank for law enforcement families in need. The access door from the outside had no lock. If there were a need, Stella damn sure wasn't going to be monitoring the flow.

"Thinking about Candy and Squirt?"

"Of course," she smiled softly. She would finally get the daughter she always wanted. "Thinking about them, starting work on the apartment in here, and I also need to get the tents delivered and set up. The vegetables are already rolling out of the fields so the gleaning will start soon. We need to have the canning kitchen set up and ready."

She headed for the door and then turned, frowning. "Where are you going to put all of this equipment when the apartment is done, and there are two or three cars in the garage?"

Hooker laughed. "Manny always wanted a barn." He pointed to the end of the driveway from where it wrapped down around the large sprawling hacienda with the huge concrete party deck. "We're going to bury it partially into the hill so it doesn't look so big."

Looking out at the hill, her mind worked in overdrive. "It might be better to make a permanent outdoor kitchen over on the side, and a larger storage area in the barn. Then you could have easier access to the gym across the way." She turned and walked across the two empty parking bays. She patted her pet Cadillac in the third bay. Her voice reverberated in the empty garage. "Ten minutes, then get cleaned up. Breakfast at nine o'clock...."

Hooker and Danny both softly echoed the rest of her spiel as she moved up the secret stairs. "If you are late, you starve." The two men chortled. Their mothers were so very much alike.

Cleaned and well-fed, Danny had taken off to get some sleep before Sweets needed to go to work for the night. The other three men gathered in Manny's office to go through the boxes of past cases of the killer secretly referred to as the Cowboy Picasso.

The boots had started it. At the third kill scene, someone had made the comment how the killer made his victims look like a Picasso painting, all torn apart. The name had stuck, but thankfully, had not made it into the papers, nor had much news of each killing. They were separated enough so the police had been able to present them as individual incidents, thus averting any public panic about a serial killer. The painted walls had never been seen by anyone from the news media. It had been one of the most closely guarded secrets of the case.

Hooker looked out the one window set mainly for light. The view through the narrow window was along the outside of the two-foot thick straw-bale and stucco wall. He could see out past the hacienda to the tan grassy hillside where the sun was pounding the South Bay Area. It was the twenty-seventh day with temperatures over the critical temperature for a crime: ninety-seven degrees, the true temperature of blood.

He knew from Manny that after six days of no relief from the heat, murders and other crimes of violence went up dramatically. He didn't watch the news or read the paper like Manny. For the most part, he had suffered enough of it in his early years and didn't need it vicariously now.

He rubbed his aching arm. Maybe it *had* been too early to take the cast off. And then there was the Danny factor. Hooker found it hard to be satisfied with working with a four-pound kettle weight when Danny was fanning himself with eighty-five pounds.

"I think Hooker would have a better take on... Hooker?"

Hooker swam back to the present. "Hmm?" he turned his head and raised his eyebrows.

Manny frowned with concern and then laughed. "Did Danny wear you out today?"

Hooker made a growling face and muttered something unintelligible.

"Paul was wondering if we might be looking at the kind of person who is technically untraceable, members of your sister's community or of that ilk."

Hooker scratched behind his right ear, and suddenly realized he was doing something he had not been able to do for the last few months. He continued scratching blissfully, then looked up, and answered. "It's possible. But then, they don't usually have any access to a car. In fact, they seem to disdain any contact with any kind of machinery. I'm not even sure they use knives, much less a small-caliber handgun."

"Hmm," Manny turned back to Paul. "I hadn't thought about that."

"Also, there is the boot issue. The lookout fits the type with bare feet, but not the cowboy with the boots. Even the Mouse doesn't wear shoes—and as a girl, she had tender feet. She at least wore sandals outside."

Paul filed the information away in his mind for later. "Okay, next in the boxes is our little friend, the raven. In going over the boxes, I found another. In kill number two, a raven bone was picked up but never cataloged. So now, we have three raven wing bones, and all of them are the leading long bone from the right shoulder to the first bend or the start of the finger bone. This makes it the..." He dug in his pocket. "Just a minute, I had it right here." Drawing out a small scrap of paper, he opened it and read, "It's the radius or the second bone. The ulna is the first."

Hooker smiled. "Just like us." He pointed to two points on his forearm. "Radius moves and the ulna is the structural bone. It could be there's something there about it being the moving bone," he pointed at the photos, "being a paintbrush and all."

Paul and Manny just stared at him. They weren't used to being taught things by a much younger man. They looked at each other and raised an eyebrow.

"Hey, I was paying attention when they were trying to put Humpty Dumpty together again."

They laughed as Paul took a set of photos from each box. "Now, what we have here is very interesting. Or, in the words of Charlie Chan, *most very interesting*."

He laid out seven photos of shoeprints and castings. "I had the lab reverse the casting photos so we would be looking at all of the same impression. I also had them adjust everything to real-life measurements."

Manny looked at all the photos. "Which kill are these from?"

Paul looked at him. "All of them."

"Can't be."

"Is."

"No boot or sole would remain the same over... what... twelve years?"

"Not if you wore them every day. No, they wouldn't. But this is 1961, here is 1964, this one is 1966, this is yours, and here is the railcar."

Manny pointed to an artifact on the prints. "This notch is the same. On a regular shoe, it would get larger until it wasn't recognizable as a cut mark."

Paul pointed along the edge of the cast print. "Notice these three little V-notches. That is from what we call kill number two. Now, look here. There are four more. This is from yours. We only know of one killing between this one and yours."

Hooker gave a low whistle. "But there are four more. Somewhere, if this guy really is putting notches on his boot, somewhere, there are three more bodies."

Paul sat down and leaned back. "Exactly. Also, there are radical separations between his kills. Either this guy is hiding some we haven't found, or he's traveling."

Manny leaned back. "A serial killer usually starts with separations of long periods, but then, as he kills, the periods between become shorter and shorter as he searches for the same high, he got from the first successful kill. That is why they also become obsessive and compulsive about their kill routine. They are always trying to duplicate the feeling they got the first time. But with this guy, we had seen a huge gap between when he attacked me and the railcar."

"And if we understand The Mouse, he has accelerated even more." Hooker pulled at his pursed lips, a mirror image of Manny's habit. "So where has he been for the last six years?"

Paul looked at Manny. "So, how do you want to cut up California?"

Manny rolled his head toward his old partner. "I'll take straight over to Tulare and up into the gold rush country and work north. I know a few of these guys from Masons, so they'll talk to me without having to pull a badge. You take the south. I don't think you would have to call any further than Riverside or San Berdoo unless you hit pay-dirt down there."

Paul nodded. "I don't know if we need to figure out where he's getting the raven wing bones, but it is curious they are all from the right-wing."

Manny looked at Hooker. "Why don't you go visit your girlfriend tonight? She knows a lot of strange people. She might know someone in the Native American mystic community who could shed some light on the bone."

"I don't know about driving the Cadillac..."

"Whimper a bit. Stella will kvetch, but she will be happy to see her sister. And you better take the mange bucket, or Dolly will just clam up."

Hooker laughed as the phone rang. They all jumped.

Manny scooped it out of the cradle. "Manny."

The conversation was short. "Where?" He rolled his eyes up into his head as the person on the other end relayed the information. "Is a car on the way?"

He swung around and looked at Hooker. "Okay, we'll be ready. And Dolly? I'm sending Hooker and the mange bucket over to see you tonight. He's bringing a chaperone, so you two can coordinate about the canning. Paul said Gwen and Peter down in Gilroy have already put up five hundred gallons of stuff. And I think the plant is kicking in a ton or something of commercially canned goods." He listened. "Okay. Love ya, sis." He placed the phone back in the cradle.

"Where?"

"Northside. The old rail docks."

Paul spat air.

Manny looked at Paul and then at the boxes of information. "They don't know this is all here, do they?"

"Hell, these new kids can barely find their asses with their hands and sniffing dogs." He shook his head. "No, they have no idea. Everything except the bones can stay here. They are all photocopies the lab-made for you. The old guy Johnson said it was the least they could do for you." He drew his lips tight against his teeth and scratched the last of the reddish hair in the gray. "They're making copies as anything comes through, but I have to take the bones back. The new guys are going to start learning soon."

Manny knew what kind of limb his old partner was out on. "Thanks, Paul. I appreciate everything you're doing here."

The man got up to leave before the deputy arrived. He put the bones in one of the boxes and put it under his arm. "Oh, and I noticed you had finally pulled the permit for the barn you busted my balls on a few years back. I look forward to finally seeing it raised."

Hooker chortled. "Heck, Paul, you can come out and swing a hammer with the rest of us."

He looked at the young man with elevated eyes. "I just might take you up on your offer. I hear there is some good food around here for an old bachelor."

Manny laughed and shook his hand. "We'll lay in some supplies."

Yellow police tape ran crazy patterns around and through the abandoned rail docks. A pathway, taped about a hundred feet wide, led out toward two large buildings about six blocks away through broken fields of concrete and old asphalt. The old sun-bleached concrete shone white-hot in the late summer sun. Hooker and Manny both squinted at the intensity of the reflection. Neither man had dark glasses to wear. Neither had had any use for them, until now.

Manny and Hooker were stationary as their eyes swept the scene. Their minds moved like the two players they now knew. They knew where the kill zone was, and so now, they were mapping out the placement of the lookout. After they found placement, they could start to map the entrance and egress routes.

"Where was the lookout?"

Hooker's head swiveled. "No real wind last night. I already called the tower at Reid-Hillview Airport. So I would go with the onshore flow off the mudflats to the north."

He looked over the wide field to the south with the eye and mind looking for a place to hide, but where he could also see everything. He looked at three clumps of low bushes. The first one looked like it was only tall enough to hide a shoebox, and it was off to the west of the kill zone.

The other two could hide Manny and him and were more to the south. He pointed to the low clump.

"Pretty small."

"I'll bet you a dollar to a donut there is a depression on the other side. It's at least a foot deep, and it's going to give up at least three good prints."

"Go get your boy."

Hooker walked off to find Harold, the casting expert he was positive would be there again.

Manny rolled along what was once a concrete road built to withstand the daily punishment of heavy trucks. The cracks, less than an inch wide, would not be open all the way to the dirt below. The heavy-duty roadway was eight to ten inches thick. The larger cracks yielded to brush, and the occasional tree start. However, long before the tree could do any damage to the concrete, the concrete had choked the life out of the tree's small trunk. The stunted three-foot-tall sticks stood here and there on the roadway.

Manny remembered this area had been part of the war effort. He looked off to the northwest as he caught a glimpse of a white P-3 Orion Sub Chaser taking off from Moffett Field. He felt old to know all of this. He remembered as a young boy, his father showing him a picture of the dirigible parked in what was fondly known around the bay as Hanger One. As a young officer, he was there for an event when a small stunt plane flew in one giant door and out the other. He was close enough to know it was a feat even a new pilot could have accomplished. The plane was small, and the doorways were five stories tall and an easy hundred or more foot wide. A real pilot could have flown one of the large Orions through it.

Manny eased the second set of yellow tapes up and over his head. He kept on pushing slowly down the road. His head was on a swivel, and his eyes were scanning for any little things out of place.

He stopped.

He looked along the broken curb. Forty feet back, a small waterway had formed. It had collected mud from somewhere. Not much, but just enough. It had flowed along the road, against the low curb. The small mudflat had only grown to about eight feet wide at the widest, then dried up, and left only a quarter inch of silt mud.

In front of Manny were seven perfectly preserved prints. Three were cowboy boots. One was a knuckle and thumbprint, and two prints of bare feet, a right, and a left.

Manny stared at the boot print in front of him. He bent forward. Captured in the perfect molding clay was a size eleven men's pointed toe cowboy boot. Along the arch were triangle notches protruding about three-eighths of an inch toward the center. They were uniform and evenly spaced. Manny counted, and his stomach rolled. There were an even eighteen. He looked at the next boot mark. It was too far away to be certain, but it looked like five notches cut into the opposite side of the opposite boot.

The white heat dimmed. All around him, clouds blocked out the sun. As the day grew dim and dark, his chest was in a vise. Each heartbeat tightened the vise. A hot brick was being pushed through his ribcage. Manny felt like he needed to throw up. He sat back and tried to call for Hooker. The breath wouldn't come. He tried to scream, but no noise came out. He tried to raise his arm and wave, but his arms wouldn't move. The world circled and became darker. He knew he should be able to see the coastal range of hills. In the dark, there was only the gray as it got darker. The brick stopped moving, and Manny could feel its hard edges. The edges scraped on his lungs with each shallow breath. He wondered why he couldn't yawn. Stella was taking a long time to bring him his soup.

The siren in his head sounded wrong. He was headed to an emergency, but he should have been driving. Paul never drove. Manny should be driving. And the stupid siren needed to be fixed. It sounded like an idiotic ambulance instead of a squad car.

Someone was talking. The radio—it wasn't Paul. The radio sounded funny. He knew the voice, but it was wrong. Hooker wasn't a dispatcher or even a cop. Why was Hooker talking to him? He was on his way to an emergency. Couldn't Hooker hear the siren?

"Pulse is 140 and thready. His blood pressure is 154 over 110. His heart sounds good, and the monitor says he has a great beat. Lungs are clear. Pupils are responsive."

"10-4, 2-7-5. Continue to monitor and fluids. We'll see you in five. Valley Medical out."

The medic tapped the microphone key twice in a fast double-tap as he turned to hang it back up.

"So it's not a heart attack, not a stroke, so what?" Hooker watched Manny with the oxygen mask and a needle in his arm. He hadn't seen him when the Cowboy Picasso had snapped a .22 slug through his spine, but Hooker's imagination drifted toward the time and thinking this was what it had looked like.

The medic kept reading the numbers as he rechecked the blood pressure. He took the stethoscope from his ears and hung them around his neck. Looking up at Hooker, he shrugged. "Hard to say. If I were a doctor, I might suggest a panic attack had caused some hysterical paralysis."

"If you were a doctor..." Hooker grimaced.

The man nodded. He leaned over. "Sir? Can you hear me?"

"His name is Manny."

The medic didn't even acknowledge Hooker's contribution. It just fed smoothly into the drill. "Sir? Manny, can you hear me? Manny?" He patted Manny on the cheek. "Manny, can you hear me? Do you know where you are?"

Manny grunted. "Where's Hooker?"

"Right here, Manny."

"Prints in the mud."

"I saw them, Manny. I got Harold on all of them before the medical pukes got there." He didn't even have to look up to know the medic didn't care. He knew the drill between departments. Only your department was the best. Everybody else was lazy and over-stuffed on donuts.

"There were more."

"I saw them.

"There were eighteen on the one, five more on the other. The guy has been busy."

"Shush," Hooker hissed.

"But..."

"Manny. Shut up before I make this poor medic knock you out."

The ambulance wallowed into the driveway, slowed, and then backed up to the doors.

Hooker got out and could only watch helplessly.

"Jeezus, Hooker. First, you go stabbing kids in the hand with forks. What now, a spoon through the heart?"

Hooker didn't need to turn around to know it was the receptionist who always looked like she just rode up on a horse, her blond hair long enough to sit on. The tight jeans flared on the sides of the thighs, with the special horse rider's muscle.

The rest of the package was sexy in a horsey sort of way. Hooker had tried to get a date for several years, but they were just acquaintances with some history of flirting. Hooker was in no mood for her scalpel between the ribs crap today. "Well, if it isn't old Cynthia Eye Candy. How are you doing, Cyn?"

The slow burn with her never took long. She spun on the toe of her ubiquitous shit-kickers, before speaking. "This best not be any of your doing, Hooker."

Hooker followed her into the maw of the large door. Thankfully, the Sunday and time of day provided an almost empty emergency room—it was one of the few times Hooker had ever seen it this way. Even with the empty waiting room, there was a certain hum in the air of moaning and a low tide ebb and flow of the sounds of people in pain.

Connie came down out of her glass booth. "How is he?"

Hooker shrugged. "He was talking. But we don't know why he keeled over like that. One of the cops just happened to look down the way. He was almost a hundred yards outside of the search area. He was lucky."

"I saw it was Jeff Kowalsky who brought him in. What did he think?"

"Maybe hysterical paralysis combined with a spike of blood pressure from a panic attack."

The older nurse pursed her lips and looked down as she thought. "Sounds about right." She looked around as if someone had more authority than she did. She pushed Hooker toward the doors leading back to the emergency area. "Go ahead. You're as close to a son as the man has. I'll go call Stella and talk her down from the tree Dolly probably talked her up."

"Thanks, Connie."

"Just take care of the man."

"Trying, Connie, trying."

By the time Dolly tracked Stella down at the grocery store, they had moved Manny up to a room.

Fortunately, or unfortunately for Manny, it was the third floor—old home week. Thankfully, it was Valley Medical instead of Good Sam and Nurse Cutter.

The older nurse spun around and glared at the man. "Gosh damn it, Manny Romero, if you don't shut up, I'm going to intubate you and then start pumping Thorazine down your IV."

He closed his mouth.

Hooker snickered. Nurse Petite spun on him, only to find a deadpan look on his face.

Stella walked through the door. "I've got this, Lydia." The nurse frowned and left.

Stella sat down next to Hooker. She softly took his hand. Hooker knew it wasn't a good sign.

She leaned over as if she were going to take comfort by resting her head on his shoulder. He did not turn his head. He knew the look in her eyes.

Her mouth was only inches from his face. The whisper probably didn't carry past a few feet. But there were large pieces of metal in the hall Hooker knew bent from the intensity.

"What... in sweet biscuits were you thinking when you left *my* man out there alone?"

Hooker tried the deadpan delivery. "There were sixty other cops..."

"How dare you talk back to me!" The tip of her finger flashed an inch from his eye.

"He sent me to do something else."

"What?"

"Get castings of the other footprints."

"Did you?" Her voice was pure glacial ice.

"I found Harold and got him started, then went looking for Manny. That's when the cop saw him."

"How long was he lying there—alone—on the ground?"

"Seconds."

She waited. He turned and looked at her. "Stella. I swear. It was only seconds. The officer saw him go down. We thought he had been shot. We ran. We all ran." He searched her hard eyes.

"Leave him alone." The croak was a whisper from the bed.

She rose. Her index finger and hard stare pointed at Hooker. She wasn't finished with him. She turned to her man.

The knock at the doorway saved Hooker. He rose and walked out to Uncle Willie. "How...?" Hooker took him by the arm and walked down the hall. "He seems okay. But nobody will let him talk. I think when he saw the fresh boot tracks, something just snapped. I think all the crap from his dance with the asshole just came rushing back."

The man with plenty of experience with bad memories and events nodded his head as he also ignored the swearing. "Sometimes it can be those stupid things like the way the string beans are arranged at the market or the smell of hot gasoline on a muggy day. You just never know."

"How did...?" Hooker frowned. His face cleared and he rolled his eyes and head on his neck in the zombie act of attrition. "Dolly."

Willie laughed at Hooker. "Wow, the boy takes a few days off and blam-o, he forgets the reach and power of his girlfriend."

"Which reminds me—she wants me back at the table on Wednesday." He looked at his adoptive uncle. "I need wheels. I can't have you and Stella schlepping me all over the place."

"I think Don's new truck just got out of paint. I'll call him in the morning."

Hooker looked hard at the man.

"Okay, okay... I'll call him tonight." The man pushed on Hooker's chest. "Just for you." A hint of the man's Nancy slipped out. Hooker knew he was relaxing.

"Thanks, Willie."

Willie nudged his chin back toward the door to the room. "So what did you guys find?"

Hooker looked down the hall. "We'll know in about sixty seconds. Did you ever meet Manny's old partner Paul?"

Willie turned. "Of course, I know Paul. How are you doing, young man?"

"Mr. Knight, great to see you again! You look younger than when I last saw you." Paul spoke as he approached.

"Well, it was with all the fretting and worrying over young Hooker and his boy Squirt. Paul, it just wears a person down. It just gets right in and grinds the soul to grist. I don't know why I worry so about this little ingrate, but I do."

Hooker rolled his eyes as Paul, and he both tugged up their pant legs. "Holy Cap'n Crunch on scrambled eggs, Willie, can you get it any deeper?"

The mock horror of suffering washed over Willie.

Paul stopped him. "Can it, William. I caught the act the first time." They all laughed.

Hooker pointed to the envelope in the commissioner's hand. "Is that what I think it is?"

The man nodded.

Hooker put his finger up for the signal for one minute. He turned and stuck his head in the door to the room. "Stella, Willie is here. We're just going downstairs for some coffee. We'll be back."

She nodded, never taking her eyes off Manny.

Hooker faced the two men. "Let's go see Walt."

"Walt?" The commissioner frowned, his freckles turned into wrinkles.

Willie slapped his arm around the man's shoulders. "The janitor—he's in the basement. He happens to be a coffee snob—so much so he roasts his own beans."

The aroma was still intoxicating twenty minutes later as they looked over the photos.

"Holy crap! I would have had a seizure too if I had seen this boot mark. This guy has been busy is an understatement. We go from five to eighteen in six years?"

"No—we go from five to twenty-three in six years. You forgot the other boot. But even that is wrong. He still gets to carve another in the boot after today." Hooker leaned his head into his hand.

"He has to have been somewhere else." The commissioner sipped on his coffee as he thought.

"Have you called around yet?"

"Started. I got five of the counties. They should have gotten back to me by this time." He turned around to look down the long room. "Hey, Walt, do you have a phone I can use?"

"Hooker can show you, sir," the man called back from the workbench with a small TV over it. Perry Mason was addressing the jury.

Hooker held one eye almost closed as he raised his eyebrows. "You don't mess with Walt's Perry Mason, even if you are a county commissioner." He laughed and pulled out a drawer of the workbench next to where they were sitting. "It keeps the phone from getting stuff on it or broken from falling tools."

Hooker could see him make a note to himself. "Willie can tell you nothing will protect a phone when you throw a three-pound piston at it." The two laughed about an incident when the phone kept ringing because Moffett Field Naval base kept looking for their construction crew. They were only supposed to assemble the former hanger—Willie's new garage —and leave. The facts of there were no end walls and Willie had a great swimming pool combined with plenty of beer and a barbecue after four in the afternoon had nothing to do with the work dragging on until the end of summer. Of course, having twenty buff young men around the place didn't exactly upset Willie either. Three phones in the shop never survived the summer.

They watched the commissioner who was rapidly running out of paper to write on. Hooker reached over and opened another drawer and pulled out a pad of yellow legal paper.

The commissioner eagerly waved it over. "Uh-huh... yeah... the date again was... okay. I'll be back in about twenty minutes. We had one of the investigators end up in the hospital this afternoon." He listened. "Yeah, Romero, Mansfield Romero—pull his file. He's retired, but we are using him as a consultant, so the department should be picking up the hospital tab on him. Also, while you're running things to ground, open a folder for the other consultant." He looked at Hooker for his real name. He just got a glare. "Just put it under 'A' period Hooker. Right. Just like the working girl." He rolled his eyes. "Right—I'll finish this when I get in."

He hung up the phone. He suspected he wasn't going to win the staring contest, but he had to try.

Willie saw what was happening and started to laugh. "Paul, you are never going to get it that way."

Hooker smiled but didn't blink. Paul finally slid his eyes over to the older man.

"Hieronymus as in Bosch the painter who painted Dante's Hell, and it couldn't have been more apropos. Octavius, as in Caesar Augustus, the first Roman Emperor, and then the name runs off the rails with O'Keller. Now, what would you call the kid—Harry or Tavi?" He looked at Hooker, who was busy trying to ignore the conversation. "What did you tell me your name was that day?"

Hooker looked at the man he loved deeply, and whom he knew every day he owed his life to this man. He thought back to the day Willie had returned to his prized convertible to find a scrawny butt in worn jeans peeking up from where Hooker was experimenting at trying to steal a car. Willie had smacked him on the butt and told him to scoot over—they were going to lunch. When Hooker had just stared at him, he had told him he was certain Hooker was starving, because he had just spent five minutes trying to hotwire the car's radio.

"Ralph."

Willie held his look for a moment then slid his eyes back to Paul with the *see what I must put up with* look. "Ralph."

Paul chuckled and eyed Hooker calmly. "Well, Ralph, you're now on the payroll for a while. Keep all the receipts if you talk to anyone over a meal or coffee."

Willie laughed. "Hooker knows where all the free coffee and meals are."

Paul stood. "Well, it looks like our boy was busy up and down the Central Valley. We even got a call from Reno. So I have some long phone calls to make." He turned and finished with, "Thanks for the coffee, Walt."

The man raised a distracted hand. There were six minutes left of Perry Mason. "Just leave a dime on the counter."

Paul looked at Hooker, who was shrugging.

"He never charged me."

The man heard more than they thought. "You weren't on an expense account like Mr. Commissioner there."

Paul laughed. "Man's got a point." He laid a ten-spot on the counter. It was always good to know where good coffee was available and better to make sure it stayed available.

They walked out to the elevator. "I wouldn't tell Manny tonight. Let him sleep."

"We'll just check-in, but since I need to talk to Dolly, I'll stay out at Willie's tonight—just to keep him honest. If you know anything before noon, that's where I'll be. If I'm on the move, Dolly or dispatch will know how to get ahold of me."

They parted at the first floor, and Hooker and Willie rode to the third. Manny was sleeping, and Stella was passed out in the chair next to him. They were still holding hands. Hooker grabbed a blanket out of the closet and covered her.

The young black-haired nurse who came on shift a little earlier, walked past as they were leaving the room. She whispered in a hushed nurse's voice. "Is she still asleep?"

Hooker nodded, knowing his voice would wake Stella.

"We'll wheel a spare bed in there in about an hour. She isn't going anywhere tonight."

Hooker took her hand and mouthed *thanks*.

13

The dim pools of light in the darkroom gave the two women at the switchboard an eerie cast as if they were witches enchanting a wall of snakes. Their disembodied conversations were an almost constant murmur. The late evening was a busy time at the dispatch, as tow companies were still busy and other responders became more active. The fever pitch would be between 10:30 and 11:40 and then die. The slow time was midnight until the drunks left the bar to start their cars or drive them into telephone poles if other drivers were lucky.

Dolly was reclining in her custom-built steel desk chair and across her expansive chest was her favorite orange fur blanket, Box.

"Stella knew you might be tied up at the hospital, and she knew she wouldn't be home to feed him, so she dropped him off for me to babysit."

Hooker took the plate from Willie and walked into the oversized kitchen with a large dining table that sat twelve every Wednesday night for dinner. Dinners were by invite only, and the players changed every week, except for Hooker, the anointed one. Everyone knew there was a reason you were invited or not. The joke was Dolly ruled San Jose by night, and only loaned it back to the minions to take care of it during the day while she slept. Hooker knew the joke was more truth than humor.

Elections and power had been won and lost around the table. Arthur in Camelot had only dreamed of such a table.

"Just put them in the sink, Hooker. I'll wash them with our dinner plates."

He rinsed them off and stacked them with the coffee mugs.

Turning off the kitchen light, he walked back into the dark room. He continued the evening's discussion. "So we thought you might know someone in the Native American community who could shed some light on the use of bird wings. If there is something more specific to a raven—that would be even better."

Dolly looked at the large school clock on the wall. "Dina, get me Doc White down in Paso Robles, would you, dear."

She looked back at Hooker. "Doc taught American Indian Anthropology at Stanford for over thirty years. He's retired now and doesn't go to bed until after Johnny."

"Line three."

"Thank you, dear." Dolly swung around and picked up the handset as she pushed the blinking light. "Yut ta hey, Doc," their standard greeting since she had taken a class from him as a young girl. She explained what Hooker was looking for.

Hooker could tell the conversation was going to run on for a while, and figured Box could use a grass break. "Box, grass?"

The cat looked at Dolly, and she heaved her chest. He jumped as much as fell out of her chest lap. The two partners strolled to the steel-clad door. Hooker checked the peephole as Dolly checked the TV monitor of the outside security camera. "You're good, Hooker."

"No, I was just telling Hooker he was clear to open the door. He had to take my cat outside."

Willie walked over to the switchboard and sat down on the third rolling chair next to Dina. He watched the routine of pulling a cord out and plugging it into a hole in the wall, throwing a switch and answering the call, then plugging another cord in another hole if she was transferring a call, or using the radio if she was dispatching a call. The night rolled on. Willie still marveled at how they could keep everything straight, no matter how many cords were plugged into how many holes, and phone calls and trucks dispatched, and where they even were.

During a brief lull, he leaned in close to Dina. "How is the baby?"

She smiled and took his hand and held it on her large tummy. "He's sleeping, but I think he's his father's son. He tosses and turns."

Willie could feel the small convulsions of the child. She was only six months along but looked more like ten. He smiled at feeling something only a father would normally feel. He knew that with Hooker, his life had blossomed into a very large family. He knew that his longest and best friend, the librarian, Maddie, felt the same. Their solitary lives had been blessed with the arrival of a young fourteen-year-old boy who only looked like a man. With Maddie's help, Hooker had become the man Willie had seen in him the first day.

Hooker knocked on the door. The thick steel on the solid oak door resounded only slightly louder than a sigh. Dolly had been watching the small security camera monitor and buzzed him and Box in.

"Just a minute, Doc, Hooker just walked back in." She lowered the handset and laid it alongside Box's body as the cat settled back in. "Hooker, he wants to know if you know which wing it was."

"Raven."

"Which side?"

"Right. It has always been the right radial bone."

"Doc, he says the right radial bone." She gave him a sharp questioning eye as to how he knew what the bone was called. He just shrugged.

She listened for a moment. "Doc, just a minute, let me put you on speaker so you can teach the whole class." She spun in the chair and punched the button, and then cradled the handset. "Doc White, this is Hooker. Hooker, Doc White."

Hooker sat on the corner of the large desk. "Glad to meet you, Doc."

"Same, son. I've heard nothing about you, so it must all be true." He laughed. Dolly rolled her eyes, and Hooker assumed it was one of the man's standards."

"So the right radial bone of the raven? How exactly is it being used?"

Hooker looked at Dolly. She held her palm out at the phone. It was as much permission Hooker needed. "He's cutting a clump of the victim's hair, and then binding it with some of their skin to the bone. He then is using it as a paintbrush to paint symbols on the wall with the victim's blood."

Over at the dispatching board, Dina turned toward Willie. Her eyes rolled into her head as she closed her eyes and wished she could close her ears. Her mouth had a full look.

Willie quickly reached down and grabbed the metal trash can full of crumpled call and run tickets. He held it up toward her.

She slowly gained control and opened her eyes. Looking into Willie's eyes, she grew a question mark on her face. He slowly nodded, confirming what Hooker was saying was true.

Karen reached over and rubbed her back.

"Can you describe the symbols?"

"They are kind of hard to describe."

"Okay, son—let's try it a different way. Do they look like numbers or something written?"

"Both, but it looks like mostly writing."

"Any other stuff, or is it just him writing in his diary?"

Hooker's eyebrows rose, and he looked at Dolly. She gripped her lips together in a smug smile. She knew her people. She petted Box.

"Man, you are good. There is a large circle with other smaller circles on the line and some other larger symbols in and out of the large circle."

"Just a minute, son." They could hear the professor had just put them on speakerphone as well. The sound of him pulling books and flipping pages was a soft background.

Dolly swung her chair around and lifted her coffee mug. She looked in it at the cold last swallow. Curling her nose, she held it out at Hooker. She slowly closed her eyes and nodded to let him know he had time. She knew the professor, and Hooker had just sent him on a hunt.

Hooker took the mug and rinsed out the old coffee. He stood leaning against the sink, thinking about the walls in the railcar. The fact of the 'ink' being the victim's blood was gruesome enough, but the writings were creepy and disturbing in a 'thing under the bed in the night' kind of way. He shook and then picked up the carafe for coffee. He put the mouth of the cup under the spigot of the large coffee urn and started to fill. The dispatch went through over a pound of coffee in a twenty-four-hour cycle. The second urn was already cleaned and ready to go when these twenty cups were low or old.

Hooker thought about his sister and what she demanded. Her minions were subservient and basically under control. But if one or two were breaking out of her control, there could be trouble that could spread through the whole community. He didn't want to think about what kind of fallout could overflow into the regular community.

He carried the carafe in his left hand. He placed Dolly's half full mug on the desk with the handle turned away from her. She drank with her whole hand, holding the body of the mug and her three fingers in the handle. Her bent pinkie finger rode stiffly on the outside of the handle.

Quietly, he filled his mug, and then the other three. He expected Willie to cut him off with only a half cup, but he took it all. Hooker suspected there was something up because Willie was not a true night owl.

Returning from the kitchen, he could hear a chair squeak and books plopped on a desk. "So, we have a few things here." The professor was still lost in his world. "If you look here, you see the..." He seemed to remember he was all alone with a phone on speaker. Hooker could imagine the man with wild hair looking over his spectacles at the empty room.

The man chuckled. "Sorry, I was talking to my cat, I guess."

Dolly and Hooker smiled as they looked at the rumbling cat on her chest. "It's okay, Doc, we have one here, too."

"Oh, Dorthia, when did you acquire a cat?"

Dolly shot Hooker a hard look before he could even think to mouth the name *Dorthia*. "It's Hooker's mange bucket, Doc. He just foists the derelict on me for safekeeping."

"Oh, I see." He fidgeted with the books. "All right now, so—are there any patterns that have an arc like a sun with rays and it's resting on a flat line?"

Hooker thought with his eyes closed. His head was turning slowly as he tried to picture the walls. A part of him swore because this was the one time he could have used the Squirt and his photographic memory. "I don't think so, Doc. Would it be big or small?"

"Um... small, I think." The sound of three large books slamming shut bounced over the speaker. "All right, we'll hold Zuni and Navaho in limbo for now. So I'm looking for objects with an arrow coming out of them. Usually, it will be pointed in an upward direction."

"Yes." Hooker sat up excitedly. "I remember there were three in the railcar. Two were smaller, but not as small as the writing. One was a little larger, near the floor, so I just thought it was easier to paint it bigger."

Two more books landed on an auditory stack.

"All right, we are not in the Pacific Northwest then. Is there any hand print or something similar to a handprint?"

"No. We would have checked it for fingerprints, and there were none."

"Good, so the Plains Indians are out now, too. I didn't want to have to go get the ladder, anyway."

Dolly licked her lips and raised her eyebrows in a memory about how the professor was so refreshing about his likes and dislikes.

"This might be taxing, but I'm looking for a specific symbol. It would be in the writing, but I think it would have stood out. As you look at it, it would be a snake-like an 'S' connected to a 'C'... or wiggle with two humps on the left and one on the right. Standing very close but not touching would be a straight line up and down, except the bottom would reach down farther like the tail on a 'g' or 'y'."

Hooker stared at the wall. The concrete melted away and became the wood of the rail car. "Could it have an arrow starting in the middle right curve that projects right through the line?"

There was silence from the speakerphone. Dolly frowned and looked over at the dispatching board and Karen.

Karen looked on the board and shook her head and shrugged.

Dolly rose to a more sitting position. Box turned his head and scowled at her. The purring stopped. She held her large hand along him as she leaned forward. "Doc? Doc, did we lose you?"

There was a pause, and then a very soft pensive voice responded. "I'm here, Dorthia... just thinking. Look, hang tight for a few minutes. I have to make a phone call, and I'll call you back in about ten or fifteen minutes."

"Okay, Doc..." She knew she was talking to a dead phone.

The clock ticked slowly as they waited. None of them wanted to talk. The last-minute had seemed to step off the sidewalk of reality into the superhighway of strange. Hooker knew they had just landed in the universe of his sister. Dolly suspected but wasn't sure if she really wanted to know.

Willie got up and stretched his legs. Looking at his coffee mug, he wandered into the kitchen. Hooker watched as he got another cup of coffee. Hooker turned and looked at the large clock. He was now positive Willie was truly up to something in the middle of the night.

"Dispatch, this is Dina… just a moment, Doc. I'll put you through."

Dolly's finger was hovering over the speakerphone button.

"What do you have, Doc?"

"I called a professor friend of mine. He has been doing some work over in Nevada and the long valley in California running along the border. They share some tribal grounds running the length of the Owens Valley, out through the many valleys north of Death Valley and into the Nevada desert. These are basically Piute Indian lands, but there are also factions. Some of these factions even reach west into the Central Valley.

"You may recall a few years ago there were some unsavory types who were rounded up out there in the desert. They called themselves a family, but they were more like a mangled collective who acted like a tribe. The leader was a guy named Manson."

He let the meaning of it soak in.

"The symbol you described would fit not only one of the more deviate factions of the Piute nation, but the Manson tribe, as well. The symbol is a hybrid of a shaman and a warrior. It represents the god of vengeance taking a mortal visage to put the world back in balance."

"By killing?"

"By not only killing, my boy, but killing in a much-ritualized manor. The entire process about creating the magic that will grant the power back to the mortal to become a god again. You said the victims were nailed up to the walls. I would hazard a statement of the number of nails always being the same, and it wasn't just the hands, but nails through the arms and legs as well."

"Correct." Hooker was drained and subdued.

"You mentioned the hair was bound to the raven's bone with a part of the victim's own skin. Would the skin have come from some sexual area such as the penis, vaginal lips, or breasts?"

"Yes."

"Then you have a very sick individual on your hands. There have been similar killings in the Central Valley. My friend was consulting on a few. They were hushed because they didn't want to frighten people about a serial killer. But you could check with the Fresno, Bakersfield, and out in Tehachapi and Mojave area."

"I thought a shaman was supposed to heal people? Like a witch doctor or something."

"Normally, they are. But with this faction, they are about the blood and killing."

"Where does the raven bone fit in to all of this?"

"The fact he uses it consistently is an indication it is a talisman for him. It is something that is very personal. If he is of the tribe, it may have been his vision quest marker. You will have to catch him and ask him to get any real definitive clarification on it."

"So, where would someone go to get a specific bone of a bird?"

"If I was one of my smartass students, I would say an ornithology supply. But I'm not, so I'm as stumped as she would have been."

Hooker looked at Dolly. She didn't acknowledge the comment, but Hooker was certain there was a glow creeping up alongside her ears.

"Do you think there would be some kind of company who could supply something like it?"

"There might be. Check with a museum. They may have a source for bones and things for restoring old skeletons or something. But I can't see them being cheap enough just to throw away every so often."

"Okay, Doc. Thanks a lot for your knowledge and research. If we need to contact the other professor..."

"You'll find him at the federal penitentiary just outside of Carson City. His last four numbers are all zeros." He laughed.

"He's an inmate?"

"Well, yes. It's a case of it takes a thief to catch a thief. He's in solitary confinement, but he has a direct phone line into his cell. He does a lot of consulting work for police and the FBI."

"Okay, Doc, you are officially a member of my family of weird people who know even weirder people. Thanks for your help."

"No problem, Hooker. Any friend of Dorthia's is like family to me. Goodnight."

Dolly poked at the phone, and it was silent.

She shuddered. Box meowed a silent protest. "Personally, I think it's creepy."

"But what Sweets had to say was creepier."

She raised her hand and pointed at Hooker. "True."

She turned slightly and peered into the darkness. "Karen, who is on the table this week?"

Karen looked up at her cheat sheet. "Drivers—Mike P, Ace, Stan, Joe, and Terry; Cops are Chet and Micha. We have a call into Whelan's office, but they said he might be back in DC still. Peter and Dutch are in, and we need them to look at the switching problem in the alarm room. Hooker is the head, and we have two opens."

Dolly swung back to the two men now standing. "Bring Sweets and Danny. On second thought, Karen, Whelan has jerked me around one too many times. He's out—and I do mean out. We aren't supporting his next election. Find someone new who will work with us."

Hooker listened and thought about how the table worked, and the power it and Dolly wielded. Every Wednesday night, there was a special mix of players at the table. Twelve, now eleven that Hooker was back, that Dolly could make or break depending on how she arranged the board. He also knew next election term, there would be a new person sitting in the seat in Congress. His rock and foundation were cast on the solid nature of the person sitting in front of him.

Dolly looked back at Hooker. "Tell Danny I want, or you want, I don't care, which ever works, all three of them to be here. We'll have Sweets fed and out the door in plenty of time for his shift."

Hooker took a mental stumble. As far as he knew, she had never invited a woman to the table. Even Dolly never sat at the table. "Tilly? A woman?"

"Sure." She gave Hooker the special look Hooker felt he should know, but it just added acid to his stomach. "It's about time I shake things up in this town. As the song goes, the times they are a-changing."

Hooker saluted his obedience. "Box…"

She placed a hand on the beast who had tensed. "You're busy. He's fine here. I have plenty of roadkill to feed the mange monster."

"Okay, it's your kitchen."

They were halfway up the hill to the giant garage with the small house attached when Willie broke the silence. "A woman… Has she…?"

"Not to my knowledge." Hooker looked out over the quiet, twinkling valley as the big car nosed onto the gas station sized driveway. Hooker tensed. The large door was slightly open.

Willie put his hand on Hooker's arm. "It's all right. Maddie rode her old Matchless motorbike up here. She's working on the Granny car. In fact, there is some stuff out in Minden-Gardnerville area I need to go pick up. If we start early, we could stop off at a certain prison."

Hooker softened and opened his door and stepped out of the car. Closing the car door, Hooker sighed with his relief. "I'll get the door."

As he pulled the large steel door all the way back, he thought about Dolly and about the coffee now sitting uncharacteristically in Willie's gut. *Something is up.*

14

The moon had finally set about the time the 1940 REO Speed Wagon truck barreled its way past Kit Carson Lake. The scenery changed to a slightly drier forest on the eastern side of the Sierra Nevada Mountains, as Willie and Hooker dropped down through the Faith, Hope, and Charity valleys. Even with all the tall pine trees, there was still high-country fall color to entertain the eyes. This beauty was not lost on either male.

Willie mused as he looked across the expanse of Hope valley. "Maybe next summer we should all come up and go camping or something."

Hooker harrumphed. "Willie, I've known you long enough to know that is code for rent a room, and maybe go take a walk around a lake like we did a few summers ago on Echo Lake. As for Maddie, I know she doesn't want to suffer through our cooking attempts over a fire pit again. We only survived because of the little diner down the road."

Laughing, Willie shot Hooker a hangdog face as he glanced over. "Well, who knew they had some good steak to offer?"

"Maybe it had something to do with the big-assed sign saying *Best Steak West of Kansas City?*"

"It was a cute place."

"I was just afraid you were going to steal some of those red and white checked tablecloths and ask Maddie to sew you up a dress or two."

Willie flashed a wide-eyed look of mock shock. Both men knew Maddie didn't even know much more than sewing on a button, and even then she would drive it over to Willie and have him do it for her.

The miles and tall trees disappeared with the teasing and remembering of times gone by. The terrain leveled out, and large ranches became the landscape as the brush was replaced by long stretches of perfectly lined barbwire fences. In the distance, the occasional large hay barn hulked near a smaller three-story farmhouse with deep-set wraparound porches. Most of them were painted red with white trim.

About every mile, a road came out to the highway. Arcing over the end of each driveway, and connecting the fences was an arch made from large old telephone poles. Hanging in the middle the arch, high enough for a stacked hay truck to pass under, was a sculpted brand or the occasional sign.

Willie slowed as he approached each ranch entrance. "It's along here somewhere. Look for a large *R* lying on its back followed by a *C*. The ranch brand is Lazy RC Ranch."

Hooker frowned. "Isn't Lazy RC the ranch you get meat shipped from?"

Willie looked over and smiled hugely.

Looking back at the road and the next arch, he recalled, "I served with Steven in Korea. He was a great cook who had a bad habit of burning field rations."

The Speed Wagon slowed, but the arch revealed only a ranch humorously named Lito Ponderosa, or Little Ponderosa. The two men laughed as Willie asked the crude question, "Who would advertise they only have a little wood?" They drove on. Not much worth seeing.

They finally found the Lazy RC and pulled into the barnyard. A large man with long gray braids strolled out of the barn door. Hooker could tell he had an educated eye as he looked over the Speed Wagon slowly curving in front of him. Willie shifted into reverse and backed toward the barn door and parked.

"The extra two inches you stuffed in the nose really looks nice,

William." The giant ran his hand along the hood. "Where did you clip it in?"

Willie winked at Hooker before he slid out of the driver's side. "Stupid asshole, you know I'm not going to tell a Ford man how to build cars right. It might upset the entire Detroit balance."

The giant laughed as he took one step toward Hooker. "Ignore him. He was always an asshole, even before Korea. The name is Chief Steven Seven Toes, but you can call me Steve or Chief." He glared at Willie. "Only my wife or another asshole can call me an asshole."

Willie laughed. "Idiot, you've met Hooker before."

The man's face exploded in shock. Snapping back to Hooker, he smiled and looked at the man Hooker. "Oh, my gee-whiz, it is. Son, you done growed up."

The memory suddenly snapped clear in Hooker's mind. "It's the beard. It was much larger then." They laughed about the mutual teasing of a brief evening when Hooker was only fifteen but already towing.

He turned to Willie. "He lies like you do."

"Nah, there is a librarian who won't let him. But he *has* learned the word elaboration."

Steven waved a large paw at the Speed Wagon. "Leave this for now. Lunch is about ready, and we can load this after."

Willie took on a serious tone. "There is a little bit of a time consideration here."

"What?"

"Hooker needs to go up to the prison near Carson and talk to an inmate."

The giant turned to evaluate Hooker. "Friend?"

"Nah, the guy is an expert on a certain serial killer we are hunting. I have some pictures requiring his knowledgeable opinion. We would normally mail them, but time is a factor."

Steven looked back and forth between the two men. "Do you have an appointment set up with the prison?"

Hooker shook his head. "Evidently, this guy is a regular consultant with the FBI and others, so we figured we'd just come on over."

The man laughed the kind of deep belly laugh only large men can do with effect. "Not fucking likely. That kind of access usually requires a couple of weeks of red tape, unless you are married to him or are a blood relative."

Turning, he shrugged. "Well, come on in, and I'll call over and see what I can work out with John Red Feather. He's the warden over there. Meanwhile, I can smell the tamales Maria is making, and it's making me some kind of powerful hungry."

Hooker looked at Willie, who was chuckling and shaking his head as he followed the man toward the house. As they drew closer to the house, Hooker picked up the delicious aroma and had to agree about the powerful hunger.

A short while later, Steven cradled the phone back on the hook. "I'll be going to Texas. John said come on down." Steven pulled his chair out and sat back at the table filled with the remains of lunch. The four ranch hands had returned to their work, leaving the three men to discuss the prison and the engine they came to get. "Evidently, you're right. This fella has people stopping by all the time. He even has a phone line in his cell so they can call him at any hour."

Hooker just nodded with a smile.

The chief grinned. "Yeah, but you already knew that."

Hooker rolled his eyes and shrugged.

Willie wiped the last piece of invisible food from his smiling mouth. He nodded toward the barn. "Shall we load the engine so we can be on our way?"

The giant rolled over to one hip and fished out a small clump of keys. Tossing them to Willie, he countered, "How about you two take my truck, and we'll load all the Mopar scrap we can find into your Speed Wagon. That way you don't have to waste time when you pass back through unless it's close to dinnertime."

Willie thought about the idea. "The keys are in the wagon. The engine is fresh, so keep it under eighty or a hundred." The two smiled, knowing their history.

"How fresh?"

"Keep it under the speed you flipped the MP's Hudson Cruiser."

The former staff sergeant saluted with two fingers as they all got up.

The chief cleared his throat. "And you remember even Nevada has the new stupid fifty-five law."

As they walked toward the barn, Willie showed Hooker the very distinctive Cobra key.

The reputation of the 427 engine was not exaggerated. Nor were the stories about the Ford Cobra. Hooker wasn't sure if his face would ever unfreeze the smile, but it was fun putting it there.

John Red Feather, who looked more like an accountant lost in some back office than the Piute Indian Hooker had envisioned, escorted them into a large interview room. The conference table had places for up to fourteen people.

"This is where the parole council meets. Usually, when Charles meets with people, they have a lot of stuff to spread out and look at. The large table helps."

Willie looked the man over. "Do you usually sit in on his consults?"

"Occasionally, I have a certain knowledge set in Piute lore and shamanism. I'm a sixth-generation shaman in our tribe." His stare was only slightly challenging, and he saw it had no effect on Willie. "When Steve told me you were coming, I had a chat with Charles. He thought I might be a bit of help."

He looked over at Hooker. "I guess he spoke to you or someone the other night?"

"Indirectly, actually, I was talking with a Doc White in…"

"San Louis Obispo… yes, Doc is an old friend of ours."

Somewhere outside the room, a bell rang, followed by a clanging, and garbled voices over speakers. The bell rang again, and a large metal door clanged shut. There was a knock on the door, and John stood up to open it.

A slender man with a mop of curly hair over thick glasses stood in the doorway. Dressed in an orange shirt and pants over a pair of fuzzy slippers, he looked more like a young child than a convicted killer.

John waved him in. "Come on in, Charles, we were just about to start."

The man entered shyly with a soft-spoken, "Hello." Hooker and Willie stood.

John performed the introductions. "Charles, this is Hooker and Willie. They're here to talk about the killer in San Jose."

Hooker sensed John was talking to a mentally challenged person, instead of a college professor. As he watched, Charles transformed physically into a more assured man. The shift was uniquely disturbing but explained something Hooker was familiar with—multiple personalities. The many facets of the man were at once explained.

"Hello, I'm Charles." His self-assured hand shot out to shake Hooker and Willie's hands. "So, my naughty boy has become busy again, I understand." Waving at the chairs, "Please, be seated."

Hooker pulled the photos out of the folder. "These are pictures of the walls of his latest kill."

The man pushed his thick glasses high on his nose and looked closely at the photos. "Good, good… I'm glad they took color this time. Those last ones you brought were useless. I need to see the blood. Anybody can paint black paint…" He shuffled the photos. His dialogue seemed to be with someone other than those in the room.

Hooker looked over at John with a frown.

John held up his palms. "He isn't here right now. We can say almost anything, but he can't or won't hear us. I'm not sure where he goes, but he is reviewing and comparing the case from the start and all the information he has gathered or has been brought since. This process takes longer and longer each time as more information is layered on top of all the previous evidence, and then is integrated. So, while we wait, can I get anyone something to drink?"

Hooker's face screwed up in curious resolve. Hooker looked to Willie. "Coffee?" The former Naval Intelligence Officer nodded as he watched the former professor.

The disjointed voice chimed in, "Yes, please. Coffee, please."

The warden patted Charles's shoulder, as the man remained bent over the photos. "Yes, Charles, of course, you want a glass of hemlock. Would you like some arsenic and old lace in the hemlock, Charles?"

The drone nodded silently.

John shrugged and quirked his face and mouth. He shook his head. "I'll be right back," as he slid out the door and a guard silently stepped inside to take his place.

The coffee was long gone by the time the 'professor' part had returned to Charles. Hooker was glad he had bought a second and third legal yellow pad as the first had filled fast.

"Wait… so you're saying even though he is presenting mostly Piute shaman characteristics, he probably didn't originally come from this area?" Hooker frowned. "How does that work?"

Charles smiled as he found the photo he was looking for. "Look at this symbol here. This circle with the arrow (which is actually called a carrot) is pure Piute. But you see this little wavy line it's resting on—it isn't Piute. It's more Chippewa. It's not even a symbol or part of a symbol, as much as it is a dialect mark."

The professor rotated his glasses up onto the top of his head. "I've heard you say the word y'all seven times while we have been talking. Willie has never said it. You also just asked the question, 'How does that work?' Based on the wording of that question, and the use of the Southern term y'all, I would say you lived in Southern California around the San Bernardino area originally, but up on the hillside like Mentone or upper Redlands, and your family work involved the orchards." He sat waiting for Hooker to confirm his theory.

Willie just watched Hooker, curious about the possibility of learning something new about his ward. The clock on the wall ticked as Hooker weighed how much he was willing to share about his personal life and past.

"I was left at an orphanage in Ramona. Most of the foster homes were in the area until I moved into the Central Valley. I never thought about it before, but we were always near some kind of agriculture."

Charles smiled softly. "Thank you for sharing something I can tell is very private with you." Leaning back in the chair to not appear threatening, he continued. "You slipped and said, 'we were near,' so you were protecting a sibling. I would assume it is female and younger."

"Older. But yes, I'm very protective of her."

"Good, but not blood-related."

Hooker nodded.

The professor watched and processed some information which was only known or important to him. "So, just like your language, these little extra pieces keep showing up in our killer's writings, and they tell a very different story than we see initially." He turned to the Warden.

"John, this block here… what is he working on?"

The warden leaned over and scanned the photo. "In Piute, this is the story of the coyote bringing fire, but he has the bear taking the fire away to the moon."

"So it would just be scrambled eggs of thought?"

Turning it around for Hooker and Willie to see, he drew his finger along the symbols. "This is the coyote and the fire. Think of the coyote as a medium-sized dog instead, much like a fox. So when we add in this mark here and here, we have a fox crossing, not the desert, but a large lake instead. He is still bringing fire to the Chippewa, but it is in the form of enlightenment instead of flames.

"The bear here works with the fox to bring enlightenment which will rival the white light of the full moon. So it's about working together in combination to produce greater power. The sacrificial body contributes the blood so the shaman can paint the symbols to create the power."

Hooker ran his fingers through his hair. All of this information was more than he had bargained for or could take in at one time. "So, what about all the rest of this—is he just saying the same thing over and over again? Is this writing 'I will not spit in class' a hundred times on the chalkboard?"

The professor had seen the overloaded student look many times. "Essentially yes, but…" He jumped up and started excitedly moving the photos around.

The other three men sensed a shift and stood.

"There. That's how he painted the inside of the boxcar."

Hooker stood stunned. He purposely had not told the man where the killing had taken place. "How did you know it was in a boxcar?"

The man turned and gave him a parental stare. "Please. I've been in my share of boxcars."

Turning back to the photos, Charles once more became the animated professor. Extending his right hand and arm with the fingers splayed as a starburst, he started. "The sacrifice, victim to you, was at this end of the car. He starts his writings close and works left, unlike a native English speaker, who would start to the right of the sacrifice, and work right."

Willie lowered one eyebrow. "So you are saying he is a foreigner?"

"No, I'm saying English is his second language. Arabic is his first language."

Hooker screwed up his face. "What? Then where does the Chippewa come in?"

Charles stood straight and buried his glasses back in the mop of curls on his head. He rolled his lips tight to his teeth and then puttered them out. "I said, Arabic was his first language. I didn't say he grew up in Arabia. Most likely he grew up in Wisconsin. His mother is Arabian, but early in his life, his Arabian father disappears. He's later replaced by a very strong figure in the Chippewa nation, probably a shaman. My guess would be this happened when he's probably nine or ten years old, a very impressionable time in a boy's life.

"Learning a new language written in a new set of symbols, such as Chipewyan, was not a hard stretch for him. After all, he has made the jump from Arabic script to Judeo-Spanish writing. The most seductive part of Chipewyan and Piute language is the power and building of strength when combined with certain other rituals."

"Such as human sacrifices." Willie looked up from the photos.

The professor pulled his glasses down and looked at Willie as if for the first time. "Well, yes… but it's not about the sacrificial body. It's about the blood." They stood looking and taking the measure of each other. The large scar across Willie's neck and up the side of his face held a fascination for the murderer, but the professor was in the forefront at the moment. "Yes, that's right, it's the blood."

He leaned over and started at the far right. "Here he is talking about the blood of a lamb. He is specific. So if we could find his original kill or kills, they would be either animals or children."

Moving to the next photo, he pointed to a small cluster of symbols in a larger circle. "Here he branched out and took two children at once. He hoped for a Gemini effect, which is more synergetic than just a doubling.

You might call it quantum mechanics in killing. It's a very advanced thought process."

Hooker wasn't sure he was listening to the detached evaluations of an academic or the salivations of an admiring devote of ritualistic serial killing. Either way, Hooker found it a bit too creepy to be comfortable.

"So he started with children, and then graduated to adults?"

The man looked up and then stood. His eyes blinked, focusing behind the glass. Hooker guessed the serial killer stepped out of the way of the professor. "Yes but think of it as driving. You start by riding a tricycle. Stop, start, and turn—it's all safe. Then you move up through bicycles with training wheels, and eventually, you drive motorcycles and automobiles. But he's even beyond that. He's up to jet airplanes now.

"Basically, killing small animals or neighborhood pets is how most start because it's safe. You don't have to explain when a cat goes missing when a raccoon could have gotten it.

"Once the dynamics of how to kill are worked out, the killer progresses onto much larger game, like a child from another part of town." Absently, the professor's hand and index finger drifted to a very specific symbol set on the third photo. The action did not escape the ever-watchful eye of the quiet warden.

Willie was becoming agitated, as well. "So what are we looking for now?"

The academic resumed in force as he scanned over the writings. "Based on his progression, I would be looking for a male with Sephardic features, in his middle thirties, probably affected clothing with a fetish for their killing knife."

He drew his face closer to the last photo in the line-up. "Based on this, he's counting his coup on his boots or shoes. He's making ritualistic cuts. He also has moved into the last phase of some kind of stars and moon alignment. He's getting close to his belief in his becoming a king, or god if it's empire-building that he is doing."

The professor rose and once again raised his glasses into his hair. "My supposition is he's very egotistical, narcissistic, and psychopathic. He may even be sociopathic, as well."

Hooker furrowed his forehead slightly. "You said 'their killing knife'—did you also mean he has multiple personalities?"

The man slowly rose, blinking rapidly. "I did? Well, I meant to say his killing knife." Hooker saw a shadow of anger hiding in the eyes of the man before him as the professor slipped the thick glasses back down to his nose.

"What about the bone from the raven's wing?"

The man snapped. "I don't know anything about birds."

Hooker decided it was best to let it go. He turned toward the warden. "John, is there anything else to add to this?"

The man hesitated, and then looked at the back of the prisoner who was markedly ignoring him. He softly shook his head. "No, I think the professor has covered everything in his usual exquisite detail. Good job once again, Charles."

Hooker noted the man barely nodded his head in acknowledgment of his prowess. He felt sure the killer part of the man's personalities now stood fully developed in their presence.

The warden opened the door and addressed the guard. "You and Paul can take Charles back home now. I'm sure he needs his rest. It's been a long day." He swung the door wide open and stepped back to give the professor a wide berth. Hooker noted the guards did not touch the man either. A ticking time bomb came to Hooker's mind.

As the door swung shut, the warden leaned his back against it. Resting, as well as waiting, listening, and counting. Outside, the voice over the speaker followed the ringing of the bell. The large steel door slammed open, and then shut. The warden's eyes remained shut. Hooker and Willie waited. The room stank of unburned fear or tension.

With a deep sigh, John finally stepped forward and pointed to the last photo. "He wasn't completely forthcoming about everything in this set of photos. Here your killer is talking about a mouse or a mouse tribe or a tribe owned by a mouse." He looked up at Hooker with a question.

Hooker nodded. "I noticed he ignored talking about the photo, and yes, thank you, the mouse is real. And she has a tribe. And I fear she's in grave danger."

15

Thanks to its oversized engine, the heavily loaded Speed Wagon easily climbed the grade on Echo Summit out of Meyers. The last of the afternoon light stretched east of them toward Lake Tahoe. Both men smiled at the decision to change the route on the way home as they snuck quick glimpses of the majestic view.

Finally, Willie gave up and pulled into the overlook.

As they walked to the thick rock retaining wall, their mouths were at half gape. The gold sparkled across the lake some five miles away. A mist or haze played through the forest to create an ethereal, dreamlike beauty.

Hooker sat on the wall. "This is the kind of view you want to show your girlfriend."

The older steely eyes never wavered from the view. "Or just someone you care about."

The air was thick between the two men. Neither needed to say more as they watched the long shadow of the mountain reach out to embrace the valley.

"So, why did you?"

Willie knew exactly what Hooker wanted to know. It was years coming. "Why did I what?"

"Why did you take me in that day?"

Willie spun on Hooker in mock horror. "You vandalized my DeSoto."

Hooker duck-lipped a raspberry. "Bull pucky!"

"With your little butt in the air, fixing to rip the wires out of the radio."

"I was trying to hotwire the car."

The older man offered out his palm. "Well, there you go. There's your answer."

"What, stealing cars?"

It was Willie's turn to duck-lip the raspberry. "You had no idea what you had in your hands. You didn't even know what to do with a stolen car —even if you could have hotwired it. But you were willing to try. You were willing to reach out and learn."

"With my tiny butt in the air…"

Willie rolled his eyes. "Oh, let's not go to any extremes. It may have been smaller than mine, but it was by no means tiny."

"But a small target of opportunity for your newspaper to smack…"

"Those papers weren't a newspaper. Those papers were my death sentence."

Hooker frowned in confusion.

Willie looked down at his hands picking at each other, and then back out at Lake Tahoe where the shadow reached out like a wraith from Hades. In his mind, it was a metaphor for the day over a decade before.

"It was the lowest day of my life. Those papers informed me I was no longer needed. I was flotsam on the sea. The Navy kicked me out. The only option I saw at the moment was to go home and crack open three or four quarts of Maddie's moonshine or drive the DeSoto off a cliff."

"Until you saw my butt…"

Willie nodded and looked back to Hooker. "Until your butt…" His lips curled in tight, white against his teeth. "I was mad already, but I got white-hot about someone trying to steal my car. You sat only a second away from me, pulling your ass out of the car and beating you to death right there in front of the post office.

"One minute, I was ready to commit suicide and the next murder. And then I saw what a screw-up you really were. I almost laughed."

"But you hit me, instead."

"I smacked your jeans… where your brains seemed to sit. I needed your attention and for you to not pull on those wires. It would have taken me hours under the dashboard to put the wires back so I could have my radio. You do realize the DeSoto is my only vehicle with a radio, don't you?"

Hooker had never thought about it. He pictured the plain expanse of smooth steel of the Speed Wagon's dashboard. As he mentally ticked through the many cars that had passed through Willie's large garage and hands, he realized all had been *radio delete*. "Yeah, why delete?"

"Because you can't have a radio on a racetrack, it would be distracting."

"Okay, but it still doesn't explain why you took me to lunch, and then gave me a home."

Willie looked at the hands continuing to pick at each other. He sighed. "As I said, you were trying. You didn't know what to do next. I didn't know what to do next. All my life, I wanted to be in the Navy, and then they didn't want me. I may have been pushing sixty, but I felt like twenty. I'd recently stopped seeing a man who wanted to try being married to his wife instead…"

"Ralph or Randy…"

Willie nodded looking back at the last light on the hills on the Nevada side of Lake Tahoe. "Randal. I didn't know what to do. Those papers were the final nail in my coffin. I knew in the moment, I would never put on my dress whites again. My daily khakis would never come out of the closet again. I was adrift, just like you, but you were down under a dashboard digging around for a new career. You were reaching out. You. All alone. You were going to take control of your destiny by your own hand.

"I guess the moment I realized what you were doing—I wanted to be a part of your life. I never thought about showing you the way. It was always about my being a part of your life. I had no idea you would turn out to be such a gearhead." He looked up and smiled warmly.

"So you adopted the screw-up."

"Ho, by no means were you a screw-up. I had years of experience of dealing with screw-ups, both below me as well as up the chain of command. Out of the gate, I just needed to show you a path and stand back. Although, I did have my doubts about securing you a bogus driver's license until you went out and got a job with it. It was a bit of a shocker.

Even Maddie raised an eyebrow, and you know how nonplussed she is about doing things."

Hooker laughed. "I think down deep, even Don knew I wasn't nineteen. But after I hooked and towed the Opel around the yard and backed it through some holes, he had to admit I drove better than at least two of his other drivers."

"Yeah, Don called me. If you had just put it in the parking spot, it would have been fine. But you had to show off by backing all the way through three rows of cars, and the holes weren't lined up."

"Oh, hell's bells, Willie, what fun would simple stuff job have been?"

"But where did you learn to tow? I sure as hell didn't teach you."

Hooker laughed. "I sat on top of the warehouse next door to the yard for a few days. I watched them hook and unhook, and the backing part… I don't know… it just seemed as natural as driving forward to me. Scary the first hole but by the third hole I was having fun."

They laughed softly and watched as the last rosy mountaintop slipped into the shadow of night. The lights of State Line were beginning to glow. As they stood to resume their travels, Willie asked the important question. "Dinner in Placerville or Strawberry?"

Hooker opened the passenger door. "I'll let you know when we get to Strawberry."

The roll down the mountain to Placerville had been quiet. Both men seemed to have a lot to think about or remember. Willie had noticed the frost already forming on the large box stuffed at the back end of the truck bed. He guessed it was probably summer hog. Steven didn't slaughter beef until after the first snow in November, then hang until the New Year. He hoped for some blood sausages, so Hank could try out his new recipe.

Placerville never seemed to change much. It was the same sleepy town it had been in the late forties when Willie first found his way around the lower Sierras. The diner along the highway was the fresh take on the old railroad car with the wheels knocked out. The quilted stainless-steel skin made it look somewhat like an Airstream trailer, a look not lost on many travelers. There had seemed to be no need to get creative with the name of the joint, as they all seemed to be called a diner. It was the food luring them in. The sandwiches were good, but the berry desserts had drawn them past Strawberry and down to the larger city.

The heavy-duty white plates sat stained with hints of black and raspberry cobbler. The ice cream tidemark was homemade French vanilla.

Willie pushed the handle of his coffee mug from finger to thumb as he stared food-struck into the dark brown liquid. He didn't have to look to know his movements were mirrored the next seat over. Stella had laughed at their unconscious mimicry.

"What prompted this sudden question about my actions?"

Hooker's finger stopped mid-track. His mind ground through the question and selected the reference. He chuckled softly. "The Squirt."

Willie looked up at the back bar of milkshake machines, coffeepots, and other food prep all neatly placed along the stainless-steel counter and back wall. He thought about how the Squirt had come into all of their lives during the spring, and ended up saving Hooker's life. He still lay in the hospital, but soon he would need a home to go home to.

Willie sipped his coffee. Slowly putting the mug down, he looked over at Hooker. "So, where are you going to stick your new child, daddy?" He smiled softly, a tease, but with an honest heart.

Hooker raised his eyebrows as he stared ahead and sipped his coffee. "It seems I have no say in the matter. Stella has all but staked her claim on the kid."

They both nodded and said in unison, "Heaven help him!" They laughed and sipped their coffee in mirror image.

As the Speed Wagon nosed out of the town limits and across the agricultural prairie of the Central Valley, Willie leaned into the open window mirroring Hooker with his arm out the other side. "So, how do you feel about being a benefactor?"

"I'm happy I have Stella and Manny to back me up, but it feels a bit daunting. I can look after myself, but to look after someone else..." He looked out the window at the rice fields whipping by in the black night. "It's why I had hoped there was some wisdom coming from you. But I think I'm far past smacking his tiny butt with some paper like a puppy."

Willie laughed at the image and analogy. "You went way past that mark the second you drove a fork into his hand in front of his sister who you hoped to take to bed. Yessirree Bob, that ship done sailed a long time ago."

Hooker groaned. "Oh, great, play the nasty memory over and over."

Willie laughed but took pity on the apple of his eye. "Look, I don't know if there is anything particularly wise I could ever tell you. When it came to you, I was making it up new every day. It scared the hell out of me. Maddie was of no help. She just kept asking why the hell I was asking her about raising up a kid. She had been the baby, and her dad just threw her in overalls and tossed her under the hood of a car like she was just another one of the boys. But what I can tell you about the Squirt is: you have your hands full. He's not like you. When he gets his head of steam up, you better give him a wide berth or hold on tight. I think he's got a whole lot of potential, and he isn't going to slow down until he fulfills it."

Hooker rolled his lips into his teeth and scratched at the new scars on his head as the nerves knit. "That's what I was afraid of. I'm glad he's going to be out at the hacienda, so Manny can fill his head with cop stuff." Hooker laughed at the memory of Squirt lying in the hospital reading his letter of acceptance into the police academy while he was petting Box and sipping the moonshine Hooker had snuck into the hospital. "You should have seen his face when he realized one way or another, he was going to get his dream of being a cop."

Willie glanced over at the man the kid had become. He smiled softly and cherished the filling ache in his chest. Yes, Willie knew a little something about dreams coming true.

1 6

W illie stood in the kitchen in a frilly apron and his favorite boxers saying "Kiss My Grits" across the back. Hooker had groaned so many times, he almost didn't see them anymore. Finally, he just stopped trying to retrain the seventy-year-old.

Hooker smelled bacon. Either Willie was feeling energetic, or Hank was coming over tonight. Either way, Hooker was just happy for him. He walked up beside him and put his arm around the naked shoulder and squeezed. He leaned over and kissed the man on the ear. The reaction was quick and predictable. Willie had the most sensitive ears. It sent shivers all the way to his toes, and he squirmed cross-legged.

"Gosh damn it, Hooker. I've told you a hundred times my neck is *not* fat. It makes me feel perverted or something." He slowly squirmed, shaking his legs back into working order and went back to his cooking.

Hooker walked away with his mug of coffee. "I've told you a hundred times not to wear them boxers... but I know you won't change, either."

Hooker could hear Willie doing something, but he wasn't going to turn around and give the man any satisfaction. He pulled the chair out and sat.

The thrown boxers landed on the table in front of Hooker. Chuckling, he took the fork from Willie's place and fished up the boxers and tossed them to the large trash can. "Besides, Willie, you already are a pervert. Just ask Hanky Panky... it's your most endearing quality."

"You, sir, are just prejudiced."

"Well, it isn't from your choice in wardrobe." Hooker looked up at the ceiling. "Although, there was a lavender dress you were sporting—that was a nice one. It brought out the highlights in your hair."

The man grumped as he turned the bacon. "It burned up Friday."

Hooker stopped and at the risk of going blind, turned around. "You sure burn up a lot of clothes."

Willie didn't turn around. "It doesn't matter. The dresses are only fifty cents or less at Goodwill."

"Why don't you buy some bib overalls like Maddie has?"

Willie served the eggs and bacon and came to the table. Thankfully, the apron was long enough. "They want two bucks for pants and three for bibs. I can buy new jeans for ten."

Hooker just nodded. He knew the rest of the story. "And they would burn up just as fast."

Willie reached out and rumpled Hooker's hair. "Oh, how cute. The boy has been paying attention."

Hooker dodged out of the head petting. "Speaking of Maddie, what time did she leave last night?"

"Who said I left?"

Hooker looked over at the usually prim and proper librarian. Her hair was a wild mess with only an attempt at control. The T-shirt only barely covered whether she was commando or not. It did nothing to hide the ropey mass of scars where the surgeons had put her legs back into some kind of working order.

The summer she had turned twenty-one, she had attempted to set a land speed record. If she had gotten to the end, she would have been the first woman to drive a motorcycle faster than one hundred and forty.

Halfway across the salt flats, the front end developed a high-speed shimmy, and she stepped off the machine as it passed down through the hundred and sixty mark. She lay crumpled in the desert heat for over six minutes until an ambulance could drive its top speed of eighty to retrieve her shattered body from the sand.

Willie had spent all of his leave time for the next three years at her side. She relearned to walk using his arm as much as a cane.

Many years later, the two had taken the Granny car to Monterey for some seafood and too much alcohol. The corner was the same corner Willie had taken many times before, but it had never been full of a deer and two fawns before. The result was Willie's retirement from the Navy and a year of Maddie learning to walk again.

Maddie petted and then kissed Hooker's head and then Willie's as she rounded the table to get herself some coffee. Sitting, she folded her hands and bowed her head. Hooker was used to her version of saying grace. "Smells good. Let us prey successfully. Amen." She raised her head and stuck out her hand in time to take the bowl of scrambled eggs from Willie. "Thank you, William."

As they ate in silence, and Hooker could feel the eyes on him. He started running his assignments over in his head. One popped up. His report on the Fall of Cromwell and the following reformation of England was a week or so past due. He looked up at Maddie in horror.

His look was enough for her. She nodded. "You have had extenuating circumstances. Please have ten pages typed and in my hands by the end of next week."

Hooker didn't know if he was lucky to have an ongoing education about seemingly random things, or whether Maddie was just a frustrated schoolteacher with a sadistic streak. But one thing he did know—he was a better person for her guiding hand, along with Willie as Sergeant of Arms, and Manny as Mentor.

Hooker took a bite of the scrambled eggs. "Oh, my, what did you put in these?" His eyes were wide open, as he reached for the glass of water.

"Some of Hanky's cardamom and chili powder—gives it a nice little kick, doesn't it?"

"Little? That's like calling Mae a midget racer." He drained the glass and got up for more. "Oh, wow. Where has Hank been all our lives? Who needs coffee when you can wake up to this?"

The man sat in his frilly apron as delicately as a debutant. He fluttered his eyes. "Exactly what I thought, too." He chewed another bite, and then drained his glass and stuck it in Hooker's stomach before he could sit. "Maybe not so heavy next time."

The two had tears in their eyes, but in a household where one wears a dress because it's a quarter the price of a used pair of jeans... food was never thrown out.

Maddie barely even blinked. Her tolerance for hot food ran in the same circle as her taste for the high-octane moonshine for which her family was known. She ignored the two men as she reached over and grabbed the tops of the salt and pepper shaker in one hand. She placed the bottoms in her other hand and upturned them over her eggs.

The day was bright and sunny, and the convertible rolled down the freeway as if it owned the world. The two men relaxed, knowing all eyes were on them and the car. Hooker guessed the reason Willie loved the old DeSoto Firedome so much was for moments like these. Every time they rode around on a day like this, Hooker allowed himself to slip back to those feelings as an almost fourteen-year-old kid, and the day he discovered someone genuinely cared about him as a human being. It took several years for Hooker to understand why Willie would take on a young boy he knew he couldn't touch, take him into his house, and raise him as his own. Hooker was the heir and validation for all the man had stood for and had given so freely to his country and to Hooker. All he asked in return was Hooker be the best man he could be.

The Congressional Medal of Honor Hooker had framed for his uncle hung by the door leading to the large garage. It reminded both men who they were.

The large chrome grill nosed into the parking lot of the hospital. The big V8 engine shuddered into silence. Willie sat a moment. He looked through the front glass at the large concrete and glass structure. There was nothing graceful about the building. It was as pretty as a cast on a leg. They both had got the job done. "I swear. Between you, Squirt, and Manny, this place is starting to feel like a second home."

Hooker gazed west along the building to the Emergency Entrance. "I know a certain blonde who would tell you it's my first home."

Willie studied Hooker's head where the hair didn't quite hide the scars on his scalp. "She might be right."

The two men were laughing as they turned in the door to Manny's room. The curtain between Manny and the other bed was pulled. They could see a foot under the blanket. They sobered up and moved beside Manny's bed.

"I see they moved Stella out and gave you a new roommate." Hooker nudged with his chin at the dividing curtain. "Was she trying to run the hospital from here?"

Manny smiled and shrugged.

Willie plowed in as he sat on the edge of the bed. "Well, this brings back memories—you in a hospital bed, unable to kick Hooker's butt, and unable to talk. They did find a heart this time... didn't they?"

The dividing curtain slid open from the wall end. Stella sat in the chair, and Squirt was sleeping in the bed. The traction on his right arm and left leg kept the young man looking like he was half tossed into the air. The look on Stella's face was anything but peaceful.

Hooker laughed. "Hello, sweetheart."

Willie smiled his canary smile.

"Not funny."

Hooker confided. "We saw Winnie on the way up. She gave us the heads up you were consolidating your chicks into one place." Hooker nodded his chin toward the kid.

"Fine." She relaxed. The mother hen was where she was the most comfortable. "They brought him up about an hour ago. He will probably be out until after dinner. They had to go back in and scrape the femur. There was a scar ball starting to stop the blood flow. He's better now, but he'll be on morphine for about a week. And just so you know—you are not allowed to make him laugh or do anything to make him cough. It is very painful and can cause him to pass out."

"But he is finished with all the surgeries?"

"They had hoped. But they will be watching to see if he is prone to growing large scar balls."

"Well, we already know he has the other kind in cast iron and huge." Hooker owed his life to the kid knocking him out of the way, taking the two loads of dimes from the shotgun and still killing the killer—all while diving out of the cab of Mae West eight feet in the air. Stella didn't reprimand Hooker for his crude reference. She simply patted the boy's hand.

"So what did Dolly say?"

Hooker looked down at the detective. "Oh, so now you can talk?"

The man chuckled. "You didn't expect me to spoil Stella's fun, did you?"

"Naw, fair is fair."

"And... did she know anyone?"

"She called an old professor of hers who used to teach at Stanford."

Stella's forehead worked into a cluster of wrinkles. "Was the guy something like White or Whites?"

"Doctor White."

"Right. Doc White. He taught Indian stuff up there. I had never seen a man wear so much silver and turquoise jewelry before in my life."

Hooker cleared his face and returned to Manny. "Where to start..." His eyes rolled up into his head as they closed. He washed his face with his hands, trying to remember it all.

"We were right about it maybe being a native Indian thing. He pretty much called it right off. It was a shaman thing going on. As we talked, we narrowed down the tribe, so we could get a handle on the kind of ritual or something.

"He asked about a snake line next to a straight line, and I remember seeing those but with an arrow in them... when I told him, he about had a heart attack. He pushed us off and called another guy who is serving time over in Carson City area but has a direct phone line."

Manny smiled. "Charles Pells. He killed his wife and her mother before hunting down five of her lovers and dismembering them. The guy is brilliant and poses no threat to anyone else, so he's given free rein to do research for police departments all over the world."

"Right. So anyway, this guy has been working on a series of kills stretching up and down the Central Valley and over many years. All of it has the raven bone and hair of the victim bound with their skin from their sex organs.

"So Willie and I went over and had a chat with him."

"You saw him?"

Hooker nodded. "The guy had some serious insight into our killer. It was as if the Cowboy was his son or something. There was some serious psycho stuff going on there, but we got our information and got out before the guy blew a mental gasket or something."

Manny thought for a minute. Finally, he looked at Hooker.

"So, now what?"

"So, tonight I go meet up with The Mouse and see what she has on her mind."

"Where?"

"The old mill."

"Think she'll be alone?"

"Pretty much. It's why we've used the mill before. It's when she wants to talk to me without the regalia of her contingent group."

"No backup. Wouldn't it be dangerous for her?"

"She knows I'm not a threat to her. But it gives her standing that she would one, meet me alone, and two, do so at the old mill."

Willie's forehead crumpled. "What makes this mill so bad news?"

Manny turned. "It was actually part of an old meatpacking plant. They also packed some fish there back in the olden days, but it is the killing floor that has them freaked."

Willie frowned even harder. Hooker picked it up. "They don't see themselves as humans. They are in touch with the animal world, so the slaughterhouse was used to kill what they think of as their kind."

"So if they take on the names of animals, and they think of themselves as animals, could this raven thing be connected?"

"It's possible."

Manny looked at Hooker. "You didn't tell Paul about The Mouse, did you?"

Hooker stood silent. Finally, he shook his head. "I didn't see any reason to get her involved before I heard her out about what she really knew, or if she was involved."

"So we know The Mouse told us when and who, just not where, and you think he doesn't think she's involved?"

"I don't know. But she's my sister."

"Okay, okay. So we wait until moonset." Willie sighed.

"No. I go alone."

17

Hooker sat at the counter of the diner. He ignored the harsh light knifing off the Formica and turned the page. The 1961 Marmon shop manual was turning out to be a better purchase than just the ten cents he had fished out of his jean pocket last summer. The man had wanted a quarter, but after seeing the yellow and blue 1959 Marmon rumbling at the curb, he must have decided Hooker was the one person who might put the book to good use.

With the giant engine for his truck, now nothing more than so much scrap metal, he needed to know more about any new engine he might find. Willie had run an ad in Hemming's Motor News, but still no phone calls. But then, the most recent edition Hooker had glanced through was dated in the latter part of 1968. Even with all the downtime he was getting, he was far behind in his reading. He also knew many of the other motorheads were just as up to date in their reading as he was.

The thin hand placed an open magazine on top of the manual. Hooker looked up at the soft but worn face of the closest thing he had going as a girlfriend. "I've told you before—I don't read Cosmo." He smiled warmly as he leaned back to look at her better.

The twenty-six years had worn hard on her, but she carried it more with pride than as yoke. Most men would walk past her on the street, but to Hooker, the quirky smile, the ropey body, and thin arms spoke more about inner strength than just another skinny girl. Her hand waved back a piece of flyaway hair at her ear.

"It's Vogue, not Cosmo."

"Same girly magazine."

"It's not about the magazine. I was thinking about cutting my hair like that."

The page had turned over, and the image was of some guy with a girl hiding behind his shoulder. Hooker laughed. "It would make you look more manly than your brother."

She looked down at the tight hair cut on the guy. She flipped the page, and it got worse with an Afro standing out past the model's shoulders.

Hooker looked at her with pursed lips, studying her face. "Yeah, that might work…"

She turned a few pages and found a model walking on what Hooker guessed to be a sidewalk in New York City. The dress and coat were hound's tooth wool, and the hair was cut scooped just below her neck, but not quite onto her shoulders. She planted her finger on the picture and glared at Hooker.

He thought about how short it was cut and how thin her neck was. He didn't have the heart to tell her the two didn't match. "I hate short hair. I like the way you have always had it. It doesn't get in the way. It makes a nice-looking ponytail, and I think it makes your… um… rear end look great."

"Men." She swiped the magazine back up and steamed off.

But Hooker watched, and he noted the playful sway of her hips was still there. She had liked that he liked her just the way she was.

Hoping to salvage some honor and tranquility, he offered. "I can bring Willie back in, and you can ask for his opinion."

Her head appeared over the waitress back station. She glared at him. "I might as well go out and ask your mother."

Hooker leaned back and thought. Maybe it was about time she *"meets the parents."*

"That's a great idea. How about Sunday dinner out at the house? I'll pick you up about four." He knew it was her one day off.

She sidestepped out from the large cabinet. "Are you serious?"

"Sure. You might as well meet the folks. If you want to stay over, you can sleep in your brother's room."

She grabbed the pot of coffee and slowly walked down the aisle toward Hooker as she thought. Her forehead worked into a frown. "Johnny has a bedroom out there?" Her one eyebrow arched up as she cocked her head and watched Hooker with the other eye.

"Where did you think he slept for the week... out under the truck? Stella fixed up the spare room the third night."

She filled his coffee cup and set the carafe on the counter. "But you said it was his room like he was living there."

Hooker realized he had let slip something that was going to be a slippery slope toward ruining a great surprise. "Well, he's not dead. He won't be in the hospital much longer. He will need a place to stay where he can be looked after. And he still owes me nine more days of slavery."

She slumped into her right hip. Her eyes wandered all over Hooker's face, looking for even a slight hint of joking. "But why would she do that?"

Hooker couldn't explain these things. The term family was an alien idea for him, as well as to Candy and her brother. A hard life and being taken advantage of had been the norm to Hooker *and* to them. To meet someone like Uncle Willie or Stella and Manny was too far out of the realm of possibility to even relate to, or for Hooker to try to explain.

"You'll have to ask her and make up your own mind about it on Sunday."

She thought quietly and then walked off to pour coffee for the other two people in the restaurant. Hooker went back to reading about how the power range could be increased by polishing the oil channels in a large diesel engine.

"Okay." She stood in front of him.

Hooker leaned back with a thin warm smile. His hazel-green eyes danced. "Good."

"What should I wear?"

He thought of several things at once. The smile probably telegraphed his thoughts. She slumped on to her right hip and closed one eye, giving him a warning look.

"Probably clothes would be a good start." He smiled with a toothy leer. "But a yellow dress would look good. It would look like you were trying to impress them." He smiled and then rolled his eyes. "But if you want to get on Stella's good side, wear some jeans, and be ready to go rooting about in the yard and storage room. She's setting up the outside canning kitchen."

Candy frowned. "I thought people canned in their kitchen in the house."

"Not when you have a dozen people peeling, washing, boiling, cooking, prepping, and bottling a few tons of produce and fruit."

"Tons?"

"They will put up well over five thousand gallons of food between now and October."

"In one kitchen? Five thou... What does that even look like?"

"Well, the storage area at the house is six hundred square feet, and the racks go eight feet with room on top for more boxes. Then there is the barn over at the Pederson place, as well as the basement at the church on third...."

"What is all the food for? An army?"

He reached over and patted her hand. "Stella will fill you in on Sunday. And if she likes you, then she will try to shanghai you into forced labor for the rest of the fall."

She closed her eyes as she raised her eyebrows until they popped her eyes open. "Okay—Sunday." She walked off to make more coffee.

She peeked back around the cabinet. "Five thousand?"

"Gallons." Hooker did the math for her. "Twenty-thousand quart-jars."

The whistle sounded like an incoming bomb. Hooker smiled. His reaction the first year had been much the same. It was a lot of food donated to support any family of a law enforcement worker who was in need. Usually, there was a fireman or two thrown into the mix along the way.

Hooker also knew there would be stacks of pallets of commercially canned goods donated from the farmers and canned gratis by the cannery. Those were held in a commercial warehouse and delivered as needed. Usually, a pallet at a time, or sometimes a truckload spread between the many pantries. It was a lot to grasp the first time around.

He would let Stella describe the non-stop around the clock trucks, and the people and the cooking running from first harvest until almost Halloween. Her telling was a lot more fun. She was a special force of nature, and this was her thing.

Hooker put his finger on the paragraph he was reading. He sensed a body standing in front of him. He looked up and smiled with raised eyebrows.

"I said, I see your uncle loaned you his car. Where are you going tonight... or was it just to come up and see me?" Her voice was playful, but her face showed she really wanted it to be about her.

Hooker leaned back and smiled; the manual forgotten. "All of these months, if I wanted to come up to see you, someone had to schlep me here. Then they would be hanging around."

"And now the cast is off, so you can drive."

"Mae still doesn't have an engine. It's really driving me nuts. Willie has the transfer case torn apart and is seeing if we can't somehow make it all work without the double-clutching." He realized he had just lost her. "It's the way I have to shift with two levers. He wants to make it faster. I keep telling him I don't care, but Willie is Willie, and we're both frustrated we don't have an engine."

"Can't you just go buy one?"

"They stopped making them in the early sixties. So anything we can get will be out of a junkyard somewhere."

"So you came up to see me and study."

"Sort of." He knew eventually, she would know about The Mouse. "I also have to go talk to my sister in a couple of hours."

"You have a sister?" She leaned in. "And I was going to hear about this... when?"

"Now." He shied back, hopefully out of hitting range. Her look was pure hard ice.

"Look, it's complicated." He thought about how to explain his sister. "You know Peter." He jammed his thumb at the door and parking lot.

She nodded slowly.

Hooker pointed toward the booth in the back room. "And you know Jerry."

She nodded.

"Jerry is a peanut butter and jelly sandwich—a little nuts and sweet. The distance from him to Peter is the lunch special with a slice of pie thrown in. To get to my sister, you would have to go to the full sixteen-course Roman orgy, and then some. She is so far out there she scares Peter. Jerry couldn't even start to understand."

"And so I wouldn't have a chance?"

"Candy, of almost everyone I know, you would have the most chance at understanding my sister. Trust me, if there was any way you two *could* meet, you would." He left out where they shared a past of foster homes which should have been havens of safety but were hells of rape and torture. "If I could rescue my sister from her life, and bring her into ours, you two would probably find you have a lot more in common than just me."

She didn't know where to take her mixed feelings. She looked toward the back of the diner at the other damaged goods frequenting the only all-night haven. It came with a waitress who understood the special and delicate needs of the denizens shuffling through the door. And then, there was the one outside, who she gave a package to every morning as she left before the sun rose.

Hooker watched her in her own special purgatory. He returned to his book, and she wandered off to clean something she had cleaned an hour before. It was her shift. Clean the clean, and mother the motherless, tend to her brood, and deal with the few drunks who could make it to Winchester Boulevard.

Hooker looked down the aisle into the back dining-room. She stood talking to Jerry. The man had worked the docks of Alameda Air Station. He had been an up and coming chief petty officer who would have made master chief.

An airplane crash had ended all of it. A small shard of shrapnel the size of a broom handle had rearranged a section of his brain. Jerry had looked up at the sound of the crash. The shard had hit him head-on and passed through the frontal lobe and all the way down one side.

The man now lived with a person he thought was his daughter. His home address and a contact phone number were always pinned to his shirt. He lived by routines you could set your watch by. Every night he would spend four hours and forty-eight minutes at the diner.

He always had coffee and white toast burned more charcoal black than white. He used half a jar of sugar, six little containers of the mixed berry jam, and three napkins. He left two quarters, one dime, three nickels, and a penny. The four-cent tip was something Candy always cherished.

Hooker always wondered what he would do if the prices went up again.

Jerry was Candy's special child. Only he was old enough to be her grandfather. Hooker smiled sadly. Candy, Stella, and Dolly—they all had a lot in common.

The clock ticked over to 1:40 a.m. Hooker looked up. The bars would be closing, and he needed to drive several miles. He started to slip a five under the glass to pay for the dinner and pie but walked toward the back instead. He found Candy sitting in one of the booths, her cheek resting on the heel of her hand.

He sat down next to her. She leaned into him. She sighed. He stroked her hair and kissed it. "I do like your hair the way it is."

They sat there for a few minutes, floating. She turned and looked at him. Her eyes wandered all over his face. She kissed him lightly on the lips. "Go see your sister. I'll be ready at four on Sunday."

He slid out of the booth. It was the best moment life was going to give him today.

The night air washed over Hooker as the glass door sucked open. The late-night summer heat left a charred tang to the more dominant odor of rotting vegetation. Hooker stopped at the car door. He listened with his whole body. It was almost two hours after their regular meeting time, but just maybe. "Peter?"

"Not for another half hour or so."

Hooker turned to see the priest pushing his wheelchair into the parking lot. It still amazed Hooker the man could maneuver the chair with one hand and a hook.

"Father Damian. It's good to see you again. I thought I had missed you."

The man rolled to a stop. "Normally, you would have. This morning came early with the call of the wild." He rolled his eyes and imitated the bad Irish brogue of his fellow priest Father McBride. "Who would ha' imagined two cats would desecrate the sanctity of it all by screwing noisily under the rectory window?"

Hooker rolled his eyes in mock horror. "Oh, the humanity of such a thing! Shocking. Shocking, I say."

The two men laughed as the priest turned toward the door. "I may have to eat the whole slice of pie I smell."

"Have a great night, Damian."

The man waved the hook over his head as he pulled the door with his hand. Hooker watched the man handle the heavy glass doors with the very fit muscles of the former Special Forces soldier.

The soft breeze rustled through the vegetation at the edge of the lot. But there was no whirlwind of dust and night trash floating across the parking lot.

Hooker opened the car door and sat down. Somehow, it had been just a hollow shell of his usual middle-of-the-night visits to the diner. He laid the book on the floor of the passenger side and turned the key. The big V8 rumbled to life. Hooker nosed the giant of another time out onto the wide boulevard. He gently mashed the pedal, and the growling car surged down the way. The deep bass of the exhaust reverberated off the buildings along the street.

The moon was perhaps a good half hour away from touching the distant tree line. Hooker stood leaning against the front left fender. He knew The Mouse was already here. he could feel it. He made a show of being alone. The driver door was open. His only nod to taking precautions was the sawed-off Remington shotgun cradled in his left arm. The shells were all stacked with thirteen dimes, his variation on the buck-forty dime-load. He had always found the number thirteen to be more lucky than unlucky.

A large shape moved across the night air. The total silence of its flight told Hooker it was a barn owl. He thought about its choice of hunting grounds. He quietly, almost to himself, offered his wishes. "Happy hunting. May your belly be full and your heart strong."

"Nathanial Hawkins never said that in the book, you know."

Hooker didn't flinch. He kept watching where the owl had gone. "I know, but it always sounded so inter-spiritual."

He turned to face his sister as she sat in the driver's seat. Her hands were delicately touching the large Bakelite steering wheel, feeling the smooth coolness. "Hello, Mouse."

She closed her eyes and leaned back into the comfort of the large seat. It almost swallowed her. Hooker thought she had become even smaller and more fragile since he had seen her in the spring. Her skin, always a problem, was now flaking off in thumbprint sized pieces. Her desquamation was getting worse. Even on her face. It looked in the moonlight like she had several eyelids." She was hugging herself to keep from picking at the skin. Her fine hair and the gauze of her clothing leant to the illusion she was all just the layers of skin floating in the air with no substance— more of a spirit than of something corporeal.

The voice was soft as a gentle summer evening. "You were hurt."

"Yes."

"They killed your truck."

He thought and then nodded. "Yes."

"Can you fix her?"

"If we can find a new engine."

"You're not the same without her."

Hooker looked out into the night. He knew she was right. He wondered if he would ever be the same again. Near-death can change a person.

Hooker thought of the Marmon—once, the most powerful truck in the five Bay Area counties, now sitting forlornly in the garage. The proud nose turned on end next to the hollow cavity where the giant engine should be. The dark impotent silence of the once-great truck had also changed its owner. For once, Hooker truly felt his mortality.

"They're not out there."

"Who?"

"My tribe."

"You're alone?"

"I didn't say who."

"The blond one... the one that is always crouched by your leg?"

"Dog." She waved a non-directional hand. "He's out there, somewhere."

"He's not afraid of the mill?"

She chortled. "He's not afraid of the silver in your shotgun either."

"It was a precaution."

"Not from me."

"No... Not from you."

"You obviously got my message."

"Peter gave it to me."

She rolled her head sideways. Her sigh was almost a whisper to herself. "Peter..."

"What about him, Mouse?"

She slowly rolled her head back and looked blankly at her brother. "You hate my name."

"Hate is a strong word. I don't like what it means—a separation between my sister and me. The name is just a name. I just like Clair better… and Sissy even more so."

Her head rolled. She was quiet. "There is a new killer stalking the night."

"You told us what would happen next, and it did. There are questions now."

"Was I part of it?"

"No. We know you weren't. Nor were any of your tribe."

"How would you know that?"

"Because he was a busy boy elsewhere. He has been counting coup on his boots, and he's up to twenty-five now. But we now know he left here and was all over in the Central Valley for the last five or six years."

"He was here before?"

Hooker frowned. "You didn't know that?"

"No."

"Manny, one of the people I live with... would have been his fifth kill, but his partner found him before the killer could carve him up."

She scooted across the seat and leaned up against the passenger door. "Come sit in here. I want to see your face." She waved him in with both of her hands. They glowed in the moonlight. It was from the abnormally high concentration of phosphorous in her skin due to a disease she had

had since they were children.

Hooker had a brief memory of being in a chair and blanket fort. A ten-year-old girl who he had started calling sister motioned with both of her hands. *Come in here. I want to watch your face when we talk.* It was the last nice home where they were dumped. He had started calling her Sissy for sister. Clair was the name the adults used.

When the abuse started, the current recipient would become the inside spoon as they comforted each other as they fell asleep, different abuse with different foster homes. But when the talk became serious, they would sit at each end of the inevitable bunk bed so they could see each other's face.

Hooker laid the shotgun on the back seat. He sat down in the driver's side and closed the door. He turned and leaned against the door and stretched out into the middle of the car.

"Just like in Riverside."

She smiled softly that he also remembered a better time. "Yes."

They sat with their memories. There was no hurry. There was no clock to watch, no radio to answer. The moon started breaking apart as it entered the trees.

"I need your help."

Hooker looked at her and waited.

"I'm dying."

He waited.

"When I become weak, they will kill me."

His heart broke.

"They will kill Dog first. They will make me watch them do it. Afterwards, they will kill me. They will tear me apart, and then eat me for my power. They will crush my bones and suck the warm marrow from inside."

Hooker strained not to flinch or show any sign.

"I will give you the killer."

Hooker waited to hear the conditions. There was always a trade.

"I will give you the killer, but you and the police must kill Dog and me. You must do it in a way there is no doubt. They will be watching."

Hooker couldn't move.

"You must shoot me with your silver bullets. You must use your shot-gun. You must stand in the open where everyone can see you kill me. After you have done this, you and the police will get the killer."

Hooker moved his hand to stop her from moving.

She rolled forward in a fluid movement as if she had no bones. The Mouse was more a snake. Her hand was cold on his hot face. She kissed his cheek as lightly as a butterfly landing. "Save me, brother. I love you." She rolled back and was outside the car. "I will come to you here in the dark of the moon. The train moans just past midnight. You have the fortnight."

And she was gone.

18

The early morning had found Hooker sitting first at Willie's, and then back at Stella and Manny's, explaining what had gone down with his sister. By the time the sun had started its predawn lighting of the sunroom, Hooker was done. Stella had barely stuffed a few bites of leftovers into his mouth before he dragged himself to his room. As he sat on his bed, he remembered making a date for Sunday. With his last energy, he yelled to Stella to remind him about Candy and Sunday later in the day. He had no memory of falling back into the bed.

Hours later, Stella checked in. She gently picked up his legs, removed the last sock, and tucked Hooker into bed. As she softly closed the door, she wondered when he had started sleeping commando.

The evening took on an almost festive flavor, as the brainstorming session turned into an all-hands-on-deck sort of affair. The crime boards had been rolled into the large sunroom and flipped over to make room for the tactical maps. Stella had laid out enough food to feed a small army and was still playing catch-up.

"Manny, I don't think you know John." Willie pointed to the other officer in a white uniform. "John and Alex over there are technically in-ground fire control out at Moffett Airbase, but they both have extensive explosive and bomb-making experience from their days as Seals."

"Glad to have you two aboard."

Manny nodded toward the three men hunkered down with Paul, balancing plates on their knees. "Those three are from the squad that is the fire department interface for the bomb squad. You five probably have a lot in common. All of my expertise was in Nam and Foo Gas."

"Nasty stuff, Foo Gas. The PD lost a couple of officers to it earlier this year." He slowly shook his head.

Manny leaned back just a little more. "My boy and I were the consults on the incident." Manny pointed out Hooker who had awakened and was just coming to the party. His uniform of the day was a crisply ironed white T-shirt, jeans, and bare feet. He was still blinking and trying to get a grasp on who was who.

"Hooker and his Squirt were the ones who finally took down the killer."

The man slapped his forehead. "Romero. Of course! Sorry, I didn't make the connection." He pointed at Hooker and back to Manny. "So the sister is Hooker's, and would make you...?"

"Someone who would like a chance to meet her..." He thought a moment. "It's complicated."

Paul returned to the room. "People, we have a lot to cover and more to figure out. So if you can wind up your sub meetings and clear the decks, we'll get started in about ten minutes. There are bathrooms in any of the bedrooms. Hooker is up and awake, so that makes three heads for use. If any of you know the way to the basement, the plumbers today plumbed out the bathroom in the area across the garage."

"Food?" Stella presented a full plate. Hooker's head swam around and looked at her and then down at the plate. He took the plate and headed back to the dining table.

Stella followed and sat with him. "Do you want some coffee? It'll be ready in a few minutes."

Hooker slowed his shoveling. He chewed and woke up some more. He wiped at his mouth.

"Who are all these people?"

"Your support team, honey." She wiped her hand down along the side of his face. The motherly thumb wiped the bit of burrito his napkin had missed. "Willie and Manny were talking this morning and thought it would be best to make an explosive kill. So they invited people who know how to stop or produce just what we need."

"Which would explain the two Seals out there and Willie?"

She nodded. "Along with a few of the guys from the bomb squad, a couple of firemen, and someone special Dolly arranged."

Hooker stopped with a fork of food almost in his mouth. He put it down. He looked Stella in the face. Her eyes were dancing between evil and merely mischievous. "Special?" He leaned back and wiped his mouth.

She smiled evilly. "Remember a few years ago, the Shriners were in town, and they couldn't get the Fire Marshal to sign off on the show because the magic act had a lot of flame and explosions?"

Hooker closed his eyes. He was looking for the answer on the inside of his eyelids. His eyes popped open. "The guy got pissed and took it outside to the Spartan arena and blew it up out there."

"No." The quiet voice approached from behind Hooker. "The magician decided to give the show away to anyone who would or could come. It just happened to be over capacity for the stadium. I only blew up the field." The small man walked around in front of Hooker. "But I did make the elephant and brand new Corvette exchange places in their crates." He stuck out his hand. "Thomas Thomason—better known as The Great Boombowski."

Hooker smiled as he remembered the show and the political fallout from it. Three long-time council members never were reelected the next year.

The two men shook. "Very glad to meet you."

"I could have just as easily made them both disappear."

"How did Dolly find you?"

"I think it had something to do with telling the local Grand Poobah he would never get a parade permit in this town again if he didn't find me. It wasn't hard. His wife and mine are good friends. We live up in Half Moon Bay."

"So you're here to make my sister and her friend both disappear."

"Well, more like a consultant. The heavy pyro-technicians are in there." He nodded at the other room. "I just do smoke and mirrors. They play with the real stuff. And if I understand the circumstance, we're going to have to put on one hell of a show."

Paul called the meeting. Hooker and the magician joined.

"What we know about the group who will be observing is there are somewhere between twenty-five and as many as a hundred of them. They tend to like the near reaches of the salt marshes out near Milpitas and moving west around the end of the bay." He indicated the location on the smaller map.

"Based on that, and looking for a place we could blow up successfully with some kind of impunity..." He placed his hand on the larger map, which looked more like a large blank sheet of paper with a few markings. "As you can see, there isn't much here." He looked up at one of the officers in Navy whites. "John?"

The man stood and stepped to the maps. "Right. What we are looking at was in 1938 an auxiliary air tie-down station for what the Navy believed would be a fleet of about twelve dirigibles. What we got was the Macon, for a short time.

"Originally, there were four of these platforms built out of the slated eight. This is the only one left not plowed over and turned into homes or truck farm. The Navy was still hopeful even after the war and airplanes had proved themselves far more capable than dirigibles. So, for our purposes this month, this is perfect in several ways."

He turned and pointed to the small square drawn in off to one side of the center. "This is the access hatch at what would have been the bottom of the mooring mast where the dirigible would have been tied. The mast is either long gone or never erected, but I checked this afternoon, and the access hatch is still there and functioning."

He reached up and curled a sheet over the top of the board. He brushed it out to hang flat. "This is the blueprint of the access area. The door is here, and as you can see, there are no stairs. It's a ramp. Even a jeep could have been driven down into the warehouse beneath the five-foot thick concrete making up the bomb-proof reinforced pad. The ware-house is about twenty-thousand square feet of space. If the helium tanks had been installed, they were probably removed during the Korean War. We were still using some weather and bombardment spotting balloons back then. So, we have plenty of room to set up a hidden control base and a recovery base where we can spend some time. Any questions?" He pointed to one of the bomb squad.

"What will the Navy let us do out there?"

"The Navy will officially see this as a training mission on an old piece of land and equipment which can be totally destroyed and not impact our mission. In other words, they won't know squat back in DC, and we aren't going to tell them."

One of the firemen raised a finger. "I know the bomb guys are under tight control. What kind of access could we have in the way of material?"

John looked to the other white uniform. "Alex?"

The other officer coughed into his hand in the universal code of every group of men. "C-4."

The group laughed.

"What about large cannon charge, and maybe something that is a lot faster burning like small arms gun powder and even detonation cord?"

Alex frowned with a questioning look. "I'm sorry, you are...?"

Manny interceded. "Gentlemen, I'd like you all to meet The Great Boombowski."

One of the firemen laughed and asked, "Was that a real elephant at the Trojan stadium?"

"Clarabelle? All two and a half tons of her. Would you like to come out to the house and muck out her stall? It will remove any doubt you may harbor about her existence."

They all laughed at the fireman putting up one index finger and crossing it with the other hand.

Alex cleared his throat. "Why cannon charge?"

The small man stepped up to the map. "If I may?"

John stepped back.

Tom circled his hand around the perimeter of the layout map. "Let's assume we have an audience completely surrounding us. There is nothing worse than to plan for your audience to all be out front, and it turns out you have people also behind or to the side of you. So we will look at a theater in the round, as it were."

He took one of the push pins and dropped it into his open hand. Slowly he closed the hand. "Now, our master of the illusion is going to be Hooker." He opened his hand, and there was a small red flower with the pushpin for a center. He took the pin and pushed it into the map. "If I understand things, he will be standing here with a very real shotgun."

He pulled two more pushpins and waved his hand over them, and they became a pink and yellow flower. "His two lovely assistants will start here and run there." He pointed at the access.

"When they are about halfway to the disappear point, he will shoot them. At that moment, it is critical to the show. First, everything must blow up, but in a progression. Let me demonstrate." He shook his body, and in his right hand, a smallish hula-hoop appeared. He shook the hoop, and a small curtain appeared from it.

Stella stepped into the room, carrying a small stand with a top hat sitting upside down on the stand. The magician showed his open palm toward Stella. "Gentlemen, our lovely hostess with the mostess—Stella Romero." They clapped and laughed.

He held up the hat. "Sorry, but there is no rabbit tonight." He placed the hoop over and around the stand and lowered it below the top of the stand. Drawing it straight up with the hoop level, he hid the hat. "If we set everything off all at once, this is what it looks like—very uniform—and very unnatural."

He pointed at Alex. "Admiral."

Alex smiled. "Thanks for the bump in rank, but it's just Captain."

Tom smiled. He knew the rank on the man's shirt. "There are sixteen-inch cannons on the Mighty Mo. How far can they throw a shell?"

"About twenty miles."

"When the trigger man pulls the firing cord, is the bullet landing those twenty miles away?" He redrew the hoop strait up.

"No."

"How long does it take?"

"About forty-five seconds for a class seven gun. Maybe a bit longer out of the Missouri."

Tom now tilted the ring slightly, and as he raised the edge past the rim of the hat, he started making little bombing sounds that grew larger and larger as more was covered. "Boom, boom, boom, boom, boom."

As he finally covered the hat from all watching, there was a flash inside the hat and a billow of white smoke boiled out of the curtain. He let the hoop fall to expose the stand with only a mouse standing on its hind legs and bottom. The hat was gone. He scooped up the mouse, petted it, and threw it in the air. And there was nothing.

"Misdirection, gentlemen." He turned back to the map with the flowers that were now moved. The two had almost made it to the square.

"As you can see, our fugitives from justice are at a critical point." Hooker raises his hand cannon and fires.

He claps his hand together. "In the control center, we set off the charges near him. Now, we don't want to injure our good magician, so we use the slower burning powder used in cannons." He pointed to Alex, who now smiled and nodded. "This looks like the explosion is coming from his magical hand cannon. The smoke and mirrors of these explosions take place each time he pumps a new round into the gun and fires. The explosion must continue around the perimeter of the kill zone—until there is nothing but fire, smoke, and a lot of noise. Inside the hat is a different story. Once the first round of the ring of fire is established, the doors are opened, and the two can run down. But remember, we must convince the audience of what they saw... really happened. So the last round of explosions must end up covering the trap door, thus sealing the illusion."

The man stepped back over to the seat just inside the room and sat down.

The room was silent. Every person was walking through what they knew how to do and how it could fit in. Hooker had never seen so many smart people so struck into silence.

John stepped back up to the center and glanced over at the now deadpan Tom. He looked back at the room, and then a quick glance back at the unmoving Tom. Slowly he looked back around the room. "Umm... uh, any questions? Comments?"

"Question?" The younger of the bomb squad members offered.

John nodded.

The man furrowed his brow. "How did you make the hat disappear?" The room looked at the small man.

He opened his mouth and then closed it. And then he simply stated, "Very well, I thought."

The group laughed at the expense of the young man, but also at the complete showmanship of the magician.

"I think," John started, "in light of the hour, we have a game plan to start with. If you bombers can get together with Alex, we can work out what we have, what we need, and how to rig it. The Seals can work on the final rigging. Meanwhile, the doors right now are mechanical. So I'll work on getting them converted to hydraulic or something that will allow them to open and close in a second or two."

Willie raised his hand. "John, I know where there are about six large rams that would do nicely. They are rated for five-ton so a bank of two on each side should do it. But add a third on each side for safety. This is one act we don't want to go FUBAR."

"Great, Will. I'll have the base maintenance guys drag some power out there. There had to be something at some time, so it can't be hard."

As the group started standing, Stella took control. "Saturday lunch is at thirteen-thirty. Those who are feeling their oats and want to help set up the outside canning kitchen, breakfast will be available, any time after oh-seven-hundred."

She turned on the small magician who still hadn't moved. He was just happy watching all the commotion. "Okay, Tom, where is the mouse?"

He chuckled silently and pointed at her left apron pocket.

Used to men and their games, she stuck her hand in but pulled it right back out. Her face went from shock to scowl. She pushed her hand back in and drew out a small porcelain mouse sitting up on his hind legs and bottom. She smiled and started to return it.

He put his hand up in the sign of stop. "It's for Hooker—to keep his eye on the prize."

19

The sunlight streamed through the giant sliding door originally made for observation balloons. The heat of the day pooled on the thick concrete slab, the large one-eared orange tabby sprawled in the center, absorbing the heat. The clanging of metal on metal and the two men talking didn't even cause the ear to twitch.

The two men looked at each other like a couple of goofy kids about to launch their first water balloon in the season's premier catapult. The two were intoxicated from working for thirty-eight hours straight. The glassy eyes and rum-punched grins were infectious.

"Hey!" The sharp voice cut through the open air as only a librarian's voice could.

The two men jerked like small boys caught about to do something they shouldn't. They wavered and turned. The cat's ear then twitched.

The thin woman in a grease-stained undershirt and bib overalls stood in the door to the house. "Not... before breakfast."

The man in the torn jeans and sweaty grease-stained T-shirt swiveled around to look at the man in the pink square-dancing dress and engineer boots. Willie wavered, blinked, and nodded as he shrugged his shoulders. "What the hell. She's probably right." Falling forward to gain momentum, they headed toward the doorway where Maddie had disappeared.

Chet scratched at the scars on his chest where the nerves were still knitting back together. He surged and stumbled after the man in the dress. He didn't have the energy to think of doing anything other than following the leader. Or, in this case, do what the librarian told them to do.

Twenty minutes later, the coffee, scrambled eggs, toast, and bacon had done nothing for their lack of sleep. They sat around the small table, looking at each other through glazed eyes.

Chet finally broke the silence that had been the conversation of the meal. "Dibs on the couch."

Willie and Maddie barely made it to the nearest bedroom. They lay face down where they fell. They would worry about the grease stains on the sheets later.

The phone rang shortly after dusk.

Willie fumbled the phone off the base in the bedroom. "Hunoo?"

"I'm just giving you a heads up if you still need to hide the new engine you kids have been playing with."

Willie was instantly wide awake. "Thanks, Dolly." He hung up the now buzzing phone. He rolled over and sat up. He decided to let Maddie keep sleeping, and then remembered what her front had looked like most of the previous day and through the night. Maddie never had a chance at being a girl. She had three older brothers and a father who knew nothing about rearing anything but grease monkeys and moonshine cooks.

She had never been shy about the oil, grease, and hot fast steel or iron of the family business, but she had the brains. She had turned into the one who called the shots. Two or four wheels, she drove the fastest and had probably accumulated the most speed records as well as the most broken bones.

He prodded her butt. "Hooker is on his way."

He went out to the general living area to find Chet was already sitting up and rubbing the sleep from his eyes. "Come on, Chet. We need to shove Hooker's engine back behind the Speed Wagon."

The two men had just wrangled the half-ton of cast iron and steel to its hiding place and covered it with a dusty old tarp when they heard Hooker pull up in the DeSoto out front. They fell into the grease-stained webbed lounge chairs. As Hooker walked in the giant door, Willie stood and carrying two bright plastic picnic tumblers, headed for the half-open door leading into the house.

"Hey, Hooker," he called out nonchalantly. "Maddie is just whipping up another batch of Hornet Slappers. You care to join us, or are you planning to drive back to Manny's tonight?"

"I'll take a sip of yours, Willie, but basically, I'm off the moonshine for a while."

Hooker saw Chet and veered off to talk to the California Highway Patrol Captain, who was recovering from the same 'dime rash' as his and the Squirt's. All three had looked into the canyon of death, courtesy of the same killer. None of the three had made out any better than the other two, just different wounds.

Hooker shook with his left and stronger hand. "How are the chest wounds?"

"Chest is fine. It's the ringing in the ears and the headaches; they still have me on stand-down. Until I go a month with no headaches, I'm on the shoulder."

"So I see you guys decided to get some time in on the MG."

Willie and Maddie returned with tumblers of mint juleps made with her family's moonshine. Hooker noted she was in clean clothes that looked like they belonged to Willie's boyfriend, Hank. The cuffs were rolled up a good seven inches.

"I'm surprised, Maddie. The boys are out here puking grease and iron, and you stayed clean."

She looked down at her clean clothes. "Oh, I was working at the library. I just stopped by with... um..." She raised a tumbler and smiled. "I just brought some dinner by."

Hooker had laid his hand on the long cold hood of her car, so he knew she had been there for several hours at least. Something was up, and he wasn't going to push it... much.

"So what did you two guys decide on the MG?" He gave Willie a hard look.

The older man in the florid dress and now exposed knobby knees sipped his drink and smiled broadly. "Oh, the Ford piece of shit two-eighty-nine has got to go. We can find a slush box anywhere, and I think it's time to let go of the three-eighteen." Hooker knew Willie was bluffing. He would never let go of any Hemi engine—especially one he had built up as a street racer engine.

Hooker raised his eyebrows and drew down his closed mouth in a wise nod. He bobbed his head and finally landed on Chet again. Chet hid his face in his tumbler.

Bingo. Hooker smiled inside. He had found the weak link, the sellout. "Did you care to raise the stack any higher in this horseshit piling contest, Chet?"

Chet flopped back in the chair. "Aw, damn it all, Hooker. Don't hang me on the meat hook." He quickly looked over at Willie and the large scar on his throat and up the side of his face. Willie's hand was up. No offense was taken.

Willie lowered his tumbler. "Okay, I can see we didn't fool you and you're obviously not going to let it go..." The man nodded at the large heap under a few tarps. "The last run we made down at the drags in Visalia last fall, Maddie blew up the three-forty. She stuck the number five piston straight through the side of the block.

"When the engine seized, it transmitted straight through the power train. I can save the axle, but the pumpkin gears are toast. So, I found a nice little straight-six we can stick in, mount it up to a standard train out of one of the yards, and the old Granny Dart GT will be ready this fall for Candy to go to school."

Maddie finished softly, with conviction. "We wanted it to be a surprise, not only her but for you as well."

Maddie reached over and laid her hand on Hooker's arm. "I'm almost sixty years old. I can give up a nine-second car that is always dreaming of an eight-second car—for a young girl to start her own dream."

Hooker saw more truth in Maddie's face than in his uncle's story. "Are you sure?"

She closed her eyes as she nodded once. She drew her lips in a tight curl against her teeth.

Quietly, Hooker thanked her but turned the all-knowing eye on his uncle. Willie squirmed, but he also knew that what he had just said had to come to pass.

Hooker stood. "I'll let you kids get back to whatever mischief you were up to. I just stopped in on my way up to have dinner with Candy and finish the old shop manual I found on Marmon engines." He turned to leave and got three steps. He turned back, and the three snapped back into their chairs as if they had been reaching for the cookie jar. "Dinner Sunday—sorry, Chet, but you're out. We don't want to overwhelm Candy on her first family date. But Willie, Stella wants you to come early and bring Hank. Maddie, if you would grace us in order to keep Willie in line?"

Maddie smiled evilly. She held the tumbler up. "It would be my pleasure. I look forward to putting a dog collar on William and meeting this young woman." She raised the eyebrow at Willie and then turned back to Hooker. "I think there may also be a few jars available by Sunday."

"Oh, I think there is more than enough moonshine out at the hacienda. Just bring yourself and the boys." He turned as he laughed all the way to the door, more maniacally with each step.

The three didn't move until they heard the DeSoto grow silent down the hill. "You think he suspects?" Chet looked over at Willie.

"Old shop manual for a Marmon, my Aunt Betty's behind!"

Maddie raised her eyebrow as she sipped. "Oh, he has one. If I remember right, it's a 1960 or '61 machining manual. So he's probably looking at the wildcat engine the government built for the Department of Energy transports. They called it the Desert Eagle. If I remember right, it muscled up in the fourteen or sixteen-hundred horse range. If we can figure a smoother through-put on the transmission, it would have more power than you could ever use, and still run some pretty tall gears in the ass-end." She worked some numbers in her head. She had always been good at math, even as a young girl building moonshine runners and racers with her father and brothers. "I'd say if we can get our hands on one of those new Spicer rigs, and load the back with an over-under, he could end up with a truck capable of hitting at least the better part of a hundred and fifty out on the new flat section of the 101 up near the airbase."

The three laid back in their chairs and thought about the eleven tons of giant yellow and blue tow truck traveling at high speed. Willie rolled his head over, at the same time as Maddie, and looked at the big yellow truck hulking in the gloom. They both smiled slowly, evilly.

"What about the engine we just got?"

Maddie laughed. "That, my dear boy, is exactly the engine they started with. And I have the blueprints to do the rest."

Willie frowned and looked at her. "Where did you get the blueprints for the Desert Eagle?"

"Umm… they floated into my hands a couple of years ago. I was just waiting to see if Hooker was grown up enough to deal with it all responsibly." She harrumphed. "Gosh knows, you aren't."

Willie looked over at the Granny car under the tarp.

Maddie smiled. "The Granny? A straight-six is sitting over at the Contra Costa yard. As far as I've heard, it's clean with low miles on it. Dolly could probably get it released tomorrow. They could probably fill the whole power train, too. And remember, the fan did take out a healthy chunk of the radiator, so we can get one of those sent, as well."

The infection was striking Willie where it always did some good. He began to softly chuckle his evil and sinister laugh. Maddie knew he couldn't control it. It was just something that happened like a cat purring or a dog's hind leg when you scratched its belly. It was just the nature of the beast.

Maddie turned up the evil stove a notch. "We can stick it all on Friday and testbed it by Friday night. It would give us Saturday for a shakedown to Monterey for some seafood."

Willie rolled his eyes, remembering the disaster the last time they had driven home drunk from Monterey in the Granny car. The engine was more than the car or driver could handle, and the black circles on the highway attested to the car spinning three complete circles before it hit the side berm and flipped four times. Both passenger and driver were thrown somewhere about midway through the second flip. Only one deer of the small herd had been hit.

"How about we keep it to lunch and some music at the Boots and Saddle over in La Honda? We can let Hanky do the driving."

The three laughed and drank some more moonshine in the night. A bat flew in the large door, flitted around, and bounced in the air out the back door. A small airplane could have done the same.

The young man out on the freeway had his left elbow on the sill of the old car. Speed was not the intent. Enjoying the evening air in the convertible was everything, as well as the woman he was heading to meet.

The last of the moon hung low over the south end of the large Bay Area. It had only four more days before it would be dark.

20

Hooker had never ridden in the back of a truck, much less a military truck. The canvas canopy reeked of wax and old diesel fumes. The truck wove its way sluggishly between piles of mechanical equipment and groups of people. It gently squealed to a halt, more from dust in the large brakes than anything resembling speed or the need for maintenance.

Hooker was dressed in the same work uniform as the Marines with who he had been riding. The two soldiers on the end unlatched and dropped the tailgate. In two files, they all jumped off the end and formed up on the old concrete airstrip. On a single command, they marched off to some undisclosed duty and not of Hooker's concern.

As they moved across the concrete pad, another group moved alongside while Hooker and one of their groups switched places.

Hooker and two others slowed, and the rest of the group kept marching. The three walked and talked quietly. All around for hundreds of yards, there were companies or groups moving or setting up and tearing down cannons, howitzers, and groups of tents along with radio equipment. The entire old balloon landing site was abuzz with the movement of military practicing being military.

The only strange activity was companies of soldiers marching four and six abreast, carrying large bags of sand or dirt. As they marched along, they were leaking the dirt where they were marching. Over to one side was a group of men filling bags from a couple of dump trucks. Hooker shrugged at the inefficiency of the whole transfer but chalked it up to the military being the military.

Hooker looked around. "Isn't this much activity bound to create a lot of interest?"

John looked around through his eyebrows as his head was down looking at a layout map. "We do something like this—two or three times a year. We could just do all of this on the bases, but this gives us all some needed practice in combined convoys and working the Navy, Marines, and those other guys from down south." The three smiled.

Alex took over. He nodded with his head at the pattern painted on the concrete—the old worn markings Hooker guessed were a carryover from the days of the dirigible. Alex dispelled the theory. They were only painted to look old. "These landing pad markings are important to you. On the night, you must be standing in this circle. Your sister must run over this circle and along this orange arrow. We put some phosphorous in the paint, and at night, it will still be glowing faintly until about one in the morning. After that, the moonlight will confuse the issue enough if the enemy comes snooping around, they won't see anything out of the ordinary."

He nodded at the area where two trucks were practicing getting over two large long humps of dirt. The ridges were about eight feet high. "Those ridges are their set up. If they run between those—they will be lined up on here. In the bay, we have a new buoy with a red over green set of lights. That will be their target. If they get to the break and then run toward the buoy, they will run straight over this arrow. You will chase them and then stop here to shoot. You must stop. This will start the timed process. Once you have stopped, you then cycle your gun. They need to be one hundred feet away from you. We figure they will be running at about four miles an hour, so when you first shoot, they will be about forty feet from the doors."

John took over. "You will know when to shoot by this small red light." He nodded over at a jeep sitting idle with just a driver. As the man pulled an imaginary shotgun up to take aim, a small red light came on. It blinked three times and went dark. "As soon as the light comes on, everything is set to roll with the pull of your trigger."

Alex resumed the explosives run-through. "The charges will ignite from only twenty feet in front of you. Those are all the special charges so they're more flash and smoke than anything else. Those are the magic of Boombowski." They all smiled. "Those lead out both ways and will run as a fan of two arms circling the door zone. As they progress, they will be getting wider and more violent. Once the ignition hits about one hundred feet from you, then the C-4 will start kicking in. This is all being buried by those men marching with the bags of dirt and sand.

"By the time we have wrapped the entire field, the second round will have already started out in front of you again. That is exactly one and a half seconds for you to cycle your gun and fire each time. It will be a fast one-two or cycle-shoot in your mind. You have five shots. The total is seven and a half seconds for everything to happen.

"The doors take one second to open or close. They will start to open one second after you take your first shot. By the second shot, your sister should be at the top of the ramp. We will close the ramp at the fourth shot. With the last shot, we have laid an extra two feet of dirt across the field. We have a field of flat explosives under everything which is timed for the grand finale. When the ring closes for the fifth time, the entire field will end up in the air. We think when it has all landed, there will be at least a foot of dirt cover over the entire door."

"That's a lot of explosives."

"Controlled explosives, but it also means when you shoot the last shot, you need to turn and start running—but you are going to trip. Stay lying down. You will be in the raining earth from heaven zone."

"Why don't I just keep running?"

"Because it's going to feel like you are at ground zero when the San Francisco earthquake hit back in '06. That was about an eight-some-thing on the Richter scale. This might feel more like a nine, and you can't run in it. Just lie down and ride it all out." He looked at Hooker's face and shrugged with a smile. "You can run if you want, but when the field goes off... everyone is going to get knocked on their asses. It's why we'll have mattresses at the bottom of the ramp for your sister and friend."

"So how do we get everyone back out?"

"Did you think we could blow up the world and nobody notices? We will have some police cars here in about fifteen minutes, followed by a couple of fire trucks. That should give the enemy a little time to snoop around, but not long enough to find anything.

"After about twenty minutes, the base will be notified there was an explosion at our old airbase. Only then will we roll a bit of equipment. As the sun comes up, we will build up the number of vehicles standing around, as well as people. There is a manhole over there about a hundred yards. We will extract everyone through it. There will be a bus sitting right over it. It has a hole we cut in the bottom this morning. They are installing sweeper curtains along the underside so nothing will show. It will just look like a shadow.

"We tried to keep you and your sister's parts really simple. We will be watching, and we will control the rest."

Hooker curled his bottom lip into his teeth as he looked around.

John finished it. "It's going to be a show The Great Boomkowski will be proud of but can never talk about. Trust us."

Hooker swung back around. "Oh, I do. I just hope my sister can keep up her end."

Alex nodded in understanding. "It will either be a thing of beauty, or it could all turn FUBAR. Only on the night will we know which way it went."

John thought. "Um, I know this is really out there, but is there any way to bring them over and walk them through it?"

"I don't know." Hooker looked around at the mass of people and equipment in a hyperactive state. "When do you guys finish and clear out?"

"They were done this morning. This was all just camouflage for your being here."

"Okay. I have my meeting with her tomorrow night. I guess I'll see if I can get her over here and run her through the plan. She's not the one I worry about, though. It's her companion. I don't know how he will react or if he can even understand what is happening." He furled his lips. "I guess we'll find out."

A jeep pulled up alongside the three. "This is us. Get in, Hooker. You get to ride like an officer this time."

They wheeled out of the area as Hooker noticed three convoys were forming out of the mass confusion. It gave him hope. Hooker thought about the games his sister used to make up for them to play. The treasure hunt was always a matter of counting. So many steps here, turn, and so many there. She could lead Hooker all over a playground and end up exactly where he needed to be. It was later when he realized that in the early years, her legs and stride would have been much longer than his. By the time you take two or four hundred measured steps, you could be off by as much as a hundred feet, but at her guidance, he always ended up where he was supposed to be.

He remembered standing on a large area laid in cobblestone bricks. To Hooker, they had all looked the same. Then he had counted out the last long set of steps. She had told him to squat, reach down, and pull up the brick. He had expected nothing, but the brick eased out of the hole and exposed a wad of cloth. He removed the cloth and unfolded it. Even today, the battered Tom Mix badge with a broken pin was in his sock drawer at Uncle Willie's house.

He had no doubts about her following directions, none at all.

John leaned forward from the back seat. "We'll let the crew in the bunker know you might be there for a dry run tomorrow night. If you want them to practice the door, then just stomp three times on it or act like you're shooting your shotgun. They will have a heat signature scan done by the Seal team by then and will open if it's all clear. If they don't open, you're being watched."

Hooker nodded.

The ride back from the base had been one of contemplation. Everything was riding on the little things, but Hooker knew if they were going to get this killer off the streets, it all had to go as planned.

Later, as he showered for his first real date, he mapped the layout of the field over and over. Finally, he just sat in the large shower on the small wooden bench and tried to focus on nothing.

Gradually, the field and plans were replaced by a soft smile and a ponytail of mousy blond hair. There was nothing special about the way she looked. Most people would never give her a second glance. She had the hollowed-out face usually associated with people from the Dust Bowl years. However, even when they had met years before, Hooker hadn't noticed her appearance. He had seen how she treated Jerry, an obvious bag of damaged goods. She had stolen Hooker's heart even before he knew her name.

The late afternoon was temperate, still nice enough to leave the top down on the convertible. The DeSoto purred its way up Stupid Hill where greedy contractors had built nothing but stupid houses on streets with even stupider names.

Hooker looked over at Candy. He liked the loose ponytail she had drawn her hair back into, along with the burnt-yellow cotton blouse—a nice touch of summer, but with deference to the coming fall colors. He smiled—the jeans weren't new.

She smiled over at him. "Approve?"

He laughed. "Tonight, I no longer count. Just remember, you can't sit in Manny's lap on the first date. Stella will love you right out of the box. It's just the way she is. Willie is a mixed bag, and I just hope he behaved himself and didn't wear a dress."

"What kind of dress?" She giggled. Her brother Squirt had told her about his first meeting with Willie and the really ugly granny dresses he wore when welding.

Hooker groaned. "Awe, beans in sauce. I don't know what to tell you. I've never brought a date home."

She reached out and put her hand on his thigh. "It's all right. I've never been brought home before either."

Hooker realized they were a lot more alike than either had realized.

The large chrome grill of the DeSoto nosed quietly up the street and onto the extra-large parking apron usually reserved for Hooker's eleven-ton girlfriend, Mae West. The large car was dwarfed by the expanse of concrete capable of holding twenty DeSotos.

"Hooker, I don't think you can park here." Her eyes grew wide as she took in the fourteen-foot stucco wall with the protruding black locust logs around the top. The large hand-hewn black walnut gates were standing open to their full nine-foot width. The twin flanking doors stood twelve feet tall. The plaza was lined by votive candles in paper sacks in the Mexican lantern style called luminaires. There was enough afternoon light even though the desired effect was somewhat diminished, it was still romantic.

The fountain glowed. Hooker suspected Stella had scrubbed and polished the tile that morning. It gleamed almost magically in the candle and early evening light. Later, it would be romantic.

"Welcome to Hacienda Romero, the only Jewish Mexican hacienda in Norte Americano."

She looked at him. "You're kidding me, right?"

He raised his eyebrow and nodded toward the equal-sized door on the inside which were the real front doors. The door was opening. There was no turning back.

"You really live here?"

"I think you better ask the lady coming this way."

Horrorstruck, Candy turned to face the smiling and waving woman in bare feet, jeans, and a Mexican peasant blouse. "Oh crap," she squeaked. "She knows you."

Hooker laughed as he got out of the car and came around. Stella stopped at the gate archway. Hooker opened Candy's door.

As they crossed the concrete, Stella solemnly stuck out both her hands toward Candy. "Let me see your hands."

She gently took them and examined them in the light from the hanging bell. The hard calluses and nicks and damage from hard work did not escape her trained eyes. "Hmm, no fork marks." She looked up and smiled. "It looks like his treatment of your brother doesn't run to the whole family." She pulled the young woman in for an official hug. Stella smiled at Hooker.

Stella pulled her arm around Candy's waist. "Come meet the rest of the crazy family."

Stella looked back over her shoulder with an evil smile as she confided, "Dolly is going to hate you for being so skinny, and she won't *even* believe you don't have a fat neck." Stella looked back at Hooker. "What do you even kiss on her? It can't be her neck." She turned back to Candy as they walked into the house, and Hooker groaned seeing Dolly through the window. "Hooker only seems to kiss us women with fat necks... don't you, honey?"

Candy didn't know whether to run screaming into the night or just wet her pants from laughing so hard. The food was amazing, and the non-stop stories, usually at Hooker's expense, were hilarious.

Candy wiped at her mouth and then leaned around Hooker and looked at Stella. "Gosh—I just can't believe we never met each other when we were visiting our boys in the hospital. I guess it was just a matter of I stopped in on my way to work, and you were probably there during the day."

Stella nodded soberly but with a devilish look at the back of Hooker's head. "Wasted time girl—just pure, unadulterated, wasted time—Hooker wouldn't have been such a moving target."

Hooker hung his face into his hands.

Somewhere between courses of the dinner part of the meal, Stella had Hooker come and help her get something in the kitchen. Once he was in the kitchen, she had him fetch something from the pantry. As soon as he started walking toward the pantry, Stella switched Hooker's and her plates and glass and sat down next to Candy. Manny had buried his face in his palm and peeked through his fingers at Willie and Hank sitting on the other end.

Willie watched Manny as he reached out with his right hand and put it on Candy's right hand. Giving Manny a reproving look, he just let a little Nancy slip out as he told Manny, "Now you just shush. We girls might need to talk a smidge." He turned back to Candy. "Now isn't that right, sugar plum?"

Hank closed his eyes and shook his head as he muttered, "Oh boy—here we go."

Hooker returned and sized up the table. He went back to the pantry and returned with two quart-jars with ceramic and wire lids. The contents looked like clear water. Hooker took his new seat next to Maddie. He weighed Candy's seatmates. "You're going to need some of this... and you'll be sleeping in your brother's room tonight." He passed the moonshine down. "Stella can decide which glasses she wants to break you in with."

Willie held up his water glass. Hooker gave him a hard look. "Even with Hank driving, you will behave to some degree tonight."

Maddie gave him an equally hard stare. She understood just how giddy her best friend probably was. He had finally met the nice girl who had seemed to steal his boy's heart. She shared much of the same mix of pride and happiness.

Hank giggled. "Oh, it's okay, Hooker. It makes it easier for me to take advantage of him later."

"Oh, you mean there is a level easier than slut?"

"Hooker!" Stella and Willie both growled a warning at the same time.

Hooker dug into his pants and pulled out a dollar. He handed it to Hank. "For the jar, I'll probably say something else tonight..." Hooker felt Maddie's slender hand patting his thigh in consolation.

Candy hid her mouth behind her napkin and giggled. She leaned over and confided in Stella. "It's too bad Dolly had to go to work."

Stella roared with laughter. "Oh, honey, when my sister and I light into Hooker, it is no laughing matter. I keep him straight, but with Dolly, the only thing he can do wrong is go nuzzle and kiss her and her girls' fat necks." She pushed her hand on the arm of the now laughing Candy. "Where he started that, I'll never know. But lord, do us fat-necked women..." she glanced over at Hooker, "think it's disgusting!" Then she leaned into Candy and murmured. "We love it."

Hank had gotten out his chef's torch and seared the canned peaches on top of the creamy rum vanilla ice cream he and Stella had churned that afternoon. There were just traces of white left in the dishes. The conversations had settled down as the moonshine had mellowed out the carnival of meeting someone new and important in their family.

Stella patted Candy on the arm and spoke quietly. "Bring your glass. I want to show you something even Hooker hasn't seen yet." The men were talking about some logistics of getting something done by the light of the moon. Candy wasn't really following, and so Stella was providing an out.

Stella calmed the look from Hooker with a mention she was just going to show Candy the luminaires and the cactus that was blooming these past three nights. The two women followed quietly by Maddie, walked out the front door. They strolled past and admired the candles and bags, but Stella kept them walking down and around the driveway leading to the large parking area below, as well as the three-car garage.

Two of the garage doors were open, and the light spilled out onto the two pickup trucks parked out in the large parking area next to a couple of very large tents with mosquito netting sides. The trucks were still full of supplies to be off-loaded in the morning.

"We have one more tent to put up. It will be out along there where the crew will prep the food and do any parboiling or blanching. Over the next month, we will generate about three dump-truck loads of peelings and skins. The pits and seeds will all be dried and crushed, but there will only be a few drums of those. All of it will be composted down the hill, and later put into any garden needing or wanting it."

"Hooker told me you did a lot of canning, but I just didn't believe him."

"We are the second-largest canning operation in the city. Metro canning is the biggest, of course, but they do it all year. They also will do about five tons of commercial style canning for us that we can't do." She pointed out toward where the hill came down to the large parking lot. "Later we're going to build a large barn out there. It will house the entire operation, including an outdoor kitchen running the full length of the barn and overlooking the valley."

She took her hand. "Here, come in here. I'll show you where we store a lot of this food." Maddie smiled warmly. They wound into the garage and around a beige Dodge Dart convertible with red leather interior.

Candy looked at the car. "What a cute car." She looked at Stella. "Is this your car?"

Stella patted the trunk of the yellow Cadillac. "This is my Buttercup. That one is for my daughter."

"Convertibles are nice with this kind of weather. It was nice riding down here in the big car of Willie's. I'd like to have a convertible someday."

Stella smiled back at Maddie and opened one side of the double doors to the storage room. She turned on the light in the almost empty room.

Their movements echoed in the large room. "By Halloween, this will be stuffed full all the way to the ceiling with boxes of canned food."

"Wow."

"Yeah, wow. There are five storage areas in San Jose. The wow part is it only lasts about one year. And then we do it all over again."

"And this is all for families of police in need?"

"All of the law enforcement—fire departments, tow-drivers, city and county workers, and the list goes on. We really don't make people in need fit any certain criteria. Goodness knows—people in need are people in need."

Stella looked at the young woman. She walked her into a big hug. "Oh, honey, don't start crying. Not yet, at least."

She turned off the light and pulled Candy back out into the garage. "I want you to see this. I need your choice on something."

As she dragged her around the cars and across the garage, she pointed up the stairs. "We've had the door locked for a week or so, in order to keep Hooker out, but he's been busy lately. The door is a secret door in the pantry. I'll show you how to open it from the other side later."

She opened the door to the apartment and turned on the lights. Maddie let out a little wow.

"Stella, they have been really moving right along on this."

"Well, all the plumbing was in, as was all the wiring. It was just the dividing walls that needed to be put in and wired. But yes, they have really moved it right along. And Hooker never suspected a thing. Poor dear has been exhausted lately."

Candy turned around in the almost finished apartment. "This is going to be where Hooker lives?"

"Not on your life," Stella growled. "He will only be allowed down here if you invite him."

Candy was still looking in the two bedrooms and the large bathroom. She came out of the small hall and looked at where the cabinets were standing to be installed for the small kitchenette. "Do the..."

She turned and frowned. "Why would I invite Hooker down here?"

Maddie quietly smiled, and Stella deadpanned as she faced Candy before stating, "Probably, because it's your new apartment, if you want it while you go to nursing school, that is. As for rent, we can talk after you have a couple of years under your uniform as a nurse."

"But...." She started to tear up.

Stella stood her ground. "Stop. You can't cry yet. Do you want the apartment? Do you want to live here? And, if so, we need to paint—so what color?"

"I like the soft yellow of butter..."

"Then Nebraska home churned butter it is."

Candy nodded numbly as she wiped at her eyes. "Now can I cry?"

Maddie calmly stepped in. Her hands were still clasped together at her legs. "No."

Candy looked with confusion at Maddie who had been very quiet all evening long. Candy knew she was a librarian and a friend of Willie's, but beyond that, she was a mystery.

"If you are going to live here, then you are part of the family." She reached out her hand, dangling a pair of keys. "Here are the keys to your home... and your car."

"But I don't have a car."

"Yes, you do. It's kind of a hand-me-down, but it will always run great. Not as fast as it once was but plenty fast for a student. It's parked right outside in your garage slot. We all call it the Granny car."

The three women came back up through the pantry after they all finished crying. They continued down the 'guest hall' that was Hooker's (and now Squirt's) domain. Maddie broke off and used Hooker's bathroom to wash her face. The other two continued to Squirt's room.

Candy turned around in the room again. "You did all of this for Johnny... for what reason?"

Stella gave her the rolled head stupid zombie act—the inside family joke for all dumb questions. "Like I needed a reason in my own home?" She slurred her answer as she thought a zombie would.

Candy giggled. She hadn't felt this good in a long time. "No, seriously. You didn't even know my brother, and you went out and bought him jeans..." She started opening drawers. "Underwear, socks ... wait... *underwear*? When did he start wearing underwear?" She looked at Stella.

Stella shrugged. "He can go commando for all I care. If he needs a dress, I'll go raid Uncle Willie's closet if it's what the kid wants. I don't care. He's now one of my brood, and I get to do what I want for them." She took hold of Candy's shoulders. "Honey, he saved my Hooker's bacon when it counted most. The kid is a saint." She hugged the girl inside of Candy. "Maybe you don't see it, but the kid is every bit as good as Hooker was at that age. He just needed to have someone tell him that." She pushed back from Candy and looked her in the eyes. "So do you."

Candy fell forward for another hug. "You just have to give us some time to get used to this."

Stella patted her on the back. "You have all the time you need. Just hurry up about it. I'm liking the idea of getting a daughter out of the deal."

They smiled as Candy took one last look around her brother's room, and then turned out the light. "And mum is the word. Hooker has no idea the apartment is almost ready... or about the car."

"I have one question." Candy and Stella stood in the darkened doorway.

"What, honey?"

Candy leaned into her. "How did you know what size jeans he wore?"

Stella let out a roar of a laugh and hung on to Candy. There was so much to teach a daughter.

Hank dragged Willie outdoors when Don and another driver showed up to drop off the new five-ton tow truck for Hooker. He went over the new features on the towing bed, and where everything was. Hooker didn't even think anything was different when Willie and Maddie were chauffeured off by Hank in the DeSoto Hooker had arrived in.

Finally, late—the lights were off. The hacienda settled, and quiet prevailed. Several minutes later, the ghostly figure crept down the short hallway in the moonlight. It slipped into the door, found its bearings, and picked up the edge of the blankets and sheets. The lithe body slid in and found the larger spoon with a small muffled giggle. Anything else in the world could wait.

2 1

Hooker stood in front of the large truck. It felt strange. Though it was a much larger truck than average, it was also much smaller than the truck he was used to driving. The moon was about a half hour from touching the trees. The hair on the back of his head began to tingle.

Hooker didn't move. "Hello, Mouse."

The voice was at the back of the truck. "It smells brand new, Hooker."

"It is. It's only a loaner until my truck is running again."

She walked around to the front and leaned against the bumper. "I love the moon when it is like this. It is so full of life."

Hooker looked at her. She was tired. It was as if there was no strength left in her. He worried.

She sensed his eyes on her. "Don't worry, Hooker. It will all be over soon."

"We have to go over what is going to happen, but we have to go there. It's at the end of the airbase—the old section."

"They were busy there the last few days. They do these things a couple of times a year. It disturbs the animals."

Hooker wondered if she meant the little fuzzy four-legged ones or the two-legged ones she called her family or tribe. He decided he did not want to know.

"Do you think anyone is watching it?"

She thought. "No." She looked over her shoulder. "It's too bright for most of them... and there would be no food anyway. Not for a few days or so."

"We need to go over there so I can show you what you have to do." He looked past her. "Will Dog be okay riding in the truck?"

She thought a moment and then nodded. "*On* the truck—he'll ride on the back."

Hooker leaned off the bumper and stood. "Well, get him, and we'll go."

She moved around Hooker and headed for the passenger side door. "You're getting slow, brother. He was on the back minutes ago."

Hooker did not even look. Somehow, he knew he wouldn't see the man even if he tried. He opened the door and climbed up into the cab. His sister oozed up into the seat. Hooker still marveled at how she could move as if she didn't have a bone in her body.

He reached for the little silver button on the dashboard out of habit. There was nothing but a new black dashboard. He swore silently and then flicked the key once. The gas engine turned over and rumbled into life. Hooker's right hand wavered in the air where gear shifters should be and then moved his right hand up to the stick on the column. He pulled... Nothing... And then he remembered to step on the brake. He pulled the selector down to drive and eased the truck out of the old parking lot.

The night air was nice as he hung his left arm out the window.

"Do you still eat ice cream with the window down in the winter?"

He smiled. For her, it would be a memory going back to when they were kids. "Sure."

The Mouse laughed. "French vanilla in a sugar cone."

He held up three fingers. "Triple scoop."

The memories with his sister were special. Of all of them, it was ones like this he loved. They were the ones Hooker held on to for dear life.

He looked at her. She was leaning against the glass, looking at the world go by a lot faster than it had been passing for her the last many years. Hooker knew the look—she was hundreds of miles away.

He parked on the old runway. The cracked concrete looked like a fili-
gree of snakes in the dimmed moonlight. The occasional truck on the
freeway from a mile away made a sighing sound. The night was alive, and
Hooker knew he probably could only grasp a tenth of what his sister was
sensing.

Her nose was slightly up. She moved more from the currents of the air
than from footsteps. Hooker saw the shadow move low about a hundred
feet away.

He spoke to the air quietly. "Dog needs to be close to hear what we
have planned."

She turned in the moonlight. Her face glowed from the extra phosphorous in her skin. With enough exposure to light, Hooker knew she would
glow in the dark. He also knew the glow was one of the special things
about her giving her control over her tribe. They were not sure if she
were human or a spirit.

"He can hear your heart beating. You're anxious, and it is very loud and
fast."

Hooker knew she was being truthful. He relaxed. "In seven days, we
will meet here at midnight. There will be a tugboat standing offshore. He
will blow his whistle three times, and then once. That is your signal to be
here in ten minutes."

She looked out into the night. Then turned and nodded.

"Dog needs to be very close. We will be meeting out here on the
airstrip, and then we will start arguing. When the argument becomes
angry, you can start backing up, back up toward those two ridges of dirt.
You are going to end up running through the gap. It is very important."

They started walking toward the gap. He pointed beyond everything
and out into the black of the brackish water of the flats. "Do you see the
buoy out there? It is the one with a red light over a green light?"

She nodded.

"The buoy is only there for you. You can only see those lights if you are
here in this cut between the two ridges. When you run through here, find
the buoy, and run toward it. You must always run toward the buoy. It is
the only safe place."

He looked at her. It was interesting to watch her. It seemed as though she was ignoring him, but he knew she was paying attention to everything he said and everything around her.

She turned back. "He finds it interesting how the lights hide."

"They are set back into a tube so you have to be looking down the tube to see them."

She nodded with a soft smile. Her little brother was telling her something she had already figured out.

Their life had always been like that. She never told him he was stupid or younger. She just nodded, and he had to accept she already knew what he was telling her, or she was acknowledging the new information. In all of the years, in good homes or ones where names like *idiot* or *stupid* were used interchangeably with your name, she had never shown Hooker anything but mutual respect and love.

He turned and walked through the gap. The dirt had been loosened up from the packing that had gone with the truck training. Hooker could imagine a company of Marines with rakes loosening the dirt, starting on the top and working down. A line of men stretched from one end to the other. He knew this would make it difficult for anyone to sneak over the ridges.

He stopped. Facing the buoy, he looked along the ground. "Can you see the arrow glowing?"

"Dog told me about it ten minutes ago." She looked at Hooker. "Yes, I see it. It is the same as my skin. In an hour, it will fade and no longer be seen."

Hooker took a deep breath and let it out slowly. "When you run this way, you have to be lined up and running on this arrow. I will stop here, at the edge of this circle. You must keep running. When you are about fifty feet away from me, I will cycle the shell into my shotgun. I know you will hear it." He pantomimed the cycling of the pump on the shotgun.

"I will know exactly when to shoot because there will be a small light on the ground facing me. When it turns on, I will shoot. I will shoot every one-and-a-half-seconds. I will have five shells in the shotgun."

A small red light, the size of a dime, came on. The Mouse twitched and whirled on Hooker.

"The light will be my signal. If you see it, it will also be your signal the world is about to end."

He walked her forward, across the lumpy dirt field. They stood looking out toward the bay. Hooker curved his hands and arms in a rising arc.

"All along here are explosives. When they get to about here, they become very large and violent. They will make an entire ring of fire and explosions seeming to come from my gun. You will, and Dog must be, in the middle to be safe."

They walked forward. "You must keep running. When I shoot the second time..." He raised his arm with the palm up.

The ground swung up, and the twin steel doors silently sprang open.

Hooker pointed. "You are running there. You have three seconds to get there and run down the ramp."

He turned to her. "When I shoot the fifth time, the entire ground will explode. Two feet of dirt will end up covering everything, especially the door."

He pointed down into the ramp where a man was standing in the dim red glow of battle station lights. "There are mattresses at the end of the ramp. Fall and lay on them. The people in the bunker are there to help you. Let them. Please."

He dropped his arm. The doors, large enough to swallow Mae West, followed suit. But for the thin metallic click, it was as if they had never existed.

She stood silent.

He waited.

"We can't do it."

"It's the only way."

"No."

"Why?"

"Because Dog goes berserk with thunder. I can only imagine what will happen when you blow up the world."

Hooker stood looking at her. He had no argument. He had expected her to accept the plan and do it. He had no plan B.

Hooker finally closed his eyes. "Ask him because there is no plan B."

She didn't move. Finally, she nodded. "Yes, it will save us."

An almost naked upright man with a glazing of dirt and sweat and air walked past Hooker. He was nothing more than a slow breeze in the night air. His white blue eyes pierced Hooker's and dredged at the bottom of Hooker's soul. Slowly, he came to a stop behind Hooker's sister. His right hand rested protectively on her shoulder. The man was as if carved of a muddy marble.

Barely perceptible, he nodded.

She looked like she was going to speak, and then didn't. Hooker knew they both knew this was it. This moment would be life or death. If it went as planned, their staged death would be the release from the life they had lived much of their lives. That life would die so they could live. Even though The Mouse said her health would eventually end, she wanted Dog to have a shot at something other than this life in the dirt. Her brother was the key to unlock the door where they now stood.

"Seven days. Midnight. When the boat horn blows three then one." She stepped forward and stood on her tiptoe. Her left hand cradled his cheek as she softly kissed the other. "Be well met, my knight." The night air shimmered, and like Dog, she was gone.

Hooker softly whispered the rejoinder from their childhood. "Or afore the dawn, we lay like scattered wildflowers on the field of battle. Our bones will till the earth, and our blood shall grow the field of honor anew."

A warm gob of spit splattered on the back of Hooker's neck. The word from his silent mouth was similar, but not the same as spit. He didn't even flinch.

The afternoon had started with strange weather and had just gotten weirder after the sun had gone down. It had not rained all day. It had just thrown the occasional spitball of warm sticky water. Hooker talked nasty at the lug bolt rusted onto the drum of the battered Impala.

Since the early hours, the weather pattern had been reversing the season's 'out to sea' flow of the steamy Sacramento River air. The Central Valley, with its heat and rotting vegetation, created some of the skankiest smelling air. Luckily, the Sierra Nevada Mountains provided a downhill push that would normally drive the fetid air out through the San Francisco Bay and into the Pacific Ocean, where it would mix and push north and back out to the giant air mass of the Gulf of Alaska.

A large storm in the Gulf of Alaska was being pushed down by the dropping jet stream and becoming a driving force of stationary air. A matching or a possibly larger tropical storm coming from the north of Hawaii was being fed by a small tropical front storm pushing up from Mexico. The result was three air masses mixing into the witch's cauldron of the San Francisco Bay. As always, with such a conflict, the riot of air got shoved into the bottom of the bay and over the greater San Jose area and as far north as Moffett Airfield.

On the mountainside of the Coast Range, the highway crossed over to Santa Cruz. The wet air hung there, trapped by the trees.

Hooker heard the gratifying groan of the rusty metal. The lug nut began to turn. The tired old Chevy was once again saved from the junk heap.

High above and almost thirty miles to the north, the Orion P-3 airplane watched the weather, as well as the infrared signatures, gathering at the target site. "Moffett control, this is Watch Eagle."

"Go, Watch Eagle."

"Be advised we have five more bogies entering the field from the southeast."

"Roger, Watch Eagle, five more players from Sierra Echo. Will advise Dugout."

All evening they had been monitoring the movement of warm bodies moving into the area. The count was now close to eighty. Everyone could feel there was another storm brewing. But this one had nothing to do with the weather.

Hooker removed the old tire and mounted the spare. He spun the five nuts on with his fingers and then threw them home by fan spinning the four-way wrench. After ten years of changing hundreds of flat tires, the sequence of one-three-five-two-four was something he did not have to think about, as his hand just automatically set-one skip, set-one skip, set-one skip, until he hit an already tight nut. Then he took one last creak on each nut, all the way around.

He stood and let the jack down. Grabbing the flat, he walked around to the trunk and threw it in. "Get this fixed or replaced in the morning, sir. In fact, we're moving into the rainy season, and these tires won't be safe. You really need five new tires."

Hooker wanted to tell the man it would be almost cheaper to get a new car, but he knew many lived very close to the edge. Although this man might be able to afford the auto club, more than one new or retread at a time might bust his budget.

The woman scowled at the sky that had just spit on her. She hung close to her husband as he handed Hooker his auto club card. "We moved here from Shreveport just to get away from weather like this. Y'all get hurricanes here?" She looked north toward the bay.

Hooker was ever helpful, but he did like to get in a dig occasionally. "No ma'am, no hurricanes. We do get a couple of small tornados out on the flats or at the airports, but no hurricanes. We're pretty uneventful around these parts—just the occasional earthquake now and then." He smiled warmly. "We need them to knock down the old buildings to make room for new freeways."

The old man smiled and tried not to laugh. He turned his head so he could enjoy the joking without being hit by his wife's purse.

Hooker split the signed receipt and handed the man his card and yellow copy. "Y'all have a great night now. Ya hear?"

Hooker smiled as he stowed the floor jack. He overheard the woman speaking to her husband as he held the door for her. "Such a nice young man, but did you hear what he said about those awful earthquakes? I just don't know about those earthquakes, Arthur."

The man wore a large smile as he came around the back of the Chevy. Hooker, leaning against the side of his truck, returned the smile as the man shot him a two-finger salute. "That will give her something to worry about for the entire winter." They both laughed.

The man opened his door. The woman looked across with a frown. "What were you two laughing about, Arthur?"

"Nothing, Gladys." He closed the door and drove off.

Hooker licked his smile and looked with a jaundiced eye at the black sky. "If this keeps up, in four more nights, the dark of the moon won't matter." He wiped his hands on the red shop rag, threw it back in the side box and closed the door.

As he stood on the running board to get into the cab of the truck, his neck received one more gob of salty gooey spit. He froze and wiped it off. Leaning out, he looked up. "Really?"

High and to the north, a young airman sat at a desk monitoring infrared scanners.

"Moffett control, this is Watch Eagle."

"Go ahead, Watch Eagle."

"We have what appears to be the formation of seventeen approaching from the northwest. I say again, diamond formation inbound from the northwest. They are about half a click out from the playing field and holding."

"Roger, Watch Eagle. Diamond formation of seventeen bogies, inbound, from November Whiskey. Will advise Dugout."

"Also, be advised, we are twenty-eight minutes from bingo."

"Roger, Watch Eagle. Night Hawk Four is on the ramp and will be on station and coordinating with you in under twenty."

The naval petty officer made a log notation and called forward to the pilot. "We will be relieved in about twenty."

"What is the count?"

"It's at ninety-five and growing. It looks like they aren't going to wait until Thursday night. It looks like the war is tonight." He looked at the digital clock above his electronics board. The clock stood at twenty-two-fourteen—still an hour and forty-six minutes until midnight.

Forty miles to the south and five thousand feet lower, the phone rang on the credenza behind Dolly. Her eyes closed, and the muscles around her large heart tightened. Her phone never rang because it was someone nice wishing her a wonderful day.

She swung around and picked it up on the third ring. "Dolly."

"Dolly, it's Danny." He sounded terrified.

"Danny, breathe honey. I'm here."

"Five minutes ago, Sweets was getting ready for work. Suddenly, he is on the floor."

"Ambulance is on the way, honey." She was snapping her fingers at Dina. It sounded more like a gunshot in the dark room.

"I don't need no ambulance. You need to call Hooker. Sweets is running his mouth about Hooker and Armageddon and the world blowing up and dead bodies flying through the air and flames every-where." He drew in a loud breath. "You need to get ahold of Hooker, and you need to do it now."

"I'm on it, Danny. You take care of Sweets."

She held the phone with her finger on the disconnect button. She let it go and dialed Willie. She let it ring five times and hung up. She grabbed the lollypop microphone off the credenza and checked to make sure she was on the right channel.

"Willie, if you don't pick up right now. I will come pull your manhood up and out through your throat."

She counted the seconds on her fingers. Her thumb and index finger were out, and the middle was twitching.

"Sounds serious, Dolly." The voice was wrong.

The voice came across on the auto club night radio.

Dolly keyed the mic. "Willie, use the mic hanging behind your head."

The female voice came out of the proper speaker. "Dolly, I tore them all out, and we're rebuilding the cab. What can we do for you?"

"Is she running? And is Betsy loaded and in her holster?"

"We are out testing her now. Stand by one."

"Betsy is ready."

"Hooker is out past The Cats on a flat tire he just finished. The meat sauce is hitting the fan, and he will need Mae. Can she go to war, Maddie?"

Willie came on the radio. "We'll meet him at the diner."

"10-4."

Dolly turned the selector to the shop line in the new truck.

"1-4-1?"

She waited. She knew if he was outside the truck, he would still have the outside speaker on.

Box returned from the office from a visit to his sandbox. He sat looking at his resting place, bouncing around and uncharacteristically moving and working. He grumbled.

Dolly didn't have time for an argument and snapped her finger at the desk. He blinked and silently ascended to the top of the desk, a new place for him. He felt the leather writing pad and then lay down. He would watch the hard work from a comfortable position.

"1-4-1?" She demanded and looked across to Dina.

Dina shrugged. "He cleared the tire ten minutes ago."

"Was he close to Henry's place?"

Dina plugged in a cord. "Teresa, is Hooker there?" She leaned back and nodded. "Yell through the door for him to slap those cheeks and pinch it short because he has a 9-9-9 call." She listened and then pulled the cord.

They waited. Dolly watched the large hand on the big schoolroom clock tick to the seven. One hour and twenty-five minutes until midnight.

"1-4-1." The radio crackled.

Dolly scooped up the lollipop and keyed the mic as she brought it to her. "9-9-9 Hooker. Meet your party at the diner. Be safe, but don't spare the gas. Don has already paid for it."

Dolly could hear the truck starting as Hooker held the mic keyed. "What's going on, Dolly?"

"According to Danny, Sweets is on the floor, foaming at the mouth and Armageddon is arriving four days early."

She could hear the blare of a horn from what was probably a cut off car. "Who am I meeting?"

"All the help I hope you need, honey. You'll know them when you see them."

"10-4. Show me 10-97 in eight minutes."

Dolly raised her eyebrows over her wide eyes as she looked at her girls. "Don must have bought himself one hot engine. Well, it will be broken in by the time he hits Winchester Boulevard."

She snapped her fingers at Karen. "Check the PD roster."

The woman looked up and over as she scanned the roster. Her eyes knew where to look for which officer. "Podel is off tonight." Officer Podel was the least liked officer in the South Bay, and he always seemed to have a hard-on to write Hooker a speeding ticket that would knock him off the street for at least a month.

Dolly smiled. She keyed the lollipop. "Hooker, the poodle is locked in the garage tonight."

She got the 'chink-chink' of a double-tap on the mic key. She could sense that if Hooker had been driving south of the hundred mark on the speedometer, he wouldn't be now. It was now a wait and listen game—her least favorite kind of night.

She leaned back and patted her large chest. Box crossed the gap in one soft jump. The purr-box actuated in mid-flight.

Out on the interstate, eleven tons of giant yellow truck was roaring down the lanes that were clearing ahead of the garish red, yellow, and blue flashing lights. "How about the siren?"

Maddie looked up from the floor where the passenger seat should have been. "We were putting in a siren?"

Willie laughed. He downshifted through the new splicer transfer gears. They had slid into the lower gear before he realized it. "I guess not on the siren." He rolled the large ivory Bakelite steering wheel as he followed Mae around the cloverleaf. The giant truck cornered like it was a slot car welded to the street. Willie smiled. He knew Hooker would love the new stabilizer bar now keeping the truck flatter in the curves. As he reached the second half of the curve, he rolled in a lot more power. The nose seemed to rise as the automatic exhaust dumps slid back with the higher pressure.

Maddie looked up. "Those work great. I couldn't even hear the PTO run."

"You should feel this new transfer gearbox. What a stroke of genius."

"Why thank you, sir. A girl gets to read a little bit every once in a while." Willie knew tthis was one librarian whose nose was always in a book, especially at home.

"What do you think of the extra horses?"

Willie upshifted and mashed the pedal down. The truck at eighty plus still seemed to lift as the enlarged power slammed into the rear end and was pushed to the asphalt.

The woman squealed with glee and clapped her palms like a little girl. "Oh, yes. Folks, we have a winner!" She didn't have to see outside to know what the sides of the freeway looked like. She had spent too much time north of the hundred mark on motorcycles and cars.

Willie smiled as he backed the truck down to shy of the hundred mark. "If I was a crude man, I would say Mae West has had a successful nose job. Maddie went back to plugging wires into the new control panel. She stood up and stuck her head out the window and looked down along the undercarriage. She flicked switches. She sat back down and smiled. "Now, if we had music, we would have the fastest calliope in the world."

"How about the floods?"

She flicked a switch and the four large high-intensity lights on top of the cab lit up the freeway wall-to-wall for over a mile. A car a half a mile away swerved and dove for the shoulder.

"How about the back ones?"

They both laughed at the thought of turning them on. Both had a warped sense of humor when it came to auto crashes. Both had their share separately from racing—and then their shared memory of the night they almost totaled the Granny car, as well as themselves, coming home from Monterey drunk, one night...

As they now raced down the freeway in San Jose, the ramp they needed was coming up fast. "Brace yourself." Willie threw on the air brakes, and the world thundered as the air flowed into the diesel engine and provided backpressure. He romped on the brakes and started jamming down through the gears.

Maddie sat on the floor and watched the shifting and the clutch work. Their week without sleep had paid off. The system was smooth and seamless. She knew Hooker would love the fact they had trimmed the twenty-four original gears down to twenty, but had given him four hundred more horses, and added at least another twenty on the top end. They had also taken out the second gear shifter and replaced the main with what was known as a knuckle buster. All the shifting happened on the one handle.

She saw Willie stomp on the brake, drop four gears, his left foot still floating in the clutch, and she braced for the turn.

Eleven tons of truck with more than half of the weight placed on the rear tires makes a very loud and ugly noise when you do a high-speed drift for a turn. Halfway through the turn, Willie dumped the clutch and mashed the fuel pedal. The driver tires lit up and smoked the asphalt in an effort to gain traction. He feathered the fuel, and all eight slowed down and hooked into the asphalt. For the first time in their lives, the front tires had six inches of air under them for over a second. The touchdown was smooth as the brightly lit, flashing truck roared down the street toward Stevens Creek Boulevard.

Maddie watched Willie's face, and she smiled. She hadn't seen him have so much little boy fun in many years. It did her heart good to see this from her childhood friend.

They swung around onto an empty Stevens Creek and roared down the yellow centerline.

The large clock on the dashboard showed an hour and fifteen minutes until midnight.

They slewed around at the driveway to the diner. The nose of the truck was out in Winchester Boulevard. Willie jammed the shifter into reverse and stomped on the fuel. Mae's tires burned rubber up into and halfway across the deep parking lot.

Candy's head snapped up at the counter. She watched the familiar giant yellow truck pull backward into the parking lot. She had never been assaulted by all of the flashing and waving lights. The red, blue, and yellow were everywhere. The tires were lit from inside the tire wells, and the colors made it look like the truck was on fire or a mechanical beast from hell.

As the truck rocked to a standstill, a smaller truck crashed up onto the parking lot. It parked at the back next to Mae West. Candy smiled to see Mae still waved from the driver's door on the giant truck.

She started toward the door as she washed her hands in her apron.

Hooker jumped out of the smaller truck and ran toward Mae's driver door as it swung open. He jumped in and closed the door. There was a brief moment, and then the rear tires lit up with smoke as Mae shot out of the parking lot and bounced heavily into the street. More rubber was left as Hooker forced the turn and headed north.

Candy could still hear the tires howling as the giant truck disappeared from her view.

She thought a moment and ran to the phone.

Manny turned down the guitar music they were listening to as Stella answered the phone.

"Hello?'

"Mama, you better call your sister. Hooker just traded trucks and raced out of here in Mae like the devil was driving."

Stella looked over at Manny. "Thanks, honey. We'll keep you posted." She hung up. She drew her upper lip into a tight roll and bit down. As the lip slowly slid out between her teeth, she looked at Manny. "It's going down."

She leaned against the counter. Her mind was a mass of thoughts. One thought came through clear as Ma Bell could make it. She smiled as she looked over at Manny. *"She called me Mama."*

To the north, the giant yellow truck skidded around the corner and lined up on the freeway entrance. The engine roared, and tires howled as the smoke poured from the wheel wells as if the devil himself were trapped there. The fire and brimstone smelled more like burned rubber as Hooker leapfrogged the gears and exploded onto the freeway.

Willie was teaching from his position in the sleeper part of the cab. "Now when you shift again, you will go back to first as you turn the whole knob right. This puts the splicer into the upper set, and you flick the lever back forward, so you are in the lower side of the upper set. Now you have ten more." Hooker listened to the engine and then made the three-move shift. The gears did not grind, and it all moved smoothly. He mashed the fuel down more and leapfrogged the next shift. As they slowed and made the large cloverleaf from the 280 to the northbound 101, Hooker could see it was all clear.

Mae was only a yellow flash of paint as Maddie had shut down the lights for now.

Hooker reached for the microphone that should have been behind his head. "Sheets of rain on the street."

Maddie offered the microphone from the dark corner she had been sitting in.

Hooker gave a double take. "Maddie?"

The woman chuckled from the dark floor where the passenger seat was missing. "Just think of me as your flight engineer."

He watched the highway and keyed the mic. "Dolly?"

"Yes, dear."

"Do we have any contact with the base?"

"We're working on it right now, honey. We'll get you patched straight through."

"Thanks, sweetie."

"Just remember, this Wednesday night you're bringing Candy."

Hooker frowned at the jump in topics. Candy was also something not allowed in the dispatch. Dolly's home-cooked food was dangerous enough for the occupational hazard of massive weight gain. "Candy?"

"Cute, scrawny little blonde with no neck but bones?"

"Candy? My Candy?"

"Yes, dear. Your Candy."

Dolly put down the microphone and resumed petting the purring chest warmer. She had a self-satisfied smile on her face. She nuzzled into Box. "Yes, sir, Box. We're going to shake things up a bit... and it's about time."

Karen raised her arm. "Yes, sir, we will be routing you in a moment. Here is Dolly."

Dolly leaned around, and her fingers danced on the keys of her large phone. She hit the red button and spoke into the air. "This is Dolly. Who am I speaking to please?"

"This is Gunnery Sergeant Cokacheck, ma'am."

Dolly frowned at Karen and Dina. They both shrugged.

"Gunny, did your mother give you a real name?"

The man laughed. "Yes, ma'am. But it's worse than Cokacheck, ma'am. You can call me Gunny or just Dan. It's short for Arachapodanacheck."

"Oh, crap." She looked deadpan with a mix of zombie at the other women.

"Yes, ma'am. That's what my mama always said the nurse said."

Dolly chuckled silently and shook her head.

"Dan, what can you tell me is going on out there? Wait, first... where are you?"

"Ma'am, I am in what we are calling the Dugout. I am the heart and soul of ground zero. We are the control center under the home plate. Everything is now routed through me."

"Are you allowed to fill me in?"

"First, I need to walk you through a series of security questions."

"Go ahead."

"Who was the first black CHP officer in the South Bay?"

"Micha Robinson."

"Is he married?"

"Tall drink of water named Bobby Sue."

"Where is she from?"

"Somewhere around the Okeefenokee Swamp."

"Close. It was the Ochekala. Just for that, you get two more hard ones."

"Where in the heck is the Ochekala Swamp?"

"I ask the questions, ma'am. Next question. Who owns and runs San Jose?"

"I do." Her patience was running thin.

"Where is the only place to be for dinner on a Wednesday night?'

"If I don't have my clearance by now, it's a table you will never sit at."

"Yes, ma'am. You were clear when you got my sister right. My brother-in-law Micha speaks of you like you're a goddess."

Dolly smiled. "Dan, we're tying you in direct to Hooker's private radio. We will back feed you constant to his other radio, so you two can have as close to a full-time conversation. Hooker, are you there?"

"Go, Dolly."

"We're feeding Dan through your sideband but picking you up on the private. You now have Dan constant."

Hooker downshifted for the off-ramp. "Dan, I'm getting off at the lower gate. What's going on?"

"Hooker, we now have over a hundred and eighty bogies showing across the zone. There is a large loose and not so loose cluster out on the end of the old airstrip. We only have minimal eyes on the area, but based on what we see and the disbursement of the infrared signatures, it looks like a confrontation of two factors. This action just started about forty-eight minutes ago. There is no violent movement yet, but the sides are definitely being drawn."

Out on the airstrip, the factions were more heated than those in the Dugout could ever know.

The Mouse stood in the center of a swirling sea of bodies who all knew tonight there would be a massive change in the structure of their lives. She watched the tall man dressed in black. Unlike the other bodies circling in this caldron, he was wearing cowboy boots.

"You dare challenge my authority when you can't even greet the earth with the skin of your feet? What have you done, Raven, joined the Other World? And now you want to bring it here?" She could hear many members of the tribe hiss, breathing with open-mouthed disdain at the mention of the outside world.

Raven preened in his killing clothes. Tonight, his knife would once again taste the blood of a woman. He slowly moved in an arc in front of the glowing Mouse. "You have become weak, Mouse. You have accused me of consorting with the Other World, but it is you who has been doing so."

He called out without turning his head. "Turtle, did you watch her here just a few nights ago with the man who kills with silver?"

The voice oozed from out of the dark. "Yes. They were here, Raven."

"And what did she do, Turtle?"

"She kissed him."

Raven smiled—the smile of a prosecutor during the Inquisition. "She kissed him."

"He is my brother. I can't kiss my own brother?" She turned as she followed the Raven's slow strut. "Who are you to talk about right and wrong? You have been driving a car—a machine."

"Lies!" he hissed. "You tell lies to cover your heresy of consorting with an Other World man with silver in his killing stick."

She seethed. "Swallow. Where are you, Swallow? Tell us about riding in the car with Raven as he went about killing people."

The child walked into the circle of conflict and stood silently. Raven stepped behind her, petted her hair, reached down, and hugged her. "She has nothing to say to you. You are nothing to her. You are like dirt under her feet, and she will drink of your blood and suck the marrow from your bones."

"She won't speak because she is afraid of you. You rule her through fear, not because you care about her."

He continued to pet the child's hair and rub her chest. "I care about my Swallow very much."

"You only care that she will lie in the dirt while you jam your man stick in her ass. That is all you care about."

"At least she is of our tribe."

"Yes, *she* is of our tribe, but you are not. You are an interloper who preys on a child. Everyone else can see it. You can't even mate with a grown female. She is only now having her first blood. I can smell it on her."

"What does it matter?"

"It matters because she isn't even old enough to realize you're only using her." She looked at Swallow's face. "Tell the tribe what you two have been doing since you came back from the other place. Tell them about riding in the car. Tell them how Raven isn't really one of us but is just a killer looking to fill his own blood lust. Tell us, Swallow... tell us or be banished."

Raven could feel the tightening in the small chest, the stiffening of the spine. He couldn't allow her to speak.

His hands jumped to her head. One swift movement of his hands and her small head snapped almost completely around. The wet snap of her neck carried through the gathered tribe. He released the small body of the child, and it crumpled to the ground like a used rag.

"Where is your evidence now, Mouse?" He laughed. "Go ahead, ask her. You are the all-powerful witch. Make her speak."

The Mouse forced herself not to react to the sudden death. She stood and listened.

If the Tribe was fractured before, it was now splintered. She knew for many, killing was only something one did as a last resort to eat. To others, the body of the tribe was sanctity itself, and killing Swallow was unforgivable. And yet there were those she knew who were ready to follow Raven no matter what.

"You killed Swallow so she couldn't testify as to the killings. But I already know. You are a wanted man. Not a god, but a man. And you will, by your own actions, bring the Other World down upon us. They will root us out of our holes and hollows. They will take us and force things upon us no Tribe member should suffer."

She pointed her finger like a sword. "You have done this to us. You have killed and done damnable things to the Other World and now here." She spread out her hands at the heap of dirt, skin, and broken bone of what had been the little girl, Swallow.

The Mouse raised her voice as she shouldered the mantle of the high priestess for the Tribe. "We have all stood witness to the evil this man is capable of..." She could feel the Tribe moving in around the center of her and Raven. The storm above only mirrored the storm on the concrete. Her arms slowly rose as she drew in strength.

Her strength was coming, but from a few miles away. The yellow Goliath lumbered around the corner and lined up.

"Ok, I just turned onto the access. I'll be there in under three. Pay attention and be ready for whatever happens." He threw the mic back down toward Maddie.

Hooker swung onto the north end of the old airstrip. He was in sixth gear. He mashed the pedal to the floor, and the front end rose. He leapfrogged the gears up to sixteenth. Eleven tons of steel rolling at one hundred miles an hour is a scary sight in itself. He reached for the dashboard switches. "Crap!" he screamed. "Where are my lights?"

Willie's evil laugh came from the sleeper. "Oh, we have better than the black-out sneak. Maddie, kill it all. Then when I say, I want only the runners." They ran black for a few breaths. Hooker pushed the shifter into eighteenth and mashed the pedal past the hundred and twenty mark. The truck was now chewing up the miles of airstrip like it was about to take off.

Quietly, Willie watched familiar territory fly by. "Okay, give us the red and yellow solids on the undercarriage."

He silently counted to three. "Add in the blues and start the red pulsing in the wheel wells."

Hooker glanced over as he listened to Willie conduct a moving light show from hell. Willie shot him an evil smile. This was his payback for all the wrongs visited on him in his life. There was a lot of payback, and it would be more than just a bitch.

"I want the ring strobes of yellows." The giant tow truck was rapidly closing on the end of the runway, and it was looking like an avenging archangel. "Give me the top strobes and rotators."

Willie counted down, "Three... Two..."

Maddie giggled hysterically.

Willie laughed evilly from the sleeper. "Light us up, Maddie!"

They were a little over a half-mile from the end of the runway and closing fast when the entire truck exploded into a light show. The final touch was when Maddie threw the last set of switches and lit up the runway and everyone on it... all the way to and past the end. A hundred and eighty denizens of the night were full of fight a moment before were now suffering under the hot searing light of a midnight sun.

The charging incarnation was floating on a cloud of light. The thick night air was now dancing with wisps of multi-colored air. The halogen lights turned the phosphorus in The Mouse's skin into a white flame. She stood with raised arms slowly turning toward her strength and salvation, embracing the light. Unlike sunshine, this light did not burn her skin.

The other denizens scattered into the safety of the night.

In the light, Hooker could see a dark figure grabbed her and flung her to the side. The dark figure started to defy the oncoming Goliath from hell but then decided to fight another day. Spinning on his toe, he reached out and grabbed at The Mouse.

She slipped through his hand as another figure raced by and seemed to slash at the taller figure. As the dark figure turned to chase the other man who had just slashed at him, Hooker was close enough to see the cowboy boots.

Hooker timed the end of the line. Stomping hard on the brakes, he whipped the steering wheel hard left, and then back right followed by three pulling turns. His right hand slipped the gears into neutral on its way to slapping the large red button actuating the air brakes all the way around.

The resulting side-slipping truck howled in a deafening anguished scream as all the tires locked in the slide and were forced to the concrete by the weight of all eleven tons of Mae. The sound spurred the runners to run faster than they had ever run before. To compound the crazy, Maddie flicked the one switch she had held in reserve. Gimbaled halogen search-lights randomly swept the area in a crazed pattern.

Hooker's hand reached back along the back of the seat and pulled the short shotgun from its holster. The door swung open with the inertia from the stopping truck. Hooker slid down and away from the rocking truck. In the crazy lights, he saw the cowboy, now pulling The Mouse by the arm.

Hooker gave chase.

The still-healing wounds in his hip and thigh screamed at his attempt to run. He had no choice. Luckily, the tussle between the Cowboy and The Mouse was slowing them down. The two were running and jerking toward the gap. Hooker stayed back just enough to push them, but as close as he would need to be. He knew he didn't dare take a shot. The dimes in his shotgun were entirely unpredictable after the first twenty feet or so.

Hooker could hear his sister screaming something at the Cowboy, and he slapped her across the face.

As she spun from the slap, he turned to face her. Dog raced down from the dirt ridge and reached out and slashed at the Cowboy along the lower back.

Hooker wasn't sure what kind of knife or blade it was, but he saw it sliced open the entire back of the man's shirt, causing the Cowboy to jump forward in pain. He spun, expecting to have to give chase. Hooker saw the empty scabbard on the Cowboy's belt. He guessed Dog had stolen the deadly blade on the first pass.

Dog had slashed and stopped, and the Cowboy turned into the waiting blade. This time Dog sliced across the face. The Cowboy roared and chased after the mostly naked blond man.

The Mouse saw Hooker coming and regained her feet and flew like the wind ahead of him. Hooker gave chase.

As they neared the circle, time and sound collapsed. Hooker saw his sister hesitate. She watched where Dog was running and leading the Cowboy. Her hand reached out hesitantly as if to stop or at least guide Dog back to safety. She looked back at Hooker, pleading.

She knew enough about life and about death. She stepped on the end of the arrow. The red light was over the green light.

She ran.

Hooker stopped. He looked at where she was. He glanced once at where Dog was leading the killer. He jerked the shotgun up and down to cycle the first shell. He aimed at his sister. He then moved the end of the gun higher, and to the right. As the tiny red light came on, he squeezed the trigger.

The world in front of him exploded. He knew as the explosions raced forward Dog had led the Cowboy directly into the line of explosives. Dog had made a choice for himself, his pursuer, and for the life of the woman who was his everything.

As Hooker pumped the next shell into the chamber, he thought he might have heard a scream. He aimed high and toward the left. He pulled the trigger.

He pumped in the next shell and pulled the trigger.

He pumped in the next shell, aimed right again, and pulled the trigger.

He pumped in the last shell. He raised the gun and fired. It no longer mattered. He was spent.

He turned to run. The world turned into white-hot noise. The dark night became the center of the sun.

Something large had pushed him thirty feet before it bounced his body off the concrete. He landed twenty feet farther.

He never heard the sirens. He never saw the cars and fire trucks. He never heard or saw the helicopters. It was Maddie who finally found his body. It just looked like another one of the lumpy mounds of loose dirt.

She sat cross-legged in the dirt, cradling his head in her lap. The man in the bib overalls stood next to them, both holding to their own thoughts.

Willie blinked and looked around in the night. His sight lit on the buoy offshore a hundred yards or so away. He thought it was curious a buoy would have two colors of light on the same side. As he watched, the red light winked out. Only the green remained steady.

2 3

She sat at the head of the table. She wasn't sure why. Some of the ten men were tow truck drivers who had worked with Hooker for years. Ace had taught him how to tow, and Hooker had taught John, the small quiet man, how to tow.

One was a tall young police officer named James Aligo. His pro-football size belied his Filipino heritage. His smile and laughter were infectious more in a steak and eggs sort of way than in a sweets sort of way. His love of life was something you wanted to fill up on—it was good for you.

There were a couple of deputies who had come up through the ranks giving Hooker tows that weren't really his.

Micha was the first black officer for the highway patrol in the Bay Area. The only other woman at the table was his wife. She too had no idea why she was there. Next to her was her brother, a Marine sergeant named Dan. He was as much of a mystery to the rest of the men as were the women at the table. Even Dolly had never sat with them.

The Marine was crystal-clear about why he was there.

Rounding out the table were two shot-up characters. The older, with the white brush cut, was the Captain on the Highway Patrol. He was the man who had hired Micha with never a single regret.

Candy smiled down the table at the other shot-up man. Squirt was out of the hospital on loan. The IV pole still contained several meds, including painkiller. Her brother smiled up the table at her with a wonky expression. She knew if they had had any serious meat, she would have to go down there and cut it for him. She noticed Dolly had cut up his spaghetti as well as the Sicilian sausage from San Jose's oldest deli, Chiaramonte's.

The conversations were subdued. Dolly was her usual self, hovering as her left hand drifted from one shoulder to the next to running her fingers through a head of hair. Her right hand was always full with a pot of coffee. Most of these men would be back at work in a few minutes.

The two hours had flown by.

The end came with Karen calling from the switchboard. "Ace, I'm holding a tow in Willow Glen going to Fremont."

"John, your back up says he is hungry. He just had a tow, and the member sounded young and sweet."

"Chet, you have meds to take before your ten o'clock bedtime."

"James, shots fired at King and Story. Please wear your vest this time."

"Micha, Good Sam called. They want to know where their patent is. Bring him in here for his hug therapy as you leave."

"Candy, it was nice to meet you finally. You're family now, so hugs are mandatory."

"Ace, I'm starting your call in three minutes. Your peanut butt best be in the truck."

Candy put her hands around the purring cat on her lap. "Here, Dolly, let me help clear..."

Everyone stopped what they were doing. Dolly froze at the coffee maker. "Micha? Would you please be so kind as to educate Candy?"

The police officer turned to Candy. He eyed the orange cat and smiled. "The rules are: you never offer to help, you never clear your place, you never get your own coffee, and you sit and act like a guest, or you never come back."

The men, who knew the routine, nodded.

Candy leaned back. "Well, that's just silly. Times are changing, and I want to help."

Dolly turned slowly on her heel. Her suddenly fierce countenance pinned Candy into her seat.

Candy's chin sunk into her chest as she squeaked in a little girl voice, "Or not."

24

The Squirt sat sprawled in the back seat of the patrol car. The IV pole lay precariously over the front seat back, still dangling his bag of medicine. Candy had squeezed in around the pole.

"How are you doing back there, Squirt?"

The young man smiled and rolled his head. "I'm doing fine."

"Bet you are. I bet you are." Bobby Sue had slipped Micha a syringe of morphine and Demerol just in case he was feeling any pain before they got back. Micha just figured why bother with carting the syringe back to the hospital. His wife would just stick it in the Squirt anyway. So he injected the load before they got out the door.

Micha pulled up to the emergency ambulance doors. Two attendants came out. He directed them to take the Squirt back up to room 324.

He parked the cruiser, took off his tie, and opened the collar on his shirt. He checked the inside pocket of his jacket. He looked at Candy. "You ready?"

"I guess."

They were walking down the hall. The elevators were ahead. "What is it we are really doing?"

The officer bit on his lower lip. He stopped and then took her arm and guided her into the small chapel. The place was as empty as it always was. He sat her down.

"It's hard to explain. Now looking back, it was just the start of another day in what we do. Not that someone dies every day—it's just not uncommon. You never get used to it, but you learn how to take it in stride and move on.

"Back when we were young, and I suspected Hooker was younger than we all thought, there was a really big accident. It was the first rain of the season. It was under the big overpasses going to nowhere, the altars to government waste and stupidity.

"The summer oils and such had built up, and then the little rain had turned it into slippery snot. There was maybe a dozen or so cars. It was a total cluster ..."

Candy nodded and smiled. "Micha, I'm a waitress. I've heard the term clusterfuck before."

If the man could have blushed, he would have. His shoulders relaxed to know he didn't need to dance prissy around things with Hooker's girl.

"Well, it was about an hour clearing things. The rotation had everyone getting a tow but Hooker. Even though he was first to get there, he was screwed by the rotation. But he was Hooker. He just didn't seem to care. He showed up and jerked a few cars around for us, and then broke out his broom. He would sweep until his trashcan was full, and then dump it in one of the other truck's cans. And then back at the cleaning. By the time we were half done, he was soaked. I think he was wearing a jean jacket back then.

"Anyway, we finally got all of the cars towed off. I think Mike told him he was going to dump a bone in one of the parking lots so Hooker could have it."

Micha noticed the frown of confusion on Candy's face. "I'm sorry. So many years, I just think everyone knows the shorthand we all use. A bone is a bonus car. One you got—just because.

"Mike didn't need the tow as much as he knew Hooker could use it. So, he threw him the bone. But as it was, Hooker got two.

"There was a sweet red restored 50's truck parked off on one side. The way it was stopped, you knew it was an accident, but it didn't fit in with the rest of the cars. All the wreck had been in the center dividing dirt. This one was on not only the shoulder, but it looked like the person was trying to drive up the hill to the top of the ramp. It just had a crazy doesn't fit kind of look about it. So after everything had been cleared, Hooker was the last tow truck out there. He waved to me he was going to check it.

"I was right behind him when he got to the door. There was a young blonde girl in the cab. Even in the pouring rain, you could tell at first glance she was a daddy's girl—one of those pretty young blondes who was a cheerleader and the prom queen of her school. Her daddy probably bought her the truck to drive to school in hopes it would scare off most of the riffraff. It was probably the sweetest thing in the school parking lot.

"When Hooker got up to the door, she turned her head and looked at him. I remember him asking her if she was all right. As he opened the door, she just folded out into his arms as she said, *'Don't let me die.'*"

Candy gasped. "She was dead."

The officer tightened his lips and nodded. "We just stood there and cried. There was nothing we could have done. Everything had been internal."

Candy held her hands to her mouth. She had never thought about what kinds of things Hooker had seen in his life and job. He just towed cars. But now she knew.

Micha could see the revelation in her face. "A few months later, I ran into Hooker at the Bold Knight. For some reason, I bought him a drink. I think I even knew he wasn't old enough at the time. It didn't matter. We were sitting there with two shots of whiskey and Hooker asked what we should drink to."

Candy finished the now understood refrain and nodded.

The room was dark, except for the monitor and the nurse's light. The tall nurse turned around at the sound of the door and automatically started her litany. "Visiting hours are over..."

Then she recognized the visitors. "But if I'm bribed with a kiss from one of California's finest, I might be persuaded to look the other way."

Micha gave her a hug and a kiss. "Candy, this is what my wife looks like at work." They laughed.

"How did you beat us over here?" She looked at Micha.

His wife then asked the obvious. "Let me guess, you gave the drunk the shot, and then tried to get him in the car?" She laughed at the stupid look on her husband's face.

Candy laughed. "It was entertaining."

The tall woman grabbed the ends of her long braids as she laughed. "Oh, I bet it was." She slapped him on the shoulder and muttered, "Dumb ass."

She turned back to her patient. "Let me get the last vitals, and then you can get him drunk." She looked back over her shoulder at her husband and then at Candy.

He nodded. "She knows."

Candy nodded.

"Is he awake?"

The white blob of gauze moved. "I'm awake."

Candy went to the side of the bed. "I'd kiss you, but I don't know where your mouth is."

Another wad of gauze came up and bumped against the lower dark slit.

"Boy, and I thought they wrapped the Squirt up. I don't know if I'm dating the Southside Hooker or the Mummy."

Bobby Sue finished and kissed Micha again. "I'll leave you two. Candy, how about I buy you a cup of coffee?"

Candy thought a moment and then looked at Micha. She knew he would not ask, but he and Hooker needed a personal moment. She turned and took Bobby Sue's arm. "Did I ever tell you how much I love coffee?"

The room was dark, except for the monitor and the nurse's light.

The two men were silent as the one opened the two little bottles. "Here." He held out the bottle where Hooker could feel it was between the two balls of gauze. Micha tapped his bottle against Hooker's.

"Here's to prom queens, may they always be pretty, and daddy's little girl."

2 5

F all in the San Francisco Bay Area can be cold, wet, and miserable. Or it can be the most pleasant place on earth.

Hooker dropped off Mae to get her oil checked and to allow Maddie and Willie to put in the new headliner with controls for all the lights and a hidden siren. Candy had dropped off the Granny car for Willie and Maddie to relive a memory by going for fish and chips at the new Monterey Cannery Fish House up on Monterey Highway.

As the sun peeked over the hills and warmed the Bay Area, the old DeSoto cruised at a leisurely fifty, befitting the style and grace of the two tons of classic ride. Hooker's left arm was on the windowsill, as he drove with his two fingers and thumb. His right arm was draped along the back of the bench seat, with his right arm around Candy's shoulder.

Stella had lent her new daughter a silk scarf Manny had brought back from Japan. The sky blue matched the canopy above and went perfectly with the ponytail. Hooker had even remembered to buy a pair of dark glasses at the Thrifty's while they were getting two triple-scoops of French vanilla in sugar cones.

The cones had almost made it to the city limits.

The new custom leather jacket he had received the previous week fit him perfectly. Danny had a tear in his eye, and Hooker had noticed it. Danny had just told him, "Shut up, fool." Everyone had laughed. But the real surprise had been when Dolly had brought out two other boxes, one for Candy, and one for the Squirt. There were few dry eyes among the eighty close friends on the party deck for Hooker's birthday.

Hooker ran his fingers over Candy's leather jacket. She put her hand up and covered his. She leaned harder into his chest and arm. He could feel her other hand lightly on his jeans. The two smiled in the sun as the deep rumble of the big V8 barely changed pace as it climbed the hill behind Stanford University.

"So, do you like your girl in a leather jacket?"

"I like my girl. It doesn't matter if she is in a leather jacket, waitress uniform, or nurse's scrubs."

She smiled coyly and looked out over the bay as it came into view. "What about in none of those?"

Hooker smiled and couldn't resist baiting the trap and teasing the tiger. "It would depend. What color of underwear?"

Candy chuckled. She had known him long enough to like his off-kilter sense of humor. She also realized he was comfortable enough in their relationship to approach joking about intimate things, something both of them were still a little gun-shy on.

"Well, I might have to consult with Willie... but I suppose they would have to be color-coordinated."

Hooker hummed and nodded. "Black leather boxers... Are you planning to borrow his...?"

She reached over and found his ticklish spot.

They rode in silence for a few miles, each lost in their own unique thoughts.

Candy shifted and snuggled down deeper into his chest. "You still haven't told me where you are secreting me away to for three days."

He considered. "It wouldn't be much of a secret if I told you when you had only asked for the ninth time, now would it?"

She settled in and feigned pouting. She had never been treated to a real surprise before. She watched the airplane taking off from the San Francisco airport. She thought that one day, they too would fly somewhere.

She didn't know where, but it sounded romantic just to fly off somewhere. Maybe somewhere exotic, like Los Angeles or New York.

The city slid by with noise and buildings as they got tall and then not. Candy sat up to watch the park drift by on both sides. The thought of the Golden Gate Park being a long and slender park pierced by major streets still seemed strange to her. She hoped one day she and Hooker could come see the zoo and other things.

She realized that doing things was something neither one of them did —they had always been working.

The Golden Gate Bridge had captured both of their imaginations. Hooker had stopped on the Marin County side, and they walked a way back onto the bridge. Alcatraz Island was a strange mix of serene living space, and a creepy prison.

They stopped in a small town for some lunch and were back on the road. The road was now only two lanes, and Candy fantasized about it being the fifties and the car was new. The large car pushed a lot of air, and they could hear the masses of fallen leaves cheering as they blew through them.

The small sign said simply, The Apple Farm. The large chrome grill slowed and nosed into the narrow driveway. The orchard on the left was large and deep. The trees were almost bare, with only spots of colored leaves hanging tenaciously from the limbs. As they rounded the curve of the driveway, the small hillside on the right gave way to the large expanse of lawn.

The three-story farmhouse rose white on the hillside. The wraparound porch was deep and filled with rockers and gliders, as well as a few tables and chairs. The clapboard siding shone in the late afternoon sun, and the windows were dark with mystery.

As they glided into the parking area next to a couple of other cars, Hooker reached up and waved to the woman hanging sheets on the long clothesline. The woman waved and started toward them. The soft halo of white hair piled high on her head, along with the long dress, gave the impression it was a different time, and the house was new. She turned her head and yelled something toward the large red barn, but they couldn't hear what she said.

"Hooker, so good to see you." The woman fell into his arms. He winced at the hug. She released and stepped back. "This episode or the dimes?"

"The dimes." He turned to open Candy's door only to find her already standing there. He turned as he slid his arm over her shoulder. "Candy, this is Aunt Claire. She is Stella's best friend since..." He frowned, fishing for an answer, "third grade?"

She pushed him aside. "Nice try. We were born in the same room one hour apart." She gently guided Candy away from the leather Lothario. "Stelly and I swore pinkie best friends for life in the nursery." She hugged Candy as she mumbled into her hair, "Welcome to the Apple Farm, Candy. Stella has told me so much of nothing about you. So it must be all true, and you can fill me in on mister silver-in-the-butt here."

She turned back toward the barn. With lungs only rural farm living creates, she called out, "Norman! Bags!" She watched as the man walked out of the gloom of the barn. She turned back to look at Hooker. "He's got himself a new Johnny Popper, and it's giving him the dickens to get running."

Hooker smiled. "I'll look at it while we're here."

As the man walked up, Hooker held out his hand. "Good to see you again, Norm."

"Likewise, Hooker. This is a very pleasant surprise." He walked toward the trunk as the women wandered arm and arm up toward the house. "Let me get those bags for you."

Hooker unlocked the trunk as the man admired the car. "Willie sure does take good care of her."

"Norm, if I didn't know any better, I would think this car was his greatest love. But then, you haven't met his Hank yet. You'll see what I mean at Christmas. You are coming down this year, aren't you?" The man nodded as he reached in for the two small bags.

"Good for him?" The man paused to look for an answer, still the clinical psychiatrist and doctor.

"Very. I don't think I have heard of any night terrors since they became serious."

"Good." He took up the bags again, refusing Hooker's hand. "Love has a curative nature for the disturbed soul."

As they walked, Hooker broke the silence. "How is she?"

The man thought a few strides. "She still has more rough days than good, but I think she also sees the light at the end of the tunnel." He stopped and looked at Hooker, studying his face. "I hope you don't think she will ever be normal—by any stretch of the imagination. The normal girl you remember, just isn't in there."

He turned and looked out toward some trees on the far lawn. "I don't think she will have to be institutionalized, but she will never be a productive member of society." He turned back toward Hooker. "She will always be frail."

"But she isn't dying."

"I can't say. She won't live a long life, but I don't think she is acutely terminal, no."

They stood looking at each other, taking measure. Finally, the older doctor flicked his head back toward the far lawn. "I think you two might want to talk a bit before she meets Candy." He raised the bags. "I've got these. Go see your sister."

Hooker reached out and grasped the man's shoulder in his hand. He bit his lip, thankful for the dark glasses. The man just nodded and turned for the house.

Hooker walked through the grass. His walk was slow and casual.

She wore a powder blue dressing gown. Her head and shoulders were covered by a straw hat with a wide brim. She lounged in the whitewashed Adirondack chair. When Hooker was still thirty feet away, she lay down her book. She looked out across the valley. Her voice was soft as a kitten's breath. "My knight returns well met."

As he came close, she raised her left hand. The white gloves covered to and over her sleeves. He took it and squeezed with the weight of a moth. Hooker bent over and kissed the fingers softly and staying for a few seconds. He could feel her collapse in on herself.

"You were hurt."

"Yes."

"They told me night."

"They shouldn't have."

"I already knew."

Hooker sat on the other chair and leaned back, letting the wood support him. He was so tired. He knew where the conversation would go next.

"Dog took Raven to hell with him."

"That was his name?"

"It was, but he had another name. The name your people are looking for. Try the name Samson Stubbs. I think he had a Bakersfield connection."

"How did you find...?"

She rolled her head and looked at him. Suddenly, her head flopped over, and her tongue lolled out. The image flashed him back to the foster home in Riverside. They had woken up in the middle of the night and turned on the television with the sound almost off. Vincent Price was the last man on earth where everyone had become a zombie.

He chuckled, and then he started laughing. The tension was too much to stop. They were both giggling with bursts of belly laughter as they made faces at each other they hadn't for almost fifteen-years. Hooker laughed, knowing now where the stupid zombie response had started.

As the sun neared the hills, they became quiet. Hooker had moved his chair closer, and they sat holding hands, watching the sun slide beyond the horizon.

"I think he loved me."

Hooker thought about the chiseled marble mud man. "He gave his life for you."

"He saw how to kill evil, and even though he knew it would cost him his life, he still felt it was worth the trade."

"No. He gave you his highest gift—his heart. Taking out the other man, Raven was just what he had to do, but he still gave his life for you."

She looked at her brother. "I can't live with that. I wasn't worth more than him."

"You don't have a choice other than to hold his gift in your heart. The choice was his. All you have to do is accept you're worth his depth of love."

"Would you do it for me? Lay down your life like that?"

Hooker thought.

"Would you do it for Candy?"

Hooker turned and frowned. "You even know her name?" He let his head fall back. "Of course, you know her name. You know Peter."

"Peter and I were... mated... for a while."

"Then...?"

"Peter is a very caring and gentle man. When I became The Mouse, I knew the Tribe would never tolerate such a fragile person. So I had to drive him off."

He listened to his sister's voice. The old connections were there still. "But you still have a fondness for him."

The forward edge of the hat dipped in the gathering dusk.

"You didn't answer me about laying down your life for Candy or me."

He looked at her. "I hope the day never comes where I have to find out. However, I would like to think I am capable of that depth of love."

His sister was quiet. He thought she might have drifted off to sleep.

Dusk was complete, and the dark drifted down on them. Hooker watched. Under the dress, and from beneath the hat, there came a faint glow.

"We should go up. They would be holding dinner for us."

She took his arm as they walked. She rubbed her hand along the leather. She leaned over and put her nose close and breathed deep. The smell of new leather was like no other.

Hooker held the door. As she stepped in the door, she removed her large hat. Her hair was gone. The treatments had started, and she had no hair or even eyebrows.

Candy stood up from the stool and placed her glass of wine on the large island. She walked over with her hands out. Her face was open. Hooker saw it was the same face she always had with Jerry, Father Damian, or even him. It was total acceptance.

He swallowed. "Candy, this is my sister..."

She stepped forward and took Candy's hands. "I've known your name for years. You have looked after so many of my... friends. Please... Call me Sissy."

UNBIDDEN GARDEN

A SOUTHSIDE HOOKER NOVEL — BOOK 3

1

THE DRIVER SWORE in the rain. Everything had gone wrong. The heist, the car, the road, and that didn't include the weather soaking the driver's clothes wet and cold.

The driver tugged on the leg, drawing the body out through the shattered window, and then taking up the second leg like a small burro with a cart. The largest of the bodies, thankfully, was tall but thin. The body bounced and tumbled along the streambed rubble. Only a slight relief came from the swelling of the small December stream. It would become larger with the winter rains. The body floated for a moment and then caught on the rocks of the other side. The driver kept dragging.

The light mist had turned the dirt road to a snotty slide now wept the blood of the driver into larger patches about the clothes the driver wore. The blood from the other man's head curled and danced down the stream, washing away into the late night, screeds of something becoming, and then disappearing.

The driver breathed hard, dragging the body up the small incline to the shallow flood-washed cliff-side cave. Pulling the taller man by the clothes and body parts, the driver fed the warm corpse into the natural tomb. The driver stopped for a moment and looked at the expensive diving watch on the body's wrist.

Quietly, the left hand smoothed over the short hair from the body's forehead. The driver sat thinking of the last few years. Better times.

In the distance, a flash of lightning cracked, and the boom of thunder rolled across the South Bay Area and up into the low coastal mountain range. It wasn't supposed to be like this.

The driver twisted and continued pushing the body into the cramped, shallow cave next to the other smaller body. Finally, the feet were needed to push and roll the larger body up and on top of the smaller to make room for what was still to come. The driver reached in and closed the now opened eye, hand hovering for a moment, and then withdrawing.

Slogging back down the damp incline, the driver once more crossed the small stream, and with dispatch, noted the volume had increased. The hills above would have been getting rain for more hours before. It was now flowing downhill.

The driver kicked at the back door of the car. With a long slender limb, the driver pried the complaining door partially open. Wedging their body into the gap, the driver began to work on widening the access. The screaming of the steel was loud. The driver wasn't worried. The nearest house was probably well over two miles away. And even if it were next door, the sound of the rain and storm would have just made it another noise during a dream in the night.

"Shit."

The last body was pounded into a ball and pummeled down into the leg area between the driver's seat and the back seat. With the car mostly upside down, it was obvious a great force had placed him there. Only the left arm hung free into the space of the car.

After stumbling among the large rocks and flood bed wastage and stubble, the driver clawed around the back of the car, pulling through to the front window. The car had spun-out above, rolled, and then flipped, causing the driver to be ejected on the second roll before the next flip had taken the car over the hundred-foot slope to the stream bed below. The driver marveled at the durability of the car. As 1937 was a great year for Chevrolet, it had also been a terrible year for Chevrolet. The cars were almost indestructible. Now, nearly seventeen years later, they were still running.

The last pitched flip had thrown the car into the ravine eighty feet below and forty feet across the stream bed for one last roll.

The driver stooped and slid upside down through the driver's window. Arching and stretching while feeling for the seat release, it was obvious nothing seemed right upside down. The mutilation on the arm didn't help.

The large black Bakelite knob felt right. The driver tugged without a result. The lever didn't move.

"Shit."

The driver hung from the knob, thinking how the car had rolled over and righted, right hand becoming the left before orientation finally became solid.

The driver's hand jerked, and then jerked harder. The lever moved. A click and the seat jumped forward an inch.

The large body thumped sickly down onto the ceiling.

The driver hung for a moment from the knob. A slight, wan smile crossed the pale, freckled face; the right, lower lip, and the left upper sucked into the teeth at the same time. The driver was still thinking.

Scooting with back down face up, the driver started moving the last body toward the other side. Pushing feet against the window post and moving the body using upper body strength—shoulders, hips, legs, shoulders—each part pushed one at a time.

Exhaustion was taking a toll.

The eyes of the driver flashed open at the sound of a rock as it rolled down the hill and splashed into the deepening water. The cold was setting in, and it hadn't helped drifting off on a nap. The driver wearily eyed the small stream. It was rapidly becoming a much larger stream now moving rapidly.

The driver rolled over, realizing sleep had come with the driver's head in the face of the last body—the face of the one person who in life had been the most repulsive.

"Shit."

Moving with renewed vigor, the driver pushed the body around until the legs were sticking out of the window. The body was now aligned to cross the now larger body of water. "You better float, you big tub of lard."

Thinking, the driver realized the body's coat was insulated and still dry. The driver stripped the body of the warm, dry shirt and jacket.

Crawling out the other window, taking up the two feet, pulling and drawing the body out and onto the water—now waist-deep, the driver was relieved as the body floated.

"Now, if you could just float up the fucking hill, you asshole."

The swearing somehow lent a certain amount of indignant strength. The body fit almost perfectly in the hole, leaving a space for the last objects.

Crawling back into the car, the driver flipped the two custom latches. The back seat swung down, and the four large bags fell from their hiding space. "Shit." The driver, picking up one of the bags and realized it would take three trips. Opening one of the bags, they looked in, and then drawing one of the objects out—the driver whistled low.

As the sun began to glow through the clouds, a lone figure plodded along the road. The driver's fingers were torn up from digging the dirt to fill in the gravesite. This caused the driver to reminisce of times making fun of all the 4-H kids in school and how dirty their hands were—which was almost as horrid as how bad they always smelled—like wet animals. The farm kids were not much better.

No, sir, the driver had never wanted any part of raising animals or growing things and had damn sure never intended to plant a garden—especially not one as unbidden as the one just planted.

The driver washed off in the now hard-moving cold river. Not even hot water and soap would be able to remove the stain of the night's planting.

The driver turned up the collar of the oversized wool P-coat. It was a very long walk to Salinas down the low coastal mountain range. With any luck, walking the road known as *The Snake* would only take a couple of days.

2

THE SEMI-COLD AUTUMN rain captured in the dark curls irritated the large scars underneath. The drizzles continued down under the leather collar to the starched white T-shirt underneath. Hooker jerked harder on the towing cable jammed under the Cadillac. Hooker and the car were in a few inches of water where the car slid its way off the dirt road and down an embankment into the creek eighty-feet below.

In disgust, Hooker yelled up the cliff to the Squirt above. "Send me down the second cable." He looked down at how the Cadillac lay on its top. "Hey, Squirt?"

His head and shoulders appeared over the top of the cliff holding the other J-hook and cable from the second boom on the tow truck. "Yeah, boss?"

Hooker smiled. He really liked how this kid was getting smart and sassy. "Clip a girdle line and two ring cinches onto the cable. I'll have to drag this bitch up on her back and flip her up there."

"10-4, Bawana. Coming right down."

Hooker shook his head. The two months in the hospital had the kid watching every single old Tarzan movie they ever made. Hooker remembered whatever the kid sees or reads, he remembers forever.

Reeling out the cable, he hooked two iron J-hooks to parts of the undercarriage he could reach. Running the ring cinches through the eyes of the hooks, he attached the girdle line. Drawing it to the end of the main cable, he attached the girdle chains to the hook on the end of the cable.

"Okay, Squirt. Slowly roll the secondary."

"Taking up slack." The cable tightened and began to pull.

Hooker could sense the tension of a snag. The grinding sound through the cable stopped. Hooker smiled. The kid was starting to sense things through his fingers on the controls and by listening to the sounds of the cable or car.

Hooker knelt down and peered through the gloom at the crap helping to bind the draw hook to the undercarriage. Fishing his hand in the cold mud and gunk, he withdrew a large bone. Examining the muddy artifact haphazardly, he sized it up as he pitched it back across the river wash toward an old rusted heap. It hadn't had the benefit of being towed. Hooker mumbled, "Somebody doesn't have a leg to stand on." Fishing around some more, he unhooked the cable and hook while watching the approaching dark uniformed figure in rain gear. As he started to rise, he noticed a quick shine in the mud. Reaching down, he picked up an oval of some kind of heavy metal. He wiped most of the mud off and stuck the oval in the front pocket of his overalls.

Hooker looked up the hill to the head and shoulders looking down. "She should come now, Squirt."

The car scraped at the mud wall but moved just fine. Hooker turned to face the officer. The officer looked at the underside of the upside-down car. "What do you think?"

Hooker wiped his hands on the large shop towel from the back pocket of his overalls. "Well, Micha, I've gotta be honest with ya. I'm pretty sure the Fly can pull the engine and transmission back out of the front seat and fix the firewall, but the upholstery is shot." Hooker's right eyebrow was cocked at an up and back angle, something the long, new scar in his scalp was doing.

"No, I meant..." The California Highway Patrol Officer and friend for over ten years stopped and gave the smirking Hooker a hard glare. "I meant, how much longer until I can clear the road?"

Feigning innocence, "Oh, give me about forty or so minutes to drag this prom queen up to the road, and maybe another ten to flip her onto a dolly, five to hook her to Mae, and she's all yours." Hooker walked back to the working deck controls and started letting the car down onto the sling. "Actually, I don't have to dolly this one. The lady left her driveline down in the creek." Seeing the raised eyebrow of the officer, he reassured him of cleaning up the wreck. "Don't worry. I threw it in the back seat with a few other pieces of metal and bones."

They climbed up out of the ravine, and both were filthy.

Re-rigging the sling for towing, Hooker set the J-hooks around the axles and cinched the chains onto the small hooks of the sling. Raising the end of the heavy car, Hooker checked around the Cadillac and tested the sling. Shutting the control compartment door and scanning the working deck, he wiped his hands one last time on the rag and pitched it into the can for dirty laundry to be done as needed. Turning back to the officer standing several yards away, he jammed his lower lip over his teeth and whistled, wheeling his right hand and index finger in a circle. "Clear, Micha."

"Thanks, Hooker. We'll see you tomorrow for dinner at Dolly's place."

Hooker waved as he shucked out of his jumpsuit overalls. Nodding to the kid, he turned and climbed up into the high yellow cab of his restored 1959 Marmon truck. The low rumble of the idling engine charged the heater blowing all winter long across the floor and the cardboard box. The box was filled with twenty pounds of yellow and scarred tabby with only one ear and one eye. Drawing in his left leg, Hooker closed the door painted with the truck's namesake: Mae West, in all her World War II pin-up glory. A small banner ram down along her body emblazoned with the slogan 'It's what's up front that counts.' This was a reference to the largest production conventional truck ever built. Its recently customized front nose contained a sixteen-hundred-horse-powered engine. Mae West was the fastest tow truck in the five Bay Area counties. Even the little two-ton Fords with their new, hot 440 engines couldn't hold a candle.

Hooker looked over at the Squirt, who was smiling with a silly smirk. Hooker nodded his head up. "What?"

Squirt laughed. "We're on the Snake." He nodded at the back end of

Micha's retreating patrol car. "Even Micha knows we have to pass Thrifty's on the way to dump the prom queen, and he doesn't even eat ice cream—much less French vanilla."

At the sound of his favorite treat, Box stood up in his box. His one ear stuck up into the draped hand and fingers. The fingers began to pull and rub at the last vestige of his ear. The purr was instant and non-stoppable.

Hooker rolled his eyes. "Ganging up on me. Jeez, mareez in the deep freeze."

Forty minutes later, with both windows rolled down, the giant truck rolled past the time and temperature sign on the bank reading twenty-eight degrees. In the night air, leather elbows stuck out of each window, triple-scoop French vanilla ice cream cones in each hand. The sounds of Tex Ritter drifted sorrowfully into the night air.

3

"Just because it's only six-ten in the morning, don't you two even *think* about sneaking in without a kiss or hello." The disembodied voice of the consummate mother hen floated from the large sunroom around the corner.

Hooker raised his right eye at his companion as the Squirt slowly closed the giant hand-hewn walnut front door to Hacienda Romero. Hooker nodded his head forward for Squirt to follow.

"Lucy, we're home." Hooker imitated Ricky Ricardo on the *I Love Lucy* show, which none of them had ever seen because it would require a television.

Stella looked over her cheater glasses and the top of the newspaper. Her mouth pursed as she examined the two men standing safely still on the slate of the dining area and inches away from her cream carpet. She slowly lowered the newspaper. "Squirt, kindly take Hooker out into the front yard and hose him down. There is mud all over his boots and lower pant legs." She raised the newspaper.

As they turned to head for their bedrooms, Hooker leveled his right eye at the younger man. "You so much as point a hose at me, and I will make sure it takes a very good proctologist to find the back end of said hose." The two smiled as they separated for some much-needed sleep.

Five tows and the long hard recovery job had taken its toll on the two still recovering men. They each had two dimes floating around in them, which were delivered by a shotgun at the hands of a killer.

Box, unaffected by the work, but always ready for some rest, searched out his patch on the queen-sized bed and settled in. Hooker was only moments behind as his pants slid down around the uppers of his boots, fireman style. His head almost bounced once on the pillow before the phone in the main room rang.

Anytime the phone rang before nine or ten in the morning was never a good sign. Hooker's mind half waited and then was gone. Moments later, Stella stood outside the cracked door. The soft snoring told her the piece of paper in her hand could wait. She padded back to her morning domain of sunshine, laying the note on the large granite island as she passed.

Three in the afternoon would be soon enough for the man on the phone. It was just about some wrecked car Hooker had towed during the night. She was sure it wasn't anything important. After all, the kid needed his sleep.

HEAVY FIESTA WARE crockery makes a very distinct, dull bell sound when placed onto thick granite. When the thick plates finally land on a thick, hand-hewn black walnut table, the sound changes to the wet thud of two fat skaters colliding on ice. In Hooker's dream, it was slow cars sliding on black ice in the fog. The thought or vision of so many cars to be towed forced Hooker to spring into action mentally. The first requirement was to wake up and smell the coffee, which meant the golden payday wreck evaporated.

Hooker groaned as his legs begrudgingly swung over the edge of the bed. His right hand smoothed along his upper thigh and the deep trough of a long surgical scar—made to find and remove three dimes. The doctor counted the surgery as seventy-five percent successful. Rising, he padded his way toward the bathroom and a quick shower. As he sat on the toilet, he could hear Squirt already in the shower in the next bedroom suite over.

Box stuck his head in the bathroom and came over to rub along Hooker's leg. The hand found the cat's one ear and rubbed it for a good morning. Hooker reached his left hand over and around the cat's head. The fingertips found the chin and gave a firm rub. "Go tell Stella I'm up and will be in for breakfast in ten minutes."

Hooker wasn't positive whether the cat truly understood him or not, but as the cat left, Hooker did know he would go check in with Manny, who would then tell Stella 'in about ten minutes.' Of course, routine had nothing to do with it.

Hooker was still blurry-eyed as he opened his bedroom door to find the other blurry-eyed zombie dressed identically in the uniform of the day—an obligatory starched white t-shirt over jeans. The other zombie mumbled something as they lined up to shuffle into the dining area.

Manny looked up and smiled. Stella turned at the stove and opened both arms wide. The two young men socketed in for their morning hug and rebounded toward the mugs of coffee standing by the percolator. Stella smiled at her two zombies. "Go sit, and I'll bring your breakfast."

With each bite or sip, the walking dead became human.

Stella slid the note into the purview of the half-alive Hooker. She was greeted with a bloodshot eyeball over the rim of the mug.

"He wanted to know if there were any other body parts he should know about." She nodded her head forward and gave Hooker the same deadeye of a zombie. Only Hooker knew where or when it had started, much less why, but the zombie look had become a family joke for dumb questions begging for dumb answers. It had all come down to shorthand for how one felt the morning after, or don't ask because Manny has been on the phone all day. Even Manny occasionally rolled his head back with a gaped mouth to comment on something as innocent as being asked what he wanted for Sunday dinner—the answer always being pot roast.

Hooker looked at the note. Allen was the 'back door' man at the Fly's auto body shop. Every wreck towed in went through Allen's hands, fell under his eye and was sorted with the same discernment he had shown as a corpsman in Vietnam—before an exploding shell had taken his right leg, leaving bits and pieces of metal in the man's body. His favorite joke about the metal floating around in his body was he had more in common with the cars than any other swinging dick in the joint. He never mentioned the large steel plate covering most of the right side of his head. The ridges were very distinct on his abnormally bald head. In fact, he had no hair left on his body anywhere. For that, his nickname was 'Dog' as in hairless Chihuahua.

Hooker laid the note down and picked up his fork in his right hand. The Squirt absentmindedly withdrew his left hand out of striking distance. The four snickered. The four tiny dot scars were still evident on the back of his hand from the night he had met Hooker. Hooker's fork had been buried in Squirt's entire hand except for the last few layers of skin on the palm. Hooker didn't know then the street tough who was trying to steal a dollar from the tip on the counter was the waitress's little brother. Candy, the waitress and the girl Hooker wanted to date, sorted everything out. Hooker and Squirt's friendship had seen rapid growth over the next week to the point where the Squirt had taken twenty-four dimes in his body and legs as he saved Hooker's life.

Manny, ever the consummate detective, nodded at the cryptic note. "Really... a skeleton hand found in the car, and you're not just a little bit curious?" The man leaned back in his custom wheelchair. Hooker continued to ignore him and kept eating.

Manny looked over at the silent Squirt, who seemed very busy examining his scrambled eggs and pancakes. He was working very hard to try to ignore Manny, as well. "Is there something wrong with your eggs, Squirt? Because, if there is, you need to speak up so either I can fire the chef or have her give you a lap dance."

The young man turned a very dark shade of red and almost choked as he focused harder on his food. Stella put her fork down and gave Manny a hard look. Picking up her coffee mug, she stood and strode to the counter to fetch the coffee percolator. Pouring some in her own mug, she stood staring out the window at the large barbecue deck, thinking.

She turned with the unplugged coffee percolator and walked over to stand next to Hooker. She stood looking down at the top of his head of wavy dark hair, parted with two large scars running the side of his head. This was where twin dimes had seared their way along his skull, slicing open the covering of both skin and hair, as they had passed at nine-hundred feet per second. "Hooker, you have two choices here. You can talk to your father, and drink this coffee, or you can start wearing all one hundred and eighty degrees."

Hooker's head snapped up and looked at Manny. "There was a leg bone at the wreck site, also. I thought about going back out today sometime and poking around with the Squirt to see what else might be there." He hadn't wanted to tell Manny and Stella because he knew the retired detective's badge was—in the words of his wife—still attached. Hooker was also hyper-aware that the last two mysteries had taken their toll on the whole family. The hot brown liquid of life at Hacienda Romero flowed unimpeded into the large mug.

There was no way in hell Manny was going to even smirk, much less smile, and lose this contest. With every bit of his decades of control in the face of adversity, or playing the deadpan face-off game, Manny asked the next question. "Right or left?"

Coffee and bits of pancake shot from the Squirt's nose. He looked up to see by the faces of the other three he had just lost the round. With the loser established, the others laughed as Stella stepped over to the large granite island and got the poor loser a towel.

Hooker wasn't about to let Manny get the upper hand, though. "It was dark, but I think it was the right tibia. I remember thinking any other remains would be all that was left."

A tiny bit of coffee missed the Squirt's rapid swallow. He mopped at it with the towel. He was still trying to choke down the last chunk of pancake.

Stella patted him hard on the back as she poured him some more coffee and glared at the two puny guys at the other end of the table. "Keep the towel. I don't think the juvenile delinquents are finished yet." She placed the carafe on the island and retook her seat.

Manny's detective gene had kicked in, and he was now ignoring the side chatter. "How old did the bone look?"

Hooker yawned and blinked his eyes. He may have made it through the shower, but Manny could see he was still having trouble getting his right hand to work proficiently enough to get his usual clean, crisp shave around the tight thin beard framing his jaw. Manny knew Stella would quietly corner him later and clean up the wandering stubble.

Hooker grabbed his mug and sipped with one eye looking hard over the rim. He slowly lowered it. "I'm not a pathologist or an archeologist, nor do I play one on television, but the bone was light-colored in the dark and rain. If I had to guess, I would say it was very probably from this era—certainly not from the Paleolithic age." His mug returned to his face. Manny knew there was a self-satisfied grin behind the stoneware.

He thought through the whole idea of a random human bone showing up at the wreck. Then what would be the odds for two bones from different limbs? The odds were beyond Manny's advanced math, even though he loved to deal with those kinds of esoteric quantifiers on a crime scene. It was the vast and fast brain of his that had established him as the top detective in half the time it took for most to even get on the squad. It also didn't hurt to have a great partner.

Manny blinked slowly. Hooker knew the tattle-tale of his. This was the wind-up, and here comes the fastball, game-winning pitch.

"How soon will you be at the Fly's?"

Hooker looked at the Squirt then stood. Looking into the sunroom for his partner, he finished the conversation as he turned. "Box, go time." The orange streak skidded to a stop at the large front door as Hooker stepped over. "Shit." He had forgotten he was barefoot. The perfect exit was now just blown into the weeds and would burn there for weeks. Hooker opened the large door for the twenty pounds of cat. "Pee, and we'll be right with you." As an afterthought, he swung the door open again. "And leave Mike alone. No beating up the poor mutt until he is at least two."

Hooker closed the door as he felt the Squirt scurry around behind him to retrieve his boots. As Hooker came out of his bedroom and headed for the door, he could hear Manny already at work in his office. His favorite weapon these days was the phone, and he was a crack marksman.

Hooker smiled as he heard Manny connect with his old partner and now a county supervisor over the different police departments, sheriff, and highway patrol. "Paul, Manny, we have a very delicate sticky situation here…"

Hooker started to close the giant front door but felt the Squirt's hand. They walked to the truck in silence. Each with his own thoughts for the day's agenda, Hooker looked to where his cat was standing straight-legged —splayed in the small patch of grass planted just for him.

The rest of the large expanse of apron and approach would be the size for a respectable filling station was all eight-inch thick concrete. The queen of this domain sat waiting in all of her yellow and blue splendor. The auto club colors, but the blue was shaded in a candy-apple, and the whole was shot over with pink and red mother-of-pearl. In the right light, the entire eleven tons would flash iridescent neon red, making the fastest truck in the Bay Area look like it wasn't going to a fire, but was the fire itself.

"Box, go time." The streak bounced off the oversized fuel tank in front of Hooker's knee, ricocheted off the heat shield of the exhaust stack and in through the open door. Hooker knew he would hit his cardboard box, circle three times, and set his butt down so Hooker's right hand could reach his right ear to rub while the radios and engine warmed up. Box may be only a cat, but he was the smartest partner Hooker could ever want.

Hooker eyed the kid as they both climbed in. He smiled to himself. *Maybe a close second, but definitely a second.*

The Squirt buckled his belt. He thought about putting on the five-point harness but figured if Hooker wasn't moving fast, he wouldn't be driving fast, especially during the daylight, when cops could see him clearly. The Squirt looked over to see a small smile.

"What?"

Hooker shoved the small silver key in the keyhole and turned the beast on. He listened as the stators took hold and warmed the glow plugs. His electric drives slowly wound the turbochargers up to speed. The whine ran from low grumble to a climbing whine. Hooker always wondered if it must feel the same for a fighter in a jet plane. As the three sounds reached perfect harmony, Hooker briefly pushed the small magical silver button. Unlike other diesel trucks not babied and watched after by a fussing mother hen named Uncle Willie—the engine exploded into its new characteristic thrumming with a low-speed whistle.

The original engine in the 1959 Marmon had only been nine-hundred horsepower. Hooker and his Uncle Willie had built the original engine up to very respectable twelve-hundred horses. Earlier in the spring, Hooker had destroyed the engine while stopping a serial killer. The result of the day was Mae West, Hooker, and the Squirt had all been sidelined and needed rebuilding. Only the truck, Mae West, had come out ahead. In the rebuild, she had lost the archaic duel-transmission system with its twenty-four gears. She was refitted with a swifter set of sixteen gears driven by a now sixteen-hundred-horse engine originally, only the Department of Energy would have ever owned. Part of the new engine was the tattle-tale whistle.

Hooker's right hand dropped with the two fingers and thumb curled to engage the ear below. If the cardboard box ever moved, Box the cat would put it right back to its rightful place next to Hooker's seat. The ear was never out of place.

Hooker rolled his head to look at the Squirt as he listened for the engine noise to change. He never had to watch the pyrometer in order to know the temperature of his engine. With Hooker, it always was about felt and hearing the changes.

Hooker nodded his head up. "What?"

The Squirt smiled. He had long gotten used to the ritual of beginning the day with Hooker, Box, and Mae West. "You were smiling like there was something funny when you climbed in."

Hooker smiled as his hand rose to move the shifter. Floating it back and forth in the neutral line, he found his balance. Stomping on the clutch, he set the gears for fifth and eased off the apron and out onto the street, taking them down The Hill of Stupid. "I was just thinking about how smart Box is. He's not like any other cat or dog I have ever heard of, and I was just marveling at how lucky I was to get him as a partner."

The Squirt held his eye for a couple of heartbeats and then slewed them back out the front and over to his side as he checked along the working bed in the rearview mirror. He knew Hooker had not lied to him —he just had not shared everything. But the Squirt was satisfied with what he had gotten. The cat was something he too marveled at, and he was happy the twenty-something pounds of orange tabby was a friend instead of foe.

4

T O CALL THE Fly's an auto body shop is to call the Queen Mary a boat. The Fly's had six entrances on four different streets and a constantly used railhead. Hooker never used any, but the tow gate, which was a two-way river of steel, glass, and rubber. If it weighed more than three tons of unladen weight, the Fly's got it. If it was a Volkswagen with half of its original length, the Fly's got it. If Hooker towed it, and it wasn't going to a place of repair a club member designated, your insurance adjuster knew where it ended its life of usefulness.

Hooker parked Mae in his usual spot along the fence. Her size would be out of the way, but it was also along the main street of business for many mechanics and people who might need a tow. Even though they wouldn't require a truck as large as Mae, it was still good advertising.

The short Asian woman who everyone called Fly, but was actually not even related, spotted Hooker walking through the front door of the business office and called out, "Hooker, you're late!" This was a standing joke among the many companies Hooker dealt with because if anything, Hooker was always early. Early to a wreck, early to get the pick of the crop, and early to get it delivered with the outside chance he might get two tows out of a wreck instead of one or none. This caused some grumbling among many of the other drivers who were not hustlers by nature, but it also created a lot of respect from the right sort of people. Fly was one of them.

"Jeez, Fly, cut me some slack." He waved his thumb over his shoulder in the direction he hoped the Squirt was still standing. "The Squirt took a while to figure out his toes went into the boots first… and then there was the whole question of the left or right thing."

If the woman came much above Hooker's belt buckle, she was wearing heels. She pursed her lips for a brief moment. "You brought me a dead bone, but it had a bone in it."

"I heard."

"It really a two-bit tow." She was referring to the two and a bit of dimes still floating around in not only Hooker but the Squirt, as well.

"Hey, Squirt was working on it too… that makes it a four-bit."

The woman who worked in the most testosterone-driven male industry grabbed near her crotch "I've got your four bits hanging right here. I think Dog is still out back in the morgue. He kept the bone for safekeeping. I didn't want somebody's ghost visiting the office and hanging around. I have enough of those of my own."

The woman stepped close to Hooker and looked up. "Don't look up; just look at me. Jessie is back there talking to the new girl, isn't he?"

Hooker nodded.

"He's been sleeping over at Mai Lin's apartment for the last few months." She hung her head, matching the hand holding a large wad of papers. "Where did I go wrong? I didn't raise my daughter to fall in love with slime buckets who cheat on her." She looked up with hope in her face. "You still single. Why don't you date her?"

Hooker put his hand on the small woman's shoulder. "I kind of like where my relationship with the Squirt's sister is going." He looked up at the body mechanic hunched over the desk and making time with some new skirt. "But just for you, I'll take care of this for you. Can you spare a mechanic?"

The Fly turned her large head of long hair done loosely in a mass bun held together with four chopsticks and a couple of pencils. She watched the subject of their discussion. Turning back, she sighed. "Just don't hurt him on my property. Otherwise, you can leave him out in the mudflats of Fremont for all I care."

"I'll go talk to Dog. That will give you enough time to get Jessie's check ready." Hooker smiled.

The Fly looked to see Hooker was serious. "On your way out, pull up by fuel dump and fill up on me."

Hooker warned her, "I'm running on less than twenty in my fourth tank."

"If you can make it stick and he leaves Mai Lin, you can fill up on me all month."

Hooker knew she would never say such a thing unless she was serious. She was known for making a nickel squeal like a dollar, but when it came time to pay for things, she bought quality, not cheap. He patted her on the shoulder as he walked past. "One step at a time, Fly, one step at a time." He didn't have to look back for the Squirt. He knew the kid was no more than six feet behind him.

The 'morgue' was where dead things ended up. People went to the one downtown while cars and trucks ended up in the large brown building near the railroad spur. There were always one or two rail cars waiting on the spur to be loaded with scrap steel. This was Dog's domain. Hooker wound his way through the large heaps of mangled auto and truck parts. He turned as a low whistle came out of the Squirt behind him. He nodded his head up at the kid, who had never seen this part of cars before.

"All of this is…"

"Scrap." Waving his hand about the basketball court-sized sorting area, Hooker explained, "This is about a week or two of sorting through wrecks. The parts that are still good are auctioned off to wrecking yards and used parts houses. The scrap metal is sorted by type and shipped out on the rail cars or sent to the crusher. Marmons become Macks and Peterbilts—they become Mopar, and after the metal has gone through Volkswagens and soup cans, they become Fords and Chevys." Hooker smiled evilly at the Squirt.

They turned and walked past two pallets of carburetors and another of shock absorbers. "Hooker, just the man I want to see."

Hooker and the Squirt turned to see the black man with Asian eyes. "Hey, Dog, what's hanging?"

"Two cheap shots and a crowbar for my date tonight. Who's the squirt?"

The Squirt hung his head. "Shit, we going to keep doing this stuff?" Hooker laughed. The poor kid had been nailed as the Squirt, a vernacular for *the new guy*, ever since he started being hauled around by Hooker during the spring.

"Dog, this is John. John, this is Dog." Hooker winked to the black man. "But he's getting used to the name Squirt. I think Dolly is embroidering "The Squirt" on his shirts." Hooker watched the kid turn even brighter red as he looked anywhere but at Hooker or Dog.

Hooker turned back to Dog. "You had a bone show up in the car?"

The man wheeled around on his one metal leg. "Not just a bone." He lumbered his way toward a bench that might pass for his office desk. "As I was hosing out the landfill you decided I needed, I came across the hand and something else."

He bounced up against the large workbench. "I know you just love a good mystery, so here is your mystery for the month." He pulled an oil pan from a small straight engine down from the shelf and handed it to Hooker. "The watch was on the hand."

Hooker looked in the pan with the Squirt looking over his shoulder. Sure enough, there were the skeletal remains of a human hand and the main bone up to the elbow. A metal band watch was still on the bone. The gray-red clay from the area had tinted the bone along with age. To Hooker's untrained eye, the bones could be ten years old or a hundred and ten years old. Only the watch made it in the last thirty or forty years. Dog had carefully cleaned the gold watch.

"If you can't find out anything, I'd sure like the watch."

Hooker was sure Dog would rather he just forget anything about a mystery and hand over the watch right there. "Give me until summer, Dog. If I find nothing and if it's okay with the sheriff, then I'm sure it can be yours. After all, you found it and could have just kept your mouth shut and not told me anything." Hooker looked at the man.

"Jeez, Hooker, what kind of guy do you think I am?"

"An honest one."

"Damn right. The Fly trusted me the second day I was out of prison. I ain't never betrayed her trust. I don't plan to start a shit now."

Hooker stuck his hand out and shook the man's hand. "Let's keep playing it, Dog, just the way you've been. I'll tell you what, if I find a rightful owner and have to let it go, I'll buy you and a lady steaks at the Bold Knight. Deal?"

"We're good." They started to break the shake.

Hooker choked back onto the man's hand and leaned in close. As Hooker talked, the man listened, with a smile slowly spreading across his face.

Dog nodded. "You got it, boss. I'll make a couple of calls. It won't cost more than a six-pack or four."

Hooker nodded. "Don't forget about Fly's daughter."

The man drew back with a struck-smitten look. "Ain't no decent man in his right mind who ever met her can forget her."

Hooker studied the man hard. "If you get a shot at her—I think you would even have the Fly's blessing."

"Consider it done by the end of the day."

Hooker turned to leave. "I'll keep in touch, Dog."

"Thanks, Hooker, you're the best."

Hooker looked at his watch and hustled. "We need to fly out of here, Squirt. We are late for our dates."

The Squirt frowned. "Da… dates? What dates? You didn't tell me anything about…"

"On the chalkboard for over a week now, my young Squirt."

"What chalkboard?"

Hooker stepped up onto the truck and opened the door. Sliding the oil pan and body parts behind his seat, he climbed in and started the engine. Squirt clawed his way in the other side. "What chalkboard?"

"Already asked that, Squirt." Hooker cleared both directions of the street and nosed Mae West out on to San Jose Avenue heading east. He would wait on the fuel and make the fill-up worthwhile—instead of only three-quarters of one tank out of his four. The day was warm for being overcast, and it felt good to hang his arm out the window. Stopping at

Monterey Highway, he turned south. Hooker leapfrogged the gears and rolled along to the highway at a quick clip. He glanced over at his passenger. "Really, you haven't been down to the mole hole to see your own sister in more than a couple of weeks?"

The apartment was in the lower level. It had been used as storage and a three-car garage. With events, Stella had turned one of the large storage areas into an apartment for Candy, who was starting nursing school. The separation of one floor accessed by a secret set of stairs everyone knew and used was not lost on Hooker or Candy. Even though the apartment was built with two bedrooms, Hooker and the Squirt still floated between their two rooms in the Hacienda Romero and the two rooms at Uncle Willie's where they were headed at the moment.

"What does my sister and her apartment have to do with anything?"

"Just outside her apartment door is a new chalkboard. You might want to get familiar with it. You have some heavy dating scheduled on it."

"Dates?"

"Why does a date seem like such an alien concept to you?"

"I've never... I mean..."

Hooker swung his head in amazement. As he stared at the kid, his mouth hung open in mock shock.

The Squirt blushed and looked out his open window. "Oh, shut up."

Hooker almost made a teasing comment, but then stopped himself out of respect for the young man who had saved his life and paid dearly for it. "Dude, you're young. Besides, how would you take a girl out, the bus? You have years of dating. Let's see how today goes." Hooker smiled. "Besides, it's not like a regular date. This one you're getting naked for."

Hooker laughed at the horror-struck face. He knew he had hit the nail on the head.

5

THE HILL UP to Uncle Willie's was only two downshifts. If Hooker wasn't taking it easy on the new engine, he could have just nailed the fuel and powered up the hill with only the single downshift at the bottom. He chuckled the whole way up the mile of hill as he listened to the new huge engine barely work. The hill was a quiet old neighborhood Willie had bought into in the late 1950s.

His property was at the end of the climb, and unlike the neighboring lots, was a full three acres dominated by a small house attached to what had started life as a hanger for a Navy blimp. The hanger was never built, and Willie had bought it for literally one cent on the original dollar. It came with full delivery, which Willie had nursed into full erection. Him having a great swimming pool and barbecue pit had the company of engineer Seabees milking the construction for the entire summer.

This didn't upset Willie one bit. In fact, he enjoyed having a hundred young, good-looking hard-body sailors strutting their stuff shirtless and in his view. A view he had to deny himself to enjoy during the decades he worked as a Navy Intelligence officer. However, as a retired old captain, he was allowed his due.

Hooker nosed Mae up off the street and onto the approach apron to the gigantic door standing sixty feet high and almost forty feet wide. The door was made for walking combat blimps or weather balloons through unscathed. Something like the eleven tons of Mae West was like a pencil through a fist-sized knothole.

Squirt opened his door and slid out. "I've got this." He entered the little man door, and moments later, Hooker heard the large klaxon horn sound and watched the door slowly roll back. The electric motor was a GE hundred-horse motor originally tasked with pulling anchor chain on a light frigate. Willie didn't like the original forty-horse motor because it took almost a full minute to open the door the entire forty feet.

Hooker stuck Mae into third gear and just let his foot off the clutch. The power eased her forward at a slow walk as they traversed the depth of the two-hundred-foot-long auto shop. Willie was standing at the end of the grease pit and guided Hooker over the pit.

Hooker slid out as Mae shuddered the last throes of life. As Hooker's feet landed on warm concrete, Box bounced off his shoulder and was across the shop headed for the grass beyond. Hooker called out at the loping cat. "No beating up any dogs, Box. I want you to have a pure record for Santa this year." The cat slowed to a walk, glanced back in what Hooker knew to be a glare, and continued out to at least use the grass.

Hooker shook his head as he turned and smiled at Uncle Willie. The man slumped down on one hip. His Navy flattop haircut never seemed to change. The large slash of a scar across his neck and up the side of his face was showing pinker today than the dead white of most days. Hooker chalked it up to the rose-colored paisley dress the man was wearing.

"Nice dress, Willie. You almost can't see the burn marks yet."

"Don't sweet talk me, young man. You know I won't be doing any welding this week." The man liked the feel of dresses. Also, it was, in his mind, justifiably economics. He bought the long granny dresses at Goodwill by the large garbage-bag full. He bought them at the going rate of rags and by the pound, which worked out in Willie's mind to less than twenty-five cents a dress. And they didn't burn up any faster than a pair of four-dollar bib overalls—when you could find any. They were frugal but with the benefit of also placating his 'Nancy' side, as well.

A low, slow wolf whistle preceded the Squirt.

Willie lost any sense of serious officiousness. His hip slung out as his face softened, and he turned to address the young man dressed in a mirror image of Hooker. "Well, John, it is so good to see a fine young man with at least some sense of taste and appreciation." He reached an arm out to solicit a hug. "You are looking and moving quite well for someone who, a short time ago, was half dead."

The young man didn't hesitate. His hug was strong and true, which he brazenly finished with a kiss on the check. "And how is the best uncle on the east side doing? I really like the deep color of the paisley. It's certainly got the *go to town and raise hell* look about it." His smile was large and sincere.

Hooker quietly placed his palm on his face. "Oh, Gawd, please don't encourage him."

"Oh, hush yourself, Hooker. Just because you don't have any taste, don't be bad-mouthing another." Turning to Squirt and sliding his hand about his waist, he guided him toward the door to the house part of the building. "Why, John, you have slipped away to mere skin and bones. Let me see if there is anything Hanky left in the refrigerator I can fatten you up with." He leaned back and winked at Hooker as he nodded his head toward the darker southwest corner of the building.

Hooker glanced over to see the tan 1963 Dodge Dart convertible, commonly known in the family as The Granny Car. Hooker smiled as the car was now possessed by his girlfriend, and the Squirt's sister, Candy. He knew Willie was now leading a lamb to slaughter.

Candy and a fellow nursing student were there to earn hours toward the massage part of their schooling. Hooker was certain the Squirt, at twenty, had never had a massage. And now he knew the boy had never been really touched by a woman. The kid was now being led to his first of many therapeutic massages at the hands of his sister and fellow students.

Willie looked back just before they entered the door and gave Hooker a large, evil, lecherous smile. He was completely enjoying having a small but fun hand in the popping of the young boy's cherry, even if it was only a massage and for Willie, vicariously. Hooker knew that just the idea of the young kid naked under a sheet—being rubbed, was a visual thought the older man would carry for months.

As they entered the domicile through the steel fire door, they were greeted by three people sitting at the dining table. The two nursing students were talking quietly over tea with the swarthy older man. The thin white pencil-line mustache matched the same white at his temples and stood out boldly on the dark Greek.

Hank sat up and leaned back in his chair. "And so we have a lamb to slaughter." He spread his arms wide, which only enhanced his broad smile. "Hello, Squirt, welcome to a whole new world." He stood. "May I introduce you to your masseuse for the day, Cynthia? Cynthia, this is the Squirt, but for today, he's just a John."

Suddenly, the smile was shaken as Hooker and Willie started to laugh. "Oh, my, that did all come out wrong, didn't it?" The man flushed with embarrassment at the sexual innuendoes of both name and nickname.

The blonde stood with a soft, tinkling laugh. "It's okay, Hank. We all knew what you meant." She stuck her hand out toward the Squirt and parlayed her own innuendo. "I'm so glad to meet you, Squirt. Candy tells me you're a virgin… to being rubbed… massaged." Her smile and eye were steady as she viewed the score she landed on the young man only a couple of years younger than her.

Willie fanned his face with his hand. "Whew, is it hot in here or is it just all the sex talk?"

Candy, used to riding herd over errant men, took control. "We only have so much time." Standing, she touched Cynthia on the shoulder. "Why don't you get the Squirt undressed in the second bedroom, and I'll go get a hammer from the shop to use on Hooker."

Willie nosed up and over as he spun back toward the shop. "I think I'm going to go massage my girl now. A man in my delicate condition can only take so much pheromone at one time." He turned toward his partner. "The soup smells wonderful, Hanky. Don't forget to give me fair warning for lunch. I think Mae is going to get me very dirty today."

The quiet, slender man pursed his lips, driving the white line askew. "More like a dirty mind if I know you, and don't you dare get that grease and oil anywhere near this god-like body." The palms of his hands gently smoothed down his physique.

Willie sing-songed his way out the door with, "Promises, promises, my Hanky-panky."

The remaining man just wagged his head and gave a knowing eye toward Hooker. The other three laughed as Cynthia pulled the Squirt away to her lair. Candy noted the look in the younger woman's eyes. "Regulation massage, Cyn, regulation massage. And use the sheet."

"Yes, mother hen." The door closed on a giggle.

Candy turned on Hooker and poked him in the chest. "Same goes for you, buster."

6

THE SOUP WAS as good as the aroma permeating the house had advertised. There were contented tummies and bodies in the kitchen, and the conversation was sparse and quiet.

Hooker had watched Willie, who had been uncharacteristically distracted during the meal. Hooker had also noticed Hank stealing worried glances as well. Hooker rinsed his and Candy's dishes and placed them on the stack by the sink. Turning, he stepped over and placed his hand on his uncle's shoulder.

Willie nodded his head toward the empty seat and pointed.

As Hooker returned to his chair, Willie reached in his pants pocket. Hooker realized then his uncle had changed from the dress to pants and shirt sometime during the day. He was prepared to go somewhere.

"As I ministered to our baby today, I found some most disturbing items." He glared at Hooker. "We will talk later about the disgusting Ford oil pan, as well as the bones." He laid the gold watch on the Formica and chrome dining table. Only Hooker and the Squirt recognized it from the morning.

Hooker wasn't sure where to start. Willie started for him. "This is a Rolex. Not just any Rolex. This is called a DateJust. It is written as two capitalized words but with no space between them. What the name means is that *just* as the hands reach midnight, the date changes. The metal band was invented by a company named Speidel. In 1947, they came out with this band called the Golden Knight. There are damn few Rolex watches with a Gold Knight band. In fact, I have only heard of one."

Willie glanced up at his partner and lover Hank, almost asking for the okay to continue. Returning his eyes to Hooker, he did. "Maddie and I had gone up to San Francisco to deliver a very fast car to a man who paid a high dollar for an untraceable car capable of outrunning anything on the road. We won't talk about how stupid he was by not paying attention to the highway patrol installing used military radios in their cruisers.

"So there we were, in San Francisco, with money burning in our pockets, and the train didn't come through until four the next morning. In those days, we didn't drink anything that didn't come from the end of a copper tube.

"Down on Market Street, there was a very nice jewelry store among the nice places to eat and just down from Saint Francis to sleep. In the window were these two items. We went in. I didn't need a watch as I was wearing whatever the Navy was giving me at the time. Maddie always wore her Cartier tank watch given to her grandmother for her grandfather's service in the Tank Corps that liberated France in The Great War. But her oldest brother had broken his watch during D-Day on Omaha beach."

Willie dabbed at the side of his eyes. The memory was as fresh as yesterday. "We went off to a long dinner while the jeweler engraved the back of the watch." He rolled the now carefully cleaned watch inside out and handed it to Hooker.

Engraved in a fine bookplate font were the words, *To My Golden Knight Brother Danny. Love, Your Little Rocket Sister, Maddie.*

The watch became very heavy in Hooker's hand, as the universe grew dark. He handed it to Candy, who read it and handed it to the Squirt. All three knew exactly who Maddie was and who she was to Willie.

The Squirt passed it back to Willie.

Willie mouthed a silent *thank-you.* He quietly stared at the engraving. He gathered the rest of his thoughts.

"When Korea started, he was still attached to the Army National

Guard. But because of his field commission in France, and the few community college courses he took, they dragged him back in.

"In 1953, the letters stopped coming, but no Army pukes showed up at the door to do Honor Duty. Eventually, two MPs showed up looking for Danny. According to them, he had been shipped to San Francisco's Letterman Hospital, but never showed up."

The man just stopped. There was no more. It was now Hooker's turn.

"The other night, some lady slid her Caddie off the edge on the Snake. The gully there is about a hundred feet, but she didn't do so bad. She went down ass first, and so her head banged on those new headrests. It took her about three hours to walk out to the Cats and a payphone. I guess Rollie went in first but knew his ton and a half would flip trying to pull the de Ville out. So I was called in. I found a leg bone and just flipped it aside. But, when I dragged the Caddy up, it must have scooped the side of the hill, and I guess it caught this. There was a lot of mud in the car, and when Dog over at the Fly's washed it out, he found the hand and this watch."

Willie rubbed his upper lip between his thumb and forefinger as he thought. He looked up at Hooker.

"Is Mae ready?"

Willie nodded.

Hooker stood and reached for the phone on the wall. He dialed without really looking at the numbers. "Hi, Karen. It's Hooker. Listen, when Dolly…" He rolled his eyes. "Yes, ma'am. Yes, ma'am. I was there already this morning. Yes, ma'am, I could see how it would upset some people. Yes, ma'am. Yes, ma'am. We just finished a little pow-wow here with Willie. The Squirt and I are going out to look around."

Hooker looked at Willie and nodded. He turned his attention back toward the phone. "Yes, ma'am. We'll meet him at the downside of the Cats. Yes, ma'am. I love you, too." He hung up and turned. The two young ladies were relaxed back in their chairs and smiling. Willie was close to laughing. Only the Squirt had a solemn look on his face.

Willie broke. "Is Dolly feeling a little mother hen needy this morning?" Dolly's day, like Hooker's, usually started around five in the evening. This was mid-afternoon, and she was already in her custom-built stainless-steel desk chair to accommodate her quarter-ton of flesh for running the city by night. A large limb lay on her desk within arm's reach. Carved into it were the words 'The Stick.' It was Dolly's to touch and use, and nobody else. It was what she used to stir the shit up with, and if she was in her desk a few hours early—there was shit flying from somewhere.

"The Fly called. Someone saw the bones Dog washed out of the car and called the PD. They came down. Dog told them it wasn't any of their business. I need to go make nice and get him out of jail. The Fly will post the bond, but the truth is the Snake isn't PD's area. So Dog was right."

"What about the highway patrol?"

"It was Micha who called me and worked the scene, but I think it was just because the woman had called from the Cats. Highway 17 is theirs, but the Snake would be more like the unincorporated area and come under the Sheriff." Willie and the Squirt booth groaned.

Willie asked, "Who are you meeting at the Cats?"

"Chet. I guess so we can go down and pop Dog out, and Chet can drive his flag into the investigation before this turns into a three-ring cluster..." Willie gave Hooker a stern look.

"There *are* ladies present."

"We'll just be leaving then. Squirt?"

The Squirt got up and shook Cynthia's hand. "Thank you for the great massage. I never knew it could feel so good."

Cynthia smiled. "I'll look forward to the next time I get you on a bed."

Candy pulled down her nose with thumb and forefinger as she looked at the other woman. There was just a hint of more than a message lurking in the smile. Maybe she had to watch whom she chose to join in on massaging the recovering hero.

Hooker bent over and kissed the top of Willie's head as the man flipped his hand at him. He blushed slightly but still smiled. Hooker gave a quick smooch at Candy, and then the two young men grabbed their matching leather jackets and donned them over their matching starched white T-shirts over matching jeans and boots. The girls giggled, but Willie saw the man of today and the man who he once had been.

The steel fire door closed solid.

They could hear Hooker yell for Box, and then the giant truck roared into life and shook the building. Candy glanced over at Willie. The man had a very satisfied, warm look on his face. He was comfortable in the life that had come to grace him.

Hank came in through the almost never used front door. "I have some good cilantro and chives. The rosemary just hasn't done well in the spot by the hose bib. But I think I can make do on the tri-tip tonight. Ladies, can you stay for dinner? There is plenty for six."

Hank stopped and counted the heads and then heard the distinct sound of Mae West as Hooker shifted for the top of the hill and the subsequent drop. "Well, I guess it just means more for four." The man smiled and danced his way toward the sink as he waved his pom-poms of herbs.

7

D OWN ON THE freeway, the eleven tons of yellow and blue steel monster was just warming up as Hooker flipped the toggle and plunged the shifter into ninth gear. He dropped the hammer and signaled into the second lane and blew past the Pontiac Firebird. The late afternoon was holding steady at cool but was always warm enough for two leather elbows out the windows. The French vanilla triple scoops of ice cream would wait until after midnight.

Hooker reached behind his head to grab the microphone off its perch. This was the personal radio, usually only going to the credenza behind Dolly. Only occasionally, after midnight, it reached out to a small version at a local radio station. The latter was for communication with one of the more bizarre lines of communication for solving problems or watching for upcoming problems.

Sweets was the night disk jockey and worked the midnight to six o'clock shift. When his sight was taken from him by a freak accident in his high school welding class, his visual sight was replaced by a sixth sense. He didn't always know what he was looking at, but he did know who it was meant for. More times than Hooker cared to remember, this sixth sense had been his protection or help in figuring out a problem.

Sweets' brother, Danny, a former lineman for USC until the accident, was now his chauffeur and protector. Danny wouldn't have it any other way.

During Hooker's recovery from the surgeries to remove the dimes a killer had left in him and the Squirt, Danny had studied texts to help in Hooker's physical therapy. The giant black man and the younger Hooker had become fast friends. Hooker knew Danny would lay down his life for Sweets and their mother and suspected he would do the same for Hooker as well.

Hooker toggled the side switch and called the woman who would qualify as his first mother behind her sister Stella. "1-4-1."

The pause didn't last more than a heartbeat. "Go ahead, Hooker."

"Do you know if Chet is in his cruiser with a radio?"

"Stand by one."

Hooker looked over at the Squirt and nodded a raised eyebrow shrug. With the mic still in his hand, he reached down and shifted down a gear.

"10-4, honey. What do you need?"

"Why not have him meet us at the jail. It will save the backtrack time."

There was a pause, and then Karen's voice took over for Dolly. "Chet says to meet him at the Whole Doughnut. He can leave the cruiser there."

Hooker laughed. "He doesn't need a doughnut in his condition. He needs to start running again. I'll be 10-97 in ten minutes."

"10-4. Dispatch out."

Hooker dropped one more gear, hung up the mic, and dropped two more as he nosed the truck into the winder cloverleaf from the 101 to the 280. They passed under the floating pieces of a future overpass everyone referred to as the Altars to Stupidity. Under Governor Reagan, the state had prospered, and many infrastructure projects were started. With the election of Jerry 'Moonbeam' Brown, the twenty-billion-dollar emergency fund for disasters had evaporated on the state's way toward bankruptcy within the year. Any and every project was stopped. So the altars stood, rotting and unfinished.

Hooker looked over at the Squirt, who was staring numbly out the window. Quietly, Hooker laughed to himself. He had seen the look before… in the mirror. He stomped on the go pedal and jumped back up the three lost gears and settled out with one extra.

"Still thinking about the massage?"

The Squirt drifted back into the cab and turned toward Hooker. He turned in the seat so his legs were in the middle, and his back was leaning against the door. The wind in the window tossed the hair on the back of his head. In a drifting but analytical voice, he reviewed the event. "Yeah… I think. First, if she's going to touch me… umm…"

"Intimately?" Hooker smiled as he glanced over.

"Yeah, intimate. So why cover you with the sheet?"

"Did you have sex?"

The kid blushed but was shocked. "No. Nothing like that…"

"Did she touch your pecker?"

"No…" John was now frowning at Hooker, who seemed to be getting a little too personal.

"But she rubbed your butt." The Squirt nodded. "And you weren't cold."

Hooker had to look over at the now silent kid. John was only twenty and had experienced a lot, but not much was nice to him.

"I think it's the law, but the sheet serves many purposes. It keeps you warm, it gives you a sense of privacy even when she's rubbing really near your hoo-hoo, but most importantly, it reminds both of you that you are there for a massage, not sex."

The kid smiled at the information. Then he decided to push the envelope with the one person who he knew it was safe to do it. "What if she is willing to—"

Hooker stopped him "Then you better negotiate it for another time. If it was to happen, she would most likely get thrown out of the program as unprofessional."

"So this would be okay?" The kid held up a small piece of paper Hooker knew probably had a phone number written on it.

"You're learning, John." He shook his head and smiled as he down-shifted to take the off-ramp. "You are certainly learning." For some reason, calling him Squirt at the moment didn't seem right.

The kid turned back around as he stashed the number in his jeans. "She said with the extent of my injuries and surgeries that I would probably need a lot of extra care." His smile was more self-satisfied than just a massage would put there.

Hooker smiled as he pulled the large white Bakelite steering wheel around to make the turn at the top of the ramp. Jamming the shifter into neutral, he toggled down to the next set of gears and pulled it back into what was now sixth gear. The thought drifted warmly across his mind, *yeah, that's what your sister told me, too.*

A short romp down the Guadeloupe Parkway and Hooker nosed Mae into the back parking lot behind the most popular doughnut place in town, The Whole Doughnut. As he set the air brakes, he heard the wooden screen door snap shut, bouncing a couple of times.

The high voice was English, with a lot of Vietnamese accents thrown in. "Why you come now, Hooker? You know missy Stella in town. My God Father, no can have cherry-filled doughnuts unless she go away."

Hooker laughed as he eased the door open and slid out for a hug. "I know, Mai Lin, but some days, the hard-working tow driver just needs something sweet... like a hug." He enveloped the small woman as he waved toward her husband, Ralph.

Ralph had fallen in love with Mai Lin in Vietnam. When he was pulled out, he told his commander they had gotten married, and she was pregnant with their child. The commander looked at the blown up soldier and to the then fifteen-year-old Mai Lin. He figured if she would have the beat-up half a man, and he was willing to take her home, who was he to come between the two?

Convincing the State Department was another matter. Eventually, it came to light that they weren't married, and Mai was not eighteen. Everything was in limbo while Ralph sat in one cell and Mai Lin in another. It was getting heated around the police department as they wanted nothing to do with the State Department or immigration problem. To make matters worse, while Ralph was in jail, the Army showed up with some medals he was due.

Manny was sitting in the office and heard the whole story from beginning to end. His only question for the State Department guy was what needed to happen to make sure she wasn't shipped back. There were only two things available considering her age—sponsorship and or adoption.

Manny told the guy to go to lunch, and then he walked down the hall to have a long talk with Mai Lin. By the time the guy came back from lunch, Manny had one of the County Clerks draw up emergency papers of foster care pending adoption, as well as a judge's signature and registered stamp. Manny sent the State Department guy packing, and the two love birds were released into his care.

He checked them into a motel up the peninsula and convinced an old friend he needed two new employees willing to work for free for a month or so. They learned everything the doughnut house had to offer, including how to treat the cops. While they were learning the business, Manny was finding them the right location, as well as taking donations from every cop, detective, street worker, fireman, or city employee who may ever chance to eat a doughnut.

The 'Whole' stood quite literally for the whole of city workers having a piece of interest in it becoming a success. The two kids opened to a daily sell-out, and they had been working hard ever since. The day Mai Lin turned eighteen was the day Manny walked her down the aisle and gave her over to Ralph. The two had been worshiping each other ever since.

"How's it hanging, Hooker?" Ralph sauntered up in his broken gait with the obligatory unfiltered cigarette hanging from his lips. He put his hand out. Hooker took it and was always amazed at the mass of scar tissue hiding a grip of steel coming from the man kneading hundreds of pounds of dough each day.

"You know, Ralph, just another day in paradise looking for something to choke down."

John had finished checking all the tires and walked up.

Ralph nodded his way and started to ask Hooker a question. John cut him off and offered out his hand. "Hi, the name is John, but everyone calls me Squirt."

Mai Lin laughed and waved her hand as she returned to the back door. The screen door slammed and then squealed back open. "Hey, Mister Squirt, what kind doughnuts you like?"

John looked at Hooker, who just shrugged. The Squirt turned, "I like the kind you choose for me."

Ralph laughed and looked at Hooker as he nodded at the Squirt. "He's going to go a long way, this one." Giving the Squirt a mock glare, he advised, "Easy on the hormones, soldier—she's my boss, and she's married."

Hooker snorted and nodded toward the Squirt. "In the spring, if he's physically able, he starts at the police academy."

Ralph's eyes lit up. The face and name finally hit home. "So you're the two-bit guy who saved Hooker's ass?"

The voice was deep and raspy. "Yes, he did—as well as putting the psycho where they belonged." The Highway Patrol Captain walked around the back end of the truck. "But before he shot her, he figured out things that broke the case." Chet put out his hand to the kid. "Good to see you up and walking around, Squirt."

"Always a pleasure to see you too, Captain." The kid beamed as they shook hands.

The screen door squealed and snapped shut. "I see you drive in, Captain. You have chocolate bar, Hooker has frog, and Squirt has two éclairs because he growing boy." Mai Lin presented the bag to the Squirt. "You guard so they don't steal your food."

The men all laughed at the obvious fondness and favoritism the small woman delivered with the heart of a tiger. Hooker and the Squirt collected their hugs and headed for Mae West, lumbering as if she were a large ticking clock.

Chet opened his arms. Mai looked sternly at him. "You no get hug. You no come see Mai enough. Mai tell you to take care of yourself." She waved her right hand up and down at the man's body. "You no mind Mai. You just stand and be target for crazy person. You retire. Then you get hugs from Mai. Mai no like man with holes in him." She crabbed over and put her arm around Ralph. "Except maybe husband." She smiled.

Chet, defeated, headed for the truck.

As Hooker drove between eating the messy doughnut called a frog, they talked strategy.

"You know they aren't just going to roll over on this and give away a juicy case."

Chet popped the last of his doughnut into his mouth and shoved it into his cheek. "Sure they will after I point out a few things. One, we have jurisdiction and two, the case is at least four decades cold—"

"Two. We know who—"

"Hush, I'm talking. And don't you dare tell them anything about the watch. But the most important thing is, even Dog doesn't know where the car went over on the Snake. Only Micha can make a positive identification as to the location."

Hooker looked at Chet. "But the Squirt and I—"

"Didn't I just tell you to hush?"

Hooker rolled his eyes and downshifted with a smile. "Right, it was a dark and stormy night. If not for the highway crew, Mae and I would have been lost." Hooker sang to the tune of *Gilligan's Island*.

The Squirt chimed in, "And they would be lost on a three-hour tow, a three-hour tow."

Chet hung his head. "Oh, Gawd, there's now two of them."

Twenty minutes later, the Gilligan crew was squared off across the table with the police. The negotiations were stalled as the police chief was under the gun by the commissioner. He said he didn't care how old the case was, and the PD needed a good, juicy case to play well in the Mercury News.

Finally, Hooker pushed back his chair and stood. All eyes were on him. "You'll have to excuse me for a few minutes." He looked at his watch. "It's after four. I need to call Commissioner Paul before I talk to Dolly at Dispatch." Everyone at the table knew Paul was Manny's ex-partner and still best of friends if not the same with Hooker. The mention of Dolly was enough to cause all four assholes to clinch shut on the PD side of the table.

Chet stood. "While you do that, I think I'll call out to Manny and ask how he's doing on the little project we talked about this morning."

The Squirt cleared his throat. Nobody expected he would have anything to contribute. Quietly, he looked the chief in the eye. "I know when you made me the offer to join your department after the shooting, you thought you were the only name in the game. But if this is the kind of pissing match that goes on here, I seriously may just have to take up the offer by San Francisco." He sat with an impassive stone face. He waited out the chief, unblinking.

Hooker paused and looked at the Squirt. The kid was no kid at the moment. "When did you get the letter?"

The Squirt never blinked. His stare was burning its way into the chief. "Last month, while Hooker was taking care of the other serial killer in your jurisdiction." The final shiv sunk home. The chief was outgunned by these two who had ended the reign of terror by not one but two separate serial killers in one year. And they had almost lost their lives in doing it: no medals, no ceremonies, no publicity. Two private citizens who did the job his department should have been able to do and hadn't.

The chief blinked. "Crap. But keep me in the loop."

Hooker was there for one thing and one thing only. "And Dog?"

The chief waved his hand backward. "Yeah, kick him loose."

Hooker pressed. "You have him on probation for another six months on a bogus DUI charge…"

The chief looked at Chet.

Chet smirked. "Welcome to the big leagues, Phil."

"Who was he arraigned under?"

"Stone."

"Oh, great. Swing 'em High Stone. Okay, I'll work it out with the DA."

Hooker knew when to close and be magnanimous. "Thank you, sir." He turned to the Squirt with a wink the PD side couldn't see. "Come on, Squirt, the Box needs to use the large lawn out here."

Neither spoke or smiled as they made their way down to lock-up and released Dog. It wasn't until they had all piled into the truck and were nosing out onto the street they finally spoke.

Hooker looked over at the Squirt "That was some great bullshit about San Francisco."

The Squirt just kept looking forward. The silence was thick.

Chet was the first to understand. "Who else did you get a letter from, son?"

The Squirt was quiet, gathering his thoughts. "Five on the peninsula, three from Contra Costa County, four from Marin County, as well as the Sheriff of Los Angeles County." He turned to look with a small smile at Chet. "I'm still leaning toward the highway patrol. They have better cars, but the uniforms suck."

They were still laughing as they dropped Dog off at the Fly's and filled the fuel tanks.

The Fly had come out to greet them, and the usually hard edge was gone. She walked right into Hooker's unsuspecting middle and hugged him firmly. "I don't know how you did it, but that asshole Steve flew out of here without his check and was gone from my daughter's life within an hour."

Hooker looked at a retreating Dog, who had his palms up. "You don't have to share the hug, Hooker... I'll get one somewhere else." The man laughed and turned on his metal leg and walked back to work.

The Fly watched him go as her arms were still around Hooker. She wasn't sure what had just happened, but she liked the excuse to hug one of the special people in her life.

"Fly, I think you just might have swapped an asshole for a really nice guy who works hard—and worships your daughter for the great person she is. If you end up with Dog for a son-in-law, I think you will all win."

The small woman looked for any joking in Hooker's face. Finding none, she buried her face back into his tummy. The hug was almost painful.

Hooker hadn't been joking about his fuel level. He took over three-hundred gallons in his four tanks. For Hooker, he was running on fumes.

Hooker reached behind his head and grabbed the mic. "1-4-1."

Dolly's smooth voice oozed out of the speakers. "Ooo, I just love hearing from my three favorite juvenile delinquents. Can any of you three spare a girl a dime?"

Hooker remembered Chet also possessed a dime floating in his body the surgeons didn't want to try to remove. "We have four and a half bits, how much do you need?"

"Just what you can spare, honey. Now, what do you need? I'm busy here, knitting a pair of booties before the kid over there becomes a stupid tow truck driver."

Hooker held his laughter at the thought of Dolly trying to knit. "Can you see if Micha is on duty yet, please?"

"Stand by one."

They waited while someone tried the radio on the highway patrol network or called the substation. Hooker loafed Mae down Winchester Boulevard. If they could get him, it would make it easier to find the crash site again. He had been there in daylight hours and then guided Hooker back in the dark.

"He says he will take Chet on tack three."

"10-4, mama."

The Squirt fished his hand under the dash near where the illegal radio used to hide.

Hooker smiled. "Maddie upgraded the whole shebang." He reached overhead and toggled a red bat-switch that now glowed. Hooker grabbed the third mic hanging under the dashboard and handed it to Chet.

Chet held it waiting for the radio to warm up, but Micha had other plans. "P-twelve to C-one." Chet looked hard at Hooker.

Hooker smiled as he nodded at the radio. "Don't get your panties in a twist. It came out of an Orion P-3 Sub Chaser out at Moffitt Field. Maddie just did some tweaking and upgraded it."

Chet's look was doubtful, but he keyed the mic. "C-one, go."

"What do you need?"

"What's your twenty?"

"I heard someone was headed for the Snake. I'm having some fine coffee and looking at two large cats."

Hooker nodded. "Fifteen." He eased down on the gas, took a right onto Hamilton Avenue, and readied for his favorite down-spiraling winder on-ramp.

"10-4, P-twelve. Give us fifteen."

Chet pitched the mic over to the Squirt—who had a seat belt on—as he braced himself in the opening to the sleeper. He had never ridden with Hooker, but he knew the young man's reputation for driving the largest tow truck like it was a sports car.

Hooker's reputation was no exaggeration. He had jumped up five more gears before the winder dumped him out onto the freeway at eighty miles an hour. Chet sat back in the sleeper and just shook his head. "I'm definitely not seeing this." Hooker knew that with Micha at the Cats, there was no other highway patrol on the weekend freeway.

8

T HE SNAKE HAD dried out some since the night before. Hooker
thought of the few moonshine runners still using it. They would
enjoy a break in the fall weather as they conducted business
during the holidays supplying the South Bay Area.

Most people thought of moonshine and runners as something from
prohibition or the thirties. Hooker knew from being around Maddie that
her family's main source of income was not from building and racing fast
cars. It came from building fast street cars with large stainless-steel tanks
with remotely triggered dumping ports. Willie once told Hooker a good
dump could put over one hundred gallons of shine on the highway in the
time it took to pull over and stop on the side of the road—about two
blocks. Hooker had Maddie's brother put two hundred gallons on the
highway in less than a hundred yards or three seconds. Pressurizing the
tanks had revolutionized the process and the amount carried at one time.
A back seat in a Lincoln Town Car might be nothing more than the thin
leather glued over a handcrafted tank. The added ton of liquid was offset
by suspension from a truck. Top to bottom, Maddie's family was creative
and full of talent.

The highway patrol cruiser pulled off to the side of the road. As
Hooker nosed Mae up to the rear end, the tall black officer eased out of

the door. The fast draw smile was one of Hooker's favorites to see at a wreck, a bar, Dolly's Wednesday night's dinner table, or anywhere else they would run into each other. Their history ran deep into the days that Hooker was towing on a bogus driver's license, saying he was nineteen. Micha had never asked how old he really was the night in the rain when they had watched a prom queen of seventeen die in Hooker's arms.

The two met and shook with grim smiles. Nothing needed to be said. This meeting was never happening, and they weren't digging up old bones. It helped that Micha's boss walked up, holding out an extra pair of overalls. "Sorry, there weren't any more rubbers." Chet smiled.

Micha looked down at his boss's ratty running shoes and paint-splattered pants. "Getting some work done around the house for the holidays, I see." The two laughed at the old department joke. One year, Chet had worked long days until December twenty-sixth, and then, to surprise his wife, bought a tree already trimmed and being thrown out by a store. Snuck it home and plugged it in. The look on his wife's face made it the best five bucks he had ever spent. The small diamond ring had only helped. Cops don't get time for holidays.

They both knew Chet being sidelined due to reoccurring massive headaches since the shooting was eating at his insides. This holiday season was no happy time for Chet—with no work and his wife passing away a few years before. "I thought I'd finally get those dime holes plugged in the living room. I even got the window replaced last week."

The Squirt strolled past with the two shovels. "You two can supervise from up here where it's not so muddy or come join in the fun." They noted from the kid's deadpan delivery he was fully aware of what they would be digging up.

Except none of them were ready for what they would find.

The small sluice of rainwater from the night before had removed a lot of the loose mud and even more of the dirt wall of the hillside. As the other three finally climbed down, they found Hooker looking over the area with his flashlight. Two arm and hand bones stuck out from the cliff.

The count was not lost on the Squirt. "Oh, crap. There is more than just Danny."

"What the hell do you think happened here?"

Hooker shook his head toward Chet. "Hell if I know, but it wasn't good." He aimed his light on what might have been some yellow cloth.

Micha kneeled and dug around it with his hands. With little work, a large basketball-sized yellowish rubberized bag rolled out into his lap. "It's a waterproof dive bag. What the hell is it doing here?" He opened it and stuck his hand in. His face swung toward the others, and it wasn't good. His hand withdrew a small cup or bowl made from what looked like tarnished gold. There were markings engraved in the metal.

Chet leaned in with his flashlight. He had seen the markings before. "Oh, crap. Those are Egyptian, like the King Tut and Mummy stuff." He settled down in a squat to think. Turning to Hooker, he looked for some guidance. Hooker shrugged, knowing they were in way over his head. They had just clandestinely disturbed a crime scene, but they didn't know what the crime was.

Hooker squinted down his face as he rubbed it with his thumb and forefinger, searching for answers. Of the four men, Hooker had the most experience walking the other side of the line of the law. The two plus one future men of the law looked to him as a leader on this.

Hooker walked back over to the bushes and tree line, where he had noticed the old upside-down car rusting into oblivion. The years of rust had taken its toll on the steel. As he played his flashlight over the brown hulk, he could tell one of the doors had been open but was now crushed along with the rest of the top by the weight of the body. He knelt down and tried to see inside. The mice and other local denizens had chewed and nested the leathers, clothes, and stuffing of the interior. Rust was working on everything else.

He stood. "Hey Squirt, let's get a line down here and flip this."

The kid walked down to the access point that was easier to climb up. A few minutes later, the line and J-hook were tumbling down the hill with Hooker's unique roller chain attached.

Hooker pulled the rigging over to the car hulk and let out a sharp whistle. The line stopped feeding.

Hooker rigged the roller chain on the few areas he thought might be still strong enough to turn the car over. Short of a net and crane, Hooker knew the hulk would never leave the ravine. Pulling on the line, he gave two short whistles. The line started taking up slack slowly. The chains dug into the rotted metal but held. Gently, the hulk slewed around to square and then slowly rolled over. As it neared the tipping point, Hooker whistled a short sharp whistle.

The metal cadaver crashed onto its frame with rotted tires and wheels. The mass didn't even rock. The roll had crushed it even more. Hooker unhooked the chains and hook, and then whistled a long call for the Squirt to haul it away.

A few minutes later, as Hooker and Chet examined where the vehicle identification number should have been in the dashboard, the Squirt slid down and walked over. "Wow… that made quick work of this prom queen." Micha gave him a questioning look and realized the kid was probably let in on Hooker and his experience.

The other two were looking at a slotted hole where a plate with a long series of numbers should have been—instead of Hooker's hand. "Without the VIN, we can't trace whose car this was."

Chet started toward the driver's door, thinking of the more modern cars. Micha shook his head. "It won't be there on this car. My guess is this is pre-1940s. They didn't put the metal sticker on until after the Korean War."

Hooker grabbed the end of the hood and pulled. The Squirt saw him struggling and jumped to the other side. Soon, all four were lifting, and the rust finally gave away. With the hood up and where Hooker had hoped for an engine number, he only swore.

"What?" Micha echoed the Squirt.

Chet nodded at the engine. "It's a Lincoln straight-eight…"

Hooker finished. "And this is no Lincoln. I'll bet there is an extra tank back there where the back seat used to be, and it's made of copper. This was a moonshine runner. There won't even be any numbers on the engine. They were etched off with acid."

Micha looked at Hooker with a drawn face and one raised eyebrow. "Why, Hooker… it is amazing the things you know." He smiled.

The Squirt laughed. "Yeah, Maddie would be so proud of you."

Chet harrumphed. "Who do you think he learned it all from?"

Hooker wasn't laughing. "And it's who we are here for." Reminding Squirt, but not ready to share about the watch.

Hooker walked to the dry streambed and looked across at the cliff in the dark. The bones shone dully in the moonlight, but the night just seemed so wrong for the respect this job deserved. Hooker turned to where Chet had walked up behind him.

Chet, with a sober face, nodded. "We have four days without rain. How about we start early tomorrow?"

"What about the bag of stuff?"

Chet waved his head over his shoulder. "Throw it in the trunk of the wreck if we can get it open. Who's coming down here in the next few days besides us?"

Hooker looked at his watch with his light. He looked over at the Squirt talking to Micha as they leaned against the rusty hulk, and then back at Chet. "I can probably get in a tow or two also before we shut it down early enough to get the kid some rest."

Chet smiled, knowing both young guys still needed sleep to recover. "Let's get the trunk open."

As the two vehicles reached the end of the Snake, Micha turned west to go get some clean uniform pants and to clean his boots. Hooker jumped up onto the freeway and took the 17 back into San Jose and dropped Chet off.

Grabbing the mic from behind his head, he keyed the red switch twice.

Dolly's voice was almost instant in response. "I have a Peterbilt sitting on Polk Street in San Francisco. It needs to come down to the Fly. SFPD says they will probably be ready to release it in about an hour or two."

Hooker looked at the Squirt, who was making duck lips and nodding with smiling eyes. Long ride and easy money. The night didn't get much better.

"Is there a trailer?"

"Just the rig."

"Just need the cross street, sweetheart."

The Squirt nodded at the street name and turned toward Hooker. "I guess Togo's is closed at this hour."

Hooker smacked his lips like he had eaten something nasty. "Closed and your sister isn't working at the diner anymore. If it was near midnight, I'd swing by and say hi to Peter, but the pig they replaced Candy with ran everyone else off."

The Squirt chuckled. "Do you think we could get away with parking Mae out in front of Sam Woo's?"

"What do you know about Sam Woo's?" Hooker frowned as he upshifted. The kid just kept amazing him with the things he knew or was learning.

"One of the nurses at the hospital said she had her best experience there."

They both laughed. "Was she talking about the food or a Chinese guy?"

The big yellow truck swung north on the 101 freeway. With two elbows encased in black leather sticking out of the windows, an eerie blue glow underneath, and yellow lights in the wheel wells—Mae West dissolved into the night.

9

THE DIGGING WAS slow and careful as the men took turns excavating the bones. They tried to dig out each skeleton one at a time so they could keep them separate. Packed in and around the legs were three—once yellow diver's bags. One had broken, and some jewelry had spilled out into the cavity.

"There's another bag here, but the top was open when it was stuffed in." The Squirt pulled it free. "Or it looks like maybe there was a tear or something. Either way, some of this is stuff is loose." The kid moved slowly with a whisk broom from the working bed of Mae. It was hard for these amateur archeologists to know what to bring. So, for the most part, the four shovels stood unused, as the small gardening trowel seemed to get the most use, along with a small hand broom.

The canopy and folding table was the base of operations for packing the four body bags. The skeletons had almost no connections left due to the twenty years of wet soil to rot the flesh and a premium breeding ground for bugs crawling about in the earth and eating the flesh. Only once did Chet start humming and then realized he was voicing the old nursery rhyme of worms and playing cards on one's nose. He looked at the others who understood but showed no signs of humor. The day's work wasn't just another wreck in the night, where gallows humor was one of the common ways of dealing with the seemingly daily carnage.

Micha stood at the table where he and Hooker had just carried the hips to shoulders, one arm, and most of the other. He pointed at the missing left arm from the elbow down. "What do you think?"

"Maybe. Looks about right. Willie said Danny was about six-foot-two or so. This table is sixty inches…"

He was cut short by the Squirt's short bark in the hole. He crawled back out with a skull and part of a chain that should have had dog tags attached. "I think we have Maddie's brother." He walked over and gently placed the skull on the table. Handing the chain to Hooker, he said, "I think you're the one to hold on to this for now. Hopefully, we will also find the tags to go with it."

Hooker nodded and started to shove the partial chain in the chest pocket of his overalls. He dropped them into his left hand and reached back in for the shining thing he had picked up the night of the tow. Rubbing the item on his pant leg to clean it, he held it out.

His palm was almost covered with a large beetle. The statuette weighed almost a pound and appeared to be almost all out of gold. Micha was the first to break his fascination. "It's called a scarab. This would probably date back to the age of King Tut, or at least, Cleopatra."

The other three looked at the officer they actually only knew from work for the most part. Hooker asked, "You study this stuff?"

"Not really, just pick up a book here or there. There is a great museum over in Santa Clara; it has all of this kind of stuff. The wife likes museums, and it's a nice, quiet place to go."

Chet raised one eye and thought. "Is that the Rosicrucian Museum?"

Micha nodded, and Chet's face cleared. "My wife asked me a few times to go with her, but we never did." The regret was written on his face. He had adored his wife, but she was gone before they had done everything they wanted to do.

"I wonder if it's where this all came from?" Hooker mused. "I mean, we haven't looked at all of the stuff, but if it is all Egypt stuff…"

Chet rested his hand on the skeleton. "Let's square Danny away here, and then we have the table to take a look."

The two body bags lay in the shade, almost as if they were empty. Micha had brought some evidence tags, and they marked what they knew of each. Danny's had his name.

The table was soon filled with bowls, urns, jewelry, breastplates, armbands, small boxes, rings, and other gold jewelry. Almost nothing had jewels. Most were painted with iridescent paints reminding Hooker of the mother-of-pearl in the clear coats of lacquer on Mae. Mae looked nice and reflective but was dull compared to the enameling on the artifacts.

As they laid out the last pieces, the four stood back and just stared at the array filling the not so small table.

"Wow."

Chet nodded with pursed lips. "You can say that again, Squirt."

"What do you think it's all worth?" Hooker mumbled.

Micha shook his head. "How's your math. It's about fourteen and a half troy ounces to a pound, and the going rate for placer gold last summer was about one-fifty an ounce."

Hooker hiccupped a chuckle and looked at the Squirt. The kid moved his mouth then looked up. "Two thousand one hundred seventy-five per pound." Hooker smiled and gently slugged the kid's shoulder in slow motion as he looked back at Micha.

Micha looked past Hooker at the kid. "How the hell do you do that?"

The kid blushed, but Hooker explained. "He saw a multiplication table once. He just pulls it back up and looks for the right answer."

Micha scoffed at Hooker and looked at the kid. The Squirt rolled his lips in tight against his teeth and nodded as he rolled his shoulders in a moving shrug. "Pretty much. With numbers, they just seem to stack up and then just fall into the right order. But I can't really explain it, so Hooker's answer makes as much sense."

With the new information, they looked back at the table. They all knew there was well over a hundred pounds on the table. Chet's eyes rolled into his head. "Just by the gold, it's a lot more than my house is worth."

Micha harrumphed. "A lot more than all of our houses… even Manny and Stella's house included."

"But for the historical value?" Hooker looked at the kid. "It's only something a museum should have." He turned to Chet for an answer.

The Highway Patrol Captain raised his hands. "Hey, you're the lead on this adventure. I'm just along for the good food."

Hooker glanced at his watch. "Crap. We have fifty-eight minutes to get to Dolly's for dinner."

The other three repacked the dive bags as Hooker scrambled up the hill to the truck. Opening the door and letting Box out to do his business, he grabbed the mic on the only radio always live—the straight line to Dolly.

"1-4-1," he called. He knew she was cooking and waited.

Dina, one of Dolly's night dispatchers, responded. "Go ahead, Hooker. Dolly is in the middle of the sauce."

"10-4, Dina. All four of us are out on the Snake and a little filthy…"

"Your mind has always been that way, Hooker." She was purring now. "So what's the problem?"

Hooker had to think about what the problem could be. Dolly knew Hooker had been with Chet and Micha all day, and they, along with the Squirt, would be his guests for the Wednesday night dinner. But she didn't know about why they were together or why Hooker was taking a few days off.

"This tow is a little more complicated than we initially thought." Hooker released the red button and hung his head. It was now dark, and he could see the glow of the South Bay Area filling the night air with light. This was one of the perks of his huge territory, which the other drivers who ran the close area of the city never saw. All they saw were the lighted streets where Hooker saw the beauty in the night sky.

Dolly's smooth, but out of breath voice came over the truck's speakers. "How many times have you sat at my table and were already filthy from an early tow?"

He knew there were too many to remember. "Ok, but we'll still be late."

"So is the other guest."

Hooker frowned. Dolly's table usually sat twelve. Who sat at the table on any given Wednesday night was up to Dolly, and they were hand-picked. Anyone who had ever sat at her table knew there was a reason they were there and on that night with those other guests. Not every evening's agenda was evident. But if you were sitting there, you were on Dolly's agenda. More promotions, contracts, or elections were won or lost at Dolly's table. It was why anyone in the know, knew the greater San Jose area was owned and run by Dolly. She knew everyone's secrets and where all of the skeletons were buried—a fact that at the moment was not lost on Hooker.

"Guest... as in singular?"

"Correct."

"We will be there as soon as we can, mama."

"Dinner will only be ready when you four are here. Oh, and Hooker... did you find who you were looking for?"

Hooker looked at the large ravine. In the dark, it was just a large winding tear of blacker black than the rest of the landscape. He slowly keyed the mic, thought a moment, and then gave her the answer. "Yes... yes, we did."

His lips rolled in as he thought about Maddie, and the special 'aunt' she had become to him of the last decade. The slight librarian who looked bow-legged and fragile had surprised Hooker time and again with her knowledge, her steel, and her resilient, tough nature and body. At sixty, she still rode an old Indian motorcycle she had ridden years before across the Bonneville Salt Flats at over two hundred miles an hour. The idea and act of which never ceased to amaze and amuse Hooker.

The voice of another strong woman in his life oozed protectively through the speaker. "You fellas drive careful. Dinner can wait. It's just food."

Hooker keyed the mic twice and hung it back up. Leaving the door open for Box, he scrambled back down the hill.

The table was empty, and Hooker could see Chet and Micha hiding the second body bag back under the brush and away from the streambed. "I guess we can just leave everything here?"

Chet stood with his hands on the small of his back stretching. The gray-haired flattop only came with age and creaky bones. "I think these will be good, but maybe the dive bags should come up, and you can stash them at Willie's until we figure out what to do with the stuff."

Micha nodded as he beat his work gloves on his overalls.

The Squirt patted Hooker on the shoulder as he walked past. "I'll send the line down with the cluster bags."

Hooker frowned after him. *What the hell are cluster bags?* His answer came minutes later.

When the wreck is so bad larger pieces become blasted off a car, Hooker had a couple of net bags he had picked up years before. The netting was made from a thin, soft bronze and lead cable that was very flexible but didn't break. Hanging from the J-hook were both bags. Hooker had never really called them anything—but you never need to name anything when you are the only person working. Hooker reflected a warm smile as he unhooked the newly named cluster bags. It was good to have the Squirt around.

Ten minutes later, the giant yellow truck followed Micha's cruiser as they wound their way down the Snake toward dinner. The three men in the truck were quiet, each lost in their own thoughts.

10

A S EACH OF THE men stepped through the large steel-plated door, they gently bent over and kissed the large woman, in the muumuu and bare feet, on the cheek. Nobody made it past Dolly without the appropriate greeting. Hooker was the last through the door as he stopped to pick up Box. Snuggling his nose and lips into her fat neck, he laid the twenty-plus pounds of scarred up orange tabby across her chest. The purring was instant. Box was in his heaven spot.

Dolly fussed like a little girl. "Hooker, damn it all, stop. You're a sick young man." As he started to pull away, her hand clamped on his neck and back of his head. "I didn't say right away." They both got the giggles, and Box mewed his discontent at their horseplay.

The man sitting in a chair by Dolly's desk, Chet had only seen once or twice before. There was not much reason for a Highway Patrol Officer to ever go up to the State Supreme Court. He had seen Chief Justice Hitchcock 'The Knife' Hack when he had to sit in on court cases for classes.

The gentleman put down his cup of tea on Dolly's desk and rose quietly as the boisterous four horsemen bubbled out of the entry hall into the main dispatch room. He dabbed at his mouth with his handkerchief and slipped it in his slacks' pocket. The pencil-line mustache was a white line across his golf-tanned face.

Chet stepped over to make introductions. "Justice Hack, I'm—"

The man smiled perfunctorily and cut him off. "Please. Tonight I'm just Hitch. I believe you would be Chet, and this man would be Michael?"

"Micha, sir, short for Malachite, the stone, not the book in the bible."

The Justice smiled. "Yes, of course. I should have remembered from when I shook your hand at the academy graduation. You told me the same exact thing at the time, as well." Turning to Hooker, "Good to see you again, Hooker, and this must be the young man everyone is talking about." Hooker was trying to place the face.

John smiled and shortcutted the judge. "John, sir, but everyone calls me the Squirt."

"Yes," the judge nodded and shook his hand, "I had heard it happened. Well, let's see if we can get you through the academy quickly and on the road back to your own name, shall we?"

He looked at the mud stains on the bottoms of the jeans and caked in the nooks and crevices of their boots and shoes. "From the looks of things, you four had a productive day." Turning to face Hooker, "Are you finished, or is there more to do?"

Hooker thought about what this man might know and what he was willing to reveal at this time. After all, as Chet had alluded, this was in the gray area of clandestine. "I think there may be more to do, sir."

"Excuse me, gentlemen." Dolly stood in the door to the large kitchen with the long dining table. "You all know where the bathroom is to wash up. Dinner will be ready in ten minutes."

The dinner had been simple and adaptive—spaghetti with Dolly's special marinara sauce with Sicilian sausages from Chiaramonte's on North 13th Street. Tiny smears of the sauce were barely visible on the five plates where the garlic bread had all but hid the evidence.

In the other room, Hooker could hear the two dispatchers taking calls between bites. When Dolly cooks, everyone within reach eats. It was one of the perks or downfalls of the occupation. For eight hours, there was nothing to do but sit, take calls, and eat. The occupational hazard was evident in Dolly's quarter-ton and Dina's rapidly approaching the two hundred mark—pregnant or not. Karen, with over ten years working for Dolly, was somewhere in between. For Hooker, all of them had one thing in common—he loved nuzzling fat necks. It made them laugh, and they loved the attention, and it warmed Hooker's heart. He wasn't sure if it was love, but he did most certainly care deeply about his extended family. With Dolly and Stella, it was flat out unmitigated love.

Dolly put a large carafe of coffee in the middle of the men clustered at one end of the table. "Gentlemen, there is no dessert tonight. If you need anything sweet, we three girls will be just outside this door." Uncharacteristically, she closed the door.

Since the start of Hooker's obligatory attendance of her Wednesday night dinner and been placed as the anointed head of the table, he had never seen her leave the room or close the door. Never.

He turned toward the judge. Up until now, the conversations had been light and covered sports or amusing little things going on in the South Bay, like shootings and which Mafia was moving into what area, and would Stanford football ever be anything other than a joke. The judge felt Hooker's scrutiny.

"You have a question, Hooker, and I'm guessing it is about my being here."

Hooker nodded. "Outside of us, there are maybe only three other people who even knew what we were doing today."

The judge looked down at his mug of cooling coffee. He thought about trust and knowledge and the power of those, as well as how fragile they could be. He looked up at Hooker. "You don't know anything about me, other than those times I stopped by the hospital after Manny had been shot. My family, well, my sister still owns about two thousand acres of truck farm down in the Hollister area. When I was a kid, we had about double the spread over near Salinas. There was a road running down the middle of our spread. Because it ran in and around homesteads, it had many very tight turns at the corners of the property. The moonshine runners used to call it El Camino d' El Diablo, The Devil's Highway. That road was the collecting road..."

Hooker finished "The south end of the Snake."

The judge nodded. "Parked outside is my Lincoln Town Car. Parked in my garage is a 1968 Road Runner with a 1970 440 six-pack Super Commander with a custom-built Max Wedge clip and shaker hood.

William and Maddie balanced the four-speed with a 4:11 rear end. William tubbed the rear and clipped the axle for an extra four inches on each side. On a piss poor night up at Fremont, I can blow the doors on some low eights. If I want the mid-sevens, I will have to insert a roller and chute. Then it would just be a factor of adjusting for the alcohol." He blinked as he watched Hooker take it all in.

"What color?"

"B-5 blue."

Hooker blinked but maintained eye contact. "The torque ripped a hole on the left side, so we welded in an eight by twelve of quarter-inch plate. The torsion bars Stimson Moly steel from Sweden, they took four months to make and get here. The pressure in the clutch is twelve pounds off a hair-trigger, and your back seat is a bucket hold for gallon bottles."

The two had just gone behind the barn and pissed as high up the wall as they could. They had compared penises, sniffed each other's butts, and come away satisfied. The judge was a silent member of the family.

Hooker looked at the other three and nodded. The tension waned as Chet reached for the coffee carafe and held it up. "More coffee… Hitch?" The man smiled and pushed out his mug.

Hooker looked at his mug and asked, "How much do you know?"

The judge sipped his hot coffee and thought. Placing his mug on the table, he frowned slightly. "Two days ago, I caught wind of a potential territorial dispute involving a found skeleton. In these kinds of matters, they usually make their way up to us in San Francisco, so it's not unusual for us to get some kind of early warning.

"Then, all of a sudden, there is no dispute. In fact, there is nothing. It was as if no skeleton had been found. That's when our antennas really go up and start to vibrate so hard the tips start hitting the walls in the hallways. Because when there is a case and then a case disappears, one of two things has happened. Either the FBI rolled into town, or the case just went underground.

"We didn't see or hear of any Feds swinging their dicks down this way, so we knew it was going dark. That, gentleman, is a very worrisome occurrence because it usually ends up with the need to fill some vacancies in the department. But then, last night I got a call from an old friend. He told me he had a hand and a watch. He also thought it would be in the interest of many to make a dinner reservation at the most powerful restaurant in the Bay Area.

"I kind of remember Danny, but he was a little older than me. I went to school with his kid sister. When I called down this morning to leave a message, Dolly was already here. She confirmed you four were out digging around. So I figured I'd come down to find out what was going on and to assure you four I have your back. From here on out, you are investigating an old case I have full knowledge of, and it is being kept under wraps and within my purview.

"Legally, as of this afternoon, you four are attached to my office and are investigating a case that may or may not exceed the boundaries of the local authority. So with all that and the powers vested in me and my office, I hereby deputize the four of you as bench investigators, and you only answer to me in these matters until we reach an agreement or resolve the case to meet with jurisprudence. Do I have your agreements?"

Micha was quick. "Does this mean I don't have to burn days off?"

Hitch smiled. "Working for me pays a lot more than you make on the street. And it also means more than just the paycheck. You are all on my office payroll for the duration. Including the Squirt..." he glared at Hooker, "especially the Squirt."

The four looked stunned at the turn of events and nodded.

The judge raised his mug to his lips and looked at Hooker. "So, where are we?"

Hooker raised his eyebrows at the other conspirators and leaned back to fish the keys out of his pocket. Throwing them across. The Squirt's hand was already in the air, "You only need to bring in one."

The Squirt rose and left, reclosing the door.

Hooker turned to the judge. "We've excavated two whole skeletons so far. The Squirt thinks he could feel at least two more. He also thinks that will be it unless there are more under those two. The cavity stops in the back with a large boulder, so we know it doesn't go back any farther. The overhead is pretty solid as well.

"There is a hulk of a late 1930 or early 1940 four-door sedan down there. We're pretty sure it's connected. The back seat is the same as your

Road Runner. It wasn't a serious shine-runner, but more of a gentleman's runner. So we're sure it was owned by someone who didn't need to run the Snake."

The judge mused. "What about the VIN numbers?"

Chet coughed. "Rusted out." He smirked at Hooker. "Hooker stuck his hand straight through the punch-out where the plate should have been."

Micha added, "And the engine was a hot-rod out of a Lincoln straight-eight."

"So if the engine was stuffed in during the war years, then there probably would be no record of sale we could use to trace it either."

Hooker wagged his head as he scratched at the long scars on his head. "No, and nothing survived to identify the other body either. If it weren't for the watch being all high-quality metal, we wouldn't have anything."

The door opened, and the Squirt slipped in with one of the dive bags. Without saying a word, he handed it and the keys to Hooker. The judge's eyebrows raised as he watched Hooker's smirk pull to one side.

Hooker stood. "There is one tiny complication to all of this…" As he up-ended the bag on the table in front of them, the gold objects flowed out. A large scarab skittered across the table and landed in the judge's lap.

Hooker sat as the judge raised the object from his lap. His eyes were huge as he looked at the unexpected sculpture. He knew what he held was well over a pound of pure gold. But the detail and craftsmanship of the sculpture went well beyond the mere value of the gold. The enameled blue iridescent wings rippled purple to red in the fluorescent light. On the belly were incised or carved ancient Egyptian hieroglyphics.

Micha sipped his coffee then commented. "We ran the math. You're holding about three grand of gold."

The judge looked up in horror. "But the value of the piece…"

He was looking at four slow nodding smirks.

"And this was in the cavity with the bones?"

Hooker nodded. "And three more bags just like this."

The judge picked up a small bowl and a chain. Looking closely, he ran his fingers over the engravings. "But these aren't just a small collection some collector would have. These are more like what you would find in a museum." He pushed his glasses up onto his head and brought the fine chain closer to his face. "A wealthy collector and I know a few in San Francisco who might have a couple of items like this along with some pottery shards…" he looked up and waved his palm at the hoard on the table, "but this alone would be a prized exhibit of any museum."

"That was our thinking," Chet said, looking over the rim of his coffee.

The Squirt mused, not sure of his position. "You mentioned you knew some collectors…?"

The judge looked up and drew down his glasses slowly. "Yes, but not ones into Egyptology. My friends run more toward more recent and local in their predilections. West Coast Indian baskets or weaponry is more their speed. Certainly, not anyone who even starts down the road toward idols or ancient art craft of this quality," he held up the scarab, "and most certainly not in such precious metals."

As he carefully placed the scarab, bowl, and chain back with the other loot, he then looked around the table. "Any ideas where you plan to proceed from here?" His eyes rested on Hooker. The judge sensed that despite his youth, Hooker was the central figurehead of the group.

Hooker watched his finger smudge along the table. "There is a museum in Santa Clara…"

11

WHEN HOOKER FINALLY pulled up out front, the museum was, in a way, what he expected—but not *where* he expected it. The last many blocks, Hooker kept frowning. The residential neighborhood was known as the Rose Garden District. With pristinely manicured lawns as display floors of specimen sized and tended shrubbery and trees, the last sort of building he expected was a large Egyptian temple with colored columns and an expanse of land.

Hooker eyed the large lawn. He swung open the door with his boot. "Go ahead, Box."

As the cat stood stiff-legged peeing on the lawn, Hooker quietly sat thinking. They had called ahead, and he had an appointment with the director of the museum, a man named James Sutter.

Box finished, scratched, and started looking around for any dogs he could tear up while he was in an easy pickings type of neighborhood. Hooker just closed his eyes and slowly shook his head. Hooker had found the large cat as a tiny kitten in a box abandoned under a stripped car behind the Almaden winery. The kitten had been badly beaten up as well as chewed up, obviously by a dog or dogs. Hooker had put the box with the kitten in his truck and hauled him to a vet. The kitten had purred the entire way and even as the vet examined him while Hooker held him. The vet had tried to convince Hooker the little life would be better off being put down. Hooker knew better, and the vet had spent hours patching him up. The cat and Hooker had been partners ever since.

"Come on, Box. There is nothing here for you to have a good fight. This kind of neighborhood is filled with nothing but bait like Poodles and Yorkies." A woman who was walking her Yorkie heard Hooker, and with horror in her eyes, scooped up her precious piece of fluff, turned around, and quickened her walk as she retreated. Hooker closed his eyes and pinched the bridge of his nose.

Box watched the retreating target with his one eye in critical evaluation, and then bound back into the truck to settle in his box. Hooker scratched Box's head and twiddled with his one ear. "I have an important meeting in here. So stay in the truck until I get back. Maybe we can get some ice cream after I get out."

He slid from the truck and closed the door with the window still open. He never believed in locking Box in. Box was his partner, and not a possession to be locked up.

As he entered the museum, he saw a small sign pointing toward the offices. The woman at a desk mulling over a document looked up surprised. "May I help you?" Hooker had the feeling the museum didn't get a lot of foot traffic.

"My name is Hooker, and I have an appointment with a Mr. Sutter…" The woman was blinking as if she were trying to see if Hooker was real or just her imagination.

Suddenly, she came to a conclusion. "Oh, yes, you called earlier." She picked up the phone on her desk and dialed a few numbers. "Yes, James, the man is here to see you. A Mr. Hooker?"

She replaced the phone in the cradle and looked up at Hooker, blinking rapidly. "He'll be right down." She blinked some more and then returned to mulling over whatever she had been reading before.

Hooker watched her with silent and hidden amusement. A deadpan face while you should be laughing was a game he learned to play with Manny and Stella. Not reacting to conversations or events had held him in good stead many times during towing—from the hilariously stupid to the tragic insanity humanity visits upon itself at high and low speeds.

"Mr. Hooker, I presume?"

Hooker turned to take in a slight mouse of a man with a bowtie. "It's just Hooker, sir."

"No first name, or is that your first name?" They shook. His grip was interestingly firm and friendly.

"Actually, a combination of all of it. Horatio Octavio O'Keller; for most people, it is just easier to use Hooker."

The man blinked a few times. Hooker was sure he must be related to the woman. "Hooker it is then. How may I help you?"

Hooker thought about the woman and what he needed to ask. His antenna was up, and he could feel her attention was more in her ears than it was toward what she had been reading. "Maybe you could show me a little bit of the museum, and we can talk as we walk."

The man glanced at his watch. Hooker was sure it was more of an affectation to let Hooker know he was a busy man, more than his checking the time. "I won't take much of your valuable time."

The man considered the young man in a leather jacket, white t-shirt, and jeans over work boots. He was certain he would not be spending much time with whatever this young man of the street wanted. He nodded and held out his hand. "Then let us start with the main gallery, shall we?"

As they entered the impressive gallery with a diorama display of an ancient Egyptian city, the man started in a routine script. "The Rosicrucian Museum was originally founded by Dr. Harvey Spencer Lewis in the early days of the 1920s. He funded several archeological digs while augmented his original collection. The collection started with a small Sekhmet statue but soon grew. In 1928, Dr. Lewis presented to the public a collection he named The Rosicrucian Egyptian Oriental Museum. It was originally housed in what is now the administration building."

Hooker looked about the main gallery. "So this is not the original building?"

"Oh, no. The collection had grown over the years, and in the sixties, Dr. Lewis's son secured the funds to build this building, as well as the gardens."

"What about the smaller items? Like the statue or jewelry? *Life* magazine did quite an issue on King Tut. There seemed to be a lot of gold artifacts."

The man blinked as he studied the young street tough dressed in a leather jacket. He wasn't sure about his safety at the moment.

Hooker sensed the man's unease. He slipped his right hand into his pants pocket and withdrew the large scarab. He held it out to the director. The man slowly took it and examined it carefully.

As the director turned the scarab over and saw the writing on the underside, Hooker spoke softly. "Let's talk about 1953."

The man looked up, almost dropping the artifact. His face was as shocked as if Hooker had just slapped him. Hooker knew he had just hit pay dirt.

"Come with me." The small man turned and walked into another gallery and stood in front of a case where there were two matching scarabs—duplicates of the one in the man's hand. The man looked to Hooker with a question on his face.

Hooker held his gaze for a few moments and then began examining each of the display cases in turn. There were a few pieces Hooker didn't recognize, but for the most part, this was the same collection he knew was in four dive bags.

He finally turned to face the man who was waiting patiently for him. He had the man's full attention as well as his curiosity. Hooker gracefully waved his palm around the gallery. "All or at least most of these are fakes."

The man stood for a moment and then silently nodded.

He held up the scarab in his hand. There was a question on his face. Hooker nodded. "By the weight, you can tell it is not a fake."

The man sagged as his hand dropped to his side. He then stepped over to Hooker and handed him the scarab back. "Maybe we should go to the administration office to have this conversation."

As they walked across the grounds, which was an Egyptian garden King Tutankhamen would have felt at home in, the man started to ask Hooker a question, then stopped. He looked about at the deserted gardens. Finally, he stopped. "You have to see this from my perspective. From out of the blue, a young man who looks like he rides a motorcycle with a gang brings me a sacred statue and then tells me all of our other treasures are fakes…"

Hooker empathized with the man. "Trust me for a little while longer. I mean no harm. I'm just looking to make something right again."

"But how did you come by…"

"For now, let's just leave it at… I found it." Hooker examined the man's pained eyes.

The man turned, and they continued toward the distant building.

As they entered the man's office, he offered a seat with his hand. "Can I get you something to drink?"

"No, I'm fine, thank you."

James picked up the phone and dialed a local number. Hooker could hear the rings on the other end. Someone picked up. "Hello, Donald, it's James over at the museum. I have a gentleman in my office who I believe you need to talk to. Could you come over, please?"

Hooker heard the sound of the response. The man thanked him and hung up.

He leaned back in his chair, looking at Hooker. Hooker was certain he was a great mystery to this man. "Donald won't be long. He only lives a block from here." His right hand waved behind him. He leaned forward to the desk. "Could I see it again… please?"

Hooker fished the scarab out of his pocket and passed it across. The man sat looking at the inscription on the underside. Hooker could tell he knew what it said and was in his own world at the moment. Hooker watched as the man became less and less attached to the room they were in. It was the kind of concentration he was familiar with watching Manny with a case or Willie with an engine or another complicated auto part. He even saw it in Maddie, as she would pour over a book containing information she wanted. It was the focus of a person who knew so much about what they were looking at it was as if it were a part of their identity.

A light rap on the doorframe startled Hooker. The elder gentleman in chinos and a sweater looked in. "Hello, you're the gentleman I am to talk to?"

James looked up and blinked several times, orienting himself. He squinted. "Oh, yes, Donald." He stood with his hand out toward Hooker, who was also rising.

Hooker stuck his hand out. "My name is Hooker."

"Pleased to meet you, Donald Phelps."

James made the connection. "Donald was the director in 1953."

The elder man's head whipped around to look at James, and then he noticed the scarab in his hand. Looking back at Hooker, there was a new light in his eye. Hooker knew the look. It was one that usually appeared in the eye of an animal who knew it was prey.

Hooker softened his demeanor. "I come in peace." They both looked at James, who was standing pinching the bridge of his nose as he held the scarab out for Donald to take.

The man took the object and gave it a cursory exam. James cinched the suspicion. "He knows. All of it."

The older man took the only other chair in the room. He collapsed. Hooker watched as the man deflated, and then became at rest as if a great weight had been lifted. He held up the scarab and looked at Hooker. "So this...?"

"Is the real one." Hooker nodded.

The man rolled his lips tight against his teeth. "So what now?"

Hooker sat as he watched James do the same. "What happens now... is you tell me what happened in 1953."

"1953..." the man's eyes became unfocused, and his head drifted off course and came to rest, looking out the second-story window, "what happened... should have never happened. I had only been recently elected to the position of director then. There were only a few paid positions in those days. A lot of the work was done by members of the society. We were basically a volunteer organization back then."

"Society?"

"The Ancient Mystical Order Roseae Crucis." He said it as if Hooker would or should have knowledge of it, so Hooker didn't ask for clarification. The education could come later at the hands of Maddie. Hooker just nodded.

"The guard duties were rotated through the membership. Mostly, it was a boring routine of wandering about the museum. Especially, the night duty—a tour of boring torture, from usually about eight at night until six in the morning when the cleaning volunteers would come to prepare the museum for guests. Even when it was in this building, the sweeping and dusting was a long and labor-intensive job for the four volunteers." Hooker could read the suffering on the man's face. Obviously, he had been a longtime volunteer before landing the job of director.

The man, laying his head back, remembered the pain or headache of the night in question. "We had a young man who was an almost regular volunteer for the night duty. We later learned he used the nights to either catch up on his rest or engage in unseemly activities with his fiancée."

He leaned his head forward to see if Hooker understood the circumstances. Hooker did.

"Well, obviously, those night forays into their indiscretions had a result, and they needed to get married. And in those days, the only place you could get married, in the middle of the night, in the Bay Area was in the Tenderloin of San Francisco. As to whether the bond was legitimate or not has no bearing on this matter. Suffice it to say, one night, this guard took the liberty of being unsupervised and ran off with his girl to elope. When he returned, about four in the morning, the one gallery had been sacked.

"There was a member who did private investigations, but there was no evidence of entry at the time. He snooped about but could never turn up any leads. It was as if the items had literally vanished in a puff of smoke."

He smiled as he leaned forward. "I can tell you… it was the spookiest thing ever. Some of the marginal members, who were only interested as a cursory association, fled. Others, seeing it as one of the great mysteries, became staunch. It had a very galvanizing effect on the select membership, who was in the know of inner workings—such as the board."

He lay back. "Years later, we had some major work done on the roof, and one of the workers discovered the pins in the hinges to one of the trap doors had been removed and then put back, thus using the lock as the hinge. The doors are large and heavily insulated with rock wool bats. The only key to the lock is kept in this office, and the lock is unique. Nobody ever suspected the weak link, as it were, was the hinge."

"Why didn't you call the police?"

"The last thing we wanted was a scandal and for the word to get out that the most valuable items in the museum had flown the coop. The membership would have had our hides for book covers and then fled with their money. You see, the membership provides and supports the museum, not the other way around."

"So you made the fakes."

He nodded. "It was the only course we could think of at the time. We closed the gallery for renovations and kept stalling the general membership about this problem until we had obtained the faux artifacts. Once we reopened the gallery, the only hard part was keeping the secret safe between these walls." He held his hands out to indicate the walls of the office.

"So the secret of 1953 was passed down from director to director." The former director nodded a mirror of the current one. Hooker pursed his lips, thinking, and then frowned. "So where do you go to get fakes made without the membership catching wind of it?"

The older man smiled, rubbed at his nose, and then tossed his hand in dismissal. "To the source, of course. We went back to Egypt with a stack of photographs. Several of the artifacts were already being knocked off by very good artisans, like the scarab, for instance. The iridescent enameling on the gold is a secret formula handed down for millennia within families of artisans there in Egypt. So we could simply look for the best representatives and purchase them as tourist trinkets."

Hooker smiled softly. "And simply re-establish the exhibit and voila, nobody is the wiser."

The man nodded. "Along with a few new flourishes to justify the long delay and renovations to the exhibit. In those days, fresh paint was enough, but when you throw in a few new artifacts, there is renewed excitement instead of suspicion or resentment."

Hooker knew he was missing something. "So did anyone ever figure out who actually did the theft?"

"Not conclusively. We had our suspicions, but we had no way to prove anything. We might have found fingerprints, but without going to the police, they wouldn't do us any good. So we never pursued any more investigations. We simply installed the fakes and carried on with our lives as if nothing had ever happened. Until today…"

"Who did you suspect?" Hooker asked.

"About time, we were having a lot of work done. There was a new roof being laid and then installation of a modern air conditioning system. With all of that, there were electricians, roofers, sheet metal men, plumbers… and the list goes on. Any one of the workers or group of workers could have done it."

Hooker thought about the different workers. "Would you still have the work orders or receipts?"

The older director looked to the newer. James frowned as he pursed his lips. "I suppose… maybe down in storage." He turned to Hooker. "Why? What good would it do? It was twenty years ago. Some or most of those companies are probably out of business by now."

"Maybe, but I have a hunch it may help me figure this all out." He glanced at his watch and stood. "I have to be somewhere else now, but if you could see about finding those records, I can see about finding more of what was stolen from you." He fished out his wallet and removed a business card. "When you find something, you can always reach me through this number." He placed the card on the desk.

The older director looked once again at the scarab then offered it to Hooker.

Hooker held up his hand in a stop. "No, keep it. It is rightfully yours. Let's call it a down payment in good faith."

The two men smiled and nodded, and then handed it back to Hooker. "We know he will come back to us… after he has gathered his friends."

Hooker knew if the receipts still existed, they would find them. After all, a museum is all about artifacts and record-keeping.

HOOKER SCRAMBLED DOWN the hillside into the ravine. The other three were under the canopy arranging bones in a body bag. Hooker noticed one more bag off to the side. He glanced over at the hole in the hillside. There seemed to be a flat, scraped-smooth floor. Even the pickiest of bears would find it in move-in condition.

"Four total?"

Chet looked up. "According to our expert excavator here, yes, it would appear so."

The Squirt looked up the ravine and wiped at his face. Turning, he looked at Hooker. His eyes were red and wet. He passed the tip of his tongue along his drawn lips. "I know I don't want to do forensics or crime scene stuff." He nodded back at the cavern. "All of the walls are firm and weren't dug at. The same holds true for the bottom." He reached in his front left pocket. "Here, I also found these this morning." He laid a pair of dog tags and what was left of the chain in Hooker's hand.

Hooker looked at the name. They were Danny's tags.

Micha cleared his throat as he began to zip up the bag. "We figure he didn't stop off when he hit the base. Probably landed in San Francisco and took a bus or something down to Ord. Somewhere along the way, he got off."

"That would explain why the family never saw him come home." Micha and Chet nodded.

Chet bent down and picked up a piece of rusted rippled metal. Anyone who drove in the United States could tell you what it was just by the shape. "The Squirt here figured out the license number. I called it in. It took a while, but they found the records in Sacramento. It was registered to a 1926 Diamond T truck."

Hooker kicked at the dirt. "Crap."

Chet chuckled. "Not so fast, and you owe the jar a few dollars by my count."

Hooker smiled up at the man. He knew Chet was right. He had been kind of gutter-mouthed lately.

Chet bent down again and came up with some old papers. "This is your employee's responsibility here."

The Squirt smiled but blushed. Shyly, he turned toward Hooker. "I got to thinking about how people are lazy. There are a lot of people who never put their front license plate on the front. So I figured most people would just put it where it would be convenient."

Hooker slapped his forehead with the heel of his hand. "The trunk."

Chet smiled. "It was still wrapped in the oil-paper they used to send them out wrapped in. The oil and wax and the fact it was above most of the flooding saved it from rusting out." He pulled the license out of the paper. The black letters still shined as did most of the yellow background.

Hooker smiled at the plate and then looked up at Chet, and then the Squirt. "Damn, kid, I might even have to start paying you a wage."

"You mean more than the two roofs over my head, food to make me fat, and all the grief you can heap on me? Oh, Massa, Squirt don't deserve such goodness." In horror, he looked over at Micha. "I didn't mean anything, Micha."

The man was looking at the kid pensively. He reached out his hand and rested it on the Squirt's shoulder. "I know you didn't. I was just thinking about how good it sounded. I wonder if I can get away with something similar with my wife."

None of them were laughing. But they did see the humor. Hooker cautioned, "We've met your wife, Micha. I don't think you had better even try it with Bobbie Sue. I don't know which I would be afraid of most, the Injun side or the Cajon."

Micha looked at Hooker with big eyes and a smirk. "Good point, Hooker. I think I'll just stick with the successful *'Yes, Dear.'*"

Hooker smiled and looked at Chet. "So did you run this plate, too?"

"Was wondering when we were getting back to the serious work at hand." He looked at the plate in his hand. "As a matter of fact, it came back to a 1937 Chevrolet Master Deluxe." He turned to look at the rusted hulk. "I would say it fits the bill. Heavy suspension, oversized brakes, and plenty of room for an extra tank or a hold box like this one. Four doors and by the end of the war, they were on used lots for two or three ten-spots. People were very tired of driving the same old car for ten or twelve years. The bulletproof rear-ends were great for making into hill climbers, too. So, if you wanted an unassuming car that would never get a second glance, and could run some great amount of moonshine, this would be your car."

"And it was registered to…"

"A Giovinito something. I think it's a Greek name. I've got it written down up at the car and the address, too." He leaned on the table with a flat hand. "No matter what, it's not going to be a very hot lead. The guy died in 1961. The car was last registered in 1952. So it's still an uphill battle."

Hooker looked at the very tired man. "If solving mysteries was easy, everyone would do it." Neither blinked nor smiled. Although it was true, it still made Hooker an outlier. But Hooker would be the first to admit—it wasn't just him—it was his family.

Hooker stood with Micha at the bottom of the ravine as they watched the last of the equipment being winched up by the Squirt. The afternoon had turned chilly, and the two were back in their jackets with four hands stuffed in pockets.

Micha waxed into common memories. "Who would have thought, all those years ago, standing in the rain with a prom queen dead in your arms, we would be digging up four skeletons and a mystery?"

Hooker thought about the defining night in their friendship as he watched the large package of tent and table slowly ascended the cliff. The chill of the evening underscored the memory.

It had been a large wreck with many cars creatively parking all over the south and northbound lanes of the 101 freeway. The last of the cars had been towed by various other wreckers when the then fifteen-year-old Hooker, driving on a bogus license, noticed a red truck parked wrong in the garden area of the cloverleaf of the two crossing freeways.

Hooker pointed out the truck in the dark and rain to Micha. They ran across the southbound lanes from the wide median. Hooker saw a young girl sitting in the driver's side. He asked if she was all right through the door. As he opened the door, she slumped over into his arms, asking him to please not let her die. She was gone by the time Micha came up behind Hooker a couple of heartbeats later. The two young men stood in the rain, letting it wash away their anguish.

Hooker watched as the Squirt reeled in the extended boom, and the package disappeared over the cliff edge. Thinking of Maddie and finding her brother Danny after all these years, he turned to the Highway Patrol Officer and friend. "Who knew a dying prom queen would be the easy one?"

With fists stuffed in their jackets, the two men strolled down the ravine to what had become the easiest access to the road above. Hooker could feel the weight of the season bearing down. It would become busier for towing as the drunks worked hard at filling his nights. People would force the smiles and joyousness into their voices with each new holiday— to suppress the disappointments, or loneliness became all too obvious. Also, would be the holes in lives—from people no longer there.

Hooker clinched the dog tags that had become hot in his pocket. And as he began to climb the hill, he thought with apprehension about the talk he would soon have to have with Maddie.

13

"HOOKER?" HOOKER GRABBED the mic from behind his head. "Go ahead, Dispatch."

Karen, the day manager's voice eased across from the speaker. "I know you vampires hate being out at this hour, but there is a tow you may have some interest in. Fly is on the line and wants an answer, toot sweet."

Hooker dropped two gears and pulled the large Bakelite steering wheel into the slow cloverleaf onto 680 headed north. He glanced over at the Squirt and the side mirror to watch the mangled bread truck wobble behind. Straightening out onto the freeway, he merged and clicked through the lost two gears, adding another.

Keying the red button, "What's the Fly got in her web?"

There was a moment's silence as Hooker signaled left and changed lanes as he overtook an empty produce-hauling trailer and tractor. The season was gone, so the wire mesh trailers were hauled north to Oregon to be filled with the Christmas trees the Bay Area consumed.

The radio sparked. "Seventy-two Mack, max twin, long boy with a nose who lost the fight with the 247 Express last night." Hooker followed the shorthand of towing large trucks. The newer Mack truck was probably a long-haul or over the road, with a driving team who didn't know where they were and had stopped on the railroad tracks to look at a map. It wasn't the first time he had seen this kind of fatal mistake, but rarely was it made by drivers with enough experience to drive overweight loads.

"What was the load?"

"Forty-two-foot Grand Banks fishing boat."

"Do I get the trailer, too?" Hooker smiled over at the Squirt and wiggled his eyebrows. "You think your sister would like to go out fishing with me?" The Squirt laughed.

"She says the boat is toast, but you get the double haul with the empty sled."

Hooker eased off the fuel as he signaled to exit. Dropping a gear, he flipped the switch on the Jake break—flooding air into the engine to create backpressure, gently slowing the rig. As he flicked off the Jake and its hammering noise—illegal on city streets, he keyed the mic.

"Where's it at, and how soon does she want it?"

"She needs the tractor before Monday morning and the trailer anytime by Wednesday."

"What's the catch?" Three days to tow a truck was too easy.

"It's in the Salinas Impound."

Hooker smiled. "Is it cleared?"

"Insurance has written off on it, so it's good to tow."

Just when he needed to go snoop in the area, it didn't get better than that. Hooker smiled. "Tell her I'll drop by later for the papers. She'll have both of them in the back lot by Sunday night."

"10-4, Hooker. Dispatch out."

Hooker double-clicked the key as he hung the mic behind his head. Thinking, he dropped four gears and wagged the gear shifter in neutral as he rolled to a stop at a red light.

"So it looks like we get paid to go track down this Giovanni guy?" The Squirt smiled out the passenger window over his leather-jacketed arm, mirroring Hooker. An early Christmas gift from their friend Sweets and his brother Danny was greatly appreciated by both the Squirt and Hooker. The uniform of the day in the truck was a black leather jacket over starched white t-shirt, jeans, and boots unless your natural uniform was orange and white striped fur.

"It would seem so." Hooker's smirk pulled to the right and away from the still fresh scars. His right hand dangled and found the single fuzzy ear. His stomach growled as he thought about lunch on the piers of Monterey's Cannery Row—*and maybe we can find Box a little fresh crab or fish for lunch, too.*

Minutes later, they stood at the back end of Mae. "Sounds like a sweet deal. We get to jerk a prom queen and a Betty to pay the fuel, and it puts us down where we need to be—to seriously do some detective work, too." The Squirt ran the levers to drop the bread truck while Hooker finished the paperwork.

"Ever have crab so fresh you choose it out of a tank, watch it boil, and then sit on the end of a wharf and eat it out of a pile of newspaper?"

The Squirt looked over as he let go of the levers. "I've never had crab before. Does it taste like shrimp? Because I've had shrimp at the diner a few times, and it was good." He went to unhook the J-hooks from the front axle of the bread truck.

Hooker watched him in horror. "You're not talking about those little things with all the breading they deep fry, are you?"

The Squirt stood up, and his eyebrows flared up, and then he frowned. "Yeah, why?"

Hooker slowly closed his eyes as his face fell forward to meet his hand as he muttered, "Oh, Saint Dolly and Willie, save me from the children." He looked up at the sound of approaching footsteps.

"They told me you were fast, but I didn't expect you until after midnight." The pudgy, balding office type strolled up with a check in his hand. He stuck out his right hand. "Joss Baker."

"Hooker. Someone broke into the crypt, and when we found out we didn't burn up in the sunlight, we figured we might as well just do some towing."

The man chuckled, and they exchanged check and bill. Hooker pointed at the large dent-gash in the side. "She was tracking with a wobble. I think you are probably looking at a bent frame."

"So it's not repairable?"

"You need to talk to your insurance adjuster. If it's worth enough, then I'll probably be back out to pull it down to the Fly in San Jose or over to

Alex's over in San Leandro. Both can take it off the frame and re-rack the frame straight. It's what they do every day." Hooker handed the man his business card, as well as the Fly's.

"We'll let you know." The man tapped the cards on his thumb holding the paperwork. "Thanks for the quick response."

The Squirt walked up, slapping his gloves in his open hand. "We're here whenever you need a quickie." The man frowned until the kid pointed out the slogan painted on the side of the towing boom: *Southside Hooker — When you need a quickie.*

The man smiled and waved as he walked away.

Hooker smiled at the Squirt.

"What?"

Hooker laughed and shook his head. "Nothing." He leaned his weight back on his heels and looked down his nose at the kid. "So, boss, where to now?"

The kid glanced at his watch. Then his face brightened. "Time for a little massage therapy."

Hooker's face pulled to the one side as he nodded in a smirk. *You learn fast, kid.*

THE LIGHT LUNCH after their massages had also been a stalling tactic. Hank liked having Candy, and whoever the other student was, around. But Willie had called Maddie to see if she could get away from the library for a while for a long lunch.

Candy and the other student had been properly hugged and sent on their way back to school. The dishes were cleared, and only the coffee mugs and carafe cluttered the table. The room was quiet, as Hank had decided he needed to run into town to get something to fix for dinner. Willie sat next to the woman, who had been his best friend for as long as he cared to remember, quietly holding her hand.

Hooker watched the woman stare at the watch and dog tags he had just placed on the table in front of her. He studied the small twitch in the jaw muscle that was there when she was figuring out things. Usually, it was about ratios in engines or rear-ends of cars to make them faster or better. This time, it was more about a weight that had been in her heart for a long time.

In the soft light coming through the north-facing window over the sink, Hooker studied the gray hairs. They had snuck in so slowly over the course of their friendship Hooker had forgotten how old she truly was. She had been about fifty when he had met her ten years before.

After taking Hooker in, Willie had told the kid he wasn't going to make him go to school knowing he would just run away again. But he did insist his education be continued. Nobody had mentioned it would also continue even after Hooker had passed his GED. Now, at twenty-five, he was still held to reading, learning, and papers or reports on as wide a range of subjects as there were aisles in the library she ran.

Hooker thought back to the first day she had sat down at the reading desk. Hooker had no idea who this slight bandy-legged older woman was. Her hair was pulled back in a hard tight bun. Hooker for years figured she had to use a come-a-long to pull it so tight until he made a smart-assed remark, and her small hand descended onto and then into his shoulder. The pain wouldn't have been as great if he had simply placed his shoulder in a bench vice and run it home until the collar-bone cracked. The small steely grip carried a lesson he never forgot. Smartass remarks were only made in jest and should never carry even a hint of malice or hurt.

Hooker harrumphed with a soft, silent chuckle. How was he to know back then he would eventually have a large extended family who held a daily interrelationship Olympics in smartass remarks? Never in malice. All jabs carried an unspoken but understood message of love, trust, and ultimate caring. As Willie had become his trusted, much-loved uncle, Maddie was his aunt.

From the first day, Hooker had learned this woman who looked frail in her demeanor and walk, slow to speak and sparse in her movements was, in fact, considered to be one of the fastest women in cars or on motorcycles. The large Indian Chief motorcycle she occasionally rode was the same one she set the land speed record at the Bonneville Salt Flats. She was the first woman to ride a motorcycle over 200 mph. Her second required pass had resulted in her having to step off the motorcycle at over 150 mph. It took two years to repair her and the motorcycle and return to lock in the title. It wasn't the first of her major accidents, nor would it be the last.

The last, she had shared with Willie in a 1963 Dodge Dart GT with a 340 Hemi engine. The resulting many loops and rolls were the result of too much wine, too late at night, too long of a day, and a slightly damp highway where a few deer stood in the headlights.

Every day, Hooker was thankful the two old birds were too tough to kill.

But now he was watching her have to deal with something she couldn't outrun or out think. Her past was rushing out to smack her as sure as an oncoming freight train.

Her free hand shook as it slowly reached out and almost touched the watch. Then it retreated to her cover her mouth. There were no tears. But her spare frame trembled with emotion that had nowhere to go. She stared at the watch and then leaned over to Willie's shoulder. Her head rested on the soft pillow at the top of his arm. Her voice was thin and distant. "We took the train up to San Francisco. I wore the canary yellow dress you like so much. You said it reminded you of the mustard blossoms in the springtime back when the hills behind Watsonville were farmed by the Japanese."

Willie squeezed her hand. "I liked the dress because it made you look like a woman. And when your father saw you dressed in it, he knew he hadn't ruined you with all the greasy iron racing and running shine. It made him happy, and I think it made him also think of your mama."

She glanced up at him with only a hint of surprise. She then snuggled her head back onto his shoulder as she started to reach for the watch again. Her hand hovered there in the air and then withdrew to rest on her heart. "We had supper while they engraved the back. To my Golden Knight, with love from your little sister…"

She drew in a fluttering breath through her half-open mouth, held it, and then slowly let out so much long endured pain.

She looked over at the silent Squirt, and then to Hooker. "How?"

Hooker sighed. "We don't know yet. There were four bodies altogether. Only this and a Timex watch body survived. The remains are up at the holding morgue in Good Sam, so they don't go through the official records until we know what happened."

Willie nudged out his chin, signaling for Hooker to share the rest.

Hooker looked down at his hands—picking at each other's cuticles. His lips were drawn back tight against his teeth.

The Squirt cleared his throat, and Maddie drew her eyes to the young man. He squirmed on the chair. "There was more."

"More bodies?" She shot Hooker a hard frown.

"No, not bodies—bags." Hooker looked up and looked soft at the Squirt for his support. "There were four dive bags full of stolen loot."

"Money?"

Hooker shook his head and reached in his pocket. He placed the large scarab on the table next to the watch. Slowly, Maddie frowned and picked up the artifact. Her eyebrows rose as she felt the weight of the gold statuette. "This is Egyptian..."

"Stolen from the Rosicrucian Museum in 1953," Hooker finished.

She gave Hooker a schoolmarm look. "Do you know that for a fact?"

"I talked to them a few days ago. At first, they didn't want to admit it, but eventually, we came to an understanding."

She studied the young man's face. Softly she asked, "Which would be...? I mean, after all, it is stolen goods."

Hooker scooted his chair a tiny bit to face her more directly. "Yes, well... there was a problem with complacency. No collusion, just not the due diligence in the job the person was tasked to."

He rolled his upper lip in and bit it in an attempt not to smile. "The long and short of it is, they will be eventually happy to replace a gallery of forged items for their real possessions, as long as there is no publicity or official involvement. They don't know how I came by it all, not about the bodies or anything else. And, I get the feeling they don't want to know."

Maddie's hand came to rest on the table with more of the weight of the circumstance than the gold bug. Her eyes slowly closed. "And Danny was involved..."

Willie put his arm around her shoulders. "It would appear so Mads. It would appear so." He looked across at Hooker. Their lips were mirrors as they drew tight against their teeth. There was nothing easy or warm and fuzzy about the whole mess.

Maddie's index finger rotated the gold bug in a slow circle. "So, Hooker... where do we go from here?"

"I was hoping you could help us with that."

There was a challenge and a mystery to solve. Hooker could see the spark galvanize the more intellectual part of her. She sat up and pushed the gold bug back to Hooker.

Hooker took out a piece of paper. "The car was a 1937 Chevy Master Deluxe. It had a Lincoln straight-eight stuffed in it. The back seat was a bucket chest partitioned off for running what looked like boxes of shine. Probably gallons would be my guess. The depth wasn't right for tall bottles, and the buckets looked like they were split into squares."

He looked over his notes. "We found a plate, and it came back registered to a Giovanni Pappas in Salinas." He glanced up to note her looking at Willie. Returning to his notes, "The county records had a Giovanni Michelangelo Pappas of Salinas pass away on the ninth of June in 1959. It seems he was survived by his wife and half of the population of the Salinas area." Hooker looked up.

Maddie and Willie both burped a small laugh at the same time. "As long as you were Greek or Italian, you were related to a Pappas. There were Pappas everywhere."

Willie continued the litany. "If you kicked over a rock, or turned over a wash pan, there was a Pappas underneath." He winked.

Maddie lowered her eyelids to half-mast. "Half the girls Danny, Ben, or Randy dated in school were Pappas." She turned to look at Willie.

Willie leaned back with his hands in front of his chest. "Whoa there, Nelly, there were none I knew of in those days," alluding to his being gay, "but there were a few I had wished were…" He smiled a lecherous grin.

She feigned disgust and backhanded his belly. "You are so disgusting some days, William." She turned and smiled with a wink at Hooker the Squirt could also see. Never lovers, but always best friends and soul mates bonded for life.

Maddie reached her hand out. "Do you have an address there?"

Hooker pushed it over. She looked it over and showed it to Willie with a frown. "That was out in the backyard, wasn't it? On the back way toward Hollister?"

Willie pulled on his pursed lips. His fingers rubbed on the stubble he hadn't shaved that morning. Hooker could hear the soft sandpaper sound. "Maybe… there was another road, too, that we used to take it ran straight into the airport…"

Hooker could tell from experience the two were about to start wandering down memory lane, and the next thing mentioned would be this car or that. He glanced at his watch. "We have to go soon and get some paperwork from the Fly before she leaves. She's got two tows to come up from Salinas by the end of the weekend, so we'll get paid to go down and snoop a bit."

"Do you remember any people Danny hung around with when he was in town?"

Maddie blinked a few times. "Umm… no… not offhand. But if you're going down, why don't you stop in and see Ben. If anyone can remember who Danny was hanging out with, he would be the one to remember."

Hooker took back the paper and stood along with the Squirt. They both stretched and yawned with a smile. The Squirt voiced their twin feelings. "Man, I could get used to this kind of day."

Hooker smiled. "Just remember, as soon as they have the hours of practice they need, the massaging stops."

The Squirt pulled a small yellow piece of paper from his pocket and smelled it as he smiled at Hooker. "Or not."

Hooker just rolled his eyes and looked accusingly at his uncle. "He must get that behavior from your side of the family."

They all laughed as Maddie leaned in for a hug from first Hooker and then the Squirt. "It's good to see you up and getting around, John. Which reminds me… "

"I know. I still owe you a paper on the Federal vs. State codes for firearms."

She patted his chest. "Good boy, I expect all five pages typed by Wednesday dinner."

Hooker frowned but didn't ask. He knew Maddie knew the Squirt would be at Dolly's for Wednesday dinner.

15

M AE IDLED ON the shoulder of the narrow two-lane country road. The only indication it was a majorly used back road was the stripe in the middle had been repainted in the last ten years, at least. There were still fades of a thicker, brighter white.

Hooker looked out his open window to the house and barns across the street. The house could have passed for an old Victorian farmhouse somewhere else, but to Hooker, it just screamed fresh as the houses on Stupid Hill. He made a mental bet with himself that there was a master suite taking up almost the entire second floor.

"Is it just me, or do the house and barn look disgustingly new and a little large for a truck farmer?"

Hooker looked over at the kid with a raised eyebrow. "A little hinky even to you, too?"

"Well, it's not like they are pot growers or something. That would be a little bold, even way out here, but the house is at least forty feet by fifty feet across and even has a third floor. So even without a basement, we're talking a farmhouse at well over five thousand square feet. Even if they're Mormons or Catholics—it's one big house."

Hooker looked back at the building in question. "Manny and Stella's house is 4,000 on the main floor and almost that much in the basement. And it was built basically for just the two of them."

"No, it wasn't."

Hooker looked back at the kid with a furrowed brow.

The Squirt shrugged. "It wasn't. I've seen the original plans and talked to Stella about it. Originally, they built your suite for his father and mine for an around the clock nurse. The downstairs was always about storing the tons of canned goods she puts up every year for the relief pantry for cops and such. They always planned on a three-car garage, and what is now Candy's apartment was going to be an office if the pantry ever needed one."

Hooker slowly remembered something along those lines being mentioned over the years. "So now we're building a big barn out in the hill just so all of the pantry stuff can be out there."

The kid shrugged. "It makes sense if you think about it. Every year, Stella and others spend days setting up the tents and stoves and such for canning literally tons of fruits and vegetables as they're harvested or gleaned from the fields. But now there will be a permanent row kitchen along the one side. The only thing not permanent will be the processing tent, and even that could be made as a gazebo. But the seventy-five hundred square feet of warehouse barn is the biggest thing. I don't even want to think about how much food can be stored there and stacked sixteen feet high."

Hooker nodded his thumb back out the window. "But it still wouldn't explain this house or what is built to look like a large horse or cow barn with an oversized hayloft on a truck farm."

The Squirt looked again at the document from the highway patrol. "But this is the address for old Giovanni."

Hooker flicked the door handle and pushed the door with his boot. He nodded his head at the Squirt. "Well, kid, we aren't going to get answers just sitting here."

Hooker left Mae in a low rumble as their four boots hit the ground. As they walked down the middle of the road away from Mae, the area's silence took over. Mae became only a distant white noise as they turned into the long driveway.

Hooker walked slowly with his head down like a tired worker. The Squirt was a mirror image. Both sets of eyes were looking around. Softly, Hooker mumbled, "Notice anything?"

"Like the fact the dirt in these fields hasn't been turned in a few years?"

"That would be it."

As they approached the house, a large man stepped out through the side screen door. He eyed the two and the large tow truck parked on the highway. "What can I do for you, fellas?"

Hooker looked up with a jerk, feigning surprise. "Oh, hey… hi." He pointed his left thumb back over his shoulder. "We towed a truck the other day for the county, and the address it was registered to was here. It was kind of old, but we have to get an owner's sign-off to collect the tow fees from the county." He pulled a slip of paper from his jacket pocket. "Are you Mr. Giovanni Pappas?"

The man couldn't figure out what was off, but he did know he was not the guy they were looking for. He stepped close to the screen door. "Hey, Fred, do you know a Geo-something Papa?"

"Giovanni," Hooker corrected him.

A scrawny guy with a gray complexion opened the door. "Who?"

Hooker studied the new guy, and then dumbly squinted at the name on the paper. "A Giovanni Papa or Pappas," he looked up expectantly.

The man thought for a moment. "You must mean old Gino. He sold the place. Well, his daughter sold the place back in 1959 or 1960."

Hooker swore and pulled his face in a side grimace as he kicked at the dirt and looked at the partially opened door to the barn. He quickly looked down at the paper and then back at the man. "Do you know where I can find his daughter… the one you bought it from?"

A man came down the stairs slowly. "I wasn't here back then. What's this about?"

Hooker wasn't sure he wanted the man too close after what he had seen through the barn door. "Well, the county had us tow an old truck last night. But because the tags had expired, we have to get the owner to sign-off on the tow for a derelict afore the county will pay for it."

The man stopped about six feet from the two. It was close enough for Hooker. The Squirt was kicking at the dirt and playing at being a step above an inbred drooling basket case. "It weren't no easy tow lass night." Even Hooker wasn't sure if the Squirt had all of his teeth or marbles.

The man rolled his eyes in commiseration at Hooker, who had just dead-panned him. Hooker wasn't going to show much more intelligence.

"I think her name is Corrina or something. Maybe it's Connie. I think she has a beauty salon down at the south end of town. I think her last name is Mannis or something."

Hooker juggled his eyebrows as he shrugged his mouth to one side. "Beauty salon at the south end… How many can there be? Thanks for the help." He turned, and they started walking.

"Hey, what kind of truck is that?"

Hooker looked back with his best deadpan. "It's a tow truck." He blinked a few times as he watched the man decide if Hooker's answer was the most intelligent he was going to get out of the two.

He waved. "Well, you boys have a good day." He turned back to the man still on the porch, and as he climbed the stairs, he smiled at the other and muttered, "Stupid fucking Okies."

As Hooker and the Squirt climbed in the truck, Hooker took one last slow look over the entire spread. No crops had grown there since the house was built. He hit the big yellow brake release and jammed the gears into fourth as he glimpsed the two men still watching from the porch. He purposely ground the gears going into the next three gears.

As Mae picked up speed, and they were a half-mile down the road, the Squirt closed his eyes and then looked over at Hooker. "Did you see the lights in the barn?"

Hooker nodded. "That small shed on the side where the power lines came in, it was a commercial 440-volt feed. The shed holds a step-down converter. They're using a lot of power to run a whole lot of lights." He looked over at the kid. "I don't think they are growing string beans."

The Squirt gave a low whistle. "Did you notice there were more than a few door panels cut in the end about fifteen feet up on the barn?"

Hooker thought a moment and then nodded. "I wonder if there is a second floor, too."

The Squirt ran his thumb and forefinger along his pursed lips. His eyebrows rose as he weighed the concept of a double-decker pot-growing barn. "The building is probably bigger than a Safeway. That's a lot of dope."

Hooker yawned and smacked his lips. "Let's go see if we can find a beauty salon owned by a Connie Mannus or something. And then we can get some lunch before we go see Uncle Ben." Hooker gave the Squirt a hard look. "You don't ever want to be on the receiving end of Ben's cooking."

"Is that why he's still a bachelor?"

"No. And if we are lucky, he might have had a bath this week."

"Ewwww." The Squirt threw his head out the window for some feigned fresh air. Hooker just laughed, but not hard. He knew the truth about Maddie's absent-minded genius brother.

There were three beauty salons in just as many blocks. The one in the middle was the one they were looking for. Carla Minton was Gino's step-daughter and sole heir. She had sold the farm in 1959 and never looked back.

The bleached blonde with the scary bee-hive hair-do and a mouth full of gum was just as snappy as her gum. "That farming shit just wasn't my thing." Her gum snapped. "My mama took to that shit like a..." She turned and pointed the scissors in Hooker's direction. "Well, like a pig in shit. She and Gino were two peas in a pod. She loved running the farm, and he loved eating her cooking. He loved making the shine, and mama was an alcoholic." She put her turned-in wrist on her hip as she looked at the stoic woman's hair. "Hell, so am I... but at least I go to meetin' once in a while to keep me on the straight and narrah."

She made the last snip on the woman's hair and patted her on the shoulder, bending close and almost yelling. "Madeline, y'all can go sit under the dryer for twenty minutes. I'll blow you out then."

The small bird lady with a full head of shoulder-length hair got up and tottered past Hooker. As she passed, she leaned in near him. She muttered softly out of the side of her mouth. "Crazy fucking bitch thinks I'm deaf... but she is the best stylist in town."

"Madeline, now you go on now. Leave them young boys alone. They be much too young for you." The blonde pushed the broom around, catching up the small pile of gray hair on the floor. She stopped and leaned against the chair. "Now, which one of you is next?"

The Squirt closed his eyes feigning sleep but knew he would be the sacrificial lamb. The silence stretched then he heard Hooker take his leather jacket off and ease into the seat.

"Just a little off the ears. But not white sidewalls."

She snapped a fresh apron and draped it over him. Pulling the strip of paper around his neck, she settled into the routine of a barber. "So, what did you want to know about old Gino for?"

Hooker went for the upfront approach. "We found his old car."

Snap! The gum had not even exceeded her mouth—she was an inside the mouth popper—a very loud, inside the mouth popper. "Which one? He had a bunch of them. Parked them all over, left the key in them, and just forgot where they were. I don't think he ever paid more than fifty clams for one." *Snap!* "One day, he came out of a store and got into a car. The key was in it, so he knowed it was his. Just drove off home." *Snap!* "The police came and got their patrol car about an hour later. I think it took the police chief that long to stop laughing."

Hooker chuckled as she snipped and snapped. "This was a 1937 Chevy Master Deluxe. The back seat was rigged to run shine." He was hoping this detail would produce some special pay dirt.

SNAP! She laughed and held onto his shoulder with both hands as she crossed her legs to keep from peeing herself. "Honey, they was all rigged for running shine. Even his three John Deere tractors had a stash box."

Hooker groaned. "So you probably wouldn't remember who might have borrowed the car to run some shine up to San Jose." He turned and looked at her.

She took his head in both hands and gently turned it back. The snap of her gum was quiet and contemplative. She snipped silently. "Half the county knew the cars had the keys in them, so they just used them as they needed. But the only people I can think of who would borrow one to run shine up to the cities would be maybe his nephew, Harold... but he blew out of this town a long time ago."

"How long ago?"

She stopped and rested her hands on his shoulder. "Oh, hell... must have been about the time I started getting serious with my husband… so about the end of the war. That's the Korean War."

Hooker waited. "So about 1953?"

She held a mirror in her hand at her hip. "Well, my Sarah Lee was born in August of '54, so… yeah, sometime in the fall of 1953 would be about right. Why?'

"Do you know if he knew a Daniel Robinson?"

She had started to hold a mirror up for Hooker to look at her work. Instead, she sat heavily down in the next chair. The wind was taken from her. "Oh, my… Now there is a name I haven't heard in a long time. Danny Robinson." She sat stewing in many mixed memories rushing back. Hooker watched her face.

"Danny was one hundred and ten percent pure steaming, sweaty, make you go change your panties after third period, kind of hunk. He was a few years ahead of me in school, but I wasn't the only girl in town who would have let him do what he wanted in the back seat of a car." Hooker could tell he had hit some kind of pay dirt. He just had to wait it out. The woman sat in her own dreamland. "He was the captain of the football team and would wear his jacket with the big red 'S' on the side. All of us girls just knew it stood for sex because nobody thought he would stop at just a kiss and some titty rubbing on a Friday night."

She looked up slowly as she struggled her way back. The blush started on her chest and didn't stop as her mind pushed the blood harder and higher. Hooker didn't smile. He wasn't going to taunt. She fanned her hands in front of her face and her exposed chest. "Oh, my."

"So you knew him." Hooker wanted to roll his head in a brainless zombie move, but he knew the behavior was restricted to home. "Do you have any idea who he used to hang out with in the fifties?"

"Sure, that's easy. He hung out with his company in Korea. He was in the reserves—Army, I think. When Korea started up, they all became active and were gone."

Hooker slowly slid the apron off his neck. He ran his hand around his head and looked in the large mirror. He glanced with a small smile at the bird lady humming happily to herself under the dryer. *Damn, the old lady was right—she really is good.*

"What was he doing before Korea?"

"I think he was driving stuff around."

"You mean moonshine?"

The infectious blonde laughed in a husky tinkle. "Well, shine too, but I seem to remember him hauling produce and anything else needed. We didn't have all the Mexicans back then, and a lot of the Okies and Arkies you wouldn't trust to drive your little girl's tricycle. So, a guy like Danny who could drive anything was in demand."

"Was there anyone he drove with or drank with?" Hooker was trying to get a feel for how old Carla actually was at the time. With the bleached blonde hair, it was hard to peg how old she was now.

"There were a couple of boys from the other Pappas families. But I couldn't tell you which. In fact, they might have been one of the Greeks. I just wasn't paying attention to other boys by then. As I said, I was already a unit short of a husband, and none of the field guys were going to get me the house I wanted."

"House?"

"You know… the American dream. White picket fence, a house at the end of the block, car in the garage…"

Hooker nodded. "Speaking of houses… have you seen the house and barn the new people built on your uncle's old place?"

She rolled her eyes and leaned in toward Hooker. "You mean the ones you never see?" She winked slowly. "Some say there are times at night if you stand along the road, and the breeze is just right… you don't need no shine to light up your night."

Hooker rolled his lips in toward his teeth and nodded. "Yeah, that's what we were thinking, too."

"So… Why all the questions about Danny anyway?" She stood and laid the hand mirror on the side counter. Turning, she looked from the Squirt to Hooker. "What's he up to these days anyway?"

Hooker bit down on his lips. The Squirt blinked slowly and said, "He's dead. He died in 1953 as best as we can tell."

Her face drained, and she stumbled to hold onto the one chair. Her breath was one long, "Nooo."

Hooker put his hand on her shoulder and guided her to sit in the chair.

"There were four bodies. We're trying to figure out who the others are."

"Oh, my."

"OH, MY?" BEN laughed. "That's all she had to say?"

Hooker was thankful they had caught Ben wet and with only a towel around him. The house was another matter. Hooker told Ben he should get some fresh clothes on and that they'd be waiting out on the side porch where the refrigerator was. The one habit of Ben's Hooker liked was his penchant for root beer. The old Frigidaire had three pull spigots coming out of the door—draft root beer, moonshine, and milk.

Hooker swallowed another large mouthful of root beer. "Pretty much. I think she was pretty shaken."

Ben put his fingers and thumbs to his pursed lips and stroked the top of his nose with the side of his index finger. His eyes were pointed out across the freshly turned fields, but Hooker could tell his sight and mind were twenty years away.

Hooker looked over at the Squirt, who was in his own world as he studied the barn and tilled earth of a true working farm. Small farms like Ben's were the backbone of the entire Salinas area. Generations of families had struggled to carve out a livelihood from the earth. Hooker finally saw what the Squirt was focused on. In one distant corner was a large live oak tree. Underneath, Hooker could see the small white chunks of marble and granite. They were headstones from generations past on the family homestead, marking heritage, as well as a signpost for the next generation.

Hooker leaned toward the Squirt and asked quietly, "The cemetery?"

The Squirt nodded. "It must be strange, and yet comforting to know you are living where generations of your family also stood, lived, worked, had children, and finally died."

Hooker thought about his life in the foster system and how it mirrored the Squirt and his sister Candy. Handfuls of years also meant handfuls of new homes. With them, there were no roots. They didn't even know who their parents had been. Hooker thought about his sister. *I don't even have a real sister. At least the kid has Candy.*

Hooker confided in the kid. "The most recent stone out there is a guy named Jethro, and he was buried in 1912. Died of an acute case of lead poisoning…"

Ben harrumphed and then started laughing. "He got all six lead poisons from the mayor, and then the mayor calmly reloaded and put all six in his wife. After that, he went outside and unloaded six more shots in old Jethro's flivver." Ben waved his hand out toward the cemetery. "If'n you want it, the car is buried right next to old Jethro. I guess, to the family, it just seemed fittin' somehow."

The Squirt thought about the car being buried with the man. And then he remembered this was a family who not only farmed, but also made and ran moonshine, and built very fast cars, raced many, and sold even more. His right cheek pulled back in a smile as his head rolled left to look at Hooker, who was also nodding at the logic of it all. The old flivver and where it ended up, summed up the entire make-up of the family, from Maddie on back.

Hooker got up and pulled himself some more root beer. Turning, he blew the foam head into the yard. "Do you remember who Danny used to hang out with after WWII?"

Ben sipped on his mug and thought. "Probably one of the Pappas kids. They were all younger than he was, but he wasn't much about age differences. There used to be a whorehouse out on the road down to Monterey. The summer before he went into high school, he walked in and looked at all the young fillies. They were all about five or ten years older than him. Then he walked over to the madam. He whispered in her ear, and she was his every Saturday afternoon for a couple of years. Never charged him, neither."

The Squirt leaned forward to look at Ben. "What did he whisper?"

Ben hiccupped a snort. "Told her he was about to turn eighteen and was a virgin. He wanted someone to teach him the ways of women." He looked down the porch and smiled a silly grin at the Squirt. "By the time she figured he was only thirteen, she knew he had balls of brass and cast iron, and it didn't matter anymore… she was in love." He leaned back in the rocker and chuckled at the old times and his brother's shenanigans.

Hooker wondered if Maddie knew the story. "So which Pappas do you think he might have been close enough to in 1953 to go get in some trouble with?"

Ben was still. His focus was across the field and back in his youth.

Hooker watched. The man could have been a statue. His shirt didn't rise and fall, like other people when they would breathe. Hooker knew this man breathed shallow. It came from tending a wood-burning still for years. Hooker watched the slight flare of the man's nostrils as he thought. This was the same as Manny playing classical music with his large head-phones on.

Slowly, the statue turned his head. "Two people... but they won't do you any good."

"Why?"

"They're gone."

"Moved away gone, or dead?"

The older man shrugged and stuck his lower lip out. "Hard to say."

"So who, then?"

"Hank and his little sister... Mary or Terry, or something." He stood up, scratching his butt through his denim. He splashed a little from each of the pulls on the cold box, swished it around in his mug, and threw the liquid mix out into the yard.

Putting the mug back on the shelf turned down, he slowly backed up and leaned his butt against the railing. He washed his hands along the stubble on both sides of his face. Hooker could hear the sandpaper from his chair.

"Hank and he used to haul a lot of everything all over the valley. There was always a demand for someone who had the intelligence to drive four gears, six tons of produce, and get there safely. Hank was another one. Both were good at the racetrack over Hollister way, too." He looked up and smiled. "Not as good as Maddie, but then, not even dad had her kind of heart. We always joked about the reason she could drive so fast was she didn't have any balls to get in the way." He chuckled at times gone by when his kid sister was the fastest woman on four or two wheels.

"The two of them never cared whose car or truck or tractor they were driving. If it had tires and an engine, they had it figured out. Hay, machin-ery, turnips, or shine, they just didn't care. It was just another chance to drive something and make some money." He looked over his shoulder at the fields and distant road where a red truck was driving by. His voice tapered off, "If it was trouble, it was most likely with Hank."

"So what happened to Hank?"

"Nobody knows." He buzzed his lips against his teeth and then made them into duck lips and blew a raspberry as he still processed his memories. "It was a big mystery around these parts. There were three or four of them… just disappeared one day. Nobody heard anything ever again from none of them."

"What about the sister?"

Ben's eyebrows rose as he looked back at the peeling paint on the clapboards of the house. "Now, there was an interesting one. Quite a looker, kind of like a Jane Russell sort of gal. She wasn't small but just nicely curvy in the right way. You could tell she had spent her time in the fields like most of us.

"She took it hard about her missing brother. After a short while, she quit her job and pulled up stakes. All of us kept waiting to see her in a movie or something. She was good looking. In fact… now as I think on it, I think she and Danny had a thing going before he shipped off to Korea."

"But he never came home."

The man shrugged his face and put out his palms. "That's what we always thought."

The Squirt was processing all of the information. One of the items floated to the top of his bubbling stewpot. He leaned forward. "Did any of the stuff on the missing guys ever make it into the papers?"

Ben fluffed his lower lip. "Sure, the Salinas paper at least. A couple of guys go missing in a small town? That will always sell papers."

Hooker stood and looked out at the afternoon sun. It was lighting the way toward dinner.

As Mae rolled, the Squirt looked over thoughtfully. "We know all of the bodies were male… What if?"

Hooker flipped the toggle and moved the gear shifter into the next level of gears. Mae surged down the highway. It had been a long day, and Hooker was hungry for crab. His lips drew in and played around his teeth.

"Okay, let's say she was with them. Why would she survive, and they didn't?"

Hooker knew the Squirt had looked up what a 1937 Chevy Master Deluxe looked like. Hooker had an idea, but he also had looked up the boxy sedan. The car was what today would be called a 'stand-up' kind of car, as in you could almost stand up in it. Its high body profile put a lot of weight at the top, which made it easy to tip over. Hooker knew a lot of the old gangsters would put large engines in them not to necessarily go faster, but to go fast with the extra half-ton of weight welded onto the frames near the ground. Later in the fifties, people like Maddie and Ben learned to lower the tops, and also make the suspension only react so far by welding in anti-sway bars. They also learned about heating the springs to lower the bodies. But the Master Deluxe they had recovered had none of that. It was just a straight-up utility moonshine runner with a fast mill—a gentleman's highway car.

Hooker could sense the Squirt lean back and smile as he relaxed and laid his elbow out of the window. He had tossed the car in his mind and had an answer.

Hooker waited and then couldn't, "Aaannd…?" He looked over at the smug young man.

"She was thrown out in the first set of rolls. The car rolled to the passenger side first, which locked the guys in, but popped the driver door."

"Then why wasn't the fourth guy, the one who was sitting behind her, thrown out also?"

"Because he was busy being the projectile killing the guy in the front seat. He was the large blow that broke Danny's neck."

"Why not the girl?"

"Because she was the only one who had something to hold onto… the steering wheel. That makes her the driver."

Hooker thought about it. No matter how he tossed it in his mind, the kid had gotten there ahead of him. He looked over and smiled at the kid.

As Hooker set the brakes and let Mae rattle down to silence, he petted Box's ear as he looked out at the large sheds of Cannery Row. His eyes drifted closed as he slowly drew in the smells of the ocean, fishing boats, and rotting kelp and other things making the area so special. He kicked open the door. "Crab for dinner, Box."

He didn't have to tell his orange partner twice about food. They all slid out of the truck and locked the doors.

Coming around the front of the giant truck, the two leather-clad men walked, bracing the large orange cat with one eye, one ear, and plenty of scars. The smell of potential drew them to dinner on the wharf with a seat by the sea.

Later, as they sat on the edge of the wharf hanging their legs over the sea lions lounging below, Hooker sucked on his fingers. "Even if she was the driver, how would we find her twenty years later in a place as big as Los Angeles? I sure as hell won't be getting a tow down there to go snooping around."

The Squirt split open his third lobster and drew out the meat. "I've been thinking about that." He dredged a thumb-sized piece through the cup of butter and slurped it in his mouth. His eyes closed as he chewed leisurely, savoring each little burst of flavor. Hooker almost laughed, but he remembered his first time, too.

Hooker looked out at the sunset shooting orange and red rays mixed with the still strong white light limned the small cloud hiding the sun. He slipped Box another finger of crab onto his paper. The cat hadn't stopped purring rough and loud since they set foot on the wharf.

The Squirt unabashedly made rude sounds as he sucked his fingers clean and leaned back. "I don't think she went that far."

"How far?"

"To Los Angeles—it wasn't her kind of town."

Hooker looked through the shells for any other large pieces of meat, and then laid it all on Box's paper. The furry man could clean the last pieces. Hooker looked up at the Squirt. "Why not? If she's built as Ben said, she could go land a waitress job and get discovered."

"But nobody ever saw her in a movie."

"Okay, so the movies are out. Why is Los Angeles—not her kind of town?"

"Because, for one, it is not a town. It's a city—a very busy, noisy city where she doesn't know anybody." He watched a bird fly by and then land on top of a boat's cabin. He turned toward Hooker. "How many generations do you think are buried out in the old cemetery?"

"The family one? Out at Ben's place? Those aren't his family."

The kid smiled in a lopsided loopy kind of smile. "It doesn't matter. How many generations?"

Hooker looked down the wharf as if there was an answer. He thought about the Californians owning the land in the early 1800s, and Steinbeck's story of the dust bowl fugitives who ended up building the large truck farms scattered across the landscape of the entire Monterey, Salinas, Watsonville, Hollister area, and ran up the 101 to Gilroy and Martinez. He looked back at the kid. "It's a small cemetery, but maybe four or five generations. Why?"

"Which is why she didn't run off to LA. There isn't a family cemetery there."

"But there's one here?"

"It doesn't matter whether there is or not. It's the roots. All of her roots are here. Ben said it showed that she had worked in the fields as a kid. I'm assuming he meant she wasn't scrawny."

"Maddie isn't a beefcake."

"Maddie didn't work in the fields."

Hooker frowned. "How would you know?"

"The way Ben talked about her. She was different, special even. She could outdrive everyone. I'll bet by the time she was old enough to see over the dashboard, she was also the better at turning a wrench, too."

"It still doesn't explain the Pappas girl."

"Sure it does."

"How?"

"Maddie went to college. She was also the fastest woman alive for a while. In theory, she could have raced anywhere. She could have taught or worked in a library anywhere."

"So?"

"She made it as far as San Jose."

"Well, because..."

"Because she married a guy and settled down there? No. Because she followed Willie there? No. Because San Jose made her the best offer? I don't think so."

"Then, why?"

"The cemetery."

"I told you the cemetery isn't theirs."

"Where is the family plot?"

"I think they own some land on Mount Angel."

"Bingo. She is the same kind of person. She's within an hour or so of her roots."

Hooker pinched his fingers to his pursed lips and watched the giant burning ball, silently slip beneath the edge of the world. The last rays of daylight splayed like a giant crown.

The kid was right. Family is a very powerful and compelling thing.

16

T HE SQUIRT SQUIRMED as he got back into the truck after they had dropped the tractor. He had been quiet most of the ride back up from Salinas Impound yard. Hooker watched him out of the side of his eye as Hooker checked his mirrors and eased Mae into gear and rolled out of the gated yard. Hooker stopped on the street and went back to close the gate and secure the lock he had the key to. It was only one of seven secure yards Hooker was trusted with a key.

Walking back toward the cab, the image of Box circling his bed at the Romero Hacienda after Stella had washed the cover was exactly how the Squirt was acting. Something wasn't settling with him. Hooker decided to check the tires and give the kid some time. Grabbing the weighted maul, he bounced it along all ten tires as he made the circle of the largest tow truck in the five Bay counties. With a top speed, thanks to the new engine and transmission, of over 150 mph, Mae West was also the fastest tow truck, too. As the motto under her figure painted waving from the engine bonnet said, 'It's what's up front that counts.'

Putting the large hammer back in its hole, Hooker climbed back up into the cab. He put the transmission in gear, hit the air brake release, and eased on down the street as his right hand fell to find empty air where he expected a fuzzy ear. Looking down, as his foot hovered over the brake pedal, he saw the shape of the large orange cat filling the box. The low snore was all he needed in reassurance. Hooker looked up into the face of the Squirt. Both were smiling.

"I think we have a Box with a very happy tummy," Squirt said as he also rubbed his own.

Hooker nodded as he spun the steering wheel through the right and immediate left to get up onto the Almaden Expressway. "Yeah, you weren't too shabby yourself on those bugs and crabs." He smiled. The dinner had cost Hooker almost a third of the tow, but it had been well worth it to introduce the Squirt to eating at the end of the wharf. Watching the sun go down over the Monterey Bay was just the dessert.

Capitol Expressway came up, and Hooker took the cloverleaf and headed east. The Squirt frowned over at his boss. "I thought we were headed home?"

Hooker leaned back tall in the seat as he tried his best imitation of Uncle Willie explaining the facts of life. "Well, John... it's like this. There are some things you should never compromise in your life. Love is one of those. Ice cream is another. And when those two things come together, it's up there with the most sacred of all things."

The kid stuck his hand out into the crisp fall air as he smirked. "It is just the right temperature for some French vanilla."

"Probably just right for even a triple scoop..."

"...in a sugar cone," the Squirt finished. They laughed, and Box just turned over but kept snoring. Hooker knew he would wake up for his dab in the bowl.

Twenty minutes later, as they headed back across the valley on Blossom Hill Road, the Squirt had the bag with the large oversized strawberry and caramel Sunday between his knees. Both windows were open to the night air, and all three tongues were busy with ice cream.

The radio speaker crackled. "Hooker, are you back in the area?"

Hooker passed his cone over to the Squirt and reached behind his head for the microphone. "Yes, I am, Dolly. How can I be of service?"

There was a long pause. "Okay, I'm going to let this one slide because I called you. Please don't talk on the radio around my girls when you are eating ice cream."

Hooker lowered and slowed his speech, knowing all six female ears were now listening to what Dolly referred to as his 'bedroom voice.'

"Gee, Dolly, whatever do you have against my ice cream voice?" He could only imagine the two younger gals squirming in their chairs while trying not to giggle.

"Just get your bodies home. And you need to back Mae into the barn. They need you to play crane or something. Other than that, you aren't even on call. Let the Squirt get some sleep."

"10-4, mama. We're gone."

Not knowing if there was a single car or forty at the bottom of the long driveway running down one side of the Hacienda Romero, Hooker backed down the wide driveway. The width of the driveway and the very large parking lot at the bottom behind Manny and Stella's house was to accommodate Stella's little brainchild that grew into a large monster.

The lower end of the Bay Area is an agricultural mecca. From the few orchards left in the south side of San Jose, down through San Martin and Gilroy and then extending through the golden truck farms of the Hollister, Salinas, Monterey, and Watsonville triangle. The area produced almost a third of California's exportable cash truck farm crops. Stella, years before, asked about gleaning the harvested fields for the left vegetables and fruits. She canned and had ready, food for families of police officers when they were in need. What started as a couple of hundred gallons of canning, with Stella and a few other wives, soon grew into a much larger resource.

When Hooker showed up on the scene, they were already putting up tons of jars. The local growers contributed harvested food that overwhelmed Stella's ad hoc system, so the local cannery in San Jose made the offer to commercially can the bulk with a private label. From trucks delivering on Saturdays and Sundays to the finished cans being loaded into trucks, all of the labor was strictly volunteers. The food now serviced not only any police families, but also fire, city, and county workers as well.

Half-buried in the hillside, they were building a large barn to hold four times as much food as they were previously able. Facing out over the Almaden Valley and running the full length of the barn was an outdoor kitchen set up for major canning.

As Hooker backed at the acres of the parking lot, there were only eight or ten trucks parked along the side near the house. Hooker saw the large rolling doors were open, so he blew his horn a few sharp blasts and backed to the door.

A large police officer dressed in jeans and a t-shirt stepped out and started waving Hooker in. Finally, with the entire truck inside, the officer held up his hand and clenched his fist for Hooker to stop. Hooker set the brake. He and the Squirt slid out and approached the back.

Hooker smiled and could not resist a tease at the tall, husky Filipino officer's expense. "Geez, James, I don't know what you are doing here. There won't be any food stored here for at least another nine or so months."

The deep voice rumbled through the smile. "Good to see you too, asshole. I see those two-bits they left in you aren't slowing down your mouth any." The three of them had worked the grisliest of the three killings.

The Squirt cleared his throat as he leaned against the back of the tow truck.

James turned. "Oh, and who do we have here? Back from the dead—and looking none the worse for wear." He reached over and shook the kid's hand. "I understand you're starting at the academy soon."

"It looks like it. There is talk that if I can pass my physical after Christmas, they might insert me mid-term in January. Chet, I mean, Captain..."

James interrupted him. "I know Chet." He pointed to the far corner and laughed. "He's the one over there with the plumber's crack and swearing at the copper pipe resisting soldering."

The Squirt smiled and rolled his eyes at the visual. "Well, he's seeing if he can get me some books so I can either catch up or challenge some of the course work."

The officer smiled. "Well, if you can study the same way you worked the burn job, I wouldn't be surprised if you weren't ready in six months. Does that recall thing work with reading books, too?"

"Eidetic memory is sometimes a tricky thing. It works best when there are more senses working than just reading. At the burn site, I could smell the torched metal, the paint, and the burned bodies. There was a very light breeze coming from the southeast. I kept hearing the squawk of the two different radio bands, and I'm especially attuned to Mae West's idle cycle sound." He gave Hooker a hard glare. "Although, with a new engine, her idle is about a hundred RPMs faster, and it's not really smooth like it was before."

James Aligo's laugh was deep and boisterous. He slapped his large hand on Hooker's shoulder. "Willie must be slipping, or you have been hard on the delicate girl."

"Hey, Aligo?"

The three turned to see the county commissioner and former detective partner of Manny's walking toward them.

Hooker smiled. "Hello, Paul. Great to see you doing something productive." They shook hands.

Paul looked around at the large barn. "Who would have ever guessed back when Manny harassed the county about the easement, he would actually be building a barn out here?"

Manny's favorite tool, since his retirement by bullet, was the phone. He heard the county was planning to run an easement through the bottom of his twenty acres. Step by step, person by person, he had worked his way from the lowest to the only person that could stop the easement—his old partner. He had calmly listened to all of the bureaucratic horse shit as he carefully kept track on his yellow pad the name and title of each functionary. The time from start to finish went with a synopsis of the functionary's final offer of what they could or couldn't do. With each call, Manny had asked who the next person up the ladder was that he needed to talk to. He was solicitous and kindly spoken, so help was at hand with the next name and phone number or a transfer.

Brick by brick, he would build his case. He never jumped the chain of command. He never pulled any kind of rank by going directly to his old friend. It wasn't so much about the results, as it was about playing the game. He fought and won each step of the battle.

Finally, he had reached Paul. They had exchanged pleasantries, and then Manny told Paul, nicely, to move the easement because he was going to build a barn where the easement would be, thus diminishing his enjoyment of his private property. When Paul started telling Manny it was out of his hands, Manny turned the phone's handset around and pounded it on a rattling board he had brought into the house specifically for the noise.

When he put the phone back to his ear, his old partner was now remembering Manny's strong-arm tactics of getting things done. Manny softly sighed and then told Paul he wasn't listening. He then proceeded to read from the four pages of specific names, times, and outcome of each conversation of the day. His tone was soft and metered. In the end, he told Paul his next phone calls would be to his sister-in-law, Dolly at Night Dispatch, and then his lawyer, the most feared shark in the South Bay Area.

He quietly hung up, looked at the clock, and went to make himself a sandwich.

The phone rang twenty minutes later. Paul contritely informed Manny the easement was moved down to the bottom of the hill onto the county property, and Manny had the green light to build whatever kind of barn and corrals he wanted.

The two longtime friends had been laughing about it ever since. Business was business, and friendship was never compromised by it.

"What did you want Mae for, Paul?"

Paul turned and guided them over to some long steel I-beams. "We have this gantry system Willie found up at Alameda air station. Evidently, it was made for moving bombs around during the war, but was never installed." He pointed high on the walls. "We've installed the studs on the walls, but we need to lift the beams into place. We looked at a larger forklift, but they only go up fourteen feet. The spuds are at twenty."

Hooker eyed the steel. "How much does the largest one weigh?"

Paul pointed at the longest beam. "The main is about a buck eighty."

One thousand eight hundred pounds, Hooker thought about the dynamics of the extended boom. "I can get it close, but we'll have to tip one end in and secure it somehow, then continue the lift on a carry trammel." Looking to the ridge beam, Hooker saw a large block and tackle hanging. "What is the block hanging up there for?"

Paul laughed. "Looks. The ridge beam is only stressed for a two-foot snow load so the block wouldn't be good for anything more than maybe five hundred pounds."

Hooker looked about. "We could point tie over on that high beam and then run to the beam and on up to the block. It would be enough for the trammel lift so I can adjust my lift point on the beam."

The Squirt unscrewed his face and opened his eyes. "The load on the tie off on the wall as well as the dead load on the block will be about four-hundred twenty-eight pounds, give or take about twenty." He looked up at Paul and smiled.

Paul looked at him with an open mouth then closed it. "Oh, you are going to be hell on the instructors at the academy."

Hooker smirked. The kid had come a long way since Hooker first met him after sticking a fork through his hand as he tried to steal a dollar off the diner's counter.

The kid turned, still smiling. "I'll get the trammel chains."

About an hour later, Candy walked up behind Hooker and put her arms around his middle as she kissed the back of his neck. "Stella said the chili is hot, and the rolls are about five minutes away from coming out of the oven. All the bathrooms are working down here, so everyone needs to wash up and come topside."

Hooker released the levers on the side of Mae and turned into his girl-friend's hug. "Hello, good looking."

Candy blushed from the top of her nurse's uniform to her hair. "You're just saying that because of the sexy uniform."

"I've always liked you in or out of uniform." Hooker turned to address the rest of the men. His whistle was sharp and reverberated in the empty space. "Chili is in five minutes in the big house, and if you need to call your wife to be able to stay—well, just whimper that Stella insisted. Wash up. There are five bathrooms and four hoses between here and the table."

Candy playfully slapped his chest as he spun her around toward the door. "Oh, you are sure the mean one. There isn't a henpecked man in this lot."

Hooker looked back at all the men as he climbed up into Mae and shut her down. Dropping to the floor, he grabbed Candy by the waist, and they continued out the large door. "There isn't a single married man here either."

She looked back and frowned. Hooker laughed. "Yeah, you can share it around with your classmates on Monday."

She looked at him, and then an evil smile crept across her face.

Hooker looked at the stars and the crisp November night. He felt the warm body that was in perfect step with him. Life was looking good. "I hope you're free for lunch tomorrow."

"Why? I need to study, but lunch sounds good."

"Good. I know a little place I want to take you to right after I spend a little time in a certain library."

"Maddie?"

"No, her hometown."

"Where is that?"

"Salinas. It's down near Monterey and lunch."

The Squirt had been following close behind. He slid up alongside them as he wiggled his eyebrows up and down. "Do I get to come, too?"

Hooker looked over. "Nope, you are taking The Granny Car over for Willie to pamper while you are spending some time with Maddie. Chet said he dropped off a stack of books for you."

"Beans."

Candy reached over and ruffled her brother's hair and smiled. She was starting to like the effect Hooker was having on him. She could have done without Hooker stabbing his hand with a fork, but if that's what it took, so be it.

Hooker steered them up the driveway instead of using the secret stairs and door in the pantry. He always liked walking in through the giant hand-hewn gates letting into the entry patio with the Mexican tiled fountain. The gentle sound of the water calmed him, and it always reinforced in him that he was home, *even if his other home was five miles away at Uncle Willie's place.*

1 7

THE QUIET OF the small library harmonized with the two scan readers. The past newspaper had all been photographed and turned into leaves of microfiche. Hooker and Candy had the year, but not the right time, so one started with December and the other with November, and they leapfrogged their way back through the year.

"I think this is it." Candy leaned over to nudge Hooker. She noticed he was looking at the cars for sale section. "I don't think you can still get... what is a Hupmobile?"

Hooker laughed. "What did you find?" He smiled at the freckles scrunched as she looked at the ad.

She leaned back and gave him a one-eyed look. "I'm looking for three missing guys, and you're shopping for cars that don't even exist anymore."

"You knew what you were getting into."

"Right," she ran her fingers up into his hair. "Just don't start wearing long dresses. They don't look good with the leather jacket."

Hooker chuckled. "Noted."

He read the article she had found. "Okay, so missing since late September." Leaning back, Hooker ran the information through his head. "The war ended at the end of July... so where was Danny for those two months?"

"Do they just one day say 'it's all over. Everybody, go home,' or does it take time to unwind a war?" She raised an eyebrow. "My guess is he was somehow involved in the wind-down."

Hooker looked for the September microfiche folder. He found the last week and slid it into the viewer. He scanned through the front pages. Candy leaned on his shoulder, watching. "Do you think it would have made the headlines? This is all about the war unwinding."

"I would think it would make at least the front..." His finger poked at the glass.

They read an article about three men who went hunting and were presumed dead. Hooker pulled up his notepad and started writing the names Hank Pappas, age 29, Zebulon Nickapopalus age 29, and Paul Giodarno age 32. The rest of the story about going deer hunting in the lower ranges near Big Sur Hooker new to be nothing more than conjecture or pure fabrication.

Candy murmured with her jaw still on his shoulder. "What do you think?"

"I think we found our guys... but who was the driver who dragged them into the cave?"

Candy stuck her finger out and touched the screen where it read 'Theresa Pappas, sister of Hank Pappas, told authorities they had gone hunting but planned to be back to work the next Monday.'

Hooker nodded. "Bingo—the only person who knew where they really went."

"So we need to track her down."

Hooker looked at his watch. "No, it's time for lunch." He smiled at her and kissed her nose.

"So where is this mysterious lunch?"

Hooker stood and rearranged the microfiche folder and leaves. He stood and smiled. He liked the way she had brought her hair down in a loose fluffy ponytail. It softened her features. "For where, you would have to ask Box because I'm not talkin'."

They rode with her nose against the door's window. "I never knew there was so much farming around here." She turned back and looked at

Hooker as Box jumped up onto the sun-drenched dashboard and stretched out. "Box certainly knows all the right places."

"If it were your brother sitting there, he would have been in the Squirt's lap the whole trip. The kid is a real sucker for Box. First Box backs him into a corner, and then they are fast friends. I just don't get it."

"Do you think he will ever warm up to me?"

"Your brother? Nah." Hooker laughed.

Candy looked around the spacious cab. "So you run the heater on high, but you don't roll the window up, and you stick your elbow out... why?"

Hooker looked over as he downshifted. "Are you comfortable?"

"I'm not complaining..."

"Well, there you go. You don't like the window open, but then, you don't have a leather jacket either. So you rolled your window up, and now you are comfortable. My legs are warm, my body is warm, and I have some wind on my face. I'm comfortable. And the Squirt runs the same way. But then, he's also weird... did you know he likes ice cream in the middle of winter?"

She laughed. "French vanilla, three scoops..."

"...in a sugar cone," they finished together.

"He told me about the ice cream. I think it was when he decided he really liked you—fork or no fork."

Hooker groaned. "Will you people ever give it a rest?"

He downshifted three gears and nosed the giant truck into a parking lot between two refrigerated trailers with large crabs painted on their sides. "Welcome to Cannery Row."

"As in John Steinbeck?"

Hooker slid out the door. Opening his arms to help her down as she slid right into him, he laughed. "One and the same."

Box led them down the wharf to the large kettle where the man was boiling the crabs or lobster you chose. His kink-tipped tail was flying like a battle banner the whole way.

Candy hung on Hooker's arm, taking in the sights and smells. "He really does know where he's going. He has walked right past three other..."

"Fishmongers."

"Fishmongers and set a beeline for this one."

Hooker stopped them thirty feet from the man and his kettle. "Watch."

Box approached the Asian man, who, upon seeing the large distinct cat, stopped his usual work and chose a part of a fish. Quickly slicing off a few choice bits of meat, he placed them on a small boat he folded a sheet of newspaper into. He stepped out toward Box and placed the small boat with both hands a foot in front of the cat. Box didn't move, just watched.

The man took a small step back, and then two more. Pressing his palms together, he raised them to his lips. With a fluid movement, Box sat back on his haunches and sat up. His left paw rested on his tummy, and he raised his right as if to wash the top of his head. His paw pads were facing the man, who now bowed deeply in mutual respect. The cat returned the respect and quickly devoured the offering of friendship.

The man watched with a sincere smile and then looked up to find Hooker. The smile grew into a brilliant row of white teeth. "Hooker-san, you grace this old man with your warrior guardian." His vision turned to Candy. He clapped his hands together and bowed. "And this beautiful lady, I can only take as the Squirt's sister. Hooker-san, you are most favored."

"Candy, this is Fuji-san. He is the only person who can feed the mange monster raw fish. Fuji-san, this is Candy, my girl."

The man took her hand delicately with a small shake. "I am honored to meet you. You are as lovely as my lotus blossom wife was."

"Did she die?" The words slipped out before she could stop them.

The solemn man rose back and laughed. "Oh, heavens no. She is now fat like a pig. And that gives me just more to love."

Candy was shocked and then laughed as she turned on Hooker. "Do you nuzzle her neck as well?"

Hooker grabbed his face as he shook his head in mock shame. Fuji laughed even harder.

"Of course he has—Hooker-san is Hooker-san. Makes her laugh and giggle like a little school girl." He waved his palm up and down at her body. "So how did a slender woman like you get his attention, much less his arm?" He leaned in with a mock confidential stage whisper. "The only woman he ever brings is his uncle and the nice Maddie-san. I don't think Hooker is interested in her." He leaned back with the smile of a naughty boy.

Candy leaned into Hooker. "So everyone else has been here but me?"

"Manny and Stella won't travel anymore. But we will be taking some crabs back for them." He smiled. "But right now, you need to pick out your dinner."

She looked in horror at the large glass tanks. Hooker hugged her. "It's okay. Fuji-san, how about four crabs and three bugs."

Candy stiffened in his hug. "What are bugs?"

Fuji held up two large lobsters, smiled, and tossed them into the boiling water. He fished one more and a couple of crabs. Reaching back in among the crabs, he nodded toward the end of the wharf. "You go sit now. Fuji brings when ready. You get your own root beer."

Hooker waved and turned Candy around, and they strolled to the end of the wharf with only a stop for two large root beers.

An hour later, Box lay curled up next to the devastated shells, snoring gently as Hooker and Candy watched the fishing boats returning across the bay. Candy wiggled over closer and rested her hand on Hooker's thigh as she leaned into his shoulder. "It's so peaceful."

Hooker looked across the bay to the north. "When things are not so calm at home, this is the place I think of—to quiet the noise."

She changed positions so she could lay with her head on his lap. "That's why you work nights—for the quiet."

Hooker smiled softly and stroked her shoulder. He knew he didn't have to answer. He could tell she had figured it out about him years ago. It was the same reason she had worked the night shift at the diner.

Just about the time Hooker thought she had gone to sleep, Candy asked, "Where do you think she is—the sister?"

"I think the Squirt has the right thought on it. She's somewhere close. Maybe as far as San Francisco, but probably closer."

"How do we find her?"

"We ask around."

"Hmm." She nodded her head in the way you adjust your pillow. Hooker knew she was going to take a nap.

"If you're going to take a nap, let's go back to the truck so I can join you in the sleeper."

She sat up with sleepy eyes, but with a smile.

The radio crackled, and then Karen's voice came through the speaker. "Hooker, Salinas Impound wants to know if you are snagging the trailer this afternoon."

The radio jarred the two awake, and Hooker reached around the small wall to grab the mic. "Just finished up in Monterey and will be there in about an hour."

"10-4. Have you been eating ice cream? You have the voice going on."

Hooker smirked. Dolly would have his hide, but he knew Karen would never talk. "No, darlin'... This is the real deal."

There was dead silence, as he knew the two daytime dispatchers would be first shocked, and then would turn into two large masses of jiggling giggles. He rehung the mic and swung his legs over the edge of the bed. He looked back as Candy rolled overtaking the rest of the blanket to herself. He reached over and tucked it up around her shoulders.

Slipping into his boots, he moved to the driver's seat and fired Mae West back into life. Slipping her into gear, he eased her out into the large lot and then nosed her out onto the street. As he cleared the main area of Monterey, he pushed the eight-track tape into the slot and turned the volume up for comfortable listening. The boys of Texas were just starting into some clear blue water.

1 8

____

WEDNESDAY NIGHT DINNER was a most unusual affair. For anyone who had ever attended Dolly's usual affairs—this one didn't make sense.

Historically, the table was a mix of males drawn from law enforcement, tow truck drivers, and political figures ranging from city officials to the occasional member of Congress. Dolly's reach was far and wide, and it was all focused on what was good for the running of the sprawling city of San Jose and the areas around, better known as the South Bay Area.

Hooker had become a weekly fixture at the head of the table. Nothing had ever been verbalized or acknowledged, but it was obvious to all Hooker was Dolly's anointed one. Dolly played close to the vest, but it was also a known fact the large lollypop microphone sitting behind her desk was a direct line to no other truck than the eleven tons of Mae West and Hooker's left ear.

The largest standout of the unusual was Willie and Maddie. Neither had much of an interest in the running of the city—other than Maddie being a librarian at one of the county libraries. Willie, retired from the Navy for over ten years, was well past any interest in any kind of politics.

Two of the three highway patrolmen were good friends of Hooker. They were the first clue to Hooker that there would be a meeting after dinner. The 'on medical leave' CHP captain sat in the middle of the table. The other, Micha, was one seat down from Hooker. On any other dinner night, either one would blend in with the mix. To have them both there, along with Willie and Maddie, was the clincher in Hooker's mind. *There had been discoveries made, and movement was in the works.*

The third officer, Steven Huggs—was the almost newbie to the table.

Hooker looked to the Squirt at the other end of the long table, seating five down each side. Hooker could tell he was trying to add up the fact of the four—especially Maddie.

Dolly had been stirring things up a bit by having, first, Micha's wife attend, and then had Candy stand in for Hooker the last time he was in the hospital. But Maddie had them both stumped.

The Squirt looked down the table at Hooker, who just shrugged. As usual, all would be revealed when Dolly decided. With these four, it would be the after-dinner meeting.

Long ago, Hooker had learned from watching Dolly that his job at the table was to listen to the conversations, not necessarily participate. He had watched how she hovered with the coffee carafe or the water pitcher. It appeared she was constantly moving, but it was where or how she was moving that had finally caught Hooker's attention. She could be attentive to a select couple or few if the conversation was of interest and to her advantage to listen in on. Even at almost a quarter-ton of mass, she had the ability to become almost invisible as she moved about the table.

Some nights were functions of small talk where she only learned more about certain men, and other nights were a rich harvest of things outside the gray concrete walls important to her Machiavellian ministrations of the city and county.

Tonight, Hooker could tell by Dolly's smooth flow about the table—it was a night of small talk and fluff. There was talk of the upcoming Thanksgiving slug-fest that started the season of blood on the streets.

Most 'civilians' would talk about the holidays and think of parties and gatherings. Law enforcement and tow truck drivers saw things from the perspective of what happens after the parties and gatherings. The only times of the year rivaling the holiday season were the Fourth of July and the two weekends of Labor Day and Memorial Day.

The little stuff like jump-starting batteries and fixing flat tires were the little things keeping Hooker and the Squirt busy while they waited for a crash involving a big rig truck. There were only a few tow companies in the South Bay who handled big trucks. The stretch of the 101, from the south end of San Jose to Gilroy, known as Blood Ally, was Hooker's domain.

One of the drivers from the north end turned to Hooker. "I understand your buddy officer Aligo just opted to transfer back to King and Story?"

Hooker frowned as he mopped up the last of the spaghetti sauce with the end of the sourdough roll. "Why would James do that? He already has lead fragments floating around in him from the Gun and Knife club."

"The way I hear it, he took it because they were looking to put a K-9 unit in there. So not only does he bump up into K-9s, but he also becomes a sergeant. I think he also speaks the languages, too."

Hooker rolled his head. "He's Filipino, but yeah, I know he speaks Spanish and Tagalog, so Vietnamese wouldn't surprise me." He stuffed the last tiny piece of food in his mouth as he pointed his finger in the air. "I think he was out there for a few years before. Every time he was shot or stabbed, they would ask him where he wanted to transfer to, and he'd tell them he had work left to do. I guess maybe he thinks he has some more work to do out there." Hooker chuckled. "Or it's just too dang boring in the south end. He's like me, a nightcrawler."

Hooker looked out the door into the dark room where Dina and Patty were sitting in their pools of light over the switchboard of snakes in holes. Dina could sense Hooker's look. It was time. Without even looking, she nodded.

A few minutes later, there was a sharp whistle from Dina, and all conversations around the table stopped. It was so sudden, Willie and Maddie were left blinking and wondering what happened. Everyone else knew at the whistle, words were cut-off, half-spoken conversations were finished, and the evening was done.

"Mike, you have a T-wonderful holding at westbound Story at the bottom of the ramp.

"Pete, your backup just went 10-7 for dinner, and the auto club is holding a T-3 for you on North Stevens Creek.

"Lupe, Jose is wondering if you died and went to heaven. There are ten pounds of sausage from Chairamonte's in the fridge unless Dolly has dropped it in your lap." Dolly picked up his plate and substituted the box of meat.

"Don, you are on duty in three more hours. Go get some sleep—and leave your home radio off."

"Steven, there is a fender bender southbound 101 at Kooser. Chip, dispatch asked if you could go take it. Probably a no report, but they want an officer to show up.

"Ace, there is a commercial waiting at the Fly's. Pack your bag. It's going to Bakersfield."

Dolly held her hand on Chet's shoulders. She nodded to Willie, Maddie, and Micha to stay seated. As the drivers and CHP officer filed out, they all got a Dolly hug, and Hooker shook their hands at the front door after he had checked the closed-circuit TV to make sure it was safe. As the more seasoned men walked up to the large steel door, they kissed their two left fingers and touched them to the badge they knew was welded just over the doorknob—badge number 701.

In the ensuing silence of the aftermath and as Dolly rinsed and placed the dishes in the dishwasher, Willie looked over at Hooker. "Well, so this is what lodge meetings look like." He smiled as he knew there was more to the dinner than met the casual eye.

Hooker looked at Dolly, who seemed to be busy and not paying attention to the table. He knew different, as she stopped for a second and then nodded as she resumed her work. Hooker had the go-ahead to reveal the inner workings. Family was family.

"Steven was here about... what? A year ago or two?"

The head and shoulders of the large woman never broke stride. "Seventeen months ago."

Hooker nodded and continued. "It was his first time at the table. Right now, he is up for promotion to sergeant. He's on the list but had never met Chet. He's a good officer, but Chet needed a closer look at the man. Roping Micha into the deal was an extra bonus as they will be sergeants together. The difference will be Micha will now be a senior sergeant." He winked at Chet, who had just had the wind knocked out of his sails.

Hooker looked over at his longtime friend, Micha. "Sorry to step out in front of you in breaking the news, but Bobby Sue looked a little tight in the pants the last time I saw her. Knowing the extra bump in pay is coming will make it easier on the little bump under her shirt." He looked at the wide-eyed officer.

Micha's gaping mouth shut, then he opened it as he leaned forward. "Man, nothing gets past you, does it? We weren't going to tell anyone until she was really showing."

Dolly turned as she dried her hands. "Oh, she's showing, Micha... that is if you're Hooker. He told me last week her scrubs were getting tighter top and bottom, but she wasn't getting a fat neck for him to nuzzle. You don't need a second opinion, not with Hooker and fat necks."

Hooker smirked and hid his face in his coffee.

Chet chuckled. "Anything else on the docket? I mean, all of my secrets are on the table now that you filled Micha in on his new promotion..."

Hooker smiled. "Other than we think Mike is carrying a diamond ring around in his pocket? Or, that Lupe is about to buy in as a full partnership with Jose? No... But I do think Pete might be about ready to get out of towing. He has been tired, and getting him to work evenings on Tuesdays and Thursdays, has been like pulling teeth for the last two years. I don't know what he's been taking, but I'm pretty sure he has been at night school. As for Ace... Ace is just always a good man to fill out the group."

Maddie looked at Dolly, who was now standing behind the Squirt pouring coffee. "And you do this every week...?" Dolly smiled and kept pouring as if to say, *welcome to my world.*

Micha leaned back. "So now that my world is blown apart, what are we four doing here?"

Hooker took the lead. "You four or more specifically, the six of us were the main event." He looked to Chet. "Chet, care to lead off with what you found?"

Chet pulled a piece of paper from his pocket and unfolded it. "Theresa Johanna Pappas moved to Saratoga, where she got a job as a cocktail waitress at first Bill's and then moved up in the world out at the Cats. Her last known address was on Trent in some apartments, which are no longer there. We have her showing eleven weeks of income at the country club and then nothing. It was as if she dropped off the face of the earth.

"Interestingly, a new gal started the next week at the country club and at the Cats with a Social Security number going nowhere. Her name was Danielle Patterson. And the address they both had was to a P. O. Box in Las Gatos. I couldn't find any bank accounts, but then over the years, banks have come and gone."

Maddie mused, "So there is no way to know if this Danielle Patterson is really Teresa Pappas or not?"

"Correct."

Micha looked up. "Unless... she got married under either name."

Willie asked, "County records?"

Micha smiled. "To start, or state—even the state would have a record."

Ever the librarian, Maddie qualified the statement. "As long as they got married in this state. But what if they ran off to Reno to get married?"

The Squirt sat up and beamed. "As I was working on one of the papers last month, I happened across another interesting note. Even if you get married in a foreign country, they will also file a conformed copy of your marriage in the state and county you reside in. So as long as she was still living here, this is where the document would be filed."

Hooker frowned. "What if she lived here and her new husband lived in, say, Contra Costa?"

"Same applies. A conformed copy would be filed in each county and another with the state of California. Otherwise, divorces would be a nightmare."

Micha muttered into his coffee. "They already are. Just ask half of any police force."

Chet nodded sadly along with him. It was a known occupational hazard of being a cop—especially the CHP. The irony of the 'nicknames 'Chips' or 'Chippy' and their connotations for 'chipping' or having sex on the side—was not lost on the rank and file.

Hooker allowed a brief time of reverence then looked at Maddie. "So we now know who and where to look. Could you do that, or should we turn the Squirt loose on bird-dogging her to the ground?"

Maddie looked at the kid. "Run her to the ground, and you're off the hook for research reports until after Thanksgiving. Bring us a valid new address, and I'll let you run naked until next year."

Hooker laughed. "Hell, I want in on that deal." Knowing what was coming next—he fished a quarter out of his pocket and slid it down the table to Willie for the swearing jar. The man just nodded and stuck it in his shirt pocket.

19

THE DRIZZLE WAS light as Hooker began dropping the chains and hooks off the Peterbilt that had seen a better day on Monday. Tuesday, it had a problem braking, and the northbound 2:45 Freight Express had sheared off about two feet of the truck's front end. A few more inches and the train would have hit the engine and completely messed up the driver's day. As it was, the guy had gotten a ride to the hospital, but only for a few nicks and cuts and a large headache.

"Hey, Hooker?"

Hooker stood up to watch the small Japanese woman bounce from island to island to miss the puddles. Hooker had once seen a television show about football players training. He snickered to think the woman everyone called 'Fly' would have done pretty well at the tire thing. She made one last hop and was on the large island with Hooker.

"What the hell you doing out in this yuck, Fly? Even Box is smart enough to stay in the cab."

"Dolly said you might be interested in a flip I have up north?" A flip is where there is a tow going out and one coming back from the same area.

Hooker hefted the loose chain into the working bed of Mae. "I'm always interested in a good flip. North, south, east, or west—as long as it isn't too far west."

"I've got a Kenworth salvage who wants to go up to Mendocino and a thirty-two-foot bus coming back down from Sebastopol for Hawkins. I think he's going to turn it into an RV or some nonsense. The bus is in a yard so you can pick it up anytime, but the Kenny wants to be there Wednesday because they are taking the four days for Thanksgiving."

Hooker pulled up the last of the chains and puddled it in the chain locker on his deck. Closing the lid, he turned. "So I can have Thanksgiving up in Marin?"

The woman smiled. "Take your girl. Show her you work for a living. Show her some pretty country and do what you want. What do I care? I'm taking six days and going over to Modesto and play with my granddaughter."

"Where is the Kenny now?"

She waved her hand out toward the south lot. "It's the blue one with the king sleeper. I'll leave the keys and paperwork in your cubby hole. You have all the keys, so take it up when you want."

"I'll talk to Candy. I think the school is closed for the whole week, so we might head up on Monday. I'll let you know so it's cleared."

The Fly was already hopping back across the yard. "It's all cleared, take it when you want."

Hooker smiled as he thought about going up to Marin. Hidden in the hills of Marin County was a place called the Apple Farm. It was owned by Stella's best friend for life—Claire and her husband, Norman. Their house guest was Hooker's sister. Norman Osofsky was a retired psychiatrist, who had specialized in psychotherapy for kidnap victims and other prisoner survivors.

Hooker's sister was also a Claire, but at sixteen, she had become a runaway with a thirteen-year-old Hooker. When they had gotten to San Jose, Hooker had been found by redemption in the form of a man who became Uncle Willie. His sister found her home first on the streets and then within a tribe of beings best described as denizens of the night. To save her life, Hooker, and others had staged her death. After some time in a hospital bed, she was released into the care of the Osofskys.

The mind is a fragile organ. Nobody knows how resilient Hooker's sister is, but if need be, she has a permanent home available to her at the

Apple Farm—a home as caring and open as the two homes Hooker split his time between. The brief visit with Candy a couple of months before had been a delicate bonding between the two women, and Hooker looked forward to them having some more time together.

Hooker climbed up into the cab of Mae West only to be staring at the single eye of a very large cat standing on the expansive dashboard. Hooker just laughed. "Okay, okay, I'll take you over to the lawn at the school."

The gigantic engine revved as Hooker slipped in the gears, released the brakes, and nosed the truck out of the muddy yard. Rolling down the back streets into the Willow Glen side of the Almaden Expressway, Hooker ran his hand over Box, still standing guard and a reminder to Hooker he needed some lawn.

Hooker never subjugated the standing of the cat or his preferences. Hooker liked French vanilla triple-scoop ice cream in a sugar cone, Box wanted lawn. Don't try to make Hooker eat Rocky Road or pistachio, and Box won't go near mud. It's not the wet because he loves to be in the really hard rain and roll in sprinklers on the grass—it was the dirt or, more specifically, the cliché clay mud sticking to his fur and especially gets up between his toes.

Hooker opened the door, and the orange streak flew through the opening. Hooker pulled the air brake knob and rolled out of the cab. Pulling the lead hammer from its hole, he started banging it on the tires to check for a flat or slow leak. By the sound alone, he could tell if a tire was just a few pounds low. The routine was several times a day. It was also a time for Hooker to think.

He was mulling over things Ben had talked about, and what the Squirt had said about family. Hooker only had Claire or the Mouse, as she had become known as, for the last ten years. They had been fostered kids together in a broken system who ended up selling them from abuser to abuser or pedophile. When they had finally run away, they ended up back together and ran as the only family they knew. When Hooker had been taken in by Willie, Claire had made it known to Hooker she knew where he was, and she was close by. Over the years, they stayed in touch through the underground telegraph of the homeless, the street urchins, and the denizens of the night. There was always some sort of connection.

Now she was only a hundred miles away or at the end of a phone call. She wouldn't talk on the phone, but Hooker could talk through Claire and Norman so there was contact—but she never seemed so distant.

Hooker glanced at his watch and noted the time. Turning, he called for Box. "Come on, Box, let's go pick up your boyfriend." Hooker still wasn't sure how he felt about the usually picky cat taking to the Squirt by the second day. They even put up with each other enough to sleep together, something Hooker would not do, as the cat had a habit of pushing Hooker out of bed or at least taking the pillow and three-quarters of the bed. Hooker had taken to closing his door, but the Squirt and Box seemed to find an agreement about sharing a bed, a couch, or even the sleeper in the truck.

Willie's boyfriend, Hank, had a feeling Box understood the Squirt needed a friend who was physically there for him. The cat filled the need. After all, the Squirt had initially started into the family when Hooker stabbed his fork through the Squirt's left hand, and then a week later, the two of them got shot full of dimes by a crazed killer with a shotgun—after that, sleeping with a cat didn't seem so weird.

Hooker closed the door behind the bounding feline. Box stepped up onto the passenger seat and shook like a dog. Hooker laughed as he was certain the Squirt wouldn't check the seat before he sat on the wet. "What? I don't let you beat up any dogs for a few months, and so you're going to start pulling pranks on poor Squirt?"

The cat looked at Hooker with a slow blink of his one eye. It was as close to the zombie head roll Hooker would ever get from the cat.

The large truck nosed out of the school parking lot and headed for the county hall of records.

"Sure. When do we leave?" Candy sat on Hooker's lap.

Hooker stared at Manny, who raised his hands up with palms out. "Don't look at me. You kids are over twenty-one and on your own. You both have keys and your own diaper drawers. I'm just a fly on the wall."

The three younger people at the table all laughed. Stella rose to hide her smile. She had never felt so full. A few months before, she felt blessed to have part of Hooker for a son. Now she had a daughter and parts of two boys.

She stacked the plates on the counter. Turning, she leaned against the sink. "How much would you lose if you took off the week?

"A few hundred, but being Thanksgiving week—maybe more."

"How much for the flip?"

"Six hundred and forty, but because it's not through Don, I get it all, less expenses. Fuel will be about two hundred, and about two hundred should go into the tire fund, so it's about a wash."

Manny joined in. "Have you talked to Don?"

Hooker looked back at Manny. "Checked in this afternoon. He's got a new guy he wants to run hard for a week and see if he can really do backup for me, so this week would be a good trial."

Manny rolled forward on his elbows and lifted his butt off the seat pad of his wheelchair. It wasn't about cooling his ass, as much as a physical manifestation of the ex-detective shifting mental gears. He dropped back down and leaned back. "What did Dolly think?"

"She'll miss me on Wednesday night for dinner, but she had decided to have the girls bring their husbands and Karen's kids for a full Thanksgiving dinner. She was going to invite Willie, Hank, and Maddie too, but I reminded her they would be here the next night along with the Sweets and a bunch of others. But as for towing, she was fine. Jose has a new Trail-All so he could flat-bed any large tractors—he just can't do any recovery so the chips would have to call down Tri-Counties for anything big."

Candy nuzzled into Hooker's neck. "So we can go for the whole week?"

"Do you have any homework?"

She slumped. "Spoiled sport. Of course, I do, and I'll take it."

Hooker looked around at the Squirt. "Speaking of homework…"

The kid sat up. "I have a few possibilities which are looking good." His eyes rolled up in his head for a moment. Hooker knew he was looking at the image of whatever he was recalling. The kid's photographic memory was a blessing as well as a curse.

The Squirt's voice took on the slight difference Hooker was coming to recognize as his robot reading the images in his brain voice. "There is a William B. Gaddis of Santa Clara who married a Daniela Quimms of San Jose, and they are now living in Fremont. There is a Feldman Yurin Slovinotskia who married a Danita Esperanza, and they still live in Los Gatos. Monty P. Helmand married Donna Schmitz, and they are in Willow Glen Cemetery—a car crash. And then there is a guy who married a woman named Dani, spelled Dani. I'm trying to track down more recent information."

Hooker laughed. "You are so full of bull pucky, Squirt."

"Why?" The kid looked hurt.

"Who names their kid Yurin?" Separated out, all five got the joke and laughed.

20

THE SQUIRT SAT at a large table, sifting through boxes of records. Occasionally, he would sneeze, and a soft voice from a few aisles over would bless him. Many of the records were not typed but, instead, handwritten in a crabbed fashion precluding comprehension. The thought of anyone in the future possibly needing the records of who married whom on what date was not what the office drone had been paid enough to even think about.

"I don't think I want to become a cop," the Squirt groused as he lifted one set of records out of the box he had just put a large stack into.

The voice had moved and now seemed to come from a much higher level in the stacks of large shelves filled with boxes. "Why not?"

The Squirt looked at the top sheet in the file. The handwriting was in pink ink and could be ancient Greek, Russian, or some form of Middle Eastern northern Arabic. He groaned and leaned back in the chair. "Because I'd rather track down all of these moron clerks and just shoot them. In 1868, three guys by the names of Sholes, Glidden, and Soule in Milwaukee, Wisconsin, built the first commercially viable typewriter. The S&G was manufactured by the sewing machine division of Remington's small arms. By 1880, the typewriter was changed by Remington, and the QWERTY keyboard with uppercase and lowercase was introduced, and the rest is history. So by the time these office idiots got their first job, the typewriter was already an office fixture..."

The young blonde in a white blouse that did nothing to hide her prodigious breasts rounded the shelves. Her glasses were shoved up into the great soft clumping of hair wound loosely onto the top of her head.

The Squirt finished, "So why the dingbats can't type the information onto the forms is beyond me or any reasonable explanation."

The blonde leaned against the towering shelf clutching a large file below her breasts. She studied the young man.

The Squirt squirmed. "What?" He blinked as he ran his hand over his head in case he had a cowlick standing up.

"How do you do that?"

"I licked my palm and just rubbed... oh, you didn't mean..." The Squirt blushed.

She smiled as her eyes lowered in a new evaluation. "No. No, I wasn't talking about your hair... and it's fine, by the way. I was talking about knowing about the typewriter."

The Squirt blushed even harder. His face dipped. "I wrote a paper on it last month."

"On typewriters? What kind of paper?"

"Regular typing paper—twenty-pound bond, soft-faced cellulose."

"No, not the paper, but the paper..." She suddenly realized he was teasing her, and it was her turn to blush. "I meant, what was the paper on and what was it for? I thought you said you didn't start at the academy until January."

"You might say I'm getting privately schooled in preparation for the academy." Thinking about Hooker and how his assignments still hadn't stopped, he groaned a little inside. "And, it might continue after, as well."

"So what was the paper on, if not the history of typewriters?"

"Actually, the history was for extra credit. But the paper was about filling out police reports dating back to the fifteenth century."

The blonde held up a large file and blew across the top, sending a cloud of dust into the air. "I think some of these files have been sitting here since the fifteenth century." She turned back to the young man. "So this *was* for the academy—police stuff?"

The Squirt leaned back in the chair. "Just as much as this investigation is police business." He rocked forward and stretched. It had been a long day chasing names through forests of bad handwriting, valleys of misfiled paperwork, and mountains of just paper forms useless to the search. "There is an old... well, older librarian who is kind of private tutoring me."

"What subject?"

The Squirt considered the young clerk. She had been the only clerk to want to assist in anything but sitting at their desk and doing as little as possible. In the Squirt's opinion, the county payroll was largely padded by large padded rear-ends that should be ejected. The exception was the blonde in front of him, Beth.

What had started with the Squirt waiting an hour at the counter for an answer, had become an invitation into the back stacks, and eventually, where they were now—the basement. Here was where the older records lay forgotten. Large cubes of paperwork sat in cardboard sarcophagi entombed in the catacombs of the county's heart and soul of dust and deterioration. But in the dead garden of the basement, there was a single spring daffodil.

The Squirt shook his head slightly, realizing he had been staring and was lost in the powder blue eyes floating above the full red lips. "I'm sorry, I was... um, and what did you ask?"

A slow smile tugged at the one side of her face. "I asked where you were taking me to dinner tonight."

The Squirt reran his trusted mental tapes. He was certain it had not been a question, but it was better than explaining the lack of a high school diploma. "How about a little Italian deli?"

She smiled. "Chiaramonte's? Sure, any day."

The Squirt looked around for a clock. Beth giggled. "We have an hour until I'm officially off." She pushed off the shelves. "I found these—and they are typed." She laid them on the end of the table. The stack was only four inches of very thin folders.

Pulling through the stack, she continued to explain. "These were misfiled for some reason. These are addendum reports for city or county employee's requests on cross transfers, and some of it is requests for special time off."

"What is special time off?"

"Having babies, death in the family, getting married, extended illnesses —stuff like that. Kind of like getting shot full of dime-sized holes." She smiled at the story he had told her earlier. After all, who is going to believe a guy could get shot full of holes the size of a dime—and still live?

"The holes were made by dimes, so think more like a slot, not a round." He held her eyes as he raised the side of his shirt. The large welts of surgical scar were still livid pink.

Her mouth dropped open and then closed as if it were holding a dime. Her eyes grew large as the red swelled up out of her blouse to her face. "I thought you were just bullshitting me to try to get in my pants..."

He dropped the edge of his t-shirt. "Why would I lie to get into your pants? They probably wouldn't fit me anyway." He sat stoic and only blinked once. Stella and Manny would be proud of him playing the deadpan face game. He enjoyed watching the young clerk become more and more flustered. For once, he wasn't the one on the end of a skewer.

He reached over and took a part of the stack. "Was this all of it, or was there more?"

Her mind had trouble shifting gears, but finally, the connection hit. "No, I mean... Yes, this is all of it. That's what made it stand out. It's not even in the right area. Some of these dates are only, umm... sixteen years old, and so they should still be upstairs in the county general area." She looked up at the Squirt. "And there should be a couple of boxes for each year." She pointed to the now two small stacks. "This is all there was—just sitting there in an unmarked box..."

The Squirt finished her thought. "Like someone had moved them here to hide them?"

"Exactly."

Johnny smiled, not feeling so much like the Squirt here. "Well, pull up a chair, partner, and let's see if we can figure out who is trying to hide what."

Much later, Beth yawned as she pushed the take-out boxes down the table. She blinked to clear her eyes and marveled as she watched the young man. She couldn't figure out which name she preferred. Johnny had an appeal, but the Squirt was a derogatory term she had heard the cops use, and Johnny owned it as an earned title. The man was a walking conundrum. His formal schooling had stopped midway through his freshman year of high school, but his love of reading, combined with his eidetic memory, pushed his learning and knowledge far beyond her two years at Santa Clara Junior College.

She leaned forward as she adjusted her glasses. Rereading the request for marital leave by an assistant district attorney, she thought it a bit quaint. The newlyweds were going to spend time in New York and visit Niagara Falls. Time requested—three weeks. She put the form on the done pile and moved to the next form.

A request for leave to give birth was accompanied by two doctors' letters describing stressful conditions requiring bed rest for the last trimester.

A request for a sabbatical leave of three years to do missionary work in Bolivia as supported by the minister and three lay ministers' letters.

The request for emergency compassionate leave was accompanied by a telegram to *'cum now—she ded.'*

Beth leaned in close and read the next request for two-week marital leave. She read it again. The names fit, as did the date. She looked up.

She cleared her throat.

The Squirt looked up. His eyes cleared. He, too, was wearing out looking through all of the forms.

Beth leaned back. "Where would you go on your honeymoon?"

He frowned. "What?"

"You heard me." She leaned forward and crossed her arms on the table and forms. "Let's say we're getting married."

"When?"

She glanced down at the form and looked back. "December twentieth."

"Hawaii, if we could afford it. At least take the train down to sunny San Diego. Where would you?"

"If money was tight—San Diego or Mexico. But if I could have my fantasy—Tahiti."

The Squirt nodded. "Those work. But what about if it was the summer?"

"Are you asking me to marry you?" She giggled. "You haven't even asked me out on a date."

Johnny smirked and pointed at the take-out containers from Chiaramontes. "I took you to one of the most exclusive places to eat in the whole South Bay Area."

They both laughed, and the connection was complete. Any future date was a given.

Beth held up the form. "This is a request for two weeks to get married and honeymoon in… wait for it… none other than sunny San Francisco."

"Who is requesting it?"

"Deputy district attorney. My question is… who the hell would spend two weeks in San Francisco over Christmas and New Year?"

"Who is the blushing bride?"

"Who said anything about blushing?"

"Because you are… and your respiration is up, too. So she is…?"

"Dani—with an 'i,'" She spun the form over to him.

He read the form, and his smile grew. He looked up. "Do you know what this means?"

Beth nodded. "More than you know—it means we're on the wrong floor, the wrong building, and looking in the wrong direction." She looked at her watch. "But if we hurry, we can maybe get some work in before the library closes."

"Library?" He watched her stand as he pushed out his chair.

"Did I mention the word *hurry*?"

The librarian stepped into the small research room. "Beth, we're going to close in ten more minutes."

The hand waved over the microfilm machines. "Thanks, Marianne, we won't be much longer."

The Squirt's head was resting on her shoulder as she moved expertly through the microfilm. The images slid past with only brief moments of hesitation. They now knew who they were looking for and who they had become in the last sixteen years. What they now looked for was recent confirmation of one other thing.

The Squirt's hand shot out. "There." He waved a finger at the screen.

"No, go back. More... more... there!" He leaned in squinting. "Can you make it..."

She expanded the view. The Squirt leaned back as the large shoulders and deep plunging V-necked dress adorned by a necklace and a large pendent swelled to fill the viewer.

Beth breathed. "Wow."

Johnny smirked. "Wow is right. I'll get you one as a wedding present."

They looked at each other.

He cleared his throat after a moment. "You asked why they would go only fifty miles away for their honeymoon—it was because it was familiar." They looked back at the picture of the couple at a gala event. "My guess is when he has to travel for his work, she doesn't go with him. Maybe fear of flying, but also maybe just uncomfortable with new surroundings."

Beth put her hand on the screen near the pendant. Her voice was soft and almost breathless. "If you're not kidding about the necklace, we can skip right to the third date."

2 1

THE DRIVE UP to Mendocino had been a smooth run. About Santa Rosa, Hooker had glanced over to see Candy nodding off, so he told her to climb into the sleeper. He slipped the eight-track of the Texas Boys Choir into the player and turned it up to just above low.

After a bit, Box thought it might be safe to go get a close look at the new person—and climbed up into the sleeper. Hooker glanced back as Box figured she might smell enough like the Squirt and settled in.

The next time Hooker looked back, Candy's arm was wrapped over the cat, and they were both either purring or dead to the world. Hooker just shook his head. There was just no figuring out his partner. The cat goes from only Hooker and Dolly can touch him to everybody skate in one brief summer. Hooker downshifted as he came into the town of Willets. *Next thing we know, Box is going to give up beating up every dog he sees.*

Hooker checked his mirrors to see how the Peterbilt was doing. *Nah, he'll never give up ripping a dog a new asshole—it's payback and too much fun for him.*

Hooker started thinking Box's love of fighting wasn't controllable—it was his nature. It was what he was used to. So if that goes for a cat that is almost human in certain ways, how much stronger would the comfort of a routine be for a human? Specifically—one Teresa Pappas—how far would she stray from what she knew?

Hooker mulled the question over until long after he had turned south in Fort Bragg. Candy had woken up, and Box shook himself as if he had never been touched by the stranger and took up a position on the dashboard to let Hooker know he needed some lawn.

Candy slid down into the passenger seat and looked about. "What did I miss?"

Hooker laughed as he saw a turn out close to some lawn. He looked over at the still sleepy-eyed Candy and teased, "Just a few herds of deer, a couple of elk, and a UFO."

Candy looked at him dully and smacked her lips and then rolled her head back in a zombie roll. Hooker groaned inside. *Oh, god, she is spending way too much time with Stella.* The zombie was the family response to stupid comments or questions.

"You must think I'm some kind of stupid, Hooker."

Hooker set the brakes and kicked his door open for the orange rocket. Sliding out of the conversation and truck was his only defense. He took it. Candy got out and stretched as she watched the strange thumping routine of checking the tires. Hooker checked the tires on the towed truck, too.

As Hooker and Box finished at the same time, they resumed their route west to the coast, and then south toward Mendocino. Candy watched as the sparsely wooded scenery turned to an ocean view. Hooker could tell she was working up to asking about something.

"Why do you do that?"

"What?"

"The big hammer on the tires." She turned in her seat toward Hooker.

"When the air pressure is correct, the hammer bounces just right in my hand. If it's too high, the hammer feels wrong on the strike. It's like hitting metal. If the pressure is low, the hammer won't bounce."

"But if you were getting a flat, wouldn't you know it?"

"Not really. Especially if it's one of the inside drivers—they can go flat and then shred, and you might never feel a thing. Meanwhile, you are throwing twenty-pound chunks of hard rubber out behind you. Those chunks can punch out a windshield and take a person's head clean off."

"You're kidding me."

Hooker looked over at her. His eyes were flat and lifeless.

"Oh, lord... you've seen it, haven't you?"

Hooker just nodded.

Candy sat back around quietly. She needed to process the new information. Hooker's hand dangled down and found the fuzzy ear. It wasn't clear to Hooker, who was more reassured by the rubbing of Box's ear, but he did know Box purred, and he felt calmer. It was a symbiotic partnership, and every time Hooker rubbed the single ear left, a part of him remembered finding the tiny bloody handful of fluff in a cardboard box stuck under an abandoned car Hooker was to tow. The chewed up thing had mewed only once, and then settled into Hooker's coat and purred all the way to the vet's office. The vet had advised euthanasia for the dog-mauled kitten, but Hooker had turned his pockets out, and emptied his wallet on the table, stating he would get more—just save the cat.

A week later, he picked up the kitten in a box. But the cat preferred being inside his leather jacket, next to the beating of Hooker's heart and the smell of the starched white t-shirt. As he grew, the box was his home in the truck and had become his name.

"She's not your real sister..."

Hooker's mind shifted. He smiled slightly as he knew this was the real thing on Candy's mind. He gently shook his head no. He glanced at the directions on the clipboard and downshifted as he flicked his left blinker.

Moving the train of two trucks into the center turn lane, he answered the next question. "I was four when we first met, and she was six."

"Where?"

"I think we were somewhere south of San Bernardino—maybe Temecula area. It was a nice couple, and they had a couple of kids of their own but were older, like ten or twelve."

"When did you start considering her to be your sister?"

"I was about six when we were moved back down the hill from a farm in Mentone. The older couple had never had kids, and they were going to try fostering. The place was in Riverside." Hooker slowed and eased off the street into a large parking lot. The signage matched up to the paperwork.

"I'll be right back." He grabbed the clipboard and slipped out of the cab. Candy watched him stride across to the building. She had never really watched him walk since being shot up. She smiled. He swaggered like Gary Cooper in High Noon.

A half-hour later, they were wheeling out of the yard. "Ready for some lunch?"

Candy kneaded the large lap full of purring orange fur. "Box and I want to know if there is a wharf with fresh crabs and lobster here too, like down in Monterey." She gave Hooker a large hungry smile. Box just looked at him with a half-closed eye.

Holding up directions. "If these are correct, I think we will be close."

The picnic bench on the lawn overlooking the ocean was its own delight. The food, on the other hand, was too much, too good, and beyond the hype by the trucking company's secretary.

Hooker leaned back and rolled his eyes. "Oh, boy, I think I need a nap."

Candy nodded down past the table at a section of the lawn. Box was stretched out sound asleep in the afternoon sun. Hooker nodded and got up to retrieve the moving blanket from the truck. The afternoon sunshine sounded better than the stagnant air in the sleeper of the truck. Hooker spent his life in the truck, so even though the fall temperature wasn't warm, a light blanket over them made for a nice nap before heading south again.

"RIVERSIDE." CANDY REMINDED Hooker where he had left off.

"Riverside." Hooker's mind spun back. "I think I fell in love with her in a pile of leaves. The couple we were with... were nice. It was the last good home. They were older, but it was still fun. They understood or wanted to understand kids in a pile of leaves. The man raked all of the leaves from the two large yards and put them in a pile in the back yard for us to play in.

"Sissy was wearing a gray sweater—probably too large for her, but then, everything was the wrong size for any of us fosters." Candy nodded —she knew.

"There was something about the softness of the sweater that matched her long hair and the way she touched. Even when we were wrestling in the leaves, she was soft and gentle. It was almost like it would hurt her if she was strong or brutal."

The dark highway miles of asphalt rolled under the truck as Hooker thought. Candy didn't push. She was involved with her own feelings and memories.

"We were rolling around in the leaves. The smells of fall were intense. People burned the leaves back then. But… then Sissy suddenly hugged me and kept holding me… She held me until I stopped squirming until I was calm. Then she whispered in my ear. She told me we would always be brother and sister, no matter whatever happened."

Hooker looked over at Candy. "I think that is when I knew I loved her. I didn't understand love… heck, I'm not sure I do even now… but I cared more about her than I did about anything else."

Candy started to speak and then cleared her throat. "Forever love." She nodded and laid her head against the window and looked out into the night. Hooker smiled sadly and echoed the words in his mind. *Forever love.*

Hooker saw the Steele Avenue exit was two miles ahead. It was a major street he had taken several times before. He knew of a Thrifty drug store about a half-mile west of the highway. It was a bit out of his way, but it was just one of those kinds of nights. He glanced over at Candy. "If I stop, do you promise not to laugh or make fun?"

She looked over and frowned. "Why would I make fun?"

"I'm just saying…"

An hour later, when they got to the Apple Farm and Hooker opened his mouth to say hello, his sister laughed. "You two stopped for French vanilla ice cream, triple scoops in a sugar cone." She looked at Candy. "Oh, tell me he hasn't got you doing it, too."

Candy laughed as she raised her cold leather-jacketed arms and hugged Sissy. "Of course not, silly… I'm a waffle cone kind of girl." Her voice had the same thick huskiness from eating ice cream while riding with the windows down—a Hooker habit. The two just giggled.

"You sound just like my brother."

22

HOOKER SNICKERED LIKE a small child. The four chairs with their backs turned toward him, and his sister towered over them. They sat between the chairs, with blankets completing the canopy. Hooker's smile mirrored the goofy smile of his sister. Neither had ever thought they would be in a blanket tent ever again, not since the second home they had been moved to in Bakersfield.

"You sound like a little boy."

Hooker laughed. "I *feel* like a little boy."

Sissy smiled softly—almost sadly. "I thought this would be the best way for us to get back to talking... just us."

Hooker knew what she was trying to say. She wanted to wipe out the years of her being the Mouse—commander or queen of a large tribe of night people, the kind creeping about the dark crevices and cracks of society. She wanted to go back to before the owners of the foster homes had turned from caring people to predatory abusers and pedophiles. To reset the clock to when they didn't have to live in fear—when they were just happy children. Or at least as happy as a couple of orphans could be as they were moved from one house to another, sometimes more than twice in a year.

Hooker's face drew back on the right side, and he cocked his head over to the left as he watched his sister. "Remember the blue quilt?"

Her eyes lit up. She pursed her lips in thought—and then a guarded smile as her eyes softened. "Maude and JT Peltson."

"Pellerson." Hooker smiled as they remembered.

"It was made from her grandmother's dresses. I never knew if she was saying her grandmother was crazy, or the pattern of the quilt was crazy." They both snorted.

"They were the first black people I remember having seen. When we first got there, I kept waiting for them to wash the color off. It never did. I think she was the only one who ever sat me on her lap and just rocked me and hummed to comfort me."

Hooker nodded. "I saw you one night when I was supposed to be in bed asleep. Something had happened at school or something. You had been crying most of the afternoon."

Sissy was silent as she picked at her bare feet. She would just pick one up an inch and let it fall. Hooker knew she was thinking.

Sissy looked up and threw her hair behind her shoulder. "Remember the peach orchard across the road?" Hooker nodded with a small smile. "Those were some big peaches."

Hooker chuckled. "They probably tasted a lot better once they were ripe."

"Oh, you were sick as a dog." She pushed at his legs laughing... and then became very quiet.

"Dog?"

She nodded.

"He loved you with all his being, Sissy. He gave his life to save yours. He knew he would, I think, before the night."

She looked up at her brother.

"I think the night I was showing you how the killing would happen—he already knew and had been planning. For him, there was no plan B. It was all about saving you—killing Raven was just a bonus."

"It doesn't hurt any less."

"I hope it never does. He was special, so very special to you. I hope you have him in your heart all of your life. To love someone that deep—to be loved that much—is something most people don't even get to think about, much less know."

She picked up her foot and let it fall. "It's a two-edged sword."

"Yes."

Sissy watched his eyes. "Tell me about Willie."

Hooker looked out the side of his shaded eyes as he smirked. "What do you want to know?"

She giggled. "I already know about the dresses. The summer you and all of those Navy men built the big barn garage, I lived some of the time on the hill behind. I would watch from the shade of the chaparral. God, it was hot that summer."

Hooker snorted. "It's why those guys worked so slowly. There was beer and the pool at the end of the afternoon. I don't know who paid for all of the steaks, but I never ate so much meat."

"In the middle of the night, I used to come down and swim. The pool was cool."

"Willie's boyfriend at the time, Danny, had insomnia. He kept saying there was a water sprite who came out of the mountain to play in the water every night. We just thought he was nipping a little too much of Maddie's moonshine."

"He was the blond who was dying."

Hooker frowned. "How could you have known? He didn't know he had cancer until that winter."

Sissy shrugged. "He came out one night. He just stood on the patio—never said a word. He just watched. I'm pretty sure I was glowing pretty bright that night. He didn't know what to make of me. After a few minutes, he just turned and walked back inside. I never saw him again. But I knew then he was dying. I think he knew it, too."

Hooker thought about the yelling matches. Everything changed that winter. As it got bad, Hooker had decamped and bunked in at Manny and Stella's house. It had been a split living arrangement ever since. It was only in the last few years Hooker allowed himself to have more than a couple of extra T-shirts and jeans at Hacienda Romero.

The deciding factor had been the day Manny had a large dog door installed in the wall of the sunroom for Box to come and go as he wanted.

Hooker had figured if they were going to make that much accommodation for a cat, then he might as well relax and be part of the family. Besides, Stella was better at ironing his white T-shirts than he or Willie was.

"You're thinking about Willie?"

Hooker duck-lipped as he shook his head slightly. "Not just Willie—Manny and Stella, too... Well, actually, all of it." He looked up.

Sissy could sense where his mind was. She reached out and stroked her hand down along his cheek. "Don't. Please. I have no regrets. I chose my life. It was the one I was comfortable with. You were offered another path."

Hooker had many years to understand this truth. He snorted. "Offered! Hell, he smacked me on the butt with his newspaper. And then forced me to go have lunch with him." Hooker lay the back of his hand against his forehead.

Sissy laughed. She could tell Hooker loved the man he called his uncle and had fun talking about him. There was just a twinge of jealousy to have the kind of relationship they had. "So—tell me about those ugly dresses..."

23

NORMAN AND HOOKER sat in the late morning sun. The Adirondack chairs were perpetual icons on the sloping south-facing lawn. The fall mist hung in wisps through the bare black limbs of the orchard. The two men were bundled in large wool overcoats and Elmer Fudd hats. As Hooker sipped on the large steaming mug of coffee, he laughed at how he must look. Norman looked the part of a farmer, but Hooker felt the sham and the warmth of the costume. He had drawn the line at the large fuzzy gloves and settled for a pair of leather work gloves out of the truck.

After about twenty minutes, Claire Osofsky, knowing her husband, had brought out two large horse-hair sleigh blankets and spread them over the men's legs. She had topped off their mugs of coffee and returned to the warmth of the kitchen to prepare the soup for lunch.

Hooker realized this conversation would not be the friendly pat on the family member's hand, telling them everything is fine. Sissy was anything but fine.

"Her skin seems to have cleared up."

The older physician and psychiatrist smiled wanly. "Yes, the extreme eczema has responded to the topical steroids. But the worry is—what is a maintenance dose for something this extreme? As for the phosphor imbalance, the steroid cream helps with the itching, so the lesions from the scratching have healed—but we have been unable to control the over productions of the phosphors, so she still glows in the dark. I'm afraid it's a genetic thing she will always suffer from."

Hooker took a sip of coffee as he thought about when his sister had started glowing. The home was on the outskirts of Bakersfield near some cotton fields. Down the road where they had better access to water, the melon fields started. Hooker had thought things might be better here. The beatings at the previous house had started to be more about having him naked than just a form of punishment. At least at the new house, there were no beatings. But there also was no door on the bathroom, and both adults would watch as the children as they used the toilet or bathed.

One night, Sissy had come to Hooker's bed. She told him to get under the covers where it was totally dark… except, this night, it was not. Sissy was giving off a soft glow. Years later, she used the glow to her advantage as the mystical witch to control her tribe of denizens of the night.

"What about… well, Sissy herself?"

"Mentally?" Hooker nodded. Norman rolled his lips—this was the tough question. "She will always be in some kind of care. At best, she might migrate into a restricted group home." Norman watched the shadows race across Hooker's face. "But, based on what you two grew up with, I would say eventually, she would be a better candidate for some kind of institution—if she lives that long."

"But she's not dying…" Hooker understood the delicate nature of the discussion.

"No, no, she's not dying—per se, but she and her organs and systems are frail. Think of her as 'a woman in her late eighties,' and you have some idea just how far removed she is from her actual age of twenty-seven. Physically, she will never get better than about eighty.

"Claire and I have always eaten a healthy diet. But now with your sister Claire here, we watch everything. In a way, it can be a strain, but we have come to find having her here as a blessing we never thought we would have."

Hooker smiled. This was an old refrain for him. "She's like the daughter you always wanted, but never even hoped to have."

Norman looked over with large eyes.

Hooker smiled. "I've heard it dozens of times from Stella, Dolly, and my Uncle Willie. Some families are just meant to be, and if it means they happen instead of being created, they are no less a family. I know I'm blessed with a large family who cares about me—and even without having ever met Sissy, they were willing to go to extremes to save her life."

Norman looked out across the orchards and thought about how true and powerful it all was. The animal nature to bond and become a collective is strong in some. He thought about his favorite time of the year when the large white boxes appeared in his orchards. He and Claire would lie on the fertile ground under the trees and listen to the masses of bees hard at work above them. It was the collective that was about the renewal of life.

"I know you said you would be coming down this year with Claire for Manny and Stella's wedding anniversary, but what about Sissy?"

Manny and Stella had gotten married on the quay in front of the troopship before he shipped out. When he kissed his bride, four thousand soldiers whooped, whistled, and clapped. Ten minutes later, Manny had walked up the gangplank headed for Korea.

Stella and Claire had stood on the quay and watched the ship until it made a left turn toward the Golden Gate Bridge. Then they had bribed a sailor to take them across in the water ferry to San Francisco's tenderloin district where they danced until dawn at the USO, celebrating the marriage. With the sun coming up, they had taken an officer up on his offer to drive them the long way back around the bay to Oakland. It was Christmas morning. Every year after, Claire came to visit. She and Stella would get dressed to the nines and then go dancing in San Francisco— without Manny. It was tradition.

Norman stirred and looked over at Hooker. "You were saying... oh, yes, your sister. We've made arrangements for her to stay with someone. It will be fine. She'll be in loving hands." The man smiled reassuringly.

FRIDAY MORNING CAME TOO FAST for Hooker, as it did for the two new sisters who stood hugging in the front hall. Hooker's heart warmed from how Sissy and Candy had bonded from the start. They both recognized they were the flipsides of the same coin. Candy hadn't known anything about Sissy but had dealt with the creatures of the night. Sissy had been the matriarch of those creatures and had known a lot about the waitress, who had looked after the extended members of her tribe. Deep down, Sissy would say it was their fate to become close bonded. Hooker was just happy to be the center of the bonding.

He cleared his throat. "Do you two need to get a room? There is fuel burning, and Mae is getting overheated."

Sissy looked at Candy and then at her brother. "Someone else is getting overheated as well." Candy giggled into Sissy's neck and then pulled away.

"Okay, mister… rip me away from my sister. Drag me back down to the hell of books and classes. I'll just probably starve away from Claire's fine food as well."

Claire and Norman laughed. "Oh, I highly doubt Stella will let you starve. She taught me everything I know about cooking." She hugged Candy and then gave way for Norman.

Norman, ever the practical one, hugged her and let go. "It's only a few weeks until Christmas, so you won't starve too much before Claire and I come down."

Candy turned toward Sissy. "I wish you could come, too." She put her hand out, and the woman took it delicately.

"Arrangements have been made. You'll be fine. You need to study, but we'll see each other again soon enough." They hugged again.

Hooker knew his sister, and he smelled a bit of overacting going on, but time was wasting, and they would have to backtrack out to the 101 to pick up the return tow. He had opened the door before there was any more hugging or sentiments.

Later, as Hooker checked the mirrors to see how the towed bus was doing, he took in the pensive look on Candy's face as she studied her textbook. "Why the serious face?"

Candy looked up with a washed-out frown. "What?"

"You're even chewing on the right side of your lower lip."

She felt the lip with her tongue. She shrugged. "I was just thinking about Sissy." Candy loosened her belt and turned in the seat. "For the last ten years of her life, she was totally free, no constraints. But now, she will always have to live with someone."

Hooker weighed the concept. "Are you free? You have no rent to make, no food bill, not even a car payment or insurance payment. So you don't have any bills, you just have to go to school merrily.

"But there is an underlying responsibility. It's not written or spoken, but it's there.

"And, it was the same with her. No, they didn't have any responsibilities or obligations of society as we know it—but she was far from free. Dog was free, most of the others were free—but she was trapped in a prison of her own doing."

"Because she was the queen, she was responsible for all of them." Candy turned and looked forward down the road. "So do you think she is free now?"

Hooker curled his lips. "No, you clearly see the future for her. She will always be dependent on someone. But she is happier now without that life and death responsibility every single minute of every day. I think it was Shakespeare who said something about 'a weary head who wears the weight of a crown.'" Hooker checked the mirrors and upshifted.

"Oh, my sweet prince, now you willst speak to me of the bard of Stratford-on-Avon?" Candy giggled. "And here I thought you were just a pretty knight in a shiny steed."

Hooker chuckled.

Candy's smile faded. "But, seriously, you think she's going to be okay? I mean long term."

Hooker glanced over at the serious face but smiled at the freckles and ponytail. "How comfortable are you with the apartment, the car, and Stella and Manny taking you and your brother in?"

Candy thought quietly. "It's still uncomfortable."

"Enough to walk away uncomfortable? Enough to move back out and give up nursing school—that uncomfortable?"

"No. But you know what I mean. It's weird. You know how we grew up..."

"Yes. You two grew up the same as Sissy and me. Sissy and I—you and the Squirt, two makes of the same movie. And that is why I understand.

"Other people just used us, beat us, shit on us, and that's what we came to expect from the world. And then along comes Uncle Willie, who slaps me on the butt and then takes me home. Not to his bed—but gives me my own bed. He bought me clothes, and fed me, and asked for nothing in return. The return was something I had to figure out when I really understood he wanted nothing from me but my wellbeing. Then when the shit hit the fan with his boyfriend at the time, Stella and Manny showed me another bed was waiting. It was unconditional. All I had to do was learn to accept it and just say thank you.

"The night I met Stella, Claire, and Manny was a Christmas eve. I had cocoa and fresh chocolate chip cookies. I took the tow and hauled the girls up to Palo Alto to drop off Stella's Caddie at the dealer, and then took them home. By the time we got down to the hacienda, it was almost dawn. Manny knew I wouldn't take payment for the tow or accept a tip. Dolly had warned him. So he told me I couldn't refuse a Christmas present Stella had gotten me the year before, and he had just been holding on to it for me."

Hooker glanced over. "You know my money clip."

"With the little knife in it? Sure."

"Christmas morning, Manny gave me the clip with a few bills in it. The one showing was a five. I started to remove the bills to give them back. Manny told me a gentleman never counts the money in front of the person giving him a gift. In the evening, I went to pay for dinner—there were two hundred-dollar bills wrapped by the five."

Candy leaned back. "Whoa."

"Yeah, it was huge then. But a few years later, I understood it was just one of the little things. It's not the T-shirts hanging in the closet—it's that Stella washes and then irons them with just the right amount of starch. It's not the food on the table. It was when I dragged home a cat who didn't like anyone else. Stella still always buys food for Box, too. Maybe someday Box will understand and warm up to her. But it doesn't matter to Stella. Box is part of me, and it's enough for her. You and the Squirt were part of me, and it was enough for them. But you two have become more than that. You are also becoming the children they have always wanted but could never have. But with you, Stella doesn't have to share you with

Willie. So she gets the daughter all to herself. And if it means I hang around a bit more, she's happy there, too."

"So with Sissy?"

"She's where you are. She trusts me. And, she is starting to trust Claire and Norman will take care of her and love her like a daughter... it just takes time for it all to soak in."

"Are we talking about Sissy or me?"

"All three of you... heck, even me. It's been ten years, and I still have to pinch myself to know this is real. This truck is in my name. The company is in my name. Willie is just a co-signer on everything. The two beds are mine. I don't know if you noticed, but there are only three keys on this ring. One is for Mae, one is for the lockbox on the back, and the other key is to both houses. Willie had them all keyed alike so I could come and go at will."

"And with all the freedom..."

"I'm still not free. Even a bird has to find a worm every day."

Candy mulled it all over as she watched the highway. Through the trees, she could see the twinkling of lights across the bay to San Francisco. She thought about finding herself a worm...

She turned. "Speaking of finding things... did you ask Sissy?"

"About the waitress, Dani? Yeah—she gave me the name of a woman who might help if the Squirt hasn't solved the problem first. You know, it was amazing how really connected throughout the South Bay Sissy was. She knew about things down in Santa Cruz and up around the San Francisco airport. Her network was a lot more extensive than I had ever imagined."

Candy nodded. "She's a pretty amazing woman, too. Did you know she read over a hundred books a year?"

Hooker turned dumbfounded. "How? Where?"

"She had people bring them to her. She even had a library card... but never used it."

"What did she read?"

"A lot of best sellers—serious stuff, but also, a lot of the classical stuff too."

"Like Shakespeare?"

"Some, she liked the dystopian nature of a lot of his works. It made her realize the things weren't just recently this way. But there was a lot of other stuff—more upbeat. Someone brought her the required reading list from Stanford, and it was just the start. She eventually got the lists from the nine colleges in the Bay Area. She said she had about nine books left to complete all of the lists. But Norman and Claire have their own lists—she has a lot of time to devote to reading."

"And here I was worried you two were just exchanging notes about me."

Candy laughed because she knew Hooker didn't have that kind of ego, just shy. "Oh, we did. She understands about you reading a lot about your truck and cars and stuff, but she thinks you should read some books like *Metropolis* and a newer one called *I, Robot*."

Candy looked to her right across the San Francisco Bay. The city was laid out like a carpet of Christmas tree lights. Her mind drifted. "Did you ever have a Christmas tree?"

Hooker thought. It was something he had never thought about or realized. The money clip in his pocket was the only gift he had ever gotten for the holiday. "No. And I had never thought about it. Manny and Stella were raised Jewish as well as Dolly. Dolly's holiday is New Year's Eve when she does up southern style ham hocks and black-eyed peas. In the south, it's all about good luck."

"But I thought Dolly was Stella's sister and Jewish? And weren't they raised in Montana or something? Where does the southern stuff come from—especially the ham?"

Hooker laughed. "I said *raised* Jewish, not practicing." He glanced over. If you talk to her much, she has a little southern twang in her speech, but where it came from is anybody's guess. But I do know that on New Year's Eve, most of the people there eating have the same twang, and they or their families are originally from Texas to the Carolinas."

"But no Christmas tree."

"No tree."

"What about Willie?"

"Bachelor—no need." Hooker glanced over. "What about you and the Squirt?"

"Never had one. Never thought about it before."

As they started across the Richmond Bridge, Candy realized where they were—or wasn't. "Why come all the way over here instead of going down the Golden Gate Bridge?"

"Not allowed to tow through the city. Those three miles could net me a two-hundred-dollar ticket."

"But you towed through the city going up."

"Had you ever been across the Golden Gate before?"

"No."

"It was worth the risk of a ticket to take you across. Besides, the cops in San Francisco at four in the morning are all over in the Tenderloin and Bay Front having doughnuts. So the risk was almost not there. But right now, the city, especially the park, is crawling with cops."

"Oh." Candy watched the bridge end as she watched the lights on the bay. "So you did it for me."

"I thought you would like it."

"I did. I liked it very much… especially because I was with you."

Hooker chuckled softly. "Merry Christmas."

THE RAIN POUNDED on the two rain slickers. The yellow had long been camouflaged with swipes of burn from hot mufflers and engines as well as smears of grease etched into the rubber. Cold hands worked the chains. The gloves had long been soaked from the December flood from the sky.

Hooker screamed into the storm at the yellow blob at the other end of the mangled tractor and trailer. The derailed train it had hit was someone else's problem. "Don't worry about the axle, its toast. Just wrap the chain around what is solid. We'll have to jerk this bastard off the rails before we can sort it out." Hooker knew he would have to split the tow. Everything about this mangled mess was screaming for a flat-bed trailer.

The Squirt backed out from under the trailer. "Jerk…"

The lightning was close enough that the crash of thunder was deafening. Hooker swore, but he knew what the Squirt had screamed. The levers in his hand were slipping, so he grabbed a rag and gripped them. Pulling them out actuated the system, pulling them up wound the cables in, and dragged the trailer around. Hooker watched the outrigger spuds. They swung out from the sides of the truck to stabilize and lift the rear tires up, so the truck became a twenty-two thousand-pound dead weight to pull from.

Even the thunder couldn't cover the scream of steel on steel as the trailer dragged off the railroad tracks. Hooker watched where the tractor had been punched into the trailer. He hoped for some movement to show them separating. They moved as one. The thunder covered Hooker's swearing. There would be no quarters dropped in the swearing jar tonight. The storm had Hooker's back.

As Hooker and the Squirt looked at the tractor half-buried in the trailer now sitting off the tracks, Hooker worked out the figures. "Jacked this way, the whole mess weighs over eighteen tons but is also almost thirty feet wide. I think we'll have to cut them apart." He looked over at the Squirt, who was leaning against the back of Mae West with his eyes closed.

Hooker was getting used to the look. The kid's mind worked in some strange but amazing ways. He was by no means the 'dumb kid' Hooker first took him for. "What are you thinking?"

"How much weight do you think a 'J' hook could take without straightening?" The kid was talking about the large hooks ubiquitous to towing. They looked like a fishing hook for catching whales and attached to twenty feet of heavy chain.

"A hell of a lot, if they are set right. I think the chain is rated for twenty or thirty tons. Why?"

The Squirt smiled evilly. "Let's tie off the front end of the tractor and the back axle of the trailer to the railroad rail. They will have to replace it after a derailment anyway." He pointed to the points and then indicated the middle. "Then we can hook into the cross-member of the tractor, right there before it disappears up into the trailer. If nothing else happens, at least we are trying to straighten the mess out."

Hooker grabbed the kid by the back of his neck through the hood of the slicker. "You sure you want to be just a dumb cop? You're good at this stuff."

The kid smiled shyly. "Let's see how it works out first."

The kid dragged out chains and hooks and set them as Hooker pulled in the outriggers. Jumping into the cab to relocate Mae for a better pull, Hooker grabbed the mic from behind his head.

"Mama?" He called over the shop radio going to Dolly's credenza.

"Go, Hooker."

"Could you please call Jose down in Gilroy and tell him we need both of his low-boy trailers. We're still working on the recovery, but these will have to be trailered."

"10-4, Hooker. I called him thirty minutes ago. The Chips called in for Tri-State to come down from Fremont, but they only have Mike and a standard. Their low-boys are on long-haul. And I figured you would want to work with the chorizo brothers anyway."

Hooker laughed at her nickname for the brothers who made some of the best Mexican pork sausages in the South Bay. Hooker had never known the brothers to be raising less than a dozen hogs at any time, with six hogs worth of sausage and hams hanging in their cool room. If you want chorizo or prosciutto ham—you give the Gomez brothers some juicy tows.

"Thanks, mama. I'll watch for Jose and Lito."

The double click came as he hung the mic.

Once the ends were chained off, the Squirt set about binding the two tow cables to the two sides of the cross-member. Hooker watched. As the configuration became obvious, the dynamics of the 'pull' also became somewhat apparent to Hooker. Geometry was a word to Hooker, but he could tell it was something alive for the Squirt.

The Squirt finished and wiped his gloves on the slicker as if it might help his wet hands inside. He moved over to the side with the levers Hooker was holding. Hooker looked at the proud kid. "Do I pull them together or one at a time?"

The kid beamed—Hooker saw his plan. "Together to start, it will apply the pressure. Then once the join is strained, we can start working the strain."

Hooker thought about the idea. He wasn't going to steal any of the kid's thunder. Smiling, he stepped aside and offered his open palms at the controls.

There was a split second of hesitation as the kid grasped what had just happened. Suppressing his smile, he stepped over to the work. Hooker watched as the kid played the levers and winches with the finesse of a concert violinist. The join moved toward them, and then stopped. From the sound of the winches, they could tell there was strain working to free the tractor.

Hooker reached out and put his hand on the Squirt's two holding the levers. "Hold it a minute. Just leave them as they are. Let the strain work for us." Then Hooker grabbed the sleeve of the Squirt's slicker, and they walked away for about fifty feet and watched.

Hooker thought about watching the original paint job on Mae dry one day in August, so many years before. The clear coat lacquer, loaded with mother-of-pearl, had shot on foggy. Hooker had started swearing, but Willie's boyfriend at the time had just held up his hand to wait. As the clear coat had dried, the fog cleared, and the pearl appeared and then disappeared. It would only reappear under the right lighting. It was the magic of mother-of-pearl in the clear paint. The candy-apple paint of the blue was static and never changed. It was the pearl that gave the truck the look of changing like a living beast of the night as she slid past neon or fluorescent lights.

As they stood watching what appeared to be nothing happening, two large trucks with low-slung flatbeds drove up. The door of the lead truck opened, and a large Mexican American dropped to the ground then clambered back up into the cab. The other, almost as tall but fatter man, walked up in his bright orange slicker. "Lito hates wearing the rubbers. Some day he will become a daddy and learn."

Hooker's grin pulled sideways. "Hola, *jefe*. Glad you two were in town."

The man smiled. "Dolly, my angel, told me some *pendejo* called for the *pienchy vatos* at Tri-State. I guess that Chip will never sit at a certain table, eh, *jefe*?"

Hooker shrugged along with an evil smile. "Some people never learn; some just never know."

The man laughed as he glanced back at what Hooker was looking at and who he really meant. His little brother was running over while he struggled to pull his slicker on.

Hooker couldn't let the chance pass to have some fun. "Lito, you might need to have your skanky sister show you how to pull a rubber on."

The kid laughed but still struggled, not realizing someone else had snapped the bottom two snaps. "Bite me, Hooker."

Jose looked down at the two snaps and smiled at Hooker, who had noticed them, too. It was an old practical joke, played in an area where the use of the jackets was a very rare occasion. "So what are we waiting for, *jefe?*"

"Waiting? We don't need no stinking waiting, Jose. We are working. Or, I should say, Mae is working. We are just supervising." Hooker smiled a large Hollywood toothy smile.

"But you are just…"

The creak and explosion came at the same time. The forty feet of run-out cable swam back toward and over the working deck and reached out for the four men.

"Jesus…" The two Mexican drivers dove into mud puddles. Hooker and the Squirt just slowly turned to look at the other two.

The Squirt, deadpan, offered, "They sure like getting all muddy."

Hooker finished the grinding. "They had a strict mother. No mud pies, no dirt. It had to come out sometime—one of those sad facts of life about them Gilroy kids."

The two muddy men harmonized, "Bite me, Hooker."

Hooker smiled lopsidedly as he turned to the kid and backhanded the Squirt's belly. "Let's go look at your handiwork."

The tractor had shifted almost six inches. With a couple of more set-ups, and pulls, the one mess became two objects they pulled and prodded up on to the two low-boy trailers. As the sun was just starting to peek over the eastern hills, the trucks were chained and ready to move. Hooker looked down the service road and could see a large crane standing by.

"*Jefe,* let me buy you both breakfast up on Monterey Highway. These bones are going in the back lot for the Fly, but Mike won't be there until eight to run the crane."

Jose leaned out of the window of his cab. "Coffee and omelets at Just Breakfast sound good to me. Lito will eat roadkill or even the asphalt, so we no have to ask him."

Hooker and the Squirt loaded into Mae, and they nosed out ahead.

"How hard is it to re-knit the loop on the broken cable?"

Hooker looked at the kid and smiled. "Don't worry about it. The cables are three years old, and this is just the right excuse for me to replace them.

I should have pulled them last spring, but I was a little short on dimes." The two laughed at the dime joke. Each of them had enough dimes and bits to be a pair of two-bit characters.

Hooker snapped his fingers. "Before I forget, how did you do with your research?"

The kid smiled and leaned back. "My next research paper isn't due until mid-January. I even have photos of the wedding and some even more recent photos you'll find very interesting."

Hooker frowned. "Recent?"

"Last month, to be exact—she's in a nice dress, but the pendant necklace you will find even more interesting."

S TELLA WALKED DOWN the hall. In the end, she knocked lightly on the door. A moment and the door cracked—the head of wild hair and blurry eyes appeared.

Stella passed through two hangers draped with a freshly ironed t-shirt and jeans. Light starch on the jean's creases, medium starch on the entire shirt. Just the way the Squirt liked it. Both being almost brand new did not escape the young man's eye.

Stella did not even pause to knock on the next door. She could hear the shower, and Box was at the door. She opened Hooker's bedroom door and let Box in. Stepping to the bathroom door, she hung the clothes on the hook.

"Breakfast is in twenty minutes, Hooker."

The response was garbled by the flood of water as he hit the valve turning on the six-head body flush for twenty seconds. Stella smiled. She remembered the first time Hooker had hit the valve. The scream had Manny throw his mug in the air just as he was taking a sip at the dining table. She chuckled. Manny had really loved that mug shaped like the torso of a naked buxom gal. The lettering simply said, 'The Three Best Things.' In sympathy for his loss, Stella had a custom mug made. It was a large black mug with his gold detective shield on it. *Gotta love those powerful six-head shower blasts.*

Manny looked up as she returned from delivering her fresh ironing. "What are you laughing about now?'

"Manny Romero, if I divulged everything, your hair would turn white and start to curl." She ran her fingers over his short curly salt and pepper hair. "Oh, I see it's already taking effect."

She swung her hip out in a dance as his left backhand just missed spanking her britches.

"Should I load the boys up on pancakes?" She sauntered into the kitchen part of the large room—her domain and queen-dom.

Manny snapped the Mercury News and folded it into quarters. "I think your sister is going to stuff them with enough carbs. You might consider packing them down with more protein. It will calm Hooker down and keep the Squirt from pissing his pants tonight."

She looked over her shoulder and frowned.

"Not at Dolly's, but after."

She turned around, still frowning. "And why would…"

Manny rolled his head, and then could not complete the zombie—he started choking on his evil laugh. "Because Candy invited four of the nursing students and three of them the Squirt was more John than Squirt with… if you catch my drift."

Stella started to laugh. "And we also extended an invitation to the new girl from the County Clerk's office…"

"Elizabeth."

"I think she goes by Beth."

The two were laughing low and evil when Hooker strolled in. Upon seeing them both doing the evil, no-good laugh, he peeled out his impersonation of Ricky Ricardo. "Lucy… you have some 'splainin' to do."

Breakfast was twenty minutes late.

Wednesday afternoons normally consisted of doing things that kept Hooker clean for Dolly's dinner at Dispatch at six o'clock sharp. Today was no exception.

Hooker and the Squirt walked through the Emergency Room of Valley Medical Center and straight to the elevators. The doors slid back at the fourth floor, and Hooker led the parade. They had to stop at three small restaurants to find someone who still had matches. Thankfully, Hooker remembered after leaving paperwork off at the Fly's that Chick-n-Ribs was right up around the corner and on the way to Valley Medical Center.

Five large women stood almost as a host as Hooker walked through the Billing Department's door with twenty-nine candles burning. "Okay, who's turning twenty-nine again this month?"

It was nobody's birthday, but it did keep Hooker on a lot of people's good side. Hooker counted on the statistic there were more fat necks to nuzzle in the billing office than any place in the hospital. Hooker knew how to be number one in their hearts and minds, if not their necks and giggles.

It also being Christmas Eve accounted for the second layer and extra frosting. There wasn't a single set of hips in the office who would ever tell him there was too much frosting.

At eight minutes before the strike of six, Hooker and the Squirt had made their Christmas rounds of deliveries, received checks, hugs, and seasoned kisses. It was a good night.

Hooker looked down the table. The table was perfect. Sitting on the left side of Hooker at the head were Micha and Bobby Sue. Sitting across were the mayor and his wife, Dani. Next pairing down the table was Ace across from the Squirt. Sitting next to the Squirt, and unsure why he was there, was the large Filipino, PD Officer James Aligo, who sat across from the Police Commissioner Paul.

Chet, a CHP captain, was still out of uniform, as he was still out on disability leave. Chet was sitting across from a blond-haired woman—who was a mystery to almost everyone but kept sneaking unsure glances at Chet. The table was finished at the end with not one but two people, as Uncle Willie and Maddie looked the quintessential outliers of the group. Hooker almost laughed when he first saw them and knew there had to be a story behind Maddie not only getting Willie into a suit, but also a tie. They looked like they were going to church somewhere in the Midwest.

With the food on the table, the soft-spoken niceties were finished, and the cross-table, as well as down-table exchanges, began. This was the nature of this table, this night, this dinner. This is where the real power of Dolly began.

Hooker sipped on his coffee to clear his mouth and tried to hold his smile in check. Only two people were supposed to know the following information. At least—before the first week in January. "I understand the city is getting a new dog next month, Paul."

Hooker's timing was to perfection. His friend almost choked on his bite of bread. The entire table watched as the flustered commissioner struggled to swallow. Dolly was standing by and reached over with a healthy whack to the back. Her filling the blonde's coffee never wavered. Dolly was an expert at what she did—running her table.

Paul looked with watering eyes down the table at Hooker. He turned his head to frown at Dolly, who was now fussing over Maddie and Willie. She looked up and then spoke up. "Don't look at me in that tone of voice, young man. I have nothing to do with this. This was all Hooker."

Paul looked back to the head of the table. "Care to fill me in on how you know about such a closely guarded piece of information?"

Hooker leaned back, pulling the napkin across his lap. "All I can tell you is I was in Marin County and beyond this last month." He strained to ignore the Squirt, who he knew was pulling a perfect deadpan. Hooker could sense the kid was continuing to eat leisurely.

"But now that the dog is out of the bag, so to speak... you want to make nice with the new K-9 officer?"

Paul looked at the squinting eyes of the affable officer. James wiped his mouth. His voice was more of a deep rumble than words. "What did he say?"

Paul smiled. "He said, you're getting the dog you have wanted for several years."

James sat up with his body shaking from a quiet laugh. His smile dragged off to the right side as he looked down the table. "I'm getting a puppy for Christmas?"

Hooker laughed and nodded. Maddie started clapping. Most at the table had no idea how many times James had submitted his paperwork for K-9.

James turned back to Paul. "Do I get to take him back to King and Story, or do I have to move?"

"I thought it was the point of you wanting a dog—to clean up the Gun & Knife club?"

James nodded. "Part of it. But, mostly, I just wanted to get a good-looking partner finally."

The table enjoyed a good laugh and enjoyed the news.

The plates were wiped clean of dinner, and the last bits of coffee were sipped. Curiosity finally got the best of Hooker. Tradition at the table was no introductions made, and for the most part, none was needed. Tonight, Hooker knew half the diners were somewhat of a mystery. The conversations had been more about the season and how commercial things had become and less about the day-to-day struggles of jobs or family. Hooker kept waiting for some clue to the mystery woman, but none was forthcoming.

"Chet," Hooker began, "there is a mystery at this table… and you know how I hate an unsolved mystery…"

Chet looked at Dolly, who had stiffened and then relaxed. After all, it was Hooker doing the asking. Chet daubed at his lips, and then pulled the napkin into a rod and laid it beside his plate. He looked at his smiling dinner guest. "This is Doctor Sylvia Stowe. She is the county shrink." He looked up to Hooker. "She holds my career in her hands. She recently suggested the reason I am so stressed and have the headaches is that I have no friends. She thinks if I had a couple of friends, I might get out more often and enjoy life."

Hooker took a measure of the man to see if the twinkle in his eye was just about having fun or if maybe something might be a little bit more. He turned his head toward the psychiatrist. "I agree, I think Dolly, Willie, and I… heck even Micha and the Squirt have been telling him the same. He just hides away in the little house of his… cleaning his guns, polishing the pine wall paneling, shampooing the carpet, mowing the lawn, and looking out big window at the gophers in his lawn. Therefore, if you can get him to meet someone or at least get a dog like James here is doing, we would really appreciate it."

The woman smiled. "I think I underestimated Chet. He does seem to have quite the support network in place already. Nevertheless, it was good to see it in action tonight and to meet all of you. I think we can look at other reasons for the headaches… maybe while he is back on duty this next year."

Hooker jumped in before Chet. "Say… in January?"

She smiled. "I'd take your advice as a good plan and doable."

From the other room, a large belt of sleigh bells rang, and all conversation was over.

Karen called out from the dispatching wall of cords snaking into holes from other holes. "Listen up. Ace, you just caught a rollover on Capital and Snell. Hooker, Don is already on his way, so stand down. Ace, you are to swing by the shop and fetch the trainee and see if you two can handle things. If not, Don will help, but you get the full ticket. Merry Christmas.

"Micha, if you would be so kind as to take that, also. 3-4-7-Alpha has a couple of drunks parked creatively at the Chesboro cut-off.

"James, you have a party getting out of hand in the Almaden Valley. I have your paperwork here. Sorry you don't have your dog or a cute partner yet.

"Bobby Sue, as always, great to see you again, but you are needed to administer to the unwell.

"Merry Christmas to all and be careful out there."

She turned back to the large board, plugged another cord into another hole, and answered another call. The table rose as a ragged host. Hugs and handshakes were exchanged as Ace headed for the door with Micha close behind.

Hooker extended his hand to the mayor. "Sir, if you and your wife would please join me for a little bit in the office, I have something to talk to you about."

The mayor's wife started to say something in protest, but the mayor squeezed her hand on his arm ever so slightly. "Of course, we will, Hooker. You have my interest piqued."

As they moved through the door, Hooker looked back at Willie and Maddie. Maddie nodded slightly as her eyes blinked gently. She confirmed the identity.

As Hooker shuffled through a couple of papers on the top of the file, the couple did what sophisticated couples do when they aren't sure of the circumstance they are in—they fidgeted with only tiny movements. From the top of his vision, Hooker caught the slight movements.

"I'm sorry. I apologize for my seeming unpreparedness." Hooker looked up at Franklin Welton, the Mayor of San Jose, and his lovely wife, Danielle—*Please, call me Dani* Welton. Hooker evaluated the fidgeting. "You see, I don't want to waste your time, but I do want to make sure I tell this story to the best of my knowledge."

The mayor glanced out of the office window. In the dark of the larger area, he could see the top of Dolly's head working at her desk. For those in the know—the custom stainless-steel chair with its four hydraulic rams supported the weight of the chair, the person who sat in it and the power she wielded—the symbolism was not lost.

He looked back at Hooker—the man who had been sitting alone at the head of the dinner table that night. With a furtive glance, his eyes danced across the dark figure of Squirt, silently buried in the gloom of the darkest corner of the office. The mayor was hyper-aware that the young man had watched everything at the table, had listened intently to every conversation, and yet had said no more than a few words the entire time. He was as much of a mystery as this clandestine meeting was.

The mayor patted his wife's hand as he cleared his throat. "Take your time, Hooker. We have no other plans for tonight," the man lied.

Hooker put the papers back into their original order and placed them on the thick folder. He rested his hands on the whole. Taking in the couple for the umpteenth time, Hooker started.

"This story starts back about 1950 when a young girl debatably turned twenty-one and started work at a local roadhouse in the Salinas valley. The bar was on one of the unmarked back roads leading out to all of the truck farms. The road was a popular shortcut between Salinas and Hollister. The bar was simply named The Mail Pouch. Why waste money on a sign when one was already painted on the one end of what used to be a grain barn."

THE ROTTING SMELL of vegetation always got worse as the summer and crops moved into the high gear of scorching heat. The lettuce, cabbage, squash, and other crops ungleaned, lay in the fields yet to be disked back under as green manure.

The lanky figure stepped down from the driver's side of the truck. Danny Robinson swung the truck door shut with a rusty protest. The latch begrudgingly caught with a greasy thud. The 1936 stake-side truck had seen better days.

The passenger and friend, Hank Pappas, came around the nose of the battered truck. What had once been a green truck was showing more signs of red undercoat and brown rust. Hank pushed his finger at the large patch of soft metal held in place by only rust. "One of these days, this chunk of rust is going to let go and fly right into the fan. Then this old girl is going to explode or just die in your hands."

"Hank, you've been poking at the soft patch all summer, and it's still there. Probably be there when we are old and gray." Danny turned toward the roadhouse front door. "Now quit your pokin' at the rust, and let's see how your sister is working out tending bar."

Hank pulled his wide-brimmed Fedora from his head and beat at his clothes. The dust seemed to swell out around him, and then as he started walking, reassumed its place back on his clothes.

Danny held the door and teased his younger friend. "You know… they have this amazing place in town. It's called a Laundromat. You can get even those clothes clean."

The younger man stuck his middle finger up and mock picked his nose as he walked past and through the door. The dim of the interior felt cooler, but only as the shade from a shade tree feels cooler.

"Hey, y'all, where's my little sister?"

The rheumy-eyed man looked up from the end of the long bar, the sudden noise waking him more than any kind of intelligent response to a question he didn't understand in his stewed condition. His fingers were frozen around a half-finished tall shot glass.

The two younger men sat down at stools in the middle of the long counter. Hank tried again to stir some life in the old man. "Hey. Old man… Hey, where is the bartender?"

The dark-haired gal came out from the back with a case of beer easily carried under each arm. Her sleeves were rolled up like most field hands. Her strong arms and shoulders were standard on most of the young men in the valley who worked the fields. They showed she had never sought out anything less than working in the fields with the rest of her family.

Danny sat at the bar and admired the ease and grace the strength brought to the attractive wide face. As she bent to shove the cases on the lower shelf in the cooler, he leaned forward to judge the fit of her denim jeans.

Hank backhanded the older man's arm. "That's my sister you're ogling."

Danny blushed for just a second as he looked at his friend. "And a nice sister she is to ogle, too."

Teresa Pappas had smiled before she stood up. After spending a lifetime in the fields tending and picking crops, it was finally nice to have a girl's assets appreciated. Even if she did know, she could arm wrestle most of the field hands in the valley, and win.

She stuck her hands into the warm wash water and stood slowly drying them on a bar towel. She studied the lanky older man with her brother. She figured he was somewhere between thirty-five and fifty, but age wasn't an issue with her. He had a certain lean, but strong look about him she found attractive.

Throwing the towel over her shoulder, she stepped over in front of the two men. "What can I get you two?"

By the third round of long necks, it hadn't surprised either Danny or Teresa when he came out of the bathroom in the back room. He ran his hands over her rear end, and it became a heated kiss. His being Army reserve, and him being called up to go far away to a place called Korea, hadn't deterred the love affair. Being twice her age had appeal for both of them.

Many letters were shuttled back and forth across the Pacific over the next three years. Then, suddenly, the Army Sergeant was standing in the doorway of a bar in Monterey. A nervous Teresa rushed to him, and they embraced, but Danny knew something was up.

She took his hand and dragged him back to the last booth. Her brother Hank stood. He, too, was acting nervously as he glanced at the other man in the booth. It had been many years since he had bent over harvesting asparagus in the Nickapopalos family farm, but the bulbous nose and scar from a thrown knife laying open the young face of the family's only son were still as identifiable as they were when they were kids.

Danny put out his hand and leaned into the table. "Hello, Zeb, it's been a long time."

Nervous, but instantly warm to the old friend, he engaged the hand. His left hand playfully touched at the nasty scar. He still smiled. "Good to see you too, Danny. I think about you every day."

Danny laughed. "But do you keep your hands off another guy's girl?"

Zebulon waved his hand. "Mostly, yes, especially when I'm going after his wallet." He chuckled nervously as he looked over at Hank.

Danny followed Teresa into the other side of the booth as his hand washed the peaked cap from his head. Giving the two Greeks the hard eye, he leaned in knowingly. "So what no good are you two up to?"

The two men acted like young boys caught sneaking a cigarette out behind the barn. Danny drilled them with his looks. Teresa squirmed in the corner.

Danny leaned back and sighed. "Oh, shit. You chicken asses are about to do something really stupid." Leaning in and serious, Danny questioned, "Have you two idiots thought about this job for more than a beer or two?"

"Hey, when did the Army hit town?" The voice was booming and with only a slight accent, but for Danny, it was as good as seeing the man walking up from behind.

Danny looked at the two across from him. "Now I know you chuckleheads are preparing to fuck up to the top degree. You're doing something with Paul."

The soldier turned slightly and looked at the man's boots. You can tell a lot about a man by what he wears on his feet. Paul Giodarno had the esteemed reputation for being the only student who dropped out in the sixth grade and never improved from there. "Hello, Paul. Now, go away, Paul. We're having a big person conversation here."

The burly man laughed as he easily swung a chair around to the end of the booth and sat down on it backward. "Well, mister high and mighty asshole, you had better leave then because we're about to go to work."

Teresa put her hand around Danny's arm. Leaning in, she warned him. "Leave it, Danny. Things have changed."

Danny swung his head and looked hard at her. "Are you sleeping with him?"

He might as well have slapped her. "No! Hell no!" She reared back, offended.

"Then what the hell has changed so much?"

Zeb coughed into his hand. "Money."

Danny looked at the two. "You have jobs. What are you talking about, money?"

Hank poked his finger at the table and rubbed at a set of initials carved there sometime in the last fifty years. "Not really."

"Not really what? A job? I saw the truck out front. One of you is still driving for old Sam. Or is it just a broken-down heap out there?"

Hank looked up. His eyes were too worn out to produce tears. "Times have been tough. The crops aren't what they used to be, and now there are large haulers who can move six times more produce up the valley to San Jose and Frisco in a single truck. They haul with a set of double trailers.

Zeb hasn't found a week's worth of work since planting. Only Paul was smart enough to go up to San Jo and get a real job."

Danny swung his head and looked at the slightly younger man with a jaundiced eye. "What kind of work?"

"Sheet metal. I'm installing heating and air conditioning ducts in buildings."

Zeb, wanting to be part of the conversation instead of the tagalong he usually was, offered more. "He also does repairs." And in a breathy hurry, before anyone could stop him, he added, "Like the museum in San Jose. That mummy place…" He stopped, knowing he had just stepped over the boundary.

Danny could feel Teresa next to him turn to stone. As he watched her brother Hank, he could see the tiny bricks of defense slowly crumble and wash away by a sea of resolve. The cat was now out of the bag.

Danny understood just how desperate people had become. None of their families ever got far enough ahead to take a deep breath. Of the three, Danny and Teresa were the winners in jobs held the longest, and for the largest paychecks. But even after twenty years and two wars as a Master Sergeant, he still couldn't walk into the bank across from Fort Ord's front gate and get a loan to buy a new Chevrolet. He looked at Zeb's mouth and could tell the hollow in his cheek was from missing teeth. Probably top and bottom. They were probably removed by Hank and a pair of pliers, the same as his family would do if they had to.

He turned to take in Paul. The man was already balding on top and probably would have a heart attack if he had to put on a rucksack and march for even ten miles. He looked at his hands. They matched the beat-up Red Wing work boots he had noticed before. They were both clean and cared for, just hard used.

Danny's eyes softened as he removed the edge from his voice. "I'm assuming you're talking about the museum belonging to the Rosicrucian church." The man nodded slowly. "So what's there?"

Paul's eyes started to slide over toward Hank—asking for permission. Danny stopped him. "Don't look to Hank for answers. His answer would be, 'Let's have another beer and think about it some more all night.' What's there?" The hard edge of a sergeant needing instant answers from his men for the last three years of life and death slid through Paul's chest like a cold shiv.

"Gold. Lots of it. A lot of jewelry, too. Big jewels the size of chicken eggs."

Danny took in the information. He now had an objective. He needed the lay of the land, and the attack response and retreat. "What kind of security?"

"None… tonight. The night guards are all church members, and it's a volunteer job. It rotates. But tonight, I know the guy is going to cut out around eight and go with his girl up to San Francisco to get married. He won't be back until around three or four. His replacement comes in about five-thirty."

Danny frowned. "What about alarms?"

"There are four doors. All of them have standard magnet switches backed up with pressure switches in the metal jams. You need a key to turn the alarms off."

"Do you have the key?"

Paul sat up and waved his hand as he scowled with his face at something repugnant. "Pfft, don't need something traceable. I have better." He held up a simple little stick of metal. "This is called a hinge key. It removes the pin from a hinge on the top of most air systems on a building. It's like having a skeleton key to any building in the city."

Danny ignored the false bravado. "Why wouldn't they suspect you of having a key if we go through this air system?"

"Because, for one, the cover is very heavy, and two, it had a lock on it the church put on there. Only they have the key. Whenever we have to go up there, they come and unlock the lock, and the guy takes the lock away until we're done. Then he puts it back on and locks it."

Danny thought about the implication of the believed perception of total security. He smiled wryly. "Except we are going to use their hasp and lock as the hinge instead."

His use of the inclusive word *we* was not lost on any of them. Teresa's hand slipped onto his thigh. Maybe it was the excitement of his joining them, or maybe it was a promise for more to come later tonight.

What Danny liked the most was—it wouldn't be a smash and grab like most robberies. For a novice group of burglars, the hours to do the job were a godsend. Danny also knew it wasn't as safe as running moonshine as Teresa and Hank's family and his family had done for extra money. But it would be the best chance Zeb and Paul would ever get to a shot of getting out of the hellhole of being dirt poor in Salinas.

He looked at his watch. San Jose was a three-hour drive. "I need to get some clothes that don't stand out. I'll meet you three in an hour at the Mail Pouch. I also need to find a car."

Teresa squeezed his thigh. "I'm the driver. The car is Uncle Gino's 1937 Chevy Master Deluxe."

Danny started to protest, but Hank cut him off. "We pulled the eighty-six horse out of her in 1943 when Gino was still driving shine over to the valley. It has a straight-eight, and the steering box is the short truck, so it's quick and responsive. The four-twenty-two is solid as we just replaced the hypoid gears last year. And Terry drives. We need all of us on the door. It weighs over two hundred pounds, and it's big."

Danny chewed on the challenge and the information. It was obvious they had been thinking about this for longer than a couple of long neck beers. He nodded as he turned back toward Paul, one last potential problem. "What if the guard gets cold feet tonight?"

Paul laughed. "He won't. She gave him only half a blow job the other night and told him he gets the rest tonight right after the papers are signed."

They all laughed. Danny even felt Teresa join in. She was little more than half his age, but she made him feel like her twenty-three more than his forty-one. "Let's hope he hasn't taken matters in his own right hand and figures he doesn't need her." As they laughed, he turned to Teresa. "I need clothes, and I can't go home now, or Maddie will be all over my ass like a June bug."

"I've got some at the apartment." She smiled. "They may be a little loose, but they'll do." She rubbed the inside of his thigh to indicate maybe more would be in the offering.

Danny smiled. "The Mail Pouch at five. We can grab some dinner up the valley."

Teresa interjected. "Mail Pouch at five-thirty. I've already packed enough food, so nobody will ever know we left town."

They all nodded and left the bar.

It had been almost nine o'clock before they arrived at the museum. The clouds were gathering thick in the late summer air. The winter cold blowing in from the San Francisco Bay was biting and harsh. Danny knew the night would end in rain. He just worried about the dirt road of the ridge route the moonshine runners called the Snake. The summer had provided a nice smooth surface coming up. Almost no dust had meant Teresa had kept the large car at a constant speed above fifty, a speed that would have had troopers on the highway eyeing them.

The museum was a large box with no windows. Bump-outs spaced along the large walls Danny knew were structural instead of decorative. Only the front entrance provided any kind of decoration to the outside. The building, even for its massive size, almost hid in the neighborhood. The four men stood on the top around the large access door. True to his word, Paul slid the hinge key through the hinges, and they were open. He placed them in his pockets with his latex gloves Teresa had obtained from her woman doctor the week before.

The door was heavy, but Danny doubted it was more than two hundred pounds. They climbed down a short ladder and then crawled through the air duct. The access screen was in the maintenance room. Paul looked carefully in the tool chest and chose a center-punch chisel and a hammer. Motioning, they filed out into a dimly lit museum. Many of the large glass cases contained mummies or miniatures of buildings Egyptians lived in thousands of years before. Danny was starting to doubt Paul's judgment until they entered the inner room.

Even in the dim light, the gold glistened and rippled. The jewels glowed with an inner fire. Everything was as Paul had promised, and more. There were vases and burial plates for a king's chest. Gold and painted helmets, rods, hook things and other items one might hold on a throne. All safe in large glass cases Danny was sure were shatter-resistant.

He turned to confront Paul only to see Hank and Zeb standing and watching a bent over Paul. Danny watched as the man inserted a large center-punch into the loop of the lock. It only fit about a third of the way.

He then struck the punch with a sharp rap of the hammer, and they all watched as the body of the lock fell to the floor.

Standing, Paul whispered, "They all do it, even the fancy expensive locks."

Emptying the cases into the four bags only took another five minutes. In twenty minutes, they were back in the Chevrolet sedan and moving south through the city. The rain was picking up, and the wipers were clicking back and forth across the window. Teresa smiled a quick draw of her cheeks, and then she was all business as she moved the heavy car through the streets. Danny marveled how she had a certain knack. If she had driven a route once one way, she could find her way back, or adapt as needed, anytime after. She also knew how many miles she was from one point to another. It was as if there was a permanent map buried under the dark curls.

DOLLY KNOCKED LIGHTLY on the door as she pushed it open. In her hands were a tray of mugs and a carafe of coffee. "I thought you folks might want to join Hooker and Squirt for some coffee about now." She placed the tray on the table. Looking at the mayor's wife, Dolly pointedly asked, "Coffee, Dani?"

The four mugs filled, Dolly withdrew.

Hooker leaned back into his seat and focused on sipping his coffee. Waiting—the game Manny had taught him so well.

The mayor blinked. "So we had a burglary. Why did I never hear about it? Something like that would have made three-inch type on the Mercury News. Hell, KLIV would have been talking about it for months. Were they ever caught?" He laughed at his un-thought-out statement. "I mean, you know their names and even what kind of car they were driving and everything... surely, they were..." He glanced at his wife, whose grip on his thigh was almost bordering on painful.

Her face was stoic. Her coffee sat on the table untouched. Her eyes lay dead, all life washed away. Fifteen years younger than her husband, the forty-four-year-old woman's usual glow of health was now blanched—

except for the remaining red rouge lips. Lacking the usual Greek glow and color, they looked garishly like fresh blood.

Quiet as a whisper, she asked Hooker to continue.

Hooker knew he now had the connection he needed. Turning to the mayor, he continued.

"They weren't caught, sir, because they are dead. They died that night. There is a road running along the ridgeback of the mountain running from south of San Jose almost to Prunedale. For the most part, it is generally straight, wide, and smooth. The county maintains it as a fire break and access road, and the State Forestry maintains it for the same reason. It's also is the fastest and most direct route from San Jose to the Salinas Valley, not patrolled by law enforcement. Which is why the moonshiners knew about and used the road called the Snake?"

Hooker opened the folder and withdrew a few 8x10 photos. He looked over at the Squirt. "John, could you close the blinds and turn on the overhead light so the mayor can see these, please." He waited for the silent man to perform the duty.

With the light, Hooker turned the first photo around and paused. "About halfway down the Snake, I would guess the rain had started to make the hard pack Caliche clay into snotty mud. There is a single nasty turn that even today catches people, and they spin out safely into the open field to the west. But if the driver is good, really good, like moonshine runner good, they will be able to catch the trouble and stay on the road. However, my guess is that on the fateful night, something else happened. I think the driver was really good but oversteered just enough. The entire weight of the three-thousand-pound top-heavy sedan leaned on the right front wheel assembly. The wheel cocked under, and the A-frame gave way —sixteen years of fatigue will do that. If Gino had swapped out the stock front end for one from a Chevy Master Supreme, it wouldn't have folded. The Supreme was a far superior framework for taking the kind of abuse running shine on those back roads."

Hooker pushed the first photo over to the mayor. It was a static photo of the cleaned up bent and broken suspension. "My guess is the car rolled in a nose roll. As it came up, the swing of the car popped the driver's door open, and they were tossed somewhat safely out onto the road. But the other four weren't so lucky. You see, in a nose roll, the next roll is the back end makes contact, and this is when it becomes what we in the towing business call an end-over-end, or becomes a mix-master or regular roll, side-top-side-bottom-side-top-side, and you get the picture.

"The big difference is not how destroyed the car becomes, but what it does to the occupants. In a standard mix-master, people are just thrown for a few feet from side to side with ricochets off the top and seats. At sixty miles an hour, a car like this can take maybe up to six or seven complete rolls on the ground. But with an end-over, the bodies are thrown not only side-to-side but from end-to-end." Hooker looked at the blanched face of the man's wife. "Thankfully, in such a crash, the occupants are killed almost outright. There is no suffering."

The mayor still wasn't catching on, but he was drawn into the story. "But someone surely would have reported a wrecked car... even way out there."

Hooker smiled and pushed over the second photo. "There was a little complication. Well, not so little. More like about eighty feet of complication," Hooker hesitated for only a beat. "What you are looking at is a photo taken from road level, looking down into the raven the car flipped into. It came to rest eighty feet down in that riverbed, and forty feet into the tree line. At the time, it might have just been a brush line. Nobody would have ever seen it lying there unless someone didn't do the same with a Cadillac about two months ago. Lucky for the insurance adjuster, there had been an eyewitness."

"So, if they're all dead..."

Hooker put up his hand. "We'll get there, Frank." Hooker stalled, and then asked, "Is it all right if I call you Frank, Frank?"

The mayor, ever the politician, felt the shift in their dynamics. He nodded instead of committing.

Hooker smiled. He knew the commitment would come later.

"The first problem was identifying the old car, and who it had belonged to. The carmakers mark a car with what is called a Vehicle Identification Number or VIN number. You're familiar with it because you have to copy it down off the dashboard when you do certain things like sell or change your license plates." Hooker watched the man as he nodded, but knew he had no idea what Hooker was talking about because he had people to do those things, or the dealer took care of it for him.

"In this case, the VIN tag had been so rusted through the last twenty years I could pass my fingers through the hole where the tab of metal should be. But in the trunk, still wrapped in the oil-paper from Sacramento, was the front license plate. Some parts had rusted, but the numbers were still good." He pushed the photo over for the two to see. "This is what led us to Salinas and Gino."

Hooker took a sip of his coffee and dove into the last part of the story of connecting lost dots.

The carafe was empty, as were the mugs of the mayor and Hooker. Dani, unmoving still, sat with a still full mug of coffee in front of her like something unbidden, which she was afraid to touch.

Frank's tie had long ago gone askew and pulled. The button was undone, and Hooker could see the mayor's Adam's apple moving as if this were more than just a simple story. Hooker could see he now realized there was more to this story of a crime gone wrong than met the eye.

Frank leaned forward, looking at the dozen or so pictures and the four small stacks of photocopies of documents. "So we have four dead bodies in a car, along with bags of loot, but nobody..."

Hooker cut him off. "The bodies were in the car for maybe a total of an hour. Across the ravine, where the small flash floods over time had washed out a small cave—the driver dragged them and the loot, and buried them."

"But you said these guys were not small men. Are you sure this little Teresa girl could drag them very far?"

Hooker glanced at the still silent Dani. He figured she stood a good five-foot-eight before she put on the low heels. With a life of working hard in the fields of Salinas, Hooker mentally bet she could have held her own against most men her size. His fine sense of noticing small things did not miss the tip of a thin, pale old scar running down her right bicep. The custom dress looked like any other nice dress, but he was sure the sleeves were extended to cover most of the long scar that was hard to hide when you reach for something in the middle of a large dining table as she had earlier.

Hooker's eyes slid back to her husband. "I didn't say she was little. She was from strong Greek stock. During the wars, even the small children were turned out into the fields to do a good day's labor. I can guarantee you the conditions were not nice, but she was more than able to get the job done."

"So how did you find the cave?"

"I didn't. The Cadillac I had to recover did. All of the windows were basically smashed out. As I dragged it up the cliff, it was upside down. The top scooped up a lot of mud and a skeleton hand and arm. Once I heard about it, I remembered finding something shiny in the mud. I had stuck it in the top pocket of my coveralls, which I hardly ever use unless the recovery is muddy. Once I cleaned it up, I started to look into everything." He pulled a large scarab beetle sculpture out of his pocket and slid it to the middle of the table. He watched Danielle *Please call me Dani* Welton as she stiffened to the state of hard stone.

The silence was palpable in the room. Hooker was sure Dani was no longer breathing, but he could imagine the gears in the mayor's head—the future election, as well as an eye toward Sacramento, and the combined reputations of one of the most respected couples in the Bay Area, who sat on many philanthropic boards. His gears turned, but there wasn't the right fit, and Hooker could almost smell the stench of searing realizations.

Hooker quietly eased the tension. "With this, we have recovered and returned to the museum all of the stolen items—all but the twin to this scarab." The scarab was about three inches long. The solid gold body was tinctured with black tars to enhance the carving. The wings were painted on with a paint made from crushed mother-of-pearl and glass made from lapis lazuli. The blue was as iridescent as Dani's dress and broach.

This time, the mayor stopped breathing. He did not have to look. He knew Dani was wearing the broach he had custom made to hold the antique scarab she had from before they were married. There was also a special pendant built the same way so she could choose which way she wished to show off her prize.

Silently, Dani finally moved. Her hands reached tenderly to the broach and removed it. Turning it face down, she slid the catch—releasing the scarab from its captivity. One last time, her fingers lovingly touched the one item she had that connected her to her brother and her first serious boyfriend. She had never stopped thinking about them or loving them both.

She softly slid the scarab to a place alongside its twin. "So now what, Hooker?"

Hooker could see the steel of her pride, but the quietness of her resolve. She had made herself into the person she could be proud of by doing good things for many people less fortunate.

Hooker reached out and covered the two treasures with his hands. As he slowly slid them back, his right hand lifted the fake the museum had given him for the real scarab he had given them. He placed the beetle on top of the now resurrected file and pushed both toward her. "This city has been doing better than it has in a long time. I think Dolly would agree with me; it not only comes from the hand of the mayor here but also from the good works you bring with your name and hard work. You two have a reputation for dealing with a fair and honest hand. You have turned down the easy but dirty money, and worked hard at doing the right thing."

Hooker paused as he looked into the soul of Dani's eyes. "This is all of the research and evidence we gathered. None of this ever was of interest to any law enforcement department. To them, it was just an accident on a country road. Those involved in the investigation were deputized and sworn in as a special squad who only answers and reports to a single judge up north.

"The Rosicrucian Museum is just happy to have their items back. They never wanted any public attention, and they still don't. But I'm sure they could find a place for a good person on their advisory board." He pointed toward the beetle resting on the file. "I believe the replica should fit in the broach cage, as well as the pendant, which looked so nice with the gown you wore at the cancer benefit last month.

"As for this folder, I don't have any use for it. It served its purpose. I think you would be the best person to know how to dispose of it."

She thought a moment of the significance of the two gestures. Her silent *thank-you* was met with a nod.

Slowly, they all rose stiffly as the clock in the other room clicked past the midnight hour. Turning to the mayor, Hooker stuck out his hand. "Mr.

Mayor, I want to thank you for taking this extraordinary amount of time from your busy schedule to hear me out."

The man was taken aback by the grace of the young man in the white t-shirt, jeans, and work boots. "Hooker, it had been a very interesting evening, as well as enlightening. If you ever need to talk, my door is always open for you. And please... it's Frank." They shook with a new understanding.

Squirt rose in the dark corner.

Ever the politician, the mayor turned toward the Squirt with his hand out. "And I think it was John?"

"Yes, sir, but I'm getting used to everyone calling me Squirt."

The mayor frowned and looked back toward Hooker as he still held the Squirt's hand.

Hooker smiled. The final brick was now in play. "Mayor, this is John or the Squirt and my right-hand man on this investigation. This next month, he will be entering the police academy as a combined guest of the San Jose PD, the CHP, and the Sheriff's Office. He's the man who performed the final takedown on the Dime Killer last spring."

The mayor turned back to the Squirt with renewed respect and cinched understanding as to why the young man was sitting in on the conversation. "Well, Squirt, I look forward to having you on our fine police force upon graduation." The man was very sincere.

As they opened the door to leave, Dani stepped over to Hooker for an almost private conversation. "Did you find any dog tags?"

Hooker swallowed and nodded. "And the watch Maddie had given him when he came home from Europe. She has both now. Danny was buried last week up on Mt. Angel. If you want, I can get you the address, or you can talk to Maddie down at the Main Library. I'm sure she would be happy to have your company and go visit."

"I'd like that." She thought a moment. "It was her at the end of the table tonight..."

Hooker nodded.

"I'll let her know to expect you. I'll be seeing her later, I think. I'm sure they're still working on some trashy Ford that they want to blow up on a race track down near Visalia this summer."

The woman smiled. "Her family never did appreciate Fords."

Dolly stood at the large steel door to usher her guest out. She stuck her hand out. "Frank, I look forward to your next term. There are still a few things to fix around here."

The mayor knew who was the real boss and smiled. "Dolly, I look forward to your vote this next election. Thank you for dinner and for a very interesting evening. But since when is the table no longer all-male?"

It was Dolly's turn to beam. "Get used to it, Frank, the times are changing." She turned to Mrs. Welton. "Dani, it was so nice to meet you finally. I have heard so many nice things about you. Please don't be a stranger."

"Dolly, someone introduced me as the most powerful woman in San Jose. I now know how silly it was, and I'm sure they have never sat at your wonderful table. The pasta was to die for, and I really do want the recipe." She glanced back at where Hooker and Squirt were going over some paperwork with Karen. "And the company was beyond expected. You have a wonderful family here."

Dolly moved in and hugged her, whispering, "Dump the stud next Wednesday and be here about three in the afternoon. We'll cook the sauce together while you write down what we add. We can get to know each other better as family should." She pulled away and could tell she had a cooking date for the next week and any other time she wanted. She smiled warmly. "Wait until you meet the rest of the family."

Ever the guardian, Dolly watched until the large Lincoln pulled safely out onto the street. She kissed her fingers and pressed them to the badge welded to the thick steel door skin as she softly closed the heavy door. The number 701 on the badge glowed dully in the dim light.

She leaned against the door as she watched Hooker explain something on some paperwork to the highly attentive Squirt. It had been an amazing eleven years since the young Hooker had stolen into her heart and created one of the most powerful and caring families along the way.

Her words were only for her, but also silently for him as well. "And that, my boy… is how you get a chip in the game."

KAREN HAD GIVEN them a call on a gold AMC Pacer with a flat tire. It was a little strange being about a mile out of Hooker's area, but a ticket was a ticket on Christmas Eve. It was a commercial call, so there was no hurry, and the back way took them past a Thrifty's.

The two young men were laughing as they enjoyed their matching triple scoops of French vanilla ice cream in sugar cones. The windows were rolled down, the heater was blasting toasty bliss, and Hooker didn't even have to feel down next to his seat to know Box had his one eye closed as he leaned into the blast of summer-like heat.

As they rolled into the parking lot, the Pacer was pretty obvious. The older man leaned against the only car in Sarah Winchester's Mystery House parking lot. The younger man dressed in a similar uniform and gently rolled himself back and forth in his chair. Both were smiling.

Hooker groaned with a smile. "Do you see a flat tire anywhere?"

The Squirt snorted. "Dude, we've been had… but I bet my knife could do some fast work on Father Damian's tires."

"I don't think either father would stoop so low or be stupid enough to drive a Pacer."

They rolled alongside but remained in the cab licking the last of the ice cream. Hooker concertedly did not look out and down, but instead kept studying the entrance to the largest attraction left standing in San Jose.

Ice cream finished, Hooker looked over at the Squirt. They both shrugged. *What the heck, it is Christmas.* They slid out the doors.

Hooker's feet hit the pavement. "Well, looky here, we have the Bobbsey Twins. Merry Christmas, boys."

Father Damian laughed as he took in the matching black leather jackets over T-shirts, jeans, and boots. "Before you start calling people twins, you should have a look in the mirror with you two."

The two tow drivers simply smirked and tipped their heads in unison.

Father McBride eased off the car. "Sorry for the ruse, my boy, but it wasn't a real lie. We just thought you would want to say hi to an old friend." He shook Hooker and John's hands. Appraising the younger, he smiled. "Well, Johnathan, you look like you've recovered well enough to take an early seat at the academy."

The Squirt smiled. "Thank you, sir, and Merry Christmas, too. The doc hasn't released me yet, but I suspect I can start the classes at least. The physical part isn't until the second cycle, and I should be up for it all by then."

Hooker shook hands with the seated father. "Did you put in any requests to Santa this year—a new set of wheels... maybe?" He nodded at the Pacer. "And hopefully not."

The two laughed. "I asked the great red-suit for a 318 Hemi for the chair..." Holding out his hands, "But, as you can see... he is still only just a good story." The young priest glanced at the back end of the large tow truck. "But the other big man gave us all a present we couldn't have even imagined asking for."

Hooker and the Squirt turned around to see what the two priests were looking at. The night urchin still bounced his fingers along the working bed of Mae West. The three one finger bounce, followed by the flourish, the double bounce, the hand clamp with a wobble spin of the hand, and then repeated. Each cycle took the exact same three feet of bed to accomplish. The first difference Hooker noticed was Peter looked like a man instead of a cluster of wind-blown detritus. He was still a homeless person living on the street, but nonetheless, a person.

Then the change hit Hooker. Peter was walking toward the four of them. The shy man seemingly afraid of everything, the man who had stayed only in the shadows, and was okay only if Hooker stayed in the cab of Mae West, was now walking in the open, with just a slight hesitation.

"Hello, Peter," Hooker called softly.

"G… goo… hello ho… Hooker." The man turned and took in the Squirt, who nodded softly with a safe smile. Peter froze. Old habits seemed to war with new trials. The twitch was physically perceptible, like a wall switch being thrown. "Yo… yo… you." Peter scrunched his eyes and face closed as he struggled. The other four waited patiently.

The face on the man only relaxed a little, but the eyes were still closed. "You… you saved Hooker." His face opened, and he smiled with open eyes.

"Yes, Peter. My name is John, but I would like to be your friend also, so you can call me Squirt."

Peter gathered his hands to the top of his chest at the sight of the offered hand. The Squirt withdrew the hand, and Peter relaxed some. "Yo… y… can… Candy…"

"Yes, I'm Candy's little brother."

"Ca… ca... Candy… Candy went away." The man frowned.

The Squirt was lost. He looked to Hooker for help.

"Peter, Candy is going to school to be a nurse so she can help people. I know you and Jerry miss her, but maybe she can come visit you on occasions."

The man smiled. "Tha… Hoo… th…" The man relaxed and sagged with a glow. "Nice."

Damian offered the explanation to Peter's transformation. "Peter is now using the rectory's back door. He's trying to make it to dinner with us on a better schedule and has started taking advantage of the temporary facilities we have set up near the alley to provide a safe place for those like Peter to clean up. Clean clothing is the next step, but one push of the wheel at a time." He smiled at Peter. A father couldn't be more proud of a child who brought home a gold sticker.

Father McBride cleared his throat.

Damian came back to matters at hand. "Peter, we will be having a special Christmas dinner later today, so please make sure to be there. I hear some of the good sisters are baking some special rolls… and I know you like a sweet roll."

"O… okay."

Hooker watched the man turn and leave… but true to the nature of the beast, he was almost invisible by the time he was twenty feet past the end of the truck. Hooker shook his head and looked back at the man in a wheelchair—the former Special Forces Ranger.

It was as if Damian could read his mind. "I don't know how he does it. He would have been extremely deadly in Vietnam." His sight moved from where the man had been to Hooker. "Have you ever noticed he doesn't make a sound? The only time you ever hear anything is when he is sort of announcing himself."

"The little rustle of leaves or something…" They nodded as all four looked back into the night.

Father McBride cleared his throat again. "I'm sorry, boys, but we have a place we need to go to before we are needed to get up in the morning."

Hooker chuckled. "I hope you weren't planning to use this car."

Damian cringed. "It just happened to be sitting here. Actually, I think it's been sitting here since last summer."

The Squirt snorted. "Someone got smart and just walked away while they could."

"We just used it because we wanted to surprise you. After all, lads, it is the night of gifts." McBride smiled.

The radio squawked in the cab of the truck. Hooker shook hands quickly as the Squirt hurried around the truck.

"1-4-1." Hooker checked in as he waved and nosed the large truck out onto the street.

Karen's voice came across the tinny speaker without any inflection. "1-4-1, you need to go to the barn at the Romero Hacienda, now."

Hooker's heart stopped. It was well after midnight. Manny and Stella would be asleep… and then he remembered what day it was.

"What's up, Karen?"

"Hooker, it's all I have. Dolly just said you were to go there now. If you plan to argue… then you need to take it up with Dolly."

"Is she there?" Of course, she was there. It was night—Dolly was always there.

"She is... indisposed."

The communication was sharp, curt, and delivered deadpan. Hooker knew the only way he could find out what was going on... was to head for the barn.

"10-4."

Hooker hung the microphone back behind his head. As he leapfrogged the gears utilizing all 1,600 horses under Mae's hood, the asphalt slid past his wheels. Soon, the white dashed lines in the center of Winchester Boulevard smoothed to a static riffle.

Quietly, the Squirt slipped his seatbelt on and pulled it tight. "What do you think?"

Hooker shook his head. He glanced over at the kid. He jammed down through the gears as he got ready for the left turn at Blossom Hill Boulevard. As he pulled the large steering wheel and danced the clutch and gears, he filled the kid in on the importance of Christmas Eve.

"Manny and Stella got married on the dock next to the troopship Manny took to Korea. It was Christmas Eve. Stella's best friend in the world, Claire, came to be her Maid of Honor. After they had watched the ship make the turn in the bay to head out of the Golden Gate, they hitched a ride on a Navy boat over to San Francisco. They danced the night away at the USO. It became their tradition while Manny was over there.

"When Manny came back, he insisted they continue... and the girls have been doing it ever since."

"Without Manny..."

"Without Manny." Hooker twitched his head and glanced over. "Back when I was... well, a kid—Willie and I had made buckets of hot cocoa and chocolate chip cookies. I was out looking for the other drivers who were working on Christmas Eve, and Dolly asked me if I'd take a special call.

"It sucked to work Christmas Eve because it usually means you either were desperate for money or you had nowhere else to go. I just thought the other guys should get a little of what I was getting with Uncle Willie. So there I was—two full thermoses of fresh hot cocoa and a few dozen warm cookies. The girls were dressed to the nines from their high heels up to the ribbons in their hair… and a conked out Caddie on the side at Guadalupe Parkway and the new 280."

The kid rolled his eyes. "Nice part of town…"

"Exactly. I think it was the first time the truck had ever been close to a hundred. It was a piece of shit Chevy one-ton.

"Anyway, Dolly never let on as to who the ladies were. Manny stayed on the phone the entire time with Dolly constantly mother henning me to death. The girls kept giggling every time Dolly would ask where I was—how were the ladies—how was the tow going—did I have an ETA…? It was annoying, but it kept the ladies amused."

Squirt chuckled. "Along with the chocolate and chocolate…"

"Exactly… But then, they don't understand French vanilla the way we do." Hooker's right hand dropped and found Box's ear. It was warm, and he could feel the deep rumble of Box's contented purr.

"So the Caddie had to go back to the dealer up in Palo Alto, so I had to take it down around the horn and up the 101. By the time we made it back to Hacienda Romero, we had sung every Christmas carol we knew at least a half dozen times, including a few with an open mic for Dolly and Karen. We didn't know Manny was also listening." Hooker looked over at the Squirt and laughed. "After I first moved in… Manny just told me never to sing again."

Downshifting, Hooker took the right and headed down Almaden Expressway. All the lights were blinking red at the intersection. Hooker figured taking the turn at thirty was close enough to stopping. "So that was how I met Manny and Stella."

"So what happened tonight?"

"I don't know. I walked out of the hacienda with some goofy assed kid this morning, and I've been going ever since." He glanced over. "Have you heard anything?"

The kid looked out of his open window and scratched the scar behind his ear. "Nah."

Hooker turned up what he called *The Hill of Stupid*. The developers had taken a single rural road and turned it into a mass of streets and houses. If the oversized English Tudor-like houses weren't stupid enough, naming the streets with Spanish names—without any knowledge of meaning—

was even worse. Hooker turned onto Calle Bonita Verde Avenida, which meant Street Beautiful Green Street... the only thing green was the money people threw away on houses built so fast they didn't work right.

Hooker recalled a bad rainstorm had resulted in him having to tow a car out of a garage at the bottom of the driveway. The runoff that should have stayed on the street was diverted down the driveway and filled the garage to the door handles of the new BMW. The developers fix afterward was to drill drain holes in the wall at the end of the garage so any new water would flood the back yard.

As Hooker pulled Mae up onto her parking pad, he was confused. The hacienda was all but dark like it normally was. Only the gate lamp and the front door lamp were lit. The interior was dark except a glow in the kitchen.

Hooker and the Squirt exchanged concerned frowns as they slid out of the truck and walked down around the driveway. The large driveway would easily hold Mae, but she had her own thick concrete parking pad. As they rounded the house, the parking lot—the size of two football fields—was full to capacity, but the lights in the barn were also dark. Hooker could see the large barn door, large enough to accommodate Mae, or any other commercial truck tractor and trailer, was slid open.

As they crossed the large parking lot, Hooker noted a small Devco milk truck parked with its nose to the basement apartment's windows. When Hooker had last seen the truck, it was white and rust in the back end of Willie's garage. Now it was red and looked brand new. There was a large bow with a large card on the back door—hiding a drop gate... *Merry Christmas, Damian.* Hooker noted the handicapped sticker next to the chaplain symbol painted prominently on the bumper. This must have been Willie's secret project.

As they approached, they could hear two soft female voices starting to sing the sleigh song. Hooker smiled. That night in the truck, nobody could carry a tune in a bucket. They still couldn't, but it was warming to hear Stella and Claire's voices. Hooker looked at the Squirt, and on the nod, they belted out the refrain as they walked through the dark doorway.

A soft glowing object floated in the middle of the dark barn. Glowing arms and bare feet stood below the face...

"Sissy...?"

The black of night shattered into many colors of light as a tall Christmas tree behind his sister, exploded in front of them. The tree appeared to be well over twenty feet tall and towered over the mass of people standing around and in front of the multitude of ornaments and lights.

In the center, walking toward them was Candy and Sissy.

As Hooker and John met them, the crowd was hushed. Candy took Hooker and John's hands as she too turned to face what Hooker had come to know as his family. Sissy snuggled in between Candy and Hooker and put her arm around Hooker's waist—leaning her head into his leather-jacketed chest. "They knew we four had never had Christmas, so they decided to have one that would be special for everyone."

Sissy put her other arm around her new sister's waist as well. It was only a second ahead of Candy's arm finding her.

As the crowd started singing *We Wish You a Merry Christmas*, Hooker leaned close to Sissy. "Have you met Danny yet?"

She softly chuckled. "I want to take him home. But he has a serious problem with my name."

"Claire?"

"Sissy." She hugged Hooker tighter. "I told him it was his problem, so he had to be the one to come up with a name he liked." She looked up and smiled at Hooker. "I gave him until next Christmas."

Hooker leaned over and lightly kissed her forehead. "Merry Christmas, Sissy."

"Merry Christmas, Hooker."

Out of the corner of his eye, Hooker saw Father McBride walk through the large door as he wiped at his eyes. Hooker knew the other priest would take a while longer in the parking lot.

BOOMTOWN

A SOUTHSIDE HOOKER NOVEL — BOOK 4

1

BOOMTOWN

ilpitas was a thug town.

The reputation didn't bother Felix. In fact, he liked it. Felix knew he was a thug, and so he fit in—disappeared.

Felix hadn't always been a thug, and he hadn't grown up in Milpitas. He found Milpitas because of its reputation, and he had worked hard to fit into the reputation.

His left hand held a winding of solder as the tip of the small soldering iron in his right hand turned the wire into a tiny bead of liquid silver. The solder melted and flowed around the connected wires to form a solid electrical bond. It became an almost indestructible joining, which only three ounces of custom cooked explosives could, and would tear apart... which was the idea. The formed wires would become so many three-inch pieces of thin metal wire... easily missed in the rubble of what used to be a building.

The cool evening was turned colder by the low mist from the San Francisco Bay. The chilly mist was pushed down the bay by the inflow of sea air squeezed between the Marin County hills to the north and the hills of the city of San Francisco, south of the Golden Gate. This natural squeeze gave the gentle breezes more power as they moved the colder air south over the late winter bay. Milpitas was aligned to receive more than its fair share of the bone-numbing chill, but Felix knew from experience the real cold weather was soon to come. Summer on the San Francisco Bay could rival the cold of many winters elsewhere.

As the light breeze blew into the screened sleeping porch where Felix worked, it drew out a rare smile from the man's face. It reminded him of the shoulder seasons in his childhood home of Colorado. He slid his bare feet into the thick wool slippers his sister had made for him, the sister who still lived on—and clung desperately to—the family ranch. The sister, who still believed, even at forty-eight, her prince would someday come and help her on the ranch, herding the cows and sheep so she could milk the goats.

Felix's toes curled and dug at the home-sheared, washed and carded wool. He humored himself to think his toes could feel the difference in the yarns where her thumbs worked the spin instead of the looser, small fingers in a trailing feed of the large wheel spinning wheel. The small upright would have given her more consistent yarn, but she insisted on using the spinning wheel, which was taller than she stood—because it was the one their grandfather had made for their grandmother when she had to leave hers behind in Boston.

The sweet smell of rosin in the soldering flux curled up from the last soldered connection.

Unplugging the small iron, Felix placed the iron in the holder and gently placed the remaining wad of soldering wire in the cubby next to the iron's cubby.

The last of the forty pieced-together wires were complete. In less than a week, they would just be small pieces of copper once again. Bits and pieces easily lost amongst the debris after an explosion in a store. He pushed them into a long cubby set into the porch's exterior wall.

Felix pulled a square box from its cubby. The box contained tiny vials made of thin glass, the size of a large vitamin pill. He withdrew the first vial and wiggled the small pea-sized drop of mercury inside. He smiled at the memory of coming up with this way to make a progressive explosion without long wires or fuses. The mine he and his father had been sealing up was over a mile long. They had wanted not just to seal the entrance but to collapse the entire tunnel.

The problem was they did not have enough wire to make the multiple runs of wire back to progressive loads of explosives. Felix figured out the small capsule of mercury inside a little plastic pouch to be nailed or stapled to the timbers. Stuck in the bottom of the pouch were two wires hooked to a battery. When the concussion wave from the first explosion hit the tiny pouch, it shattered the glass capsule, and the mercury closed the connection between the wires.

This set off the next explosion, which set off the next—until the entire mine tunnel had been destroyed with less than one hundred feet of wire and a few small batteries.

Felix had soldered the short wires to a small stack of watch batteries. These would be connected to the blasting caps during the setup. There was just enough energy to set off the tiny blasting cap igniting the larger package of explosives. Felix smiled as he slipped each glass vial into the plastic pouch, sealing it all with a touch of clear fingernail polish, completing the small pressure switches.

This next job would only require sixty of the small compression switches and a few of the larger explosive triggers. The bottles of propane and white gas in the sporting goods store would do the rest of the job for him. The idea was to create many small indistinct explosions, which would become untraceable, instead of one or two large explosions that would leave a traceable starting point at the center of a blast ring. Felix's success came from his explosions going unexplained—unlike arson that would reek of accelerant and have definite start points.

Felix looked at the clock, stood up, and pulled on a brown uniform shirt over his white sleeveless undershirt. He checked the polish on his boots and picked up his keys. Putting the last items in their proper cubbies, he placed the sections of boards back on the wall. He felt as much as heard the click of the small, rare earth magnets drawing the boards into place. The wall looked as it had for the last sixty or eighty years... once painted but now left to chip and weather. He peeked in his now empty coffee mug. He had hoped for one last swallow.

He would pick up a couple of donuts and more coffee on his way to work.

Walking in front of the old dining table pushed to the wall and used as his workbench, he pulled the strings on the two old gooseneck desk lamps. Reaching the door, he turned back for one last check. Everything looked the same. It was a musty, almost bare, seldom-used screened porch just like dozens of other porches rimming the bay.

He turned off the overhead light and gently closed the door. The key clicked in the lock, and then the house joined the early morning silence, muffling the retreat of the crepe-soled boots down the hall toward the front door.

The stork standing on the end of the grass fluffed its feathers about its head and resumed sleeping. Dawn was still hours away. The foghorn on the Golden Gate Bridge started its early morning ritual. The long lonely sound echoed down the bay and blended with the engine of the old panel truck starting and finally crunching its way down the gravel driveway.

2

DRUNKS AND ICE CREAM

The cross wrench spun in Hooker's left hand then stopped. He moved it to the next lug nut and spun it with his right hand again. This was quiet work Hooker did without looking. Spin one, skip one, spin one, skip one, and one around the wheel. He looked up at the man weaving drunkenly. Even at quarter past four, the man was well past the limit of anything close to preserving composure. Hooker figured the man had hit close to toxic levels at two o'clock when some bar threw him out. With luck, he would get back behind the wheel and simply pass out before he could start the car.

Hooker let down the jack and restored it to the back of his truck. The giant vehicle was three times longer than the man's Chevelle and weighed six times more. To someone who didn't understand Hooker, they would have thought the truck, nicknamed Mae West, was overkill for a flat tire, but for an auto club driver, these 'T-1' calls were the 'T-wonderful' butter and jam lining the bread of Hooker's living. Hooker only got $3.12 for the tire change while Mae burned through almost a gallon—or sixty cents of fuel—but it all added up at the end of the night. The dead batteries, flat tires, and 'locked my keys in the car' were the auto club calls keeping Hooker busy during the night when he didn't have a wreck or commercial, and therefore, more profitable tow.

Lately, his nights had been nothing but the sparse butter and not much bread. The dead business wasn't what was eating at him—it was the quiet.

Hooker dropped the trunk on the Chevelle and turned toward the drunk. "Okay, sir. You're all set except twenty-six bucks."

The man fished some wadded bills from his pocket, leaning back against the car. He fingered through the money. Finally, looking up, he held out two twenties. His speech was massively slurred.

"Does this cover it?"

Hooker realized the man could not even tell what the bills were. He sighed. The man was beyond redemption. Still, Hooker could hear Candy's voice comforting these same kinds of people where she worked at the all-night diner. It was one of the main reasons Hooker had been drawn to her.

He leaned into the fog of alcohol from the man's lungs. "Let's see what you have here," Hooker said, not unkindly, as he fished through the man's bills and found the five and one to go with one of the twenties. Gently taking the rest, he pushed the bills down into the man's pants pocket so they did not end on the ground.

"Here, let's get you into the backseat for a nice nap, shall we?" He started to guide the man into the back of the two-door. It would make it harder for the guy to get back into the driver's seat.

"I have to be at work at eight o'clock," the man slurred.

"I think this is going to be a sick day for you today." Hooker watched as the man took the direction and stretched out on the small bench seat in the back. The first snore was wafting its way out the door as Hooker quietly eased it shut after sticking the keys on top of the visor.

Hooker grabbed the microphone from behind his head as he drew his left leg up into the cab of the truck.

"1-4-1."

"1-4-1?"

"Show me 10-97 on this red Chevelle, and you might advise PD, I put the guy in the backseat to sleep it off. Hopefully, he'll stay there until the afternoon brings him a huge headache. If an officer checks on him, warn them not to be smoking within twenty feet of the guy's breath."

The young dispatcher giggled. "10-4, Hooker... drunk at Pearl and

Blossom Hill. Will advise PD and at least, have them watch so the car doesn't wander off. We aren't holding anything for you at this time. Dolly says Stella and Manny are playing gin right now, so you have a choice of breakfast with them or leftover beef stew here."

Hooker dropped his right hand and found the single ear of his partner. The twenty-plus pounds of orange tabby started to purr. Hooker looked toward the eastern hills. He knew there would be nothing left for the night unless someone decided to park creatively on the freeway.

He keyed the mic. "10-4, Dina. Tell Dolly thanks for the offer, but I think Box and I will mosey on down to the hacienda and see what creative thoughts Stella has in mind with last night's leftover barbecued pork."

Dolly's voice came back over the speaker. "If you're thinking of stopping by Thrifty's for any French vanilla ice cream—don't call back. I don't want Dina to go mush-brained on me her first week back."

Hooker snorted. The ice cream gave Hooker what Dolly called 'bedroom voice' and made the dispatch girls squirm in their seats. Dina had been out for a few months while she had her baby. Hooker was surprised to hear her voice back so soon, but he guessed the rumor might be true about IBM going through another round of layoffs.

"10-4, Mama. I wasn't thinking about ruining my breakfast with the folks."

Hooker hung the mic back behind his head and squeezed his left foot down on the clutch as he set the truck in sixth gear. Looking down at his partner, he smiled evilly. "How about it, Box? Should we go get some ice cream and then call Dina from the payphone?"

Box was always ready for his dab of ice cream in his small red bowl while Hooker usually got a triple scoop in a sugar cone. There were a few things Box always seemed ready for in life. Ice cream was right up there with beating the snot out of a dog or two and lying draped across the expanse of Dolly's chest. At nearly a quarter-ton, Dolly's exposed chest above her perpetual Muumuu was a perfect fit for a large cat and produced a lot of heat. Dolly was one of the few who could touch the cat —much less pick him up. Box was his own man and had very established preferences.

Hooker nosed the eleven tons of Mae West out onto the street and headed for Monterey Highway and their twenty-four-hour ice cream pit stop. The cops all joked (especially when the weather was bitter cold), about it being perfect weather for Hooker to show up at an accident with a triple scoop of French vanilla ice cream in a sugar cone with the window rolled down in the truck. Winter was when Hooker was at his most memorable.

Tonight, the window was down, and Hooker reached toward the small rack of eight-track tapes. His fingers hovered over Tex Ritter and then moved to the Riders. His forefinger and thumb even embraced the cassette, but then he leaned back in the seat, opting for the quiet of Mae West's 1,600 horsepower and the matching purr from below and beside his seat. He knew Box had his only eye closed and was leaning into the blast of heated air.

Hooker felt out of sorts.

A short but eventful year had started with him jamming his fork into a street punk's hand, which was stealing tips from Hooker's girlfriend. The punk turned out to be her younger brother, and Hooker ended up having to pack the kid around while his hand healed. Those fourteen days had been cut short when the kid saved Hooker's life. The indentured help eventually became the second set of intelligent hands and was now sleeping in a bed ten feet from one of Hooker's beds. Now the Squirt was attending the police academy, compliments of the San Jose Police, the Santa Clara sheriff, and the California Highway Patrol. All had lost officers to the serial killer the Squirt ended up killing.

Hooker was happy for the kid, and he would make a great cop... but now Hooker missed the warm body in the other seat.

As Hooker pulled up in front of the Thrifty Drugstore, he could see the only two people standing at one of the check stands, talking. Hooker was sure the topic of conversation was either how the 49ers had been robbed or how the Oakland Raiders had become nothing more than thugs on the field. The manager was the 49ers fan, and the night cashier's uncle had once played a short career with the Raiders. For Hooker, it was the green light to break the health code law and let Box come in with him.

The manager, Randy, had heard stories about Box eating ice cream but had never met him. Holly had seen Box and always loved watching him delicately slurping his share.

Hooker grabbed the little red dish and swung open the door. "Come on, buddy. Show time."

The large cat slid between Hooker's legs and seat, beating him to the door. Holly was standing at the open glass door as Box strolled up.

"Well, hello, Box... Your place awaits." Looking up, the tall, athletic young woman smiled at Hooker. "We were just talking about beat-up street tuffs."

Hooker snorted. "Raiders tonight, eh? You know you'll catch your death of cold standing out here in the freezing weather."

Holly snorted a muffled laugh. "I love winter. I don't celebrate it with French vanilla ice cream and drive around with my window down, but it's my favorite time of the year." Hooker stopped and frowned. He could tell she was serious.

Still sober, she summed up her childhood. "When everything is cold or frozen, there are no rows to hoe, no smell of steer-blood or shit on the fields, and my hands are clean—or at least not stained black from gathering those stinking black walnuts." She followed Hooker into the store. "Nope, winter is my time to relax and enjoy—cold, rain, snow and all."

Randy chuckled as Hooker walked in with Box. "Actually, it's not the Raiders at all, this time. The ruling came out tonight and should be in the mercury this morning. They're going ahead and fining the Steelers and Green Bay for some of the underhanded stuff they pulled this year." He eyed the large orange body of fur and scars. "So this is Box?"

Hooker offered the man the small red bowl. "And this is the famous dish."

"Of course..."

Holly took the dish and headed for the ice cream counter. Hooker watched the way she moved. At almost six foot, she flowed with the fluid nature of a surfer who logged thousands of hours of water time off Capitola Point, except her hair was dark instead of blonde. Hooker knew her seemingly constant tan came more from working on the family truck farm in Gilroy since she was a tiny child, instead of any time floating around on a surfboard in the sun.

Hooker nudged Randy softly with his elbow. "How's the anatomy class coming, Holly?"

She looked up and smirked as she rolled her eyes. "Candy told you about...?" Looking down at the ice cream, she shook her head. "Yeah, of course, she would."

She set the dish down for Box and handed the cone to Hooker. "It was horrible *and* embarrassing. I don't skip lunch anymore. I'm sure they're already making up a nickname like Faint Girl, or something equally mean."

He gave her the famous Hooker one-sided smile. "Nah, I think you're good there. Nurses aren't mean by nature. After all, you didn't faint on the Squirt or anything like that." He watched as the deep red flushed up from under her shirt.

"What did John say?"

"Nothing. However, the day *he* was your massage body—he was very quiet for the rest of the day... So what did happen?"

Holly glanced at Randy, who held up his hands and rolled his eyes. "We're all adults here, Holly, and you know you don't have to share anything you don't want to. After all, I'm happily married, and it probably isn't anything I haven't experienced before."

Hooker could see her stiffen. "It wasn't anything sexu—well, you know. It was his scars." She blushed again. "I've never seen so many and so fresh... I-I urped."

Hooker stopped mid-lick. "You threw up? Where...?"

Holly was now in full flush. "In his pants." She realized how it sounded and rushed to explain. "They were on the floor."

Hooker pictured the scene and drew the final conclusion. "Which means he shucked them down around his boots..."

Holly buried her face in her hands and nodded, her voice muffled as she finished.

"I filled his boots as well."

BREAKFAST AT THE HACIENDA

Hooker parked the large truck on the thick driveway pad specifically built for her 22,000 pounds. As he grabbed his paperwork, he could feel Box's tail rubbing under the back of his knees as he absently opened the door. Set into the concrete pad the size of a gas station was a small patch of lawn. There was only one reason this existed. Box, hopping down, made it clear it was his turf.

Two doors down, the man who lived there had a young dog, barely more than a pup. For whatever reason, the dog's name was Mike. The owner had already suffered through Box coming down and beating the snot out of his previous older Doberman. Mike was a beautiful yellow Lab, and the man did not want cat scratches all over the young dog's mug. So the agreement was he would mow and edge the patch, and Hooker would keep Box at bay until Mike turned at least two.

Hooker hesitated to tell the man about Mike coming down, and Box taking a liking to the pup. Hooker had caught them more than once, wrestling quietly on the grass, which upfront to perfection. To keep up appearances, Hooker still called out loudly for Box to leave Mike alone until he was at least old enough to know fear.

Box threatened, Mike shied, Hooker bellowed, and the lawn stayed mowed and trimmed to excellence. Life was good in the neighborhood, except for the familiar '63 Dodge Dart convertible parked up close to the wall on the driveway instead of down in the garage where it belonged. At five in the morning, there had to be an explanation. Hooker looked at the heavy morning dew collected on the cold car.

As he walked through the front plaza with the fountain, Hooker could see it had been another one of those nights. Eight years since a bullet shattered its way through his spine, putting him in a wheelchair, and ending his career as a police detective, Manny was still dogged by nightmares.

As he reached the door, the angle was just right. Stella could see him from the kitchen counter, and she reached for his mug. Hooker knew she had heard the heavily baffled exhaust of Mae West and was prepared.

When Hooker remembered, he switched the exhaust to the 'silencer' as they climbed the hill filled with expensive homes. But as he settled her in on the parking pad, he ran her in standard exhaust for a minute to clear her pipes and make it easier to start.

Hooker opened the heavy front door, and the orange streak beat his foot to the interior of the slate floor.

"Lucy…you have some 'splainin' to do…" His Cuban accent was terrible, but his imitation of Ricky Ricardo never missed securing at least one smile from the family.

As he closed the door to the silence of being ignored, a slender hand grabbed his left butt cheek.

The immediate laughing of the three others helped to mask his high-pitched squeal of fear. Spinning, he found Candy still in pink pajamas with little red hearts. He settled down and grabbed her laughing neck in the crotch of his elbow and drew her in as she tried to wiggle out of his grasp. The giggling got worse as his right boot tried to swing up in a good-natured backhand slap. They danced in the entry much to the amusement of Manny and Stella. It was good to see the two having some pure laughter. Hooker knew, all too often, it was just the opposite.

"What are you doing up this early, you little scamp?"

Stella put his mug of coffee down on the table next to Candy's. "She was in your room…"

Hooker looked up and over at Manny. The man was nodding and no longer smiling. It was his 'I'm not going to talk about this' face. Hooker eased the arm grip on the now messed up head of hair. He leaned over and kissed the top.

Quietly, he muttered only for Candy, "It's something we all have to get used to around here."

Candy looked Hooker in the eyes and nodded slightly as he let her go.

Hooker frowned as he looked back down toward the hall leading to his bedroom suite as well as the Squirt's room at the end.

Candy snorted. "Are you kidding? The Squirt wake up from just a tiny little scream? Hah! Try a bomb, maybe."

The sound of the muffled zombie came through the door as it opened. "I heard that, sis, and for your information, I was already up and studying."

Hooker spun around and laughed. The Squirt had not come from his bedroom but had been in Manny's office. "Good morning, sweet cheeks. Holly says hi."

The kid blushed but smirked as he carried a large coffee mug toward the dining and kitchen area. "She owes me a massage… and dinner." He shuffled over to side-hug Stella and got a kiss on the top of his head as he poured more coffee. Turning, he looked at Manny as Hooker and Candy —still playing mild grab-ass—took the morning side of the table. "If I place the evidence bag on my desk and go to the bathroom for a couple of minutes, the chain of evidence is broken… but if I throw it in the bottom drawer, and leave on vacation for two weeks, it's not."

"Implied reasonable circumstances of security."

"But if I didn't lock the desk, where is the security?"

"I said, *implied*. I did not say it *was* secure."

"…and so it's defendable in court?"

Manny leaned back in his chair. Hooker knew the Squirt being at the academy invigorated the old detective as nothing else could. The man's eyes were electric with possibilities and training.

"I can think of a couple of great lawyers in the counties who I wouldn't try to run this past, but for most of the bucket-scum oozing through the courts today… sure, I'd run it."

Candy looked at Hooker. Hooker shrugged and wobbled his open spread hand. The meaning was maybe he understood and maybe not.

There were a lot of cop protocols Hooker had picked up over the years. Some of those were the fine details of being a cop that did not matter to Hooker's job, but he still picked up from being around Manny, as well as other cops, for so many years.

"It's like if I tow a car and leave it on the street outside a shop's fence, then someone breaks in and steals the radio or something, it's on my insurance. But if I park it in their parking lot, the implied is, I left it in their care—even though I didn't stick it in their locked yard."

The Squirt snorted a laugh. "What about stashing trailers and cars in Safeway's parking lot?"

Hooker shot him an evil smile. "As long as I don't leave a trailer full of color TVs in the median dirt area in the middle of the 101. But then it goes on the trucking company's insurance. Their assurance was for the driver not to break down and to safely deliver the TVs to the stores—which he didn't."

Manny laughed as he remembered the incident. "Wasn't it Ace who left it there after the Chips had cleared it?"

Hooker laughed then saw Candy was lost. "Ace got a tow. The Chip hauled the driver away because he found a second time-log in the cab—that he searched after the guy failed to walk the white line. Drunk or too many hours on the road still makes you a ticking time bomb.

"Anyway, the Chip had pulled the guy over because he was high-balling in the fast lane on the 101 in the section where they have to stay in the two slow lanes. So the guy pulls off into the middle play area. The truck Ace is driving is only a deuce and a half—a two-and-a-half ton truck, and can only take the tractor and trailer one at a time. He uncouples the rig and hauls off with the tractor to go stash it somewhere close. He gets back, and the back doors are swung open... and a whole lot of tire tracks everywhere. He was gone, maybe twenty minutes..."

Manny snorted. "Which was about ten more than was needed."

Hooker tried to calm down and finish, but he was laughing too hard.

Stella just wagged her head. "There were just nine TVs left in the whole trailer." She held up her hands about a loaf of bread apart. "You know those little black and white TVs you get for a kid's room or something?"

The Squirt finished the punch line. "Only then was when Ace looked at the side of the forty-foot trailer. The whole thing was one big billboard. It said 'Another Load of Fine Zenith Color Televisions.'"

It was not clear if everyone was laughing at Candy's horror-struck face or the story, but Stella could not get up to start breakfast for at least five minutes.

As she stepped to the sink and from the corner of her eye, she saw a person just leaving from the front door across from the entrance plaza. She stepped over to the next window to see them walking out through the front gates, which pierced the fourteen-foot tall wall enclosing the plaza.

"Hooker, the Sunday Missile just got hand-delivered to the front door. Would you be a dear and find out why?"

The Sunday Missile was the only newspaper they got all week. Mostly, it was because Stella did not want Manny to cruise all the crime news. He was seven years retired with full disability, and still, the urge to figure out crimes was only held below the surface by his thinning skin. It was bad enough Hooker occasionally dragged home cases the police had no competence or interest in solving.

Stella saw Hooker glance at the newspaper and then run toward the street. A few minutes later, he returned, picked up the paper, and came back in.

Stella's question was written on her face as she stood with her hands splayed on the large stone island's top. Hooker deadpanned and quietly offered out the large roll of newspaper in the plastic condom. They stood staring—both holding deadpan faces—the battle was on.

Finally, Stella realized she would have to heighten the conflict. "Did you want breakfast with your girlfriend?"

"Remember Lloyd Summers?"

She nodded. "Retired about two years ago… What about him?"

"He's your new missile boy. He got bored with fishing every day… and wanted something exciting to do. Out of respect, your missile will be placed, not thrown, at your doorstep every Sunday. I'm sure if you want, he'd even bring it in and place it in your hands. But then, you might have to give him coffee, and the others would get their paper late." Hooker smiled his quirky grin. He knew he had won the battle, and he loved stroking Stella's heart at the same time.

"I'll call his wife later. If the door's open, he's always welcome to coffee. He and his wife have done their share of canning in our backyard."

Hooker's face collapsed. "He got the job because… she passed away a few months ago. He sold the boat and moved back up from Monterey. Evidently, he fished because she loved to fish."

Stella looked at Hooker as she thought. "The door will always be unlocked on Sunday mornings." She looked over at Manny, who just nodded with his eyelids. Cops were always family. It was the reason Stella started what had become a huge canning project involving hundreds of volunteers. Every year, they helped can many tons of food, which was then stashed in large storage larders about the city—for those in need. What had started for comrade cops in need had grown larger through firefighters, city workers, county workers, and other civil servants. As Stella always told people, those in need are the only family ties needed.

With breakfast finished and cleared, the household settled down into a quiet routine. The Squirt was sequestered back in the office. The large, professional reel-to-reel tape recorder oozed out classical music into the equally professional-grade headphones. Pages of textbooks were turned and memorized. There were four large stacks of books. As the Squirt memorized a book, it went into the correct box to be returned. The boxes were labeled: County Library, Paul—the County Commissioner over all police matters, Chet—a California Highway Patrol captain, or he simply stood and returned the book to the proper space on the office's bookshelf.

With his photographic memory, he had no reason to mark them up or keep them or bother with reading them in any certain order. Every book was read, memorized, and ready for almost instant recall. What the Squirt would like to happen was to forget most of his growing up with his sister as much-abused foster children.

What the two had stumbled into was Hooker—and his family. Hooker and his sister had also grown up in the worst the foster care system had to offer. Like the Squirt and Candy, Hooker and his sister had ended their torture in foster care at the ripe age of fourteen and sixteen respectably. John was uncertain, but he had a feeling it was the commonality which first drew Hooker toward Candy at the all-night diner she was working at then.

On the other side of the wall, Hooker slept the sleep of the dead, with a soft slender arm thrown over his side. Candy had her nose buried in the back of his neck and hair and behind her knees, curled into a large orange furry package, lay Box. Even as a small kitten—which had not lasted long—he had a way of taking over the bed, and Hooker had taken to closing the door so he could have the bed to himself.

The large sunroom was off the dining area. Manny and Stella had designed it for afternoon lazy lounging days. The custom-made couch was a large "L" shape running for fourteen feet along the solid wall and then hooked left, running another twelve feet under the south wall of windows. The floor-to-ceiling wall of glass looked east across the Almaden Valley, and the south looked down the valley. The two had bought the large property back when the road was nothing but a dirt track. They would bounce their way up to their knoll just to picnic and gaze upon the unmolested valley. Later, they built their dream home, as did so many others. Eventually, the developers came and overbuilt the beautiful valley into just another tract of ticky-tacky boxes. However, the Romeros had their slice of heaven and were not interested in leaving. Therefore, they had designed the hacienda with its two-foot thick adobe walls and windows open to the expansive view and morning sun. The large expanse of lounging area, enough for the whole family, was a bonus.

"Huh." Manny almost sat up. The effort was too much, and he resumed his relaxed state. He waited.

The large grandfather clock in the dining and entryway great room ticked with its dull metered pace. Manny pinched his thumb on the line of news and continued to read. A few minutes later, he heard the other section of the newspaper slowly fold down at one corner.

He never had to look to know his wife's eye was studying him through the space where the corner of newsprint had been a moment before. She waited.

"It says here the old sporting goods store out on the Guadalupe had a gas explosion last night. Evidently, one of the propane canisters was defective and blew up. It must've set off a chain of other stuff because it's a total loss."

The newsprint in Stella's hand curled the rest of the way down into her lap as she reached out to the coffee table for more of what she called *her thinking liquid*. She sipped slowly as Manny waited.

The two had married just at the beginning of the Korean War. They were married on the dock by an Army Padre right before Manny boarded the troopship. On his return, they had slowly gotten used to the mechanics of how they collectively thought about things. As Manny's old partner used to tease, Manny got more productive deducing accomplished on a Sunday afternoon at home with Stella—than he did with the whole squad all week.

Manny never told Paul just how close to the truth he was.

"About two months ago…" Her hand and mug hovered in the air.

"…upper Stevens Creek Boulevard area…"

"… a machine shop or something?" Stella took another sip.

"Some kind of manufacturing…"

"…but it was natural gas or something…" She put her mug on the table and then leaned back into the couch.

The clock ticked. The minds both ground along.

"But it never caught fire… just exploded."

There were a couple of minutes of silence, and then the newspapers returned to their positions.

Across the valley, a bald eagle searched one of the last fields, hovering and watching for the tiny spot of red that meant movement. The predator was patient as he waited for the mouse or mole to move again. The wan winter sun did not heat the ground anymore, so the bird would only need the last twitch or step to zero in its targeting. The rodent was caught— they just didn't know it yet.

4

ANOTHER BOMB

Felix slid the key into the door. Through the tiny window, he could see there was another fat envelope. Two in one month—someone was in a hurry. He didn't mind the extra money, but there was always the risk someone would put explosions together and see patterns.

He opened the mailbox door and withdrew the envelope. This was the only reason he had this mailbox account—fat envelopes with instructions and money—lots of money.

Felix closed the little door and turned the key. Slipping the large envelope under his shirt and down the back of his pants, he fluffed the tail of his work shirt and walked out of the store. He wouldn't look at the envelope again until he was on his screened porch and safe from prying eyes.

The afternoon hadn't improved the light drizzle. Felix guessed there must be a large storm coming out of Alaska, pushing the cold down into the Bay Area. The weather in February usually could get nicely calm and allow the sun to bring the temperatures up into the balmy fifties. Felix thought of it as T-shirt weather.

The 1949 Ford panel truck squealed and creaked as the man nosed it off the street and up the gravel driveway. The salt air didn't help any of the offenses visited on the old truck, but they did no worse than the once or twice a year hosing down Felix squandered on what had once been his work truck. The house paint slapped on the side panels barely hid the old signage of *Rocky Mountain Mine Services*. Even the lead paint was taking a beating from the Back Bay's brackish salt air. The truck's once glossy finish had taken on a matching appearance to the house.

Felix turned the key to the left, and the old engine chugged and rattled its way to silence. The man's hands hung in his lap. His shoulders curled from a long-endured weight. He was home, and there was no joy in it. He looked over at the equally battered Volkswagen. He ran his fingers through his already graying hair. At forty-seven, Felix felt he and the two vehicles had seen better days. His left hand pulled the door handle up as his right hand grabbed his lunch pail, just another battered reminder from a better time.

As Felix walked the short walk to the entrance, the door opened. The scrawny woman in the threadbare coat with hair to match jerked her way out as she pulled the door closed behind her.

"I got her fed and bathed today. She be 'n fresh diapers now and was already sucking at her blanket when I leaved her. Sorry I can't stay longer, but I'z gots ta get home to my babies."

Not once did the woman look up. Her sunken features were as thread-bare as her clothes. Felix called over his shoulder. "Thanks, Edwina. See you tomorrow."

The rusted German relic rattled to life with a few pops, and the transmission whined as she backed out of the driveway onto the road. She ground the gears like every day and then drove off down the road just as fast as she had backed out of the driveway.

Felix closed the door. Not much ever changed.

He looked into the small room. He would turn off the tiny nightlight later. He stood listening to what was left of his wife of twenty-nine years as she suckled on the corner of one of the blankets. In an hour or two, she would be mercifully asleep. He drew the door mostly closed so the light from the other room would not intrude.

Almost to himself, he whispered to his love, "Sleep well, Thelma."

Felix stepped out onto the screened sleeping porch. He pulled the strings on the two gooseneck lamps. Drawing the envelope out from his back, he settled heavily onto his chair. He looked at the return address. The man or the address had moved from Fremont to San Leandro. Felix guessed neither was true. The pinched handwriting was the same as when it made out paychecks to the miners in Colorado.

Felix absentmindedly reached under the table. His fingers curled around to the backside of the table's apron and found the knife held there by two magnets. He slit the top of the large envelope and carefully poured out the contents. He fished about the pile with the knife. There was nothing there that could hurt him—just all of it. He placed the knife back on the magnets and began to read.

An hour later, he folded up the letter and maps and placed them in the envelope. He removed the boards from the wall and stuck the folded envelope into an empty cubby. Fanning through the three bundles of bills, he then stuck the $30,000 into another cubby and sealed up the wall.

Turning off the two lights, he rose and walked to the end of the porch. The iron bed squeaked as he sat to take off his boots. As he stretched out, pulling the two blankets over himself, he listened to the night noises of the bay.

There would be a lot of work to do in the next week.

5

BLOOD ALLEY

Bill Talbert walked through the large entryway of the main offices. He waved at the guard who was always there. They changed, but on Sundays, they seemed always to be the same—the stupid one, the old one, the zit-faced one, or they simply drew the short straw. It had to be a mind-numbing boring job... the job a person would have to be severely desperate to take.

Bill turned right down the second hall. He chuckled sadly about the guards. Since graduating from MIT, he never had to take a job he did not want. The recruiter came to him from Advanced Systems when he was a senior. When Connie was pregnant with their first child, she did not want to deal with the snows in Boston anymore. They had taken a vacation once to San Francisco, and she had fallen in love with the Bay Area. Bill picked up the phone, and two weeks later, IBM was moving their new engineer across the continent.

At the end of the long hall, he fumbled with his key to the Ram Core Design wing. Entering the large open area used for brainstorming, he walked along the southern row of small offices. Sundays were his time to get some serious work done in the silence. He reached his office and opened the door.

Putting his briefcase and coat on the couch, he turned to his desk.

There was an envelope in the middle of the desk. Typed in the middle was his name. He opened the envelope and withdrew the letter and check. He glanced at the letter and then sat down heavily in the chair and reread. He looked up at the large clock in the main room, positive the long blur was both hands pointing in the two o'clock position.

Three o'clock was early for the phone to ring at the Romero hacienda. Manny mumbled into the wireless extension in the sunroom. He listened as he saw the door to his office open. He nodded his head toward the hall at the Squirt. "Yeah, Karen. The Squirt is getting him now. How bad…?"

He reached over. Pulling and dragging, he sat up with his legs hanging over the couch edge. Stella had one eye half-open—watching him. She never trusted phone calls at the wrong hours.

Hooker walked into the office with only his jeans on. His voice joined the conversation. "Hooker."

"Hooker, Karen. CHP rolled up three minutes ago. A single car heading south—crossed the line into a set of doubles. First response says at least a dozen vehicles and three are rigs."

"Blood Alley again… "

"10-4, Hooker, just south of IBM. I'll call Jose for you—the car punched a cab-over, and witnesses estimate he was going well over eighty. The cab-over sounds like toast, but there are also the other two rigs—"

Hooker didn't even listen to the last part. He hung up on her and moved to his bedroom. As he turned into the room, the end of the hall caught his eye. The Squirt was already dressed and pulling on his boots… not the police academy boots, but his real work boots.

Candy lay curled in the blankets, but both eyes were open.

"Large pile-up out by IBM…"

"Blood Alley…" Nobody lived in the South Bay for longer than a month before they knew and understood the name applied to the worst eight miles of highway—two lanes of highway separated by a set of double six-inch yellow lines. The new 55mph speed limit did nothing to slow down the drunks, sleepers, or suicides who had no respect for the people on the other side of the lines. When a car crosses the line traveling at 60mph and slams into another going in the opposite direction at 60mph, the combined kinetic energy is five tons of steel moving at 120mph comes to an instant rest at zero. The energy has to go somewhere. Hooker knew from street education the smaller energy would now be buried and flattened into the tractor of the truck and trailers. The engine of the truck would be pushed up into the cab or possibly out the back of the cab if it were one of the thin cabs called stand-ups.

Hooker dropped a fast kiss as he slid his feet into the boots with the tops of the socks turned over the rims of the top. He didn't even check to see if his T-shirt was fresh—it wasn't. It was the same one he had worn all day and night from the previous day.

Turning, he strode through the door as his left hand grabbed the leather jacket off of the hook. The Squirt strode by in identical uniform—black leather jacket over a starched white T-shirt, tucked into jeans over eleven-inch-tall engineer boots.

The Squirt made the corner and grabbed the doorknob. "Box. Go time." He looked back with a self-satisfied smile at Hooker with his lips poised to say the same thing.

The large orange streak was out the door before either of them.

Hooker smiled back at Candy as she stood hanging in the corner at the end of the hallway. She blew him a kiss with her hand. Hooker watched the Squirt grab the hammer and start pounding a fast route on the tires, checking for flats or wrong inflation. Even in a hurry, it is an important job taking less than a few seconds. Hooker shook his head and smiled. *I missed this kid.*

Candy watched from the long floor-to-ceiling windows making up the south wall of the hallway and the north wall of the plaza. Stella watched from the small observation window set in the wall of the kitchen. Together, they were thinking the same, simple caution—*be safe.*

The whine of the turbo had only run up about halfway when Hooker pushed the small silver button—lighting the controlled explosions in the engine. Mae West's 1,600 horses roared to life. Hooker blipped the throttle a couple of times as he passed the gears into sixth. He thought about the late afternoon and Sunday. The traffic would be heavy on Blossom Hill Road, but it would be several extra miles to go down and around through Uvas Road. The choice of route determined which way he dropped off the hill and into the Almaden Valley.

Hooker pulled the mic from behind his head. "1-4-1," he called the night dispatch as he glanced at his watch. He knew, at this hour, it could go either way. Karen was managing the day shift, but Dolly may be an hour or so early taking over command of the city.

"Go ahead, Hooker." Dolly was in. It told him the wreck was bigger than they do not just seal the entrance thought. Dolly's house was only a mile from the office, but she lived in the gray pumice brick building with the thick armor-plated steel door.

"Better from the Hill or Uvas?"

"The entire southbound is backed up past the 280, but they have it blocked, so the lanes are open to the south. I'd run Uvas and just open her up. Jose and Manual are on their way, and they're bringing both lowboys just in case."

Mae had already started rolling south down the street, dumping them out a short distance from the Uvas turnoff. Hooker shot the Squirt a glance. The young man had a look on his face, which could have been Box at go time.

"10-4, Mama. Let's have a great Sunday."

"Let's keep it safe, Hooker. Keep your powder dry."

Hooker hung the mic behind his head and jumped two more gears. He loafed the truck down the back road filling up with new homes. Every one of them larger than the next, and none of them looked like they belonged.

Glancing at the kid, he smiled. "How's school?"

"Finals for this section are next week. I'll be glad when they're over." The Squirt turned his head to the open window. The day had warmed up to a pleasant forty degrees. In the Squirt's world, as well as Hooker's, this meant it was just about right for leather over T-shirts with the heater running full bore. The winter wind through the open window felt good. He had missed his time in the truck.

"Tough classes?"

The Squirt snorted and looked over at Hooker with a sneer. "More like boring. I could have taken these tests two weeks ago. I'm just ready to move on to some of the more practical classes, like the shooting range and physical training." He smiled down where Box was leaning into the blast of the heater. "Heck, I think Box could take these courses and pass."

Hooker glanced over as he rolled to the stop sign. "Not everyone can read a book only once and have it memorized for life." Hooker set the gears into fifth and turned right, falling in behind a Camaro.

The Squirt watched how close Hooker rolled out behind the muscle car. The Camaro was smaller than the working bed on Mae West and barely stood taller than her wheel wells. He started to chuckle. He knew Hooker could not resist showing a Ford or Chevy what the real muscle on the road looked like.

The guy in the Camaro thought he was safe when he took a power turn onto Uvas Road. Eleven tons of yellow and blue rear end drifted in the corner. The back eight drivers howled.

As Mae straightened, the full force of the enormous engine churned the rubber—now gripping the asphalt—the front end rose.

Hooker hit the switch to move the exhaust dumps. Underneath the cab, the cylinders rotated, and the exhaust took the nine-inch shortcut— pounding the asphalt directly below. Mae responded to the lack of back-pressure, and the tachometer jumped 380 RPMs. Hooker shifted to keep up with the new power range and eased into the oncoming lane. The Camaro aired out his exhaust the best he could, but the giant lady danced past him like it was a wallflower at the barn dance. Long before the back hook cleared the front nose of the Chevy, Mae was dancing a high-step. Hooker shifted twice more as Mae left the 120mph mark in the dirt with the Camaro.

The Squirt giggled harder as he cinched his belt tighter and considered reaching behind the seat and pulling the shoulder straps out for the four-point harness. Hooker grinned. *The kid had missed this girl, too.*

Hooker reached over his head and hit a large red button on the new header console. "1-4-1."

"Go, son." The Squirt marveled at the new hands-free radio mic.

"We're on Uvas—ETA is sixteen—any updates?"

"Hooker, you are breaking up, nine-by-nine. I hate the new mic Willie installed—but I can only guess as to why you are using it. The total looks like twenty-six shorts, four talls, and seven blackouts."

Hooker's throat filled. Dolly had just given him their shorthand for the number of small vehicles, rigs, and deaths. He knew the statistic with a wreck this big. The number of people who didn't get to emergency care in time would drive the last number up by at least another fifty percent.

"10-4, Mama." He hit the red button again.

The silence in the truck was a blessing.

The dangerous curves were coming, and Hooker did not have time to drop down to the recommended forty-five. He drifted down to seventy and held it at the top of the power band. Cycling the exhaust dump gave him back the Jake-brake that fed air into the engine and let the backpressure slow down the truck the same as a regular gas car does. The curves were not banked right and could take a person unfamiliar with them through the curve and continue across the field in one curve or up a sand hill with another. Hooker became familiar with them by towing drunken locals off the hill and out of the field when it became an overflow for the creek running through it.

As Hooker wrestled with the snaking flat track, he remained calm. "So, after finals, are they giving you wannabe cops a break?"

The Squirt looked back into the cab. He wasn't sure Hooker was seriously asking about school when he was hauling eleven tons through some nasty road. Then he looked down at Box. The cat hadn't changed. His single eye was closed as he leaned into the hot air. As the truck shifted, he just leaned into the turn. Nothing seemed to faze the cat. Rolling his eyes behind his closed lids, the Squirt took his cue from the expert and flowed with the go.

"We have two weeks off. You need some help?"

Coming out of the curves, they raced around the top end of the small lake. At the near midpoint, Hooker stomped on the brake and clutch. Dropping the transmission five gears, he mentally lined up on the next turn—a sharp left onto the road leading them out to the bottom end of Blood Alley.

Hooker reached to the top of the large steering wheel boosted by two instead of only one power steering boosting pumps. This gave him the steering of a sports car at a tenth of the weight and a dozen times smaller than Mae. He flinched the wheel to the right, and then pulled down hard and around left. He mashed harder on the brake for a brief second, which broke the rear end loose. The view in the cab became a carnival ride as the back of the truck slewed around on the sand and gravel covered the intersection.

"Nah, it's as dead as a door knocker in a mausoleum." He dumped the clutch and tromped on the throttle as the truck lined up on the new road. Mae responded, and the tires bit into the asphalt, and the sliding truck became the usual yellow and blue missile. Hooker glanced over at the kid.

"I'm so bored that I was thinking the three of us could go and invade the Apple Farm and see Sissy."

The Squirt pursed his lips into a prune to keep from screaming. As he watched the posts on the barbed wire fence turn into a blur, he knew they were traveling at speeds most police cars could never obtain.

"Sure," he squeaked. "Sounds good."

Hooker took his last chuckle. In a few minutes, he knew they would be awash in a sea of sorrow. He wouldn't know any of the brain donors, but it was the sadness of how something could have been fixed with a simple fence of concrete down the middle. Something the state of California said it was too broke to do even if it meant saving lives.

As they rolled up to and into the carnage, Hooker and John were both evaluating the wrecks. In Hooker's mind, John had long ago stopped being the Squirt or a know-nothing new guy when it came to working an accident. In fact, the kid's first accident had been about half this size only a couple of miles north.

The kid pointed to a farm road breaking through the fence line and over the railroad tracks. About a hundred yards in, there was a large flat area where the farmer would park his trucks and tractors. Hooker nodded. They would stash tows there and come get them later when the mess was cleared.

Hooker snatched the mic from behind his head. "1-4-1."

"Hooker…"

"Who are the little trucks coming to the party?"

"Ace is returning from Gilroy and is behind the brothers. Mike and one of their new guys are coming in from uptown. Stan just picked up the Chevy and will be out in about ten. Don is on his way in to get their two-ton, and Karen says there are a few more, but they're coming from Clara."

"Hit Ace and Mike on their sidebands, and tell them there's a large stash lot just at the bottom end and to the west of the mess. Warn them it's over the tracks so they don't try it with any dollies. With luck, we'll have this all cleaned up for the Monday morning slugfest."

"10-4. West of the south end of the mess."

"Thanks, Mama."

He hung the mic and looked along the road littered with twisted metal. The stench of spilled gasoline and oil hung heavy in the air.

"Where do you want to start?"

The Squirt pointed at the steel pipe truck trying to mount a Monte Carlo. "Let's back the truck off... the drivers still look good, and we can recharge the air hoses for the brakes if we have to. We can stash the prom queen before the others even know we're here. If we have time, we can bone the Monte Carlo in the field and throw it to someone for a favor, but let's clean our way into the shit storm so we have some breathing room. We already know the crap upfront is two pieces of toast. We may or may not get a payday out of the trailer."

Hooker wound Mae around in a left arch and began to back her into the nightmare. The Squirt jumped out to guide him. As the afternoon dark became cold night black, the sky began to weep. Hooker did not have to explain how to do something, or what was next—even once. While Hooker shuttled twisted steel and rubber into the distant field, the Squirt worked the broom, shovel, and pail. Every small tow truck pulling out with a car also had a full debris pail. As the wrecks disappeared, so did the debris of shattered glass and peeled bits and pieces of what was left of the cars.

As they were down to a few last problematic hulks, the CHP captain showed up. Hooker was raising the busted end of a trailer as the captain walked up and quietly looked back down where the wreck had been.

Hooker looked at the man and then down the highway. He knew what the man was thinking, so he just shook his head. "It wasn't me, Chet. I've been jerking steel all afternoon." He nodded his head at the dark figure on the side of the highway, sweeping.

Chet snorted. "Is that the Squirt? Why isn't he studying?"

Hooker gave him a stupid face and hound-dogged his eyes. "He's bored. He reads the books and remembers them word for word. Dinner at Monterey Steak House says he aces every single test."

The captain just laughed. "No way am I taking a rigged bet. I've seen how his mind and memory work." He watched the kid as he swept and then dumped the pail in someone else's debris bucket. "Bored, huh? I guess maybe it's time to find some more classes he can challenge."

"Good to see you, Chet, but I need to jerk this Prom Queen and stash her. I think I saw Taylor over near the fire truck."

"Thanks, Hooker. I guess I'll be seeing you Wednesday night for dinner at Dolly's?"

"10-4. Dolly mentioned getting some salad fixings for you." The two laughed about the three pounds he had gained while he was off active duty.

Hooker looked at his watch several hours later. "Holy beans in sauce, Squirt. Do you have any idea what time it is?"

The kid rolled his eyes into his head, "Time for a nap?"

Hooker thought about the appeal of a nap. In another hour, the sun would be coming up. "Well, maybe… but first, it's time for ice cream."

6

BREAKFAST AT SWEETS

The drizzle had dithered about all week. It was as if the clouds were thinking about raining, but maybe not. This afternoon it decided a little ray of sunshine on the South Bay would lull the inhabitants into a sense of safety so the streets could become snot rinks in the evening. Hooker had one of those feelings about plenty of work during the Friday night date time. Even if it were dead batteries, it would still put fuel in the tanks.

Mae pulled up along the curb. The excellently tended front yard and the house stood out as the step above the neighborhood. It had nothing to do with a black family living in a mostly white neighborhood. This was the work of the oldest son, Danny. Everything about and around him was as well cared for or detailed as the 1968 Lincoln Town Car in the driveway. Hooker knew without looking there was not even a fingerprint on any of the chrome—even the door handles were clean and polished. Hooker believed it was the only reason Danny carried a handkerchief in his left back pocket. He had seen the giant of a man pull it out and make a final wipe every time he used the doors.

Mae's large engine, as quiet as it was when running, though, the dampening exhaust was noisy in the quiet neighborhood, so Hooker shut her down. The last vibrations echoed through the empty working-class neighborhood in the dying light of the winter day. Breakfast at the Sweets' was the same time as Hooker's beginning of the day—mid to late afternoon.

Sweets was the youngest son's name as well as the family name. In a high school accident during metal shop, Sweets traded eyesight for a unique set of other skills. He had always loved music, but in his blindness, he could remember all the liner notes and all the statistics of all the artists he had ever heard or even heard of. His skillset for talk and knowledge of music lead him to a career as a disc jockey for a local radio station. His shift started at midnight. Danny was his driver, caretaker, bodyguard, and minder. He was also Sweets' personal attendant when it came to clothes. Even though Danny's uniform of the day varied little beyond the black dress pants and shoes below the heavily starched white French-cuffed dress shirt and brown leather sports coat, Sweets dressed like a fine dandy. Danny's eye of décor prevailed everywhere within his reach, except for their much-loved mother.

The door swung open as Hooker reached for the doorbell. "Tilly, my dear."

"Hooker? Oh, my stars and garters—I almost didn't recognize you. You are simply wasting away from lack of food. Get in here. This is an emergency intervention."

Hooker laughed at the family joke for all of them and stepped into the same padding Stella provided with hugs. Tilly wasn't quite the level for him to snuggle into a fat neck, but he knew she giggled anyway.

"Stop that, Hooker. It just isn't decent. I'm an old woman." Hooker started to withdraw, and she grabbed the back of his head and pulled him back in. "I didn't say for you to stop now... just sometime in the far future." She giggled and squirmed some more.

A deep rumble like a mountain moving echoed with the giggles. "Are you molesting my mother?"

Hooker didn't stop. He turned himself and the focus of his attack to the left so he could stick his right hand and arm out.

Danny took the smaller hand and shook it. "You two hurry up with this foolishness. The neighbors are going to talk, and this hand is nothing but bones."

A voice of pure warm molasses came from the dining room. "I hope we're having more than bones for breakfast. I could swear I heard a sound like Hooker at the door—but it sounded weak and distant."

The teasing never stopped through the entire meal. It was always like this when the four got together. Hooker had been adopted into the family long before he was eighteen and legal to drive a commercial tow truck. He first met the two Sweets men one night outside the radio station when he was fifteen and driving with a bogus license.

Sweets had introduced Hooker to his other questionable gift from the injury—or skill set, depending on your perspective. Sweets could not see Hooker visually, but he could see Hooker was much younger than he was projecting. Sweets had a sixth sense or saw visions. He didn't know how to interpret them, but he knew who they were for. Hooker didn't always like what he heard, but he did pay close attention.

"How has the business been, Hooker?" Sweets touched lightly with his two smaller fingers for the edge of the plate as he put the knife down. Tilly's biscuits were legendary.

Hooker mumbled around the last bite. "Goomf." He swallowed with a sip of coffee. "

Good, Sweets."

Danny snorted.

Sweets nodded toward his brother and smiled. "Even Danny doesn't need my sight to see there was a stumble of the truth."

Hooker blushed. "Okay, slow."

Danny was the moneyman. He told Hooker the first night when he handed him his card, 'If you get in trouble, you call Dolly. If you need money, you call me.' The man now stared at Hooker. "Do you need anything?" The unspoken yet understood word was *money*.

Hooker thought about his large family. Above all else, they were always looking out for everyone else. Family—by blood or bond. Hooker laid his napkin on the table. "Nah, I kissed Uncle Willie on the ear last Monday and hugged and nuzzled Stella this morning, so all the rents are up-to-date. I need fuel, but I've got some credit left with the Fly."

Danny smiled. He knew about the credit and why. "How are her daughter and Dog getting along?"

"I'd give them until this spring or maybe summer before they find a place together."

"Good to see both of them finally find the right person."

Hooker started to ask how Danny knew the man who worked sorting the vehicle cadavers for the Fly, much less the Fly's daughter, and then he remembered Danny was the same as Hooker—he knew everyone worth knowing, whether it be in high places, in the gutter, and everywhere between. Hooker just nodded, agreeing.

Sweets laced his fingers together in a tent over his empty plate as Danny silently cleared the table. "How much do you know about explosives?"

Hooker thought about where the question may have come from. "The dime killer used napalm the one time—"

"That would be more about flames."

"Well," Hooker continued delicately, "there were a lot of explosions out at the base when I killed my sister…"

"Close, but still not large enough."

"Then I would have to go with the answer of nothing." He frowned at the line of questioning. "Survey said?"

Sweets sat still. His face was passively quiet. "I'm not sure, but there wasn't fire… just one drawn out explosion or explosions."

"Did you see anything else?"

"Trees, but they didn't make much sense. They were too close together."

"How close?"

"Like they were touching… Like a fence made out of trees, but I could see the explosions like there were windows through the fence. It was like a large building, and I was looking in all the windows, but the explosion went from right to left instead of all at once."

Hooker looked at Danny, who just shrugged. Hooker looked back toward Sweets. "Usually, when they blow up a building, there are some smaller explosions all over inside, so the walls collapse down into the building area and don't blow out into the neighborhood."

Tilly laughed. "Kind of like you boys growing up. The explosions were all in the house."

Sweets snorted with an evil smile. "Except when Danny ate too many beans—"

"You want me to rearrange the furniture on you?" The bigger brother growled, but all four could tell it was hiding a laugh.

Tilly slapped his arm but still shook with a silent giggle.

Sweets looked in her direction. "You do know I can hear the wet slap of your teats when you giggle, don't you?"

The four burst into laughter.

It was breakfast at the Sweets' house, after all.

FRONTIER VILLAGE

"Squirt, Box—Go time." Hooker hung up the phone at the Whole Donut. Turning, he found himself in a hug with Mai Lynn, the owner. Her head barely reached his chest, but her hugs were always as welcome as any other hug he received in the Bay Area.

"Cherie, I gotta go to work. Besides, your husband might catch us." He looked up and reached out to shake Ralph's hand. The man smiled at his wife.

"She knows we never know when you'll leave and return or if we have to go up to the hospital to see you again." Hooker shrugged at the truth of the statement. Everyone joked about Hooker's third home being the Valley Medical Center and its emergency room.

Mai Lynn pushed back and shook her finger in his face. "You go to hospital. Very expensive for Ralph and Mai Lynn to come see you—we have to bring many dozen donuts to bribe our way in."

Hooker laughed at the tiny woman who had stolen Ralph's heart in Vietnam. He had convinced his superiors he had knocked her up and, subsequently, was married by the village priest. The State Department let her come to America, but they couldn't marry for three years—until she was eighteen. Manny had signed on as her godfather and guardian and then gotten them jobs up the peninsula working in a bakery.

To raise money, Manny and Stella had spoken to every cop, fire-fighter, nurse, and doctor. The donations had come in pocket-change and small bills. Eventually, they raised enough to buy the land and build with a parking lot big enough to hold many cop cars and fire trucks, as well as entire county work crews. Everyone had bought in to sponsor a donut shop for the madly in love couple. The donut shop was not about the couple or a few interested friends. It was about the whole situation and what they represented. The walls were plastered with nothing but photos of all the city, county, and state workers who frequented the shop.

The only thing on the one wall—other than photos—was a large saying in a simple frame:

No matter where your travels wend,
And take you in your life, my friend.
No matter where be your travel,
No matter what be your toll,
Keep your eye upon the donut,
And not upon the hole.

Ralph's long recovery had never reached completion. He still moved with hitches and stutters in his muscles and bones—but he had never lost his focus on the whole donut or on his wife.

As Hooker and Squirt moved past her, she popped a round donut hole in each of their mouths. Ralph and Mai Lynn followed the two men out the back door and stood by the screen door, waving as the large yellow truck drove away. The painting of Mae West as a pin-up on the driver's side waved back.

"What do we have?"

Hooker pulled on the steering wheel as the truck followed the cloverleaf up and onto the 101.

"A bobtail delivery truck broke down this afternoon in the back parking lot of Frontier Village. The driver caught a ride, but they want the truck hauled up to Ivankavitch's so he can work on it first thing in the morning."

"I thought the Frontier Village was dead and gone…"

Hooker snorted dryly as he cleared his side mirror and rolled onto the freeway. "Probably should have been years ago, but there are people who went there as kids and who now take their kids there."

"But isn't it closed in the winter?"

"Maybe the guy was just driving by, and this is where he broke down."

"Or this is where he left it to go *meat* someone... and where it was when he got caught." The Squirt held his two fists next to his waist and pumped them back and forth.

Hooker laughed at the Squirts double-entendre. "How did you spell the word meet?"

"Just the way he was using it..." The kid laughed and played his hand in the wind out of the window. Distractedly he asked, "Have you always had your window down?"

Hooker had never thought about it. "When I started driving, they gave me the junkiest truck. They figured I'd wreck it anyway. I didn't know if there was a window in the door or not, but it never rolled up. By the end of the year, I got into the six-year-old Ford. I never even tried to see if it had a window. The little trucks never get a break. Your whole shift demands your butt in the seat, so you never have a reason to roll up the window and lock the rig."

The delivery truck was full of auto parts. Hooker looked over at the Squirt and smiled. "Looks like you nailed the Lothario to the bed."

"Why wouldn't they just come down and drive it back themselves?"

They slid out of the cab and headed toward the back end of the two trucks. "Maybe it did break down, and there's some face-saving going on. Either way, we get paid a commercial job out of it."

The kid slung the J-hook and chain under the back end of the bobtail and followed it in. Hooker threw his hook and chain so the kid could hook it all up while he was underneath and turned toward the utility door covering the controls for the working bed and boom.

The echo gave the Squirt the sound of almost being the size of Danny. "Were you serious about going up to see your sister this week?" He slithered out from under the truck and nodded. The chains were all hooked and secure.

Hooker pulled on the twin levers and started the cables lifting the back end of the truck. With trucks, it was always slow work in the raising. As the truck changes attitude, the driver has to listen carefully for any creaks or snaps that could be a problem. Hooker quietly told the kid to go check the steering to see if they would need to tie it off. The weight on the rear tires of the truck reached zero. Hooker could see the tire move sideways a half-inch as the truck settled into the towing sling.

Waiting for the kid, he looked along the extended building, which stretched for a city block. During the summer, the many large doors would be open to allow people to drift in and out as they moved from one carnival-like game to the next. The large windows dotting the length of the building were set into the fake log cabin walls. These narrow logs were vertical, like the fort walls instead of horizontal like a real log cabin.

Hooker was wondering what was taking the kid so long, but also half of his brain was filled with red lights flashing and the dull sound of klaxon alarms going off. Something was there just outside of his grasp...

The kid was sitting in the small truck. The steering was locked and, therefore, good to tow. As he started to slide back out of the cab, his height advantage allowed him to look over a low fence. An old white panel truck was parked on the end of the building—like it was hiding.

In the last window, there was a flash. The yellow flash turned into a white-hot flash growing into the next window. Then another flash joined the first flash and grew into the next few windows. A new flash continued within a split second joining it.

Out of the corner of his eye, the Squirt saw the panel truck pull out. It hesitated when it came into full view and then turned and drove away. By then, the noise of the explosions had become deafening and had his complete attention. The white panel truck was just a memory—a momentary distraction gone as quickly as it was seen.

Hooker watched what Sweets was seeing. Right to left, the whole series of explosions had not taken more than a couple of seconds or even one very long second. The speed of sound deafened him, and he dove for safety as the windows of the building all reached out in shards of glass searching for something to burrow into.

Hooker's face pushed against the damp asphalt. Something was wrong.

An explosion rips through a building hundreds of yards long should have deafened the bum on upper Ninth Street twelve miles away. It should have rocked Mae West from the concussion. And yet, she stood solid and unmoving.

"Squirt?" Hooker called out. His hearing was ringing, but he could hear.

"Yeah…" The kid tumbled out of the passenger side door of the smaller truck. "I'm good. I ducked, but the other window wasn't so lucky." He stood up, dusting off the crystals of tempered glass. He looked back into the cab. "Holy fireworks, what happened?"

Hooker stood. Shards of glass had knifed their way over and under Mae. Hooker looked back at the building seventy feet away. The distance of the thrown glass was also wrong for an explosion. The shards should have been thrown at least a hundred yards or more. And then there was the building. It stood there silent, still structurally sound in appearance, and not burning.

Hooker walked around the front of Mae. The 1950s heavy metal skin had turned most of the assault away from everything else behind her. A couple of the larger shards had the energy to puncture the working deck box doors. Hooker and Uncle Willie had folded the custom doors out of only twenty-two-gauge sheet steel, similar to the skin on the bobtail truck's cab. The large cargo box on the other truck was covered with thin twenty-eight-gauge sheet metal and now looked like the nose of a dog who kissed a porcupine. There was a shard for every six square inches. Even small, thumb-sized shards had planted themselves in the skin.

Hooker let out a low whistle. "Man, the Fly is going to love this." He turned to look for the Squirt.

The kid had taken a glance at the prickly scene and had then gone into cop mode. He was already walking the scene. Hooker watched the measured steps. He knew they were preliminary to the kid figuring out the energy spent throwing the shards and to still have the energy to plant them into the truck's steel skin.

Hooker leaned against the back corner of Mae to watch him work. In six short weeks, the kid had grown way beyond any other rookie in the academy. This was the result of spending so much time with Manny and Paul, as well as his other friend and CHP officer, Micha. Hooker knew he was done for the night. The trucks were part of a crime scene or, at least, a scene of an explosion. There would be no hurry to do anything but wait.

He watched as Officer Squirt walked to the end of the building and peeked into each window—or the hole where a window had been only a few minutes before. Hooker knew what was next. He turned and walked to the passenger side of Mae's cab. Tucked behind each entry door was a small hatch. He opened the door and reached in, grabbing the familiar long tube containing six D-cell batteries. Glancing at the orange blob of fur leaning into the hot air, he turned and handed the flashlight to the Squirt before the kid could ask. Both smiled at the silent teamwork.

As Officer Squirt walked back to the building to restart his exam, Hooker walked around the nose of Mae. He patted her on the heavy bar rails of her four hundred-pound front bumper. "Sorry, girl. We'll make this right."

Climbing into the cab, he grabbed the mic from behind his seat. "1-4-1."

Dina's voice giggled out of the speaker. "Why, Hooker, I'm shocked. It's after the witching hour, and you're calling me without your French vanilla ice cream voice."

"Give us a few hours. We'll be here for a while. Could you please call PD, and I think they may have to send the bomb investigation team as well. The bomb went off, so they won't need Max."

Dolly's voice took over. "Hooker?"

"We're fine, Mama. The explosion was in the long building at Frontier Village. It went the entire length. I've never even heard of anything like it, but the PD will have to cordon off the area, and the bomb guys will need to do their thing. I'm going to need some downtime, though. Mae got hit and needs some bodywork done. Maybe it's time to get some touch-up paint done, too. I didn't get to it last year."

"Hooker... Are you sure you're okay? You're running off at the mouth."

"I'm fine, Dolly. We're just a little shaken up."

"We...? Where's the Squirt?" By her voice, Hooker could see her head down on her arm and desk. The knock of the lollypop microphone tapping the top of the desk confirmed it.

"Oh, crap, Mama… you should see him. He picked himself up, dusted off, and went right into investigation cop mode. If Manny were dead, you would think it was reincarnation."

"Don't let him screw up the scene…"

"He knows what he's doing. Just get the PD out here. Tell them if they take too long, the Squirt will have it all figured out, and he'll take the information to the sheriff himself."

"10-4." The radio shorthand still couldn't mask the sound of Dolly laughing at the idea of the Squirt figuring it all out in a few minutes. But then again, he was very instrumental in breaking the last three cases Hooker had worked on—even though the first case almost killed both men.

Hooker hung the mic and went back out to watch the Squirt work. The Squirt was standing back up near the start with both hands holding the large flashlight across his thighs. He was looking at Hooker.

Hooker smirked and rolled his eyes. Walking over, he noticed the interesting pattern of the glass. He stopped.

"It's okay. You're still in the path I took to get over here, and you don't scuff your feet. The patterns are consistent all the way down. It's thirty-seven or thirty-eight small bombs. They went off in sequence, so I'm sure we'll find the wires once they start digging through the debris. You're okay on the porch here. The first throw pattern starts out there about twenty-nine feet."

"Not twenty-eight? Not thirty? How can you be so exact?" Hooker smiled at the younger man.

"Laugh it up, chuckles. The deck here is sixteen feet. The overhang is an extra four for shade. The first small shards are out another twelve feet."

"Which makes a combined thirty-two feet, not your twenty-nine?"

"But where they're lying is not where they first hit. The scatter pattern of the close pieces did not have the high-energy to throw them far, but glass always hits and then skips. In the professional investigation community, we have a specific term for the shattered-glass phenomenon called 'hit and skip.' It even has changing parameters like hitting concrete, dirt, asphalt, or your fault." The kid stood with a solid deadpan face.

Hooker held his face as a mirror for only about three seconds. Laughing, he turned and looked down the long porch. "Get your best jokes in now, because PD will be here shortly, and you'll have to have this all figured out by then. Why? Because you know they won't let you near it again." He looked back at the Squirt—sober and serious. They both knew how true it was. Three times, they had broken the case ahead of the PD, which did not sit well with the current officers. Their attitudes would now be even more hostile, with the Squirt being an academy snot.

John waved his head back toward the end. As they got to the last window, he shined the powerful flashlight at the wall. "See where it looks like a phone once was?" Hooker nodded. The Squirt moved the bright center of the light about eight feet over to a warped metal sign. "The metal sign is where it started. My guess is there was a small timer attached to the face of the charge. The metal plate directed the blast. The timer vaporized in the first five feet."

He walked down about sixteen feet and pointed the light at a support column. "The next charge was attached to the face of this post facing down the building. If the first charge had been bigger, the crack in the post would be on the other side. But the next explosive was on the downside and cracked the post this way."

He pointed the focused beam of the flashlight down to each of the upright support posts. "The same is true for all the rest down the line. Every single post is cracked—with the crack on this side and the blast facing the other way. This is the good news. As each blast went off, the blast radius behind was preserved. If the guy had put even a smaller charge on this side of the posts, it would have messed up and confused all the evidence."

He turned to face Hooker. "This building is toast. Those supports can never be safely replaced. I'm not even sure if this building will remain standing through the week. We get little earthquakes through here every day. All it would take would be one aligned north and south and be enough for us to feel."

"So it was intentionally set."

The Squirt nodded.

"Motive?"

"You said it yourself… the place should have gone belly-up a long time ago."

"But kids love this place."

"Sentiment goes only so far. This is business." He stepped over to the wall and knelt down. "Let me see your knife."

"I don't carry one."

"Sure you do. Manny gave it to you years ago for Christmas. And if you don't trust me, take the money out."

Hooker smiled and fished the money clip out of his pocket. He left the money in as he handed it to the kid.

The Squirt pulled the tiny knife blade out of the clip. He tested the edge on his thumbnail. It was sharp but not as sharp as he had seen it. He took the tip and pushed it against the faux log. A solid board would have stopped it after an eighth of an inch—but the blade sunk in almost the entire two inches. He pulled it out and continued to sink it into the boards until he met resistance, about four feet up.

"A good piece of lumber comes from the heart of a tree where there's some hardness. The entire outside of the tree is new wood and very soft— which makes it useless for lumber—but explains why these fake logs are made from the trash part of the log. The soft outside is susceptible to bugs and rot." He folded the blade back into the clip and handed it to Hooker as the first police car drove up and right into the glass scatter pattern.

The Squirt leaned close and muttered. "We won't tell them about the dry rot."

The two men stood there like a matched pair of mannequins—engineer boots, jeans, starched T-shirts, and leather jackets. Only Hooker's beard was the general difference. The spotlight seared the night as the officer focused on the two men, then stepped out onto the slippery glass shards. He immediately slipped and fell on his butt.

Hooker leaned close to the Squirt and muttered, "We do get to talk about this, don't we?"

The Squirt didn't show any sign of moving or talking. "Oh, hell yes. Chet and Micha will love this. Maybe Dolly will invite this crime scene spoiling rookie for dinner one night—for a nice roasting." They both knew almost all of the Wednesday night dinners were spaghetti with Dolly's secret marinara sauce with Sicilian sausage from Chiaramontes.

Hooker could not resist. "I hope he didn't hurt himself. We already know he's going to be a pain in the ass."

The Squirt shook silently.

"How did you spell it... p-a-i-n or p-a-n-e?"

8

MILPITAS REGRETS

Felix sat in the panel truck cursing. His hands gripped the steering wheel. His fingers and knuckles were the same aged-white of the Bakelite.

"Damn it to hell." His mind replayed looking over the fence into the face of the man sitting in the broken-down truck. The truck he had left there to draw any attention while he worked. Rigging the succession of explosions took him over an hour. Even though it was a simple rig, the sheer quantity had taken time.

The small trigger went on the side receiving the blast from the previous charge. The new charge was on the side facing the building toward the end. A small piece of tape for the trigger, and a thumbtack or more tape for the small charge, and a tiny battery—all would be destroyed by the blast.

The battery was bonded inside the plastic explosive, which was in the small baggie. The baggie was just a convenient way to carry the pre-made bomb. The short, constructed wire was wound up and stuck in the baggie. As long as the glass vial didn't break, the rig was safe. On-site, he would pull out the wire and trigger, then nail, tack, or tape the baggie to the post or wall. He would then run the short wires and pressure switch to the other side of the post and tape or pin the small plastic bag.

Felix had carried the entire thirty-seven charges in the cotton duct grip bag. The Gladstone bag had been his father's tool bag in the mines. In the old days, his father would carry the dynamite or TNT in the Gladstone and stick six or eight blasting caps between his lips and teeth like a carpenter does with nails. Sometimes, ignition fuses would be hanging from the caps in small coils. On large jobs such as this, the mass of caps and white fuses made the man with prematurely white hair look like a malevolent Santa Claus.

Thinking of his father did nothing to ease Felix's mood. He knew the driver in the truck had seen the distinctive panel truck. Felix waited for the first explosion, hoping the attention would be on the bright light, not on his license plate. But he also knew he would now have to get rid of the last vestige of his father and better times in Colorado's high country.

He sat in the truck as if an extra few minutes would be enough to soak up the essence of the memories embedded in the walls, seats, and floorboards of the truck. His father had been using a stripped out old Chevy sedan from the 1930s. Mining was never a game of much money, other than with some of the big corporations or a lucky wildcat miner who had hit a valuable vein, or series of veins, in one of the metals having paid a decent day. Even gold wasn't much of a payday unless the ore was rich or a visible vein could be worked to produce heavyweight, instead of just dust or tiny nuggets in a cold-cream jar.

Most of the hard-rock mining was coal and salt on very large scales. Whole mountain tops were removed in some states, but in Colorado, the veins had to be chased inside the mountains. Felix knew from personal experience there were many seemingly large mountains, which were nothing but a large pile of Swiss cheese. He and his father had collapsed tunnels only to find they had done nothing but open an even larger cavern. A web of tunnels, drifts, and shafts fed these caverns running not only below the tunnel they'd tried to collapse but also above.

One series of tunnels they had blown up in the mid-sixties became a cavern over a half-mile in height with a floor covering twenty acres. The mining company sold it to a storage company and then contracted to clear the debris. The last Felix heard before moving to California was the mining company was still cleaning the chamber and processing the silver, gold, and mercury along with other trace minerals. He and his father worked for three long, backbreaking weeks. They were paid less than what the company was taking in each day from the residual work.

Felix wasn't mad about the inequity of the income, but he did miss his father. Being a powder monkey and setting charges paid more than most other jobs in the industry, but it hadn't protected him from the black lung, which took so many miners. In the end, his father would review the plans with Felix—between the coughing and hacking that would turn the man's face purple with strain. But, in the end, it was Felix alone who carried the bags into the mine and set the charges. Luckily, he never had to use a hammer and star drill chisel to bore holes into the rock faces like his father. The fine dust blowback went straight to the lungs and stayed there.

Felix was tired, and he would have to be up early in the morning for his shift. He pulled on the door handle, and the door of the Ford truck creaked open. His body felt the same as he crossed the front yard in the dark.

He checked on his wife. She was hours past sucking on the corner of the blanket, and he could hear her little squeak as she breathed in her sleep. If not for the memories of their life together, it could have been him checking on a small child. He turned off the nightlight, knowing she wouldn't wake up again until morning when it was time to change her diaper and feed her. Tomorrow would also be bath day. She fussed about the water.

He retreated from the room and drew the door almost closed.

He unlocked the back porch door and stepped out into the screened area that defined his life. He sat heavy on the chair and slowly removed his boots. Moving them near the bed, he then pulled the board from the wall. He counted out six of the hundred dollar bills and put the rest back in the cubbyhole. Replacing the board, he looked at the bills. They were used, but still too close to new. He began to wad and rub them on the underside of the table where there was a thin layer of axle grease and caliche clay with a touch of lampblack soot. The mix transferred to the bills and then got rubbed in. He picked at a corner on some of the greasy bills with his fingernail and made a crease more prominent in others. In a few minutes, the bills looked well abused, probably more than any respectable bank would ever let back into circulation, but for the street, they were perfect. He placed the bills in a used envelope and set it aside for tomorrow to pay for his wife's care. The sum was three times the monthly rent on his house, but Felix knew it was the woman's only income.

He slid into bed and pulled the blankets over his body. He looked at the alarm clock. Five hours of sleep. He pulled the button up. He reached over and pulled the string on the lamp. The dark settled in. Out across the bay was a glow as light as the predawn before sunrise. The light caused gray shadows on the lighter gray wall.

Felix was used to the gray. His life was gray. His eyes drifted closed. The gray heron at the end of the lawn shook its feathers to fluff.

9

GOING NORTH

The Speedwagon was the vehicle of choice for the three. The backseat provided the Squirt room to read the new stack of books his cheer-squad had provided him. What had started with the librarian Maddie, the Police Commissioner Paul, and the California Highway Patrol Captain Chet had now grown by a sergeant in the Sheriff's department and three of the professors at the police academy, one of which was the director. If the Squirt was successful in challenging the next round of courses, the thought was he could possibly graduate with the class ahead of his normal cycle. As if he was not unique enough, he would be the first to have ever succeeded in jumping their graduation class cycle.

Hooker glanced back at the kid, hunched against the side. His book was face down on his lap. His eyes were closed, but his face was working through gyrations of thought. "How are you doing back there?"

There was silence.

Candy turned and looked behind her. "John?"

His eyes fluttered open, and he turned and sat up. "I'm fine. I was just thinking about the other night."

"The explosion...?"

"Nah... the truck."

Hooker glanced back. "What truck?"

"There was a whitish panel truck parked behind the short fence at the end of the building. As the explosion started—it left." The Squirt looked up at the rearview mirror. "I've been trying to see the license plate, but it's all wrong."

"Wrong how?"

Candy's head moved back and forth through the volley of the conversation. She had never seen how the two worked almost like a single brain.

"The color…it should be yellow letters on black. But I keep seeing white letters, same as the truck."

"Can you see any numbers or letters?"

The kid shook his head. "Nah, it was too dark. It's why I'm not completely sure about the plate. Color washes out in the dark." He pulled his legs and feet up and leaned his back against the other side. Picking up his book, he went back to reading.

That night, the four sat around the small table in the heated porch. The cheery fire dancing lazily in the wood stove was more than enough heat for the large porch. The storm windows had been hung over the panels of screened mesh months before.

Sissy suggested playing cards. Hooker and Candy had said nothing but looked at each other. The silent communication wasn't complete, but it was getting there. Hooker had no personal experience with the Squirt and cards, but he could imagine. Candy's glance all but confirmed it.

The hand was halfway played when the Squirt spoke up. Sissy had just led with the king of spades. The Squirt laid his cards face down on the table. "You have five of the lesser hearts, and you're fishing for the Queen." The Squirt pointed at Hooker, and then Candy. "They each have a heart. Hooker picked up the king when Candy ran out of diamonds. Candy got her nine of hearts when I ran out of diamonds. You may think you're strong enough in diamonds, but no matter what you played—even if you had the two hearts they have—Hooker is still holding the Ace of hearts I passed to him."

Sissy slowly put her cards down as she examined the kid's face. She turned deadpan toward her brother. "Let's take him to Reno."

Hooker shook his head.

Sissy frowned. "Why not?"

Candy started laughing. "The table limits are too low."

As the laughter settled down, Sissy slurped the last of her cocoa. "So what games can we play where Mister Super-brain doesn't have an advantage?"

The Squirt smiled but with a slight blush. "Anything with dice."

"Why dice?"

"Because every roll is random—there is nothing there for me to memorize."

"So the cards you memorize?"

"If I've seen it, I've memorized it."

"Seriously?" She looked at Hooker and Candy, who were both nodding.

"So if I wrote down a string of numbers twenty-six numbers long..." The kid nodded.

Hooker thought a moment. "What was the book Maddie gave you last fall? The poetry book..."

The kid rolled his eyes toward the ceiling for a moment. "The Collected Poems of Robert Service, published by Dodd, Mead, & Company in New York."

Candy turned over her hand and counted the cards. "Page thirty-three."

John's eyes rolled up, and he lost any life in his face for a moment. Hooker and Candy were used to this face of his recalling. His voice had a faraway quality about it as he began to read the page, burned forever, in his mind. 'The Cremation of Sam McGee.' His head rotated forward as he recited:

There are strange things
done in the midnight sun
By the men who moil for gold;
The Arctic trails have their secret tales
That would make your blood run cold;
The Northern Lights have seen queer sights,
But the queerest they ever did see
Was that night on the marge of Lake Lebarge

I cremated Sam McGee.

The kid opened his eyes and smiled softly at Sissy. She sat quiet—digesting. It had been many years since she had heard any poetry. This was not dainty woman poetry; this was the kind men forged from a hard life spent on the razor's edge—something she could relate to.

Candy and Hooker watched her.

Finally, her voice was more of an echo of a lover's sigh, something more a part of the night air than a voice. "Was there more?"

Claire and Harold listened from the other room as the young man recited of the Yukon and men struggling and dying in the snow or on battlefields. Claire had looked toward the wisdom of the former psychiatrist in her husband. He had covered her hand with his and nodded with his eyes. The shared time with her brother and growing family would heal old wounds more than any number of hours talking with Harold in sessions. Therefore, they leaned back and listened.

10

QUIET ON THE HOME FRONT

Manny put his pencil down. He had been trying to write down some notes on something, but the lack of noise distracted him.

He looked up. Stella shook the Sunday newspaper in the sunroom. Everything was as it should be. Peace, quiet, good coffee, and the newspaper after a late Sunday breakfast.

Manny looked about the room. The dishes were rinsed and in the dishwasher. His mug was still half-full of coffee. The grandfather clock was ticking, and he had drawn the weights up yesterday, which meant it was wound for the next eight days. Stella had her coffee and newspaper. Even a slim patch of blue sky was helping with some sun in the large sunroom. He looked toward his office... the door stood open to the darkened room.

Manny picked up his pencil to write. Staring at the paper, he realized he had forgotten what he was going to write. He gently placed the pencil down and pushed the pad away from his eating area. He pushed back from the table. Turning his chair, he moved to the archway defining the boundary between the dining area and the sunroom.

He sat staring at the two hands and the newspaper they were holding.

The clock ticked.

Slowly, the one corner of the paper curled down. Stella's right eye became visible.

"I don't like it," Manny grumped as he pushed down on the arms of the wheelchair. The weight of his butt lifted from the seat. It wasn't about comfort because he couldn't feel his rear end—it was about adjusting his mental state.

The paper curled down a tiny bit more.

"Do you want me to bring the Caddie up, and we'll go for a drive?"

"No..." His voice trailed off before it turned into a whine. He turned and gave a halfhearted push on the wheels. "I just don't like it."

Stella laid the paper in her lap and watched her retreating husband, best friend, and love. She closed her eyes in commiseration. "The kids will be home tonight."

"I just don't like it when they're gone." He disappeared into his sanctuary and office.

Stella stretched her legs out on the couch. She knew he would swap out the large sixteen-inch reel on the professional tape recorder for something more violent like Vivaldi or Frank. He had been listening to Brahms the night before. On a day like this, it would not suit his mood. She thought about the music. "Put on the Vivaldi and leave the speakers on. I want at least an eight on the volume, Mr. Romero."

She was rewarded with a soft chuckle. She knew he would turn the volume up closer to halfway and come back out to lie in the sun and maybe nap. It wasn't the sound of the kids, but it helped. She didn't like the silence either. It was the wrong kind of silence.

The shadows in the sunroom had long changed sides of the room and disappeared with the early sunset. The sound of two soft snores vibrated through the room. The Vivaldi tape had only lasted for three hours and twenty-nine minutes. As designed, the phone rang in the office first. The distance softened the awakening tone ringing next in the sunroom.

Stella's hand reached behind her head at the buzzing wireless handset phone. As she pulled it back to her head, the thumb finding the button with the green phone icon. "This better be good," she growled.

Her matched voice growled right back. "Oh, shut up. I'm in early. Where's Hooker?"

Stella relaxed, but her entire body went on high alert. Her sister didn't start work on a Sunday until what most people would consider a late dinner. "What time is it?"

"Almost four."

Stella swung her legs over the edge of the couch and sat up in the gloom. She looked over at the other stretch of couch. She could see movement. "My guess is somewhere around the city, maybe even up or down."

"He's not answering the radio." Dolly was irritated, and Stella could hear her fussing with papers on her desk. A few years separated the two, but for the way they read each other's voices, they may as well have been twins.

"They took Willie's truck. Mae was getting a facelift this week." By the little sounds in the room, Stella didn't have to look up to know Manny was making ready to transfer into his chair.

"They should have been down by now. We woke them at four this morning."

Stella stopped herself. She almost asked why but stopped because she didn't want to know. She leaned forward and put her face in her left hand —thinking. "Did you call Willie?"

There was silence. Either she had just tripped up her sister, or she had asked a stupid question.

"Gotta go." The metallic click vibrated around the room. Stella smiled. It was a great day when she could trip up the great Dolly at her own game of communication.

"What do you think she—"

"Manny Romero, you know I don't want to know. It's Sunday, and I was having a great dream where I was shopping for a wedding dress with my daughter."

Manny smiled. It was less than a year, and mama bear was already protective of her new cubs. He remembered when Hooker first landed in their guest bedroom. There ensued a certain love and hate relationship in the house for all of them.

Stella loved her quiet house, but Hooker's schedule of towing at night, coupled with Manny's detective shift during the day, filled the hacienda with another breathing soul in residence at all hours. It never had time to irritate her, though; she had quickly taken to mothering Hooker as much as she did Manny.

Hooker, on the other side of the coin, was a distant, reserved entity, who was uncomfortable with close contact. He had become accustomed to Willie, but when the household went to war, it was hit the streets and find shelter. Dolly vehemently told him he had no choice—if he didn't bunk at Hacienda Romero, he could go find some other state to live in— because the Bay Area just wouldn't be big enough for her and him. Luckily, he chose to become family.

But the new children had turned on a new side of Stella that Manny liked seeing. The Squirt was actually young enough (and innocent enough) to be mothered. His sister had done a great job with what she had, but it was more of a child raising another child.

However, it was Candy who opened Stella's heart to full motherhood. She finally had a daughter that she could be a mother and a friend. Manny quietly hummed to himself, for he was also content at the blend the large household had become. He just wasn't sure whether they were part of Stella's and his family or if they were all part of Hooker's family. Either way, it all worked for him. He pushed his way to the office.

Across the valley, Hooker nosed the Speedwagon onto the approach apron large enough for most small airplanes. The gigantic door was built for small lookout dirigibles. The oversized motor quietly rolled the monolith of corrugated steel back from the closed position.

Uncle Willie walked out as the door rolled back. His dress of the day was florid pink and lavender paisley floral pattern. The burn marks and small holes bore testimony that it had also been a welding day. The holes were consistent with not only a torch but also either the heliarc or the standard stick arc welder—Hooker didn't want to look close enough to find out which. Willie smiled as he grabbed the long dress and pulled it out as he took a curtsy.

Candy stepped out of the passenger side. "Oh, now Willie, those are definitely your colors. The lavender really sets off your highlights, and the pink just adds a certain *devil be damned* flair."

Hooker reached out and grabbed the last of the Squirts leather jacket and pulled him back into the Speedwagon. The Squirt turned around with an evil, mischievous smile on his face.

Hooker looked at him and growled. "If you encourage him, I swear... I'll stick a fork in you. *Again.*"

The Squirt snorted. "Oh, look at it. You know you didn't have to tell me. Good gosh, it's paisley, for God's sake." He continued to climb out of the backseat of the Speedwagon.

Willie smiled as he hugged Candy. Willie was always happy to see the young man. His right hand stuck out, but his left arm didn't let go of the Squirt's sister. "It is always a pleasure to see you, Jonathan."

He took the man's hand and winced as the man squeezed. His smile turned to a quiet chuckle echoing his sister. Willie pulled the young man in closer and whispered, "Hooker hates the dress, doesn't he?"

Candy shook even harder and pressed her face into both the dress and Willie's chest.

The Squirt nodded slightly and chortled. "Willie, it's hideous. Good job."

The older man smiled broadly. "I searched through the entire bag of dresses from Goodwill this morning. Many of 'em had potential, but I just knew this was the winner."

The three watched as Hooker slowly pulled the Speedwagon into the giant air hangar-turned-into-an-acre of garage. Willie called out, barely in control of his voice. "Go ahead and take it all the way back to the grease rack, Hooker." He knew they needed the extra minute to get the laughs out of him and the other two. As they stood laughing, the large DeSoto convertible pulled up.

Willie's boyfriend, Hank, sat staring at the dress. Slowly, he rolled the window down. "William, I'll be forced to take your Goodwill privileges away from you if you insist on wearing only the ugliest of the dresses. Now please, go put on a nice rose color or at least a blue. I bought wine, and we have company."

Candy put her finger to her lips. "Hanky, shh. Hooker is parking the Speedwagon."

The man rolled his eyes and pulled the DeSoto through the door. "I have wine...children"

Willie called after the car, "I have shine..."

The glasses were mixed. Hank and Willie shared the vino while Candy sipped on the moonshine Willie had mentioned. His childhood friend and fellow car fanatic came from a family of moonshiners, but recently, her brother had been branching out from the standard mash and had been mixing in some of the local fruits. This one happened to have a distinct peach flavor with an apricot aftertaste.

Hooker was on the phone with Dolly. He and the Squirt were holding off on any drinking until it was determined if the early morning wake up had been resolved. The conversation was going a lot longer than Hooker's usual talks with Dolly.

To not feel useless, the Squirt sat doodling what he had been thinking about. What he saw in his mind was the cartoon face of a Chinese dragon. The truck had been in the dark, and when the front came out from behind the fence, he only had a split second of a look. He was looking at the round eyes, but they were wrong—they were below the nostrils. Then, too, the teeth were wrong...

Willie leaned over and looked over his shoulder. "It's a fucking Ford. Don't buy it."

Hank's hand reached out and slapped the other man's arm. "William!" Willie looked at him from the bottom of his second water glass of wine.

"You owe Hooker's swear jar a quarter for the word, and a quarter because you said it in front of the children." Hank's pencil line of a white mustache twitched. He was also drunk. "I don't care how you feel about the cars from Dearborn, we have rules, and you are not above them."

Willie smirked and growled at the slightly younger man. "You know I can still take you."

Hank drew himself up straight. "We will not be discussing our bedroom activities in front of the children either."

Candy giggled, and the Squirt blushed. Willie glared at Hank and then returned his attention to the drawing as he laid his head on the Squirt's shoulder.

"At least someone still loves me." He pointed at the semi-teardrop nostrils. "Those are the vents they put on some of the late 1940s Ford trucks. If the grill ran horizontal, as you are intimating here, then it's 1949. It actually wasn't a bad truck."

The Squirt snorted. "It just wasn't a MOPAR."

Willie rested his hand on the Squirt's arm and pouted at Hank. "See… at least *he* gets it."

Hooker hung up the phone and looked at the table arrangement. Hank, Candy, and Willie draped all over the Squirt's arm. "What's going on?"

They all stiffened into a guilty silence. The Squirt broke the stall. "What about the wreck."

Distracted, Hooker sat. "They got it handled. A car cut off a small bobtail truck in the early morning. The truck flipped and scattered the box all over the 680. They found some bodies, but there was evidence there were several other people in the back of the truck."

Candy frowned. "The truck was hauling bodies?"

"No… people." Hooker sagged at the implication of what he had just spoken.

Willie whispered, "Who?"

Hooker was slow to look up. "Asian. Probably Vietnamese…"

Hooker and Willie had spoken about slavery in the Asian cultures before. Chinese and Japanese workers brought over as little more than indentured workers built California in the early years of the gold rush. What followed were the women in the form of sex slaves along with the opium. San Francisco's Chinatown was built on the needs of the Chinese workers, and eventually, the needs of the white residents of the city. Asia provided the cooks, maids, laundry workers, seamstresses, and sex workers, along with the means to forget your cares in the opium dens.

The Squirt leaned forward. "Where on the 680?"

Hooker looked at the Squirt. He could tell it was the future cop asking.

"Near King and Story." It was the new center for the Vietnamese gangs or the Mafia.

The Squirt thought for a moment. He picked up the mason jar of clear liquid and held it up toward Hooker. Hooker almost laughed at the look on the kid's face. It was almost more eager than asking. Hooker nodded, and the top was off with a single twist.

Hooker stood and stepped to the phone. He knew Stella and Manny would want to know their plans.

As the phone rang, Hooker looked back at Willie. "When do you think I can have Mae back?"

The man closed his eyes to clear his thinking. Hank's hand had slid up inside his shorts. The evening of entertaining was rapidly ending for the two older gentlemen.

"Um, I believe she called…yes, the Fly called, and said they couldn't match the pearl flake in the clear coat until at least next week. However, if you need her now, the color is all shot and pinstriped. I think this would also be a good time for Candy to add the two dimes on the tote board. And if she's up to it, not that I'm an expert on womanly anatomy, I've always felt Mae looks slightly under-endowed."

Hooker nodded and turned toward the wall to hide his laughter at seeing Hank invading Willie's privates. He had to give it to his uncle… he hadn't broken under fire. He could hear the two chairs slide back as the phone picked up on the other end.

"Romero's… Okay, Hooker… What's so funny?"

Hooker giggled harder.

"Willie and Hank are plowed and just beat a fast retreat. Listen, Manny, we're staying here tonight so I can pick up Mae in the morning." He turned back toward the Squirt as he spoke. "Could you put in a call to Paul and have people start looking for a—"

The Squirt chimed in, "A 1949 Ford F-1 panel truck with a funky white paint job. License plate is not California. It's white letters on a black back."

The former detective, on the other end, mumbled while he wrote.

"Got it. Anything else?"

"Just a squeeze for Stella."

"Got it. A major suck up for not calling earlier."

"Thanks, Manny. You're a champ." Hooker hung up.

11

ANOTHER ENVELOPE

The new envelope was fatter than any Felix had received as a down payment. This one had almost not fit in the large mailbox. Any larger, and he would have drawn attention to himself by having to ask for the package. He didn't like the size. He could feel there were five bundles of money instead of the usual three. The sheaf of information was also much thicker than usual.

He sat on the screened porch without any lights. Only the dim light from across the bay illuminated the envelope dully.

Felix did not like this one bit.

He thought back to what the woman said when she'd left. *That man from the county was here again today. He's not just going to disappear. They are going to take her.*

He moved from Colorado because they had tried to take his Thelma away from him. In his soul, he knew the woman he fell in love with and married so many years before was no longer in the shell lying on the bed, ten feet away. The body suckling on the corner of a blanket until she drifted off to sleep only looked similar. He had resolved himself to this fact many years before. The accident took all of her away from him. She was never coming back. However, it did not mean some soulless state facility could warehouse what was left until it expired from lack of food and attention. Felix would rather die than let such a thing happen.

Reaching out, he pulled the strings on both of the lamps. The envelope looked even larger in the bright light. The yellow-cream was wrinkled where the center bulged. The large stone in Felix's stomach sunk lower and rattled somewhere near the pit. Whatever his old boss had contracted for him to blow up was large or important. The usual half down payment, as well as the twenty-five percent for expenses, was normally twenty plus ten thousand—three stacks. These lumps were thicker, and he was looking at five distinct lumps.

His right hand moved under the table to the commando knife. One smooth pass and his hand returned the blade back to the magnets behind the table's skirting.

His hands rested on the table, bracketing the envelope. He closed his eyes and drew in an even slow breath. Pinching the two back corners, he lifted as his eyes opened. A sheaf of papers slid out with the ten packs of hundred dollar bills. One hundred thousand dollars—the job wasn't small or huge but rather, it was complicated—so it was also important.

Twenty minutes later, Felix started rereading the instructions. He had done something like this only once before in Colorado. Actually, the job had been in Amarillo, Texas, just across the border.

The job then was a car dealership. Felix didn't understand why they wanted him to blow it up. The people who usually hired Felix were the sort of people who had been cooking the books on a business in trouble, or they were skimming so hard it was about to be in trouble. The idea was a large insurance payday to make it all go away or to cover everything needed to restart the clock ticking on the scammed business.

Felix did his research on the car dealership. The dealer was anything but in trouble. In fact, he was making money at such a rate he was paying out bonuses to even the receptionists. The dealer supported three little league teams, had just installed lights at the local high school so they could play night football and had a new hospital wing named after him and his wife. He wasn't hurting, but someone wanted to hurt him.

Felix leaned back as he thought about the long-ago night. It was more than just to hurt the guy's business—it had been much more.

It was Christmas Eve. Felix thought it was from the owner because they provided keys and security alarm codes. The lot was loaded with cars, and he had set lines of detonation cord wound into a rope of five lines. In confined spaces or wrapped around something, each of the cords burning at the speed of sound provided an explosion. Then multiple cords were wound into a rope around a thin line of Felix's homemade plastic explosive, and the cars over the rope lifted forty feet in the air before crashing to the ground. To hide the evidence, Felix had hosed out thin pools of diesel fuel. The fuel burns slower than gasoline, so it was a confusing curative instead of an added explosion. The fires also guaranteed the cars and trucks were a total loss instead of repairable.

Felix didn't like the idea of explosions in the open air. However, with all of it contained within the area of the car lot, he figured it would be okay. Only he was set up by someone who had shown up shortly before he had. Many of the cars had been bathed down with gasoline in the engine compartments, or fuel lines were shaved where they would be slow leaks under the outer perimeter cars.

The building had a whole different gemstone of things wrong. Felix was to set up the showroom and the cars there. Usually, he would use low-grade explosives, which would cause massive damage but would be contained within the building. If a window blew out, it would be from the rapid expansion of the explosion, not by the explosion itself. This time, it was different.

The payloads were almost three times the size he felt would have done the job—but the instructions had been explicit. Where the explosives were to be placed, the size, the blast spread, and even what chemistry to use. Felix had the feeling whoever had ordered the job was also an explosives expert. Felix had been so right.

At exactly 3:41 in the morning on Christmas day, the local radio station played Elvis's *Heartbreak Hotel*. The start of the song was obvious, but the disk jockey even announced it. The song was Felix's signal to explode the dealership. The total time for all the explosions to go off was forty-three seconds.

While Elvis sang, nineteen telephone switching stations tasked with routing telephone, radio transmissions, alarms for security systems, and a myriad of other transmissions vaporized. The plastic explosives planted in those switching boxes the previous day left nothing but bits of twisted copper, steel, and aluminum. Fifty-nine windows, a motorcycle illegally chained to one box, and a row of prized Texas yellow roses had also ceased to exist.

What nobody knew until two days later was sometime during the explosion, which lit up the sky and captured everyone's attention, the floors in the vaults of seven local banks also turned to rubble from below. By Boxing Day, or as the locals would call it, the day after Christmas, the local banks were drained of over eleven million dollars and heaping mounds of personal possessions once filling the hundreds of violated safe-deposit boxes.

The local media had tried to keep some lid on the banks being breached, but eventually, the word spilled out. Keeping quiet about a bank staying closed longer than three days is next to impossible, especially when businesses need to deposit their holiday receipts.

The firestorm that followed never even got close to looking at the car dealer with anything other than an after-mention. The focus was all on the banks. The funds Felix was paid provided what he needed to find and purchase the house on the bay using a fake identity.

Moving his wife had been more problematic than the complicated explosion. Wiping out a car dealer with over two hundred cars and trucks was child's play in comparison. By the time Felix was ready to move her, Thelma had the mental acuity of a one-year-old. Still, Felix and Thelma had disappeared only one step ahead of the law. Colorado felt Thelma's care was not up to the standards of a state institution, which would be covered by Medicare.

Felix put the paper down on the desk and looked out into the gloom sprinkled by the distant twinkling lights from across the bay. His hand went to the scar on his forehead, which continued into his thick head of dark hair. His left ring finger found the furrow and rubbed it as he thought. The wording was similar—too similar. He had trouble remembering names, but patterns he recognized—the patterns of speech, the details of the explosives, how much and where were the same. Even down to a specific record, playing at a fixed time on a named radio station in the middle of the night was the same, or it was close enough.

It had been five years since the job in Texas. Felix now wondered where he would have to run to next. He knew he couldn't do this job and not to be swept up in the resulting investigation. You don't get lucky the second time, and whoever these guys were—he had a feeling he was going to be the patsy this time.

1 2

BITS AND PIECES ON THE MUDFLATS

"Hooker." The small Asian woman yelled across the muddy parking lot. She wasn't getting any closer to the mud than the doorway, porch, and two steps. The deep overhang of the roof over the porch was designed for sunshade during the long hot summers. The Fly knew, in the bottom of her heart and soul, it was to protect her from the nuisance of the South Bay Area rain, which begets mud.

She turned in the doorway and spied one of the new workers. The man was already dressed in his rain gear and mud boots.

"Hey, slug."

The man looked up. She called all the new guys slug or slug-bait until they proved themselves—in her eyes and on the balance sheet.

"Go tell Hooker that Dolly try to get him on radio for twenty minutes. CHP and Sheriff have panties in twist… they screaming for him."

The man lumbered out the door and across the nasty mud lot and rain. He never looked to pick a dryer path. He just went straight to work. His only nod to the rain was wearing a stupid Dodger's hat. Everyone knew she was a Giant's fan, but she liked how he was about his job… straightforward and to the point.

One of the office assistants walked by and glanced out. "Looking ugly today, Fly—don't go out there."

The Fly turned slowly with her smartass scowl prepped. The young woman was chuckling and had beaten her to the scowl. Everyone knew the Fly hated this time of year. "Okay, smartass—who is slug I just sent out there?"

The young woman peeked to confirm her suspicion. "Bradley. You hired him last fall when Spider took to the wind. I think he is one of Dog's nephews or cousins or something. He's a nice kid. Smart too." The woman took one more peek as she set the Fly up for the punch. She looked over her shoulder as she walked away. "You should fire him… so he can go find a better job."

The Fly muttered as she looked out at the young kid walking back into the yard. Hooker was climbing into his cab and then waved. Her job was done. She shivered and closed the door.

Hooker grabbed the mic from behind the seat. "Go, Dolly."

"Head for the flats at the south end of Moffett field, I think they meant where you killed your sister last year. When you get close, find Chet on tack five. Your number will be Tango-Tango 4-1. He's in the command car, so he's Charlie Alpha One."

Hooker put the mic up to his mouth, but before he could key—she walked on him. "Just so you know, this call is now twenty-eight minutes old. Your perfect record this week is shot to slime and guts on toast."

Hooker chuckled. "10-4." He had taken three calls so far this week since picking Mae up. All three had problems in the front end, which started them already running late. He was also still waiting for at least one commercial tow—something to start putting a down payment on the new paint job. The insurance would only cover so much. The fancy layers of clear coat with mother-of-pearl floating in it—giving Mae her iridescent look—were never covered on a commercial truck and were expensive as hell.

The afternoon traffic had started. Monterey Highway was still the fastest way up through San Jose to grab the Guadalupe Parkway and out to the 101 North. Hooker was starting to understand all the work Willie and his lifelong friend Maddie had done when they revived Mae the last time. The 1,600 horsepower engine with the top end of over a hundred and sixty was a gas for sure, but the special rig Maddie cooked up took the cake every time Hooker got stuck in traffic.

Maddie was a slight built librarian by day, but it was the other side where she shined. She was born into a family who knew three things—driving moonshine, driving fast, and building the right car for the job. When she left Salinas for a more respectable life, she had never stopped loving the last two. Being a librarian meant nothing more than ready access to more knowledge of how to go faster and better.

Hooker had seen Maddie covered in more grease than he'd seen on Willie, and when it came to the quarter-mile speed, they were equaled no matter what the bracket. However, for overall crazy top-end speed—Maddie won hands down. For eight years out of eleven, she held the title of the fastest land speed record holder in her brackets on two or four wheels. The only endeavor better than Maddie's racing as the years started to take their toll was her family's other product—moonshine.

Hooker rolled to a stop at the light. Flicking the small lever down, he shifted the large shifter from the twelfth gear to the sixth. Maddie's research had removed the transfer case with an extra gearshift and dropped the gears from twenty-four to sixteen. The important differences were how the gears were laid out, and the new engine with an increase of four hundred horsepower. A large conventional Peterbilt with high-weight load dual rear end now towed like a lightweight Cadillac.

The light changed, and Hooker rolled forward behind the stock-blue Nova. He knew the young kid driving the Chevy was staring at the four hundred pounds of chrome ramming bumper in his rearview mirror.

"Hook?"

Hooker smiled. Danny was the one person who did not see a reason to waste energy on words, even to the extent of shortening his name. The former most promising lineman for USC had been scouted by the NFL when he was still playing for the blue and white of Branham High Bruins. He was now his brother's bodyguard, driver, and caretaker of anything other than the music his brother lived and breathed.

His little brother, Sweets, had been hit in the head during an accident in high school. Danny walked away from a full scholarship and a promising career. He stepped on the train, and seven hours later, he was walking the head nurse of the ICU backward because they had entered his brother's name wrong. He never stopped being the man he had chosen to be.

Hooker grabbed the mic and shifted again. "Go, Danny."

"Mama says, breakfast tomorrow. Bring Candy, and I have your grand."

Hooker frowned. "Grand?"

"Sweets says you need a grand for the new paint."

"10-4, Danny. See you three at three, and thanks."

Three clicks rattled over the speaker. Danny had reached the end of his word limit.

Hooker shook his head as the Nova turned and left the road onto the parkway clear. Hooker up-shifted as his face pulled into his trademark quirky smile.

He knew nobody had told Sweets about the damage to the truck or about Mae getting a new paint job out of the deal. Sweets *knowing* was just part of the package deal known as Sweets.

When the welding gas cylinder hit Sweets in the head, it took his sight. What replaced it was a second kind of sight as well as a memory for everything music. Sweets knew who made what, who really wrote the song, or who had done the lyrics, and who had done the music. He knew every word printed on all the liner notes of all the records. He was a walking encyclopedia when it came to music. Billboard writers regularly called him for interviews or background information. The checks were an endless stream of cash flowing to the young black disc jockey. Sweets the man went to work at midnight and played old country and western music on a rock and roll station... and got paid top dollar for breaking the rules.

Twenty minutes later, Hooker took the off-ramp leading to what used to be the southern part of the Moffitt Field Air Base. The old part had originally been part of the large push for dirigibles. The largest two were the Akron and the Macon. The original thought was for the Macon and a newer ship to be stationed here at Moffitt. The first hangar was built and still stood. It was named creatively, Hangar One. The Macon did come and did not fit. Today, the building housed a large office building and the entire squadron of P-3 Orion Subchasers. Each of the airplanes was the same size as PSA's commercial jets flying up and down the coast.

Hooker turned right at the cross street, away from the southern entry gate. A mile south, he rolled out onto a three-mile-long runway he had blasted down the previous summer. His speed, while over the state limit, was much more docile this trip. From his vantage point high in the large cab, he could look across most of the open area and spotted the red domestic fire engines as well as the lime green or fluorescent orange base emergency response team trucks. Mingling in the static scene were smaller cars of the familiar black and white variety.

Hooker nosed the large truck left and across the last of the large balloon tie-down stations. Parking at the edge of the large gathering, Hooker checked in with Dolly and then slid out into the light mist.

"What's the matter, Hooker? Couldn't you find any ice cream on the way over?"

Hooker veered toward the familiar voice. What Chet missed was it being before eight at night. Hooker rarely stopped for a triple scoop of French vanilla in a sugar cone before eight at night. Usually, it was after midnight, but always when the temperature had dropped down to a low enough temperature to guarantee cops would be stomping the feeling back in their feet as they cringed at the sight of Hooker enjoying his large slurp of pleasure.

"I picked up some street mackerel on the way. Probably wasn't killed more than a week ago, still a little squishy on the inside, but the outside has the tasty asphalt tough crust you like so much." He offered the CHP captain and friend a piece of the strange-looking homemade salmon jerky one of Dolly's friends had given her.

The man didn't even look. His hand was already out. If Hooker was eating it, it was good enough to eat. He had seen it in Dolly's refrigerator but wasn't going to be the first to try it. He chewed as they both looked across a field dotted with dozens of little yellow plastic tents. He was hyper-aware of the rookie PD standing on the other side. He thought he had heard a muffled 'urp' as Hooker was describing the food. He thought it was his duty to urge things along.

Chet leaned to Hooker, and in a loud grumble, commented, "I saw this on the way over. I thought it could use a few more days to rot before I'd pick some up. I see I was right. You did leave the rest to age up, didn't you?"

Hooker glanced leisurely behind Chet as he watched the young cop run for the distance. The kid made it almost twenty yards before all parts of the last three meals reminded him he was just a rookie.

Hooker smiled and bit off another piece. "Well played."

"Oh, I wasn't just going to leave it lying on the table. I heard him flinch as you were walking up. I think he is of the mind…" Chet waved his hand at the field, "…out there, in all this mess, is a possible body."

Hooker looked at the field of short winter-burned grass and bits and pieces of twisted steel. "What am I doing here, Chet? This is something for a skip loader and a dump truck."

The man started walking. "Let's go take a look."

As they walked, Chet thought out loud, "Where do you think the Squirt is about now?"

Hooker looked at his watch. "The Hacienda… having dinner. Why?"

"Let's take a look and see if we need him or not."

The debris field and little yellow plastic crime scene numbered tents covered the better part of a pair of football fields. Everywhere Hooker looked were small pieces of twisted sheet steel and some recognizable auto parts. The two started by walking around the perimeter, but Hooker still scanned outside the specified area just to make sure nothing had been missed.

Hooker stopped and knelt down to examine a piece of twisted steel the size of his hand. Chet handed him a pair of latex gloves. Hooker looked around as he pulled the tight gloves on before picking up the piece of sheet steel. One side was a thin, smooth coat of white paint, the other a thick white paint with brush stroke marks.

"I believe you are looking at the Squirt's funky white color paint."

Hooker frowned as he looked closer. "It looks like—"

"House paint. There's some writing underneath, but it's anybody's guess if we can put Humpty Dumpty together again. The explosion did a real number on the body."

Hooker slowly flipped the piece over as he examined the ripped steel edges. "It looks like the explosion came from inside this. But this piece wasn't blown in the center of the piece, just the edges."

"The bomb squad from up at Moffitt—who worked on the thing with your sister last summer—they said it looked like cordite or detonation cord. It burns at the speed of sound and is sometimes used to cut metal. But they all agreed this would have taken a hell of a lot of det cord."

"Sure cut the truck up into tiny pieces." Hooker carefully put the piece back next to the little tent with the number 217 on it. He let out a winded whistle as he stood up.

Chet snorted. "Not all the pieces were so little." He pointed then walked downfield, carefully picking his way through the little markers.

In the distance, Hooker could see two guys working with a camera and a large clipboard. "Who're the two file clerks?"

Chet looked over and smirked. "You know when you really screw up? I mean screw up so bad Dolly won't talk to you for a year or even a lifetime?" Hooker started chuckling quietly. "Well, this is the job you end up with. They're charting every single piece and where it fits on the grid, which is about a hundred and fifty yards each way. Those guys are the newbies of the bomb squad and have either unsteady hands or just sweat too much."

Hooker thought about what some of the graphing and mapping Chips had done at wrecks when someone dies. "Tedious work."

Chet raised an eyebrow. "Don't ever screw up this bad." He pointed to the hunk of metal they had been walking toward.

Hooker frowned, and then slowly realized what he was looking at. "How in the pickled peach soup can you cut an engine block like...?" The chunk of metal was the front four cylinders and the top half of a straight-six engine. The rest of the engine had been cut away explosively. Hooker could see the fracture marks from the instantaneous beheading of the engine.

"The guy looped a couple of wraps of det cord over the engine and hoped it would destroy the top part. They almost succeeded."

Hooker and Chet turned toward the voice and watched the man in khaki slacks and a leather flight jacket approach. The sewn-on nameplate read Cpt. J. Thack. Hooker smiled. "Hello, John. Good to see you again."

"Better to see you survived the last time you came out here, Hooker." They shook hands.

"Chet, this is Captain John Thack. His people were the ones who blew me up the last time I was out here."

"Glad to meet you, John. I'm glad your crew was a bunch of screw-ups, and Hooker is still dodging bullets and bombs."

John laughed. "Yeah, I hear the only thing he can't dodge is a dime or three."

Chet's eyes lowered as Hooker laughed. "Yeah, well, Chet has the same affliction."

John turned with the light going on in his eye. "So you're the matching two-bit—"

Chet cut him off. "Nope, I'm just a one-bit. The Squirt, who is also a John, is the other bookend to Hooker. He was also the one who ended the rampage."

The naval officer turned on Hooker. "I'm not so sure if it's safe to be friends with you."

Chet leaned over the engine part. "Oh, I can guarantee it isn't safe…but it is interesting." He leaned close. "Hooker…?"

Hooker stepped over and looked at the area where Chet was pointing. The raised area was dirty and flash-smeared from the heat of the explosion. Hooker squinted—all the serial numbers were there.

Hooker turned his head to smile at Chet. "Unlike Giovanni and his Chevy, this guy screwed the pooch."

They stood as Chet shook his head. "I'm telling you, some criminals just want to get caught."

The Navy captain smiled. "It gets better. Take a look at this over here." He led them over to where four men in dark blue jackets were working among the pieces. John passed his outstretched hand around an area. "These guys are the Navy's answer to the ultimate jigsaw puzzle—putting crashed airplanes back together to find out what went wrong. The first thing Poncho and the guys saw was a field of glass scatter. This large field is where the front windshield went. About thirty yards is a fine spread of the left window and about forty yards over there where the yellow pole is —is the other side window. So working within those boundaries, they could start narrowing down to find this." He knelt and picked up a small twist of sheet steel and handed it to the gloved hand of Hooker.

Hooker laughed. He was looking at the stamped piece of tin every car after 1954 contained. Henry Ford had started the original number system for his Model A. When he started churning out cars from different assembly lines—and different plants—he wanted a way to trace where a specific car was made, on which day, which line, and presumably, by whom. Soon, the other automakers in Detroit saw the advantage and adopted their own. In 1954, the federal government saw an advantage to the system and standardized it to seventeen numbers.

The vehicle identification number—more generally known as the VIN —became universal. The tin was intact in the oval opening stamped into the dashboard. Hooker knew this would tell them who was supposed to own the car. He handed the metal shard over to Chet.

13

SLOP IN THE STREETS

When the jet stream pushes down at steep angles, the storms come straight out of the Gulf of Alaska. When there's a large tropical depression off Hawaii, the rotation drags moisture up out of Mexico and creates fire-hose-like rain. Mix the two together, and you have a Monday like no other.

This Monday morning had been nonstop for three days, except for the occasional short nap in the sleeper. Hooker pushed the broom along the highway. With each reach of the arms, it opened his leather jacket just enough to take in air. When he brought them back, the expelled air could just about knock over a horse with the stench.

Hooker was starting to have fantasies about getting a break long enough to go grab a shower and fresh clothes. He knew if he were at Willie's, the clothes he was wearing would be washed with a cutting torch. Realistically, he didn't care. He had just gotten another whiff.

Hooker laughed at the thought of Willie. The man had spent so much time in the jungles of Korea and Vietnam and, as a POW, had gone weeks without any kind of reference to hygiene. And yet, as frugal as he was, if an article of clothing were passed a certain point, he or his boyfriend Hank would rather burn it than allow it to enter his clean washing machine.

As he once told Hooker, his machine was for *soiled* clothing, not dirty street grim. Hooker knew if he made it past soiled point, it was far wiser and frugal to take it to a laundry or have Stella do it. Even Maddie had been known to carry a pair of jeans out into the garage area at the end of a stick. Once there, she would take vicious pleasure at striking a three-foot flame on the cutting torch, her flame of choice.

The trick would be how to sneak into the house, get fresh, and escape with the dirty clothes without being caught by Willie or Hank. The latter had been spending more time at the house lately while he changed the whitewashed walls to a new paint palate he called Tuscan Morning. Hooker thought the new color looked like it was a little smudged with dirt but still basically white.

The whistle bridged the time gap between the flare of lightning and the crash of the resulting thunder. Hooker pushed one last sweep at the pile and turned. The CHP officer in the yellow slicker wound his finger in the air—he was releasing the traffic. Hooker waved and grabbed the dustpan out of his back pocket. He carried the small pile scooped up back to the working deck of Mae. As he passed the crushed Gremlin, he reconsidered, and his hand flashed. The dustpan was empty, and there was a little more weight when the AMC car went on its journey to the crusher. Dog wouldn't even bother taking the seats out. Only the rubber tires would be removed. Nobody wanted the clown-car rims.

As Hooker closed the door, he glanced at his watch. It was half-past three. Sticking the truck into gear, he looked across the freeway. He evaluated the off-ramp on the other side—leading straight up to Willie's place.

Hooker looked in the mirrors for the CHP officer. He was looking north at the oncoming traffic. Hooker and what he was doing was the least of his concern. Hooker smiled and reached to the large new overhead command board Maddie had built and installed for him. He would be safe, as long as he stayed away from triggering the siren.

Facing the two lanes of oncoming traffic from the south—the front of Mae West lit up in red and blue rotating lights. Hooker had chosen a break in the traffic, which had a little stopping room. The mass reared in panic at the monster truck and stopped. Hooker spun the wheel and stomped on the go-pedal. As he invaded the space of the two lanes, he reversed the switches, so when the officer looked around, it just looked like a bunch of kind drivers had been nice and gave Hooker the right-of-way.

Hooker bounced over the low break curbing separating the freeway from the off-ramp and turned the nose up the hill. The traffic resumed, and two minutes later, Hooker pulled up in front of Willie's giant garage.

Even with the cold of the storm, the door was half-open for ventilation. The heat in the acre of garage was provided through the thick concrete floor courtesy of the hot water artesian well in the side of the mountain.

Hooker hurried quietly along the one wall as he kept his eye on the hunkered form bent over the blue-white glow of a welding arc. It was too big for Maddie, and he knew Hank would never get close to something so potentially dirty. Hooker figured it was his uncle, and he just might not lose a set of clothes today.

As much as Hooker wanted to curl up on the floor of the shower and let the water beat him into sleep, he knew he had a car to drop before his compulsory appearance at the Wednesday night dinner at Dolly's. Turning off the water and grabbing the plush white bath sheet, he dried his hair and started down. As his eyes cleared the towel, he noticed the empty floor. His wallet, money clip, change, and keys were on the counter. He closed his eyes and kept drying off.

Dressed, with hair brushed and a semi-decent shave, he walked out into the general living quarters. Hank sat at the large dining table, sipping his tea and reading the racing forum. He never bet, but he loved handicapping the ponies. On occasion, Hooker had placed a two-dollar bet at Hank's suggestion and came away a winner almost every time. If Hank ever caught wind of Hooker betting any real money, he would never speak of the ponies again. However, the occasional nice dinner paid with a two-dollar bet was okay in his book. With his knowledge, it wasn't like it was gambling or anything.

"William is washing your rags out on the concrete." Hank didn't even look up.

Hooker remained silent and headed for the garage. He knew Hank would not take his pleasure and smile until after Hooker had cleared the door to the large garage.

As Hooker stepped out into the garage, two things were askew. Willie was standing over a smoldering heap of rags while wearing a short square dance dress. Hooker assumed the burn pile had been his clothes, but the hulking form in the welding booth was still welding.

Hooker shielded his eyes and saddled over to Willie. "Who's burning the arc?"

"The Squirt."

Hooker frowned and started to look.

"Don't look. It makes him nervous."

The static snarling stopped. Hooker could hear the strikes of the welding hammer breaking off the slag. The pounding went on for a couple of minutes. It was a very long weld.

"You want to check this, Willie?"

Willie smiled at Hooker and swooped his turn with an arm up like a dancer. "Coming, dear…"

The two men walked over to where the Squirt was standing next to two long pieces of railroad rails—now attached. Hooker didn't ask—he knew the railroads never sold their rail. They smelted them back down and made more. Therefore, it was illicit to be in possession of any rail… but the steel made a nice anvil. Hooker recognized the two-foot-long double-width form.

"Planning on doing some bodywork, Squirt?"

The Squirt smiled. "Nah, I just wanted to learn the welding. But I think Chet and Willie are planning on some bodywork."

Willie bent over to examine the weld. "We found the frame for a 1929 AC Runabout."

Whatever he was saying after that was lost in Willie's mind. Hooker knew he was already folding and pounding into shape sheets of steel. The short dress and petticoats exposing most of the man's legs—was not lost on Hooker. Long past any stage of being repulsed by the sight, he was also long past any compunction at using it to get his uncle's attention back.

Hooker grabbed the large industrial drill with no bit in it. After checking to make sure it was plugged in, he started to place the drill between the man's legs. The hand on his arm stopped him. Hooker jumped and looked into Hank's face. The man had pure devil in his eyes. Hooker handed the drill to his uncle's boyfriend.

The one-second goose of the electric drill produced a reaction none expected.

The man didn't jump. He didn't scream. He just started to straighten and then spoke in a slightly higher octave, "It must be Hank. Because that Jacobs Chuck is way too large to be Hooker."

The four were laughing twenty minutes later as Hooker and the Squirt were leaving for Dolly's and the Wednesday night dinner.

As the two young men stood poised at the large garage door, the two older men stood with their one arms around each other's shoulder or waist. Willie snapped his finger and looked at Hank. "The phone call."

Hank raised both eyebrows, which lifted his forehead. "Oh, yes, Hooker. A very nice Lieutenant named Miller called today from up at Moffitt Field." Hooker stepped back into the garage, and the Squirt followed. "He said the explosive cord the person had used was a unique kind… it was only used in hard mining or something."

The Squirt stepped forward and stood next to Hooker. "Did he say hard-rock mining?"

Hank snapped his fingers and pointed at the Squirt. "Exactly the term he used. Very good, Jonathan. I'm proud of you."

Hooker muttered with a teasing bored smile, "Get over it. He read it somewhere once."

Willie growled.

The Squirt ignored them both. "It means the mining is done in a confined space, and the explosion needs to be constrained or restrained. Making a large explosion is not the objective, but instead, is made to be used for precision."

Hank rolled his shoulder. "Well, I don't know about that. It sounded like a big bang was the idea. They estimated he used about one hundred pounds of the rope. This Miller fella seemed to think he glued up a cord every six-inch square. It sounds to me like he wanted more than just a quiet whoop-de-do."

Hooker gave a low whistle. "Wow. What kind of person is this?"

Willie had a serious look on his face, and his arm around Hank's waist applied a little bit more squeeze. "This is a very dangerous person, Hooker. You be very careful… which goes double for you, Squirt."

The two young men saluted the former Navy Seal and recipient of the Congressional Medal of Honor hanging ten feet away. Hooker placed it there to remind everyone Willie had earned his right to be the man he wanted to be—the hard way. If any person had the right to speak of danger, Willie held the honor—in spades.

Turning, the matched set of black leather jackets, starched white T-shirts, jeans, and boots sauntered out into the midwinter drizzle. Hooker grabbed the large hammer and bounced it down on every one of the ten tires. Dropping it into the bucket, he climbed up into the cab of his first love—the giant truck known as Mae West. As he closed the door, Willie smiled at the new rendition of the early screen star waving from the side of the truck.

Hank purred his approval. "Oh, those new extra-large bumpers are just perfect."

Willie leaned into his boyfriend. "So she doesn't look like some anemic adolescent tenth-grader anymore?"

Hank slapped him on the chest. "Just stop. I never said such a thing. She just didn't look so…well, Mae West."

The two men waved as the truck rolled, and leather-covered arms waved from both windows.

They turned, and Willie hit the switch. The pig-sized electric motor across the large doorway started to close the forty-foot tall and wide corrugated tin door. He knew the boys wouldn't be back until after the storm was gone, he just hoped Hooker would get some rest.

Willie caught Hank staring at him. "What?"

"Nothing… other than the kid looked like hell warmed over."

Willie's lips rolled into barrels. "It's the job. You make hay while the sun don't shine."

14

DOLLY'S TABLE AND A COLORADO PLATE

The seating arrangement at Dolly's table on any Wednesday night was up to Dolly. One phrase a guest would never hear Dolly say is, "Oh, just take a seat anywhere!" It just would not happen. Everyone knew the seating was part and parcel of Dolly's selection of who was invited for a certain night.

Until the previous year, no woman had ever sat at the table—not even Dolly. Those few women who had broken the tradition were powerfully connected women in their own right.

Tonight's agenda was even obvious to the Squirt, who sat at the foot of the table. Hooker, quietly amused, sat at the head. There were five seats down each side. Sitting in the middle seat on Hooker's right was the Highway Patrol Captain, Chet. Hooker was silently enjoying watching the man squirm. Dolly had let Hooker know the local CHP office had six new openings for patrol officers. Hooker was aware the official title was Patrolman, but if Dolly had her way, it would become patrol officer or just officer.

Seated down Hooker's left side were two field officers from the sheriff's office, two patrol officers from the San Jose police department, and a Deputy Fire Chief from Moffitt Field Air Base. The five women smiled prettily at the Squirt, Hooker, and especially Captain Chet Davis.

Flanking Chet was the county commissioner Paul, who kept watching his plate for fear he would start laughing at the uncomfortable spot Chet was now in. Nothing official would happen tonight, but Paul and Chet knew the pressure from Dolly's table could be worse than an investigation from Internal Affairs. Both of their careers had experienced and enjoyed the power of the table.

Sitting between Paul and the Squirt was the large mass of the happy Filipino, Officer James Aligo. His right hand slid a small snapshot of his new partner, a black German Shepard, over to the Squirt. The man was positively radiant... like a proud new father.

The deputy on the end leaned forward as she recognized the type of photo. "New K-9?"

Aligo beamed. "Zaafir. She's just a year old. I start training next week. Her name means—"

"Victorious." The black eyes flared.

Aligo smiled.

The female deputy continued. "My mother is from Lebanon. They met when my father went to Israel on a sabbatical to study in the original scriptures. She was on holiday. It was love at first sight. Her parents said it would never work because of the differences."

"Because he was Jewish...?"

The deputy laughed. "Oh, no. Jewish would have been fine. My mother was Jewish. No, it was because he was an American."

The Filipino frowned, as did the others who were now listening. "Your mother was Jewish, but from Lebanon?"

"Certainly. Why not? There were large Jewish ghettos in both Beirut and Tripoli. Most of the major cities of the Muslim world had large Jewish populations and ghettos. Usually, they were the commanding population in the medina or old central district of a city." She passed the dog photo down the table on the female side.

Chet was happy the object of discussion and focus was off him. "So the only problem was your father was from America?"

She chuckled, "No, because he was married."

The table was silent. She continued to explain. "Nobody thought to ask about the ring on his finger. Even my mother wanted to ignore the ring.

In those days, jewelry was something most people in the region couldn't afford. So for the man to have a wedding ring… it spoke volumes about the importance of the marriage."

The lieutenant in the Navy whites leaned forward on his elbows and rested his turned head on two fists. "So, obviously somehow, they resolved the issue of this marriage which was in the way of their own, otherwise… he wouldn't be your father."

She blushed. "Well, if he had been married, he would still be my father. The truth came out after my mother had discovered she was pregnant with me. The wedding ring was just a ring. When my father was only nineteen, his parents had died in a train derailment. They were in New York on the elevated train over Jamaica Bay. The train plunged into the deepest part of the bay. After the bodies had been recovered, my father was given their jewelry. It was their simple thin rings and her gold earrings. He had them melted down and made into a ring for him to wear and remember them by. He just never thought about it being on his wedding finger—honoring their marriage."

The Navy captain in khakis mused, "It's amazing sometimes how wrong, or misplaced beliefs can be… when understanding can sometimes be as close as a simple question."

Chet shifted in his seat and cleared his throat. Then he looked up to see Dolly with two hot plates in her hand. "Incoming. Nobody move."

Dolly nodded a thank you and started placing plates of her spaghetti with dispatch-cooked marinara sauce and a Sicilian sausage from Chiaramontes in the north end of the city in front of each of them. The banter changed, as Chet relaxed and did what was expected of him. He asked the female officers about their experiences with being a female in the field.

The conversation led to the many factions of the law enforcement culture, and how it was changing. The consensus was slowly and not often for the better. Chet and Paul both got the full blast of the female viewpoint. All five of the officers had been coached on the nature of the table. Nothing in conversation went beyond the door, and even then, it always answered to Dolly. Hooker was enjoying his dinner. He was certain a few —if not all—of the officers would be seen at the table in the future. He gave Dolly a knowing smile. They both liked the idea of change.

Dina called from the other room, "Aligo, your watch commander wants to know if you will be swinging by the precinct. I believe he has someone for you to meet."

"Ladies, it has been a pleasure to meet you this evening. We hope to get to know all of you better. Hooker and Squirt, I have a commercial in San Francisco going to Auburn. Pack an extra T-shirt."

Hooker stood first, with Aligo a fast second. "James, as always, it's been grand. Good luck with your new girlfriend. She looks a little young for you, but I'm sure it will all work out. Please keep her safe out there in the Knife & Gun Club of King and Story."

Turning to the left side of the table, Hooker smiled winningly. "Ladies, the protocol is you do not touch your plate." The deputy quietly placed her plate back on the table. "Thank you. You place your napkin on the table, push your chair in, and thank Dolly for dinner. Hugs are optional and your choice. However, I recommend considering them. We'll clear the security cameras and meet you at the door. Gentlemen, please be seated once the ladies are gone. I'll be right back."

Hooker cleared the monitors and gave Dolly the nod. Dolly opened the door and received five hugs. She enforced the exchange by telling each she would be in touch. The last was one of the deputies, and she held her hand to keep her a moment. Quietly, she leaned in. "I know you're getting the promotion you put in for and heading for Sacramento."

"The selection hasn't been released from—" She frowned at Dolly. "Not even my supervisor knows I put in for the position." Her voice trailed off as she remembered where she just had dinner.

Dolly had waited to see the light of understanding cross those deep, black eyes. She smiled as she recognized she had just secured the friendship she was looking for.

"I wanted you to know your new job doesn't let you off the hook with my table. Whenever your new schedule involves the South Bay, you make sure it also involves dinner on a Wednesday night—just let me know you're coming. I also don't want you to think this is about you being special. Besides, I need a set of eyes and ears in Sacramento attached to a sharp working mind."

The woman hugged her again. "Thank you again. The dinner was fantastic..." She stopped and struggled with what she needed to say next. "All my life, I have lived and eaten halal. Halal means I don't eat pork... But after tonight..."

Dolly smiled as she put a finger to the young woman's lips. "This is our secret. The dinner tonight was kosher. I knew about you. I made... um... accommodations. Nobody comes to my table without me knowing how they eat and a lot more about them."

The woman slumped. "Of course, you would. It was silly of me—"

Dolly cut her off again. "Never think less of your beliefs or who you are, and so you know where you stand in my eyes, say hello to Lynnette when you get home tonight. Give her a large hug for me. If I thought I could do her any good, I would bring her to the table also. I understand your relationship will be a strained long-distance one with her. But I've also heard there may be a need for a good nurse at Central Valley."

The two smiled as the understanding sunk in. Sarah leaned in for a last hug. "Of course, you would know about us. Thank you for being a friend. When the announcement comes out next week, I'll remember to act very surprised."

Dolly squeezed a little tighter. "You have my numbers."

Dolly watched as the woman crossed the parking lot and safely drove off. As she closed the door, she kissed her two fingers, and then pressed them to the badge welded to the thick steel plate door just above the doorknob. She could hear the men going over the strange new case taking up Hooker's attention. She knew they would need more coffee.

Captain Thack leaned forward and looked down the table at the Squirt. They were chuckling at Chet, who had asked, "How many feet of det cord was used, John?" The two Johns had started to answer at the same time.

The Squirt settled it. "Let's just stick with Squirt and captain. That way there's no confusion."

Paul snorted and muttered. "At least, for now, there's just one captain."

Chet cleared his throat, and they all laughed.

Hooker leaned back as he realized his mug was empty. "Okay, Squirt, as you seem to have the answers... how many feet of cord?"

The kid walked them all through the problem, and it became obvious he had not previously worked out the answer. The two naval officers had never watched the Squirt's mind work like the other three had. Even Dolly had not seen him crunch information and stood amazed as she leaned against the counter with the coffee carafe floating ineffectively in midair.

"Assuming the box of the interior was roughly twelve feet long and five feet wide… the walls in a standard panel truck are almost five and a half feet tall. The end-for-end runs would be twenty-nine feet. Accounting for the way he cut up the dashboard and firewall, let's use an integer of thirty because he used more under the dash, but he didn't need any for the glass. There would be eleven of those runs if we assume one running at the edge of the walls.

"The inner circumference of the cylinder would be twenty-one with a basic sum of fourteen runs. All of this gives us eight hundred and eighty-five feet… but that is the bare minimum. As we didn't find much in the way of seats and other interior parts, I would assume the bomber used at least an extra hundred and forty feet, wrapping extra loops under the dashboard, around the seats, and the steering column. The drive train didn't receive as much attention. From what I could see from the photographs, it would appear he made several loops over the rear end and suspension, as well as down the driveshaft. I would estimate he used only an extra couple of hundred feet there. The transmissions condition, or the mess of the gearbox, would suggest he made several loops about six feet each and draped them over the transmission. My guess is there were two sets of loops—one in front of the shifter and one behind. All total, about an added hundred feet." He paused a moment to take a sip of his coffee. In the room, a pin could have dropped and startled the listeners.

"The blast deformation changes with the engine compartment, the front end, and the fenders. The blast shifts from inside to dual blast and or shell compression." He looked at the two naval officers. The man in white smiled and nodded.

"He wanted the front end of the truck to be obscured. He knew it was a unique shape and design, so he used most of his remaining charge line to destroy the shape. I'm going to go with about two hundred feet of cord, which… out of a pair of one-thousand-foot rolls of mining detonation cord, he only had a few long hanks left to try to blow the engine. My guess is we are dealing with someone who knows their way around a mine and explosives but is not automotive inclined."

Paul leaned back with the thumbnail of his left hand pushed into his lips. Where Dolly's mind was stunned into a stall, his was whirling with information. "So two-thousand feet...?"

The Squirt looked at Dolly and held out his coffee mug. Dolly jerked back to the world she knew and started pouring. The Squirt looked at Paul. "Two-thousand would be my guess. I did a little digging around, and a regular person can buy small rolls of two-hundred and fifty feet or even five-hundred feet if they have a blasting license like a farmer would have for clearing trees and such. However, someone who knows explosives, especially if it is their profession, would be buying the more economical roll of a thousand feet. So, two rolls."

He looked back at the lieutenant. "But there was something I was curious about. The pieces of the hood and inner panels of the engine compartment seem inconsistent with the shearing of the body. There wouldn't be a change of the metal's thickness. So, did your squad have any conjectures about what would account for the change in the deformation?"

"We thought maybe your figure of two thousand might have been close, but not close enough. We think in the front he used a smaller roll of the more common form of cord—which would be standard use with the farmers you mentioned. The cord would be tighter and less contained in its explosive nature. It wouldn't be used in a mine but would be the right thing for use on a stump or large boulder." He leaned back as Dolly filled his cup. "We think he ran out of the cord he normally used and had to supplement it with a two-fifty roll. We're hoping the police can find a roll bought locally in the last few weeks."

Hooker smelled his fresh coffee and took a sip. Setting the mug down, he weighed in. "So how did we do with the numbers, Chet?"

"A strange mixed bag there also. The truck was last bought by one Helmut Lysander. However, it seems Helmut died in 1968 in a mining accident, but he continues to drive and register his truck each year in

Colorado. I've reached out to the sheriff in a place called Fairplay—he hasn't gotten back to me yet."

The Squirt pinched the bridge of his nose. The information was not making sense, or whatever he was processing, and it seemed to hurt. Speaking into his hand, he continued to pinch his nose.

"In 1963, a woman in Tulsa, Oklahoma, was found guilty of fraud. Her husband had died the year after returning from the war in the Pacific where he had been injured. She buried him in the backyard and continued to receive his disabled veteran benefits checks. When the VA required a check-up, she convinced her brother to stand in. Nobody at the VA hospital noticed the blood type had changed. It was only when someone took an x-ray of his gut they saw the lower half of the left lung as well as the kidney had grown back. The woman had maintained the ruse by continuing to pay the registration fees on his truck, which sat disused in the barn. She also paid his Masonic Lodge dues as well as his Shriner dues. The Master of the Masonic Lodge was reported as saying they regretted hearing of the brother's passing as he had been a regular attendant of the lodge, and he would be missed." The Squirt released his nose and looked up.

Hooker looked at him with a deadpan face. "Did they charge the Master with collusion?"

All five of the men laughed. Hooker, Dolly, and Paul knew the Squirt had just read something he had seen at some time. The Squirt shrugged. "It didn't say."

The other five stopped laughing. Captain Thack opened his mouth, thought, and then shut it. "That was real?"

The Squirt nodded. "The point being—we're looking for a relative."

15

HELMUT'S SON

Helmut Lysander's son sat on the screened porch and looked across the bay. The panel truck was history, but he had a bad feeling about it. The two large rolls of det cord weren't beyond his budget, but they also were not cheap. His supplies came through strange roundabout routes to hide their final destination and took time. With this new job, time is what he did not have.

In addition, the new van was a connection he did not like. He had to buy it in his own name… a name where, for the last five years, had all but remained outside the system of records in California. Even his work shirt only had Jake stitched on the breast.

His right hand reached out and grabbed the soldering iron from its stand. The left fingered the wad of solder and fished out a longer end. The two met on the small asbestos mat. The flux seared, and the tendril of smoke enveloped Felix in memories.

Felix could still smell the wet, pungent odor of the rotting timbers mixed with the damp earth and leaking seams of sulfur in what was left of the coal. He held his father's left hand, and the man carried the large canvas bag in his right. It was Felix's seventh birthday, and he had wanted to see what his father did with all the stuff in the large locked shed behind the house. He had always known it was dangerous, or he and Tommy

Campbell would have broken into the shed a long time before—as they did with Tommy's older brother's room. At the time, the two boys did not understand the pictures of the women who were not wearing clothes... but it was only a matter of time.

The old mine was large to the seven-year-old, but later, Felix knew it had been just a short walk into the mountain. It was only a test hole. The entire shaft did not run a thousand feet or more. His father had spent the week before pounding on a two-foot-long rod with a hardened end in the shape of a cross. The rod was called a star drill. One man can drill a hole in rock wall by hitting on the rod, and between hits, turn the rod an eighth of a turn. Then two hits and turn. Two hits and turn. The first hit would break the nodes from the previous beats, and the second would drive a new star into the bottom of the hole—which created four new nodes.

With each hit, a small puff of stone dust would eject from the hole. Not enough to notice, but just enough to be breathed in. Over the course of a decade or two, the tiny pieces of stone would make tiny cuts in the lungs where they came to rest. Those cuts would fester and heal, fester, and heal. With age, the scars lose elasticity, and the lungs cannot expand and contract like they needed.

With the lack of fresh air to the lungs, combined with a daily pack of unfiltered cigarettes, the damage becomes either black lung or cancer. Either one was a short death sentence to a miner. Many like Felix's father had first gone in a mine not much older than Felix was on his seventh birthday. Many of those miners, like his father, had retired because they could no longer breathe—and would never leave the hospital where they ended up.

By the time his father fell in the mine and rushed to the hospital, Felix was already in the family business with enough experience to be running most of the day-to-day work. He had watched his father fade away. When he was young, he was in little league. In the summer evenings, his father and he would throw the ball. Nobody ever said anything, but if you stood quiet-like, you could hear the echo of leather balls smacking into leather mitts.

Few fathers could afford or felt a need to buy a glove for themselves.

Most were just grateful they could watch their boy play high school ball. Some didn't even last long enough. The mines gave up their riches grudgingly, and occasionally, extracted a high price. Later it would extract a high price from all the miners—it was just a matter of when.

Felix counted the four-foot lengths of pieced wire... one hundred and seven. He banded the hundred and placed the packet on the shelf. Turning back to the table desk, he started making the next hundred. He would need seven bundles for the next job and one more for any unforeseen problems that may arise. The wires were always the same and adaptable as to length due to their construction.

Felix looked out across the black expanse he knew was lawn—or what passed for the lawn. Even in the cold of winter, Felix could feel the fresh-cut grass between his toes. The summer he played left field in the city league, he could feel the strength leaving his father. The mitt didn't sting anymore. They threw the ball until his father's television shows were on instead of until it was too dark to see. It was also in his step. He had caught his father sitting on a rock or old timbers, catching his breath. He took two days to set up a job instead of the morning to set up and then would blow the job when the four o'clock whistle blew.

When Felix was twenty, the two of them would go over the plans, outlining the job. Felix would then set the charges, and his father would come to examine the first few hundred feet. His pat answer was spoken with a shortness of breath. He would wave his large hand in the air, saying, *Felix, you set it up just fine. I don't know why you insist on my checking your work.* Then he would shuffle back out of the mine. As the years and stone dust took their toll, his shuffling became slower and longer.

One day, the shuffling stopped. The man collapsed, and Felix almost left him in the mine. The man had no one, but his son left. The woman he loved and thought loved him had left him with a six-year-old boy to rear on his own. For a moment, as Felix knelt there in the dark of the mine, he could feel the new radio detonator in his jacket pocket. It would have been so easy to simply carry his father deeper into the mine where the charges were larger—sit with him and hold his hand while he pushed the little button.

Felix had only dated Thelma a few times by that day. He had no plans.

Felix stuck the iron in the holder and gently placed the small loop of solder on the table. He leaned back in the chair with his eyes closed. This is what his father must have felt. Life had started with such promise—and then a little stone dust here, a bump there, and things turn out not like you had thought, even if you had planned.

Felix pushed back the chair as he stood.

He turned off the last lights in the house. He wouldn't need any to see his way around a house he knew so well. For a man who had spent most of his life in dark mines, the house in the middle of the night was almost like daylight.

He checked at the bedroom door. The cover was askew, so he went in. He straightened the sheet and folded the top three inches down over the blanket. He knew she would find the satin binding in the night and stick the corner of the blanket back in her mouth like a baby. He pulled back the quilt square to her shoulder, leaving just the top inch out to the cool of the night.

He ran his hand down along the quilt—feeling the pattern. Thelma and her mother had pieced the top from four generations of their family's clothes. When Thelma and Felix were first married, she could point to a tiny piece of cloth and tell him who had worn it and what it had been. It was a graph of her history. She was the smart one. She had even studied at the junior college in Boulder. A misplaced charge and a two-inch stone to the front of her head had taken it all away from her— had taken her away from him.

Felix ran his hand down along her shoulder and arm. There was almost nothing left of the woman. She would hardly take any food or water. She was disappearing in front of him, but his guilt and grief couldn't let her go.

The Colorado hospital had sent a nurse out to check on her condition and the condition she was living in. Felix hadn't blamed them. Even in the best of times, mining towns were not sanitary or comforting places. People were busy trying to dig a living out of the side of a mountain— even though the living they were digging was at the bottom of the barrel.

With Felix's side money, they were building a nest egg they thought would one day set them free. They dreamed of a day when they could just live in a clean town somewhere—somewhere they could both work nice clean jobs. Things like a fine new home and cars were never part of the dream. Their dreams were simple and down to earth—same as they were.

Felix looked at the small line of a rise in the quilt. The moonlight through the window barely cast any shadows on the bed. Like their dreams—the day at the mine having ended in the hospital had wiped out their savings and left only a small lump casting almost no shadow on a bed.

Felix walked back out to the screened porch. Glancing at his watch, he started putting the equipment back in the wall. In six hours, he would have to become Jake Smalley again.

As he removed his boots, he thought about the fateful night in the bar in North Platte, Nebraska. He had finished a job earlier in the evening, further east in Chapman. The old wood grain silo had blown just the way the man had described an old silo would explode if the heat built up in the grain. Felix had laughed. The site was instantaneously ready for an over-sized cement pond.

He had stopped in at the roadhouse because most bars had some generally decent food to go with their watered-down drinks and cheap beer. The food was better than expected, and the beer was damn good.

Felix had ordered and then gone into the men's room to freshen up. When he returned, the waitress looked surprised. She stepped back a few paces and grabbed a plate a man was starting to reach for. She told the man sorry and brought the sandwich back over to Felix. Then she kept looking at him and then the other guy. Finally, she asked if they were brothers or something.

The two men looked at each other. In a rough sort of way, they could have been twins. The joke about *who's your father* was as instantaneous as the *let me buy you a beer*. Felix had long known about the existence of an estranged sister… but had never heard about a brother. This wasn't, but their lives would become perversely intertwined moving forward.

Felix wasn't forthcoming about what he was doing in the left armpit of the country. Jake, on the other hand, by the third beer, had mapped out a life gone all shades of wrong. He had a decent job, but he was dating the boss's seventeen-year-old daughter. Next thing everyone noticed, she couldn't fit in her ass-tight flowered jeans anymore. Her daddy had a shotgun, and soon, Jake found himself on the road with his thumb out headed west from Fort Wayne, Indiana. A trucker here and a drunken territory salesman there had landed him in North Platte. He was hoping to land a job on a tramp freighter in Seattle. If not, he would continue up to Alaska and the pipeline.

Felix had given his doppelganger a thousand dollars the next morning as traveling money and then explained how to get fake identification in a large city like Seattle. The man would no longer need his real driver's license and had given it to Felix. In exchange of good faith, Felix had promised he would run the trail cold.

True to his word, Felix had washed the ID through the Texas system, rinsed it in Utah, and dried it in Colorado. By the time anyone asked in California if he was Jake Smalley from Terra Haute, Indiana—he could honestly look the man in the eye and tell him he had never been in Indiana. It was a simple truth.

As Felix pulled the light cord and pulled the blankets over him, he was hoping Jake had found his freighter. He just hoped he wouldn't have to do the same.

16

CAN YOU TOW A TRAIN?

Hooker leaned over and felt in the rack. Along the right outer edge were bumps on a tape that Sweets had put there for Hooker. Each of the eight-track tapes had a unique set of bumps. Hooker just needed to learn the Braille. They were the same bumps Sweets had on all the eight-track tapes at the radio station. Being blind for Sweets was the same for Hooker when it would be dangerous to take his eyes off the road at sixty while running up a dark 101.

Dinner had been a few hours before in San Luis Obispo across from where he had dropped a Mack tractor with a cracked engine block. The hotdog stand was everything the man had told him. What the man hadn't mentioned was the woman who owned it also loved cats. Box had gotten a dish of fresh caught Rock Cod. He had also failed to mention she served soft frosty. It wasn't his usual French vanilla, but neither he nor Box had a problem with any of it.

The tow was a special deal with the Fly. She wanted it towed on Sunday so she could charge weekend rates, and to force Hooker to take it, she had handed him the key to the lock on the fuel depot. Her instructions were to give it back sometime next week. He would have made the tow for just the three hundred plus gallons of fuel, but she also was implying a refill when he got back, on top of the long green for the tow. She knew he was working to pay Danny back for the extra special pearl paint job—Mae West's signature look.

Tex Ritter's boy was just starting into the steel guitar solo Hooker liked so much. Hooker smiled. The song would take him all the way to the top of the grade, climbing out of the coastal plain. The rest of the album would see him past Atascadero, and by then, he could pick up Sweets at shortly after three-thirty.

Hooker rubbed his face with his right hand. It had been a long day, but worth it.

The red lights swung onto the highway just after Hooker passed the cutoff to Santa Margarita. The cruiser fishtailed and then became steady. Hooker expected the Chip to pass him, but the officer tucked in behind Mae. Hooker looked at his speedometer. He was only about twelve over the limit. Hooker could smell chicken manure growing all over this.

Mae nosed onto the shoulder, and Hooker set the brakes. He considered making the officer work for the ticket by having him climb up and down to get to Hooker's window but then thought about the fairness. He had been speeding—a little. Which was nothing compared to what he had been doing when he dragged the dead tractor down, or what he was going to open up and do after Atascadero…

Hooker pushed open his door and slid down the side of Mae. He met the officer at the end of the working bed. The man was all smiles. Hooker could feel the weight of a rural ticket.

"Are you Hooker?"

Hooker stopped. "Yes, sir…"

The man turned and headed back to his cruiser. "You'd better come on and set in the passenger seat. Y'all ain't gonna believe this."

Hooker slid down into the low-slung cruiser, which sat purring a little rough. Hooker frowned and looked over at the man. "Do you take this home at night?" Hooker nodded his head toward the car's front end— which was not running a stock engine.

The man chuckled. "Sure."

"440?"

The look on the man's face soured. "Panty-attack crap? No way. I ripped that out years ago, son. That there is the sweet sound of pure

Mopar. My buddy races and we built out a 340 Hemi to a 390 and got a sinker manifold to mount the twin quad Hollys. If I could get away with it, I'd trick out a shaker hood with a stack of six-pack."

Hooker stared at the man as he thought about the engine the man had just described. It was a unique design meant for only two cars.

"Did you pull this engine out of a Belvedere that went sideways on the Visalia drags and ended rolling through the weeds?"

The man laughed. "Y'all know Ben Robinson?"

Hooker smirked. "Sure—but I know his sister better."

"It were Maddie's boyfriend done rolled the sum-bitch."

Hooker nodded. "My uncle."

The man laughed and stuck his hand out. "Wa'll hell, son—that there makes you family. Chester. Chester Duggins. Ben's daddy and mine done run shine together. They runned north, and daddy runned south." The man leaned back and just slowly shook his head. "Shoot… small world."

"Sure is." Hooker gave him a moment and then started to open the door. It reminded the officer of the unfinished business.

"Let's get dispatch on the horn here." He took the mic off the holder on the dashboard. Reverently he called his dispatcher. Hooker was amazed they had one at this time of night.

"Alpha 2-4."

The female voice crackled: "Go ahead, Alpha 2-4."

He turned toward Hooker. "Oh, good. She's still awake. I was expecting you an hour ago. They said you had a mean mill in that there rig." He keyed his mic. "Sugar, I have that there tow guy they was looking for."

"10-4. Let me call them back, honey."

Hooker looked at the man. "Honey?"

The smile was pure pride. "As you can guess, there ain't much out here in the weeds at night, so we have the phones and radio switched over to my house. My wife is a light sleeper and a hair-trigger. It don't hurt none that the phone and radio is right thar by the bed." The man blushed. "Of course, it makes being out here even harder knowing that there radio is a direct connection to the prettiest pink baby doll."

"Honey, they want to know if you have a *hooker*?"

"It's the man's name, sweet pea—and yes, he's here."

"The lady said to use the top four gears and head for Fremont... he has a train to tow. Something about trying a county that don't work or something. Honey, I was in the middle of a nice dream, and then you called... I don't understand any of this... Oh, wait. She wants more."

Chester just smiled as his yoke was showing. "She's not the brightest star in the night..."

Hooker smiled. "But she's your star."

"You got that right."

"Honey, I think I get it now. They want him in Fremont code-three. There was some big train wreck, and he's the closest crane."

"10-4, Sugar. I'll talk to you in the morning."

"Love ya, honey."

The man hung the mic and looked at Hooker. He frowned. "Code three?"

Hooker rolled his eyes. "Trust me. You don't want to know. What can I expect between here and San Jose?"

"Cop wise?" Hooker nodded.

"I'm it until you hit Gilroy. Battle, Henry Battle, will come on at King City about five, but I'd 'spect y'all will be long gone by then."

Hooker stuck out his hand and shook. "Long gone, Chester... long gone. Thanks for the pullover. Good to know the killer engine is being put to good use. Also, it's always good to know more of the family."

He backed out of the car and loped back to the cab of Mae.

Chester tried to keep up but finally fell off at Atascadero.

17

COG IN A LARGER CRIME

Felix sat in the bar. The place smelled worse than the most disgusting mine he had ever been inside of. One would expect the bathrooms to smell of old urine and maybe even shit… However, when sitting at the bar, or even shooting balls on what was passing for a pool table, a person would expect to smell only stale beer and possibly vomit. Even Felix's nose could smell all four mixed with what he knew to be the coppery smell of old blood mixed with semi-fresh blood.

Someone recently bled more than just a nosebleed or small cut. Felix guessed it had been in the last few hours.

Felix chose the bar a few times in the last five years simply because of all the filth and neglect. Anonymity also came with the territory. The skanky barmaid with the skewed false eyelashes and a bra she should have upgraded three sizes ago—would never remember him. He would try hard never to remember her or her bad dental habits that matched the men's room and the corner of the bar. Felix could feel the wobble in the fourth leg of the stool. It had probably been the strike-point too many times. The repairs were getting sloppier and sketchier with each bar fight.

Felix didn't care. He was watching the ten o'clock local news. The flashing lights of police and fire were everywhere the reporter and the cameraman panned the camera. Felix inwardly smiled. *It must be tough to report on such a train wreck. Just point the camera everywhere and keep saying things like horrible and disastrous.* He raised the long neck to his lips. The cheap beer was biting in his mouth. He kept watching the television hanging off the side of the wall in the corner.

The scene changed back to the station's newsroom. The guy with the bad wig was talking to the young woman who was struggling to not look at his hair. Felix would have thought it was a comedy skit from Saturday Night Live, but he knew it was local talent.

In the corner, a large building appeared. Felix recognized the building. The caption read there had been a catastrophic failure of the floor in the building's parking structure. The TV switched to the reporter on the scene. To Felix, the guy appeared to have been either pulled out of bed or told to get out of his janitor's uniform and put on the company's jacket. He was having several problems with his microphone. It all seemed to match the fact his fly was open, and the cameraman either hadn't caught it or didn't care.

Felix didn't care either. His focus was on what news crews called the "B" roll. It was the footage of the destruction, which they had been allowed to shoot sometime in the previous hour.

The walk-up showed a secured loading dock surrounded by a heavy steel-barred fence and electric gate. There was only room for one truck at the dock at a time. Looking through the bars of the fence, the camera looked down into the large hole which seemingly had swallowed an armored truck whole. The concrete dust was still hanging in the air. A light powdering was everywhere the camera looked.

What the camera did not see, but Felix knew, was the back door of the truck was also blown. He hadn't been there for the door part of the job, but he had supplied the special charges and left them in the sub-basement. It was a simple peel-and-stick charge. It was one of his specialty charges.

He had seen enough. He threw a five on the bar and left knowing he would never walk into this bar again.

The underground parking with the secure loading dock was the transfer station for the Bay Area's Federal Reserve. Every bit of new money and every bit of old, used, untraceable money processed through the dock. Felix had no idea how much or what was in the armored truck, but he guessed there were pallets of conveniently wrapped large bundles. The news over the next week would give at least some idea of what had really been in there. A tingling in the back of his neck told Felix—moving to another state would not solve his problem this time.

As he drove the van, he repeatedly stretched and clenched his hands. Making the C-4 the way he did required him to knead the dough by hand. Once the mixing began, it could not be stopped until it reached the right color and consistency, telling him it had stabilized.

His special recipe malleable plastic was easier to mold and shove into cracks than a child's plasticized clay—which plastic explosives were named after. Felix's father had worked out the recipe when he was in the paratroopers in the Pacific. There were many ways to make the explosives known as plastic. The material went back to the late 1870s, but the clay Felix and his father always used was known as C-4—short for Composition-4.

Felix raised his right hand to his upper lip and smelled. The corn oil he used instead of the motor oil the paratroopers had used gave it the extra smooth thinner consistency. Felix was sure it might take a few hundred miles per hour off the 26,000 feet a second the shock wave was supposed to travel at, but even at 25,000 feet a second, the destruction was enough.

Felix learned to be a minimalist. Where a one or two-pound block of C-4 would be more than satisfactory to take out an eight-inch thick steel I-beam, many explosive technicians would go for the overkill and belt the beam with an eight or ten-pound satchel to leave no doubt of getting the job done. Felix believed in knowing exactly what the job would take and only adding an extra ten percent.

Where others would lean a case of dynamite against a twelve-by-twelve Ponderosa pine timber having rotted in a mine for sixty years—Felix would jamb a pound of C-4 between the timber and the stone of the wall. When the dynamite would blow, most of the force would be wasted in the air where the box was facing. When Felix's charge would blow, the force blew into the stone, amplifying the push toward the timber. The early force would crack the timber, but the rebound force would push the broken timber into the middle of the mine.

The frugal nature of his father and Felix brought them much work.

Not because they were a bit cheaper than others were, but because they showed up on time, did not wreck the rest of the mine, and were always sober on a job. Even in the bar, Felix had only taken a few sips of the one beer.

Felix knew there would be a package or large envelope at the mailbox store. It would be either new bills he would have to wash and age or old used bills. Either way, it would be his last job. He had a large nest egg now. It was just a matter of Thelma and how to transport her.

He turned the lights off as he nosed the van into the driveway. It wasn't because the lights might disturb Thelma—she was beyond that. It was just habit. He jingled the keys in his left hand as he walked toward the door—one of his other habits. Thelma used to know whether it was Felix or his father who was coming up the walk. If there were keys jingling, it was Felix. If it was silent, it was his father who lived with them after Felix's mother passed away.

Felix tucked the one leg back under the covers and straightened them. His hand rested on her shoulder as he lightly bent over and kissed her hair. He could tell that somewhere in there, she had heard his keys jingle and would now sleep peacefully through the remainder of the night.

18

PULLING RAILCARS

Hooker eased Mae down into the mess. One look and he started missing the Squirt.

Hooker was on the outer perimeter of the response to the carnage. A fast count of what he could actually see was seventeen freight cars. Some had held new cars, some had boxes, and three contained, so far, unlabeled canned goods. Hooker wondered if any of the cans would make their way back to Stella's wonder rooms of food. The four Hooker had a feeling about were the tank cars. From experience, Hooker knew a standard railcar weighed thirty tons empty. The same held true for a tank car, but then you start putting liquids in a tank, and the weight starts to approach the weight of the locomotive engine—at a hundred tons.

Mae could not lift the railcar, but she could lift or shift one end at a time. Set with holdouts stacked or chained off to something large, her twin pulling power was rated at over one-fifty. This meant Hooker could roll a tank car, or even move it around, which was something a Class-A crane could not do.

Hooker's only worry was his cables were at the end of their lifespan. He had meant to get new cable wound last year, but a little problem had come up just before the holidays, and everything slipped his mind.

The scene looked like chaos, but to the eye of someone who worked in the middle of disasters, there was a system to the madness. Hooker scanned the workers. He was looking for the one person who did not have dread in how they were moving. This would be the person who had seen so much that they were in charge—if not for the whole event, at least some of it.

The yellow hardhat had thrown Hooker off. Yellow was usually the color worn by workers, where supervisors wore the clean, seldom worn white plastic hard hat. The man stood looking at the large tow truck. His eyes traveled over the massive scale from the diamond-plate front fenders to the oversized working bed on the back. His eyes did not miss any detail of Mae West or the slogan painted on the boom.

"I don't need a quickie, but I understand you know how to roll a tank car and do it carefully."

Hooker's head ground around to look at the man. Hooker almost laughed. Not only did the man sound like Wally Cox, but he also was the same size and even built like him. The thought of this small man behind a standard desk brought up the idea of him sitting in Dolly's oversized chair. He figured both of them would be uncomfortable in those situations.

Hooker looked back in the cab. "Box, stay. I'll find you some dry grass later."

Only the single ear twitched to signal the cat had heard him. Box leaned forward a little harder, maybe to get closer to the heat coming out through the vent.

Hooker slid down the side of Mae. He stuck his hand out. "The name is Hooker. What are we looking at?"

"Victor Mayhew. What we have is a very delicate situation. Are you familiar with caustic soda?"

Hooker looked down the jumbled line of mayhem chopped up by more and more work lights being set up. He looked back at the man who looked like he should be sleeping after a long day as an accountant. The only piece missing was the bow tie.

"Other than… it can strip the meat off a bone in seconds rather than hours… no, not much."

"That's probably the most important thing to know. The other is about a hundred yards and some. Over there in the dark are the title flats. In about five hours, the bay water will be at its high point. If one of these tanks were to rupture, the resulting fish kill would stretch up past Alcatraz by early spring. By the end of summer, there wouldn't be anything alive in the bay."

"What about boom barriers?"

The man smiled. "So, you've done this before."

Hooker nodded. "A couple of times."

"Good. I like experience. The barrier trucks are coming down from Richmond. They should be here in the next half hour. Arco is sending down skid diapers as well. We have forty tank trucks coming from all over the Bay Area, plus a pumper. This means we can only clean one car at a time. While waiting for you, we went ahead and surveyed the conditions of the cars. There is one with an expanded weld near the neck. I want to roll it first, but it's number three in line."

"How soon can I get Mae in there?"

"Probably not for another hour or so… I'm sorry… I know you rushed up here from somewhere down south, but there's nothing to do right now but hang tough and wait."

"I was in San Luis Obispo this evening. If it's all the same to you, I'll just get some sleep, but I'm going to call in my assistant. He's the only person I'm going to trust on this."

"That's fine." The man looked around. "If you want, you can park over there near those warehouses. I'll come get you when we can get you in."

Hooker climbed back in the cab and called Dolly.

"Ask him to borrow the Granny car and get up here. Stella can take Candy to school in the morning."

"Got it. Now get some sleep, and we'll talk to you when you know more."

About an hour later, the Squirt crawled in on the passenger side. "Go back to sleep. They still haven't cleared the way through. I just wanted to let you know I was here, but I'm going to go scout along the site. I'll come get you when they're ready for us."

John listened for the mumble or acknowledgment, but only got a couple of low snores harmonizing with the slow lope of Mae's engine.

Quietly, he slid out and closed the door. Putting his hood up on his poncho, he faded into the dark and light misting drizzle.

After talking to a couple of men in white hardhats, he finally found the yellow hat with the VM on the back. "Victor Mayhew?"

The man turned, "Yes?"

The Squirt stuck his hand out. "Squirt... I'm Hooker's, um... consultant."

The man looked at the youth in the poncho. "Son, I don't know who you think you are, but this is an extremely dangerous—"

The Squirt cut him off. "I understand you have three tank cars running fifteen to eighteen tons over the legal limit, which I understand is one-thirty on these rails. Once you go past marker 741, which this engineer was just twenty-two minutes away from doing, it drops to one-fifteen. We have a low-pressure cell settling in, and this nice tropical evening we are enjoying right now is about to get train-wreck ugly. Pardon the euphemism. At this moment, Northern Pacific is only facing a $75,000 fine for each of those rail tankers, and if one splits, the fine will run into the millions before the caustic soda hits the bay. If the CS spreads north into the bay—by four this afternoon, the die-off of the fisheries will extend up past Antioch as the tide comes in." He paused for a moment as Victor Mayhew could only stare at the young man.

The Squirt continued. "Now, you can stick your head up your ass about my age and waste precious time, or you can stop being an asshole and help me do my job. It's your choice.

"Personally, I don't give a shit. Until you opened your mouth, NP was on the hook at a thousand an hour. You just removed any goodwill you might have enjoyed, and we are now standing at two thousand an hour from when you put the call in for us to come save your ass. Now, are you going to help us help you, or did you want to explain to your review board how you hired and wasted the only team who could save the bay and your job... and still got charged five thousand an hour starting from the time your engineer ran this hunk of shit off the rails?"

The man stood with his mouth hanging.

The Squirt gave it the old Dolly five-count and then turned to walk off. "Fine, I'll go find someone who knows what the hell is going on..."

It took Victor almost five heartbeats and the young man covering almost twenty feet before he could find his voice. "Where's Hooker?"

The Squirt only half turned—still negotiating through body language. "I have him working on some other logistics. There is a hell of a lot more going on tonight than your party."

The man thought and looked up into the dark sky. True to the kid's word, the rain was beginning to feel a little heavier. "Fine, let's look at the tankers."

Forty minutes later, the Squirt was directing Hooker as he maneuvered Mae up into a pocket where there were three large concrete bunkers. Set on the top of each bunker was a two-inch-thick steel loop. Originally, the loop was used to crane the bunkers into place. They had been the foundation for one of the log loading cranes used until the late 1950s. It became cheaper to build a smaller mill and rough lumber near the source, and then rail from there. After the timber was no longer trucked and railed, the bunkers were the only parts left standing.

Once the Squirt had seen them, he knew the fourth lay buried in the hillside. The three visible six-foot-high bunkers were only the top third. The other two-thirds were twelve feet deep, and each weighed close to twenty tons. They were perfect for what they wanted.

The two men stood in the rain as Hooker listened to the Squirt. "The smaller car only has a skin about a half-inch thick. She is the one we need to handle gently. This one in front of us is the prom queen with the stretched weld. The flaking paint is about six inches, so the stretch is probably a foot long—eighteen-inch at the most. The good news is she's the prom queen. Her maker mark is Gunderson up in Portland. She's one of the new double walls, and the outside is just under three-quarters of an inch, so we can manhandle her, and she won't whine. The third one with the graffiti on the belly is the lightest of the four, and we can turn her after these two. I think the cables will still reach, but we'll be at the limit if we still want to belay off these bunkers." He jerked his thumb behind them.

Hooker half turned. "And you knew about these... um, things, how?"

"Paper for Maddie last November had some information about the rails and why they run up both sides of the bay. Stanford was running food and people up the peninsula, but he was grabbing logs here from

Oregon and then trucking them out to Pleasanton and the old mill. These bunkers were just part of the research, and there were some old photos of the cranes. I think there's another set about a hundred yards down south of here, but it useless for the fourth car—that one, we will have to snatch straight off Mae. I'm sure Mae is fine with the hundred and forty tons to roll, but it's the cables I'm worried about. You didn't get it replaced last fall, and they're stretched and worn out. Therefore, I figured we would leave it for last. We can take it from close in and do a loop-tie. But it's still the biggest risk."

Hooker looked at him. He studied the kid who had become a man.

The Squirt fidgeted. "What?"

Hooker laughed. "You really told him two grand an hour?"

The face was deadpan. "From when you got the call or cleared San Luis Obispo."

"I wouldn't charge the travel time, and I damn sure don't charge a grand an hour—much less two."

The Squirt looked over the long jagged line of tossed about railcars. "You do today." He looked back at Hooker and winked. "Are we finished screwing around?"

Hooker thought a moment, then put two fingers to his forehead and saluted the kid. "Yes, boss. Let's earn some easy money."

The weather had other plans. There was nothing easy about any of it.

A soaked Hooker looked at the wheel assemblies called the 'trucks.' They had leveraged the first and lighter car back onto the rails, but this one wasn't even close. The lead truck was at least twelve feet away from the rails and cocked.

"Hey, Squirt?"

The kid came around the head of the car. He nodded his jaw up in the dark and then realizing Hooker couldn't see the nod, called out. "What?"

"When we pull this up, she's not going to be even close to the rails."

The Squirt kept coming. "It won't matter. Not only does it not matter about the rails, but also we aren't going to right her completely. The weld stretch is on the downside of the manhole on the top. All we have to do is get the load chemicals down below the stretched weld." He pointed at the valves and pipes running along the underside of the car. "Once we have it done, they have trucks that will hook up to those nipples and suckle the tits until they get almost everything out. When she's empty, the car will only weight thirty-tons with maybe a couple of tons of soda left. From there, they can crane her with ease."

Hooker smirked. "I suppose you have some blocking material coming?"

"Eight to ten trucks with self-loading arms are bringing rail sleepers. They should be here by now." He looked around at the perimeter of the mass of trucks and equipment. "They were coming down from Antioch."

Hooker pointed out through the rain at a tractor-trailer making its way down along the other side. "While you go talk to the driver, I'm going to go put on the spare jumpsuit. This one's soaked."

The kid nodded. "You might think about hitting up one of these rail guys near their trucks. They have the heavy-duty work rain slickers. They don't tear every time you fart in them. I'm sure they'd let us borrow a couple."

Five minutes later, Hooker came back with two insulated jumpsuits, mud boots, and two sets of slightly used rain gear. They took turns changing in the cab of Mae. The warm-up break combined with dry clothes helped. The other critical ration was the hot coffee and sandwiches Hooker was already scarfing down in the backseat of Chet's cruiser.

The Squirt slid in. "We have a savior from the south?"

"Dolly figured Hooker would at least need coffee, and the food is always good. How's it going with the cars?"

Hooker swallowed. "The easy one is done, but we're just starting on the scary one. If we're lucky, we should have it up enough by sunrise for them to start emptying it."

Chet frowned. "Dolly wasn't sure what was in them."

The Squirt swallowed his coffee. "Caustic Soda—highly corrosive and deadly—if we get a spill out here, the fumes alone will require everyone to suit up in re-breathers and protective suits." He took another bite of his sandwich as if he was talking about flipping a Volkswagen back over with a full tank of gas.

Chet looked at Hooker. Hooker duck-lipped his mouth and rolled his eyes up toward his one raised eyebrow. They were both noticing how much the kid had matured in less than a year. Maybe having twenty-eight dimes shoved into you with a shotgun will do that to you.

Chet stayed and kept his distance in his cruiser. He watched the painfully slow dance of rolling the tank car back upright or close to it. The sky eventually lightened. Although filtered through the clouds, which, thankfully, had stopped raining, it still helped everyone to see. The work up and down the wreck site seemed to pick up the pace.

Chet wiggled the last thermos. There was less than a swallow left. He started the cruiser and backed off the outcropping, which had given him the vantage point. Like most highway patrol officers, he knew where he could get more coffee and maybe even some donuts. The sugar would help with the waning energy. Hooker had to be on the back end of at least twenty-four hours—if not thirty-six.

19

COFFEE RUN

Chet placed the three thermoses on the counter. The man in the rumpled white shirt, pants, and apron didn't even blink. As Chet looked over the early morning offering of donuts, the man refilled the thermoses.

"Do you want me to leave room for cream in any of these?"

Chet looked up. "No, thanks… black all around."

The man placed the thermoses on the counter. He reached behind him to a large stack of already made-up boxes. His hand paused, "One dozen or two?"

Chet held up his index finger, and the man swung around with a box. "Are you out at the train or the bank?"

Chet looked up at the man with a frown. "Bank?"

The man rolled one eye at him. Chet realized the weepy eye was glass.

The man tossed his head toward the left. "The feds have been through here all morning. I thought cops ate a lot of donuts and coffee, but you guys can't hold a candle to the feds. They've been grabbing the two-packs and a large thermos load. They tend to go for the fluffy with high sugar while you guys down at the train have been sucking up all of my old-fashioned and cakes."

"What bank?" Chet pursued.

"Actually, it's the transfer station for the Federal Reserve. It's where they take all the money they have to destroy, but also where they deliver out to the banks in the East Bay and maybe down south."

Chet was getting a bit exasperated with the guy's lack of information. "So, what happened over there?"

"Oh, it's been all over the news… "

"I don't have a TV in my cruiser—but I do have handcuffs, a nightstick, and if I need it later, a shotgun, and shovel to bury you." He glowered at the man. "Now what the hell happened?"

The man blinked. "Someone robbed one of the armored trucks. Blew up the floor under it and then blew the back door of the truck. I overheard a couple of the Feds talking, and one guy said it was three pallets of new hundreds. Millions."

Chet wasn't a banker, but he knew the man could only guess at what Federal Reserve pallets looked like. Chet had firsthand knowledge—there was an extra zero stuck in there. He threw a ten on the counter and grabbed the coffee. "I'll be back for the donuts. You know what we're eating."

He strapped the thermoses into the passenger seat then turned the selector on his radio to one of the tactical bands.

"C-C-1-4."

"1-4?" The voice was the day shift. Chet swore silently.

"Karen, is Dolly still there?"

"No, hun… but there is a large blob doing a mountain of paperwork over there in the dark. What can we do for you?"

"This is going to sound strange, but… how many explosions have you guys heard about in the last couple of years?

"Explosions?" Dolly's voice sounded tired and harried.

"Morning, sunshine… yes, explosions. Ones like… what was it… um, Frontier Village. I'm talking about businesses that went out of business—because they had some mysterious freak explosion."

There was silence. Chet watched the traffic with the eye of a longtime officer. The deep cloud cover was slowly burning off or seemed to be. Maybe they would catch a break today at the wreck and not have to work with yuck in the air, just the mud the rain had left.

Chet felt as much as he heard the cruiser's back door open and close. The donut guy never said a word.

"Chet, we think it's maybe about six or seven made the paper. Why?"

"Someone blew the Federal Reserve transfer station up here. I don't think it was the only place blown up last night."

There was dead air for a minute. Chet could smell the donuts, but he started the car instead. Swinging out onto the road, he headed back toward the train wreck.

"Mike at Alonge's mentioned a couple of phone company crews out… In fact, Fremont Alarm has a couple of crews out checking why they had a whole bank go down this morning."

Chet grabbed his mic. "Can you ask Mike the locations and see if they overlay Fremont's dead zone?"

"We'll get back to you."

"I'll put the outside speaker on, but I think we may be taking a break here in the big yellow schoolhouse. The Squirt is here…"

Dolly knew he was talking about tapping into the kid's freaky memory. Anything the kid had ever seen, heard, or read was his for total recall. He also had a strange way of seeing math or geometry. "A good mind is a thing to use."

Chet chuckled. "C-C-1-4, out."

The radio clicked twice as Dolly or Karen double keyed the mic.

Chet pulled up near the giant yellow and blue tow truck. He could see Hooker at the controls and knew the Squirt was around somewhere close. He opened the door and started to get out.

"Oh, my, I smell donuts."

Chet laughed. Turning, he faced the Squirt, deadpan. "Nope, only day-old coffee."

"Uh-huh, and Mae West is a Volkswagen." The kid rolled his head in a shortened zombie roll.

They laughed and pulled the breakfast out of the cruiser. Hooker walked over, and they climbed up into the heat of the cab, exchanging places with an orange streak. Mud or no, Box needed his morning run and dump. The Squirt kept his foot bracing the door open halfway until Box returned.

Hooker sunk his teeth into a donut as he poured dry cat food into the little red bowl. The water bottle was always strapped to the gear shifter and handy for Box to lick the nipple from his place in his own box next to the driver's seat.

With Box taken care of, Hooker sat up. The crack and crunch, along with the deep rumble of purring, were music to Hooker's ears. "Thanks for breakfast, Chet." The Squirt also raised his cup while he quietly chewed.

"Oh, I brought you more than just coffee and donuts…" The man smiled and raised his half-eaten donut.

"What?"

"Just relax. Enjoy the break. It'll all be coming soon."

The radio crackled. "1-4-1?" Chet pointed at the radio with his donut and then took a bite.

Hooker reached over and grabbed the microphone from where it hung behind his head when he was driving. "1-4-1, go." His eyes were fixed on his friend—who ignored him.

"The Fed, the phone work crews, and dark alarms are all in a one-square-mile area. You are a mile and a half away from the center of the dark target zone. The train had derailed twenty minutes before the power, and phone lines went out. Nobody is giving out any information from the Fed."

Hooker looked at Chet and mouthed *fed?*

"Uh, 10-4." Chet was nodding.

"Fed?"

Chet nodded and swallowed. He took a sip and swallowed again. Hooker could see his mind was doing the same thing he was used to seeing in the Squirt.

Chet cleared his throat as his eyes rolled up into his head—looking for the information. "Let me see if I have this all straight. The train derailed. Twenty minutes later—while the police and fire trucks are making a lot of noise and racing here—several phone lines and alarm lines go down at the same time. Meanwhile, someone blew their way into the Federal Reserve Bank and popped an armored truck for several million bucks."

The Squirt choked, "Too much of a coincidence. The odds of even two of them happening on the same day are close to eleven million to one. Not going to happen naturally." The Squirt sipped his coffee and then closed his eyes as he bit into a chocolate-covered old-fashioned.

Hooker watched the kid. Finally, the kid opened his eyes with a sly smile. "That was so much bullshit. You just made up those odds."

The three laughed. The kid raised his mug to his lips. "You don't like my odds… make up your own number."

Hooker thought a moment. "I think for all three to happen together would be in the billions. It all smells rotten." He reached and grabbed the mic.

"1-4-1."

Karen's voice was laughing, "Took you long enough. Dolly's on the phone to them now."

"Fremont PD?"

"Oh, no… she's done with those idiots. She called the governor's office. She decided to start working top-down. I have a call holding for the Assistant Field Director of the FBI for the west coast down in Los Angeles. His secretary was a little snippy, so we're letting him cool his heels before I swap him out for the bozo answering the phone at the governor's mansion this morning."

"How did she get the mansion's phone number—oh, never mind. I'm sure I don't even want to know this story. Tell her we're headed out and are going to go walk the rails. I'm in a betting mood, and I'm willing to lay down good money on us finding something long before those transportation fools catch wind of this."

Hooker hung up and looked at the kid. "Where are the locomotives?"

The kid pointed up the bay. Hooker looked and pointed down. "Let's take a stroll."

He grabbed the long black flashlight from its holder next to the sawed-off shotgun. The kid nodded and grabbed the matching one from the holder on the passenger seat.

Even though it was daylight, it was still overcast. As they piled out of the truck, Chet stepped over to his cruiser. "I'll get mine too."

Forty minutes later, they stood with three officers from the transportation board and four supervisors from Northern Pacific. All eyes were on a small mangling of the wooden railroad ties. All it had taken was probably thirty feet of small explosives to blow out the bedding under the ties, then some explosive charges placed first on the ties where the rails were tied, and then along the outside of the rail to push it in.

Once the width of the rails had been compromised, the locomotive's wheels had jumped the track. Where the heavy wheels dug through the rail, the next dozen had cut the rail in half and started to work on the unsupported ties. A nine-inch square piece of wood cannot support twenty tons of railcar. They were quickly cut and torn apart with each consecutive car derailing. Effectively, the cars derailing at thirty-miles-an-hour had all but destroyed the evidence.

The one man knelt to look closely at where the bright flashlights were shining. He removed his helmet and ran his fingers through his hair.

"I would have never seen that." He looked up at the Squirt as he fingered the helmet with the VM painted on the back. "I've been at this game longer than you've been alive…" He stood and put his hand out. "I owe you an apology, young man. I would say you have earned every bit of the four-thousand an hour you last quoted me. I'll make sure the check gets cut this afternoon when you know all of your hours."

Chet snorted. "And that's why he'll be graduating from the police academy in half the time of the other cadets. The bottom line is—we cannot wait for him to turn twenty-one or lollygag around in school. We need him out here on the street where he can do some good."

Victor chuckled. "You're not even twenty-one?"

"Twenty, sir… and the two is enough."

"Not today, son. Not today. You just took this crap dump out of my hands and gave it to them and the FBI. My wife would insist on the extra. My vacation starts on Friday, and I'm taking her to Paris for our twenty-fifth."

The spare looking man in the blue jacket with the letters NTSB looked hound dog at Victor. "Thanks a lot, Mayhew… you just reminded me… today is my wife's birthday."

"Well, cripes sake, Neal. Just get her something on your way home and tell her it was in the car for a week. I love my sister dearly, but she isn't sharp enough to figure out you forgot a national holiday like her birthday."

Hooker laughed. "So this is a family affair?"

They grimaced and nodded. Then together, they said, "I got him his job." Obviously, this was an old routine.

Victor laughed. "If there was an opening, and he didn't like the politics so damn much, I have a brother with the FBI back in DC."

The brother-in-law laughed. "He's a pansy. He doesn't appreciate our beautiful weather we get to work in." They both nodded and then wagged their heads.

"He's right. Teddy would rather fly a desk for twenty straight hours than be out here in the elements for twenty minutes."

Hooker and the Squirt begged out of further discussion as they still had two railcars to roll. The sun was threatening to break through in the east, but the clouds over the coastal hills were looking darker. Hooker and the Squirt both were eyeing the leading edges of the cloudbank for telltale wisps indicative of the clouds moving their way.

"How did the cables feel on the roll?"

"They were both warm, but not hot. I think we can get this done and be fine, but the last one, we'll need to do a loop pull. But I'm telling you, it's time to get Mae re-wound."

"Yeah, yeah, I know. Things just got a little busy."

"Well, four-thousand an hour will pay for a lot of cable rewinding."

Hooker stopped stunned. His head ground around to look at the Squirt. "Thousand? You told him thousand?"

"He was being a jerk."

Hooker read the kid's face. He could imagine what kind of jerk the guy had been to a mere kid. "Even so, my billing is only eighty an hour on a complicated tow, and one-fifty flat if it goes back to the Fly."

"Well, you heard the man. You can drop it to hundreds, but it's still four hundred an hour. What time did you clear SLO town?"

"Nine-twenty, but I stopped for some pizza and got pulled over by a Chip in Atascadero. I don't charge for inbound."

"This was the only way these could get rolled last night. They needed you no matter where you were at the time. For all they know, you were headed down to Los Angeles to go see what the big deal was about the Sunset Strip. They called—you came. End of story—four hundred an hour. Now let's go earn some paint and fuel."

Seven hours later, Hooker handed Victor a bill under the watchful eye of the Squirt. The man read it through and looked up at the kid.

"You read this over?"

The Squirt nodded.

"You approved it?"

The kid jerked his thumb back over his shoulder at the truck. "It's his name on the truck."

Victor looked at Hooker and then at the truck. Smiling, he looked back at Hooker. "So your real name is Mae West?"

He bent over the checkbook and dashed out a number closer to the Squirt's original statement. He tore it out and tossed the book back in the car. Handing the check to the Squirt, he showed a deadpan face. "I stand by my statement. You both were worth every penny."

The Squirt didn't even look at the check. He folded it and stuck it in his back pocket. The arguing could come later… or not. He stuck his hand out and shook the man's hand.

"Have a great time in Paris. There's a restaurant named Tour d'Argent. It means the silver tower; it's the oldest restaurant in the world. It's probably expensive, but they are known for their duck and the view of Paris. It's probably the best place to take her for your anniversary."

"You've been there?"

"Read about it somewhere. It was Victor Hugo's favorite restaurant, as well as Charles the first."

"…and someday…?"

The kid nodded. "Someday… When I have someone worth taking."

2 0

THEY TOOK HER

Felix gave the woman the pink notice from his box. He tried to look as bored as she did. She shuffled over to a large set of shelves and found the box. It looked like it had been used a few times or had gone a few times around the planet. Felix knew inside the box was a brand new and much sturdier box. However, even the outside box was new—just made to look as worthless as the millions of other boxes in the postal system too worthless to insure. She started to lift it and quickly adjusted her grip. Felix knew it probably weighed at least twenty-five pounds.

She plopped it on the counter, ignoring the fragile stickers. "There you go. Tell your boy to have a happy birthday from me, too."

Felix picked it up, nodded, and walked out. It was not the first time the package came addressed to a made-up son from his made-up grandmother with birthday stickers attached. What adoring grandmother would send some kid twenty-five pounds of cookies?

He placed the box on the floor of the van, went around to the driver's side, and got in. As he started the van, the news came on. The lead story was still the train wreck. Felix knew the next story would be the armored truck heist. The T-shirt at his neck seemed to get tighter.

As he nosed the van into the gravel driveway, he saw Edwina sitting on the front porch. Her face was down in her hands. Her duffle bag of a purse was next to her. There was also a large paper cup with a lid and straw next to her. Obviously, she had been out at some time during the day.

Felix slowly got out of the van. The woman, who normally wasted no time leaving, was now sitting. He could hear her soft sobbing from the driveway.

"Edwina, what's wrong? What happened?"

The sobbing turned to wailing, and Felix confirmed his long-held belief. There wasn't a tooth in the woman's head. Everything in her mouth was pink with dark splotches.

He sat down next to her and waited the hysterics out. It was his experience from mine accidents that, after a few minutes of wailing, a woman who had been crying for an extended time would settle down and would finally be able to talk.

Eventually, the lips began to suck in and out. The blubbering turned to hitched sucking of air and moaning.

"What happened?" He knew it had something to do with Thelma, but he could feel the cowardice in his guts—the last thing he wanted to do was go check a dead body.

"There… there was nothing. Nothing I could do."

"It's okay. I'm not blaming you for anything. I just need to know what happened."

"They came. I… I couldn't… I couldn't stop them." She looked up at him. Her eyes were red like a forest fire sunset. She whispered, "Thems had papers this time."

She rolled up on her one butt cheek and slid the papers out from under the other. Felix was almost certain she couldn't read. These could have been work orders for furnace repair or even his daily delivery logs. She would never know.

He unfolded the four pages. It was a court order from Weld County, Colorado. There were conforming stamps from Contra Costa and Santa Clara counties. They had run him to ground and bracketed him. He read through. Thelma was to be transferred to a locked care facility to wait for medical clearance before transporting her back to Weld County.

He stood. "Edwina, stay right here. You understand? I'll be right back." She nodded, and he entered the house.

He had never thought about not leaving fingerprints, but for some reason, he now didn't touch a thing. The quilt lay puddled mostly on the floor. Only one corner had enough weight to still be on the bed. The blanket lay pushed up against the wall. It lay bunched like a boa constrictor. The tongue was a frayed corner of saliva stained satin. It was all Felix had left of his wife.

"Dan?" The voice was more of a moan than a wail. Felix realized he had been standing, looking at the empty bed and room for more than just a few minutes. It was almost dark.

"Sorry, Edwina. Give me a couple of minutes more. I'll be right there. Don't leave." He rushed to the back door. His hand fumbled in his pants pocket. He stood with his head against the door as he thumbed to the right key and felt the ridges to know which side was up.

The door swung open. Three steps and he stood at one of the older hiding panels. He stuck the key in the crack and used it like a pry. The board bent and then came loose. He reached forward to one of the many bundles stacked in the wall. He knew each bundle was twenty-thousand dollars in twenties and fifties. Each one was an old, untraceable bill. He stood and left the wall open. He knew he would be opening it later, anyway.

He walked out and sat down on the porch.

"Edwina, this is very important. Do you have anyone you can go live with for a while?"

"My husband's old girlfriend." Nervously, she sucked her lips back and forth over her gums.

Felix felt the ground beneath him sway. "Where is your husband?" She had never mentioned anyone before—other than her babies, which Felix knew were stray cats in the back alley or something similar.

"Dead," she blinked.

Felix frowned. "When did he die?"

"After I shooted him."

Felix's stomach took a flop and a roll. He wasn't sure he wanted to go down this road, but he had to know, and now he was glad he had never really interviewed her in the beginning.

"Um…how long ago?"

"Boat maybe ten years or so." Felix sighed.

"What did the police say?"

"Never knowed about it—I jus' buried him in the backyard and moved."

"And where were you living then?"

"Black Water, Mississippi."

"Is that where his girlfriend lives now?"

She snorted and screwed her face up into an ugly rendition of a smile. "No… course not. After we had done buried him and his brother, we lit out of there. She were here for a while, but she don't like the fag and cold, so she live now down Las Vegas way."

"You mean she didn't like the fog."

The woman frowned ugly. Her whole face was loose skin and seemed to move about. "Nah, she like the fog good enough."

"But you said—"

"No, the fag—the queer. The man we live withs. He lacks kissing other mens and thems parts."

Felix felt like he was losing ground. "So if I put you on a bus to Las Vegas, do you think you can find her?"

"Sure. I have her number in my purse if you can dial it." She reached for her bag.

He put his hand on her bag to stop her from searching. "It's okay, Edwina. I just wanted to make sure." He paused and thought a moment. "Listen, your car… is it registered in your name?"

She waved her finger and hand. "The bug? Oh, hell no. I found it one night a few years ago. It had the key in it and so I drived it home. No bodies looked for it, or found it, so I keeps just drivin' it."

Felix got up and went to look at the license plate. Sure enough. The registration was six years out-of-date, and it was an Idaho plate. He had never noticed it with all the mud splattered on and about the body and plate.

Felix wondered if the mud splatter and placement were by happenstance or design. Either way, he didn't care. It was about to become abandoned again. He sat back down on the porch. Edwina had been silently staring with giant eyes at the bundle of money he had left on the concrete.

"Okay, Edwina. I need for you to think real hard. Is there anything at your house you feel you simply cannot leave behind?"

"My..." She started to wail.

"I know—the cats. I'll have them taken care of. Anything else? This is very important. I don't want you to go back to your house. I'm going to take you to the bus station and get you on the bus to Las Vegas and your girlfriend. But I need to know now if there is anything you might think later was important enough to go back for."

The woman sat and rocked. Felix wasn't sure if she was thinking or had gone into shock. Finally, she gently shook her head. "I don't really got much. Jus some clothes."

"Nothing else?"

Her shoulders slumped when she realized her sum total amassment of wealth was basically her purse. "No... Nothing."

Felix brought the four-inch-thick block of money around. "Okay, listen. This is twenty-thousand dollars. This is enough for you to start a new life. If I thought you could do it, I would tell you to go to Mexico, but maybe Las Vegas is good enough. I'm going to put you on the bus. You need to think of another name you want to be. Those men today probably know your real name by now."

She shook her head. "No... no, they don't. My real name is..." she leaned in as she looked out toward the street, "Vesta Conworthy." She sat back and smiled. She just shared the biggest secret she had ever held with this man.

Felix felt the ground under him become a little more solid. He smiled back at her. This might just work. "Great, but you can't be Edwina anymore. They might look for you by that name."

"I had an aunt once I liked. Her name was Bina. I kinda liked that name."

"Okay... Bina, it is. So here's the money. I'll take you to the bus and see you off. Then you never come back here again. Okay?"

"Okay." Her hands started to shake as she touched the money. However, a second later, it disappeared into the bag.

"I need the keys to the car."

"I always just leaved it in the little hole so I knowed which way it go."

The system made sense to Felix. He had watched many miners use similar systems to order their lives.

Felix stood and locked the front door. "I need to move my van. I'll be right back, and we will take your car."

"Okay."

REVENGE

The bus to Las Vegas was a connection through Reno. Felix hoped Edwina, now Bina, would be able to make it to Las Vegas. They had spent the two hours with a bunch of rubber bands, making smaller, more usable bundles of the bills. When Felix suggested hiding some of the bundles in her underwear and bra, she had started to giggle. He realized she didn't own something so frivolous.

They backtracked to the drugstore a few blocks away and bought some underwear and a tight T-shirt-like top. She said it worked. Felix didn't want to know, but she finally looked like she had a female figure—bumps and all.

Felix hugged her when he said goodbye. He felt more like a parent sending a child off to summer camp than getting rid of a witness. Felix never had to kill anyone who wasn't already dying, but he didn't want any loose ends either.

As he drove, he finally let himself get angry. In his soul, he knew Thelma would be looked after better than anything he had ever provided, but it was the taking away from him that made him mad. He knew she was alive, but he would never again touch her arm, hold her hand, or kiss her head goodnight. He would never again be able to tell her how sorry he was for the day at the mine. He would never again just be able to sit in the room and listen to her breathe as she slept.

He went into the garage and brought out the two-gallon can of gas. He shook it. About a gallon and a half... more than enough. He took some rags and the cheap cotton work gloves out of the van. There was a place about a mile away he knew where only kids came, and even then, mostly just on Friday and Saturday nights to drink stolen liquor, smoke stolen cigarettes, and tell stolen stories.

He could see lights ahead. He pulled over to the side. Opening the gas can, he soaked a rag damp and then started wiping every surface he thought Edwina might have ever touched. The doors were open, and yet the car reeked of gasoline. After a few minutes, the car was wiped clean.

Felix drove through the collective of street toughs. He knew what he was looking for. It would be the kid who was the hanger-on. He didn't have enough to be a real player in the club, but he felt if he hung around long enough…

Felix pulled up. The thin, short kid would be perfect. Felix got out, pulling the key from the ignition at the same time. His left hand reached into his pocket and pulled out the two thousand. He walked over to the kid and shielded the kid from the other toughs. He showed the kid the wad of money and then shoved it in the kid's front pants pocket. He grabbed the kid's right hand and turned it palm up. Felix dropped the key in the hand and rolled the fingers closed. "Don't get caught."

Turning, Felix walked off into the night. The crowd behind him was eerily silent as they gathered around the new cool kid. Felix smiled as he walked. He knew a place on the way home that he could get a burrito. It had turned out to be a nice evening for a walk. Tomorrow would be a lot different.

The sun came up in the screened-in porch. Almost all the wood paneling was off the low wall. The amount of money would pose a problem with Felix's travel. No matter how you break it up, six hundred and forty-seven grand was a large package. Felix knew he would have to stash large chunks of the money at places he could have access to at later dates.

He had tried to sleep, but the idea of how *they* had come into *his* home and taken *his* wife from *him* had him back up by two. The wiping down of all surfaces had started with rubbing alcohol and gin. The areas open to the outside, he switched to a mix of acetone and benzene gas. From now on, he would be wearing gloves as he got ready.

Felix stood in the phone booth. "No, Bill, I'm fine… It's my wife who's very ill. No, it doesn't look good for the rest of the week." He looked around at the street while his boss talked.

"Bill… Bill… how much personal time do I have built up? Okay, fine, I'll take the three weeks. Yes, I know how busy we are. I'm one of those idiots out there on the street for ten or twelve hours a day."

A large set of doubles rolled down the road past the gas station. Felix didn't need to hear his boss to know the man was getting mad. But he wasn't getting his way—not today.

"Bill? Bill… I think maybe you need to go out to the dock, put on one of those itchy stupid-looking shirts, and go drive my truck up your ass."

He held out the phone.

"Bill… whether you like it or not, my wife is dying. I'm not going to let her die alone."

Felix let the man run his mouth in a quieter tone.

"She has spacious parietal encephalitis. It means she got hit in the head, and now she's dying. I've lost my wife and the only friend I ever had. I don't care if I lose my job. You can't compete. All I'm asking is for the three weeks off. I doubt she'll last that long, but you know doctors. As soon as I've buried my wife, I'll be back. Then I won't ever need another day off."

Felix looked at the woman in the car with three kids. She needed gas, but the kids needed a minder. Felix missed the days when gas station attendants helped people—especially people like her.

"Bill… Bill, they're calling me. I've gotta go. We'll talk soon." He hung up.

"Hi, ma'am. What kind of gas y'all need, and how much?" Felix calmed down as he pumped the woman's tank full. She'd asked for only three dollars' worth. She had no idea how far her three dollars were going to go in a twenty-gallon tank. While he watched the pump dial turn, he peeled off five hundred-dollar bills and folded them in his right hand.

"Thank you, ma'am—that will be three dollars even."

As she handed him the bills, he pointed at the little girl in the passenger seat. "Those sure are pretty curls there, little girl." As the mother turned to look at her daughter, Felix dropped the money and walked away.

He was around the corner of the building before the woman could come to her senses and get out of the car. Felix knew she would be stuck with the kids instead of being able to chase after the stranger. He hopped over the low fence and walked down the hill into the bushes. He had parked the white van on the other side.

Three hours later, he walked into the mining and hardware supply in Mokelumne Hill. The town was tiny, but it had what every dry gulch and hard rocker needed... dynamite or the fixing to make your own explosives.

"Hey, Pete. Long time since you worked on the hole."

Felix slipped into his identity of Peter Farnham. "You know how it is, Steve. I have to put in the time working for the man before I get to come up here and throw my life savings down some money pit."

"You still working the drift over by Shingle Springs?"

"Nah. The ore never came back to pencil out, so I'm working an old straight back just southeast of Grizzly Flats. It's around the face from the old Mailbox mine. I figured they stripped the face of the mountain, but I'd be sneaking out the back door. Who knows... and I've got a month to find out if I'm wasting my time."

"Well, what can we set you up with today?"

"How about three hundred pounds of Royal DX, a twenty can of sebacate, and a ten weight of polyiso to start. I should still have some left up at the cabin, but who knows if it's any good. The raccoons tend to like it once they get a taste of it."

"What kind of primers are you looking for?"

"You know I'm old school. I think I have a roll of det left, but how about throwing say, six rolls in and a case of caps."

"Low knock on the caps?"

"Sure, that's fine."

Felix looked around as if he was either shopping or trying to remember something. The next item on his list was highly controlled. "Hey, Steve. Do you got any of the new cutting det cord?"

"The high mag or the phosphorous?"

"Which works best on metal, and which will work on cutting logs?

"You'd want the phosphorous for the wood, but the magnesium can't be beat for metal. Iron or steel?"

"Mostly old steel, but I also have some trees I want to turn into firewood. You can only imagine what I look like trying to drive a chainsaw. It's your worst nightmare."

The man stopped at the door leading into the back. "How much you want of each?"

"How big are the rolls?"

"Two-fifties."

"Hmm... How about three of each, and I can come down next week when I know how much I'll need total."

"We have you on file, right?"

"You'd better… I've been coming up here for how long?"

The man knocked his knuckles on the door jam. "One of these days, you'll hit some serious gold and never go back to that shit hole in San Diego."

"Hey, I'm going to run over to Mabel's and grab some grub. I'll be back in a few."

The man called back from the storage room. "Sure thing. I'll have it ready on the dock."

By shortly after nightfall, Felix was passing back through Pleasanton and rounding third base headed for home. It was a long drive, but a necessary separation from his real life.

He would begin to cook the explosives in the morning, but there was a lot more items on his list to get. This explosion was a lot different from what he would normally do. This one was for revenge.

WORD FROM COLORADO

Sundays were the traditional day for rest, family, friends, and food —or as Manny put it, the Four *F's*. Only, for him, it was family, friends, food, and fun. Somewhere down deep in the man, he missed the days of standing hip to hip in the kitchen with Stella. The giant brick barbecue on the patio was his to command. As Stella and Dolly would say, it was a testosterone reality. The more men knew about barbecues, the less they knew about the controls on a stove.

There had been parties as intimate as just Manny, Stella, and Hooker. Then again, the house had seen over four hundred people, before the police and fire department showed up for Stella's birthday party with a live band they'd arrested the night before. The drunk and disorderly charges were lost when the band agreed to meet their van at a private party.

The neighbors gave up when the police told them there were no officers available to go settle a noise abatement problem. They were told half of the night force was at a riot in the Almaden Valley. The neighbors knew which riot it was, and finally pulled on their clothes and went to party with the Romero family until dawn. Sunrise was about the time Manny stoked up the barbecue and laid a large steel plate down to become the griddle. Three not-so-drunk firefighters eased Manny aside and told him this was what the fire department was expertly trained for.

They had raided the last of the giant larder, and Stella was Queen Bee for the day. Many at the party had never been there before, which meant they did not know about the larder she had started for them and others for when they were in need. That day, Stella gained hundreds of more volunteers for her giant canning fest, which would run for three months as food became available.

It was also the first time Hooker realized just how big of a family he had fallen into. He just didn't understand he would become the center the family would grow and orbit around.

With Hooker usually waking up around three in the afternoon, Manny and Stella's clock had also shifted. The afternoon meal was usually break-fast for Hooker and some snack or meal for Stella and Manny. The days flowed with whatever was up. What never flowed into the house were phone calls.

With Manny retired from the police force because of his injury years before, the two parents' lives rolled with the punches of Hooker's life on the days or nights he was encamped at the Hacienda Romero. Same as during Manny's career, a phone call was hardly ever a welcome event.

When he worked the streets, and he was home, it would mean over-time or to come fill in because something had gone horribly wrong. When he was at work, it only meant Stella needed to grab her purse and head for the Valley Medical Center where they'd taken him.

On a Sunday morning at eleven after ten, no good could come of the phone ringing.

Stella's heart clenched.

Manny rolled his head over and looked at the offending piece of plastic and electronics. Even though it was his favorite weapon or tool, it had rung before he wanted to use it.

His right arm flopped out next to the wireless handset resting in its charger. He looked at Stella. Her eyes burned back at him. They both held their breaths as he scooped up the handset and brought it toward his ear. On the way, his thumb pushed the green button.

"Romero."

Stella watched him carefully. He rarely reacted. There were tragic times she almost had to beat him to get him to tell her what was going on.

"Uhum… how bad?"

She watched him talk with his eyes closed. His voice was dull.

"Did he actually use the word critical, or are you…?"

Stella picked up her coffee mug. She looked at the cold dregs left in the bottom half. She hated wasting good coffee—but this may be one of those times when she didn't mind.

"Well, I don't think I would use a siren or lights… it could make things worse…"

Stella started to rise. This conversation had just stepped back at least fifteen years when Manny worked the streets. Detectives never used lights and sirens. She sat.

"I think it's time to bring in the commander on this. Just a minute, Danny…" Manny laid the phone on his chest. Rolling his head toward Stella as he opened his eyes, he asked. "How are we set for eggs?"

"Manny Romero, I am going to skin you alive." She pointed. "Is that Danny Sweets?"

She rose, and he smiled softly as he held out the phone. She took the phone gently but with pure threat in her eyes.

She put the phone to her ear. "Hello, Danny." She closed her eyes. "Is your mama home, or are you two just latchkey kids?"

Manny could hear the big man on the other end of the line laugh… then obey the silent command.

"Tilly… What in Hades are these men-children trying to cook up? I love you dearly like a sister, but I was lying here making wonderful sweet love to my man when your boy decided it would be just wonderful to call his extra mama…"

The two giggled as she carried the phone into the kitchen. Stella knew she would need more coffee.

"No, I think we're pretty low on almost anything. I was just going to whip up some gruel and slop it onto some trencher boards and call it good."

Manny loved hearing her talk to Sweets' mother, Tilly. They were more alike than Stella was with her blood sister, Dolly.

"You figure the menu and get what we need, and we'll see you three about two or so. Hooker is not going anywhere this evening. I need him and the Squirt down in the barn to move some pallets of canned goods around. I have three care vans showing up at nine tomorrow morning."

She listened, and then again noticed a note she had left yesterday for Hooker. "Honey, I just remembered something. We have a few others coming. Make it four or five more, I think the men are going to do the man thing, but Candy is here, and Willie will bring Hank, so there's plenty of girl stuff. Maddie can choose for herself which room she wants to be in."

Manny pulled himself up. Things just got interesting.

"We'll see you about two-thirty-ish." Stella hung up as she walked back in and placed the phone in the charger. She returned to her place on the long side of the giant couch and sat down. She sipped her coffee as she found where she had left off in the paper.

Manny just sat and stared at the paper she had between them. The silence was enough. Finally, she couldn't stand it and folded down the one corner.

The right eye showed, and Manny started. "Willie, Hank, Maddie… this slipped your mind?"

"And Chet and one of those guys from up at Moffett… I think he's a captain or something."

"Captain John Trask, the explosives expert?"

She moved the corner of the newspaper back up. "See, you're already up to speed. Brunch is at three."

WITH ALL FOUR leaves installed and turned sideways, the table extended out into the vestibule. The thirteen were comfortable around the table, which fully extended, could fit sixteen. When Stella ordered the table to match the size and look of the gigantic front doors, Manny thought she had slipped a gear. In those days, they thought they didn't know fourteen people to invite over. Between his work and Stella taking care of those in need, they never found the time or reason to gather in many people—even though they had designed the house around entertaining large groups.

After Hooker had become a fixture and Manny retired with a bullet to the spine, there seemed to be a pent-up bucketful of reasons. This close family was only one reason.

"Now, Stella, you just quit your Jack-in-the-box jumping up and down. I've got the coffee covered." She reached across the table as if to cover Stella's hand with hers. Between the wide table and both women possessing well-endowed chests, it was more of a gesture than a real reach out.

Stella settled back down and watched Tilly. She could see the devil twinkling in those eyes, even if the face was relaxed into an almost sanguine deadpan.

"Now there… doesn't that just feel better?" But Stella pointed behind her at the coffee carafe.

Tilly nodded as she settled even deeper into her seat. "Uh-huh, I've got this." Without breaking eye contact, she continued. "Danny, sweetheart…"

The man jumped up with a smile as if he had been waiting for the request he knew was coming. Tilly smiled and nodded. Stella quietly jiggled with laughter. Sweets hung his head down onto the back of his propped-up hand. He heard it coming for the last twenty years. His mama was Queen Bee. What Sweets could do, he did. Everything else was on Danny. Even with Sweets' blindness, he knew his brother did it with grace, a smile, and looked good doing it—whatever she asked.

Sweets raised his head toward where he knew the Navy captain was. "So the bombs were—"

Dolly cut him off. "Sweets, honey… not at my table. After you men have enjoyed the company of us ladies, you can go into the office and speak of the crudities of this world all you want. Even the swear jar doesn't apply in the man room if the door's shut. But here, at this table—my table—only things of pleasant and kindness are spoken about."

"Yes, ma'am." Even Sweets didn't have to have sight to know she had spoken with a warm yet firm smile. Sweets knew his Queen Bee.

Maddie cleared her throat as she placed her carefully folded napkin on the table. "How do you like the Granny car in the rain, Candy?"

"It's noisy when it rains hard. I can barely hear the radio."

Maddie and Willie both frowned. "But the Dart is radio delete. It doesn't have a radio." Hooker and the Squirt laughed. Candy had delivered the best punch with a completely innocent face. She was definitely learning to fit into the fighting ranks of the family.

Sweets got the joke but wanted to continue the subject. "Don't you have to be sometimes driving after midnight?"

"Yes. Sometimes we shadow the swing shift at the hospitals. They're the most informative about patient care. As we get people ready to sleep for the night, many need drug doses, narcotics for sleep, pain meds, and diaper changes. The difficult ones with dimes in them just need to have their pulse taken and heads examined."

Chet snorted. "Careful there, little nursey. We have you surrounded."

Candy grew big eyes. "Ooo, spoken with five bits of wisdom…" The table laughed. Hooker and the Squirt had each two dimes and some pieces, where Chet only had some pieces still floating around in him.

Candy turned back to Sweets. "To answer the question you were really asking, Hooker got me a little battery radio, so I could listen to my favorite disc jockey after midnight. I think his name is Wolf Man Joe or something."

The table roared at Sweets' expense.

As the noise settled down, Sweets mumbled clearly, "Yeah, I think that's the show Danny listens to back there with the engineer."

The table erupted with laughter as they all rose to clear plates and get ready for the second part of the day. Cooking would be in the kitchen, and bombs would be dropping in the office. Maddie took the easy way out and chose the man-talk. Hank was always up for the kitchen. Everyone knew it was a fair exchange.

Not everyone would fit in the office, so they opted for Candy's front room in the apartment built in the basement just off the three-car garage. Instead of taking Manny out in the heavy rain, Hooker pushed his empty chair down the secret stairs while Manny clung to the large back of Danny. Hooker knew Manny was well under a hundred-twenty-pounds— as the lower half had atrophied.

Hooker started the coffee percolator in the small kitchenette area. Chairs were brought from the storage room across the garage as people found places to settle in.

"Before we get to the explosives, let's cover what we got from Colorado. Chet, you spoke with the sheriff out there?" Manny rolled forward on his forearms—to adjust his attention.

"Yes, at length, actually—the guy was born and raised in the house he lives in. He is the third generation to the area and the only one who didn't go into the family business of mining." Chet looked at his fingernails and smiled. "He said even as a kid, he liked his fingernails clean."

The CHP captain opened a thin manila folder and looked at his notes. His eyes scanned the pages until he was oriented.

"To understand what we're dealing with today, we need to understand the father—Helmut Lysander." Chet flipped back a few pages. "According to immigrations, he came to America, running away from Hitler in 1936. He was young and knew explosives. He approached the American team at the Olympics and asked for asylum. Later, he worked as a cannon charge expert for the Pacific fleet in Pearl Harbor. After the attack, he moved, along with many others, to Alameda, and then eventually, down to Long Beach in California. He spent the rest of the war shuttling back and forth from Long Beach and San Diego's North Island. After the war, he moved to the mining areas of Colorado and worked as a…" Chet laughed. "This has to be wrong… but it says 'powder monkey.'"

Captain Trask and the Squirt both at the same time, "It's right." They looked at each other. Trask held his palm out to the kid.

The Squirt nodded and offered the explanation. "This really is in the Navy's wheelhouse—as it's an old naval term. Back in the heyday of sail and mass destruction of beautiful sailing ships, the powder monkey—or powder boy—was a small boy who shuttled gunpowder from the hold to the cannons. Later, the term was applied to someone who worked with explosives. They were also known as blasters."

Trask smiled and nodded with a satisfied look on his face. "And you know this why?"

The Squirt nodded the top of his head in Willie's direction.

Willie squirmed a tiny bit. "Well, when we started working with you on the big bang thing, Maddie thought a little research into naval explosives would be in order. So when the Squirt was free to move around in a library, Maddie turned him loose."

The Squirt added in, "It was very interesting to find explosives—well, firebombs at least, dated all the way back to the Phoenicians and the Henweighs." He waited with a deadpan face.

Trask frowned, but he wasn't going to get caught in his lack of knowledge. "And what's a Henweigh?"

Hooker snorted as Willie answered the old gear-head joke. "About two to three pounds."

The room groaned.

Sweets still had his face down in his hand. The thumb and forefinger were pinching the bridge of his nose. New to the workings of these campfire meetings to hash out information and see what everyone is thinking, he wasn't sure if he had a place in the discussion. Danny rested his hand on the younger brother's shoulder and leaned over. "Are you okay, man?"

Sweets shook his head but sat up. "What I'm hearing is this man comes to America with valuable knowledge. Then during the war effort, we give him even more knowledge. This man has a son, whom I assume went into the family business... so he buys explosives and blows things up. Am I up to speed here?"

Trask and Chet both grimaced. Trask took the lead. "Not exactly—but you have the basics. If all he did were to purchase five hundred pounds of dynamite, we'd have a way to track the sale. However, this man has knowledge of not only how explosive materials work, but also how to make them the way he wants them to work. In the pharmacy world, these kinds of people are called compounders. They take a little of this and a touch of that combined with a smidge of other and pretty soon, you have a drug nobody makes commercially. This is what the man can do."

He paused to make sure this sank in before going on. "Let's say you have a case of eighty-percent dynamite. You put it under a Lincoln Towncar..."

Danny rumbled. "Make it a Cadillac."

Manny laughed. "Just don't tell Stella."

Trask massaged his face. He knew he was in a room full of car guys. He looked over at Maddie.

Maddie smiled. "Ford LTD. It's essentially a wannabe and weighs about thirty-seven pounds lighter, but with a crap engine."

Trask laughed. He now knew who was probably the expert in the room... or in this case, the mistress of knowledge. "Okay, we have this puke green old LTD and a case of dynamite." Everyone nods. "We want to make the car blow or be thrown forty feet in the air. The case of dynamite will get it to about thirty-seven, but it isn't forty. This guy knows how to mix chemicals he can buy, semi-unrestricted, to make the green lemon reach forty feet. Not forty-two and not thirty-eight, but forty. Which... is the real reason why this guy is so very scary. He knows what to do.

"We now know he blew the entire guts of the main building at Frontier Village. The glass blew out, but nothing collapsed. Well, until a little shaker a few days later. We also know he wiped the walls of the hardware store clean and didn't break a single window. He retarded the explosion and redirected the concussion. Then there's the floor of the Federal Reserve transfer station. He placed fifty-some charges which cut the floor out from beneath the armored truck. Then he blew the back doors in such a way as to take the doors off but left the sides of the truck in essentially normal condition. They'll only need to weld on new hinges. Oh, and did I mention when the doors blew? They were sucked out of the truck and thrown to the two sides, so they were out of the way for a forklift to take the pallets of money?"

Sweets held up his two hands in surrender. "I get it. I get it..." His voice trailed off.

Hooker knew the look. "What have you got, Sweets?" The look was when the man had tapped into his other sight and didn't know where it fit in.

"There is a truck..."

"Yes, he blew it up."

"That was last week... too small. This one is larger. Delivery van... square..."

Five stomachs in the room churned, knowing the visions Sweets sees —are somehow true.

23

THE DELIVERY VAN

Felix stood at the back end of the delivery van. His trained eye measured the long cavity of the cargo area. The van was rated to carry more than ten thousand pounds of newspapers. He knew the load he would put in the van would only fill the cargo area about six feet deep and weigh much less than a load of newspapers. The only problem was the newspaper's name painted on the sides and back door.

He turned toward the balding man in the cardigan sweater. "Eight-hundred, you said. How does it run? I have to drive all the way to Texas with the load."

The man scratched his head and lied. "Oh, no problem there. They just took her off the line, and she was the main truck down Salinas' way."

Felix looked at the rust edging along the wheel wells and anywhere the metal ended. It was obvious to him this truck had sat idle for a few years. He thought about sticking the liar in the back of the van and burying him in the fertilizer he would have to pick up soon. He handed the bills to the man in exchange for the keys.

"You'll need to twiddle with the gas a bit to get her started. These Detroit engines are kind of fussy that way."

Felix didn't even look at the man. He now knew the man was praying the truck would start. He probably had never seen the truck even run.

Rolling his eyes and closing his eyelids, Felix pulled open the door and stepped up into the stand-up driver's area. He pulled down the jump seat and sat. He looked for the keyhole.

"I think it's over there on the right."

Felix found it. He pumped the gas twice and turned the key. The battery had enough power to crank the starter, and in a few heartbeats, the engine caught and coughed into some likeness of life. Felix figured it would live for as many miles as he needed it to.

He waved at the bald man who was counting his money. Felix didn't think about it. The money came from another twisted dealer and another shady deal. The seamy underside of the world wasn't Felix's to clean up. His mind was more biblical—they had taken his wife and his reason for living. The extra money from his explosive work had started as a means to retire. After the accident, it became a means to keep his wife with him and to provide for her care—something Felix felt the system had never done —care.

The large van rattled down the forgotten highway. The faster interstates and freeways produced many such pockets of long-forgotten culture and civilization. As the world went zipping by a mile away, the calmer, quieter old road wound between the mounds of small hills, straightened through the meadows and pastures, and wiggled through the groves of trees. Tucked here and there were former homes—now just so many boards waiting for a strong windstorm to scatter what was left of lives and dreams.

Felix eased the step-van onto the abused gravel approach to the battered Atlantic Richfield gas station. The metal skin was showing signs of a metropolis of rust under the faded paint—cancer under the makeup of an old whore. The three windows remaining stood cracked and sprawled from a former neighborhood kid's BB gun. The surrounding trees stood shriveled from the years of drought. The dry had only been good for the mesquite, which survived more from the humidity in the sea air than anything in the ground. The recent winter rains, sparse as they were, had washed the leaves, adding some darker green.

Felix stepped down from the van and walked to the new lock he had installed a few years before. He cupped his hand under the lock as he lifted it. The penny trapped there by the weight of the lock—dropped into his hand. The old station with its two work bays sat tucked into a pocket, keeping it out of any serious wind. Over the years, the penny never dislodged from any of the powerful storms ravaging the Bay Area. The low hills protected the small valley from the rage of any storms, but also prevented much of the rain from reaching the surrounding trees and ground.

Felix rolled the door up on the second bay. The rough rumble startled a sparrow, which flew out from under the small metal eaves where it had found a rust hole large enough to nest in. Felix smiled knowingly as he watched the bird fly away. The Bay Area was just warm enough that the small birds did not migrate with the winter. They just hunkered into smaller holes and wintered over. Thelma would have said they know where to seek out a place where the love is just closer to them.

As he walked back to the van, he looked up-country. Through a sparse smattering of trees, one could see a small clearing—if there were enough rain, it would be a small meadow.

Felix stopped at the van door. The meadow in his mind was decades before and a thousand miles away. The young girl had been wearing a yellow dress. Her legs churned as she ran through the new high mountain flowers. Tiny blue blooms speckled the low grass of the sloping meadow. Yellow buttercups washed like tiny rivers cutting through the miniature grasses. A single flower would start the meandering stripe of yellow and flood into thousands as they ran like a stream of butter, and then they would peter out to a single flower—and then they were gone.

A seven-year-old Felix stood in the hard-nailed shoes marking him as an immigrant. His shorts were leather lederhosen with integrated braces and a small placard across the chest. Only the white shirt was a nod to being in America. A little girl with long blonde hair glowing in the sunshine spun and ran like one of the angels his grandmother had told him about. He knew they were standing on a very high mountain, so they must be closer to his grandmother's heaven than the adults thought.

The girl spun with her arms outstretched. Her hair floated in a slower arch but nearly touched her outstretched trailing hand. Her circling the meadow finally drew her near to Felix.

"Vas ist dein name?" He asked her name.

The little girl spun one more time and stopped. She looked at the funny boy in the shorts. "You talk funny."

"Wie ist dein name?" He wanted her to say more. Her voice sounded like the tinkling of the tiny harp hanging on the back of their front door. When the door opened or closed, the little balls on strings played the harp by knocking on the strings.

The girl took another step forward and pointed to the flowers painted on the placard crossing his chest from suspender to suspender.

"Those flowers are pretty."

"Wer bist du?" Who are you?

She touched the tiny blue and black flower on his chest. She looked into his eyes. "I know where that flower is." She took his hand. "Come on. I'll show it to you."

He followed her—and never let go.

Until they took her away from him.

His face darkened as he stepped up into the van. Putting it in gear, he eased the Ford step-van into the garage bay. He was aware of the tight clearances the large square shape of the commercial truck created. When the nose of the van was about two feet from the narrow workbench, he stopped. Stepping down, he moved toward the back of the van to check the clearance between the back and the door. Felix knew he would need at least two feet. He eyeballed the distance from the back of the bumper to the metal meet-plate where the door locked down to... the three feet would be more than enough.

He returned to the cab and turned the engine off. Habit had him close the van's door. Walking to the large roll-up entrance, he pulled the chain, drawing it down. He gazed through the trees as the door rumbled down. In a moment, the metal severed his vision of the field and the memory. The memory and the woman had been removed by a system with no heart or compassion. Like his father, Felix never rose to anger. It only seethed in his gut as his mind stepped through the paces of what was needed for revenge.

Felix looked at the large empty metal cylinder in the corner. It would take hours for the tank to reach full pressure. Felix ran his hand over many areas of the van's body. He knew he had at least a day of sanding to do. He could only work in the daylight. Any light at night would draw attention to the old abandoned gas station, as well as to him. He flipped the circuit breaker and heard the compressor start to hum within the insulated box he had built. Under normal conditions, sound suppression is never used. It overheats the compressor, and after a short while, the compressor motor dies, or the compressor cylinders overheat and seize.

Felix rechecked the stacks of sanding disks for the pneumatic sander. The sanding wouldn't have to look professional, but the job did have to have a certain finish to it to pass casual scrutiny. His mental checklist had him kick the new five-gallon can of acetone and tip back the four gallons of paint. The paint was enamel house paint for trim but flawlessly mixed to match the needed look. Felix's eyes passed over the two boxes of other supplies, as well as the valuable roll of white paper containing layout drawings with small holes pricked along the lines.

Felix walked back to the far corner and out the small door. Turning, he locked up. Walking to the second bay door, he picked up the large lock that was painted to look old—snapping it shut in the hasp. Reaching into his left pocket, he drew out the penny and slipped it behind the lock. It stayed.

Straightening up, he glanced back at the trees. The meadow now hid in the freshening gloom. Felix knew in his heart—the important meadow was now gone forever. With a drooped face, he turned back south and walked out to the road. His home was a couple of hours away walking, but the Volkswagen, now painted tan, was only a mile away. He would be back in the morning.

24

WAKE UP THE NEIGHBORS

ooker had been mildly aware of a moving van across the street sometime during the last few weeks. He wasn't certain if it was about moving stuff out or if there was a new neighbor. Either one would come to surface only when Stella knew she had his attention and would remember what she was saying. Five-forty in the morning after hauling a smashed bobtail down to Salinas was not the time. Because of the emergency work on the 101 around Prunedale, Hooker had taken the long way home by means of Santa Cruz and up over the 17 to Saratoga. At the crest, Dolly had asked him to take a tow for Central Tow going to Daley City. The miles had taken their toll, and he was ready for a fluffy pillow. Even Box was moving slowly at the end of their day. The cat had taken a paused stop on the gas tank before jumping to the ground. At three years old, Hooker knew age hadn't stopped the large cat—it had just been a long day.

Hooker dropped to the ground and turned to close and lock the door. He ran his hand over the new paint. The enamel was smooth, but he knew the clear coats would be even smoother when they were all done. It was just a matter of finding the time to schedule the week or so of paint.

Hooker turned at the sound of Box growling. The mangled cat didn't have a normal voice box of a cat. His growl was more like Hooker missing a shift and the gears clashing in the transmission. It was more of a series of chopped growls instead of one long, drawn out growl. The cat stood stiff as he looked intently at the neighbor's front yard.

Hooker knew the neighbor had recently installed a doggie door for their young yellow Lab named Mike. The dog had the run to relieve himself in the early morning.

"Box… Leave Mike alone."

The sound of two dogs growling ended in yelping and a whine—Box exploded. The orange streak was almost impossible to follow with the eye. Hooker spun and started running—he knew this would not end well and would require his hand in the fight.

The mass of fur was more dark brown and black than the yellow of Mike. Hooker hadn't seen a new German Shepherd in the neighborhood. He glanced over at the dark house across the way as he ran.

The orange missile hit the mass of fur. Even moving in a whirling mass, Box had targeted the interloper. The first hit looked to be only a glancing blow. Hooker was sure what was tossed from Box's mouth was a dark brown and black ear. Box landed, turned, and aimed. A split second, and he sprang for the second hit. This time, he stayed in the mix.

Hooker stopped. He could see Box had his mouth sunk into the large dog's remaining ear. His front paws, the size of fifty-cent pieces each, were on each side of the head with claws anchored into the face just behind the eyes. Box's body was a machine. The hind legs were a blur and working on fur—still connected to chunks of skin. Pieces of the large dog flew out behind Box like a lawnmower throwing grass.

The large dog shifted from attacking the young Labrador to defending itself from the unseen demon. It threw its head from side to side to dislodge the cat. Once free, it could attack. Except the orange demon was Box.

The cat had stripped the entire back and neck of fur. Box bunched at the head. With a raking upward sweep of the front paws, he peeled the face from behind the eyes and into the ear holes. As Box released the ear from his mouth, he continued into a forward flip and landed five feet away from the large dog still straddling Mike. Box crouched and waited.

The low growl had turned to a chuffing Hooker had only heard twice before. Box was not going to let this dog live.

The dog hesitated for only a heartbeat and then sprang. As he came in from the top, Box charged from underneath and then did a backflip. The dog tried to respond by arching as it landed. Its face came in and was within its defensive front legs. Box was waiting.

The dog's lower jaw landed in Box's mouth. Hooker could hear the teeth grinding into the jawbone as the large paws reached expertly into the eye sockets. Both eyeballs exploded at the same time. Box's powerful hind legs shredded deep through the soft neck. The sound of the dogs howling seemed to stretch for miles in every direction and then snapped back to a wet boiling as the dog collapsed.

Less than the three racing heartbeats of Hooker's, the fight was over. The large dog lay heaving. Its last breaths gurgled through the bloody mass that had been its throat. The large mangled dog was incapable of even whimpering. The mass lay heaving on the concrete like so much half-ground hamburger.

Box stood over the mass and then raised a leg and pissed.

Hooker turned back to his truck. He returned with a short pipe, usually only used as a cheater extension for the four-way star lug wrench. It was now a tool of euthanasia. He looked up for Box.

Box was licking and checking his friend and neighbor, Mike. The young dog had suffered only a few bites before the avenging missile had struck. Hooker didn't want to think about what could have happened if they had stopped to get another call or just taken a little longer. He thought about Uncle Willie's favorite saying: *There are no accidents in this universe; things are meant to happen.*

Hooker looked at the large body. He looked around in the growing light of the early morning. There was no evidence of a collar. He felt around what remained of the neck. There was no hollow even suggesting a collar. It was not uncommon. Even Box didn't wear a collar. But then again, Box was Box and not one of the foo-foo cats living down the street in one of the big houses.

Hooker looked Mike over. The young Lab was lying stretched out and enjoying the open administrations of his secret friend. "I'll wake your dad in a few minutes, Mike. I need to handle this first." He pointed to the body of the dog, which was well over a hundred pounds. Hooker knew a dog this size would not go unnoticed in the neighborhood for more than a day. He stood and walked across the street.

Hooker stood at the door and pushed the button again. He could hear the set of obnoxious chimes ringing in probably the hall of the house. He thought about them and chuckled silently, knowing if Stella had ever installed something so ridiculous, Manny would have shot them the second time they chimed. Luckily, they all had the same taste in their door announcement. There was an eight-pound rot-iron knocker on the giant doors of Hacienda Romero.

Hooker saw a face peek out of the tall window next to the door. The man opened the door. Hooker took in the whole picture. The fuzzy pinkish bathrobe, the fuzzy light blue slippers, and the small poodle dyed pink with light blue ears. Hooker didn't have to see to know the tail was also blue to match the ears and blue pom-poms shaped at the tiny feet.

The man's comb-over was standing almost straight up. He blinked, which didn't help the look of the owl-like face. "Yes?"

Hooker coughed the laughter out of his throat and pulled his best deadpan face. "Um, sorry to wake you, but there was a serious dogfight…"

The man was horror-struck. "Oh no… Mr. Puddles is strictly an inside dog."

"Yes, I see it now. It wasn't a dog I recognized—and with you being new to the neighborhood, I thought I'd better check."

The man frowned, which did not help with the look of his face with the large hooked beak of his nose. "And you are…?"

A female voice whined from somewhere back in the house. Hooker figured from a warm bed. "Who is it, Bill, and what do they want at this hour?"

The man's face slumped, and he rolled his eyes. Hooker could see the long-suffering familiarity etched in his features.

He stuck his hand out. "My name is Hooker. I live in the large hacienda across the street with Manny and Stella Romero."

The man offered him a limp, dead fish of a hand. "You must be the owner of the big yellow noisy truck."

Hooker knew down deep he and this couple would not become the best of friends. "Yes, sir. It's my living, and I try to keep things as quiet around here as possible. I work nights and usually gone from late afternoon until the morning."

The man was already closing the door. "Well, just be mindful. You have neighbors now."

Hooker crossed the street steaming.

He knelt next to the young yellow Lab—still being licked by Box. "How are you doing, kid? Can you walk? Want to go back in?" Hooker looked at the area still oozing a little blood near where the neck met the shoulder. "Come on, Mike… Let's go wake your daddy up."

For the second time, Hooker stood pushing a button at a door. This time, thankfully, the bell was the old-fashioned dingdong. Hooker smiled. He thought ya gotta respect a guy who is a dingdong and proud enough to show it.

The door swung open, and Ray stood in the doorway with nothing but his smile.

Hooker laughed. "Well, good morning to you too, sunshine."

Ray snorted and smiled. "You need a jumpstart, Hooker?" The man was one of the coaches at San Jose City College, but he could moonlight as a stand-up comedian or heckler. He had one of the fastest minds and mouths Hooker knew.

"Nah, I'm good, Ray… but Mike here got attacked…"

"Not by Box, those two little fuckers sneak around here and hang out together."

"Nah, it wasn't Box—for once. The body is out here. I've never seen the dog before." He waved his thumb back toward the street.

Ray started to step out into the tiny courtyard running the length of his garage. Hooker put up his hand to stop him. "Um, Ray…" He waved at the man's privates.

"What time is it?"

"Not quite six."

"Nobody will be up for—"

"I woke the new guy. I'm sure he's fully awake now."

Ray frowned. "Yeah, I met the panty-waist and his harridan from Houston. Give me a minute. I'll be right out."

Minutes later, they stood over the carcass. Ray shook his head. "Nope, can't say I've ever seen this one. What did it look like before the freight train hit it?" He looked over where Box was still taking care of the young Lab.

"Like a very large German Sheppard, but with all the parts in the right places."

"Hmmm…" The man thought with his braced arm and hand to his chin. His lips were screwed into a prune. "Looks more like German sausage now."

Ray looked down the street, and Hooker could tell he had just gotten serious. It was like a switch the man threw back and forth.

"Give me a few minutes," he said and took off running in a lazy loping way. Even though it looked almost like he was running in slow motion, Hooker could see he was eating up serious ground. He turned into the pinkish house at the crest of the hill. A few minutes later, he returned with another person in a bathrobe walking along beside him. They were talking animatedly. As they got closer, Hooker could see longer, dark hair in a ponytail.

"Hooker, this is Dalia—like the flower. She's Mike's personal girlfriend."

The woman smiled as she stuck out her hand. "Glad to finally meet the famous son of Manny and Stella. I've seen your truck, and I've heard some wild stories…"

"Don't believe a word of them—they're all true." Hooker smiled and shook her hand.

"Is it true about getting shot up by the killer last year?"

Ray snorted. "If it's change you want, Hooker has… what, about two or three dimes still in you?"

"Two and a half dimes…"

Ray pointed to the dead dog. "What do you think, Doll?"

She knelt down and was not hesitant to push and move the head. "I think he got into it with a mountain lion." She started to look up at the men and then noticed the twenty-plus pounds of Box still working over an almost purring Mike. "Oh."

Ray chuffed. "Doll, meet Box. Just don't try to shake hands with him." He looked at Hooker and pointed at the carcass. "This took how long?"

Hooker thought about how much time. "Three, maybe four seconds—five seconds would be tops."

The vet slowly rose as she pulled her robe tighter. "Alone?"

"Box doesn't need backup. Last year I watched him take down a full-grown man in less than two."

"Killed him?"

"If I had let him…"

She thought for a few heartbeats. "I don't think I want to be his vet."

Hooker smiled. "He's only needed one vet, who is Connie over at South County Services. She saved his life three years ago—and he's never forgotten her. When he walks in and jumps up on the counter, all the others clear the room. Even I wouldn't be allowed to hug him the way she does." He nodded at the carcass. "Have you've seen this dog around?"

"Seen this around? Yes. Dog... no. This is what is known as a Kai-dog. A dog runs away and gets knocked up by a coyote. The litter is a straight cross between those two, but when a pack produces generations, you get all the strong traits of the more powerful dogs." She knelt and rubbed back the fur. "This hair shows the undercoat of some large winter dogs like Newfoundland, Saint Bernard, Husky, Great Pyrenees and a few other breeds which all run well over a hundred pounds. Cross them with other dogs and the small forty or fifty-pound coyote, and you get a powerful wild dog like this. My guess is he left the pack to start his own. I've seen him around for the last few months." She stood back up. "My personal feeling is your cat did the neighborhood a favor."

Ray stared at the large dog. "Thanks, Doll." He looked up at her. "Sorry for waking you at this hour."

She opened her bathrobe to disclose the running shorts and T-shirt that said UCD Track. "Are you kidding? You almost missed me. I was heading out to run the hill."

The man smiled. "You run the hill? Shoot, give me a few minutes, and I'll go with you."

"I'll call the county and get this picked up while I wait for your slow old butt. I know I can smoke a tweety-bird from Stanford."

Hooker held up his hands. "I'm out of this fight. Dalia, it was nice to meet you, and thank you for taking care of this."

"Please, everyone calls me Doll. My last name is Hause." She smiled.

Hooker chuckled. "Okay, Doll, it is." He turned for the hacienda. "Let's go, Box. Mike is plenty washed." He turned back as he remembered the one wound on the neck. The vet was already looking the pup over. Hooker smiled. He liked this woman's style. Obviously, Ray did too.

25

NEW DEVELOPMENTS

The tapping on the door was light but sufficient. Hooker stirred.

Hooker didn't have to open his eyes. He didn't have to look at the clock. He just instinctively knew it wasn't three in the afternoon yet. Somewhere deep in his body, there was a clock that knew certain times, like, at three in the afternoon, it was time to get up. At midnight, the radio dispatch changed from the auto club to Dolly. Ten after midnight and Sweets took his first break in the music to tell you it was KLIV in San Jose—the world's best place to live. One-forty, Dolly will put her feet up on the desk, close her eyes, and wait for the first drunk wreck. Karen says she's even seen her not move anything but her arm to pick up the lollipop microphone to call Hooker. Three in the morning and the first batch of apple fritters hit the hot oil at the Whole Donut—seven days a week. The two people watching the run of the number-one seller among the night shift cops were Ralph and Mai—the co-owners. Four-fifteen and the blinking red light at Monterey Highway and Alma stops blinking red and turns to blinking yellow for the next thirty-four minutes.

Hooker knew it was before noon.

He swung his legs over the edge of the bed and padded into his bathroom. A small sound announced the arrival of Box. Halfway across the expanse of white onyx tile, the deep rattle of the cat's purr started to echo in the room. Hooker's right hand hung beside the toilet. The large cat turned, sitting so the single ear protruded into the knuckles of Hooker's hand—which automatically started to massage it. Hooker thought about the morning's event. "You did great this morning, Box. Sorry about Mike getting bit, but I think it's for the good your relationship is now out in the open."

Hooker flushed and splashed his face with some water. He would take a shower later.

Walking into his dark bedroom, he moved with the confidence of knowing everything was where it was supposed to be. He stuck his left foot down into the boot and followed with the right. Reaching down on both sides of the boots, he grabbed hold of the belt on his pants and drew them up in one movement. Three deft movements later, and they were zipped, buttoned, and belted. He stepped to the closet and drew a T-shirt from one of the hangers. Slipping it on, he stepped to the door. Time from the quiet knock to his opening the door had been three minutes.

He stepped into the hallway. A movement to his right caught his eye. The Squirt was walking out of his room while reading a thick book. Hooker noticed the slight twitch of the head bobbing up, recognizing Hooker's presence. The Squirt was studying. Hooker turned left, and the two zombies headed for the kitchen area.

Hooker looked at Stella standing by the large stone-topped island. Her right hand was pointing back at the office. Hooker changed course, and the Squirt followed.

Manny was at the desk but turned sideways and backed up to the wall. Hooker looked at the couch just inside the door. Chet sat in full uniform.

"Is this an official visit, or are you here to arrest me for all the times I exceeded the speed limit?" Hooker had never seen the man in his official dress uniform. The man was overwhelming with officialdom.

Chet didn't smile at the playful banter. "There have been some developments."

Hooker took a seat in one of the club chairs, and the Squirt closed his book and sat. "The bomber...?" Chet nodded.

"Four days ago, the Department of Human Services received a request for assistance in a seizer by a peer department in Colorado. The Colorado department had been tracking down Felix Lysander and his wife Thelma for over four years. They tracked them to a location in Milpitas."

The Squirt coughed. "Written or phone?"

Chet frowned. "Written or phone, what?"

"The request—did they make the request officially by sending a conformed notice of intent, or was the request made verbally by phone? How the request is made makes a difference."

"They showed up in person."

The Squirt duck-lipped and nodded his approval. "Qualifies as very official..."

Hooker sat back and leaned on the arm of the chair—still not quite awake. "What happened?"

Chet opened a slim folder on the desk. "They took the wife, Thelma, into protective custody. Evidently, she is in a vegetative state and should be under constant care. Five years ago, Felix removed her from the county hospital in the middle of the night and disappeared into the night with her. They had been looking for them since."

Manny rocked forward on his forearms. "Where is she now?"

"Back in Colorado—in a locked ward."

"So the case is closed." Hooker was still wondering why he was awake at... he looked at the reflection in the glass covering a photo taken of Manny, face down in a dark ally. The reflection was of the clock behind his head. In his mind, Hooker reversed the image and came up with eleven-twenty or so.

"No. Well... yes and no. Thelma is in Colorado—that part is closed. We're still looking for Felix for the bombings."

"And I'm awake because...?"

"The people from Colorado said Felix was not known as a hothead or a violent man—other than being someone who plays with explosives. But to their knowledge, he has never killed anyone before..."

Hooker rolled his hand in the air. "But...?"

"Nobody had ever taken his wife away before. So they don't know how he'll react."

The Squirt frowned. "But she was in a hospital before... in Colorado..."

Chet pulled the file toward him and looked at some notations. "Yes, following an accident at a mine where she was struck in the head by a piece of flying rock. She was taken to a hospital and placed on a respirator in..." He pulled the folder closer and then turned a page. "That was in 1968. A year later was when Felix busted her out, and they fled."

"So she had basically recovered."

Chet read through the notes. "No... according to the medical examiner at the time, she was basal responsive. In other words—one step above a coma. She was off life support and could be spoon-fed. The examiner had recommended transfer to a state care facility. Felix took her and disappeared the night before she was to be transferred."

Hooker's voice was from a long way off, and a long time ago. "If she had transferred, he would have lost her forever."

The four digested the observation. The clock on the wall ticked, echoing the deeper tone of the tick in the tall grandfather clock in the other room.

Manny eased cautiously onto his forearms and then settled back. "I think we can assume we're no longer dealing with a rational person." He looked to Chet.

The officer shook his head. "No telling what he's capable of now. Maybe he never killed before, but I would assume now all limiting factors are wiped from the playing field, as it were."

Hooker shifted. "So, what are we looking out for now?"

The Squirt grumped, "Anything and everything. The guy blew up the whole inside of Frontier Village and only blew out half of the windows. He cut a perfect hole through twenty-two inches of reinforced floor and then blew the hinges off a federal armored truck—while derailing a freight train. Heck, this guy could probably drop all four corner buildings at First and Stevens Creek and still leave the streetlights working."

Chet thought as he listened. "I think he would probably do something a lot more personal than some random buildings."

26

PAINT AND DECEPTION

The whole interior of the bay hung in diffused plastic. There was clearer plastic sheeting, but Felix wanted the obscuring quality as well. By wetting the windows, he had also lined the glass with the same plastic. From the outside, it increased the dirty windows to add to the lack of being able to see in. The side effect was the light inside the old gas station evened into a soft illumination without shadows.

He had attached a makeshift sound absorber to the random orbital sander. He wasn't sure how much the sound would be dampened, but anything would help. The result was enough for him to hear the sand-paper grit grind against the paint. The full-face rebreathe mask also had its own sound of the air pressurizing the mask to his face after filtering out the dust, and eventually, the paint particles.

This was not the first vehicle he had painted. Shortly after the wedding, Thelma had gotten a job as a secretary over in the next town. Because of Felix and his dad's work, the panel truck was sometimes needed to drive long distances for work. They needed a second car. The state highway troopers were having an auction of their old fleet of cars. Felix had secured the winning bid on a 1946 Studebaker sedan.

The car spun out and rolled down a small grassy hill in a high-speed chase reaching speeds of over eighty miles per hour. The smaller deuce coupe had made the curve. The driver had gotten away to run moonshine another day. The patrol car had its police lights removed and put up for auction with one cracked window. Felix and his dad sanded the entire black and white car by hand. They filled all the bolt holes and then painted the body with some barn-red paint they had found. Thelma had called it her Cherry. The Cherry had lasted her for almost six years. Each year, Felix carefully brushed out another coat of red paint. The fact that the car was painted with barn paint—applied with a four-inch brush never bothered Thelma. It was her first car, and Felix not only bought it but also painted it for her in her favorite color. To her, the color and Felix painting were the only points of importance.

Now, as he sanded with a much faster sander, Felix still thought about all the fun the two shared on the roads and highways of Colorado and New Mexico. Sometimes, they would just drive until they were tired and then climb into the large backseat to sleep. The next day, they would look on the map and find a different way home. By the time they sold the car, Felix had replaced the tires three times.

He turned the sander over as he released the switch. The sandpaper was loaded with the old paint. There was no running water in the gas station, so he had to do the sanding dry. Dry meant he would go through many 120-grit paper disks. Felix stared out the window at the light fog as his fingernail found the edge of the paper and peeled it off the sander. His mind was only a few dozen miles away. He was starting to plan. This time, he did not have directions. This time, he did not have schematics. This time, like in the mines, it was all his own show—and he knew what he wanted to do. It was just a matter of figuring out how to do it.

The last disk started to load with paint. Felix stopped and walked around the entire van. It was good enough for what he had planned.

Winding up the air hose, he detached the sander and put it back in the small box. It would not get used again. He placed the box in the backseat of the Volkswagen van. The new license plates on the small car had come off a Datsun pickup lying at the bottom of a small wash. The shape of the engine dented the hood from the underside. The large boulder the truck came to rest on might have had something to do with it. The registration stickers had been courtesy of a Ford parked at a supermarket about eleven the night before.

Felix turned to the large can of acetone. Splashing some out in a can, he began to wash down the entire van—inside and out. From now on, he would be wearing latex gloves or leather gloves any time he touched the van. Fires have a cleansing effect—but explosives leave much, which he did not want to leave.

As he washed, he remembered the trial. He had thought it was a legal job. The man had filled out all the paperwork and even had what Felix thought was the legal permit to blast the mine. As it turned out—the mine did not belong to the man. As best as Felix could find out later, the mine belonged to an ex-partner who had run off with the man's wife.

Because some of the timberings in the mine were steel, and the man had said he wanted all the shafts, drifts, and winzes dropped at the same time, Felix had overcharged the explosive load. The result was the entire mine had all but disappeared inside the mine, but places Felix had touched were still found.

The police pulled fingerprints and matched them to Felix's explosives credentials. They had prints for seven of his fingers.

If Felix had been a party to the criminal side of the job, he would still be in Colorado State Penitentiary, but when they started looking for him, he was easy to find. Everyone in the mining community knew he was at the hospital, sitting, waiting for his Thelma to wake up. The Grand Jury held a meeting and found he had no knowledge of the duplicitous nature of the crime. He was an innocent dupe.

The now not-so-innocent man took the small can of acetone-drenched rags covered with paint dust out the back door and into the small forest. In the clearing, he laid them out on the patch of ground he had cleared the day before. There was three feet of raw earth cleared around all the rags laid out flat. Felix lightly dusted dirt over the rags— just enough to cover them. From experience, he knew the acetone would wick up through the thin blanket of earth and evaporate by the next morning. The last thing Felix wanted was a small forest fire, a bunch of fire trucks, and people crawling all over the area.

Felix went back into the station and began cleaning up everything. The few noisy pieces of equipment he could not afford to ignore were the exhaust fans he had mounted in the ceiling with ducting out through areas disguised in the eaves. He had not planned on painting anything, but when he mixed up his C-4, he had to vent the fumes with an explosion-proof fan.

The fan had been running all during the washing stage. With his walk out to the clearing, he had cleared the smell from his nostrils and could now smell if there were any residual fumes. There didn't seem to be, so he shut down the fans.

Felix checked the supplies for the paint one more time. He didn't want to have to go get more supplies in the middle of the day.

With everything in place, he sat down in what had been the office at one time and waited for the night to become dark. Only then, would he open the back door and push the Volkswagen out and leave. He knew the police would be watching his home by now, but they would never think about him camping out.

Two long days of driving had seen Felix through stashing money and reserves in preparation for his final departure. He had come to feel fondly toward the bay and the scenery. However, for Felix, people come and go. Now with them stealing Thelma from him, he was willing to go. But, first, there was his complaint he needed to file. It would have his signature on it.

In three days, he would start bringing the fertilizer to the gas station.

WHERE DID HE GO?

The roll-over had only started the mess on the 101. The early morning commute got out of hand as people got great jobs in what some people were calling the Silicon Valley. With the larger income, those people wanted larger houses than their neighbors had or at least larger than the house they grew up in. With most of the land already developed decades before, the orchards and farmlands to the south never stood a chance. The 'Hill of Stupid' Hooker drove up to get to Manny and Stella's was a great example—but it was only the start.

The farther south, the cheaper the land, and the more house you could buy. Who cared if the only difference between your pink house and their tan house was your garage was on the left, and theirs was on the right: next two houses—the same. Next two, same again, and so it went until you found yourself two hundred homes later, back on the same street at the beginning home.

The news of some poor, working stiff at the end of a lot of days of overtime would come home and get shot coming through what he thought was his front door—but was actually three blocks over and two streets south—was only a matter of time. When it did happen, everyone would just nod and say, *yup...it was bound to happen.*

The hard pounding rain never made it easier. When the computer worker usually left their house at five in the morning, they would leave at four-thirty and drive aggressively as they prayed they would make it to work before their boss. Hooker was always amazed he never found steering wheels twisted out of shape from people grabbing them in a death grip.

Through the rain, he watched another slow line of cars crawling by the wreck, single-file, in the breakdown lane. The faces were lost in the pre-five o'clock in the morning dark, but the white knuckles always stood out at the top of the steering wheels. Their color drained and now replaced by the jaundiced yellow of his flashers and the white of his work lights. The color flowed yellow, white, yellow, white… their wipers keeping a back-beat while their blood pressure and heart took the beating.

Hooker looked down the long jumble of the wreck. It looked like a yard sale gone horribly wrong. He counted five auto club trucks and three commercial. Without asking Dolly, he already knew they had drained the entire towing fleet of the South Bay.

The evidence would eventually be stacked in a long line of cars parked parallel with large yellow oil cake markings as to which car belonged to which towing company. One of the trucks was marked for Tri-County, who was rushing to get back from a haul out to Lodi. Hooker smirked and hummed the tune, *Stuck in Lodi Again*. If the driver didn't get back when CHP cleared the scene, they would throw it to Hooker.

It was going to be a great day for Hooker. He had already stashed two small bobtail trucks, and this tracker guaranteed the trailers were his as well. He would come back for the rolled over bobtail with its nose still slammed into the back of the Pacer, which died suddenly from driving through a large lake of a puddle. He could see Don dragging the other two box vans into the center, which would keep the scene working while Hooker grabbed what he could.

Hooker pulled the levers, and the rear end of the smaller truck rose until there were about six inches of clearance. Rushing back around the nose, he checked the steering rope secured in the driver's door. The rope, looped in and around the steering wheel, would hold the front wheels running semi-straight. A slight cock on a car of a box van was no more than a foot or so running out of the straight, but okay. On a larger truck,

Hooker had a special rig that could freeze the steering in perfect alignment. On a thirty-six-foot-long truck, the slight cock could put the frontend running in half of the next lane.

Hooker had only seen it happen once. He had vowed in his second month of towing it would never happen with any of his tows. Eleven years in, concerted watching every detail and no jokes about towing wrong had ever been made at Hooker's expense.

On the other hand, other disgruntled tow drivers who lost tows to the quicker kid started calling him a whore by the moniker of mockery—Southside Hooker. Hooker took to the name and painted it on his rig's tow cranes. The subtext told it all. *When you need a quickie.* The following year at the Tow Truck Rodeo, he proved five times over, he was the fastest, and he had the fastest truck.

As Hooker scrambled into the cab of Mae West, he whistled between his teeth. The CHP wound his finger over his head and stopped the traffic.

Mae nosed out into the lanes and shot down the one mile to the next off-ramp. Hooker watched the bobtail as it tracked behind. There was going to be no problem parking it in the Safeway parking lot overlooking the freeway.

As he pulled into the large lot, Hooker could see his other three trucks lined up as if they had been parked there overnight. He drew in and unhooked number four and headed back for number five of seven or eight —if he could beat Tri-County's driver to the last bone.

Much later in the day, Hooker was unhooking the last of the eight vehicles lined up in the Fly's back lot. He would get all the tows, Fly would get any storage, and if she converted any or all into bodywork, Hooker would get a thin slice of the residuals. Very likely, this long day would make his month—if nothing bad happened.

Hooker didn't have to look to know the footstep he was hearing. The walk of only one leg and a mass of aluminum and titanium on the other side was distinct. "Who let the dog out in the yard on a beautiful day like today?"

"Well, at least the rain has lightened…"

Hooker dragged the chains out from under the box van and poured them into the back of the working bed of Mae. "It was pig ugly this morning on the wreck. Forget cats and dogs—it was Chips and taxicabs." Hooker wiped his hand and stuck out his fist. The man bounced his on top of Hooker's hand. Hooker felt the sluggishness in the man's hit and studied his face. "Gee, sunshine... you look radiantly like shit."

"Jeez, Hooker, I don't know whether to thank you or just take you out and shoot you. That Mai is a shooter. She shoot her eye at you, and you are dead. Dead at the wall, dead in the shower... Do you have any idea how hard it is to take a shower with only one leg as it is? Then the crazy woman gets that look in her eyes and starts talking sexy baby talk... and do you think she would let me lie down or something? Noooo... she wants to do it standing up. And then she hooks one leg straight up and over my shoulder—"

Hooker closed his eyes and held out his two hands with index fingers making the sign of a cross. "Hang on, super stud... you are talking to a man here with virgin ears. Last week, Candy and I moved up to holding hands for more than ten minutes, and then she kissed me on the ear. Dog, I'm telling you—I almost passed out from the excitement."

He opened his eyes. The man had a confused look on his face.

"Dog, what you and Mai do is none—and I do mean none—of my business. You have been around the world a good bunch, but I'm still at home. I am still trying to figure out the simple stuff—do not be telling me the college stuff. I might want to take it home and take it out for a spin— which might just freak Candy and me both out. I don't want to lose her."

The man raised his shoulders and took a deep breath, held it as if he needed to say something, and then let it out slowly. "I'm sorry, dude. I didn't mean to lay that all on you. You're right. It's my stuff..."

"Dog, talk to her. Just talk. Tell her what's going on. I think she's just so excited to get a guy who doesn't treat her like crap. You're a stand-up guy. You just don't want to. She hasn't been around a gimp and doesn't know your boundaries." Hooker thought about the small wooden stool in his shower. "Maybe what you also need is a small wooden shower stool. Ask her or the Fly—it's a Japanese thing. They might know where to get one, along with a soap bucket and sea sponges and brushes. If Mai likes being in the shower with you, get a bigger shower and put her to good use washing your back."

The man studied Hooker. "You know, for a cocky kid, you make a lot of sense. I'll talk to her tonight—hopefully before she attacks me at the door."

Hooker closed his eyes and hung his head. He wasn't going to win this one. "What did you come out here for, Dog? I know it wasn't to stand in the rain and talk about your sex life."

The man smiled his big toothy smile. "Nah... it was to tell you there is a CHP officer waiting for you in the office." The man turned on the metal leg and wobbled off.

"Thanks, Dog." Hooker closed the side door on the toolboxes. Turning, he smiled evilly. "Hey, Dog?"

The man turned around.

"So doing it in the shower is a nice thing?"

The man laughed from the bottom of his last foot. "For me, it's either going to be a heart attack... or just fall and bust my ass. For you... try it. You may just find you like swimming upstream." He waved and continued into the building he ruled.

Hooker climbed into the truck as he thought about the effect of the six large showerheads pumping five hundred gallons a minute, and what it would feel like at the right moment. He ground his head around and felt the stiffness in his neck. It had been a long night.

Hooker slid out the door of Mae and looked at the CHP cruiser. He didn't recognize the tail number painted on the back bumper panel. It wouldn't be either of his friends Micha or the captain, Chet. He leaned forward in the rain and headed for the office.

Stepping into the office, he fanned his rain jacket. He didn't mind the rain, but the nonstop fire hose of the last ten hours was too much. The two large storms the radio had been talking about for days had decided to have a convention in San Jose.

"Hooker." The nasal tone of the Japanese woman was distinctive. By the echo, Hooker could tell she was in her office—a place she avoided more than bill collectors. Hooker swung through the low gate and headed down the short hall.

"Hooker, this is Officer Pool, I'll leave you two. Whatever CHP track Hooker down for, the Fly no want to know." Hooker could hear her giggling as she walked down the hall. He knew her ears would be tuned to the finest of noises coming from this office.

Hooker sat on the corner of the almost unused desk. "What can I do for you, officer?"

The man looked back around to see if it was okay to talk.

Hooker snorted. "She isn't standing anywhere you'll see her. Besides, she had this office bugged—don't you, Spider-Woman?" His voice had never risen.

"You leave me out of your mess, Hooker." The voice had come from the other end of the main office. Hooker just deadpanned the officer as if to say, *see, I told you so*. "So, what are you here for? Are you here to arrest me?"

"No." The man thought a second about how it all looked, clandestine and all. "Oh, heavens no… It's not like that at all." He was flustered and out of his element.

"Okay, I didn't get caught—again. So what do you need? And by the way, I need another couple boxes of thirty-minute flares. The guys last night used every one, and so did I."

"I've got three fresh boxes in the…" The officer realized he had just been roped into giving up flares. Flares were the universal bargaining chip in the world of towing, and the thirty-minute CHP flares were the gold standard. His shoulders slumped. "Sure, I'll get you some flares. The captain should have warned me about you."

"What does Chet want?"

The man fished a piece of paper out of his shirt pocket and handed it to Hooker. "He asked me to track you down on the QT and have you meet him there. He said to go ninety-seven and then silence."

Hooker looked at the address. It looked like a residential area in Milpitas. He looked at the large map the Fly had as a back wall. It covered the area from Fremont down to Gilroy and across to the coast range. He stepped to the list of streets and found the one he was looking for. Cross-referencing it to the vertical and horizontal of the map, he found the small street. It was only four blocks long. From what he could tell, the address would be near the end. From the street number, he figured it looked north to nothing but the San Francisco Bay.

Hooker muttered, "Nice view—but a lousy neighborhood." Turning to the officer, he held up the note. "Thanks, Pool. Now let's go shopping in your trunk." He smiled. The patrol knew most of the drivers were fast to pop flares to keep accidents safe to work in. If it looked like it was going to be a long hard wreck, they would build Vs and Ws out of the flares so the one would light the next as it burned down. CHP offices stocked thousands of boxes of flares, and their trunks held at least one unused box. If a driver asked nicely, the officers would dig out a couple of hand-fuls. If the driver was known as there to help with the larger accidents... they were usually rewarded with more. Hooker usually found a box or two on the working bed of Mae. However, the morning's wreck had stripped every cruiser and tow truck of flares.

The officer softly groaned as he opened his trunk. Hooker smiled down on the glory of a full back trunk. He patted the young officer on the shoulder. "You just made my day. Are you at the beginning or end of your shift?"

"End. I'm off at one."

"I'll leave you two boxes just in case." He leaned in and embraced four of the unopened boxes and walked off to store them in Mae. Thinking, he turned as he laid the boxes on the bed. "Did you load up before you saw Captain Davis or after?"

"After. He said you would strip anything I had."

Hooker laughed and waved. "Thanks, Pool. I owe you a donut at the Whole Donut." The officer waved and slid into his cruiser.

Hooker stowed the flares and locked the side box. He knew the same positioned box on the other side was still empty, but he had another CHP officer to see.

He pulled out the Thomas book and found the same street. He figured out the route in and put the book on the dashboard. It was rare he had to check for addresses because he had almost been everywhere he towed—to, or from. However, with the twists and turns of a town laid out by drunks and roads made by crazy people, Milpitas would require the map book.

Some of the twists and turns had even Hooker backing up and taking a second run at the turn. The streets were never the problem. It was how people parked or simply left a vehicle. Some were nothing more than a hulk—gutted long ago by some gang and now just a shade stop for cats and dogs roaming freely about the neighborhood.

Finally, he was at a point where he was looking at the bay, which started no more than a hundred yards in front of him. He looked right and saw a lone CHP cruiser sitting in front of a house. Hooker thought about the position, and then jockeyed a three-point turn, which had him backing Mae down the street to the cul-de-sac. He parked ten yards in front of the cruiser.

He knocked on the screen door. "Chet?"

"In the back, Hooker."

Hooker walked through a sterile house. There was only a rocking chair facing a small black and white television on a couple of milk cartons in the front room. The kitchen had a small dining table with only two chairs. None of them matched. He stepped through to a screened porch. He could tell the crime scene boys had been here. The black fingerprint dust was everywhere.

"Luuucy, you forgot to dust..." Hooker looked up at his friend, who was sitting on a bed. "Anything?"

The man shook his head and duck-lipped just short of a raspberry. "Our boy was interesting. From rent receipts, they lived here for about five years. He always paid a month in advance and always cash. The property management company said he was paying two hundred dollars, but I'm guessing he might have paid four hundred so the property owner would never come around.

"Neighbors we interviewed said they rarely saw the guy, but during the day, there was always a yellow VW bug here. They described a woman as about five-two and maybe a hundred pounds. It was hard to know as she was always wearing a down coat—winter and summer. The sketch artist was out, and the three gave close descriptions, so they're canvassing the area. The plate numbers matched a Volkswagen stolen about six years ago. We don't hold out much hope in finding the car or the woman."

"I see there're some prints near the outside door..."

"We're guessing they're not our guy. We think he trained himself to touch only in certain areas. It means less cleaning up after yourself, and you don't have to remember everywhere you might have touched. We figured this is where he slept and worked. The entire table and the walls in this area match the area around the keyed doorknob—wiped clean with acetone. Notice the lamps are pull string, not the original chain."

Chet got up and pulled a knife from his pocket. He opened it and leaned toward the wall. "This is an extremely interesting wall."

Hooker glanced around the room. "Looks like it was built maybe as an addition to the screened in the porch."

"Hmm, we'll get to the screen in a moment." He started prying the boards off and revealing the cavities behind. When he was finished, half the wallboards were stacked on the table. Hooker studied the series of shelves.

"What the heck? Why is there a stud missing there by the table, but—" He stopped as he was about to touch the four strange shelves. Chet nodded that it was okay.

"They're all dished. What would you put on a dished shelf?"

Chet reached over onto the bed. His hand returned holding a wire. Hooker looked at the spliced wire. Each piece of copper was only about two inches long—soldered to the next and the next until it made a wire about twenty inches long.

Chet raised his one eyebrow. "Remember at Frontier Village, the inspector had asked if they had some electrical work done recently? It was because he kept finding tiny pieces of wire with solder on the end." Chet pointed at the pieced wire in his hand. "He must have made hundreds of them and stacked them in there. The bomb guys were impressed. They said if he had gone with long conventional runs of wire, they would have spotted it and figured out things from there. There's a coding labeled on the wire every so often they can trace where it came from and finally figure out where it was sold and maybe who to. But with this guy, he used stripped wire, and took the time to splice together something the bomb would blow apart and become just background debris lost in the rubble."

"All of this for what?"

Chet held up his right index finger. "Ah, and that is the sixty thousand dollar question. Or maybe should I say the eighty-five thousand..." He sat back down on the bed. "As I waited here over the last hour, I got to thinking about him living out here, and his wife, an invalid, in the bedroom. The man was making a living wage at De Salvo driving a local delivery truck—"

"Pick up or dropping?"

Chet frowned. "Why?"

"It makes a huge difference. Delivery trucks work a certain area—say the southwest quarter of downtown. However, the trucks doing pickups would cover all of downtown. It's a much larger area, but you still get to know everything about the area."

"I'll check." He laid back and stuck the knife in the wall between two boards. "I figured if he had rigged all of those boards with magnets, why would he stop there?" The lower board popped off the wall as Chet moved to the next one down. "I figure this is the original stash hole, but he stopped going to it and maybe in his hurry forgot about it."

Hooker stared at the stacks of money still in the bank wrappers. "How much did you…"

"Eighty-five grand—all in fifties and twenties and not in sequential numbers—they were rewrapped by a bank. Rewrapped by hand… by a bank in Texas." He sat back up. "I'll bet we find some interesting explosions in Texas too."

Hooker sat on the desk table. His eyes were dancing all around the room, looking for answers. Chet had seen this with Hooker before.

"So the bills are not fresh, crisp, and clean."

"No. They're old and used."

"It's his running money." Hooker focused and looked at Chet. "He still might have to come back for it. He hasn't flown the coup."

Chet pointed to the three-feet-tall wall, running nearly fifteen feet. "That's a lot of room for money."

Hooker frowned—his mouth drew to one side. Waving Chet out of the way, Hooker laid face down across the bed.

"Just don't touch…" Chet regretted saying it as he did.

Hooker shot him a disgusted look. Both knew he had been around enough crime scenes to know what to do.

Hooker reached in his pants pocket and slid out his new commando knife. He held the safety and slid the button. The blade slicked out the end—six inches of thin double-edged death. Hooker carefully slid the blade between the top two stacks and the third. Lifting the money, he slid it out and carefully set it on the bed as if it were a bomb. He looked in the cavity. "Do you have the little pocket flashlight you carry in your jacket?"

The officer handed him the light. Hooker turned it on and illuminated the back wall of the cavity. He studied the smoothness and thought about it. Getting up, he went over and examined the other cavities in the long wall. He looked at the exposed money and then about half of the cavities on the long wall.

He stood. "I was wrong. He won't need to come back. In fact, I think he may have just forgotten about this wall stash."

Chet sat back and smiled. He loved watching Hooker and the Squirt figure problems out. The Squirt had the freaky memory, but Hooker had an uncanny way of seeing details most people don't. "So what makes you think he's going to walk away from eighty-five thousand dollars?"

"He doesn't need it."

"Who doesn't need eighty-five grand when they're on the run?"

"Someone who needs to run light." Hooker pointed at the money. "Look at it. There's at least a briefcase worth of money there. Maybe even a small suitcase... like an overnight bag."

"Okay, so why is it a problem?"

"It's not. It's the other eight hundred grand he has with him now. It's a lot to carry."

Chet started to say something smart, but then stopped and tried to figure out what Hooker had figured out in minutes—but he had missed. "Okay, you got me. Explain how you figure this."

Hooker smiled. He only wished Manny was here, but he figured word would get back to him and Dolly both.

"We know he's storing his parts for the bombs here." He waved his hands along an area near and over the table. Chet nodded.

"We know what he makes—he plants only C-4, which is like plastic." He waits for the nod. "And the other parts are the wires and some kind of trigger. My guess is the trigger is as susceptible to moisture as the wire." He looked at Chet and waited for the nod.

"So, what does he store in the wall that would be sensitive to the moisture coming off the bay?"

"The money."

"And we know he stored it in the wall for years. Long enough, unless protected, for mold and mildew to set in and destroy his stash." He climbed back over the bed and showed Chet the walls of the cavity.

"What is the coating?"

"My guess is sandwich bags."

"It's what?" The man's face folded up in a scowl.

"Plastic sandwich bags..." Hooker sat up, went over to the other wall, and directed the flashlight along the much larger areas. "See, he sealed these as well. All told, I think the holding capacity here is close enough to ten times the little hole over there. But I also think he has much larger bills. My guess is more than half of what he has is in hundreds. With Benjamins, you can stick twenty grand in your front pocket. So maybe he even has a million to do with what he needs to do."

"Okay, but get back to the sandwich bags..."

"Have you ever left a sandwich in a bag on your dashboard during the summer? It melts the bag, and the bag welds itself to the dashboard."

"Okay, I can see that. But lining the wall...?"

"Easy. I'm assuming he probably knows his way around some kind of torch. After all, we know he can solder." Chet nodded at the wire.

"So you hold a single layer of the bag against the area you want it to bond with and run the torch near it until the bag melts just enough to bond, but not burn up. He probably pushed on it with a block of wood— maybe wrapped with aluminum foil or something so it wouldn't stick to the block he was using as an iron. Because remember, he wants the whole compartment sealed."

Chet stared at the man that he kept mistaking for *the kid*.

"What?"

The older man just shook his head and laughed. "Being around you this last year gives me mixed feelings."

Hooker leaned back with dramatic horror on his face. "Is this an Uncle Willie talk?"

The two busted up laughing. "No. Oh, God, no. I've known about you from almost the day you started pulling wrecks for Don. I just actually met you this last year with the shotgun whacko. I'm not far from retirement age…" He looked down at his hands picking at each other.

Hooker could tell the man was deep in a serious emotional state. He asked softly, "So what's the problem?"

The man lifted his head and looked the other way out the screen toward the bay. "I don't know what I would want most—a do-over of the last ten years to watch you grow into the man you've become or just an extra ten years in this job to see where you go from here."

He turned back, and Hooker could see the wet in his eyes. The man was at peace with finally understanding where he stood in his world… but there was still a haunting.

Hooker almost whispered as he said softly, "It's okay, Chet. Neither one of us is going anywhere. We have as much time as you want. Heck, look at Manny—he never stopped. But I don't think this is all about doing this stuff or about me… I think you're missing Carol." The man nodded and wiped at his eyes. "It's called companionship. It's been almost four years since she passed away. I think even she would tell you it's okay to move on. You aren't a solitary guy. You do better when you have someone to do things with."

Chet looked where the bedroom was in the house. He thought about the man who slept out here with his wife in there. He had her possessively, but if the reports were right, he had lost her years before they moved here. The man had already lived in a prison of his own making for almost a decade… and now, they were working to stick him in a different prison.

He turned back to Hooker. "You really think Carol would approve?"

"I'll let Dolly kick your ass tomorrow over dinner."

"I wasn't invited."

"I'll make room."

Chet studied the young man's eyes and realized just what kind of man he had become. He was a long way from the snot-nosed run-away kid hauling garbage and jumping batteries with a bogus driver's license. He now fully understood where Manny and Willie stood on Hooker.

Hooker surveyed the room and then looked out the screen toward the bay. He thought about the choice to live here. The bay stretched to the hazy, thin line horizon of Marin County. The house and neighborhood were hard-beaten old houses built before the Great War to End All Wars. They were worker housing then, and marginal now. It was a great place to hide, where there were no nosey neighbors—and hell, everyone had something to hide. When people are beaten up by life, they look for other outlets, and not many of those are legal. Hooker guessed it was a little moonshine here, a pot plant or two there, and maybe someone was cooking up drugs. LSD was all but out of favor now. Hooker guessed the neighborhood probably had a meth cook stamping out powder for drug-gies and little white pills for waitresses working two jobs, truck drivers running double logs, and cops working as much overtime as they could stay awake for. Hooker knew cops were no angels. They were just working stiffs with a badge and gun who were willing to run toward trouble instead of away.

He frowned and realized what he had just watched. A small bug landed on the screen and vaporized with a sizzling snap. He turned with wide eyes.

Chet smiled and wiggled his eyebrows. "Impressive, isn't it? But don't touch it. He wired it to the 220 instead of the 110." He pointed out to the small dock with a tiny rowboat tied to it. "I don't know if he had to or not, but he had a ready-made body dump out in the marsh. If anyone lays their whole hand on the copper screening, they either get thrown a few long yards on their ass, or it will just stop their heart where they stand. Lucky for the investigators, the first one had barely set foot in here when a fly landed on the screen. Word got passed quickly to watch for any booby-traps. There weren't any others, so I figured this was his form of security. Although, looking in here, there's nothing but the bed, desk, chair, and the two lamps. He hired some woman to watch his wife while he was at work, so someone was here most of the time. I don't know why he went to the trouble and expense to screen the porch in copper and then paint it to look like regular screening. We haven't found the switch to turn it off yet."

Hooker thought. "Hmm, did you check the front door to see if it's also wired?"

"Damn." The man got up and went to the front door.

Hooker pointed at the striker plate after a few minutes. "Right there. It only works when the door is closed. I'll bet we'll find a hidden switch outside. It'll be where he normally walks when he comes home." They went outside, and Hooker went through the movements a few times, reenacting coming home and parking, and then walking to the front door. Finally, he thought about the panel truck.

He shifted his thinking and started from the far side of the driveway. He walked around the imaginary truck backed into the drive, right up to the house. The ruts in the gravel were deepest and were formed by habit. The gravel leading to the beaten-down garage was smooth but disturbed as if a light car had parked there, albeit randomly.

The house had the cheapest form of siding—batten over a wide board. There was a batten every foot with a count of twenty. The switch was just above Hooker's hanging hand. The man was taller than he was. It was a simple rocker switch buried into the batten. Hooker followed the batten up with his eye and along the header board. The painted over wires peeked out here and there, but not so it would draw any attention. He showed the setup to Chet.

"Think there is a switch to find in the screened porch?"

"I doubt it. I think he wired it straight into the fuse... so it was always on."

They both turned as a loud motorcycle roared down the street. Slowing at the end of the cul-de-sac, it turned. The rider sat on the chopper studying the CHP car and the large tow truck. The rhythmic thumping of the large engine pulsed in the neighborhood.

Chet looked at Hooker. "I think my presence is making the natives restless."

Hooker was studying the way the rider held their arms. One draped— at rest while the other was cocked out stiff. Hooker knew the set of arms. He turned slightly and quietly nodded, "Give me a minute."

Hooker walked to the street and stood at the back end of Mae. He leaned against the corner of the working deck and crossed his legs, relaxed and watchful.

Carefully, the biker drew in the clutch and heel-kicked into first gear. Easing down the street, the biker tossed their head, and a large thick braid pulled up out of the front to fly around to the back. Hooker smiled. Not *his* head...*her* head. His memory hadn't failed him.

The bike chuffed to a coasting stop in front of Hooker.

"Afternoon, Max... It is Max, isn't it?"

The woman smiled, "Only if you're the towing whore who works the south side of San Joe." She pulled her glove off the right hand. Hooker knew she wouldn't take the glove off the injured left. He had seen what had become of it when he pulled it from the wreck a few years before.

They shook. "You're a long way from your territory, Hooker." She reached over and turned off the bike. It chuffed in protest and settled into silence.

"I'm a whore, Max. I go where the money is."

She turned and looked at the cruiser and officer. "The house was crawling with cops yesterday, and I thought they'd left this morning."

Hooker could sense the unease. He didn't know what she was into, but it probably wasn't printing names on pencils to sell on the corner downtown. "You can relax, Max. This investigation only has to do with this house and the person who lived here."

"The guy was pretty much a ghost. Stuck to his own business."

Hooker looked around. "Seems like that pretty much sums up the entire neighborhood." He looked back at the large woman as she pulled the braid that looked more like a lethal weapon than hair back around to hang down her front. "Is this where you call home, Max?"

The woman weighed the man she hardly knew.

"Jeez, Max, you can trust me. You trusted me to save your clutch hand from the wreck..."

She seemed to settle. "Yeah, you're right." She looked around. "It ain't pretty... but it's home."

"See... that wasn't so hard. We're not here sniffing around the neighborhood. Chet couldn't care less what you're doing in the privacy of your own home. His only concern would be if you were pushing this hog down his highway at twenty over."

"Why would I be going so slow? The engine would overheat." She smiled.

Hooker laughed. "Now there's the Max, who gave the nurses conniption fits and liked the moonshine I snuck into the hospital." He gently reminded her she might owe him some grace.

She smiled at the memories. "There was one little redhead. She had the nicest little…" She looked back at Chet and then up at Hooker. She moved the wrap-around dark glasses up onto the top of her head. "I don't know much about the guy. Like I said, Dan kept to himself."

"What do you know?"

She rubbed her lower lip and jaw. "He drove an old panel truck. The plates were from Colorado. The paint wasn't car paint. It looked like he just used what he had to paint over some old signage. It was something about mines or mining. His wife must have worked nights or something. Her yellow Volkswagen was always here during the day. It was the screwiest thing. His panel had Colorado plates, and the tabs were up-to-date, but the VW, those plates were years out-of-date. She was a squirrel. I saw her a few times. Same as Dan—kept to herself. Kind of hunched over, and she looked like she could have been his mother."

Hooker thought about the power of sharing information. "Thanks, Max. It doesn't add really to what we know, but it does confirm a few things. First off, the guy's name was Felix—Dan was the name he'd taken. They were hiding out in plain sight. The woman you saw was looking after Felix's wife, who was invalid while he was at work. The rest we'd pieced together." Hooker stuck his hand out. "It was good seeing you again." He nodded at the left hand that never left the handlebar. "How's the hand and arm?"

She screwed her face into a shrug. "Eh, it's stiff like the doctors said it would be, but I can still pull the clutch… so I get by."

"I wasn't sure who you were until you whipped the big-ass braid around." He smiled.

She lowered her glasses and smiled with a nod at the truck. "Some big-assed things are sometimes our signature trademark. I see you around now and then. You don't see me, though, because I'm most times in my car."

"What do you drive?"

"A '70 Roadrunner—black primer, shaker hood with a six-pack."

Hooker snorted. "Got a skull and crossbones on the back right bumper?"

She raised her glasses and looked at him.

"Oh, beans and wieners, Max...It is Mopar, after all. Of course, I'm going to notice. It sits down at a bar just off Willow Glen most nights."

"Stop in some night. I'll buy you coffee. Just ignore the girls. The Balls & Sticks is only about the pool tables. The others aren't allowed. You, I'll make an exception for."

"What about my partner?"

"You don't have a partner."

Hooker smiled and walked to the door. He opened it as he watched Max. "Box. Grass."

The orange streak was on the street and only paused for a second to look at the motorcycle. As he stood stiff-legged on the grass, he watched the woman laughing.

"Now I don't know why, but it is the perfect partner for you. It looks like he's good in a scrap too."

"More than just good. I watched him drop a full-grown man in under three seconds last year. Just the other day, he took on a hundred-pound Kai-dog."

"How did he do?"

"Didn't even breathe hard... it was all over in about five or six seconds."

"Hurt the dog?"

"Nope... killed the dog. Tore up its back before ripping out its throat."

Max whipped her braid around through the air as she looked back at Box. "You're shittin' me."

Hooker just stared and then, with a deadpan look, slowly ground his head back and forth.

"Why would he take on, much less kill a dog the size of a man?"

"The dog was wild and was attacking our neighbor's young yellow Lab. I think Box is sweet on the kid."

The woman pursed her lips and nodded. She watched the large cat walk back over and sit down next to Hooker's leg. "I think I can understand that."

RIGGING

Felix fingered the switch. The light turned on.

The step-van was all painted and just needed a day before putting on the decals. The brown was not a color most people would paint a house, and Felix had to get it custom mixed. The man had been a little nosey for Felix's taste, but then he was in the tiny town of Sebastopol, and the man did not know him. Felix pled being new to the area.

The paint shot on better than he thought it would. Having a matching primer had certainly helped. He only half chuckled about how much easier it was to spray on paint than painting a car with a four-inch house painting brush, but times were always tough, and you did with what you had. His chest ached about his Thelma having never seen the good days.

His hand felt along the bottom of the rail for the roll-down door. He felt the roller button depress—a small green light lit. He moved his finger back up, as the door would do if opening—the green light winked out, and the small red light went on.

Eventually, when everything was ready, there would be a series of nine green lights set in a box pattern glowing like a monochromatic tic-tac-toe board. The board was set high on the back of the one side. This time, Felix didn't worry about leaving only tiny debris to be scattered among the rubble. This time, he was leaving a statement. Everything would be straight out of the box perfect.

When all nine of the green lights in the box were on, he started preparing the rest of the van. The whole job would take two days, even though it was just about placing all the parts. The construction adhesive was the hard part.

He picked up the yardstick and started laying out the six-inch grid on one wall. In the sequence, the explosives forming the grid on this side would be the second thing to happen. The first trigger would ignite four runs of the fast detonation cord. These four lines ran in layers of the sodium nitrite fertilizer. The fertilizer burned slower or exploded and expanded slower than the detonation cord. As the one-ton of mass slowly reached its critical mass, the cord burned ahead at the speed of sound. The four lines crossed each other on the way to their final destination. This was a fail-safe in case one of the lines had not burned its way to the crossover.

Once the burn was past the crossover, it split into forty lines racing up the center of the wall and then flashing out across the grid. Meanwhile, another four lines ran under all the fertilizer to ignite a series of other detonation lines. These triggered the shaped forms of C-4 to push the entire mass out of the now-opened wall of the van. The result was in the form of two hundred tiny bombs of C-4 connected directly to their own miniature compression triggers. These tiny bombs would speed up the mass of the now flying fertilizer and cause a double-tone concussion within the one explosion.

The high brisance of the C-4 would crack concrete and shatter windows, and the slower bass explosion of the fertilizer would deliver the mass concussion driving the shattered face of the building into and through the rest of the building, in effect—destroying the building. It would just have to wait for the demolition crews to finish the job.

Felix ran a bead of the construction adhesive down the pencil line. Putting down the tube gun, he picked up the end of the detonation cord and pushed it into the adhesive. It stuck perfectly. Only detonation would knock it loose. He repeated the process with the rest of the lines and then did the horizontal lines. The tails of the horizontal draped over the hook he had suspended until the adhesive dried. The tails of the odd lines hung on the left and the evens on the right.

Every other one of the tails on each side gathered to its own detonation point. In theory, the four sets of runs would start burning within a hundredth of a second of the others, cutting an identical pattern of metal squares.

Felix thought back to his childhood. His father had sat him on his knee and showed him a hand grenade. His father had slowly taken it apart and showed the young Felix how it all worked. He had explained how the cuts in the shell were the weak parts, and therefore, the grenade would turn into little square pieces of metal shrapnel when it exploded. Later Felix understood the true power and theory—only close concussion resulted in death by a grenade—it was the shrapnel doing all the widespread destruction.

In the mines, there were many pieces of machinery they used, much like a grenade to wreak havoc on the mine walls. Much as the bomb in the van would do, the shrapnel and high-energy explosives did the setup, and the mass explosives did the deep trauma, which would bring the mine walls down—closing the cavern or shaft.

A geologist had once explained to Felix what he was replicating in the mine was the same devastation happening with an earthquake. The first shockwave to hit is the high-frequency wave, which races to the surface and then radiates out from the surface epicenter. Because it's high frequency, it's much faster. It's called the 'S' wave for sound or snap. It is the first to hit a building, and it jars the foundation away from the center, causing micro cracking in foundations and stiff walls.

The second wave travels through the rock strata and is called the 'P' wave for pulse or power. It is coming directly from the fault slip and has all the mass of the earthquake behind it. It is what pushes back and forth, and up and down as wave after wave hits. This is what causes the weakened building to fall.

Felix looked at the wall and ran his eyes over every inch of every run of the detonation cord. He reached over and started separating the tails out to the end of where they would start. There would be four start points for the wall. From those points, all the remaining action would flow.

He braided the many cords together into one. He remembered how she had taught him how to braid her thick, long hair with the multiple strands instead of the usual three. The result was a braid hanging flatter down the back of her head. His hands hung helplessly in the air. So much was no longer his.

Sluggishly, he started moving again and bound each of the braided ends to a low exploding blasting cap with electrical tape. He then slid a thick piece of pipe over each of the caps and braids and taped them in place. This would restrict the small explosion inside the pipe and ignite only the braid.

Backing out of the van, he visualized the next step. He had done the process thousands of times. You take the explosion you want, walk it backward into the components you need, and how and where they need to be laid out.

He walked around the van to a small roll-around table. He picked up the mug and drank some of the tepid coffee. He thought about using the torch to warm it up, but he now had the bags of fertilizer in the building. What he did, what he used, and what he created were now restricted. No sparks, no flames... nothing that could ignite the explosive nature of the fertilizer. The fumes hung threatening in the air.

His left hand felt in the paper wrapping and found the second half of the sub sandwich he had bought this morning. He bit off a small bite and chewed mindlessly. His eyes were wandering awash across the many components left to place, but his mind was in a meadow of small mountain flowers. All the smells of the explosives drove his memories of those flowers, the girl, the day, and all the days after. All the years that had followed. All of his life—now gone.

He laid the last part of the sandwich down in the paper. He glanced in the mug—one last swallow of the now cold coffee. He swallowed and turned back toward the one wall. He picked up the rough leather work gloves. Pulling them on, he looked at two piles of steel plates. The quarter-inch mild steel would lie across the floor of the van. The three-eighths armor plate would stand up the wall. The flooring was in one-foot squares. There was also a series of plate-only six-inch wide and twenty inches long—those would start the second layer.

Carrying the squares two at a time, Felix layered the floor of the van. The next layer he glued with dots of the construction adhesive. This made a half-inch thick, dull cushion for the explosive. It would uniformly push down, resulting in the axles and wheels collapsing as they all worked together in directing the force. The van would be one giant shape charge like a stand-up claymore mine. The force of the explosion is directed toward the enemy—the ones who took the only person who made his life worth living.

With the floor in place, he started with the long narrow strips. The strips were only four inches wide but stood almost the entire height of the inside of the van. He glued each of the plates to the wall of the van. A few dots of glue between each plate held them as a single unit. Running over the wheel well, he had ordered the plates cut first at an angle, and then just eleven inches short.

The second and third layers would overlap the seams of the previous by one and a half inches to build as close to a solid hard wall as possible without welding. The layered wall would also defuse any backfire explosion so as not to injure innocent people or structures. Felix's target was not random, and therefore, his weapon was just as targeted.

Once the wall was up and all glued in place, he layered the eight blankets he had made from lead cold shot for reloading shotgun shells. The birdshot made a compact heavy blanket and would do more absorbing of the backblast than directing the forward destruction. They formed easily over the wheel well of thin metal.

The standing seams of the wall reminded him of the first house Thelma, and he had moved into when they got married. The wind of the Colorado plains came like a flood out of the plains of Canada and straight through the pasteboard walls of the shack. Felix had bought a roll of tarpaper and glued it to the outside wall. It helped, but it wasn't enough. There were some old boards used for cribbing the walls of mines. They were thicker than regular boards, but they were free. The two had spent a long weekend between nailing up two layers of boards and snuggling under the pile of quilts to get warm. Being naked under the covers helped, but trying to nail up boards naked didn't. Thelma had made him put his pants on when he got a splinter in his privates. He caught himself smiling at the memory and came back to where he was. The smile bled into the cold and mixed with the coming night.

As Felix took off his gloves, he looked at the gathering gloom through the windows. He brought nine of the bags of fertilizer over arranging their contents and decided because he was having trouble seeing in the dark; it would be dark enough to leave. The small Volkswagen was now parked a mile away in a clearing popular as a parking spot for day hikers. He would be the last to get back from his hike. He shouldered an old daypack as he closed and locked the door.

He looked about and then hiked in long loping strides out through the trees to the small meadow behind. His route would take him around and back to one of the longer trails people used for hiking.

He thought about the arrangement of the small tiny bombs. He would have to drive to San Jose and look at exactly where he would be parking and the building. The placement of the bombs in the six feet of fertilizer was as critical as conducting a symphony—a little too much brass could drown out the clarinets. Too many violins and cello would make the tympani drums sound wrong. Everything must be played just right to make the music sound the way it should, and everything must explode at the right time—and way—to direct the destruction of the place and people who had taken his Thelma.

Monday would be a day to remember.

WHAT TO DO WITH A 3-DAY WEEKEND

Saturday nights were usually hit-and-miss with a touch of weird mixed in. Throw in a three-day weekend with a constant drizzle, and you can count on it being a definite hit and no miss. It was just a matter of waiting for the alcohol to set in.

Unlike the Fourth of July, and its heat to drive the start-drinking time to somewhere before lunch, the winter has its own schedule. Usually, the colder the wind, the sooner the drunks hit the bars. A nice day and the bars load up later. This drizzle was not the cold out of the Alaskan Gulf or a sub-Artic creeper mixed with something up out of Mexico—this drizzle was all San Francisco Bay born and bled.

The onshore breezes push against the downhill fall of the air off the Sierra Nevada Mountains. The blend could go two ways. The famous February 'summer' with every sailboat out on the water, or the cold convinces the moisture-rich sea air to drop its load. Unfortunately, for the holiday, the load had lasted for five days and was looking the same for the next five days.

Hooker did not care either way. With holidays and alcohol—he got tows and made money. The money was great and paid the bills, but sometimes, it was about keeping busy too. The Squirt was on a break with the academy, and for once, had no studying, so the two men were hanging out in the dark confines of dispatch.

The two had stopped in, and Dolly had strong-armed them to stay for dinner. With still no calls, the two settled into the office. They processed paperwork, which had gotten away from Hooker the previous month. Dolly was also shuffling through her never-ending river of paperwork. Almost every company or department using a radio in the South Bay— flowed through dispatch. This created a mountain of billing. Even some of the law enforcement communication went through her switchboard and radios—creating a small molehill.

Dina had brought the new baby to work, and with the calm of the radios and phone calls, she had the little one in her lap for a feeding. Karen was cooing and making the noises most aunts without children made. They were random baby talk words but were also the same silly talking she made when she got home and snuggled with the husky.

"Hooker?"

"Yeah?"

"How much is it to haul a… just a minute." She ducked back down to the board and wrote what the guy said.

"How much to tow a four-ton trailer up to eighty miles northwest of Portland…? He says it's a cogeneration plant—if it makes a difference."

"Does it have wheels and registered to be on the highways?"

"He says it does and has its co-rate registration and plates."

Hooker looked at the numbers guy. "How far to Portland?"

"Roughly nine-hundred-forty miles—depending on how you go. With the extra eighty, you're right at one-thousand-fifty. You'll have Interstate carriage fees at the border. Last I saw, they would run one hundred-eighty."

Hooker blinked. He did not want the tow. It was too long. He watched the Squirt while he answered Karen. "If it's under eleven-foot, nine-inches, I'll move it for twenty-eight hundred. The site must be accessible for a flatbed."

They listened to the conversation from their perspective, low mumbling. Hooker could see the Squirt trying to work out how Hooker was going to move it when the height would be taller than regulation for a standard travel-all trailer.

"When can you pick it up?"

Hooker smiled. "Where is it?"

"Gilroy… across from the Shilling plant."

"Get his number, and I'll call him in about thirty minutes. But… probably tonight."

Hooker leaned back with his hands laced behind his head and a wider smile on his face. Quietly, he asked the kid, "Have you figured it out yet?"

"Tri-County has a Land-All, but with those numbers, he wouldn't fit the fifteen-foot of clearance. He'd be dodging all over the place, and the over height is the same as a wide load… they want some heavy fees."

Hooker's trained ears could tell the conversation was over in the other room. "Karen?"

"He said its eleven-foot four-inches."

Hooker kept watching the kid. Watching his face as the gears churned the mountains of information was a truly amazing thing to watch. Finally, he was ready to spill the beans. "Dina?"

"Holding on line three…" Hooker had seen the button light up, but the desk phone was turned where he knew the Squirt could not see it.

Hooker's hand hovered over the phone as he watched the kid. "Five… Four… Three…"

The Squirt's face lit up. "Jose."

Hooker smiled, pushed the button for line three, and pushed the button for the speakerphone. "Hola, jefe. Thanks for holding."

The big man on the other line laughed. "Chew want something, Hooker? I know chew. You no call for maybe at least a month. Now you have you white ass in a penche vey, and you needs the magnifico Garcia to come rescue chew."

"Oh, heck no, Jose… I just wanted to know if my chorizo is ready to pick up. I've run out of good things to feed my cat, and I figured when your skank sister comes up to work First Street—she could drop it off." They both laughed at their standard, 'take no prisoners' approach to humor—even if it was at the expense of the man's sister, who was second in line to be the next District Attorney in Santa Clara County.

"Give it a week more on the sausage, Hooker. I just let the flies in, and they no have finished making the taste perfect yet. So how you been?"

"A little busy but not too much. You…?"

"I no have accidents like you, but we be doing okay."

"So, let me ask you this… how low is the new lowboy of yours?"

"Sixteen inches and bridged for eighty-K."

Hooker rolled his head to face the Squirt. The young man was nodding.

Hooker raised his one finger for the Squirt to wait. His smile turned mischievous and evil. "How lazy is that new partner of yours?"

The man rattled off a line or two of pure Mexican swearing. He and his brother were fifth-generation Mexican-Americans, but their language sounded more like they just swam the Rio Grande last year. Finally, the swearing stopped when the laughing got in the way. Hooker and the Squirt could hear the younger brother protesting in the background. "I try to wake him up at decent time each morning, but you know how lazy he is. He go see a girl in San Martin, and he be weak knees *por tres* days until I force him to eat good meat."

"So, it sounds like maybe a few days away from the Chica would be good for the boy?"

"Whatz chew got?"

"Four-ton trailer going from Gilroy to Portland, Oregon area."

"Dat a beeg area, jefe…"

"About eighty miles northwest up the river is my guess."

"How much chew leave por the starving Mexican?"

"Sixteen plus two hundred to cover the Interstate Carriage fees."

"When?"

"How soon can your bambino have the trailer across from the Shilling plant and be ready to roll out to the new interstate?"

Hooker could hear the conversation between the two brothers. Hooker knew the money would cover the fuel, rubber, and food and still leave the month's payment on the trailer. It was a good deal to cover the payment in the front of the month.

"Hooker?"

"*Si, jefe.*"

"He says he no go for less than two grand. But for two, he can be there in an hour."

"You have a smart partner, Jose. You take care of him. Is he okay to pull it all tonight?"

"No, no jefe. He already have a four-hour tow on his log, so he make Medford den shut down for a nap. He be on site midnight tomorrow."

"Okay, let me get you the information, and I'll get back to you before he rolls. Does he need travel money?"

"No, he has a new Bank AmeriCard, and we have four fuel cards. But thank chew for the offer."

"I wasn't offering—I was going to tell him where a few liquor stores were to hold up."

They laughed and hung up.

The light on two was lit. Hooker picked up the handheld and took down all the information. The man would meet the driver and give him all the maps he would need, as well as the information to cross the state lines.

As he hung up from relaying the information to the older Garcia, he looked at the now smiling Squirt.

"What?"

The Squirt laughed. "You worked your hind-end off to earn just six hundred. I'm proud of you."

Dolly snorted as she stood in the doorway. She had a small catalog in her hand. "He just spent it too. The new cables for Mae will run you just under eight-hundred—each. But they are a business expense and will go under schedule C on your taxes."

Hooker leaned back with a sigh and looked at the kid. "What the big letters giveth, the fine print taketh away."

Dolly leaned against the doorframe. "Amen."

Karen interjected, "Hooker, roll-over, big rig, set of tandems under the Alters—southbound 101. Micha is on-site, and fire is on the way. Looks like a car hit and torched."

The two men exploded into action. Dolly hugged Box but knew the large cat was itching to be out in the air.

Dolly checked the security monitor viewing the parking lot. She nodded, and the three men in her life strolled out the heavy steel door. Two kissed their fingers and touched the 701 badge as they moved past the door. The door thudded shut, and the silence descended like a blanket.

Dolly sat for a moment and then leaned forward to her paperwork. "And so the weekend begins."

DIRT AND BOMBS

Felix was damp but not from the rain. The rain had dried out shortly after he arrived at the old gas station. The rain was still to the south, but the last half-mile of the morning's hike had been under gray clouds but no rain.

The still air had reminded him of the fall days in Colorado when he and Thelma had taken short walks because they never knew when an overcast sky would become rain or snow. Some people said they could smell the rain or snow coming hours in advance, but Felix couldn't smell anything in advance except an explosion in a mine. As the years had gone on, Thelma teased she had to go from rubbing the bottle of perfume on her breasts to spritzing herself down like a Nevada whore at a rodeo. Felix wasn't sure if it was true or not, but he could still remember the way she smelled. She had never changed her brand of perfume.

They were in high school, and the Spring Ball was coming up. Felix and his dad had to go into Bolder to get some spare parts. His mother had decided to tag along and to go shopping at one of the department stores. She had invited Thelma. With a smile, Felix's father had grumbled to Felix out in the garage about the girls being up to something—but it was a man's duty to never ask what. Asking was the road to denial and a spoiled dinner. The easiest and most peaceful way was just to ignore them and wait for the surprise.

The surprise was worth the wait. The dress they bought was as summery as a spring alpine meadow. Thelma simply floated in the soft fabric. The petticoats had rustled like a soft breeze through the Aspen trees on a summer afternoon. As she had walked close, Felix lost a friend and fallen in love. It was the moment he smelled her perfume as she stood on her tiptoes to kiss him lightly on the cheek. It was the first kiss he ever remembered. He knew his mother probably kissed him on the head, but he didn't remember. His mother was caring but was not demonstrative in her affections. Even his father only got a called out cautionary to take care as he left for a mine. Thelma's soft lips hovered at his cheek like a butterfly—and then like a butterfly, they were gone. And so was his heart.

The same month, he had bought a new pair of boots. As he put them on, he told the man he needed them one size larger so he could stuff some paper in the toe and grow into them. He had sworn he would not buy another pair until he married Thelma. It was a promise he kept to himself, even when the cobbler in town told him he couldn't fix them again... that when the soles wore out, they would be finished. Felix was twenty, sixteen days shy of his twenty-first birthday.

A few days later, Thelma met him at a mine he and his father were working on. She brought them lunch—something they hardly ever ate. They sat on a large flat rock outcropping and looked out over the large valley containing Boulder and Denver. The day was light with a breeze, which hinted at a coming fall. Thelma asked him what he wanted for his twenty-first birthday. He thought about it as he chewed the sandwich. Finally, he took a drink of water, and as he put the sandwich back toward his mouth, he said, *'For you to marry me.'*

Thelma stopped taking a bite of her sandwich. She replayed the words in her head. He had not stumbled, mumbled, nor stuttered. She took a bite and slowly chewed. Finally, she took a sip of water. Two can play this game. As she put her sandwich up to her mouth, she answered, *'I guess I need to go to town and buy a dress.'* She then took a bite and quietly chewed.

After a moment, she leaned into his arm. He put his arm around her, and she moved closer. Their love and life were like that—easy and matter of fact. When the justice of the peace started to ask the question, *do you…* they had answered in unison—yes. It was all they needed to say.

When she had gotten the job down in the city, she told Felix she needed a car. She was standing at the sink, washing dishes. He was drying. There was no discussion. It was just a fact. He asked what kind. She had told him red. Red it was—barn red.

Felix wiped at his brow and picked up another bag of fertilizer. He dragged it over to the back of the step-van. It was the last layer of fertilizer. Carefully crawling along the wall with the detonation cord attached, he carried the large scoop of fertilizer. The points at both ends were packed down firmer and formed higher. This built more of the nitrate into the overall shaping of the charge.

Of the five parking places he knew he could park the fake delivery van in, the shape of the charge would be the same. At the two extreme ends, the building would only sustain damage to half of the building, but because of the age of the building, it would probably collapse entirely. The three spaces in the middle would be the most effective and were usually the last to be used on any given workday. The commercial deliveries to the county building came and went all day. Usually, they were little more than couriers making a single drop or pick up from only one office. The turnover was rapid and allowed Felix to wait for a space.

The result of the explosion at the center of the building would be catastrophic and probably drop the face of the structure within seconds. Felix almost wished he could wait around and watch. Every single explosion of his had been contained in a mine or a building. The only explosion he had ever watched in its entirety was the planning that went on in his head. Those were silent, nondestructive, and always moved in reverse—explosion to placement to parts. The only one to happen where he could watch would happen when he was already miles away. The same as when the people in the county building took his love and life away from him—he would again be miles away.

Felix sat in the step-van. Everything was ready for Monday—the next day.

31

BOOM

Hooker swung the rope over his head and gently let the loop follow his hand as he threw and let go. The lasso caught the Squirt as he walked by. The two laughed. They had been watching some old western movie the night before, and Hank had shown them how to make a lasso. The rope was wrong, but the idea was fun.

"Are you two cowboys just going to horse around today, or are you up for some pancakes?" Uncle Willie stood in the doorway to the house part of the structure.

"Let me at least hog-tie this steer, or he will eat us out of feed in the barn." Hooker laughed and quickly looped a few turns around the Squirts head and neck, who was doing his best to scurry after Willie.

The door was automatically closing on Willie's voice. "Hank slaved long and hard on this…" The fire door closed as the Squirt reached for the knob.

Shrugging his way out of the loops, he let the rope fall to the ground. The Squirt opened the door and bowed his hips forward as he quickly stepped out of the reach of the boot headed for his butt. The two burst into the kitchen dining room, laughing at the ill-fated kick and the abandoned horseplay.

The Squirt draped his arm over Hank's shoulder as the man served up the homemade pancakes. "You are an evil man, Hank."

"Why? Because I like to feed you kids or because I put chocolate chips in my pancakes?" The man smiled with wild eyes at the young man.

"No. Because you taught Hooker how to use the dumb rope—now he's going to keep playing spaghetti western for weeks." Giggling, he kissed him on the neck. The man froze—then started laughing and shied away.

"I told you… I'm Greek, not Roman. There's a big difference."

The kid held up his two index fingers crudely four inches apart with a questioning look on his face.

"No, that would be Sicilian." The two laughed as the Squirt reached over, grabbed the coffee carafe, and felt it was already full. Hank picked up the large plate of pancakes, and the two turned to the table and the other two. Morning had broken.

Later, as Hooker finished the last pancake, Willie sipped his coffee and then put the mug down. Leaning back, he relaxed. Life had taken its time but had turned out good. "Can you be in the north end today?"

Hooker swallowed and wiped his mouth with the napkin. "Why, do you need some Sicilian sausage from Chiaramontes?" He glared at Hank and the Squirt, who were chuckling about something he was sure he didn't want to know.

Willie glared at his partner out of the side of his eyes. "No, I'm fine in the sausage department." He cleared his throat—which set off the other two again. "Ben has my new cutting torch, and I'd like for you to pick it up, please."

"What's wrong with the old one? I mean, you can only burn up so many dresses…"

"It has a double head." This set off Hank and the Squirt even worse. Willie just folded his arms and glared at the both of them. "Can we have an adult breakfast, please?"

Hank just waved his two hands, got up, and headed for the bedroom. The Squirt figured it was the only safe refuge and headed for his room, also. The other two men just watched them go.

Hooker finally turned around and looked at his uncle. "Really…? Double head…?"

The man was turning red. "Oh, hush, and you owe the swear jar a dollar for even thinking like Hank."

The two stared at each other until the giggles set in. Then Hooker couldn't stand it any longer, "Sicilian sausage?" They both broke into laughter.

Finally, with a sense of decorum returning, Willie explained. "It had two full sets of valves and hoses, so you can have a cutting head on one and brazing on the other, instead of having to swap out everything back and forth."

"Slick. Sure, we can head up there."

An hour later found them at the back of Mae West, stowing the tanks and carrier with the new valves already rigged. The streets were all but empty as offices were closed for the holiday. Hooker always felt a little creepy when the traffic was down. For years, he thought it was because he knew he wouldn't be getting any tows, but then one late night, he was waiting out a slow night over at Ace's house, and they were watching old movies. Vincent Price's movie *The Last Man on Earth* came on, and Hooker knew why he hated holidays—there was no traffic. He had gotten up and driven over to Dolly's and slept on the couch until he got a flat tire at four in the morning.

As he finished cinching down the ropes on the tanks, he grabbed the lead hammer from out of his permanent hole. He started toward the rear tires to check the air pressure when he noticed the kid just standing and staring down the street. He slowly walked around the working bed of the tow truck.

Hooker looked down the street where the Squirt was looking. "What's up?" he asked quietly.

"What day is this?"

"Monday...?" Hooker frowned as he watched the Squirt scan the empty street.

"What is the day about?"

"It's President's Day... why?" Both were still looking down the street.

"What offices would be open?"

"None..." Hooker's eyes started scanning rapidly. Something was really wrong, and he didn't see it.

"Then who would the UPS truck be delivering to on this block?"

"Maybe he just—"

The Squirt started walking. "It was parked there when we got here. They're on a very tight schedule."

Hooker followed. The truck was definitely wrong… even if UPS delivered on holidays. "What are you thinking?"

The Squirt started walking faster. "Radio for a bomb squad. It's a Ford van—UPS only uses Chevy vans made by Grumman. That is *not* a real UPS truck."

Hooker changed course. Running to the cab, he climbed into Mae and grabbed the microphone from behind his seat.

"Dolly, we're at the old county building just off Guadalupe Parkway. We have a bogus UPS truck, and it may be a bomb. We need to get the area blocked off, and the bomb squad rolled."

"10-4, Hooker. We're on it. You get out of there. I don't want to lose you to something stupid. Let the police do their job."

"One of them is here right now."

"Crap. You tell the kid to stop playing cowboy and get out of there."

Hooker looked in the mirror and could see the kid standing on the front bumper of the truck. He was pumping his fist in the air—it was their private code for *danger and hurry.*

Hooker slammed Mae into reverse and dumped the clutch as he hit the air brake release. Mae spun both sets of rear tires as she slewed backward into the street. Hooker could smell the burned rubber as he closed on the scene in the rearview mirrors. He backed and then slowed as he lined up with the front of the step-van.

As he stopped, he saw the Squirt hit the side box holding the hand tools. Hooker slid out and ran toward the back.

"What…?"

"It's full of fertilizer. One wall is laced with cord to blow. There's a box with nine green lights. I can only imagine the doors are booby-trapped." The kid fell on the ground and rolled under the truck. Hooker could hear him continue. "There's a digital clock on the dashboard with wires running back into the cargo area. It is counting down—there're only twelve minutes left."

Hooker could hear the kid working the ratchet wrench on something. "What are you…?"

"Dropping the driveline…"

Hooker looked down the street the way Mae was pointed. The map scrolled out in his mind. Even though this wasn't his territory, he was nonetheless very familiar with where things were and where they led. He spun around and opened the door to the levers controlling the booms and towing equipment. He lowered the sling in preparation for the tow. The kid was right—they could not leave the van there, and the bomb squad would never make it in time.

Hooker ran to the cab and swung up into his seat. He backed the sling up under the front end gently. He saw the kid roll out.

The Squirt threw the wrench in the toolbox and slammed the door shut with a kick of his boot. He raced back to the sling and Hooker.

"We set the J-hooks like usual but only run the chains under the roller bar. Don't lock them on the tie-off hooks. We cross the chains over the front and set them on the opposing boom cable. When we get up to the run-out area of the airport, we can kick them loose and leave it in the middle of the runway and let it blow."

Hooker looked at him as they started setting the hooks on the front steering. "How are we going to let them run out? I'm not stopping and then get blown to Texas."

The kid hesitated and returned to setting the chain. "I'm thinking."

They tied off the chain, and Hooker started bringing the front end off the ground. Neither one stopped to think the van or the frontend might be booby-trapped.

The van rose and did not blow.

The Squirt suddenly jumped in the back of the working bed. He scrambled up to where the welding rig sat secured. He looked at the cutting torch and then pawed around in the box. He found another cutting head and screwed it into place. "I need duct tape."

Hooker opened the side box and grabbed a roll. "Here."

The Squirt caught the roll and taped the handles of the cutting torch heads to the uprights guiding the cables coming off the two large spools. The torch tips were now pointed directly at the cables two inches away. "I need some cord—about ten or twelve feet lengths—two of them if you have it."

Hooker reached in another box and drew out lengths of half-inch nylon cord. He did a fast shuffle of his arms and cut the lengths. He now knew what the Squirt was doing.

"Time?"

Hooker ran to the back and jumped up on Mae's bed so he could see the clock. "Five minutes and thirty seconds on my mark... four, three, two, mark." He could hear the Squirt start the torches. The flames sounded angry.

As Hooker jumped down and ran for the cab, he saw the kid pull the two cords and test the loops taped to the handles of the cutting torches. The flames constricted to pencils of blue super-hot flames. They hit the cables direct. He released the cords, and the gentle flames wafted in the morning air. As Hooker clambered in the cab, the Squirt swung around the heat shield of the exhaust stack.

"Damn."

"What?"

"Go! I just burned my hand on the exhaust stack." He never thought about the heat on a half-inch nylon cord.

As they pulled away, the driveline of the step-van came loose and lay were the bomb van had been. The bomb squad was two minutes away.

TEN BLOCKS AWAY, Felix was looking down the street and then at his watch. The sign on the post said the bus should have been there seven minutes before. He was worried.

"Holiday," the woman said.

Felix spun. "Did you say something?"

The woman looked up from her knitting. "I said, the bus don't run on that schedule. It's a holiday. The number fo-teen done come but every hour on holidays. It won't be here none for at least another half hour. We be lucky if it come then." She went back to her knitting and ignored the man who was dancing around the bus-stop sign.

She had seen her share of antsy kids, and this one had never grown up.

Felix knew if he started to run, she would remember him. If he stayed, he ran the risk of getting caught when the bomb blew. Then the weight of what the woman had said hit him.

"Which holiday?"

The heavyset dark woman took a couple of more stitches. Then her hands lowered to her lap. "Hmm… I think they call it just President's day now. Used to be Washington and Lincoln's birthdays, but you know them politicians out there in Washington. They just love to have long weekends and vacations. So they done take away the fine men's birthdays and just made them share a single day." She shook her head as her knitting resumed. "Just a terrible shame if you asked me. But do they ask poor Laretta Walters, no sir, they do not. Just a cryin' shame."

Holiday. A Federal Holiday. Offices would be closed. Nobody would be working. It was all a waste. Felix sagged onto the other end of the bench. He had lost.

Laretta Walters looked at the man at the other end of the bench. "You okay, young man? You don't look so good. It's only a bus, for gosh sakes."

Felix slowly looked up at the woman. He blinked and thought about what she had said. Dejected, he rose and wandered off. He had become adrift.

32

END OF THE LINE

Mae West roared down the street, slowly building speed. Hooker was highly aware of the nature of the bomb tied to the end of his truck. He had turned on all the lights, rotators, and flashers. He considered using the siren but was afraid the bomb might be booby-trapped for sirens.

"Mama, the bomb is on the move. I'm hauling it down the Guadalupe to the north end of the airport. Call the airport and tell them a bomb will be going off at the end in less than four minutes. This is not a threat—this is a promise."

"Hooker, damn it all. I told you to wait for the police. They are almost there."

"Dolly, this time, the boom is happening on its clock, not yours."

The Squirt chimed in as he counted. "Two-fourteen."

"The Squirt says about two minutes. Gotta go."

The gate at the end of the runway where the parkway curved did not have a chance. The front bumper the size of a Volkswagen and backed by eleven tons of angry woman blew the gate nearly forty feet in the air and threw it for at least forty yards. Mae never quivered.

Hooker made a giant slow loop to line up with the runway.

"Starting the burn now." The Squirt pulled on the two cords. In back, the two cutting torch pencils of blue death raced out. The stretched cables turned red and then started to melt.

The nylon cords were pulled tight around the exhaust stacks heat shield. The shield did what it was designed to do. It had absorbed heat and was slowly giving it off into the air—but not before it had started to melt the cord caught under the other one. The lower cord went to the cutting torch on the passenger side. The cord stretched, and the nylon loop loosened. The hard blue flame fluttered with some yellow.

The service road looped around so a large airplane could use it as an emergency taxi, and they occasionally did. Hooker guided Mae around the large loop.

The cutting flames melted through the cables as, strand by strand, they began to pop. Stretching, pulling, straining, melting…

The nylon cord stretched thinner. The blue flame fluttered into yellow as the hard force of oxygen was shut off.

Mae took the last turn left and began to line up with the runway.

The Squirt started counting down. "Ten, nine…"

The blue cutting flame leaped through what was left of the cable. The weight of the overloaded van did the rest. The one cable snapped. The cable whipped through the pulleys in the boom. The chain slid down and around the roller bar and bounced on the tarmac as the van—still tied to the passenger side of the towing arm—slewed. The left front tire with the fresh breaks touched down.

With the last left turn, the weight of the van pushed hard against the turn. The front tire touching in a locked position forced the van to push harder.

Eleven tons of Mae West and Hooker felt the backend being pushed sideways for the first time. With all the towing of heavy trucks, he had never felt this. He thought to straighten the truck out, but in forcing the new turn, the rear tires broke traction on the smooth landing strips numbers. Mae slewed, and the step-van's rear tires howled as it was whipped around on the overloaded tires. The leading tire pinched as the weight transferred. The single-chain—still wrapped around the cables suspending the roller bar pulled the front corner. The van tipped toward where it was pulled and slammed into the back of Mae West.

Five of the nine green lights turned red. The clock still had four seconds left to count down. Twelve volts raced through wires to sixteen small blasting caps.

To the naked eye, Mae West disappeared into a fireball the size of Candlestick Park. The entire end of the airport became a boiling mass of red, orange, yellow, and black.

An explosion only takes less than a second to happen, but the expansion can take up to a few seconds to reach the entire area of the expanding gasses. Then, as the now vaporized air becomes a void, everything rushes back in, and the secondary concussion occurs.

In the first hundredth of a second, the side of the van was cut and opened up into shrapnel. The load of fertilizer split into two bombs. The upper freeload pushed its way out of the canister of the van and took most of the paint, rigging, and small items off the working bed as it passed at the eighteen-hundred miles per hour mark. The tiny bombs within the fertilizer exploded and ignited the larger mass. Unrestrained, the larger mass snapped the towing booms from their mounts and threw them back past the Guadalupe Parkway—three hundred yards away. Windows rattled as far away as the east side and downtown. Windows facing the airport became shard of glass buried in living-room walls and office cubicles as far away as a mile in any direction.

The lower half of the fertilizer had been compressed when the van snapped around and slammed into the working bed of Mae. Seemingly taking retribution, the small bombs within the larger bomb built up a static explosion. Once released, the rear half of the working bed, as well as the top of the van and armored wall, became flying shrapnel.

The armored wall became lances—turned the old DC-3 sitting out near the end of the runway for years—into a sieve. The holes punched through instantaneously, showing daylight as the two main landing gears were hit, and the whole plane flattened like a pancake to the ground.

Mae's tandem rear axles almost stayed together as they passed through a large control box across from the taxiway. The landing lights would have to wait while the whole was replaced. The new combined mass of metal, switches, gears, axles, and what was left of wheels and tires came to rest in the middle of the southbound parkway.

The tempered glass of the control tower did not stay inside the tower. The leading crystals hit the four men and knocked them against the far bank of desks. One died instantly when his head struck the edge of the desk and snapped his neck as the body passed under. The other made it through the explosion only to suffer the insult that comes at the end of a career of sitting and eating. The heart raced against the blood clot stopping the flow to the brain. The heart pushed harder against the clot, and the arteries exploded.

Everyone exposed on the airfield was knocked about and deafened.

In the silence—the music of tin and steel parts finally falling to the ground prevailed. It would take almost twelve seconds for everything to return to earth.

Four miles away, the trained ear knew the explosion had not occurred where he had left it. Felix kept walking. The train station was at least a thirty-minute walk away. He would stop for the bag in Sacramento. Seattle was two days away.

33

WHAT TO DO ABOUT MAE

Willie stood in the mud. He had been there before. If he closed his right eye and held his head just right—everything would look almost all right. *Almost.*

The back of Mae's sleeper had taken the brunt of the concussion. The custom ribbing to make the sleeper soundproof had held the crushing box away from the cab. The spools of coiled cable had become ovals of heat-welded cable. Effectively, the cab and forward were salvageable—everything else was gone or soon to be.

"What you think, Mr. Knight... time to get a new truck? I have nice five-year-old Peterbilt. It has long frame. I make into max-weight tow truck for when doctors through with Hooker—again... this time."

Willie looked into the mangled and misaligned eyes of Mae West. If he had been dreaming, he knew she would be giving him a wink. There was no other machine like Mae. It may be true about it being what's up front that counts, but Willie had just had an idea of how to make it also about the rest of the machine. He turned with a shy smile and looked down at the Japanese woman with the false eyelashes.

"No new truck, but throwing her onto a new frame for a max-weight rig sounds good, and while we're stretching her, let's add some inches to the sleeper. Sometimes Hooker doesn't travel alone—thirty inches of sleeping space is a little tight."

The Fly looked at him with one of her more evil smiles. "That cat not that big."

Willie snorted. "You haven't tried to share a bed with him."

The Fly snorted. "Hooker or cat?"

———

Two miles away, Hooker laid in one bed and the Squirt in the other. They were both sleeping thanks to large doses of painkillers and sedatives.

The nurse turned to the two students shadowing her. Her long braid whipped up and over her shoulder. Bobby Sue smiled at Candy and Holly. "At least, this time, they didn't end up with more metal shoved into them."

Holly blushed. "There're already enough scars."

Candy harrumphed. "Which one?"

The three chorused, "Both."

The blonde civilian adjusted her tight sweater. Beth smiled… she found the scars to be sexy.

ONE DAY UNDER THE GRASS

A SOUTHSIDE HOOKER NOVEL — BOOK 5

WORKING DOWNTOWN

If the girls had been a little younger, a little classier, a little prettier, and a little smarter, even as streetwalkers, they would work San Francisco or Los Angeles. But everyone has to be somewhere. Even in the night in downtown San Jose, there was a little something for almost any taste or preference.

The johns circled in their seven-year-old family cars—some too lazy to remove the child's booster seat from the backseat, others not caring. The color of their money and how fast they finished was everything to the girls.

The sidewalks were barely clean during the day. By night, the gutters collected fortified wine-laced puke, urine, feces, used condoms, and broken syringes, each a gemstone, jewelry of the broken dreams decorating the lives of those at the bottom, who only had lower to look forward to with each passing day.

The girls all knew each other, at least in passing. They knew who did what and who was really what or not. They all knew which block was theirs to walk. They also knew what was semi-clean to wear—and got the best responses—both in stops and spurts. They knew each other's names… most by their street names, some even by their real names. Some even shared cheap hotel rooms together—as the years, drugs, alcohol, and trade all took their toll.

The one female there night after night was the one who seemed least affected by it all. Pete, short for Petunia, worked but not in the sex trade.

The dirty blonde ponytail hung to her shoulders. The gray-blue uniform jumpsuit matched her one blue eye. The red-brown of the thread on her nametag—Pete—matched her other eye. The uniform was loose and baggy—even on the woman her size. Her large pendulous breasts swayed unrestrained in the suit — her work-battered hands raw, callused, and with ropey muscle. The muscles played like piano strings as her hands moved, guiding the three-wheeled Westcoaster scooter, a dump bed on the back.

The mail carriers had the same scooter, but a shell protected them from the winter weather. Pete also knew, during the summer, the heat made the shells almost unbearable to drive in. The fiberglass shell also made them loud inside. Pete hated noise.

When she had originally gotten the job, she worked during the day. The noise and smell of the traffic made her almost quit. But, when a night shift came open, she begged for the job. By ten o'clock, downtown San Jose mostly slept—except the ten-block area where the girls walked.

Pete pulled the cart over to the curb in front of Original Joe's. Her eyes continuously moved. She took in everything around her. She once spotted a sparkle on the sidewalk, forty feet away. The streetlight had refracted through the stone—the diamond almost three and a half carats. The pawnshop traded it straight across for an eighteen-foot aluminum canoe someone had painted black.

The new concrete trash cans lining the streets of downtown had beauty tops. Pete found them to be an added annoyance. Every single can, she had to take the lid off, pull the liner up from between the concrete shell and the metal trash can, tie the bag off, and then lift and throw it into the back of her scooter. Then she had to lift the can out to put the new plastic bag liner on, stick it back in the concrete shell, and put the beauty top back on.

If anything was broken, she had to fill out a form to request the day unit come and replace the broken piece. Some nights she wanted to take the short pipe she carried for protection to the beauty top of every single one of the one hundred and fourteen trashcans.

The city-smart guys had mapped out her area and figured she could process one can every five minutes. This gave her plenty of time in her ten-hour shift to handle even the forms. It had not taken her long to figure out which cans were full, which cans were always only half-full, and even better—those which required changing once a week. Pete hated nosy people and hated worse those people who told her how to run her life or do her job.

The only manager who worked the night shift was under a truck or car in the garage. Pete knew him. Most of the night, he was asleep on the creeper. If he processed more than two or three vehicles in a shift, he had consumed too much coffee and needed to work it off. The paperwork was also pushed off onto the day shift. Pete had seen him rearrange the vehicles in the lot to make it seem like a lot was done—but mostly, it had been sleep.

With a boss like him, she didn't feel bad about how she did her job of collecting the city's trash.

Can after can, she moved methodically through the city. By ten o'clock, she was in the busy section with the working girls. This block was a quieter part on the north end. Pete knew the six girls who worked the block from Monday night to Saturday night. Her night off during the week had floated up and down from Tuesday to Friday. The one thing a woman in the city could never get was two days off in a row. Her boss never worked on Saturday or Sunday. One was sports night, and the other was the Sabbath. She was never sure what religion he claimed to be, so she didn't know or care which day was his religious day. Her lack of religion didn't matter—she got Sunday off because there wasn't enough garbage to collect.

Pete pulled the scooter to the curb. She turned the engine off and just sat looking down the street. Her eyes scanned the street, but a part of her mind was twelve hours and twelve miles away. The car pulled up at the end of the block—a 1960 Buick, four-door, a family man who should be using his money to buy better food instead of a blowjob on a Friday night. Pete could see the head of hair in the passenger seat.

Pete turned and opened the small utility box. Pulling her Roy Rogers lunch pail out, she got off the scooter and sat on the bus stop bench. The last bus was at nine-fifty. The next one would come just before dawn.

Her right hand reached into the back pocket of her overalls and withdrew the latex gloves. On the street, it was easier to put on clean gloves instead of finding somewhere to wash her hands. The leather work gloves lay on the seat of the scooter.

She opened the lunch pail and withdrew the thermos. She removed the top and set the cup down. Reaching into the lunch pail, she removed the sandwich and then the still cool can of cola. Prying off the pop-top, she dropped it into the can. Aside from the bubbles, the cola looked just like coffee when she poured it into the cup. Chugging the last of the can, she pitched it into the back of the scooter.

Pete pulled the sandwich out of its baggie and leaned back. Taking a bite of the sandwich, she chewed slowly and waited.

The footsteps were light, but the sound of how the heels thudded on the sidewalk disclosed the exhaustion. Pete knew the woman was only a little over five feet tall and wore a size four dress. The extra padding and breasts helped her fill out the stretchy dresses she liked. From the back, she was alluring, but her face showed her age and drug abuse. The woman was well past her street prime—but had nowhere else to go.

"Hi, Pete..." The voice was a little girl but was husky from age and alcohol.

Pete looked up at her. "Oh, oh, hi... um... Star. How are you?"

The woman came around and plopped mid-bench. Her sigh deep and mournful, she replied, "You know... same old same old."

Pete took a bite of her sandwich and slowly chewed as she leaned back on the bench and nodded. She nudged her chin at the scooter half full of bags of garbage. "Picking up for me... how about you?" She looked over at the woman. Again, she thought about how the body package was great, but the face was just a hole in the package where someone had scribbled crayon over the face, drawing Groucho Marx eyebrows and the hint of a mustache. Even the eyes were slightly crooked.

"Two so far..."

Pete took another bite. *Hope springs eternal.* Ten o'clock—the woman's chances of one more blowjob tonight were between slim and never going to happen. Two or three ten-dollar blowjobs a night was what the woman averaged and lived on. She shared an eight-dollar room with another whore who used it until midnight. The services she offered didn't work well in the front seat of a car.

"I don't know, Pete…" The woman sighed deeper as she looked up and down the almost empty street. "Sometimes, I just want to lie down and just never wake up."

"That's kind of a depressing thing to say…"

The whore looked at Pete. "It just doesn't matter anymore—my prince is never going to come and sweep me off my feet. Watch…" She saw a few cars coming. She hooked both thumbs in the stretchy top of her dress and pulled it down and under her teats. She sat back with both hanging out with no bra.

The three cars passed without so much as a head turned. The two women watched as the taillights flashed bright red for half a second when they got to the end of the block where two hookers with long legs and not much else but a smile stood.

Pete looked back at Star. The whore was pulling herself back in her top. "See… nothing."

Pete thought a moment and then pulled the flipper on the rubber stopper of the thermos. She pulled the stopper out and passed it over to the woman. "Here, you can have the rest of my coffee. I'm not going to finish it." She held up her red lid-cup.

Star took a sip. "It's a little old, but it tastes good after the last guy. I swear… I don't know what the hell people eat these days. His sperm tasted like a bad poop in a goat barn."

Pete continued to eat. She didn't want to know how the woman knew about goats—much less the taste of the animal's poop.

The occasional car drove past. Pete sipped on her soda and finished her sandwich. She reached over and carefully picked up the thermos where it had fallen on the bench. She poured out the remaining warm coffee and cyanide. She packed it in the lunch pail with the baggie.

Pete put the pail back in the utility compartment. Turning, she took the beauty lid off the concrete trash bin and pulled up the plastic bag. She tied off the half-full bag, pulled it out, and placed it on the end of the bench. She pulled the metal can out, inserted the new bag, and then put the can back into the concrete shell. Replacing the beauty top, Pete pressed her hands against her back and bent backward, stretching her sore back—as she looked around. The street was empty.

Bending, she pushed her shoulder into the dead woman's gut. She was lighter than Pete thought. She stood, took two steps, and tossed her into the area between the carefully arranged bags of trash. She reached and grabbed the other bag and tossed it on top.

Sliding down onto the seat of the scooter, she glanced at the large watch on her wrist. It had taken almost twenty minutes less than she had planned on. She turned the key and pushed the silver button. The scooter chugged and shuddered to life. Pete put the scooter in gear and eased from the curb. Looking in the rearview mirror, she hung a U-turn in the middle of the empty block. At the corner, the traffic lights had just started to flash red. Moonrise was still an hour away. The temperature sign on the Woolworth's building read eighty-one degrees.

The tiny red taillights of the scooter disappeared up Stevens Creek Boulevard. The whore on the second corner thought it was strange for Pete to be heading north when Pete was usually working south at this time of night. The end of the cigarette swelled hot red as she took another drag. By the time she breathed the smoke out toward the street, a car was coming, and everything else forgotten.

THE MORNING SUN was only half up as the heat of the day started to rise. The barrel-chested man stood in the black aluminum canoe as he pushed on the long pole. The sea of tan grass slid quietly past him. He stood steady in the boat—he had been standing in canoes and pirogues all of his life. The Everglades in Florida, the bayous of southern Louisiana, the sea of grass in the South San Francisco bay, all of them to Lane were the same —grass above, water, and mud below.

Lane saw the world as night and day. The sky, grass, and areas he moved in were day. The surface of the water was the demarcation border leading into the night. Lane remembered his mother telling him as a boy

—when a body slides into the water, they are sliding into night. All the water in his life had been dark. His momma never lied.

He tugged at the binding bandage around his chest. He hated his chest. As a man, it betrayed him. The bandage helped flatten the shape, but at times, he felt like he couldn't breathe. He pulled the long-billed hat closer to his eyes. The shadow was dark, but in the early sunlight on the water, the reflection played in the blue and brown eyes. In school, he was teased about how he must be from Australia. Rarely did those mean children ever tease him again.

The canoe flowed on the freshwater river, which ran between the two saltwater marshes and grew full of salt grass and bulrushes. He knew what he was looking for, the area where the most crabs and ghost shrimp were —under the trestle. He tossed his head, and the short ponytail flipped off his shoulder and hung down the back of his neck to his shoulders.

He switched sides with the pole and started to turn the canoe into the grass. He looked up at the timbers of the trestle. He hadn't been to this spot since just after the New Year. He could name what was under the sea of grass—they had all been friends. Now they slept in the night of the water.

The back of his hands was ropey with muscle. He pulled back the trap. The woman quietly lay as if she were asleep.

Lane reached down and lifted the slightly built body to the edge of the canoe. Placing his left hand in the middle of the crossbeam, he lightly jumped the gunwale and stood in the shallow water and mud to just above his waist. The water wasn't cold, but it wasn't warm. He reached in for the body. Lifting, he turned and then slowly pushed the body under the grass and into the night of the dark water.

He watched the last of the legs and feet slip into the shadows and night. He whispered, "Sleep... Sleep well, Star."

FUNCTIONAL FORENSICS

Hooker, still a bit blurry-eyed, opened his bedroom door. The silence had woken him.

The morning was his time to sleep since he worked at night. Certain noises in the house were missing. No matter where he was sleeping—certain noises of life reassured him and kept him asleep. The silence wasn't one of them. The only sound was something irregularly and lightly hitting metal…

He rolled over, looking at the dimly illuminated clock. The forty-four card flipped over, making it nine-forty-five. No tiny red dot glowing —*morning*. Hooker lay listening. No murmurs of people talking. With four others in the house, there should have been talking.

Hooker swung his feet over the edge of the bed. Running his right hand over his face, he rubbed his eyes. He grabbed his pants off his socks and boots as he rose. Dragging his pants, he walked into the dark bathroom adjoining his bedroom, which made up his private suite.

He raised his arms and smelled his pits—he'd shower later. Flushing, he pulled on his pants and brushed his teeth. He stood looking into the mirror, remembering he no longer drove Mae West—his giant 1959 Marmon tow truck. He thought about the five-ton truck parked out front. He groaned, turning off the light.

So much changed since he and the Squirt blew up the end of the San Jose airport, along with Mae West. The time in the hospital had been fairly short. The only surgery, this time, removed a large piece of cable shrapnel, which had whipped around and pierced his door and calf. The scar occasionally itched but didn't hurt.

He scratched at the old scars on his chest where the dimes had gone in. Padding out of his door, he still rubbed at his eyes as he took in three of the four other residents sitting silently at the table.

Manny leaned back and quietly sipped his mug of coffee as he watched the Squirt work on the toaster. Stella looked up. At seeing Hooker, she stuck her arm out for a hug—Hooker was capable of getting his own coffee.

Hooker folded over, hugging Stella and added a kiss on the top of her head. "Is the toaster broken?"

"Shhhh…"

Hooker put up his hands in surrender. Turning, he got his coffee. As he glanced at the clock, he remembered he was starting early for Don. His usual six-ish start would be when he got his first call after two. He looked out the window—thinking about working during the day. It paid better—but there were more people to deal with. More people meant more traffic in the way and more breakdowns and small accidents. The big stuff in the night had been his real meat and potatoes for over ten years.

Mae West had been the fastest of any tow truck in the five counties. Her booms and four-footed outriggers made her the most mobile crane for dead-drag recoveries and rollovers. She had proved her mettle on a recent train derailment with cars full of toxic chemicals. Even the Burlington Northern Railroad's twenty-ton Manitowoc rail crane couldn't do the rollovers needed, nor could it have lifted the hundred and forty-ton overloaded tank cars.

His golden girl had seemed almost indestructible—until the explosion ripped her into nothing left but the cab and front-end. The banner draped over the pin-up painting of the actress on the front read 'It's What's Up Front That Counts' never rang so true before. He was going to miss those eleven tons of hot, fast mama.

He returned to the arm of his other mama, or at least the one still here.

His other surrogate mother, Stella's sister, wouldn't be up for another four hours to run the Night Dispatch as well as the city of San Jose. She only lent it back to the regular people to take care of it during the day…

Hooker leaned over and kissed Stella on the head again.

She didn't look up. "Hooker, you are either still asleep or slipping. You already gave me my morning kiss."

"This one was for being who you are."

Manny grumped at the other end of the table. "Then why are you stopping?"

"Manny T. Loverbe, you leave my boy alone. Some of these things take time to learn. In fact, I remember a day in 1956—it was a Tuesday in May, you left the house without kissing me goodbye."

Manny hid his face in his mug. Eighteen years and he still had never heard the end of it.

"You didn't come home either." She looked up at Hooker as the Squirt looked up from the toaster. "He was resting up at his other home—*the hospital*. A knife in the back can do that to you."

Hooker and the Squirt looked toward the retired detective in the wheelchair. Manny snorted. "Not up for the retelling. Let it be."

Stella wasn't about to stop. She leaned her head against Hooker's hip. "My lips ached that day—all day. And then there was still no relief while they had him in an oxygen tent."

"She went and kissed one of the K-9 dogs—ruined him from ever working again."

The Squirt coughed. "Okay, you just got a little too deep. I might have to go put my boots on."

Hooker frowned. The probing of the toaster had removed its bottom. Spread over a large sheet of white paper laid all the crumbs that had been in the appliance. The Squirt worked with tiny spatulas, brushes, and tweezers placed next to various magnifying glasses and a notepad.

"What is it you're doing, Squirt?"

Manny snickered. "It's a pop final exam in forensics."

Stella nodded as she got up to fix Hooker some breakfast. "I had the police lab clean the toaster out a few months ago—while you two were lounging about at Good Sam, chatting up all the wrong nurses." She gave him a stern eye.

She continued as she pulled out the omelet pan. "I have kept a record of everything I ever put in there. Now the Squirt has to replicate the list and the percentages of what was toasted."

Hooker moved around to look at the Squirt's list so far. The tiny crumbs were sorted into areas on the large white sheet of paper where he had labeled—white, wheat, sourdough, bagel, oat bran, and other. His notes were just thoughts about certain characteristics of the different breads toasted and why.

Hooker picked up a large magnifying glass and looked at the single curved seed in the area marked *other*. The side of his mouth facing Manny curled up. Manny cleared his throat, and Hooker put the glass down. He returned to one of the chairs on the other side and sat to watch the process.

Every crumb or crumb particle was examined, qualified, and sorted to its designated area. Some of the pieces were small enough to require the Squirt to pull down his head magnifier to look through for a super-enlargement. More than half of the tiny specs on the paper Hooker wouldn't even qualify as dirt—they were fine enough to be more like dust.

Knowing how Manny and his lessons were always about a much bigger picture than just crumbs in a toaster—Hooker was curious. He looked at the intent young man working. He had seen the look overtake the Squirt many times and knew he was beyond any distraction.

He turned to Manny and asked in a low voice. "This isn't about crumbs, is it?"

Manny put his mug down and braced his forearms on the armrests of the wheelchair. He pushed up and adjusted his body. Hooker waited as the retired detective became the teacher.

"When you go into a room having been trashed—you see a trashed room. With training, you start to see how it might have gotten trashed. A single person who searches a room methodically will leave a room trashed in a methodical trail. Two people create havoc, but it is a formal havoc. When there is a violent fight, there is nothing sacred, and so everything is swept up in the tornado of violence. With time and even finer training, the tornado aftermath can reveal how many people were in the fight, and even sometimes, the size of the combatants, or even their sex. Women fight a lot different from men."

"How so?"

"When they get angry, they throw stuff, but always in their mind, they are cleaning up after." He looked up at his wife. "Have you ever thrown any plates or crockery?"

"Only those ugly square Melmac we used to have." She held the heavy plate of her cherished Fiestaware to her chest. Her right hand absent-mindedly stroked the smooth glaze.

Manny held out his hand to the proof. "They usually throw things they know won't break. Throwing dishes at a husband is something Holly-wood made up. It's dramatic and shocking—but not based in reality—as a general rule. If the fight is for one's life, then all the rules are thrown out the window. Anything goes."

"So the crumbs?" Hooker took a sip of his coffee as Stella placed the plate in front of him.

"Once you determine what kind of a fight had ensued, you need to also see all the tiny details, right down to a hair on the carpet."

Hooker took a bite of the omelet and chewed. Swallowing with a sip of coffee, he frowned. He knew when Manny mentioned a detail, it was important—not a throwaway.

"You mentioned a hair on the carpet. It could have just been a hair. They fall out every day…"

Manny smiled. "So we know the fighters were a large man and a woman. The occupant of the apartment is a woman with short dark brown hair. A witness saw a bald man entering the apartment shortly before a neighbor called the police to report screaming. We presumably now have our two fighters. But what if the hair on the floor is about seventeen inches long and blond?"

"We have a third person of interest…"

"Bingo." Manny smiled and took back his mug as he leaned back in the chair.

Then all watched as the Squirt sorted out the last few chunks. He moved a sizable black something into the area marked other. He then grabbed his mug and sat back, evaluating his work.

Manny smiled. "Well?"

The Squirt pointed to each of the marked areas as he spoke. "Almost every day, ten pieces of wheat toast are made. Manny is diabetic, and the whole wheat provides the lowest glycemic problem. There are no crumbs from white bread because they don't have a heat tolerance and would be black char. You toasted sourdough about three times, which would match the three times in the last two months we have had French toast made with the thick-sliced sourdough. So you were toasting off the leftovers. The oat bran comes from Candy. She brings up her own bread the two days a week we all eat together."

He touched his tweezers to the large chunk of black. "The raisin is from raisin toast, which you got especially for Sissy when she came down with Claire and Norm to visit us in the hospital." He looked up at the smiling Stella. "You sent them back with the rest of the loaf to one, get rid of the evidence, and two, you hate raisins."

Stella clapped as she laughed. "Very good."

The Squirt turned to Manny. "And so we have come to the final. What would have thrown me was this." He pointed at the tiny seed. "At first look, I thought it was a caraway seed. Logically it would have come from rye toast. The toast would fit with you two being Jewish, but I have never seen Stella slice a brisket thin enough to make a Rueben sandwich. Plus, I know you don't like sauerkraut, so Stella doesn't use it. The seed is similar to caraway, but the light and dark lines with stripes running the length are not color differences—so the seed is not caraway. I can only assume it is a wild card and was only thrown into the toaster to confuse or trip me up." He stood and walked toward the pantry.

Stella chuckled as Manny frowned at not understanding. She called out as he reached the door. "It should be the second shelf down and about the third one over from the left."

The Squirt returned a moment later. Opening the jar, he tumbled out a few seeds. With tweezers, he picked one up. With a magnifying glass, he took a quick look. He set it back down and smiled at Stella. "Bravo. Very close and easily confused, but fennel would never be used in rye bread. But it would be used for dill bread."

Stella, the consummate cook, frowned. "How would you make dill bread?"

The Squirt watched her with a deadpan face. "With some naughty dough..."

It took a few seconds until Manny started snickering. Hooker's mind wasn't far behind. Stella looked at her youngest baby and realized he was always a man—he just hadn't grown into his pants yet.

"You owe the swear jar fifty-cents... make it a dollar. You can pay for my having to repeat it to my sister." The four chuckled at the great but naughty pun.

IN THE SWING OF SUMMER

Stella picked up the phone and talked softly. The two men ignored her. Stella looked at the ceiling. "Sure, he can make it. He's in the shower, but he only takes a few minutes anyway. I'll tell him." She paused. "Okay, thanks, Karen." She hung up.

As she started to walk away, she felt the four sets of eyes on her. If she didn't know Box was outside lying on the deck sleeping in the sun, she knew she would have been feeling five. She laughed as she walked, shaking her head. "Stand down, gentlemen. It's only a flat tire."

"Yeah, that's how it all started with the shotgun…"

She froze, turning, her finger up and facing out. Her one eye was down, and her lips were set. "Don't you dare jinx this day…"

She pushed her way into Hooker's suite.

"Sweetheart, you have a T-wonderful. Karen is giving you three to get in the truck before she bangs it and starts the clock."

"Thanks, Mom…" The voice echoed off the tile walls. She knew if she didn't leave instantly, his naked body would be pushing her out of the way.

She stood at the front door and waited. She counted the seconds, and she hadn't hit ninety when he came bustling out of the bedroom.

"I'll keep in touch, and if I'm clear, I'll pick you up a bit after seven, and we can eat at the hospital if you want."

The Squirt looked up at Stella. She snorted. "Leftover lasagna."

"Sure, seven sounds great."

Hooker kissed her on both cheeks and the forehead. As he walked through the plaza to the front gates of the hacienda, he called for his cat. "Box—go time." Stella watched the orange streak flash past the front arch and stop. He still looked for the giant Mae instead of just a large truck.

At least the large bench seat fit the box the twenty-pound cat rode in. The two were inseparable.

Hooker grabbed the strange mic. "1-4-1. I'm 10-8."

"10-4, 1-4-1, your T-1, flat tire is the right rear on a 1970 El Dorado, white. The woman member will meet you inside the Marie Calendars. She called this one direct to the shop, so it's a shop call." Hooker smiled. $9.57 straight in his pocket instead of only half of the usual $7.41, plus the fuel and truck was on Don instead of coming out of Hooker's half.

"10-4. Any word yet?"

"Hooker, you asked the same question at two this morning. When they locate him, they will let you know."

Hooker hung the mic looking at the cat already close to sleep. "Beans and wieners, Box. Willie should have told me where he was running off to."

The cat half-opened his one eye and then rolled over to ignore Hooker. He had serious napping to do, and Hooker needed to stop whining. Neither one of them was happy with the truck—even if it was brand new. Don, his boss, had ordered it up for Hooker while he and the Squirt were in the hospital this last time. The part about them blowing up Mae West all over the north end of the airport, which shut the entire airport down for almost eleven days, was beside the point.

The city was still trying to figure out how to repay Hooker and the Squirt for saving a few dozen lives and one of the major county office buildings. The airport was screaming for Hooker's head, skin, and anything else. The city informed the Port Authority if they tried to sue Hooker, the city would pull the port's charter, or at least make any ideas of expansion difficult. The lawyers for American Airlines and PSA put it more succinctly—shut up, or they would both pull out.

Hooker couldn't figure out how the city could threaten the port when they owned it. It would be like holding a knife to your own throat, and then, with the other hand sticking a gun to your heart and saying... *go ahead, try it, and I blow a hole through your middle.* It just didn't make much sense. Dolly tried to explain it to him, and then, even she gave up.

The Cadillac sat near the front door. The heat was already in the high nineties, if not over one hundred. Hooker didn't blame the member for not standing outside to wait for the tow truck—even if they knew one would show up in fewer than twenty minutes.

There were few cars in the parking lot in the afternoon. The bar crowd would start in an hour, seniors the following hour, and finally, the dinner rush after six. Even with the solid air conditioning, Hooker knew people's appetite dropped off in the summer heat. He pulled into the two spaces next to the flat tire.

He left the air conditioner running as it was blowing into Box's face. The cat had his one eye closed and was leaning into the air. Hooker smiled as he left his partner to his comfort.

Stepping into the restaurant was a thirty-degree drop. The large muscular woman standing at the receptionist desk had a distinctive leather-braided ponytail. Hooker hadn't noticed any choppers in the parking lot, so he was a little confused.

"Did you put on training wheels, Max?"

The woman laughed and turned. "You're late, Hooker."

He glanced at his watch. *Eighteen minutes—slow but on time.* "Nope. Right on time."

"Your truck says if I want a quickie—"

Hooker's face turned sour. "Not driving my truck. I'm in a pig with only five hundred horses. The bean-herder can barely get out of its own way. I feel like you would if you had a Moped loaner."

Max laughed. "I heard. Sorry about your big truck. I liked the look of her. It fit you."

"Yeah, well..." He shrugged. "So is the Caddie yours?"

Max showed her hand at the tiny woman sitting on the long bench.

"Hooker, meet my great-aunt Poppy. Her parents were some of the first florists west of St. Louis. They were in Hollywood when it started and were the florist to the stars. Poppy, this nice young man is Hooker."

The woman stood and smiled. "You're a hooker? Are you my birthday present also?"

Max laughed. "Poppy, behave. His name is Hooker."

Hooker laughed as he shook the elderly woman's hand. "I'm also a hooker, but not in the Hollywood sense of the word. I drive a tow truck, and it has a hook on the back."

"Well, then, let's stop flapping our lips and go flip the Firestones." She laughed at Hooker's face. "I may be eighty-four, sonny, but I know my way around a car or two."

Hooker smiled as he thought of a few people he knew she would fit in with.

As Hooker placed the flat in the trunk, Max handed him a twenty.

"I don't have change. Let me go inside—"

Max cut him off. "I was counting on it—in case you have a date for tonight. Stop by on Monday. I'll have chili, and it's slow—we can talk."

"Thanks, Max. I'd like that." Turning to the woman sitting in the seat with the door open. "It was very nice meeting you, Poppy. If you ever get up to the main library, you ought to look up a librarian named Maddie Robinson."

"Is she from the Salinas area?"

Hooker smirked and hung his shoulders. "Yeah, you probably already know her."

"Only know of her. For a number of years, she was the fastest woman in the world. I think her family built race cars or something. I would love to meet her."

Max looked at Hooker with a raised eyebrow. "And you know this woman…?"

"She's my aunt." Hooker smiled as he now knew what the topic of conversation would be the next night.

Hooker climbed back in the truck and rolled up the window as he did the paperwork. The truck may be a slow pig, but it did have a top-notch air conditioner.

"1-4-1." He called Night Dispatch for any commercial calls.

It was still the day shift, and Karen answered. "1-4-1, we have nothing, but I think the club just got one for you."

"10-4." Switching microphones to the auto club radio, Hooker checked in. "1-4-1, show me 10-98 on Blossom Hill."

The auto club was rarely busy on Sunday afternoons, so Jake was right back in his clipped rapid file style. "10-4, 1-4-1, holding T-3 at Granny's Attic, going to member's mechanic on San Jose Avenue. Red, AMC Pacer. Timeout: four-twenty-four."

Hooker was tempted to ask if it was okay to just drive the truck over the lemon car, but he was civil. "10-4, Pacer at the Attic."

The traffic was sparse on Blossom Hill and only slightly more once he turned onto Almaden Expressway. The real crowds would not be coming back from Calero reservoir for at least another hour or two. The heat would keep them in or on the water. The heat of summer kept many people indoors, out at the lakes, or away on vacations. Hooker still hated working during the daylight hours—it just meant more people, more traffic, and with the heat, heated tempers.

Hooker pulled up to find one such temper boiling over and kicking at not only tires, but the fenders, doors, and anything they could dent but not break. Hooker didn't even need to get close to hear the man swearing at the car.

"1-4-1, show me 10-97 at the Attic. I have a member, or at least someone kicking this car into just dents."

"10-4, 1-4-1. Member is male with the last name of Michaels." Hooker smiled at the syrupy voice that sounded almost like a twelve-year-old girl. He had met Bethany. She was built just like her uncle—who played for the San Francisco 49ers.

Hooker double-clicked the key on the microphone and slid out of the truck. He worked hard at restoring his deadpan face. With a Pacer, Gremlin, or Pinto, it was a hard thing to do.

"Are you the auto club member?"

Hooker eyed the dented panels of the car as he waited for the man to finish fuming. Some of the dents had rust along the creases—this was not the first time at the kicking rodeo.

The man fished the card out of his wallet. "You know Nick, up on San Jose Avenue?"

"Sure, he's right across from the Fly. An easy push when Nick can't fix it."

The man's head snapped up. Hooker swallowed. He knew he best remain quiet. Some people were sensitive about their cars.

The man leaned back against his Pacer, folding his arms across his chest. "Let me ask you. How many of these do you tow?"

Hooker's mouth drifted closed. With Mae West, the man would have been wondering why a truck nine times as big as his car responded to the tow. But Hooker knew what the man's question truly was.

"Compared to Fords and Chevys, they didn't make very many of these."

The man knew he would have to work for the right answer. "How many of these do you tow, straight to the scrap heap, instead of a repair place?"

Hooker was now in the corner. "About half."

The man curled his lips against his teeth. "My dad always drove Ramblers..."

"Good cars. Built like a brick. Simple and made for work. They ran like a Sherman tank—sometimes dependable and sometimes..." Hooker waited.

The man's smile was slow to come but finally got there. "Let's let Nick give the last rites."

"Where can I drop you off?"

The man looked at the sky, evaluating the day. "I live about a mile from here... I think I need the walk... and time to think. I need a dependable car. Nothing fancy, but it needs to run when I need it."

Hooker rubbed his jaw. "Nick knows a lot of people and a lot of cars. You tell him what you want to spend and what kind of car you need by nine tomorrow morning, and I'll bet he has three cars by noon for you to go look at."

The man was a little surprised. "Nick...?"

Hooker nodded. "It's his business... and he would want you in a car he knows will make you happy and will bring to him for oil and tune-ups."

"I never thought... makes sense. I'll call him tomorrow morning. God knows I certainly don't want to be taking the bus to Santa Clara every day for very long."

A half an hour later, Hooker was backing the car into Nick's apron. There were already three other cars on the large apron with only room for two more. Monday would be a busy day for the man.

"1-4-1."

"Go ahead, 1-4-1."

"Show me 10-98 on the Pacer."

"Did you get it started?"

Hooker laughed. "It was a T-7. It went to Nick Ivankovitch on San Jose Avenue."

"10-4. I have a T-5 stall... Might be a T-7 at Branham High. Don was going to get it, but his T-1 turned into a seven."

"Go ahead. Give it to me."

"It's a 1964 Corvair, red with white sidewalls. Member will meet you at the car."

Hooker pinched the bridge of his nose—it was turning into one of those days...

Actually, the little Chevy wasn't half bad. As Hooker nosed the large truck into the parking lot, the sun flashed off many afternoons of polish. The chrome package had been installed correctly and with flare. The young man was standing, not leaning against the car—a true sign of respect for his many hours of effort making the most of his car.

Hooker slid down from the cab. Box took the opportunity to use the large lawn. Hooker looked the car over. "This has got to be the nicest Corvair I have ever seen... You really take care of it."

The slight young teen smiled. "Thanks, I try."

"Well, it shows... which says a lot these days. What's the problem?"

"Twice today, when I went to accelerate, the car just dies. I wait a little bit, and it starts right up. I go gentle, and she runs fine. If I go up an incline or need to goose it to go around someone..."

Hooker thought a moment. "Did you install any extra fuel filters?"

"No, I've tried to keep it just the way I got it."

"Let's take a look."

A few minutes later, Hooker had the rear end up on the jack. He slid under and a minute later, slid out. In his hand was a small glass cylinder with two metal ends. The filter was inside. "Just as I thought... Whoever had this before you put in this little in-line fuel filter just in case. There is no fuel filter until you get to the engine—which is a bugger to get to. This one is a snap to clean while you change the oil."

A few minutes with the air, some gas, and the filter was clean and returned to its place. The kid had slid in from the other side, and Hooker showed him where it was hiding so he could clean it when he did the other maintenance.

Hooker tore off the receipt and handed the card and paper to the member, using his name. "Is Roc short for something?"

"Nope, just Roc. There was a boxer back in the fifties who my dad liked. Not a big one like Rocky Marciano, Battling Hays, or Max Baer, but good enough in the Bay Area. Dad just liked the name."

Hooker stuck his hand out. "Well, Roc Reed, it's been a pleasure to meet someone who likes their car enough to take good care of it. I apologize... I might have left a fingerprint or two on the paint."

The kid whipped around. "Where...?" He turned back around with a crooked grin and a chuckle. He knew he had been had.

Hooker was halfway up into the truck's cab. "You take care, Roc. I don't want to tow the bomb."

The kid waved and smiled.

4

———

HOW LONG IS YOUR CABLE

Hooker woke to the soft tapping on the door. "Yeah…?"

Manny opened the door and pushed in. The cordless phone was in his lap. He handed Hooker the phone.

Hooker sat up with his legs over the edge of the bed. He glanced at the clock—*7:43 in the morning.* "Maybe I need to drag a line into here…"

He put the phone to his ear. "Hooker… "

The conversation was short and sweet. "I'm pretty sure it's five-hundred feet, but even if it says three, I know they would wind more like four and call it shorter. I'll be in the truck in five." He hung up and handed the phone to Manny. "Someone drove off into the seagrass out near Milpitas way."

Manny nodded. "Stella already put some tuna on the floor, and she's wrapping bacon and scrambled eggs into some burritos. The thermos is already full."

Hooker started toward his bathroom. "Sorry to have woken…" He turned back and looked at Manny. By the face, he knew it had been one of those nights. "When…?"

Manny shrugged. "About three or so." The nightmares would wake him up, and the screaming would wake Stella up, and they would get up and play Gin until the sun rose, and the night terrors stopped. Hooker had his own terrors now to deal with. They had gotten good at playing three-legged Gin.

Hooker nodded and headed into his bathroom. "Tell Stella to give me about three minutes. I need to brush my teeth." He knew it was not going to be a short day.

"1-4-1, I'M 10-8 on Commercial, sheriff."

"10-4, Hooker. Captain Davis said he'll meet you at the bird sanctuary. There is a pumping station just north of there, and then the road continues north where the railroad tracks cross over to a ghost town named Drawbridge. He thought you might know where he was talking about. It seems there is a large rock or something out there..."

"10-4, I know the area intimately."

"He thought you did. Evidently, someone tried to cross on the rails last night. It seems they figured if they did it fast enough, it wouldn't be so rough on the trestle."

"How far across did they get?

"Into the seagrass, and the deputy figures it's a hundred yards to the dry land."

"He must have played football in high school."

"Played for the Raiders."

"I hope he wasn't a lineman."

"Running back... It's my second cousin, but we all call him Uncle Fester."

Hooker hung up the microphone. "Oh, great, Box. We have us an athlete."

The Night Dispatch radio squawked, "I heard that, Hooker. He actually has some brains, and he's a nice guy."

Hooker laughed. He thought about how he wanted to get to the bird sanctuary. There were areas Mae West, his usual eleven tons of sixteen-hundred horse-powered diesel truck, could go, but he wasn't sure he wanted to get Don's new baby stuck. He figured going in at Zanker Road was safer than where he used to go in just southeast of Moffett Field.

His sister and tribe roamed the entire mudflats, salt marshes, seagrass lands, and the buildings around there. Sometimes, he could talk to some of the street people in town, and they would know where she was—because they didn't want to be near her and her tribe of night denizens. Most were closer to the animals whose names they took, some a little more primal. His sister took the name Mouse—and like the old movie, *The Mouse That Roared*, she roared—making her the supreme power over the others known.

Hooker hauled on the steering wheel. The truck, a quarter the size of his big rig, was four times harder to steer, shift, or move down the road. He pitied the man who would eventually drive this truck—year after year.

Box got tired of being where he couldn't get his ear rubbed and jumped up on the bench seat. Hooker smiled, and his knuckles found the ear. The purring was almost instant.

The wildlife refuge was more like a mud bath stop on the west coast flyway for migrating waterfowl. At times, Hooker had been tempted to bring some shotgun shells loaded with birdshot instead of his usual dime load of a buck-forty in each barrel. But he also knew birdshot coming from the twelve-inch cut-down barrels of his Betsy would only be effective for about eight or ten yards, beyond which, the geese would just laugh at him.

He drove along the mudflats. If a person didn't know they were in the San Francisco Bay, they would have just thought the fields were some farmer's property. The smell was the only giveaway. Everything was rotting, especially the mud.

Hooker wasn't happy about coming out here in the heat of summer. The heat just made the small boring bugs, worms, and microorganisms more active eating and pooping. Sissy had explained it as a cycle. The big bugs rotted the big grass, the little bugs feasted on the rotting grass and the big bug poop, and then they pooped too, which fertilized the mud, and the grass grew better… a cycle. She was good at explaining those things, but he was sure she would get lost figuring out how the city and county were suing each other and themselves over Hooker blowing the runway up. A lot of things in Hooker's life made sense—and then there was the other stuff.

Hooker saw Chet standing out by the road, his cruiser parked and locked. Hooker smiled. They both knew every time they worked together, his cruiser got muddy, dented, or broken. Today, the CHP captain wasn't taking any chances. But why he was here in sheriff territory was beyond Hooker.

Hooker stopped. The passenger door opened. The older officer climbed slowly up into the rig. "I knew you probably got pulled out of bed, so I swung by the Whole Donut for some food. Mai Lin says you don't love her anymore. So how the hell are ya?" The friend and officer looked around the cab of the truck. "I hate what you did with the place."

Hooker grumped at the obvious. "Don't listen to him, Box... He's always Mister Grumpypants. He just doesn't know this fine piece of shit like we do. He'll learn to hate it like a reasonable human being. Just give him time." Hooker looked up at Chet. "What kind of donuts?"

They eased down the road as it turned from asphalt to dirt to something little more than a track in the short grass. Hooker jammed the last half of the French cruller into his mouth and wrestled with the wheel. The truck lumbered off the road and around the pumping station and back up onto the small track, which ran around the slough pond covering a square mile.

"Is he this side or the Drawbridge side?"

"I think he said on the south side. The guy was coming from this side, and I don't think there is any way to tow him out of there going north..."

Hooker thought about the maze of tracks and roads laced in and around the ponds, flats, and sloughs of the bay.

"From Drawbridge, there are three ways to get out to Fremont. Two cross the floating island, and the other we would be walking the last five miles or so. This pig has no guts and only six wheels to carry the weight."

Hooker looked over at his friend. "I used to bring Mae in here all the time looking for Sissy. There were a couple of years they were north of Fremont and Newark. Most of the time, they were straight out from Union City. Occasionally, they would be up around Hayward because the salt crabs are cleaner there."

"How did you find them?"

"Mostly, I could get good information from Peter. Occasionally, I would take some food and troll north on Thirteenth or even go up to

Newark. It's amazing what some of the broken bums would come up with for a warm meal. Usually, if the information was good, I'd go back and take them several days' worth of food. The food usually lasted about ten minutes. They aren't greedy—if they have food, they share with everyone else. They really understand what it means for all of them being in it together." Hooker nodded his chin at the officer who stood leaning against his squad car.

Chet laughed, knowing the nature of cars parked in nasty wet places. "There's your swimming partner."

Hooker glanced over with a smile. "Think he brought his wet suit?" Then Hooker remembered he was not in Mae West. His wetsuit vaporized into thin air along with the working deck of the truck when the bomb went off. *Beans in sauce, I'm going skinny-dipping.*

Chet read the sudden change of Hooker's face. "Did you just remember what part of the airport your wetsuit turned into?"

Hooker shot the laughing captain the bird as he slid out of the cab.

"What are we looking at?"

The deputy pointed out into the expanse of tan saltwater grass. It took Hooker a few moments to finally see the trunk and red plastic taillight of the white Cordoba peeking out of the grass.

"The guy had to be going well over a hundred when he hit the hump." They all looked at the tire tracks where they burst the top of the hump of dirt on the edge of the solid ground and road. The top of the hump was about seven feet above the top of the grasses. There was no track from the berm to the burial site. The car had gone airborne—flying at least two hundred feet.

Never to give a deputy a break, Hooker deadpanned the deputy who still looked like he was playing in the NFL. "I thought you called it in as one hundred yards?"

The man smirked. "I said approximately one hundred yards. The only thing to ever count is making a first down, which is only ten."

Chet chimed in and let his captain's bars carry the weight. "Did you bring your wetsuit?"

The deputy rolled his head to the side and smiled slightly. "Water temp is sixty-four. If I put my wetsuit on, I'd be overheated when I got out there. But it would probably fit you if you CHP pukes are so pansy." He started unbuttoning his shirt. Hooker noticed his black shoes were actually diver's booties.

"Rescue and recovery?"

The deputy wiggled his eyebrows as he opened his back door and laid his uniform on the seat. "I have an extra pair of booties, size twelve if you need them."

"Thanks. Mine are still at the airport."

The man stood up and looked at the young man as if for the first time. "You must be Hooker." He stuck his hand out and looked at the long scars racing into Hooker's hairline. "I'm Dina's Uncle Frank, but everyone calls me Uncle Fester." He finally took off the optional Smokey Bear hat to reveal a bald head. The smiling face took on a perfect mock of the TV character.

Hooker pulled the jumpsuit out of the side box on the truck. He looked in and saw there was another one in there too. He turned. "I have an extra jumpsuit if you want it."

The deputy stood in his bathing trunks and booties. "I'm good. The leeches and I are old friends. I used to keep a few dozen at home. Feeding them controlled my polycythemia. Now I just go bleed once a month at the Red Cross."

Chet frowned. "I thought you could only donate once every eight weeks."

"They only take the red cells. I produce too many, which is no good, and the cells can collect and cause a blockage."

"Clot?"

"No. Clotting is coagulation. This, they crowd the artery to a standstill. So they take out the extra and give it to other people who need them, like people with anemia."

Hooker swallowed. "But you put leeches on you to purposely suck the blood out?"

"Sure. They've been doing it for centuries. And because I did it at home, there was no doctor record of it, and I could play ball."

Hooker finished tucking the pant legs into the booties. "Let me pull up here, and if you can bring your cruiser down here about thirty yards, I can turn this pig around."

"Aren't you glad you don't have the big rig right now?"

Hooker looked the man in the eye. "If Mae was here, I'd just drive her out there, snag on, and haul the Prom Queen off to the dance."

Fester held his look for the count of three. He wasn't sure if Hooker was pulling his leg or if he really was crazy enough. The big truck was amazing enough to deal with two feet of muck under three feet of water. He took the low road and moved the cruiser.

Chet chuckled as he watched the two vehicles swap places. He wasn't sure if Mae could or couldn't, but he knew better to not bet against Hooker and the amazing Mae West.

The sun was low, but the heat was still working. Chet climbed up into the cab and grabbed some more coffee and a donut to watch the show from a safe perch. Box barely opened his one eye at the sound of the door. He was happy in the cool cab with the air conditioner running.

The water wasn't warm, but it wasn't the coldest Hooker had endured. The hot water bottle ballooned up with air and kept the heavy cable eye afloat after Hooker ran out a hundred feet of cable and coiled it at his feet. He swung the cable and heavy-duty balloon over his head in an ever-widening arc and finally threw the cable almost halfway to the car.

Hooker laughed at where the cable end landed with the balloon. "Hah, two hundred twenty feet at the most." The deputy in retribution had pushed him into the bay water. Hooker swam through the sea of grass. It was like a frog walking the mud and pulling himself along with the grass. Suddenly, there was a canal of open water. He looked down the canal both ways.

"They call it a river in the grass." The deputy swam up alongside him. "There are some old-timers still paddling canoes through the rivers for shrimp and to fish for crabs. The rivers are where the fresh water doesn't mix with the saltwater of the bay, and it just cuts through. The grass lives on the salt and alkali, so where the freshwater is, the grass doesn't grow."

"Personal experience?"

"Third-generation crabber from Hayward."

"Make money at it?"

"Not a real living—not anymore. The Dungeness crab was once plenti-ful, but overharvest has killed off much of the population. We used to have a good-sized shrimp, but now it's just the smaller ghost shrimps and tiny ones like the flea shrimp. There is a growing population of the Mitten crab, but not enough beyond maybe just sport-crabbing. Plus, the restau-rants have to want the crab to make it marketable to go after."

Hooker finally grabbed hold of the back bumper of the Cordoba. He tried to push and wiggle the wreck, but it didn't budge. "Looks like I'll need to get the shovel and release some of the mud suction. The mud cushioned the landing, but also stuck it too."

"What can I do?"

"Maybe see how bad it is on the downside. See if the tire is buried while I wrap the cable around the pumpkin and axle. I don't want to have to come back out here when I start pulling."

Hooker moved the tie on the blown-up water bottle. He figured about twenty feet of cable should make a complete figure-eight around the differential. He took a deep breath and closed his eyes. He knew he could open his eyes in saltwater. He just didn't like the idea of trying to see in the muddy water. He felt his way to the pumpkin and started feeding the cable end around and over the axles.

As he hooked the fast clips to secure the cable, he knew his time was up. He reached for the back of the gas tank and pulled his way to air. As he stood in the mud up to his knees, he pulled on the cable. The wrapped cable cinched and held. He was ready to pull.

"Hey, Fester… what did you find?" He pulled himself around to the side of the car.

The bear of an officer stood in water to his waist. His demeanor was a calm tension. His tanned face was now blanched white.

"What's wrong?"

"I don't think we can tow the car…"

Hooker frowned. "Because it's connected to a submerged train…?" The old trestle ran almost overhead, but Hooker knew smaller trains still ran across the flats once a day.

Fester bent down and felt in the water. As he rose, his hands were full of a blob somewhat in the shape of a basketball, but with long stringy hair. "No... I think we have a crime scene."

Hooker could see flesh was still attached to the skull. The ghost shrimp, leeches, worms, finger crabs, and spider crabs were still busy on the surface as well as in and out of the openings, which had once been eyes, nose, and mouth.

The man dropped the head. "The rest of the body is under the car—I felt her. The car cut the head off or just disturbed it. We need divers out here."

Hooker's detective mind took over from the shock of going from a tow to a crime scene. "How long do you think it's been underwater?"

The officer thought, but Hooker knew the third-generation crabber answered. "With all of these guys feeding—not more than maybe a few days... a week at the most."

Hooker thought and then pulled himself back under the car to unhook his cable. He wouldn't be towing this Prom Queen any time soon. The water recovery team wouldn't touch it until the sun was up.

As Hooker stood winding the cable back in, Fester explained the situation to Chet. They dried in the last of the sunshine and then just wiped the last of the goo off. Hooker called Dolly at Night Dispatch while Fester called the sheriff's office. They both knew dinner was going to be late.

5

WE HAVE ANOTHER BODY

Ace and Hooker sat on the back of his working bed. Ace drove a one-ton, so it was easier for them to get up on it. Chet and Fester stood as they all chewed on large Togo's sandwiches.

Hooker washed his mouthful down with some chocolate milk. "How did you hear about us out here?"

Ace smiled with his huge teeth. "I had a commercial up to Sacramento. I had just cleared the curves out of Pleasanton and had reception, so I grabbed the mic. Only, I grabbed the shop mic instead of the club. I called in, and Dolly knew what had happened. She asked me if I wanted to come over for Wednesday night dinner, and if so, I needed to run by Togo's tonight. I knew where the tracks run across because my great-uncle lived over there in Drawbridge. I used to fish those rushes for crab and shrimp when I was a kid." He pointed out where a team of six divers was searching the area for any other parts or clues."

"How much do I owe you?"

Ace wagged his head. "Did you know Dolly has a tab at Togo's?"

"No."

"Neither did I, but we know it now." He wiggled his eyebrows.

"That is the last tab I would want to mess with if you know what I mean." Hooker took another bite and chewed while he looked out across the grass.

The sun was down, and the gloom was setting in. The divers had water lights and would work through the night if need be. The Sheriff Tactical Support truck had shown up over an hour before and backed the mile up the road because the officer did not think he would find a place to turn around. They shifted vehicles around, and the support truck now had a rack of large field lights run up and would soon light up the area like a baseball diamond.

One of the divers surfaced, and a red balloon popped to the surface next to him. He was about twelve feet from the corner of the car. Fester hung his head. Hooker could tell he was swearing.

Ace leaned over. "What happened?"

Hooker pointed at the diver and the balloon. "The second balloon means they found another body. It just went from homicide to serial killer."

Ace looked at Hooker. "Isn't that where you take over?"

Hooker gave him a dirty look. *The truth was...*

Both of their attentions were distracted by the sound of another diver standing up. He was almost sixty feet from the car. There were two red balloons floating near him.

Chet turned around and looked at Hooker. There wasn't going to be a recovery tow tonight—probably not even this week.

The diver in the support truck, who was taking a mandatory rest period, started pulling down the yellow nylon cord used to grid off a large crime scene. Hooker knew the ten-foot-long orange stakes would come out next. He was afraid to guess how big the grid would become. His night was done. All he needed was to have the original deputy release him.

Fester walked along the tow truck. His face was dark and angry. "Hooker, they have five bodies now. Your tow is now the center point of a crime scene. We'll send you a letter when we either finish here or retire."

Hooker's head ground around to face the bald deputy. "Sorry about the events. I know you don't get relief until the big boys get here."

Fester scowled and flipped his head toward the support truck. "There are bunks in there..."

"I'm headed back…" Hooker glanced at his watch in the stadium brightness. "At this hour, probably to Dispatch… You want me to let anyone know where you are?"

"Nah, we'll keep a lid on this until we know what's going on. Maybe we get lucky, and the killer tries to stash another body…"

"Makes sense." Hooker backhanded Ace's shoulder. "You off or on?"

"Off."

"Want to go get some ice cream and call the girls?"

The two laughed about the effect the French vanilla ice cream had on their voices. Dolly hated it and called it the bedroom voice. She knew it made her girls squirm and get distracted, which made Hooker do it even more.

When Hooker had started towing, his mentor, if he had one, was Ace. The man had taught him a lot about what to do and what not to do. But they both had the habit of driving with the window open and the heat on full blast—all winter long. It was Hooker who got Ace started on eating ice cream in the middle of the night. They both had a reputation for showing up at a crash while just finishing a large cone.

Of course—when they show up on a call, they are required to call in their position…

They had dumped Ace's truck back at the tow yard, and the two were having fun like old times. The tape deck Don had ordered in the new truck ran through the stereo with an extra speaker. Ace had brought one of his new mixed tapes, and it was filled with all the old songs and singers. The two drivers caterwauled about sixteen tons of coal as they finally cleared a locked car and made it to Thrifty's for some ice cream—just before midnight.

Ace grabbed the auto club mic and called them in. "1-4-1."

The new dispatcher, Stephan, answered. He learned the voices, and even with Ace using Hooker's numbers, he knew who was who. "Go ahead, 1-4-1, Hooker Ace… or is it the Ace Hooker?"

"10-4. Show us 10-98 on our T-6. Also, put us in the log for an El Dorado in under ten seconds. Note it as a fully enclosed window with a Slim-Jim down the glass."

"You two do know we don't keep records like—"

Ace laughed. "Please. And Andy only weighs in at one-twenty."

"Does Hooker confirm the time?"

Ace tossed the mic into the air as he laughed. They both knew Andy would still be there and the last man out the door. Hooker snatched the mic out of the air.

"I confirm Andy is a slender three-hundred, and it was actually just over six seconds. My hand was on the handle as I watched the clock. Ace beats Mike's time by three seconds for any El Dorado newer than 1972. Also, show us 10-7 for a short coffee break."

"10-4, Hooker... and just for the record... has anyone tried to beat your record on opening a hotrod Plymouth?

"Not enough nuns driving those around..."

"Good thing... and good night in 5-4-3-2..." The radio squawked a double click of his microphone key as he signed off the auto club. For the rest of the night, all the calls would go through Dolly's company—Night Dispatch.

Dina's voice from Night Dispatch tinkled through the cab. "Midnight, Night Dispatch." The baton had been passed. Hooker looked over at Ace. The two giant smiles were evil—like two little boys getting into trouble. It was time for ice cream.

Hooker reached down and picked up the little red dish as his left foot nudged the door open. The orange streak knifed between the seat and his calf. Box was looking for a patch of grass.

"Did you wash your truck in hot water and tumble dry on high heat?" The tall young woman stood in the open doorway. Holly was studying to be a nurse along with Hooker's girlfriend, Candy. Raised on a truck farm, she had a tight strength about her, but Hooker always thought she looked more like a surfer with her liquid movement and the slightly splayed legs and hips. They looked like she rode a surfboard—or horses. He had never thought what the rotation of the hips from bending over could do when you spend hours a day planting and then weeding.

Her hips were the only thing giving her body curves. The rest was as straight up and down as a water glass. But her quick undercutting humor was her best feature—in Hooker's opinion.

"Mae overheated, and now I'm trying to get this little pup raised up with all the cold air you're letting out."

"Just waiting for my boyfriend..."

Hooker frowned, and his head snapped around and looked at the huge toothy smile of Ace.

"Oh, in your dreams, tow boy. I only have love for a man who wears a fur coat on a hot day and never sweats."

Box walked past the two men. His tail was straight up and waving like a flag—except for the kink at the tip. Holly bent over and put her hand out with the palm down. Box sniffed and then let it pass from the top of the head, down the back, and loosely up the tail.

"Good evening Mister Box... Your reserved spot on the floor awaits you."

She stood with her hand out for the little red dish. Her smile was as large as Ace's, but the teeth were smaller. Hooker still found it warm and inviting. He was glad she and Candy were becoming fast friends. Their studies to be nurses had brought their two worlds together—Holly's large family working on a collective family farm, and Candy's scattered, anything but family foster homes, and worse—the two had grown to understand a larger universe through understanding each other.

Hooker followed the parade of Box and Holly. Ace brought up the rear. "Where's Randy?"

Holly waved her head toward the back. "Trying to figure out the day shift's inventory sheets." She placed Box's dish in the same spot she did any night they showed up.

She stood and watched Hooker as she scooped triples of French vanilla into sugar cones. There were certain things you could always rely on—the sun rising in the east, pumpkins harvest after corn, and a triple French vanilla in a sugar cone. As long as she had known Hooker and Ace, their order never changed. If it ever did, she or anyone who works the night shift would know right away that something was wrong, and the world was coming to an end.

"Sorry about your truck. I know you loved her. But how are you and John doing?"

Hooker took his cone and put the dollar bill on the counter. "Thanks, maybe someday she will live again... but for now..." He looked out the window at the seemingly tiny truck, which was a beast by most standards.

"And John?"

"Oh, he's on the final parts of the academy."

She frowned. "I thought he graduated last month?"

"He did... but he's doing some extra work most only come back to. He wants it all out of the way before he makes his choice."

Ace took his cone and left his bill. "Is he still leaning toward the PD over the highway?"

"It looks that way. Manny has him figuring out all sorts of stuff, so I don't know if he's interested in ballistics, forensics, or he's just going to ask straight up for a gold badge."

Holly cocked her head as she closed the ice cream case and took up the two dollars. "Gold badge?"

"Detective's badge—something you might get after many years of fieldwork..."

Holly chuckled, "But because he hangs out with you..."

"Hey, he's worth more than a couple of plugged nickels..."

Ace snorted. "Yeah, not a bad tow bunny for such a two-bit kid."

Holly stiffened. "He may be only a little more than a pair of dimes, but he is a stand-up guy and a gentleman when someone throws up in his boots." She turned red under her jaw, but Hooker was proud to see she was becoming less embarrassed by her slip when she saw the fresh scars laced across the kid's body.

"Holly?" The voice came from the rear of the store.

"Yeah, Randy?"

"Is Hooker there?"

"He's just leaving..."

"Tell him he has a roll-over northbound 101, just north of Story. Tell him Dolly said he isn't supposed to even touch the mic until all of the ice cream is out of his mouth."

"10-4, Randy." He stooped to fish up the red bowl. Hooker and Ace pushed through the door. "Next time, Holly."

"Good to see you too, Ace—stop in more often."

Hooker looked at Ace as they got in the truck. "Doesn't she know you're on days now?"

"Guess I might have to start making some late-night ice cream breaks."

Hooker looked over with an evil smile. He handed Ace the mic. "Dolly only said I'm not supposed to call in…"

Ace controlled his laughter and breathing. He rumbled up his deeper voice and keyed the mic. "1-4-1, 10-8 for 101 rollover."

They only got a stutter of mic keys in answer. It sounded like both women on the board had keyed over each other. Both men knew there would be some hell to pay on Wednesday night after dinner—but some things were worth it.

6

WEDNESDAY DINNER

Candy rolled over to find a warm bed and pillow, but no Hooker. She listened, and then the shower started. She didn't need to be up for a while yet, but a shower that starts with sitting on a wooden stool either scrubbing Hooker's back or him scrubbing hers sounded like a reason to get up. She padded into the bathroom to find Hooker standing naked—waiting for the water to get hot.

She bent to get a closer look. "I think before you get in the shower, you might want me to get those leeches off your back."

He turned and then looked in the mirror. Four large engorged leeches were attached to the area he couldn't feel—right where the bra hooks would be—if he wore one.

"And I took at least two dozen off last night…"

Candy took the rubbing alcohol out of the cabinet. "I guess I better check you all over…"

As Hooker strolled into the kitchen, he was smiling. Stella gave him a side hug as she was scrambling the eggs. "Looks like a good long shower this morning did you some good."

Manny looked up to see Candy coming out of his bedroom, buttoning the last couple of buttons. Manny laughed. "Looks like your shower theory just got blown out into the back forty."

"Hush your mouth, and clean up your mind." She turned and folded Candy's head into her large chest. "This is my favorite daughter you are talking about."

Hooker wasn't sure who was doing the laughing to cause both of them to jiggle. He turned and ignored them all and poured two mugs of coffee. A hand reached over his shoulder and took one of the mugs. "Candy might want a mug also." Hooker glanced back. He hadn't even heard the Squirt walk in.

Hooker poured another mug and turned to give it to Candy. As he leaned back against the counter, he took in the white sidewall haircut and the slick-sleeve blue uniform with no designations. "Boy, they are still putting you in the yoke? At least towing, I allow a white T-shirt."

Stella rolled her head over and gave Hooker a stern look. "A white T-shirt *is* your uniform."

Hooker laughed. It was true. "At least I am lax about whether he uses starch or not."

Stella laughed. "You think I have your shirts marked. You both wear the same large shirt. I throw a dozen into the wash and iron a dozen with light starch. Six go in his closet, and six go in your closet. The same goes for your pants—you two are a matched set, right down to your socks and underwear. Only thing changed is now he has a real uniform, which just makes me feel young again. I get to pretend I'm ironing Manny's uniform when he was just back from Korea."

She scraped the eggs out of the pan into the large orange Fiestaware serving bowl. She nodded at the bowl and at the table. Candy pulled the last of the four pieces of toast out of the new commercial-sized toaster, and they all gathered around the table and sat. Other than silverware on Fiestaware, the room was silent. Manny and Stella were in heaven—breakfast with all of their children at the table at one time. Everyone healthy, happy, and...

The phone in the office rang.

A second later, it was echoed in the sunroom.

Hooker rose and headed for the office. Stella laid her fork down. The phone ringing in the morning was never a good sign. She sipped her coffee as she eyed the Squirt. The tempo of his fork had increased in speed and the size of the bite.

"You do know you're going to school today and not out to play with Hooker?"

The Squirt hesitated for only a half-second and then continued.

Candy gently put her mug of coffee down. "John?"

Her brother looked up.

"Our mother is talking to you."

He shoveled the last bite into his mouth, and while he was chewing, he stood, took up his plate, kissed Stella on top of her head, and put the plate in the sink. As he passed the table, he grabbed his coffee mug. As he walked toward the office, he sang out, "Manny, could you please explain the nuances of forensic investigation." The office door closed quietly behind him.

Hooker was just hanging up the phone and turned to face the Squirt. His face was deadpan.

The Squirt sat and sipped on his coffee. Neither one was going to blink. The first to open their mouth was the loser.

Finally, the Squirt lowered his mug. "Seven hundred forty-two million, fifty-one, and twenty-three."

Hooker knew it was a puzzle he should know how to answer. He knew it had nothing to do with anything other than the two of them. It was a Squirt-Hooker puzzle. "Fifty-one is how much change we share."

"The turns of Mae West's tires we have shared... The amount of change that almost killed us... and how many times we have stopped for French vanilla ice cream in a sugar cone." He didn't have to say anything about the four tiny white scars on the back of his left hand. They had started everything—Hooker burying his fork through the Squirt's hand. They had shared a lot. More than most friends share in a lifetime.

"How did you figure the revolutions?" He knew if the Squirt said it was true, it was true. Hooker didn't question the figure. He was only curious about the math and how the kid got there.

"Miles divided by the circumference of the thirty-six-inch tire. Give or take about one or two miles."

"I don't keep a log."

The Squirt tapped his head. Hooker smirked. He knew if the kid had seen it, it was forever in his memory bank and ready for quick, if not instant, recall.

The kid looked at the phone and then back at Hooker.

Hooker had stalled long enough. "It's not a call out. It was just an update. You rushed through your breakfast for nothing." Hooker stood. "Now I'm going in and finishing my breakfast and enjoying my family." He opened the door.

As he walked through, the Squirt rose and muttered, "Good luck with that."

Hooker's eyes went to Manny. The man had his elbows on the table and the coffee mug to his lips. He was working hard at ignoring anything near his office door.

Hooker started silently counting down from sixty. The two men returned to the table and sat. As Hooker silently hit three, Manny cleared his throat. Stella put her fork down next to the last three bites.

Hooker glared at Manny. "Jeez in the breeze... you couldn't let her finish this one time?"

"Is she going to get upset?"

"No."

"Are you going to share about the phone call from Dispatch?"

"No, it was just an update. They still don't know where Willie is." He looked over at Stella. "You can finish eating. I'm just worried."

Stella looked up at the large grandfather clock. It was nine-seventeen. She knew she had just been lied to, and she wanted Hooker to know she knew and was remembering the time.

Hooker slumped back into his chair. Candy watched the battle that only these two could play. The Squirt sensed a shift and rose to get the coffee carafe—breakfast just got longer.

Hooker slid down in his chair—defeated. "Karen also gave me this morning's body count."

Manny sat up, and the Squirt froze halfway through filling Stella's mug. "Body count for what?"

Hooker turned as Stella slowly put her fork down. There was one bite left on her plate. He turned to Manny. "Are you familiar with the old ghost town out in the seagrass off Milpitas and Fremont?"

"Where the old train trestle crosses and heads over to Newark? Sure, there was a shooting out there in 1958. The guy killed three people and then wounded four officers before they got him. What about the place?"

"There's a body dump just east of the trestle, just north of the bird sanctuary."

Manny's first urge was to ask how many bodies, but he could feel the anger radiating from the other end of the table. He sipped on his mug. "And why are they calling you?"

"I have an El Dorado nosed into the grass and mud about seventy-eight yards into the grass. It's the hub of the search."

Candy snorted, "And where those leeches came from…"

"You had leeches?" Stella started to rise.

Hooker waved her down. "They went down the toilet. The nurse gave me a clean bill of health."

Manny laughed. "Very clean."

Stella growled. "Manny P. Romero, you now owe the naughty thought jar a full buck."

"Why a full buck?"

"To cover me telling Stella later." She turned. "You too, Hooker—you are up to a buck, also."

They all laughed as the Squirt fished out a dollar, and Candy threw out two dollar bills. The goodness of the morning was restored… right up until the Squirt tripped getting up and spilled coffee all down the front of his uniform. He never even yelped. But he did fish into his pocket and added another dollar to the pile.

A few minutes later, he returned wearing his other uniform. As he threw the leather jacket over his shoulder, he looked at Hooker. "My other uniforms are in the wash. Karen can call the academy and let them know."

Hooker sighed and stood. He kissed Stella on the head and walked around the table to Candy's head. She remained deadpan as he kissed her neck. Fishing for a laugh, he placed his hand on top of Manny's head and then kissed the back of his hand. There was only a small chuckle from

Stella. Hooker knew Candy had seen right through his talk about the body dump.

"Box, go time."

The two men and cat walked out the large hand-hewn door. The sunlight in the courtyard already had the heat up over a hundred—it wasn't even noon yet. The peak would hit about five. The summer heat of San Jose was fierce and unrelenting, even though Hooker's leather jacket was already in the truck.

Hooker drifted the truck down off the Hill of Stupid. The five-ton truck was a third the size of Mae West, but stock, it was a pig to drive. It made Mae's eleven tons and twenty-eight feet handle like a sports car in the curves. He and Uncle Willie had worked to make the giant truck the most nimble as well as the fastest in the five counties of the Bay Area. Hooker knew there would never be another truck like her. The other big diesel rig tow trucks made the five-ton look like a Chevy Nova—not great,or easy to drive.

The Squirt cleared his throat. Hooker had been waiting for it.

"Twenty-seven and thirty."

The kid watched the fake English Tudor manors slip by as they rolled down a street with a Spanish name. His mind was not even registering the houses. "Bodies and feet or yards?"

"Yards—they were just starting the next ring this morning at daybreak."

"And we are headed...?"

"Coroner's office. They found something on one of the bodies."

"What?"

"Her driver's license."

The kid leaned his head back. "Tracking down Willie, my ass."

Hooker's head snapped. "You owe—"

"I paid ahead." They both laughed at the idea of paying in the morning and having free rein in the afternoon when you need it.

Later, as they drove down Stevens Creek, the Squirt looked longingly out the window. "We need a better tape deck in here. Tex Ritter sounds like Roy Orbison."

Hooker laughed. "Ass... it is Roy."

7

WHO IS JOYCE JACOBSON?

"Jesus, Hooker." The man in the white smock pulled him over against the wall. The man held his head down, and his voice barely more than a harsh whisper. "What the hell are you doing bringing *that* kid here? Do you even know who he is?"

Hooker looked at the assistant coroner. The frazzled mess almost vibrated. His long hair hung stringy and greasy like he hadn't showered in days. As Hooker got a good whiff of the guy, he changed his estimate to at least a week. "He's my brother. Who do *you* think he is?"

"He's been burning up the academy and pushing..." The guy's eyes popped wide. He looked at the Squirt and then back at Hooker. "Your brother...?"

"Well, sort of. His sister is my girlfriend, and our parents are... Well, it's complicated. What did you want to show me? And don't worry about the Squirt. He is mine, and nobody else's unless we agree."

"But he's—"

"Going to be a cop... Right now, he is my partner. What I learn—he learns. It's how we solve problems. My mind works one way and his works... Well, different. Forget what you've heard and just tell us what you've got."

"If he knows every—"

"Quinton, you're talking eight years ago. The kid was eleven and didn't even live here then. There is no reason—yet—that he would know about the dope in your trunk, the meth in the glove box, or the six grams—"

"Okay, okay... In here." He led them through a back hallway to the examining room. The room's temperature hovered in the fifties. But even the chill did nothing to mask the smell in the room, and what it was used for by the second day it was running—thirty years before. One of the old cops explained the facts about morgues to Hooker—they never stop using old morgues. They just burn them to the ground and move on. Standing in the room, Hooker could believe the truth in the joke.

The Squirt leaned in close to Hooker. "Why is he so squirrely?"

Hooker silently harrumphed as they watched the man open one of the refrigerator doors and pull out the cadaver tray. "Meth, cocaine, dope, too much coffee, and he recognized you from the academy."

The Squirt looked at Hooker with a face of horror. "There is such a thing as too much coffee? Say it's not so."

Hooker remained deadpan as they stepped over to the body. Quinton drew back the sheet. "We haven't done an autopsy yet for a good reason— as you can see, there are no GSWs, ligature marks, lacerations, or punctures. By the swelling and deformation, we estimate the body to have been in the water since either Saturday or Sunday." He smiled and stepped back and stood silently.

Hooker's mind raced. A lot of information there—for having not done an autopsy yet, but also, what wasn't being said. He looked at the Squirt. The kid stood with one eyebrow raised watching Hooker.

"You've already figured this one out, haven't you?" The kid nodded slightly. "And you're just going to stand there and watch me screw it up."

"What is the obvious question?"

"What's the cause of death...?" Hooker frowned as the kid just kept moving his head back and forth.

"He told you what wasn't there... but he also gave you some hard facts."

There wasn't much the assistant coroner had said... Hooker's eyes opened wide as he snapped his fingers. "Saturday or Sunday... and we pulled her out yesterday... so how do you know?"

Quinton pointed at Hooker and smiled. He turned to the Squirt, "Care to tell him? While I push her back in and turn on the fans…"

The Squirt smiled. "Take a last smell."

Hooker frowned. "It smells like Stella baking for Christmas."

"Chanukah, but same season… what is she making?"

Hooker tried to remember the few baked goods Stella made to give away. Sweets in the house stopped at small amounts of tidbits, and the orange sherbet because of Manny's diabetes. One of the few cookies she made and also allowed Manny to eat—the cookie with a nut in the middle of the top. "Almonds." And as he said it, he realized how strong the odor was.

The Squirt grabbed at his sleeve as he guided them away from the area. "And…?"

"Cyanide… cyanide poisoning."

Quinton smiled. "Exactly, but with the body being in water, there was no telltale white foam about the mouth. So when the examiner started to perform the gross exam, he became overcome by the cyanide off-gassing and collapsed. Lucky for him, I came in when I did and found him on the floor."

"He died from breathing in the cyanide gas from the body?"

"He didn't die… but yes. There are high levels of cyanide in the body. He will, however, be at Valley Medical for a couple of days in an oxygen tent until his system is flushed."

"So let's go back to how you figured out when she died."

"Oh, time of death is still undetermined. But we do know she was in the water more than a day and less than three."

Hooker looked at the Squirt with a frown.

The kid smiled softly. "Because of the Fiddle crab. There are no marks from her being chewed on. The cyanide was still toxic, so she was oozing poison and killing the crabs who wanted everything off her bones. In the saltwater, the cyanide is toxic for about seventy-two hours. But the saltwater also causes other abuses to the flesh, so they knew she had been in for at least a day, but the crabs hadn't started in on her—so it was less than three."

"So, boy genius, what is your best guess at the time of death?"

"I want to know what they found in her clothing first."

The examiner smiled. "Now I see why you are striking fear into the black hearts of the academy. This line of question is exactly the right idea." He turned to a file cabinet and opened the middle drawer. He took out a box and opened it on the desk. Reaching in, he withdrew a plastic bag with a driver's license in it. "We found this stuffed in her panties, under her pantyhose."

The Squirt snapped his fingers. "TOD was late Friday night."

Hooker lowered one eyelid. "How did you figure…?"

"After further examination and investigation, they will find she worked the downtown area of San Jose as a streetwalker. My guess would be her stock-in-trade was the blowjob. So they need to start asking around near Stevens Creek and First, and then circle out."

Quinton leaned back against the wall. There was a short smile on his face. "Yes, they figured she was turning tricks—but how would you know the rest?"

"Her ID was in her panties. If she turned regular tricks, she would have a purse, and the ID would have been in it. But she didn't have or need a purse. She had a great hot body, but you saw her face… it was a train wreck looking for a place to happen. So the john gets to look at her great body and behind while he gets sucked off—and never has to look at the face."

"But how do you come up with Friday, and why late?"

"If she died Thursday, she would have had the crabs start working the body over. With early Friday, it might have attracted attention… but late…"

Quinton chuckled. "The crabs don't work on the weekends?"

Hooker snorted and mock punched at the kid. The Squirt knew it was also Hooker's way of showing he was proud of him. *They had come so far together.*

"The fiddler crab is very sensitive to toxins. They would wait for the cyanide to leach out into the saltwater before they would go near her. The mud worms, on the other hand, went straight to work and died. I noticed tiny bite holes on her underside, but they had not lived long enough to get around to the top."

The Squirt turned to Hooker. "The killer buried her under the water so she could, in theory, see up through the water. He didn't dig in the mud and then just throw her in. She was on top of the mud, under the grass..." He nodded for Hooker to continue.

Hooker would have expected the same from Manny, but from the kid, he was caught off-foot. "Could see the sky... umm..." He searched his memory for all the lessons learned from Manny and Willie... and then he remembered his first conversation with Dolly. He had to drop off some paperwork. He didn't expect a woman three times his size and a couple of inches shorter. Her muumuu and bare feet caught him off-guard. Her voice over the radio sounded like warm honey, but standing with her nose two inches from his, he could taste the razor-sharp teeth in the honey.

In his youthful way, he became bored waiting for her to finish talking to someone on the phone. She kept calling them *hon* and *sweetheart* as he snuck glances at the size of the woman. He wasn't sure he wanted to even know who she was talking to. As kids will do, his fingers danced along the edge of her oversized desk. And then he actually wrapped his hand around the handle end of the large limb on her desk. Carved into the limb were the words 'The Stick.' It was the stick Dolly—and only Dolly—used to stir shit up.

He never heard her say good-bye. She simply hung up and then appeared in front of him. She never huffed or puffed. Her voice didn't raise. In fact, it lowered—somewhere down into the bowels of the earth.

Quietly, she explained about respect and honoring other's property. He never touched the stick again.

"He respected her, or at least, had empathy for her. He didn't bury her. He laid her to rest in a spot where he could show he respected her. Where she could watch the sky."

Quinton frowned—the side of his mouth curled up in a snarl. "She was dead. How was she supposed to watch anything? Especially under the muddy water?"

The Squirt sighed. "Brackish... not muddy."

"What?"

The Squirt turned from watching Hooker. He looked at the assistant coroner, who was only maybe a year or two older than Hooker. "You said muddy water… the water in the south bay is brackish saltwater. For the most part, it will be hazy to clear."

"But we cleaned a lot of mud off her, and there was muddy water in her mouth and upper throat—"

Hooker held up his hand to hold off the Squirt. "John is right. The water was clear… until I put my foot into the mud. By the third step, it's all just muddy water as the mud floated in the disturbance I had created. Some of the other remains probably won't show as much mud since the guys were floating as they looked and worked the grid."

"Oh." The hand stroked the stubble just above the white smock. He looked up. "What kind of mud?"

The Squirt stepped in. "It's called float mud because of its tendency to float. The sediment is so vegetation dense that it should be called grass clippings or something. But it captures the fine silt, which will stir up with the least movement of the water. Once it is trapped by the vegetation fibers, the color is the mud, but it all floats like the grass clippings. The reality is it never packs down because most of what we see as two feet deep of mud is only about four inches' worth if you took a core sample and dried it out. But what you would find is about six-inches of worms, beetles, sea mites, slugs, leeches, and other hen ways."

The examiner furrowed his brow. "What's a hen way?"

Hooker laughed as he slapped the Squirt's chest. They needed to go. As they walked out, Hooker called back, "About two or three pounds." The large doors swung shut on the young examiner's swearing.

In the truck, Hooker looked out at the large parking lot. He sat quietly thinking.

The Squirt clicked his seat belt. "What…?"

Hooker turned the key. "Did you get the name and address?"

The Squirt pulled his hand out of his pocket and held up the driver's license.

Hooker took it and looked at the photo. "We need a good photo, man."

"There's a guy at the academy, but then, I'd have to say where the ID came from."

They sat at the light. The heat of the day allowed for no breeze. The fan in the truck was going full blast but barely pushing cooled air. Hooker looked at Box, who was draped upside-down in the box, trying to get rid of his body heat through the moving air over his tummy.

"My next truck is going to have real air-conditioning."

The Squirt snorted. "Heavy-duty enough to run with both windows still open?"

Hooker laughed because it was so true about him. "Of course."

The Squirt pointed at the white airplane a few thousand feet above them. There was a large dish floating above the fuselage. Everyone in the South Bay knew what an Orion P-3 Sub Chaser looked like. It was headed for a landing at Moffett Field Naval Air Base.

"You could be up there—the temperature, while they are on station, is about minus twenty degrees. They turn on the heaters once they clear land and don't turn them off until they land."

Hooker watched the white plane with the red tail as it crawled along the sky. They were pointed in the same direction. The light changed, and he turned right on the parkway. He pulled the auto club mic from its clip. "1-4-1."

The new voice of the club radio came back. Hooker knew it sounded like an eight-year-old girl, but he was willing to bet lunch at Togo's that she was over thirty and at least a hundred pounds larger than her voice sounded like. "1-4-1, go ahead…"

The tiny woman released the wiggle key. Her feet didn't reach the floor, and she had just celebrated her twentieth birthday. Hooker would have lost on all accounts but would still buy her lunch.

"Show me on a commercial T-5. Can't start at Moffitt Field."

"Can the toy truck you're in jump-start one of those sub hawks?"

"One engine at a time, Jenny. One engine at a time." He hung the mic and smiled at the Squirt. "She sounds like something you might date."

"I'll stick with Beth right now, thank you."

THE TINY WOMAN spun sideways on her swivel chair. Her arms were outstretched to grab the armrests. She looked at Jake—the old hand at the club.

He noticed the change out of the side of his eye. His head snapped over to confirm the change and then snapped back to scanning the three calls in front of him they were currently working. Nothing was running the clock—he could talk.

He turned back. "What's the question?"

"What does Hooker look like?"

He laughed. Few club dispatchers ever meet the drivers and the other way around. "How do you picture him?"

She thought a moment. "How I imagine him and what he looks like is probably the same difference of what he thinks I look like, and me."

Jake thought as he acknowledged the voice on the radio calling to say he was 10-97 or finished with his call. "10-4, 1-7-1, board is clear at this time."

The radio squawked. "10-4, dispatch. Show me 10-7 for lunch at Chiaramontes."

Jake wiggled the double key to give two clicks on the radio. The one-second delay from broadcast to receive and back into the dispatch gave a static echo to the two clicks of his key. He turned back to the young woman.

"You've handed off the radios to Dolly—try her."

"Voice alone… she sounds about average height, say about five-foot-six, but she has some husky power there, so I'd say about one-sixty or one-eighty."

"How old?"

"Forties, but then, her voice has some edge… so I'm going to hedge at young fifties. Have you met her?"

He nodded. "Night Dispatch, for years, has thrown an open house from about eleven-thirty until about two in the morning, on New Year's Eve. If you wait for midnight, there isn't a parking spot within two blocks of the building. I've seen cop cars and tow trucks from as far south as Salinas and north of San Francisco. One year, I met one of the senators there. Everyone here is invited, but few make an effort."

"So was I close?"

"Not even… you're off about three-hundred pounds, and I think she's in her sixties. She's taller than I am, and I'm five-eight with shoes. She's always barefooted." He looked at the dwarf next to him, and how she sat in the chair. "You could use her custom chair as a bed."

"Whoa." The word was barely stronger than an exhale. Her eyes were wide. She knew exactly where she wanted to be on New Year's Eve.

"So try Hooker…"

"Kind of a mix of Mickey Dolenz and Michael Nesmith—tall, but has some thick muscle to him. He has a certain… um… seriousness about him, but also, he has a fun laugh in his voice." She looked over at the frown on Jake's face as he sat back, staring at the run sheets. "What?"

His face cleared, and he looked over. "Nothing… I just never thought about Hooker and his voice. For the playful side, throw in Davy Jones, but only part of Peter… Hooker is no goofball. The guy is one of the smartest drivers out there. And if you ever meet his partner—the human one—the Squirt, hang onto your hat. The guy is a walking landmine of knowledge."

"Landmine?"

"Poke his mind, and the eleventh-grade science department will blow up, and you get the whole years' worth in ten minutes. It's freaky."

"So if he's the human one…?"

"Biggest orange cat you've seen who wasn't a lion or tiger. Actually, I'm not sure he doesn't have some tiger in him. Rumor had it a few months ago, he attacked a hundred pound Kai dog, and in less than two seconds, the throat of the wild dog was missing."

The radio squawked. Jenny and Jake listened. Jenny took the call and pulled the slip of paper, passed it through the time stamp, and spun it into the done box.

8

MOFFETT FIELD PHOTOGRAPHERS

The gate at Moffett Field was the usual small white building with glass all the way around. Hooker always wondered if there was a short toilet in the back somewhere—just in case. But with two people running the gate, he figured they just ran somewhere or used the small shrubs along the fence line.

The khaki dressed guard stepped out of the booth. Hooker squinted as they rolled up. The man looked familiar, somehow.

Hooker was expecting to be asked about his business, but instead, his truck fell under immediate exam. Both guards began to look the truck over. The second had brought out a measuring tape and started checking the height of the tires. He shook his head at the first guard.

Finally, the man looked up at Hooker. The blackout wrap-around glasses showed no sign of the eyes, only reflections of Hooker in the window.

"Did you wash this truck, sir?"

Hooker frowned. "Hmm… yes… Of course. It gets dirty every day. I like a clean truck."

"Did you wash the truck with extremely hot water, sir?"

"No. I used the hose… What's this about… um… Sergeant?"

The Marine continued. "Have you recently put this truck on a diet, sir?"

"Diet?"

"Can you explain the unusually small size of the tires, sir?"

"They are standard for a truck this size..."

"Yes, about that, sir... can you explain why the paint job is not the regulation nature with a hot woman draped along the door? Or did she take off when you blew the other half off the truck?"

Hooker squinted at the man as the guard removed his dark glasses, and the smile swept across his face. Hooker was fairly sure who the man was. He turned back into the truck. "How much did we throw into the swear jar this morning?"

The kid began to laugh. "More than enough..."

Hooker's head ground back around. "Screw you, Marine. You have been twisting your fucking hat on too tight." He smiled broadly and was mirrored by the marine.

"You've been hanging out with my brother-in-law and Willie Knight way too much." He stuck his hand up. "I heard about you blowing your girlfriend up. Sorry about your loss."

Hooker bit on his lip. "We saved many lives that day." He didn't mention the two who had died.

"I take it you're here to see the captain?"

"Actually, I need help with some photography."

"Best to see the captain first..." He glanced at his watch. "Chow call is in about twenty minutes. He can introduce you to Snaps over some good old Navy chow." He pointed at the low white building at the north end of the base offices.

Hooker saluted with a Cub Scout two-finger and let the clutch slip as he edged off. He parked at the far end of the building, and they walked back up toward the entrance.

"The guy is..."

"Sue's brother. Micha is his brother-in-law. I met him a few years back when he was out for their tenth of July barbecue. I think he had just gotten out of boot camp or something. He was a lot thinner then."

"Tenth? You mean the fourth?"

"Nope—we all work on the drunk days. The tenth is their anniversary."

They entered the cool building. No matter how tight budgets got, the government always had solid air conditioning.

The yeoman at the desk looked up and smiled. "You look just like a guy we blew up last summer." He stood and stuck out his hand. "Sorry about killing your sister."

Hooker smiled. He figured the whole Navy base had been in on the performance. "She's in a far better place now."

"It still sucks about her friend."

"I think he did what he planned to do all along. It wasn't like he was ready to settle down in the suburbs with a car, wife, and the two point five kids, including the dog."

"Do I see a dead body walking?" The voice boomed down the hallway. The khakis had crisp knife-edge creases, and the man walked with a smile.

Hooker turned. "Hello, Captain."

"Hooker, how are you?"

"Alive and well, John. John, I'd like you to meet my Squirt. John, this is John—also known on base as Captain Jacobs. He's the one who worked hard to kill me while I was killing Sissy, and you were chasing nurses."

The Squirt stuck his hand out. "Just call me Squirt, it's easier. And don't pay attention to the man. He hasn't been the same since he died… again."

"Great to finally meet the famous two-bit Squirt. How are the classes at the academy going?"

"Done and almost done. I'm staying on for the extra credit in forensics. I figure it will help when I interview."

"You're planning on skipping patrol and just jump right to detective?" The man laughed until he noticed the Squirt wasn't. He sobered. "You're serious."

Hooker notched up his one eyebrow. "We told you he was special, John." Then thinking, he smiled. "How many bills do you have in your front pocket?"

The man frowned. "A few." his hand dipped into his right front pocket and fished out three ones, a five and two tens.

Hooker nodded to hand them to the Squirt. "Now, your driver's license, a military ID, and maybe a credit card." Hooker looked at the Squirt, who nodded as he looked over the last bill and folded them and exchanged them for the man's wallet. He opened the leather, and his eyes scanned over the information on the two forms of identification. He pulled out the three credit cards and the base PX card. He glanced at both sides and returned them to the wallet. Folding the wallet, he held it out.

The captain smiled as he took it back. "We had a professional magic guy here who memorized three or four bills… so this will be amazing if you do as much."

Hooker ignored the Squirt. "Did we catch you before your lunch?"

"Was just going to go roust Alex and head over to Capri's for lunch. They have a great chef's salad we both like."

"Can we talk a moment before we go?"

"Sure. What do you need?"

The Squirt held out the driver's license. "About twenty eight-by-tens of just the photo."

He looked at the ID. "Is she missing?"

"No… dead."

The captain held Hooker's eyes for a few heartbeats. Without looking away, he held out the card. "Yeoman, we need headshot only, standard print. Tell Snaps I need one-hundred prints right after lunch."

"Color or black and white, sir?"

Hooker swung his head around to the yeoman, who was already turning to walk away. "Black and whites are just fine, thanks." The yeoman was already through the back door and gone.

Captain Jacobs bit his lip. "Let's go get Alex."

As they waited for their food, the Squirt made a fast pass at Captain Alex Romanoff's wallet as well. The two captains were smiling. They were keen to see how well the Squirt did. Everyone loves a show.

Lunch was bright and lively as the two captains enjoyed telling the Squirt about setting the stage to blow up the world and help Hooker kill his sister. The Squirt kept sneaking glances at Hooker. He could tell Hooker liked hearing how it had been set up, but he also knew there was still some leftover trauma from the fatal night.

He looked at the ribbons on John's blouse. "You were a SEAL?"

The captain nodded. "It's where I know Bill Knight from—he was my commander."

Hooker chuckled at the Squirt's frown of confusion. "Uncle Willie."

The Squirt's face cleared, and then he dug back in. "Did you ever lose anyone?"

The man held up three fingers.

The Squirt nodded. "You don't talk about them." The man slowly shook his head, and his eyes lowered. "Yeah, sorry... but you see, the night... Hooker was there to save two people. No matter what the man named Dog had in mind, Hooker's mission was clear... and he lost a man."

The point hung in the air.

"Okay, who had the grilled cheese sandwich, and who had the barbecued beef?" The two salads dropped where they always did on a Wednesday, and the other two were sorted. "Anything else?"

The Squirt cleared his throat. "Could I see your order book a moment?"

"This?" The woman screwed up her face. The Squirt took it and looked at the back, and then peeked at the inside of the back.

Handing it back, he winked. "Thanks. How many dollar tips have you gotten today?"

She reached in her apron and took out four. He took them, looked at each, and returned them. "Thanks."

She smiled, but she wasn't sure what had just happened.

As the Squirt picked up his fork, he turned to Alex. "Did you opt for a Corvette or a Camaro?"

Alex laughed. "Neither. I already had a Nova with a 327, which was blown and polished. I wasn't interested in a slow car." He pointed at the other uniform.

The Squirt laughed. "No, John is too easy. He didn't do Annapolis. He was up through the ranks, so he has a low-end Hemi—probably a 340 in a Dart."

"You pegged me for a Chevy and nailed him with a slow car?"

The Squirt looked at Jacobs, who was very busy eating his salad. The Squirt reevaluated. "Actually, I think I have to go with no flash, so it would be a Belvedere, but it has a 383 Willie reworked for you."

The man laughed as he wiped his mouth. "Close… it's a 340 made into a 390. I would have gone for the 440s, but it would have made the engine a little too… um, weak—easier to break."

Hooker smiled. "I remember the discussion with Willie and Maddie. She took it out to Stockton when they were finished with it."

Jacobs smiled. "I was there. She brought home some good money from Stockton. First, she won the bracket, then there was some kind of open run, and then, finally, she staged against a rail job and still won."

Hooker nodded. "The open was a challenge from one of the guys she eliminated earlier, but they were friends. He just didn't want to pack it in for the day. The rail job was a not so friendly grudge match, which had been brewing for a few months. She would have preferred to run the race on a motorcycle, but Willie had taken it down to LA and sold it to some undercover cop friend of his to use as a fast chopper."

The rest of lunch danced quickly through gears, tires, and gasoline. There was no more talk of blowing things up or killing people. Hooker watched the Squirt—the kid was still over a year away from buying a legal drink, but he had developed into an adroit guide of conversation and people.

The waitress brought the check. She held it to her chest. "So, what was the business about looking at my ticket book?"

The Squirt smiled and nodded that it was time. "Gentlemen, time to get your wallets out." He started with Captain Jacobs.

"Wait, that's not one of the numbers," the man protested.

"Look between the PX card and MasterCard. There is a county library card."

John looked. "Not the number either…"

"No… the library card number is seven-three-zero-two-five-eight. The number I told you before is the phone number for Sally on the back of the library card."

The man looked and turned red. "Oh, so that's where I wrote it down. No joy now—it was a year ago."

The Squirt smiled and turned toward Alex. First came his ID card information and then the PX and credit cards. The Squirt smiled and then continued through the man's insurance card, two business cards, and the name and address on a receipt, as well as what the man bought and how much. Turning, he started with the information on the back of the waitress's book, then stopped. "Let's leave the man's name and phone number out of it. But the other numbers are interesting."

The waitress roared with laughter. "It's my new son-in-law, and those are the measurements I needed to rent the tuxedo he's wearing for my son's wedding next week."

The Squirt chuckled and then recited another phone number.

"It's our phone number here…" She looked at her ticket book.

"It's on the back of the menu." Hooker laughed.

The Squirt smiled and pointed a finger at Hooker and rattled off a medium number, and then a long number.

Hooker's eyes got big. "The first is my driver's license, but the second…." His mouth dropped open. "Bells in the wind… Mae's VIN number?"

"How do you…?" Alex was astounded.

Hooker snorted. "Pay the bill, and he'll tell you."

The captain reached out. "Oh, no. This was too enjoyable. I've got this lunch."

Thirty minutes later, Hooker swung the five-ton up onto the freeway. The Squirt was looking at the enlarged photo. "This guy did really great work. He cleaned it up too. She almost looks happy."

Hooker looked over. "Maybe it was just one of those days…"

The Squirt looked out the window. The large photo hung in his hand. "Yeah… the kind everyone should get… more than they do."

9

WORKING THE STREET

"Where do you think we should start?"

"Let's start by returning the driver's license and handing over most of the prints. I don't know about you, but my math says there are only three of us in this truck."

The Squirt started laughing.

"What?"

The kid leaned over and held one of the photos up for Box to look at... the cat rolled over and went back to sleep. The Squirt sat up. "He wasn't impressed and doesn't want to ask around."

Hooker snorted with an upturned smirk. He leaned forward and grabbed the shop microphone. "1-4-1."

"Go ahead, Hooker."

"Any PD at the table tonight?"

Karen chuckled as she looked at the ten people on the dinner roster other than Hooker and now the Squirt. "You mean other than the Squirt?"

Hooker pulled the key on the mic once—his only response to honor the comment.

"Aligo and his girlfriend..." Sergeant James Aligo, notorious for serving many tours of the King & Story Road turf wars. When he finished his one year and was given his choice of any duty he wanted, he said he already had a beat and home—just needed a partner. The man was a giant Filipino who made most Irish look small. He had a quick smile and a bigger heart that had turned to affection for the beaten-down area of the city. When he finished his third year staked out at the Gun & Knife Club, they asked again—his answer was still a dog. Now he had a partner he could respect.

He hadn't liked the long Phoenician name. He reached an agreement with her, and she became Zap.

Mexican, Vietnamese, White, or any other language, they all understood the power and meaning of Zap. Zap was rarely on leash. The gangs knew and respected her as much as her partner.

"1-4-1?"

"Go ahead, Karen…"

"Did you need someone else? Because there's a pair of fillers on here who can be—"

"No… we're good, Karen. See y'all in about an hour." He knew who the fillers might be, and he didn't want them getting away.

He swung the truck toward the off-ramp and, at the bottom, turned right. He wanted a little time to sit and think without driving. He looked over at the Squirt. "Do you shoot pool?"

The kid wrinkled his upper nose. "I can sink a ball or two, but it's a motor skill set I haven't really mastered. Why?"

"We're going to go shoot some pool."

The Stick and Balls was a low-lying bar with a large parking lot in the front and an even larger one in the rear. It was Hooker's guess most of the patrons preferred to park out of sight in the rear. This left the front with plenty of room to park the large tow truck.

As they slid down out of the truck, Hooker sized up the one section of the parking lot. If the coffee and food were as good as Max promised, Mae West would have no problem snuggling up into the wide berth at the end of the building.

Hooker looked back in the cab. "Well? You need grass or not?"

Box rose from his place on the seat, thought, and almost shrugged as much as a cat can. He strolled to the edge of the seat and slid over more than leaped. Hooker chuckled softly at the casual masculinity of the twenty-some pounds of orange tabby.

After a brief stop on the tiny strip of grass, Box caught up with the men as they entered the door.

The dim interior was brighter than Hooker expected. Each of the eight tables was lit by their own low hanging table light. Hooker wasn't an expert on tables, but to his eye, they were all high quality. One thing he noticed was the lack of any quarter eating hardware. Gentlemen's tables, you pay the house for your time.

Hooker's eyes flowed down the row of tables. Every table was different —some heavily ornate, a plain-Jane, and the rest in between. As his mind figured out the differences, the Squirt muttered a low warning. "I don't think we're welcome here."

Hooker saw a dozen women slowly moving down the room. Some with pool cues held at a casual ready, and two slowly spun their sticks in a show of weaponry. Hooker held his hands up in front of him but said nothing. The air rapidly grew thick with tension.

The Squirt was nervous, and his mouth started muttering smartness as fast as his mind worked. "Let's go play some pool, he said. Just a friendly game with some friends, he said. Maybe have some coffee with our cracked skull, he forgot to mention. Hooker, don't you think it's time we backed out of here?"

Box slid between their legs and advanced. His saunter was of a wildcat ten or twenty times his size and weight. The tail whipped back and forth. It had been more than a few months since he killed or beat-up anything at least four times his weight. Hooker could see the bunching in the shoulders —Box's tattletale he was ready. The cat was looking forward to the fight mere seconds from starting—and a few seconds more from being over. The approaching woman in the work shirt, jeans, and biker boots had no clue how close her life, or at least her face, was now hanging in the balance.

Hooker decided to end the standoff. His voice was calm but loud enough to reach everywhere in the building. "Max... does your liability insurance cover death by twenty-pound cat? Because you're about to lose one of your customers, and by the look of her clothes—a fellow biker."

Everyone froze as they heard the heavy desk phone slam down in the office. "God damn it, Hooker, don't… I'm coming." The large woman whipped around the corner. Her massive gray braid continued and swept the air to circle around her neck, with two feet continuing around to fall onto her chest.

Max took in the scene of her patrons. They thought they were about to take apart two men who stupidly walked into a lesbian bar. It was not common, but usually, the fantasy of stupid men who hazarded the thought, *If only they tried me just once, they would go back,* ended more often than not with a trip to a hospital for the man. It had happened only four times in the fifteen years she had owned the bar. Usually, it was just broken bones, but twice, there were knife wounds. The cops searched for the long thin knives, but nobody ever thinks about an old woman hiding throwing knives in her braid. The six knives were what made the braid move and swing so heavy. In a close-quarter fight, Max had even used the weighted braid as a bludgeon.

"Girls, meet my good friend Hooker. The cat is named Box, but I would not suggest trying to snuggle with him. He killed a man-sized wolf-dog a few months ago. It only took him about…" She looked to Hooker.

Hooker blinked. "Five seconds… plus or minus a second. His favorite signature—dog or man—neither hits the ground with their throat in place. Box usually drops it on their chest as they lie gasping on their end, right before he stands over them and pisses where the air is trying to be drawn in."

The woman in the lead smirked. "That is so much bull shit."

"I'd be more than happy to give you the name and phone number of the vet who pronounced on the last dog. As for the two men, I can give you the name of four county coroners who can show you photos. We had to knock Box out to pull dental impressions that matched the few bite marks, but it wasn't until I watched him kill the wolf-dog I understood how he rips the throat out. He sinks his claws into the sides of the eyeballs or ears and shreds the throat out with his hind legs."

"A cat doesn't have enough strength." She was now leaning on her pool cue instead of getting ready to use it as a weapon.

Hooker looked at the sturdy chains supporting the large lights running two-thirds the length of the tables. The top of the old stained glass fixtures was almost seven feet above the floor. To get to the fixture, Box would have to clear the end of the table so the jump would be almost ten feet of vertical angle.

"Box… top of the lights over the table… Do not touch the tables."

The orange fur shimmered and then was a flash. The hindfoot touched the edge of the light fixture as the rest of the cat streaked out in a show of energy. He raced down the five-foot fixture and leaped into a high arch carrying him to the next fixture twelve feet away. Fixture by fixture, he raced to the end of the building. At the end, he leaped out directly toward a stunned woman who shrieked and dropped.

Box hit the wall behind her. The weight of his impact knocked a cube of chalk into the air. As he backflipped off the wall, his hind paw smacked the cube, and it flew into the air in a higher arch.

As the cube arched toward the second table's light fixture, Box dove under the first table. The orange exploded out from under the other end, only to arch up and land on the second table's light fixture just as the chalk cube arrived. He caught it in his mouth and raced once more the length of the fixture, only to dive to the floor. He disappeared under the third table, back to the top of the fixture of the next, and then repeated the up and down until he got to the last fixture. As he leaped off, he leapt over the head of the woman he had been kept from fighting. As he flew over her, he spit out the cube. It hit her in the face as she ducked. If she hadn't flinched, it would have only hit her shoulder. He knew she would flinch.

He bounced off the floor and landed on the bar. He stopped next to the woman he recognized as in charge. He sat and started cleaning his paws as if to say *the top of the fixtures needed dusting*.

Max smiled at Box's style and size. Slowly, she looked back at the stunned group. "Any more stupid questions?"

A tall, good-looking blonde near the front of the group notched her chin up. "If the cat is Box, and he is Hooker… who's the squirt?"

The Squirt snapped out his hand onto Hooker's chest as if to say *I've got this*. He smiled at the woman. "Exactly, my name—the Squirt."

The woman next to the blonde laughed and jabbed at her shoulder. "He got you on that one Mindy."

The blonde ignored her friend and stepped forward. "Is that true?"

The Squirt nodded with a quirky smile and a shrug. "Real name is John, but everyone calls me the Squirt. It's slang for—"

She cut him off and stuck out her hand. Her voice was lower. "The fucking new guy in the cop car." She smiled. "Are you a cop?"

"Not yet. I'm just finishing the academy. You?"

"Nah, I went the nurse and EMT route. My dad and his two brothers are cops. Two of my cousins are cops up in the city, and one is a firefighter in Santa Clara. I figured one of us needed to learn how to patch up the rest of them."

The Squirt snorted. "Sounds like my sister." He jerked his thumb at Hooker who was talking to Max. "And his girlfriend." He shook her hand. "It was Mindy?"

"Yes, nice meeting you. A bit bizarre—but nice. What are you guys doing in here, anyway?"

"You mean because it's a… girl-girl bar?" He shrugged. "You'd have to ask Hooker. He told me we were going to shoot some pool and have some coffee… but I think there is more to it."

Max looked up and spotted Mindy. She waved them over as she looked for another. "Hey, Carol." The brunette who had been teasing Mindy looked up and laid her pool cue down.

They stood around as Max showed them the blown-up photo. "You ever see this woman up at Valley Med or over at Joe's?"

Hooker helped. "We think she worked the streets downtown."

Mindy looked up and studied Hooker's face. She reached over and moved some of his hair to reveal the long scars running back along his scalp. She smiled. "I thought I recognized your voice." Then her eyes got really big as she turned on the Squirt. "That's who you are. You're the two-bit kid. You have dimes and pieces in you too."

Her shoulder's sagged. "It's also where I've seen this cat before…" She glared at Hooker. "You left the Squirt catatonic one night."

Hooker laughed as he remembered visiting the Squirt with Willie and they had snuck Box into the hospital in a shopping bag. The blonde nurse caught them. "A small world."

Mindy pointed back at the photo. "She's dead?"

Hooker nodded.

The blonde turned and looked at the room again. Not seeing who she was looking for, she turned and tapped the photo. "Can you leave this here? If Sonia comes in—it won't be until after eight tonight—maybe she knows something."

Max lowered her voice. "I thought she worked up around Stanford or the city?"

"Not since she lost her driver's license."

Hooker could see on Max's face the same look he often saw on Dolly and Stella's—all mother hens with huge hearts looking out for their broods. She would make three in his life, but he knew the world was short too many. So many chicks fall through the floor of the coop only to get drowned in the waste below.

"Sure, and if it would help, we have a few dozen more in the truck."

Max's eyes slowly left the photo and softened around the edges. "Any idea on the cause?"

Hooker nodded. "She was murdered. Cyanide."

Hooker noted a collective pause in the heartbeats of the two women. Violence, car accidents, and gunshots—those areas the two had intimate familiarity with. A specific poison so targeted is a wild card usually only experienced in a movie—and even then, rarely.

"Are you sure? Cyanide?"

The Squirt nodded. "They recovered the body soon enough, but even with the other bodies, they were able to pull trace from the bones."

"Other bodies?" Max's eyes were surrounded by compressed dark. "Where?"

Hooker glanced at his watch. "Up near Bridgetown, in the seagrasses. Look, we've got to go, but you can have a handful of photos to ask around. We need to know what happened the last night."

Max smiled wanly. "Thanks. I'll walk out with you."

The three walked across the front parking lot toward the tow truck. Max glanced with a smirk at Hooker as she looked at the size of the five-ton truck.

"This is going to get some getting used to. Do both of you fit in the clown car?"

Hooker turned to the Squirt. "Do I have any credit left in the swear jar?"

"Nope." The kid laughed. "You used it all up on the jarhead."

"Well, he deserved it."

He turned back to Max as he opened the door. His face took on the look of Uncle Willie at his sweetest intoxicated level when his Nancy was dancing as hard as his dress was ugly. "Sweet thing, you certainly are special." He stalled. Finally fishing into his pants, he pulled out a wadded bill and threw it at the kid. "Fuck you, Max. It hurts enough as it is."

Max smiled. "Dude, been there. I'm sorry about you losing her. We followed it all in the paper. But you two saved many lives that day. If I thought I could help, I would… a lot of us would."

Hooker sagged. "Thanks, Max. I know you were just teasing, but it really does hurt. I miss her like you could never know."

She nodded as she took the stack of photos. "If you ever just need to talk… or just coffee…" She rested her hand on his upper arm and squeezed gently. "And as for the swear jar? Leave the civilized crap at home. Around here, everyone would be broke by Tuesday if we threw a buck in."

"Hey!" They all looked back at the bar's door. Mindy stood there as Box sauntered toward them. "I don't think anyone wants to play pool with him. He doesn't use the chalk fairly."

They all laughed as the three males climbed up into the cab of the truck.

Max raised her hand. She watched them leave. She turned back to her bar and shivered as ice ran down her spine, even though the day's heat was still over ninety-seven degrees. Even at three in the morning when she finished closing, it would still be over eighty degrees, but she shivered from the cold thought of poison.

10

WHERE HAVE YOU BEEN?

Wednesday evening dinner at Dolly's was a dance of politics, power, and friendship. Dolly's needs or wants dictated a person getting an invitation to be one of the anointed at her long table. Dolly positioned and paired until the seating met her critical orchestration. Many political careers began or ended at the table.

On her desk lay the stick Dolly used—and only Dolly—to stir shit up within the South Bay Area. Most people focused on the stick as her scepter of power—but they were wrong. The table and Wednesday night dinner were the true embodiment of her power.

Dinner was at six sharp. Don't be late.

If you ever decline an invitation—and aren't in the hospital—don't ever expect another.

Hooker sat at the head of the table as Dolly's anointed one and complaisant ringmaster. His only nod to the warm season—his leather jacket hung on the back of the chair. Summer dinner attire—starched white T-shirt. Along one side sat the Squirt, but almost everyone else was an interesting mix.

The previous year, Dolly started mixing things up a little. She called it stirring. What had once been a table of testosterone now occasionally enjoyed the spice of hormone harmony. Tonight was more than a spice—more like a dose.

The two sheepish diners were at the sacrificial end of the table. They sat the farthest away from Hooker, but still under his direct view. Uncle Willie and his constant cohort, Maddie, squirmed just a little. Some would even find it interesting the two squirmed at all.

William Knight was a retired Naval Intelligence Captain. As a SEAL, he led an escape from a Vietnamese prison camp. After hanging from a meat hook for four days, he worked himself loose, killed the guards, and led the rest of prisoners over one hundred miles to safety. Six commanders of the returned prisoners, and every prisoner, to the man, wrote letters directly to the Joint Chiefs of Staff recommending him for the highest honor the country could bestow.

Hooker found the medal and sky blue ribbon in the back of a drawer one day. Willie had left the White House, took off the medal, and he never wore it again. Personal grandeur was not his style.

Hooker had the medal and certificate framed then hung it by the door they used the most. Hooker did it to remind Willie—and everyone else—he had paid the price and earned the right to wear any dress he wanted, love the man he wanted, and be the person he took pride in being. Not one person in the land could say else wise.

Maddie, a librarian, grew up wearing bib-overalls more than anything resembling a dress. Her father and three brothers raised her in the family business, making fine moonshine, building fast race cars, and driving them even faster. For a few years, she held the world speed record as the fastest woman. She enjoyed it at the time but knew technology and younger women would eventually take the title away. With only a summer sprinkle of salt in her pepper hair, she was still the only woman Hooker knew who was as comfortable driving a car at two hundred as she was going to the store for milk and eggs.

To the others, the couple sat calmly. To Hooker's trained eye, they would give anything to be elsewhere.

Along the one side sat the anomalies. The table's normal mix of guests were officers of the law, politicians, firefighters, tow truck drivers, or other customers of Dolly's answering service or radio dispatching. Rarely did anyone fall outside this scope.

Hooker watched the small, yet powerful, Japanese American woman everyone knew as The Fly. Her wrecking yard and truck repair had grown into the largest auto body repair shop in the South Bay—possibly the entire Bay Area. The back storage yard, Hooker's impound, and the haul-to yard were over three-acres alone. The building hulking between the yard and the rail docks was another two acres under one roof and the kingdom of the one-legged yard boss commonly known as Dog.

The fluorescent light reflected softly off the pecan-colored bald head of Dog. His goofy smile told Hooker he had no idea why he got cleaned up and escorted The Fly and her daughter Mai Lynn—his live-in girlfriend. All he probably cared about was the dinner in the offering.

Mai Lynn, more Americanized than her mother, was tall enough to have played basketball for Branham High. Her taste in colors still ran to the blue and white of the school she graduated from over ten years before. Her voice was like honey, as she small-talked with the other person of Asian descent in the room—Officer James Aligo.

The large Filipino had a booming quality about his voice, which could make you feel good and warm with his friendship or freeze you in your tracks when he caught you on the street. The dog at his feet was only there for back up. Zap didn't give a rip about the dinner. She knew when and where her dinner would be placed and in what bowl. Everything else was work or didn't concern her.

The Fly sat chatting with one of the usual suspects and close friend of Hookers. Ace almost went to work for The Fly more than a few times. Like Hooker, towing was the only job Ace had ever worked. Even mowing his small lawn, he hired a neighbor kid.

The two men at the end of the table next to Uncle Willie were the ones Hooker couldn't figure out. The older one wore a red and white checked seersucker shirt. The fringe of white hair ringed his head. His voice was low as he talked to Willie, and the younger man with the butch cut hair just sat and listened. His white short-sleeve shirt looked like it was usually pinched at the throat by a tie. By the strained edge of their seats demeanor, Hooker could tell they were also clueless about their presence at the table.

Hooker looked up at Dolly, making herself busy ignoring Hooker as she served up the plates of spaghetti with Sicilian sausages from the deli on North 13th Street. Hooker would just have to let the evening play out.

As the dinner wore on, the talk landed on fishing. At first, it was innocent enough as the conversation involved pulling ten-inch stocked trout from Calero Dam. The conversation changed when the man in the seersucker shirt asked Aligo if he had ever done any deep-sea fishing.

"I've gone out a few times."

"Where?"

"I have a cousin down in San Diego, and we've gone out of there, and a small place in the Baja."

The younger Texan drawled, "Ensenada or San Felipe?"

Aligo's eyebrow rose with interest. The man knew of both places. "We usually make a long weekend of it and went out of San Felipe."

The man swallowed his mouthful of sausage and wiped his lips on his napkin. "Gotta love the long, slow ride down the sea of Cortez—sand on both sides of the dead flat sea—unless y'all are with Zeb here. He gets antsy and opens up all four diesel engines. Thirty-two hundred horses and our old PT boat flies down the Cortez. We usually clear the end in about ten hours."

Uncle Willie gently put his fork down and patted at his lips. He watched the older man named Zeb turn red as he tried to ignore Willie. "You told the Navy the PT sank."

The man whined. "Jeez, Bill, they'd just scuttle her anyway. She's the best the Navy ever had."

"Where did you hide her?"

"Con Son Island off Bac Lièu down in the Mekong. I friended a couple of French pirates who needed a boat for a while. If it happened to have some machine guns and a torpedo or ten—so much, the better."

"And they gave it back?"

"By sixty-nine, things heated up all over the peninsula, and they needed a bigger rig. One day, they asked where I wanted it parked. I thought they were joking… so I said San Felipe. When I got home a month later, in the mail was a picture of her, parked in a slip for life. At first, I was afraid to go near her. She sat for six months." He jammed his thumb at the younger man. "One day, Junior here said he wanted to go fishing. I figured what better trolling machine than an old PT boat. At worst, we just kick off a depth charge or two and see what floats to the surface."

Hooker choked as Dolly walked by and slapped his back. She leaned in near his ear. "Keep up, Hooker. This man is the mirror of Willie, Maddie, and Manny."

Hooker took a sip of his coffee as the entire table looked after his well-being. "They left live depth charges on the boat?"

Junior snorted. "Oh, they was just the starter package. I'd just gotten back from 'Nam, and there was stuff I never seen on even the new Surface Effect boats. Even the heavier armed Swift boats, which replaced the old PT boats, didn't have this stuff."

He smiled at his father. "The racks of torpedoes were larger and held about four extra. They installed a shielding on the outside of the racks the Navy never even thought about. The old twin-thirties were replaced by a pair of mini-guns off a gunship or Cobra."

Willie smirked. "What did the locals think?"

"They paid the local police captain to clean and take care of it for us. We figured they went out for the occasional joyride, but they worried about who we were. They never shot the guns or touched off a fish or can."

Junior snorted. "They also never tried to pick the lock on the forward locker."

Aligo laughed. "What was so important in a locker?"

The father and son looked at each other and sized up where they were. "Because the rent was in there."

"Rent?"

"For the use of the boat."

"I assume more than a couple of baskets of old fish…"

"Hardly. It was more than any bank would loan us to start our business."

The Fly was quickest with the smart mouth. "Which wasn't a sport fishing business done with explosives?"

The younger turned toward the woman. "No, ma'am. We design and build prototype specialty vehicles—usually for the government, or mining and exploration."

The man's voice was soft and quiet, but for Hooker, he might as well have screamed it at the top of his lungs. The weight of his words cleared up many questions.

Hooker leaned forward as he watched both heads of Uncle Willie and Maddie drop. "And how long is it going to take to build the special new tow truck?"

The Fly swore softly in Japanese, and Mai Lynn's head snapped up in shock to look at her mother. Hooker had his confirmation the small woman was in on the surprise. He ignored the woman, as well as the glowing red faces at the end of the table.

"Well, shoot... Mr. Knight here said we had until about Thanksgiving. We could even have until the first part of December if we did the wild custom paint job he gave us photos of—"

Zeb backhanded his son's chest. "You can stop talking any time now."

Junior frowned at his father, then seeing Willie and Maddie blushing and not looking up the table, he looked at Hooker. "Oh, shoot. I done ate the wrong end of the armadillo, didn't I?"

Hooker nodded with a smile. He was just happy to get his girl back—even with a new dress. Revealing Willie's disappearance was only a bonus. "I'm assuming you have done a little work with Marmons before?"

"Yes, sir. We designed the slip-shift for the Desert Eagle. We had a bunch of other modifications the government never seemed interested in looking at, but we still wanted to test bed." He looked back at his father and then looked down. "I think I'm going to say a bunch of hush-up now."

Dolly patted him on the shoulder as she poured him more coffee. "It's okay, Junior. You aren't the first to lose the lock on your lips around this table. And just so you know... nothing ever leaves this room—or the person would answer to me."

"Yes, ma'am. Very good, ma'am."

Dina's whistle shrilled from the other room. "I have calls."

"Ace, you have a T-Wonderful in Willow Glen.

"Aligo and Zap are needed at the academy, and please take the Squirt with you.

"Micha, your backup just went 10-7 at the Monterey Steakhouse for dinner. Your dispatch requests you head for the north 101 and work from Story to the breakers.

"Fly, Mai Lynn, and Dog, nice to finally meet you three. Please, do not touch your dishes. Monitor is showing clear. Oh, and Hooker, you have a phone call on line two from a woman named Max." The Squirt and Hooker looked at each other. The pleading was in the kid's eyes. Hooker gave him a *shooing* motion with his two hands.

The slow, gentle rumble of laughter migrated from the large Filipino as he hid his face and bent over to collect his partner.

The table erupted in directed chaos as Hooker left for the inner office.

Uncle Willie started to move. A growl from behind him settled him back down. "I think you four could use some more coffee. It may be a long night." Dolly smiled at the two gentlemen from Texas. They both recognized where command stood and who was on the working end of the shit-stick.

Hooker hurried past the door. "Dolly, cut 'em loose. Karen, I'll call you in about an hour to go 10-8." The door opened and closed in one heartbeat. The Squirt stood with his mouth open, and his finger outstretched—he had just been cut out of the investigation.

11

WE WORKED TOGETHER

Hooker backed the tow truck into the end of the parking lot. A few cars sat in the front lot as he walked across. He figured many more hid in the back lot. The music was thumping on the wall. As he opened the door, he realized the walls were thinner than they looked, and the music wasn't as threatening as it sounded.

The general attitude had changed in the few hours. Some of the women stood with their hands draped from their pool cues. Others glanced up and went back to shooting the balls on the table. The hostility toward a man walking in ratcheted down. Hooker still felt sensitive to being the interloper.

"Where's your cat?"

Hooker sized up the stocky woman. The haircut almost as short as his, but the bulging arms revealed a much more physical day's labor than his. Hooker recognized the work shirt and figured her for a yard worker or drove one of the larger forklifts at the canning plant.

His glance took in the tattoo on the right forearm. He smiled at the logo for the Arm Wrestling Association. "Box doesn't arm wrestle… and you beat my right arm before I got through the door." He stood passive waiting for the response.

The woman thought and then smiled. She turned her forearm in and rubbed at the tattoo. "Made it to the finals five years running." She pointed at the large lightning bolt scar running up her left arm from the mid-forearm and into the short-sleeved shirt. "I used to be a lefty—until they chased my bicep back up into my shoulder. When the muscle is under tension and tears away from the elbow…"

Hooker smiled. He understood pissing on the backside of the barn. He sloughed off his jacket and pulled up his shirt to expose several scars, and then ran his hand up along the scars leading into his hairline. "Dimes— from the mouth of a shotgun."

She laughed, and her chest shook but didn't jiggle. "You win. And, yes, I already knew who you were… as well as the dimes." She stuck her hand out. "Tawny. I'm Max's little sister."

"Hooker, and I left Box with his girlfriend. He and I both hate the truck I'm driving… for now."

Max came out of the office. "Oh, good. Now you know the whole damn family." She flipped her braid around to her back. Hooker got the distinct feeling it was her way of uncocking a gun. She lowered her voice. "Tacky, can you go quietly get Shawna, please? Bring her into the office— it'll be quieter."

She waved Hooker into the back. "You want some coffee?"

"I'm good."

Hooker took the offered chair. "Can I ask a question?"

Max sat and gently drew her braid around where she could reach all parts of it. In the light, Hooker could see the leather bindings dyed to match and blend into the hair and hide the arsenal of knives. "Sure… but I'm assuming it's about Shawna hanging out here, but her working as a prostitute. You're wondering if she's a lesbian."

He nodded.

"The short answer is yes. The longer answer is—you should never confuse a person's sexual leanings with what they need to do sexually to make a living—or for many, to stay alive. When I was in my twenties, I was married. The man was my closest friend in high school. We knew each other's secrets, and we loved each other."

"What happened?"

"One night, he was leaving a bar up in San Francisco, and four thugs jumped him for his jacket. I sat in the hospital, holding his hand for two days while they tried to control the bleeding in his brain."

"I mean… you were married?"

"Conveniences—society said you marry—my mother wanted a son-in-law. Harold needed a wife who understood, and I needed a husband who also understood. A little two-bedroom house in Milpitas can go a long way toward hiding many secrets."

Tawny knocked at the door. Max waved them in.

Shawna was already made up for work. Only the short dress was needed. Hooker rose and put out his hand. "I want to thank you for talking to me. My name is Hooker." Suddenly, he started to blush as he realized, for the first time, his name could be awkward.

The woman laughed. "Down, sport. Every working girl in town knows about you, who you are, and the big-assed tow truck with Mae West on the side." She sat down. "So, what's on your mind?"

Max pushed the photo across her desk. The woman glanced at it and then picked it up. "This is Star." Her face crushed in realization. She looked up at Hooker. "What happened?"

"We're trying to figure it out."

"But you're not the police."

Max interceded. "No. No, he's not. But tell me… would you rather talk to the police about work and how you know her?"

The woman thought it over. She looked sadly back at the blown-up driver's license photo. "This is an old picture of her. She was prettier then."

"It was the driver's license she had on her."

"I remember thinking then how young she was. But then… we all started young." She cautiously looked up at Max for support. "I was fourteen when I ran away. I met my first pimp the next day at the bus station in Salt Lake City. Two fast years before I was in San Francisco." She rested her elbow on the desk and her head in her hand as she softly rubbed or scratched at the pancake makeup on her forehead. "It seems like a couple of lifetimes ago."

Max pushed her hand out flat on the desk. She didn't touch the woman, but the gesture was there. The woman read the offer. She looked up at Hooker. "What do you want to know?"

"We're trying to figure out when she went missing and from where."

The woman looked at her small silver watch and thought. "I need some food, and then Toni will be uptown about nine or so."

Hooker stood. "This guy Tony is her pimp?"

"She's too… she doesn't have a pimp. Toni is another girl—they room together." She didn't have to explain why a forty-two-year-old woman didn't have a pimp—there wasn't the potential for enough money.

"What do you want for dinner?"

"Food."

Hooker looked to Max for guidance. She only shrugged one shoulder. He smiled back at the woman. "Steak at the Bold Knight or pizza at VIP?"

"Pizza. Too much meat upsets my stomach."

"VIP, it is."

She knew who she was and what it could look like. "Are you sure?"

"Unless you prefer Original Joe's."

"No, nothing uptown." He knew she was thinking about being seen. He gave her a warm smile.

"What kind of pizza do you like?"

"Anything out on the by-the-slice table."

"I think I can spring for something more than just a slice. I'm hungry myself," he lied.

WEDNESDAY NIGHTS WERE NORMALLY slow nights, especially after the usual dinner hours. A couple of other tow truck drivers still hung out and shot pool in the backroom. Some old black and white movie played on the screen. Hooker focused on the woman, ignoring the screen. Knowing the owner, it was an early Hitchcock mystery. They took a quieter seat, Hooker knew.

The leftover of a medium mushroom, ham, and olive pizza, sat next to a half-full pitcher of root beer. The two talked sparingly about life on the streets for the working women. Hooker knew some and wasn't really surprised by the new revelations. What surprised him were the backgrounds of the girls who drifted into the world.

Shawna sipped and then blotted her lips. "You would think broken homes, foster kids, and beaten or molested girls would be the majority... and in a way, they kind of are. But there are also ones like me—a good home, bored, and running away to seek excitement. I was probably looking just to make my parents pay attention—but what I got was a pimp and turned out by five businessmen by the end of the next night. Afterward, I was afraid to leave. I didn't even think making a phone call from a payphone would be safe. It wasn't until Michael got stabbed to death by my next pimp I realized he didn't have real control over my life.

"But to answer your question, girls aren't always in trouble when they walk away from home—but trouble finds them. Once a girl in San Francisco—a rich trust baby going to Stanford—worked along Polk St. She worked Polk dressed like a young boy. Her johns were businessmen in town for meetings or conventions looking for something they would never get in Ohio."

"A young boy?"

"Exactly, and she was good. They never knew the boy blowing them was really a girl."

"What if they wanted more?"

"That's how we found out. The john beat her because she wouldn't have anal sex. If she'd just dropped her jeans enough in a dark alley, everything would have been fine. But when the guy didn't find a young boy, she ended up in the hospital."

Hooker frowned in confusion. "Were you working Polk Street?"

"No. I was the other hospital bed in the room. They were putting my jaw and seven broken ribs back together."

"Your pimp?"

"Wrong pimp—jumped by four other girls who wanted me off Market Street."

"Tough competition."

She snorted. "They were nothing compared to your sister and gang."

Hooker froze—a small piece of pizza halfway to his mouth. "My sister?"

"Your sister… The Mouse… wasn't she…"

Hooker returned the pizza to the plate. His interest in food finished. He nodded. "How would you know my sister… or she being my sister?"

Shawna leaned back and thought. She realized Hooker had no real idea of the darker side of the streets and how his sister and her army of cockroaches worked.

"When I was young, I wouldn't talk to the person panhandling for dimes and nickels. As you get older, you realize you're just another animal on the street. When you're so old, a pimp won't keep you—your only defense is every set of eyes on the street. We older girls look out the best we can for each other, but the invisible people are the best watchers."

"But how did you know about her being my sister?"

"Those little tow trucks… what? Fifty or sixty in this city?" Hooker nodded, and she continued, "The size you're driving now…?"

Hooker thought a moment. There were only a few big rigs in the four counties. "Seven or eight… maybe."

"And how many trucks the size of Mae West dolled up like she was?"

"One."

The woman put her finger on the tip of her nose as she laughed. "Everyone on the street at night knows your truck. At first, you recognized the yellow, then just the size and shape of her as she slides by. After a while, I could hear you, two or three blocks away, and know it was you. Most of the girls do. We call you the Knight in Yellow Shining Thunder."

"And the Mouse?"

"The members of her army knew you too. They always kept tabs on you. After a while, I asked why. I knew who The Mouse was—she preserved a certain quiet on the night streets. The lack of violent types was good for us, but even more so for her people. The quiet left them unmolested as they could scurry about and collect food and stuff. I miss those times. We miss your sister and what she did for the city."

"Has it gotten more dangerous?"

Shawna twisted her mouth around her answer. "After…"

"She was killed."

Shawna studied his face. "There were stories about how…"

Hooker realized the street had its news, and the woman looked for full honesty from him. "I shot her, and well... a big explosion."

She nodded. "If they weren't afraid of your shotgun before, they have no doubts now."

Hooker wound his finger in the air. "You were saying about after..."

"There was quiet for several months. But this spring, things are changing. Much of the army doesn't come into town anymore. But those who do are, well... skittish. There is something out there they are afraid of, which is strange because they used to be the scariest thing on the streets at night."

"How so?"

She studied his face for any duplicity. "You do know they're cannibals, don't you?"

He thought and nodded. "Not all." He shrugged. "Or at least, I don't think they all partook."

"Your sister...?"

He rolled his lips into his teeth hard. "I would be just lying to myself and you if I said not. She may have even started it."

"See? Worse than getting beat up. They made people disappear."

"Is Star the first you can think of to have disappeared from the streets?"

The woman shrugged as she rolled her eyes and head. "Girls come and go. If they moved to LA or up to the city, did they disappear? Or did they just move?"

"So how would you know?"

"All of us have friends. If I moved, say, down to LA and Hollywood, I'd tell my friends Connie or maybe Tawny and Max. It's a safety net of sorts. Once I got there, I would call back and give Max my phone number in case anyone needed to get ahold of me."

"Like my sister and her people keeping track of me."

Shawna smiled. Her eyes wandered all over his face as she took her time. "I think she loved you more than you knew."

"I knew." He looked toward the unmoving front door.

"It... it must have been hard to kill her."

Hooker nodded and looked back at the woman.

His damp eyes were not from what he knew the woman would think, but it would work.

Even so, he missed his sister.

"We should go."

Hooker looked at his watch. It was late enough. The woman Toni would be working the street.

1 2

—————

WHAT HAVE WE GOT?

Manny sat in the office with his giant professional-grade headphones on. Hooker glanced in and guessed Brahms was rolling on the large tape recorder with the sixteen-inch reels. Sweets got Manny the tape deck while he recovered from the gunshot wound ending his detective career.

The professional set-up was a few years old, so the radio station replaced it. Sweets told the owners about Manny, and they sprung for brand new headphones, and a lot of music Sweets knew Manny would like. Sweets and his brother Danny spent days and nights putting together several dozen tapes containing eight hours of music each—almost all classical.

Hooker wandered into the kitchen, finding Stella pulling the last loaves of fresh bread from the oven. The smell filled the large hacienda.

Hooker snickered as he kissed the top of Stella's head. There was a voice—seeming to come from the large pantry, "Do we smell fresh baked bread down here?"

"The children are restless… and when did you start baking bread?"

Stella turned on Hooker and gave him a stupid look without the zombie head roll. "When I was about six."

"No, I mean… Oh, never mind. It smells amazing." He looked at her with eager eyes.

She pointed at the Squirt just coming out of the pantry. "You better go bring your posse up to speed. I'll bring some in when it's cool enough to slice."

His shoulders sagged, and he put on a grumpy face but turned. She popped the towel on the back of his jeans and made him laugh. It felt good to come home to a busy house.

Hooker pointed at the office but looked at the pantry and the Squirt.

"We're going through the anatomy. They have a test tomorrow."

Hooker knew any book the Squirt read was committed to ironclad photographic recall. The Squirt probably read Candy's nursing textbooks out of boredom, but would now be a great study partner for his sister and any other nursing student.

"Are you two going to talk out there all night, or are you coming in here like gentlemen?"

Hooker lowered one eye looking at the Squirt. They both smiled. The Squirt held up his one finger. "His voice is louder than needed—which meant, the music is still playing, and his headphones are on."

Hooker nodded.

"But standing here, he can't see us or even know we are here."

Hooker snorted. "Trust me—he knows. It's a Manny thing. And if I drive the rig up to the Bold Knight without ever saying anything, I can count on the phone ringing before my steak gets there."

The Squirt nodded in resolve. "Because it's a Dolly thing."

"Welcome to the family."

They turned to find the man in the wheelchair sitting in the doorway. "Well, we having a meeting or not?"

"Just working out logistics, Manny."

Stella walked up behind Hooker and took his left hand. She slipped the syringe into his hand as she looked him in the eye and smiled. "I always wanted to say this—shoot him." She turned to retrace her steps back into the kitchen. She called over her shoulder, "Challah bread and fixings in ten minutes."

The bread, cream cheese, jam, and butter left only tiny marks on the plates or at the edge of a lip. A moment of reverent silence descended over the three men. But as long as they kept staring at the squiggles and lines on the chalkboard, they could pretend they were still brainstorming.

Stella knew better, as she gathered the evidence of her fourth superpower—the ability to knock out a whole brain collective with her cooking. At the door, she decided it was humane to turn the mental switch back on. "Anyone ready for seconds?" She was met with six glassy eyes. She made a mental note to check Manny's blood sugar in another half hour. *Let him fly with the kids for a little bit.*

The Squirt was the first to re-track. "So Toni saw Star get to her block around nine, and then Toni hooked up with three businessmen who wanted her kind of party." He turned and frowned at Hooker. "Which is exactly...?"

Hooker looked over at Manny, whose head was back, and his sight was down his cheeks, and over one of his famous Manny teaching smirks. He waited to hear Hooker explain the extreme level of what the street offered —without providing a number to call for an appointment to a specially rigged house or basement.

The Squirt continued naively, "Three guys on one woman sounds like gang-rape to me..."

Hooker snorted. "You have your penetration and receivers all backward. Toni is just short of six foot before she put on her tight thigh-high black boots with nine-inch heels and four-inch toes. Then there is a tight one-piece leather swimsuit thing laced up the back. Hanging off her Sam Brown belt is a curled six- foot whip and a shorter cat-o-nine-tails. I didn't want to know the contents of her large black leather bag. I imagined a portable dungeon gear set or some such equipment. She was reaching into her bag and talking about a perfect mask for me when I asked her not to. I just needed to ask her about Star."

Manny just smiled as the Squirt did the three-second catch-up and snickered.

Hooker growled. "I set you up with a date for Saturday night at ten to go over the contents of the bag. She promised she would let you go by Tuesday."

The Squirt squirmed and blanched, but still giggling, "Can I bring Beth along?"

Manny and Hooker's mouths popped open in round exclamations. They were either bested in a comeback or made privy to his love life. They both knew there would be no confirmation either way.

Manny cleared his throat first to stop the laughing. He loved getting out of hand with the boys, but he also knew they had serious work to do.

"So Friday night, and you found the body on…?"

"Tuesday." Hooker pointed to the redheaded pin in the marsh. "Where the train trestle crosses over to the old ghost town of Drawbridge. Last I heard—twenty-seven skeletons or, at least, those are the complete ones. The skeletons a little east of there, bits and pieces having been worked over for many years. Those might go back fifteen or twenty years."

The Squirt added, "Toxicology on the ones they looked at so far have high traces of cyanide in the bones. The older the bones, the more leach, but they're checking the sternums as well as the rotators of the shoulders and hips."

Manny nodded. "As the blood stops pumping, the highest concentration is in the arterial. If the lungs survived, they're high in the exchange. Next are the extremities where it makes it to the pinch-points of the shoulder and the hips. The concentration of blood leaks into the bones as the cyanide breaks down the platelets and the blood thins. The cyanide binds with the thin plasma, leaking through the artery wall and finally pooling in the joints—forming the concentration they're looking for. Once they knew it was cyanide, they look in the joints… any joint. If it had been arsenic in slow doses, they would be looking at hair and fingernails. Every poison has its tattle-tell. People think it's clean, but there is just as much trace as the lands and grooves on a bullet."

Going back to the downtown map, "So maybe from ten o'clock on she's on…?"

Hooker stopped mid-sip. "Santa Clara. Just off First."

Manny studied the photo. "Hmm, still a good body but needed the darker to hide the face. Do we know what she was doing?"

"Oral."

Manny nodded. "The john can touch and watch the back and legs but doesn't see the face. It's the end of a career. When they're down there, the better money is gone. If you're lucky, you're making rent in a cockroach motel off Monterey Highway or in Milpitas."

Hooker rubbed his face to stay awake. "I think she was moteling with Toni. Toni needs someone dependable to lace her into her rig. I didn't notice any side zippers or anything—she's the real deal. Plus, she was angry she'd been in the rig for four days straight. She had me loosen the laces right there on the street."

The Squirt snickered. "And that's all?"

Manny smiled at Hooker's expense.

"So Star getting into a car for a date. This gets her off the street and away from prying eyes. But how do we slip her cyanide? In my years, hookers weren't the most trusting people—especially with johns."

Hooker's lips rolled in. "I think if we figure it out, we will have our killer. So who do you think the girls trust?"

The phone on the desk made them all jump. Hooker frowned, and Manny looked at the clock. The Squirt raised his hands as if to say it wasn't for him.

Manny swept the hand unit off the base halfway through the second ring. "Romero."

There were a couple of heartbeats of silence. "What time?" Manny nodded. "He'll be there." He hung up.

Hooker knew of only one other person so short in words. "What time is breakfast?"

"Three."

The disc jockey Sweets was blind. His brother Danny was his bodyguard, driver, and anything else he needed. Hooker once joked Danny was rationed to only seventy words a day. His joke didn't go down well, but they were all good since.

Because Sweets worked from Midnight to six, he went to work around nine in the evening. His mother, Lovey, would make breakfast for her three sons—her two biological black sons and the one she referred to as her ghost son. Because Hooker usually worked the night shift, he never had a tan of any kind.

Hooker pushed his T-shirt up his arm. The tan line was more of a shadow and only visible in the right light.

Manny snorted. "Nope—you're still a ghost."

13

BREAKFAST WITH SWEETS

Hooker's head was buried down in the dark cleft of Tilly Sweets' chest. He could feel a laugh or giggle working its way north. But for the moment, she was looking at the tow truck parked at the curb.

The colors were right. But the size...

She held onto Hooker's head harder. "Danny... Danny, you get out here right now."

"What, Mama?" The giant of a man loomed up behind her.

"Look out yonder. What do you see?"

"An itty-bitty tow truck?"

"And I have your ghost brother, my ghost child, clenched to my breast." Hooker squirmed with her laughter, even though it was at his expense. She clenched her large arms even firmer. "Hush, Hooker. I'm talking here with your brother."

She looked back at Danny. "So if Hooker is in my breast, what is at the curb, and what does it mean?"

"Means someone stupidly washed Mae West in very hot water and then dried her on high heat. She done shrunk, Mama."

Tilly grabbed the back of Hooker's hair and pulled his head out of her breast. "Shrunk is exactly what it looks like. Did you not pay attention to our years of explaining the facts of real life, and you done washed her in hot water?"

Hooker was laughing so hard, he fell into her and nuzzled her fat neck until she giggled and started pounding his back.

Danny, understanding his job as straight man for his mother tormenting Hooker, was done, turned, and returned into the depths of the house. Ever the logical man, he growled back at his mother, "You're letting the expensive air-conditioned cold air out the open door."

Laughing, the two closed the door and supported each other down the hall. Tilly finally turned serious. "I am awfully sorry about Mae. Can they fix her? I heard she was cut in half."

"Oh, the whole back two-thirds were vaporized by the blast. Her rear-axle cluster took out the runway light controller, went through the storm fence, and ended blocking traffic four football fields away on the parkway. The sleeper on the back of the cab was what saved me and the Squirt from being flattened like little bugs."

Danny stood his full height as he held four large plates. "You are a little bug."

"Says the man who never eats enough so he shrivels away until his mother can hardly recognize him…"

The voice from the other room was accompanied by the sounds of a braille book being dropped on a coffee table. "Did I hear some strange skinny guy say breakfast was served?"

Hooker could hear the crinkle of the starched white dress shirt before Sweets came around the corner. The man turned as his tongue clicked its ubiquitous sounding tick as he located where people were. He stuck out his hand—directly at Hooker.

The fact a totally blind man knew exactly where he was had long ago stopped unnerving Hooker. He took the man's hand. "How's it hanging, Sweets?"

"Bright, sweet, and beautiful, Hooker, like it should be." They shook and then sat down at the table. There was not much protocol in the Sweets house. This was breakfast. Tilly cooked, Danny served and cleared, and the guest was expected to only be there.

Hooker looked at his plate as Danny set it down. "Oh, Tilly, I don't know how you knew what I woke up this morning thinking about. Stella was cooking bacon, but Candy had some flowers in the bedroom or something, and quiche floribunda was all I wanted."

"My sister Stella didn't make it for you?"

"When I got out to the kitchen, the bacon was gone, the eggs were gone, and she was headed for town. I thought about stealing a piece of bacon off Manny's plate… but you do know he still hides his 357 bulldog under his crotch."

The three snickered at the thought of Manny stuffing his old service revolver between his crotch and the wheelchair seat. Sweets was the first to sober. "I thought his nightstand weapon was a Glock 17, nine-millimeter automatic?"

Hooker smiled at being called out on his joke. "Hmm, yeah, I guess it wouldn't fit, would it? What with them giant cast-iron detective balls of his."

Tilly leaned over and placed her hand gently on Danny's arm. "Honey, after breakfast—not now, but after breakfast, call Willie and let him know the swear jar is a dollar richer."

Hooker protested. "I don't owe a dollar. I only used the word balls once."

She smiled evilly as she held up her two fingers. "What about the other fifty cents?"

"Oh, honey… I'm going to use it up when I talk to Stella later this afternoon."

Sweets held his napkin up to his mouth to laugh. "Hooker, you never learn. You were had the moment you met Mama. She is always going to win."

Hooker growled as he took another bite. "Nothing new in my life, Sweets. Dolly, Stella, Maddie, and now Candy—these women are all on the same team, and we are just the water boys."

Tilly smiled and nestled her hands under her chin as she made goo-goo eyes at Hooker. And then she sat up as she snapped, "Nope… the line sounded good, but you still owe the dollar."

Sweets tapped his finger on the table near Danny's right hand. The big man growled, "What?"

"Give Hooker a buck. It was a great line, and it did make up for the balls line."

Hooker protested, "I don't need—"

"Shut up, skinny," Danny growled with a wink as he tossed a ten over from his pocket. "The man has spoken."

Hooker held up the bill. "But this…" The look on Danny's face had snapped to cold and hard. Hooker gave up.

Turning to Sweets, Hooker took a sip of coffee to wash down the last bite of quiche. "I know I wasn't invited here just because you needed a sparring ball to bounce back and forth."

Sweets calmly wiped his mouth and refolded his napkin. Feeling for the edge of the plate, he aligned the cloth to the knife and plate edge. His left hand found his coffee mug, and his index finger dipped in and found the mug empty. He pushed it toward his brother, who filled it from the carafe and placed it back in Sweets hand. Sweets head dipped almost imperceptibly as he raised the mug to his lips. Sipping, he placed it back on the table.

"I'm not sure where to begin. None of what I have been seeing makes any sense. I almost dismissed it, but then, it started to repeat."

Hooker cleared his throat. "What was first?"

"Mud. To be more exact, it was you covered in mud."

"Mud?" Hooker knew better than to help.

"I could taste salt… but it tasted nasty like it was old or contaminated."

"So salty mud."

"No. Like saltwater and mud. There was grass or something, also… but it was gray or brownish tan like it was dead or at least not alive. It wasn't green."

"Could you see what I was doing?"

Danny growled quietly. "Towing a crab."

Sweets' head swiveled loosely toward his brother. The face never changed. Danny got the hint and retreated into silence. Sweets' attention returned to Hooker.

"You were supposed to tow… but you didn't. There was something in the grass."

Hooker watched the man. It was time. "Bodies."

Sweets' head rose less than an inch. "Ah…"

Hooker cleared his throat. "Well, actually skeletons… and remains."

Tilly held her fingers to her lips as she gently closed her eyes. Hooker knew this part of her *adopted* son made her uncomfortable, but she was coming to grips. It was just the fact of it coming to roost in her dining room and at her table. Hooker knew she loved him as she loved her sons by birth, but he also knew this side of Sweets' life only came with him and his involvement with crimes, as they seemed to find him.

Hooker's voice softened. "Anything else?"

"Plenty. There are scattered dots of things. I feel a woman who is also a man… or is it a man who is really a woman? I am above the water, gliding along…"

"Like a bird?"

"Closer to the water, but not too close… It's like a small river in the grass… it winds."

The slender black man shifted in his chair. "I can feel… It's like I have been here before… the internal war, the hatred, the self-loathing… I can feel the large stick in my hand… I'm pushing…"

Sweets sat back. His shoulders droop as if his strength has suddenly drained out of his feet. Like a deflated balloon. Hooker knew to wait.

The voice was Sweets but from a great distance. "You need to go talk to your sister."

Hooker thought about his sister. The marshlands and the salt flats of the edge of the bay had been her domain—her empire. She had ruled upward of a hundred people society would not recognize as one of their own. She was the manifest of a goddess, a queen, and a mother to all who had been cast aside. The reach of her minions had ceased to amaze Hooker. From the depths of the salt marshes in the southernmost tip of the bay having stretched sixty miles north, she had exhibited knowledge of things going on in the northern parts of Marin County and as far up the Sacramento River as Sacramento itself.

Hooker had figured out over the recent years why he never saw more than a few dozen of the tribe at a time—because the others were traveling and gathering information. His sister was intelligent and knew information was power. He recently discovered she even had a resource for checking out and reading hundreds of books from the Santa Clara County Library system each year. He remembered her capacity to consume vast quantities of the written word, but never thought, while living among the scrub brush in a hole or cave, how she would continue to devour so much information.

Hooker thought about the sea of grasses and the nature of Star's work and life. Maybe it was time to go up to sit in the cool shade of a large tree and pick his sister's wealth of information.

Hooker looked to Sweets. "Anything else?"

The man nodded slow and slight. "This is the part I have a problem with. I have a sense of a ponytail. Not a big one, but just long enough to be one—but I have no sense of it being a man or a woman."

"Any color?"

He shook his head. "No... but for the first time... even right now, I keep getting a smell. Not solid, but just whiffs here and there."

"What kind of smell?"

Sweets turned to his brother. "Danny, could you go get the garbage from under the sink and take it to the front door? Not just the bag, like you usually do—but the whole can."

The man rose and silently followed his brother's bidding. He walked past the table carrying the can—with the garbage exposed to the air. He reached the front door and stood.

"Okay, now slowly take it back to the kitchen."

As Danny passed the table, Sweets' finger came up and pointed at where the man and garbage had been a second before. "There. *That* is the smell. Just like the smell of the garbage can—a little... and then more. It's not old and rotting, like when we are near the dump or when a garbage truck passes with all the old smell and rot... but the fresh smell. Fresh garbage—but it comes and goes... "

Hooker's nose wasn't as sensitive as Sweets, but he did finally get the smell. "And this is the first time you ever had a smell connected to one of your visions?"

"Well, yes and no. Back when I was in the hospital, I was getting crazy memories and kept smelling oranges and occasionally, grapefruit."

Danny snickered.

Sweets' head jerked, and then he snickered and was followed by Tilly. "One morning, I was still asleep. But for some reason, I always knew and still know when Danny is in the room or close. In my sleep, I knew he had come in and quietly sat down. I didn't know Mama was with him.

"Suddenly, I got a strong smell of—" he looked at Danny, "How much did you give Hooker just now?"

"A five or something..."

"Good, because... I smelled a lot of shit." They all laughed. "I woke up and asked Danny if he had just shit his pants or only farted. I was only seventeen and still had a high school smart-assed mouth on me."

Danny snorted, and Tilly continued with a smirk. "He didn't know better. During the night, he had gotten a roommate. The old man had one of those bags on his stomach because they cut into his bowel."

Hooker nodded at what was coming next.

"The poor man had something wrong, and he blew the bag open, and it was all over him, the bed, and the floor. He was so embarrassed."

Sweets wiped down his face with his one hand. Hooker had seen him do this at the radio station when he needed to be serious and maybe do the news. At times, it was scary to watch. Hooker had watched him go from a full belly laugh with tears in his eyes to reading the news about someone killed in an auto accident, in the space of a couple of heartbeats and a hand swiping down his face. *Training and focus.*

"It was the last time I smelled anything when I was seeing something... until now. My guess is—it must be important."

Hooker shrugged and played down the heavy nature of what they were talking about. "Or it means I forgot to take out the trash this morning and will pay dearly later when I get home. Maybe I should go stay with Willie for a few days."

Sweets snorted, and then he was serious again. "Or maybe you better go see your sister."

"It's been a few months."

Sweets leaned back. "Any word on Mae West?"

Hooker looked at the blind man hard. "What do you see?"

Sweets shrugged with a twisted mouth. "Bits and pieces, but she is coming together. It's strange. Some of it's close, and some feel far away."

"The new frame and stuff are being custom-built in Texas. I can only assume the Fly is working on the body here."

"When?"

"By Christmas, I think."

Sweets pursed his lips and pulled at the cluster with his one hand. "I have a feeling… you're going to need her sooner."

"How soon?" Hooker knew in his heart he needed to, and *would*, trust in what Sweets was seeing—in his strange way of seeing—what was happening or what was coming. Those visions had never been wrong, nor had they let Hooker down.

"I can feel Halloween. Not in the past, but close."

"October?" The sooner timeframe was sounding better and better to Hooker, but only if Mae was ready in time. Hooker knew what Sweets was seeing was not the completed Mae, but Hooker's need for her. The two could be mutually exclusive—or have no relationship at all.

Sweets nodded. "I don't feel a conflict, but I also don't see why either."

"But… I need to go see Sissy." Hooker's head snapped up at the sound of Danny's low growl. Hooker focused on the large man whose shoulders and upper arms looked more like someone had parked a large steer in his starched white shirt. "You may not like her name, but she has granted you until this Christmas to come up with a name you like better. I don't get a say. She doesn't get a say… but until then, she can be Mouse, Clair, or Sissy, and you have nothing to say about it… nor are you allowed to growl or grumble. So you either play by her rules, or I will let her know you're misbehaving when I see her soon."

Hooker held the man's hard look. Finally, Danny sat back and held his hands up in surrender.

Hooker nodded. "Good… because I certainly don't want to be the one who has to tell her something that could really piss her off."

Sweets snorted a short laugh and then thought about Hooker's world. He was surrounded by women who it'd be wrong or dangerous to anger. Sweets moved to defuse the situation. "Give her our love when you see her."

14

APPLE FARM WITH SISSY

The working masses of San Francisco, and the elite who manage them, herd them, prey on them, or provide legal ramifications for or against them are separated by the long expanse of the Golden Gate Bridge. The living refuge to the north is where the three-piece suits slip off their Bill Blass slippers and strap on their heavy hiking boots. For many, the shoes are changed in the city to the south before the march to their BMWs or Porsches. Then it is a race to the snail line of metal coffins being pushed north by the thoughts of a glass of wine, a joint, and a soak in their hot tub.

Many workers were painfully aware of the true separation being a few minutes before four in the afternoon. With still a full hour of work for the working bees—the Marin County evening migration begins to build up mass. In the middle of the early wave of German sports cars, the fire engine red of the 1938 REO Speedwagon stood out among the muted greens, silver-grays, blues, and blacks.

When Hooker asked Uncle Willie for the use of a car to run up and see his sister, Willie took the opportunity to have Hooker also deliver an engine to a client in Santa Rosa. The large eight-hundred horse-powered engines with all of its shining parts—either powder painted or chromed—rested snug in its transport crate under the secured tarp.

Hooker glanced right at the side mirror and saw the self-important black Porsche attempting to pass the *old* truck. He smiled at the sleeping bundle in the seat next to him. Box had his form of fun, and Hooker had his. The ramp ahead narrowed from two lanes to only the one. The three-piece suit in the sports car didn't want to be slowed by some old codger in a broken-down piece of old Detroit iron.

Hooker looked back at the empty ramp with a nasty fifteen miles per hour right hook at the end. He was sure the sports car could take the corner at maybe twenty or even twenty-five if the guy was good. Hooker also knew, even with the massive engine in the back of the truck, he could drift the Speedwagon through the turn at well over thirty.

The German car dipped its nose as the maladroit driver downshifted to make his move. Hooker snorted and just mashed down the gas pedal. The five-hundred horses grunted a muted roar, and the red truck shot toward the turn. As the truck's rear end started to drift, Hooker snuck a peek at the mirror—he was almost fifty yards ahead. As he cleared the curve, Hooker shot ahead to merge with the light traffic. Glancing in the mirror as he blended, he snorted when he saw the black Porsche almost spin out as it tried to take the corner too fast. Hooker's smile pulled to one side as he thought about the driver trying to explain to his insurance broker how a fifty-year-old truck could make the curve, but he fish-tailed and smashed into the signpost that said fifteen miles per hour. Box, Hooker, and the old truck calmly rode north to Santa Rosa.

IN THE EVENING, after dinner, Hooker took his sister's hand. They strolled through the long grass toward the two Adirondack chairs under the gigantic Queen Anne cherry tree on the west slope of the large yard. The long grass of the lawn felt good between Hooker's toes. He couldn't remember the last time he had walked barefoot on a lawn—but he was sure his sister might be able to tell him.

"Remember the last time we walked in tall grass?"

"Together?"

"Okay…"

Her laughter tinkled in the dusk air. Hooker smiled. It felt so complete

—her laugh, the smell of the grass mixed with scents from the apple orchard, and the wet grapevines. The evening air was thick with information for all of his senses. Even his eyes were tantalized by the twinkling flights of a few early bats.

"You don't know, do you?"

His silence was covered by his smile. They eased into the chairs. Both of their heads fell back against the gray wood of the rustic furniture.

"Fifty-six."

Hooker thought a moment. "Mentone."

Sissy nodded in the gathering gloom. They rarely used the names of the foster people who had cared for them. The few names they used had been special people, and from a young age—before they were sold into abusive and twisted circumstances.

"The man left to take care of his mother somewhere, and the lawn grew long and un-mowed."

"She lived in San Diego. He went for almost a month. But he had to go back, which is why we moved down to Redlands."

Hooker sat silent. They didn't have to say anything. They both knew when their foster care became abusive—the man who paid extra attention to the nine-year-old Sissy, and the woman with a penchant for using a wide leather belt on the young Hooker. The same year the blanket tent thrown over four chairs became a fort and refuge.

The two were only beginners at preying on children. Mostly, they were agents of a sort—they found children in the system they could make disappear into an underground organization. The children were sold from one pedophile to another, if not to another torturer.

They sat under the giant tree like it was their old blanket tent. Hooker's hand curled to hold the tips of his sister's hand, which was stretched over his. Even in the dusk, Hooker could see the glow of her skin begin to show in the last light of day. *She must have been out in the sun today—to glow this bright.*

The two drifted in their silence, letting go of the old and bad, celebrating their bond and being together. The few bats became many as the summer evening dimmed. Tiny bits of darker dusk flittering about in the only slightly lighter dusk. The occasional tweet of a tree frog syncopated with or counterpointed the rhythm of the night's cricket choir.

"Neither one could have children." Her voice sounded like part of the valley breeze. Hooker's thoughts froze. He wasn't sure he heard the words. "He studied mental health because both of his parents had become so bad, they were institutionalized. He was afraid it was hereditary—he volunteered to be sterilized at nineteen."

Hooker realized she meant Norm Osofsky, who she now lived with for his medical and psychological expertise and care. Norm married Clair, Stella's best friend and maid of honor. The bonds of family and friendship ran deep. As Manny and Stella became Hooker's family, Sissy's problems meant she would always be Norm and Clair's family.

Hooker cleared the stiffness in his throat. "But he is fine…"

"Time occasionally has a way of proving you right or wrong."

"They could have adopted."

"Still would have been a gamble. What if he provided a nice home only to become deranged?"

"But they always wanted kids?"

"It wasn't an option… until now."

"You." Hooker's head rolled toward her as she nodded. He squeezed her glowing hand lightly.

Her face was self-illuminated from the phosphors her body produced. It made her soft smile literally glow. "Now I know how you feel about your Uncle Willie, Manny, Stella, and everyone else. I feel so complete now. More complete than when I was the goddess and mistress of a hundred minions."

Hooker wanted to pull her back from where he would need to take her later. "Don't forget my brother Danny…"

"Ho no." She giggled. "Danny is mine now. I'm counting the days until Christmas when he is to give me my new name."

Hooker mused about the deal she had struck with Danny the previous Christmas. Her real name was Clair, the same as Norm's wife. Hooker had always called her Sissy for sister since he was only four. When she became the goddess of her tribe of night people or animals, she became The Mouse.

Danny hated the name Sissy and became agitated when Hooker used it. He believed it was disrespectful because of the other connotation of the word. So when she finally met Danny, she gave him until the following Christmas to come up with a name he liked. She would officially change her name, and all would abide by his choice. Hooker was sure she had also been a bit captivated by the giant of a man and his quiet calm manner.

A thought formed in Hooker's mind. "What do Norm and Claire call you? I mean, wouldn't it be a bit confusing to use Clair?"

"At first, it was strained, but then I just told them Sissy was good. After all, my middle name is Lucinda. But it just seemed… family, and I said it was similar to Scout… as in the book *To Kill a Mockingbird*. Then one night, Norm pinched me and said, 'Go to bed, Scout.' I jumped and squealed, Clair laughed, and Norm laughed so hard he choked. They both said he had never had the nerve to do something so improper… and they have been calling me Scout ever since."

From the way she told it, he knew she was good with the pinch, and it hadn't been abusive. "So… did you go to bed?"

She laid her head back as she recalled the night. "No." Hooker watched the long slow sigh. Her whole body now glowed through the thin shift. "I don't know who or how the conversation started, but soon, the deck of cards came out. We drank jackrabbit and chamomile tea until breakfast. Clair never sat in on my sessions with Norm, but it seemed like a group catharsis—it was when I learned he couldn't have kids."

"It sounds like many good things happened that night."

She held up her arms and looked at the strength of the phosphor glow. "Coming to accept and even love my inner light was one of them."

Hooker smiled. "Your skin doesn't seem to flake anymore."

"Norm got me on a test drug to control it. There's a little flaking—but using a sea sponge in the shower with some cream after takes care of it. We ran out of the drug once. Within a week, I was back to the large flakes. So if you ever need me to play a snow fairy in a play… I'm your girl."

She stood, and as she did, her shift came off with a wave of her hand. The thin formfitting slip allowed all of her body to glow through as she danced and jumped in the night air. Hooker hadn't watched her dance with abandon since their childhood. It was truly a release of her inner fairy or night spirit. He watched, mesmerized as she floated over the dark lawn… only where her feet came to rest did the grass turn green for a moment. And then it would return to black as the fairy of light danced back into the air, only to reveal other tiny spots of green.

She spun about in a last wild pirouette and collapsed into Hooker's lap. Her legs were curled in, and she was half the size she usually projected. Her head lay nestled in his neck as her arms and hands were folded hovering on his chest. She weighed almost nothing. He had never realized how tiny she was; she had always seemed so much larger than life.

The back screen door spring squealed softly in the night. "It's ten o'clock, Scout."

"Thank you, Papa." She softened her voice as she giggled. "It's past my bedtime… and I'd bet it's really closer to ten-thirty." She nuzzled her head down into Hooker's neck. Hooker glanced at the glowing hands on his watch. It was ten-forty-seven.

Hooker leaned his head over onto hers. "Papa?"

"They call each other Mama and Papa, and I just fell into it." She wiggled as if to get closer to Hooker. "I love my life now. I love my family and, most of all… I love the fact my family is part of my brother's family… especially my new sister."

She kissed his neck with force and then jumped up and ran toward the house.

Hooker sat, taking it all in as the moon rose behind him and lit the top of the cherry tree, creating patterns of light green and black. Dealing with his sister was much the same way—patterns of light and dark. Hooker's questions would have to wait until the morning.

The Apple Farm at one time was over four hundred acres. The fruit supplied the Northern Pacific Railroad as well as the commissary of the owner's little experiment into higher education—Stanford University. Over the years, shipping apples from the state of Washington and better oranges from Southern California resulted in the parceling and selling off most of the farm. Norman had salvaged the last parcel of eighty acres and bought back another hundred that had not been converted to houses during the expected housing boom of the late 1950s.

His colleagues from various colleges had led him to convert to diverse plantings. Many of them were planted by colleges as test groves or vineyards to evaluate the region for future agricultural development. The fruits of the varied trees and soil lay about the morning table.

Hooker rested back in his chair. His head rolled over to look at his sister. "If you ate like I just did, you'll look like Dolly by next summer."

Clair snorted. "You weren't paying attention. She takes in more calories than you do. She just doesn't, and never will have, a fat neck for you to nuzzle."

Sissy smiled at her brother and drew another large slice of homemade bread from the basket and continued to layer slices of banana onto the toasted bread. When the toast was full, she drizzled honey over the banana slices.

Norm smirked as he turned to the amazed face of Hooker. "And I will have to remind her to also have a snack again before lunch. The biochemistry that produces the phosphorous burns an enormous number of calories. It mostly demands the faster-burning carbohydrates in the bread and fruits. So she feeds the production with the foods it needs, and we also slip in more of the protein she needs to produce more body mass, such as meat and beans—foods she didn't get during the last ten years. So it's a balancing act."

Sissy popped the last bit of toast into her mouth. "As you saw last night, it feeds my nightlight. But, with Norm's help, I have come to accept, and even enjoy, being a firefly. The hard part will always be putting meat on my bones."

Folding his napkin and placing it next to his plate, Hooker cleared his throat. "Speaking of bones…"

Clair pushed her chair back and stood as she took up his plate. She gave Hooker a hard look. "You waited until breakfast was over?" She held his gaze. Hooker felt his insides squirm the same as if it was her best friend, Stella.

"I didn't know—"

She cut him off. "I've been around Manny and Stella a lot longer than you've been alive. Back home, a normal Sunday dinner table topic was the best way to kill a given animal—wild or farm. I remember one Christmas dinner gathering, the men discussing the new way of field dressing and deboning an elk so a single man could pack out all the meat. We watched the local minister trying to keep his dinner down while his wife all but passed out. We found it funny and laughed for years about it. So next time you have some gory thing to ask your sister… don't wait. Now I need to make another pot of coffee… so give me a minute before you get to the goo and guts."

Hooker looked at Norm. The man nodded. "She is serious. So if the guts are first, you had better just go open the door for your cat. He's been knocking for almost five minutes."

Sissy whipped out of her chair and was at the door before Hooker could turn. She cracked the door, and as the large cat strode in, she scooped him up and snuggled her face into his side. She didn't have a huge shelf to lie on like Dolly, but as they came close, Hooker could hear the picky cat had lost himself to a fourth person.

Box's head lolled out of her arm. The single eye was already half-closed as he looked at Hooker.

Hooker chuffed. "Slut."

The cat rolled in on himself and snuggled his face into her neck—ignoring Hooker. She giggled as she sat back down, and Box's purr deepened and slowed as it got louder.

"First, you lay claim to Danny, and now you steal my cat…"

She giggled. "He started it by crawling into my bed."

"Danny or Box?"

Clair snorted as she returned with a fresh carafe of coffee. "He's got you there, Scout."

Sissy nuzzled her face down into the body of the large cat. "I rather like the idea of not designating which male. It's good to keep a little brother guessing."

Hooker snorted over his steaming mug of coffee. "The purring screws your scheme of intrigue."

Clair sat and looked at Hooker. "So, where were we about bones, and knowing you—dead bodies?"

Hooker told them about the body dump, his interview with the street-walkers, and breakfast with Sweets. Part of the way in, Norm went to a drawer and got some paper and a pencil and two pens— red and blue. He started graphing out the information, and occasionally, a thin hand would surface out of the depths of orange fur to point to a couple of things to connect.

Hooker was relying on his sister's amazing ability to see patterns and paths where others saw only random information. By the end of the hour, Norm had redone the information in four different ways with path connections in red and blue arrows covering all of them. Hooker sat back and waited for the questions or answers to flow. It started from a place he hadn't expected.

Clair had been glancing at the growing graphs and lists, but not necessarily paying attention. She sipped from her mug and then quietly put it down. "Are all the bodies female?"

Norm and Sissy looked up and then at Hooker.

"I'm…" He thought a moment. "Can I use your phone?"

A few minutes later, he came back. "The count is thirty-two, and three are male. But the coroner is not so sure about those bones. They're older and could be just others dumped there from the days of when Drawbridge was a real town."

"So what we potentially have is a killer who only preys on women. And is probably targeting prostitutes."

Hooker looked at Claire. "But only one confirmed identity is a prostitute."

Norm took over. "Have you ever been driving in the afternoon and watched a guy at the stoplight who is picking his nose? I'm not talking casually… I'm talking about really mining at the back of his sinuses."

Hooker nodded with a smirk.

"Do you think the guy does it all the time… or did you just happen to see the one and only time he did it?"

Now Hooker snorted. "All the time and twice on his morning drive."

"In the psychological profession, we call it a pattern of one. You only observe it once, but you know it is a pattern. I think if you ask around, you will find many streetwalkers have disappeared over the years. And yet, we only have one… but the rest are also."

Sissy spoke with her mouth, barely out of hiding in the fur of Box. "I think, as they examine the bodies… well, bones, they will find no incidents of violence. No gunshots, no knives, no bats, no broken bones, no strangulations… nothing."

"Why?" Hooker frowned.

Claire looked at Norm. "Because the killer is a woman. She's only using poison." Norm nodded.

Hooker looked at Sissy. The liquid blue eyes opened and looked back, half-hidden by the fur. She nodded. "It's because it isn't violent and rude—poison is passive, clean, and dignified."

"What about Sweets seeing two people—a man and a woman?"

Sissy poured down the now aqucous cat. "According to you, he didn't." She checked one of Norm's notes. "He saw both, but they weren't separate… and he only saw one ponytail."

Hooker sat back, thinking. "So where to now?"

Sissy looked at the graphs. "You need to go talk to the older girls, the ones who have been around the longest. Try to get a feel for who is missing, and let the police go from there."

She sat back and sighed. Hooker knew what would come next was not easy for her. He knew the sigh.

"Do you know how to get ahold of Peter still?"

"Sure, he's spending more time around the parish with Father Damian. Why?"

"He used to know a man named Tess. She was a mess. She only wore a dress, but her real heart was her crest. Yes, it's a terrible rhyme, but the woman is a man in a dress. She dives garbage bins, but she also loves shrimp and crabs, so she works the bins behind seafood markets and restaurants. But more importantly for you—she knows many watermen working the flats of the south bay. She'll know about someone we called the Waterman, but he was different from the rest. He was like a ghost. But he stood in his boat when every other waterman sat and rowed—as if he was uncomfortable sitting. He moved very stiff in his body. I always thought he'd been in an accident. Maybe there's more to it."

She shifted in her seat, and Hooker knew she had just curled her legs up under her. The act was subtle, but like a snake coiling its base weight so it could strike.

"The few times I saw him, he poled a long canoe instead of rowing. But he had a certain delicate nature about him—even with the massive upper body. The one thing was he wore a few layers of T-shirts—almost like armor—even if the temperatures were climbing into the high nineties or hitting a hundred. But the one thing that always struck me as odd was his ponytail—it was more girl length than those short guy head whips."

Hooker looked at Norm, who shrugged. *It wasn't his department.* He turned back to Sissy. "Where did you see this guy?"

"Occasionally, we were up around the rim on the east side. He might be putting in around south of Fremont. With a canoe, you don't need a ramp or any other public place. It's not really a far stretch to boat, but we would catch glimpses of him when we would winter out in the old buildings on the island. There is a small ghost town out there called Drawbridge. The train trestle running across the island has no drawbridge, it's just the name."

"Do you remember what time of day you would see him?"

"Sure, the bird girls used to twitter about him being the dawn patrol. It was like he rose up out of the water with the early fog. Just as silent too. Paddling can make noise, but the pole never leaves the water. It makes a very spooky sight to watch him glide by through the soft fog wisps. Just his body was visible above the seagrasses—just gliding along."

Hooker shivered. "I think that's what Sweets saw. The view from standing in the boat, gliding through the grasses. I'll go find Peter."

Sissy rocked on her chair and sat up straight, leaning forward as she took up her coffee mug. Her face had changed to pure glowing delight. "How is my sister?"

Hooker knew her feet now lay flat on the floor—a safe topic to talk about. Some of her old physical tells would never leave her. He smiled softly, knowing he knew her so well, and forever, the best parts would be there.

He thought about the first time he realized when they talked about scary things that she would pull her feet off the ground. In their blanket tent forts, one chair always had the seat facing into the fort. If she slith-ered up onto the seat, drawing up her legs, they were talking about scary things.

"She's doing great. The classes are long and hard, but she is working at Good Sam as a nurse's aide, so she gets great practical knowledge and experience. The Squirt teases her about taking so long, but she teases back—she has so much to learn about why two guys keep landing in the hospital—shot up or blown up."

Norm snorted. "Tell her it's on-the-job training for marriage."

Hooker blanched, and Norm realized he had raced well past the level of Hooker and Candy's relationship. "You two haven't thought about…?"

Hooker's gut knotted, but he remembered who he was with. It still only made it tolerable to talk, but not easy.

"We're still trying to figure out the love part. Neither one of us had the greatest of loving track records to copy. And as for my last ten years, there is a lot of love, but no examples to see how they all got there. You two, Manny and Stella, Dolly, and even Uncle Willie and Maddie have a long history at how you relate to each other. We don't have a clue how to get there. The first night Candy snuck up to my room, we were so scared we just cuddled until we fell asleep in the early dawn. We don't know what we're doing now… much less thinking about something like getting married."

Clair reached across the table and put her hand on Hooker's hand. "Honey, nobody comes to a relationship perfect—if we did, you would have to wonder what happened to the last one. In the beginning, there are many questions—you just need to find the person you are comfortable talking to. Even your Uncle Willie has answers… or at least Hank will have them for him. They are a newish couple, but they understand the loving part. The sex part is just mechanics. Hell, talk to Dolly—you two are cut from the same cloth. You just don't see it."

Hooker harrumphed. "We're nowhere near the same—"

"Horseshit." The woman cut him off. "Why do you think you sit at the head of her table on Wednesdays… because you look pretty? No. It's because you truly are an extension of her. She's not grooming you to take over when she's gone—she just wants you comfortable sitting on the throne she's built in San Jose. And from what I hear, you have already built quite a war chest of markers and chips for the big game, in your own right. Talk to her. If there is one thing I know about Stella and her sister, their hearts are bigger than their bodies."

"I'm not the one in line to take over when she's gone... but I'll talk to her."

"You talk to her, and I'll have a little chat with Stella."

Sissy giggled. "And then, you can always send my sister up here to visit me."

Hooker gave her a zombie roll of the head. "I may be dumb sometimes, but I'm not stupid."

Box poured his way back up onto Sissy's lap and leaned into her chest as he looked back at Hooker. Hooker recognized the *I'm bored with all the talking* stance, but it looked more like he was also laughing at Hooker.

Sissy pushed her face down into the neck of the large cat. The squirming stopped and then turned into a purr. Hooker knew his sister had awesome powers nobody understood. Box was a force of nature and had his own will, but Hooker had just watched him become a quiet kitty instead of the swaggering stud. They all sat quietly watching and listening to Box purr. It was like watching Mae West idling at the curb, and just as loud.

15

CHECKING IN WITH WILLIE

The barnlike garage originally designed to house large blimps stood dark. The three-story-tall sliding door was rolled back—waiting for Hooker to get home. Hooker scratched Box around the cat's single ear as they both reluctantly got out of the Speedwagon.

"I know, boy. But we can't run tow calls in the Speedwagon, and Mae isn't back together yet." They strode across the acre of floor like a couple of Wild West gunslingers. Hooker continued, "I hate the stinking dinky truck as much as you do, but it is what we've got for now. It's either the dinky toy and keep working or sit on some ugly beach in Mexico."

Hooker had never been to Mexico, but sitting on a beach was something he thought about with the summer heat. Sitting next to Candy, watching the ocean.

Hooker reached for the door to the house.

"The fun is all out here, Hooker." The matching giant door, out to the backyard, was also rolled open.

Hooker and Box both froze in the dark. Hooker didn't want to turn around. "Are you two naked, Hank?" With the summer heat, Willie and Hank sometimes enjoyed the night air in the buff as they got drunk on moonshine. Even Maddie occasionally joined them—but wore a long T-shirt. *Some decorum had to be preserved.*

"Oh, heavens to Betty in a broken Bonneville, Hooker—you are such a priss." Willie's speech was only slightly slurred. Hooker guessed they were only on the first fruit jar of moonshine.

"Well? Are you naked or not?"

Maddie giggled as she asked quietly, "Is he always this skittish, or is this something new?"

Willie moaned. "I tried to raise him up with an open mind, you know I have. But lately, it is like he is a different person. I don't know whether to chalk it up to not having Mae around, or his new girlfriend living under the same roof—"

Hooker growled, "Willie…"

Candy giggled. "We all be naked as little jaybirds."

Hooker now knew both of his legs had been pulled. Candy was barely up to being naked with him—much less being so in public. He turned and made his way toward the voices and dark shapes.

Willie clicked on a work light. They were all dressed in work clothes. Nurse, librarian, retired schoolteacher in a bow tie, and the former Navy intelligence officer in an extremely ugly plaid granny dress with burn holes and scorch marks among the grease stains. Hooker figured Willie or Hank would put the cutting torch to the rag before Willie would be let back into the house.

The small Ball fruit jars sat beside each of their empty plates with dark crumbs and forks.

"Any cake left?"

Hank rose and pointed at his seat. "Sit. I'll fix you a plate."

"I stopped for a hotdog in San Mateo, but Box could use some tuna."

Hank pointed toward the roll-around workbench. "The shine is over there. Cake for you and fillet of fish for the big guy."

"Thanks, Hank."

"Don't thank me. Maddie brought the fresh salmon from up the coast. She can have my kiss. Just save my hug for later."

Hooker sat down and glared at Willie and Maddie. The staring contest was off to a great start because Hooker was most of a fruit jar behind in the drinking. Maddie got the giggles. Hooker snorted as he thought about this giggling woman stepping off a motorcycle on the Bonneville Salt Flats at well over a hundred miles per hour.

"And you were planning to tell me about Mae… when?"

Maddie made an attempt to act serious. "Don't get your boxers in a bunch, Hooper… I mean Hooter." With each attempt at his name, Willie got closer to wetting his dress, Candy a close second, and Maddie's speech got worse. Hooker thought about revising his estimate about the amount of alcohol floating around the giant garage.

Hooker warned with only a slightly straight face, "Don't anyone light a match."

Uncle Willie was the first to recover. "We were going to tell you, but it wasn't a done deal when we left for Texas. The Challenger with the eight-hundred horse motor cinched the deal."

"You sold the Challenger?"

The door to the house opened as Hooker's mouth hung open. Hank snorted as he crossed the garage. "You must have told him about the tinker toy."

Hooker turned and frowned. "*Tinker toy?*"

Maddie sighed. "The Challenger. We were only tinkering around with it. The drags are full of them out here on the coast, so they force them to bracket in the nines. At the horsepower we were throwing into the beast, she would have turned closer to six or seven seconds with ten percent alcohol." She lifted her fruit jar and took a sip and then held it up to look at the clear liquid. "And that's with regular stuff… just think what this would do."

As Hooker finished the last of the chocolate cake, he glanced at his watch. He looked over at Candy, who had a silly smile on her face with the rosy cheeks. "I need to go over to Father Damian's tomorrow around dinner to see if I can find Peter. Do you want to go?"

Her eyes rolled, and her smile spread wider. "Remind me in the morning what you asked me…"

Hooker knew he would have to carry her over his shoulder into the house.

Maddie patted his hand as she watched Candy start to snore. "Just put a blanket over her. And while you're at it, I'll take one too."

Hooker stood and went to retrieve four blankets.

THE MORNING FOUND the five bodies in various positions, covered and uncovered. Everyone had their clothes on except Hooker. Even Hank still had his bow tie on, but Hooker had only his swim trunks—the urge for a midnight swim in the hot summer night was too delicious to pass up.

Candy woke to find Maddie looking at Hooker. Maddie's smile was the woman's silent laugh. She looked over at Candy and jerked her head out the back door toward the swimming pool. Candy thought about how devilishly naughty it sounded. They silently rose and, padding on bare feet, headed for the large open maw of the back door.

Hank's voice froze them halfway out the door. "The kid up the hill has his Cub Scout den over, and they are all over the hill watching for birds with their binoculars."

Maddie glared conspiratorially at Candy. "Just showing Candy the area I think would make a great barbecue. Oh, and Hank," she turned, "could we have some breakfast soon? I know Hooker needs to do some work today, and I need to run up to Emeryville for some parts for the Matchless."

Hank chuckled. "Pancakes with all the fixings coming right up." He mumbled to himself, "It will soak up the hangovers." He reached out with his sock-covered foot and nudged Willie. He addressed the one open eye. "Breakfast in thirty… just in case you want to burn your dress. I laid out a nice neon-lime one earlier."

The dresses were not always about the cheap nature of buying them by the large garbage bag full at twenty-five cents a bag, but mostly, it was about the uglier, the better to tease Hooker's senses. All other kinds of teasing were either off-limits or had stopped working long before. Hank had been offended by the ugly nature of his boyfriend's taste until he warmed up to the nature of the family's inner workings. Once he understood the *take no prisoner* level of teasing—and the truth of Willie's sense of taste being much finer than the ugly dresses—he was a willing participant. Hank was a quiet, behind the scenes, and protective body of his partner—but a willing, and sometimes devious, participant.

Willie rolled back and forth as he loosened his stiff body. His eyes never left the backside of his partner. The smirk on the ex-spy, ex-POW, ex-Navy SEAL pulled jagged by the scars on his throat and neck, but no less appreciative of the devious nature Hank currently showed.

Willie's head ground around as his soft giggle only slightly shook his body. Maddie had seen the look many times.

She stretched her own scarred body as she mouthed, "What?" Candy still looked with longing at the pool—and up the hill. *Someday.*

Willie looked over at the still sleeping Hooker. "I was thinking about April first and Hank's biscuits stuffed with cotton balls... Hooker had been tired and heading for bed. He slathered butter and some jam through the side of one and shoved the whole into his mouth. The reaction came after he made it into his bedroom and wearing nothing but his angry face. He caught Hank, threw him over his shoulder, and didn't stop until they were both in the pool."

The laughter of Maddie and Willie woke Hooker, who looked at them with bloodshot eyes. He didn't participate in the worst of the drinking but was purely exhausted.

"What?"

The door from the house opening cut Maddie off. Candy stood in the opening. "Breakfast is almost ready."

Hooker closed his eyes against the pain and stood. The jolt of grimace did not escape the two older walking scar-bodies. They exchanged knowing looks and followed the younger stiff-walking zombie. Food is a motivator; good food is a powerful motivator. Breakfast cooked by Hank can raise the dead—the three filing through the door past Candy were living proof. Each received a kiss on the side of the head as they stumbled past.

HOOKER PUSHED the last piece of bacon into his mouth and washed it down with more coffee. The four were looking more alive.

Willie put his coffee mug down. "She knew her killer."

Candy thought a moment. "How can you be sure?"

Maddie leaned back. She had been around Willie the longest and had even done research for him back in the day. "Because there was no evidence of a struggle."

Willie smiled. "And you know this... how?"

"She was still dressed."

"But the dress was torn up."

Maddie leaned in and faced her mentor as the others enjoyed watching the two engage in mental tennis. "The dress wasn't the important part. The waist of her pantyhose was the only important part."

"Why?" Candy couldn't stand the drawn-out dialogue of discovery.

Willie and Maddie both turned on her. Willie was first, "If she had been in a fight, her pantyhose wouldn't be in place. How often do you pull your hose up?"

"Often..."

Maddie finished. "In a fight, her pantyhose would have come down, and her driver's license would have fallen out." She smiled. "It hadn't and was still on her hip in her pantyhose. She trusted her killer and didn't know she was being poisoned."

Hooker leaned in. "Do you think she would trust a john that much?"

Hank sat up and primped at his bow tie. "It would be highly unlikely."

"Why?"

"To acquire so much trust, the john would have to spend a great deal of time with her. By doing so, he would risk drawing a high degree of unwanted attention from the other streetwalkers. After all, girls do talk. So highly unlikely. I think you need to be looking elsewhere."

Hooker rubbed at the scars along his head. "But who else spends time with them—other than the other girls? Are we thinking one of the girls is taking out the competition?"

Hank sipped on his coffee. His eyes traveled over Hooker's face. He gently placed the coffee cup back on the only saucer on the table. "You tell me. Do you only spend time with other tow truck drivers?"

"Hardly any time at all..." His voice faded off. "But cops are a different story. There are always cops who have a beat, and they know everyone and everything they can about those people."

Willie grunted grumpily. "This isn't a cop."

Maddie turned on her oldest friend. "Why so quick to judge? Or in this case, to give a free pass?"

"Poison is not the act of a cop. They are more forthright, more direct with physical and brutal methods."

"Not all cops are brutal."

"No, but when they go off the reservation and turn to killing, they are. Their weapon of choice is what they know the most—guns and truncheon."

Hank pulled himself up. "Experience, William?"

Willie stared with a thousand-mile stare at the table. *He did not need to nod.*

Hooker broke the thick silence. "So not another working girl and not a cop. Who else would they know?"

Candy cleared her throat. "Waitress, waiter, or even the owner of a restaurant they frequent for food." She looked at Hooker. "You talked to a couple of the girls. Go ask them who they talk to and have become friends with."

"I don't think—"

The loud klaxon horn honked in the shop garage area just before the phone rang on the counter and in Hooker's bedroom. Hooker, Willie, and Candy all glanced at their watches.

Hank answered the phone and listened. "Thank you, Karen. I'll have him ready. Say hello to your wonderful mother. Good-bye." He turned to Hooker. "Your truck is about five minutes away… or less."

Hooker looked at his watch again.

Hank sunk back against the counter. "It's down here in Blood Alley—about fourteen cars and some trucks. Wear your dirty clothes, and I'll just burn them when you come back all bloody."

Hooker rose, kissed Candy on the top of the head, and turned for his bedroom. He looked at the jeans draped around his boots. He had yet to have a pair of jeans last more than three or four months. Usually, they got torn, but also, they disappeared at the hand of Hank doing the laundry. If they were only soiled, they got washed, but anything Hank didn't want in his sparkling clean machine got washed from the earth by Willie's cutting torch—the closest Hank got to tools.

Hooker's arm draped over Candy's shoulders as they walked out into the sunshine. The five-ton truck pulled up the last of the hill and nosed into the large concrete apron poured to accommodate the much larger Mae West. The apron made the large truck appear even smaller. Hooker frowned at the size and then smiled when he saw who was driving the truck.

The Squirt slid out the door and onto the apron. Candy gave her brother a hug. "Are they giving you some time off?"

"I turned in my last paper yesterday, and it will take them about a week to sort through the eighty pages, and sixty-seven bibliographies." He smirked. "Who knew doing all those research papers for Maddie would pay off in time off?"

"How did you get the truck?"

"I ran calls yesterday while you were traveling. Also, I was up at Dolly's doing paperwork this morning when the call came in." He hugged Candy one more time and kissed her on top of her head. "Gotta go."

As they climbed into the truck, the Squirt filled Hooker in on the accident. Hooker thought about the commercial tows that would have to go to someone else. He missed Mae.

16

THE WORK IS THE WORK

Working an accident is much like triage during a war, or a train wreck—sometimes small and manageable, and other times, spread over an area the size of a football field, or larger.

Being high up in a cab of a large truck can give a better advantage to see across a large area of carnage. With the shorter truck than his usual, Hooker chose to first drive up on a small hill.

He saw no other way to get to the back of the accident, so a short stop on the way to working the accident from both ends seemed like a great idea.

"Fudge… still not good enough." Hooker hit the steering wheel.

The Squirt snorted with a smile—he understood Hooker's frustration. "Don't blame the tool; blame the person who isn't using it right."

He slithered through the window and stood on top of the cab before Hooker figured out what he was doing.

As Hooker worked his way out of his window and onto the top of the truck, the Squirt had already started mapping the large accident. The report of only fourteen cars needed updating.

"We're going to have to take out some fence, but we need to get down at least where the white van is on its side. The best would be to use the field we used last year to stash a bunch of cars. It's only a half-mile down the road, but I remember it wasn't even half-full with seventeen cars. We can just do a pass-through and drop them as we feed through the line-up."

Hooker scanned the length of the whole wreck. "What about the other end?"

The Squirt laughed. "Do you see who the chip is?" *Micha.* "Knowing him, he'll make any of the rigs coming down the 101 grab a tow and leave. If they head up Blossom Hill and stash a car or three, they will be smarter than I think."

Hooker smiled at the kid but pointed at a distinctive auto club rig. "There's the stash king himself. How do you like Ace's new rig?" He pointed at a five-ton truck similar to the one they stood on.

The Squirt snorted with a laugh. "How big is his engine?"

Hooker laughed. "They thought they got a monster at just under four hundred horses." The Squirt and Hooker both knew they stood on closer to five-hundred and was still a wallowing pig.

The kid laughed again. "Let's go jerk some prom queens out of this barn dance."

As the cars were hauled away, and the highway slowly cleared, the day turned ugly. A rare summer squall blew in with enough wet to dampen everything. Within minutes, the clouds were squeezed dry and blew away. The sun seared the damp and turned it into mugginess as the temperature soared again.

Micha walked up to Hooker as the man crawled out from under a delivery van with its engine now pushed into the cargo hold. The paramedics had long removed what was left of the driver. Hooker had seen the man's injuries before. He knew the man would only be good for parts donation when they got him to Valley Medical.

"Hooker, what should we do with the prom queen?"

Hooker knew his friend was talking about the one vehicle Hooker would have gotten with Mae—the real money job in the whole mess.

Hooker and the Squirt looked at the payday twisted in the slow lane. The truck tractor was a conventional Peterbilt with high capacity dual driving axles. The set of double trailers suffered a few scratches in the melee, but it was basically good to roll with some new paint. The Squirt had peeked into the cab after they took the driver to the hospital from hitting the windshield. It hadn't knocked him out, but his vision was blurred. The tractor still had paper license plates in the back window, and less than ten thousand miles on the odometer—even the bent frame wouldn't total the tractor. It was at least a hundred hours of work for the Fly. Hooker's cut would have paid his basic bills for the month or more.

Hooker wiped his hands on the grease rag as he thought about the larger tow rigs on the scene earlier. "Did Tri-Counties take the Mack in front?"

"They were early and only got the short-bob, and it went up on Guadalupe. I think Miller got the Mack—and it's headed for South Bay Auto in Daily City."

"See if Karen can get Tri-Counties back here. I might be able to pull the back trailer with the tongue on the jeep, but if I can talk them into taking the whole enchilada to the Fly, then it would make my time here worthwhile." Hooker tried to look hangdog as he cocked his head, looking at his friend.

Micha shaded his eyes as he looked south toward the field where Hooker had been stashing cars for the last three hours. "And you have how many cars parked down near the rail spur?" Micha laughed as he glanced at his watch. "Dolly is there now. How about you powwow with your partner in crime while stashing this one—let her strong-arm Tri-Counties."

Hooker smiled. He knew Micha would casually tell the Tri-Counties driver the rig was headed for the Fly's repair yard. All Hooker had to do was pre-arrange the slots in the backyard.

As Hooker and the Squirt headed for the truck cab, the Squirt turned and looked back at the retreating Highway Patrol Officer. "Hey, Micha... what was the count?"

The man turned. His face was sober in the hot sun. "Four and twenty-three… so far…" *Four dead and twenty-three critical enough to be taken to the hospital. The final death toll may be another twenty-four hours away.*

The kid mused, "It would be nice if the state could find some money to put up at least a dividing barrier."

Micha nodded as he turned. "Seat belt law would have helped too… especially with the little kid."

The accident started with a couple of beers in the middle of the day. Those beers and the heat led to the man falling asleep and crossing the two yellow paint lines separating his car from the oncoming lane full of cars and big rigs.

The southbound lane was only a single lane, but the northbound was split into two lanes a half-mile before. It was natural for drivers to speed up in anticipation of entering the new freeway. The combined force was over one hundred miles per hour coming to a dead stop. The car had caromed off the short-bob truck and angled into the Mack, flipping the tractor and its long trailer full of pipes.

The pipes had split their constraints and boomeranged into the oncoming traffic. The total carnage covered a quarter-mile and spread across all three lanes. Nine tow trucks had worked the scene, along with five fire vehicles and twelve ambulances. Hooker knew the photos of the wreck would be above the fold on tomorrow's front page of the Mercury News. Hooker stopped saving clippings of the wrecks he worked long ago. Someone would be screaming for the state to do something about Blood Alley by noon the next day.

He slipped the truck into gear and watched his mirrors as he began towing the small truck down to the field. The highway was empty. Hooker knew the CHP had the entire highway blocked off to allow access for emergency vehicles. He glanced at his watch and knew the highway would be closed for at least two more hours while the last was towed away. Only then would the forensic guys wrap up the entire scene.

The four-man crew would carefully walk the length of the accident, spread across only one lane at a time. There would be three very slow trips. But first, all the vehicles had to be removed.

Hooker grabbed the microphone and called Dolly. The day had only started, and it wouldn't be over until every car and truck was towed to where they were going. Hooker knew their day wouldn't be over until well after midnight.

He glanced at the Squirt. Hooker knew if he were hungry, the Squirt was too. On the seat between the men, Box was snoozing, but Hooker knew he would like some food as well.

"1-4-1."

Dolly sounded agitated and in rare form. "Go 1-4-1… and I better get the count."

Hooker passed the microphone to the Squirt as he pulled into the field. He drew the short truck up to the end of the row of eleven cars and three trucks.

"Four and twenty-three, Dolly… but we think the four might be only wishful thinking."

Hooker slid out of the cab. "Ask her if she can order some lunch to go at Chick-n-Ribs. We'll be there in about an hour."

The Squirt waved his hand and returned to the microphone.

When Hooker climbed back into the cab, the kid had a thousand-mile stare as he looked north toward San Jose. "What?"

"She's holding a long tow for tonight or tomorrow."

"Where?"

"Lake Tahoe… and they found another girl… stuffed behind a trash bin…"

"How many days do you have off?"

"A few… but I'll only take the tow to Tahoe with you if I also get to work the case."

"The boys in blue downtown won't like it."

"Their boss won't like it worse when we break the case, and I tell him I'm taking the job with the DOJ in Sacramento." He ground his head around as he leaned back. His face rolled into the family zombie pose.

"Did you get an offer in Sac?"

The kid held up three fingers… and smiled.

Hooker had missed the kid.

As Hooker pulled back onto the highway for the last tow, he smirked and shot the kid a glance. "Sometimes, it pays to get your hand in the way of a fork."

The Squirt held up his hand and examined the four tiny scars on the back of his left hand. "Yeah, well… it was a two-bit stunt."

They both laughed as they pulled up alongside the set of double trailers.

17

WHO?

Dolly looked up from her paperwork. She heard the armor-plate front door swinging open. She glanced over at the small black and white television attached to the cameras looking out to the parking lot and at the front door. It took her a moment to remember who was driving the new five-ton truck, but the second camera revealed two leather jackets and a large cat.

Box slid through the legs and stalked into the large room. His target was sitting where expected. With little effort, he landed in the middle of the big desk and walked onto the top of Dolly's large chest. He snuggled the side of her head as she chuckled, and then he poured himself onto her lumps and into her hands. The French vanilla ice cream had been tasty, but this was worth purring about.

Dolly put her face down into the large cat's side and muttered dove coos and other messages of love. He was the only animal who got her unmonitored affection... everyone else got grief with an occasional hug.

Dolly's head leaned back as she addressed the two men. "You're late."

The two men looked at each other and smiled. In unison, they both rumbled, "We had a stop to make..."

The ice cream voices were stereo and caused the two women at the switchboard to go into instant fits of laughter. Dolly's head snapped up, only an inch from the fur, as she gave them both a hard look. Both men were constantly warned about stopping for French vanilla ice cream and then calling the switchboard. All the girls squirmed and giggled at what Dolly called the bedroom voice. Everyone knew it only made Hooker stop for ice cream more often.

"Go drink some warm water… both of you." Dolly's growl made the women laugh even harder. Everyone knew it was bluster. The girls also knew when the guys called in with ice cream voices, Dolly's work suffered for a brief while after. Dolly's right eye followed the two men returning from the kitchen. The two had scamp written all over their faces, but she was sure they had minded and washed the cream from their throats.

"How was Tahoe?"

Hooker sat next to the desk as the Squirt went over to look in the playpen at Dina's sleeping baby. Dina had made noises about staying off work longer, but Dolly had put her foot down to get back to work and bring the little one. Dolly had already bought the playpen. The kid had inherited a nickname of Dee—short for dispatch. The little bundle had become the company mascot.

Hooker stretched. "Tahoe was an easy in and out. Their new impound yard has some solid features the Fly could implement…"

"I hear a *but* in there."

"That truck is a piece of—"

"Hooker…"

"Piece of a tin dog toy."

"And it is Don's new toy, not yours."

"He'll never drive it more than a hundred miles… maybe." Hooker stuck his thumb in his mouth and pushed on his upper teeth. "Crossing Vacaville to Sacramento, it liked to shake my upper teeth loose."

Dolly rolled her eyes at his exaggeration. She looked over at the younger hoodlum. "You got a complaint too, Squirt?"

The kid looked up. "No, ma'am… but I do think my liver is where my spleen is supposed to be, and my kidneys played square-dance with a foxtrot…"

"You two whiners need to go get some sleep. Don't get up before three this afternoon, and be clean when you come to dinner."

Hooker nodded. It had been a long twenty-two hours. It wasn't until he got to the front door he remembered it was daylight and he was going home. "Box… Go time."

The sleeping cat roused and slid out of the already closing door.

Dolly turned to Dina. "Grab the kid and go home."

The young woman started to protest about not being off for another hour. Karen gave her a stern look. Dina unplugged her headset and, with a *yes ma'am*, was gone.

Karen gave it a few minutes before she turned to face her mother.

Dolly eased herself forward in the chair. "I want her to take the night off. Get Toni in here instead. Also, find Fester and get him here for dinner. Tell his commander he will be held a little late after dinner."

"Anything else?"

"Have Mike pick me up an extra twenty pounds of sausage at Chiaramontes. Call your aunt after one this afternoon and tell her I have the sausage, we need to have a Sunday barbecue. I think the Sweets would be nice to have out also."

Karen knew, even in her sister's home, Dolly had no qualms about arranging people who needed to meet or see one another. The politics of running the county from behind the scenes never stopped.

"Anybody else you want there?"

Dolly thought as she rose from the chair. "Chet… and the nice girlfriend he's seeing. It has been way too long since we've seen him… or them."

Karen thought about the mix for the night's dinner and the Sunday dinner. There were always two sides of the same investigation when it came to the police—and Hooker. "What about Willie, Hank, and Maddie?"

Dolly chuckled, her daughter was learning well. "You mean they don't automatically come with Hooker?"

"Goodnight, Mama." Karen swung her chair around as she gave Dolly one last smirking look. They both looked at the movement on the monitor. The yellow Super Bee had just pulled in. *June.*

As the new gal on the day shift, June pulled the first in slot. By seven-thirty, there would be five snake-wranglers for the patch lines on the answering service's busy switchboards.

Dolly's day finished as Karen's just got warmed up. Their long hours overlapped at both ends. Dolly would be back around three in the afternoon to start dinner, and Karen would usually run the floor and board until the dinner finished.

Without Dina, Karen knew her day would end sometime around nine or ten at night, but Dina would work long the next day while Karen had a day off.

Karen watched the monitor as her mother got into her Cadillac. She knew the last time the woman had taken a day off was when the doctors sent an ambulance to pick her up. Dina had called Valley Med and asked what to do—Dolly was at her desk, panting for breath.

Two days later, the doctor told Dolly she'd had congestive heart failure. Dolly waited for the doctor to leave and then called for a tow truck. She was back running the city after taking a thirty-four-hour vacation.

Karen waited for June to plug into the board then she toggled the shop radio. "1-4-1?"

"1-4-1."

"Your boss said to remind you not to get up before three this afternoon. You are also to be clean and presentable tonight. Where are you and the Squirt going to be?"

"The Hacienda—Hank was up to the city yesterday and didn't do wash. We need fresh shirts."

Karen smirked as she looked up at a schedule Hooker didn't know she had. Candy got off work shortly after midnight.

"Right... Hank... 10-4, 1-4-1."

She wrote a note on her 'hot-board' to call her aunt around one—to tell her about Sunday and Hooker sleeping until at least three.

Well, at least not come out of his room.

She pulled a cord up and plugged it into one of the holes. "Good morning, San Jose Plumbing..."

Fourteen hours later, Karen was still plugging holes on the board, and the dining room was aglow with her mother and the select participants at the table. She gathered the small stack of notepapers and blew a police whistle. She checked the roster again real fast to make sure she had remembered correctly about it being an all-men night. Without turning, she called out the messages to the men seated at the table.

"Ace, you have a commercial holding. See me. I have all the information about the tow—it is going up-country to Santa Rosa. Make sure you get your fuel at the yard.

"Mike, your wife says don't forget to bring the jerky. I think this is code for don't forget your puppy is at your brother's house, and he is holding some homemade jerky for you.

"Fester, the lieutenant said to stay for the meeting, but come see him at home after. You are rover until midnight and then will be working the 17 from the Cats up.

"Don, it was good to see you again. Hooker doesn't let you out enough. Now go home and pack. Your flight is early in the morning. Aloha.

"Steve, you have a T-wonderful. It's now twelve minutes old. You are two minutes out and looking.

"Paul, call your shop. They want you to swap trucks for the night.

"The rest of you men can have more coffee, but you might want to use the office.

"Those leaving—the yard is clear. Don't forget to hug Dolly at the door. Keep it safe."

Hooker pushed back his chair and stood. "Gentlemen..." He shook hands as the men left or moved into the office. The Squirt finished the line.

"Seems like old times..."

"Squirt, you haven't missed many dinners... but your presence has been missed." Hooker tossed his head toward the office. "Let's go fill you in."

As they entered the office, the three other men were just getting comfortable. Hooker took the lounge chair near the desk and pointed at the large desk chair. The Squirt started to object, but Hooker gave him a hard look.

"Que jefe?" The kid took the hint and sat in what would usually be the seat of power.

Hooker gave the Squirt a bland look of mild expectation as he sipped on his coffee. He was amused to see the small signs of the kid uncomfortable at being thrown into the lead position. Hooker also watched the casual adjustment with interest.

The Squirt spread his hands out on the desktop as if feeling the power of the desk and its place in the city and county, as well as its place in Dolly's purview. He looked at the stately gentleman he knew.

"Your Honor, it's good to have you down from the big city to see us again… but I have a feeling this isn't just social. Would you care to introduce your friend…?"

The Superior Court Judge nodded with a smile. "If it would please the desk, we can do without formal titles tonight." He stretched his hands up and out. "After all, we are among friends here, are we not?"

The Squirt nodded with a chuckle. "And we are gathered as brothers in the innermost sanctum sanctorum…"

"Exactly to my way of thinking, Squirt." He smiled and turned to the slight man with the pencil-line mustache, which reminded Hooker and the Squirt of Hank. "This is the man with the most titles, but it's just easiest to say Francis is the foremost authority on the marshes of the San Francisco Bay. Francis, this young man is named John but is ironically known as Squirt. Squirt… Francis d'Bois de la Champagne, of the San Francisco Bay aquarium."

The man had only a slight French accent, but his air and how he sat was very continental. "When I came here to San Francisco, I lived in the dormitory reserved for marine biology students. Because of my fear of being underwater—in a culture that is almost exclusively diving, I was nicknamed Bubbles because of my last name—Champagne. But also, a tease for the one thing I would never do—make bubbles. But you can call me Frank or Frenchie, I respond to those as well as Puddles." He hung his head. "I have a strong love for tide pools."

The Squirt snorted with a laugh. The man fit right in with the usual motif of humor among the extended family of Hooker. "I think we can be comfortable with Francis."

The judge turned with a laugh and poked his fist at the other man's shoulder. "See, Crabby, I told you they were great guys." The man groaned with mock suffering while the judge laughed. Obviously, they were old friends.

The Squirt raised his eyebrows. "And your other friend, Hack?" Feeling comfortable, he used the judge's preferred nickname.

Hooker leaned forward. "Um, Fester is family here, Squirt. He's Dina's uncle." He waved his finger back and forth between the judge and the officer. "But you two know each other?"

"Only recently... I met Francis out in the marsh because I was the officer of record on the wreck and the resulting homicide investigation. The judge… I only met yesterday up at the aquarium."

Francis re-crossed his legs as he leaned toward Fester. "The duties of a crime scene investigator in the wetlands include taking water and mud samples. Those samples were sent to us at the aquarium for analysis. The extremely high content of cyanide was, to say the least, very alarming. I arranged to take my own samples with the help of an experienced diver. Sadly, we found the fresh samples as alarming as the original ones. Subsequently, we have spent the last two weeks taking counts and samples of the fauna as well as the seagrasses and other flora." Fester rubbed his bald head. As it turns out, the studies have been fortunate in explaining some of the abnormalities in all the skeletons. We scratched our heads about some of the decomp and raw rotting, as opposed to the chew marks we expected from the local crabs and bugs—but only found them in the older bones.

"*Oui*, it appears the poison was in high levels, and because of the stagnant nature of the wetlands, the cyanide concentrated in pockets and either killed off much of the aggressive bio population. A few of the more sensitive yet hearty beetles were driven away. Eventually, if this keeps happening, there will be no more fauna, and from lack of stimulation and diversification, the flora will also die off."

"Are there any measures of mitigation we can take?" Hooker's head snapped around to look at the kid almost as fast as the smirk of pride washed over his face.

The kid ignored his friend and raised his eyebrows toward the scientist.

"*Oui*, stop this killer from putting bodies in the bay. But I know this is already on everybody's mind—we are just here to add an urgent reason to catching this person, *n'est-ce pas?*"

Hooker's head ground back around. "Persons—as in plural."

The judge gasped. "Two? Do we know who they are?"

Hooker and the Squirt started at the same time. "Sort of..." They stopped and snorted. *Great minds...* Hooker nodded for the Squirt to continue.

"We have a lead on the person who's dumping the bodies. Our sources suggest a man referred to as The Waterman. He has been seen in a canoe he poles standing up. Given the area, it makes a lot of sense. All we know is the area he operates in, and a description of a short blond ponytail, and muscular—or at least has a barrel chest, which could just be an abnormality stemming from chronic childhood asthma in a high altitude or several other medical conditions.

"The poisoner is still a mystery. We are canvassing the downtown area as well as putting the word out for the street workers to be very careful and work or hang out in teams. They are our best bet to watch over one another, and they know it."

"What is being done about finding this Waterman?"

Hooker cleared his throat. "Um… I have a lead… my sister gave me a… she told me there is a vagrant—goes by Tess. She dives the dumpsters behind seafood restaurants on the east side. My sister said this Tess might know more about the guy…"

The judge asked quietly, "Your sister?"

The Squirt came to the rescue. "She has many… um… unorthodox connections and sources for information in the entire Bay Area. She has proved to be reliable and instrumental in solving several investigations. It was her information that led to the wrapping up of the cold case last Christmas as well as critical aid with the mutilator and the shotgun killer cases."

He held the judge's stare until the older man nodded. "Then, let's see where your sister's information leads us."

18

TESS

ooker sat on the toilet—still half asleep. His right hand curled with the two first knuckles mindlessly rubbing the solo fuzzy ear. The deep purr rumbled in the tiled bathroom. Images of the coming day tumbled loosely in Hooker's mind.

The east side of the lower bay was a hodgepodge of industrial areas. In the early years of industry in the south bay, the manufacturing relied on flat-bottomed boats and barges. The alternative to getting your goods to San Francisco entailed a long trip down and around the bay by wagon. The other involved freighting the goods on the train up to Oakland and then ferry across to the docks in the Barbary Coast. Many of the original entrepreneurial boatmen had worked in their youth on riverboats on the Mississippi or the Ohio. A wind-powered skiff or barge can haul a lot of cargo and not worry about snagging on seagrass.

Later, as steam changed boating, the channels became formalized, and centers popped up along those shipping avenues. Tiny clusters named after the original dock owner—now became towns and cities. Between larger known towns or cities, like Milpitas, Fremont, and San Lorenzo, there were tiny enclaves named for more colorful reasons. Union City had been one of the first to ban the Bars and Stars of the rebels who had broken away from the United States. There had been no other group or town who thought to align with the new federation—most were more concerned with getting the last money of the gold rush and looking forward to what was next for the state.

Another enclave named Newark—for a castle in Scotland. Originally, a broad flatland enjoyed by the Ohlone Indians. Then came Mission San Jose, and the Indians were put to work on the same land, now claimed by the padres. The land wasn't the most fertile, but the fish, crabs, and shrimp were put to good use—mostly feeding the padres' pigs.

An enterprising young man named Mowry dug out a shallow area and diked off the water. Once flooded, he would stop any new water for a few days of hot sun and then refill the shallow basins. Eventually, the basins would dry, and he would have his workers harvest the raw salt. This salt would then be loaded into bags, ferried out along Mowry's slough, and then across to the waiting ships. The salt was sold around the world.

Hooker stood in the cool fall of shower water as he thought about Mowry's slough, and the small crab shacks dotting the shoreline. The crab was better in Monterey, but it would be a good place to start looking for a man in a dress named Tess.

"Good morning, sunshine." Stella looked at the foggy eyes as she poured Hooker a large mug of coffee. She wanted to laugh, but at a quarter till noon, she knew he was not in his usual routine. "Manny and the Squirt are going over some maps and details in the office. Do you want me to start making you something to eat?"

Hooker leaned his hip against the counter with his eyes closed. Stella wasn't sure if he had fallen asleep or just thinking. "Um… when did you plan to eat next?"

"We can have lunch in about an hour. Manny will need food then." She was timing his blood sugar levels in her head.

Hooker took the mug and gently sipped. Stella watched his shoulders relax. He turned toward the office and then turned back and kissed her on the cheek. "Thanks. I can wait, and we can all eat together."

She watched the bare feet padding across the slate floor as the zombie in a white T-shirt and jeans walked with his nose in the coffee vapors. He paused for a larger sip before entering the office.

Absentmindedly, Stella dialed the number she called at least once a day.

Karen's voice reminded her Dolly wasn't up yet. It didn't matter. Her niece would do just fine. This was just silly girl stuff anyway. "When did he become such a man?"

Karen chortled. "Hooker? You obviously haven't been paying much attention these last... what, ten years?" She sighed. "Auntie Stell, I think he was a man before he got his real truck. We just weren't paying attention."

"The one-ton Don gave him... or Mae?"

"Take your pick. I think Don knew he was underage back then. But he wouldn't have given the new Ford to someone who wouldn't respect the opportunity. I think Don always saw the man in Hooker. It just took the rest of us time to catch up."

Stella ran the cold water and stuck her left hand in the stream. "Well, I'm sure glad my daughter Candy saw the man in him. Sometimes a jacket can hide a lot of adult."

Karen snorted. "He tries to... but there is nothing he can get away with around here. Sweetie, the boards are on fire this morning. I gotta go help out. Love you."

"Love you too—" Stella pulled the buzzing dial tone away from her ear. "—sweetheart." She hung up the phone and leaned against the counter, sipping her coffee. Her sense of need had only been partially placated. She hated when the ogres of her childhood would sneak back into her heart when she was supposed to stand strong for her family.

She thought about lunch and gently poured the last of the coffee from her cup into the pot of the coleus plant hanging near the window. Even the tiny plant she bought only six months before—now the size of a beach ball—proved coffee was good for you.

Manny was calmly reading with the headphones on. Hooker glanced over at the large reels on the tape recorder. The sixteen-inch reels moved slow enough for Hooker to read the word Bach on the label. He knew Manny was truly relaxing and working hard at not being interested in the Squirt methodically going over a couple of detailed auto club maps.

"Did Manny breakout water charts for the bay, as well?"

The Squirt put his finger on where he had last studied. He looked up and smiled.

"No need. I memorized those when we rolled the train with the caustic soda. At the time, I also needed the tide flowcharts to know where the currents would eventually take the soda—and what it would end up killing."

"What a waste of time… "

"No… I knew we could roll the cars over and not leak a drop—we had done it too many times to screw up. No, I needed the information to solidify my credentials."

Hooker chuckled. "And jack the poor railroad guys up for an unwarranted payday."

The Squirt rolled his eyes as he returned to the map. "Yeah, I noticed how polished and shiny Mae looks out front. Even if she also looks like you shrunk her in the spin cycle."

Manny slipped his headphones down and turned his chair around. "Where do you plan to start?"

Hooker pointed at his chest. "Excuse me? Are you talking to the one person who hasn't got the slightest clue as to where we're going?" He pointed at the Squirt. "Why don't you ask the driver?"

The Squirt's head snapped up, and his look volleyed back and forth between the other two. "Since when do I get to drive?"

"The question is more like do you know how? I mean, you did drive the five-ton over and pick me up… but then, you could have just gotten lucky."

"I've been practicing on the skidpad at the academy if it counts for anything?" He looked at Manny for support.

Manny shrugged and mewed his lips. "I guess if the street just happens to be all hosed down with soapsuds and it's raining." He smiled at Hooker.

Hooker gave the kid a cold look. "So where are we going? Or have you worked it out yet?"

"Mostly." He grabbed one of the more detailed water depth maps and folded under the bay water section—leaving the shoreline and land. He took the auto club map and laid it out the same way. With the auto club map on top, he started pointing at the channels.

"I've been looking for areas containing small food joints which might overlook public put-in ramps or docks. In the water, I've also been looking at where the channels lead from the body dump to the east side of the bay. Now the distance by small boat being paddled or poled is quite a ways, but if the guy is on the water all the time—the distance won't matter." He washed his hand along the shoreline. "I think our best chance of finding Tess is in this twelve miles. It sounds like a lot, but I'm guessing there are only seven or eight crab shacks at the most." He sat back.

Hooker looked at the area. He hadn't wanted to start down in Fremont and work north, looking for a crab shack, sandwich hut, or food joint along the shore. He could just feel how tedious the hunt could be.

The Squirt's plan would cut to the heart of the southeast shoreline and trim the work in half or less. He looked up at the Squirt and smiled. He then looked at Manny and started to laugh.

Hooker could hear the insecurity in the kid's protest. "What...?"

Hooker put his hand up. "No, really, kid. You did great. You already cut at least half of the search area out. And in this? That's huge." He turned toward Manny. "What is your favorite most powerful weapon or tool?"

Manny started to laugh as he picked up the phone to show. "But I don't have the phone book for those areas."

Hooker held his hand out for the instrument. "No, but dispatch does. And more than that, they have phone numbers and radios straight to the guys who tow those areas and would know all of those shacks."

Stella called from the other room. "Boys, your powwow is over. Wash your hands. Lunch is ready."

Hooker nodded his head sideways. "Go ahead. I'll be quick..." He started dialing

19

FROM OUT OF THE GRASS

Lane poled slowly. The late grass grew high enough above the waterline to hide all but his head. As his canoe slid silently over the water, he scanned the grass and beyond. He rarely looked at the open water of the rivers through the grass. In the black water, he only ever saw the night sky. It disturbed him to think of the other part.

The sunshine burned on his back. The three layers of cotton shirt and undershirts, although hotter, were necessary. He picked at the binding layers with his off-poling hand as he switched the pole to the other side. The few crabs in the bottom of the canoe crawled slowly in the heat and made a scratching noise on the aluminum. Lane knew the water kept the floor of the canoe cool because his bare feet rested there. He liked to think he could feel the water flowing under the metal even though he knew it was just in his imagination. His eyes burned darkly under the long-billed hat as he watched the distant shoreline.

Lane did not need to be close to know what the bearded woman in the filthy baggy dress was telling the two men. Her fat arms waved back and forth as she pointed at the sea of grass. She pointed north where the river of freshwater came from, where the crayfish were sweeter, where Lane usually hid his canoe. Her arm moved south to where the river wound into the grass, and with three chops of her hand and arm, she told them about the three passages Lane used the most to get out to the island.

Lane watched as the woman's hand fanned out as she described the spread of the smaller streams of sweet water wandering out toward the trestle. His eyes rolled up into his head as he silently hacked up some bile and spat into the water near the grass. He slowly sank down onto the seat in the middle of the canoe. His hand slowly slid down on the pole shoved into the mud. He leaned into the pole and his hand. *That nosey fucking woman...*

Lane's breathing was raspy. He was becoming agitated. Even as a child, his mother would see him this way and take his hand, guiding him into the house and onto her bed, where she would rub his chest until he calmed down. The rubbing had been reassuring and calming as a small child, but as an older child, it became another form to cause agitation. The rubbing became more than just to calm the chest.

With a bible in one hand, scripture spewing rapid-fire from her mouth between the panting breaths that turned to moans—Lane was introduced to tantric hellfire and brimstone salvation and sex. As the body matured, and the chest grew large, the ritual took on even more grotesque machinations. None of which had anything to do with calming or religious salvation—but everything to do with sexual deviancy.

Lane's eyes rolled, and his breathing turned to panting. His pupils looked out from the edge of his upper eyelids as his head lowered. The hand on the pole pulled down as the body slowly rose. The eyes, hidden in the dark shadow of the long bill of the waterman's hat, focused across the tips of the grass. The loose hand slowly rubbed and stroked the large breasts under the binding as the one side of the mouth twitched and jerked gradually into a sardonic smirk.

Pete's voice growled deep in the throat, "Tonight, bitch... tonight."

Slowly, Lane took back his body and face. His breathing was calmer. Everything would be taken care of... tonight. Under the night sky, the same sky he saw when he looked into the water. The sky of his other half...

Unhurriedly, he crouched slightly, his head just below the level of the grass. His hands gripped the pole and worked it—silently walking the tip in the mud.

The canoe turned and drifted back through the rivers of the grasses. The sun overhead danced in the wavering heated air. The summer sun drove the crabs and shrimp to find safety in among the grasses... in among the dead... in among... the two's mother. Lane pushed on the end of the pole. Tonight would come. *Their mother would be fed.*

THE SQUIRT PUT his hand up to shade his eyes as he looked west across the grass. Slowly, his eyes panned across an area Tess had pointed out.

"What do you see, Squirt?"

He shook his head as his hand dropped. He turned and looked at Hooker and Tess. "Probably a bird or something."

Tess harrumphed. "The grass will do funny things to you. You think there is something there... and then you really look... and it's nothing." He looked at Hooker. "Or it's the waterman..."

"So you think he's in the area?"

Hooker raised an eyebrow.

"If the sun is up—he's on the water. It's always just a matter of where. Like I was saying, he moves around a large area. I mean... not large like the whole bay, but for a man in a canoe... the grass lakes are large." Tess hitched at the shoulder of his muumuu. Hooker heard the metallic sound again like muffled tin.

"You used the term before—lakes of grass. What do you mean by it?"

Tess pointed out across the bay with his hand spread out flat. "When you look out there, you see grass. When you think of the bay from here to, say, the place where the white airplanes fly—"

The Squirt cut in. "The Navy base... those are submarine chasers—P-3 Orion." He could see on the man's face that none of the information was making sense to him. He shook his open palm back and forth. "Never mind. Continue."

Tess grabbed his chest with both palms and moved his breasts or whatever was under the large dress, side to side. He closed his eyes, and as he opened them, he was looking back at Hooker. "When you think of the bay, you think of it as one large body of water. But what you don't know, unless you have been out there, is there are large areas which have water, but there are also areas of land."

"Like the island the trestle runs across."

"Yes. And on the island, there's a lake, as there are other lakes. There are paths of land between those lakes, and the only breaks are the rivers of freshwater running through everything. But the areas between the levies, pathways, roads, or just dirt, make those lakes. But when I say lake, you think of a large area of open water. But what I'm talking about is a body of water consisting of mud below, grass above, and the water between the two."

Hooker pointed at the clear water in front of them for all of twenty feet and then the field of grass. "So you are saying this area in front of us is one lake, and the one way down there is another lake…"

Tess smirked. "Almost. Way down there is just a salt marsh—not much water." He turned, pointing further north of them. "That… is another lake —of grass."

The Squirt was having a hard time with the concepts. "But why say grass instead of a lake of water with grass in it?"

"Because… the grass is everything here.

"I've been up North Bay. I've seen what they have there. Until you start up the river… there is no grass. Sure, there is some little grass growing along the shore. But no lakes of grass—not like here."

Hooker was starting to understand the weight or meaning of the grass. "So, without the grass…?"

Tess's head began to bob, and his long stringy beard crinkled and folded below his chin. "… ever'thin' be dead." He pointed out across to where he knew the ghost town was. "Dead like that there Drawbridge town." He shook with a muted sound of metal. "Dead like them women you said they pulled out from under the old trestle."

Hooker glanced at his watch. "Tess," he stuck his hand out, "we would like to thank you for taking the time to talk to us. Is there anything we can do for you… buy you some seafood from the shack or anything?"

"Don't like no fresh food. Better to get it out of the barrels—too hot otherwise. But if you have any empty cans…" He smiled and patted his hips. The muted sound of tin cans rattled under his hands. No clarification.

Hooker softly shook his head. "If we had any, they would be yours. If we come back, I'll remember to bring some... any particular size you want?"

"Naw... any size will do."

"I'll remember that."

2 0

NIGHT ATTACK

The crescent moon left only an eerie ghosting glow around objects. The collective trash heap of shipping pallets, packing crates, and tin cans were squeezed into what had once been a loading dock before a fire removed the old wooden warehouse. Layers of smashed tin cans littered the top of the heap—showing leaden in the soft light.

A dark figure moved from deep shadow to deep shadow. It crept along the alley, which once had been lined with busy trucks of commerce. The crumbling ruins were now a reflection of the broken dreams of better times.

The large breasts swung loosely in the shirt as Pete crept to the piled trash where Tess lived. Pete squatted to see in the low hooch.

The lumps of darker shapes in the gloom of the structure were the focus of her intent. Her hands absentmindedly snapped open the commando knife. Gripping the knife with both hands, she began stabbing the shape in a rage.

"Hey." The voice bounced muffled off the alley structures.

Pete jumped erect—frightened. She flipped the knife, face forward in her hand. The heap she dismissed before as trash rose. *Tess*. Pete charged and stabbed at the woman's chest. The knife met with hard resistance.

Pete became enraged and stabbed over and over—all ending with the tip of the knife hitting a hard surface or being deflected.

Tess began hitting at the attacker's head. It wasn't the first time Tess had been attacked. But once he started making his tin-can armor, the attacks had become less successful. His fists were telling as he hit the head and shoulders.

Finally, realizing the stabbing wasn't successful, Pete focused on the head and arms. But even those became difficult as the intended victim seemed adept at defending those areas not protected by the dress of armor plate.

The battle raged, crashing among the trash. The two stumbled in amateurish combat for their lives. Tess grabbed and threw trash as ammunition, most of which just bounced off the attacker. Occasionally, some trash was heavy enough to take a toll. The blood flung about as the knife slowly took its toll on the exposed flesh.

Pete dodged a large wet object and made one last slash at Tess's neck, connecting. The blade bit deep at the side of the neck and slid forward. Grabbing at her neck, Tess stumbled backward and fell, screaming into a pile of trash. Pete fled.

Gasping for breath, Tess rolled over and began to crawl. The trail of blood smeared blackly in the dim light. Tess's vision blurred, but a glow of light blossomed into a peony of yellow, and then contracted to a dim forty-watt bug light a few blocks away.

Tess knew nobody would be in the small machine shop at this hour, but she clung to the hope—*someone would at least find her body.*

FORTY MILES, and hours later, the phone rang in the sunroom. The walls were still yellow with the dawn light. The phone rang a second time as the phone in the office echoed the ring.

The third ring was cut short. "Hello?" Hooker stood naked in the office.

"Hooker?"

"Yes...?"

The female chuckled as Dolly joined the conversation. "Where are you?"

"Hacienda..."

Dolly cleared her throat. "Where are you standing?"

"In the office..." Hooker's mind was catching up to his standing and talking on the phone. "I'll be right back." He put the phone down and stalked out of the office. He resisted the urge to look down the other short hallway to see if Stella was standing in her and Manny's bedroom doorway. This would be one of those things they would never talk about.

A slender milk-white arm and hand poked out of his bedroom door—holding his pair of jeans. As he took them, he heard the door down the other hall snick quietly closed. Candy's muffled giggle was cut short by the door closing. The thick doors in the Hacienda were almost soundproof. The sound of Candy laughing hysterically was only in Hooker's mind. *Or not.*

"What?"

There was a silent dead pause Hooker recognized as Dolly's finger holding down the mute button on her desk phone. The usual static of empty air in the Dispatch office returned. "Do you have... are you wearing—"

Hooker saved both of them by cutting her off with a growl. "It is six-twenty-seven in the morning, Dolly. I don't work today, and you have woken your sister. This had better be good."

Hooker was sure he had just heard Dolly open and close her mouth at least three times in the ensuing minute of silence. He didn't care. Only now did he have any scrap of decency with his jeans on. He did not turn at the sound behind him. He heard his boots settle on the floor and something soft being placed over the back of the chair beside the doorway.

"Were..." She still had to take a moment. "Were you out near Fremont yesterday?"

"We tracked down a man named Tess..." Hooker rubbed at the large scars along his right side, where the dimes had entered and been removed the year before. The nerves were always knitting.

"She was admitted to Fremont Memorial this morning. When they found her, they thought she was dead."

"She is a he…"

"He is a she… despite the beard."

Hooker's mind skidded on strange ice. He turned slowly at another sound. The Squirt was fully dressed and leaning against the doorway.

The Squirt raised one eyebrow as he continued. "Tess is female…"

Hooker covered the phone and looked hard at the young man. "How do you know?"

The kid, now the teacher, ran his finger down his throat. "She doesn't have an Adam's apple… therefore, a female."

Hooker grumped as he turned. "It doesn't matter." He held the phone to his ear. "We're on our way."

"Take your time… she's in surgery. But the sheriff's deputy is there and wants to talk to you. Just make sure you get something to eat—it might be a long day."

Hooker thought about the time as he hung up. "I need coffee…"

The Squirt harrumphed. "Too early. The new coffeemaker doesn't go on until eight."

Hooker leveled half an eye at the young man. "We'll get some on the way." Hooker grabbed his boots and the T-shirt as he slid past the Squirt. He opened the door to his bedroom to find Candy pulling on her espadrilles.

She looked up and paused. "Are you off or not?"

"Off… but the Squirt and I are going to the hospital in Fremont."

She stood and growled. "Oh, no, you aren't. Not without me. I'm not letting you anywhere near a hospital unsupervised. Knowing you two— you would check yourselves in."

"What are you doing about breakfast?" Hooker turned to find Stella in her bathrobe and bare feet.

"Nothing which concerns you… go back to bed. You two get the house to yourselves today." He smirked and winked. Leaning back into their surrogate mother, he kissed her on the cheek. "If I have to stay on days much longer… I'm pulling another phone line direct into here… or moving downstairs."

Stella grabbed him with both arms around his neck as she laughed.

"Don't even joke about keeping my daughter locked up down there and away from me…"

Candy kissed her on the other cheek. "I'll pay for the phone line. It can ring both places for all I care. I'm going to be wherever stinky is, anyway." She laughed and danced away toward the pantry as Hooker's hand grabbed for her jeans.

The three disappeared down the secret stairs to the garage. As the door swung back closed, Stella laughed as she heard the Squirt call back, "Don't wait dinner, Mom."

The silence settled down around her. The house was still full of the kids' noise. Stella smiled as the grandfather clock began to chime. She had hours of sleep left. She shuffled down the hall and swayed her hips as she hummed a tiny happy tune.

The Squirt backed the Granny car out of the garage. Hooker and Candy rode in the back. Candy giggled as she watched Hooker try to get comfortable. "Have you ever even been in the backseat of a car before?"

Hooker blushed. "Sure… as a kid."

As the Granny eased up the driveway to the street, Candy remembered who wasn't in the car. "Where's Box?"

The Squirt snorted. "At the curb." He pulled up and stopped at the street for only a second. The orange avenger crested over the door and stepped down and across to sit next to the Squirt. The young man nosed the car out onto the street and headed north. His right hand curled around the fur body, and his fingers found the softest fur of the cat's chest. Hooker and Candy weren't sure which was doing the purring. They leaned back and enjoyed being chauffeured in the early sunshine.

They ended at the table in the front window of the Whole Donut. As the other daughter in the family, Mai fussed over Candy and left serving the men to her husband, Ralph. "You live in big house with too many men." She moved to present her rear end just as her husband came with a plate of donuts. He knew it was coming and came to rest gently. "Just one big clumsy oaf in house enough… and sometimes too much. You take Hooker. He strong and have good teeth. He enough." She reached behind her and grabbed at her husband's crotch but only came away with a loose apron.

"Woman, you are slow. I should have used faster bait when I went fishing for a wife." Ralph sat down next to Hooker. He leaned over with a conspiratorial whisper they could all hear. "I think she is trying to kill me. She makes me run all day and then expects me to rub her feet at night. What is it with their feet?" He looked at Candy, who was now blushing.

Hooker smirked and nodded. "It's a woman thing, Ralph... it's a woman thing. I'm just happy I only have to rub Mae West's feet once every three-thousand miles."

Candy's eyes opened wide as her mouth formed a large O. "Oh, so now my feet are to be equated with big fat tires?"

Mai patted her on the shoulders. "Oh, maybe Mai be wrong about Hooker. Mai find you nice Vietnam boy. They work hard... unless they are lazy. I no find you American boy. You already have brother... if Mai have little sister—he no run far." She winked at the now blushing Squirt.

Everyone laughed at the Squirt's expense. Ralph enjoyed the moment of sitting. It was rare Hooker ever stayed more than a few moments in the back lot to pick up some donuts or the occasional stop to just say hello. The couple met in Vietnam, and when he brought Mai home with him, it was learned she was still only sixteen. They waited out the two years working in a donut shop near the VA hospital at Stanford.

Once Ralph had finished with his medical recovery, the local police and fire pooled money to buy the donut shop with its large parking lot. The police departments, fire departments, and others related to law enforcement had created pools the whole office or department had poured coins and dollars into. Once the young couple found out how it wasn't just a few special people—but the whole community who pooled together—they named the shop for the greater city of new friends.

The wall behind Ralph and Hooker was a mass of photos already layers thick of those people who helped make the shop happen, and now enjoyed the fruits of the couple's labor. Hooker's photo was in many of the photos and newspaper clippings of accidents.

Ralph leaned toward Hooker as he watched his wife and Candy. "To what do we owe the pleasure of the three of you for more than a few minutes?"

Hooker put down his mug. "We have to run up to Fremont Memorial.

Someone we interviewed yesterday was attacked last night. We think they are related."

"And Candy is along to keep the two of you out of the hospital beds?" Ralph started to chuckle.

Hooker gave him a hard look. "Is my reputation that bad? That is exactly what she said she came along for."

Ralph roared and almost fell out of his chair.

"It's not funny…"

Gaining control, Ralph pointed his finger between Hooker and the Squirt. "But you have to admit…"

The Squirt rolled his eyes and raised his eyebrows. "They do have a point…"

"Oh, don't you start in on this. I can always replace you with a brick in the seat."

Ralph snorted. "Speaking of Box… didn't you bring the man?"

Hooker gave him a look. "It's a food joint."

"And?"

"It gets full of cops…"

"And?" Mai stood with her fists on her hips as she joined in. Turning, she marched to the back door where they could all hear her open the whining screen door and call once for the cat.

Box strolled in with his tail straight up to the tip where it crooked at the last inch. The front door opened. Two motorcycle cops—a CHP and a San Jose officer—walked in. The chip slowly pulled his helmet off and looked at the cat. "Good morning, Box. Where is your—" He then saw the table full of people. "Oh…"

Hooker winked. "Good morning, Bill. We're not here."

"Heck no… You're out there on the wreck on 101, with the four over-turned rigs and six cars." He smiled at pulling Hooker's chain. Everyone knew it was killing Hooker to be driving a smaller tow truck, as well as pulling a standard day shift.

Hooker's middle finger mirrored the Squirt's as they slid slowly up the sides of their noses. The two officers saw the two fingers and laughed.

Ralph looked at the chest and head of the now purring cat. He could tell Candy's hands were busy massaging the large cat. "As you can see, the regular clientele have no problem with your partner being in here. We don't see enough of any of you, so getting to see Box is a bonus."

Hooker thought about what was on many people's minds. "You two need some employees so you can come out for a Sunday barbecue."

"We have a new guy. He helps do the prep in the morning as well as the clean up after. But you know how she is about the baking." He nodded at his wife serving the two cops. "But we do talk about it. It has been six years, and we do more than enough business… and it would be good to come out to the big house and visit with Manny and Stella."

"Look, how much business do you really do on the Fourth of July?"

Ralph duck lipped a raspberry.

"Right, so you use the day as an excuse to just clean. So put a sign up today saying you'll be closed on the Fourth. Everyone will expect it anyway. Besides, you know where all of your customers will be from about eleven o'clock on." Hooker raised his eyebrow. "We expect you two no later than noon… and no donuts. Mai is only allowed to bring some hugs. Gosh knows we always have more food than we can eat… or the few hundred people who will be there."

Ralph looked at his wife returning to the table. "Honey, we're going to be closed on the Fourth of July."

"Good, you need to clean the oven racks… they start to turn brown. And, then—"

He cut her off—probably for the first time. "Good thing we will be closed on the third as well. As for the cleaning, I'm sure Manuel has a cousin or brother he can bring along. We're going to let them clean from the Wall of Fame to the street. You and I can watch or go have a nice lunch somewhere and maybe go see a movie." He looked hard at his wife.

Finally, her shoulders sagged, and she sat down. Carefully, she reached out and gently tried one cautious pet of the large cat. She watched her hands fold down into her lap. Looking up, she looked at Ralph with a slim smile. "Okie dokie, husband." She turned and smiled at Candy.

Ralph looked at a stunned Hooker. His face was a surprised relief. "Well, that went well."

Hooker snorted softly. "Noon, no later…"

"Noon."

Mai leaned over and asked quietly, "Where I make him take me for lunch?"

Candy chuckled softly. "You call Stella, and if she can't tell you—you call Dolly." The two smiled at the thought of the two powerful women in their lives, and in Hooker's life.

21

INTERVIEW AT THE HOSPITAL

"Officer Stafford?" Hooker stepped over to the officer standing behind the nurse's station. "My name is Hooker. The Squirt here and I talked to Tess about a possible suspect in the body dump out in the grasses."

"Thanks for coming out. I rolled out on the report of a dead body in the front door of a local machine shop. Lucky for the lady, machinists have a habit of working in the cool of the early morning."

Hooker pointed out the others. "This is my girlfriend, Candy, and her brother John—but he responds faster to Squirt. This isn't the first time we've worked a case."

The officer shook hands with Candy as he eyed the Squirt. He leaned in. "Is this the same snot-nosed kid who is upsetting everyone at the academy?"

Candy snorted and nodded. The Squirt opened his mouth with mock offense in a silent protest.

Hooker chuckled. "Save it, Squirt. Word travels fast."

The officer smirked. "So… making you the two-bit towing whore."

The Squirt held Hooker's hand up, and they all laughed at Hooker's chagrin. Candy smiled at the establishing credentials. "You almost sound like you're related to Dolly."

The man smiled softly. "Dispatch Dolly? She almost became my mother-in-law, but Karen ran a little too fast. But at least I attended the wedding. She graduated the year ahead of me in school."

Hooker glanced down the hall at an orderly pushing a heavily draped gurney. "Is that…?"

The officer glanced at the gurney. "Nah, she got out of surgery over an hour ago." He looked over at the nurse. "When do you think we can have a minute with her?"

The nurse stood. "Let me go check." She held her finger up. "But only a minute."

Candy snorted softly then growled. "I'll keep them on a short leash, but it is important." The nurse nodded and left.

The officer nodded. "She lost a lot of blood. The EMTs said if the machinist found her just twenty minutes later… we would be having this conversation at the morgue.

"Her wounds are all consistent with a knife attack. The lacerations are light to deep, mostly along the fronts of her forearms, so she participated in the fight. From the looks of her knuckles, our guess is she gave almost as good as she got. The final blow is the deep slash to her neck. It missed the carotid artery—but barely. Another millimeter and she would have bled out at the scene of the fight."

Hooker shifted and leaned against the desk. "So they didn't find her where she was attacked?"

"She left quite a trail. It was about two long blocks away from the machine shop. If she had died there, she would have never been found. The blocks were warehouses back during the war—"

The Squirt frowned. "Korea?"

"Maybe as late as Korea… but it was more like manufacturing munitions to support Alameda Naval Station during the first and second war. I think it was some of the artillery stuff that started the blaze—it took out over a square mile. The area never really recovered. Manufacturing moved down into Fremont or up to Emeryville. The Navy wanted things closer, and the stuff like regular machining, tooling, and warehouses needed to be closer to the workers' homes."

The Squirt liked the history lesson, but it chaffed his cop side. "So the area is burned out and empty?"

"For the most part. There is a little rebuilding. Land is cheap, and tilt-ups are easy to build. But around where the lady set up her hooch is still pretty empty—except where people just dump stuff, which, in her case, is camouflage. It took us several minutes to realize the pile of trash, heaped in an old loading dock bay, was her hooch. The only thing that gave it away was the layers of flattened cans attached as a roof. It looked the same way she had built her dress of armor."

"Armor?"

The officer nodded. "Damnedest thing I'd ever seen. It reminded me of some of the suits of armor I saw in a German museum when I was stationed there. She had three or four layers of flattened cans held together with a network of plastic rings from six-packs of beer. We would have laughed it off like a guy with tinfoil in his hat, but we could tell by how torn up her dress was it saved her life."

"Was there anything in her… hooch?" The Squirt's face wound into his face of not quite understanding. "I mean where she was living… anything of value?"

The officer chuckled. "Hooch… it's a term from Vietnam. The guys would stack things and make underground living shelters, much like the bums do under bridges, in doorways, old buildings… where they can feel safe and return to night or day. Some of them roam at night, and others move about panhandling and such during the day."

Hooker looked at Candy. She smiled back softly. The man was talking about family.

"There wasn't anything of real value we could figure out. But the bedding told us a lot. Whoever attacked her did so at the point of rage, but was also methodical in their attack. Most of the violent stabbings centered where a person's middle would be. It's the least defensible and the softest target. After five fast stabs—very close together, the stabs become random as if searching for a body the original attack didn't find. Under the bedding, there were some pallets. Where the original five stabs had hit, four broke the boards underneath. The power needed to do such damage tells us we're looking for a man with developed upper body strength.

From my experience with knife fights and wounds, I would say we're looking for a man between five-eight and six foot. But I don't think they're really comfortable with knife fights."

"Why do you say that?"

"If you know knife fights, the blade is held down like you're using an ice pick. The edge faces away from you. This way, you can use your fist or hit and slash. Also, with a longer knife, the blade somewhat protects your forearm. But the edge cuts in the bedding were on the side toward the person kneeling there, and all the slash wounds on the woman are blade forward, edge down cuts. The person doesn't know how to fight... but they do understand a sturdy knife. Their knife did some serious damage on those boards, and the armor was bent pretty bad... I wouldn't be surprised if she has some internal damage."

"What about a waterman—someone who makes their living out there in the grass and bay?"

"Crabbies? Sure... they'd fit the bill. Pulling even small nets and poling small boats around... takes upper body strength. Shucking clams and busting up crabs takes a thick, sturdy knife. What made you think of them?"

"Call it a hunch." Hooker looked up to watch the nurse return.

"Come this way. She's still groggy from the anesthesia, but you can have a brief moment." She led the way.

"Hey, Tess..." Candy took the lead. "Hooker and the Squirt are here. They want to ask you a couple of questions. But if you start to feel woozy or tired, you let me know, and I'll send them packing."

The woman, laying quietly—more bandages than skin—waved her left arm of white gauze. Hooker leaned close.

Her voice was little more than a soft breeze rustling across the seagrass. "It was the waterman's sister..." She swallowed hard. Hooker reached over and grabbed the bottle with the straw. She took a few sips. "She looks like him. She must be a twin... but I felt her tits."

Hooker patted her on the shoulder gently. "You rest, Tess... We got all we needed. The information and to know you're all right." He leaned in close to the woman's ear. "The Mouse says to say hello." He drew back, expecting to see shock in the woman's eyes. There was none.

"I just knew it…" Softness appeared at the edge of her eyes. "You tell your sister I said hello. She always treated me with respect. She also thought, because of the beard, I was a man. You can tell her you know the truth now."

Hooker smiled and squeezed her shoulder softly. "I'll tell her next month when I go to see her."

"Is she doing okay?"

He nodded as the nurse came in. "You get some sleep now. You're safe here." He watched for the soft blink of acknowledgment. They left Tess to the nurse who pushed a syringe into the IV tube. They all knew she would be asleep before they made it to the hall.

The Squirt looked at Hooker as they walked down the hall. "I couldn't quite make out…"

"It's the waterman's twin or sister. She said she could feel the woman's tits." He looked over at the Squirt. "How big do you think they would have to be—when you can feel them during a fight for your life?"

The Squirt was almost analytical, but he had a smile. "Probably bigger than Beth's…"

Candy slugged the kid in the shoulder.

"Hey… He asked."

"Well, you didn't have to… Well, Beth is… Well, I like her." Candy grumped and folded her arms across her own chest. She knew she was nowhere near what the conversation was about—but nonetheless felt a little self-conscious.

"I like her too… but she's not as big as she likes to show. There is a little push and pad in there. Not much—but a little."

Hooker looked at the ceiling as they neared the intersection of the halls. "So, would you say maybe as big as—"

Candy cut him off. "Do you two want to catch a bus home… because, in case you didn't remember—the car was given to me?"

The men laughed and changed the subject to their favorite. The Squirt gave Hooker the eye. "Do you know where to get some ice cream around here?"

Hooker chuckled. "What do you think I am… braindead? Of course, I do." His head rolled in the zombie flop... which was mirrored by the Squirt.

"A couple of children." Candy rolled her eyes as they hit the door to the outside. She flipped around and banged the door with her butt as her head rolled back and down onto her shoulder with her mouth open and tongue slewed out. The quintessential Stella zombie roll. *She was studying her mother well.*

Hooker laughed as they spilled out into the small parking area. His eyes scanned along the strips of grass until he saw the familiar feline. "Box —go time."

22

FOURTH OF BARBECUE

The lower parking lot was full. The large doors on the food barn were wide open, and people spilled out under the large tents erected over the long tables and chairs. The canning kitchen, along the south side of the barn, was put to use as the cook stations for everything coming out of the giant barbecue trailer.

What looked like a large watering truck tank on its own set of wheels was parked along the southeast rim of the parking lot—overlooking the Almaden valley. The attending firefighters had one of the large doors up and were loading the first half of four dozen tri-tip roasts, a dozen hams, and four racks of fresh-made Sicilian sausages from Chiaramontes.

"You guys going to have enough meat?" Hooker stood with a carafe of coffee in one hand and a stack of white foam cups in the other.

The redhead, going gray, turned. The small burn patches on his face were white on his florid face. "Oh, thank the saints, Ax. The rescue is at hand." He patted the other man.

Hooker laughed. "I don't know if I would go so far as to call it a rescue, Sparks. This tainted water is only a few minutes old. But we did start a whole pot, which will be more to your tastes in about four hours." He handed each of the men a foam cup and started pouring. Stella had known to ladle half a cow of cream and a field of cane sugar into the carafe for her two favorite firefighting brothers.

Ax took a sip and smiled. "Ah, I taste the touch of a sweet woman in these grounds." The man had never been closer to Ireland than Reno, Nevada—but Hooker had never heard him speak any other way than if he was from the green isle. *Father McBride and he must be best friends.*

"How much meat are you putting up in this monster?" Hooker looked into the large cavity and the rotating racks.

Sparks grabbed up a clipboard and glanced down the list. His lips moved as he did the math in his head. He sipped at the coffee as the totals rattled and then dropped into place. "Looks like we'll end with three-hundred-eighty or three-ninety, depending on how long the hams and sausage cook. But we filled this monster with over eighteen hundred pounds in tri-tips for the benefit last week." He waved over at the closed door. "We have the burners off on this side for a gentle heat. So we'll put the sausage and corn in there."

Hooker's smile pulled sideways as he pulled his head out of the giant barbecue and looked at the twins. "I think you two found your new careers for when you retire."

Ax grumped. "Hardly. This we do for fun… but we did buy a metal shop over in Milpitas. We already have orders for six of these. The boys down in Slow Town are drawing up plans for one to cook off well over a ton of tri-tips. They said they'd put the word out and think they can even get us some orders from back east."

Hooker continued to listen to the brothers as they talked about their favorite pastime. Inside, he chuckled. Listening to these two was almost like listening to Uncle Willie and Maddie talk about the heart and soul of a fast car or motorcycle. He thought about the motorcycle Maddie had recently let go to an undercover cop in Los Angeles. He needed a faster machine. The cop mentioned he also might need one to fit his seventeen-year-old daughter—who needed something to go to college on but also needed to keep up with dad's machine.

Hooker's attention drifted down along the ridgeline where Candy was talking to a few of the nurses she was going to school with. She seemed to be fitting into the medical world as if she had been doing it for years instead of taking care of the night creatures at the diner.

The blonde in the summer dress snapped her fingers in remembering. "Bernie, did you start reading that book yet? Because… I'm dying to read it as soon as you're finished with it."

Maddie, wandering by, perked up at the mention of a book. She swung back and gently put her arm around Candy's waist in a side hug. "Did someone say book?"

Candy laughed. "Girls, this is my aunt, Maddie. She is the head ass-kicker at the county library. And if you didn't notice the black bike over there—it's hers. And it can go over one-sixty." Maddie held up two fingers as she winked with a smile. Candy gawped. "Two hundred?"

Maddie nodded as she turned back to the nurse with the book. "Which book?"

"Sybil—about a woman who has something called multiple personality disorder," Candy explained. "One of the teachers in nursing school had mentioned the disorder and suggested the book. I haven't had time—yet."

Maddie nodded. "We have a few copies at the library. I've read it. It's very interesting. I'm not sure it's totally on the up and up, but then there are some strange things in this world. As well as stranger people… just ask Candy." She hugged the younger woman and wandered off.

The other two nurses watched her move off with her broken gait. Her affected walk made her appear older than she was.

"Wow, imagine riding a motorcycle at her age…"

Candy snorted. "Don't count her out. I think she is only sixty, but even at fifty, she was the fastest woman in the world on two wheels."

The brunette was still watching the librarian walk. "She looks like she broke her hip once."

"Probably a couple of times, at least… and her back, legs, arms, head, and even her butt." The nurses laughed, but Candy knew what she said was true and couldn't be understood by someone not in the family. At the thought, a wave of warm happiness washed through her as she realized what her thought had really meant—*she was part of a family*. She smiled as she looked over her shoulder and across to where Stella and Dolly were sitting with their bare feet up on a bench and tall glasses of iced tea in their hands. The two women were laughing and animatedly poking at each other.

"You did not… Mother came and got you…"

"Hah. It was Dad, and he was coming by in the truck while I was walking."

Stella snickered, anyway. "But you have to admit, the Taylor boy was some good-looking chunk of teen boy."

Dolly held the back of her hand against her sister's shoulder. "Which one—there were five Taylor boys, and then out Clear Waterway there were the Tailor boys…"

"Oh, God… I had forgotten about the Tailors." Her eyes got huge as she turned toward Dolly.

They both said, "Hugh Tailor…" and swooned at the same time… and then broke into a rolling round of giggles.

Uncle Willie stood with his glass of pure iced tea. His body was ramrod straight. "It would appear your wife and Dolly have started in on the moonshine a little early."

Manny rolled his eyes against his half-closed lids. "You're already up… You go tell them to behave." The moment was frozen, and then both sets of shoulders and chests started to bounce with their common silent laughing.

Hooker stood leaning on the railing. The sea of family and friends spread out below.

"Is it my imagination, or has this family grown since last year?"

Hooker looked at the Squirt with a jaundiced eye. "This time last year? This time last year, you were going in for your fourth surgery, and I could never have gotten Candy to come down then." He turned and looked back at the sea of humanity. "But to answer the question… yes, there are a lot more people here this year. You were here for Christmas—but it was cold then." They both laughed.

The Squirt snorted. "Just the right temperature for ice cream."

Hooker laughed and then looked at the couple walking down the driveway. The look on their faces was one of surprise or disbelief. Hooker muttered as he pointed out Ralph and Mai. "This ought to be interesting."

"Haven't they ever been to one of these?"

"A few years ago… back when the whole party only filled most of this deck. You remember last spring. We considered Sunday dinner to be a large party… Then last summer, things got a little out of hand. And after the Christmas party…" He turned and leaned his butt against the rail as he smiled. "The parties just got better… Hello, ladies."

The Squirt glanced over his shoulder and then turned around with a large open smile. Candy escorted Beth out through the glass door.

"We're two lost sheep… looking for a place to graze while being protected by a big strong man or two." Beth moved into a hug from Hooker before turning and kissing the Squirt.

Candy watched the heat and length of the kiss. "Well, I guess I can tell the nurses they need to start looking elsewhere."

Beth broke the kiss and fell around into the Squirt's left arm as she became even more molded to his body. "They were even looking?" She smiled. "Do I need to gouge some eyes out?"

Hooker choked. "Easy, kitten. If there is any catfighting to be had, we'll let Box do the work."

Beth looked up at the Squirt as she pushed her tightly stretched angora sweater into his stomach. "Did the cat really kill a large dog?"

The Squirt nodded.

"It must have been some fight to see."

The Squirt snapped his fingers. "It was all over in a flash…"

"Wow…" She breathed. "You were there…?"

Hooker almost choked—he couldn't miss the twin blossoms of her excitement became obvious in the stretched summer-weight sweater. He glanced at Candy who was also staring at the rapid change.

"No… but I do know Box quite well." The hitch in the Squirt's voice belied he was also feeling the young woman's excitement.

Hooker ran the tip of his tongue along his dry lips as he winked to Candy. "Maybe you can introduce Beth to Box."

The Squirt looked up at his friend with the look of a trapped animal… torn by its acceptance and eager willingness to be in the position of inability to escape. "Good idea. Let's go see where he might be hiding."

Hooker couldn't help himself. "He looked kind of tired earlier. I think he headed up the hall for a nap."

The Squirt rested his chin on the top of Beth's head as he rolled his eyes larger. Candy almost choked on a giggle, and Hooker just made a turn of his index finger in the air. *Go for it.*

As they watched the two younger ones as they beelined for the back bedroom, Candy fell laughing into Hooker's side. "You are awful. We won't see them for at least an hour."

"Or three." Hooker laughed and turned her toward the outside stairway. "Come on, mother hen. We have a party to mingle in. Someone has to be responsible around here." Hooker felt the side of her foot almost side-slap up to his butt. His boot showed her how it was done, and they laughed the whole way down the stairs.

The late evening settled in on the large group. The louder band finished. A soft trio of Navy firefighters playing a fiddle, a plucked cello, and a slide steel guitar took over. The odd mix was from Moffett field and called themselves The Black Sheep Yeomen. None of them had been west of the Mississippi before joining the Navy. All three grew up in musical families where they considered them to be black sheep—because they no longer played classical music.

The music was natural with no amplifiers—soft and gentle. Hooker could tell Sweets was tuned into the music instead of the conversation. The man played all kinds of music, as long as it was an old-style country. The western twang of a cowboy was his love, but his appreciation ran deeper into the country's mountain music from the Smokey Mountains to the Appalachians. His expertise also extended into swamp-music or the Creole music called Zydeco.

Hooker leaned over. "You've been quiet tonight. If your toe wasn't twitching ever so slightly, I would think you were sleeping behind those shades."

The blind man remained unmoving. "I've been trying to make heads or tails about something."

Hooker snorted softly. "Let me help you out. The guy on the steel slide is Puerto Rican from New York, the white guy on the fiddle is from somewhere near Kansas City, and the cello is from somewhere up around Motor City. They all have classical training, but don't play classical or their instruments the way they were trained…"

Sweets started silently chuckling. His head turned halfway toward where he knew Hooker was. "You are the fastest mouth to wise-ass, I know. How in the world did you get this old?"

"Luck, speed, and I tease blind men who can't see where I am."

Sweets' hand was fast, and his forefinger touched the tip of Hooker's nose and recoiled before Hooker could react.

"Okay, sometimes I'm faster, but most of it came from luck." He held up his own index finger and gave Sweet's brother a mock hard look. "Don't say it, Danny… I'll break you down like a shotgun and load you up like a cannon."

Everyone within hearing broke up in laughter. The only person not laughing was Danny, whose smile was larger than Sweet's usual megawatt smile. At almost double the size of Hooker, he knew it was one of the funniest sayings to fall out of the smaller man's mouth.

"Before Danny folds you up like a cheap wallet and puts you in his hip pocket, tell me if this sounds wrong…" He paused with his hand out flat. Hooker knew the look and what could be coming.

"I have growing live grass—but it is tall and brown. There are people in the grass, but it feels like they are under the grass. The sun is hot, but my body or their bodies are cold. There is a man, but I also feel a woman. But even though I can see the sun, I know it's night. There is killing, but not there…" His voice trailed off.

"Can you see the man's face? Or the woman?"

"No, but they're the same. I can feel the tightness of a ponytail gathered tight at the base of the head. But it is the dark-light, day-night, man-woman, cold-hot thing I'm having trouble with. I'm not even sure if it has to do with you…"

Hooker closed his eyes and thought. "Have you ever told me anything you have seen—and it wasn't for me or about something I was involved with?"

He watched the black man's face. There were little twitches and muscle pulls Hooker had come to know about Sweets and his thinking.

"No."

"And it's true this time too. This all has to do with what we went over at breakfast the other day." Hooker told him about the body dump, Tess, and the waterman. He watched the man's face as he talked, waiting for a twitch of recognition or a touch on a memory.

As he spoke, Candy came and sat on the arm of Hooker's Adirondack chair. "You know... we were just talking about a new book—one that's popular..."

Hooker paused and looked at his girlfriend. He waited.

Sweets was not as patient. "And...?"

She twitched. Hooker was now sure she had indulged in more than her share of moonshine. "Um... it's called Sylvia... or something. It's about a woman who has a bunch of people living in her—"

Danny cut her off. "Excuse me, but it's called multiple personality disorder. The book's title is Sybil."

Sweets' head rolled his brother's way and stopped. Danny sighed and continued. "They are whole personalities or people who live in the one body. They don't, for the most case, know about the other people. The case study the book is written about—Sybil had over sixteen personalities."

Hooker sat up and frowned. "How does... um... a personality exist in a body and not know if someone else is in the body?"

Danny looked at him hard. He was deciding if Hooker was just trying to draw him into talking more than a few words or if he really wanted to know.

They all looked over at the wheelchair moving rapidly backward. Just before it hit them, it spun around. Manny leaned forward. "Yes, I read the book when it first became available in the library, but I still don't really understand how they don't or can't know about the other. The woman had many blank spaces in her different lives."

Danny shifted mental gears. He pointed toward the east, where the moon was just cresting the east hills. "If the moon is a dead ball of rock, how does it glow?"

Candy giggled, and Hooker chuckled and rubbed her back as she answered. "It reflects the sun."

"But the sun went down an hour ago..."

She opened her arms wide with her fingers held as if she was holding the moon and sun in a pinch hold. "They are so far apart, it all works except when there's an eclipse."

"Correct. So during the day, the moon is behind the earth... sort of. And at night, the sun is behind, and we see the moon. During those days and nights, we have the two which don't know the other exists... just for our purposes of this explanation. So if our sky is their lives, this is what they know... but don't know about the other." He looked for nodding heads. "They can't look in the mirror and see the other person—because they're both on the inside—so the mirror only reflects the same person they always see—themselves."

Nobody laughed at the idea of Danny holding forth on something as odd as this. All except Candy knew good and well Danny had gone off to USC on a football scholarship, only because it also covered his housing. The scholastic scholarship for USC would have covered everything but his housing. His walking away from a winning year—which took USC to the Rose Bowl, a shot at the NFL, and him becoming a psychiatrist or college professor—surprised nobody.

Danny came home to take care of his brother and family. It was just a different path to his happiness—not a lesser one.

In his days of waiting while his brother worked as a respected radio personality, Danny read. Possibly more than Manny or Maddie combined. His weekly order at the library Maddie ran was a dozen books of the combined librarian's choosing. If it was in the pile, Danny read it. Maddie's only concern was someday, Danny would run out of library, or librarians. The only thing Danny didn't do was written book reports.

Manny rocked forward on his elbows as he shifted his thoughts. "But a few of her personalities knew about one another."

Danny smiled. "Correct. They did. How often in the evening are they both in the sky at the same time?"

"Enough..."

Danny looked around at Hooker, and Candy laughed as she slipped down onto his lap. "Don't ask Hooker—he's a vampire and only knows about the night."

Danny snorted. "She does have a point there, Casper." Everyone laughed at Hooker's nocturnal nature.

"So… with the two in the sky at the same time—those two would know about each other."

Danny nodded as he looked back at Manny. "Exactly. Now in the book, they know about each other through inference only. One of them knew of several of the others, but the guy was a snoop and tracked down all the clothes and notes and such until he had figured out who the others were."

Hooker harrumphed, and Candy giggled. "Going back to the night and day thing… We have a person stashing bodies during the day. He is a known person in the area. But the guy or woman in the hospital swears it was the guy or his twin, but is a female because they felt the chick's…" he looked at Candy and realized she was too far gone to care, "…boobs."

"So what are you asking?"

Hooker started to talk, and then he frowned. His mouth closed, and then he looked up. "I'm not sure… but Tess swore the person who attacked her or him looked exactly like the waterman—"

"Except for teats."

"Yeah." Hooker leaned back, exhausted.

Danny stroked his chin. "You seem confused about the person in the hospital. Is it a man or a woman?"

Candy giggled. "They said she is a she… but the person lying in the bed definitely has a beard. You could put him on the cough drop box or make the Grateful Dead guy look clean-shaven."

Manny interjected. "I got the fill-in—Hirsutism. She is definitely female but suffers from extreme Hirsutism, which displays in beard and body hair."

Danny rocked as he registered the information. "It fits what I was just thinking… classic case of the sideshow's bearded woman."

He turned back to Hooker. "When was the attack?"

"At night…"

Danny was catching onto the question trail to an answer or solving a crime, which Manny usually led. "But the waterman is usually only seen during the day?"

"Only seen during the day… from what I understand."

Danny leaned back and thought. His right arm flopped out, and his finger touched his silent brother. "Which this would explain your problem of them being male and female, but the same person."

Sweets nodded. "I've been thinking about that."

Danny continued, "And if the guy you said is only around during the day—he isn't the killer personality. Which means the night personality is the one who showed up to kill your friend. Only the killer is a female personality."

Candy leaned over—or fell over—onto Hooker's chest. "So explain how the guy—the waterman guy—when the sun goes down… grows boobs." She giggled softly at saying the word boobs. Hooker knew the evening was coming to a close… soon.

"He doesn't. But during the day… she binds her chest so it looks like a guy."

The simple answer had them all nodding in silence. Sweets was the first to hear the soft little snort of a delicate snore. He started to rise. "Manny, it was a delightful party. I need to gather my mother so we can trundle her off to go sleepy bye."

"I'd get up and give you guys a hug, but I probably had a shot too many, so give me a shake, man." The blind disc jockey laughed at the old joke about Manny being paralyzed. In other's eyes, they were disabled, but they both knew and respected they were simply alternately abled.

They shook as Danny moved off like a silent ship in the night to fetch their mother. Returning, he lifted Candy so Hooker could get up, and then placed her on Hooker's body so he could carry her into her apartment a few dozen feet away. Hooker wasn't getting up early the next morning so he would stay with her. They all watched as Candy clutched with her legs around his waist with her arms and head draped over his shoulder. Her lips smacked in her sleep.

With Candy draped on his body and shoulders, he stuck his right hand out. "Thanks for the information as well as the explanation, Danny… Sweets." He turned and gave a partial hug to their mother. "Thanks for coming, Mom. We don't see enough of you three. And you can always come out alone. I know Stella would love the help in keeping Manny in line."

"Hooker, we already made plans for Wednesday. While you menfolk have your secret dinner—we women can have some fun too." She kissed him on the cheek and let him go. She could tell Candy wasn't heavy, but she also wasn't light like a child either.

TO FIND THE FEMALE

Max swung her ponytail around to her back. The first time had almost caught Candy on the side of the head. The glancing blow had been a fair warning to duck when the large woman moved her head down and hitched up her shoulder—the deadly weapon was about to move. Candy hadn't noticed the series of knives secreted in the braid, but she rubbed her head and wondered if there was a hammer hidden in the braid or if the woman had too much iron in her diet. Either way, she was leery and had changed sides with Hooker.

The rust faced woman in the work uniform smiled. She could wish Candy just wanted to be closer to her, but she could tell she was definitely attached to Hooker.

"So really… all you have is the woman is blonde, built to eat oats and draw wagons, and has a rack of large bazoombas. Hell, Hooker… the only thing keeping me out of the line-up is my tiny braid is too long." To highlight her point, she tossed her head, and the long braid swept a circle in the air. Candy and Hooker both ducked. Laughing, Max stopped the cudgel in midair with her left hand and guided it down her chest.

"Not to be rude, Max… but I think you may be a little more than what we are looking for, too."

She leaned forward and planted her forehead and nose an inch away from Hooker's nose. She growled. "Are you saying I don't have a delicate girly figure?"

Candy caught her breath. "Eep." She was afraid something involving blood was about to happen.

Max's eyes shifted right and took in the frail-looking woman who, even when scared, hadn't twitched to move from Hooker's side. Her sight ground back to Hooker's face an inch away. A growl rumbled somewhere deep. "I like this one. She's going to run you ragged. You need to bring her and the cat around more often."

Hooker didn't blink. "What about the Squirt?"

Max stood to make room for her laugh. "The smartass can come by anytime—on his own time. I like a man who can remember things." She nodded her head sideways at Tawny. "It reminds me of our father. If he read it, he remembered it. He was a pisser at Scrabble. How is the Squirt at Scrabble?"

Hooker looked in surprise at Candy.

Candy shrugged. "I don't know. We've never played. But don't play cards with him. He cheats."

Max roared as she held her belly. "So do I."

Hooker snickered. "But he knows if you added a card or two."

Max toyed with her braid. "And that counts... how?"

At Candy's horrified face, Tawny leaned over. "Don't put too much into my sister's threats." Candy relaxed and looked to Tawny for her reassurance. Tawny's smile drew back lopsided. "She's only killed a few people."

Max snorted. "That you know of... and all seven deserved it."

Hooker washed his face in his hands. "Oh, God. It just keeps getting deeper and deeper."

"What?"

"Last week, you told me it was only five... and now it's up to seven?"

"This month..."

Candy pinched the bridge of her nose as she closed her eyes and gently shook her head. "Oh, my gawd—she's as bad as Willie."

Max laughed as she pointed. "She knows Willie?"

Hooker closed one eye and looked at the woman. She held both hands up and stepped back half a step before she swung her braid to her back. "Okay, I'll behave."

She splashed some brown liquid into a glass and put it on the bar in front of Hooker. He looked at it with a frown and question. Max nodded for him to go ahead. "Tell me what you think."

Hooker sipped cautiously and then slurped the rest down. "Good... very good... but it's not commercial root beer."

"Nope, but it might become commercial. A friend grew up in New Orleans, and he said this is the root beer of choice down there. He's working on reproducing the bite, which only comes from the sarsaparilla."

"Why not just get the stuff they sell down in New Orleans?"

"Because it's only made and sold down there."

Hooker thought about the strange divergence from their discussion. "So what does this have to do with the killer?"

Max smirked and leaned hard against her hands spread along the backside of the bar. "Sometimes, you have to go where the root beer is, and sometimes you have to go where the killing is." She stood back up and smiled. "And there she is."

Hooker turned to look at Shawna walking through the door.

She saw who was at the bar, and her mouth pulled up to one side in a quirky smile. "Hello, Hooker." She spotted Candy and changed the side she was headed for. She lounged her arm over Tawny and gave Hooker a smoldering look. "Who's your friend?"

Hooker chuckled at the dynamics. "This is my girlfriend, Candy. Candy, this is Shawna."

Candy smiled knowingly, and she put her hand out, but as the woman started to shake her hand, Candy drew her into a hug. "I'm so glad to meet another friend of Hooker's." And then she whispered in her ear, "We need to talk... I need some tips."

The woman froze and then softened as she realized Candy wasn't talking about the sex trade, but an open woman-to-woman talk about what to do. She drew her in fully. "Anytime, girlfriend."

They parted, but only enough to turn around as they stayed draped with an arm around the other. Hooker's eyes rose, but he knew better than to ask. He knew when he was outgunned.

Max snorted, then pulled out a glass and filled it with cola. She pushed it forward and reached for a couple of lime pieces. Twisting them into the glass, she announced, "Cola, no ice, with a twist of lime."

"Thanks, Max. I've been having fantasies about this for the last hour on the bus." She had drained half before she started to put it down. Looking at Candy, she took another sip and then put it down.

"I don't think you should take your girlfriend out slumming to places like this."

Max protested… weakly.

"We have some information, and Candy has the day off, so she's been tagging along."

"New information?"

"We had a lead for someone to talk to. After we had talked to her, she was attacked and almost killed."

"That's horrible. Do they have any idea who attacked her?"

"A good suspicion, but we have nobody who matches the description."

Max leaned forward on the bar. "That's why they're here to talk to you."

"How would I know—"

Candy rested her hand on the woman's upper chest. "Nobody is accusing you of anything… We just think you might be able to help us think of a person you and the other women might know, fitting the description. We think the person who is doing the killing is a female you girls might know."

"But we already went through this… Well, sort of. But none of us hook anything but straight-up guys looking for girls. Maybe in San Francisco, there is some girl on girl. There are certainly guys for guys, but I don't know of any girls for girls." She looked around the bar. "It's… Well, just not our style."

Hooker cleared his throat. He was still playing catch-up with Candy suddenly friendly with this other woman. "Um, we don't think it's another."

"Working girl?"

Hooker blushed and nodded. "We do think it's a female, but one who knows all of you, and more importantly, all of you know well enough to be comfortable around her. Maybe like a waitress… who works where you all go at the end of the night?"

"So what does she look like?"

"Blonde with a small ponytail. We're assuming she's about five-eight or so and muscular."

"Which would describe more than a few women I know." She looked at Max, and they all laughed.

Hooker snorted. "I said a small ponytail, not a flail attached to an anchor rope."

Shawna thought about the description and shook her head. "All the waitresses who work the restaurants we go to—or are allowed into—are my size or smaller, unless you're talking a couple who are Max's size but make her look slender."

Hooker glanced toward Max. "Well, it is someone you know, or at least, knows you. Maybe this requires some sitting and watching."

Shawna and Candy both frowned. "Sitting and watching." The words were perfect unison, and the two giggled. Candy hugged her tighter. "I knew I liked you…" And then she remembered where she was and the kind of women who were the customers. Her eyes flew open as her mouth made a small O. "I didn't mean… I mean… oh, this isn't going right." She blushed.

Shawna gave her a squeeze. "You're safe. I knew what you meant… and yeah, I like you too. But watch out for Tawny—you're definitely her type."

Max laughed, and Tawny snorted. "Not hardly. She doesn't have any meat on those bones."

Shawna giggled and leaned into Candy. "They tell everyone they're sisters… but really, they're girlfriends."

Max growled with a twinkle in her eye. "You want to get eighty-sixed from here?"

Hooker cleared his throat. He could feel the girl play could rapidly slip out of hand, and they had crimes to solve, and possibly people to save.

"We know the killer is someone who knows all of you. So we just need to watch all of you and see who's there—who you're so used to—you don't see them."

Max raised her eyebrows and toyed with her braid. Hooker braced to duck if she flipped it around again. He could sense Candy ready also. "So you're saying this killer is *yahoody?*"

"Who?"

Tawny snorted. "Kids these days... nobody reads, nobody respects the old poems."

She turned and recited the poem.

YESTERDAY, upon the stair,
  I met a man who wasn't there.
  He wasn't there again today,
  I wish, I wish he'd go away...

WHEN I CAME HOME last night at three,
  The man was waiting there for me,
  But when I looked around the hall,
  I couldn't see him there at all!
  Go away, go away, don't you come back any more!
  Go away, go away, and please don't slam the door...

LAST NIGHT, I saw upon the stair,
  A little man who wasn't there.
  He wasn't there again today.
  Oh, how I wish he'd go away...

CANDY HUNG ON SHAWNA. "Sounds more like someone with hallucinations."

Shawna mumbled, "Yahoody is an old Jewish folktale about the little guy who does things nobody sees… like when you close the refrigerator door—he's the one who turns the light off."

Candy snickered. "Or leaves the toilet seat up?"

"Hey… not me."

Conspiratorially, Candy turned in toward Shawna. "It's true, he sits."

"For both?"

"For either one." They both snickered.

Hooker growled. "I'm standing right here, you know."

Max grunted. "Dude, you don't count in this conversation."

Hooker turned to make like he was leaving. "I'm going to go find a killer."

Tawny snorted. "Dude… you leave now, you ain't ever getting her back."

He turned. "The killer?"

Tawny stood up off the stool and draped her arm over Candy's shoulders—making the three a Candy sandwich. "No… someone more important."

Candy caught the drift of the innuendo and slipped out. She hit Hooker's arm and spun around, smiling. "Fun thought, but maybe another time." She winked with the eye Hooker couldn't see. The three women laughed at Hooker's struck look.

Max stood and swung her braid. "Say good-night, Hooker. Take your woman home before someone else does."

Hooker knew when he was outgunned. He spun Candy around, and they headed for the door. "Good-night, ladies." His arm waved over his head as he kissed the top of Candy's head.

He froze. He stood staring at the top of Candy's head as it rotated up to look at him. "Hooker, what's wrong?"

He smiled. "Nothing… now." He turned back.

"Shawna… around where you…"

"Work?"

He nodded. "Are there any buildings, say… two or three stories?"

"Sure. We look at a three-story office building all night. It's the Taylor building. Why?"

"Because we are going to stake it out and watch you. What is commonplace and unnoticed to you will be new to us. We'll see what you don't." His slim smile was more satisfaction for figuring out a course of action than being happy. They turned and left.

Max turned to Shawna. "What do you think?"

"I think he is one smart guy… and she is one lucky girl."

Tawny snorted as she leaned her arm on the bar and ran her fingers through her hair as she looked longing at the closed door. "I think he's the lucky one. There is something very special about her. It's very soft and subtle and still hiding from even her."

Max nodded. She made her living at reading people and saw Hooker and Candy as a great match—both damaged goods but made for each other.

24

STAKEOUT

Manny shifted in his chair. The Brahms concerto drifted from the large headphones. He studied the three young people he and Stella had come to think of as their children. He, of all people, knew the dangers of even a simple stakeout. It was a stakeout that ended his career and his ability to walk. *The stakeout... and a bullet to the spine.*

"The first thing about a stakeout is… it is—"

The Squirt coughed. "Never done alone." He had covered his mouth with his fist. He looked over the fist. The man's face was only slightly red but was rapidly growing darker. "Excuse me… a bit of dust. Please continue." The red was creeping up the young man's neck. He had forgotten he could not overstep with Manny like he could with Hooker.

Manny gave it a slow five-count, and then his eyes slid over to Hooker. "As it was so rudely put… you have to work as a team. The second you go gonzo Steve McQueen—things turn bad." He patted his chair's arms. He rolled up on his forearms as he looked at the few papers on his desk. "If you can work out the timing, I would suggest the three of you watch from the top of the building here. The last woman killed that we know of was taken from along here. Her beat was along this block, so the killer is somewhere around there."

Chastised, the Squirt was back in learning mode. "Why all three of us? Why not just Hooker and me? I mean, why put her in danger?"

Manny smiled. It was at these kinds of moments the most important lessons of police work were learned. He turned to Candy. He nodded at the Squirt.

"What can you tell me about John's clothes?"

Candy thought a moment, and then she peeked to make sure. "When we stopped for a few minutes at Willie's, the Squirt changed his pants."

"Were his pants from this morning somehow soiled?"

"On *Mister, I Aced the Academy*? Never. If they had been, he would have changed them here."

"So he soiled them later in the day?"

"Not that I observed… no."

Manny and Candy were both smiling at their knowledge and how the other two had not figured it out. Manny raised an eyebrow and looked at Hooker.

Manny motioned for the kid to stand. "Hooker, take a good look. How did Candy know the Squirt changed his pants at Willie's—instead of here?"

They waited as Hooker had the kid gradually turn around. Finally, Hooker saw it and chuckled. He leaned over toward Candy and stage-whispered, "Do you want to tell Hank, or should I break his heart?"

Candy gave him a horrified look. "Oh, there is no way I'm telling Hank how to do his laundry. He would just put a blowtorch in my hand and tell me to have at it."

They all laughed. Hank's fondness for "laundering" very soiled clothing with a blowtorch and a long stick was infamous. Hooker had taken to carrying an extra pair of pants and a white T-shirt in his truck after a particularly nasty and filthy week of towing had cost him all but the pants and shirt he was wearing.

Hank was extremely picky about just how dirty something could be and still be washed in his sparkling and hand waxed washing machine and dryer set. Uncle Willie joked about Hank and the Maytag man being on a first-name basis, and Hank could give the repairman tips on the best wax for the white boxes of his cleaning empire.

The Squirt took one last look at his pants and sat down in wonder. "Okay, we've all had a great laugh. Now how did you know?"

Hooker pointed. "Lift your right leg and cross it semaphore on your left knee." The young man did. "Now what is wrong?"

The Squirt's left hand absentmindedly straightened the curled cuff. He continued to look for something wrong enough to see from a few feet away. "Nothing…"

Manny smiled. "What did you just do with your left hand?"

"Nothi… I just smoothed out the hem. Why?"

Manny closed his eyes as he thought about what day Stella had done laundry.

He opened his eyes. "Stella hung six pairs of jeans in your closet yesterday—please bring me two pairs."

The kid returned a moment later with a pair in each hand, still on their hangers. "I don't see it…"

Candy snorted. "She really does iron them flat."

Manny chuckled. "A dozen years of ironing my uniforms. The old habit dies hard. Well, actually, she can't stand the thought of the boys being out there looking any less than what she is capable of doing." He turned back to the Squirt. "Stella mentioned it about four minutes after you three got home. Actually, her observation was more in the vein of going over and teaching Hank how to properly do laundry."

Hooker mused. "I remember Willie being such a stickler about ironing his pants and shirts. I guess it was from many years of having a perfectly pressed uniform." He looked up. "But now he doesn't seem to care as much, except I do notice the difference when he irons my T-shirt and when Hank does. Hank only shows the bottle of starch to the shirt, where Willie gives the shirt a whole new backbone."

The kid sat down—thinking. "So with three sets of eyeballs, one might see something the other two would miss."

Manny nodded. "More importantly, Candy has a woman's eye. She might see something you two see but will assign a different importance to it… like the cuff having curled."

The Squirt looked to Hooker. "So when did you want to do this?"

"Tonight. Tomorrow is Wednesday, so the load for me will be light, and we should be out of dinner by nine." He looked at Candy.

"I'm good. I have tonight and tomorrow night off... but I work a double on Thursday. As long as I can get about eight hours of sleep before five, I'm good."

Hooker nodded. "Let's get a couple of hours rest, and then we can be on the roof by, say... nine-thirty."

Manny leaned back. "We'll wake you at nine, and Stella can have some food and a thermos packed."

They stood. "Thanks, Manny—sounds good."

Candy leaned over and kissed Manny on the top of his head as they shuffled out of the office. Stella stood in the kitchen leaning with one hand on the island. Hooker pushed his thumb back toward Manny and then put his hands together by his head.

Stella nodded. She knew she would be filled in and would have suggested they take a nap anyway.

THE TWO BACKPACKS leaned bloated against the parapet wall. The three snickered at the size of *I packed you a bit to eat*—Stella style.

"Does she ever do just a small snack like a few stalks of celery with peanut butter on them?"

Hooker rolled his head in a shortened zombie roll. "Probably the last day she squeezed into a training bra."

The Squirt blushed and mumbled as he pointed at the farthest end of the building. "I'll... um... just be down here." He grew his eyes big at Hooker and walked away. Candy snickered at her brother being still uncomfortable at the mention of a woman's undergarments. For all the grown-up he had become, there was still the boy in him. She also knew the same went for all three of them.

She wrapped her arms around Hooker's one arm and kissed him on the cheek. "I'll be at this other end." She picked up one of the bags and started toward the closer end.

Hooker looked at the two others and mumbled quietly to himself, "If anybody cares, I'll just be right here." He sat down on an old tar bucket he had turned upside-down.

Hooker's eyebrow rose, surprised at the traffic on the streets at ten-thirty at night. San Fernando ran across in front of them. From Candy's corner, she could look north up First to Santa Clara and south as far down as San Carlos. Hooker knew the Squirt worked the same range up and down Second.

From their perches on top of the bank building, they could watch most of the night action—according to Shawna. Hooker smiled at the small marker of neon green dress Shawna said she would wear. Hooker found her in his binoculars and wondered if the skirt covered anything below the edge of her bottom. As for the top, it was mostly what would be expected on a warm, humid night.

Hooker lowered the binoculars and scanned the large parking lot the bank shared with the rest of the building's tenants on the north end. There were only a few cars left parked. They looked like they would prob-ably be there in the morning, as well. Cars moved on the street at the speed limit. The heat of the evening tempered any urgency people might feel—getting to wherever they were going.

Looking east down San Fernando, he looked for any foot traffic coming from the San Jose State housing he knew was only a few blocks away. Going for a walk or a woman could make for a nice study break. The college was full almost all year long. Summer was only a shorter semester and student load for the university. Most of the students lived at home in the area and usually took the summer off. But there was always a small group who were in a hurry to graduate and move on with their advanced education or their lives.

Three young men in T-shirts and shorts approached from the college. Judging from the arm gestures and body language, the topic of conversa-tion started in a classroom. They were out to carry on the conversation and maybe get something to eat. Some quick sex wasn't on their minds.

The small voice in the back of Hooker's head was keeping his usual count. On San Fernando, there were three Fords, one beat-up VW bug, a Dodge Super Bee, two Chevrolets, and a Pacer he wondered about making it home. The offending gold car was smoking as if it had blown at least three of its ring sets and probably, had burned the edges of at least four valves. Of all the cars, the self-destructing Pacer, and the sanitation three-wheeler made enough noise to be heard on top of the two-story building.

The three-wheeler stopped at the garbage can at the corner of Second and San Fernando. The guy driving wore the city's loose-fitting blue jumpsuit and a Spartan's ball cap. The short ponytail stuck spiky out the hole over the size adjusting tabs. Part of Hooker's mind watched the smooth dance of the lid removed with one hand, and the other whipped around the inner can—gathering the plastic bag liner. One-handed, the worker pulled the bag of garbage out of the can.

Leaning the lid against the concrete shell, the worker kicked the bag to spin. As it slowed, they pushed down—compressing the contents and air. With a flourish, the bag was tied and slung onto the pile on the back of the cart. A fresh bag appeared from somewhere and was snapped open, hung in the can, the top turned over the can's rim, and the lid replaced.

The city worker drew a squirt bottle from where it hung in their side pocket and with a rag, spritzed and wiped the lid down—clean and ready for the denizens of the day. They jumped back on the three-wheeler, put it in gear, and moved to the next stop. The process from stop to go had lasted less than a couple of minutes. Hooker smiled. It was all automatic— just like he was when changing a tire.

Movement to his right caught his eye. In the dark of a doorway, the red of a cigarette flared. Someone was in the doorway. Hooker raised the binoculars and searched the depth of the dark area. Shapes moved in the dark recess. Hooker wished he could get his hands on at least one of the Starlight scopes Willie had shown him a few years before. The dark doorway would have been a green light, but he could then see everything in there like it was daylight.

The cigarette flared again, and Hooker could see from the glow a man's face. He also could see the red glow lit up enough of the bobbing blond hair at the man's waist. The man was taking a smoke break and getting a blowjob at the same time. He watched to see if he could see the man's face better, but the flare of the cigarette was never enough. Hooker waited, hoping they would walk out into the street when they finished.

Hooker watched the traffic gradually become sparse. Occasionally, a car would slow, look at the girl walking, and then think better of it. One pulled to the curb, and Shawna sauntered over along with another girl called Tiny—who was anything but. If she had ever seriously been called Tiny, it was long before her chest blossomed. They bent over and talked with the driver. Tiny stood up and arched her back. Shawna stood, they conferred, and they both piled into the car. It was going to be a party.

Hooker focused on the doorway. The cigarette flared and then arched through the air out into the street. A few minutes later, the blonde stepped into the light of the street—straightening her dress. There wasn't much there to straighten. She smoothed the tight clinging material down along her hips. She waved back into the dark without even looking back and walked east along the street. Hooker saw a slight reflection as if a glass door had opened and closed—reflecting some of the streetlight. The man had entered the building. Hooker made a note of the blonde and the doorway in his book.

By midnight, the traffic was down to the occasional car. Most were passing through on their way to somewhere else. Only a rare one would slow for one of the girls. Tiny and Shawna had returned and gone at least five more times. Hooker sat watching as he quietly chewed his way through one of Stella's kosher ham sandwiches. It was she and Manny's joke. The sandwich was full of mayo, cheese, pickles, lettuce, and, of course, the ham. Manny said he would marry her if she knew how to make a kosher ham sandwich. The half-done dill pickles were the only kosher part to the sandwich. The two spears of pickle were enough for Manny.

Hooker looked in the sky to the northwest and watched the large PSA 727 letting down for a landing at the airport. The distance muted the sound of the jet engines. A Lincoln drove almost silent along San Fernando. Hooker could hear the distinct sound of the horizontally opposed two-cylinder engine of the garbage collector a few blocks away to the north. He figured they probably picked up most of the garbage from the downtown area every week. With the use of the three-wheeler, the whole of downtown would only take two or three workers.

Hooker fished through the bag looking for the thermos. Coffee sounded good right then—he noted the Squirt probably had the same idea. The young man was picking his way along the parapet.

"I thought you might want some coffee…"

The kid sat on the parapet. "Eighty-seven Fords, forty-three Chevys, nineteen Mopars, a dying Pacer, and a Westcoaster garbage cart. There were ninety-one walkers, two bicycles, and a blowjob over there in the doorway." He shook his head. "Who would have guessed the Pacer would have made it up past San Carlos?"

Hooker laughed at the young man's avoidance of the blowjob. He handed him the second thermos. "How many working girls could you see?"

"Four. Shawna and Tiny here, and two more up Second… but I did find it interesting nobody is working down this block."

Hooker knew the answer, and it drew a smile from him. "What kinds of streetlights do you see out there?" He pointed toward the street.

The kid looked and then shrugged. "I don't know… some variety of incandescent or halogen, I guess."

"The color is…?"

"White…?"

Hooker nodded and then nodded toward the parapet. "And the lights in the parking lot?"

The kid glanced. "Yellow." The Squirt snapped his fingers. "Same as that place we got the burrito for the guy up in Contra Costa last year."

Hooker smiled. "They're called low-sodium. They are much cheaper to run than those halogens. The problem with them is they make a woman's makeup look like Halloween horror makeup. So you take a nice girl to dinner, and then just when you're feeling the romance—you leave the restaurant—right into a street filled with low-sodium lights. *Bam!* Your Farrah Fawcett turns into Medusa."

The kid took a sip as Hooker pointed down into the parking lot.

"So you have a nice place for kids to hang out. But because you don't want them to hang out and maybe cause some mischief, you want to discourage them. Well, young guys like to hang out where there are girls… and girls only want to hang out where they'll look good. It only takes a sixteen-year-old one walk under the yellow lights to know she's never going there again. So… no girls, no boys—problem solved."

"So how about Second and First?" Candy wasn't getting left out of a little conversation after being bored out of her mind for two hours.

Hooker turned as she walked into his arm. They tapped heads lightly. "Nobody was working the street on this block, either?"

She poured herself some coffee from Hooker's thermos as she shook her head. "All I saw on First were the two working the west side up toward San Carlos. There was nobody down here."

Hooker continued. "The bank owns the building. They paid the city to put in the yellow lights all around the three sides, just to deter people from hanging around hoodlums or hookers." He took the last sip from the cup-top of the thermos and poured the last little bit. He looked at the bag Candy had taken.

She shook her head. "Long gone. I'm up past my bedtime—I needed some coffee."

The Squirt was still studying the parking lot. "So it really works?"

Hooker nodded. "Well enough—the city is considering retrofitting all the streetlights downtown to the low-sodium."

"But why—would the energy savings be enough to justify the retrofit?"

"It doesn't need to be. Even if each light could save them, say… twenty-eight cents a week… it's enough. What they really can't say is—they are doing it to discourage the girls from working the city."

The Squirt looked out at the lime green dot across the street. "So a guy gets a blowjob in a dark alley or some motel room. Who really gets hurt?"

"Well, why we are here is maybe a real wild card—but we still don't know how many women were taken from these streets and killed. On the other hand, there are drugs, pimps, and a whole handful of other crimes that circle around the simple blowjob in the doorway. But the biggest crime—in the city's eyes—is it's a business they can't collect taxes on."

Candy smirked. "So much for capitalism and the American spirit of entrepreneurialism."

Hooker bobbed his head slightly. "I'm just like Shawna and the rest—but they can tax me, so I'm allowed to still hook." He looked out across the street. The two girls got into a cab without its light lit. He knew they were calling it an early night. He looked back at Candy.

"Did you see anything of note?"

"Nothing really stood out. When the girls got picked up, it didn't look like they knew the person. It was very strange to watch. We are raised not to talk to strangers and don't get in the car with a man you don't know, and yet, this is the very nature of their business."

"So nothing stood out?"

She shoved the thermoses in the bag as she thought. She stopped, and she cocked her hip and head. "There was one thing. How often do you think the garbage person comes by?"

Hooker splayed his face. "Once or twice a week, maybe. Why?"

"Do you think it would always be the same guy?"

"I don't know." Hooker looked at the Squirt, who rolled his shoulders.

"Because one of the girls waved to him."

"Calling him over? Soliciting? What?"

"No… just a wave… like a hello or something."

Hooker looked at the kid. The Squirt shrugged and poked out his lower lip. The nod was one Hooker recognized as *I need to think about it…*

25

MEETING CRICKET

Hooker unwound the chain from around the axle of the service truck. The driver had said there was a loud whining noise that turned to gravel-in-a-cement-mixer—right before the back of the truck crashed to the asphalt after the bump in the road where Snell and Blossom Hill crossed. Hooker didn't have to look at the street to know the dip had shattered the last of the axle. The six-inch dip, designed for rain run-off that almost never came, had claimed many differentials, oil pans, engine mounts, and mufflers. As a small truck tow driver, Hooker almost wanted to kiss the designer of the dip for keeping him in constant money. But while driving the small truck, he was also susceptible to the same design. He had never consciously noticed the dip when he drove Mae, but the first time he hit it in the small truck at real speed, he hit his head on the ceiling. Lately, he had taken to wearing the seat belt.

"What you got, Hooker?" The short Japanese woman was third-generation American born in Watsonville, but the Fly found she could get away with more if she only spoke in pigeon English.

Hooker just shook his head before he turned around with a smile. "Fly, you aren't going to believe this… but I finally brought you a piece of shit. You slap a new rear end under this heap, and she will be as good as last Thursday."

She eyed the three or four-year-old service truck with her accountant's eye. Hooker almost swore he could hear the abacus beads clicking back and forth.

Finally, she waved her finger at the truck. "You take truck out. You go beat it up. Truck driver, he bad driver. You go sideswipe a few telephone poles then you bring back. Fly no want just rear-end job—no money for new shoes."

Hooker laughed. "I think Dog was parting out one of these service trucks just last week. Same year and model—heck, same company... but it was the one who got hit in the nose." He silently referenced the rear end still being good. He knew she would still charge for a new one.

"Okay, you leave here. Dog come get. I have car. It need go to Palo Alto. I only give you half—it a forty-dollar jerk job."

"North Palo Alto or south end?"

"Palo Alto—what difference?" Hooker knew full well she knew the difference was a ten-mile spread or a forty or fifty-mile tow. The difference could mean five to eight gallons of gas.

"I'm getting low on fuel..."

She glared at him, but the twinkle was always there. They knew each other too well. He knew she would always try to chisel, but he also knew she had a warm spot for him in the place her heart should have been—if it hadn't been replaced by the abacus.

She flipped her hand in the air as she turned back to the office. "Go fill up. But I only pay you twelve."

"Eighteen and a full tank it is."

She never turned around as she opened the door. "I said only fourteen—"

"Sixteen and a tank it is."

They both knew he would get paid fifteen.

Hooker chuckled as he threw the chains on the working deck and ran the boom up. The sparring on price and pay had started the first day they met. Hooker was new to the job and a fifteen-year-old filled with enough bluster to pull off making everyone believe he was nineteen or twenty. Nobody had warned him about the woman known as The Fly. He had pulled in a wrecked but repairable year-old Cadillac.

The bodywork alone was worth at least a grand, but there was also damage to the front axles that could add another grand. It was a cherry piece.

The Fly looked over the new kid and read him the riot act for dragging in a total wreck only worth fifty bucks to her. Hooker stood quietly. She had no idea he was scared. He blinked a couple of times, quietly turned, and got back in the truck.

She watched in amazement as a thousand-dollar job rolled back out the door.

Hooker drove around the corner to a phone booth he had seen earlier. He called his boss, Don.

"What do you want me to do with this Cadillac, Don?"

"Are you sure it's repairable?"

"Don, it got smacked on the left front quarter panel. It moved the grill and bumper. All of it has to be replaced. I think she could even sell a whole front clip. The damage to the front left axle will need a complete front suspension along with a new rim and tire. She might even sell a new right to balance the alignment that could be affected. Jeez mareez, Don, Willie could have this back on the road in a week for under two-hundred in used parts and a paint job."

Hooker heard the radio in the shop and his truck squawk at the same time.

"Just a minute, Hooker. She's on the radio. I guess she forgot you had a shop radio too."

Hooker listened to the radio conversation. If he didn't like Don before, he did after the conversation.

"Don… your new idiot… where he take my Cadillac?"

"Fly, you said you didn't want it… it was a total."

"I maybe figure something out… where he go?"

"He hauled it over to Capital Cadillac."

"You tell him to bring back now. I no want Capital get my wreck."

"I think he already dropped it, Fly."

"He not that fast. He new idiot. He no last. He stupid and don't know where he supposed to go with wrecks. He no good for you, Don. You call him and tell to bring car back to Fly, I make it worth you while."

"Well, Bill already called and said he would pay me three-fifty for it. There may even be something on the back side."

"You know Bill have no back side. Only Fly have back side. You bring back car."

"I don't know, Fly. My boy is probably in the office, and Bill is counting out seven Grants into his left hand right now."

"I know drivers. You call him. You get him back. I do better."

"How much better, Fly?"

"I pay you boy eight Grants."

"Well, let me see what I can do, Fly."

Hooker heard his main radio squawk, and then the shop radio rattled with static proceeding Don's voice. "1-4-1?"

Hooker slowly walked to the truck and leaned in. Grabbing the mic, he keyed the talk button. "1-4-1, go ahead?"

"What's your status on the Cadillac...?"

"I was just walking into the office to get the four hundred and eighty dollars. When he quoted you before, he didn't realize how new it was."

The silence on the radio was deafening. Hooker knew Don was laughing four miles away.

"Umm... 10-4. Umm... hold on a minute. I need to make a phone call before you get paid."

"10-4. Standing by. 1-4-1 out."

The Fly squealed the radio as she was nearly swallowing the microphone. "Don, you tell you boy bring it back. You no more play games. I give you ten Grants. He be back here in ten minutes."

Don ignored the woman. "Um, Hooker, how are you set for fuel? You might have to haul the Cadillac down to Gilroy."

"Let me see, Don... but I think I was down under a quarter tank... you know how these Chevys love to just suck gas."

The Fly was almost apoplectic. "Don, you no fool around anymore. You tell him bring to Fly. He be here in under ten minutes, Fly pay six hundred."

"He needs fuel too, Fly."

Hooker could almost hear the woman choking in the silence.

"Yeah, yeah... fuel too. He have nine and a half minutes left."

"Cash, Fly. And he gets the whole ten minutes."

Hooker took the turn onto San Jose Avenue. "1-4-1, show me 10-97 at the Fly body shop."

Hooker backed the car into the same spot it had been in only thirty minutes before. He got out of the truck and stood with his hand out. He expected the woman to come out screaming mad. He did not expect the woman who came out with the cash in her hand.

"You good. What you name?"

"Hooker."

"No, I know you a whore in a tow truck. What your name… what I call you?"

He stared her down, thinking about how much he would give away. "Horatio Octavius O'Keefer." Their eyes were locked.

"The Hor fits, but so does Hooker. You're smarter than you look. Why are you towing for Don?"

"Your pigeon English is slipping. You make a lot more money than you let on… so why are you trying to bust my chops? Don's a nice guy. He told me about his arrangement with you. If I bring you a piece of shit dog bone, you don't have to pay me. I'll try to pass those somewhere else. If it makes you money, you'll get it. But you treat Don and me right. The day you screw me or Don is the last day you will see a wreck on the end of my truck."

She smiled. "I knew it. I grew up in Watsonville. My great grandparents came here from Japan. I was born in Watsonville but learned how to talk in the camps." She wagged a finger back and forth between them. "You keep our secret, we get along."

"Deal. Now, where do you want this brick of gold, and where do I fill the tank?"

She pointed deep into the yard. "Stick the Caddy next to the white Ford truck, and the fueling is over near the gate. No more than twenty gallons. I'm not made of gold, you know."

Hooker smiled. "I'm only about half down. You got lucky today."

Hooker chuckled about the Cadillac day over ten years before. He clicked the nozzle a few times and topped off the second tank. The Fly had never let her pigeon English slip again—except when they were alone.

She had always haggled with Hooker, but never maliciously. They had always worked to better both of their bottom lines.

He walked into the office and sat down next to the desk she was sitting at. He knew she moved around the six desks in the office just to throw other people off. Hooker knew it had nothing to do with him.

"How bad?"

"I took thirty-four gallons."

"No… the truck."

"Like I said—three or four hours. Pull the rear-end off the other service truck. There is no way the insurance will ever sign off on fixing it. So the busted rear-end will fit right in with the rest of the scrap."

She always marveled at how much Hooker knew about fixing cars and how he could size wrecks up in a glance. She knew almost all of his knowledge he learned from his adoptive uncle. "How's Willie doing?"

"He's great. He and Hank just got back from relaxing up near Lake Tahoe. There is a small lake with some cabins. They like the rustic stuff."

She snorted. "Is rustic the code word for no room service?"

Hooker laughed. "Not after midnight."

"So the new man is working out okay for Willie?"

Hooker nodded with a soft smile. "Yeah, Hank is good for Willie. I think he has a good calming effect on him. I also haven't heard about Willie having the nightmares like he used to have."

She mirrored his smile. "He deserves some good in his life. He is one very special man. When are you seeing him next?"

"I need to take some paperwork up to him this afternoon. He's going down to Texas, and they want the specs on the new engine."

"I thought the engine had survived the explosion?"

"It did, but these friends of his want to put some new experimental oversized engine in her. They figure she's going to be a great test bed, and I'm a good test monkey."

The Fly knew her men. "How big of an engine?"

"Bigger than the sixteen-hundred I had before." He rolled his eyes huge and smiled.

She laughed and slapped his shoulder. "Oh, crap, Hooker. How we ever going to keep you down on the farm when you done seen the elephant?"

Hooker stood. "You won't, and I'll let Willie know you owe the swear jar fifty-cents."

"Only a quarter, but you give him a big hug for me."

"Should I kiss him behind the ear too?"

She laughed and shook her head. "I'll do the kissing part myself. Now get out of here so I can get some work done."

He was almost out the door when she added her usual money-grubbing line. "And you bring Fly more wrecks."

"I bring you all there are."

"Then you go make some more, Hooker. You slacking off."

He let the door slam before he started to laugh.

HOOKER NOSED the truck up onto the oversized concrete apron the size of most backyards. He eyed the two motorcycles parked in front of the giant door to the barnlike garage. He had never thought much about how his world consisted of large items. The scale of the two motorcycles heightened the domination.

The garage originally was designed to hold large dirigibles at the start of the century. The Navy built two of the larger hangers at Moffett Field, of which only Hanger One still stood. The eight smaller hangers, which were only an acre in footprint, were never erected. After Willie's retirement from the Navy—and feeling a need for a large indoor space to work on many auto projects at one time, he pulled strings and bought one of the hangars, which had been mothballed for well over twenty years. Almost burning down his house only led to the excuse to build an entire remodel of the structure.

The construction started with an old buddy with some old toys bought at a government auction. The D-8 Cat had made quick work of what was left of the house, and the man's new company of ex-Seabees soon had the property prepared for the new structure. The two items left in place and in working order were the swimming pool and the propane barbecue newly rigged to a five-hundred-gallon tank. The rest was just home remodeling.

The concrete pad for the new house was nothing more than a bump off the acre of twelve-inch thick concrete for the approach apron and the garage. All the concrete had suspended loops of copper pipe, which were eventually filled with hot, warm, or cool water—depending on the temperature needed for comfort and the season.

Once the concrete was ready, the area flooded with young sailors from the base who knew about construction. Some had erected one of the hangars before. Ostensibly, they were there to erect the hanger and leave —a job which should have taken a couple of weeks. The presence of a nonstop barbecue and a ready swimming pool had a delaying effect lasting the entire summer. Nobody cared if they were swimming in their undershorts or commando—Willie liked the look either way.

Willie's being well-liked on Moffett Field helped with the young Seabees and engineers borrowing needed materials from the base as they needed them. The base commander turned a blind eye to the requisitioning of material from the other four hangers stacked at the end of his runway. As a control measure, he also found time to come supervise from the shade of the large tent erected along the pool and next to the barbecue. A pint jar of clear liquid or a set of tongs for turning steaks was usually close at hand.

The acre of backyard had turned into a tent city of canopies. There were plenty of cots for those who took part in the clear liquid and spent the night.

By the first rains, the three-bedroom house was snugly overshadowed by the garage with giant doors forty feet square at both ends. By Halloween, the temperature in the garage was a toasty seventy-two degrees provided by a floor whose temperature neared ninety. Willie and Hooker were happily in new beds in a new home much to their liking. The true celebration for William Knight and his best friend Maddie Robinson was in the proper living room—an acre of concrete, filled with everything cars, trucks, and motorcycles.

Hooker parked the tow truck next to the motorcycles. As he walked toward the open door, he studied the motorcycle he had never seen before. The motor was a Triumph, but the frame was all wrong. It was low-slung like an older Harley or Indian. The back had a spring set-up providing a softer ride. The whole was modified and on the verge of being a hybrid of a racer like Maddie's Matchless and a chopper—right down to the short sissy bar on the back. There was a small roll tied down over the small front light, and a larger pack affair bungee strapped to the sissy bar. Hooker knew it wasn't one of Maddie's motorcycles because of the road grime that looked over a week old.

Willie's voice echoed in the garage, "We have shine..."

Hooker could tell Willie was already rosy-cheeked deep into the moonshine. Whoever had come with Maddie obviously didn't care if Willie was in pants or his usual dress—ugly, paisley, with burn holes from sparks picked up from welding or body grinding on one project or another.

Hooker took one more look at the black with red flames Triumph. He tucked the engine schematics under his left arm and rested his hands in his pockets as he walked into the dark garage. From thirty feet away, Hooker could tell the dress was one of the more offensive ones Uncle Willie had dragged home from the Goodwill store in a long time.

"Interesting new motorcycle you dragged over, Maddie. It looks like it was designed by Datsun and Leland but built by Fiat. Does it actually run?"

"Be nice, Hooker. We have a guest."

The young woman rose. Hooker was wondering where they made cute looking miniatures of Max. From the black cowboy boots to the white T-shirt over the jeans, she could be Hooker's relative. But the leather jacket stuffed into a cutoff jean jacket with patches screamed biker. The softly held reddish-brown ponytail fell just below her shoulders. Her face was young with a hint of freckles, but her stance was of someone much older —experienced.

He stuck his hand out. "Hi, I'm Hooker."

"Cricket, Cricket Street... happy to finally meet the topic of our conversation."

Hooker groaned. "Don't believe anything these two tell you. It's probably all true, but blown way out of proportion."

She snorted. "Yeah, I bet that's just as much bullshit as what they were slinging."

Hooker stopped pumping her hand. "Do you have a quarter?"

"Sure..."

"It goes in the swear jar."

She held his gaze as she thought for a moment and then pulled a wallet from her hip pocket. Pulling a hundred dollar bill out, she handed it to Hooker. "I live with two bikers who are undercover cops. About a hundred cops and firefighters wander in and out of our house twenty-four seven, and the place is a sea of high-test macho testosterone. Besides which, I sleep with a fourteen-foot-long snake who outweighs me by at least sixty pounds. I don't think I'll be changing my language anytime soon. If this doesn't cover everything by the time I leave, let me know—I have more where that fucking came from."

Hooker broke her gaze and looked to Willie. The man was unfazed. He simply nodded his head toward the door to the house as if to say *Go stick it in the jar. You just got one-upped.*

Hooker took the bill and turned for the house. "I'll leave the schematics in on the table."

Maddie stopped him. "Just leave them here. I want to go over them before we eat. Hank is out on the barbecue. Go say hi after you change the filthy shirt."

Hooker pulled his shirt around and looked at the large grease mark. "Damn..."

Cricket giggled. "You can take the quarter out of my hundred."

Hooker looked back at her and saw no malice. He bobbed his head. "Thanks."

The plates were cleaned, and the five sat around the large table made from a tail wing off a P-3 Orion sub chaser. The gift came from Moffett field flight wing as a belated retirement memento, and a thank you for the continuing friendship Willie showed the base and all who worked there.

Cricket pushed her plate a small bit forward and sipped on her lemonade. "Wow... the food was perfect, Hank. And I finally got a whole steak to myself."

Hooker frowned. "Why don't they let you have much meat?"

She laughed. "We have a big-assed commercial refrigerator-freezer at the house. The freezer is stuffed with steaks and some fish or hamburgers for the wimps."

"Then why not have a whole steak?" Hooker noticed the other three were holding their mouths—trying not to laugh.

"Because I always end up sharing it with the snake I sleep with."

"You were serious about the snake…"

Both Willie and Maddie nodded. "We've seen her. And she wasn't exaggerating about any of it… not the cops, not the refrigerator, and certainly not about the size of Gertie."

Hooker's mouth fell open. "What kind of cage do you keep her in?"

Cricket wagged her head as she chuffed a laugh. "The house and yard. They are hers to roam. She has never crossed the street or gone over the fence. The people who feed her are where she is, and the kids in the neighborhood come to her in the front yard—so she doesn't have to chase them. She is happy where she is."

"Does she eat the kids?"

"They don't taste good. She just stretches out on the grass after we mow it, and the kids love to pet her."

"What do the mother's think about her? I mean… she is one big snake."

"For the most part, they don't come close. Gertie is a lesbian… a very aggressive lesbian. She loves the smell of females, which is why she sleeps with me. I also think she would protect my father or me if she needed to."

"You mentioned your father before…"

"He's an undercover special investigator for the US Attorney General in Los Angeles. He just looks like a six-foot-six three-hundred-pound biker."

"Which would explain your bike out front and…" Hooker slowly waved his hand up and down pointing out her clothes.

"Both carry a certain understanding."

"Nobody asks you out?" Hooker snickered at his teasing.

Her face was anything but amusement. "Exactly."

He thought for a moment. "Seriously…"

Maddie slurred only slightly. "Why not. She's cute and obviously alone… and she will be going to a big college next month…" She left the obvious hanging in the air.

"So you're just up here taking a break before school?"

"Visiting Maddie and learning…"

"Library stuff…?"

Willie broke his silence with a hacking laugh. He looked at Cricket. "Can I borrow some of those hundred dollars?" She nodded, so he turned to Hooker. "So there, my boy is where you just screwed the pooch."

Willie's swearing set Hank to laughing. Hank's laughing set off Maddie, and as much as Hooker liked seeing the three have a good laugh —he knew it was at his expense.

He looked at the only other person—and she wasn't laughing. "Obviously, I misspoke."

"It's okay. That is exactly why I dress like my dad and ride the most kick-ass bike I can get my legs over. Perception is sometimes more powerful than reality. You see the wild chopper and the hard-assed biker bitch… and then just assume…" She smiled sweetly, and Hooker realized he had misjudged her age.

"You're not my age at all." He glared at the other three who were still trying to get themselves under control.

"No, I'm not. I turned seventeen only two months ago."

"And… my mistake was assuming you were learning something feminine from Maddie—such as working in a library." He put his face in his hands as she nodded.

Maddie snorted a half-drunk growling laugh.

"Without my boots, Maddie is four or five inches taller than me. I'm only five-foot—with two pairs of thick socks. I weigh just under ninety-four pounds, but I'm working on it with many steaks and weight training. But no… I don't want to work in a library. I'm challenging as many courses as I can at UCLA, and I hope I can start law school next fall. I'm sure I will have to take a few classes before then."

"Wait… you're challenging four years of college courses?"

She laughed. "In high school, I was a straight four-point-oh student. I have already taken some advanced placement classes at Pasadena City College. But my future uncle challenged all of his high school in a summer and most of his undergraduate work in the fall. He started med school at age sixteen. I have a great tutor to prep me."

"So what do you want to do?"

"First, I want my law degree…"

"And then what?" The other three were now working hard to learn about this enigma of a young girl.

"I don't know. My dad has his degree—he even finally took the bar exam—but is still doing what he did before."

Willie cleared his throat. "Undercover." She nodded. "I met him when he was fresh out of the Marines. He bought Maddie's old bike the night I met him. He took it for a test ride up the LA River toward Sylmar."

Cricket snorted. "I hate those tar seams. They liked to tear me up the first time I ran the Triumph up there."

Maddie smiled. "How fast?"

"First couple of times I kept it around ninety. The speedometer was the original off a Norton and only went to one-twenty. When I made the last run, I broke it."

Maddie nodded. "What's Roscoe building for you now?"

Cricket smiled. "Of course, you would know Roscoe and Honey. He has a bottom end of an old K-1, and he's casting new heads to make it around eighty-inches with Shovelhead tops. He's doing some horse-trading to get me a late forties Indian Scout frame and front-end. He thinks by stretching it about two inches, he can shoehorn it all in and add an oil radiator. It should be good for about one-seventy or one-eighty—good enough to keep up with Dad and Uncle Rabbit."

Hooker snorted. "You're here to learn how to ride fast bikes."

The freckled cheeks pooched up with her smile. "Actually, I'm here to learn how to crash safely."

Maddie nodded soberly. "Any fool can go fast. The real trick is knowing how to survive."

"Like stepping off in the salt flats at a hundred miles-per-hour."

Cricket chimed in, "Roscoe said it was more like one-fifty."

Maddie mumbled something as she waved her hand in dismissal.

Willie, without thinking, added the definitive answer. "The crash froze the speedometer at one-eighty-seven."

When Maddie backhanded Willie's chest, Hank knew it was time to put them all to bed. He stood and drew Willie up. "Cricket, if you would, Hooker can help you bring the motorcycles inside. You can use the Squirt's bed, and Maddie can use Hooker's. I washed all the sheets yesterday, so they are nice and clean." He straightened and blinked to clear his vision. "G'night." They stumbled off.

Cricket sat and watched Maddie follow the two men into the house part of the complex. She turned back and frowned at Hooker.

"You sleep with Maddie?"

Hooker chuckled once softly. "Not hardly. I live in two places. My other family and bed are across the valley." He realized what he was saying was even more complicated. "It's complicated, but nobody is really *family*. Uncle Willie more like took me under his wing than adopted me. A couple of years later, things were kind of rough around here. I was taken in by a couple—Manny and Stella. Manny was a detective on San Jose Police. They took me in because I wasn't given a choice. Stella's sister is, if anyone is, my mother, and she demanded I go live there. Maddie can explain it all sometime when she's sober... or better yet, if you're still around this Sunday, we can have a family barbecue out at the Hacienda, and you can meet the whole family."

"Whose?"

"Whose what?"

"Whose family?"

Hooker sat back. He had never thought about it. He thought about all the connections, and the only single lynchpin was him. "I guess… it would be mine. But we are all one family."

"So you're adopted, but not legally?"

"I was just going on fourteen when I tried to hot-wire Willie's DeSoto. He smacked me on the butt with his mail and told me to scoot over. He took me to lunch because if I were trying to steal a car—I must be hungry. It was the most official we ever made it."

"And the dress?"

Hooker put his face in his hands. "Oh, gawd. He always chooses the ugliest ones. He does it because he thinks it bothers me—it doesn't. But he buys them by the garbage bag full at Goodwill. They cost him about a quarter each. He pays rag price. So when he burns one up, it's not a big deal. A pair of bib-overalls cost about three dollars and jeans are two."

"Makes sense."

"If I remember right—and possibly don't, but the cop who got Maddie's bike down in LA is not much older than me…"

Cricket smirked. "So how does he have a seventeen-year-old daughter?"

"Yeah…"

"It's more complicated than you and Willie… but he adopted me two days after my seventeenth birthday. The same day I got emancipated from my birth parents." Hooker could tell by her face, the original family was not a pleasant affair.

He nodded gently. "My sister and I grew up in the dark side of foster homes and were sold from abusers to abusers until we ran away. My girl-friend, Candy, and her little brother, Squirt had the same—I guess it's why we understand each other so well."

"Abuse, beatings or…"

"All the above."

"I'll be around for a couple of weeks. Your family is the kind I think I would like to meet."

Hooker stood. "Just don't bring the snake."

They laughed as they went to move the motorcycles.

"So only five-foot, huh?"

"I hear you have a big truck… when you aren't blowing it up."

"You're going to fit into the family just fine."

"That's what Hank said."

"Hank is a smart man."

"So tell me about the scar on Willie's neck."

"You can ask Maddie about the medal just inside the door when she's sober in the morning."

"So what were they drinking, Vodka?"

"Worse… White Lightning. Maddie's family makes it down Salinas way."

"I think I'm liking this family more and more…"

"They grow on you."

"I've got room to grow."

26

OUT ON THE DECK AT THE HACIENDA

The heavy metal of the industrial barbecue was ticking as it cooled down. The dinner, for the most part, was done. Only the watermelon-strawberry mousse dessert was left to serve and eat.

Stella came through the door with a small tray of only six cut-crystal glasses. "Here we are… Mom's famous all summer mousse." Each of the delicate glasses full of the whipped pink mousse had a pair of handmade chocolate antlers stuck in the pudding.

A few of the diners looked at the small tray of only six delicate crystal parfait glasses with longing faces. Stella ceremoniously set one of the glasses in the center of each round table of eight dinners. "First person to touch one of my masterpieces of delicate work which took me all day to make… has to wash the dishes."

All eyes snapped back to the door with Danny's booming rumble of a voice. "But who wants some dessert?" His arms were spread wide with a large serving tray filled with larger bowls. Each heaped with the fluffy delight, which some risked putting coins into the swear jar by calling pink farts. As delightful the taste, there seemed the whipped gelatin desert had no body to it—but it did taste like summer. Maddie and Candy jumped up to help pass out the large colorful Fiestaware bowls. Cricket wasn't sure if it was her place but joined in. As she started to place the dessert in front of certain people, they laughed and covered their placemats. Finally, she noticed they would take it from Maddie or Candy… but instead of getting mad, she asked Manny why he wouldn't take it from her.

Manny laughed and reached out and grabbed her waist. Reeling her in for a hug, he started pointing out the guys who wouldn't take it from her. "He's a cop, he's a cop, he's a cop, he's an ex-cop, he's a fireman, he's close to being a cop, and the Squirt we're not sure about." He looked up at her and smiled. "I'm diabetic, and if I'm going to eat one, it's going to be the tiny centerpiece. But those guys… no cop wants to be served by a lawyer —even if she is years away from being one." The party erupted in laughter.

Being a good sport, she leaned over and gave him a hug. "Thanks. I guess I broke the first rule of litigating. I didn't know the answer before I asked the question."

"You're going to be fine. Now leave the bowl and go tell on me to Stella so she can bring me some insulin. Tell her I snitched both antlers off the centerpiece."

"But they're both there…"

"Not for long… so run along." He swatted her bottom, and she giggled. As he watched her wend through the crowd, he thought, *another kid*. It put a smile on his face.

Paul looked down at his bowl and spoke as much to the dessert as he did to his old partner. "There is a lot to like there…"

Manny nodded. He knew their conversation was theirs alone as their low voices were lost in the rest of the conversations. "Ever think about not having kids?"

"I used to… but not anymore."

Manny looked over at the county supervisor and closest friend. "Why not now?"

He gently smiled as he nudged his jaw toward the young girl returning with the insulin kit. "Because when I feel like having some, I know I can borrow some of yours." He chuckled silently as he turned and smirked at his friend.

Cricket stopped and held onto the kit. "Where do you want it… butt, thigh or arm? I can do it between your toes also."

Manny frowned. "Are you diabetic too?"

"Nah, but a few of the cops are. I was thinking about becoming a doctor, so they thought it was good practice. Actually, most doctors don't even know how to give a shot or draw blood. I know how to do all three."

Now Paul frowned. "Shot or draw blood is only two. Where do you get three?"

She counted on her fingers. "Shot is one, draw a blood sample is two, and..." Her right hand flashed to her belt just right of her buckle, and there appeared a thin four-inch blade in her hand. "And then, there is spilling blood."

Manny and Paul both looked at the blade and the implication of it even being secreted on her body. Her only being seventeen spoke, even more, volumes about the nature of the defensive tactic. The way she had produced it showed this not to be a childish show-off trinket or whimsy.

Manny rubbed his chin. "I'll take the needle in the arm, please. How many knives do you have?"

She stepped over and took out the already measured syringe. She peeled open the alcohol patch and rubbed down his deltoid muscle toward the back. As she stuck the needle in, she answered softly. "Only the one... for now. A guy across the street is a Marine but used to be in a street gang. He's been teaching me how to use the knives and throw them. He's working on a belt that will give me four, and maybe I'll get some boots made giving me four more."

Paul rolled to one side to better look at the small young woman. "Is there a need?"

She sat down and closed the insulin kit. "I don't know... but it's a feeling I have. It is the same sort of feeling, and why I'm up here learning how to crash and ride fast from Maddie. I mean... who learns how to have an accident?"

"It's not learning to have one. It's learning to be prepared when one occurs." They all looked up at Hooker and the Squirt. The Squirt leaned over with his hand out. "Hi, we weren't introduced earlier. My name is John, but everyone calls me the Squirt."

She smiled. "The fucking new guy."

He nodded. "But it just seemed to fit. So I'll probably be like the seventy-year-old guy they call Junior or JR."

She screwed up her face with her eyes closed and began to recite a long string of numbers. "One point six, one, eight, zero, three, four." She opened her eyes and looked at him.

He smiled. "It was the Golden Mean of Euclid as confirmed by Aristotle. Leonardo De Vinci called it the Divine Proportion. Later, it was used to define the Golden Rectangle, which is the most pleasing proportions to the eye in architecture and shape of a painting."

She smiled and shied her face in query. "But...?"

He laughed. "The modern painters' canvases are the right proportions, but when you put them in a picture frame, the proportions are destroyed."

"Eidetic memory is very rare. Maddie showed me the paper you wrote on the Golden Rectangle... it was impressive. I wrote a similar one a year ago... I got my knuckles rapped with a ruler for heretic ascription for one of God's beauties." She rolled her eyes. "Someday, you will have to come to Los Angeles and meet my future uncle. Do you have to read the address or can I just tell you?"

He smiled. "You can just tell me. What does he do?"

"He just started med school."

"So he's Hooker's age..."

"No, he's my age. He challenged all of high school and most of his undergraduate work. He has been prepping me to challenge at least the first two years of undergrad work. But he is visual, so he has to read it or at least see it. He learned most of the American Sign Language in two days."

The men all gave a low whistle. She nodded and then gave the Squirt the address and phone numbers for the house and the restaurant.

Hooker cleared his throat. "Listen, you said something the other night —about perception."

She nodded. "About it being more powerful than knowing... yes, I remember."

"Well, we have this case we're working on—"

She cut him off. "The body dump in the bay. Yes, Maddie spoke some about it, but we also stopped in to meet Dolly. There was a bald Sheriff's deputy—"

"Uncle Fester. He was the first responder. Well, he was there for the wreck… then we found the skeleton together."

"But there is another person who is the killer?"

Hooker held up his finger and looked down a couple of tables. He clicked his tongue and watched as Sweets' head jerked around as well as Danny's. Hooker crooked his finger at Danny. Danny leaned over and spoke to Sweets. The two rose as one and came over.

"Sweets, Danny, I think you met Cricket earlier. Pull up a seat. We're going over the case and what we know and observed. I hope she can see what we are not seeing." Sweets turned and gawped at Hooker in mock shock.

Hooker growled. "Oh, shut up and sit down. I'll go get Candy."

Cricket snickered. "Make mine chocolate, please."

Hooker scowled at her in misunderstanding. And then rolled his head in zombie fall and walked off.

Cricket turned to Manny. "What was the head and dead look thing?"

Manny rolled his eyes. "It's shorthand around here for a stupid question or not realizing the chocolate and Candy reference. Some of us have been damaged enough, and so we don't like smacking ourselves in the forehead. Ask Hooker. It was something he and his sister started as small kids."

"With a family gathering this big—I expected to meet her."

"She'll come down for Christmas. She lives with friends about a hundred miles north of here."

Cricket slumped slightly. "I think we are going to be in Brazil then."

Hooker and Candy returned holding hands. Cricket sized up the body posture. It wasn't your usual relationship handhold. It had a lot more *us against the world* than just lovebirds. It was as if they drew strength from each other's presence. She could relate, and her lap suddenly was missing the heavyweight of her snake. Hooker sat, and Candy snuggled between Hooker and her brother. Cricket recognized a wall of force when she saw it.

"So, we will start with what we know, and as we go through it, stop us at any time and ask questions or make suggestions."

Manny pushed up on his chair. "Wouldn't it be better to have the whiteboard?"

The Squirt jumped up. "Good idea. I'll get it as you go over the initial discovery."

Soon, the large gathering had pushed tables around and rearranged the deck so they could all see the whiteboard and the rapidly growing lines of information. Cops, firefighters, or those just loosely associated with law enforcement made up most of the gathering. No matter their job, the detective work and how it developed through Hooker and the family was of interest to all.

Cricket pulled her legs up into the large chair as she leaned forward. "So wipe out all the cars driving by. What we need is who stopped—someone they might know—regular customers. And what is a Cushman?"

Candy looked back and smiled. "It's one of those little three-wheel carts like a golf cart. Only, instead of golf bags, this one has a truck bed kind of thing the garbage man puts the bags of garbage in and takes them to a larger collection place."

"Oh... Thanks. I think it's the same system they have in San Marino. They have a fleet of little carts running up the long driveways of the mansions—so the rich people don't have to haul their trash to the curb or suffer seeing their neighbor's garbage. Okay, so we have someone getting a blowjob while they have a cigarette break. Some people from the college walking around. Several cars driving through the area—few stop, and a garbage man collecting the day's trash before it starts to stink up the area. But no one they seemed to know."

Candy started to put up her finger... but her face was still screwed up trying to work out what it was Cricket had said... wrong... or not quite right.

Sweets' head suddenly twitched, and Danny jerked and studied him. Sweets reached out and held on to Danny's arm and just softly hummed to himself. Danny knew he was working through a memory or something he had seen in one of his visions.

Sweets' head swiveled. "What did you just say?"

Candy jumped. "I didn't…"

"No, the other… Cricket. What did you say about the garbage man?"

"I said he drives around and puts the garbage in the cart and hauls it away?"

Sweets was disturbed. It wasn't right… he searched. His head swung about. "Squirt?"

"Yeah?"

His head swung around and locked on. "What exactly did she say?"

The Squirt's eyes rolled back, and he searched for the right moment. "The blowjob, the cars, nobody stopping… and then a garbage man collecting the day's trash before it starts to stink up the area."

Sweets rolled his finger and hand in the air, "But after… "

"But no one they seemed to know…"

Sweets pointed. "Which… is wrong. Candy said the garbage dude waved to the girls on First."

Candy stiffened. "Oh, my lord. The one girl did wave back. But it seemed so natural. It was like a side wave from her hip. It was a… a… friendship wave, not a flirty wave."

Sweets leaned back and smiled. "And I told you about the smell. It was the same as when Danny took out the garbage from under the sink every day… it's fresh…" He pointed directly at Cricket. "Before it stinks up the place."

"But how would you know about the smell?" Cricket furrowed her brow.

Manny leaned over and rested his hand on her arm. Quietly, he muttered, "It's a very long story for another time."

Sweets smiled. "Because I smelled it before. There is your killer—the garbage dude."

Hooker wasn't convinced. "What about what Tess said about the Waterman having a female twin? She was the one who attacked Tess."

Chet looked up from where he had been quietly enjoying the evening with his blonde date. "Maybe there is a third person in this party…"

Cricket had talked with Chet and the shrink for a while when they first arrived. She liked the man and his lady friend. "Captain, do you have any female officers?"

Micha snorted and called out to his boss. "She sounds a lot like Dolly."

Chet rolled his eyes and nodded with a lopsided smile of agreement. "We are implementing new guidelines from Sacramento with some of the new recruits from this new hiring cycle."

Cricket swung around. "Candy, are there any male nurses or female doctors?"

"Both."

"So why assume a garbage collector you only saw from... what? A block away—is a dude?"

Paul's one eyebrow rose as he looked past Cricket at his old partner. But he addressed the young woman. "Are you sure you want to become a lawyer? You think more like a cop."

Her head ground around as she growled. "I'm also only five feet tall. And they don't make bulletproof vests in size zero."

"Pity... I'm just saying."

"You change the requirements and give me a call. The Squirt has our number at the frat house."

"Frat house?"

Manny leaned back and looked to his partner. "The house she lives in has a commercial coffee pot and a large freezer full of steaks and no lock on the back door. The local LEOs are in and out around the clock."

Paul smiled. "Frat house."

Hooker cleared his throat and pointed at the whiteboard.

Cricket nodded. "Any way to find out who the garbage person is?"

Stella stood. "On it..." She padded into the house. Six minutes later, she came out reading from a small piece of paper. "Her name is Petunia Scarsdale, like the city in New York. She goes by the name Pete."

Later, as the party was breaking up and people were leaving, Hooker sat down next to Cricket. "It's a shame you aren't staying. You do have a good mind for this stuff."

"I think you're selling your family short. I don't think any major crimes unit in any large city has the experience, talent, and special skills of the team or family you have surrounded yourself with. Manny told me about Sweets and how he sees things. That is amazing enough, but then you live with the Squirt and Manny, which is not to dismiss Willie and his intelligence background."

"Don't leave out Maddie…"

"I've adopted her as my official aunt. There is a lot there that I'm sure most of us will never know. My time here has been amazing."

"When do you head back?"

"I'll catch the train tomorrow night."

"Why so soon?"

"Roscoe said he will have my new chopper ready Wednesday. And you can only crash a Triumph so many times. The last one this afternoon—the asphalt and wall won. Maddie didn't think there were any parts to salvage… but you never know about Willie and his creative welding."

"Are we going to see you again?"

"I'd like to bring Dad up. I think he would enjoy spending some time picking Manny's brain. And the ride was nice."

"We have room to put you guys up, downstairs. When I'm here, Candy doesn't spend much time in her apartment. So you two can stay as long as you want. If it's cop talk and investigation, the time would be good for Manny, as well. Just don't bring the snake."

Cricket snorted a giggle. "Gertie doesn't travel. She has a house full of cops to keep straight. But the family may soon be four or five of us."

"Well, you are welcome anytime. Two or six… we'll find room here or at Willie's."

"So you really do float back and forth?"

"Not as much as I used to. I like being here with Candy, and the Squirt has pretty much made his nest here too. But I still stay over at the boy shack enough to keep Willie and Hank on their best behavior."

She gave an amateurish zombie roll of her head. "Right, but at least the dress tonight wasn't one of the ugly paisley ones."

Hooker lowered his one eye. "The jean patchwork dress was the Squirt's idea. He told Willie it had more of the go-to town look."

She laughed. "Panache."

Hooker looked at his watch but then remembered it was Sunday. Shawna probably didn't work, and it was too late to go by the Stick and Balls. He would swing by Monday evening.

27

BUT FIRST

ooker was a mile away. Fewer than five minutes even with the traffic. The right turn was in his sight.

"1-4-1, I'm holding a multiple-vehicle pile-up… Southbound 101, just south of Blossom Hill, but Micha says to forget trying to get there from Blossom Hill. He suggests dropping to Santa Teresa and come back. You will have to come up on the southbound lanes as the northbound is already jammed up halfway to Coyote."

Hooker had reached for the switches for the lights and siren before he realized those were only in Mae West. His right hand pawed useless on the smooth metal under the dashboard.

"Oh, hell." He grabbed the mic as he took a right. "10-4, it's going to take a while. I'm in the pig."

"10-4, Hooker—we feel the frustration from here. Chet just called and said Almaden to Santa Tee and out, was clear, but to please keep it under sixty or so."

"Thanks, Karen. Tell auto club I'm probably done for the day."

"We already told Motorbody and the club dispatch. Don is picking up the Chevy just in case. There are a couple of elephants in the zoo, so I called Jose, and he's on his way up the back way. He said to get started, and he'll be there in an hour."

Hooker straightened out on Almaden Expressway and switched on his rotating yellows and the flashers. "Micha, have a count...?"

"Rapid read was double arms and three legs. We have seven meat wagons coming to the party and fire is just arriving. Five known log-outs so far."

"10-4." He hung the microphone. He turned the volume down on the auto club radio. He knew the only radio he wanted to hear was the shop. It was the only one Dispatch, and he could talk freely on.

The double arms meant over twenty cars with the legs being larger trucks or buses. Seven ambulances meant there would be many injuries and five dead bodies with just the first look-over. The elephants or large trucks were usually double trailers, which could mean some serious money. Late in the summer, the crashes are few, and real money starts to look like something a tow driver won't see until the rains come. This large of an accident on clean hot pavement was rare and always serious.

Every tow driver out there feels for the people involved, but to keep it from becoming overwhelming, they only think about the money and how to tow what, and how many they can get. Hooker had once even watched a driver hook up the back end of a CHP car with the light bar lit up. The guy tried to explain he had been tired and wasn't paying attention.

Hooker wound through the traffic and crossed Blossom Hill. Two lights further down, he would then turn left.

"1-4-1, pull over."

What? He snapped the mic up and keyed it. "1-4-1, say again?"

"1-4-1, we didn't say anything."

The siren behind him blipped. Hooker looked in the mirror. He realized the talking wasn't over the radio at all.

"Pull over, Hooker."

He nosed to the curb. In his right rearview mirror, he saw the Squirt jump out of the squad car. He ran to the passenger door and jumped in. "You thought you could go to a big hoedown without me?" Hooker liked his smile.

Hooker cleared the mirrors as the squad car pulled out in front of them with lights and siren.

"Bill is going to clear Santa Teresa for us, but the new rules say he has to keep it under eighty."

Hooker snorted as he jammed the gears into third. "Man, I hope this pig can keep up."

The Squirt grunted. "So have you thought about stepping on the gas pedal?"

Hooker blew a raspberry with his lips as he watched the creeping needle claw its way to the midpoint marked with a large sixty. He knew the manufacturer had been dreaming or just laughing when they installed a speedometer marked to one-twenty.

"When does the new rendition of Mae West rise from the ashes?"

"They decided the new Desert Eagle engine wouldn't perform as well with the new configuration of triple axles—so they're building an engine from the ground up. They won't even know what the true horsepower is until…" He paused as he wrestled the truck around a large sweeping curve he had driven Mae around many times with a single finger. "This pig wallows like a whale… I sure hope Don likes it." He downshifted as he saw the patrol car turn left to head for the highway. "So they have to get the engine in Mae and throw it all on some giant dyne-o-tune machine to even find out what the horsepower is at the rear end."

"What are they hoping for?"

A FEW MILES LATER, they slowed to turn north onto the southbound lanes of the highway. They both glanced south. They could see over a mile of standing traffic. People stood in small groups—talking and looking north.

They had seen this before. "It's going to be a long day."

"Maybe it won't be so bad."

As they came around the one last jog in the highway, their view was of static mass pandemonium. Hooker let out a low whistle. "Dante painted this."

The Squirt's eyes danced over the mass and calculated cars, directions, towing lanes. "No—right idea, just the wrong painter. This work is pure Hieronymus Bosch."

Hooker glanced at the Squirt. He wasn't sure if the kid knew his true name… but he didn't put it past him. He smiled and returned his attention to the officer waving them down. "Yeah, I should be more mindful of keeping my names straight."

They pulled alongside the black officer sweating like a pro basketball player in the final minutes. "Hey, Micha, I thought you were used to this heat."

Micha bit his lower lip. Hooker noted the strained look around his eyes. He had a job to do and would never shy from his responsibility, but Hooker saw his friend was now hurting.

Hooker lowered his voice. "How bad?"

Micha glanced north into the carnage. "Too many prom queens, and this one… we have a baby… the mom was holding it in her arms."

Hooker knew the dynamics of an eight-pound baby becoming a one-ton projectile at the sudden stop from thirty or forty. He could only imagine what would happen with a car traveling at sixty. He scanned over the field of twisted metal.

"Where did it end up?"

"On the dashboard… of the camper they rear-ended…" Micha's voice was shaky, and he looked away. He and Hooker had too much history for his hiding his tears, but…

"Where do you want us to start, Micha?"

The man indicated their area and south. "We need to build a buffer zone."

"10-4." Hooker cleared his mirrors and started backing to turn around. He backed onto the side and turned the truck south. As they came to the last damaged car, he pulled onto the shoulder.

Both dropped open their side compartments and pulled out the large boxes of thirty-minute flares. "Stuff your pockets, but let's hold off lighting them up. We'll turn this herd around and head them back toward Coyote Road, and the Chips can set up the detour later."

Hooker took the newish Ford pickup truck with the young couple in work clothes. The Squirt in his uniform took the white Cordoba and its beefy driver with an angry red face. Reluctantly, the line started making the U-turn and headed south to the exit.

As they slowly walked south, waving the retreating line into a continuous U-turn, they continued their personal conversation.

"Is it possible to get that much horsepower out of a standard-sized engine?"

"You tell me. Maddie had you do some wild research reports."

"Nothing I ever ran across. The stuff I was researching sounded more like the racetrack crazy Maddie and Willie would be doing. Those monster engines are built for speed—but with short lifespans."

"I don't know… it is beyond my understanding too. Maddie went over the schematics the other night and again the next day. She talked to her brother Ben… and they seem comfortable with the whole idea. Either way, we will always have the Eagle here as a swap-out backup."

"Hmm…" The Squirt stared at the woman in the Corvette, who seemed to have a hard time understanding why she couldn't just drive straight. After all, she was headed to San Jose or San Francisco… and she was in her expensive car, with her hair all done up in the new style giant Dutch-boy flip…

Hooker was holding the VW, waiting on the Corvette as she finally huffed and puffed herself into turning around… but she wasn't going to like it.

"Did you hear anything new this morning up at the office about finding the garbage collector?"

"They went to the address she had on her application and her driver's license—"

Hooker snorted. "Empty building, wrong person, or no such address…?"

The Squirt chuffed. "You've been at this way too long—electrical transfer station."

"So what now?"

The Squirt glanced over at Hooker and gave him a smarmy smile.

"What?"

"CHP and the Sheriff want to throw it back into our hands."

Hooker took a double-take. "Are you serious?"

"We do have a certain reputation… and we don't care about county lines or jurisdictions…"

The CHP cruiser pulled out from Coyote Road and onto the shoulder. The officer stepped out and opened his trunk. Grabbing a box of flares, he walked over to Hooker and the Squirt.

"Hey, Heinz, did they wake you up or just call you back from fishing?"

"Neither. The wife's cousin wound up at Good Sam early this morning with some kind of woman issues, and so I was there with them." He handed the box to the Squirt and jabbed his chin up the highway. "How bad…?"

The Squirt turned around so the man could pull the four flares out of his back pocket. Hooker growled softly. "You don't want to come up. Just stay here in the sun. You'll be better off tonight."

The man grabbed the four out of Hooker's pocket as well. "There are six more boxes in the trunk—leave me at least two."

"I'll leave you four. You're going to need them before midnight."

The officer sighed. "Thanks."

Hooker was wrong. The traffic finally started crawling by in restricted lanes shortly after two in the morning. The Squirt sat on the running board. Hooker gave up and simply stretched out on the highway. There was a problem, and they couldn't hook onto their last car until the fire guys cleared it.

"Do you think we can come get all those stashed cars later this morning?"

Hooker smiled. "Don has already got us covered. He's having the two new hires shuttle everything up to the Fly for us. It's actually kind of smart. They get a week's worth of experience blowing-and-going with turds they can't damage—and we get paid for the tows."

"What about those six pancakes needing a dolly?"

"The sleds too."

The kid leaned back against the door. "Wow… Sleep…"

"Someone here order some French vanilla ice cream, triple-scoops in sugar cones?"

The two men looked up at a paramedic holding two cones. Her smile was as refreshing as the ice cream looked.

Hooker rolled up and stood stiffly. "Hello, Holly. You look like an angel standing there." He took the offered cone.

The Squirt stood with a smile. "Hello, Chuck."

She blushed. "You promised you wouldn't call—"

"I promised not to call you Vomit Comet." He ran his tongue around the top scoop and smiled at her.

Hooker snickered. "Hmm, Comet Chuck… has a certain ring to it."

She turned on him. "And this coming from a certain man who has a reputation for being a quickie?"

Hooker smiled drunkenly tired. "Yes, ma'am."

She growled.

The Squirt talked around the last of the top scoop. "Thanks for the first aid. How do you like working the ambulance?"

She blushed. "I like the siren. I like being out."

Hooker and the Squirt looked up as they saw the other driver walking up. The woman was shorter than Holly but blonde with a nice shape, which did good things for the uniform.

Hooker smiled. "And you like your partner?"

Holly blushed and looked back. Turning, she looked at Hooker and gently nodded. Hooker gave her a wink. *Good for you.*

She looked at the Squirt. He nodded a small nod and smile. He also approved of the partner.

"Am I interrupting?"

"Kam, this is Hooker and the Squirt. Guys, this is my partner, Kam— and behave."

Kam leaned over with her hand out. "Mr. Quickie and Mr. Scar tissue… Yup, I've heard all about this team." Her smile was disarming. She looked close at the Squirts' hand. "How is the paw?"

"How do you know about his hand?"

She smiled. "Where you forked him to the counter?"

Holly looked at Hooker. "You did what?"

Hooker waved it off. "Old story and it was nothing."

Kam laughed. "No… that came later. What? About two bucks of dimes shoved in you?"

Holly blanched.

"And you are…?"

"My cousin is, um, what do you call her… Cynthia Eye Candy?"

Hooker and the Squirt both laughed. "Yeah, then you would know about all the stuff."

"Yeah, Cyn and I go way back on the stories about you bringing in body parts."

"Do you ever talk to Max up at the Stick and Balls?"

The woman didn't even flinch. "Her hand is doing pretty good. At least it didn't stop her from riding the motorcycle... but she can't throw the knives two-handed like she used to."

"I wish I could have seen that."

"She'll still whip your ass at darts if you don't make her use darts."

They all turned at the sound of the shrill whistle. The fireman in the dirty yellow turnouts was winding his finger over his head. Hooker waved and headed for the cab of the tow truck. "Duty calls. Thanks for the ice cream, Holly and nice meeting you, Kam. Maybe we'll run into you two at the Stick and Balls some night." He jumped up in the cab and started the truck.

Kam looked back, and Hooker watched her in his side mirror as she smiled and then told Holly something as they walked back to their rig. He would miss Holly at the Thrifty's when he stopped for ice cream, but he was glad she had found her niche.

28

GETTING WET

"You two were out late last night." Hank sat sideways in the chair as he leaned over the morning newspaper. His socks were on, but no shoes. His chinos had knife-edge creases as crisp as his starch-stiffened white dress shirt. Hooker knew the bow tie and freshly polished shoes would be the last items to go on. Hooker shuffled to the coffeemaker.

"We wanted to give you two enough time alone to be nasty and run around the shop naked and go skinny-dipping." He turned to find a single eye drilling holes in him. He grabbed the carafe and held it out. "More coffee?" He hoped his smile appeared disarming.

Hank moved his coffee cup as he pretended to read the Dear Abby column. "You need to show a little more respect. Your uncle is getting up in years. He is no longer capable of running wild through the garage." He softly turned the page. "We creep."

The Squirt kissed him on the top of the head and silently sat down, burying his nose into his coffee mug. Hooker watched—afraid he had fallen asleep and might drown.

Without looking up, Hank reached over, and grabbing a handful of hair, lifted the head out of the mug. Coffee dripped from the end of the nose. The zombie mumbled, "I'm good…" and returned to sipping his coffee.

Hank closed and creased the Mercury News. Shuffling the parts back together, Hooker could have sworn it had never been read.

Hank took up his mug and rose. "I can hear the grizzly bear crashing about his cave, so I'll start breakfast."

Hooker looked at the clock. Two-forty-three… there had been much creeping going on the night before. "Do I need to vacuum the pool this afternoon?"

Willie's voice croaked with the early morning dryness affecting his scarred throat. "No need to be crude, Hooker. We have a new pool boy for that. Augustus is a respectful, quiet, young man who doesn't make vulgar comments about his elder's nightlife." He wandered past Hank and grabbed his butt. The other man jumped only slightly and nodded at the coffee. Willie poured his own mug full and topped Hank's off as well.

Willie parted his bathrobe to reveal standard white Navy swim trunks, and sat heavily. "Maybe Augustus can come tomorrow instead."

Hooker's one eyebrow moved. "Is Augustus feeling under the weather?"

Willie looked at him with only one eye over the top of the mug. "Just old…"

Hooker closed his eyes and then stood. Silently, he walked into his bedroom, and a minute later returned. In his hand, he held a large pink envelope. He kissed Willie behind the ear and laid the card in front of him.

He whispered with a laugh, "You thought we forgot…"

As Hank stood behind him, Willie opened the birthday card. The card folded out to over four feet long. Whatever had been printed on the inside —had long been written over with signatures. His laughter sounded like a coughing lion after swallowing a driving range bucket of balls. Hank patted him on the back and kissed him on the forehead as he looked up.

His eyes were wet as he looked up at two blurry blobs across the table. His smile crinkled and finally, he just sagged back. Nothing needed saying.

Hooker mopped up the last few bites of pancakes and eggs as the phone rang. The Squirt, standing closest as he poured more coffee into four mugs, answered the phone.

"Good evening, Chez Menz."

He stood for a second and then turned and looked at Hooker. "10-4, we'll take it in the truck. We're out in three… I need a shower." He hung up laughing. "The new girl." He checked to make sure Hooker had his boots on. Both had taken advantage of the warm summer night and bathed in the swimming pool at quarter past three in the morning.

Hank patted the air. "Leave it all. Go…"

He found himself talking to the air as the fire-rated door to the garage slammed shut.

Hooker started the truck and nosed it off the apron and down the street. The Squirt looked around. "Where's Box?" Hooker slammed on the brakes. They sat in the middle of the afternoon street thinking.

Hooker grabbed the shop mic. "Karen, is Box there with you?"

"Negatory, Hooker. Do I need to check if he is out running calls in another truck all by himself?"

Hooker knew she could barely keep from laughing.

Hooker pinched the bridge of his nose. He left the mic unkeyed and muttered to himself or the Squirt, "What day is this?"

The silence was deafening. The small tin speaker rumbled and vibrated with Dolly's voice. "You left him here when you ran out so fast on Wednesday night. If you have missed a step or six… this is Saturday."

Karen's voice bled in, "Squirt?"

The Squirt took the mic. "Go ahead."

"See Fester at the crab shack near Tess's camp. And from what I gather… you need to step on it."

Hooker dumped the clutch and the truck shot forward two feet and stalled. He turned the key and restarted the engine. The silent growl was enough. The Squirt didn't even smile. He rolled down his window and hoped for some cooling. They were four minutes away from the freeway.

The Squirt got an evil look in his eye. The truck lumbered down the hill. Gaining speed, he and Hooker both knew could not be used in a drifting slide to make the left turn at the bottom. "Um… 10-4… Show our ETA at four hours and twenty-eight minutes."

"10-9?" Dolly's voice had an edge to it.

The Squirt still wasn't done. "We're in the High-Speed Wonder, not the svelte demure Ms. West."

"The High-Speed Wonder… 1-4-1, which vehicle are you in?" Don must have been listening on the shop radio or out running a call.

Hooker grabbed the mic from the Squirt. "Your new baby… and when you get her back, you too will be wondering where they hid the high-speed gears."

"They said the truck could hit at least one-twenty…"

"Capable and able to do so are two different universes. They travel in deep space on TV, but us getting there is another story."

Hooker glanced at the Squirt before he stomped on the breaks and manhandled the truck around the turn. "Before you get it back, Don, you might want to let Willie have it for a few months."

The radio was silent as they rode the distance to the next sharp turn onto the freeway on-ramp.

"Calling the reservation into William right now…"

"You might make it for after the holiday wrecking party." Every tow truck driver knew from the first rains until a week after New Year's Day, all moving trucks were busy.

"That's what Willie just said."

The two in the tow truck chuckled. Hooker tossed the mic in the air, and the Squirt caught it as he watched Hooker muscle the right turn. He keyed the mic. "Willie's a smart guy."

"I think it runs in the family. Don out."

Hooker and the Squirt cleared their mirrors as they settled into the long drive to Fremont. Hooker tried to push the truck past seventy-five, but the shimmy affected the steering, so he held it at seventy and relaxed in the wind of the window.

Hooker left the yellow flashers off. Nobody would have paid attention, and the drivers were all lethargically numb from the heat and driving on autopilot. *Sunday and a hot afternoon—drones going nowhere.*

Fester checked his wristwatch when he spotted the medium-sized yellow blob of a tow truck turn the corner four blocks away. Dispatch hadn't been far wrong. This was not the fast truck Hooker got his reputation with. They were only off by a couple of hours.

The Squirt dropped from the truck first. "What have we got?" He held the double-barreled sawed-off shotgun at his side.

"Suspect went out on the water about two this afternoon. The witness, who called it in, said they thought he had a large and long garbage bag over his shoulder. Could be we have another body."

Hooker came around the nose of the truck. "Who's the witness?"

Fester pointed to the crab shack. "Waitress named Joan or Joanne."

Hooker and the Squirt looked out across the miles of grass. They both had seen aerial photos of the fine spider-web of freshwater rivers running through the grass like streets in a crazy laid-out city. If you didn't know where you were going, it would be easy to get lost—*or hide.*

"We have two fast-assault pontoon boats coming down from Alameda. The SEAL teams come down here to train so they won't get lost."

Hooker looked up the long street to the north.

Fester laughed. "Are you kidding, Hooker? I said SEAL."

The Squirt snorted. "They're on the water." He turned. "I'm going to go talk to the waitress."

Hooker looked at the kid. "Yeah, coffee sounds good."

As the three walked to the shack, Fester glanced at Hooker and the drained look of his shoulders. "What time did you clear the wreck yesterday?"

"Three… this morning… "

"I'll buy."

THE WAITRESS HAD nothing more to add, except some carrot cake. She said she and the owner were like many of the people in the area. At first, they were leery of Tess and her strange habits, but then they got to looking after him. Hooker didn't think it his place to set her straight about Tess being a woman. He could tell the young woman really was protective, if not fond of her.

Hooker assured her Tess would be back, but not until it was safe.

"Gentlemen, it looks like your rides are here."

The three turned to look out the window as the two insertion boats nosed up onto the launch ramp. The heavily muffled engines were noiseless through the window. Hooker was pretty sure they would have still been surprised if they had been sitting out on the deck.

Fester passed a ten across the counter, and they left. The waitress sang them out with a longing call to three good-looking men, "Y'all come back soon now. Ya hear?"

The SEALs had chart maps showing all the rivers or lanes as they called them. Hooker and Fester showed them where the body dump had been. The two team leaders quickly assessed the route to go in and see if the suspect had gone home to what he knew. They also looked at a pincher assault to Bridgetown by coming in from the south and north. This would be their search area B. If both of those failed, they would start a quadrant search and call for some air support from Moffett. If night fell, they would switch to Hueys with spotters using infrared and starlight scopes that could spot the heat of a man.

The temperature drop surprised Hooker the moment they left the shallows and ran along the grass line just offshore. The twin outboard motors were quieter than most cars with their windows closed. The team members wore a dark-water camouflage Hooker had never seen before. Each man intently searched the grass and lanes as they glided down the waterway. Even though Hooker searched also, he felt like a billboard in his white T-shirt and also felt out of his league in the search department. Tell him to find the dead AMC Pacer in the middle of a fifty-car pile-up, and he's your man. But grass, water, the sun, and looking for someone who lives in this condition—Hooker felt like a tourist.

They turned west and ran down a narrow lane, which let out onto a wider lane Hooker would have called a freeway. The two pontoon boats ran side by side. With all eleven men searching, the drivers ran the boats up closer to thirty. Hooker could feel the boat rise out of the water and assumed it now only ran on the narrow part of the V in the bottom. The ride had become as smooth as Sweets' Lincoln Town Car. The water seemed like a flat glass mirror of the summer's dead air. The grasses along the north side seemed darker—like they held a secret.

As Hooker looked forward, he spotted the trestle and knew why the grass seemed so foreboding. *Because the secret was death.* He turned to the driver and patted his hand down in the air. The driver throttled back as the other boat responded the same. Hooker pointed to the car trunk with the police ribbon still attached. The team members started spotting the fiberglass orange marker sticks standing six-feet out of the water, and a foot or so above the grass.

The other boat surged ahead. It threaded through the trestle and around the corner. The radio squawked. "The Sheriff said the body dump extended back to the next lane. We're going to work the north end," the driver responded and then turned the boat around.

"This is all clear, but there's a narrow alley back there we can get up."

Hooker nodded. He knew, eventually, they would probably drive up, down, through or around every acre of the south bay. This tedious crime-solving he didn't usually do—usually, it came to him.

As they slid tightly through the grass in the narrow alley, Hooker slumped down into the bottom of the boat. He rested against the round of the pontoon. The low hum of the engine and the hiss of the boat slipping past the grass created a powerful sleep aid. The heat from the sun didn't help. The radios were turned down and became only a small distraction as Hooker drifted in and out with the heat.

The boat slowed. The pressure of the grass pushing against the sides had become a large drag. If need be, the SEALs will start hacking back the grass to clear a passage, or just push harder. Hooker slid down further and finally rolled over onto his side.

His head had just dipped below the edge when the other men started yelling. Hooker's eyes flew open—looking at a knife, tied to a pole, thrown like a spear. A few seconds earlier and the knife would have been in his back or neck. As it was, the jerry-rigged spear stuck into the side of the pontoon.

One of the SEALS dove to the floorboard and grabbed a small kit. He drew out a rubber patch and peeled the tape off. Pulling the spear out, he inserted the patch and worked it with his finger. He withdrew his hand, and the sound of escaping air stopped. The man rolled over.

"Are you okay?"

"I'm good." Hooker's guts were shaking, but he knew he could function.

The boat had slid to a stop, but nobody moved. The driver quietly spoke into his walkie-talkie, "We just took assault from out in the grass to the east of us and south of you."

The radio squawked. "Roger, we're coming down the north border lane."

Hooker watched as two of the SEALs rolled over the side of the boat and slid into the water and grass without a splash or rustle. Hooker sat on the bottom of the boat and leaned against the other side—his shoulders covering the patch. His head swiveled as he kept watching the grass for something, anything. His mind worked in overdrive with more than just a hint of panic. A part of him started expecting another spear to fly out of the grass and pin his chest to the side of the boat.

He was wrong.

The hand came from behind him. Before he could scream or anyone knew what was happening, he was pulled up and over the pontoon. He had a second to take a last breath.

Under the boat, a murky person attacked Hooker. As they fought, the silt clouded the water. Old nightmares of drowning flashed through Hooker's mind. The beast in front of him would give him even more. The light-colored shirt wavered in the water and left the impression of an indistinct shape—maybe a human or maybe a shark. Hooker struck out with his fist.

Nothing there.

A sudden pain shot through his thigh. As he looked down, he could just make out a dark trail leaving his leg. The warm water numbed the pain, but he knew it was either cut or stabbed. He feathered his legs, turning his body in place. The water swished—too deep to stand up.

Out of the corner of his eye, he saw a movement of light color. He fanned his hands up and pushed his body down. The knife aimed at his throat was a glancing slash across his forearm. *Another trail of blood in the water—are there sharks in the bay?*

Hooker punched up with his right fist. He struck something soft and forgiving. He didn't think it had any effect. He tried to grab a leg or arm or something to no avail.

Hooker touched the bottom, but his attempt to push off only resulted in his boots sinking deeper into the mud and silt. The suction stopped him from leaving to the air above. *He stood floating in the water—trapped.*

The white shark came out of the dark murk. Hooker bent sideways away from the knife glinting in the water. His right foot slipped out of its boot. The pain in his back spun him around. The feet were kicking as the body moved back into the murk. Hooker lurched right and released his left foot.

He pushed off as best he could in the direction the fiend had gone. He clawed at the water as his lungs clawed at his chest—he knew he needed air. As he cleared the shadow of the boat, he grabbed the grasses and pulled himself up in one desperate lunge.

The water in the grasses ruptured as Hooker gasped for air. A thick rope struck him around the shoulders. "Grab the rope…"

He wrapped the rope around his arm as he felt it being pulled back to the boat. In his blurred vision, he could see the two seamen hauling him in.

Just as he cleared the grass, the form reared out of the grass and fell on his legs. The right hand drove the knife into Hooker's back. The hilt of the large knife slammed to a stop on his shirt. Hooker screamed and letting go of the rope, twisted around to try to remove the knife. His right hand fanned at his lower back as he sank back into the water.

Against protocol, the second SEAL dove in after Hooker. The team leader stared, helpless. He had no idea where his other two SEALs were. Now, it was just him. He called out. Nobody answered.

The SEAL clawed through the muddy water. His eyes stung. He looked for anything that could be Hooker or the other thing. As he looked down, he thought he saw a foot disappearing into the grass. He folded up and dove after it.

The other boat maneuvered into the alley, hanging nosed in with the other half out in the wider lane. The four SEALs and the Squirt stood in the boat looking into the grass. They could see movement in the tops. Fester finished getting his pants off and his tech-belt on. He checked the knife on each side and then dove out into the grass. Two of the SEALs followed. They all knew with the water muddied, they could end up swimming right over who they were looking for.

Fester stuck closer to the bottom as he pulled his way through the grass. His head swung a constant pendulum of motion. As he slid toward where they had seen movement, he saw a light shape. Grabbing the grass to his right, he pulled his way down to the body. The SEAL hung in the water suspended—motionless—a foot or two above the silt. Fester recognized the position of the short stick protruded from the man's back. A small area of silver hung at the man's skin. Fester knew it would be duct tape, holding a blade to the end of the short spear. The loop of the surgical tubing attached to the end had provided the propulsion of the handheld spear. He had used such a rig for years instead of a spear gun. He rolled the SEAL over. The man's throat gaped open—*coup d grace*.

Fester gently pushed the man up toward the light and air. Breaking the surface, he found himself turned around in the grass. "Call out…"

"Over here."

Fester started swimming in a sidestroke as he dragged the body. He got to the boat, and the SEALs leaned over and silently pulled in their teammate. Their mutual silence spoke volumes. Fester turned to go back.

In the grass, someone thrashed and a scream—mixed with gasping for air.

The Squirt called out, "Hooker, this way. Over here, Hooker. Swim to my voice."

They could hear the grass whipping about as the person thrashed toward the sound of Squirt's voice. The movement and sound were not smooth but the sound of desperation.

"Keep coming…"

One of the SEALs stood with a hank of line ready to throw. As the grass parted, he threw it hard. Most of the hank hit Hooker on the back and the back of his head. His one arm swung up and wound around, trapping the line around it. The SEAL pulled hard. Hooker surged out of the grass as an arm swung through the air. The short spear was buried into Hooker's ribs. The knife still protruded from his back. The fiend grabbed the knife and hung on as the SEAL pulled Hooker's body up onto the pontoon.

Fester surged from the side of the pontoon where he had been hanging. The knife in his hand flashed as he buried it into the armpit of the white shirt. The fiend screamed and bared her teeth. The eyes were wild with bloodlust. Her hands worked on Hooker's back. Her left grabbed into his shirt as the right pulled the knife from his body and drove it in again.

As she pulled the knife out again, she rose. She looked into the bottom of the boat. Her eyes locked with the eyes of the Squirt.

He smiled. "Oh, hell no, bitch…"

She looked down at the large openings of the shortened twelve-gauge shotgun. The Squirt rested the end on the top of Hooker's head as his thumb moved the selector to the middle.

"You're going straight to hell…" He pulled the trigger on both barrels. Her head—a foot away… disappeared.

29

———

THE HOSPITAL AGAIN?

The headless body floated half in the grass. The body still convulsed with muscle contractions as the heart worked pumping life-sustaining blood to a head no longer there.

In the boat, the men worked rapidly. "Stay with us, Hooker. Just hang on, buddy. We're getting you to a doctor."

The radio squawked. "SEAL two, go ahead."

"This is team leader Chief Sanchez, requesting immediate medical evac. I have two men in their mid-twenties with multiple stab wounds. Both have lost a lot of blood. BP is dropping. Pulse is rapid but thready. Helo can set down at the crab shack parking lot. We will clear it."

The team leader turned to the driver. "Get us the hell up there now, Chief."

The boat surged and straightened in the lane, as it began to hydroplane, the chief switched the radio. "Team two to team one."

"Team one."

"We have Hooker and the Squirt. Hooker is badly wounded. Roberts is dead, say again, Roberts is dead. We are making our way to the shack for dust off. Round up the rest and meet us there."

"Roger, team two. We have just Porter to get in, and we'll be right there. The sheriff will need the evac, as well."

"Roger."

As the driver ran the pontoon up the launch ramp, the chief looked up. The helicopter came across the grass tilted forward. He figured the pilot kept it at fast attack angle the entire way from Alameda.

As they hoisted Hooker, the helicopter flared and started to settle on its skids. The side doors opened, and one medic jumped to the ground.

The other medic shoved out a stretcher, and they laid Hooker on it and shoved it back in. The diver with the arm wound rolled in.

The other boat raced out of the lane, already turning. The driver aimed for the launch ramp and the helicopter. The boat slid the entire length of the ramp—coming to rest twenty feet from the helicopter.

The two SEALS grabbed Fester and ran him over. They rolled him onto the chopper's floor as the one medic yelled, and the machine lifted off. It turned in the air and nosed over. The hospital was four minutes away with a ticking clock.

"Where to?" The Squirt stood watching the helicopter become a dot in the sky.

"Moffett is the closer of the two." The man pointed where the helicopter had gone—out over the grasses. "It's straight across. Alameda would be another five or ten minutes. But because Hooker's a civilian, they will probably take him straight to Stanford."

The Squirt mused as he watched the now empty sky. "With stab wounds, why not straight to Valley Medical?"

"Even five minutes can make a difference. Stanford will at least stabilize him and then later move him either down to Valley or up to San Francisco. Either one is expert when it comes to stabs and gunshot."

The Squirt turned and looked at the SEAL. "What about your guys?"

The guy shrugged and waved his hand in dismissal. "As soon as they got in the chopper, they probably handed him a roll of duct tape and put him to work."

The Squirt snorted. "Yeah, sounds like something Uncle Willie would do..."

"Rear Admiral William Knight? Cutthroat Willie?"

"I think he was only a captain. But the cutthroat thing fits."

The guy was excited. "You're talking about William Knight who builds fast cars?"

The kid grunted with a smirk. "And drinks moonshine, wears a dress, and is Hooker's uncle."

"The gentleman is no captain. I don't know what he's told you, but the man saved my uncle and a couple dozen other guys from a POW camp. They made him a Rear Admiral and got put in for a Medal of Honor. The guy is a legend." The guy stopped. "What do you mean he wears a dress?"

The Squirt smiled. "If Hooker survives this one, we'll have you guys down for a barbecue. The medal and citation hang by the door into an acre of garage. Next to it, hangs a picture of him in the hospital with tubes everywhere, and the President shaking his hand and looking like an idiot. The dresses are just cheap and burn up or get greasy a lot."

The man laughed. "He always did march to a different orchestra..."

"But he followed regulations. Give the man a pennywhistle and a place to walk, and he's happy—which is all we care about." The Squirt felt in his wet pockets in panic and then relief as he pulled out the key to the truck. "For a moment there, I thought I had given the key back to Hooker after I got Betsy Ross." He held up the shortened shotgun.

The man looked at the wild pistol grip 12-guage shotgun. "I saw the head disappear—double-aught buck doesn't act like—"

The Squirt held up the shotgun he had become so entwined with. "No, but a buck-forty of dimes in each barrel does—especially from a foot away."

The radio squawked. "Helo six-eight to SEAL two."

"SEAL two, go ahead."

"Hooker and the sheriff are down at Stanford. We'll take your diver back to Alameda. He says he wants to sleep in his own bed. Helo six-eight out."

The SEAL nodded at the Squirt. "Roger six-eight. Franco just got married last month. I will advise Hooker's partner, and thanks for the lift. SEAL two out."

He gazed across the grass to an unseen distant hospital. Looking back at the Squirt. "You won't know anything for several hours or tomorrow even. We'll round up the Coasties... the body is in the bay, and they will want to see it. We probably need the sheriff out here as well. They get whiney when you move a body and don't tell them."

The Squirt tossed the key in the air and caught it. "I'll handle the law enforcement end while you get the Coast Guard down here. I'm sure the sheriff has several questions for all of us... even if they didn't want to do their job in the beginning."

Both men nodded with grimaces. The diver pointed his radio up at the young woman watching them from the deck of the crab shack. The Squirt nodded. He would join them in a few minutes.

"1-4-1."

"Go ahead, Squirt." Dolly's voice had a strained edge to it. It was not going to be a good night.

"We're going to need some sheriff out here. They need to send the crime scene unit. I also think it would be best to advise the Transportation Department—the body is under the trestle and in the railroad easement."

"10-4, Sheriff and Cal Trans... on their way."

The Squirt looked out across the grass. The late afternoon's golden light was just starting to settle in over the waves of tan grass—turning it to a warm fire in the late summer heat. He didn't want to think of anything at the moment. He slid out of the truck and walked across the parking lot.

The closed door muted the radio, but the tears came anyway.

"1-4-1... Where is Hooker?"

"1-4-1?"

"1-4-1... Are you there?"

"Squirt...?"

30

JUDGE'S CHAMBERS

"We won't know for a while. He was in surgery for sixteen hours the first round…" An exhausted Squirt looked over at the Superior Court Judge.

The man lowered his glasses from the top of his head. "Have you slept at all?"

"I've dozed a bit at the hospital…"

Hack leaned back in his chair. "So I'll take it as a no…"

The Squirt shrugged his eyes and nodded.

"So what now… for you…?"

The young man hesitated, and then his hand unclasped in a manual shrug.

The judge eased forward and looked at the large pile of files open and spread across his desk. "I've been going over… well, for no other word for it… your resume."

"Resume?"

"If you could boil down a couple of years of taking down killers, solving cold cases and murders, and the bombing, and anything else you two did… outside the academy. And then there is the impressive work inside the academy…" The man gently pulled his horned-rimmed glasses from his face and tapped the files.

Laying the glasses down, he leaned back in his large chair. A thin knife of light through the vertical shutters traced a line across the thinning hair. He closed his eyes as his left hand gently scratched the length of his nose.

"Can you actually picture yourself in a uniform for the years it would take to make detective?"

The Squirt sat back in his chair. What had once been a fantasy for a career had been made available as reality. But along the way, it had become other than what he found interesting or exciting. His joke of going straight to detective was just that—a joke. He knew in his heart that he would have to serve the trial of being a uniform and serve out his time as well as test for the position. He also knew his activities of solving major crimes had created some ill feelings toward him. And he knew those ill feelings could cause political roadblocks on his road for future advancements.

He bit his upper lip as he rubbed his thumb over the four small scars on his left hand. *Four tiny dots... where everything had started—a lifetime ago.*

He sighed as he looked up. "I'm adrift… if you have any suggestions."

"I spoke with Russell over at Department of Justice in Sacramento… He said you have received more than a few offers outside the Bay Area—apart from his office. But anywhere you go, they all would involve a uniform of sorts. Even if you landed with Russell, you would be in a uniform suit with a tie and tight shoes."

The kid nodded. "I've been thinking about all of those things this summer."

"Which is why you have delayed graduating from the academy by taking all the higher courses? Courses which others return over the years to take?"

The Squirt's lower lip pushed up against his upper in a shrug. His eyes wandered over the judge's wall of legal reference books.

Hack slowly closed the files and stacked them. The final pile was several inches thick. He rested his folded hands on top. "I think you have already found your place—we just need to find a legal way to use that unique position and resource."

The kid looked up through his eyebrows. His head gently rose in interest.

"How soon is the giant truck getting back on the road?"

"Last we heard, they were putting the final pieces together down in Texas."

The judge glanced at the small calendar on his desk. He ran the edge of his index finger along his curled lips. "Maybe we need to send you down to Texas to oversee the final construction—and learn how to drive her."

"Who, exactly, are we…?"

"For now… my office. It wouldn't be the first time you worked for me. But, for the future, we'll figure it out when the time comes."

BAER CHARLTON

ABOUT THE AUTHOR

BAER CHARLTON

Baer Charlton graduated from UC Irvine with a degree in Social Anthropology, monkeyed around for a while, and then proceeded onward with a life of global travel, multi-disciplinary adventure, and meeting the memorable array of characters he would come to describe in his writing. He has ridden things with gears, engines, and sails, and made things with wood, leather, and metal. He has been stitched back together more times than the average hockey team; his long-suffering wife and an assortment of cats and dogs have nursed him back to health after each surgery.

Baer knows a lot about many things in this world. History flows through his veins and pours out of him at the slightest provocation. Do not ask him what you may think is a simple question unless you have the time to hear a fascinating story.

You can find more about Baer at his website.
www.baercharlton.com